HOLT Science Spectrum®
Physical Science
with Earth and Space Science

TENNESSEE EDITION

HOLT McDOUGAL
a division of Houghton Mifflin Harcourt

About the cover: The cover image shows a racing bicycle's back wheel in motion. The chain running through the gear assembly (derailleur) is labeled with the basic equation for speed. By convention, speed is indicated by the letter "v" (velocity) even when the only component being considered is the magnitude.

Copyright © 2010 Holt McDougal, a division of Houghton Mifflin Harcourt Publishing Company. All rights reserved

Warning: No part of this publication may be reproduced or transmitted in any form or by any means, electronic or mechanical, including photocopy, and recording, or by any information storage or retrieval system without the prior written permission of Holt McDougal unless such copying is expressly permitted by federal copyright law.

Requests for permission to make copies of any part of the work should be mailed to the following address: Permissions Department, Holt McDougal, 10801 N. MoPac Expressway, Building 3, Austin, Texas 78759.

Original edition ©1995, 1996 by Ken Dobson, John Holman, and Michael Roberts.

This adaptation of Nelson Balanced Science and Nelson Science is published by arrangement with Thomas Nelson & Sons Ltd., Walton-on-Thames, UK.

HOLT MCDOUGAL is a trademark of Houghton Mifflin Harcourt Publishing Company.

LIVE INK is a registered trademark of Walker Reading Technologies, Inc., licensed for use by Holt McDougal.

SCILINKS is a registered trademark owned and provided by the National Science Teachers Association. All rights reserved.

The trademark **SCIENCE SPECTRUM®** is used under license from Science Spectrum, Inc., Lubbock, Texas.

Printed in the United States of America

> If you have received these materials as examination copies free of charge, Holt McDougal retains title to the materials and they may not be resold. Resale of examination copies is strictly prohibited.

> Possession of this publication in print format does not entitle users to convert this publication, or any portion of it, into electronic format.

ISBN-13: 978-0-55-402281-9

ISBN-10: 0-55-402281-8

2 3 4 5 6 0914 11 10 09

Unpacking Physical Science Standards

Tennessee

As you read the following pages and work through the Tennessee Physical Science Standards, you will discover the big ideas and key concepts that your teacher expects you to learn and understand.

You will see three things:

1 >
what the standard actually says

2 What's it mean?
an explanation to help you understand the big ideas within the standard

3 Review Question
a typical standards review question

Tennessee
Volunteer State

State capitol, Nashville

Deer, Great Smoky Mountains

Beale Street at night

Discipline: Physical Science

Inquiry

Conceptual Strand
Understandings about scientific inquiry and the ability to conduct inquiry are essential for living in the 21st century.

Guiding Question
What tools, skills, knowledge, and dispositions are needed to conduct scientific inquiry?

>CLE 3202.Inq.1 Recognize that science is a progressive endeavor that reevaluates and extends what is already accepted.

What's it mean?
Know that science is an ongoing effort that looks at what people already understand about the world and tries to improve upon that understanding. Go to Chapter 1, Introduction to Science, for help.

Review Question During the development of the periodic table, many scientists built on the work of other scientists. Which of the following statements shows scientists not reevaluating or extending what is already accepted in the development of the periodic table?
 A. Mendeleev predicts the existence of an element based on a hole in the pattern of elements and properties he studied.
 B. A new column is added to the periodic table because the new elements have properties that differ from the properties of all known elements.
 C. Each element that has an atomic number less than 100 has been identified, so scientists do not look for any unknown elements.
 D. The determination of atomic numbers allows scientists to explain why the atomic masses of some elements seemed out of place.

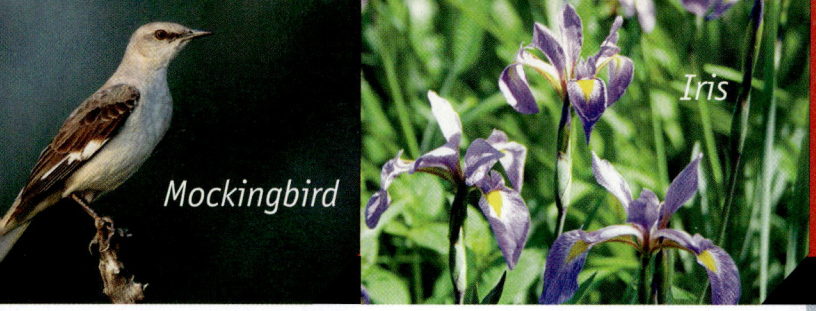

Mockingbird
Iris
Smoky Mountains

⟵ Unpacking Physical Science Standards

>CLE 3202.Inq.2
Design and conduct scientific investigations to explore new phenomena, verify previous results, test how well a theory predicts, and compare opposing theories.

What's it mean?
Plan and carry out experiments to study new facts, check other people's findings, see how well a scientific explanation describes what will happen, and find out how different scientific explanations are alike and different. Go to Chapter 1, Introduction to Science, for help.

Review Question You are designing a controlled experiment to explore a new phenomenon. In your experiment,
  A. the outcome is controlled.
  B. all variables except one remain fixed.
  C. all variables are held constant.
  D. one outcome is decided, and the conclusions are controlled.

>CLE 3202.Inq.3
Use appropriate tools and technology to collect precise and accurate data.

What's it mean?
Handle proper equipment to gather information that is both exact and true. Go to Chapter 1, Introduction to Science, for help.

Review Question A balance is a scientific tool used to measure
  A. temperature.
  B. time.
  C. volume.
  D. mass.

Answers: Inq.1) C; Inq.2) B; Inq.3) D

Tennessee
Volunteer State

>CLE 3202.Inq.4 Apply qualitative and quantitative measures to analyze data and draw conclusions that are free of bias.

What's it mean?
Use different ways of gathering numerical and non-numerical information, study that information, and come up with fair explanations for it. Go to Chapter 1, Introduction to Science, for help.

Review Question The graph below shows the average use of various energy sources in the United States. British thermal units (Btu) are commonly used to express energy usage. Use the graph to answer the following question.

Which of the following is a factor that is a likely source of bias for conclusions drawn from these data?

A. the change in the population of the United States
B. the use of multiple sources to compile the data
C. the identity of the group that gathered the data and created the graph
D. the change in the value of United States currency during the time shown

The Mississippi and Memphis

Unpacking Physical Science Standards

>CLE 3202.Inq.5 Compare experimental evidence and conclusions with those drawn by others about the same testable question.

What's it mean?
Look at how data and findings from a scientific study are alike and different from what other studies have found. Go to Chapter 1, Introduction to Science, for help.

Review Question In his gold-foil experiment, Ernest Rutherford noted that most of the beam of positive particles which he aimed at the foil seemed to pass through the foil untouched and that a small portion of the beam passed through but was moved aside from a straight path. Which of the following statements is not a reasonable conclusion based on the experimental evidence?

A. The foil had a small hole in it, which let the beam of particles through. The deflected particles grazed the edges of the hole and were deflected.
B. The atoms in the foil were made up of mostly empty space, which allowed most of the particles to pass through.
C. There were small places in the foil where positive charges were closely packed and which caused some particles of the beam to be deflected.
D. The matter that made up the atoms in the foil was evenly distributed throughout the foil.

Answers: Inq.4) C; Inq.5) D

TN7

Tennessee
Volunteer State

Ruby Falls, Chattanooga

> **CLE 3202.Inq.6** Communicate and defend scientific findings.

What's it mean?
Tell about and present arguments for scientific explanations. Go to Chapter 1, Introduction to Science, for help.

Review Question A company determines the compositions of several ores. In the report of the findings, the results are best represented using which kind of visual representation?
- A. a pie graph
- B. a line graph
- C. a bar graph
- D. a scatter plot

Embedded Technology and Engineering

Conceptual Strand
Society benefits when engineers apply scientific discoveries to design materials and processes that develop into enabling technologies.

Guiding Question
How do science concepts, engineering skills, and applications of technology improve the quality of life?

> **CLE 3202.T/E.1** Explore the impact of technology on social, political, and economic systems.

What's it mean?
Look at how new tools and ideas affect communities, governments, and money. Go to Chapter 1, Introduction to Science, for help.

Review Question In the mid 1800s, aluminum metal was rare because it was difficult and expensive to produce. As a result, the price of aluminum was greater than the price of gold at that time. In 1886, a cheaper way to produce aluminum was developed. Which of the following effects is the least likely result of the new process?

Unpacking Physical Science Standards

A. The price of aluminum dropped below the price of gold.
B. The number of products made from aluminum increased.
C. Governments stockpiled aluminum rather than gold.
D. Companies that produced aluminum were created.

> **CLE 3202.T/E.2** Differentiate among elements of the engineering design cycle: design constraints, model building, testing, evaluating, modifying, and retesting.

What's it mean?

Describe each step in the invention process: listing what is needed, making a test version, trying it out, looking at how well it did, making a better version, and trying it out again. Go to Chapter 1, Introduction to Science, for help.

Review Question A team of students is working to enter a robotics competition. Which statement correctly describes elements in their engineering design cycle?

A. After making modifications to their design, the students should not retest the design because the robot might be damaged during retesting.
B. After making a model, the students should identify the design constraints they will need to apply.
C. The evaluation of the test results should be compared with the design constraints and should be the basis for any modifications made.
D. The final design should be determined before the model is made to help conserve materials.

Answers: Ing.6) A; T/E.1) C; T/E.2) C

Old Town, Nashville

Tennessee
Volunteer State

> **CLE 3202.T/E.3** Explain the relationship between the properties of a material and the use of the material in the application of a technology.

What's it mean?
Connect the characteristics of what a new tool is made of with how that new tool will be used. Go to Chapter 2, Matter, for help.

Review Question Which material would be the best to use in a technology that requires a good conductor of energy?
- A. plastic
- B. water
- C. wood
- D. metal

> **CLE 3202.T/E.4** Describe the dynamic interplay among science, technology, and engineering within living, earth-space, and physical systems.

What's it mean?
Explain the changing connections among experimentation, invention, and design within studies of living things, earth and space, and different materials. Go to Chapter 1, Introduction to Science, for help.

Review Question Spider silk is strong enough to support the spider and has enough elasticity to absorb the energy of the collision of a flying insect. The strength comes from the covalent bonds between units of the amino acid polymer of which spider silk, a protein, is made. The elasticity is the result of interactions between different parts of the molecule. Coils or folds in the protein expand on impact. Which of the following statements is not a description of the dynamic interplay among science, technology, and engineering that is likely to happen in the study of spider silk?
- A. Scientists identify some of the structures that account for silk's properties and find ways to mimic the properties in synthetic fibers.
- B. Spider silk research involves only scientists who have an interest in life science and who have no chemistry or engineering background.
- C. Technology to control the addition of amino acids in the building of spider silk might also be used to make other proteins for medical research.
- D. Research into the chemical composition of spider silk could lead to improved products, such as ropes or bungee cords.

Great Smoky Mountains National Park

Unpacking Physical Science Standards

Embedded Mathematics

Conceptual Strand
Physical science applies mathematics to investigate questions, solve problems, and communicate findings.

Guiding Question
What mathematical skills and understandings are needed to successfully investigate physical science?

>CLE 3202.Math.1 Understand the mathematical principles behind the science of physics.

What's it mean?
Know how math helps to describe the science of physics. Go to Chapter 1, Introduction to Science, for help.

Review Question The equation below relates the initial velocity, v_i, the final velocity, v_f, the acceleration, a, and the time, t, for an object. Use the equation to answer the following question.

$$v_f = v_i + at$$

Based on the equation, which of the following statements is correct?

A. The final velocity is equal to the initial velocity plus the acceleration when the time is 0 s.
B. The initial velocity can be greater than the final velocity if the acceleration is a positive value.
C. The final velocity can be 0 m/s if the initial velocity is a positive value and the acceleration is a negative value.
D. The initial velocity is equal to the final velocity divided by the product of acceleration and time.

Answers: T/E.3) D; T/E.4) B; Math.1) C

Tennessee
Volunteer State

>**CLE 3202.Math.2** Utilize appropriate mathematical equations and processes to solve basic physics problems.

What's it mean?
Use the correct equations and math skills to answer simple problems in physics. Go to Chapter 1, Introduction to Science, for help.

Review Question The graph below shows the results of a test that used a car and a truck. Use the graph below to answer the following question.

What conclusion about the motions of the car and of the truck is supported by the graph?
  A. The truck's final speed is greater than the car's final speed.
  B. The car's initial speed is greater than the truck's initial speed.
  C. The truck took 1.5 times longer to stop than the car.
  D. The car slowed down at 2 times the rate at which the truck did.

Standard 1 – Matter

Conceptual Strand 1
The composition and structure of matter is known, and it behaves according to principles that are generally understood.

Guiding Question 1
How does the structure of matter influence its physical and chemical behavior?

>**CLE 3202.1.1** Explore matter in terms of its physical and chemical properties.

What's it mean?
Learn about materials based on their physical properties and their chemical properties. Go to Chapter 2, Matter, for help.

Review Question Which of the following properties is a chemical property?
  A. density
  B. flammability
  C. malleability
  D. conductivity

Nashville music scene

Unpacking Physical Science Standards

Parthenon, Centennial Park

>CLE 3202.1.2 Describe the structure and arrangement of atomic particles.

What's it mean?
Describe how protons, neutrons, and electrons, the particles that make up atoms, are put together and arranged to make different atoms. Go to Chapter 4, Atoms, for help.

Review Question Xenon has an atomic number of 54. A particular isotope of xenon has a mass number of 131. Which answer lists the correct numbers of protons, neutrons, and electrons in each atom of this isotope?
- A. 77 protons, 131 neutrons, and 77 electrons
- B. 54 protons, 131 neutrons, and 185 electrons
- C. 185 protons, 54 neutrons, and 77 electrons
- D. 54 protons, 77 neutrons, and 54 electrons

>CLE 3202.1.3 Characterize and classify elements based on their atomic structure.

What's it mean?
Put elements into different groups based on the way in which the particles that make up their atoms are arranged. Go to Chapter 5, The Periodic Table, for help.

Review Question The graphic below shows the upper right portion of the periodic table. Use this graphic to answer the following question.

13	14	15	16	17	18
					2 He 4.00
5 B 10.81	6 C 12.01	7 N 14.01	8 O 16.00	9 F 19.00	10 Ne 20.18
13 Al 26.98	14 Si 28.09	15 P 30.97	16 S 32.06	17 Cl 35.45	18 Ar 39.95

Which pair of elements would most likely have a similar arrangement of outer electrons and have similar chemical behaviors?
- A. boron and aluminum
- B. helium and fluorine
- C. carbon and nitrogen
- D. chlorine and oxygen

Answers: Math.2) C; 1.1) B; 1.2) D; 1.3) A

Tennessee
Volunteer State

Sun Sphere, Knoxville

>CLE 3202.1.4 Investigate chemical and physical changes.

What's it mean?
Study chemical changes, which change the identity of the material, and physical changes, which do not change the identity of the material. Go to Chapter 2, Matter, for help.

Review Question Which of the following is an example of a chemical change?
- A. gasoline evaporating into the air
- B. sugar dissolving in a cup of water
- C. iron rusting in a damp garage
- D. water freezing in a freezer

>CLE 3202.1.5 Evaluate pure substances and mixtures.

What's it mean?
Tell whether a material is a pure substance, (an element or a compound), or a mixture, (a combination of two or more pure substances). Go to Chapter 2, Matter, for help.

Review Question Which of the following is a mixture?
- A. air
- B. salt
- C. water
- D. sulfur

>CLE 3202.1.6 Distinguish between common ionic and covalent compounds.

What's it mean?
Tell whether a compound is made up of charged ions or of molecules in which atoms are sharing electrons. Go to Chapter 6, The Structure of Matter, for help.

Review Question Crystals of table salt, sodium chloride, are made up of
- A. atoms whose electrons are free to move between atoms.
- B. molecules in which atoms share electrons.
- C. atoms that have all of their original electrons.
- D. ions that formed when atoms transferred electrons.

Unpacking Physical Science Standards

>CLE 3202.1.7 Construct chemical formulas for common compounds.

What's it mean?
Write the correct formulas for some everyday compounds. Go to Chapter 6, The Structure of Matter, for help.

Review Question The chemical formula for calcium chloride is
- A. CaCl.
- B. $CaCl_2$.
- C. Ca_2Cl.
- D. Ca_2Cl_2.

>CLE 3202.1.8 Investigate relationships among the pressure, temperature, and volume of gases and liquids.

What's it mean?
Learn how the volume of a gas or liquid changes as either the pressure or the temperature changes. Go to Chapter 3, States of Matter, for help.

Review Question A gas has a volume of 2.0 L. What is the new volume if the pressure of the gas doubles and the temperature is held constant?
- A. 1.0 L
- B. 2.0 L
- C. 3.0 L
- D. 4.0 L

Answers: 1.4) C; 1.5) A; 1.6) D; 1.7) B; 1.8) A

Memphis Skyline at dusk

Tennessee
Volunteer State

>CLE 3202.1.9 Apply the Laws of Conservation of Mass/Energy to balance chemical equations.

What's it mean?
Explain how a balanced chemical equation, in which the numbers and kinds of atoms are the same on the left side as on the right side, shows that neither mass nor energy can be made or destroyed. Go to Chapter 7, Chemical Reactions, for help.

Review Question In hydrogen fuel cells, a catalyzed reaction between hydrogen and oxygen gases forms water. The diagrams below show models of the chemicals involved in this process. Use these diagrams to answer the following question.

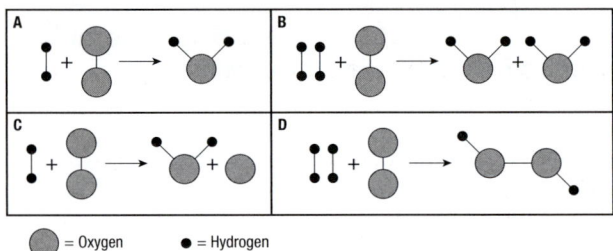

Which of the diagrams represents the balanced equation for the reaction of hydrogen gas with oxygen gas to form water?
- A. A
- B. B
- C. C
- D. D

Rural Tennessee

Unpacking Physical Science Standards

> **CLE 3202.1.10** Distinguish among acids, bases, and neutral substances.

What's it mean?
Tell whether a compound is an acid, a base, or neither. Go to Chapter 9, Acids, Bases, and Salts, for help.

Review Question You think that a substance is neutral. What pH value would you expect this substance to have?
- A. 3
- B. 5
- C. 7
- D. 9

Standard 2 - Energy

Conceptual Strand 2
Various forms of energy are constantly being transformed into other types without any net loss of energy from the system.

Guiding Question 2
What basic energy related ideas are essential for understanding the dependency of the natural and man-made worlds on energy?

> **CLE 3202.2.1** Investigate the properties and behaviors of mechanical and electromagnetic waves.

What's it mean?
Study mechanical waves, which need to travel through a material, and electromagnetic waves, which do not need to travel through a material, in terms of what they are like and what they can do. Go to Chapter 15, Waves, for help.

Review Question A sound wave is an example of
- A. an electromagnetic wave.
- B. a transverse wave.
- C. a longitudinal wave.
- D. a surface wave.

Answers: 1.9) B; 1.10) C; 2.1) C

Highway to Nashville

Tennessee
Volunteer State

>CLE 3202.2.2 Explore and explain the nature of sound and light energy.

What's it mean?
Study what sound energy and light energy are like and describe each kind of energy. Go to Chapter 16, Sound and Light, for help.

Review Question Sound waves travel faster through liquid water than through air because
- A. water is hotter than air.
- B. water is less dense than air.
- C. the particles in the liquid vibrate more than the particles in a gas.
- D. the particles of the liquid transfer energy better than the particles in a gas.

>CLE 3202.2.3 Examine the applications and effects of heat energy.

What's it mean?
Study how heat energy is used and how materials change when they absorb or give off heat energy. Go to Chapter 14, Heat and Temperature, for help.

Review Question A mercury thermometer measures temperature based on the height of a column of mercury inside a glass tube. Which of the following statements correctly describes how the thermometer works?
- A. As the thermometer gets hotter, the glass absorbs heat, contracts, and squeezes the mercury higher in the column.
- B. As the thermometer gets hotter, the mercury absorbs heat, expands, and the column gets higher.
- C. As the thermometer gets colder, the glass gives off energy, contracts, and squeezes the mercury higher in the column.
- D. As the thermometer gets colder, the mercury gives off energy, expands, and the column gets higher.

Tennessee farmland

Unpacking Physical Science Standards

>CLE 3202.2.4 Probe the fundamental principles and applications of electricity.

What's it mean?
Explore electricity based on what it is, how it works, and how it is used. Go to Chapter 17, Electricity, for help.

Review Question The schematic diagram below depicts an electric circuit. Use this schematic to answer the following question.

LIGHT BULB CIRCUIT

No current could exist in the circuit if which bulb burned out?
- A. bulb A
- B. bulb B
- C. bulb C
- D. bulb D

>CLE 3202.2.5 Distinguish between nuclear fission and nuclear fusion.

What's it mean?
Describe the differences between nuclear fission, in which the nuclei of atoms split, and nuclear fusion, in which the nuclei of atoms join together. Go to Chapter 10, Nuclear Changes, for help.

Review Question Which of the following is a correct statement that describes the generation of energy using nuclear changes?
- A. Nuclear fission uses hydrogen as fuel.
- B. The fuel for nuclear fusion is rare.
- C. Nuclear fusion generates more radioactive waste than nuclear fission does.
- D. Nuclear fission is currently used to generate electrical energy.

>CLE 3202.2.6 Investigate the Law of Conservation of Energy.

What's it mean?
Explore the fact that energy cannot be created or destroyed, but it can change form. Go to Chapter 13, Work and Energy, for help.

Review Question Which of these statements describes the law of conservation of energy?
- A. No machine is 100% efficient.
- B. Energy is neither created nor destroyed.
- C. The energy resources of Earth are limited.
- D. The energy of a system is always decreasing.

Standard 3 – Motion

Conceptual Strand 3
Objects move in ways that can be observed, described, predicted, and measured.

Guiding Question 3
What causes objects to move differently under different circumstances?

>CLE 3202.3.1 Investigate the relationships among speed, position, time, velocity, and acceleration.

What's it mean?
Explore how speed, position, time, velocity, and acceleration are related to one another. Go to Chapter 11, Motion, for help.

Review Question If you jog for 1 h and travel 10 km, 10 km/h describes your
- A. velocity.
- B. average speed.
- C. displacement.
- D. acceleration.

Answers: 2.2) D; 2.3) B; 2.4) A; 2.5) D; 2.6) B; 3.1) B

Tennessee
Volunteer State

Chattanooga architecture

>CLE 3202.3.2 Investigate and apply Newton's three laws of motion.

What's it mean?
Explore the three laws that help to describe motion and use them to help explain the motion of objects. Go to Chapter 12, Forces, for help.

Review Question Based on Newton's first law of motion, balanced forces acting on an object in motion will cause the object to
- A. come to rest.
- B. speed up.
- C. maintain its motion.
- D. change direction.

>CLE 3202.3.3 Examine the Law of Conservation of Momentum in real world situations.

What's it mean?
Look at events that happen in the real world and describe them in terms of the fact that the total momentum before and after a collision must be the same. Go to Chapter 12, Forces, for help.

Review Question Railroad car A is heading east at 5.0 m/s when it hits and joins to railroad car B which was at rest on the track. If the masses of the railroad cars are the same, which statement best describes the ideal motion of the cars after the collision?
- A. Car A will come to rest, and car B will move east at 5.0 m/s.
- B. Car A will move east at 5.0 m/s, and car B will move east at 5.0 m/s.
- C. Car A will move west at 2.5 m/s, and car B will move east at 2.5 m/s.
- D. Car A will move east at 2.5 m/s, and car B will move east at 2.5 m/s.

Unpacking Physical Science Standards

Standard 4 – Forces in Nature

Conceptual Strand 4
Everything in the universe exerts a gravitational force on everything else; there is interplay between magnetic fields and electrical currents.

Guiding Question 4
What are the scientific principles that explain gravity and electromagnetism?

>CLE 3202.4.1 Explore the difference between mass and weight.

What's it mean?
Study the difference between mass, which is a measure of how much matter is in an object, and weight, which is a measure of the gravitational force exerted on the object. Go to Chapter 12, Forces, for help.

Review Question Which statement best describes what happens to the mass and weight of an object when it is taken from Earth and is placed on the moon?
- A. The object's mass increases; the object's weight stays the same.
- B. The object's mass stays the same; the object's weight decreases.
- C. The object's mass stays the same; the object's weight stays the same.
- D. The object's mass decreases; the object's weight decreases.

Memphis

Answers: 3.2) C; 3.3) A; 4.1) B

Tennessee
Volunteer State

>CLE 3202.4.2 Relate gravitational force to mass.

What's it mean?
Describe how the force that objects exert on one another due to gravity is based on the masses of the objects. Go to Chapter 12, Forces, for help.

Review Question Gravitational force between two masses _____ as the masses increase and rapidly _____ as the distance between the masses increases.
- A. increases, increases
- B. decreases, decreases
- C. decreases, increases
- D. increases, decreases

>CLE 3202.4.3 Demonstrate the relationships among work, power, and machines.

What's it mean?
Show how machines, such as levers and pulleys, help to make work easier and how power is a measure of how fast work is done. Go to Chapter 13, Work and Energy, for help.

Review Question A machine cannot
- A. change the direction of a force.
- B. multiply or increase a force.
- C. redistribute work.
- D. increase the total amount of work done.

Discipline: Earth Science

Standard 1 – The Universe

Conceptual Strand 1
The cosmos is vast and explored well enough to know its basic structure and operational principles.

Guiding Question 1
What big ideas guide human understanding about the origin and structure of the universe, Earth's place in the cosmos, and observable motions and patterns in the sky?

>CLE 3204.1.1 Explore theories for the origin and evolution of the universe.

What's it mean?
Look at different ideas that explain how the universe began and how it changes. Go to Chapter 20, The Universe, for help.

Review Question Which of the following is a possible age of the universe, according to the big bang theory?
- A. 4.6 million years
- B. 13.7 million years
- C. 4.6 billion years
- D. 13.7 billion years

Memphis skyline

Unpacking Physical Science Standards

> **CLE 3204.1.2** Examine the components of the solar system.

What's it mean?
Describe the different parts that make up the solar system, including the sun, planets, comets, and asteroids. Go to Chapter 19, The Solar System, for help.

Review Question Between the orbits of Mars and Jupiter is an orbital ring consisting of what?
- A. asteroids
- B. comets
- C. meteors
- D. nebulae

> **CLE 3204.1.3** Explore the sun, earth, and moon relationships and their gravitational effects.

What's it mean?
Describe events, including seasons, eclipses, and tides, based on the positions, motions, and forces due to gravity of the sun, Earth, and the moon. Go to Chapter 19, The Solar System, for help.

Review Question The graphic below shows the positions of Earth, the sun, and the moon during two eclipses. Use the graphic to answer the following question. (Diagrams are not to scale.)

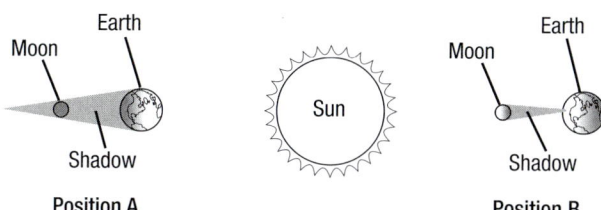

Which statement correctly identifies the eclipse and the phase of the moon during that eclipse?
- A. Position A shows a solar eclipse when the moon is in first quarter.
- B. Position A shows a lunar eclipse when the moon is in third quarter.
- C. Position B shows a solar eclipse when the moon is new.
- D. Position B shows a lunar eclipse when the moon is full.

Answers: 4.2) D; 4.3) D; 1.1) D; 1.2) A; 1.3) C

Tennessee
Volunteer State

Great Smoky Mountains National Park

> **CLE 3204.1.4** Investigate the history of space exploration.

What's it mean?
Describe how people have studied space during different periods of history and how their understanding of space has changed as a result. Go to Chapter 19, The Solar System, for help.

Review Question Which statement best describes the current view of our solar system?
- A. Earth and the planets move around the sun in elliptical orbits.
- B. Earth spins on its axis while the moon and the sun are motionless.
- C. The planets move around the sun in circular orbits.
- D. The sun, the moon, and the planets move around Earth.

Standard 2 – Energy in the Earth System

Conceptual Strand
Energy cycles drive the earth system.

Guiding Question
What are the scientific explanations for how energy cycles through the earth system?

> **CLE 3204.2.1** Investigate the principal sources of energy.

What's it mean?
Describe what the main sources of energy are. Go to Chapter 23, Using Natural Resources, for help.

Review Question Fossil fuels consist mostly of what elements?
- A. carbon and hydrogen
- B. carbon and calcium
- C. calcium and hydrogen
- D. potassium and chlorine

Unpacking Physical Science Standards

>CLE 3204.2.2 Explore pathways of energy transfer.

What's it mean?
Trace the paths of how energy moves and changes from one form of energy into another. Go to Chapter 23, Using Natural Resources, for help.

Review Question What energy source results when energy from the sun is stored in plant and animal matter which is prevented from decomposing in air?
- A. hydroelectric power
- B. geothermal energy
- C. nuclear energy
- D. fossil fuels

>CLE 3204.2.3 Evaluate alternative energy sources.

What's it mean?
Compare alternative sources of energy. Go to Chapter 23, Using Natural Resources, for help.

Review Question Changes to the centers of atoms are the basis of an alternative source of energy called
- A. fossil fuels.
- B. hydroelectric power.
- C. geothermal energy.
- D. nuclear energy.

Answers: 1.4) A; 2.1) A; 2.2) D; 2.3) D

Nashville skyline

Tennessee
Volunteer State

Standard 3 – Cycles in the Earth System

Conceptual Strand
The earth system consists of interrelated subcycles that act over extended periods of geologic time.

Guiding Question
What are the subcycles of the earth system and how do they interact?

>CLE 3204.3.1 Explain the components of the tectonic cycle.

What's it mean?
Explain what causes the motion of large parts of Earth's surface and what happens as a result of that motion. Go to Chapter 21, Planet Earth, for help.

Review Question Which geologic feature is least associated with places where tectonic plates meet?
   A. rifts
   B. plains
   C. volcanoes
   D. mountains

>CLE 3204.3.2 Investigate the rock cycle.

What's it mean?
Explore the three main types of rock and how rock changes from one type to another. Go to Chapter 21, Planet Earth, for help.

Review Question High pressure and high temperature can cause igneous rocks to change and become
   A. sedimentary rocks.
   B. physically weathered.
   C. metamorphic rocks.
   D. chemically weathered.

>CLE 3204.3.3 Analyze the hydrologic cycle.

What's it mean?
Explain how water changes near Earth's surface and trace the steps of the water cycle. Go to Chapter 22, The Atmosphere, for help.

Review Question Clouds form when water vapor in the air condenses as
   A. the air is heated.
   B. the air is cooled.
   C. snow falls.
   D. snow forms.

Tennessee river

Unpacking Physical Science Standards

>CLE 3204.3.4 Interpret data related to the atmospheric cycle.

What's it mean?
Collect and use information about conditions in the atmosphere to make an informed prediction about what is likely to happen. Go to Chapter 22, The Atmosphere, for help.

Review Question Interpret the data shown in the weather map below to answer the following question.

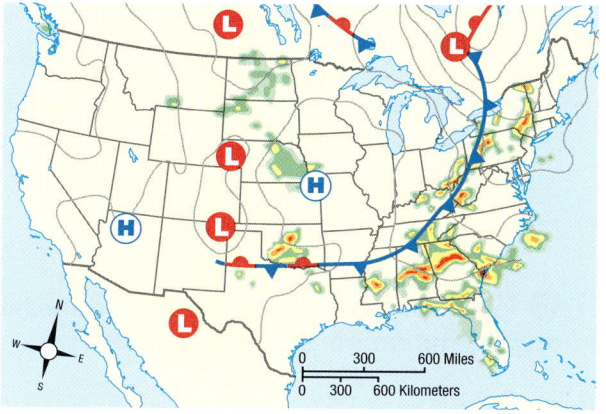

Which of the following statements best describes the weather that people in Tennessee can expect?
- A. A warm front is moving through, so they can expect high-level clouds followed by lower-level clouds and perhaps a day or two of steady rain.
- B. A warm front is moving through, so they can expect high winds, thunderstorms, and perhaps even tornadoes.
- C. A cold front is moving through, so they can expect high-level clouds followed by lower-level clouds and perhaps a day or two of steady rain.
- D. A cold front is moving through, so they can expect high winds, thunderstorms, and perhaps even tornadoes.

Answers: 3.1) B; 3.2) C; 3.3) B; 3.4) D

TN27

Tennessee
Volunteer State

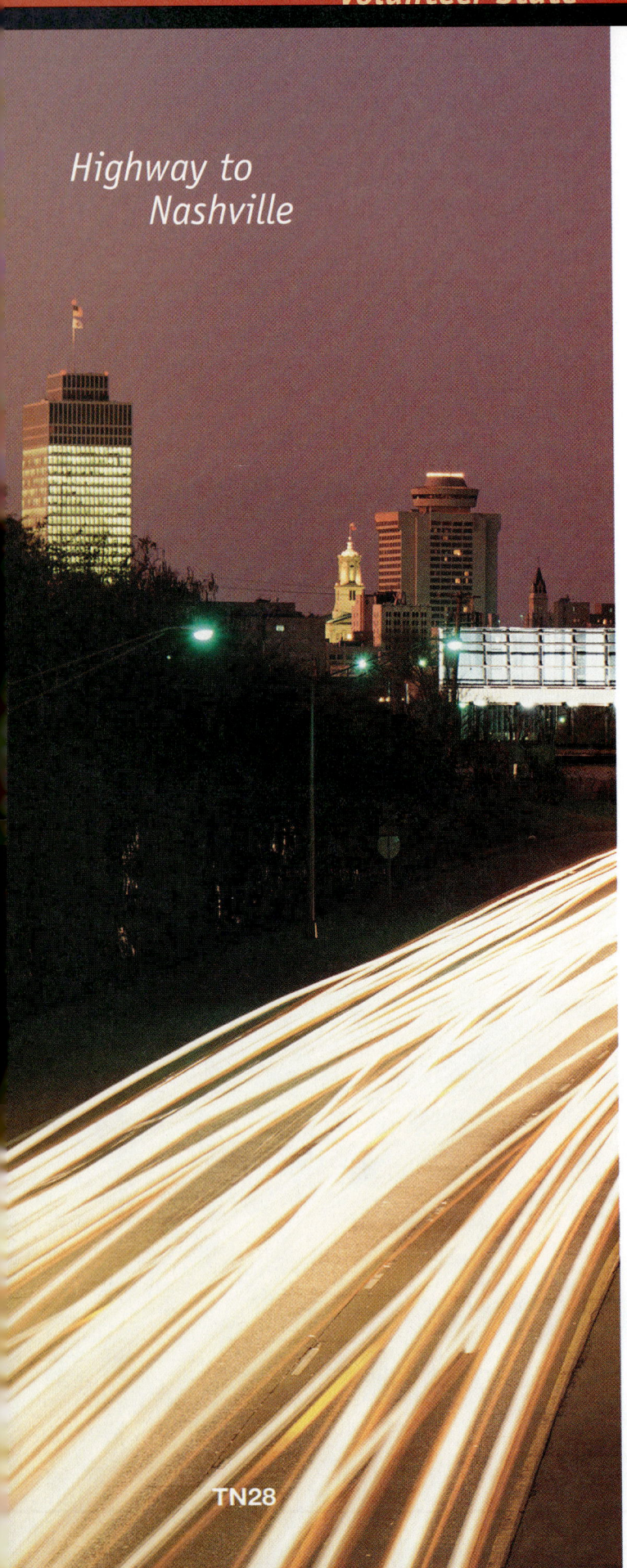

Highway to Nashville

>CLE 3204.3.5 Differentiate among the geochemical cycles.

What's it mean?
Describe the steps that different substances go through during geochemical cycles, including the oxygen–carbon dioxide cycle, the nitrogen cycle, and the carbon cycle. Go to Chapter 22, The Atmosphere, for help.

Review Question Which of the following statements describes part of the oxygen–carbon dioxide cycle?
- A. Plants release carbon dioxide that animals need for respiration.
- B. Animals take in oxygen by eating plants.
- C. Plants release oxygen during photosynthesis.
- D. Animals release oxygen that plants need for photosynthesis.

>CLE 3204.3.6 Evaluate the impact of living organisms on earth system cycles.

What's it mean?
Consider how living things affect cycles, such as the water cycle or the carbon cycle, on Earth. Go to Chapter 22, The Atmosphere, for help.

Review Question Without the evolution of photosynthesis, which gas would still be missing from Earth's atmosphere?
- A. oxygen, O_2
- B. nitrogen, N_2
- C. methane, CH_4
- D. carbon dioxide, CO_2

>CLE 3204.3.7 Investigate how maps can be used to interpret changes in the earth system.

What's it mean?
Use maps to study changes on Earth and to make reasonable explanations for those changes. Go to Chapter 21, Planet Earth, for help.

Unpacking Physical Science Standards

Review Question The map below shows Earth approximately 18,000 years ago. Use the map to answer the following question.

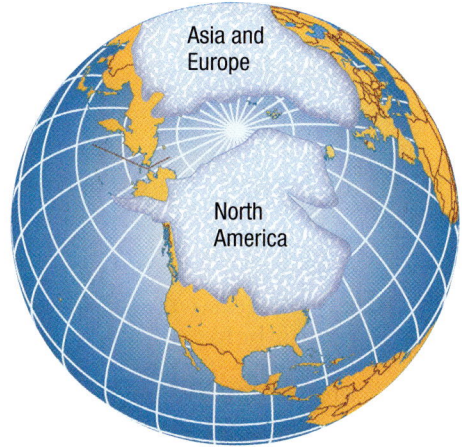

Which of the following is a reasonable interpretation of the change that has happened since the time represented by the map?
  A. The amount of land covered by glaciers has decreased.
  B. More water has been locked up in ice.
  C. The average temperature in North America has decreased.
  D. North America drifted south away from the glaciers.

>CLE 3204.3.8 Relate earth system cycles to past and current patterns of global change.

What's it mean?
Describe how patterns of changes that are happening in the world now and that happened in the past are connected to cycles on Earth. Go to Chapter 22, The Atmosphere, for help.

Review Question Which statement describes the effect that the burning of fossil fuels has on an Earth system cycle?
  A. Less water is available for the water cycle.
  B. More carbon dioxide enters the oxygen–carbon dioxide cycle.
  C. More nitrogen enters the nitrogen cycle.
  D. Less carbon is available for the carbon cycle.

Smoky Mountains

Answers: 3.5) C; 3.6) A; 3.7) A; 3.8) B

Tennessee
Volunteer State

Standard 4 – Geologic History

Conceptual Strand
The earth has changed over a long period and global change is a continuation of this evolutionary process.

Guiding Question
What is the scientific evidence for the evolution of earth and life on earth?

>CLE 3204.4.1 Interpret the nature of geologic time.

What's it mean?
Describe the history of Earth, known as geologic time, using laws that describe how events happened in the past and using different methods to tell the age of past events. Go to Chapter 21, Planet Earth, for help.

Review Question While examining a road cut, you find a fossil clam in a layer of limestone 1 m above the road. You find a fossil oyster in a layer of sandstone 2 m above the clam. Which statement best describes their relative ages?

A. The clam died after the oyster died.
B. The sandstone was deposited after the clam died.
C. The oyster died before the limestone formed.
D. The limestone was deposited after the sandstone formed.

>CLE 3204.4.2 Investigate the evolution of the earth.

What's it mean?
Describe how Earth has changed over time. Go to Chapter 21, Planet Earth, for help.

Review Question Which statement about the evolution of Earth's atmosphere is correct?
A. The first atmosphere was made up mostly of nitrogen and oxygen.
B. High oxygen levels existed before photosynthesis began.
C. The ozone layer formed from oxygen gas in the atmosphere.
D. The level of carbon dioxide is higher now than in the early atmosphere.

Great Smoky Mountains National Park

> ⋯ **Unpacking Physical Science Standards**

>CLE 3204.4.3 Interpret the fossil record for evidence of biological evolution.

What's it mean?
Use the remains of living things that are preserved in rocks as support for the idea that living things change over time. Go to Chapter 21, Planet Earth, for help.

Review Question Which statement best describes the use of the fossil record as evidence of the evolution of living things?
- A. Fossils of a particular clam can be found in only one rock layer.
- B. Fossils of mammals and fossils of trilobites are never found together within a single rock layer.
- C. Fossils of the bones of a fish match the bones of a living example of the fish.
- D. Fossils of leg bones of similar organisms found in rock layers from different times show a gradual elongation of the bones.

>CLE 3204.4.4 Demonstrate the impact of environmental change on the origin and extinction of plant and animal species.

What's it mean?
Show how different kinds of plants and animals can begin or can die off as a result of changes to environments. Go to Chapter 23, Using Natural Resources, for help.

Review Question A rare kind of salamander lives only in a small network of caves which are located on a ranch just outside of a small town. Which of the following environmental changes is likely to cause the extinction of this salamander species?
- A. A brush fire burns the pasture near the cave mouth.
- B. A severe draught drains the cave system of water.
- C. Erosion opens a passage to an additional cave.
- D. A rock slide divides the population into two groups.

Answers: 4.1) B; 4.2) C; 4.3) D; 4.4) B

Tennessee
Volunteer State

Hernando Desoto Bridge

TN32

HOLT Science Spectrum®

Physical Science

with **Earth** and **Space Science**

HOLT, RINEHART AND WINSTON
A Harcourt Education Company
Orlando • **Austin** • New York • San Diego • London

About the cover: The cover image shows a racing bicycle's back wheel in motion. The chain running through the gear assembly (derailleur) is labeled with the basic equation for speed. By convention, speed is indicated by the letter "v" (velocity) even when the only component being considered is the magnitude.

Copyright © 2008 by Holt, Rinehart and Winston

All rights reserved. No part of this publication may be reproduced or transmitted in any form or by any means, electronic or mechanical, including photocopy, recording, or any information storage and retrieval system, without permission in writing from the publisher.

Requests for permission to make copies of any part of the work should be mailed to the following address: Permissions Department, Holt, Rinehart and Winston, 10801 N. MoPac Expressway, Building 3, Austin, Texas 78759.

Original edition ©1995, 1996 by Ken Dobson, John Holman, and Michael Roberts.

This adaptation of Nelson Balanced Science and Nelson Science is published by arrangement with Thomas Nelson & Sons Ltd., Walton-on-Thames, UK.

HOLT and the "**Owl Design**" are trademarks licensed to Holt, Rinehart and Winston, registered in the United States of America and/or other jurisdictions.

The trademark **SCIENCE SPECTRUM**® is used under license from Science Spectrum, Inc., Lubbock, Texas.

SCILINKS is a registered trademark owned and provided by the National Science Teachers Association. All rights reserved.

Printed in the United States of America

> If you have received these materials as examination copies free of charge, Holt, Rinehart and Winston retains title to the materials and they may not be resold. Resale of examination copies is strictly prohibited.

> Possession of this publication in print format does not entitle users to convert this publication, or any portion of it, into electronic format.

ISBN-13: 978-0-03-067213-2

ISBN-10: 0-03-067213-9

6 032 10 09 08

Acknowledgments

Authors

Ken Dobson, MSc FInstP
Former Head of Science
Thurston Upper School
Suffolk, United Kingdom

Professor John Holman
Director, The National Science Learning Centre
University of York
York, United Kingdom

Michael Roberts, Ph.D.
Science Writer
Bristol, United Kingdom

Contributing Authors

Robert Davisson
Science Writer
Albuquerque, New Mexico

Mary Kay Hemenway, Ph.D.
Research Associate and Senior Lecturer
Department of Astronomy
The University of Texas at Austin
Austin, Texas

Doug Jenkins
Adjunct Professor
Department of Physics and Astronomy
Western Kentucky University
Bowling Green, Kentucky

William G. Lamb, Ph.D.
Winningstad Chair in the Physical Sciences
Oregon Episcopal School
Portland, Oregon

Lab Writer/Reviewer

Marlin L. Simon, Ph.D
Associate Professor of Physics
Department of Physics
Auburn University
Auburn, Alabama

Reviewers

G. Fritz Benedict, Ph.D.
Senior Research Scientist
McDonald Observatory
The University of Texas at Austin
Austin, Texas

Thomas J. M. Connolly, Ph.D.
Assistant Professor
Department of Mechanical Engineering
The University of Texas at San Antonio
San Antonio, Texas

Glenn Dolphin
Earth Science Teacher
Union-Endicott High School
Endicott, New York

Hima S. Joshi, Ph.D.
Assistant Professor
Department of Chemistry and Biochemistry
California Polytechnic State University, San Luis Obispo
San Luis Obispo, California

Joel S. Leventhal, Ph.D.
Research Scientist Emeritus
U.S. Geological Survey
Denver, Colorado

Sten Odenwald, Ph.D.
Astronomer
Department of Space Physics and Astronomy
NASA-QSS Corporation
Greenbelt, Maryland

James L. Pazun, Ph.D.
Professor and Chair, Chemistry and Physics
Department of Chemistry and Physics
Pfeiffer University
Charlotte, North Carolina

H. Michael Sommermann, Ph.D.
Professor
Department of Physics
Westmont College
Santa Barbara, California

Larry Stookey, P.E.
Physics and Chemistry Teacher
Antigo High School
Antigo, Wisconsin

Raymond Turner, Ph.D.
Professor Emeritus of Physics
Department of Physics and Astronomy
Clemson University
Clemson, South Carolina

Reading Specialist

Robin Scarcella, Ph.D.
Director and Professor, Academic English and English as a Second Language
University of California, Irvine
Irvine, California

Inclusion Specialist

Joan Altobelli
Special Education Director
Austin Independent School District
Austin, Texas

Contents in Brief

Safety in the Laboratory ... xviii
How to Use Your Textbook ... xxii
Chapter 1: Introduction to Science ... 2

Chemistry ... 41

Chapter 2: Matter ... 42
Chapter 3: States of Matter ... 74
Chapter 4: Atoms ... 110
Chapter 5: The Periodic Table ... 142
Chapter 6: The Structure of Matter ... 174
Chapter 7: Chemical Reactions ... 216
Chapter 8: Solutions ... 256
Chapter 9: Acids, Bases, and Salts ... 290
Chapter 10: Nuclear Changes ... 324

Physics ... 361

Chapter 11: Motion ... 362
Chapter 12: Forces ... 394
Chapter 13: Work and Energy ... 428
Chapter 14: Heat and Temperature ... 470
Chapter 15: Waves ... 502
Chapter 16: Sound and Light ... 540
Chapter 17: Electricity ... 582
Chapter 18: Magnetism ... 616

Earth and Space Science ... 649

Chapter 19: The Solar System ... 650
Chapter 20: The Universe ... 690
Chapter 21: Planet Earth ... 726
Chapter 22: The Atmosphere ... 770
Chapter 23: Using Natural Resources ... 804

Reference Section ... 841

Appendix A: Reading ToolBox ... 842
Appendix B: Science Skills ... 862
Appendix C: Useful Data ... 880
Appendix D: Selected Math Answers ... 887
Appendix E: Answers to Reading Checks ... 890
Glossary ... 898
Index ... 919

Contents

Chapter 1: Introduction to Science — 2

- **Section 1:** The Nature of Science — 5
- **Section 2:** The Way Science Works — 14
- **Section 3:** Organizing Data — 22
- **Standardized Test Prep** — 38

Why It Matters
- Millennium Bridge — 11
- Leonardo da Vinci — 13
- How Was the Gateway Arch Built? — 29

Labs
- Measuring Area — 3
- Making Observations — 16
- Precision Vs. Accuracy — 27
- Making Measurements — 30

Chemistry — 41

Chapter 2: Matter — 42

- **Section 1:** Classifying Matter — 45
- **Section 2:** Properties of Matter — 51
- **Section 3:** Changes of Matter — 59
- **Standardized Test Prep** — 72

Why It Matters
- Aerogel — 53
- Identifying Mystery Substances — 57
- How Is Glass Made? — 65

Labs
- Finding Density — 43
- Mystery Mixture — 48
- Density of Water — 55
- Reactivity — 58
- Can You Separate a Mixture? — 63
- Physical Properties of Metals — 66

Chapter 3: States of Matter — 74

- **Section 1:** Matter and Energy — 77
- **Section 2:** Changes of State — 84
- **Section 3:** Fluids — 89
- **Section 4:** Behavior of Gases — 96
- **Standardized Test Prep** — 108

Why It Matters
- Plasma — 82
- Why Do People Sweat? — 85
- How Do Submarines Work? — 95

Labs
- Changes in Density — 75
- Hot or Cold? — 81
- Boiling Water — 86
- Density and Shape — 91
- How Are Temperature and Volume Related? — 99
- Boiling and Freezing — 102

Chapter 4: Atoms — 110
Section 1: The Development of Atomic Theory — 113
Section 2: The Structure of Atoms — 119
Section 3: Modern Atomic Theory — 128
Standardized Test Prep — 140

Why It Matters
- How Do Televisions Work? — 116
- Nuclear Medicine — 123
- How Do Fireworks Work? — 133

Labs
- Making a Model — 111
- Evidence for Atoms — 114
- Modeling Isotopes — 122
- Electron Levels — 131
- Building Isotopes — 134

Chapter 5: The Periodic Table — 142
Section 1: Organizing the Elements — 145
Section 2: Exploring the Periodic Table — 151
Section 3: Families of Elements — 156
Standardized Test Prep — 172

Why It Matters
- Mercury in Fish — 147
- How Are Silicon Chips Made? — 165

Labs
- A Periodic Table — 143
- Elements in Food — 158
- The Cost of Metals — 160
- Exploring Periodic Trends — 166

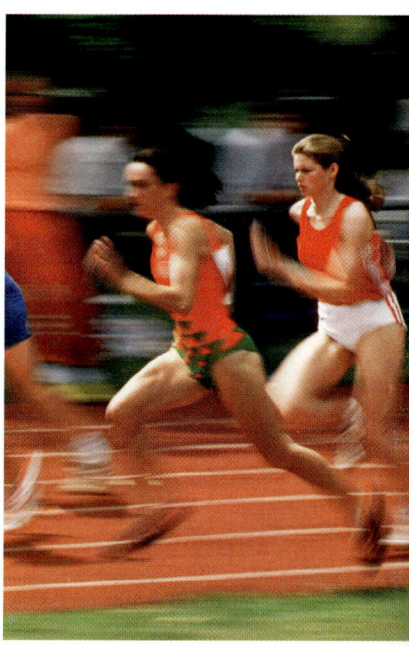

Chapter 6: The Structure of Matter — 174
Section 1: Compounds and Molecules — 177
Section 2: Ionic and Covalent Bonding — 183
Section 3: Compound Names and Formulas — 191
Section 4: Organic and Biochemical Compounds — 197
Standardized Test Prep — 212

Why It Matters
- How Is Clay Molded? — 179
- How Do Gas Grills Work? — 198
- DNA Fingerprinting — 205
- Careers Using Chemistry — 214

Labs
- Melting Sugar and Salt — 175
- A Close-Packed Structure — 188
- Polymer Memory — 201
- What Properties Does a Polymer Have? — 203
- Comparing Polymers — 206

Chapter 7: Chemical Reactions — 216
Section 1: The Nature of Chemical Reactions — 219
Section 2: Chemical Equations — 225
Section 3: Reaction Types — 230
Section 4: Reaction Rates and Equilibrium — 238
Standardized Test Prep — 254

Why It Matters
- Bioluminescence — 223
- How Are Fires Extinguished? — 232
- Ozone — 236
- What Kinds of Chemical Reactions Happen in the Human Body? — 242

Labs
- Matter and Chemical Reactions — 217
- An Endothermic Reaction — 222
- Balancing Chemical Equations — 228
- Determining the Products of a Reaction — 235
- What Affects the Rates of Chemical Reactions? — 239
- Catalysts in Action — 241
- Rate and Temperature of a Chemical Reaction — 248

Chapter 8: Solutions — 256
Section 1: Solutions and Other Mixtures — 259
Section 2: How Substances Dissolve — 267
Section 3: Solubility and Concentration — 276
Standardized Test Prep — 288

Why It Matters
- How Is Crude Oil Turned into Gasoline? — 265
- Blood Substitutes — 274
- Fluoride in Water — 281

Labs
- Dissolving Salt and Sugar — 257
- Making Butter — 262
- What Will Dissolve a Nonpolar Substance? — 270
- How Temperature Affects Gas Solubility — 282

Chapter 9: Acids, Bases, and Salts — 290
Section 1: Acids, Bases, and pH — 293
Section 2: Reactions of Acids with Bases — 302
Section 3: Acids, Bases, and Salts in the Home — 307
Standardized Test Prep — 320

Why It Matters
- Acid Rain — 301
- How Does Soap Remove Grease? — 308
- Chemistry Connections — 322

Labs
- Acid-Base Reaction — 291
- Which Household Products Are Acidic, and Which Are Basic? — 296
- Detergents — 309
- What Does an Antacid Do? — 312
- Quantities in an Acid-Base Reaction — 314

Chapter 10: Nuclear Changes 324
Section 1: What Is Radioactivity? 327
Section 2: Nuclear Fission and Fusion 337
Section 3: Nuclear Radiation Today 344
Standardized Test Prep 358

Why It Matters

Discovering Nuclear Radiation 332
The Power of Fission 343
How Do PET Scans Work? 347

Labs

Radiation and Film 325
Modeling Decay and Half-Life 335
Modeling Chain Reactions 341
Simulating Nuclear Decay
  Reactions 352

Physics 361

Chapter 11: Motion 362
Section 1: Measuring Motion 365
Section 2: Acceleration 372
Section 3: Motion and Force 380
Standardized Test Prep 392

Why It Matters

Accident Reconstruction 378
How Do Brakes Work? 383

Labs

Motion on Motion 363
Measuring Speed 368
Friction 384
Static, Sliding, and Rolling
  Friction 386

Chapter 12: Forces 394
Section 1: Newton's First and Second Laws 397
Section 2: Gravity 403
Section 3: Newton's Third Law 412
Standardized Test Prep 424

Why It Matters

How Do Air Bags Work? 399
Black Holes 411
How Do Rockets Work? 416
Careers Using Physics 426

Labs

Earth's Attraction 395
Newton's First Law 398
Action and Reaction Forces 414
Building a Catapult 418

Chapter 13: Work and Energy — 428

- **Section 1: Work, Power, and Machines** — 431
- **Section 2: Simple Machines** — 438
- **Section 3: What Is Energy?** — 444
- **Section 4: Conservation of Energy** — 453
- **Standardized Test Prep** — 468

Why It Matters
- What Machines Are Used on Bicycles? — 435
- Energy Stored in Plants — 451
- How Do Engineers Use Conservation of Energy? — 458

Labs
- Kitchen Tools — 429
- Power Output — 433
- A Simple Inclined Plane — 441
- Energy Transfer — 454
- Is Energy Conserved by a Pendulum? — 457
- Energy of a Rolling Ball — 462

Chapter 14: Heat and Temperature — 470

- **Section 1: Temperature** — 473
- **Section 2: Energy Transfer** — 480
- **Section 3: Using Heat** — 490
- **Standardized Test Prep** — 500

Why It Matters
- Why Does the Wind Blow? — 483
- How Are Homes Heated and Cooled? — 488

Labs
- Color and Temperature — 471
- Sensing Hot and Cold — 474
- Temperature and Energy — 478
- Absorption of Radiated Heat — 482
- Conductors and Insulators — 484
- Conduction of Heat by Metals — 494

Chapter 15: Waves — 502

- **Section 1: Types of Waves** — 505
- **Section 2: Characteristics of Waves** — 514
- **Section 3: Wave Interactions** — 524
- **Standardized Test Prep** — 536

Why It Matters
- How Does Mountain-Bike Suspension Work? — 510
- How Are Good Surfing Waves Formed? — 517
- Physics Connections — 538

Labs
- Making Waves — 503
- Particle Motion in a Wave — 509
- Polarization — 511
- Wave Speed — 520
- Transverse Waves — 530

Chapter 16: Sound and Light 540

Section 1: Sound 543
Section 2: The Nature of Light 552
Section 3: Reflection and Color 560
Section 4: Refraction, Lenses, and Prisms 566
Standardized Test Prep 580

Why It Matters
What Are Sonograms? 550
How Do Cell Phones Work? 559
Detecting Counterfeit Money 572

Labs
Colors in White Light 541
Sound in Different Mediums 544
Frequency and Pitch 547
How Can You Amplify the
    Sound of a Tuning Fork? 548
Echoes and Distance 551
Curved Mirror 563
Filtering Light 564
Water Prism 570
Lenses and Images 574

Chapter 17: Electricity 582

Section 1: Electric Charge and Force 585
Section 2: Current 593
Section 3: Circuits 600
Standardized Test Prep 614

Why It Matters
Benjamin Franklin 587
Miniaturization of Circuits 604

Labs
A Simple Circuit 583
Charging Objects 590
Using a Lemon as a Cell 595
How Can Materials Be
    Classified by Resistance? 598
Constructing Electric Circuits ... 608

Chapter 18: Magnetism 616

Section 1: Magnets and Magnetic Fields 619
Section 2: Magnetism from Electric Currents 626
Section 3: Electric Currents from Magnetism 632
Standardized Test Prep 646

Why It Matters
Earth's Changing Magnetic Field 625
Airport Security 629
How Do Electric Guitars Work?   635

Labs
Magnetic Levitation 617
Magnetic Poles 621
Magnetic Field of a File Cabinet 623
Electromagnet 628
Can You Demonstrate
    Electromagnetic Induction? ... 633
Making a Better Electromagnet   640

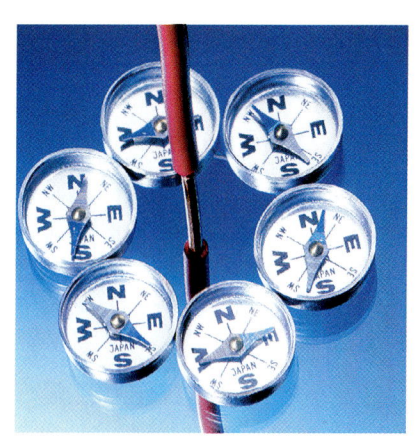

xi

Earth and Space Science

Chapter 19: The Solar System 650
- **Section 1: Sun, Earth, and Moon** 653
- **Section 2: The Inner and Outer Planets** 661
- **Section 3: Formation of the Solar System** 671
- **Standardized Test Prep** 686

Why It Matters
- A Return to the Moon 659
- Exploring Planets 665
- Where Are Earth's Craters? 677
- Careers Using Earth Science 688

Labs
- Observing Stars 651
- Modeling Eclipses 658
- Planetary Distances 668
- Estimating 4.6 Billion 672
- The Size and Power Output of the Sun 680

Chapter 20: The Universe 690
- **Section 1: The Life and Death of Stars** 693
- **Section 2: The Milky Way and Other Galaxies** 702
- **Section 3: Origin of the Universe** 708
- **Standardized Test Prep** 724

Why It Matters
- Constellations 697
- Any Aliens Out There? 706
- We're All Stars! 714

Labs
- Constellation Names 691
- Modeling Fusion 695
- An Expanding Universe Model 711
- Types of Galaxies 718

Chapter 21: Planet Earth 726
- **Section 1: Earth's Interior and Plate Tectonics** 729
- **Section 2: Earthquakes and Volcanoes** 738
- **Section 3: Minerals and Rocks** 748
- **Section 4: Weathering and Erosion** 756
- **Standardized Test Prep** 768

Why It Matters
- Volcanoes and Humans 747
- What Are Rocks Good For? 755

Labs
- Observing Changes in Rocks 727
- Convection and Plate Tectonics 733
- Tectonic-Plate Boundaries 736
- Seismic Waves 739
- Rock Formation 753
- Finding the Epicenter of an Earthquake 762

Chapter 22: The Atmosphere ... 770
Section 1: Characteristics of the Atmosphere ... 773
Section 2: Water and Wind ... 781
Section 3: Weather and Climate ... 789
Standardized Test Prep ... 802

Why It Matters

Harnessing the Wind ... 788
Surviving Natural Disasters ... 793

Labs

Making a Rainbow ... 771
The Greenhouse Effect ... 779
Measuring Rainfall ... 784
Thunder and Lightning ... 791
Effects of Temperature on the Buoyancy of Air ... 796

Chapter 23: Using Natural Resources ... 804
Section 1: Organisms and Their Environment ... 807
Section 2: Energy and Resources ... 815
Section 3: Pollution and Recycling ... 824
Standardized Test Prep ... 838

Why It Matters

A Natural Cooler ... 823
What Is Recycling? ... 830

Labs

Using Energy at Home ... 805
Why Do Seasons Occur? ... 812
Observing Air Pollution ... 827
How Can Oil Spills Be Cleaned Up? ... 829
Designing a Windmill ... 832

Reference 841

Appendix A: Reading ToolBox ... 842
Appendix B: Science Skills ... 862
Appendix C: Useful Data ... 880
Appendix D: Selected Math Answers ... 887
Appendix E: Answers to Reading Checks ... 890
Glossary ... 898
Index ... 919

Why It Matters

Have you ever wondered why you need to learn science? Check out these short, interesting articles to learn how science relates to the world around you.

Real World

How Was the Gateway Arch Built?	29
How Is Glass Made?	65
Why Do People Sweat?	85
How Do Submarines Work?	95
How Do Televisions Work?	116
How Do Fireworks Work?	133
How Are Silicon Chips Made?	165
How Is Clay Molded?	179
How Do Gas Grills Work?	198
How Are Fires Extinguished?	232
What Kinds of Chemical Reactions Happen in the Human Body?	242
How Is Crude Oil Turned into Gasoline?	265
How Does Soap Remove Grease?	308
How Do PET Scans Work?	347
How Do Brakes Work?	383
How Do Air Bags Work?	399
How Do Rockets Work?	416
What Machines Are Used on Bicycles?	435
How Do Engineers Use Conservation of Energy?	458
Why Does the Wind Blow?	483
How Are Homes Heated and Cooled?	488
How Does Mountain-Bike Suspension Work?	510
How Are Good Surfing Waves Formed?	517
What Are Sonograms?	550
How Do Cell Phones Work?	559
How Do Electric Guitars Work?	635
Where Are Earth's Craters?	677
Any Aliens Out There?	706
What Are Rocks Good For?	755
What Is Recycling?	830

Weird Science

Aerogel	53
Plasma	82
Bioluminescence	223
Blood Substitutes	274
Black Holes	411
Earth's Changing Magnetic Field	625
We're All Stars!	714

Forensics

Identifying Mystery Substances	57
DNA Fingerprinting	205
Accident Reconstruction	378
Detecting Counterfeit Money	572

Science & Society

Millennium Bridge	11
Nuclear Medicine	123
Fluoride in Water	281
The Power of Fission	343
Miniaturization of Circuits	604
Airport Security	629
A Return to the Moon	659
Constellations	697
Harnessing the Wind	788
Surviving Natural Disasters	793
A Natural Cooler	823

Eye on the Environment

Mercury in Fish	147
Ozone	236
Acid Rain	301
Energy Stored in Plants	451

Careers

Careers Using Chemistry	214
Careers Using Physics	426
Careers Using Earth Science	688

History in Science

Leonardo da Vinci	13
Chemistry Connections	322
Discovering Nuclear Radiation	332
Physics Connections	538
Benjamin Franklin	587
Exploring Planets	665
Volcanoes and Humans	747

Science Skills

Science Skills will help you succeed in your science class by allowing you to practice a variety of skills used in science.

Math Skills

Conversions Within SI	19
Writing Scientific Notation	25
Using Scientific Notation	26
Significant Figures	28
Density	54
Converting Units	68
Pascal's Principle	93
Boyle's Law	98
Converting Moles to Grams	126
Writing Ionic Formulas	193
Finding Empirical Formulas	196
Balancing Chemical Equations	227
Using Mole Ratios to Calculate Mass	250
Molarity	280
Determining pH	299
Nuclear Decay	331
Half-Life	334
Counting Nuclear Decay	354
Velocity	369
Acceleration	375
Newton's Second Law	401
Momentum	415
Rearranging Equations	420
Work	432
Power	434
Mechanical Advantage	436
Potential Energy	446
Kinetic Energy	448
Efficiency	460
Temperature-Scale Conversion	477
Specific Heat	486
Solving Problems	496
Wave Speed	519
Using Fractions	576
Resistance	597
Electric Power	606
Finding Percentages	798

Graphing Skills

Interpreting Graphs	101
Making Graphs	104
Making Pie Charts	284
Interpreting Titration Curves	304
Calculating Slope	370
Graphing Acceleration	376
Graphing Motion	388
Graphing Mechanical Energy	455
Graphing Waves	532
Making Bar Graphs	720

Scientific Methods

Forming a Hypothesis	34
Testing a Hypothesis	136
Understanding Symbols	208
Making Measurements and Observations	464
Making Predictions	642
Making Models	764

Technology Skills

Reading Web Addresses	168
Finding Reputable Sources	316
Learning Internet Terminology	610
Using Search Engines	682
Recognizing Bias	834

READING TOOLBOX

Reading a textbook is different from reading a novel. The *Reading ToolBoxes* suggest ways to help you organize the concepts in each chapter to get the most out of your reading.

Analogies	112, 584
Cause and Effect	396, 618
Classification	4, 292, 504
Comparisons	326, 472
Describing Space	692
Describing Space and Time	364
Describing Time	806
Fact, Hypothesis, or Theory?	76, 728
Finding Examples	44, 258
FoldNotes	76, 112, 176, 218, 258, 326, 364, 396, 542, 584, 618, 692, 772, 806
Frequency	176
Generalizations	144
Graphic Organizers	4, 144, 292, 430, 472, 652, 728, 806
Mnemonics	542, 652
Note Taking	44, 76, 258, 396, 504
Predictions	772
Reading Equations	218
Science Terms	4, 292, 364, 430, 692
Word Families	472, 584
Word Origins	112, 326, 652
Word Parts	44, 144, 176, 218, 504, 542, 618, 728, 772
Word Problems	430

Labs

Safety in the Laboratory xviii

Short Labs

These short *Inquiry Labs* and *QuickLabs* are designed to be done quickly during any class period (or at home!) with simple materials.

Inquiry Labs

Measuring Area	3
Finding Density	43
Can You Separate a Mixture?	63
Changes in Density	75
How Are Temperature and Volume Related?	99
Making a Model	111
A Periodic Table	143
Melting Sugar and Salt	175
What Properties Does a Polymer Have?	203
Matter and Chemical Reactions	217
Determining the Products of a Reaction	235
What Affects the Rates of Chemical Reactions?	239
Dissolving Salt and Sugar	257
What Will Dissolve a Nonpolar Substance?	270
Acid-Base Reaction	291
Which Household Products Are Acidic, and Which Are Basic?	296
What Does an Antacid Do?	312
Radiation and Film	325
Motion on Motion	363
Earth's Attraction	395
Kitchen Tools	429
Is Energy Conserved by a Pendulum?	457
Color and Temperature	471
Temperature and Energy	478
Absorption of Radiated Heat	482
Making Waves	503
Colors in White Light	541
How Can You Amplify the Sound of a Tuning Fork?	548
A Simple Circuit	583
How Can Materials Be Classified by Resistance?	598
Magnetic Levitation	617
Can You Demonstrate Electromagnetic Induction?	633
Observing Stars	651
Constellation Names	691
Observing Changes in Rocks	727
Making a Rainbow	771
Using Energy at Home	805
How Can Oil Spills Be Cleaned Up?	829

QuickLabs

Making Observations	16
Precision Vs. Accuracy	27
Mystery Mixture	48
Density of Water	55
Reactivity	58
Hot or Cold?	81
Boiling Water	86
Density and Shape	91
Evidence for Atoms	114
Modeling Isotopes	122
Electron Levels	131
Elements in Food	158
The Cost of Metals	160
A Close-Packed Structure	188
Polymer Memory	201
An Endothermic Reaction	222
Balancing Chemical Equations	228
Catalysts in Action	241
Making Butter	262
Detergents	309
Modeling Decay and Half-Life	335
Modeling Chain Reactions	341
Measuring Speed	368
Friction	384
Newton's First Law	398
Action and Reaction Forces	414
Power Output	433
A Simple Inclined Plane	441
Energy Transfer	454
Sensing Hot and Cold	474
Conductors and Insulators	484
Particle Motion in a Wave	509
Polarization	511
Wave Speed	520
Sound in Different Mediums	544

Frequency and Pitch	**547**
Echoes and Distance	**551**
Curved Mirror	**563**
Filtering Light	**564**
Water Prism	**570**
Charging Objects	**590**
Using a Lemon as a Cell	**595**
Magnetic Poles	**621**
Magnetic Field of a File Cabinet	**623**
Electromagnet	**628**
Modeling Eclipses	**658**
Planetary Distances	**668**
Estimating 4.6 Billion	**672**
Modeling Fusion	**695**
An Expanding Universe Model	**711**
Convection and Plate Tectonics	**733**
Tectonic-Plate Boundaries	**736**
Seismic Waves	**739**
Rock Formation	**753**
The Greenhouse Effect	**779**
Measuring Rainfall	**784**
Thunder and Lightning	**791**
Why Do Seasons Occur?	**812**
Observing Air Pollution	**827**

Chapter Labs

Each chapter includes an in-depth, hands-on lab that lets you experience science first-hand.

Skills Practice Labs

Chapter 1: Making Measurements	**30**
Chapter 4: Building Isotopes	**134**
Chapter 9: Quantities in an Acid-Base Reaction	**314**
Chapter 10: Simulating Nuclear Decay Reactions	**352**
Chapter 13: Energy of a Rolling Ball	**462**
Chapter 15: Transverse Waves	**530**
Chapter 17: Constructing Electric Circuits	**608**
Chapter 19: The Size and Power Output of the Sun	**680**
Chapter 20: Types of Galaxies	**718**

Application Labs

Chapter 2: Physical Properties of Metals	**66**
Chapter 6: Comparing Polymers	**206**
Chapter 8: How Temperature Affects Gas Solubility	**282**
Chapter 11: Static, Sliding, and Rolling Friction	**386**
Chapter 16: Lenses and Images	**574**
Chapter 21: Finding the Epicenter of an Earthquake	**762**
Chapter 23: Designing a Windmill	**832**

Inquiry Labs

Chapter 3: Boiling and Freezing	**102**
Chapter 5: Exploring Periodic Trends	**166**
Chapter 7: Rate and Temperature of a Chemical Reaction	**248**
Chapter 12: Building a Catapult	**418**
Chapter 14: Conduction of Heat by Metals	**494**
Chapter 18: Making a Better Electromagnet	**640**
Chapter 22: Effects of Temperature on the Buoyancy of Air	**796**

Lab Safety

In the laboratory or in the field, you can engage in hands-on explorations, test your scientific hypotheses, and build practical lab skills. However, while you are working, it is your responsibility to protect yourself and your classmates by conducting yourself in a safe manner. You will avoid accidents by following directions, handling materials carefully, and taking your work seriously. Read the following safety guidelines before working in the lab or field. Make sure that you understand all safety guidelines before entering the lab or field.

Before You Begin

- **Read the entire activity before entering the lab.** Be familiar with the instructions before beginning an activity. Do not start an activity until you have asked your teacher to explain any parts of the activity that you do not understand.
- **Wear the right clothing for lab work.** Before beginning work, tie back long hair, roll up loose sleeves, and put on any required personal protective equipment as directed by your teacher. Remove your wristwatch and any necklaces or jewelry that could get caught in moving parts or contact electrical connections. Avoid or confine loose clothing that could knock things over, catch on fire, get caught in moving parts, contact electrical connections, or absorb chemical solutions. Wear pants rather than shorts or skirts. Nylon and polyester fabrics burn and melt more readily than cotton does. Protect your feet from chemical spills and falling objects. Do not wear open-toed shoes, sandals, or canvas shoes in the lab.
- **Know the location of all safety and emergency equipment used in the lab.** Know proper fire-drill procedures and the location of all fire exits. Ask your teacher where the nearest eyewash stations, safety blankets, safety shower, fire extinguisher, first-aid kit, and chemical spill kit are located. Be sure that you know how to operate the equipment safely.

While You Are Working

- **Always wear a lab apron and safety goggles.** Wear these items while in the lab, even if you are not working on an activity. Labs contain chemicals that can damage your clothing, skin, and eyes. Aprons and goggles also protect against many physical hazards. If your safety goggles cloud up or are uncomfortable, ask your teacher for help. Lengthening the strap slightly, washing the goggles with soap and warm water, or using an anti-fog spray may help the problem.
- **NEVER work alone in the lab.** Work in the lab only when supervised by your teacher.
- **NEVER leave equipment unattended while it is in operation.**
- **Perform only activities specifically assigned by your teacher.** Do not attempt any procedure without your teacher's direction. Use only materials and equipment listed in the activity or authorized by your teacher. Steps in a procedure should be performed only as described in the activity or as approved by your teacher.
- **Keep your work area neat and uncluttered.** Have only books and other materials that are needed to conduct the activity in the lab. Keep backpacks, purses, and other items in your desk, locker, or other designated storage areas.
- **Always heed safety symbols and cautions listed in activities, listed on handouts, posted in the room, provided on equipment or chemical labels (whether provided by the manufacturer or added later), and given verbally by your teacher.** Be aware of the potential hazards of the required materials and procedures, and follow all precautions indicated.
- **Be alert, and walk with care in the lab.** Be aware of others near you and your equipment and be aware of what they are doing.
- **Do not take food, drinks, chewing gum, or tobacco products into the lab.** Do not store or eat food in the lab. Either finish these items or discard them before coming into the lab or beginning work in the field.
- **NEVER taste chemicals or allow them to contact your skin.** Keep your hands away from your face and mouth, even if you are wearing gloves. Only smell vapors as instructed by your teacher and only in the manner indicated.

- **Exercise caution when working with electrical equipment.** Do not use electrical equipment with frayed or twisted wires. Check that insulation on wiring is intact. Be sure that your hands are dry before using electrical equipment. Do not let electrical cords dangle from work stations. Dangling cords can catch on apparatus on tables, can cause you to trip and can cause an electrical shock. The area under and around electrical equipment should be dry; cords should not lie in puddles of spilled liquid, under sink spigots, or in sinks themselves.

- **Use extreme caution when working with hot plates and other heating devices.** Keep your head, hands, hair, and clothing away from the flame or heating area. Remember that metal surfaces connected to the heated area will become hot by conduction. Gas burners should be lit only with a spark lighter, not with matches. Make sure that all heating devices and gas valves are turned off before you leave the lab. Never leave a heating device unattended when it is in use. Metal, ceramic, and glass items do not necessarily look hot when they are hot. Allow all items to cool before storing them.

- **Do not fool around in the lab.** Take your lab work seriously, and behave appropriately in the lab. Lab equipment and apparatus are not toys; never use lab time or equipment for anything other than the intended purpose. Be considerate and be aware of the safety of your classmates as well as your safety at all times.

Emergency Procedures

- **Follow standard fire-safety procedures.** If your clothing catches on fire, do not run; WALK to the safety shower, stand under it, and turn it on. While doing so, call to your teacher. In case of fire, alert your teacher and leave the lab.

- **Report any accident, incident, or hazard—no matter how trivial—to your teacher immediately.** Any incident involving bleeding, burns, fainting, nausea, dizziness, chemical exposure, or ingestion should also be reported immediately to the school nurse or to a physician. If you have a close call, tell your teacher so that you and your teacher can find a way to prevent it from happening again.

- **Report all spills to your teacher immediately.** Call your teacher rather than trying to clean a spill yourself. Your teacher will tell you whether it is safe for you to clean up the spill; if it is not safe, your teacher will know how to clean up the spill.

- **If you spill a chemical on your skin, wash the chemical off in the sink and call your teacher.** If you spill a solid chemical onto your clothing, using an appropriate container, brush it off carefully without scattering it onto somebody else and call your teacher. If you spill corrosive substances on your skin or clothing, use the safety shower or a faucet to rinse. Remove affected clothing while you are under the shower, and call to your teacher. (It may be temporarily embarrassing to remove clothing in front of your classmates, but failure to thoroughly rinse a chemical off your skin could result in permanent damage.)

- **If you get a chemical in your eyes, walk immediately to the eyewash station, turn it on, and lower your head so your eyes are in the running water.** Hold your eyelids open with your thumbs and fingers, and roll your eyeballs around. You have to flush your eyes continuously for at least 15 minutes. Call your teacher while you are doing this.

When You Are Finished

- **Clean your work area at the conclusion of each lab period as directed by your teacher.** Broken glass, chemicals, and other waste products should be disposed of in separate, special containers. Dispose of waste materials as directed by your teacher. Put away all material and equipment according to your teacher's instructions. Report any damaged or missing equipment or materials to your teacher.

- **Even if you wore gloves, wash your hands with soap and hot water after each lab period.** To avoid contamination, wash your hands at the conclusion of each lab period, and before you leave the lab.

Safety Symbols

Before you begin working on an activity, familiarize yourself with the following safety symbols, which are used throughout your textbook, and the guidelines that you should follow when you see these symbols.

 ## Eye Protection

- **Wear approved safety goggles as directed.** Safety goggles should be worn in the lab at all times, especially when you are working with a chemical or solution, a heat source, or a mechanical device.

- **If chemicals get into your eyes, flush your eyes immediately.** Go to an eyewash station immediately, and flush your eyes (including under the eyelids) with running water for at least 15 minutes. Use your thumb and fingers to hold your eyelids open and roll your eyeballs around. While doing so, call your teacher or ask another student to notify your teacher.

- **Do not wear contact lenses in the lab.** Chemicals can be drawn up under a contact lens and into the eye. If you must wear contacts prescribed by a physician, tell your teacher. In this case, you must also wear approved eye-cup safety goggles to help protect your eyes.

- **Do not look directly at the sun or any intense light source or laser.** Do not look at these through any optical device or lens system. Do not reflect direct sunlight to illuminate a microscope. Such actions concentrate light rays to an intensity that can severely burn your retinas, causing blindness.

 ## Clothing Protection

- **Wear an apron or lab coat at all times in the lab to prevent chemicals or chemical solutions from contacting skin or clothes.**

- **Tie back long hair, secure loose clothing, and remove loose jewelry so that they do not knock over equipment, get caught in moving parts, or come into contact with hazardous materials or electrical connections.**

- **Do not wear open-toed shoes, sandals, or canvas shoes in the lab.** Splashed chemicals directly contact skin or quickly soak through canvas. Hard shoes will not allow chemicals to soak through as quickly and they provide more protection against dropped or falling objects.

 ## Hand Safety

- **Do not cut an object while holding the object in your hand.** Cut objects on a suitable work surface. Always cut in a direction away from your body.

- **Wear appropriate protective gloves when working with an open flame, chemicals, solutions, or wild or unknown plants.** Your teacher will provide the type of gloves necessary for a given activity.

- **Use a heat-resistant mitt to handle resistors, light sources, and other equipment that may be hot.** Allow all equipment to cool before storing it.

 ## Hygienic Care

- **Keep your hands away from your face; hair and mouth while you are working on any activity.**

- **Wash your hands thoroughly before you leave the lab or when you finish any activity.**

- **Remove contaminated clothing immediately.** If you spill corrosive substances on your skin or clothing, use the safety shower or a faucet to rinse. Remove affected clothing while you are under the shower, and call to your teacher. (It may be temporarily embarrassing to remove clothing in front of your classmates, but failure to thoroughly rinse a chemical off your skin could result in permanent damage.)

 ## Sharp-Object Safety

- **Use extreme care when handling all sharp and pointed instruments, such as scalpels, sharp probes, and knives.**

- **Do not cut an object while holding the object in your hand.** Cut objects on a suitable work surface. Always cut in a direction away from your body.

- **Do not use double-edged razor blades in the lab.**

- **Be aware of sharp objects or protrusions on equipment or apparatus.**

Glassware Safety

- **Inspect glassware before use; do not use chipped or cracked glassware.** Use heat-resistant glassware for heating materials or storing hot liquids, and use appropriate tongs or a heat-resistant mitt to handle this equipment.

- **Notify immediately your teacher if a piece of glassware or a light bulb breaks.** Do not attempt to clean up broken glass or remove broken bulbs unless your teacher directs you to do so.

 ## Proper Waste Disposal

- **Clean and sanitize all work surfaces and personal protective equipment after each lab period as directed by your teacher.**

- **Dispose of contaminated materials (biological or chemical) in special containers only as directed by your teacher.** Never put these materials into a regular waste container or down the drain.

- **Dispose of sharp objects (such as broken glass) in the appropriate sharps or broken glass container as directed by your teacher.**

 ## Electrical Safety

- **Do not use equipment with frayed electrical cords or loose plugs.** Do not attempt to remove a plug tine if it breaks off in the socket. Notify your teacher and stay away from the outlet.

- **Fasten electrical cords to work surfaces by using tape.** Doing so will prevent tripping and will ensure that equipment will not be pulled or fall off the table.

- **Do not use electrical equipment near water or when your clothing or hands are wet.**

- **Hold the plug housing when you plug in or unplug equipment.** Do not touch the metal prongs of the plug, and do not unplug equipment by pulling on the cord.

- **Wire coils in circuits may heat up rapidly.** If heating occurs, open the switch immediately and use a hot mitt to handle the equipment.

 ## Heating Safety

- **Be aware of any source of flames, sparks, or heat (such as open flames, electric heating coils, or hot plates) before working with flammable liquids or gases.**

- **Avoid using open flames.** If possible, work only with hot plates that have an on/off switch and an indicator light. Do not leave hot plates unattended. Do not use alcohol lamps. Turn off hot plates and open flames when they are not in use.

- **Never leave a hot plate unattended while it is turned on or while it is cooling off.**

- **Know the location of lab fire extinguishers and fire-safety blankets.**

- **Use tongs or appropriate insulated holders when handling heated objects.** Heated objects often do not appear to be hot. Do not pick up an object with your hand if it could be warm.

- **Keep flammable substances away from heat, flames, and other ignition sources.**

- **Allow all equipment to cool before storing it.**

 ## Fire Safety

- **Know the location of lab fire extinguishers and fire-safety blankets.**

- **Know your school's fire-evacuation routes.** Always evacuate the building when the fire alarm is activated.

- **If your clothing catches on fire, walk (do not run) to the emergency lab shower to put out the fire.** If the shower is not working, STOP, DROP, and ROLL! Smother the fire by stopping immediately, dropping to the floor, and rolling until the fire is out.

 ## Safety with Gases

- **Do not inhale any gas or vapor unless directed to do so by your teacher.** Never inhale pure gases.

- **Handle materials that emit vapors or gases in a well-ventilated area.** This work should be done in an approved chemical fume hood. Always work at least four to six inches inside the front edge of the hood.

 ## Caustic Substances

- **If a chemical gets on your skin, on your clothing, or in your eyes, rinse it immediately (shower, faucet or eyewash fountain) and alert your teacher.**

- **If you spill a chemical on the floor or lab bench, alert your teacher, but do not clean it up yourself unless your teacher directs you to do so.**

How to Use Your Textbook

This textbook might seem confusing to you when you first look through it. But by reading the next few pages, you will learn how the different parts of this textbook will help you to become a successful science student. You may be tempted to skip this section, but you should read it. This textbook is an important tool in your exploration of science. Like any tool, the more you know about how to use this textbook, the better your results will be.

Step into Science

The beginning of each chapter is designed to get you involved with science. You will immediately see that science matters!

Chapter Outline You can get a quick overview of the chapter by looking at the chapter's outline. In the outline, the section titles and the topics within that section are listed.

Why It Matters The photo that starts each chapter was selected not only to be interesting but also to relate to the content you will learn about in the chapter. The photo caption lets you know how this content applies to the real world.

Inquiry Lab This lab gives you a chance to get some hands-on experience right away. It is designed to help focus your attention on the concepts that you will learn in the chapter.

Read for Meaning

At the beginning of each chapter you will find tools that will help you grasp the meaning of what you read. Each section also introduces what is important in that section and why.

Each **Reading Toolbox** contains a variety of learning tools that will help you better understand the content of the chapter.

The **Key Ideas** ask the important questions that you will be able to answer after learning about the science in each section.

The **Key Terms** are science words that you may not be familiar with but that are important to understanding the section. Pay special attention when you see them highlighted in the pages that follow.

Why It Matters This gives at least one reason that you might be interested in the subject of the section. Often, this topic is covered in more detail with an article later in the section.

Keep an Eye on Headings

Notice that the headings in this textbook are different sizes and different colors. The headings help you organize your reading and form a simple outline, as shown below.

> **Blue:** Section titles
>> **Red:** Key-idea heading
>>> **Blue:** Topic sentences

The paragraph under each red heading contains an answer to a **Key Idea** question from the section opener. These key-idea answers are indicated with a red arrow and are printed in bold.

How to Use Your Textbook **xxiii**

Science Is Doing

You will get many opportunities throughout this textbook to actually do science. After all, doing is what science is about.

Almost every section in the textbook has at least one **Quick Lab** or slightly more-involved **Inquiry Lab** to help you get real experience doing science.

SciLinks lets you use the Internet to link to interesting topics and activities related to the section.

The **Chapter Lab** at the end of the chapter helps you build your understanding of scientific methods. These labs reinforce the chapter with hands-on activity.

Work the Practice Problems

Build your reasoning and problem-solving skills by following the example problems in **Math Skills**. Then, you can practice those skills in the Practice problems that follow.

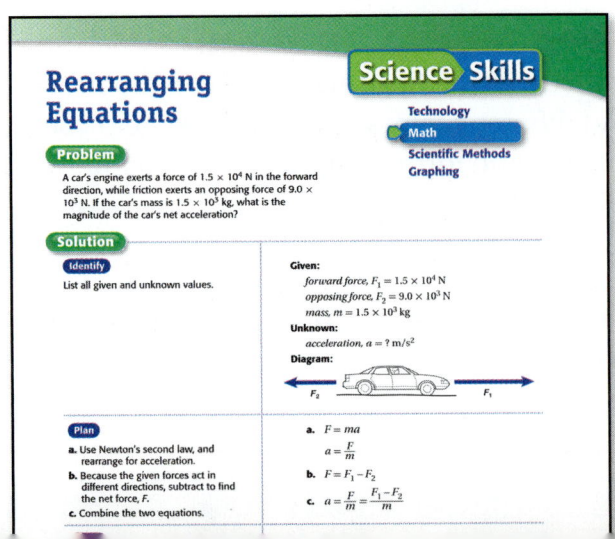

xxiv How to Use Your Textbook

Review What You Have Learned

You can't review too much when you are learning science. To help you review, a **Section Review** appears at the end of every section and a **Chapter Summary** and **Chapter Review** appear at the end of every chapter. These reviews not only help you study for tests but also help further your understanding of the content.

Just a few clicks away, each **Super Summary** gives you even more ways to review and study for tests using a computer and the Internet.

Be sure to read the **Key Ideas** to see how they all fit together. If you need to recall any of the **Key Terms,** the page number on which they appear is given.

When it is time for a chapter test, don't panic. The **Chapter Review** helps you get ready by providing a wide variety of questions. Many of these questions help you develop a better understanding of the content. Once you understand the content, you will be ready for any test!

Mastering science standards takes practice. The **Standardized Test Prep** at the end of each chapter helps you practice questions about the chapter in a format similar to formats you may see on standardized tests.

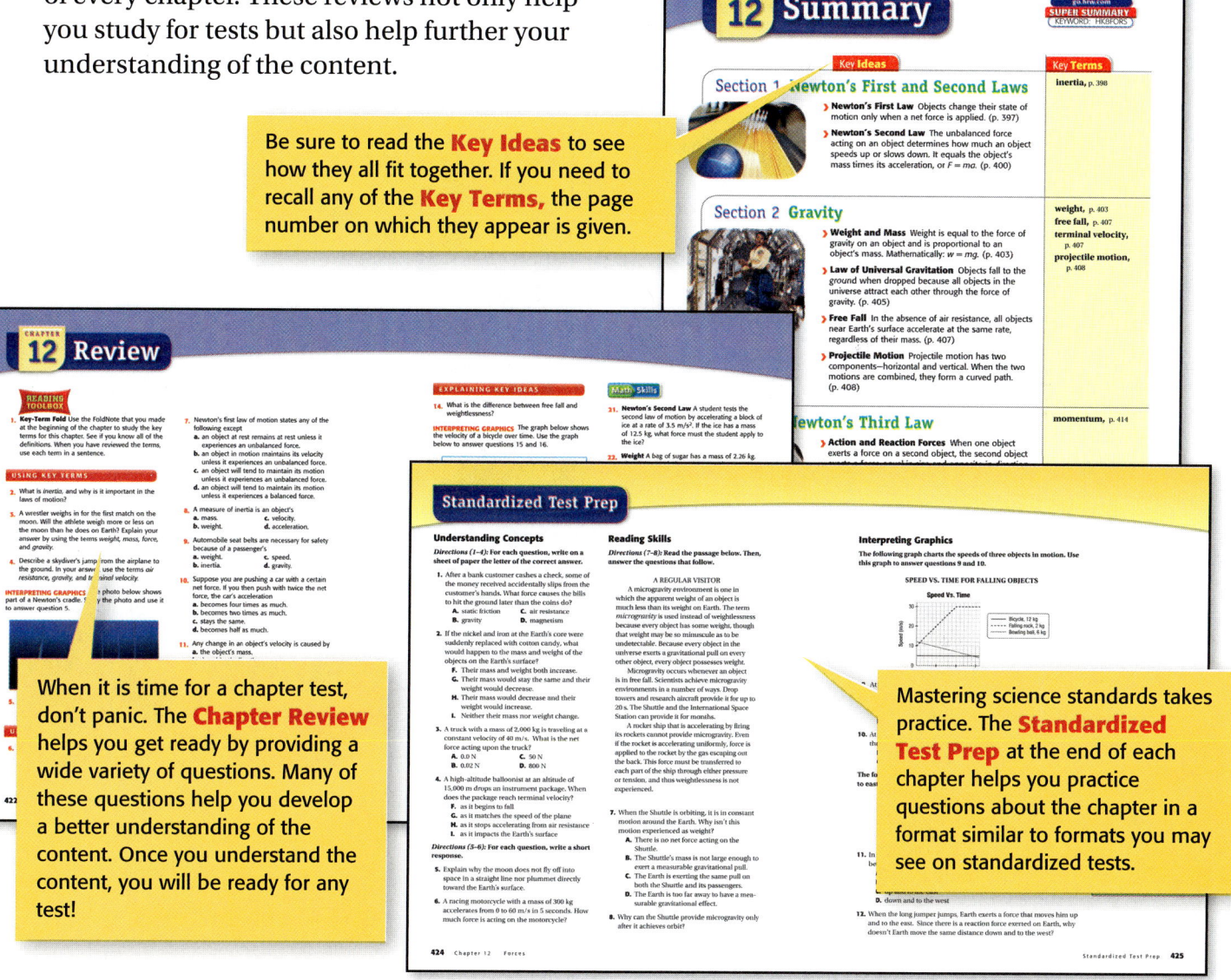

Be Resourceful—Use the Web!

More Practice
Each Math Skills example is followed by Practice problems. However, you may want more practice than you find in this book. You can find more practice online at **go.hrw.com.** There, type in the keyword **HK8MP,** and find more practice problems for your chapter.

Your Online Textbook
If your teacher gives you a special password to log onto the **Holt Online Learning** site, you will find your complete textbook on the Web. In addition, you will find some great learning tools and interactive materials. You can now access your textbook anywhere and anytime via the Internet.

Take a Test Drive
How well can you use this book now? Take Chapter 1 out for a spin and see how you do. Log onto **go.hrw.com** and enter the keyword **HK8 TEST DRIVE** for a short list of questions that will test your ability to navigate this book.

How to Use Your Textbook **XXV**

CHAPTER 1
Introduction to Science

Chapter Outline

1 The Nature of Science
How Science Takes Place
The Branches of Science
Scientific Laws and Theories

2 The Way Science Works
Science Skills
Units of Measurement

3 Organizing Data
Presenting Scientific Data
Writing Numbers in Scientific Notation
Using Significant Figures

Why It Matters
Many inventions, such as cars, would not exist today if scientists did not understand how to use scientific methods and how to perform experiments. For example, a model of a car can be tested in a wind tunnel to perfect the car's design.

Tennessee Course Level Expectations (Physical Science)

CLE.3202.TE.1 Explore the impact of technology on social, political, and economic systems; **CLE.3202.4.1** Explore the difference between mass and weight; **CLE.3202.Inq.1** Recognize that science is a progressive endeavor that reevaluates and extends what is already accepted; **CLE.3202.Inq.2** Design and conduct scientific investigations to explore new phenomena, verify previous results, test how well a theory predicts, and compare opposing theories; **CLE.3202.Inq.3** Use appropriate tools and technology to collect precise and accurate data; **CLE.3202.Inq.4** Apply qualitative and quantitative measures to analyze data and draw conclusions that are free of bias; **CLE.3202.Inq.5** Compare experimental evidence and conclusions with those drawn by others about the same testable question; **CLE.3202.Inq.6** Communicate and defend scientific findings; **CLE.3202.TE.2** Differentiate among elements of the engineering design cycle: design constraints, model building, testing, evaluating, modifying, and retesting; **CLE.3202.TE.4** Describe the dynamic interplay among science, technology, and engineering within living, earth-space, and physical systems.

Inquiry Lab
10 min

Measuring Area

Using a **meterstick,** measure the length and width of the top surface of a rectangular **table.** Multiply your two measurements to calculate the surface area of the table. Compare your results with those of other students.

Questions to Get You Started

1. To what fraction of a unit can you reliably measure?
2. How can you explain any differences between your results and those of your classmates?

READING TOOLBOX These reading tools can help you learn the material in this chapter. For more information on how to use these and other tools, see **Appendix A.**

Science Terms

Everyday Words Used in Science All of the key terms that you will learn in this book are used by scientists. Many words used in science are also words used in everyday speech. You should pay attention to the definitions of such words so that you use them correctly in scientific contexts.

Your Turn As you read the chapter, make a table like the one below for the terms *scientific law*, *scientific theory*, and *scientific notation*. Include the everyday meaning of the word that comes after the word *scientific*.

TERM	SCIENTIFIC CONTEXT	EVERYDAY MEANING
scientific method	a series of steps used to solve problems or answer questions in a scientific way	method—a way of doing something

Classification

Branches of Science Classification is a logical tool for organizing ideas. Classification involves grouping things into categories. The example below shows that you do a lot of classifying without even realizing it.

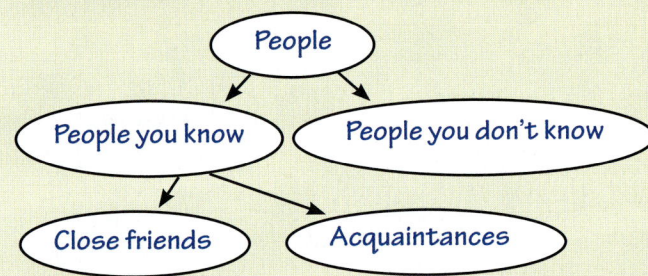

Your Turn Figure 3 in Section 1 shows how branches of science can be classified. Write down the definitions of the branches of science included in the figure. Explain why astronomy, geology, and meteorology are classified as types of Earth science, and explain why physics and chemistry are classified as types of physical science.

Graphic Organizers

Spider Maps Graphic Organizers are drawings that you can make to help you organize the concepts that you learn. A spider map is a Graphic Organizer that shows how details are organized into categories that relate to a main idea.

Your Turn As you read Section 2, complete a spider map like the one started here to organize the ideas that you learn about SI units. You may also create more spider maps to organize the science skills that you learn in this chapter.

SECTION 1: The Nature of Science

Key Ideas

> How do scientists explore the world?
> How are the many types of science organized?
> What are scientific theories, and how are they different from scientific laws?

Key Terms

science
technology
law
theory

Why It Matters

Science is applied to the technologies that are used to build many important things, such as bridges and vehicles.

When you have a question about how something works, how do you find the answer? Generally, scientists describe the universe by using basic rules, which can be discovered by careful, methodical study.

Tennessee Course Level Expectations (Physical Science)
CLE.3202.TE.1; CLE.3202.Inq.1

How Science Takes Place

> **A scientist may perform experiments to find a new aspect of the natural world, to explain a known phenomenon, to check the results of other experiments, or to test the predictions of current theories.**

Imagine that it is 1895 and you are experimenting with mysterious rays known as cathode rays. These rays were discovered almost 40 years earlier, but in 1895 no one knows that they are composed of electrons. To produce the rays, you pump the air out of a sealed glass tube, which creates a vacuum. An early version of this type of tube is shown in **Figure 1.** You then connect rods inside the tube to an electrical source. Electric charges flow through the empty space between the rods and produce the rays.

Figure 1 An early cathode-ray tube is shown on the left. A television picture tube, on the right, is a form of the same cathode-ray tube.

Academic Vocabulary

conduct (kuhn DUHKT) to do

Integrating Biology

Penicillin In 1928, the Scottish scientist Alexander Fleming was investigating disease-causing bacteria. He saw that one of his cultures contained an area where no bacteria were growing. An unknown organism was growing in that area. Rather than discard the culture as a failure, Fleming investigated the unfamiliar organism and found that it was a type of mold. This mold produced a substance that prevented the growth of many disease-causing bacteria. What he found by questioning the results of a "failed" experiment became the first modern antibiotic, penicillin. Major discoveries are often made by accident when scientists are trying to find something else.

READING TOOLBOX

Spider Map
Create a spider map that explains the steps that happen when science takes place. Use the blue heads in the section as the branches of your map.

Scientists answer questions by investigating.

As a scientist, you have learned from the work of other scientists and have conducted your own experiments. You know that when certain minerals are placed inside the tube, the cathode rays make them glow. Cardboard pieces coated with powder made from these minerals are used to detect the rays. If a very high voltage is used, even the glass tube glows.

Other scientists have found that cathode rays can pass through thin metal foil, but the rays travel in our atmosphere for only 2 or 3 cm. You wonder if the rays could pass through the glass tube. Other experiments have shown that cathode rays do not go through glass. You think that scientists may not have been able to see the weak glow from the mineral-coated cardboard because the glass tube glowed too brightly. So, you decide to cover the glass tube with heavy black paper.

Scientists plan experiments.

Before experimenting, you write your plan in a laboratory notebook and sketch the equipment that you are using. You make a table in which you can record your observations and your variables—the electric voltage used, the distance from the tube to the cathode-ray detector, and the air temperature. You state the idea that you are going to test: At a high voltage, cathode rays will be strong enough to be detected outside the tube by causing the mineral-coated cardboard to glow.

Scientists observe.

You are ready to start your experiment but want to be sure that the black-paper cover does not have any gaps. So, you darken the room and turn on the tube. The cover blocks all of the light from the tube. Just before you switch off the tube, you glimpse a light nearby. When you turn on the tube again, the light reappears.

You realize that this light is coming from the mineral-coated cardboard that you planned to use to detect cathode rays. The detector is already glowing even though it is almost 1 m away from the tube. You know that cathode rays cannot travel 1 m in air. You suspect that the tube is giving off a new type of ray that no one has seen before. What do you do now?

Wilhelm Roentgen (RENT guhn) pondered this question in Würzburg, Germany, on November 8, 1895, when he did this experiment. Should he call the experiment a failure because the results were unexpected? Should he report his findings in a scientific journal or ask reporters to cover this news story? Maybe he should send letters about his discovery to famous scientists and invite them to come see his experiment.

6 Chapter 1   Introduction to Science

Scientists always confirm results.

Because Roentgen was a scientist, he first repeated his experiment to be sure of his observations. His results caused him to think of new questions and to do more experiments to find the answers to these questions.

He found that the rays passed through almost everything, but dense materials absorbed some of the rays. When he held his hand in the path of the rays, the bones were visible as shadows on the detector, as **Figure 2** shows. When Roentgen published his findings in December, he still did not know what the rays were. He called them *X rays* because *x* represents an unknown in a mathematical equation.

Within three months of Roentgen's discovery, a doctor in Massachusetts used X rays to help set the broken bones in a boy's arm. After a year, more than a thousand scientific papers about X rays had been published. In 1901, Roentgen received the first Nobel Prize in physics for his discovery.

Reading Check How did Roentgen confirm his observation? (See Appendix E for answers to Reading Checks.)

Figure 2 Roentgen included this X ray of his wife's hand in one of the first papers that he wrote about X rays.

The Branches of Science

Roentgen's work with X rays shows how scientists work, but what is science about? **Science** is observing, studying, and experimenting to find the nature of things. You can think of science as having two main branches: social science, which deals with individual and group human behavior, and natural science. Natural science tries to understand how "nature," or "the whole universe," behaves. ❯ **Most of the time, natural science is divided into biological science, physical science, and Earth science.** **Figure 3** shows how science is divided.

science (SIE uhns) the knowledge obtained by observing natural events and conditions in order to discover facts and formulate laws or principles that can be verified or tested

Figure 3 This chart shows one way to look at science. Modern science has many branches and specialties.

Section 1 The Nature of Science

The branches of science work together.

The classification of science seems to be very simple. For example, life science is *biology*. Biology has many branches, such as *botany*, the science of plants, and *ecology*, the science of balance in nature. Medicine and agriculture are also branches of biology.

Physical science has two main branches—chemistry and physics. *Chemistry* is the science of matter and its changes. *Physics* is the science of forces and energy. Both depend greatly on mathematics.

Two branches of Earth science are *geology*, the science of the physical nature and history of Earth, and *meteorology*, the science of the atmosphere and weather.

But the branches of science have become more mixed. For example, some chemists study chemicals that make up living things, such as the DNA shown in **Figure 4.** This branch of science is *biochemistry,* the study of the matter of living things. It is both a life science and a physical science. Other branches of science are also mixed. For example, *geophysics*—the study of the forces that affect Earth, is both an Earth science and a physical science.

Figure 4 This model shows the structure of DNA (deoxyribonucleic acid), which makes each of us unique.

Science and technology work together.

Scientists who do experiments to learn more about the world are doing *pure science*. **Technology** is the application of science for practical uses. Engineers apply scientific knowledge and methods to design products people use. Advances in science and technology depend on one another. The first computers, such as the one shown in **Figure 5,** often filled up a whole room. But advances in science have led to smaller computers that are both faster and cheaper. Modern computers also help scientists. For example, computers help scientists make complex calculations quickly.

Figure 5 Advances in science have greatly reduced the size of and increased the availability of computers. **What devices that use computer technology do you use?**

Scientific Laws and Theories

People sometimes say things like, "My theory is that we'll see Jaime on the school bus," when they really mean, "I'm guessing that we'll see Jaime on the school bus." People use the word *theory* in everyday speech to refer to a guess about something. In science, a theory is much more than a guess. ❱ **Theories explain why something happens, and laws describe how something works.**

Experimental results support laws and theories.

When you place a hot cooking pot in a cooler place, does the pot become hotter as it stands? No, it will always get cooler. This example illustrates a scientific law that states that warm objects always become cooler when they are placed in cooler surroundings. A scientific **law** describes a process in nature that can be tested by repeated experiments. A law allows predictions to be made about how a system will behave under a wide range of conditions.

However, a law does not *explain* how a process takes place. In the example of the hot cooking pot, nothing in the law tells why hot objects become cooler in cooler surroundings. Such an explanation of how a natural process works must be provided by a scientific **theory.**

Scientific theories are always being questioned and examined. To be valid, a theory must continue to pass several tests.

- A theory must explain observations clearly and consistently. For example, the theory that heat is the energy of particles in motion explains why the hot cooking pot gets cooler when it is placed in cooler surroundings.

- Experiments that illustrate the theory must be repeatable. A cooking pot always gets warmer when placed on a hot stove and always gets cooler when placed in cooler surroundings, whether the pot is moved for the first time or the 31st time.

- You must be able to predict results from the theory. You might predict that anything that makes the particles in an object move faster will make the object hotter. Sawing a piece of wood, as shown in **Figure 6,** will make the metal particles in the saw move faster. If you saw rapidly, the saw will get hot to the touch. The theory can explain both why the saw gets warmer and why the cooking pot gets cooler.

Reading Check How does a scientific law differ from a scientific theory?

technology (tek NAHL uh jee) the application of science for practical purposes

law (LAW) a descriptive statement or equation that reliably predicts events under certain conditions

theory (THEE uh ree) a system of ideas that explains many related observations and is supported by a large body of evidence acquired through scientific investigation

Figure 6 The kinetic theory of energy explains many things that you can observe, such as why a saw blade gets hot when used.

Mathematics can describe physical events.

How would you state the law of gravitation? You could say that something you are holding will fall to Earth when you let go. This *qualitative* statement describes with words something that you have seen many times. But many scientific laws and theories can be stated as mathematical equations, which are *quantitative* statements.

> **Rectangle area equation** $A = l \times w$

The rectangle area equation works for all rectangles, whether they are short, tall, wide, or thin.

> **Universal gravitation equation** $F = G \dfrac{m_1 m_2}{d^2}$

In the same way, the universal gravitation equation describes how large the force will be between two galaxies or between Earth and the sky divers shown falling to Earth in **Figure 7**. Quantitative expressions of the laws of science make communicating about science easier. Scientists around the world speak and read many different languages, but mathematics, the language of science, is the same everywhere.

Theories and laws are always being tested.

Sometimes, theories must be changed or replaced when new discoveries are made. More than 200 years ago, scientists used the *caloric theory* to explain how objects become warmer and cooler. Heat was thought to be an invisible fluid, called *caloric,* that flowed from a warm object to a cool one. People thought that fires were fountains of caloric, which flowed into surrounding objects and made them warmer. The caloric theory could explain all that people knew about heat.

During the 1800s, after doing many experiments, some scientists presented a new theory based on the idea that heat was a result of the motion of particles. Like many new ideas, this new theory was strongly criticized and was not accepted at first by other scientists. But the caloric theory could not explain why rubbing two rough surfaces together made them warmer. This new theory, the *kinetic theory,* could be used to explain why the surfaces became warmer—rubbing the surfaces together caused the particles in the surfaces to move faster. The kinetic theory was accepted because it explained both the old and new observations, and the caloric theory was no longer used.

Figure 7 The gravitational force of attraction between Earth and these sky divers varies depending on the mass of the sky divers and their distance from Earth.

Models can represent physical events.

When you see the word *model,* you may think of a small copy of an airplane or a person who shows off clothing. Scientists use models, too. A scientific model is a representation of an object or event that can be studied to understand the real object or event. Sometimes, models represent things that are too small, too big, or too complex to study easily.

A model of a water molecule is shown in **Figure 8.** Chemists use models to study how water molecules form ice crystals, such as snowflakes. Models can be drawings on paper. Real objects can also be used as models to help us picture things that we cannot see. For example, a spring can be used as a model of a sound wave. A model can also be a mental "picture" or a set of rules that describes how something works. After you have studied atoms, you will be able to picture atoms in your mind. You can use these pictures to figure out what will happen in chemical reactions.

Figure 8 Models can be used to describe a water molecule (top right) and to study how water molecules are arranged in a snowflake.

Reading Check What are three types of models?

Why It Matters
Millennium Bridge

SCIENCE & SOCIETY

Computer models are important tools for scientists and engineers. Computers process long, complicated calculations to predict how the system being modeled will behave under various conditions. This type of modeling is an essential part of designing massive structures such as the Millennium Bridge in London.

Engineers used computer models to predict the strength and stability of the Millennium Bridge. The 320 m bridge was built so that people could walk over a river in London, England.

YOUR TURN

ONLINE RESEARCH
1. Research how computer models were used by the engineers who worked on the Millennium Bridge.

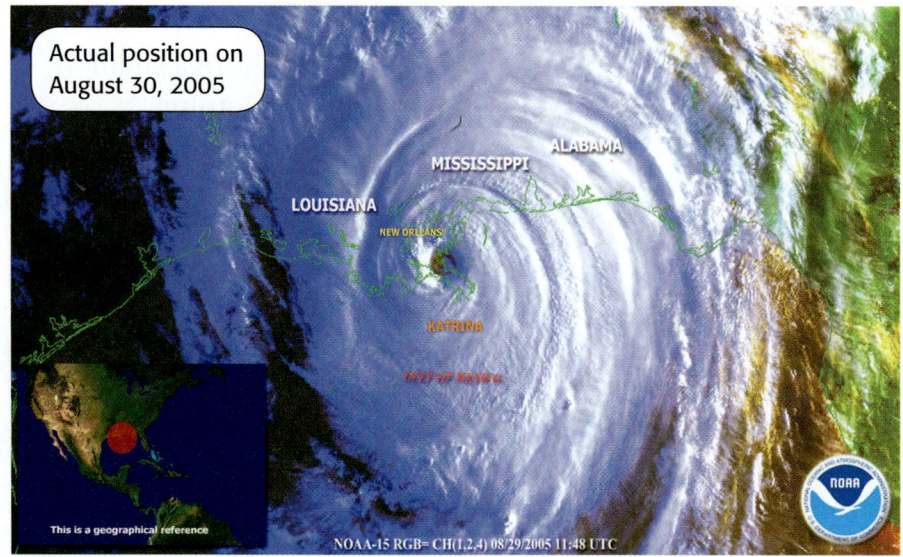

Figure 9 Models help forecast the weather. The black lines in these models indicate the projected path of Hurricane Katrina days before the eye of the storm made landfall. The satellite image shows the actual location where the eye of the storm hit land.

We use models in our everyday lives.

Computer models have many uses. For example, they can be used by *meteorologists* to help forecast the weather. Meteorologists use computer models that use information about wind speed and direction, air temperature, moisture levels, and ground shape. **Figure 9** shows how a model was used to predict the path of a hurricane.

The outcome of a model depends on the information that is put into the model. Notice that in the first model of the hurricane path, the predicted area where the eye of the hurricane would hit land is very large. As the hurricane got closer to land, more data were collected and added to the model, and the area of the potential landfall was smaller. The satellite image of the actual hurricane shows that this model did a very good job predicting where the hurricane would hit land.

Section 1 Review

KEY IDEAS

1. **Compare** the two branches of physical science.
2. **Explain** how science and technology depend on each other and how they differ from each other.
3. **Define** *scientific law,* and give an example.
4. **Compare** a scientific law and a scientific theory.
5. **Explain** why a scientific theory might be changed.
6. **Describe** how a scientific model is used, and give an example of a scientific model.

CRITICAL THINKING

7. **Applying Ideas** How may Roentgen's training as a scientist have affected the way that he responded to his discovery?
8. **Analyzing Ideas** Explain how a scientific theory differs from a guess or an opinion.
9. **Forming Hypotheses** Pick a common occurrence, develop an explanation for it, and describe an experiment that you could perform to test your explanation.

Why It **Matters**
Leonardo da Vinci

HISTORY IN SCIENCE

Science and technology depend on each other. Basic scientific research is needed to obtain the knowledge to develop technology. However, technology is also needed to advance scientific ideas. Sometimes, great thinkers use their knowledge of science to invent new things that are "ahead of their time." Leonardo da Vinci was such a thinker. He designed many things, including a forerunner to the modern-day helicopter. But in the 15th century he did not have the technology available to make his ideas work. For example, he did not have the engine technology that would give his machine enough lift to get it off the ground.

Leonardo da Vinci was a master artist, a creative inventor, and an engineer.

In 1480, Leonardo da Vinci used his knowledge of physics to create a design for a helical air screw. He thought that if the screw turned fast enough, the air would be compressed enough to lift the machine off the ground.

Modern helicopters use rotating propeller blades and powerful engines to obtain vertical lift. Because helicopters can take off vertically, they can be used for remote rescue operations.

SCILINKS
www.scilinks.org
Topic: Leonardo da Vinci
Code: **HK80869**

YOUR TURN

UNDERSTANDING CONCEPTS
1. Explain how technology depends on science.

WRITING IN SCIENCE
2. Research another invention by Leonardo da Vinci. Write a short report explaining how science and technology were important for this invention.

13

SECTION 2 The Way Science Works

Key Ideas
› How can I think and act like a scientist?
› How do scientists measure things?

Key Terms
critical thinking
scientific methods
variable
length
mass
volume
weight

Why It Matters
Thinking logically, like a scientist, can help you solve problems that you face in your daily life. For example, you can use critical thinking to help you find the best deals when shopping.

Tennessee Course Level Expectations (Physical Science)
CLE.3202.Inq.1; CLE.3202.Inq.5

In our society, riding a bicycle or driving a car is considered almost a survival skill. The skills that we think are important, however, change over time, as society and technology change.

Science Skills

Pouring liquid into a test tube without spilling it may be a useful skill in the lab, but other skills are more important in science. › **Identifying problems, planning experiments, recording observations, and correctly reporting data are some of the most important science skills.** The most important skill is learning to think creatively and critically.

Critical thinking helps you solve problems logically.

Imagine that you and a friend want to buy some popcorn but also want to save money. Would you buy the large container of popcorn, shown in **Figure 1,** and share? Or would you buy two small containers of popcorn? We often assume that products in larger packages are a better value than products in smaller packages. However, we need to make observations and compare data to see if this assumption is true.

How many ounces are in each container of popcorn? What is the price of each container? How many ounces would you get if you bought two small containers? How much would two small containers cost? If you approach the problem by asking questions, making observations, and using logic, you are using **critical thinking.**

Figure 1 Logical decision making is important in scientific processes and in everyday life. **Which size of popcorn is the better deal?**

Figure 2 A scientific method is a general description of scientific thinking rather than an exact path for scientists to follow.

Scientists use scientific methods to solve problems.

Critical thinking is used to solve scientific problems as part of scientific methods. **Scientific methods** are general ways to help organize your thinking about questions. Using scientific methods helps you find and evaluate possible answers. Scientific methods are sets of procedures that scientists use, as **Figure 2** shows, but the steps can vary.

Although the set of procedures used depends on the nature of the question to be answered, most scientific questions begin with observations—simple things that you notice. For example, you may notice that when you open a door, you hear a squeak. You ask the question, "Why does this door make noise?" You may gather data by checking other doors. You form a hypothesis, a possible answer that you can test. For example, you may think that the doorknob is the source of the squeak. Your hypothesis might then be: The doorknob makes this door squeak.

 Reading Check Do you have to use exactly the same steps every time that you use a scientific method?

Scientists test hypotheses.

Scientists test a hypothesis by doing a *controlled experiment*. In a controlled experiment, **variables** that can affect the outcome of the experiment are kept constant, or controlled, except the one(s) that you want to measure. Only the results of changing the given variables are observed.

The more things that you change at a time, the harder it is to make reliable conclusions. You may stop the squeak if you remove the knob and oil the hinges, but you will not find the cause of the squeak. You may not find the answer on the first try, even if you test one thing at a time. If the door makes noise after you take the knob off, was your experiment a failure?

READING TOOLBOX

Spider Map
Create a spider map for scientific methods. Label the center "Scientific methods," and create a branch for each step.

critical thinking (KRIT i kuhl THINGK ing) the ability and willingness to assess claims critically and to make judgments on the basis of objective and supported reasons

scientific methods (SIE uhn TIF ik METH uhdz) a series of steps followed to solve problems including collecting data, formulating a hypothesis, testing the hypothesis, and stating conclusions

variable (VER ee uh buhl) a factor that changes in an experiment in order to test a hypothesis

Section 2 The Way Science Works

QuickLab

Making Observations

1. Get an ordinary **candle** of any shape and color.
2. Record all the observations that you can make about the candle.
3. Light the candle, and watch it burn for 1 min. Use caution around open flame.
4. Record as many observations about the burning candle as you can.
5. Share your results with your class, and find out what other types of observations were made.

Experiments test ideas.

Even if an experiment does not give the desired results, it is not a failure. All observations of events in the natural world can be used to revise a hypothesis and to plan tests of a different variable. For example, once you know that the doorknob did not cause the squeak, you can change your hypothesis, "Will oiling the hinges stop the noise?" Often, as with Roentgen's X rays, experimental results are surprising and lead scientists in new directions.

Scientists always keep in mind the question to be tested. To keep from making false conclusions, they must carefully search for <u>bias</u> in the way that they plan and analyze their experiments. Scientists who work together tend to see things the same way. So, it is important for them to publish their results in scientific journals, where other experts can review the work. Research that has been examined by other scientists is said to have been *peer reviewed.*

Scientists should keep in mind their personal bias and report conflicts of interest. Government agencies, private foundations, and industrial interests often fund scientific research. Scientists must guard against reaching false conclusions that may be desired by the groups that give them money.

Some questions, such as how Earth's climate has changed over millions of years, cannot be answered by doing experiments in the laboratory. Instead, geologists make observations all over Earth. As **Figure 3** shows, scientists collect many samples to study so that they can form conclusions based on a convincing amount of data.

Reading Check Why should scientists publish their results?

Figure 3 Researchers can analyze the chemicals that are trapped inside the many ice-core samples they collect to learn about past climates on Earth.

Scientists use special tools.

Logical thinking is not the only skill used in science. Sometimes, scientists make observations by using tools made through advancements in technology. Scientists must know how to use these tools, what the limits of the tools are, and how to interpret data from them.

Astronomers, for example, use *telescopes* with lenses and mirrors. Some of the observatories shown in **Figure 4** hold telescopes that magnify objects that appear small because they are far away, such as distant galaxies. Other observatories contain telescopes that do not form pictures from visible light. *Radio telescopes* detect the radio waves given off by distant objects. Some of the oldest, most distant objects in the universe have been found with radio telescopes.

Chemists use *spectroscopes* to separate light into a rainbow of colors. By using this tool, chemists can learn about a substance from the light that it absorbs or gives off. Physicists use *particle accelerators* to make fragments of atoms move very fast. Then, they let the pieces smash into atoms or parts of atoms. Scientists learn about the structure of atoms from the data that they collect.

Figure 4 Kitt Peak National Observatory in Arizona has a large assortment of telescopes that can be used to study distant galaxies or the sun. This photograph of the Fireworks galaxy (NGC 6946) was taken with an optical telescope. This spiral galaxy is almost 20 million light-years from Earth.

Academic Vocabulary

bias (BIE uhs) a way of thinking that favors one outcome or interpretation

detect (dee TEKT) to discover the presence of

www.scilinks.org
Topic: SI Units
Code: **HK81390**

Units of Measurement

Mathematics is the language of science, and mathematical models rely on accuracy. ❯ **Scientists use standard units of measure that together form the International System of Units, or SI.** *SI* stands for the French term *le Système Internationale d'Unités*. This system allows scientists around the world to compare observations and calculations.

Section 2 The Way Science Works

SI units are used for consistency.

Suppose that one of your classmates estimates that she drinks three gallons of water in a week. Another classmate thinks that he drinks about 350 ounces of water in a week. Who drinks more water? When all scientists use the same system of measurement, sharing data and results is easier. SI is based on the metric system and uses the seven SI base units that are listed in **Figure 5.**

You may have noticed that the base units do not include area, volume, pressure, weight, force, speed, and other familiar quantities. Combinations of the base units are called *derived units* and are used for these measurements.

For example, suppose that you want to order carpet for a floor that measures 8.0 m long and 6.0 m wide. You know that the area of a rectangle is its length times its width.

$$A = l \times w$$

The area of the floor can be calculated as shown below.

$$A = 8.0 \text{ m} \times 6.0 \text{ m} = 48 \text{ m}^2 \quad \text{(or 48 square meters)}$$

The SI unit of area, m^2, is a derived unit.

Figure 5 SI Base Units

Quantity	Unit	Abbreviation
Length	meter	m
Mass	kilogram	kg
Time	second	s
Temperature	kelvin	K
Electric current	ampere	A
Amount of substance	mole	mol
Luminous intensity	candela	cd

SI prefixes are used for very large and very small measurements.

Look at a meterstick. How would you express the length of a bird's egg or the distance you traveled on a trip in meters? The bird's egg might be 5/100 m, or 0.05 m, long. The distance of your trip could have been 800,000 m. To avoid writing a lot of decimal places and zeros, you can use SI prefixes to express very small or very large numbers. These prefixes are all *multiples* of 10, as **Figure 6** and **Figure 7** show.

If you use the prefixes, you can say that the bird's egg is 5 cm (1 *centi*meter equals 0.01 m) long and your trip was 800 km (1 *kilo*meter equals 1,000 m) long. Note that the base unit of mass is the kilogram, which is a multiple of the gram.

It is easy to convert SI units to smaller or larger units. Remember that for the same measurement, you need to use more of a small unit or less of a large unit. For example, if a person's height is 1.75 m, the same height in centimeters would be 175 cm, a larger number. But 1.75 m and 175 cm express the same quantity.

Figure 6 Prefixes for Large Measurements

Prefix	Symbol	Meaning	Multiple of base unit
kilo-	k	thousand	1,000
mega-	M	million	1,000,000
giga-	G	billion	1,000,000,000

Figure 7 Prefixes for Small Measurements

Prefix	Symbol	Meaning	Multiple of base unit
deci-	d	tenth	0.1
centi-	c	hundredth	0.01
milli-	m	thousandth	0.001
micro-	μ	millionth	0.000001
nano-	n	billionth	0.000000001

Reading Check Why are SI prefixes used?

You can convert between smaller and larger numbers.

To convert to a smaller unit, multiply the measurement by the ratio of units so that you get a larger number. For example, to change 1.85 m to centimeters, multiply by 100.

$$1.85 \text{ m} \times \frac{100 \text{ cm}}{1 \text{ m}} = 185 \text{ cm}$$

To convert to a larger unit, as in the question in **Figure 8**, divide the measurement by the ratio of units so that you get a smaller number. To change 185 cm to meters, divide by 100.

$$185 \text{ cm} \times \frac{1 \text{ m}}{100 \text{ cm}} = 1.85 \text{ m}$$

Figure 8 The size of bat that a player uses depends on his or her height. If a bat is 0.81 m long, it is 81 cm long. **If you use a bat that is 76 cm long, how long is your bat in meters?**

Math Skills — Conversions Within SI

The width of a soccer goal is 7 m. What is the width of the goal in centimeters?

Identify
List the given and unknown values.

Given:
length in meters (l) = 7 m
Unknown:
length in centimeters = ? cm

Plan
Determine the relationship between units.

Look at **Figure 5** through **Figure 7**. You can find that 1 cm = 0.01 m. So, 1 m = 100 cm.
You must multiply by 100 because you are converting from meters, a larger unit, to centimeters, a smaller unit.

Solve
Write the equation for the conversion.
Insert the known values into the equation, and solve.

$$\text{length in cm} = \text{m} \times \frac{100 \text{ cm}}{1 \text{ m}}$$

$$\text{length in cm} = 7 \text{ m} \times \frac{100 \text{ cm}}{1 \text{ m}}$$

length in cm = 700 cm

Practice

1. Write 55 *deci*meters as meters.
2. Convert 1.6 *kilo*grams to grams.
3. Change 2,800 *milli*moles to moles.
4. Change 6.1 amperes to *milli*amperes.

For more practice, visit **go.hrw.com** and enter keyword **HK8MP**.

Practice Hint
> If you have done the conversions properly, all the units above and below the fraction will cancel except the units that you need.

Figure 9 Quantitative Measurements

	SI unit	Other units	Examples
Time	second (s)	millisecond (ms) minute (min) hour (h)	Stopwatches measure time precisely.
Length	meter (m)	millimeter (mm) centimeter (cm) kilometer (km)	Many diving boards are as long as 4.9 m.
Mass	kilogram (kg)	milligram (mg) gram (g)	A CD in its case has a mass of about 100 g. Mass can be measured by using a triple-beam balance.
Volume	cubic meter (m^3)	cubic centimeter (cm^3) milliliter (mL) liter (L)	A liquid's volume can be measured by using a graduated cylinder. You can find the volume of a dresser by multiplying the length, width, and height.

Chapter 1 Introduction to Science

Measurements quantify your observations.

Many observations rely on quantitative measurements. Basic scientific measurements usually answer questions such as "How much time did it take?" and "How big is it?"

Often, you will measure time, **length, mass,** and **volume.** The SI units for these quantities, examples of each quantity, and some of the tools that you may use to measure them are shown in **Figure 9.**

Although someone may say that he or she is "weighing" an object with a balance, **weight** is not the same as mass. Mass is the quantity of matter, and weight is the force with which Earth's gravity pulls on that quantity of matter. Your weight would be less on Mars than it is on Earth, but your mass would be the same on both planets.

In the lab, you will use a graduated cylinder to measure the volume of liquids. The volume of a solid that has a specific geometric shape can be calculated from the measured lengths of its surfaces. Small volumes are usually expressed in cubic centimeters (cm^3). One cubic centimeter is equal to one milliliter (mL).

Scientific instruments can measure quantities that are very small. You cannot see the tiny guitar shown in **Figure 10** with the unaided eye. But by using an electron microscope, the width of the strings on the tiny guitar can be measured. At only about 50 nanometers (nm) wide, these strings are more than 1,000 times as thin as one of your hairs.

Figure 10 This tiny guitar is made of silicon and is only about 10 micrometers long.

length (LENGKTH) a measure of the straight-line distance between two points

mass (MAS) a measure of the amount of matter in an object

volume (VAHL yoom) a measure of the size of a body or region in three-dimensional space

weight (WAYT) a measure of the gravitational force exerted on an object

Section 2 Review

KEY IDEAS

1. **Describe** a hypothesis and how it is used. Give an example of a hypothesis.
2. **Explain** why you should not call any experiment a failure.
3. **Explain** the difference between SI base units and SI derived units. Give an example of each.
4. **List** three examples each of objects that are commonly measured by mass, by volume, and by length.

CRITICAL THINKING

5. **Applying Concepts** Explain why scientific methods are said to involve critical thinking.
6. **Summarizing Information** Why do you think that it is a good idea to limit an experiment to test only one variable at a time whenever possible?
7. **Understanding Relationships** Using scientists' tools as an example, explain how science and technology depend on each other.
8. **Drawing Conclusions** An old riddle asks, "Which weighs more, a pound of feathers or a pound of lead?" Answer the question, and explain why you think that people sometimes answer incorrectly.

Math Skills

9. Convert the following measurements to grams.
   a. 50 kilograms
   b. 4,630 micrograms
10. Convert 0.42 kilometers to meters.

SECTION 3
Organizing Data

Key Ideas
- Why is organizing data an important science skill?
- How do scientists handle very large and very small numbers?
- How can you tell the precision of a measurement?

Key Terms
scientific notation
precision
significant figure
accuracy

Why It Matters
Measurements must be reported correctly when building structures such as the Gateway Arch in St. Louis, Missouri.

Tennessee Course Level Expectations (Physical Science)
CLE.3202.4.1; CLE.3202.Inq.1; CLE.3202.Inq.2; CLE.3202.Inq.3; CLE.3202.Inq.4; CLE.3202.TE.2; CLE.3202.TE.4

Being able to read about the experiments that other scientists had performed with the cathode-ray tube helped Roentgen discover X rays. He was able to learn from the data.

Presenting Scientific Data

Suppose that you are trying to determine the speed of a chemical reaction that produces a gas. You could let the gas push water out of a graduated cylinder, as **Figure 1** shows. You read the volume of gas in the cylinder every 20 s from the start of the reaction until there is no change in volume for three readings. You make a table to organize the data that you collect in the experiment. ❯ **Because scientists use written reports and oral presentations to share their results, organizing and presenting data are important science skills.**

Because you did the experiment, you saw how the volume changed over time. But how can someone who reads your report see how the volume changed? To show the results, you can make a graph.

Experimental Data

Time (s)	Volume of gas (mL)
0	0
20	6
40	25
60	58
80	100
100	140
120	152
140	156
160	156
180	156

Figure 1 You can find the volume of gas that a chemical reaction produces by measuring the volume of water that a gas displaces in a graduated cylinder.

Line graphs show continuous changes.

There are many types of graphs that you could use, but which one best shows how the volume changed over time? A *line graph* is a good choice for displaying data that change continuously. Our example experiment has two variables, time and volume. Time is the *independent variable*—you chose the time intervals to take the measurements. The volume of gas is the *dependent variable*—its value depends on what happens in the experiment.

When you make line graphs, you should put the independent variable on the *x*-axis and the dependent variable on the *y*-axis. **Figure 2** is a graph of the data that is in the table in **Figure 1**.

Line graphs clearly show how the data changed during an experiment. A person who has not seen your experiment can look at this graph and know how much the volume of gas increased over time. The graph shows that gas was produced slowly for the first 20 s. From 40 s to 100 s, the rate increased until it became constant. The reaction then slowed down and stopped after about 140 s.

Reading Check When should you use a line graph?

Figure 2 Data that change are best represented by a line graph. Notice that many in-between volumes can be estimated.

Bar graphs compare the values of items.

A *bar graph* is useful when you want to compare similar data for several individual items or events. If you measured the melting temperatures of some metals, your data could be presented in a table. **Figure 3** shows the melting temperatures of five metals presented in a table and as a bar graph. The bar graph clearly shows how large or small the differences in individual values are. A bar graph is a better choice than a line graph for showing single values for many items.

Figure 3 Data that have specific values for various items or events should be represented by a bar graph.

Melting Points of Some Common Metals

Element	Melting temperature (K)
Aluminum	933
Gold	1,337
Iron	1,808
Lead	601
Silver	1,235

Pie graphs show the parts of a whole.

A *pie graph* is ideal for displaying data that are parts of a whole. Winter jackets, such as the one shown in **Figure 4**, are made of various fabrics that help keep you warm and dry. A jacket may contain 66% nylon, 30% polyester, and 4% spandex. As **Figure 4** shows, you can draw a pie graph that shows these percentages as a portion of the whole pie. In this case, the pie represents the jacket. To construct a pie graph, refer to Graphing Skills in Appendix B.

Writing Numbers in Scientific Notation

Sometimes, the value of a measurement is very large or very small. For example, the speed of light in space is about 300,000,000 m/s. Suppose that you wanted to calculate the time required for light to travel from Neptune to Earth when Earth and Neptune are 4,500,000,000,000 m apart. To calculate this time, you would divide the distance between Earth and Neptune by the speed of light, as shown in the equations below.

$$t = \frac{\text{distance from Earth to Neptune (m)}}{\text{speed of light (m/s)}}$$

$$t = \frac{4,500,000,000,000 \text{ m}}{300,000,000 \text{ m/s}}$$

There are a lot of zeros to keep track of when performing this calculation. ❯ **To reduce the number of zeros in very big and very small numbers, you can express the values as simple numbers multiplied by a power of 10, a method called scientific notation.** Some powers of 10 and their decimal equivalents are shown below.

$$10^3 = 1,000$$
$$10^2 = 100$$
$$10^1 = 10$$
$$10^0 = 1$$
$$10^{-1} = 0.1$$
$$10^{-2} = 0.01$$
$$10^{-3} = 0.001$$

In scientific notation, 4,500,000,000,000 m can be written as 4.5×10^{12} m. The speed of light in space is 3.0×10^8 m/s. Refer to Math Skills in Appendix B for more information on scientific notation.

✓ **Reading Check** When should you use scientific notation to express a quantity?

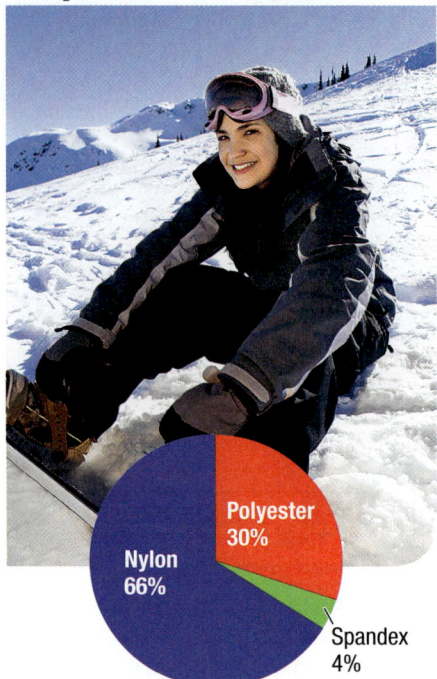

Figure 4 A pie graph is best for data that represent parts of a whole. This pie graph shows the composition of a winter jacket and gives the percentage of each type of fabric in a jacket. **If you add the percentages of each material, what is the total?**

scientific notation (SIE uhn TIF ik noh TAY shuhn) a method of expressing a quantity as a number multiplied by 10 to the appropriate power

www.scilinks.org
Topic: Presenting Scientific Data
Code: HK81213

Use scientific notation to make calculations.

When you use scientific notation in calculations, you should follow the math rules for powers of 10. For example, when you multiply two values, you add the powers of 10. When you divide two values, you subtract the powers of 10.

Using these rules can help you calculate more easily the time required for light to travel from Earth to Neptune.

$$t = \frac{4.5 \times 10^{12} \text{ m}}{3.0 \times 10^8 \text{ m/s}}$$

$$t = \left(\frac{4.5}{3.0} \times \frac{10^{12}}{10^8}\right) \frac{\text{m}}{\text{m/s}}$$

$$t = (1.5 \times 10^{(12-8)}) \text{ s}$$

$$t = 1.5 \times 10^4 \text{ s}$$

READING TOOLBOX

Everyday Words Used in Science
As you read this section, make a list of scientific words that you have heard before, such as *precision*. Then, compare the familiar meaning of the word with the scientific meaning.

Math Skills — Writing Scientific Notation

The adult human heart pumps about 18,000 L of blood each day. Write this value in scientific notation.

Identify
List the given and unknown values.

Given:
$\text{volume } (V) = 18{,}000 \text{ L}$
Unknown:
$\text{volume } (V) = ? \times 10^? \text{ L}$

Plan
Write the form for scientific notation.

$V = ? \times 10^? \text{ L}$

Solve
First, find the largest power of 10 that will divide into the known value.
Then, write that number as a power of 10.
Insert the values that you obtained into the form.

Divide 18,000 L by 10,000. The result is 1.8, leaving one digit before the decimal point. So, 18,000 L can be written as $(1.8 \times 10{,}000)$ L.
Because $10{,}000 = 10^4$, you can write 18,000 L as 1.8×10^4 L.
$V = 1.8 \times 10^4 \text{ L}$

Practice

1. Write the following measurements in scientific notation.
   a. 800,000,000 m
   b. 0.0015 kg
2. Write the following measurements in long form.
   a. 4.5×10^3 g
   b. 1.99×10^{-8} cm

For more practice, visit **go.hrw.com** and enter keyword **HK8MP**.

Practice Hint

> To use a shortcut for scientific notation, move the decimal point and count the number of places it is moved. To change 18,000 to 1.8, move the decimal point four places to the left. The number of places that the decimal is moved is the correct power of 10.
>
> $18{,}000 \text{ L} = 1.8 \times 10^4 \text{ L}$

> When a quantity smaller than 1 is converted to scientific notation, the decimal moves to the right and the power of 10 is *negative*. To express 0.0000021 m in scientific notation, move the decimal point to the right.
>
> $0.0000021 \text{ m} = 2.1 \times 10^{-6} \text{ m}$

Math Skills: Using Scientific Notation

Your county plans to buy a rectangular tract of land measuring 5.36×10^3 m by 1.38×10^4 m to establish a nature preserve. What is the area of this tract in square meters?

Identify
List the given and unknown values.

Given:
   length $(l) = 1.38 \times 10^4$ m
   width $(w) = 5.36 \times 10^3$ m
Unknown:
   area $(A) = ?$ m^2

Plan
Write the equation for area.

$A = l \times w$

Solve
Insert the known values into the equation, and solve.

$A = (1.38 \times 10^4 \text{ m})(5.36 \times 10^3 \text{ m})$
Regroup the values and units as follows.
$A = (1.38 \times 5.36)(10^4 \times 10^3)(\text{m} \times \text{m})$
When multiplying, add the powers of 10.
$A = (1.38 \times 5.36)(10^{4+3})(\text{m} \times \text{m})$
$A = 7.3968 \times 10^7$ m^2
Round the answer.
$A = 7.40 \times 10^7$ m^2

Practice Hint

> Because some scientific calculators and computer math software cannot display superscript numbers, they use E values to display numbers in scientific notation. A calculator may show the number 3.12×10^4 as 3.12 E4. Very small numbers are shown with negative values. For example, 2.637×10^{-5} may be shown as 2.637 E–5. The letter E signifies exponential notation. The E value is the exponent (power) of 10. When writing this number on paper, be sure to use the form 2.637×10^{-5}.

Practice

1. Perform the following calculations.
   a. $(5.5 \times 10^4 \text{ cm}) \times (1.4 \times 10^4 \text{ cm})$
   b. $(4.34 \text{ g/mL}) \times (8.22 \times 10^6 \text{ mL})$
   c. $(3.8 \times 10^{-2} \text{ cm}) \times (4.4 \times 10^{-2} \text{ cm}) \times (7.5 \times 10^{-2} \text{ cm})$
2. Perform the following calculations.
   a. $\dfrac{5.2 \times 10^8 \text{ cm}^3}{9.5 \times 10^2 \text{ cm}}$
   b. $\dfrac{6.05 \times 10^7 \text{ g}}{8.8 \times 10^6 \text{ cm}^3}$

For more practice, visit **go.hrw.com** and enter keyword **HK8MP**.

Using Significant Figures

The **precision**, or exactness, of measurements can vary. What would you use to measure the distances of two long jumps that are very close? If you use a tape measure that is marked every 0.1 m, you could report that both measurements were 4.1 m. But if you use a tape measure that is marked every 0.01 m, you could report more precise values—one jump was 4.11 m, and the other was 4.14 m.

> **Scientists use significant figures to show the precision of a measured quantity.** The distance of 4.1 m has two significant figures because the measured value has two digits.

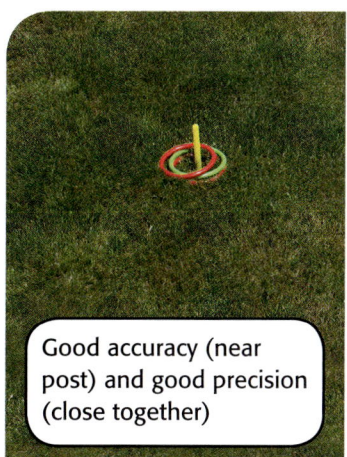
Good accuracy (near post) and good precision (close together)

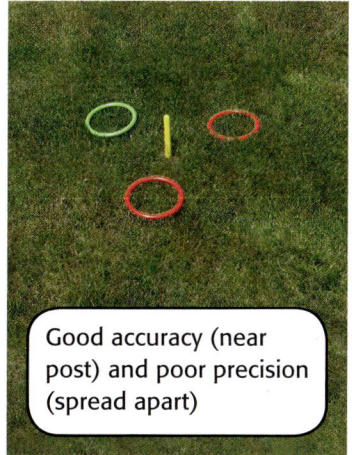
Good accuracy (near post) and poor precision (spread apart)

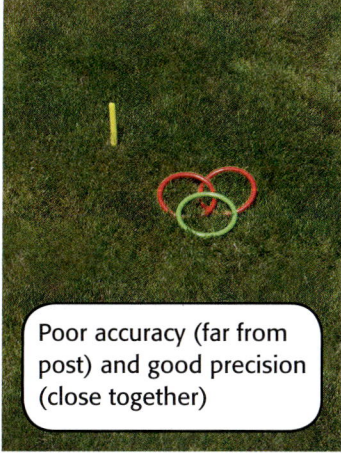
Poor accuracy (far from post) and good precision (close together)

Poor accuracy (far from post) and poor precision (spread apart)

Figure 5 This ring toss can help you visualize how accuracy differs from precision.

Accuracy differs from precision.

Precision and **accuracy** do not have the same meaning, as **Figure 5** shows. If you measure the long jump with a tape measure that has a broken tip, you can still read 4.14 m precisely. But that number is not accurate because it is not the actual distance of the jump. A measured quantity is only as accurate and precise as the tool used to make the measurement. Significant figures tell you how precise a measurement is, but they do not tell you how accurate the measurement is.

Round your answers to the correct significant figures.

When you use measurements in calculations, the answer is only as precise as the least precise measurement used in the calculation—the measurement with the fewest significant figures. For example, suppose that you are going to paint a mural on a wall. To figure out how much paint you will need for your project, you need to know the area of the wall. The measured dimensions are reported to be 8.871 m by 9.14 m.

If you use a calculator to multiply 8.871 by 9.14, the display may show 81.08094 as an answer. But you do not know the area of the room to the nearest 0.00001 m^2, as the calculator showed. To have the correct number of significant figures, you must round off your results. The answer should have the same number of significant figures as the least precise value in the calculation. In this case, the value of 9.14 had three significant figures, so the correct rounded result is $A = 81.1$ m^2.

When adding or subtracting, use this rule: The answer cannot have more decimal places than the least number of decimal places in the calculation. A calculator will add 6.3421 and 12.1 to give 18.4421 as a result. The least precise value was known to 0.1, so round the answer to 18.4.

> **Reading Check** When you add measurements, how many significant figures should the result have?

precision (pree SIZH uhn) the exactness of a measurement

significant figure (sig NIF uh kuhnt FIG yuhr) a prescribed decimal place that determines the amount of rounding off to be done based on the precision of the measurement

accuracy (AK yur uh see) a description of how close a measurement is to the true value of the quantity measured

QuickLab   10 min

Precision Vs. Accuracy

1. Crunch **five pieces of paper** into five paper balls.
2. Try to throw the balls into a **trash bin** that is 2 m in front of you.
3. Move the trash bin 2 m farther away, and try to throw the balls into the bin.
4. How accurate were your throws when the bin was 2 m away? How precise were your throws?
5. When the bin was moved farther away, were your accuracy and precision better or worse?

Section 3   Organizing Data   **27**

Math Skills: Significant Figures

Calculate the volume of a room that is 3.125 m high, 4.25 m wide, and 5.75 m long. Write the answer with the correct number of significant figures.

Identify
List the given and unknown values.

Given:
  length (l) = 5.75 m
  width (w) = 4.25 m
  height (h) = 3.125 m
Unknown:
  volume (V) = ? m^3

Plan
Write the equation for volume.

volume $(V) = l \times w \times h$

Solve
Insert the known values into the equation, and solve.

V = 5.75 m × 4.25 m × 3.125 m
V = 76.3671875 m^3
The value with the fewest significant figures has three significant figures, so the answer should have three significant figures.
V = 76.4 m^3

Practice Hint

› When rounding to get the correct number of significant figures, do you round up or down if the last digit is a 5? The correct way is to round to get an even number. For example, 3.25 is rounded to 3.2, and 3.35 is rounded to 3.4. Using this simple rule, you will generally round up half the time and will round down half the time. See Math Skills in Appendix B for more about significant figures and rounding.

Practice

1. Perform the following calculations, and write the answer with the correct number of significant figures.
   a. 12.65 m × 42.1 m
   b. 3.244 m ÷ 1.4 s

For more practice, visit **go.hrw.com** and enter keyword **HK8MP**.

Section 3 Review

KEY IDEAS

1. **Describe** the kind of data that you would display in a line graph.
2. **Describe** the kind of data that you would display in a pie graph. Give an example of data from everyday experiences that could be placed in a pie graph.
3. **Explain** in your own words why scientists use significant figures.

CRITICAL THINKING

4. **Applying Concepts** You throw three darts at a dartboard. The darts all hit the board near the same spot close to the edge but far away from the bull's-eye. Were your throws accurate or precise? Explain.

Math Skills

5. Convert the following measurements to scientific notation.
   a. 15,400 mm^3
   b. 2,050 mL
6. Make the following calculations.
   a. 3.16×10^3 m × 2.91×10^4 m
   b. 1.85×10^{-3} cm × 5.22×10^{-2} cm
7. Make the following calculations, and round the answer to the correct number of significant figures.
   a. 54.2 cm^2 × 22 cm
   b. 23,500 m ÷ 89 s

Why It Matters

How Was The Gateway Arch Built?

At 192 m high, the Gateway Arch in St. Louis, Missouri, is the tallest monument in the United States. The architects and structural engineers who designed and planned the construction of this massive steel arch needed to make very accurate and precise measurements and calculations.

REAL WORLD

The arch was built by adding sections onto each of its legs. If the dimensions of any one of the 142 sections had not been accurate, the results could have been disastrous.

Although the arch is 192 m wide at its base, the builders had to make sure that the final connecting piece of the arch fit perfectly. When they were building the arch, they had to make sure that the two sides were aligned precisely.

YOUR TURN

UNDERSTANDING CONCEPTS
1. Why was it important for the measurements of the building blocks of the arch to be accurate and precise?

CRITICAL THINKING
2. Do you think that it is important to make accurate and precise calculations when designing a skyscraper? Explain why or why not.

www.scilinks.org
Topic: Measurements and Data
Code: HK80925

Skills Practice Lab

⏱ 50 min

Making Measurements

In scientific investigations, you must collect data accurately so that you can reach valid conclusions. In this laboratory exercise, you will practice this skill by using laboratory tools to measure familiar objects.

What You'll Do
- **Measure** temperature, length, mass, and volume.
- **Organize** data into tables and graphs.

What You'll Need
- balance, platform or triple-beam
- basketball, volleyball, or soccer ball
- beaker, small
- block or box, small
- graph paper
- graduated cylinder, 100 mL
- meterstick or metric ruler, marked with centimeters and millimeters
- rock or irregularly shaped object, small
- sodium chloride (table salt)
- sodium hydrogen carbonate (baking soda)
- string
- test tubes (and test-tube holder)
- thermometer, wall

Safety

Procedure

Preparing for Your Experiment

① In this laboratory exercise, you will use a thermometer to measure temperature, a meterstick to measure length, a balance to measure mass, and a graduated cylinder to measure volume. You will then determine volume by liquid displacement.

Measuring Temperature

② At a convenient time during the lab, go to the wall thermometer, and read the temperature. Be sure that no one else is recording the temperature at the same time. On the board, record your reading and the time at which you read the temperature. After you have finished taking your lab measurements, you will make a graph of the temperature readings made by the class.

Measuring Length

③ Measure the length, width, and height of a block or box in centimeters. Record the measurements in a table like the one below. Using the equation below, calculate the volume of the block in cubic centimeters (cm^3), and write the volume in the table.

$$volume = length\ (cm) \times width\ (cm) \times height\ (cm)$$
$$V = l \times w \times h$$
$$V = ?\ cm^3$$

④ Repeat the measurements two more times, and record the data in your table. Find the average of your measurements and the average of the volume that you calculated.

Sample Data Table: Dimensions of a Rectangular Block

	Length (cm)	Width (cm)	Height (cm)	Volume (cm³)
Trial 1				
Trial 2		DO NOT WRITE		
Trial 3		IN BOOK		
Average				

30 Chapter 1 Introduction to Science

5. To measure the circumference of a ball, wrap a piece of string around the ball and mark the end point. Use the meterstick or metric ruler to measure the length of the string. Record your measurements in a table like the one shown below. Using a different piece of string each time, make two more measurements of the circumference of the ball, and record your data in the table.

6. Find the average of the three values, and calculate the difference, if any, of each of your measurements from the average.

Sample Data Table: Circumference of a Ball

	Circumference (cm)	Difference from average (cm)
Trial 1		
Trial 2	DO NOT WRITE IN BOOK	
Trial 3		
Average		

Measuring Mass

7. Place a small beaker on the balance, and measure the beaker's mass. Record the value in a data table like the one below. Measure to the nearest 0.01 g if you are using a triple-beam balance and to the nearest 0.1 g if you are using a platform balance.

8. Move the balance rider to a setting that will give a value 5 g more than the mass of the beaker. Add sodium chloride (table salt) to the beaker a little at a time until the balance just begins to swing. You now have about 5 g of salt in the beaker. Wait until the balance stops moving, and record in your table the total mass of the beaker and the sodium chloride (to the nearest 0.01 g or 0.1 g). Subtract the mass of the beaker from the total mass to find the mass of the sodium chloride.

9. Repeat steps 7 and 8 two times, and record your data in your table. Find the averages of your measurements, and record them in your data table.

10. Make another data table like the one below, but change the name of the substance to "sodium hydrogen carbonate." Repeat steps 7, 8, and 9 using sodium hydrogen carbonate (baking soda), and record your data.

Sample Data Table: Mass of Sodium Chloride

	Mass of beaker and sodium chloride (g)	Mass of beaker (g)	Mass of sodium chloride (g)
Trial 1			
Trial 2		DO NOT WRITE IN BOOK	
Trial 3			
Average			

Measuring Volume

11 Fill one of the test tubes with tap water. Pour the water into a 100 mL graduated cylinder.

12 The top of the column of water in the graduated cylinder will have a downward curve. This curve is called a *meniscus* and is shown in the figure below. Take your reading at the bottom of the meniscus. Record the volume of the test tube in a data table like the one below. Measure the volumes of the other test tubes, and record their volumes. Find the average volume of the three test tubes.

Sample Data Table: Liquid Volume

	Volume (mL)
Test tube 1	
Test tube 2	DO NOT WRITE
Test tube 3	IN BOOK
Average	

Measuring Volume by Liquid Displacement

13 Pour about 20 mL of tap water into the 100 mL graduated cylinder. Record the volume as precisely as you can in a data table like the one below.

14 Gently drop a small object, such as a rock, into the graduated cylinder. Be careful not to splash any water out of the cylinder. To prevent splashing, you may tilt the cylinder slightly and let the object slide down the side. Measure the volume of the water and the object. Record the volume in your data table. Determine the volume of the object by subtracting the volume of the water from the total volume.

Sample Data Table: Volume of a Solid

	Total volume (mL)	Volume of water only (mL)	Volume of object (mL)
Trial 1		DO NOT WRITE	
Trial 2		IN BOOK	
Trial 3			
Average			

Meniscus

Analysis

1. **Graphing Data** On a sheet of graph paper, make a line graph of the temperatures that were measured with the wall thermometer during the class. Did the temperature change during the class period? If so, find the average temperature, and determine the greatest number of degrees above and below the average.

Communicating Your Results

2. **Drawing Conclusions** On a sheet of graph paper, make a bar graph using the data from the three calculations of the mass of sodium chloride. Indicate the average value of the three calculations by drawing a line across the individual bars that represents the average value. Do the same for the sodium hydrogen carbonate masses. Using the information in your graphs, determine whether you measured the sodium chloride or the sodium hydrogen carbonate more precisely.

3. **Applying Concepts** Suppose that one of your test tubes has a capacity of 23 mL. You need to use about 5 mL of a liquid. Describe how you could estimate 5 mL.

4. **Analyzing Methods** Why is it better to align the meterstick with the edge of the object at the 1 cm mark than at the end of the stick?

5. **Analyzing Methods** Why do you think that using string to measure the circumference of the ball is better than using a flexible metal measuring tape?

Extension

In this lab, you did not investigate time, another basic measurement of science. Design an accurate and precise method for measuring the time required for a certain pendulum to swing back and forth once.

Forming a Hypothesis

Science Skills

Technology
Math
▸ Scientific Methods
Graphing

One important step of any scientific method is forming a hypothesis. A *hypothesis* is a possible answer to a question. A hypothesis is an educated guess that can be tested with experiments. A good hypothesis attempts to account for any known data and observations. The steps below show you how to form a hypothesis.

❶ Making Observations
Suppose that you baked some bread, but it did not rise. You want to form a hypothesis about what happened. First, you need to make observations.

Observations
- The kitchen is drafty.
- The dough was left to rise in a covered, porcelain bowl.
- The oven was set to 350 degrees.
- The yeast is several months old.

❷ Evaluating Observations
Think about which observations from step 1 may offer clues to the cause of the problem.

> You have heard that bread dough must rise in a warm room, so the draft could be one reason the bread did not rise.

> Old yeast may not work very well.

Observations
- The kitchen is drafty.
- The dough was left to rise in a covered, porcelain bowl.
- The oven was set to 350 degrees.
- The yeast is several months old.

❸ Forming Explanations
Use the list of observations that you made in step 2, and think of some possible explanations about why the bread did not rise.

Possible hypotheses
- The temperature in the room was not warm enough to allow the bread to rise.
- The yeast was too old to work properly.

❹ Determining Which Explanations Are Hypotheses
Examine the possible solutions that you listed in step 3. A hypothesis can be tested by an experiment. Because both of these explanations can be tested with experiments, both are valid hypotheses.

Testing my hypotheses
- Experiment 1: Turn up the thermostat, and block any drafts in the kitchen.
- Experiment 2: Use new yeast.

Practice

1. Suppose that your computer printer is not able to print. Make a list of the observations that you might make. Then, follow the steps above to form a hypothesis about what is wrong with the printer.

2. Think of a question that you can investigate by using a scientific method. Follow the steps above to form a hypothesis that may help answer the question.

CHAPTER 1 Summary

go.hrw.com
SUPER SUMMARY
KEYWORD: HK8INTS

Key Ideas

Key Terms

Section 1 The Nature of Science

- **How Science Takes Place** A scientist may perform experiments to find a new aspect of the natural world, to explain a known phenomenon, to check the results of other experiments, or to test the predictions of current theories. (p. 5)

- **The Branches of Science** Most of the time, natural science is divided into biological science, physical science, and Earth science. (p. 7)

- **Scientific Laws and Theories** Theories explain why something happens, and laws describe how something works. Theories and laws are supported by scientific experiments. (p. 9)

science, p. 7
technology, p. 8
law, p. 9
theory, p. 9

Section 2 The Way Science Works

- **Science Skills** Identifying problems, planning experiments, recording observations, and correctly reporting data are some of the most important skills in science. Scientists use scientific methods to find answers to their questions. (p. 14)

- **Units of Measurement** Scientists use standard units of measure that together form the International System of Units, or SI. (p. 17)

critical thinking, p. 14
scientific methods, p. 15
variable, p. 15
length, p. 21
mass, p. 21
volume, p. 21
weight, p. 21

Section 3 Organizing Data

- **Presenting Scientific Data** Because scientists use written reports and oral presentations to share their results, organizing and presenting data are important science skills. (p. 22)

- **Writing Numbers in Scientific Notation** To reduce the number of zeros in very big and very small numbers, you can express the values as simple numbers multiplied by a power of 10, a method called *scientific notation*. (p. 24)

- **Using Significant Figures** Scientists use significant figures to show the precision of a measured quantity. Precision is the degree of exactness of a measurement. (p. 26)

scientific notation, p. 24
precision, p. 26
significant figure, p. 26
accuracy, p. 27

Introduction to Science   **35**

CHAPTER 1 Review

READING TOOLBOX

1. **Everyday Words Used in Science** In everyday speech, the words *precision* and *accuracy* are often used interchangeably. When these terms are used in science, are their meanings the same as their everyday meanings?

USING KEY TERMS

2. *Physical science* was once defined as "the science of the nonliving world." Explain why that definition is no longer sufficient.

3. Explain why the observation that the sun sets in the west could be called a *scientific law*.

4. Explain why the following statement could be considered a *scientific theory:* The rotation of Earth causes the sun to set.

5. What is *mass,* and how does it differ from *weight*?

6. Some features on computer chips can be as small as 35 nm. Explain why you would use *scientific notation* to express this quantity in meters.

7. The mass of a certain elephant is 3,476 kg. A zoologist who measures the mass of that elephant finds that the mass is 3,480 kg. Is the mass measured by the zoologist *accurate*?

UNDERSTANDING KEY IDEAS

8. Which branch of science is not included in physical science?
    a. physics
    b. chemistry
    c. astronomy
    d. zoology

9. Which science deals most with energy and forces?
    a. biology
    b. physics
    c. botany
    d. agriculture

10. Using superconductors to build computers is an example of
    a. technology.
    b. applied biology.
    c. pure science.
    d. an experiment.

11. A balance is a scientific tool used to measure
    a. temperature.
    b. time.
    c. volume.
    d. mass.

12. Which unit is an SI base unit?
    a. liter
    b. cubic meter
    c. kilogram
    d. centimeter

13. The composition of the mixture of gases that makes up our air is best represented on what kind of graph?
    a. pie graph
    b. bar graph
    c. line graph
    d. variable graph

14. In a controlled experiment,
    a. the outcome is controlled.
    b. one variable remains fixed, and the other variables are changed.
    c. you change one variable throughout the experiment, and the other variables remain fixed.
    d. results are obtained by computer models.

15. Written in scientific notation, 0.000060 s is
    a. 60 s.
    b. 6.0×10^{-5} s.
    c. 6.0×10^{-6} s.
    d. 6.0×10^{4} s.

16. When studying a molecule, a chemist might make a model of the molecule to
    a. know the outcome of the experiment.
    b. help visualize the molecule.
    c. measure the mass of the molecule.
    d. observe the results of a chemical reaction.

17. The maximum depth of a certain lake is 244 m. What is the depth of the lake in kilometers?
    a. 0.0244 km
    b. 0.244 km
    c. 24,400 km
    d. 244,000 km

EXPLAINING KEY IDEAS

18. Do scientific laws ever change? Explain.

19. Explain whether or not scientific methods are sets of procedures that scientists follow.

INTERPRETING GRAPHICS The graph below shows how temperature changes during a chemical reaction. Use the graph to answer questions 20–21.

20. Which variable is the dependent variable, and which variable is the independent variable?

21. Why was this data presented in a line graph?

CRITICAL THINKING

22. **Applying Ideas** Today, scientists must search through scientific journals before performing an experiment or making methodical observations. Where would this step take place in a diagram of scientific methods?

23. **Evaluating Assumptions** At an air show, you are watching a group of sky divers when a friend says, "We learned in science class that things fall to Earth because of the law of gravitation." What is wrong with your friend's statement? Explain your reasoning.

24. **Applying Concepts** You report that a friend can go exactly 500 m on a bicycle in 39.46 s. But your stopwatch runs 2 s fast. Explain how your stopwatch affects the accuracy and precision of your measurement.

Graphing Skills

25. **Bar Graphs** The bar graph below summarizes how a consumer magazine has rated several stereos by price and sound quality. Use the graph to answer the following questions.

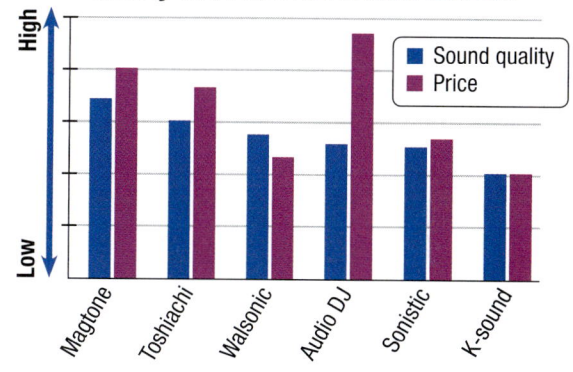

   a. Which brand do you think has the best sound for the price?
   b. Do you think that sound quality is truly related to price? Explain your answer.

26. **Pie Graph** The composition of silver solder is 40% silver, 40% tin, 14% copper, and 6% zinc. Show this composition in a pie graph.

Math Skills

27. **Writing Scientific Notation** Write the following measurements in scientific notation.
   a. 22,000 mg   b. 0.0000037 kg

28. **Using Scientific Notation** Write the answers to the following calculations in scientific notation.
   a. 37,000,000 A × 7,100,000 s
   b. 0.000312 m^3 ÷ 486 s

29. **Significant Figures** Round the following measurements to the number of significant figures shown in parentheses.
   a. 7.376 m (2)   b. 362.00306 s (5)

30. **Significant Figures** Write the answers to the following calculations. Be sure to use the correct number of significant figures.
   a. 15.75 m × 8.45 m   b. 5,650 L ÷ 27 min

Standardized Test Prep

Understanding Concepts

Directions (1–4): For each question, write on a sheet of paper the letter of the correct answer.

1. How many milliwatts are there in a kilowatt?
   - **A.** 100
   - **B.** 1,000
   - **C.** 1,000,000
   - **D.** 1,000,000,000

2. A student is trying to decide what subject to study. The student is most interested in the way that molecules of living things interact. What should the student study?
   - **F.** botany
   - **G.** biology
   - **H.** geophysics
   - **I.** biochemistry

3. An astronomer is measuring the distance between a comet and the sun. What units of measurement should the astronomer use?
   - **A.** miles
   - **B.** centiliters
   - **C.** kilometers
   - **D.** micrograms

4. The universal gravitation equation describes how the gravitational attraction between two masses is inversely proportional to the distance between them squared. What is the universal gravitation equation?
   - **F.** a hypothesis
   - **G.** a scientific law
   - **H.** a scientific theory
   - **I.** an experimental result

Directions (5–6): For each question, write a short response.

5. Density equals mass divided by volume. If a chemist is calculating the density of a substance with a known mass of 23.523 g and a known volume of 17.5 L, how many significant figures will the result have?

6. A demographics researcher needs a graph comparing the populations of the 10 largest cities in the world. What would be the best type of graph to use?

Reading Skills

Directions (7): Read the passage below. Then, answer the question that follows.

AIR MAY BE HEAVIER THAN YOU THINK

In 1642, the Italian scientists Rafael Magiotti and Gasparo Berti attempted to produce a vacuum. They filled a long tube with water and plugged both ends. Then, they placed the tube upright into a basin of water and opened the bottom end of the tube. Only a portion of the water in the tube flowed out, and the water still inside the tube stayed at the level of 10.4 m. Air could not have filled the empty space in the tube because no air had been in contact with that space. This result seemed to suggest that a vacuum existed in the space above the water. Magiotti and Berti theorized that the attractive power of that vacuum caused some water to stay in the tube.

Evangelista Torricelli had a different opinion. He hypothesized that air must have weight and that the weight of the air pressing down on the water in the basin kept all of the water in the tube from draining out. He performed the same experiment using mercury, which is 14 times as heavy as water. Mercury stopped flowing out of the tube when the level in the tube reached a height 14 times lower than the height at which water stopped. Thus, Torricelli's idea seemed to be confirmed.

7. What was the initial hypothesis of Magiotti and Berti?
   - **A.** A long tube filled with water, with both ends plugged, was placed in a basin of water.
   - **B.** The weight of air on the basin kept all of the water from flowing out of the tube.
   - **C.** The attractive force of the vacuum drew the water up the tube.
   - **D.** A vacuum can exist.

Interpreting Graphics

The graphs below show two sets of data. Use these graphs to answer questions 8–9.

UNDERSTANDING TYPES OF GRAPHS

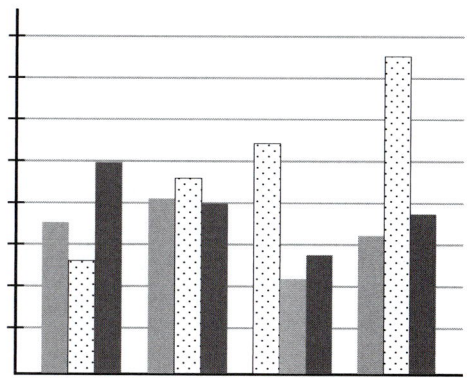

8. One of the graphs shows the percentage of the total mass of each of four compounds in a mixture. If there is more water than any other compound in the mixture, what is the percentage of water in the mixture?
   - **F.** 100%
   - **G.** 83%
   - **H.** 48%
   - **I.** 25%

9. One of the graphs shows the results of a fertilization experiment in which four types of fertilizers were applied to groups of three kinds of plants. The plants' average height increase was measured. Was there a single fertilizer that worked best on every plant? How do you know?

The graphic below displays the projected world population in the year 2012, along with the average number of cells in the human body. Use this graphic to answer question 10.

PROJECTED WORLD POPULATION

10. In the year 2012, how many human cells will there be in the world?
    - **A.** 7.0×10^7
    - **B.** 7.0×10^{22}
    - **C.** 1.43×10^7
    - **D.** 1.43×10^{22}

> **Test Tip**
>
> When answering short-response or extended-response questions, be sure to write in complete sentences. When you have finished writing your answer, be sure to proofread for errors in spelling, grammar, and punctuation.

Chemistry

Chapter 2	**Matter**	42
Chapter 3	**States of Matter**	74
Chapter 4	**Atoms**	110
Chapter 5	**The Periodic Table**	142
Chapter 6	**The Structure of Matter**	174
Chapter 7	**Chemical Reactions**	216
Chapter 8	**Solutions**	256
Chapter 9	**Acids, Bases, and Salts**	290
Chapter 10	**Nuclear Changes**	324

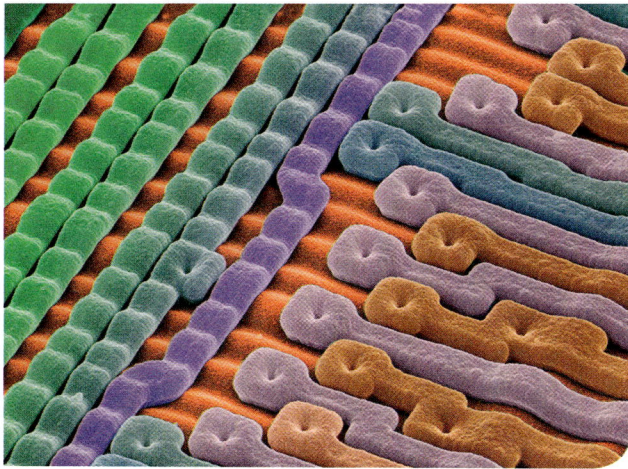

CHAPTER 2 Matter

Chapter Outline

1 Classifying Matter
What Is Matter?
Elements
Compounds
Pure Substances and Mixtures

2 Properties of Matter
Physical Properties
Chemical Properties

3 Changes of Matter
Physical Changes
Chemical Changes
Breaking Down Mixtures and Compounds

Why It Matters
This glass is part of a sculpture by artist Dale Chihuly. He blows the glass while it is hot and nearly liquid. Then, he controls its shape as it cools and becomes solid.

Tennessee Course Level Expectations (Physical Science)

CLE.3202.TE.3 Explain the relationship between the properties of a material and the use of the material in the application of a technology; **CLE.3202.1.1** Explore matter in terms of its physical and chemical properties; **CLE.3202.1.4** Investigate chemical and physical changes; **CLE.3202.1.5** Evaluate pure substances and mixtures; **CLE.3202.1.7** Construct chemical formulas for common compounds; **CLE.3202.Inq.1** Recognize that science is a progressive endeavor that reevaluates and extends what is already accepted; **CLE.3202.Inq.2** Design and conduct scientific investigations to explore new phenomena, verify previous results, test how well a theory predicts, and compare opposing theories; **CLE.3202.Inq.3** Use appropriate tools and technology to collect precise and accurate data; **CLE.3202.Inq.4** Apply qualitative and quantitative measures to analyze data and draw conclusions that are free of bias; **CLE.3202.Inq.5** Compare experimental evidence and conclusions with those drawn by others about the same testable question; **CLE.3202.Inq.6** Communicate and defend scientific findings.

Inquiry Lab
⏲ 30 min

Finding Density

Add some **water** to a **cup,** and begin adding **salt.** Use a **spoon** to stir the salt into the water. Place an **egg** in the cup. Continue adding salt and stirring until the egg begins to float. Remove the egg. Pour the solution into a **graduated cylinder** until you measure 25 mL of solution. Then, use a **balance** to find the mass of the 25 mL of solution.

Questions to Get You Started

1. The density of an object is equal to the object's mass divided by the object's volume. What is the density of the saltwater solution?

2. Find the mass and volume of the egg. Use the method of liquid displacement to find volume. What is the density of the egg?

3. Compare your measurements for the density of the solution and the density of the egg. What conclusions can you draw from this comparison?

These reading tools can help you learn the material in this chapter. For more information on how to use these and other tools, see **Appendix A**.

Word Parts

Suffixes The suffixes –ity and –ness usually change adjectives into nouns that denote a state, condition, or property. The root can help you understand the word's meaning.

Your Turn Two key terms in Section 2 use the suffix –ity. (Key terms in sections are indicated by bold text with yellow highlights.) On a sheet of paper, complete the table below for the missing key term. Then, think of two nouns that have the suffix –ness, and add those to your table.

WORD	ROOT	SUFFIX	DEFINITION
density	dense	-ity	the quality of being dense; the ratio of mass to volume
		-ity	

Finding Examples

Words that Signal Examples Examples can help you picture an idea or concept. Certain words or phrases can serve as signals that an example is about to be introduced. Such signals include
- for example
- such as
- for instance

Your Turn Make a list of the key terms from Section 1. See the sample list below. As you read Section 1, add examples that correspond to each key term. If a word or phrase in the text signals the example, add that word or phrase:

KEY TERM	EXAMPLES	SIGNAL WORDS
• element	• carbon • copper	(none)

Note Taking

Two-Column Notes Two-column notes can help you learn the main ideas from each section.

Your Turn Complete two-column notes for the Key Ideas in this chapter.
1. Write one Key Idea in each row in the left column.
2. As you read the chapter, add detailed notes and examples in the right column. Be sure to put these details and examples in your own words.

KEY IDEA	DETAIL NOTES
How can matter be classified?	• Matter is either an element, a compound, or a mixture. • Every sample of matter can be classified into one of these three groups.
Why are carbon and copper classified as elements?	• Each element is made of one kind of atom. • Diamonds are made up of carbon atoms.

44 Chapter 2 Matter

SECTION 1
Classifying Matter

Key Ideas
> How can matter be classified?
> Why are carbon and copper classified as elements?
> How are elements related to compounds?
> What is the difference between a pure substance and a mixture?

Key Terms
matter
element
atom
molecule
compound
pure substance
mixture

Why It Matters
By letting a charcoal grill rust outside, you are making a compound. By making a glass of iced tea, you are making a mixture. Understanding matter helps you understand your world.

What do you have in common with this textbook? You are made of matter, and so is this textbook. Your pencil and paper are also made of matter.

Tennessee Course Level Expectations (Physical Science)
CLE.3202.1.5; CLE.3202.1.7; CLE.3202.Inq.1; CLE.3202.Inq.2; CLE.3202.Inq.3

What Is Matter?

All of the materials that you can hold or touch are matter. **Matter** is anything that has mass and takes up space. The air that you are breathing is matter even though you cannot see it. Light and sound are not matter. Unlike air, they have no mass or volume.

The study of matter and its changes is what chemistry is about. When chemists study matter, they explore the makeup, properties, changes, and interactions of matter. Chemistry is an important part of your daily life. Many items that you use each day, from soaps to foods and from carbonated drinks to gasoline, are chosen in part for their chemical properties.

One important part of chemistry is classification. The compact discs in **Figure 1** are easy to find because they are classified into groups. All classical music is grouped. Likewise, all pop music is together. Matter can be classified into groups in a similar way. One useful way to classify matter is based on what makes up the matter. > **Every sample of matter is either an element, a compound, or a mixture.** For instance, gold is an element, water is a compound, and a vegetable salad is a mixture. You will learn more about each of these types of matter in this section.

matter (MAT uhr) anything that has mass and takes up space

Figure 1 Compact discs are classified by music type. **What is one way to classify matter?**

Section 1 Classifying Matter 45

element (EL uh muhnt) a substance that cannot be separated or broken down into simpler substances by chemical means

atom (AT uhm) the smallest unit of an element that maintains the chemical properties of that element

molecule (MAHL i kyool) a group of atoms that are held together by chemical forces; a molecule is the smallest unit of matter that can exist by itself and retain all of a substance's chemical properties

compound (KAHM pownd) a substance made up of atoms of two or more different elements joined by chemical bonds

Elements

When wood gets too hot, it chars—its surface turns black. Its surface breaks down to form carbon, whose properties differ from the properties of wood. The carbon will not decompose further by normal chemical processes. Carbon is an **element,** a substance that cannot be broken down into simpler substances by chemical means.

The smallest unit of an element that keeps the element's chemical properties is an **atom.** ❯ **Each element is made of one kind of atom.** As a result, every known element is unique. The elements carbon and copper are shown in **Figure 2.** Carbon has multiple forms, including diamond and graphite, but each form is made of carbon atoms.

✅ **Reading Check** Can elements be broken down into simpler substances? (See Appendix E for answers to Reading Checks.)

Elements are represented by symbols.

Each element is represented by a one- or two-letter symbol that is used worldwide. Symbols for elements are always a single capital letter or a capital letter followed by a lowercase letter. For example, the symbol for carbon is C, and the symbol for aluminum is Al. The periodic table on the inside back cover of this textbook shows all of the elements and the symbols used to represent them. The elements that make up the human body are shown in **Figure 3.** For example, nitrogen, N, makes up 2.4% of the total weight of the human body.

Figure 2 Every element is made up of a single kind of atom. Both copper and carbon are elements.

Copper wire is made up of copper atoms.

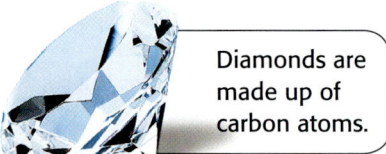

Diamonds are made up of carbon atoms.

Figure 3 The human body is made up of many elements. **Which element makes up the largest percentage of the total weight of the body?**

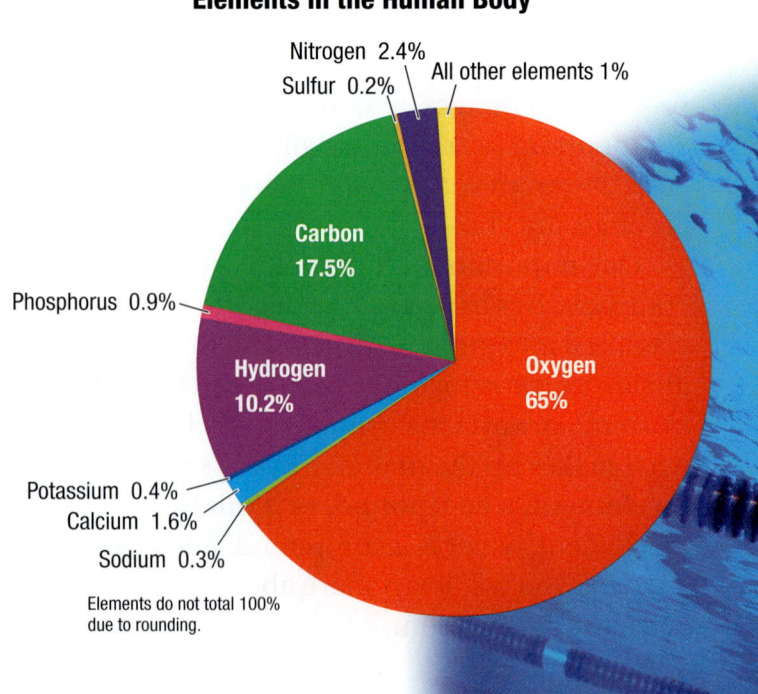

Elements in the Human Body

- Nitrogen 2.4%
- Sulfur 0.2%
- All other elements 1%
- Carbon 17.5%
- Phosphorus 0.9%
- Hydrogen 10.2%
- Oxygen 65%
- Potassium 0.4%
- Calcium 1.6%
- Sodium 0.3%

Elements do not total 100% due to rounding.

Atoms that make up a molecule act as a unit.

Atoms can join to make millions of molecules just as letters of the alphabet combine to form different words. A **molecule** is the smallest unit of a substance that behaves like the substance. The atoms of some elements, such as neon, are found uncombined in nature. Other elements, such as oxygen, form molecules that have more than one atom. **Figure 4** shows some molecules that are made of atoms of the same element.

Compounds

One substance that you are familiar with is water. When oxygen and hydrogen atoms combine to form a molecule of water, the atoms act as a unit. Water is an example of a compound. A **compound** is a substance made up of atoms of different elements. ❯ **Each molecule of a compound contains two or more elements that are chemically combined.**

When elements combine to make a certain compound, they always combine in the same proportions. For example, a water molecule is always made of two hydrogen atoms and one oxygen atom, as **Figure 5** shows. The compound iron (III) oxide, which is often seen as rust, always has two atoms of iron for every three atoms of oxygen.

Compounds have unique properties.

Every compound differs from the elements that it contains. For example, the elements hydrogen, oxygen, and nitrogen are colorless gases. But they combine with carbon to form nylon, a flexible solid. Likewise, the properties of water differ from those of hydrogen and oxygen, which make up water.

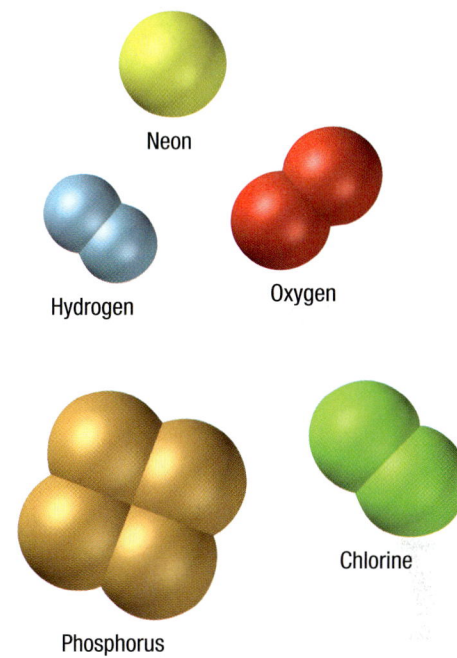

Figure 4 Each of these molecules is made of atoms of the same element. **How many atoms are in one phosphorus molecule?**

Figure 5 Water is an example of a compound. Each water molecule is made up of two hydrogen atoms and one oxygen atom.

Figure 6 The chemical formula for a molecule of indigo shows that it is made of four elements. **How many atoms are in a molecule of indigo?**

pure substance (PYOOR SUHB stuhns) a sample of matter, either a single element or a single compound, that has definite chemical and physical properties

mixture (MIKS chuhr) a combination of two or more substances that are not chemically combined

Chemical formulas represent compounds.

Indigo is the dye first used to turn blue jeans blue. The *chemical formula* for a molecule of indigo, $C_{16}H_{10}N_2O_2$, is shown in **Figure 6**. A chemical formula shows how many atoms of each element are in a unit of a substance. The number of atoms of each element is written as a *subscript* after the element's symbol. If only one atom of an element is present, no subscript number is used.

Numbers placed in front of a chemical formula show the number of molecules. So, three molecules of table sugar are written as $3C_{12}H_{22}O_{11}$. Each molecule of sugar contains 12 carbon atoms, 22 hydrogen atoms, and 11 oxygen atoms.

Pure Substances and Mixtures

The word *pure* often means "not mixed with anything." For example, pure grape juice contains the juice of grapes and nothing else. In chemistry, the word *pure* has another meaning. A **pure substance** is matter that has a fixed composition and definite properties.

The composition of grape juice is not fixed. Grape juice is a mixture of pure substances, such as water and sugars. A **mixture** is a combination of substances that are not chemically combined. ▶ **Elements and compounds are pure substances, but mixtures are not.** A mixture can be physically separated into its parts. The parts of a pure substance are chemically combined and cannot be physically separated.

✓ **Reading Check** Why are compounds classified as pure substances?

QuickLab

Mystery Mixture

 10 min

Procedure

1. Place a **pencil** on a **clear plastic cup**. Use **scissors** to cut a strip of paper (3 cm × 15 cm) from a **coffee filter**. Wrap one end around the pencil. Attach the paper with **tape**.
2. Take the paper out of the cup. Using a **water-soluble, black marker**, make a dot in the center of the strip, 2 cm from the bottom.
3. Pour **water** in the cup to a depth of 1 cm.
4. Lower the paper into the cup. Keep the dot above the water.
5. Remove the paper when the water is 1 cm from the top of the paper. Record your observations.

Analysis

1. What happened as the paper soaked up the water?
2. Which colors make up the black ink?
3. Is the ink-making process a physical change, or is it a chemical change? Explain.

Mixtures are classified by how well the substances mix.

There are several examples of mixtures in **Figure 7.** Mixtures are defined by how well their substances are mixed. The salad is a mixture of lettuce and vegetables. The shirt is a mixture of cotton and polyester fibers. The vinegar in the dressing is a mixture of water and acetic acid. The water is not a mixture. Water is a pure substance because it has a fixed composition and definite properties.

The vegetables in the salad are not evenly distributed. One spoonful may contain tomatoes. Another spoonful may have cucumber slices. A mixture such as a salad is a *heterogeneous mixture*. The substances in a heterogeneous mixture are not evenly distributed. Some heterogeneous mixtures are harder to recognize. The shirt is a heterogeneous mixture because the cotton and polyester fibers are not evenly distributed.

In a *homogeneous mixture*, the components are evenly distributed. The mixture is the same throughout. For example, vinegar is a homogeneous mixture of evenly-distributed water molecules and acetic acid molecules.

Gasoline is a homogeneous mixture of at least 100 liquids. The liquids in gasoline are *miscible,* or able to be mixed. On the other hand, if you shake a mixture of oil and water, the oil and water will not mix well. The water will settle out. Oil and water are *immiscible*. You can see two layers in the mixture.

Figure 7 Mixtures are all around you. **What is the difference between the mixtures and the pure substance shown? What is the difference between the two types of mixtures?**

Integrating Biology

Indigo The pure substance indigo is a natural dye made from plants of the genus *Indigofera*, which are in the pea family. Before synthetic dyes were developed, indigo plants were widely grown in Indonesia, in India, and in the Americas. Most species of indigo are shrubs that are 1 to 2 m tall and often have small flowers in spikes or clusters. The dye is made from the leaves and branches of the shrubs. Today, most indigo dye is synthetic rather than natural.

Section 1   Classifying Matter   **49**

READING TOOLBOX

Finding Examples
Make a list of all of the examples given on this page. Use signal words such as *for example,* but also look for unmarked examples. Next to each example, write the general idea that the example represents.

Gases can mix with liquids.

Carbonated drinks are homogeneous mixtures. They contain sugar, flavorings, and carbon dioxide gas, CO_2, dissolved in water. This example shows that gases can mix with liquids. Liquids that are not carbonated can also contain gases. For example, if you let a glass of cold water sit overnight, bubbles may form inside the glass. The bubbles form when some of the air that was dissolved in the cold water comes out of solution as the water warms up.

Carbonated drinks often have a foam on top. The foam is a gas-liquid mixture. The gas is not dissolved in the liquid but forms tiny bubbles in the liquid. The bubbles join to form bigger bubbles that escape from the foam and cause it to collapse.

Some foams are stable and last for a long time. For example, if you whip egg whites with air, as shown in the photograph on the left in **Figure 8,** you get a foam. When you bake the foam, the liquid egg white dries and hardens, as shown in the photograph on the right. The solid foam is meringue.

Figure 8 The meringue in this pie is a mixture of air and liquid egg white that has been beaten and then heated to form a solid foam.

Section 1 Review

KEY IDEAS

1. **Describe** matter, and explain why light is not classified as matter.
2. **State** the relationship between atoms and elements. Are atoms and elements matter?
3. **Define** *molecule,* and give examples of molecules formed by one element and molecules formed by two elements.
4. **State** the chemical formula of water.
5. **List** the two types of pure substances.

CRITICAL THINKING

6. **Classifying** Classify each of the following as an element or a compound.
   a. sulfur, S_8
   b. methane, CH_4
   c. carbon monoxide, CO
   d. cobalt, Co
7. **Making Comparisons** How are mixtures and pure substances alike? How are they different?
8. **Drawing Conclusions** David says, "Pure honey has nothing else added." Susan says, "The honey is not really pure. It is a mixture of many substances." Who is right? Explain your answer.

SECTION 2
Properties of Matter

Key Ideas
> Why are color, volume, and density classified as physical properties?

> Why are flammability and reactivity classified as chemical properties?

Key Terms
melting point
boiling point
density
reactivity

Why It Matters
Properties determine uses. For instance, the properties of a substance called *aerogel* enable it to trap fast-moving comet particles.

When playing sports, you choose a ball that has the shape and mass suitable for your game. It would be hard to play soccer with a football or to play softball with a bowling ball. The properties of the balls make the balls useful for different activities.

Physical Properties

Shape and mass are examples of *physical properties*. Some other physical properties are color, volume, and texture. The balls in **Figure 1** have different physical properties. > **Physical properties are characteristics that can be observed without changing the identity of the substance.** For example, you can determine the color, mass, and shape of a ball without changing the substance that makes up the ball.

Physical properties are often very easy to observe. For instance, you can easily observe that a tennis ball is yellow, round, and fuzzy. Matter can also be described in terms of physical properties that are not as obvious. For example, a physical property of air is that it is colorless.

Physical properties can help identify substances.

Because many physical properties remain constant, you can use your observations or measurements of these properties to identify substances. For example, you recognize your friends by their physical properties, such as height and hair color. At room temperature and under atmospheric pressure, all samples of pure water are colorless and liquid. Pure water is never a powdery green solid. The physical properties of water help you identify water.

Tennessee Course Level Expectations (Physical Science)

CLE.3202.1.1; CLE.3202.Inq.1; CLE.3202.Inq.2; CLE.3202.Inq.3; CLE.3202.Inq.4

Figure 1 The physical properties of these balls make the balls useful in different sports. **How many physical properties can you observe?**

Finding Examples
As you read this section, find examples for each property that is discussed. Don't forget to use signal words as clues. Make a table of properties and examples.

melting point (MELT ing POYNT) the temperature and pressure at which a solid becomes a liquid

boiling point (BOYL ing POYNT) the temperature and pressure at which a liquid becomes a gas

Academic Vocabulary
durable (DUR uh buhl) able to withstand wear or damage
flexible (FLEK suh buhl) capable of bending easily without breaking

Figure 2 Aluminum is light, strong, and durable, which makes it ideal for use in foil.

Physical properties can be observed or measured.

You can use your senses to observe some of the basic physical properties of a substance: shape, color, odor, and texture. Another physical property that you can observe is *state*—the physical form of a substance. Solid, liquid, and gas are three common states of matter. For example, water can be in the form of solid ice, liquid water, or gaseous steam.

Other physical properties, such as melting point and boiling point, can be measured. The temperature at which a substance changes from a solid to a liquid is the **melting point.** The temperature at which a liquid changes to a gas is the **boiling point.** A characteristic of any pure substance is that its boiling point and its melting point are constant if the pressure remains the same. At sea level, water boils at 100 °C and freezes at 0 °C. At constant pressure, pure water always has the same boiling point and the same melting point. Regardless of the mass or volume of water, the physical properties of the water are the same. This principle is true for all pure substances.

Other physical properties that can be measured are strength, hardness, and magnetism. The ability to conduct electricity or heat is also a physical property. For instance, copper conducts electricity well, while plastic does not.

Reading Check Name five examples of physical properties.

Physical properties help determine uses.

Every day, you use physical properties to recognize substances. Physical properties help you decide whether your socks are clean (odor), whether your books will fit in your backpack (volume), or whether your clothes match (color).

Physical properties are often used to select substances that may be useful. Copper is used in power lines, telephone lines, and electric motors because it conducts electricity well. As **Figure 2** shows, aluminum is used in foil because it is lightweight yet durable and flexible. Car frames are made of steel, which is a strong solid that provides structure. Tires are made of a flexible solid that cushions your ride. Antifreeze is used in car radiators because it remains a liquid at temperatures that would freeze or boil water.

Can you think of other physical properties that help us determine how we can use a substance? Some substances have the ability to conduct heat, while others do not. Plastic-foam cups do not conduct heat well, so they are often used for holding hot drinks. What would happen if you poured hot tea into a metal cup?

Why It Matters

Aerogel

WEIRD SCIENCE

Aerogel, nicknamed "solid blue smoke," is a substance with unique physical properties. For instance, aerogel has the lowest density of any known solid. Air makes up 99.8% of one form of aerogel. Glass is 1,000 times as dense as aerogel! NASA's *Stardust* mission, shown below, used aerogel to trap thousands of tiny, fast-moving comet particles. Aerogel's unique properties enabled it to capture the particles without damaging or vaporizing them.

This collector contains the aerogel that trapped comet dust as the *Stardust* spacecraft passed through comet Wild 2. The spacecraft returned successfully in January of 2006. Scientists all over the world are studying the particles to learn more about comets.

Aerogel can withstand very high temperatures. These crayons are not melting because aerogel protects them from the flame below. Aerogel is also very strong. It can support 4,000 times its own weight. These properties make aerogel ideal for space missions.

YOUR TURN

UNDERSTANDING CONCEPTS
1. What are some physical properties of aerogel?

CRITICAL THINKING
2. NASA used aerogel to protect the *Sojourner* rover from the cold environment on Mars. What property makes aerogel useful for this purpose?

SCLINKS.
www.scilinks.org
Topic: Aerogel
Code: HK81695

density (DEN suh tee) the ratio of the mass of a substance to the volume of the substance

Density is a physical property.

Another physical property is *density*. **Density** is a measurement of how much matter is contained in a certain volume of a substance. The density of an object is calculated by dividing the object's mass by the object's volume.

> **Density equation** $D = \dfrac{m}{V}$ $density = \dfrac{mass}{volume}$

The density of a liquid or a solid is usually expressed in grams per cubic centimeter (g/cm³). For example, 10.0 cm³ of water has a mass of 10.0 g. Thus, the water's density is 10.0 g for every 10.0 cm³, or 1.00 g/cm³. A cubic centimeter has the same volume as a milliliter (mL).

Reading Check What is the density of water in grams per milliliter?

Math Skills Density

If 10.0 cm³ of ice has a mass of 9.17 g, what is the density of ice?

Identify
List the given and the unknown values.

Given:
mass, $m = 9.17$ g
volume, $V = 10.0$ cm³
Unknown:
density, $D = ?$ g/cm³

Plan
Write the equation for density.

$density = \dfrac{mass}{volume}$
$D = \dfrac{m}{V}$

Solve
Insert the known values into the equation, and solve.

$D = \dfrac{9.17 \text{ g}}{10.0 \text{ cm}^3}$
$D = 0.917$ g/cm³

Practice Hint

▶ Problem 3: You can solve for mass by multiplying both sides of the density equation by volume.

$D = \dfrac{m}{V}$

$DV = \dfrac{m\cancel{V}}{\cancel{V}}$

$m = DV$

Practice

1. A piece of tin has a mass of 16.52 g and a volume of 2.26 cm³. What is the density of tin?
2. A man has a 50.0 cm³ bottle completely filled with 163 g of a slimy, green liquid. What is the density of the liquid?
3. A piece of metal has a density of 11.3 g/cm³ and a volume of 6.7 cm³. What is the mass of this piece of metal?

For more practice, visit **go.hrw.com** and enter keyword **HK8MP**.

QuickLab

Density of Water

⏱ 20 min

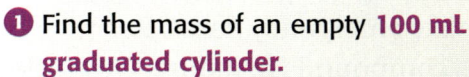

Procedure
1. Find the mass of an empty **100 mL graduated cylinder**.
2. Pour 10 mL of **water** from a **250 mL beaker** into the graduated cylinder. Use a **balance** to find the mass of the graduated cylinder that contains the water.
3. Repeat Step 2 for several different volumes of water.
4. Use **graph paper** or a **graphing calculator** to plot volume (on the x-axis) versus mass (on the y-axis).

Analysis
1. Estimate the mass of 55 mL of water and 85 mL of water.
2. Predict the volume of 25 g of water and 75 g of water.
3. Use your graph to determine the density of water.

Density is different from weight.

A substance that has a low density is "light" in comparison with something else of the same volume. The balloons in **Figure 3** float because the denser air sinks around them. A substance that has a high density is "heavy" in comparison with another object of the same volume. A stone sinks to the bottom of a pond because the stone is denser than the water.

The brick and sponge shown in **Figure 4** have similar volumes, but the brick is more massive than the sponge. Because the brick has more mass per unit of volume than the sponge does, the brick is denser. If you held the brick in one hand and the sponge in the other hand, you would know instantly that the brick is denser than the sponge.

Although the denser brick feels heavier than the sponge, weight and density are different. In the example of a brick and sponge, both objects have about the same volume. But compare two objects that have different volumes. Two pounds of feathers are heavier than one pound of steel. But the feathers are less dense than the steel, so two pounds of feathers have a greater volume than one pound of steel does.

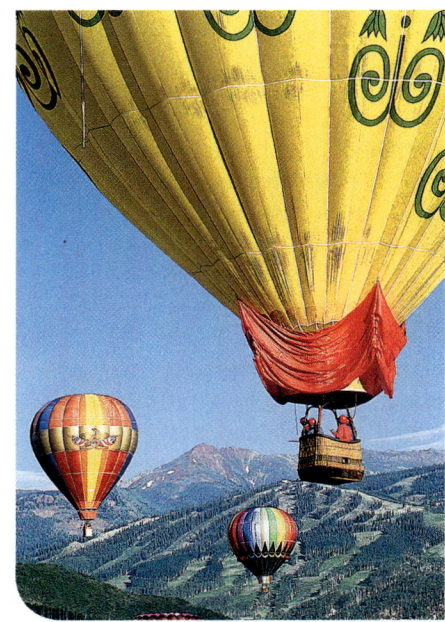

Figure 3 Helium-filled balloons float because helium is less dense than air. Hot-air balloons rise for a similar reason. **Which is less dense: hot air or cool air?**

More mass · Denser

Less mass · Less dense

Figure 4 This brick is denser than this sponge because the brick has more matter in a similar volume. **If a brick and a sponge have equal masses, which has less volume?**

Section 2 Properties of Matter **55**

Chemical Properties

Some elements react very easily with other elements. For example, because magnesium is very reactive, it is used to make emergency flares. Reactive elements are usually found as compounds in nature. Other elements, such as gold, are much less reactive. These elements are often found uncombined. Light bulbs are filled with argon gas because it is not very reactive.

These properties are examples of *chemical properties*. ▶ **A chemical property describes how a substance changes into a new substance, either by combining with other elements or by breaking apart into new substances.** Chemical properties are related to the specific elements that make up substances. Chemical properties are generally not as easy to observe as physical properties.

Flammability is a chemical property.

One chemical property is *flammability*—the ability to burn. For example, wood can be burned to form new substances that have new properties. So, one chemical property of wood is flammability. Even when wood is not burning, it is flammable. A substance always has its chemical properties, even when you cannot observe them. A substance that does not burn, such as gold, has the chemical property of nonflammability.

Reactivity is a chemical property.

Another chemical property is the reactivity of elements or compounds with oxygen, water, or other substances. **Reactivity** is the capacity of a substance to combine with another substance. For example, although iron has many useful properties, its reactivity with oxygen is one property that can cause problems. When exposed to oxygen, iron rusts. You can see rust on the old car shown in **Figure 5.** Why does rust occur? The steel parts of a car rust when iron atoms in the steel react with oxygen in air to form iron(III) oxide. The painted and chromium parts of the car do not rust because they do not react with oxygen. In other words, the elements in steel, paint, and chrome have different chemical properties.

Reading Check Name two chemical properties.

reactivity (REE ak TIV uh tee) the capacity of a substance to combine chemically with another substance

Figure 5 One chemical property is reactivity. **Which reacts more easily with oxygen: iron, paint, or chromium?**

This hole started as a small chip in the paint, which exposed the iron in the car to oxygen. The iron rusted and crumbled away.

Paint does not react with oxygen, so paint provides a barrier between oxygen and the iron in the car's steel.

This bumper is rust free because it is coated with chromium, which does not react with oxygen.

Why It Matters

Identifying Mystery Substances

Forensic scientists use physical and chemical properties to identify substances, such as paint, glass, or fibers. For instance, paint chips from an accident can be analyzed to learn about the car from which the paint came. Although this method does not always provide conclusive evidence, it can be used to support further investigation.

1 The first step is to collect the paint chips. This forensic investigator is using a scraping tool to collect paint from a car.

2 This scientist is studying a sample under a microscope to look for small traces of paint left by another car.

3 The next step is to study the collected sample's physical and chemical properties. Physical properties include color, layer sequence, and layer thickness. Chemical properties include pigments and additives.

4 The physical and chemical properties can then be compared with a database of paint properties for different makes and models of automobiles. The investigators can use this information to determine from what kind of car the paint sample most likely came.

YOUR TURN

UNDERSTANDING CONCEPTS
1. Why is layer thickness a physical property?

CRITICAL THINKING
2. What is one situation in which the database of automobile paint would not provide information about the unknown car?

QuickLab

10 min

Reactivity

1. Measure 4 g each of **compounds A** and **B**. Place them in separate **clear plastic cups**.
2. Observe the color and texture of each compound. Record your observations.
3. Add 5 mL of **vinegar** to each cup. Record your observations.
4. Baking soda reacts with vinegar, but powdered sugar does not. Which of these two substances is compound A, and which is compound B?

Physical and chemical properties are different.

It is important to remember the differences between physical and chemical properties. You can observe physical properties without changing the identity of the substance. But you can observe chemical properties only in situations in which the identity of the substance changes.

Figure 6 summarizes the physical and chemical properties of a few common substances. Some substances have similar physical properties but different chemical properties. Other substances have similar chemical properties but different physical properties. For example, wood and rubbing alcohol both have the chemical property of flammability, but they have different physical properties.

Figure 6 Comparison of Physical and Chemical Properties

Substance	Wood	Iron	Red dye
Physical property	has a grainy texture	bends without breaking	has red color
Chemical property	is flammable	reacts with oxygen to form rust	reacts with bleach; loses color

Section 2 Review

KEY IDEAS

1. **List** two physical properties and two chemical properties.
2. **Identify** the following as physical properties or chemical properties.
   - a. reacts with water
   - b. is red
   - c. is shiny and silvery
   - d. melts easily
   - e. boils at 100 °C
   - f. is nonflammable
   - g. has a low density
   - h. tarnishes in moist air

CRITICAL THINKING

3. **Applying Concepts** Describe several uses for plastic, and explain why plastic is a good choice for these purposes.
4. **Making Inferences** Suppose that you need to build a raft. Write a paragraph describing the physical and chemical properties of the raft that would be important to ensure your safety.

Math Skills

5. Calculate the density of a rock that has a mass of 454 g and a volume of 100.0 cm^3.
6. Calculate the density of a substance in a sealed 2,500 cm^3 flask that is full to capacity with 0.36 g of a substance.
7. A sample of copper has a volume of 23.4 cm^3. If the density of copper is 8.9 g/cm^3, what is the copper's mass?

SECTION 3
Changes of Matter

Key Ideas
- Why is a getting a haircut an example of a physical change?
- Why is baking bread an example of a chemical change?
- How can mixtures and compounds be broken down?

Key Terms
physical change
chemical change

Why It Matters
The process of making glass—for practical applications or as art—involves both physical and chemical changes.

Leaves change color in the fall, an ice cube melts in your glass, and bread dough turns into bread when it bakes in the oven. Such changes occur in matter as a result of physical or chemical changes.

Tennessee Course Level Expectations (Physical Science)

CLE.3202.1.1; CLE.3202.1.4; CLE.3202.1.5; CLE.3202.Inq.1; CLE.3202.Inq.2; CLE.3202.Inq.3; CLE.3202.Inq.4; CLE.3202.Inq.6; CLE.3202.TE.3

Physical Changes

If you break a piece of chalk, you change its physical properties of size and shape. But no matter how many times you break the chalk, its chemical properties remain unchanged. The chalk is still chalk, and each piece of chalk would produce bubbles if you placed it in vinegar. Breaking chalk is an example of a **physical change**. ▶ **A physical change affects one or more physical properties of a substance without changing the identity of the substance.**

Figure 1 shows several examples of physical changes. Some other examples of physical changes are dissolving sugar in water, sanding a piece of wood, and mixing oil and vinegar.

physical change (FIZ i kuhl CHAYNJ) a change of matter from one form to another without a change in chemical properties

Figure 1 Examples of Physical Changes

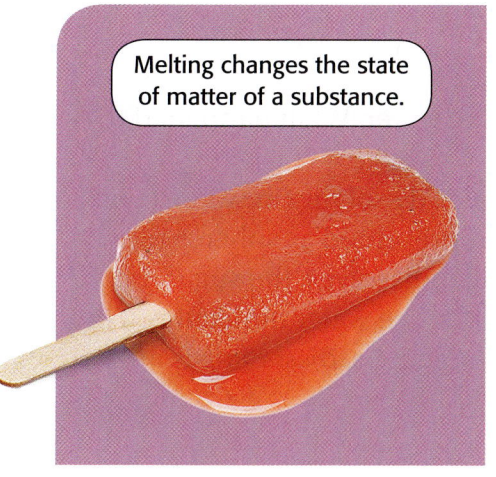

Melting changes the state of matter of a substance.

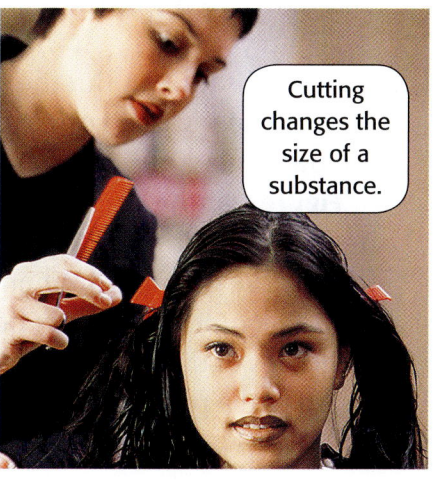

Cutting changes the size of a substance.

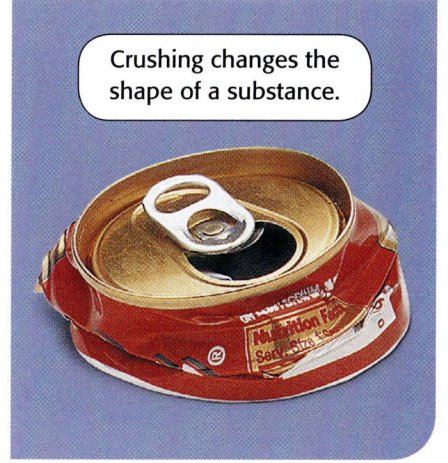

Crushing changes the shape of a substance.

Figure 2 One way to form gold rings is to melt the gold and then pour it into a mold. **What physical properties of gold change during this process?**

Figure 3 When sugar dissolves in water, the water molecules attract the sugar molecules and pull them apart. As a result, the sugar molecules spread out in the water.

Keyword: HK8MATF3

Physical changes do not change a substance's identity.

Melting a gold nugget to form a gold ring involves several physical changes, as **Figure 2** shows. The gold changes from solid to liquid and then back to solid. The shape of the gold also changes. The gold nugget becomes a ring of gold. But these physical changes do not change all of the properties of the gold. For example, the gold's color, melting point, and density do not change.

During a physical change, energy is absorbed or released. After a physical change, a substance may look different, but the arrangement of atoms that make up the substance is not changed. A gold nugget, molten gold, and gold rings are all made of gold atoms.

Dissolving is a physical change.

When you stir sugar into water, the sugar dissolves and seems to disappear. But the sugar is still there. You can taste the sweetness when you drink the water. What happened to the sugar?

Figure 3 shows sugar molecules dissolving in water. (The sugar and water molecules are represented as spheres to simplify the diagram.) When sugar dissolves, the sugar molecules become spread out between the water molecules. The molecules of the sugar do not change. So, dissolving is an example of a physical change.

Chemical Changes

Some materials are useful because of their ability to change and combine to form new substances. For example, the compounds in gasoline burn in the presence of oxygen to form carbon dioxide and water. The burning of the compounds is a **chemical change.** ▶ **A chemical change happens when one or more substances are changed into entirely new substances that have different properties.** The chemical properties of a substance describe which chemical changes can happen. You can learn about chemical properties by observing chemical changes.

Reading Check What is the difference between a physical change and a chemical change?

Chemical changes happen everywhere.

You see chemical changes happening more often than you may think. When a battery dies, the chemicals inside the battery have changed, so the battery can no longer supply energy. The oxygen that you inhale when you breathe is used in a series of chemical reactions in your body. After the oxygen reacts with molecules containing carbon, the oxygen is then exhaled as part of the compound carbon dioxide. Chemical changes occur when fruits and vegetables ripen and when the food you eat is digested. **Figure 4** shows some other examples of chemical changes.

chemical change (KEM i kuhl CHAYNJ) a change that occurs when one or more substances change into entirely new substances with different properties

www.sclinks.org
Topic: Physical/Chemical Changes
Code: HK81145

Figure 4 Examples of Chemical Changes

Chemical reactions produce pigments that give leaves their colors. In the fall, green leaves change colors as different reactions take place.

When effervescent tablets are added to water, the citric acid and baking soda in them react to produce carbon dioxide, which forms bubbles.

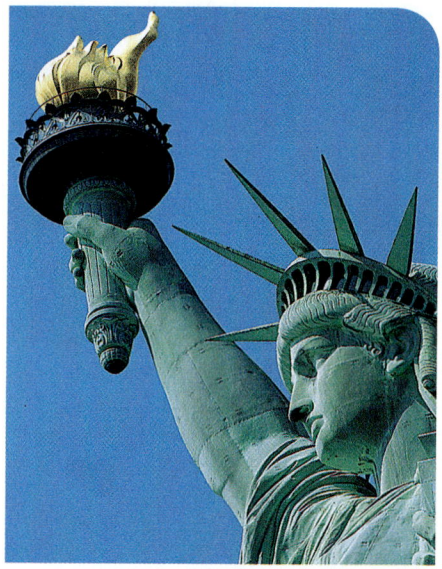

The shiny, orange-brown copper of the Statue of Liberty has reacted with carbon dioxide and water to form green copper compounds.

Figure 5 These ingredients are combined and baked to make French bread. **What evidence shows that chemical changes occurred?**

Academic Vocabulary
interaction (IN tuhr AK shuhn) the action or influence between things

Chemical changes form new substances.

When you bake French bread, you combine the ingredients shown in **Figure 5**: water, flour, yeast, and salt. Each ingredient has its own set of properties. When you mix the ingredients and heat them in an oven, the heat of the oven and the interaction of the ingredients cause chemical changes. These changes result in bread, whose properties differ from the properties of the ingredients. This is an example of how new substances are formed by chemical changes.

Chemical changes can be detected.

When a chemical change takes place, clues often suggest that a chemical change has happened. A change in odor or color is a good clue that a substance is changing chemically. When food burns, you can often smell the gases given off by the chemical changes. When paint fades, you can observe the effects of chemical changes in the paint. Chemical changes often cause color changes, fizzing or foaming, or the production of sound, heat, light, or odor.

Figure 6 shows table sugar being heated on a dessert to form a thin caramel layer. How do you know a chemical change is taking place? The sugar has changed color, bubbles are forming, and a caramel smell is filling the air.

Chemical changes cannot be reversed by physical changes.

Because new substances are formed in a chemical change, a chemical change cannot be reversed by physical changes. Most of the chemical changes that you observe in your daily life, such as bread baking, milk turning sour, or iron rusting, are impossible to reverse. Imagine trying to unbake a loaf of bread! However, under the right conditions, some chemical changes can be reversed by other chemical changes. For example, the water that forms in a space shuttle's rockets can be split into hydrogen and oxygen by using an electric current to start a reaction.

Figure 6 Table sugar is a compound made of carbon, hydrogen, and oxygen. When table sugar is heated, it caramelizes.

Breaking Down Mixtures and Compounds

You know that a mixture is a combination of substances that are not chemically combined. A compound, on the other hand, is made up of atoms that are chemically combined. As a result of this difference, mixtures and compounds must be separated in different ways. ❯ **Mixtures can be separated by physical changes, but compounds must be broken down by chemical changes.**

✓ **Reading Check** Why must mixtures and compounds be separated in different ways?

Mixtures can be physically separated.

Because mixtures are not chemically combined, each part of a mixture has the same chemical makeup that it had before the mixture was formed. Each substance keeps its identity. Thus, mixtures can be separated by physical means.

In some mixtures, such as a pizza, you can see the components. You can remove the mushrooms on a pizza. The removal results in a physical change. Not all mixtures are this easy to separate. For example, you cannot pick salt out of saltwater. But you can separate saltwater into its parts by heating it. When the water evaporates, the salt remains.

If components of a mixture have different boiling points, you can heat the mixture in a distillation device. The component that boils and evaporates first separates from the mixture. Another technique for separating mixtures is to use a centrifuge, which spins a mixture rapidly until the components separate. **Figure 7** shows blood separated by a centrifuge.

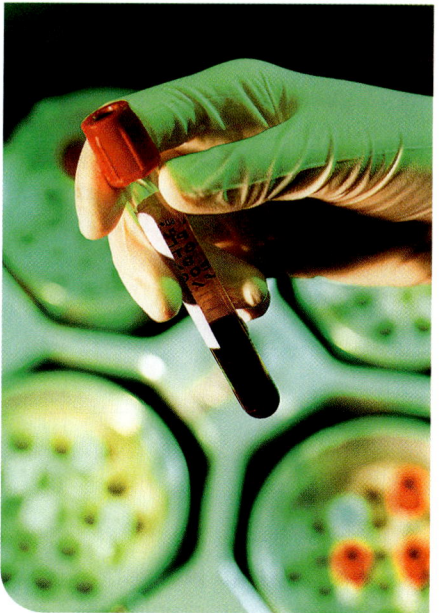

Figure 7 You can see layers in this blood sample because it has been separated into its components by the centrifuge. **Is blood a mixture or a compound?**

InquiryLab Can You Separate a Mixture? 30 min

Procedure

1. Study the **sample mixture** provided by your teacher.

2. Design an experiment in which the following materials are used to separate the components of the mixture: **distilled water, filter funnel, filter paper, magnet, paper towels, clear plastic cup,** and **plastic spoon.** Consider physical properties such as density, magnetism, and the ability to dissolve.

Analysis

1. What properties did you observe in each of the components of the mixture?

2. How did these properties help you to separate the components of the sample?

3. Did any of the components share similar properties?

4. Based on your observations, what items do you think made up the mixture?

Section 3 Changes of Matter

Figure 8 Heating the compound mercury(II) oxide breaks it down into the elements mercury and oxygen. **Is this change a physical change or a chemical change?**

Some compounds can be broken down through chemical changes.

Some compounds can be broken down into elements through chemical changes. For instance, when the compound mercury(II) oxide is heated, it breaks down into the elements mercury and oxygen. This process is shown in **Figure 8.** Electric currents can be used to separate some compounds. For example, if a current is passed through melted table salt, which is a compound, the elements sodium and chlorine are produced.

Other compounds undergo chemical changes to form simpler compounds. When you open a bottle of soda, compounds in the soda break down into carbon dioxide and water. The carbon dioxide escapes as bubbles. The escaping carbon dioxide is the reason that a soda bubbles when you open it. Through additional chemical changes, the carbon dioxide and water can be further broken down into the elements carbon, oxygen, and hydrogen.

READING TOOLBOX

Two-Column Notes
Create two-column notes to review the Key Ideas for this section. Put the Key Ideas in the left column, and add details and examples in your own words in the right column.

Section 3 Review

KEY IDEAS

1. **Define** *physical change* and *chemical change,* and give examples of each type of change.
2. **Explain** why changes of state are physical changes.
3. **Describe** how you would separate the components of a mixture of sugar and sand. Would your methods result in physical or chemical changes?
4. **Explain** why physical changes can easily be reversed but why chemical changes cannot.
5. **Identify** two ways to break down a compound into simpler substances.
6. **List** three clues that indicate a chemical change.

CRITICAL THINKING

7. **Classifying** Classify each of the following as a chemical change or a physical change.
    a. sugar being added to lemonade
    b. plants using carbon dioxide and water to form oxygen and sugar
    c. water boiling
    d. an egg frying
    e. rust forming on metal
    f. fruit rotting
    g. salt being removed from water by evaporation
8. **Making Inferences** Describe the difference between physical and chemical changes in terms of what happens to the molecules.

64 Chapter 2 Matter

Why It Matters

How Is Glass Made?

REAL WORLD

People have been making glass for thousands of years. The raw materials of sand, limestone, and soda ash are heated and turned into glass through chemical changes. Several physical changes, including changes in state, shape, and size, also occur. There are different ways to shape the glass once it has been made. One method, called *glass blowing,* is illustrated below.

1. Glassmakers often purchase the raw ingredients—sand, limestone, and soda ash—mixed together in a form called *batch*. When the batch is heated to about 1,500 °C, the mixture becomes transparent and flows like honey.

2. A glass blower dips a hollow iron blowpipe into the hot mixture and picks up a gob of molten glass. The blower occasionally reheats the glass to keep it soft.

3. By turning the sticky glob and blowing into the tube, the glass blower creates a hollow bulb that can be pulled, twisted, and blown into different shapes. When the finished shape is broken from the tube, a work of art has been created.

YOUR TURN

UNDERSTANDING CONCEPTS

1. After the molten glass has been shaped, it cools and solidifies. Is this a physical change or a chemical change?

WRITING IN SCIENCE

2. Research another method of shaping glass, such as pressing, drawing, or casting. Write a paragraph describing this method.

SCILINKS
www.scilinks.org
Topic: Glass
Code: HK80678

Physical Properties of Metals

Some properties are shared by all metals, but not all metals are exactly alike. As a materials engineer at a tool manufacturing company, you have been asked to determine which of several metals would be the best to use as plating on heavy-duty drill bits. The main requirements are that the metal be dense and hard. It is also desirable for the metal not to conduct too much heat and not to be affected by magnetism.

What You'll Do

> **Measure** the physical properties of various metals.

> **Compare** possible applications for the metals that you test based on the properties of the metals.

What You'll Need

balance
beakers (several)
graduated cylinder
hot plate
ice
magnet
metal samples: aluminum, iron, nickel, tin, and zinc
ruler, metric
stopwatch
water
wax

Safety

Procedure

Testing the Properties of Different Metals

1. You will be comparing the four properties of the five metals in the sample data table below. You will be able to measure some of the properties directly. For other properties, you will rank the metals from most to least (1 through 5).

Sample Data Table: Physical Properties of Some Metals

Metal	Density (g/mL)	Hardness (1–5)	Heat conductivity (1–5)	Affected by magnetism (yes/no)
Aluminum, Al				
Iron, Fe				
Nickel, Ni		DO NOT WRITE IN BOOK		
Tin, Sn				
Zinc, Zn				

2. Density is the mass per unit volume of a substance. If the metal is box shaped, you can measure its length, width, and height, and then use these measurements to calculate the metal's volume. If the shape of the metal is irregular, you can add the metal to a known volume of water and determine what volume of water is displaced.

3. Relative hardness indicates how easy it is to scratch a metal. A metal that is harder can scratch a metal that is less hard, but not vice versa.

4. Relative heat conductivity indicates how quickly a metal heats or cools. A metal that conducts heat well will heat up or cool down faster than other metals.

5. If a magnet placed near a metal attracts the metal, the metal is affected by magnetism.

Designing Your Experiment

6. With your lab partner(s), decide how you will use the materials provided to determine the properties of each of the metals to be tested. There is more than one way to measure some of the physical properties that are listed, so you might not use all of the materials that are provided.

7. In your lab report, list each step that you will perform in your experiment.

8. Have your teacher approve your plan before you carry out your experiment.

Performing Your Experiment

9. After your teacher approves your plan, carry out your experiment. Keep in mind that repeating your measurements will help ensure that your data are accurate.

10. Record all of the data you collect and any observations you make.

Analysis

1. **Making Comparisons** Which physical properties were the easiest for you to measure and compare? Which properties were the most difficult to measure and compare? Explain why.

2. **Describing Events** What happens when you try to scratch aluminum with zinc?

3. **Applying Ideas** Suppose you find a metal fastener and determine that its density is 7 g/mL. What are two ways that you could determine whether the metal in the fastener is tin or zinc?

4. **Applying Concepts** Suppose someone gives you an alloy that is made of both zinc and nickel. In general, how do you think the physical properties of the alloy would be similar to or different from those of the individual metals?

Communicating Your Results

5. **Organizing Data** In a data table like the one provided in this lab, list the physical properties that you compared and the data that you collected for each of the metals.

6. **Evaluating Methods** What are some possible sources of error in the measurements that you made? What could you have done differently to minimize those sources of error?

Application

Which of these metals would you recommend as the best one to use as plating on heavy-duty drill bits? Justify your answer.

Converting Units

Science > Skills

Technology
▶ Math
Scientific Methods
Graphing

Problem

Density can be expressed in grams per cubic centimeter (g/cm^3). The density of lead is $11.3\ g/cm^3$. What is the density of lead in grams per cubic millimeter (g/mm^3)?

Solution

Identify

List the given and unknown values.

Given:
$$\text{density},\ d = 11.3\ g/cm^3$$

Unknown:
$$\text{density},\ d = ?\ g/mm^3$$

Plan

a. Determine the relationship between units. Because cm is cubed, the conversion value must also be cubed.

b. Write the equation for the conversion. Use the units as a guide. If the units don't cancel properly, you may have the conversion equation backwards.

a. $1\ cm = 10\ mm$

$1\ cm^3 = (10\ mm)^3 = 1{,}000\ mm^3$

b. $\text{density in } g/mm^3 = \text{density in } \dfrac{g}{\cancel{cm^3}} \times \dfrac{1\ \cancel{cm^3}}{1{,}000\ mm^3}$

Solve

Insert the known values into the equation, and solve.

$$\text{density in } g/mm^3 = \dfrac{11.3\ g}{\cancel{cm^3}} \times \dfrac{1\ \cancel{cm^3}}{1{,}000\ mm^3}$$

$$d = 0.0113\ g/mm^3$$

Practice

Use the table to answer the following questions.

1. Find the density of dry air in the following units:
   a. grams per cubic millimeter (g/mm^3)
   b. grams per cubic meter (g/m^3)
2. What is the density of water in grams per cubic millimeter?
3. Find the density of helium in grams per cubic meter.
4. Will the density of gasoline in grams per cubic meter be greater than or less than the value given in the table? To see if you are correct, convert the value given in the table to grams per cubic meter.
5. What is the density of iron in grams per cubic meter?

Substance	Density (g/cm^3)
Air (dry)	0.00129
Brick (common)	1.9
Gasoline	0.7
Helium	0.00018
Ice	0.92
Iron	7.86
Lead	11.3
Nitrogen	0.00125
Steel	7.8
Water	1.00

CHAPTER 2 Summary

go.hrw.com
SUPER SUMMARY
KEYWORD: HK8MATS

Key Ideas

Section 1 Classifying Matter

- **What Is Matter?** Every sample of matter is either an element, a compound, or a mixture. (p. 45)
- **Elements** Each element is made of one kind of atom. (p. 46)
- **Compounds** Each molecule of a compound contains two or more elements that are chemically combined. (p. 47)
- **Pure Substances and Mixtures** Elements and compounds are pure substances, but mixtures are not. (p. 48)

Section 2 Properties of Matter

- **Physical Properties** Physical properties are characteristics that can be observed without changing the identity of the substance. Examples include color, mass, melting point, boiling point, and density. (p. 51)
- **Chemical Properties** A chemical property describes how a substance changes into a new substance, either by combining with other elements or by breaking apart into new substances. Examples include flammability and reactivity. (p. 56)

Section 3 Changes of Matter

- **Physical Changes** A physical change affects one or more physical properties of a substance without changing the identity of the substance. (p. 59)
- **Chemical Changes** A chemical change happens when one or more substances are changed into entirely new substances that have different properties. (p. 61)
- **Breaking Down Mixtures and Compounds** Mixtures can be separated by physical changes, but compounds must be broken down by chemical changes. (p. 63)

Key Terms

matter, p. 45
element, p. 46
atom, p. 46
molecule, p. 47
compound, p. 47
pure substance, p. 48
mixture, p. 48

melting point, p. 52
boiling point, p. 52
density, p. 54
reactivity, p. 56

physical change, p. 59
chemical change, p. 61

Matter **69**

CHAPTER 2 Review

READING TOOLBOX

1. **Finding Examples** Review Section 3. As you review, list at least five examples of a physical change and at least five examples of a chemical change.

USING KEY TERMS

2. For each pair of terms, explain how the meanings of the terms differ.
   a. *atom* and *molecule*
   b. *molecule* and *compound*
   c. *compound* and *mixture*

3. When wood is burned, new substances are produced. Describe this reaction, and explain what type of change occurs. Use the terms *flammability, chemical property,* and *physical change* or *chemical change*.

4. When sugar is added to water, the sugar dissolves and the resulting liquid is clear. Do the sugar and water form a *pure substance,* or do they form a *mixture*? Explain your answer.

5. When water is mixed with rubbing alcohol, the two liquids completely dissolve. Are the two liquids *miscible,* or are they *immiscible*? Explain the difference between the two terms.

6. The photograph shows magnesium burning in the presence of oxygen. Give some evidence that a *chemical change* is occurring.

7. Make a table that has two columns. Label one column "Physical properties" and the other "Chemical properties." Put each of the following terms in the correct column: *color, density, reactivity, magnetism, melting point, corrosion, flammability, dissolving, conducting electricity,* and *boiling point*.

UNDERSTANDING KEY IDEAS

8. What is matter?
   a. any visible solid that has mass
   b. any liquid that takes up space and has mass
   c. anything that takes up space and has mass
   d. any liquid or solid that takes up space

9. What is the chemical formula for iron(III) oxide?
   a. Fe^{2+} c. I_2
   b. NaCl   d. Fe_2O_3

10. Which of the following is a mixture?
    a. air   c. water
    b. salt   d. sulfur

11. Compounds and elements are
    a. always solids.   c. pure substances.
    b. mixtures.   d. dense.

12. Which of the following is an example of a physical change?
    a. melting ice cubes
    b. burning paper
    c. rusting iron
    d. burning gasoline

13. Which of the following is a pure substance?
    a. grape juice   c. table salt
    b. saltwater   d. gasoline

14. If you add oil to water and shake the liquid, you will form a
    a. pure substance.
    b. miscible liquid.
    c. heterogeneous mixture.
    d. homogeneous mixture.

EXPLAINING KEY IDEAS

15. List four properties that can be used to classify elements.

16. Describe a procedure to separate a mixture of salt, finely ground pepper, and pebbles.

INTERPRETING GRAPHICS The graph below shows mass versus volume for two metals. Use the graph to answer questions 17–19.

17. What does the slope of each line represent?

18. Which has a greater density: silver or iron? Explain how you can answer this question without doing any calculations.

19. What is the density of silver?

CRITICAL THINKING

20. Analyzing Data A jar contains 30 mL of glycerin (mass = 37.8 g) and 60 mL of corn syrup (mass = 82.8 g). Which liquid is the top layer? Explain your answer.

21. Applying Concepts A light green powder is heated in a test tube. A gas is given off while the solid becomes black. What type of change is occurring? Explain your reasoning.

22. Making Inferences Suppose you are planning a journey to the center of Earth in a self-propelled tunneling machine. List properties of the special materials that would be needed to build the machine, and explain why each property would be important.

Graphing Skills

23. Constructing Graphs Use the data below to make a graph that shows the relationship between the mass and volume of aluminum samples of different sizes. Plot mass on the y-axis, and plot volume on the x-axis. What does the shape of the graph tell you about the density of aluminum?

Block number	Mass (g)	Volume (cm^3)
1	1.20	0.443
2	3.59	1.33
3	5.72	2.12
4	12.4	4.60
5	15.3	5.66
6	19.4	7.17
7	22.7	8.41
8	24.1	8.94
9	34.0	12.6
10	36.4	13.5

Math Skills

24. Calculating Density A piece of titanium metal has a mass of 67.5 g and a volume of 15 cm^3. What is the density of titanium?

25. Calculating Density A sample of a substance that has a mass of 85 g has a volume of 110 cm^3. What is the density of the substance? Will the substance float in water? Explain your answer.

26. Calculating Volume The density of a piece of brass is 8.4 g/cm^3. If the mass of the brass is 510 g, find the volume of the brass.

27. Calculating Mass What mass of water will fill a tank that is 100.0 cm long, 50.0 cm wide, and 30.0 cm high? Express the answer in grams.

Chapter Review **71**

Standardized Test Prep

Understanding Concepts

Directions (1–3): For *each* question, write on a sheet of paper the letter of the correct answer.

1. Which of the following is an example of a chemical change?
   - **A.** gasoline evaporating
   - **B.** sugar dissolving in water
   - **C.** a metal surface rusting
   - **D.** a mixture separating into its components

2. Which of the following terms most accurately describes carbon dioxide?
   - **F.** element
   - **G.** compound
   - **H.** mixture
   - **I.** solution

3. An experiment shows that the element mercury has a density of 13.57 g/cm^3. What is the volume of 1.000 kg of pure mercury?
   - **A.** 0.7369 cm^3
   - **B.** 13.57 cm^3
   - **C.** 73.69 cm^3
   - **D.** 1,357 cm^3

Directions (4–6): For *each* question, write a short response.

4. At 4 °C, the volume of 15 g of water was 15 cm^3. At 20 °C, the volume of the same 15 g of water was 15.03 cm^3. What effect did the increase in temperature have on the water's density?

5. If the density of water changes because the temperature of the water changes, is this change a physical change or a chemical change?

6. Study the graph below. Which has a greater density: water or gasoline?

Reading Skills

Directions (7–8): Read the passage below. Then, answer the questions that follow.

METAL ALLOYS

When a metallic element is combined with one or more other elements and the resulting combination has metallic properties, that combination is known as an *alloy*. Metals are most often alloyed with other metals, but other elements and compounds can also be included in an alloy to give it particular properties. For example, blending small amounts of manganese and carbon with iron creates a substance known as *carbon steel*. Carbon steel is harder and more corrosion-resistant than pure iron.

Some alloys are compounds. One example is cementite, Fe$_3$C. Other alloys, such as bronze and brass, are solutions of two or more metals dissolved in one another. Alloys that are mixtures of several compounds may not have a single melting point. Instead, they may have a melting range, in which the material is a combination of a solid and a liquid.

7. Which of the following is an alloy?
   - **F.** iron
   - **G.** carbon
   - **H.** bronze
   - **I.** manganese

8. An alloy of aluminum is observed to have a melting range instead of a single melting point. What can be concluded from this observation?
   - **A.** The alloy is a compound.
   - **B.** The alloy is probably a mixture of different compounds.
   - **C.** The other components in the alloy have higher melting points.
   - **D.** Each individual molecule of the aluminum alloy has all of the properties of the alloy.

Interpreting Graphics

The tables below give the chemical formulas for some common substances. Use the tables to answer questions 9–11.

Substance	Chemical formula
Ethanol	C_2H_6O
Baking soda	$NaHCO_3$
Hydrogen gas	H_2
Oxygen gas	O_2

Substance	Chemical formula
Ozone	O_3
Table salt	$NaCl$
Solid sulfur	S_8
Water	H_2O

9. Which of the following substances is classified as a compound?
   - **F.** water
   - **G.** ozone
   - **H.** hydrogen gas
   - **I.** solid sulfur

10. A mixture contains 100 molecules of table salt, 30 molecules of baking soda, 20 molecules of ethanol, and 10 molecules of water. Atoms from which of the following elements make up most of the mixture?
    - **A.** sodium, Na
    - **B.** oxygen, O
    - **C.** hydrogen, H
    - **D.** carbon, C

11. A scientist discovers a way to easily combine molecules of ozone and molecules of hydrogen gas to make molecules of water. To create 300 molecules of water, how many molecules of ozone and how many molecules of hydrogen gas would the scientist need?

A geologist who is studying rocks found on an expedition places a 25 g graduated cylinder on a scale and adds 100 cm³ of water to the cylinder. Then, the geologist places the rocks in the cylinder one at a time, as shown below. Use the graphic to answer questions 12 and 13.

12. Which rock or rocks have the greatest density?

13. Which rock or rocks will float to the surface of the water in the cylinder? Why?

Test Tip

On a standardized test, take time to read completely each question, including all of the answer choices. Consider each answer choice before determining which one is correct.

CHAPTER 3
States of Matter

Chapter Outline

1 Matter and Energy
Kinetic Theory
States of Matter
Energy's Role

2 Changes of State
Energy and Changes of State
Conservation of Mass and Energy

3 Fluids
Pressure
Buoyant Force
Pascal's Principle
Fluids in Motion

4 Behavior of Gases
Properties of Gases
Gas Laws

Tennessee Course Level Expectations (Physical Science)

CLE. 3202.1.8 Investigate relationships among the pressure, temperature, and volume of gases and liquids; **CLE.3202.1.9** Apply the Laws of Conservation of Mass/Energy to balance chemical equations; **CLE.3202.Inq.1** Recognize that science is a progressive endeavor that reevaluates and extends what is already accepted; **CLE.3202.Inq.2** Design and conduct scientific investigations to explore new phenomena, verify previous results, test how well a theory predicts, and compare opposing theories; **CLE.3202.Inq.3** Use appropriate tools and technology to collect precise and accurate data; **CLE.3202.Inq.4** Apply qualitative and quantitative measures to analyze data and draw conclusions that are free of bias; **CLE.3202.Inq.6** Communicate and defend scientific findings.

Why It Matters

This temporary art exhibit, called "100,000 Pounds of Ice and Neon," was on display for a weekend at an ice rink in Tacoma, Washington. Colorful gases inside solid blocks of ice illustrate two states of matter.

Inquiry Lab

 20 min

Changes in Density

Fill an **empty, 2 L plastic bottle** with **water.** Fill a **medicine dropper** halfway with water, and place it in the bottle. The dropper should float with part of the rubber bulb above the surface of the water. (If the dropper floats too high, remove it and add more water. If it sinks, try less water.) Place the cap tightly on the bottle, and gently squeeze the bottle. Watch the water level inside the dropper as you squeeze and release the bottle. Try to make the dropper rise, sink, or stop at any level.

Questions to Get You Started

1. How do changes inside the dropper affect its position in the water?
2. What is the relationship between the dropper's density and the dropper's position in the water?
3. How could a submarine use changes in density to move up and down?

READING TOOLBOX

These reading tools can help you learn the material in this chapter. For more information on how to use these and other tools, see **Appendix A.**

FoldNotes

Key-Term Fold A key-term fold can help you learn the key terms in this chapter.

Your Turn Make a key-term fold, as described in **Appendix A.**

1. Write the key terms from the summary page on the front of each tab. The first few terms are shown on the right.
2. As you read the chapter, write the definitions under the tabs for each term.
3. Use this FoldNote to study the key terms.

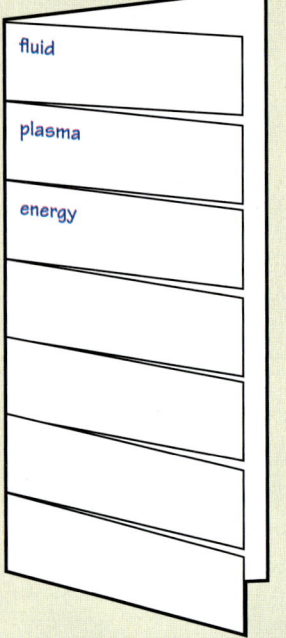

Fact, Hypothesis, or Theory?

Laws and Principles A scientific law or principle describes how nature works. The following describe laws and principles:

- They are general descriptions of what happens in nature.
- They differ from theories.
- They have been confirmed by experiments.
- They can be mathematical equations.

Below is a common form of laws and principles.

| Law or principle | "If X happens, then Y happens." |

Your Turn As you read Sections 3 and 4, add to the list of laws and principles below. Include the conditions under which the law or principle is true.

| Pascal's principle | A change in pressure at any point in an enclosed fluid will be transmitted equally to all parts of the fluid. |

Note Taking

Comparison Table You can use a comparison table to organize your notes as you compare related topics. A table that compares the states of matter described in Section 1 has been started for you. It includes the following:

- topics that you are going to compare
- specific characteristics that you are going to compare

Your Turn As you read Section 1, complete the table. Add columns and rows as needed.

	SOLIDS	LIQUIDS
Shape and volume	have definite shape and volume	have definite volume; shape changes to fit container
Behavior of particles	vibrate around fixed positions	

76 Chapter 3 States of Matter

SECTION 1
Matter and Energy

Key Ideas
- What makes up matter?
- What is the difference between a solid, a liquid, and a gas?
- What kind of energy do all particles of matter have?

Key Terms
- fluid
- plasma
- energy
- temperature
- thermal energy

Why It Matters
When you can see your breath on a cold day, you are watching gaseous water turn into liquid water.

When food is cooking, energy is transferred from the stove to the food. As the temperature increases, some particles in the food move very fast and spread through the air in the kitchen. The *state,* or physical form, of a substance is determined partly by how the substance's particles move.

> Tennessee Course Level Expectations (Physical Science)
>
> CLE.3202.Inq.1; CLE.3202.Inq.2; CLE.3202.Inq.3

Kinetic Theory

If you visit a restaurant kitchen, such as the one in **Figure 1,** you can smell the food cooking even if you are a long way from the stove. One way to explain this phenomenon is to make some assumptions. First, assume that the atoms and molecules within the food substances are always in motion and are colliding with each other. Second, assume that the atoms and molecules move faster as the temperature increases.

A theory based on these assumptions is called the *kinetic theory of matter.* **According to the kinetic theory of matter, matter is made of atoms and molecules. These atoms and molecules act like tiny particles that are always in motion.** The following are observations of particles in motion.

- The higher the temperature of the substance is, the faster the particles move.

- At the same temperature, more massive particles move slower than less massive ones.

For example, consider a cup of hot tea. At first, the particles move very quickly. As the tea cools, its particles begin to slow down. As you will see, the kinetic theory can help you understand the differences between the three common states of matter: solid, liquid, and gas.

Figure 1 The ingredients in foods are chemicals. A skilled chef understands how the chemicals in foods interact and how changes of state affect cooking.

Section 1 Matter and Energy 77

Particles of a gas, such as carbon dioxide, move fast enough to overcome nearly all of the attraction between them. The particles move independently of one another.

Particles of a liquid move fast enough to overcome some of the attraction between them. The particles are able to slide past one another.

Particles of a solid, such as ice, do not move fast enough to overcome the strong attraction between them, so they vibrate in place.

Figure 2 Three Familiar States of Matter

READING TOOLBOX

Comparison Table
Complete a comparison table for the three common states of matter as you read these pages. See the Reading Toolbox on p. 76 if you need help getting started.

States of Matter

Three familiar states of matter are solid, liquid, and gas, as **Figure 2** shows. Notice the differences in the atomic models for each state. Particles in a solid vibrate in place. In a liquid, the particles are closely packed, but they can slide past each other. Gas particles are in constant motion and do not usually stick together. **❱ You can classify matter as a solid, a liquid, or a gas by determining whether the shape and volume are definite or variable.** Most matter found naturally on Earth is either a solid, a liquid, or a gas, although matter can also be in other states.

Solids have a definite shape and volume.

An ice cube removed from an ice tray has the same volume and shape that it had in the ice tray. The structure of a solid is rigid, and the particles cannot easily change position. The particles are held closely together by strong attractions, and they vibrate in place. Because of the strong attractions between the particles, solids have a definite shape and volume.

Liquids change shape, not volume.

The particles in a liquid move more rapidly than the particles in a solid do. The particles move fast enough to overcome some of the forces of attraction between them. Thus, liquids flow freely. And liquids are able to take the shape of their containers. Although liquids change shape, they do not easily change volume. The particles of a liquid are close together and are in contact most of the time. Thus, the volume of a liquid remains constant.

Gases change both shape and volume.

Like liquids, gases do not have fixed shapes. Liquids and gases both can flow. Because the particles in liquids and gases can move past each other, liquids and gases are **fluids.**

But gases change more than shape—they change volume, too. If you leave a bottle of perfume open, particles of the liquid perfume will escape as gas, and you will smell it around the room. The particles of a gas move fast enough to break away from each other. So, the amount of empty space between the particles changes, and the gas expands to fill the space.

For example, consider the cylinder of helium shown in **Figure 3.** It can fill about 700 balloons. The helium atoms in the cylinder have been forced close together, or *compressed.* But as the helium fills a balloon, the atoms spread out, and the amount of empty space between gas particles increases.

Reading Check What is one difference between liquids and gases? (See Appendix E for answers to Reading Checks.)

Plasma is the most common state of matter.

Scientists estimate that 99% of the known matter in the universe, including the sun and other stars, is made of plasma. **Plasma** is a state of matter that does not have a definite shape or volume. Particles in plasma are electrically charged, or *ionized.* Natural plasmas are found in lightning, fire, and the aurora borealis shown in **Figure 4.** The glow of fluorescent light is caused by artificial plasma, which is formed by passing electric currents through gases.

Plasmas are similar to gases but have some properties that are different from the properties of gases. For instance, plasmas conduct electric current, while gases do not.

Figure 3 The particles of helium gas in the cylinder are much closer together than the particles of the gas in the balloons.

fluid (FLOO id) a nonsolid state of matter in which the atoms or molecules are free to move past each other, as in a gas or liquid

plasma (PLAZ muh) a state of matter that consists of free-moving ions and electrons

Figure 4 Auroras form when high-energy plasma collides with gas particles in the upper atmosphere. **What other states of matter do you see in the photograph?**

Energy's Role

What sources of energy would you use if the electricity were off? You might use candles for light and batteries to power a clock. Electricity, candles, and batteries are sources of energy. The food you eat is also a source of energy. **Energy** is the ability to change or move matter, or to do *work*. The energy of motion is called *kinetic energy*.

According to kinetic theory, all matter is made of particles—atoms and molecules—that are constantly in motion. ❯ **Because they are in motion, all particles of matter have kinetic energy.** Figure 5 compares the kinetic energy of the particles in a solid, a liquid, and a gas.

Temperature is a measure of average kinetic energy.

Do you think of temperature as a measure of how hot or cold something is? Specifically, **temperature** is a measure of the average kinetic energy of the particles in an object. Particles of matter are constantly moving, but they do not all move at the same speed. As a result, some particles have more kinetic energy than others have. When you measure an object's temperature, you measure the average kinetic energy of the particles in the object. The more kinetic energy the particles of an object have, the higher the temperature of the object is.

Reading Check What does temperature measure?

Academic Vocabulary

constant (KAHN stuhnt) without interruption; continual

Figure 5 Kinetic Energy of Solids, Liquids, and Gases

Solid

The particles in an ice cube vibrate in place. Compared to the particles in liquids and gases, they have the least kinetic energy.

Liquid

The particles in ocean water move around. They have more kinetic energy than the particles in a solid but less than those in a gas.

Gas

The particles in steam move around rapidly. Compared to the particles in solids and liquids, they have the most kinetic energy.

QuickLab

Hot or Cold?

⏱ 10 min

Procedure

1. You will need **three buckets:** one with **warm water,** one with **cold water,** and one with **hot water.** **CAUTION:** Test a drop of the hot water to make sure that it is not too hot to put your hands into.
2. Put both of your hands into the bucket of warm water, and note how the water feels.
3. Now, put one hand into the bucket of cold water and the other into the bucket of hot water.
4. After a minute, take your hands out of the hot and cold water, and put them back in the warm water.

Analysis

1. Can you rely on your hands to determine temperature? Explain your observations.

Thermal energy depends on particle speed and number of particles.

The temperature of a substance is not determined by how much of the substance you have. For example, a teapot holds more tea than a mug does. But the temperature, or average kinetic energy, of the particles in the tea is the same in both containers. However, the total kinetic energy of the particles in each container is different. The total kinetic energy of the particles that make up a substance is **thermal energy.**

Because particles of matter move faster at higher temperatures than they do at lower temperatures, the faster the particles in a substance move, the more kinetic energy they have. However, the *total* kinetic energy (thermal energy) of a substance depends on the number of particles in that substance. Look back at **Figure 5.** Although the individual particles in the steam have the most kinetic energy, the ocean has the greatest thermal energy because it contains so many more particles.

> **energy** (EN uhr jee) the capacity to do work
>
> **temperature** (TEM puhr uh chuhr) a measure of how hot (or cold) something is; specifically, a measure of the average kinetic energy of the particles in an object
>
> **thermal energy** (THUHR muhl EN uhr jee) the total kinetic energy of a substance's atoms

Section 1 Review

KEY IDEAS

1. **List** three main points of the kinetic theory of matter.
2. **State** two examples for each of the four states of matter.
3. **Compare** the shape and volume of solids, liquids, and gases.
4. **Describe** the relationship between temperature and kinetic energy.

CRITICAL THINKING

5. **Compare and Contrast** Compare the temperature and thermal energy of hot soup in a small mug and that of hot soup in a large bowl.
6. **Applying Concepts** Which particles have the strongest attraction between them: the particles of a gas, the particles of a liquid, or the particles of a solid?
7. **Making Inferences** Use the kinetic theory to explain how a dog could find you by your scent.

Why It Matters

Plasma

We are surrounded by matter in one of three states: solid, liquid, and gas. But 99.9% of all matter in the universe, including the sun and all other stars, is plasma. Matter in the plasma state is a collection of free-moving electrons and ions, or atoms that have lost electrons. Plasmas conduct electricity and are affected by magnets. They require an energy source to exist. This energy may be a heat source, such as the heat of the sun; an electric current; or a strong light, such as a laser.

The sun is a giant ball of superheated plasma. On its surface, violent eruptions send waves of plasma streaming out into space at high speeds. Earth is bathed in waves of plasma known as solar wind. After periods of disturbance on the surface of the sun, strong solar winds can disrupt radio and telephone communications, damage orbiting satellites, and cause electrical blackouts. Scientists are working to understand the forces behind solar wind and hope to better forecast damaging solar wind that is headed toward Earth.

Some plasmas, including lightning and fire, occur naturally on Earth. Artificial plasmas, including fluorescent and neon lights, are created by running an electric current through a gas to change the gas into a plasma that emits light. When the current is removed, the plasma becomes a gas again.

WEIRD SCIENCE

Scientists hope to someday harness nuclear fusion—the process that powers the sun and other stars. Fusion occurs at very high temperatures, so the fuel for fusion is a plasma. In the Tokamak Fusion Reactor, shown here, the plasma is heated in a ring-shaped vessel. Strong magnetic fields keep the plasma from touching the walls. Scientists study the plasma to learn more about fusion as a possible future energy source on Earth.

YOUR TURN

CRITICAL THINKING
1. Why do you think scientists want to predict solar winds in Earth's atmosphere?

ONLINE RESEARCH
2. Research the Tokamak Fusion Reactor, and answer the following questions: What do scientists hope to achieve with this research? What challenges do scientists face when studying plasma?

www.scilinks.org
Topic: Plasma
Code: HK81169

SECTION 2
Changes of State

Key Ideas
> What happens when a substance changes from one state of matter to another?

> What happens to mass and energy during physical and chemical changes?

Key Terms
evaporation
sublimation
condensation

Why It Matters
The evaporation that occurs when you sweat helps to keep your body cool in warm weather.

Tennessee Course Level Expectations (Physical Science)
CLE.3202.1.9; CLE.3202.Inq.1; CLE.3202.Inq.2; CLE.3202.Inq.3; CLE.3202.Inq.4

What causes dew drops to form or causes ice to melt? These changes of state—conversions of a substance from one physical form to another—are caused by energy transfers.

Energy and Changes of State

Five changes of state of water are shown in **Figure 1**. The ice, liquid water, and steam are all the same substance—water, H_2O. But they all have different amounts of energy. > **The identity of a substance does not change during a change of state, but the energy of a substance does change.**

If energy is added to a substance, its particles move faster. If energy is removed, the substance's particles move slower. For instance, the particles in steam have more energy than the particles in liquid water. A transfer of energy known as *heat* causes the temperature of a substance to change. If enough energy is added or removed, the substance will change state.

evaporation (ee VAP uh RAY shuhn) the change of state from a liquid to a gas

sublimation (SUHB luh MAY shuhn) the process in which a solid changes directly into a gas

Figure 1 Water can undergo multiple changes of state. The red arrows represent changes that require energy, and the blue arrows represent changes that release energy.

Some changes of state require energy.

A solid changes to a liquid by melting. Heating a solid transfers energy to the particles, which vibrate faster as they gain energy. Eventually, they break from their fixed positions, and the solid melts. The *melting point* is the temperature at which a substance changes from solid to liquid. Melting point depends on the pressure.

Evaporation is the change of a substance from a liquid to a gas. Boiling is evaporation that occurs throughout a liquid at a specific temperature and pressure. The temperature at which a liquid boils is the liquid's *boiling point*.

Solids can also change directly into gases in a process called **sublimation.** In **Figure 2,** solid carbon dioxide (dry ice) changes into gaseous carbon dioxide. Ice cubes in a freezer will eventually get smaller, as the ice sublimes. Note that melting, evaporation, and sublimation all require energy.

Reading Check What is one example of sublimation?

Figure 2 Solid dry ice changes directly into a gas. **Which change of state is shown here?**

Why It Matters
Why Do People Sweat?

REAL WORLD

You can feel the effects of an energy change when you sweat. Energy is needed to separate the particles of a liquid to form a gas. As you sweat, energy from your body is transferred to sweat molecules as heat. This energy transfer cools your body.

Nitrogen molecule in air

Water vapor in air

The molecules in sweat on your skin gain energy from your body and move faster. Eventually, the fastest-moving particles break away, and the sweat evaporates. This loss of energy by the body makes the body feel cooler.

Sweat droplet

Oxygen molecule in air

YOUR TURN

CRITICAL THINKING
1. Does your body take in energy or give off energy during sweating? Explain.

QuickLab: Boiling Water

⏱ 10 min

Procedure

1. Remove the cap from a **syringe**. Place the tip of the syringe in **warm water**.
2. Pull the plunger out until you have 10 mL of water in the syringe.
3. Tighten the cap on the syringe. Hold the syringe, and slowly pull the plunger out. This decreases the pressure inside the syringe.
4. Observe any changes you see in the water. Record your observations.

Analysis

1. Water usually boils at 100 °C. Why are you not burned by the boiling water in the syringe?
2. What effect does a decrease in pressure have on the boiling point of the water?

---

condensation (KAHN duhn SAY shuhn) the change of state from a gas to a liquid

READING TOOLBOX

Comparison Table
Make a comparison table for five changes of state that water may undergo. Include information about the states of matter involved and about the direction of energy transfer.

Energy is released in some changes of state.

When water vapor in the air becomes a liquid, as **Figure 3** shows, energy is released from the water to its surroundings. This process is an example of **condensation,** which is the change of state from a gas to a liquid. For a gas to become a liquid, large numbers of gas particles clump together. Energy is released from the gas, and the particles slow down.

Condensation sometimes takes place when a gas comes in contact with a cool surface. For instance, drops of water form on the outside of a glass that contains a cool drink. The *condensation point* of a gas is the temperature at which the gas becomes a liquid.

Energy is also released during freezing, which is the change of state from a liquid to a solid. The temperature at which a liquid changes into a solid is the substance's *freezing point*. Freezing and melting occur at the same temperature. For example, liquid water freezes at the same temperature that ice melts: 0 °C. For a liquid to freeze, the attractions between the particles must overcome their motion.

✓ **Reading Check** What is the relationship between the freezing point and the melting point of a substance?

Figure 3 Dew drops can form overnight. Water vapor from the air turns into a liquid when it contacts a cool surface such as grass or a dragonfly's wings. **Which change of state is shown here?**

Figure 4 Temperature remains constant when matter changes state. **Why are the arrows on each side the same length?**

① Energy is released when water freezes and is absorbed when ice melts.

② Energy is released when water vapor condenses and is absorbed when water vaporizes.

Temperature is constant during changes of state.

When a substance loses or gains energy, either its temperature changes or its state changes. But the temperature of a substance does not change during a change of state, as **Figure 4** shows. For example, if you add energy to ice at 0 °C, the temperature will not rise until all of the ice has melted.

Conservation of Mass and Energy

Look back at the changes of state shown in **Figure 4**. When an ice cube melts, the mass of the liquid water is the same as the mass of the ice cube. This change of state is an example of a physical change. Mass is conserved for all physical and chemical changes.

Likewise, energy can change forms during physical and chemical changes, but the total amount of energy present before and after a change is the same. The amount of energy in a substance can change, but this added energy must come from another source. ❯ **Mass and energy are both conserved. Neither mass nor energy can be created or destroyed.** These principles are fundamental laws of physical science.

Integrating Space Science

The Mass of the Universe Studies of the chemical changes that stars and nebulae undergo are constantly adding to our knowledge. Current estimates are that hydrogen makes up more than 90% of the atoms in the universe and makes up about 75% of the mass of the universe. Helium atoms make up most of the remainder of the mass of the universe. The total mass of all of the other elements is a very small part of the total mass of the universe.

Section 2 Changes of State 87

www.scilinks.org
Topic: Conservation of Energy
Code: HK80345

Mass cannot be created or destroyed.

In chemical changes, as well as in physical changes, the total mass of the substances undergoing the change stays the same before and after the change. In other words, mass cannot be created or destroyed, which is the *law of conservation of mass*.

For instance, when you burn a match, it seems to lose mass. The ash has less mass than the match. But the oxygen that reacts with the match, the tiny smoke particles, and the gases formed in the reaction also have mass. The total mass of the reactants (the match and oxygen) is the same as the total mass of the products (the ash, smoke, and gases).

Energy cannot be created or destroyed.

Energy may be changed to another form during a physical or chemical change, but the total amount of energy present before and after the change is the same. In other words, energy cannot be created or destroyed, which is the *law of conservation of energy*.

Starting a lawn mower, as **Figure 5** shows, may seem to violate the law of conservation of energy, but that is not the case. It is true that for the small amount of energy needed to start the mower, a lot of energy results. But the mower needs gasoline to run. Gasoline has stored energy that is released when it is burned. When the stored energy is considered, the energy present before you start the lawn mower is equal to the energy that is produced.

Some of the energy from the gasoline is transferred to the surroundings as heat, which is why the lawn mower gets hot. The total amount of energy released by the gasoline is equal to the energy used to power the lawn mower plus the energy transferred to the surroundings as heat.

Figure 5 Energy is conserved when gasoline is burned to power a lawn mower.

Section 2 Review

KEY IDEAS

1. **Describe** the following changes of state, and explain how particles behave in each state.
   a. freezing
   b. boiling
   c. sublimation
   d. melting

2. **State** whether energy is released or whether energy is required for the following changes of state to take place.
   a. melting
   b. evaporation
   c. sublimation
   d. condensation

3. **Describe** the role of energy when ice melts and when water vapor condenses to form liquid water.

4. **State** the law of conservation of mass and the law of conservation of energy, and explain how they apply to changes of state.

CRITICAL THINKING

5. **Drawing Conclusions** If you used dry ice in your holiday punch, would it become watery after an hour? Why or why not?

SECTION 3
Fluids

Key Ideas
- How do fluids exert pressure?
- What force makes a rubber duck float in a bathtub?
- What happens when pressure in a fluid changes?
- What affects the speed of a fluid in motion?

Key Terms
pressure
pascal
buoyant force
viscosity

Why It Matters
A submarine crew knows how to change the density of its boat, and this is how the crew controls the submarine's depth.

As you have learned, liquids and gases are classified as fluids. The properties of fluids allow huge ships to float, divers to explore the ocean depths, and jumbo jets to soar across the skies.

▶ Tennessee Course Level Expectations (Physical Science)
CLE.3202.1.8; CLE.3202.Inq.1; CLE.3202.Inq.2; CLE.3202.Inq.3

Pressure

You probably have heard the terms *air pressure, water pressure,* and *blood pressure.* **Pressure** is the amount of force exerted on a given area of surface. ▶ **Fluids exert pressure evenly in all directions.**

For instance, when you add air to a bicycle tire, you push air into the tire. Inside the tire, tiny air particles push against each other and against the walls of the tire, as **Figure 1** shows. The more air you pump into the tire, the greater the number of air particles pushing against the inside of the tire and the greater the pressure is. Pressure can be calculated by dividing force by the area over which the force is exerted.

pressure (PRESH uhr) the amount of force exerted per unit area of a surface

pascal (pas KAL) the SI unit of pressure; equal to the force of 1 N exerted over an area of 1 m² (symbol, Pa)

▶ **Pressure**

$$pressure = \frac{force}{area} \qquad P = \frac{F}{A}$$

The SI unit of pressure is the **pascal.** One pascal (1 Pa) is the force of one newton exerted over an area of one square meter (1 N/m²). The newton is the SI unit of force.

Figure 1 The force of air particles inside the tire creates pressure, which keeps the tire inflated. **How does the pressure change if you remove some of the air?**

Buoyant Force

If you push a rubber duck to the bottom of a bathtub, the duck pops to the surface when you release it. A **buoyant force** pushes the duck up. ❯ **All fluids exert an upward buoyant force on matter.** When you float on an air mattress in a swimming pool, the buoyant force keeps you afloat.

Buoyant force results from the fact that pressure increases with depth. The forces pushing up on an object in a fluid are greater than the forces pushing it down. Thus, there is a net upward force: the buoyant force.

buoyant force (BOY uhnt FAWRS) the upward force that keeps an object immersed in or floating on a fluid

Archimedes' principle is used to find buoyant force.

Archimedes, a Greek mathematician in the third century BCE, discovered a method for determining buoyant force.

| Archimedes' principle | The buoyant force on an object in a fluid is an upward force equal to the weight of the fluid that the object displaces. |

For example, imagine that you put a brick in a container of water, as **Figure 2** shows. The total volume of water that collects in the smaller container is the displaced volume of water from the larger container. The weight of the displaced fluid is equal to the buoyant force acting on the brick.

You can determine whether an object will float or sink by comparing the buoyant force on the object with the object's weight, as **Figure 3** shows. Note that the seagull is only partly underwater. The seagull's feet, legs, and stomach displace a weight of water that is equal to the seagull's total weight. So, the seagull is *buoyed up* and floats on the water's surface.

Figure 2 Archimedes' Principle

An object is lowered into a container of water.

When the object is completely submerged, the weight of the displaced fluid equals the buoyant force acting on the object.

Figure 3 Comparing Weight and Buoyant Force

The buoyant force acting on the seagull is equal to the weight of the displaced fluid, so the seagull floats on the surface.

The buoyant force equals the fish's weight, so the fish is suspended in the water.

The weight of the shell is greater than the buoyant force, so the shell sinks.

QuickLab

Density and Shape

⏱ 10 min

Procedure

1. Roll **two equal pieces of clay** into two balls (the size of golf balls). Drop the first ball into a **container of water.** Record your observations.
2. Flatten the second ball until it is thinner than your little finger, and press it into the shape of a canoe.
3. Place the clay boat gently into the water. Record your observations.

Analysis

1. How does the change of shape affect the buoyant force?
2. How is the change of shape related to the overall density of the boat?

An object will float or sink based on its density.

You can also determine if a substance will float or sink by comparing densities. For example, the density of a brick is about 2 g/cm^3, and the density of water is 1.00 g/cm^3. The brick will sink in water because it is denser than the water. On the other hand, helium has about one-seventh the density of air. A given volume of helium in a balloon displaces a volume of air that is much heavier than helium, so the balloon floats.

Steel is almost eight times denser than water. And yet huge steel ships cruise the oceans with ease. They even carry very heavy loads. But substances that are denser than water will sink in water. Given this, how does a steel ship float?

The shape of the ship allows the ship to float. Imagine a ship that was just a big block of steel, as shown on the left in **Figure 4.** If you put that steel block into water, it would sink. But ships are built with a hollow shape. The amount of steel is the same, but the hollow shape decreases the ship's density. Water is denser than the hollow ship, so the ship floats.

✓ **Reading Check** How can you use density to determine if an object will float?

Integrating Biology

Swim Bladders Some fish can adjust their density so that they can stay at a certain depth in the water. Most fish have an organ called a *swim bladder*, which is filled with gases. The inflated swim bladder increases the fish's volume, decreases the fish's overall density, and keeps the fish from sinking. The fish's nervous system controls the amount of gas in the bladder based on the fish's depth. Some fish, such as sharks, do not have a swim bladder. So, they must swim constantly to keep from sinking.

Figure 4 Despite its large size and mass, this ship floats. **How does the ship's density compare with the density of the water?**

A block of steel is denser than water, so the block sinks.

Shaping the block into a hollow form increases the volume occupied by the same mass, which results in a reduced overall density.

Topic: Pascal's Principle
Code: HK81116

READING TOOLBOX

Laws and Principles
Write down all of the scientific laws or principles that are covered in this section. State each one in your own words, and list the conditions under which the law or principle is true.

Pascal's Principle

What happens when you squeeze one end of a tube of toothpaste? Toothpaste usually comes out the opposite end because the pressure you apply is transmitted throughout the toothpaste. So, the increased pressure near the open end of the tube forces the toothpaste out. This phenomenon is explained by Pascal's principle, which was discovered by the French scientist Blaise Pascal in the 17th century.

Pascal's principle | A change in pressure at any point in an enclosed fluid will be transmitted equally to all parts of the fluid.

❯ **In other words, if the pressure in a container is increased at any point, the pressure increases at all points by the same amount.** Mathematically, Pascal's principle is stated as $P_1 = P_2$. Because $P = F/A$, Pascal's principle can be expressed $F_1/A_1 = F_2/A_2$.

Hydraulic devices are based on Pascal's principle.

Hydraulic devices use liquids to transmit pressure from one point to another. Because liquids cannot be compressed into a much smaller space, they can transmit pressure more efficiently than gases can. Hydraulic devices can multiply forces. For example, in **Figure 5,** a small downward force is applied to a small area. This force exerts pressure on the liquid in the device, such as oil. According to Pascal's principle, this pressure is transmitted equally to a larger area, where the pressure creates a larger force. Note that the plunger travels through a larger distance on the side that has the smaller area.

Reading Check How does a hydraulic device multiply force?

Figure 5 Because the pressure is the same on both sides of the enclosed fluid in a hydraulic lift, a small force on the smaller area (left) produces a much larger force on the larger area (right).

Math Skills: Pascal's Principle

A hydraulic lift uses Pascal's principle to lift a 19,000 N car. If the area of the small piston (A_1) equals 10.5 cm² and the area of the large piston (A_2) equals 400 cm², what force needs to be exerted on the small piston to lift the car?

Identify
List the given and unknown values.

Given:
$F_2 = 19,000$ N
$A_1 = 10.5$ cm²
$A_2 = 400$ cm²

Unknown:
$F_1 = ?$ N

Plan
Start with Pascal's principle, and substitute the equation for pressure. Then, rearrange the equation to isolate the unknown value.

$$P_1 = P_2$$
$$\frac{F_1}{A_1} = \frac{F_2}{A_2}$$
$$F_1 = \frac{(F_2)(A_1)}{A_2}$$

Solve
Insert the known values into the equation, and solve.

$$F_1 = \frac{(19,000 \text{ N})(10.5 \text{ cm}^2)}{400 \text{ cm}^2}$$
$$F_1 = 500 \text{ N}$$

Practice

1. In a car's liquid-filled, hydraulic brake system, the master cylinder has an area of 0.5 cm², and the wheel cylinders each have an area of 3.0 cm². If a force of 150 N is applied to the master cylinder by the brake pedal, what force does each wheel cylinder exert on its brake pad?

For more practice, visit **go.hrw.com** and enter keyword **HK8MP**.

Practice Hint

> The pressure equation
$$pressure = \frac{force}{area}$$
can be used to find pressure or can be rearranged to find force or area.
$$force = (pressure)(area)$$
$$area = \frac{force}{pressure}$$

Fluids in Motion

Examples of moving fluids include liquids flowing through pipes, air moving as wind, or honey dripping, as **Figure 6** shows. Fluids in motion have some properties in common. Have you ever used a garden hose? When you place your thumb over the end of the hose, your thumb blocks some of the area through which the water flows out of the hose. Because the area is smaller, the water exits at a faster speed. > **Fluids move faster through small areas than through larger areas, if the overall flow rate remains constant. Fluids also vary in the rate at which they flow.**

Figure 6 Dripping honey is an example of a fluid in motion.

viscosity (vis KAHS uh tee) the resistance of a gas or liquid to flow

Viscosity depends on particle attraction.

Honey dripping from a spoon flows more slowly than lemonade poured from a pitcher. A liquid's resistance to flow is called **viscosity**. In general, the stronger the attraction between a liquid's particles is, the more viscous the liquid is. Honey flows more slowly than lemonade because honey has a higher viscosity than lemonade.

Fluid pressure decreases as speed increases.

Imagine a waterlogged leaf being carried along by water in a pipe, as **Figure 7** shows. The water will move faster through the narrow part of the pipe than through the wider part. Therefore, as the water carries the leaf into the narrow part of the pipe, the leaf moves faster.

If you measure the pressure at different points, you would find that the water pressure in front of the leaf is less than the pressure behind the leaf. The pressure difference causes the leaf and the water around it to accelerate as the leaf enters the narrow part of the tube. This behavior illustrates a general principle, known as *Bernoulli's principle,* which states that as the speed of a moving fluid increases, the pressure of the moving fluid decreases. This property of moving fluids was first described in the 18th century by Daniel Bernoulli, a Swiss mathematician.

Figure 7 This leaf speeds up when it enters the narrow part of the pipe, where there is less pressure. **How does this example illustrate Bernoulli's principle?**

Section 3 Review

KEY IDEAS

1. **Explain** how differences in fluid pressure create buoyant force on an object.
2. **State** Archimedes' principle, and give an example of how you could determine a buoyant force.
3. **State** Pascal's principle. Give an example of its use.
4. **Compare** the viscosity of milk and the viscosity of molasses.

CRITICAL THINKING

5. **Applying Concepts** An object weighs 20 N. It displaces a volume of water that weighs 15 N.
   a. What is the buoyant force on the object?
   b. Will the object float or sink? Explain.
6. **Drawing Conclusions** Iron has a density of 7.9 g/cm^3. Mercury has a density of 13.6 g/cm^3. Will iron float or sink in mercury? Explain.
7. **Making Inferences** Two boats in a flowing river are sailing side-by-side with only a narrow space between them.
   a. What happens to the fluid speed and the pressure between the two boats?
   b. How could the changes in fluid speed and pressure lead to a collision of the boats?

Math Skills

8. A water bed that has an area of 3.75 m^2 weighs 1,025 N. Find the pressure that the water bed exerts on the floor.
9. The small piston of a hydraulic lift has an area of 0.020 m^2. A car weighing 12,000 N is mounted on the large piston (area = 0.90 m^2). What force must be applied to the small piston to support the car?

Why It Matters
How Do Submarines Work?

REAL WORLD

A submarine is a type of ship that can travel both on the surface of the water and underwater. Submarines have special ballast tanks that control their buoyancy. The crew can control the amount of water in the tanks to control the submarine's depth, as shown below.

The first submarine was used in 1776 during the American Revolution. It was a one-person, hand-powered, wooden vessel. Most modern submarines are built of metals and use nuclear power, which enables them to remain submerged almost indefinitely.

When a submarine is floating on the surface, its ballast tanks are filled mostly with air.

Ballast tanks

When the submarine dives, the ballast tanks are opened to allow sea water to flow in. This water adds mass and increases the submarine's density, so the submarine descends into the ocean.

YOUR TURN

UNDERSTANDING CONCEPTS
1. How do submarines use ballast tanks to control their depth?

CRITICAL THINKING
2. Identify the advantages of using metals instead of wood in the construction of today's submarines.

To bring the submarine through the water and to the surface, compressed air is blown into the ballast tanks to force the water out.

SCLINKS
www.scilinks.org
Topic: Submarines and Undersea Technology
Code: HK81474

SECTION 4
Behavior of Gases

Key Ideas
> What are some properties of gases?
> How can you predict the effects of pressure, temperature, and volume changes on gases?

Key Terms
gas laws

Why It Matters
The expanding gas in a car engine's cylinder provides the energy for motion.

Tennessee Course Level Expectations (Physical Science)
CLE.3202.1.8; CLE.3202.Inq.1; CLE.3202.Inq.2; CLE.3202.Inq.3; CLE.3202.Inq.4; CLE.3202.Inq.6

Because many gases are colorless and odorless, it is easy to forget that they exist. But every day, you are surrounded by gases. Some examples of gases in Earth's atmosphere are nitrogen, oxygen, argon, helium, and carbon dioxide, as well as methane, neon, and krypton. In chemistry, as in everyday life, gases are very important.

Properties of Gases

As you have learned, gases are fluids, and their particles move rapidly in all directions. Many properties of gases are unique. **› Gases expand to fill their containers. They spread out easily and mix with one another. They have low densities and are compressible. Unlike solids and liquids, gases are mostly empty space.** All gases share these properties.

Gases exert pressure on their containers.

A balloon that is filled with helium gas is under pressure. Helium atoms in the balloon are moving rapidly. They are constantly hitting each other and the walls of the balloon, as **Figure 1** shows. Each gas particle's effect on the balloon wall is small, but the battering by millions of particles adds up to a steady force. If too many gas particles are in the balloon, the battering overcomes the force of the balloon that is holding the gas in, and the balloon pops.

If you let go of a balloon that you have pinched at the neck, most of the gas inside rushes out and causes the balloon to shoot through the air. The balloon shoots through the air because a gas under pressure will escape its container if possible. For this reason, gases in pressurized containers, such as propane tanks for gas grills, can be dangerous and must be handled carefully.

Figure 1 Gas particles exert pressure by hitting the walls of a balloon. **What happens if the pressure becomes too great?**

Gas Laws

You can easily measure the volume of a solid or liquid, but how do you measure the volume of a gas? The volume of a gas is the same as the volume of the gas's container. But there are other factors, such as pressure, to consider. Gases behave differently than solids and liquids. The **gas laws** describe how the behavior of gases is affected by pressure, volume, and temperature. ❯ **The gas laws will help you understand and predict the behavior of gases in specific situations.**

gas laws (GAS LAWZ) the laws that state the mathematical relationships between the volume, temperature, pressure, and quantity of a gas

Boyle's law relates the pressure of a gas to its volume.

A diver at a depth of 10 m blows a bubble of air. As the bubble rises, its volume increases. When the bubble reaches the water's surface, the volume of the bubble will have doubled because of the decrease in pressure.

The relationship between the volume and pressure of a gas is known as Boyle's law. Boyle's law is stated as follows:

| Boyle's law | For a fixed amount of gas at a constant temperature, the volume of a gas increases as the gas's pressure decreases. Likewise, the volume of a gas decreases as the gas's pressure increases. |

Boyle's law is illustrated in **Figure 2.** Each illustration shows the same piston and the same amount of gas at the same temperature. These examples show that pressure and volume have an inverse relationship: one increases when the other decreases. Note that the temperature is not changing.

READING TOOLBOX

Laws and Principles
Write down all of the laws in this section. If possible, write the law in the form "If X happens, then Y happens," and state the conditions under which the law is true.

✓ **Reading Check** What two variables are related by Boyle's law?

Figure 2 Boyle's Law

Lifting the piston decreases the pressure. The gas particles spread farther apart, and the volume increases.

Pushing the piston increases the pressure. The gas particles are pushed closer together, and the volume decreases.

The product of pressure and volume is constant.

Boyle's law tells you that when pressure increases, volume decreases, and vice versa. In mathematical terms, pressure multiplied by volume is constant (if temperature is constant). This is expressed as follows:

> **Boyle's law** $(pressure_1)(volume_1) = (pressure_2)(volume_2)$
> $P_1V_1 = P_2V_2$

P_1 and V_1 represent the initial volume and pressure, while P_2 and V_2 represent the final volume and pressure.

Academic Vocabulary
initial (i NISH uhl) first
final (FIEN uhl) last

Topic: Gas Laws
Code: HK80637

Math Skills — Boyle's Law

The gas in a balloon has a volume of 7.5 L at 100.0 kPa. In the atmosphere, the gas expands to a volume of 11 L. Assuming a constant temperature, what is the final pressure in the balloon?

Identify
List the given and unknown values.

Given:
$V_1 = 7.5$ L
$P_1 = 100.0$ kPa
$V_2 = 11$ L
Unknown:
$P_2 = ?$ kPa

Plan
Write the equation for Boyle's law, and rearrange to solve for P_2.

$P_1V_1 = P_2V_2$
$P_2 = \dfrac{P_1V_1}{V_2}$

Solve
Insert the known values into the equation, and solve.

$P_2 = \dfrac{(100.0 \text{ kPa})(7.5 \text{ L})}{11 \text{ L}}$
$P_2 = 68$ kPa

Practice Hint

> Problems 2 and 3: The equation for Boyle's law can be rearranged to solve for volume in the following way.
>
> Start with the equation for Boyle's Law:
>
> $P_1V_1 = P_2V_2$
>
> Divide both sides by P_2:
>
> $\dfrac{P_1V_1}{P_2} = \dfrac{\cancel{P_2}V_2}{\cancel{P_2}}$
>
> After you cancel like terms, you are left with the final volume.
>
> $\dfrac{P_1V_1}{P_2} = V_2$

Practice

1. A flask contains 155 cm³ of hydrogen at a pressure of 22.5 kPa. Under what pressure would the gas have a volume of 90.0 cm³ at the same temperature? (Recall that 1 cm³ = 1 mL.)

2. If the pressure exerted on a 300.0 mL sample of hydrogen gas at constant temperature is increased from 0.500 kPa to 0.750 kPa, what will be the final volume of the sample?

3. A sample of oxygen gas has a volume of 150 mL at a pressure of 0.947 kPa. If the temperature remains constant, what will the volume of the gas be at a pressure of 1.000 kPa?

For more practice, visit **go.hrw.com** and enter keyword **HK8MP**.

Gay-Lussac's law relates gas pressure to temperature.

What would you predict about the relationship between the pressure and temperature of a gas at constant volume? Remember that pressure is the result of collisions of gas molecules against the walls of their containers. As temperature increases, the kinetic energy of the gas particles increases. The energy and frequency of the collision of gas particles against their containers increases. For a fixed quantity of gas at constant volume, the pressure increases as the temperature increases. This property of gases is sometimes known as Gay-Lussac's law.

| Gay-Lussac's law | The pressure of a gas increases as the temperature increases, if the volume of the gas does not change. The pressure decreases as the temperature decreases. |

If you often measure the pressure in your bicycle tire, as **Figure 3** shows, you may notice that the tire pressure in the winter is lower than it is in the summer. As the temperature outside decreases, the tire pressure also decreases. When the temperature outside rises, the tire pressure rises. Notice that in this example, the volume is constant.

If pressurized containers that hold gases, such as spray cans, are heated, the containers may explode. You should always be careful to keep containers of pressurized gas away from heat sources.

Figure 3 The pressure in a bicycle tire increases when temperature increases. **Which gas law does this illustrate?**

✅ **Reading Check** If volume is constant and temperature decreases, how does pressure change?

InquiryLab

How Are Temperature and Volume Related?

⏱ 30 min

Procedure
1. Fill an **aluminum pan** with 5 cm of **water.** Put the pan on a **hot plate.**
2. Fill a second **aluminum pan** with 5 cm of **ice water.**
3. Blow up a **balloon** inside a **250 mL beaker.** The balloon should fill the beaker but should not extend outside it. Tie the balloon at its opening.
4. Place the beaker and balloon in the ice water. Record your observations.
5. Remove the balloon and beaker from the ice water. Observe the balloon for several minutes, and record any changes.
6. Next, put the beaker and balloon in the hot water. Record your observations.

Analysis
1. How did changing the temperature affect the volume of the balloon?
2. Is the density of a gas affected by temperature? Explain.

Figure 4 Charles's Law

When the temperature is decreased, the gas particles move more slowly and hit the sides of the piston with less force. As a result, the volume decreases.

When the temperature is increased, the gas particles move faster and hit the sides of the piston with more force. As a result, the volume increases.

Charles's law relates temperature to volume.

Another gas law, Charles's law, is shown by the model in **Figure 4.** Each illustration shows the same piston and the same amount of gas at the same pressure.

| Charles's law | For a fixed amount of gas at a constant pressure, the volume of the gas increases as the gas's temperature increases. Likewise, the volume of the gas decreases as the gas's temperature decreases. |

Because of Charles's law, an inflated balloon will pop when it gets too hot. Or, as **Figure 5** shows, if the gas in an inflated balloon is cooled (at constant pressure), the volume of gas will decrease and cause the volume of the balloon to shrink. You can observe another example by putting an inflated balloon in the freezer and waiting about 10 minutes to see what happens.

Figure 5 This experiment illustrates Charles's law.

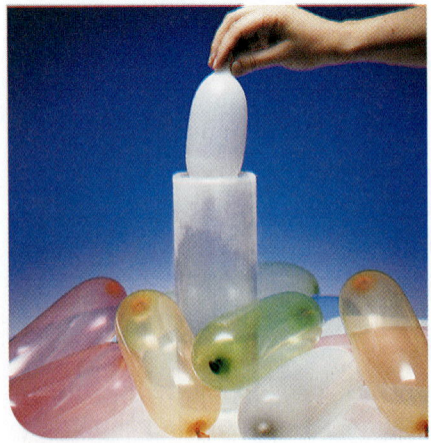

Air-filled balloons are exposed to liquid nitrogen.

The low temperature of the liquid nitrogen makes the balloons shrink in volume.

When the balloons are removed from the liquid nitrogen and warmed, they expand to their original volume.

Graphing Skills: Interpreting Graphs

The top graph shows volume versus temperature for a gas at a constant pressure. What can be determined from this graph about the relationship between volume and temperature?

1 Determine whether the relationship is direct or inverse.

In a *direct* relationship, the two variables change in the same direction. In an *inverse* relationship, they change in opposite directions. In this graph, temperature increases as volume increases, so the relationship is *direct*.

2 Study the shape of the line.

If a graph is a straight line, one variable is directly or inversely *proportional* to the other. If a graph is a curve, the relationship is more complex. Because this graph is a straight line, temperature is *directly proportional* to volume.

Practice

1. Which gas law does the straight-line graph represent?
2. Is the relationship shown by the curve in the bottom graph a direct relationship or an inverse relationship?
3. Is this relationship proportional?
4. Which gas law is represented by the curved graph?

Section 4 Review

KEY IDEAS

1. **List** four properties of gases.
2. **Explain** why the volume of a gas can change.
3. **Describe** how gases are different from solids and liquids, and give examples.
4. **Identify** what causes the pressure exerted by gas molecules on their container.
5. **Restate** Boyle's law, Charles's law, and Gay-Lussac's law in your own words.

CRITICAL THINKING

6. **Applying Concepts** Identify a real-life example for each of the three gas laws.
7. **Making Inferences** Why do gases have low densities?
8. **Relating Concepts** When scientists record the volume of a gas, why do they also record the temperature and the pressure?
9. **Making Predictions** Predict what would happen to the volume of a balloon left on a sunny windowsill. Which gas law predicts this result?

Math Skills

10. A partially inflated weather balloon has a volume of 1.56×10^3 L and a pressure of 98.9 kPa. What is the volume of the balloon when the balloon is released to a height where the pressure is 44.1 kPa?

Inquiry Lab

 50 min

Boiling and Freezing

Adding or removing energy from a substance often causes its temperature to change. But does the temperature of a substance always change when the substance's energy changes? In this lab, you will investigate this question with a common substance—water.

Ask a Question

When you add or remove energy from water, does its temperature always change?

Forming and Testing a Hypothesis

① Make some predictions. What happens to the temperature of boiling water as the boiling process continues? What happens to the temperature of freezing water as the freezing process continues?

Boiling Water

② Prepare two data tables like the one below. (Note that you can also use Time and Temperature as column headings, to create a vertical table.) You will need to add additional cells for the time measurements.

Sample Data Table: Temperature of Water

Time (s)	30	60	90	120	150	180	etc.
Temperature (°C)	DO NOT WRITE IN BOOK						

③ Fill the beaker about one-third to one-half full with water.

④ Put on heat-resistant gloves. Turn on the hot plate, and put the beaker on the plate. Put the thermometer in the beaker. Use the clamp on the ring stand to hold the thermometer so that it does not touch the bottom of the beaker. **CAUTION:** Be careful not to touch the hot plate. Also, be careful not to break the thermometer.

⑤ In your first data table, record the temperature of the water every 30 s. Continue doing this until about one-fourth of the water boils away. Note the first temperature reading at which the water is steadily boiling.

⑥ Turn off the hot plate. Let the beaker cool for a few minutes. Then, use heat-resistant gloves to pick up the beaker. Pour the warm water out in the sink, and rinse the warm beaker with cool water. **CAUTION:** Even after rinsing the beaker with cool water, the beaker may still be too hot to handle without gloves.

What You'll Do

› **Test your hypothesis** by measuring the temperature of water as it boils and freezes.
› **Graph** data, and interpret the slopes of the graphs.

What You'll Need

beaker, 250 mL or 400 mL
clamp
coffee can, large
gloves, heat-resistant
graduated cylinder, 100 mL
hot plate
ice, crushed
paper, graph
ring stand
rock salt
stirring device, wire loop
stopwatch
thermometer
water

Safety

Freezing Water

7. Put approximately 20 mL of water in the graduated cylinder.
8. Put the graduated cylinder in the coffee can, and fill in around the graduated cylinder with three to four alternating layers of crushed ice and rock salt.
9. Slide the tip of the thermometer through the loop on the wire-loop stirring device, and put the thermometer and the wire-loop stirring device in the graduated cylinder.
10. As the ice melts and mixes with the rock salt, the level of ice will decrease. Add ice and rock salt to the can as needed.
11. In your second data table, record the temperature of the water in the graduated cylinder every 30 s. Stir the water occasionally by moving the wire-loop stirring device up and down along the thermometer. **CAUTION:** Do not stir in a circular motion with the thermometer.
12. Once the water begins to freeze, stop stirring. Do not try to pull the thermometer out of the solid ice in the graduated cylinder.
13. Note the temperature when you first notice ice crystals forming in the water. Continue taking temperature readings until the water in the graduated cylinder is frozen.
14. After you record the final reading, pour warm water into the can. Wait until the ice in the graduated cylinder melts. Remove the thermometer. Pour the water out of the cylinder, and rinse the cylinder with water. Pour out the contents of the can. Rinse the can with water.

Analysis

1. **Graphing Data** Make a graph of temperature (y-axis) versus time (x-axis) for the data on boiling water from the first table. Indicate the temperature at which the water started to boil.
2. **Graphing Data** Make a graph of temperature (y-axis) versus time (x-axis) for the data on freezing water from the second table. Indicate the temperature at which the water started to freeze.
3. **Interpreting Graphs** What does the slope of the line on each graph represent?
4. **Analyzing Data** In your first graph, compare the slope when the water is boiling with the slope before the water starts to boil.
5. **Analyzing Data** In your second graph, compare the slope when the water is freezing with the slope before the water starts to freeze.

Communicating Your Results

6. **Drawing Conclusions** What happened to the temperature of water while the water was boiling or freezing?
7. **Interpreting Graphs** Explain what happens to the energy that is added to the water while the water is boiling.

Extension

When water freezes, energy is removed from the water. How do you think this energy affected the water before the energy was removed? What happens to the energy when it is removed?

Making Graphs

Science Skills

Technology
Math
Scientific Methods
Graphing

Problem

Suppose that 100 g of ice is heated in a pan on a stove. The initial temperature of the ice is −25 °C. The temperature rises steadily to 0 °C in 1 min. The temperature then remains at 0 °C for 6 min as the ice melts. The temperature of the water then steadily rises to 100 °C in another 7 min. After that, the temperature remains constant. Make a graph that shows the temperature of the water as a function of time.

Solution

① Determine the *x*-axis and *y*-axis of the graph.	The *x*-axis is time in minutes. The *y*-axis is temperature in degrees Celsius.	
② Determine the range of each axis, and add tick marks.	The time ranges from 0 to 14 min. Add and label marks on the *x*-axis for 0, 5, 10, and 15. The temperature ranges from −25 °C to 100 °C. Add and label marks on the *y*-axis for −25, 0, 25, 50, 75, 100, and 125.	
③ Mark all of the key points described in the problem.	The key points are (0, −25), (1, 0), (7, 0), and (14, 100).	
④ Fill in the lines between the points.	Because the temperature changes were steady, straight lines connect the points. Add a horizontal line after the last point.	

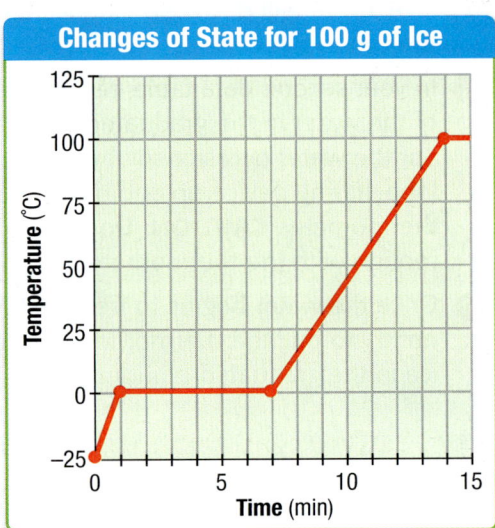

Changes of State for 100 g of Ice

Practice

Use the graph to answer questions 1–4.

1. Was energy released or absorbed during the process shown in the graph?
2. During what time intervals did changes of state happen?
3. What changes of state happened during those time intervals?
4. Describe what happened to the temperature during those time intervals.

Based on what you have learned, answer questions 5–7.

5. Suppose the hot water at the end of this process is put in a freezer with a temperature of −25 °C. Sketch a graph that shows the temperature of the water as a function of time until it reaches −25 °C.
6. Identify and label any changes of state that are represented on your graph.
7. Is energy released or absorbed during the process shown in your graph?

CHAPTER 3 Summary

go.hrw.com
SUPER SUMMARY
KEYWORD: HK8STAS

Key Ideas

Section 1 Matter and Energy

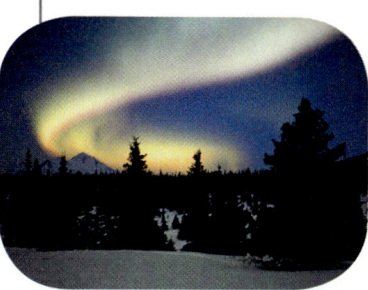

- **Kinetic Theory** All matter is made of atoms and molecules that are always in motion. (p. 77)
- **States of Matter** You can classify matter as a solid, a liquid, or a gas by determining whether the shape and volume are definite or variable. (p. 78)
- **Energy's Role** Because they are in motion, all particles of matter have kinetic energy. (p. 80)

Section 2 Changes of State

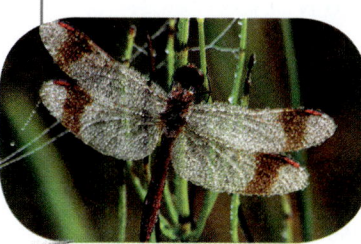

- **Energy and Changes of State** The identity of a substance does not change during a change of state, but the energy of a substance does change. (p. 84)
- **Conservation of Mass and Energy** Mass and energy are both conserved. Neither mass nor energy can be created or destroyed. (p. 87)

Section 3 Fluids

- **Pressure** Fluids exert pressure evenly in all directions. (p. 89)
- **Buoyant Force** All fluids exert an upward buoyant force on matter. (p. 90)
- **Pascal's Principle** If the pressure in a container is increased at any point, the pressure increases at all points by the same amount. (p. 92)
- **Fluids in Motion** Fluids move faster through small areas than through larger areas, if the overall flow rate remains constant. (p. 93)

Section 4 Behavior of Gases

- **Properties of Gases** Gases expand to fill their containers. They have low densities, are compressible, and are mostly empty space. (p. 96)
- **Gas Laws** The gas laws will help you understand and predict the behavior of gases in specific situations. (p. 97)

Key Terms

fluid, p. 79
plasma, p. 79
energy, p. 80
temperature, p. 80
thermal energy, p. 81

evaporation, p. 85
sublimation, p. 85
condensation, p. 86

pressure, p. 89
pascal, p. 89
buoyant force, p. 90
viscosity, p. 94

gas laws, p. 97

CHAPTER 3 Review

READING TOOLBOX

1. **Comparison Table** Make a comparison table to compare the five changes of state that are described in this chapter.

USING KEY TERMS

2. Describe four states of matter by using the terms *solid, liquid, gas,* and *plasma.* Describe the behavior of particles in each state.

3. Describe how *pressure* is exerted by fluids.

4. Describe the *buoyant force,* and explain how it relates to *Archimedes' principle.*

UNDERSTANDING KEY IDEAS

5. Which of the following assumptions is *not* part of the kinetic theory?
   a. All matter is made up of tiny, invisible particles.
   b. The particles are always moving.
   c. Particles move faster at higher temperatures.
   d. Particles are smaller at lower pressure.

6. Three common states of matter are
   a. solid, water, and gas.
   b. ice, water, and gas.
   c. solid, liquid, and gas.
   d. solid, liquid, and air.

7. During which of the following changes of state do atoms or molecules become more ordered?
   a. boiling   c. melting
   b. condensation   d. sublimation

8. Which of the following describes what happens as the temperature of a gas in a balloon increases?
   a. The speed of the particles decreases.
   b. The volume of the gas increases.
   c. The volume of the gas decreases.
   d. The pressure decreases.

9. Fluid pressure is always directed
   a. up.   c. sideways.
   b. down.   d. in all directions.

10. Matter that flows to fit its container includes
    a. gases.   c. gases and liquids.
    b. liquids.   d. liquids and solids.

11. If an object that weighs 50 N displaces a volume of water that weighs 10 N, what is the buoyant force on the object?
    a. 60 N   c. 40 N
    b. 50 N   d. 10 N

EXPLAINING KEY IDEAS

12. State the law of conservation of energy and the law of conservation of mass. Explain what happens to energy and mass in a change of state.

13. For each pair, explain the difference in meaning.
    a. *solid* and *liquid*
    b. *Boyle's law* and *Charles's law*
    c. *Gay-Lussac's law* and *Pascal's principle*

INTERPRETING GRAPHICS Use the graph below to answer questions 14 and 15.

14. What type of relationship does the graph represent: direct or inverse?

15. To which law or principle does the graph apply?

CRITICAL THINKING

16. Inferring Relationships Explain what happens to the pressure of a gas if the volume of the gas is tripled. Assume that the temperature remains constant.

17. Drawing Conclusions Why are liquids instead of gases used in hydraulic brakes?

18. Applying Concepts After taking a shower, you notice that the mirror is foggy and covered with very small droplets of water. Explain how this happens by describing where the water comes from and the changes the water goes through.

19. Making Inferences An iceberg is partially submerged in the ocean. At what part of the iceberg is the water pressure the greatest?

20. Applying Concepts Use Boyle's Law to explain why bubbled packing wrap pops when you squeeze it.

21. Making Predictions Will a ship loaded with plastic-foam balls float higher or lower in the water than an empty ship? Explain.

22. Applying Concepts All vacuum cleaners have a high-speed fan. Explain how this fan allows the vacuum cleaner to pick up dirt.

Graphing Skills

23. Graphing Data Kate placed 100 mL of water in each of five different pans. She then placed the pans on a windowsill for a week and measured how much water evaporated. Graph her data, which are shown in the table below. Place surface area on the *x*-axis.
  a. Is the graph linear or nonlinear?
  b. What does this answer tell you?

Pan number	1	2	3	4	5
Surface area (cm²)	44	82	20	30	65
Volume evaporated (mL)	42	79	19	29	62

24. Interpreting Graphs The graph below shows the effects of heating on ethylene glycol, the liquid commonly used as antifreeze. Before the temperature is 197 °C, is the temperature increasing or decreasing? What physical change is taking place when the ethylene glycol is at 197 °C? Describe what is happening to the ethylene glycol molecules at 197 °C. How do you know this is happening?

Heating of Ethylene Glycol

Math Skills

25. Pressure Calculate the area of a 1,500 N object that exerts a pressure of 500 Pa. Then, calculate the pressure exerted by the same object over twice that area. Express your answer in the correct SI unit.

26. Pascal's Principle One of the largest helicopters in the world weighs 1.0×10^6 N. If you were to place this helicopter on a large piston of a hydraulic lift, what force would need to be applied to the small piston to lift the helicopter? The area of the small piston is 0.7 m², and the area of the large piston is 140 m².

27. Boyle's Law A sample of neon gas occupies a volume of 2.8 L at 180 kPa. What will its volume be at 120 kPa?

28. Boyle's Law At a pressure of 650 kPa, 2.2 L of hydrogen is used to fill a balloon to a final pressure of 115 kPa. What is the balloon's final volume?

Standardized Test Prep

Understanding Concepts

Directions (1–3): For each question, write on a sheet of paper the letter of the correct answer.

1. An industrial thermometer is heated until the mercury inside it is exerting 400 N of force against the inner surface. That surface has a total area of 200 cm². How much pressure is the mercury exerting against the inner surface of the thermometer? Note that 1 Pa = 1 N/m².
   - **A.** 800 Pa
   - **B.** 2,000 Pa
   - **C.** 8,000 Pa
   - **D.** 20,000 Pa

2. A sealed refuse container is buried near a fault line, and seismic activity brings the container close to an underground source of geothermal energy. As the container gets warmer, what happens to the internal air pressure of the container?
   - **F.** The internal air pressure decreases.
   - **G.** The internal air pressure increases.
   - **H.** There is no effect on internal air pressure.
   - **I.** There is no air pressure inside a sealed container.

3. In the year 2032, a space probe investigating Neptune scoops up a load of solid frozen oxygen from the planet's atmosphere. Upon re-entry into Earth's atmosphere, some of the solid oxygen immediately changes into a gas. Which of the following processes happened?
   - **A.** evaporation
   - **B.** condensation
   - **C.** sublimation
   - **D.** melting

Directions (4–5): For each question, write a short response.

4. Plastic is put into molds to create specific shapes. In what state of matter should the plastic be when it is put in the mold, and why?

5. A kitchen scientist combines 5.0 g of baking soda with 100.0 g of vinegar, which causes a gas (carbon dioxide) to be given off. After all of the gas has escaped, the liquid has a mass of 102.4 g. What is the mass of the escaped gas?

Reading Skills

Directions (6–8): Read the passage below. Then, answer the questions that follow.

SPECIFIC GRAVITY

Buoyancy makes a piece of wood float in water. It also makes a battleship float on the high seas and makes a block of steel float in a pool of liquid mercury. The first principle of buoyancy is simple: if a solid immersed in a fluid weighs less than an equal volume of the fluid, the solid will float. Another way of saying the same thing is the following: if a solid has a lower specific gravity than a fluid, then the solid will float in that fluid. Specific gravity is defined as the weight of a substance divided by the weight of an equal volume of pure water.

If an immersed solid floats, the level at which the solid floats is determined by the second principle of buoyancy: a floating object will displace its own weight in a fluid. The percentage of the volume of the solid immersed in the fluid will be equal to the specific gravity of the solid divided by the specific gravity of the fluid. If a block of wood that has a specific gravity of 0.3 floats in water (specific gravity = 1.0), 30% of the volume of the block will be below the water's surface.

6. A cruise ship has a volume of 100,000 m³ and possesses an overall specific gravity of 0.4. If the density of sea water is 1,000 kg/m³, what is the mass of the sea water displaced by the cruise ship? Note that 1,000 kg = 1 metric ton.
   - **F.** 40,000 kg
   - **G.** 60,000 kg
   - **H.** 40,000 metric tons
   - **I.** 60,000 metric tons

7. If 90% of a floating iceberg is underwater, what is the specific gravity of the ice?
   - **A.** 0.2
   - **B.** 0.9
   - **C.** 20
   - **D.** 90

8. If a substance is compressed, what happens to its specific gravity?

Interpreting Graphics

The graphic below shows the water cycle. Note that the water in the clouds is in liquid form. Use this diagram to answer questions 9–11.

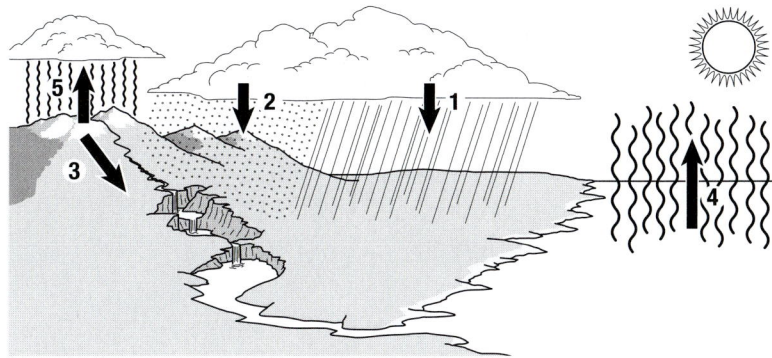

9. Which arrow indicates evaporation?
- F. 1
- G. 2
- H. 3
- I. 4

10. Which arrow indicates sublimation?
- A. 2
- B. 3
- C. 4
- D. 5

11. Which three arrows indicate a phase change that occurs at 0 °C?

The following graphic shows a full tank of helium, the same tank after it has filled 10 balloons, and then the same tank after it has filled 20 balloons. Use this graphic to answer questions 12 and 13.

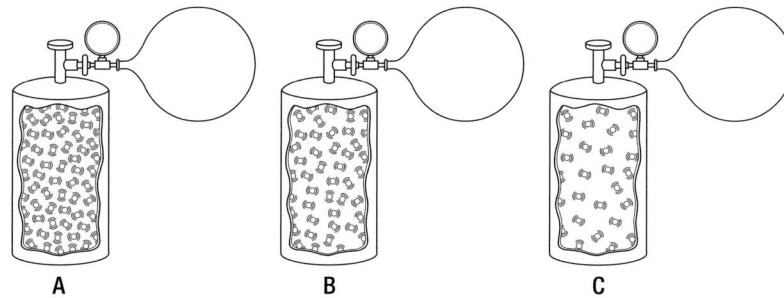

12. In which tank is the greatest pressure being exerted on the tank's inner surface?

13. As more helium is released from the tank, the person who is inflating the balloons notices that the tank has become cold to the touch. Why does this happen?

> **Test Tip**
>
> When answering short-response questions, be sure to write in complete sentences. When you finish, proofread for errors in spelling, grammar, and punctuation.

Standardized Test Prep   **109**

CHAPTER 4 Atoms

Chapter Outline

❶ The Development of Atomic Theory
The Beginnings of Atomic Theory
Dalton's Atomic Theory
Thomson's Model of the Atom
Rutherford's Model of the Atom

❷ The Structure of Atoms
What Is in an Atom?
Atomic Number and Mass Number
Isotopes
Atomic Masses

❸ Modern Atomic Theory
Modern Models of the Atom
Electron Energy Levels
Electron Transitions

Tennessee Course Level Expectations (Physical Science)

CLE.3202.TE.3 Explain the relationship between the properties of a material and the use of the material in the application of a technology; **CLE.3202.1.2** Describe the structure and arrangement of atomic particles; **CLE.3202.Inq.1** Recognize that science is a progressive endeavor that reevaluates and extends what is already accepted; **CLE.3202.Inq.2** Design and conduct scientific investigations to explore new phenomena, verify previous results, test how well a theory predicts, and compare opposing theories; **CLE.3202.Inq.3** Use appropriate tools and technology to collect precise and accurate data; **CLE.3202.Inq.4** Apply qualitative and quantitative measures to analyze data and draw conclusions that are free of bias; **CLE.3202.Inq.5** Compare experimental evidence and conclusions with those drawn by others about the same testable question; **CLE.3202.Inq.6** Communicate and defend scientific findings.

Why It Matters

Tiny robots, such as this microsubmarine shown inside a human artery, may be used for medical purposes someday. Although each layer of this submarine is smaller than a period on this page, each layer is much larger than an atom.

Inquiry Lab
⏱ 30 min

Making a Model

A scientific model is a simplified representation that shows how an object, system, or concept looks or functions. In this activity, you will construct your own model. Obtain from your teacher a **can** that is covered by a **sock** and sealed with **tape.** An **unknown object** is inside the can. Without uncovering the can, try to determine the characteristics of the object inside the can.

Questions to Get You Started

1. Examine the object through the sock. What is the object's mass? What is its size, shape, and texture? Record all of your observations in a data table.
2. Using the data that you have collected, draw a model of the object.
3. Remove the object to see what it is. Compare the model that you made with the actual object that the model represents.
4. How is the process that you used to observe the unknown object similar to the ways that scientists study atoms?

READING TOOLBOX

These reading tools can help you learn the material in this chapter. For more information on how to use these and other tools, see **Appendix A.**

Word Origins

Subatomic Particles Before atoms were understood, people discovered that they could generate static electricity by rubbing fur against amber (tree resin). This is where the word *electron* comes from:

- The word *electricity* is derived from the ancient Greek word *elektron*, which means *amber*.
- The word *electron* was later formed by combining this same root (*electr-*) with the suffix *–on*, which means *particle*.

Your Turn When you learn about protons and neutrons in this chapter, guess at the root meanings of the words *proton* and *neutron*. Look up the etymology (word origin) of the words in a dictionary to see if you guessed right.

Analogies

Making Comparisons An analogy compares two things that may seem quite different. Analogies are often formed by using the word *like*, as in "X is like Y." Other words or phrases that signal analogies include *as, just as, is comparable to,* and *resembles.* An analogy can be modeled as follows:

Your Turn In this chapter, you will learn about several models of the structure of atoms. Analogies are often used to describe these models. Make a list of analogies as you come across them. For each analogy, write down ways in which the two things compared are alike, and ways in which the two things are different.

FoldNotes

Pyramid Pyramid FoldNotes help you compare words or ideas in sets of three.

Your Turn Create a Pyramid FoldNote as described in **Appendix A.**

1. Along one edge of one side of the note, write "Atomic number."
2. On another side, write "Mass number."
3. On the third side, write "Average atomic mass."

As you read Section 2, fill in for each term the definition and an example. Use this FoldNote to review these terms.

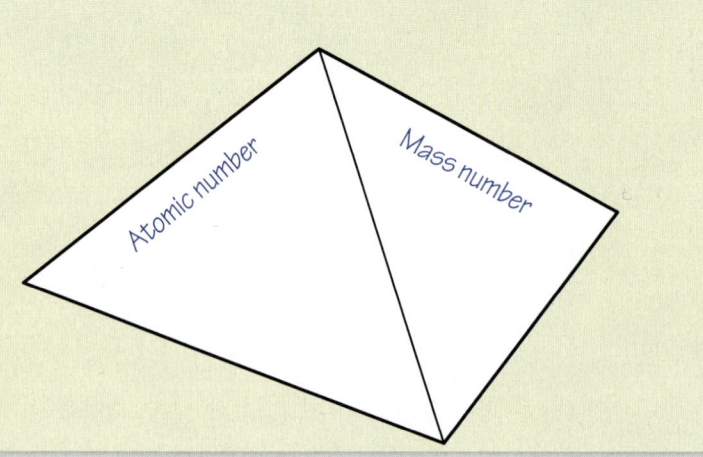

SECTION 1
The Development of Atomic Theory

Key Ideas

> Who came up with the first theory of atoms?
> What did Dalton add to the atomic theory?
> How did Thomson discover the electron?
> What is Rutherford's atomic model?

Key Terms

electron
nucleus

Why It Matters

The electrons stripped from atoms are used in television tubes to help create the images on a television screen.

Atoms are everywhere. They make up the air you are breathing, the chair you are sitting in, and the clothes you are wearing. Atoms determine the properties of matter. For example, the aluminum containers shown in **Figure 1** are lightweight because of the properties of the atoms that make up the aluminum.

Tennessee Course Level Expectations (Physical Science)
CLE.3202.Inq.1; CLE.3202.Inq.2;
CLE.3202.Inq.3; CLE.3202.TE.3

The Beginnings of Atomic Theory

Today, it is well known that matter is made up of particles called atoms. But atomic theory was developed slowly over a long period of time. The first theory of atoms was proposed more than 2,000 years ago. > **In the fourth century BCE, the Greek philosopher Democritus suggested that the universe was made of indivisible units.** He called these units *atoms*. "Atom" comes from *atomos*, a Greek word that means "unable to be cut or divided." Democritus thought that movements of atoms caused the changes in matter that he observed.

Democritus did not have evidence for his atomic theory.

Although his theory of atoms explained some observations, Democritus did not have the evidence needed to convince people that atoms existed. Throughout the centuries that followed, some people supported Democritus's theory. But other theories were also proposed.

As the science of chemistry was developing in the 1700s, the emphasis on making careful and repeated measurements in experiments increased. Because of this change, more-precise data were collected and were used to favor one theory over another.

Figure 1 The properties of aluminum containers come from the properties of aluminum atoms, shown magnified here in an image from a scanning tunneling electron microscope.

QuickLab

⏲ 10 min

Evidence for Atoms

1. Your teacher will provide **two cups** that contain a mixture of **pennies** and **marbles**.
2. Use a **balance** to find the total mass of the pennies in the first cup. Then, find the mass of the marbles.
3. Repeat step 2 for the second cup.
4. Compare the composition of the "compounds" in the two cups in terms of the proportions of marbles and pennies by mass. Do the cups contain the same "compound"?
5. What can you deduce from your results?

Dalton's Atomic Theory

In 1808, an English schoolteacher named John Dalton proposed a revised atomic theory. Dalton's theory was developed on a scientific basis, and some parts of his theory still hold true today. Like Democritus, Dalton proposed that atoms could not be divided. ❯ **According to Dalton, all atoms of a given element were exactly alike, and atoms of different elements could join to form compounds.**

✓ **Reading Check** How are Dalton's and Democritus's atomic theories similar? (See Appendix E for answers to Reading Checks.)

Dalton used experimental evidence.

Unlike Democritus, Dalton based his theory on experimental evidence. For instance, scientists were beginning to observe that some substances combined together in consistent ways. According to the *law of definite proportions,* a chemical compound always contains the same elements in exactly the same proportions by weight or mass. For example, any sample of water contains the same proportions of hydrogen and oxygen by mass, as **Figure 2** shows. This and other evidence supported Dalton's theory.

Dalton's theory did not fit all observations.

Today, Dalton's theory is considered the foundation for modern atomic theory. Some parts of Dalton's work turned out to be correct. However, as experiments continued, Dalton's theory could not explain all of the experimental evidence. Like many scientific theories, the atomic theory changed gradually over many years as scientists continued to do experiments and acquire more information.

Figure 2 The Law of Definite Proportions

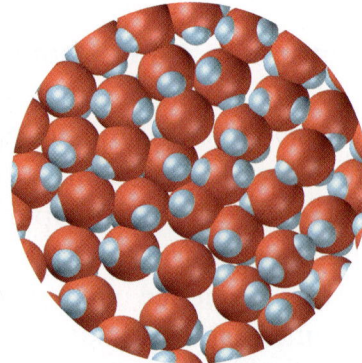

Water Composition by Mass

Hydrogen 11%
Oxygen 89%

For any given water sample, the proportions of hydrogen and oxygen by mass are constant.

This fact suggests that water molecules are made up of atoms that combine in simple whole-number ratios to form compounds.

Figure 3 Thomson's Cathode-Ray Tube Experiment

- The cathode has a negative charge.
- The beam is straight when no magnet is present.
- The anode has a positive charge.
- The air was removed from the tube by a vacuum pump.
- The beam is deflected by the magnet. Electric charges behave in this way. So, the deflection suggests that the beam is made of charges.

Thomson's Model of the Atom

In 1897, J. J. Thomson, a British scientist, conducted an experiment that suggested that atoms were not indivisible. Thomson wasn't planning to learn about the atom. Instead, he was experimenting with electricity. He was studying *cathode rays,* mysterious rays in vacuum tubes. ❯ **Thomson's cathode-ray tube experiment suggested that cathode rays were made of negatively charged particles that came from inside atoms.** This result revealed that atoms could be divided into smaller parts.

Thomson developed the plum-pudding model.

An experiment similar to Thomson's is shown in **Figure 3.** The two metal plates at the ends of the vacuum tube are called the *cathode* and the *anode.* The cathode has a negative charge, and the anode has a positive charge. When a voltage is applied across the plates, a glowing beam comes from the cathode and strikes the anode.

Thomson knew that magnets deflected charges. He reasoned that because all of the air was removed from the tube, the beam must have come from the cathode or from the anode. The direction of the deflection confirmed that the beam was made of negative charges and thus came from the cathode. Thomson had discovered **electrons,** negatively charged particles inside the atom.

Thomson proposed a new model of the atom based on his discovery. In this model, electrons are spread throughout the atom, just as blueberries are spread throughout the muffin in **Figure 4.** Thomson's model, often called the *plum-pudding model,* was named after a dessert that was popular in his day.

electron (ee LEK TRAHN) a subatomic particle that has a negative charge

Figure 4 This blueberry muffin is similar to Thomson's atomic model. **What do the blueberries represent?**

Section 1 The Development of Atomic Theory

Why It **Matters**
How Do Televisions Work?

REAL WORLD

How does your television screen display images? Television images are made up of thousands of tiny pixels. Your brain puts the pixels together and interprets them as images. How the pixels are created depends on the type of television.

In any television set, red, green, and blue colors combine in different proportions to produce the entire color spectrum.

Some televisions use cathode-ray tubes, like the one in Thomson's experiment. Color TVs contain three electron beams—one for each primary color of light. CRT televisions are deep because they hold the cathode-ray tubes behind the screen.

Electron gun

Electromagnets

Pixel

Grille

The television screen is coated with *phosphors,* which glow when struck by the electron beams. The phosphors are arranged in groups of three. Each group makes up a pixel.

Electron beams

Phosphor-coated screen

Flat-panel televisions use various technologies, including plasmas, to produce pixels. Because these TVs do not contain large cathode-ray tubes, they can be very thin.

SCLINKS
www.scilinks.org
Topic: Television Technology
Code: HK81501

YOUR TURN

UNDERSTANDING CONCEPTS
1. How are CRT televisions and flat-panel televisions similar?

ONLINE RESEARCH
2. Use the Internet to learn more about how flat-panel televisions work. Choose one type of flat-panel technology, and create a poster that illustrates how it works.

Rutherford's Model of the Atom

Shortly after Thomson proposed his new atomic model, Ernest Rutherford, another British scientist, developed an experiment to test Thomson's model. Rutherford found that Thomson's model needed to be revised. ❯ **Rutherford proposed that most of the mass of the atom was concentrated at the atom's center.** To understand why Rutherford came to this conclusion, you need to learn about his experiment.

Rutherford conducted the gold-foil experiment.

In Rutherford's experiment, shown in **Figure 5,** two of Rutherford's students aimed a beam of positively charged alpha particles at a very thin sheet of gold foil. In Thomson's model of the atom, the mass and positive charge of an atom are evenly distributed, and electrons are scattered throughout the atom. The positive charge at any location would be too small to affect the paths of the incoming particles. Rutherford predicted that most particles would travel in a straight path and that a few would be slightly deflected.

The observations from the experiment did not match Rutherford's predictions. As **Figure 5** shows, most particles did pass straight through the gold foil, but some were deflected by a large amount. A few particles came straight back. Rutherford wrote, "It was quite the most incredible event that has ever happened to me in my life. It was almost as incredible as if you fired a 15-inch shell at a piece of tissue paper and it came back and hit you."

Reading Check Why were Rutherford's results surprising?

READING TOOLBOX

Pyramid FoldNote
Create a Pyramid FoldNote to compare the atomic models of Dalton, Thomson, and Rutherford. Be sure to note the similarities and differences between the models.

www.scilinks.org
Topic: Atomic Theory
Code: **HK80120**

Figure 5 Rutherford's Gold-Foil Experiment

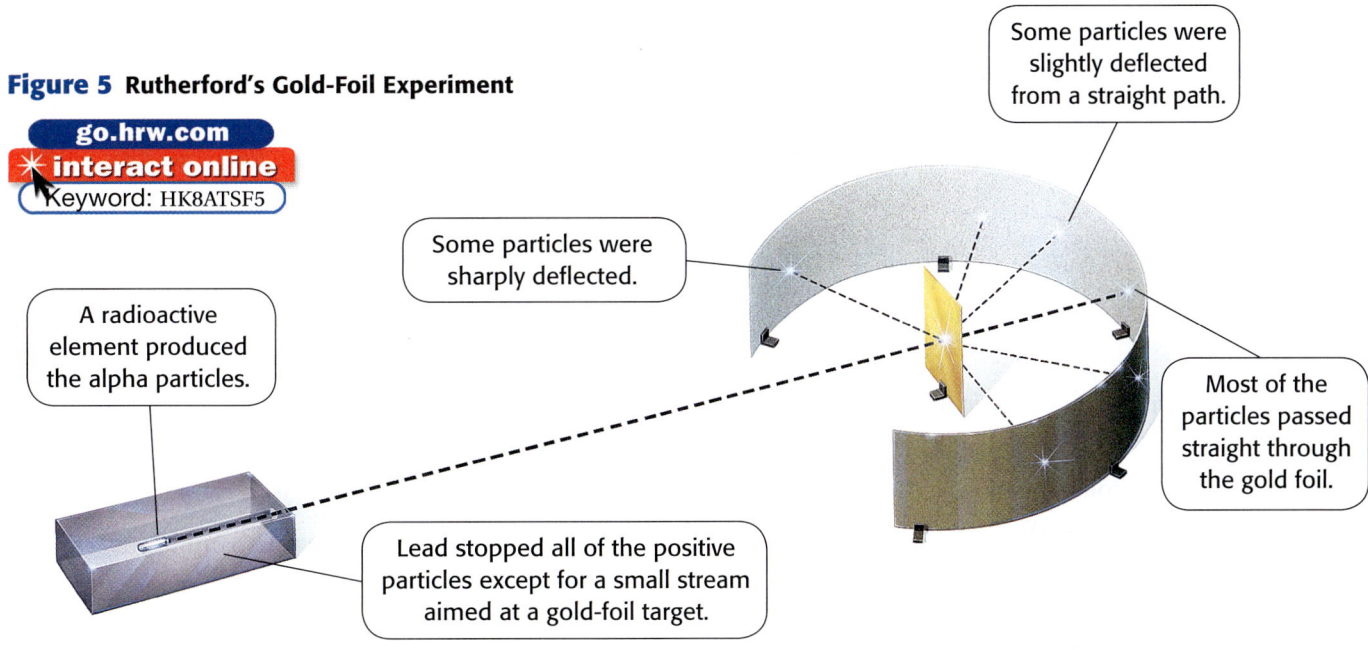

Figure 6 If the nucleus of an atom were the size of a marble, the whole atom would be the size of a football stadium!

nucleus (NOO klee uhs) an atom's central region, which is made up of protons and neutrons

Figure 7 In Rutherford's model, electrons orbit the nucleus. (This figure does not accurately represent sizes and distances.) **Is the nucleus positive, negative, or neutral?**

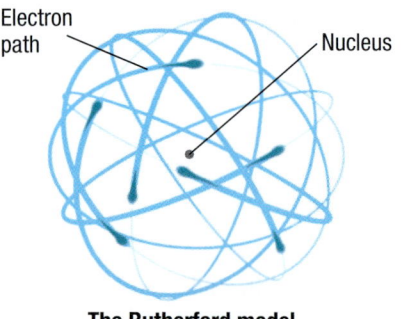

The Rutherford model of the atom

Rutherford discovered the nucleus.

Rutherford's experiment suggested that an atom's positive charge is concentrated in the center of the atom. This positively charged, dense core of the atom is called the **nucleus.** In the gold-foil experiment, incoming positive charges that passed close to the nucleus were deflected sharply. Incoming positive charges that were aimed directly at the nucleus bounced straight back. Data from Rutherford's experiment suggested that compared with the atom, the nucleus was very small, as **Figure 6** shows.

Rutherford's results led to a new model of the atom, shown in **Figure 7.** In Rutherford's model, negative electrons orbit the positively charged nucleus in much the same way that planets orbit the sun. Today, we understand that the nucleus contains particles called *protons* and *neutrons.* Protons have a positive charge, and neutrons have no charge. You will learn more about these particles in the next section.

Section 1 Review

KEY IDEAS

1. **Describe** Democritus's atomic theory.
2. **Summarize** the main ideas of Dalton's theory.
3. **Explain** why Dalton's theory was more successful than Democritus's theory.
4. **Compare** Thomson's atomic model with Rutherford's atomic model.

CRITICAL THINKING

5. **Analyzing Experiments**
   a. How did the cathode-ray tube experiment lead to the conclusion that atoms contain electrons?
   b. How did the gold-foil experiment lead to the conclusion that the atom has a nucleus?
6. **Making Inferences** Does the term *indivisible* still describe the atom? Explain.

SECTION 2
The Structure of Atoms

Key Ideas

> What is the difference between protons, neutrons, and electrons?

> What do atoms of an element have in common with other atoms of the same element?

> Why do isotopes of the same element have different atomic masses?

> What unit is used to express atomic mass?

Key Terms

proton
neutron
atomic number
mass number
isotope
unified atomic mass unit
mole

Why It Matters

Radioisotopes emit energy when they decay. To diagnose and treat diseases, doctors use this property of radioisotopes to track where in the body certain atoms go.

Less than 100 years after Dalton published his atomic theory, scientists determined that atoms consisted of smaller particles, such as the electron. In this section, you will learn more about the particles inside the atom.

> Tennessee Course Level Expectations (Physical Science)
>
> CLE.3202.1.2; CLE.3202.Inq.1; CLE.3202.Inq.2; CLE.3202.Inq.3; CLE.3202.Inq.6; CLE.3202.TE.3; CLE.3202.TE.4

What Is in an Atom?

Atoms are made up of various subatomic particles. To understand the chemistry of most substances, however, we need to study only three of these particles. **> The three main subatomic particles are distinguished by mass, charge, and location in the atom.** **Figure 1** compares these particles.

At the center of each atom is a small, dense *nucleus*. The nucleus is made of **protons,** which have a positive charge, and **neutrons,** which have no charge. Protons and neutrons are almost identical in size and mass. Moving around outside the nucleus is a cloud of very tiny, negatively charged *electrons*. The mass of an electron is much smaller than that of a proton or neutron.

proton (PROH TAHN) a subatomic particle that has a positive charge and that is located in the nucleus of an atom

neutron (NOO TRAHN) a subatomic particle that has no charge and that is located in the nucleus of an atom

Figure 1 Subatomic Particles

Particle	Charge	Mass (kg)	Location in the atom
Proton	+1	1.67×10^{-27}	in the nucleus
Neutron	0	1.67×10^{-27}	in the nucleus
Electron	−1	9.11×10^{-31}	outside the nucleus

Figure 2 Helium atoms, including the ones in this helium blimp, are made up of two protons, two neutrons, and two electrons. **Which of these particles defines the element as helium?**

Academic Vocabulary
overall (OH vuhr AWL) total; net

Each element has a unique number of protons.

A hydrogen atom has one proton. A helium atom, shown in **Figure 2,** has two protons. Lithium has three protons. As you move through the periodic table of the elements, this pattern continues. Each element has a unique number of protons. In fact, an element is defined by the number of protons in an atom of that element.

Unreacted atoms have no overall charge.

Even though the protons and electrons in atoms have electric charges, most atoms do not have an overall charge. The reason is that most atoms have an equal number of protons and electrons, whose charges exactly cancel. For example, a helium atom has two protons and two electrons. The atom is neutral because the positive charge of the two protons exactly cancels the negative charge of the two electrons, as shown below.

Charge of two protons:	+2
Charge of two neutrons:	0
Charge of two electrons:	−2
Total charge of a helium atom:	0

If an atom gains or loses electrons, it becomes charged. A charged atom is called an *ion.*

The electric force holds the atom together.

Positive and negative charges attract each other with a force known as the *electric force.* Because protons are positive and electrons are negative, protons and electrons are attracted to one another by the electric force. In fact, the electric force between protons in the nucleus and electrons outside the nucleus holds the atom together. On a larger scale, this same force holds solid and liquid materials together. For instance, electric attractions hold water molecules together.

Atomic Number and Mass Number

Atoms of different elements have their own unique structures. Because these atoms have different structures, they have different properties. Atoms of the same element can vary in structure, too. ❯ **Atoms of each element have the same number of protons, but they can have different numbers of neutrons.**

The atomic number equals the number of protons.

The **atomic number** of an element, Z, tells you how many protons are in an atom of the element. Remember that most atoms are neutral because they have an equal number of protons and electrons. Thus, the atomic number also equals the number of electrons in the atom. Because each element is defined by its unique number of protons, each element has a unique atomic number. Hydrogen has only one proton, so $Z = 1$ for hydrogen. The largest naturally occurring element, uranium, has 92 protons, so $Z = 92$ for uranium. The atomic number of a given element never changes.

The mass number equals the total number of subatomic particles in the nucleus.

The **mass number** of an element, A, equals the number of protons plus the number of neutrons in an atom of the element. A fluorine atom has 9 protons and 10 neutrons, so $A = 19$ for fluorine. Oxygen has 8 protons and 8 neutrons, so $A = 16$ for oxygen. The mass number reflects the number of protons and neutrons (and not the number of electrons) because protons and neutrons provide most of the atom's mass. Although atoms of an element have the same atomic number, they can have different mass numbers because the number of neutrons can vary. **Figure 3** shows which subatomic particles in the nucleus of an atom contribute to the atomic number and which contribute to the mass number.

✓ **Reading Check** Which defines an element: the atomic number of the element or the mass number of the element?

> **atomic number** (uh TAHM ik NUHM buhr) the number of protons in the nucleus of an atom
>
> **mass number** (MAS NUHM buhr) the sum of the numbers of protons and neutrons in the nucleus of an atom

READING TOOLBOX

Pyramid FoldNote
Create a Pyramid FoldNote for the terms *proton*, *neutron*, and *electron*, and describe which can vary for a given element. Also include the terms *atomic number* and *mass number* in your notes.

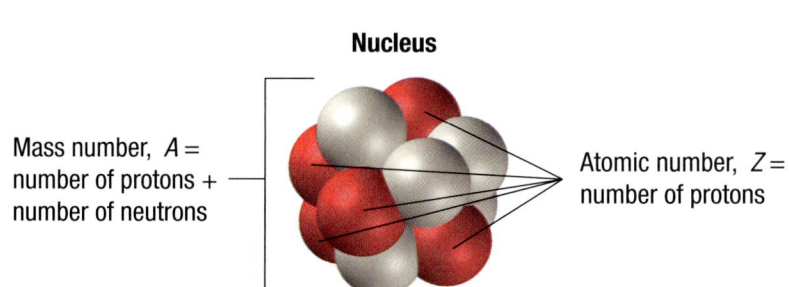

Mass number, A = number of protons + number of neutrons

Atomic number, Z = number of protons

Figure 3 Atoms of the same element have the same number of protons and thus the same atomic number. But because the number of neutrons may vary, atoms of the same element may have different mass numbers.

QuickLab

Modeling Isotopes

⏱ 20 min

Procedure

1. Use **gumdrops of three different colors** to represent protons, neutrons, and electrons. Use **toothpicks** to hold the gumdrops together.
2. Create atomic models for the three isotopes of hydrogen: protium ($A = 1$), deuterium ($A = 2$), and tritium ($A = 3$).
3. Create atomic models for helium-3 ($A = 3$) and helium-4 ($A = 4$).

Analysis

1. How do the isotopes of hydrogen compare to one another?
2. How do the hydrogen isotopes differ from the helium isotopes?
3. Which isotopes have the same mass number? Which isotopes have the same atomic number?

SCLINKS
www.scilinks.org
Topic: Isotopes
Code: HK80820

isotope (IE suh TOHP) an atom that has the same number of protons (or the same atomic number) as other atoms of the same element do but that has a different number of neutrons (and thus a different atomic mass)

Isotopes

As you have learned, atoms of a single element can have different numbers of neutrons and thus different mass numbers. An **isotope** is an atom that has the same number of protons but a different number of neutrons relative to other atoms of the same element. Because they have the same number of protons and electrons, isotopes of an element have the same chemical properties. However, isotopes have different masses. ▶ **Isotopes of an element vary in mass because their numbers of neutrons differ.**

Each of the three isotopes of hydrogen, shown in **Figure 4**, has one proton and one electron. The most common hydrogen isotope, protium, does not have any neutrons. Because it has one proton in its nucleus, its mass number, A, is 1. Deuterium, a second isotope of hydrogen, has one neutron as well as one proton in its nucleus. Its mass number, A, is 2. A third isotope, tritium, has two neutrons. Because its nucleus contains two neutrons and one proton, tritium has a mass number of 3.

✓ **Reading Check** Which hydrogen isotope has the most mass?

Figure 4 Each isotope of hydrogen has one proton, but the number of neutrons varies. **What is the atomic number, Z, of each isotope?**

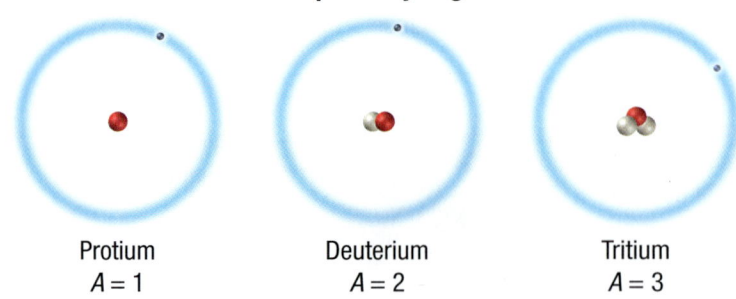

Isotopes of Hydrogen

Protium $A = 1$ Deuterium $A = 2$ Tritium $A = 3$

Some isotopes are more common than others.

Hydrogen is present on Earth and on the sun. In both places, protium is most common. Only a small fraction of the hydrogen found on Earth and on the sun is deuterium. For instance, only 1 out of every 6,000 hydrogen atoms in Earth's crust is a deuterium isotope. Similarly, on the sun, protium isotopes outnumber deuterium isotopes 50,000 to 1.

Tritium is an unstable isotope that decays over time. Thus, tritium is the least common isotope of hydrogen. Unstable isotopes, called *radioisotopes,* emit radiation and decay into other isotopes. A radioisotope continues to decay until the isotope reaches a stable form. Each radioisotope decays at a fixed rate, which can vary from a fraction of a second to millions of years.

www.scilinks.org
Topic: Radioisotopes
Code: HK81260

Why It Matters
Nuclear Medicine

Radioactive isotopes, or radioisotopes, are widely used in medicine. They are used to diagnose and treat certain conditions. Some isotopes are used to create images similar to X-ray images. Doctors interpret the images to study organ structures and functions. Radioisotopes are also used to study organ metabolisms and to identify and treat cancer.

In the full-body image shown here, the radioisotope *technetium-99m*, along with a biological agent that localizes the radioactivity in the bones, was injected into the body. The image, called a *colored gamma scan* or *scintigram,* shows a healthy human skeleton.

A radioisotope that has been injected into the body emits small amounts of radiation. A special camera, such as the one shown here, detects the radiation. A computer uses the information from the camera to create the image. The image is often interpreted by a radiologist, a doctor who specializes in imaging technologies.

YOUR TURN

CRITICAL THINKING
1. Will radioisotopes injected into the body remain in the body forever? Explain.

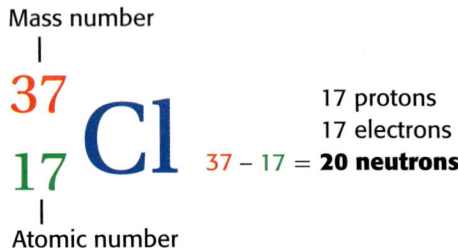

Figure 5 One isotope of chlorine has 18 neutrons, while the other isotope has 20 neutrons.

Figure 6 The average atomic mass of chlorine is closer to 35 u than it is to 37 u. **Which chlorine isotope is more common?**

Isotopes of Chlorine

^{37}Cl 24%

^{35}Cl 76%

17
Cl
Chlorine
35.453

Note: Calculations using the values from the pie graph do not give a result of exactly 35.453 u because of rounding.

The number of neutrons can be calculated.

To represent different isotopes, you can write the mass number and atomic number of the isotope before the symbol of the element. The two isotopes of chlorine are represented this way in **Figure 5.** (Sometimes the atomic number is omitted because it is always the same for any given element.)

If you know the atomic number and mass number, you can calculate the number of neutrons that an atom has. For example, the isotope of uranium that is used in nuclear reactors is uranium-235, or $^{235}_{92}$U. Like all uranium atoms, this isotope has an atomic number of 92, so it has 92 protons. Its mass number is 235, so there are a total of 235 protons and neutrons. The number of neutrons can be found by subtracting the atomic number from the mass number, as shown below.

Mass number (A): 235
Atomic number (Z): − 92
Number of neutrons: 143

Atomic Masses

The mass of a single atom is very small. The mass of a single fluorine atom is less than one trillionth of a billionth of a gram. ▸ **Because working with such tiny masses is difficult, atomic masses are usually expressed in unified atomic mass units.** A <mark>unified atomic mass unit</mark> (u) is equal to one-twelfth of the mass of a carbon-12 atom. (This unit is sometimes called the atomic mass unit, amu.) Carbon-12, an isotope of carbon, has six protons and six neutrons, so each individual proton and neutron has a mass of about 1.0 u. Recall that electrons contribute very little mass to an atom.

Average atomic mass is a weighted average.

Often, the atomic mass listed for an element in the periodic table is an average atomic mass for the element as found in nature. The *average atomic mass* for an element is a weighted average. In other words, commonly found isotopes have a greater effect on the average atomic mass than rarely found isotopes do.

For example, **Figure 6** shows how the natural abundance of chlorine's two isotopes affects chlorine's average atomic mass, which is 35.453 u. This mass is closer to 35 u than it is to 37 u. The reason is that the atoms of chlorine that have a mass of nearly 35 u are more common in nature. Thus, they make a greater contribution to chlorine's average atomic mass.

The mole is useful for counting small particles.

Because chemists often deal with large numbers of small particles, they use a large counting unit called the **mole** (mol). A mole is a collection of a very large number of particles.

1 mol = 602, 213, 670, 000, 000, 000, 000, 000 particles

This number is usually written as 6.022×10^{23} and is called *Avogadro's number*. The number is named for Italian scientist Amedeo Avogadro. Why is 6.022×10^{23} the number of particles in one mole? The mole has been defined as the number of atoms in 12.00 grams of carbon-12. Experiments have shown this value to be 6.022×10^{23}. So, one mole of a substance contains 6.022×10^{23} particles of that substance.

The following example demonstrates the magnitude of Avogadro's number: 6.022×10^{23} popcorn kernels would cover the United States to form a pile about 500 km (310 mi) tall! So, Avogadro's number is not useful for counting items such as popcorn kernels but is useful for counting atoms or molecules.

✓ **Reading Check** How many particles are in 1 mol of iron?

Integrating Space Science

Counting Stars How many stars are in the universe? In 2003, a group of astronomers estimated that the visible universe—the portion that our telescopes can reach—contains 70,000,000,000,000,000,000,000 stars, or 7×10^{22} stars. This quantity is about one-tenth of Avogadro's number! Of course, this estimate is based on observations from existing telescopes. As improvements in telescopes occur, the estimate could increase. Perhaps the estimate will reach Avogadro's number someday.

Moles and grams are related.

The mass in grams of one mole of a substance is called *molar mass*. For example, 1 mol of carbon-12 atoms has a mass of 12.00 g, so the molar mass of carbon-12 is 12.00 g/mol. **Figure 7** shows the molar mass of magnesium.

In nature, elements often occur as mixtures of isotopes. So, a mole of an element usually contains several isotopes. As a result, an element's molar mass in grams per mole equals its average atomic mass in unified atomic mass units, u. The average atomic mass of carbon is 12.01 u. So, one mole of carbon has a mass of 12.01 g. Because this mass is a weighted average of the masses of several isotopes of carbon, it differs from the molar mass of carbon-12, which is a single isotope.

unified atomic mass unit (YOON uh FIED uh TAHM ik MAS YOON it) a unit of mass that describes the mass of an atom or molecule; it is exactly 1/12 the mass of a carbon atom with mass number 12 (symbol, u)

mole (MOHL) the SI base unit used to measure the amount of a substance whose number of particles is the same as the number of atoms of carbon in exactly 12 g of carbon-12

Figure 7 One mole of magnesium (6.022×10^{23} Mg atoms) has a mass of 24.3050 g. Note that the balance is accurate only to one-tenth of a gram, so it reads 24.3 g.

You can convert between moles and grams.

Converting between the amount of an element in moles and the mass of an element in grams is outlined in **Figure 8**. For example, to determine the mass of 5.50 mol of iron, first you must find iron, Fe, in the periodic table. The average atomic mass of iron, rounded to the hundredths place, is 55.84 u. So, the molar mass of iron is 55.84 g/mol. Next, you must set up the problem by using the molar mass as if it were a conversion factor, as shown below.

Figure 8 The molar mass of an element allows you to convert between the amount of the element in moles and the mass of the element in grams.

Math Skills — Converting Moles to Grams

Determine the mass in grams of 5.50 mol of iron.

Identify
List the given and unknown values.

Given:
amount of iron = 5.50 mol
molar mass of iron = 55.84 g/mol
Unknown:
mass of iron = ? g

Plan
Write down the conversion factor that converts moles to grams.

The conversion factor you choose should have what you are trying to find (grams of Fe) in the numerator and what you want to cancel (moles of Fe) in the denominator.

$$\frac{55.84 \text{ g Fe}}{1 \text{ mol Fe}}$$

Solve
Multiply the amount of iron by this conversion factor, and solve.

$$5.50 \text{ mol Fe} \times \frac{55.84 \text{ g Fe}}{1 \text{ mol Fe}} = 307 \text{ g Fe}$$

Practice Hint

▶ Remember to use the periodic table to find molar masses. The average atomic mass of an element is equal to the molar mass of the element. For consistency, this book rounds values to the hundredths place.

▶ Follow the procedure shown in the sample to convert grams to moles, but be sure to reverse the conversion factor, as shown in Figure 8. You can convert grams to moles to check your answers to the practice questions.

Practice

1. What is the mass in grams of each of the following?
   a. 2.50 mol of sulfur, S
   b. 1.80 mol of calcium, Ca
   c. 0.50 mol of carbon, C
   d. 3.20 mol of copper, Cu

For more practice, visit **go.hrw.com** and enter keyword **HK8MP**.

Compounds also have molar masses.

Recall that compounds are made up of atoms joined together in specific ratios. To find the molar mass of a compound, you can add up the molar masses of all of the atoms in a molecule of the compound. For example, to find the molar mass of water, H_2O, first you must find the masses of hydrogen and oxygen in the periodic table. Oxygen's average atomic mass is 16.00 u, so its molar mass is 16.00 g/mol. The molar mass of hydrogen is 1.01 g/mol. You must multiply this value by 2 because a water molecule contains two hydrogen atoms. Thus, the molar mass of H_2O can be calculated as follows:

molar mass of H_2O = (2 × 1.01 g/mol) + 16.00 g/mol = 18.02 g/mol

What does this value tell you? As you learned earlier, molar mass equals the mass in grams of 1 mol of a substance. Thus, the mass of 1 mol of water is 18.02 g. In other words, the total mass of 6.022×10^{23} water molecules is 18.02 g. Take a look at **Figure 9.** Then use information in the caption to find the molar mass of carbon monoxide, another common compound.

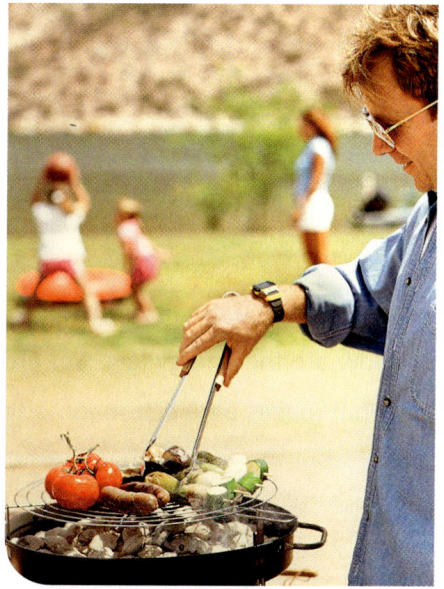

Figure 9 Burning charcoal produces carbon dioxide and carbon monoxide, CO, which is a colorless, odorless gas. **What is the molar mass of CO?**

Section 2 Review

KEY IDEAS

1. **List** the charge, mass, and location of each of the three subatomic particles found in atoms.
2. **Explain** how you can use an atom's mass number and atomic number to determine the number of protons, electrons, and neutrons in the atom.
3. **Identify** the subatomic particle used to define an element, and explain why this particle is used.
4. **Explain** why the masses of atoms of the same element may differ.
5. **Calculate** the number of neutrons that each of the following isotopes contains. Use the periodic table to find the atomic numbers.
   a. carbon-14
   b. nitrogen-15
   c. sulfur-35
   d. calcium-45
6. **Identify** the unit that is used for atomic masses.
7. **Define** Avogadro's number, and describe how it relates to a mole of a substance.
8. **Determine** the molar mass of each of the following elements:
   a. manganese, Mn
   b. cadmium, Cd
   c. arsenic, As
   d. strontium, Sr

CRITICAL THINKING

9. **Making Inferences** If an atom loses electrons, will it have an overall charge?
10. **Making Predictions** Predict which isotope of nitrogen is more common in nature: nitrogen-14 or nitrogen-15. (Hint: What is the average atomic mass listed for nitrogen in the periodic table?)
11. **Applying Concepts** Which has a greater number of atoms: 3.0 g of iron, Fe, or 2.0 g of sulfur, S?
12. **Drawing Conclusions** A graph of the amount of a particular element in moles versus the mass of the element in grams is a straight line. Explain why.

Math Skills

13. What is the mass in grams of 0.48 mol of platinum, Pt?
14. What is the mass in grams of 3.1 mol of mercury, Hg?
15. How many moles does 11 g of silicon, Si, contain?
16. How many moles does 205 g of helium, He, contain?

SECTION 3
Modern Atomic Theory

Key Ideas
› What is the modern model of the atom?
› How are the energy levels of an atom filled?
› What makes an electron jump to a new energy level?

Key Terms
orbital
valence electron
photon

Why It Matters
Modern atomic theory explains why different elements produce different colors in fireworks.

Tennessee Course Level Expectations (Physical Science)
CLE.3202.1.2; CLE.3202.Inq.1; CLE.3202.Inq.2; CLE.3202.Inq.3; CLE.3202.Inq.4; CLE.3202.Inq.5; CLE.3202.Inq.6; CLE,3202.TE.3; CLE.3202.TE.4

Dalton's theory that the atom could not be split had to be modified after the discovery that atoms are made of protons, neutrons, and electrons. Like most scientific models and theories, the model of the atom has been revised many times to explain new discoveries.

Modern Models of the Atom

The modern model of the atom, which accounts for many new discoveries in the early 20th century, is very different from the model proposed by Rutherford. › **In the modern atomic model, electrons can be found only in certain energy levels, not between levels. Furthermore, the location of electrons cannot be predicted precisely.** This model is not as easy to visualize as the earlier models that you have studied.

Electron location is limited to energy levels.

In 1913, Niels Bohr, a Danish physicist, suggested that the energy of each electron was related to the electron's path around the nucleus. Electrons can be in only certain energy levels. They must gain energy to move to a higher energy level or must lose energy to move to a lower energy level. Bohr's description of energy levels is still used by scientists today.

One way to imagine Bohr's model is to compare an atom to the stairless building shown in **Figure 1.** Imagine that the nucleus is in a deep basement. The energy levels begin on the first floor, above the basement. Electrons can be on any floor, but they cannot be between floors. Electrons gain energy by riding up the elevator and lose energy by riding down.

Figure 1 The energy levels of an atom are like the floors of the building shown here. The energy difference between energy levels decreases as the energy level increases.

Electrons act like waves.

By 1925, Bohr's model of the atom no longer explained all aspects of electron behavior. A new model, which no longer assumed that electrons orbited the nucleus along definite paths in the same way that planets orbit the sun, was proposed. According to this new atomic model, electrons behave more like waves on a vibrating string than like particles.

Reading Check How does the electron-wave model of the atom differ from earlier atomic models?

The exact location of an electron cannot be determined.

Imagine the moving propeller of a plane, such as the one shown in **Figure 2**. If you were asked to identify the location of any of the blades at a certain instant, you would not be able to give an exact answer. Knowing the exact location of any of the blades is very difficult because the blades are moving so quickly. All you know is that each blade could be anywhere within the blurred area that you see as the blades turn.

Similarly, determining the exact location of an electron in an atom and the speed and direction of the electron is impossible. The best that scientists can do is to calculate the chance of finding an electron in a certain place within an atom. One way to show visually the likelihood of finding an electron in a given location is by shading. The darker the shading, the better the chance of finding an electron at that location. The shaded region is called an **orbital.**

Academic Vocabulary
assume (uh SOOM) to accept without proof

Making Comparisons
As you read this section, make a list of comparisons that you find. For each pair of items, write down ways in which the two items are alike and ways in which they differ.

orbital (AWR buh tuhl) a region in an atom where there is a high probability of finding electrons

Figure 2 The exact location of any of the blades of this airplane is difficult to determine. Likewise, pinpointing the location of an electron in an atom is difficult.

The shaded region, or orbital, shows where electrons are most likely to be.

Electron Energy Levels

Within the atom, electrons that have various amounts of energy exist in different energy levels. There are many possible energy levels that an electron can occupy. **Figure 3** shows how the first four energy levels of an atom are filled. ❯ **The number of energy levels that are filled in an atom depends on the number of electrons.** For example, a lithium atom has three electrons: two in the first energy level and one in the second.

The electrons in the outer energy level of an atom are called **valence electrons.** Valence electrons determine the chemical properties of an atom. Because lithium has one electron in its outer energy level, it has one valence electron.

There are four types of orbitals.

Within each energy level, electrons occupy orbitals that have the lowest energy. There are four kinds of orbitals: s, p, d, and f orbitals. **Figure 4** shows the s and p orbitals.

The s orbital is the simplest kind of orbital. An s orbital has only one possible orientation in space because it is shaped like a sphere, as the figure shows. An s orbital has the lowest energy and can hold two electrons.

A p orbital, on the other hand, is shaped like a dumbbell and can be oriented in space in one of three ways. The axes on the graphs in **Figure 4** can help you picture how these orbitals look in three dimensions. Imagine that the y-axis is flat on the page. Imagine that the dotted lines on the x- and z-axes are going into the page and the darker lines are coming out of the page. Because each p orbital can hold two electrons, the three p orbitals can hold a total of six electrons.

The d and f orbitals are much more complex. There are five possible d orbitals and seven possible f orbitals. Although all of these orbitals are very different in shape, each can hold a maximum of two electrons.

Figure 3 Each energy level holds a certain number of electrons. **How many total electrons can the first four energy levels hold?**

www.scilinks.org
Topic: Atomic Orbitals
Code: HK80118

Figure 4 The s and p Orbitals

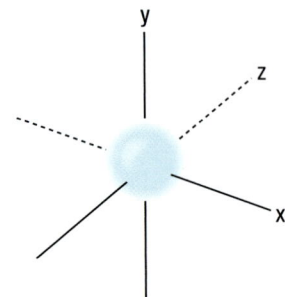

An s orbital is shaped like a sphere, so it has only one possible orientation in space. An s orbital can hold a maximum of two electrons.

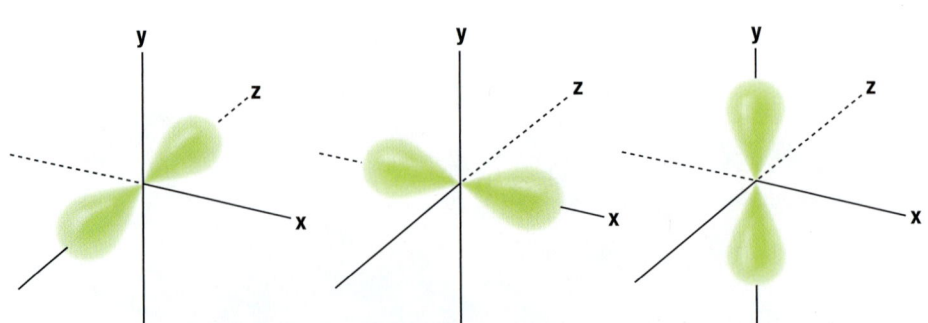

Each of these p orbitals can hold a maximum of two electrons, so all three p orbitals can hold a total of six electrons.

Orbitals determine the number of electrons that each level can hold.

You have seen that each energy level contains a certain number of electrons. The orbitals in each energy level determine the total number of electrons that the level can hold, as **Figure 5** shows. For instance, you learned earlier that the second energy level can hold eight electrons. The reason is that this level contains four orbitals: one s orbital and three p orbitals. Because each orbital can hold two electrons, the second energy level holds $4 \times 2 = 8$ electrons.

Figure 5 Orbitals and Electrons for Energy Levels 1–4

Energy level	Number of orbitals by type				Total number of orbitals		Number of electrons
	s	p	d	f			
1	1				1 = 1	×2 =	2
2	1	3			1 + 3 = 4		8
3	1	3	5		1 + 3 + 5 = 9		18
4	1	3	5	7	1 + 3 + 5 + 7 = 16		32

Electron Transitions

As you have learned, the modern model of the atom limits the location of electrons to specific energy levels. An electron is never found between these levels. Instead, it "jumps" from one level to the next. What makes an electron move from one level to another? ▶ **Electrons jump between energy levels when an atom gains or loses energy.**

The lowest state of energy of an electron is called the *ground state.* At normal temperatures, most electrons are in the ground state. However, if an electron gains energy, it moves to an *excited state.* It gains energy by absorbing a particle of light, called a **photon.** The electron may then fall back to a lower level. In doing so, the electron releases a photon.

Photons of light have different energies. The energy of a photon determines to which level the electron will jump. Think back to the elevator analogy. When an electron absorbs a photon, it gains energy and "rides up the elevator." The energy of the photon determines the level up to which the electron rides. When the electron loses energy and "rides down the elevator," a photon is released. In this case, the change in levels determines the energy of the emitted photon. Electrons can move between any two levels of the atom.

✓ **Reading Check** What makes an electron jump from the ground state to an excited state?

QuickLab

Electron Levels

1. Make a table that has 10 columns and 4 rows. Label the first cell "Energy level." Label the remaining cells in the first row "s" (1 cell), "p" (3 cells), and "d" (5 cells). Label the remaining cells in the first column "1," "2," and "3."

2. For each energy level, place an *X* in cells that correspond to orbitals that are not found in that level.

3. Place **pennies** in empty cells to represent electrons. Each "orbital" can hold two "electrons."

4. Draw Bohr models of atoms whose atomic numbers are 3, 5, 10, and 20. For each model, fill in the cells with the correct number of pennies (in order) to see how the electrons are located in the energy levels.

valence electron (VAY luhns ee LEK TRAHN) an electron that is found in the outermost shell of an atom and that determines the atom's chemical properties

photon (FOH TAHN) a unit or quantum of light

Integrating Space Science

Spectral Analysis Astronomers use the principle that every element emits a unique set of wavelengths to learn about elements in space. This method, called *spectral analysis,* has been used to identify elements in stars. The element helium was discovered through spectral analysis of light from the sun. It was named *helium* because the Greek word for "sun" is *helios.* Helium was later found on Earth.

Atoms absorb or emit light at certain wavelengths.

You have learned that photons are particles of light. The energy of a photon is related to the wavelength of the light. High-energy photons have short wavelengths, and low-energy photons have long wavelengths. Because atoms gain or lose energy in certain amounts, they can absorb or emit only certain wavelengths.

Because each element has a unique atomic structure, the wavelengths emitted depend on the particular element. For instance, the set of wavelengths emitted by hydrogen differs from the set of wavelengths emitted by any other element. For this reason, the wavelengths can be used to identify the substance. They are a type of "atomic fingerprint."

The emission of photons produces the light in neon signs. The wavelength of visible light determines the color of the light. For instance, the wavelengths emitted in neon gas produce the red color shown in **Figure 6.** Gases of other elements produce other colors.

Figure 6 This neon sign lights up because atoms first gain energy from electricity and then release this energy in the form of light. **What happens to the electrons as the light is released?**

Section 3 Review

KEY IDEAS

1. **State** two key features of the modern model of the atom.
2. **Explain** what determines how the energy levels in an atom are filled.
3. **Describe** what happens when an electron jumps from one energy level to another.
4. **Identify** how many electrons the third energy level can hold, and explain why this is the case.

CRITICAL THINKING

5. **Analyzing Models** Compare an atom's structure to a ladder. Identify one way in which a ladder is not a good model for the atom.
6. **Making Comparisons** Explain how Bohr's model and the modern model of the atom differ in terms of the path of an electron.
7. **Applying Concepts** How many valence electrons does nitrogen ($Z = 7$) have?

Why It Matters

How Do Fireworks Work?

REAL WORLD

Today's firework displays often feature complex patterns and vivid colors. The colors in fireworks are produced by the emission of photons. The photon wavelength—and thus the color—depends on the compounds that are used. Just as neon gas produces red light, various compounds create specific firework colors. For instance, sodium salts produce yellow, and magnesium and aluminum produce white. These coloring agents are packed into the "stars" inside the shell, often by hand.

④ The second shell continues to shoot into the air. When the time-delay fuse reaches the black powder in this shell, the second set of fireworks explodes.

- Main fuse
- Stars
- Black powder
- Time-delay fuse
- Lift charge

③ The time-delay fuse inside the shell eventually ignites the black powder in the lower shell, which creates the first set of fireworks.

① At the push of a button on a master control board, the main fuse ignites and moves down toward the lift charge. When ignited, the stars in each shell burst into dazzling displays of color. Black powder, or gunpowder, is used as the explosive.

② The main fuse quickly ignites the lift charge, which shoots the firework into the air. At the same time, the time-delay fuse begins burning slowly. This system of fuses creates two sets of fireworks from this multibreak shell.

www.scilinks.org
Topic: Fireworks
Code: **HK81697**

 YOUR TURN

UNDERSTANDING CONCEPTS
1. How is a firework similar to a neon sign?

ONLINE RESEARCH
2. Use the Internet to learn about the history of fireworks. Create a visual timeline based on the results of your research.

133

Skills Practice Lab

Building Isotopes

Imagine that you are an employee at the Elements-4-U Company, which custom builds models of elements. Your job is to construct a model of the atomic nucleus for each element ordered by your clients. You were hired for the position because of your knowledge about what a nucleus is made of and your understanding of how isotopes of an element differ from each other. Now, it's time to put that knowledge to work!

What You'll Do

> **Build** models of nuclei of certain isotopes.

> **Use** the periodic table to determine the composition of atomic nuclei.

What You'll Need

periodic table
plastic-foam balls, blue, 2–3 cm in diameter (6)
plastic-foam balls, white, 2–3 cm in diameter (4)
toothpicks (20)

Procedure

Making the Simplest Nucleus

1. Copy the sample data table onto another sheet of paper.
2. Your first assignment is the nucleus of hydrogen-1. Pick up one proton (a white plastic-foam ball). Congratulations! You have built a hydrogen-1 nucleus, the simplest nucleus possible.
3. The atomic number of an element is the number of protons in an atom of the element. In your data table, record the atomic number and the number of neutrons for hydrogen-1.
4. Add the atomic number and the neutron number together to determine the mass number of hydrogen-1. Record this information in your table.
5. Draw a picture of your hydrogen-1 model.

Building More-Complicated Nuclei

6. For the next part of the lab, you will need to use information from the periodic table of the elements. You can find the atomic number of any element at the top of the element's entry on the periodic table. For example, the atomic number of carbon is 6. Find the atomic number for each remaining isotope in the data table, and add this information to your table.
7. The name of the isotope tells you the mass number. For instance, the mass number of hydrogen-2 is 2, and the mass number of helium-4 is 4. Determine the mass number for each remaining isotope in the data table, and add this information to your table.
8. Subtract the atomic number from the mass number to find the number of neutrons for each remaining isotope in the table.

Sample Data Table: Nuclei of Various Isotopes

	Hydrogen-1	Hydrogen-2	Helium-3	Helium-4	Beryllium-9	Beryllium-10
Atomic number (*Z*)						
Number of neutrons			DO NOT WRITE IN BOOK			
Mass number (*A*)						

9 In a nucleus, the protons and neutrons are held together by the strong nuclear force, which is represented in this activity by toothpicks. Protons and neutrons always form the smallest arrangement possible because the strong nuclear force pulls them together. Using a toothpick, build a model of the nucleus of hydrogen-2.

10 Draw a picture of your hydrogen-2 model.

11 Repeat steps 9–10 for the remaining isotopes in your table. Remember to put the protons and neutrons as close together as possible—each particle should attach to at least two other particles.

Analysis

1. **Interpreting Data** Why do different isotopes of the same element have the same atomic number?
2. **Applying Concepts** If you know the mass number and the number of neutrons of an isotope, how can you determine the atomic number?

Communicating Your Results

3. **Applying Conclusions** Look up uranium on the periodic table. What is the atomic number of uranium? How many neutrons does the isotope uranium-235 have?
4. **Evaluating Models** Compare your model with the models of your classmates. How are the models similar? How are they different?

Extension

Create a new nucleus by combining your model with another student's model. Identify the new element (and isotope) that you have created.

Testing A Hypothesis

Science > Skills

Once you have formed a hypothesis, the next step is to test it. To test a hypothesis, you need to create an experiment that will clearly show whether the hypothesis is true or false. The steps below show you how to test a hypothesis.

Technology
Math
▶ **Scientific Methods**
Graphing

1 State the hypothesis.
A hypothesis is formed from observations that you have made or data that you have already collected. Sometimes, scientists test a hypothesis that was formed by another scientist.

> Ernest Rutherford wanted to test J. J. Thomson's model of the atom. Rutherford's hypothesis was: Atoms consist of negative electrons embedded in a cloud of positive charge.

2 Design an experiment.
To think of an experiment that will test the hypothesis, you can start by asking yourself, "What can I do that will give me one result if the hypothesis is true and a different result if the hypothesis is false?"

> In Rutherford's experiment, positively charged alpha particles were fired at a thin sheet of gold foil. A detector showed the angles at which the particles left the foil.

3 Make predictions.
Your predictions should state what the outcomes of the experiment would be if the hypothesis were true. You may also want to state what the outcomes would be if the hypothesis were false.

> If positive charges are spread throughout the atom, then most alpha particles would pass straight through the foil. A few would be deflected, but not at very large angles.

4 Do the experiment, analyze the results, and draw conclusions.
Analyze the results of the experiment to see how they compare to your predictions. If your original hypothesis was false, you may need to form a new hypothesis and begin the testing process again.

> A few particles were deflected at large angles, and some even came straight back. This result did not match the prediction. Thus, the hypothesis was incorrect.

Practice

1. Suppose that you have a flashlight that does not work. You form the hypothesis that the batteries are dead. Describe an experiment that you could do to test this hypothesis. Predict what the results of the experiment will be if the hypothesis is true and what they will be if it is false.

2. Suppose that you get a stomachache every time you eat a hot dog with chili. Form a hypothesis to explain this observation. Then, describe an experiment to test the hypothesis. Predict what the results of the experiment will be if the hypothesis is true and what they will be if it is false.

Chapter 4 Summary

Key Ideas

Section 1 The Development of Atomic Theory

- **The Beginnings of Atomic Theory** Democritus suggested that the universe was made of indivisible units called *atoms*. (p. 113)
- **Dalton's Atomic Theory** According to Dalton, all atoms of a given element were exactly alike, and atoms of different elements could join to form compounds. (p. 114)
- **Thomson's Model of the Atom** Thomson's cathode-ray tube experiment suggested that cathode rays were made of negatively-charged particles that came from inside atoms. (p. 115)
- **Rutherford's Model of the Atom** Rutherford proposed that most of the mass of the atom was concentrated at the atom's center. (p. 117)

Section 2 The Structure of Atoms

- **What Is in an Atom?** The three main subatomic particles are distinguished by mass, charge, and location in the atom. (p. 119)
- **Atomic Number and Mass Number** Atoms of an element have the same number of protons, but they can have different numbers of neutrons. (p. 121)
- **Isotopes** Isotopes of an element vary in mass because their numbers of neutrons differ. (p. 122)
- **Atomic Masses** Atomic masses are usually expressed in unified atomic mass units. (p. 124)

Section 3 Modern Atomic Theory

- **Modern Models of the Atom** Electrons can be found only in certain energy levels. The location of electrons cannot be predicted precisely. (p. 128)
- **Electron Energy Levels** The number of energy levels that are filled in an atom depends on the number of electrons. (p. 130)
- **Electron Transitions** Electrons jump between levels when an atom gains or loses energy. (p. 131)

Key Terms

electron, p. 115
nucleus, p. 118

proton, p. 119
neutron, p. 119
atomic number, p. 121
mass number, p. 121
isotope, p. 122
unified atomic mass unit, p. 124
mole, p. 125

orbital, p. 129
valence electron, p. 130
photon, p. 131

CHAPTER 4 Review

READING TOOLBOX

1. **Word Origins** The word electron was formed by combining the root *electr-*, meaning amber, with the suffix *–on*. List at least three other words that include the root *electr-*.

USING KEY TERMS

2. How many *protons* and *neutrons* does a silicon, Si, atom have, and where are these two types of subatomic particles located? How many *electrons* does a silicon atom have?

3. Explain why different atoms of the same element always have the same *atomic number* but can have different *mass numbers.* What are these different atoms called?

4. What does an element's *molar mass* tell you about the element?

5. What is an *orbital*?

UNDERSTANDING KEY IDEAS

6. Which of Dalton's statements about the atom was proven false by J. J. Thomson?
   a. Atoms cannot be subdivided.
   b. Atoms are tiny.
   c. Atoms of different elements are not identical.
   d. Atoms join to form molecules.

7. What did Rutherford learn about the atom from his gold-foil experiment?
   a. Atoms have electrons.
   b. Atoms have a nucleus.
   c. Atoms have negative charge embedded in a sphere of positive charge.
   d. The nucleus is most of the atom's volume.

8. If an atom has a mass of 11 u and contains five electrons, its atomic number must be
   a. 55.   c. 6.
   b. 16.   d. 5.

9. Which statement is not true of Bohr's model of the atom?
   a. Electrons cannot be between energy levels.
   b. Electrons orbit the nucleus.
   c. An electron's path is not known exactly.
   d. Electrons exist in energy levels.

10. According to the modern model of the atom,
    a. moving electrons form an electron cloud.
    b. electrons and protons circle neutrons.
    c. neutrons have a positive charge.
    d. the number of protons for a given element varies.

11. Carbon has six protons. How many valence electrons does carbon have?
    a. 2   c. 6
    b. 4   d. 12

12. The second energy level has 1 s orbital and 3 p orbitals. How many electrons can this energy level hold?
    a. 2   c. 18
    b. 8   d. 32

13. An electron moves from the ground state to an excited state when it absorbs
    a. a proton.   c. a photon.
    b. a neutron.   d. an isotope.

EXPLAINING KEY IDEAS

14. Study the graphic below of Rutherford's gold-foil experiment. Which of the deflections, A or B, was a surprise to Rutherford? Why?

138   Chapter 4   Atoms

15. Identify the particles that make up an atom. How do these particles relate to the identity of an atom?

16. Determine the atomic number and mass number of an isotope that has 56 electrons and 82 neutrons.

17. Why do most atoms have no charge even though they are made up of positively charged protons and negatively charged electrons?

INTERPRETING GRAPHICS The diagrams below show three atoms. Use the diagrams to answer questions 18–20.

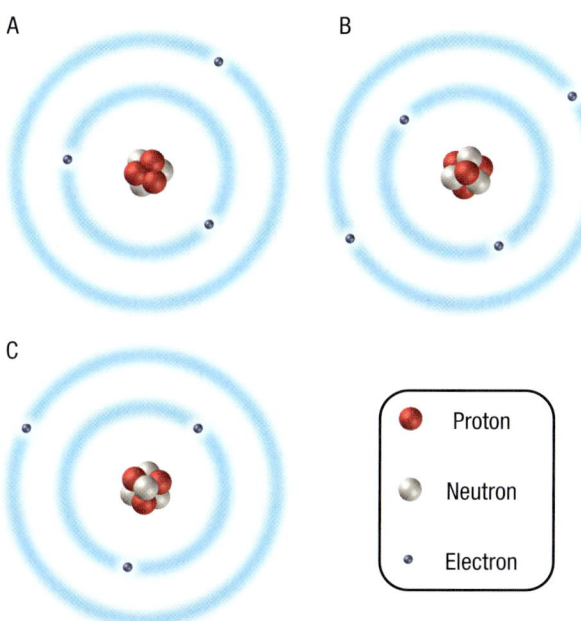

18. Which diagrams represent the same element?

19. What is the atomic number for atom A?

20. What is the mass number for atom B?

CRITICAL THINKING

21. **Applying Ideas** Particle accelerators are devices that speed up charged particles in order to smash them together. Scientists use the devices to make atoms. How can scientists determine whether the atoms formed are a new element or a new isotope of a known element?

22. **Making Inferences** Why is measuring the size of an atom difficult?

23. **Drawing Conclusions** Are hydrogen-3 and helium-3 isotopes of the same element? Explain.

24. **Making Inferences** Some forces push atoms apart, and other forces pull atoms together. Describe how the subatomic particles in each atom interact to produce these forces.

25. **Analyzing Methods** If scientists had tried to repeat Thomson's experiment and found that they could not, would Thomson's conclusion still have been valid? Explain your answer.

Graphing Skills

26. **Interpreting Graphs** Study the graph of mass (g) versus amount (mol) for iron.
    a. Is the relationship between the two variables direct or inverse?
    b. How many particles are there in 111.6 g of iron?

Math Skills

27. **Converting Grams to Moles** For an experiment you have been asked to do, you need 1.5 g of iron. How many moles of iron do you need?

28. **Converting Moles to Grams** Robyn recycled 15.1 mol of aluminum last month. What was the mass in grams of the aluminum she recycled?

Chapter Review **139**

Standardized Test Prep

Understanding Concepts

Directions (1–4): For each question, write on a sheet of paper the letter of the correct answer.

1. When electricity is connected to a neon sign, an atom of neon inside the sign emits a photon. What has happened within the atom to allow the emission of light energy?
   - **A.** An electron has moved to a lower energy level.
   - **B.** Two electron orbitals have collided.
   - **C.** A proton has been lost from the nucleus.
   - **D.** The atom has gained a positive charge.

2. After a single subatomic particle is removed from an atom of helium, the helium atom becomes an atom of hydrogen. What subatomic particle was removed?
   - **F.** an electron
   - **G.** a proton
   - **H.** a quark
   - **I.** a neutron

3. Gold has an average atomic mass of 196.97 u. Approximately how many atoms of gold are there in 100 g of gold? Note: there are 6.022×10^{23} atoms in a mole.
   - **A.** 3.0573×10^{19}
   - **B.** 3.0573×10^{23}
   - **C.** 1.1862×10^{24}
   - **D.** 1.1862×10^{28}

4. What subatomic particles can be found in regions called *orbitals*?
   - **F.** protons
   - **G.** neutrons
   - **H.** electrons
   - **I.** photons

Directions (5–6): For each question, write a short response.

5. Xenon has an atomic number of 54. A particular isotope of xenon has a mass number of 131. How many protons and how many neutrons does each atom of that isotope have?

6. Suppose that a team of chemists discovered that lead has the following composition: 80% of lead is an isotope whose mass number is 207, and 20% of lead is an isotope whose mass number is 208. What would they determine the average atomic mass of lead to be?

Reading Skills

Directions (7–8): Read the passage below. Then, answer the questions that follow.

THE BOHR MODEL OF THE ATOM
In the Bohr model of the atom, electrons can be found only in certain energy levels. Electrons "jump" directly from one level to the next level; they are never found between levels. When an electron moves from one level to another, it gains or loses energy, depending on the direction of its jump.

Bohr's model explained an unusual event. When electric charges pass through atoms of a gaseous element, the gas produces a glowing light, like in a neon sign. If this light is passed through a prism, a pattern of lines appears. Each line has a different color. The pattern depends on the element—neon has one pattern, and helium has another. In Bohr's model, the lines are caused by electron jumps from higher to lower energy levels. Because only certain jumps are possible, electrons release energy only in certain quantities. These "packets" of energy produce the lines that are seen.

7. In the Bohr model of the atom, which of the following characteristics of electrons is limited?
   - **A.** the number of electrons in an atom
   - **B.** the location of the electrons
   - **C.** the size of electrons
   - **D.** the speed of electrons

8. What causes the colored lines that appear when the light from a gas is passed through a prism?
   - **F.** packets of energy released by electron jumps
   - **G.** electrons changing color
   - **H.** atoms of the gas exchanging electrons
   - **I.** There is not enough information to determine the answer.

Interpreting Graphics

The graphic below shows how electron orbitals around the nucleus of an atom are organized into energy levels. Each orbital holds 2 electrons. Use this graphic to answer questions 9–11.

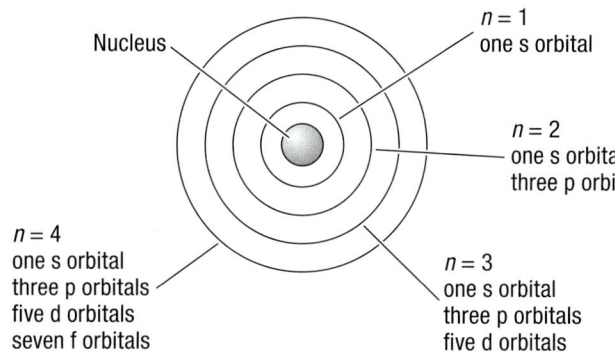

9. If every orbital of an atom's $n = 4$ energy level was full of electrons, how many electrons would there be in that energy level?
   A. 7
   B. 14
   C. 16
   D. 32

10. The atomic number of sulfur is 16. If energy levels are filled with electrons from the innermost level to the outermost level, how many electrons are in the $n = 3$ energy level of a neutral sulfur atom?

11. Every known element has seven or fewer energy levels. How many orbitals would there be room for in energy level $n = 7$?

The table below gives information about the subatomic particles in six atoms. Use this table to answer questions 12–13.

	Protons	Electrons	Neutrons
Mystery atom #1	15	15	15
Mystery atom #2	17	16	15
Mystery atom #3	23	23	23
Mystery atom #4	23	24	22
Mystery atom #5	42	43	52
Mystery atom #6	51	51	41

12. Which two atoms are isotopes of the same element?
    F. #1 and #2
    G. #2 and #3
    H. #3 and #4
    I. #4 and #5

13. What is the mass of one mole of the heaviest atom in the table?

Test Tip

For multiple-choice questions, try to eliminate any answer choices that are obviously incorrect, and then consider the remaining answer choices.

CHAPTER 5
The Periodic Table

Chapter Outline

1 Organizing the Elements
Recognizing a Pattern
Changing the Arrangement

2 Exploring the Periodic Table
The Role of Electrons
Ion Formation
How Are Elements Classified?

3 Families of Elements
Classifying Elements Further
Metals
Nonmetals
Semiconductors

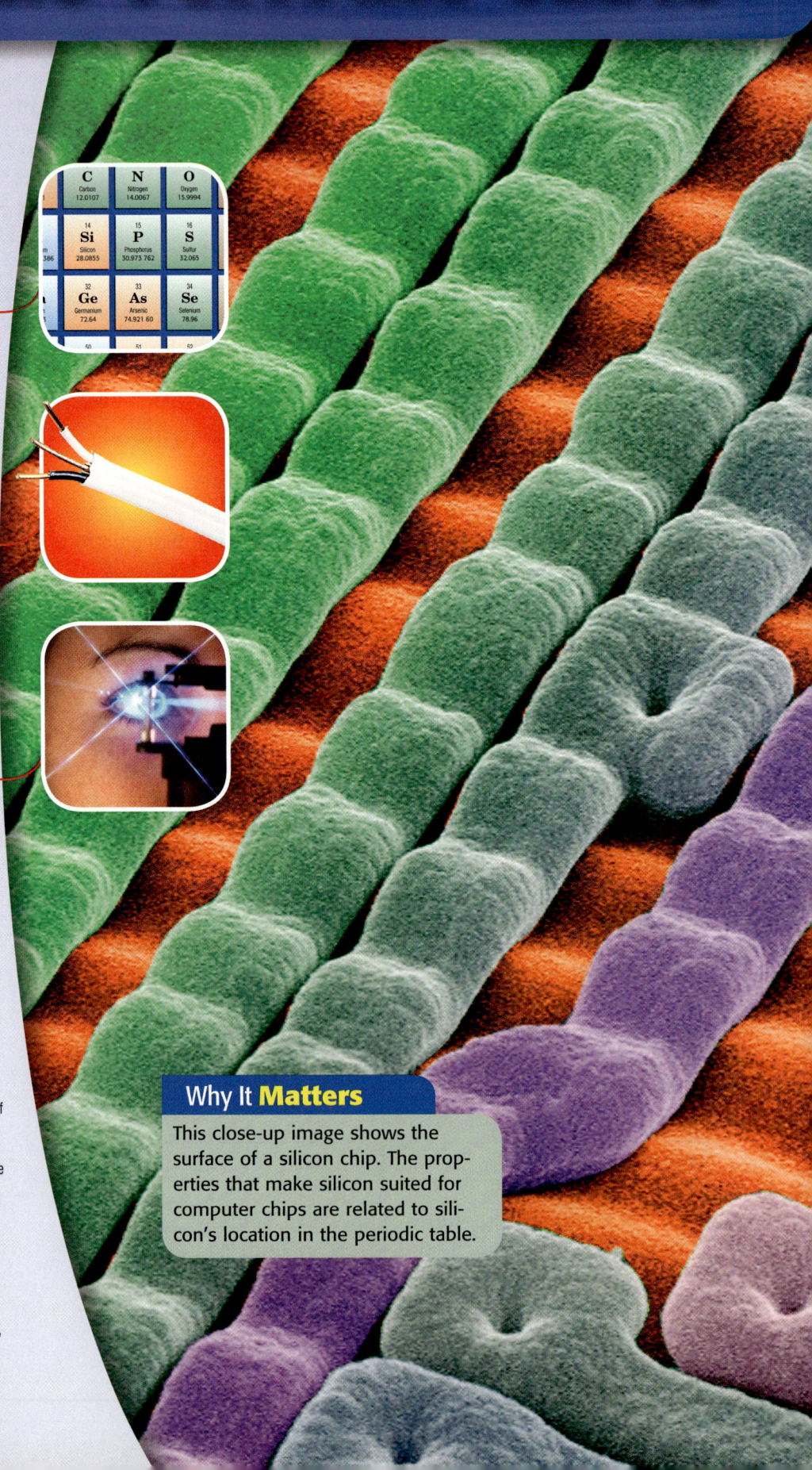

Tennessee Course Level Expectations (Physical Science)

CLE.3202.TE.3 Explain the relationship between the properties of a material and the use of the material in the application of a technology; **CLE.3202.1.3** Characterize and classify elements based on their atomic structure; **CLE.3202.Inq.1** Recognize that science is a progressive endeavor that reevaluates and extends what is already accepted; **CLE.3202.Inq.2** Design and conduct scientific investigations to explore new phenomena, verify previous results, test how well a theory predicts, and compare opposing theories; **CLE.3202.Inq.3** Use appropriate tools and technology to collect precise and accurate data; **CLE.3202.Inq.6** Communicate and defend scientific findings; **CLE.3202.TE.4** Describe the dynamic interplay among science, technology, and engineering within living, earth-space, and physical systems.

Why It Matters

This close-up image shows the surface of a silicon chip. The properties that make silicon suited for computer chips are related to silicon's location in the periodic table.

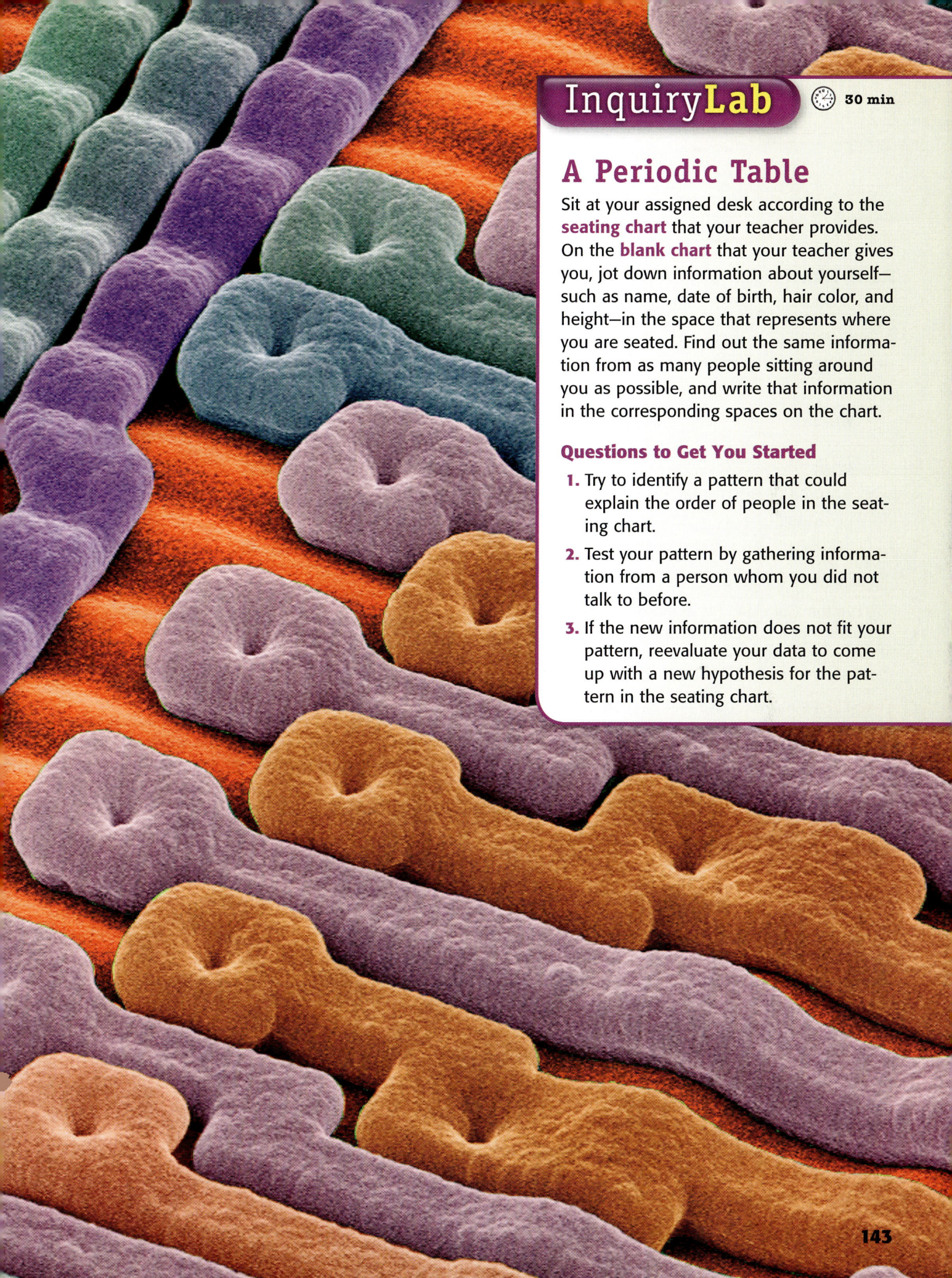

Inquiry Lab ⏱ 30 min

A Periodic Table

Sit at your assigned desk according to the **seating chart** that your teacher provides. On the **blank chart** that your teacher gives you, jot down information about yourself—such as name, date of birth, hair color, and height—in the space that represents where you are seated. Find out the same information from as many people sitting around you as possible, and write that information in the corresponding spaces on the chart.

Questions to Get You Started

1. Try to identify a pattern that could explain the order of people in the seating chart.
2. Test your pattern by gathering information from a person whom you did not talk to before.
3. If the new information does not fit your pattern, reevaluate your data to come up with a new hypothesis for the pattern in the seating chart.

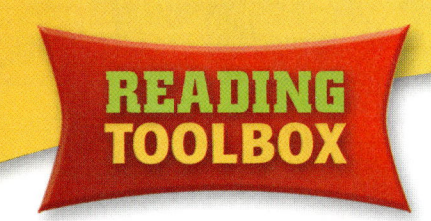

READING TOOLBOX

These reading tools can help you learn the material in this chapter. For more information on how to use these and other tools, see **Appendix A**.

Word Parts

Root Words Many scientific words are made up of word parts derived from ancient or foreign languages. Understanding the meanings of these word parts can help you understand new scientific terms. Here are two examples from this chapter:

WORDS	alkali metal / alkaline earth metal
ROOT	alkali
SOURCE OF ROOT	Arabic "al-qali"
MEANING	ashes of plants grown in salty soil

You can think of elements in these groups as elements that are likely to be found in ashes. Alkaline-earth metals have low solubility, so they are more likely to be found in solid—or earthy—form.

Your Turn After you have read Section 3, look up the roots *hal-* and *halo-* in a dictionary. Then, explain why you think the word *halogen* is appropriate for the elements in Group 17 of the periodic table.

Generalizations

Properties of Groups Generalizations are general statements or principles applied to a large set or group of things (or people).

- Generalizations are sometimes signaled by words such as *most, mostly,* or *generally,* or by phrases such as *in general* or *for the most part*.
- Most generalizations, however, are not signaled by any telltale phrases.

> **Example of a generalization:**
> For the most part, pure metals are solid at room temperature.

This example statement is a generalization because
- the statement applies to most but not all metals.
- mercury, which is a liquid at room temperature, is an exception.

Your Turn As you read about the properties of groups of elements, make a list of generalizations that you find in the text. If there is a word or phrase that signals the generalization, underline that word or phrase in the generalization.

Graphic Organizers

Spider Maps Spider maps show how details are organized into categories, which in turn are related to a main idea.

To make a spider map, follow the steps.
1. Write a main topic title, and draw an oval around it.
2. From the oval, draw legs. Each leg represents a category of the main topic.
3. From each leg, draw horizontal lines. Write details about each category on these lines.

Your Turn As you read Section 3, use a spider map to organize the information that you learn about families of elements in the periodic table.

144 Chapter 5 The Periodic Table

SECTION 1
Organizing the Elements

Key Ideas
- How did Mendeleev arrange the elements in his periodic table?
- How are elements arranged in the modern periodic table?

Key Terms
periodic law
period
group

Why It Matters
Gold and silver—both used in jewelry—have similar properties and are, therefore, located in the same column of the periodic table.

Scientists in the 1860s knew some of the chemical and physical properties of more than 60 elements. However, there was no general system of organizing the elements. To find a way to organize the elements, scientists studied the elements and the properties of the elements.

Recognizing a Pattern

Dmitri Mendeleev, a Russian chemist, was one of the first scientists to design a way of organizing the elements. He studied the properties of the elements and looked for patterns among the properties. He found that if the elements were listed by increasing atomic mass, certain properties appeared at certain intervals within the list.

In 1869, Mendeleev published the first periodic table of the elements. ▶ **In this periodic table, Mendeleev arranged elements in rows by increasing atomic mass.** He started a new row each time the chemical properties of the elements repeated. So, for any column, all of the elements in that column had similar properties. **Figure 1** shows Mendeleev's handwritten list of the elements and a copy of his published table.

Figure 1 The Russian scientist Dmitri Mendeleev published the first periodic table in 1869. **How did he organize the elements?**

READING TOOLBOX

Spider Maps
Create a spider map that has two legs and several lines on each leg. Use the map to compare Mendeleev's periodic table with the modern periodic table.

Mendeleev was able to predict new elements.

When Mendeleev arranged the elements in a list, he left gaps in the list. When he used his list to construct a table, he included these gaps in the table. **Figure 2** shows that he put question marks in these gaps. The question marks indicate places where there was no known element whose properties fit the pattern. He predicted that new elements would be discovered that would fill those gaps. He used each new element's position in the periodic table to predict some of the properties of the element.

For example, Mendeleev left a space for an element after silicon. He predicted that this element would be a gray metal that has a high melting point. In 1886, the element germanium was discovered. As **Figure 2** shows, the properties of germanium are very similar to those predicted by Mendeleev. Also discovered were two other elements that closely matched Mendeleev's predictions: gallium and scandium.

Mendeleev was not the only person to develop a periodic table, but he was first to use the table to make predictions. Mendeleev is often considered to be the father of the periodic table. The element *mendelevium* was named in his honor.

✓ **Reading Check** Why did Mendeleev leave gaps in the periodic table? (See Appendix E for answers to Reading Checks.)

A few elements did not fit the pattern.

Mendeleev found that some elements did not quite fit the pattern. For example, he had to reverse the positions of the elements tellurium and iodine. When he did so, they were in columns with similar elements. However, they were no longer in order of increasing atomic mass. Mendeleev thought that perhaps the values of the masses were not accurate, but later experiments proved that the values were correct.

Figure 2 Mendeleev's periodic table left a question mark for germanium, which was discovered in 1886. Germanium's properties are similar to those predicted by Mendeleev, as shown in the table.

Properties of Germanium

	Mendeleev's prediction	Actual property
Atomic mass	70	72.6
Density*	5.5 g/cm^3	5.3 g/cm^3
Appearance	Dark gray metal	Gray metalloid
Melting point*	High	937 °C

*at room temperature and pressure

Changing the Arrangement

As scientists learned more about the structure of the atom, they improved Mendeleev's table. About 40 years after Mendeleev published his table, the English chemist Henry Moseley arranged the elements by atomic number rather than by atomic mass. As you learned earlier, an element's atomic number is the number of protons in an atom of the element. Most elements did not change their location in the table, but a few elements did. This new arrangement fixed the discrepancies with elements such as tellurium and iodine.

Today's periodic table, which includes more than 100 elements, is shown on the next two pages. ❯ **The modern periodic table organizes elements by atomic number. When the elements are arranged in this way, elements that have similar properties appear at regular intervals.** This principle is known as the **periodic law.** The periodic table in this book lists the atomic number, the symbol, the name, and the average atomic mass of each element.

Academic Vocabulary

discrepancy (di SKREP uhn see) disagreement or difference between apparent facts

periodic law (PIR ee AHD ik LAW) the law that states that the repeating chemical and physical properties of elements change periodically with the atomic numbers of the elements

Why It Matters
Mercury in Fish

EYE ON THE ENVIRONMENT

The element mercury can be toxic. Some mercury occurs in nature, and some is added to the environment by industrial activities. Methylmercury, the most dangerous compound of mercury, can build up in fish tissue. Most commercial fish have low levels, but there are higher levels in fish at the top of the food chain, such as shark and swordfish. People can become exposed when eating contaminated fish.

Mercury, a metal, is a liquid at room temperature. Toxic mercury compounds can damage the human nervous system.

The FDA recommends specific limits for the consumption of certain fish, such as canned and fresh tuna. You can check the fish advisories in your area for information about local fresh fish.

YOUR TURN

CRITICAL THINKING
1. Why do fish at the top level of the food chain have higher concentrations of methylmercury than fish at lower levels?

- Hydrogen
- Semiconductors
  (also known as metalloids)

Metals
- Alkali metals
- Alkaline-earth metals
- Transition metals
- Other metals

Nonmetals
- Halogens
- Noble gases
- Other nonmetals

Group 10	Group 11	Group 12	Group 13	Group 14	Group 15	Group 16	Group 17	Group 18
								2 **He** Helium 4.002 602
			5 **B** Boron 10.811	6 **C** Carbon 12.0107	7 **N** Nitrogen 14.0067	8 **O** Oxygen 15.9994	9 **F** Fluorine 18.998 4032	10 **Ne** Neon 20.1797
			13 **Al** Aluminum 26.981 5386	14 **Si** Silicon 28.0855	15 **P** Phosphorus 30.973 762	16 **S** Sulfur 32.065	17 **Cl** Chlorine 35.453	18 **Ar** Argon 39.948
28 **Ni** Nickel 58.6934	29 **Cu** Copper 63.546	30 **Zn** Zinc 65.409	31 **Ga** Gallium 69.723	32 **Ge** Germanium 72.64	33 **As** Arsenic 74.921 60	34 **Se** Selenium 78.96	35 **Br** Bromine 79.904	36 **Kr** Krypton 83.798
46 **Pd** Palladium 106.42	47 **Ag** Silver 107.8682	48 **Cd** Cadmium 112.411	49 **In** Indium 114.818	50 **Sn** Tin 118.710	51 **Sb** Antimony 121.760	52 **Te** Tellurium 127.60	53 **I** Iodine 126.904 47	54 **Xe** Xenon 131.293
78 **Pt** Platinum 195.084	79 **Au** Gold 196.966 569	80 **Hg** Mercury 200.59	81 **Tl** Thallium 204.3833	82 **Pb** Lead 207.2	83 **Bi** Bismuth 208.980 40	84 **Po** Polonium (209)	85 **At** Astatine (210)	86 **Rn** Radon (222)
110 **Ds** Darmstadtium (271)	111 **Rg** Roentgenium (272)	112 **Uub*** Ununbium (285)		114 **Uuq*** Ununquadium (289)		116 **Uuh*** Ununhexium (292)		

The discoveries of elements with atomic numbers 112, 114, and 116 have been reported but not fully confirmed.

63 **Eu** Europium 151.964	64 **Gd** Gadolinium 157.25	65 **Tb** Terbium 158.925 35	66 **Dy** Dysprosium 162.500	67 **Ho** Holmium 164.930 32	68 **Er** Erbium 167.259	69 **Tm** Thulium 168.934 21	70 **Yb** Ytterbium 173.04	71 **Lu** Lutetium 174.967
95 **Am** Americium (243)	96 **Cm** Curium (247)	97 **Bk** Berkelium (247)	98 **Cf** Californium (251)	99 **Es** Einsteinium (252)	100 **Fm** Fermium (257)	101 **Md** Mendelevium (258)	102 **No** Nobelium (259)	103 **Lr** Lawrencium (262)

The atomic masses listed in this table reflect the precision of current measurements. (Each value listed in parentheses is the mass number of that radioactive element's most stable or most common isotope.)

Figure 3 Titanium, arsenic, and bromine are in Period 4. **Which is most metallic, and which is least metallic?**

Elements become less metallic across each period.

Each row of the periodic table is a **period**. The periodic table, which is shown on the previous pages, has seven periods. **Figure 3** shows three elements in Period 4. As you move from left to right across a period, properties such as reactivity and conductivity change, and elements become less metallic.

Elements in a group have similar properties.

Each column of the periodic table is a **group**. For each group, all of the elements in that group have similar chemical properties. For example, helium and neon, in Group 18, are both unreactive elements. That is, under normal conditions, these elements do not join with atoms of other elements to form compounds.

The periodic table on the previous pages shows color-coded categories. Many of these categories are associated with a certain group or groups. You will learn more about specific groups of elements later in this chapter.

period (PIR ee uhd) a horizontal row of elements in the periodic table

group (GROOP) a vertical column of elements in the periodic table; elements in a group share chemical properties

www.scilinks.org
Topic: Origin of Elements
Code: HK81082

Section 1 Review

KEY IDEAS

1. **Describe** how Mendeleev organized his periodic table.
2. **Explain** why Mendeleev left a space for the unknown (at the time) element germanium in his periodic table.
3. **State** the property used to organize elements in the modern periodic table.
4. **Identify** the following on the periodic table.
   a. the chemical symbol for mercury
   b. the period and group of gold
   c. the atomic mass of iron
   d. the atomic number of neon
   e. the element represented by Cu

CRITICAL THINKING

5. **Applying Concepts** Metals conduct electricity well, while nonmetals do not. Which element should conduct electricity better: germanium, aluminum, or helium?
6. **Drawing Conclusions** Are the properties of sodium, Na, more like the properties of lithium, Li, or magnesium, Mg? Explain your answer.
7. **Making Inferences** Before 1937, all naturally occurring elements had been discovered, but no one had found a trace of element 43. Chemists predicted the chemical properties of this element, now called *technetium*. How were these predictions possible? Which elements would you expect to be similar to technetium?

SECTION 2
Exploring the Periodic Table

Key Ideas
- Why do elements within a group of the periodic table have similar chemical properties?
- What happens to an atom that gains or loses electrons?
- What are the three main categories of elements?

Key Terms
- ion
- metal
- nonmetal
- semiconductor

Why It Matters
The properties of metals make metals useful for conducting electricity. For example, wires that carry electricity are made of metal.

Why is neon an unreactive element? Why is sodium so reactive that it reacts violently with moisture and oxygen in the air? These chemical properties are related to the number of electrons in each element.

> Tennessee Course Level Expectations (Physical Science)
> CLE.3202.1.3

The Role of Electrons

The periodic table is organized by atomic number, which is the number of protons in an atom. For a neutral atom, the number of protons equals the number of electrons. ▶ **The periodic trends in the periodic table are the result of electron arrangement.** Specifically, the chemical properties of each group are largely determined by the number of valence electrons. These electrons are closest to the outside of the atom and are sometimes considered part of an outer "shell" of electrons.

Valence electrons account for similar properties.

The number of valence electrons determines many of the chemical properties of an element. The diagrams in **Figure 1** show atoms of two elements from Group 1: lithium and sodium. Because they each have one valence electron, lithium and sodium have similar chemical properties. In general, elements in a group have chemical and physical properties in common because they have the same number of valence electrons. Of course, elements in a group are not exactly alike. They differ in numbers of protons in their nuclei and in numbers of electrons in their filled inner energy levels. As a result, the properties of elements in a group are not exactly the same.

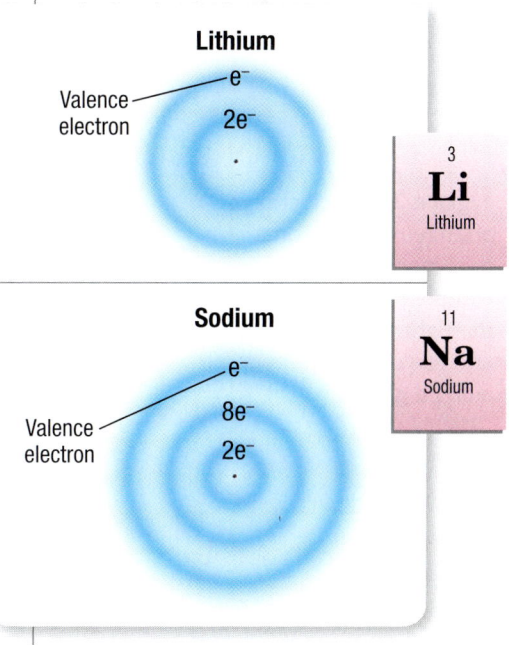

Figure 1 These two elements in Group 1 each have one valence electron. **What is the difference in the location of these electrons?**

Root Words
Use a dictionary or the Internet to find the root words for *hydrogen*, *helium*, and *lithium*. Explain how each root is related to the properties of that element.

www.scilinks.org
Topic: Periodic Table
Code: HK81125

An element's location in the periodic table is related to electron arrangement.

You can find out how the electrons are arranged in the atoms of an element if you know where the element is located in the periodic table. Hydrogen and helium are in Period 1. **Figure 2** shows that a hydrogen atom has one electron in an s orbital and that a helium atom has two electrons in an s orbital. Lithium is located in Period 2. Like helium, lithium has two electrons in an s orbital. But lithium has a third electron, which is in an s orbital in the second energy level. The table below shows the electron arrangement of lithium.

Element	Energy level	Orbital	Number of electrons
Lithium	1	s	2
	2	s	1

As you move to the right in Period 2, electrons begin to fill the p orbitals. For instance, a carbon atom's six electrons are in two s orbitals and one p orbital, as shown in the table below.

Element	Energy level	Orbital	Number of electrons
Carbon	1	s	2
	2	s	2
	2	p	2

A nitrogen atom has three electrons in p orbitals, an oxygen atom has four, and a fluorine atom has five. **Figure 2** shows that a neon atom has six electrons in p orbitals. Each p orbital can hold two electrons, so neon's three p orbitals are filled.

Figure 2 The electronic arrangement of atoms becomes increasingly complex as you move to the right across a period and as you move down along a group.

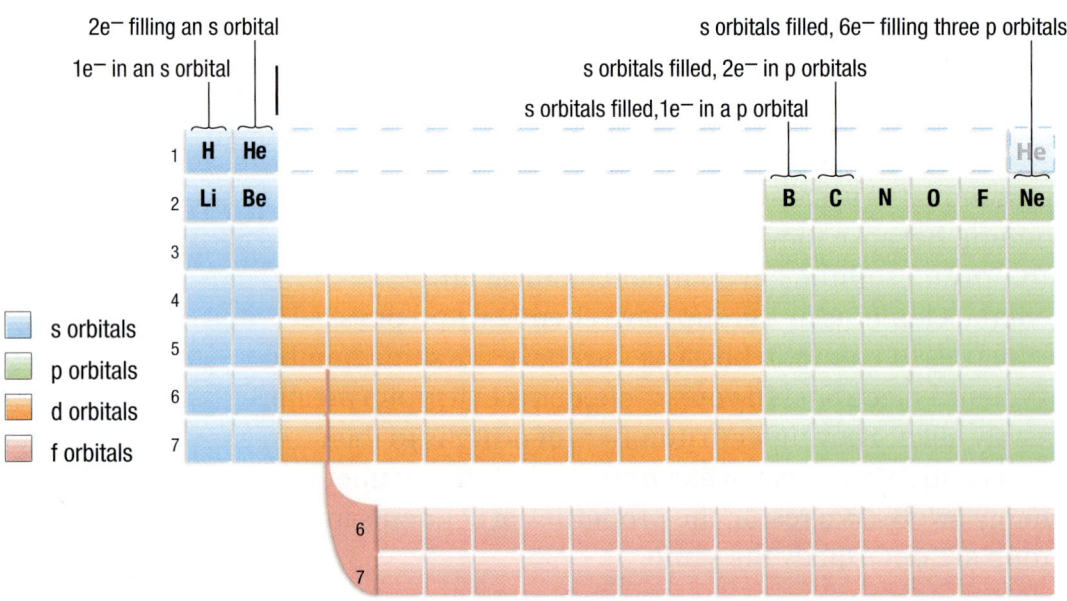

Ion Formation

Atoms whose outermost orbitals are not filled may undergo a process called *ionization*. That is, such atoms may gain or lose valence electrons so that they have a filled outermost orbital. ❭ **If an atom gains or loses electrons, it no longer has an equal number of electrons and protons. Because the charges do not cancel completely, the atom has a net electric charge.** A charged atom is called an **ion**.

ion (IE AHN) an atom, radical, or molecule that has gained or lost one or more electrons and has a negative or positive charge

Group 1 elements form positive ions.

Lithium is a Group 1 element. Lithium is reactive in air, in water, and especially in acid. The atomic structure of lithium explains lithium's reactivity. A lithium atom has three electrons, as shown in the upper left diagram in **Figure 3**. Two of these electrons occupy the first energy level in the s orbital, but only one electron occupies the second energy level. This single valence electron is easily removed, which makes lithium very reactive. Removing this electron forms a positive ion, or *cation*, as shown in the upper right diagram in **Figure 3**. A lithium ion, written as Li$^+$, has a filled outer s orbital.

Atoms of other Group 1 elements also have one valence electron. These elements are reactive and behave similarly to lithium.

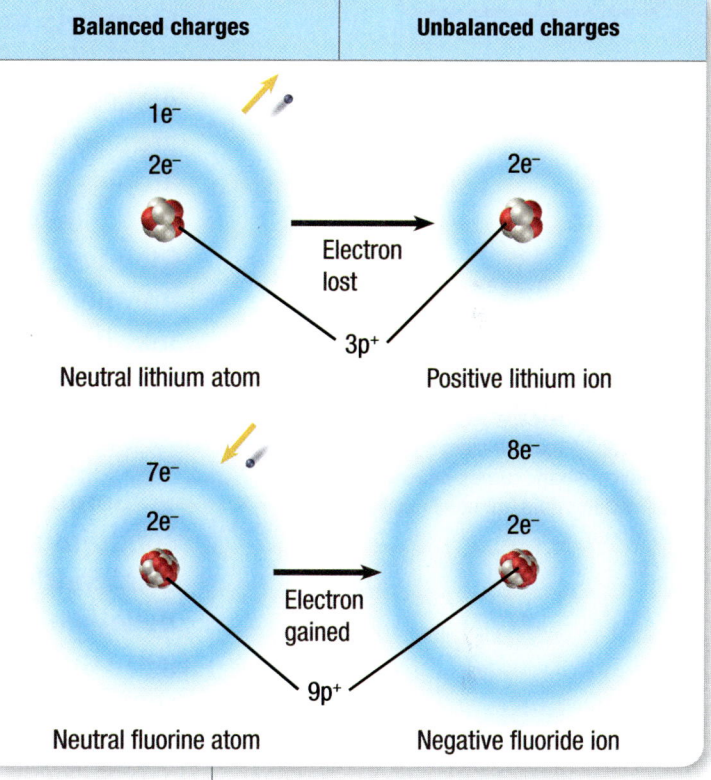

Group 17 elements form negative ions.

Like lithium, fluorine is very reactive. Each fluorine atom has nine electrons. Two of these electrons occupy the first energy level. The other seven electrons—the valence electrons—are in the second energy level. A fluorine atom needs only one more electron to have a filled outermost energy level. An atom of fluorine easily gains this electron to form a negative ion, or *anion*, as the bottom diagram in **Figure 3** shows. Because an ion of fluorine has a filled outer energy level, the ion is more stable and less reactive than a fluorine atom.

Ions of fluorine, which have a 1– charge, are called *fluoride ions*. The symbol for the fluoride ion is F$^-$. Because atoms of other Group 17 elements have seven valence electrons, other Group 17 elements are reactive and behave like fluorine, too.

Figure 3 The valence electron of a lithium atom may be removed to form a lithium ion, Li$^+$, which has a 1+ charge. A fluorine atom easily gains one valence electron to form a fluoride ion, F$^-$, which has a 1– charge.

Keyword: HK8PTAF3

✓ **Reading Check** Why do Group 1 and Group 17 elements easily form ions?

Topic: Metals/Nonmetals
Code: HK80948

metal (MET'l) an element that is shiny and that conducts heat and electricity well

nonmetal (nahn MET'l) an element that conducts heat and electricity poorly

semiconductor (SEM i kuhn DUK tuhr) an element or compound that conducts electric current better than an insulator does but not as well as a conductor does

How Are Elements Classified?

As you have learned, elements within a group have similar chemical properties. In addition to being organized into groups, the elements in the 18 groups in the periodic table are further classified into three main categories. These three categories are based on general properties that the elements in the categories have in common, as shown in **Figure 4.** ▸ **All elements are either metals, nonmetals, or semiconductors.**

Elements in each category have similar properties.

As shown in **Figure 4,** most elements are **metals.** Most metals are shiny solids that can be stretched and shaped. They are also good conductors of heat and electricity. Some examples of metals are gold, platinum, and copper.

Figure 4 shows that all **nonmetals,** except for hydrogen, are found on the right side of the periodic table. Examples of nonmetals include carbon, oxygen, and helium. Nonmetals may be solids, liquids, or gases at room temperature. Solid nonmetals are often dull and brittle. They are poor conductors of heat and electricity. Materials that do not conduct heat or electricity well are sometimes called *insulators.*

Some elements can conduct electricity under certain conditions. These six elements, shown in **Figure 4,** are called **semiconductors.** Semiconductors are also sometimes called *metalloids.* Two common semiconductors are silicon and germanium. The main properties of metals, nonmetals, and semiconductors are summarized in **Figure 5** on the next page.

✓ **Reading Check** Which category contains the most elements, and which category contains the fewest elements?

Figure 4 Classification of the Elements

■ Metals
■ Nonmetals
■ Semiconductors

154 Chapter 5 The Periodic Table

Figure 5 Three Categories of Elements

	Metals	Nonmetals	Semiconductors
Properties	• Metals are good conductors of electricity. • Metals are good conductors of heat. • Metals are ductile (easily drawn into thin wires) and malleable (easily shaped or formed). • Most metals are shiny.	• Nonmetals are poor conductors of electricity. • Nonmetals are poor conductors of heat. • Nonmetals are not malleable or ductile. • Most nonmetals are not shiny.	• Semiconductors share properties with metals and nonmetals. • Semiconductors can conduct electricity under certain conditions. • Semiconductors are the main components of chips in computers and in other electronic devices.
Examples	Copper Lead	Carbon Sulfur	Tellurium Silicon

Section 2 Review

KEY IDEAS

1. **Explain** why elements in a group on the periodic table have similar chemical properties.
2. **Compare** the number of valence electrons in an atom of oxygen, O, with the number of valence electrons in an atom of selenium, Se. Are oxygen and selenium in the same period or group?
3. **Explain** why some atoms gain or lose electrons to form ions.
4. **Describe** why lithium and other Group 1 elements usually form positive ions, while fluorine and other Group 17 elements form negative ions.
5. **List** the three main categories of elements, and give an example of each.

CRITICAL THINKING

6. **Making Predictions** Predict which ions cesium forms: Cs^+ ions or Cs^{2+} ions.
7. **Drawing Conclusions** Determine whether elements that fit the following descriptions are more likely to be metals or nonmetals:
   a. a shiny substance used to make flexible bed springs
   b. a yellow powder from underground mines
   c. a gas that does not react
   d. a conducting material used within flexible wires
   e. a brittle substance that does not conduct heat
8. **Making Predictions** Predict the charge of a beryllium ion.

SECTION 3
Families of Elements

Key Ideas

> What does each element family have in common?
> What are the families of metals?
> What are some of the families of nonmetals?
> What are semiconductors?

Key Terms

alkali metal
alkaline-earth metal
transition metal
noble gas
halogen

Why It Matters

The tiny chips in electronic devices contain semiconductors, such as silicon. Semiconductors give chips properties that allow computers to work.

Tennessee Course Level Expectations (Physical Science)

CLE.3202.1.3; CLE.3202.Inq.1;
CLE.3202.Inq.2; CLE.3202.Inq.3;
CLE.3202.Inq.6; CLE.3202.TE.3;
CLE.3202.TE.4

Sometimes, one or more groups in the periodic table are categorized as being members of a unit called a *family*. Consider your own family. Each member is unique, but you all share some features. For example, family members often have a similar appearance, as **Figure 1** shows. Likewise, members of a family in the periodic table have properties in common.

Classifying Elements Further

You learned earlier that elements can be classified as metals, nonmetals, and semiconductors. **Figure 2** shows how elements are further categorized into five families. ❯ **The elements in a family have the same number of valence electrons**. This section explores some of the shared physical and chemical properties of elements in each family.

Figure 1 Just as the members of this family have similarities, elements in a family on the periodic table have similarities.

Figure 2 Element Families

Group number	Number of valence electrons	Name of family
Group 1	1	alkali metals
Group 2	2	alkaline-earth metals
Groups 3–12	varied	transition metals
Group 17	7	halogens
Group 18	8*	noble gases

*except helium, which has two electrons

Metals

Many elements are classified as metals. All metals conduct heat and electricity. Most metals can also be stretched and shaped into flat sheets, or pulled into wires. ❯ **Families of metals include the alkali metals, the alkaline-earth metals, and the transition metals.**

The alkali metals are very reactive.

Sodium is found in Group 1 of the periodic table, as shown in **Figure 3**. Like other **alkali metals**, it is soft and shiny and reacts violently with water. Alkali metals are often stored in oil to prevent them from reacting with moisture in the air.

An atom of an alkali metal is very reactive because it has one valence electron that can easily be removed to form a positive ion. You have already seen how lithium forms positive ions that have a 1+ charge. Similarly, when its valence electron is removed, a sodium atom forms the positive ion Na^+.

Because alkali metals such as sodium are very reactive, they are not found in nature as uncombined elements. Instead, they are found combined with other elements in the form of compounds. For example, the salt that you use to season your food is the compound sodium chloride, NaCl. In addition to having similar reactivity, many alkali metals have similar melting points, boiling points, and densities.

Reading Check Why are alkali metals very reactive?

Topic: Element Families
Code: HK80494

alkali metal (AL kuh LIE MET'l) one of the elements of Group 1 of the periodic table

Potassium is an alkali metal.
Which property of alkali metals is illustrated here?

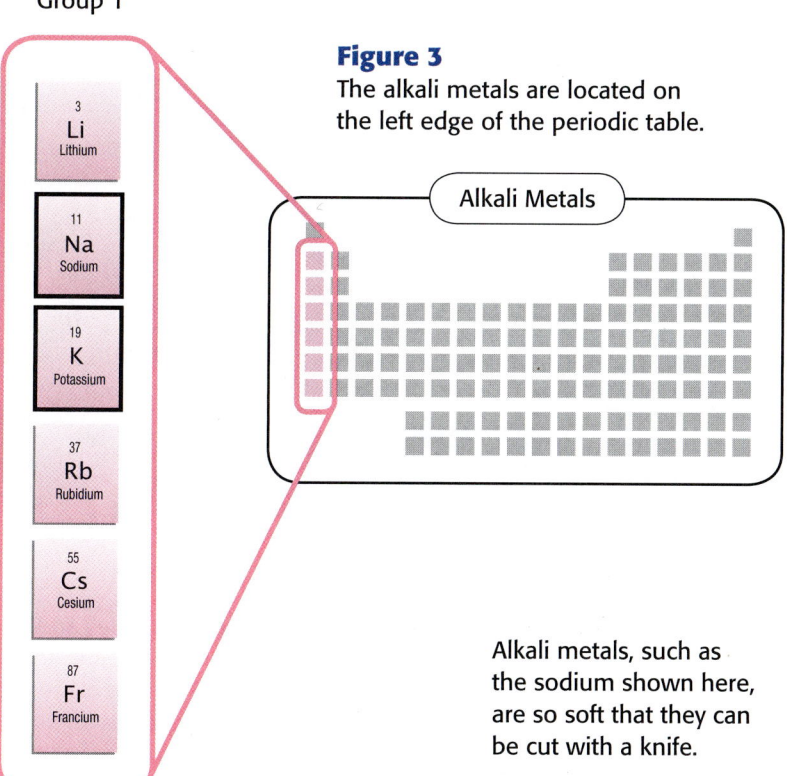

Figure 3
The alkali metals are located on the left edge of the periodic table.

Alkali metals, such as the sodium shown here, are so soft that they can be cut with a knife.

QuickLab

Elements in Food ⏲ 20 min

1. For 1 day, make a list of the ingredients in all of the foods and drinks that you consume in that day.
2. Identify which ingredients on your list are compounds.
3. For each compound on your list, try to figure out which elements make up the compound.

Alkaline-earth metals form compounds that are found in limestone and in the human body.

Calcium is in Group 2 of the periodic table, as shown in **Figure 4**. Calcium is an **alkaline-earth metal.** In general, alkaline-earth metals are harder, denser, stronger, and have higher melting points than alkali metals.

Atoms of alkaline-earth metals, such as calcium, have two valence electrons. Alkaline-earth metals are less reactive than alkali metals, but alkaline-earth metals still react to form positive ions. These ions have a 2+ charge. When a calcium atom loses its two valence electrons, the resulting ion, Ca^{2+}, has a filled outer energy level. Alkaline-earth metals, such as calcium, combine with other elements to form compounds.

Calcium compounds make up the hard shells of many sea animals. When the animals die, their shells settle to form large deposits that eventually become limestone or marble, both of which are very strong materials used in construction. Coral is one example of a limestone structure. The limestone skeletons of millions of tiny animals combine to form sturdy coral reefs that are the habitats of many fish. Your bones and teeth also get their strength from calcium compounds.

Magnesium, another alkaline-earth metal, is the lightest of all structural metals, or metals used as part of a structure. Magnesium is used to build some airplanes. Magnesium, as Mg^{2+}, activates many of the enzymes that speed up processes in the human body. Two magnesium compounds are commonly used in medicines—milk of magnesia and Epsom salts.

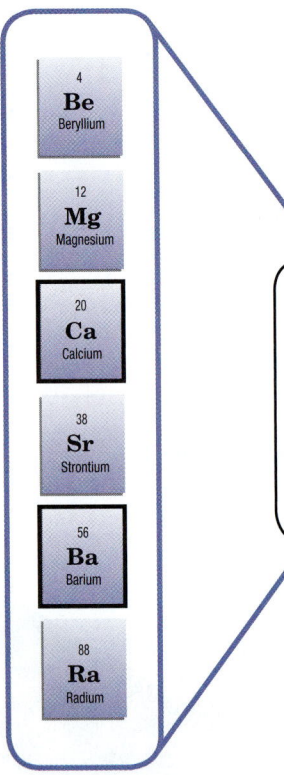

Group 2

Figure 4
The alkaline-earth metals make up the column that is second from the left edge of the periodic table.

Barium is used in medical imaging. This X-ray shows the colon outlined in barium contrast material.

The stalagmites and stalactites in limestone caves contain calcium carbonate deposits.

The transition metals platinum, gold, and silver are often shaped to make jewelry.

Transition Metals

Groups 3-12

Figure 5
The transition metals are located in the middle of the periodic table.

This artificial hip component is made of titanium, which is light, strong, and nonreactive.

Transition metals are in the middle of the periodic table.

Gold is a valuable **transition metal**. Figure 5 shows that the transition metals are located in Groups 3–12 of the periodic table. Unlike most other transition metals, gold is not found in nature combined with other elements.

Transition metals, such as gold, are much less reactive than sodium or calcium. But transition metals can lose electrons to form positive ions, too. There are two possible cations that a gold atom can form. If an atom of gold loses only one electron, it forms Au^+. If the atom loses three electrons, it forms Au^{3+}. Some transition metals can form as many as four differently charged cations because of their complex arrangement of electrons. With the exception of mercury, transition metals are harder, more dense, and have higher melting points than alkali metals and alkaline-earth metals.

Because gold, silver, and platinum are shiny metals, they are often molded into various kinds of jewelry, as shown in **Figure 5.** There are many other useful transition metals. Copper is often used for plumbing or electrical wiring. Light-bulb filaments are made of tungsten. Iron, cobalt, copper, and manganese play important roles in your body chemistry. Mercury, the only metal that is a liquid at room temperature, is sometimes used in thermometers.

✅ **Reading Check** What are some examples of transition metals?

alkaline-earth metal (AL kuh LIEN UHRTH MET'l) one of the elements of Group 2 of the periodic table

transition metal (tran ZISH uhn MET'l) one of the metals that can use the inner shell before using the outer shell to bond

Section 3 Families of Elements **159**

QuickLab: The Cost of Metals

 20 min

Procedure

1. The table gives the abundance of some metals in Earth's crust. List these metals in order of abundance, from most abundant to least abundant.
2. List the metals in order of price, from cheapest to most expensive.

Analysis

1. If the price of a metal depends on the metal's abundance, you would expect the order to be the same on both lists. How well do the two lists match? Mention any mismatches.
2. A list of these metals in order from most reactive to least reactive is as follows: aluminum, zinc, chromium, iron, tin, copper, silver, and gold. Use this information to explain any mismatches that you noticed in item 1.
3. Create a spreadsheet that can be used to calculate the number of grams of each metal that you could buy with $100.

Metal	Abundance in Earth's crust (%)	Price ($/kg)
Aluminum, Al	8.2	1.55
Chromium, Cr	0.01	0.06
Copper, Cu	0.006 0	2.44
Gold, Au	0.000 000 4	11 666.53
Iron, Fe	5.6	0.03
Silver, Ag	0.000 007	154.97
Tin, Sn	0.000 2	6.22
Zinc, Zn	0.007	1.29

Some elements are synthetic.

Technetium and promethium are two synthetic elements (elements made in a laboratory). They are both *radioactive*, which means the nuclei of their atoms are continually decaying to produce different elements. There are several isotopes of technetium. The most stable isotope is technetium-99, which has 56 neutrons. Technetium-99 was used to create the image shown in **Figure 6**. Doctors use scans such as this to diagnose cancer as well as other medical problems that occur in soft tissues of the body.

When looking at the periodic table, you might have wondered why part of the last two periods of the transition metals are placed toward the bottom. This arrangement keeps the periodic table narrow so that similar elements elsewhere in the table still line up. Promethium is one element found in this bottom-most area. Its most useful isotope is promethium-147, which is an ingredient in some glow-in-the-dark paints.

All elements that have atomic numbers greater than 92 are also synthetic and are similar to technetium and promethium. For example, americium, another element in the bottom-most area of the periodic table, is also radioactive. Tiny amounts of americium-241 are found in most household smoke detectors. Although even small amounts of radioactive material can affect you, americium-241 is safe when contained inside your smoke detector.

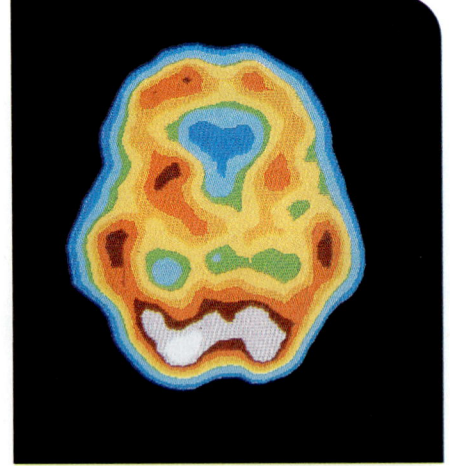

Figure 6 By using the radioactive isotope technetium-99, doctors are able to create brain scans, such as the one shown, that help confirm that a patient has a healthy brain.

Nonmetals

Except for hydrogen, nonmetals are found on the right side of the periodic table. Nonmetals include some elements in Groups 13–16 and all of the elements in Groups 17 and 18.
❯ **Families of nonmetals include the noble gases and the halogens.**

The noble gases are relatively inert.

Neon is one of the **noble gases** that make up Group 18 of the periodic table, as shown in **Figure 7**. Neon is responsible for the bright reddish orange light of neon signs. Mixing neon with other substances can change the color of a sign.

The noble gases are different from most elements that are gases because noble gases exist as single atoms instead of as molecules. Like other members of Group 18, neon is *inert,* or unreactive, because its s and p orbitals are filled. For this reason, neon and other noble gases do not gain or lose electrons to form ions. Also, under normal conditions, most noble gases do not join with other atoms to form compounds.

Helium and argon are other common noble gases. Helium is less dense than air and is used to give lift to blimps and balloons. Argon is used to fill light bulbs because its lack of reactivity prevents the bulbs' filaments from burning.

noble gas (NOH buhl GAS) one of the elements of Group 18 of the periodic table

Academic Vocabulary
normal (NAWR muhl) usual; typical

✓ **Reading Check** Why are the noble gases unreactive?

A neon sign is usually reddish orange, but adding a few drops of mercury makes the light a bright blue.

Figure 7
The noble gases are located on the right edge of the periodic table.

Argon lasers are used in some eye surgeries.

161

halogen (HAL oh juhn) one of the elements of Group 17 of the periodic table

The halogens combine easily with metals to form salts.

Chlorine and other **halogens** belong to Group 17 of the periodic table, as **Figure 8** shows. The halogens are the most reactive nonmetals. Halogens have seven valence electrons. With the addition of a single electron, halogens become stable. For this reason, the halogens combine easily with alkali metals. Halogens can also combine with other metals. Compounds that result from such combinations are called *salts.*

You have probably noticed the strong smell of chlorine in swimming pools. Chlorine is widely used to kill bacteria in pools, as well as in drinking-water supplies. The chlorine in most swimming pools is added in the form of the compound calcium hypochlorite, $Ca(OCl)_2$. Elemental chlorine is a poisonous yellowish green gas made of pairs of joined chlorine atoms. A chlorine atom may gain an electron to form a negative chloride ion, Cl^-. The attraction between Na^+ ions and Cl^- ions forms sodium chloride, NaCl, which is table salt.

Fluorine, bromine, and iodine are also Group 17 elements. Fluorine is a poisonous yellowish gas, bromine is a dark red liquid, and iodine is a dark purple solid. Atoms of each of these elements can also form compounds by gaining an electron to become negative ions. A compound containing the negative fluoride ion, F^-, is used in some toothpastes and added to some water supplies to help prevent tooth decay. Adding a compound containing iodine in the form of the negative iodide ion, I^-, to table salt makes iodized salt. You need iodine in your diet for proper thyroid gland function.

Integrating Earth Science

Elements in Seawater Eighty-one elements—including magnesium and bromine—have been detected in seawater. To extract an element from a sample of seawater, you must evaporate some of the water in the sample. Evaporation causes sodium chloride (NaCl) to crystallize, which raises the concentration of bromide, magnesium, and other ions in the water that remains. The rise in concentration makes the extraction of the elements easier.

Iodine solution can be used as a skin disinfectant and to treat wounds.

Figure 8
The halogens are in the second column from the right of the periodic table.

Group 17

Chlorine keeps pool water bacteria free for swimmers to enjoy.

Nonmetals and their compounds are plentiful on Earth.

In addition to the noble gases and the halogens, six other nonmetals are on the right side of the periodic table, as shown in **Figure 9.** Oxygen, nitrogen, and sulfur are common nonmetals. These three nonmetals may form compounds or may gain electrons to form negative ions. Oxygen forms oxide, O^{2-}, nitrogen forms nitride, N^{3-}, and sulfur forms sulfide, S^{2-}. The most plentiful gases in air are nitrogen and oxygen. Sulfur is an odorless yellow solid, but many sulfur compounds, such as those in rotten eggs and skunk spray, have a terrible smell.

Carbon can form many compounds.

In its pure state, carbon is usually found as graphite (pencil "lead") or as diamond. The existence of *fullerenes,* a third form of carbon, was confirmed in 1990. The most famous fullerene, a cluster of 60 carbon atoms, is called a *buckminsterfullerene.* It resembles a geodesic dome, which is a structure designed by the American engineer and inventor R. Buckminster Fuller.

Carbon can also combine with other elements to form millions of carbon-containing compounds. Carbon compounds are found in both living and nonliving things. Glucose, $C_6H_{12}O_6$, is a sugar in your blood. A type of chlorophyll, $C_{55}H_{72}O_5N_4Mg$, is found in all green plants. Many gasolines contain isooctane, C_8H_{18}, and rubber tires are made of large molecules that have many repeating C_5H_8 units.

Reading Check What are some examples of carbon compounds?

> **READING TOOLBOX**
>
> **Spider Maps**
> Create a spider map for element families that has one leg for each family. To each leg, add examples of the family and a description of the family's shared properties.

Sulfur is a solid yellow powder at room temperature. Sulfur is found in meteorites, volcanoes, and hot springs.

Graphite and diamonds are both forms of carbon.

Figure 9 The remaining nonmetals are carbon, nitrogen, oxygen, phosphorus, sulfur, and selenium.

Section 3   Families of Elements   **163**

Semiconductors

The six elements sometimes referred to as *semiconductors* or *metalloids* are shown in **Figure 10.** Although these elements are not metals, they have some properties of metals. ▶ **As their name suggests, semiconductors are elements that are able to conduct heat and electricity under certain conditions.**

Silicon atoms, usually in the form of compounds, account for 28% of the mass of Earth's crust. Sand is made of the most common silicon compound, called silicon dioxide, SiO_2. Small chips made of silicon are used in the parts of computers and other electronic devices.

Boron is an extremely hard element. It is often added to steel to increase steel's hardness and strength at high temperatures. Compounds of boron are often used to make heat-resistant glass. Arsenic is a shiny solid that tarnishes when exposed to air. Antimony is a bluish white, brittle solid that also shines like a metal. Some compounds of antimony are used as fire retardants. Tellurium is a silvery white solid whose ability to conduct increases slightly with exposure to light.

Hydrogen is in a class by itself.

Hydrogen, which has just one proton and one electron, does not behave like any of the other elements. As a result, hydrogen is in a class by itself in the periodic table. Hydrogen is the most abundant element in the universe. About three out of every four atoms in the universe are hydrogen atoms, mostly in the form of clouds of gas and stars. With its one electron, hydrogen can react with many other elements, including oxygen. The compound water, H_2O, is essential to life and is present in all living organisms.

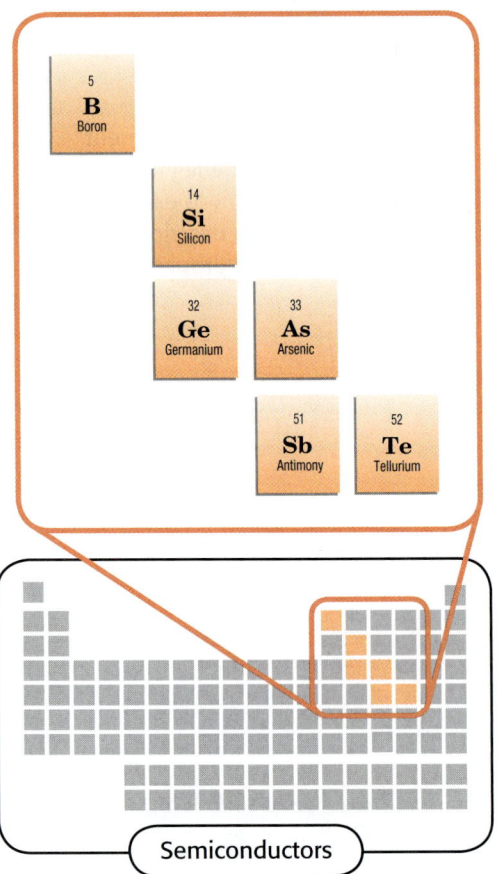

Figure 10
Semiconductors are located toward the right side of the periodic table.

Section 3 Review

KEY IDEAS

1. **Classify** the following elements as alkali, alkaline-earth, or transition metals based on their positions in the periodic table:
   a. iron, Fe
   b. potassium, K
   c. strontium, Sr
   d. platinum, Pt

2. **Describe** why chemists might sometimes store reactive chemicals in argon, Ar. To which family does argon belong?

3. **Describe** why atoms of bromine, Br, are very reactive. To which family does bromine belong?

4. **Identify** which element is more reactive: lithium, Li, or beryllium, Be.

CRITICAL THINKING

5. **Creative Thinking** Imagine that you are a scientist who is analyzing an unknown element. You have confirmed that the element is a metal, but you do not know which kind of metal it is: an alkali metal, an alkaline-earth metal, or a transition metal. Write a paragraph describing the additional tests that you can do to further classify this metal.

Why It **Matters**

How Are Silicon Chips Made?

Silicon is an important component of semiconductor chips, which are used in computers, cell phones, and many other electronic devices. Each silicon chip is a tiny electronic circuit. Impurities such as boron, aluminum, phosphorus, and arsenic are added to the silicon to increase its ability to conduct electricity.

The most sophisticated chips, called *microprocessors,* can execute hundreds of millions of instructions per second. The chip-making process involves hundreds of steps. Some of the main steps are shown below.

REAL WORLD

❶ First, pure silicon is melted down in a crucible. A large crystal cylinder of silicon is extracted, and thin discs called *wafers* are cut from it. The wafers are then ground, polished, and cleaned.

❷ Materials are precisely added to, removed from, and shaped on the wafer through chemical and photographic processes. These processes create a complex set of layers, as shown in this side view. These layers make up the circuitry of a chip.

❹ Several microprocessors are created from a single wafer. When the wafer is finished, the circuitry of each microprocessor is tested. Then, the wafer is cut with a diamond saw. The final result is a computer chip like this one.

❸ Silicon chips are made in the world's cleanest environment: clean rooms. Air in these clean rooms is highly filtered, and workers must wear clean-room suits, sometimes called "bunny suits."

YOUR TURN

UNDERSTANDING CONCEPTS
1. Why are impurities such as boron added to the silicon?

CRITICAL THINKING
2. Why must semiconductor chips be made in clean rooms?

www.scilinks.org
Topic: Silicon
Code: HK81393

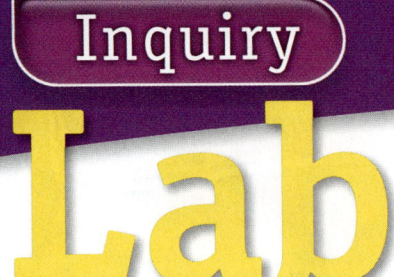

Inquiry Lab

50 min

Exploring Periodic Trends

Many element properties vary predictably according to the position of the element in the periodic table. In this lab, you will make a model that represents the periodic trends in the atomic radii of the elements.

Asking a Question
How do the atomic radii of the elements vary with atomic number?

Forming and Testing a Hypothesis

1. Hypothesize about how atomic radius varies with atomic number.

Performing Your Experiment

2. Using the data in the table below, graph the atomic radius (in picometers, pm; 1 pm = 10^{-12} m) versus atomic number on a sheet of graph paper. Use a ruler to help you scale the graph. Choose a scale for the largest radius that is less than the length of one straw.

What You'll Do:

- **Form a hypothesis** describing how the radius of an atom depends on the atomic number of that atom.
- **Graph** atomic radius as a function of atomic number on regular graph paper (data provided).
- **Create** a three-dimensional model of the periodic trend in the radius of atoms using the well tray, straws and the modified periodic table template.

What You'll Need

marker, permanent, fine point
paper, graph
ruler, metric
scissors
straws, 1/4 in. outer diameter (25)
well tray, transparent, 96-hole

Safety

Atomic Radii of the First 40 Elements

Atomic number	Element	Atomic radius (pm)	Atomic number	Element	Atomic radius (pm)
1	H	37	21	Sc	162
2	He	50	22	Ti	147
3	Li	152	23	V	134
4	Be	111	24	Cr	130
5	B	88	25	Mn	135
6	C	77	26	Fe	126
7	N	70	27	Co	125
8	O	66	28	Ni	124
9	F	64	29	Cu	128
10	Ne	70	30	Zn	138
11	Na	186	31	Ga	122
12	Mg	160	32	Ge	122
13	Al	143	33	As	121
14	Si	117	34	Se	117
15	P	110	35	Br	114
16	S	104	36	Kr	109
17	Cl	99	37	Rb	244
18	Ar	94	38	Sr	215
19	K	231	39	Y	178
20	Ca	197	40	Zr	160

3 Cut a straw to represent each element where the length of the straw represents the atomic radius of the element. To do this, place one end of the straw on the graph at the value of the radius plotted for that element and cut the straw where it crosses the graph's *x*-axis. (**Hint:** First, cut straws for the elements whose radii are largest, and then use the straw scraps for the elements that have smaller radii. This will allow you to represent 40 elements with just 25 straws.) With a fine point marker, label each straw with the element symbol.

4 Place the transparent well tray on top of the modified periodic table template below and insert each straw into the well that is over the symbol of the element that the straw represents.

H 1																	He 2
Li 3	Be 4											B 5	C 6	N 7	O 8	F 9	Ne 10
Na 11	Mg 12											Al 13	Si 14	P 15	S 16	Cl 17	Ar 18
K 19	Ca 20											Ga 31	Ge 32	As 33	Se 34	Br 35	Kr 36
Rb 37	Sr 38																
		Sc 21	Ti 22	V 23	Cr 24	Mn 25	Fe 26	Co 27	Ni 28	Cu 29	Zn 30						
		Y 39	Zr 40														

Analysis

1. **Analyzing Methods** What trends in atomic radius are more visible in the three-dimensional model that you built with straws than they are in the two-dimensional graph that you drew?

Communicating Your Results

2. **Drawing Conclusions** Does the model that you built confirm your hypothesis? Explain why or why not.

Extension

As you move down a group on the periodic table, each successive element has one more filled main energy level than the previous element has. Which trend that your model showed does this explain?

Reading Web Addresses

Science Skills
- Technology
- Math
- Scientific Methods
- Graphing

The World Wide Web is one of the most frequently used parts of the Internet. Every page on the Web has a unique address, called a *uniform resource locator* (URL). A URL locates a certain file.

1. **Protocol** The protocol tells you what method is used to transfer the information between computers on the Internet.
   - The protocol for most Web pages is **http,** which stands for *hypertext transfer protocol.*
   - The *file transfer protocol,* or **ftp,** is used for downloading files.

2. **Domain** The domain specifies the computer or server on the Internet that contains the Web site. The domain often tells you the name of the company, organization, or institution that owns the Web site.
   - The last part of the domain, called the *top-level domain,* is the broadest level of organization. Top-level domains include
     - **.com** (commercial sites)
     - **.net** (Internet service providers)
     - **.org** (nonprofit organizations)
     - **.edu** (educational institutions)
     - **.gov** (the U.S. government)

3. **Path** The path specifies the file's location on the server.
   - The path consists of directory and subdirectory names that are separated by one or more forward slashes (/).

4. **File Name and Extension** The file name identifies the file, and the extension tells you the file type. If no file name is specified, most servers will look for index.html, default.html, or home.html.
   - The extensions **html** and **htm** indicate that a Web page is written in HTML, which stands for *hypertext markup language.*
   - Image files may have the extensions **jpg** or **gif.**
   - Documents often have the extensions **pdf, doc,** or **txt.**
   - Files with the extension **exe** are executable files that can install software, some of which may be unwanted, on your computer.

Practice

1. Consider the following Web address:
   http://www.smithsonianeducation.org/students/index.html
   a. What is the server name?
   b. What does the top-level domain tell you about the Web site?
   c. What kind of file is this? How do you know?

2. Consider the following Web address:
   http://www.science.doe.gov/feature/WFD/CollegePlanGuide_WEB1.pdf
   a. What does the top-level domain tell you about the Web site?
   b. What is the name of this file, and what type of file is it?

CHAPTER 5 Summary

Key Ideas | **Key Terms**

Section 1 Organizing the Elements

> **Recognizing a Pattern** Mendeleev arranged elements in rows by increasing atomic mass. He started a new row each time the chemical properties of the elements repeated. (p. 145)

> **Changing the Arrangement** The modern periodic table organizes elements by atomic number. When the elements are arranged in this way, elements with similar properties appear at regular intervals. (p. 147)

periodic law, p. 147
period, p. 150
group, p. 150

Section 2 Exploring the Periodic Table

> **The Role of Electrons** The periodic trends in the periodic table are the result of electron arrangement. (p. 151)

> **Ion Formation** If an atom gains or loses electrons, it no longer has an equal number of electrons and protons. Because the charges do not cancel completely, the atom—now called an ion—has a net electric charge. (p. 153)

> **How Are Elements Classified?** All elements are metals, nonmetals, or semiconductors. (p. 154)

ion, p. 153
metal, p. 154
nonmetal, p. 154
semiconductor, p. 154

Section 3 Families of Elements

> **Classifying Elements Further** Elements can be grouped into families. The elements in each family have the same number of valence electrons. As a result, they have similar chemical properties. (p. 156)

> **Metals** Families of metals include the alkali metals, the alkaline-earth metals, and the transition metals. (p. 157)

> **Nonmetals** Families of nonmetals include the noble gases and the halogens. Other nonmetals are carbon, nitrogen, oxygen, phosphorus, sulfur, and selenium. (p. 161)

> **Semiconductors** As their name suggests, semiconductors are able to conduct heat and electricity under certain conditions. (p. 164)

alkali metal, p. 157
alkaline-earth metal, p. 158
transition metal, p. 159
noble gas, p. 161
halogen, p. 162

CHAPTER 5 Review

READING TOOLBOX

1. **Prefixes** The prefix *semi-* means "half," "partially," or "somewhat." Explain why this prefix is appropriate for the term *semiconductor*.

USING KEY TERMS

2. Compare the following terms:
   a. an *atom* and a *molecule*
   b. an *atom* and an *ion*
   c. a *cation* and an *anion*

3. List several familiar *transition metals* and their uses.

4. How is the *periodic law* demonstrated in the halogens?

5. Explain why the name *semiconductors* makes sense.

6. Distinguish between *alkali metals* and *alkaline-earth metals*, and give several examples of how they are used.

UNDERSTANDING KEY IDEAS

7. How did Mendeleev arrange atoms in the periodic table?
   a. by atomic mass
   b. by atomic number
   c. by the number of electrons
   d. by the number of neutrons

8. Which statement about atoms of elements in a group of the periodic table is true?
   a. They have the same number of protons.
   b. They have the same mass number.
   c. They have similar chemical properties.
   d. They have the same total number of electrons.

9. The majority of elements in the periodic table are
   a. nonmetals.   c. synthetic.
   b. conductors.   d. noble gases.

10. An atom of which of the following elements is unlikely to form a positively charged ion?
    a. potassium, K   c. barium, Ba
    b. selenium, Se   d. silver, Ag

11. Which of the following statements about krypton is not true?
    a. Krypton's molar mass is 83.798 g/mol.
    b. Krypton's atomic number is 36.
    c. Krypton forms ions that have a 1+ charge.
    d. Krypton is a noble gas.

EXPLAINING KEY IDEAS

12. Explain why magnesium forms ions that have the formula Mg^{2+}, not Mg^+ or Mg^-.

13. Why did Mendeleev leave a few gaps in his periodic table? What eventually happened to these gaps?

14. Compare the meanings of *period* and *group*, in terms of the periodic table.

INTERPRETING GRAPHICS The figure below shows a sodium atom and a chlorine atom. Use the figure to answer questions 15 and 16.

Neutral sodium atom   Neutral chlorine atom

15. What types of ions will sodium and chlorine each form? Explain.

16. Sodium ions bond with chlorine ions to form table salt, NaCl. Explain why one sodium ion bonds with one chlorine ion.

CRITICAL THINKING

17. Forming Hypotheses Why was Mendeleev unable to make any predictions about the noble gas elements?

18. Identifying Relationships When an element whose nucleus has 115 protons is synthesized, which type of element will it be: a metal, a nonmetal, or a metalloid? Explain your answer.

19. Making Comparisons How is the periodic table like a calendar?

20. Applying Concepts Your classmate offers to give you a piece of sodium that he found on a hiking trip. What is your response? Explain.

21. Making Inferences Identify each element described below.
  a. This metal is very reactive, has properties similar to those of magnesium, and is in the same period as bromine.
  b. This nonmetal is in the same group as lead.

22. Evaluating Data The figure shows relative sizes of ionic radii for ions of elements in Period 2 on the periodic table. Why do the negative ions have larger radii than the positive ions do?

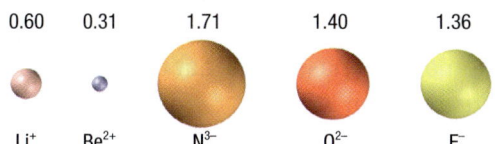

23. Analyzing Information You can keep your bones healthy by eating 1,200 to 1,500 mg of calcium a day. Use the table below to make a list of the foods that you might eat in a day to satisfy your body's need for calcium. How does your typical diet compare with your list?

Item, serving size	Calcium (mg)
Plain lowfat yogurt, 1 cup	415
Ricotta cheese, 1/2 cup	337
Skim milk, 1 cup	302
Cheddar cheese, 1 ounce	213
Cooked spinach, 1/2 cup	106
Vanilla ice cream, 1/2 cup	88

24. Problem Solving Suppose that the following alterations are made to poisonous chlorine gas. How will the identity and properties of the chlorine change in each case?
  a. A proton is added to each atom.
  b. An electron is added to each atom.
  c. A neutron is added to each atom.

25. Applying Knowledge You read a science fiction story about an alien race of silicon-based life-forms. Use the periodic table to hypothesize why the story's author chose silicon over other elements. (**Hint:** Life on Earth is carbon based.)

Graphing Skills

26. Interpreting Graphs The pie chart shows the elements in the Earth's crust. Examine the chart, and then answer the questions.
  a. What is the most abundant element in Earth's crust?
  b. Excluding the category *Other*, what percentage of Earth's crust is alkali metals, and what percentage is alkaline-earth metals?

Elements in Earth's Crust

27. Constructing Graphs Use a graphing calculator, a computer spreadsheet, or a graphing program to plot the atomic number on the *x*-axis and the average atomic mass in u on the *y*-axis for the transition metals in Period 4 (from scandium to zinc). Does the graph show a trend? Is there a break in the trend near cobalt? Explain why elements that have larger atomic numbers do not necessarily have larger atomic masses.

Standardized Test Prep

Understanding Concepts

Directions (1–4): For each question, write on a sheet of paper the letter of the correct answer.

1. What group of elements is the least reactive?
   - **A.** halogens
   - **B.** alkali metals
   - **C.** noble gases
   - **D.** semiconductors

2. What does the symbol Li^+ represent?
   - **F.** a lithium isotope
   - **G.** a lithium atom
   - **H.** a lithium ion
   - **I.** a lithium molecule

3. What information about an element is most crucial for locating that element in the periodic table?
   - **A.** the element's atomic number
   - **B.** the element's electric charge
   - **C.** the element's most common isotope
   - **D.** the number of orbitals the element has

4. Carbon, whose atomic number is 6, has four valence electrons. Sulfur's atomic number is 16, and sulfur is located two columns to the right of carbon and one row down on the periodic table. How many valence electrons does sulfur have?
   - **F.** 4
   - **G.** 6
   - **H.** 7
   - **I.** 14

Directions (5–7): For each question, write a short response.

5. Why are the elements in Group 1 the most reactive?

6. If the element ununoctium is ever synthesized, it will be located directly under radon, xenon and krypton on the periodic table. What would ununoctium's atomic number be? Predict ununoctium's properties.

7. What group of elements has some properties of metals and some properties of nonmetals? How does the periodic table reflect this fact?

Reading Skills

Directions (8–10): Read the passage below. Then, answer the questions that follow.

MENDELEEV'S DISCOVERY

On March 6, 1869, Mendeleev made a formal presentation to introduce his new periodic table. He explained that elements that have similar chemical properties either have atomic masses that are nearly the same value (as have Os, Ir, and Pt) or have atomic masses that increase regularly (as have K, Rb, and Cs). Arranging the elements in rows, within which they are in order of their atomic masses, creates columns corresponding to electron valences. The elements whose particles are the most widely diffused—gases—have small atomic masses. Mendeleev told scientists that they should expect the discovery of some new elements. Two of the elements whose existence he predicted are gallium and germanium. Based on their location in the periodic table (directly below aluminum and silicon), he accurately predicted their atomic masses to be between 65 and 75.

8. Based on the passage, what does the word *diffused* mean?
   - **A.** close together
   - **B.** spread apart
   - **C.** a high temperature
   - **D.** a low temperature

9. What is one of the widely diffused elements Mendeleev was likely referring to in his presentation?
   - **F.** bromine
   - **G.** iodine
   - **H.** helium
   - **I.** uranium

10. When Mendeleev predicted the existence of the elements gallium and germanium, he temporarily named these elements *ekaaluminum* and *ekasilicon*. What does the prefix *eka-* mean, in terms of the layout of the periodic table?

Interpreting Graphics

The graphic below shows the bonding of sodium and chlorine to form sodium chloride, NaCl. Use this graphic to answer questions 11–12.

SODIUM CHLORIDE

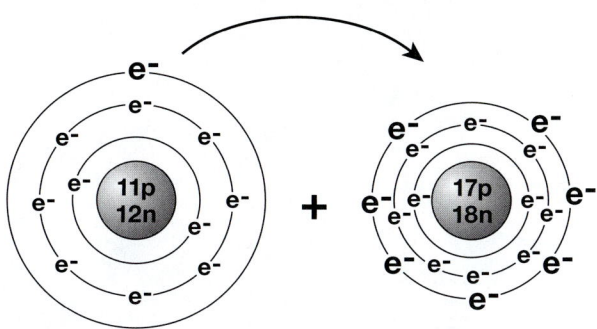

11. How many total valence electrons do the two atoms have?
- **A.** 0
- **B.** 1
- **C.** 7
- **D.** 8

12. What is the mass of one mole of NaCl molecules?
- **F.** 28 g
- **G.** 58 g
- **H.** 1.68×10^{25} g
- **I.** 3.49×10^{25} g

The graphic below shows the upper right segment of the periodic table. Use this graphic to answer questions 13–15.

SEGMENT OF THE PERIODIC TABLE

13	14	15	16	17	18
					2 He 4.00
5 B 10.81	6 C 12.01	7 N 14.01	8 O 16.00	9 F 19.00	10 Ne 20.18
13 Al 26.98	14 Si 28.09	15 P 30.97	16 S 32.06	17 Cl 35.45	18 Ar 39.95

13. Which pair of elements would most likely have a similar arrangement of outer electrons and have similar chemical behaviors?
- **A.** boron and aluminum
- **B.** helium and fluorine
- **C.** carbon and nitrogen
- **D.** chlorine and oxygen

14. What is the atomic mass of helium?

15. How many neutrons does the average helium atom contain?

> **Test Tip**
>
> For multiple-choice questions, try to eliminate any answer choices that are obviously incorrect, and then consider the remaining answer choices.

CHAPTER 6
The Structure of Matter

Chapter Outline

1 Compounds and Molecules
Chemical Bonds
Chemical Structure
How Does Structure Affect Properties?

2 Ionic and Covalent Bonding
Why Do Chemical Bonds Form?
Ionic Bonds
Covalent Bonds
Metallic Bonds
Polyatomic Ions

3 Compound Names and Formulas
Naming Ionic Compounds
Naming Covalent Compounds
Empirical Formulas

4 Organic and Biochemical Compounds
Organic Compounds
Polymers
Biochemical Compounds

Tennessee Course Level Expectations (Physical Science)

CLE.3202.TE.1 Explore the impact of technology on social, political, and economic systems; **CLE.3202.1.6** Distinguish between common ionic and covalent compounds; **CLE.3202.1.7** Construct chemical formulas for common compounds; **CLE.3202.Inq.1** Recognize that science is a progressive endeavor that reevaluates and extends what is already accepted; **CLE.3202.Inq.2** Design and conduct scientific investigations to explore new phenomena, verify previous results, test how well a theory predicts, and compare opposing theories.

Why It Matters
All properties of matter depend on the structure of the elements and compounds that make up matter. The patterns in this diamond crystal come from the bonding patterns of its carbon atoms.

Inquiry Lab

⏱ 20 min

Melting Sugar and Salt

Sugar and salt are both white, granular substances. You know they taste different, but are their other properties different? Make a hypothesis about whether sugar or salt will melt more easily.

To test your hypothesis, place **1 mL of sugar** in a **test tube.** Use **tongs** to position the test tube over a **Bunsen burner** flame, as shown below. **CAUTION:** Tie back long hair and confine loose clothing. Use tongs and heat-resistant gloves to handle hot glassware. When heating a test tube, always point the open end of the test tube away from yourself and others.

Move the test tube back and forth slowly over the flame. Use a **stopwatch** to measure the time it takes for the sugar to melt. If the sample does not melt within 1 min, remove it from the flame. Next, place **1 mL of salt** in a test tube. Repeat the steps that you followed for the sugar.

Questions to Get You Started

1. Which compound melts more easily? Was your hypothesis right?
2. How can you relate your results to the structure of each compound?

READING TOOLBOX

These reading tools can help you learn the material in this chapter. For more information on how to use these and other tools, see **Appendix A.**

Word Parts

Suffixes The suffix *-ic* usually changes a noun to an adjective and adds the meaning "pertaining to" or "having characteristics of" to that noun. For example, *periodic* is an adjective formed from the noun *period*. It means "pertaining to a period." The suffixes *-al* and *-ar* affect a noun in much the same way. When you see a word that uses one of these suffixes, look at the noun at the root of the word. It can help you understand the word's meaning.

Your Turn In Section 2, there are three key terms that contain words with the suffix *-ic*. For each of these words, write the word, the noun the word is related to, and the word's definition. Then, do the same for three more words that you can think of that have the suffixes *-ic* or *-ar*. The example below is for the word *molecular*, which is in the key term *molecular formula* in Section 3.

WORD	RELATED NOUN	DEFINITION OF WORD
molecular	molecule	pertaining to molecules

Frequency

Always, Sometimes, or Never? Many statements include a word that tells you how often that statement is true. Examples include words such as *always*, *sometimes*, and *never*. Words such as *some*, *many*, and *most* tell you about frequency in number.

Your Turn As you read this chapter, make a list of statements that contain frequency words. For each statement in your list, underline the word or phrase that tells how frequently the statement is true. An example is given at right.

Frequency Statement: A compound is <u>always</u> made of the same elements in the same proportions.

FoldNotes

Layered Book FoldNotes are a fun way to help you learn and remember ideas that you encounter as you read.

Your Turn As you read the chapter, make a layered book, as described in **Appendix A.** Label the tabs of the layered book with "Chemical Bonding," "Naming Compounds," and "Organic Molecules." Write notes on the appropriate layer as you read the chapter.

SECTION 1
Compounds and Molecules

Key Ideas

> What holds a compound together?
> How can the structure of chemical compounds be shown?
> What determines the properties of a compound?

Key Terms

chemical bond
chemical structure
bond length
bond angle

Why It Matters

Understanding the structure of compounds can help you understand changes in matter, such as in molding clay.

If you step on a sharp rock with your bare foot, your foot will hurt. It hurts because rocks are hard substances. Many rocks are made of quartz. Table salt and sugar are both grainy, white solids. But they taste very different. Quartz, salt, and sugar are all compounds that are solids. Their similarities and differences partly come from the way their atoms or ions are joined.

Chemical Bonds

A compound is made of two or more elements that are chemically combined. > **The forces that hold atoms or ions together in a compound are called chemical bonds.** **Figure 1** shows that when a mixture of hydrogen gas and oxygen gas is heated, a fiery chemical reaction takes place. Chemical bonds are broken, and atoms are rearranged. New chemical bonds form water, a compound that has properties very different from the properties of the original gases.

chemical bond (KEM i kuhl BAHND) the attractive force that holds atoms or ions together

Figure 1 Placing a lit candle under a balloon that contains a mixture of hydrogen gas and oxygen gas ignites the gases, and water vapor is produced.

Oxygen gas, O_2

Hydrogen gas, H_2

Water vapor, H_2O

Section 1   Compounds and Molecules   **177**

Academic Vocabulary

structure (STRUHK chuhr) the arrangement of the parts of a whole

chemical structure (KEM i kuhl STRUHK chuhr) the arrangement of atoms in a substance

bond length (BAHND LENGKTH) the average distance between the nuclei of two bonded atoms

bond angle (BAHND ANG guhl) the angle formed by two bonds to the same atom

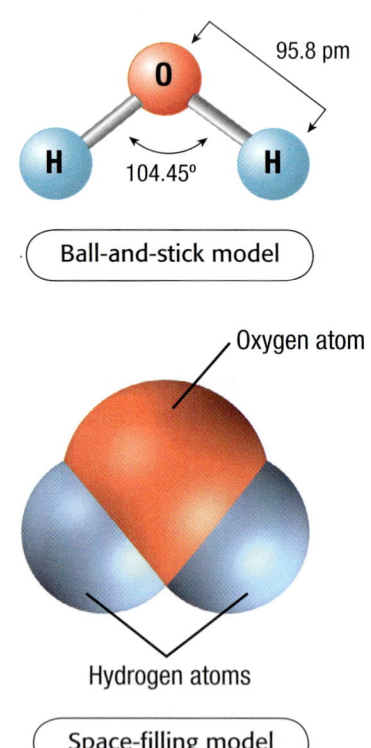

Ball-and-stick model

Space-filling model

Figure 2 The ball-and-stick model (top) shows the bond angle in a molecule of H_2O. A picometer (pm) is equal to 1×10^{-12} m. The space-filling model of water (bottom) shows that each hydrogen atom takes up less space than the oxygen atom.

Chemical Structure

Water's chemical formula tells us what atoms make up water, but it does not tell us anything about the way the atoms are connected. The structure of a building is the way the building's parts fit together. Similarly, a compound's **chemical structure** is the way the compound's atoms are bonded to make the compound. ❯ **Just as the structure of buildings can be represented by blueprints, the structure of chemical compounds can be shown by various models. Different models show different aspects of compounds.**

Some models represent bond lengths and angles.

In the ball-and-stick model of water shown in **Figure 2,** the atoms are represented by balls. The bonds that hold the atoms together are represented by sticks. Although bonds between atoms are not as rigid as sticks, this model makes it easy to see the bonds and the angles they form in a compound.

Two terms are used to specify the positions of atoms in relation to one another in a compound. **Bond length** is the distance between the nuclei of two bonded atoms. When a compound has three or more atoms, a **bond angle,** the angle formed by two bonds to the same atom, tells which way these atoms point. A ball-and-stick model helps you understand a compound's structure by showing you how the atoms or ions are arranged in the compound. In **Figure 2,** you can see that the way hydrogen and oxygen atoms bond to form water looks more like a boomerang than a straight line.

Structural formulas can also show the structures of compounds. Notice that water's structural formula, shown here, is a lot like water's ball-and-stick model. But in the structural formula, chemical symbols are used to represent the atoms.

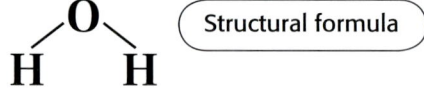

Space-filling models show the space occupied by atoms.

Another way that chemists represent a water molecule is shown in **Figure 2.** The model below the ball-and-stick model is called a *space-filling model* because it shows the space that the oxygen and hydrogen atoms take up, or fill. A space-filling model shows the relative sizes of atoms in a compound, but not bond lengths.

✓ **Reading Check** Name an advantage to each model: the ball-and-stick model and the space-filling model. (See Appendix E for answers to Reading Checks.)

Why It Matters

How Is Clay Molded?

Clay has a layered structure of silicon, oxygen, aluminum, and hydrogen atoms. Artists can mold wet clay into any shape because water molecules hold the clay together loosely, which allows layers of clay to slide over one another. After the artist has gotten the clay into just the right shape, a series of chemical changes have to be made to clay for it to harden. These changes to the chemical structure of the clay molecules make the molded clay into something durable and useful.

When clay dries, the water molecules that had kept the clay soft evaporate and leave the clay dry and crumbly. This is one step in finishing a clay pot, but you wouldn't want a crumbly pot!

The last step in making a clay pot is to fire it in a kiln. Heating the clay causes bonds to form between the molecules of the clay, which makes the pot hard so that you can use it.

YOUR TURN

UNDERSTANDING CONCEPTS
1. Name two other substances that can be shaped when they are wet and then set when they are dried or heated.
2. Suggest what happens to these substances when they dry and set.

Bonds can bend, stretch, and rotate without breaking.

Some chemical bonds are stronger than others. But bonds themselves are not really like the sticks in a ball-and-stick model. If the ball-and-stick model was more accurate, bonds would be represented by flexible springs, as **Figure 3** shows. Bonds can bend, stretch, and rotate without breaking. The atoms can move back and forth a little, and their nuclei do not always stay the same distance apart. In fact, most reported bond lengths are average distances. Although bonds are not rigid, they hold atoms together tightly.

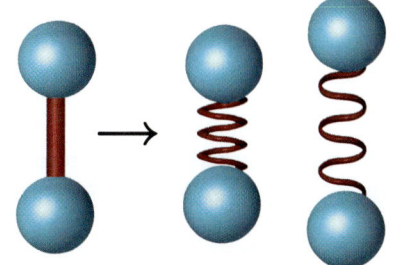

Figure 3 Chemists often use a solid bar to show a bond between two atoms, but bonds are actually flexible, like springs.

SCLINKS
www.scilinks.org
Topic: Structures of Substances
Code: HK81470

READING TOOLBOX

Always, Sometimes, or Never?
As you read this section, make a list of frequency statements that describe the structure of various kinds of chemical compounds.

How Does Structure Affect Properties?

Some compounds, such as the quartz found in many rocks, form a large network of bonded atoms. Other compounds, such as table salt, are also large networks but are made of bonded positive and negative ions. Still other compounds, such as water and sugar, are made of many separate molecules. ❯ **The chemical structure of a compound determines the properties of that compound.**

Compounds with network structures are strong solids.

Quartz is sometimes found in the form of beautiful crystals, as **Figure 4** shows. Quartz is made of silicon dioxide, SiO_2. Every silicon atom in quartz is bonded to four oxygen atoms. The bonds that hold these atoms together are very strong. All of the Si–O–Si and O–Si–O bond angles are the same—109.5°. This arrangement is the same everywhere in silicon dioxide and holds the silicon and oxygen atoms together in a strong, rigid structure.

The chemical structure of the silicon dioxide determines the properties of the quartz. Silicon dioxide has a very rigid structure, so rocks that contain quartz are hard and inflexible solids. It takes a lot of energy to break the strong bonds between silicon and oxygen atoms in quartz. The strong bonds also make the melting point and boiling point of quartz and other minerals very high, as the table in **Figure 4** shows.

✓ **Reading Check** How is the hardness of minerals explained by minerals' chemical structure?

Figure 4 Quartz is made of silicon and oxygen atoms bonded in a strong, rigid structure.

Some Compounds with Network Structures

Compound	State (at 25 °C)	Melting point (°C)	Boiling point (°C)
Silicon dioxide, SiO_2 (quartz)	solid	1,700	2,230
Magnesium fluoride, MgF_2	solid	1,261	2,239
Sodium chloride, NaCl (table salt)	solid	801	1,413

Some networks are made of bonded ions.

Table salt—sodium chloride—is found in the form of regularly shaped crystals. Crystals of sodium chloride are cube shaped. Sodium chloride is made of a repeating network connected by strong bonds. The network is made of tightly packed, positively charged sodium ions and negatively charged chloride ions, as **Figure 5** shows. The strong attractions between the oppositely charged ions give table salt and other similar compounds high melting points and high boiling points.

Some compounds are made of molecules.

Salt and sugar are both white solids that you can eat, but their structures are very different. Unlike salt, sugar is made of molecules. A molecule of sugar, as **Figure 6** shows, is made of carbon, hydrogen, and oxygen atoms that are joined by bonds. Molecules of sugar attract each other to form crystals. But these attractions are much weaker than the attractions that bond carbon, hydrogen, and oxygen atoms to make a sugar molecule.

We breathe nitrogen, N_2, oxygen, O_2, and carbon dioxide, CO_2, every day. All three substances are gases that you cannot see or smell, and are made of molecules. Within each molecule, the atoms are so strongly attracted to one another that they are bonded. But the molecules of each gas have very little attraction to one another. Because the molecules of these gases have weak attractions to one another, they spread out. Thus, gases can take up a lot of space.

Figure 5 Each grain of table salt, or sodium chloride, is made of a tightly packed network of Na^+ ions and Cl^- ions.

Figure 6 Sugar, $C_{12}H_{22}O_{11}$, is made of molecules.

Section 1 **Compounds and Molecules** **181**

Some Molecular Compounds

Compound	State (at 25 °C)	Melting point (°C)	Boiling point (°C)
Sugar, $C_{12}H_{22}O_{11}$	solid	185–186	–
Water, H_2O	liquid	0	100
Dihydrogen sulfide, H_2S	gas	–86	–61

The strength of attractions between molecules varies.

Compare sugar, water, and dihydrogen sulfide, H_2S, in the table in **Figure 7**. Although all three compounds are made of molecules, their properties are very different. Sugar is a solid, water is a liquid, and dihydrogen sulfide is a gas. Thus, sugar molecules have a stronger attraction for each other than water molecules do. And dihydrogen sulfide molecules have weaker attractions for each other than sugar or water molecules do. The fact that sugar and water have such different properties probably does not surprise you. Their chemical structures are not at all alike. But think about water and dihydrogen sulfide, which have similar chemical structures.

Because water has higher melting and boiling points than dihydrogen sulfide, we know that water molecules attract each other more than dihydrogen sulfide molecules do. **Figure 7** shows an oxygen atom of a water molecule attracted to a hydrogen atom of a nearby water molecule. This attraction is called a *hydrogen bond*. Water molecules attract each other, but these attractions are not as strong as the bonds holding oxygen and hydrogen atoms together within a molecule.

Figure 7 Water is a liquid at room temperature because of the attractions between water molecules.

Strong bonds within each water molecule

Weaker attractions between water molecules

Section 1 Review

KEY IDEAS

1. **Classify** the following substances as mixtures or compounds:
   a. air
   b. CO
   c. SnF_2
   d. pure water

2. **Draw** a ball-and-stick model of a boron trifluoride, BF_3, molecule. In this molecule, a boron atom is attached to three fluorine atoms. Each F–B–F bond angle is 120°, and all B–F bonds are the same length.

3. **Explain** why silver iodide, AgI, a compound used in photography, has a much higher melting point than vanillin, $C_8H_8O_3$, a sweet-smelling compound used in flavorings.

4. **Explain** why glass, which is made of mostly SiO_2, is often used to make cookware. (**Hint:** What properties does SiO_2 have because of its structure?)

5. **Predict** which molecules have a greater attraction for each other: C_3H_8O molecules in liquid rubbing alcohol or CH_4 molecules in methane gas.

CRITICAL THINKING

6. **Analyzing Relationships** A picometer (pm) is equal to 1×10^{-12} m. The O–H bond lengths in water are 95.8 pm, while S–H bond lengths in dihydrogen sulfide are 135 pm. Why are S–H bonds longer than O–H bonds? (**Hint:** Which is larger: a sulfur atom or an oxygen atom?)

SECTION 2
Ionic and Covalent Bonding

Key Ideas

> Why do atoms form bonds?
> How do ionic bonds form?
> What do atoms joined by covalent bonds share?
> What gives metals their distinctive properties?
> How are polyatomic ions similar to other ions?

Key Terms

ionic bond
covalent bond
metallic bond
polyatomic ion

Why It Matters

Chemical structure explains matter's properties, such as why metals like copper conduct electricity.

In many of the models that you have seen so far, the bonds that hold atoms together are represented by sticks. But what bonds atoms in a real molecule?

Tennessee Course Level Expectations (Physical Science)

CLE.3202.1.6; CLE.3202.Inq.1; CLE.3202.Inq.2; CLE.3202.Inq.3

Why Do Chemical Bonds Form?

Atoms bond when their valence electrons interact. You have learned that atoms with full outermost *s* and *p* orbitals are more stable than atoms with only partly filled outer *s* and *p* orbitals. **> Generally, atoms join to form bonds so that each atom has a stable electron configuration.** When this happens, each atom has an electronic structure similar to that of a noble gas.

There are two basic kinds of chemical bonding: ionic bonding and covalent bonding. **Figure 1** shows some differences between ionic and covalent compounds. The way that a compound bonds determines many of the properties of that compound.

www.scilinks.org
Topic: Chemical Bonding
Code: HK80264

Figure 1 Comparing Ionic and Covalent Compounds

	Ionic compounds	Covalent compounds
Structure	network of bonded ions	molecules
Valence electrons	transferred	shared
Electrical conductivity	good (when melted or dissolved)	poor
State at room temperature	solid	solid, liquid, or gas
Melting and boiling points	generally high	generally low

Ionic Bonds

Atoms of metals, such as sodium and calcium, form positively charged ions. Atoms of nonmetals, such as chlorine and oxygen, form negatively charged ions. ▶ **Ionic bonds form from the attractions between such oppositely charged ions.**

Ionic bonds are formed by the transfer of electrons.

Some atoms form bonds because they transfer electrons. One of the atoms gains the electrons that the other one loses. The result is a positive ion and a negative ion, such as the Na^+ ion and the Cl^- ion in sodium chloride shown in **Figure 2**.

Each positive sodium ion attracts several negative chloride ions. These negative chloride ions attract positive sodium ions, and so on. A crystal of table salt is made of a large network of oppositely charged ions. Two atoms tend to form an ionic bond when one atom has more attraction for electrons than the other. Chlorine has much more attraction for electrons than sodium. So, neutral chlorine atoms react with neutral sodium atoms to form sodium chloride.

Reading Check What holds two ionically bonded atoms together?

ionic bond (ie AHN ik BAHND) the attractive force between oppositely charged ions, which form when electrons are transferred from one atom to another

Integrating Social Studies

Achievements of Linus Pauling
American scientist Linus Pauling studied how electrons are arranged within atoms. He also studied the ways that atoms share and transfer electrons. In 1954, he won the Nobel Prize in chemistry for his valuable research. Later, Pauling fought to ban nuclear weapons testing. Pauling won the Nobel Peace Prize in 1962 for his efforts. A year later, a treaty outlawing nuclear weapons testing in the atmosphere, in outer space, and underwater went into effect.

Figure 2 Ionic bonds form when one atom transfers one or more electrons to another atom. The result is two ions with opposite charges, which attract each other. **In sodium chloride, which ion is negatively charged and which ion is positively charged?**

go.hrw.com
interact online
Keyword: HK8STRF2

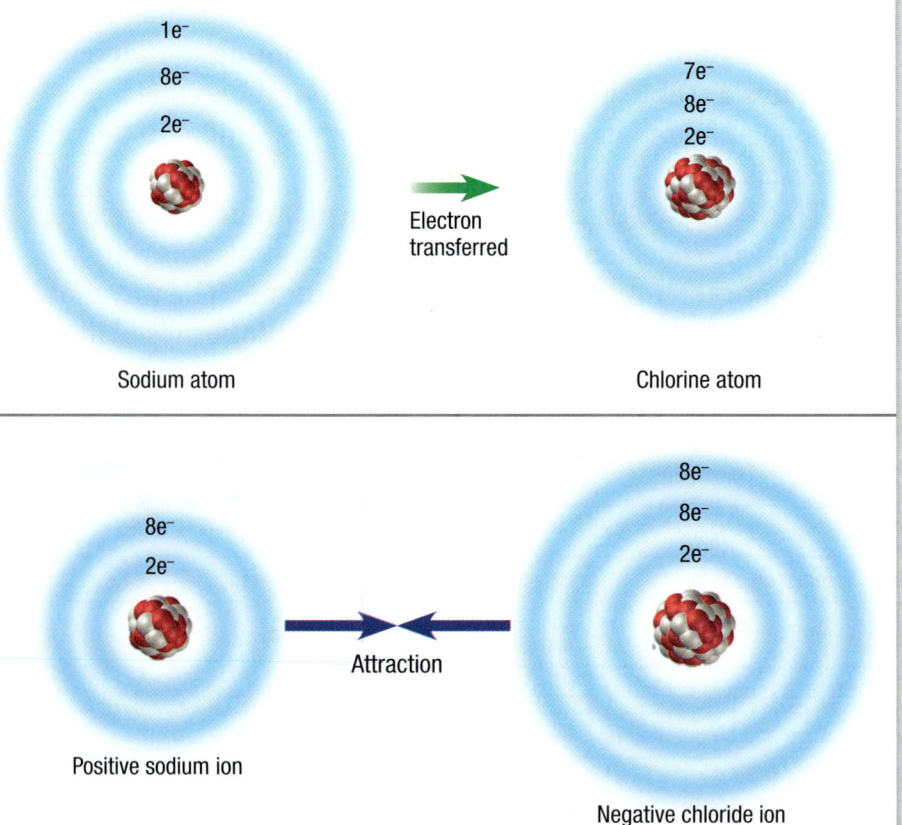

Ionic compounds are in the form of networks, not molecules.

Because sodium chloride is a network of ions, there is no such thing as "a molecule of NaCl." Sodium chloride is a network because every sodium ion is next to six chloride ions. Therefore, chemists talk about the smallest ratio of ions in ionic compounds. Sodium chloride's chemical formula, NaCl, tells us that there is one Na^+ ion for every Cl^- ion, or a 1:1 ratio of ions. Thus, the compound has a total charge of zero. One Na^+ ion and one Cl^- ion make up a *formula unit* of NaCl.

Not every ionic compound has the same ratio of ions as sodium chloride. An example is calcium fluoride, which is shown in **Figure 3.** The ratio of Ca^{2+} ions to F^- ions in calcium fluoride must be 1:2 to make a neutral compound. Thus, the chemical formula for calcium fluoride is CaF_2.

When melted or dissolved in water, ionic compounds conduct electricity.

Electric current is moving charges. Solid ionic compounds do not conduct electric current because the charged ions are locked into place. But if you dissolve an ionic compound in water or melt it, it can conduct electric current. This is because the ions are then free to move, as **Figure 4** shows.

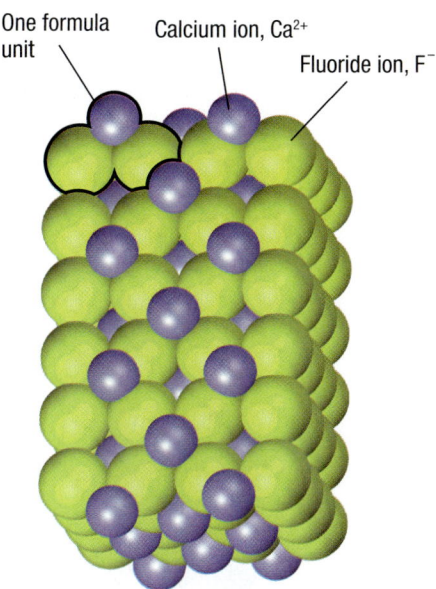

Figure 3 There are twice as many fluoride ions as calcium ions in a crystal of calcium fluoride, CaF_2. So, one Ca^{2+} ion and two F^- ions make up one formula unit of the compound.

Figure 4 Conductivity of an Ionic Compound

As a solid, an ionic compound's particles are fixed in place and cannot conduct electric current.

When an ionic compound is melted, ions can move more freely and conduct electric current.

Ions dissolved in water can move freely and conduct electricity.

Section 2 Ionic and Covalent Bonding **185**

Covalent Bonds

Compounds that are made of molecules, such as water and sugar, have **covalent bonds**. ❯ **Atoms joined by covalent bonds share electrons.** Compounds that are networks of bonded atoms, such as silicon dioxide, are also covalently bonded. Covalent bonds usually form between nonmetal atoms.

Covalent compounds can be solids, liquids, or gases. Most covalent compounds that are made of molecules have low melting points—usually below 300 °C. Molecules are free to move when the compound is dissolved or melted. But most of these molecules do not conduct electricity, because they are not charged. Chlorine, Cl_2, is a covalent compound that is a gas at room temperature. **Figure 5** shows how two chlorine atoms bond to form a chlorine molecule. Before bonding, each atom has seven electrons in its outermost energy level. If each atom shares one electron with the other atom, then both atoms have a full outermost energy level. That is, both atoms have eight valence electrons.

The structural formula in **Figure 5** shows how the chlorine atoms are connected in the molecule that forms. A single line drawn between two atoms shows that the atoms share two electrons and are joined by one covalent bond.

Reading Check What holds two covalently bonded atoms together?

> **covalent bond** (koh VAY luhnt BAHND) a bond formed when atoms share one or more pairs of electrons

Chlorine gas

Figure 5 Two chlorine atoms (above) share electrons equally to form a *nonpolar covalent bond*. Covalent bonds are often shown as a single line drawn between two atoms. The model at right shows that the two chlorine atoms share two electrons. Dots represent electrons that are not involved in bonding.

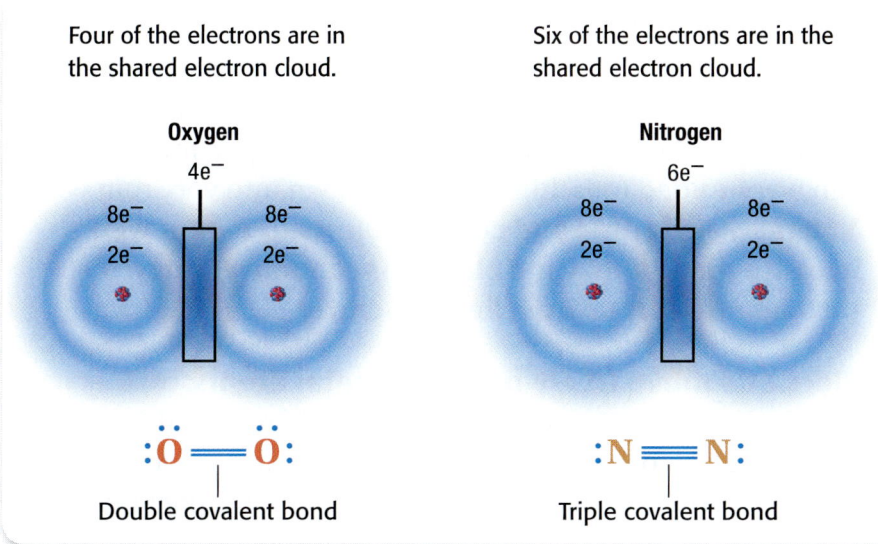

Four of the electrons are in the shared electron cloud.

Six of the electrons are in the shared electron cloud.

Double covalent bond

Triple covalent bond

Figure 6 Molecules of oxygen and nitrogen have covalent bonds. Electrons that are not involved in bonding are represented in these structural models by dots.

Atoms may share more than one pair of electrons.

Covalent bonding in oxygen gas, O_2, and nitrogen gas, N_2, is shown in **Figure 6.** Notice that the bond joining two oxygen atoms is represented by two lines. Two lines show that two pairs of electrons (a total of four electrons) are shared to form a double covalent bond.

The bond that joins two nitrogen atoms is represented by three lines. Two nitrogen atoms form a triple covalent bond by sharing three pairs of electrons (a total of six electrons). More energy is needed to break a triple bond than to break a double bond. So, the triple bond between two nitrogen atoms is stronger than the double bond between two oxygen atoms. Triple and double bonds are shorter than single bonds.

Atoms do not always share electrons equally.

Any two chlorine atoms are identical. When the atoms bond, electrons are equally attracted to the positive nucleus of each atom. Bonds, like this one, in which electrons are shared equally are called *nonpolar covalent bonds*.

When two atoms of different elements share electrons, the electrons are not shared equally. The shared electrons are attracted to the nucleus of one atom more than to the nucleus of the other. An unequal sharing of electrons forms a *polar covalent bond*.

Usually, electrons are more attracted to atoms of elements that are located farther to the right and closer to the top of the periodic table. An example is nitrogen in an ammonia molecule, NH_3, shown in **Figure 7.** The shared electrons in an ammonia molecule are more attracted to the nitrogen atom than they are to the hydrogen atoms.

Figure 7 In a molecule of ammonia, NH_3, electrons are more attracted to nitrogen atoms than to hydrogen atoms. So, the bonds in ammonia are *polar covalent bonds*.

Always, Sometimes, or Never?
As you read this section, make a list of frequency statements that describe different ways that electrons can be shared within a chemical compound.

Section 2   Ionic and Covalent Bonding   **187**

Metallic Bonds

Metals, such as copper, shown in **Figure 8,** can conduct electricity when they are solid. Metals are also flexible, so they can bend and stretch without breaking. Copper, for example, can be pounded into thin sheets or drawn into very thin wire.
❯ **Metals are flexible and conduct electric current well because their atoms and electrons can move freely throughout a metal's packed structure.**

Electrons move freely between metal atoms.

The atoms in metals such as copper form **metallic bonds.** The attraction between an atom's nucleus and a neighboring atom's electrons packs the atoms together. This packing causes the outermost energy levels of the atoms to overlap, as **Figure 8** shows. Thus, electrons are free to move from atom to atom.

Academic Vocabulary
conduct (kuhn DUHKT) to be able to carry

Figure 8 Copper is a flexible metal that melts at 1,083 °C and boils at 2,567 °C. Copper conducts electricity because electrons can move freely between atoms.
What is one property of metals that you can see in this picture?

QuickLab

A Close-Packed Structure

 10 min

Procedure

1. Place **three books** flat on a table so that their edges form a triangle.
2. Fill the space between the books with **table tennis balls.**
3. Adjust the books so that the table tennis balls, or atoms, make a one-layer, close-packed pattern.
4. Build additional layers on top of the first layer. Each ball should be as close as possible to those around it.

Analysis

1. The structure you have made represents the close-packing structure of metal atoms. How many other atoms does each atom touch?
2. Is the structure that you have made packed as closely as it could be? Explain.
3. Where have you seen other patterns in daily life that are similar to this one?

Polyatomic Ions

Until now, we have talked about compounds that have either ionic or covalent bonds. But some compounds have both ionic and covalent bonds. Such compounds are made of **polyatomic ions,** which are groups of covalently bonded atoms that have a positive or negative charge as a group. ▶ **A polyatomic ion acts as a single unit in a compound, just as ions that consist of a single atom do.**

There are many common polyatomic ions.

Many compounds that you use either contain or are made from polyatomic ions. For example, baking soda is a compound that has polyatomic ions. Another name for baking soda is sodium hydrogen carbonate, $NaHCO_3$. Hydrogen carbonate, HCO_3^-, is a polyatomic ion. Sodium carbonate, Na_2CO_3, is often used to make soaps and other cleaners. It contains the carbonate ion, CO_3^{2-}. Sodium hydroxide, $NaOH$, has hydroxide ions, OH^-, and is also used to make soaps. A few of these polyatomic ions are shown in **Figure 9.**

Oppositely charged polyatomic ions, like other ions, can bond to form compounds. For example, ammonium nitrate, NH_4NO_3, and ammonium sulfate, $(NH_4)_2SO_4$, both contain positively charged ammonium ions, NH_4^+. Ammonium nitrate contains one ammonium ion, and ammonium sulfate has two ammonium ions. Nitrate, NO_3^-, and sulfate, SO_4^{2-}, are both negatively charged polyatomic ions.

Parentheses group the atoms of a polyatomic ion.

You might be wondering why the chemical formula for ammonium sulfate is written as $(NH_4)_2SO_4$ instead of as $N_2H_8SO_4$. The parentheses remind us that ammonium, NH_4, acts like a single ion. Parentheses represent the group that the atoms of the ammonium ion form. The subscript 2 outside the parentheses applies to the whole ion. Parentheses are not needed in compounds such as ammonium nitrate, NH_4NO_3, because there is only one of each ion.

Always keep in mind that a polyatomic ion's charge applies not only to the last atom in the formula but to the whole ion. For example, the 2– charge of the carbonate ion, CO_3^{2-}, applies to carbonate, CO_3, not just the oxygen atom. A polyatomic ion acts as a single unit in a compound.

✓ **Reading Check** Why are parentheses used in a chemical formula for a compound that contains more than one of a particular polyatomic ion?

---

metallic bond (muh TAL ik BAHND) a bond formed by the attraction between positively charged metal ions and the electrons around them

polyatomic ion (PAHL ee uh TAHM ik IE ahn) an ion made of two or more atoms

Hydroxide ion, OH^-

Carbonate ion, CO_3^{2-}

Ammonium ion, NH_4^+

Figure 9 The hydroxide ion, OH^-, carbonate ion, CO_3^{2-}, and ammonium ion, NH_4^+, are all polyatomic ions.

Section 2   Ionic and Covalent Bonding   **189**

Integrating Space Science

Ions and Molecules in Space Most of the ions and molecules in space are not the same as the ions and molecules that are found on Earth or in Earth's atmosphere. C_3H, C_6H_2, and HCO^+ have all been found in space. So far, no one has been able to figure out how these unusual molecules and ions form in space.

Some names of polyatomic anions relate to the oxygen content of the anion.

You may have noticed that many polyatomic anions are made of oxygen. Most of their names end with -ite or -ate. An -ate ending is usually used to name an ion that has more oxygen atoms, while ions that have fewer oxygen atoms associated with the same positive group usually end in -ite. **Figure 10** lists several common polyatomic anions. Notice that hydroxide, OH^-, is a polyatomic ion that is not named in the way that other ions that contain oxygen are named. Hydroxide and cyanide, CN^-, are examples of polyatomic anions that have unique names and are not named according to any general rules.

Figure 10 Some Common Polyatomic Anions

Ion name	Ion formula	Ion name	Ion formula
Acetate ion	$CH_3CO_2^-$	Hydroxide ion	OH^-
Carbonate ion	CO_3^{2-}	Hypochlorite ion	ClO^-
Chlorate ion	ClO_3^-	Nitrate ion	NO_3^-
Chlorite ion	ClO_2^-	Nitrite ion	NO_2^-
Cyanide ion	CN^-	Phosphate ion	PO_4^{3-}
Hydrogen carbonate ion	HCO_3^-	Phosphite ion	PO_3^{3-}
Hydrogen sulfate ion	HSO_4^-	Sulfate ion	SO_4^{2-}
Hydrogen sulfite ion	HSO_3^-	Sulfite ion	SO_3^{2-}

Section 2 Review

KEY IDEAS

1. **Determine** if the following compounds are likely to have ionic or covalent bonds.
   a. magnesium oxide, MgO
   b. strontium chloride, $SrCl_2$
   c. ozone, O_3
   d. methanol, CH_3OH

2. **Draw** the structural formula for acetylene, C_2H_2. The atoms of acetylene bond in the order HCCH. Carbon and hydrogen atoms share two electrons, and each carbon atom must have a total of four bonds. How many electrons do the carbon atoms share?

3. **Identify** which two of the following substances will conduct electric current, and explain why.
   a. aluminum foil
   b. sugar, $C_{12}H_{22}O_{11}$, dissolved in water
   c. potassium hydroxide, KOH, dissolved in water

4. **Explain** why electrons are shared equally in oxygen, O_2, but not in carbon monoxide, CO.

5. **Predict** whether a silver coin can conduct electricity. What kind of bonds does silver have?

6. **Identify** which of the bonds in calcium hydroxide, $Ca(OH)_2$, are ionic and which are covalent.

CRITICAL THINKING

7. **Applying Concepts** Does dinitrogen tetroxide, N_2O_4, have covalent or ionic bonds? Explain how you reached your conclusion.

8. **Applying Ideas** An atom of the element iodine, I, has much more attraction for electrons than an atom of strontium, Sr, does. What kind of bonds are likely to form between atoms of the two elements?

9. **Compare and Contrast** How are metallic bonds similar to covalent bonds? How are they different?

SECTION 3
Compound Names and Formulas

Key Ideas
> How are ionic compounds named?
> What do the numerical prefixes used in naming covalent compounds tell you?
> What does a compound's empirical formula indicate?

Key Terms
empirical formula
molecular formula

Why It Matters
Knowing how compounds are named can help you recognize them in food ingredients.

Just like elements, compounds have names that distinguish them from other compounds. Although the compounds BaF_2 and BF_3 may seem to have similar chemical formulas, their names make it clear that they are different. BaF_2 is *barium fluoride*, and BF_3 is *boron trifluoride*. You can see that the names of these compounds come from the elements that make up the compounds.

Tennessee Course Level Expectations (Physical Science)
CLE.3202.1.6; CLE.3202.1.7

Naming Ionic Compounds

Ionic compounds are formed by the strong attractions between oppositely charged particles, cations (positive ions) and anions (negative ions). Both ions are important to the compound's structure, so both ions are included in the name. > **The names of ionic compounds consist of the names of the ions that make up the compounds.**

Names of cations include the elements of which they are composed.

In many cases, the name of the cation is just like the name of its element. For example, when an atom of the element *sodium* loses an electron, a *sodium ion*, Na^+, forms. Similarly, when a *calcium* atom loses two electrons, a *calcium ion*, Ca^{2+}, forms. And when an *aluminum* atom loses three electrons, an *aluminum ion*, Al^{3+}, forms. Common cations are listed in **Figure 1.** The periodic table can be used as a tool for figuring out what ions are formed by different elements. Notice that ions of Group 1 elements have a 1+ charge and that ions of Group 2 elements have a 2+ charge. In many cases, you can tell what charge an ion will have by looking at where the element is located on the periodic table.

Figure 1 Some Common Cations

Ion name and symbol	Ion charge
Cesium ion, Cs^+	1+
Lithium ion, Li^+	
Potassium ion, K^+	
Rubidium ion, Rb^+	
Sodium ion, Na^+	
Barium ion, Ba^{2+}	2+
Beryllium ion, Be^{2+}	
Calcium ion, Ca^{2+}	
Magnesium ion, Mg^{2+}	
Strontium ion, Sr^{2+}	
Aluminum ion, Al^{3+}	3+

Figure 2 Some Common Anions

Element	Ion	Ion charge
Fluorine, F	fluoride ion, F^-	1–
Chlorine, Cl	chloride ion, Cl^-	
Bromine, Br	bromide ion, Br^-	
Iodine, I	iodide ion, I^-	
Oxygen, O	oxide ion, O^{2-}	2–
Sulfur, S	sulfide ion, S^{2-}	
Nitrogen, N	nitride ion, N^{3-}	3–

Figure 3 Some Transition Metal Cations

Ion name	Ion symbol
Copper(I) ion	Cu^+
Copper(II) ion	Cu^{2+}
Iron(II) ion	Fe^{2+}
Iron(III) ion	Fe^{3+}
Nickel(II) ion	Ni^{2+}
Nickel(III) ion	Ni^{3+}
Chromium(II) ion	Cr^{2+}
Chromium(III) ion	Cr^{3+}
Cadmium(II) ion	Cd^{2+}
Titanium(II) ion	Ti^{2+}
Titanium(III) ion	Ti^{3+}
Titanium(IV) ion	Ti^{4+}

Names of anions are altered names of elements.

An anion of an element has a name similar to that element's name. The difference is the name's ending. **Figure 2** shows how some common anions are named. Like most cations, anions of elements in the same group of the periodic table have the same charge. NaF is made of sodium ions, Na^+, and fluoride ions, F^-. Therefore, its name is *sodium fluoride*.

An ionic compound must have a total charge of zero.

If an ionic compound is made up of ions that have different charges, the ratio of ions will not be 1:1. Calcium fluoride is made of calcium ions, Ca^{2+} and fluoride ions, F^-. For calcium fluoride to have a total charge of zero, there must be two fluoride ions for every calcium ion: $(2 \times -1) + (+2) = 0$. So, the formula for calcium fluoride is CaF_2.

Reading Check What determines the amounts of each ion in an ionic compound?

Some cation names must show their charge.

Iron is a transition metal. Transition metals may form several cations—each with a different charge. A few of these cations are listed in **Figure 3**. Think about the compounds FeO and Fe_2O_3. According to the rules you have learned so far, both of these compounds would be named *iron oxide*, even though they are not the same compound, as **Figure 4** shows. They are different compounds and should have different names.

The charge of the iron cation in Fe_2O_3 is different from the charge of the iron cation in FeO. In cases such as this, the cation name must be followed by a Roman numeral in parentheses. The Roman numeral shows the cation's charge. Fe_2O_3 is made of Fe^{3+} ions, so it is named *iron(III) oxide*. FeO is made of Fe^{2+} ions, so it is named *iron(II) oxide*.

Fe_2O_3, iron(III) oxide, is a component of rust.

FeO, iron(II) oxide, is a black powdery substance.

Figure 4 Iron can form different cations, which then form different compounds.

Determine the charge of a transition metal cation.

How can you tell that the iron ion in Fe_2O_3 has a charge of 3+? Three oxide ions, O^{2-}, have a total charge of 6−. Thus, the total positive charge in the formula must be 6+ so that the total charge can be zero. So, each of the two iron ions must have a charge of 3+.

Write formulas for ionic compounds using names.

You can find the charge of each ion in a compound if you are given the compound's formula. You can find the formula for a compound if you are given the compound's name.

www.scilinks.org
Topic: Naming Compounds
Code: HK81010

Math Skills — Writing Ionic Formulas

What is the chemical formula for aluminum fluoride?

Identify
List the given and unknown values.

Given:
Symbol for an aluminum ion from **Figure 1:** Al^{3+}
Symbol for a fluoride ion from **Figure 2:** F^-
Unknown:
chemical formula

Plan
Write the symbols for the ions, with the cation first.

$Al^{3+}F^-$

Solve
Find the least common multiple of the ions' charges.

Write the chemical formula. Show with subscripts the number of each ion needed to make a neutral compound.

The least common multiple of 3 and 1 is 3. To make a neutral compound, you need a total of three positive charges and three negative charges.
You need only one Al^{3+} ion because $1 \times (+3) = +3$.
You need three F^- ions because $3 \times (-1) = -3$.
AlF_3

Practice Hint

> Once you have determined a chemical formula, always check the formula to see if it makes a neutral compound. For this example, the aluminum ion has a charge of 3+. The fluoride ion has a charge of only 1−, but there are three of them for a total of 3−. $(3+) + (3-) = 0$, so the charges balance, and the formula is neutral.

Practice

Write formulas for the following ionic compounds.

1. lithium oxide
2. beryllium chloride
3. titanium(III) nitride

For more practice, visit **go.hrw.com** and enter the keyword **HK8MP**.

Figure 5 Prefixes Used to Name Covalent Compounds

Number of atoms	Prefix
1	mono-
2	di-
3	tri-
4	tetra-
5	penta-
6	hexa-
7	hepta-
8	octa-
9	nona-
10	deca-

N_2O_4

Dinitrogen tetroxide

Figure 6 One molecule of diitrogen tetroxide has two nitrogen atoms and four oxygen atoms.

Naming Covalent Compounds

Covalent compounds, such as silicon dioxide, SiO_2 and carbon dioxide, CO_2, are named using rules that are different from rules used to name ionic compounds. The main difference from ionic compounds is the use of prefixes. ❯ **For covalent compounds of two elements, numerical prefixes tell how many atoms of each element are in the molecule.**

Numerical prefixes are used to name covalent compounds of two elements.

Some prefixes used in naming covalent compounds are shown in **Figure 5**. If there is only one atom of the first element, the name does not get a prefix. The element farther to the right in the periodic table is named second and ends in *-ide*.

One boron atom and three fluorine atoms make up *boron trifluoride*, BF_3. *Dinitrogen tetroxide*, N_2O_4, is made of two nitrogen atoms and four oxygen atoms, as **Figure 6** shows. Notice that the *a* in *tetra* is dropped to make the name easier to say.

Empirical Formulas

Emeralds, shown in **Figure 7,** are made of a mineral called beryl. The chemical formula for beryl is $Be_3Al_2Si_6O_{18}$. But how did scientists determine this formula? It took some experiments. Chemical formulas that are unknown are determined by figuring out the mass of each element in the compound.

Once the mass of each element in a sample of the compound is known, scientists can calculate the compound's **empirical formula,** or simplest formula. ❯ **An empirical formula tells us the smallest whole-number ratio of atoms that are in a compound.**

For most ionic compounds, the empirical formula is the same as the chemical formula. Covalent compounds have empirical formulas, too. The empirical formula for water is H_2O. The formula tells you that the ratio of hydrogen atoms to oxygen atoms is 2:1.

Reading Check What is an empirical formula?

Figure 7 Emerald gemstones are cut from the mineral beryl. Very tiny amounts of chromium(III) oxide, Cr_2O_3, in the gemstones gives them their beautiful green color.

Different compounds can have the same empirical formula.

Empirical formulas show only a ratio of atoms, so it is possible for different compounds to have the same empirical formula. Formaldehyde, acetic acid, and glucose all have the empirical formula CH_2O, as **Figure 8** shows. However, these three compounds are not alike. Formaldehyde is sometimes used to keep dead organisms from decaying so that they can be studied. Acetic acid gives vinegar its sour taste and strong smell. And glucose is a sugar that plays a very important role in your body chemistry.

Molecular formulas are determined from empirical formulas.

Formaldehyde, acetic acid, and glucose are all covalent compounds that are made of molecules. They all have the same empirical formula, but each compound has its own molecular formula. A compound's **molecular formula** tells you how many atoms are in one molecule of the compound.

As **Figure 8** shows, formaldehyde's empirical formula is the same as the molecular formula. The molecular formula for acetic acid is two times the empirical formula, and the molecular formula of glucose is six times the empirical formula.

Masses can be used to determine empirical formulas.

You can find the empirical formula of a compound if you know the mass of each element present in a sample of the compound. Convert the masses to moles. Then, find the molar ratio, which will give you the empirical formula.

> **READING TOOLBOX**
>
> **Suffixes**
> Find two adjectives on this page that end in the suffix -ar. For each one, tell what noun is its root, and give the meaning of the phrase in which it appears.

> **empirical formula** (em PIR i kuhl FAWR myoo luh) the composition of a compound in terms of the relative numbers and kinds of atoms in the simplest ratio
>
> **molecular formula** (moh LEK yoo lur FAWR myoo luh) a chemical formula that shows the number and kinds of atoms in a molecule, but not the arrangement of atoms

Figure 8 Empirical and Molecular Formulas for Some Compounds

Compound	Empirical formula	Molar mass	Molecular formula	Structure
Formaldehyde	CH_2O	30.03 g/mol	CH_2O	
Acetic acid	CH_2O	60.06 g/mol	$2 \times CH_2O = C_2H_4O_2$	
Glucose	CH_2O	180.18 g/mol	$6 \times CH_2O = C_6H_{12}O_6$	

Math Skills: Finding Empirical Formulas

One mole of an unknown compound contains 62 g of phosphorus and 80 g of oxygen. What is the empirical formula of this compound?

Identify
List the given and unknown values.

Given:
62 g phosphorus, 80 g oxygen
Unknown:
empirical formula

Plan
Write the atomic masses.

phosphorus: 30.97 g/mol
oxygen: 16.00 g/mol

Solve
The molar ratio of elements in the compound will be the compound's empirical formula.

$$\frac{62 \text{ g P} \times 1 \text{ mol P}}{30.97 \text{ g}} = 2.0 \text{ mol P}$$

$$\frac{80 \text{ g O} \times 1 \text{ mol O}}{16.00 \text{ g O}} = 5.0 \text{ mol O}$$

empirical formula: P_2O_5

Practice Hint

▸ An empirical formula must have whole numbers of elements. If the molar ratio of elements has a decimal in it, you will need to multiply the ratio by a whole number to make the ratio consist of only whole numbers.

$1.5:1 \times 2 = 3:2$

▸ An empirical formula must represent the simplest possible molar ratio between the elements in the compound. If a molar ratio can be reduced to a simpler fraction, divide it by a whole number.

$10:4 \div 2 = 5:2$

Practice

1. One mole of an unknown compound has 36.04 g of carbon and 6.04 g of hydrogen. What is the compound's empirical formula?
2. A sample of a compound contains 3.6 g of boron and 1.0 g of hydrogen. What is the compound's empirical formula?

For more practice, visit **go.hrw.com** and enter keyword **HK8MP**.

Section 3 Review

KEY IDEAS

1. **Name** the following ionic compounds, and specify the charge of any transition metal cations.
   a. FeI_2
   b. MnF_3
   c. $CrCl_2$
   d. CuS

2. **Find** the charge of the cadmium cation in cadmium bromide, $CdBr_2$. Explain your reasoning.

3. **Name** the following covalent compounds:
   a. SeO_2
   b. SiI_4
   c. As_2O_5
   d. P_4S_3

CRITICAL THINKING

4. **Analyzing Data** A mole of a certain compound contains 207.2 g of lead and 32.00 g of oxygen. Without doing any calculations, tell whether a formula unit of the compound contains more atoms of lead or more atoms of oxygen. Explain.

Math Skills

5. Determine the chemical formulas for the following ionic compounds:
   a. magnesium sulfate
   b. rubidium bromide
   c. chromium(II) fluoride
   d. nickel(I) carbonate

6. What is the empirical formula of a compound that contains 4.03 g of hydrogen per mole, 64.14 g of sulfur per mole, and 128.00 g of oxygen per mole?

7. A sample of a compound contains 160 g of oxygen and 20.2 g of hydrogen. What is the compound's empirical formula?

SECTION 4
Organic and Biochemical Compounds

Key Ideas
> What is an organic compound?
> What is a polymer?
> What organic compounds are essential to life?

Key Terms
organic compound
polymer
carbohydrate
protein
amino acid

Why It Matters
Your body is made of organic compounds, which play important roles in keeping you alive.

The word *organic* has many different meanings. Most people associate the word *organic* with living organisms. Perhaps you have heard of or eaten organically grown fruits or vegetables. They are grown using fertilizers and pesticides that come from plant and animal matter. In chemistry, the word *organic* is used to describe a type of compound.

Tennessee Course Level Expectations (Physical Science)
CLE.3202.TE.1; CLE.3202.1.6; CLE.3202.1.7; CLE.3202.Inq.1; CLE.3202.Inq.2; CLE.3202.Inq.3; CLE.3202.Inq.4; CLE.3202.Inq.6; CLE.3202.TE.4

Organic Compounds

> **An organic compound is a covalently bonded compound that contains carbon.** Most organic compounds also contain hydrogen. Oxygen, nitrogen, sulfur, and phosphorus, can also be found in organic compounds.

Many ingredients of familiar substances are organic compounds. The active ingredient in aspirin is a form of the organic compound acetylsalicylic acid, $C_9H_8O_4$. Sugarless chewing gum also contains organic compounds. Two of its ingredients are the sweeteners sorbitol, $C_6H_{14}O_6$, and aspartame, $C_{14}H_{18}N_2O_5$, both of which are shown in **Figure 1**.

organic compound (awr GAN ik KAHM POWND) a covalently bonded compound that contains carbon, excluding carbonates and oxides

Figure 1 The organic compounds sorbitol and aspartame sweeten some sugarless chewing gums.

Sorbitol

Aspartame

SC/LINKS.
www.scilinks.org
Topic: Organic Compounds
Code: HK81078

Carbon atoms form four covalent bonds in organic compounds.

When a compound is made of only carbon and hydrogen atoms, it is called a *hydrocarbon*. Methane, CH_4, is the simplest hydrocarbon. Its structure is shown in **Figure 2**. Methane gas is formed when living matter, such as plants, decay, so it is often found in swamps and marshes. The natural gas used in stoves is also mostly methane. Carbon atoms have four valence electrons to use for bonding. In methane, each of these electrons participates in a C–H single bond.

A carbon atom may also share two of its electrons with two from another atom to form a double bond. Or a carbon atom may share three electrons to form a triple bond. However, a carbon atom can never form more than four bonds at a time.

Alkanes are hydrocarbons that have only single covalent bonds. Methane is the simplest alkane. It has only C–H bonds. But alkanes can also have C–C bonds. You can see from **Figure 2** that the two carbon atoms in ethane, C_2H_6, bond to each other. Note how each carbon atom in both of these compounds bonds to four other atoms.

Methane   Ethane

Figure 2 Methane and ethane are the two simplest hydrocarbons.

Why It Matters

How Do Gas Grills Work?

REAL WORLD

Many gas grills are fueled by the alkane propane, C_3H_8. Propane is a gas that is stored in tanks at high pressure. When the valve to the tank is opened, the gas comes out in small amounts to the burner, where it is ignited. Like other hydrocarbons, propane undergoes combustion and releases a lot of energy as heat.

This man is preparing his dinner on a gas grill that is fueled by propane. Propane is an alkane that has two C–C bonds and eight C–H bonds.

YOUR TURN

ONLINE RESEARCH
1. Find one other compound besides propane that is used as a fuel for outdoor grills. What does it have in common with propane? How is it different from propane?

Arrangements of carbon atoms in alkanes may vary.

The carbon atoms in methane, ethane, and propane are all bonded in a single line because that is their only possible arrangement. When there are more than three bonded carbon atoms in a molecule, the carbon atoms do not have to be in a single line. When they are, the alkane is called a *normal alkane*, or *n-alkane*. **Figure 3** shows chemical formulas for the *n*-alkanes that have up to 10 carbon atoms. *Condensed structural formulas* in the table show how the atoms bond.

The carbon atoms in any alkane that has more than three carbon atoms can have more than one possible arrangement. Carbon atom chains may have branches, and they can even form rings. **Figure 4** shows some of the ways that six-carbon atoms with only single bonds can be arranged.

Reading Check What is the shortest chain of carbon atoms that can have more than one arrangement? Explain.

Figure 3 The First 10 *n*-Alkanes

n-Alkane	Molecular formula	Condensed structural formula
Methane	CH_4	CH_4
Ethane	C_2H_6	CH_3CH_3
Propane	C_3H_8	$CH_3CH_2CH_3$
Butane	C_4H_{10}	$CH_3(CH_2)_2CH_3$
Pentane	C_5H_{12}	$CH_3(CH_2)_3CH_3$
Hexane	C_6H_{14}	$CH_3(CH_2)_4CH_3$
Heptane	C_7H_{16}	$CH_3(CH_2)_5CH_3$
Octane	C_8H_{18}	$CH_3(CH_2)_6CH_3$
Nonane	C_9H_{20}	$CH_3(CH_2)_7CH_3$
Decane	$C_{10}H_{22}$	$CH_3(CH_2)_8CH_3$

Alkane chemical formulas usually follow a pattern.

Except for cyclic alkanes, the chemical formulas for alkanes follow a special pattern. The number of hydrogen atoms is always two more than twice the number of carbon atoms. This pattern is represented by the general formula C_nH_{2n+2}. Look at the six-carbon alkanes shown in **Figure 4**. All of the alkanes except for cyclohexane have the chemical formula C_6H_{14}, which is what you get when you replace the variable *n* in the general formula C_nH_{2n+2} with the number 6.

Figure 4 Hexane, 3-methylpentane, 2,3-dimethylbutane, and cyclohexane are some of the forms that six-carbon atoms with single covalent bonds may have.

Some Six-Carbon Alkanes: Hexane, 3-Methylpentane, 2,3-Dimethylbutane, Cyclohexane

Section 4 Organic and Biochemical Compounds

Figure 5 The peaches in this plastic container, which is made by joining propene molecules, release ethene gas as they ripen. **To what class of hydrocarbons do ethene and propene both belong?**

Figure 6 Many products, such as the sterno in a buffet heater, contain a mixture of the alcohols methanol and ethanol. This mixture is called *denatured alcohol*.

Alkenes have double carbon-carbon bonds.

Alkenes are also hydrocarbons. Alkenes are different from alkanes because alkenes have at least one double covalent bond between carbon atoms. This bond is shown by C=C. Alkenes are named by replacing the *-ane* ending with *-ene*.

The simplest alkene is ethene (or ethylene), C_2H_4. Ethene is formed when fruit ripens. Propene (or propylene), C_3H_6, is used to make rubbing alcohol and some plastics. The structures of both compounds are shown in **Figure 5**.

Alcohols have hydroxyl groups.

Alcohols are organic compounds that are made of oxygen as well as carbon and hydrogen. Alcohols have *hydroxyl*, or –OH, groups. The alcohol methanol, CH_3OH, is sometimes mixed with another alcohol ethanol, CH_3CH_2OH, to make denatured alcohol. Denatured alcohol is found in some familiar products, as **Figure 6** shows. Isopropanol, which is found in rubbing alcohol, has the chemical formula C_3H_8O, or $(CH_3)_2CHOH$. You may have noticed how the names of these three alcohols end in *-ol*. This is true for most alcohols.

Alcohol and water molecules behave similarly.

A methanol molecule is like a methane molecule except that one of the hydrogen atoms is replaced by a hydroxyl group. Like water molecules, neighboring alcohol molecules are attracted to one another. Because of the attractions many alcohols are liquids at room temperature. Alcohols have much higher boiling points than alkanes of similar size.

Polymers

What do rubber, wood, plastic milk jugs, and the DNA inside the cells of your body have in common? They are all made of large molecules called polymers. ❯ **A polymer is a molecule that is a long chain made of smaller molecules.**

Polymers have repeating subunits.

Polyethene, which is also known as *polyethylene* or *polythene,* is the polymer that makes up plastic milk jugs. The name *polyethene* tells polyethene's structure. *Poly* means "many." *Ethene* is an alkene that has the formula C_2H_4. Thus, *polyethene* means "many ethenes," as **Figure 7** shows. The smaller molecule that makes up the polymer, in this case C_2H_4, is called a *monomer.*

Some polymers are natural, and others are artificial.

Rubber, wood, cotton, wool, starch, protein, and DNA are all natural polymers. Human-made polymers are usually either plastics or fibers. Most plastics are flexible and easily molded, whereas fibers form long, thin strands.

Some polymers can be used as both plastics and fibers. For example, polypropene (polypropylene) is molded to make plastic containers, such as the one shown in **Figure 5,** as well as some parts for cars and appliances. It is also used to make ropes, carpet, and artificial turf for athletic fields.

✓ **Reading Check** What is the relationship between a monomer and a polymer?

A polymer's structure determines its elasticity.

As with all substances, the properties of a polymer are determined by its structure. Polymer molecules are like long, thin chains. A small piece of plastic or a single fiber is made of billions of these chains. Polymer molecules can be compared to spaghetti. Like a bowl of spaghetti, the chains are tangled but can slide over each other. Milk jugs are made of polyethene, a plastic made of such long chains. You can crush or dent a milk jug because the plastic is flexible. Once the jug has been crushed, though, it does not return to its original shape. It cannot be reshaped because polyethene is not elastic.

When the chains are connected to each other, the polymer's properties are different. Some polymers are elastic, like a volleyball net. An elastic polymer can stretch. When the polymer is released, it returns to its original shape. Rubber bands are made of elastic polymers. As long as a rubber band is not stretched too far, it can go back to its original form.

Figure 7 Polyethene is a polymer made of many repeating ethene units. It is used to make various plastics, such as the plastics in this milk jug.

polymer (PAHL uh muhr) a large molecule that is formed by more than five monomers, or small units

QuickLab   10 min

Polymer Memory

1. Polymers that return to their original shape after stretching can be thought of as having a "memory." Test the memory of a **rubber band** and that of the **plastic rings** from a six-pack of cans.
2. Which polymer is easier to stretch?
3. Which one has better memory?
4. Warm the stretched six-pack holder over a **hot plate.** Be careful not to melt it. Will the six-pack holder return to the shape it had before it was heated? Explain.

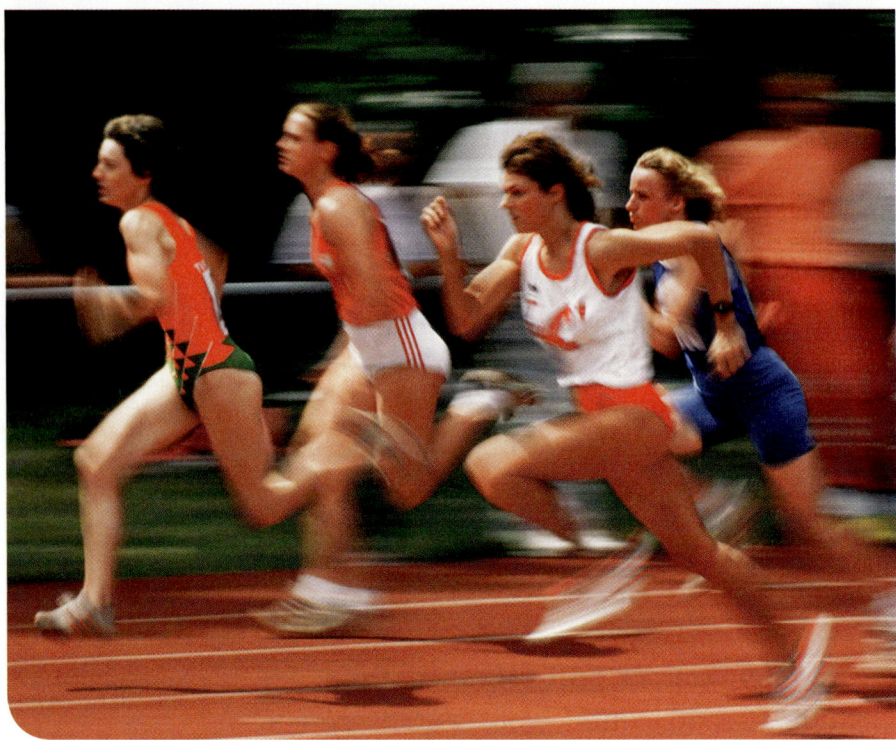

Figure 8 Athletes often eat a lot of foods that are high in carbohydrates the day before a big event. Carbohydrates provide them with a ready supply of stored energy.

READING TOOLBOX

Layered Book
Make a layered book FoldNote, and label the tabs with "Hydrocarbons," "Carbohydrates," "Proteins," and "DNA." Write notes on the appropriate tab as you read this section.

carbohydrate (KAHR boh HIE drayt) a class of molecules that includes sugars, starches, and fiber; contains carbon, hydrogen, and oxygen

protein (PROH teen) an organic compound that is made of one or more chains of amino acids and that is a principal component of all cells

amino acid (uh MEE noh AS id) a compound of a class of simple organic compounds that contain a carboxyl group and an amino group and that combine to form proteins

Biochemical Compounds

Biochemical compounds are organic compounds that can be made by living things. ❯ **Biochemicals, which are essential to life, include carbohydrates, proteins, and DNA.** Burning carbohydrates gives you energy. Proteins form important parts of your body, such as muscles, tendons, fingernails, and hair. The DNA inside your cells gives your body information about what proteins you need. Each of these biochemical compounds is a polymer.

Many carbohydrates are made of glucose.

Biochemicals called **carbohydrates,** which include sugars and starches, provide energy to living things. Sucrose, table sugar, is made of two simple carbohydrates, glucose and fructose, bonded together. Starch is made of a series of bonded glucose molecules, and is therefore a polymer. You get energy from the chains of starch stored in certain plants.

When you eat starchy foods, such as potatoes or pasta, enzymes in your body break down the starch. This process makes glucose available as a nutrient for your cells. Glucose that is not needed right away by the body is stored as *glycogen,* a polymer of glucose. When you become active, glycogen breaks apart into glucose molecules, which give you energy. Athletes often eat starchy foods so that they will have more energy when they exert themselves later on, as **Figure 8** shows.

✓ **Reading Check** Why do people need carbohydrates in their diets?

202 Chapter 6 The Structure of Matter

Proteins are complex polymers of amino acids.

Starch is made of only glucose. **Proteins**, which provide structure and function to parts of cells, are much more complex. Proteins are made of many different molecules that are called **amino acids**. Every amino acid contains an amino group ($-NH_2$), a carboxyl group ($-COOH$), and a side group that gives the amino acid its unique properties. There are 20 amino acids found in naturally occurring proteins. Each protein is made of a specific combination of a certain number of amino acids. The amino acids that make up a protein determine the protein's structure and function.

Proteins are long chains made of amino acids. A small protein, insulin, is shown in **Figure 9**. Many proteins are made of thousands of bonded amino acid molecules. Thus, millions of different proteins can be made. When you eat foods that contain proteins, such as cheese, your digestive system breaks down the proteins into individual amino acids. Later, your cells bond the amino acids in different ways to form the proteins that your body needs.

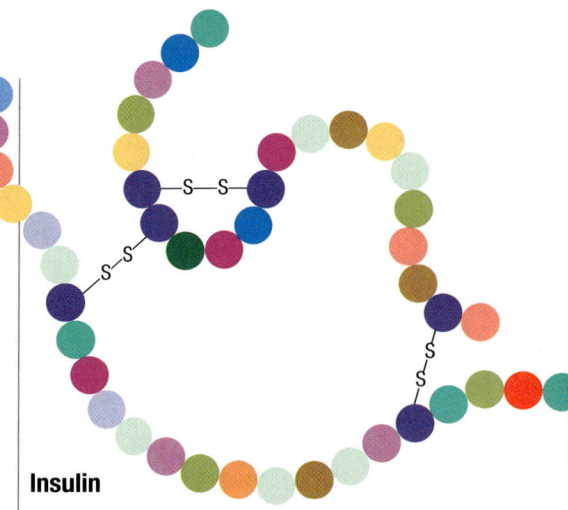

Insulin

Figure 9 The protein insulin controls the use and storage of glucose in your body. Each color in the chain represents a different amino acid. Disulfide bridges between certain amino acids link different chains and provide additional structure.

Inquiry Lab

What Properties Does a Polymer Have?

 30 min

Procedure

1. In one **250 mL beaker**, mix **4 g borax** with 100 mL **water**, and stir well.

2. In a second **250 mL beaker**, mix equal parts of **white glue** and water. This solution will determine the amount of new material made. The volume of diluted glue should be between 100 mL and 200 mL.

3. Pour the borax solution into the beaker containing the glue, and stir well using a **plastic spoon**.

4. When the solution is too thick to stir, remove the material from the cup and knead it with your fingers. You can store this new material in a **plastic sandwich bag**.

Analysis

1. What happens to the new material when it is stretched or rolled into a ball and bounced?

2. Compare the properties of the glue with the properties of the new material.

3. The properties of the new material resulted from the bonds between the borax and the glue particles. If too little borax were used, in what way would the properties of the new material differ?

4. Does the new material have the properties of a polymer? Explain your conclusion.

Section 4 Organic and Biochemical Compounds **203**

DNA is a polymer that stores genetic information.

All of your genes are made of DNA molecules. DNA is a very long molecule made of carbon, hydrogen, oxygen, nitrogen, and phosphorus.

Figuring out the complex structure of DNA was one of the greatest scientific challenges of the 20th century. Instead of forming one chain, like many proteins and polymers, DNA is in the form of paired chains, or strands. It has the shape of a twisted ladder known as a *double helix*.

Sugar molecules that are bonded to phosphate units correspond to the ladder's sides, as **Figure 10** shows. Attached to each sugar molecule is one of four DNA monomers—adenine, thymine, cytosine, or guanine. These DNA monomers pair with DNA monomers that are attached to the opposite strand in a predictable way, as **Figure 10** shows. Together, the DNA monomer pairs make up the rungs of the ladder.

Most cells in your body have a copy of your genetic material in the form of chromosomes made of DNA. When a cell in your body divides, copies of your chromosomes are made. This process happens when DNA strands separate and a new strand is made from of the old strands.

DNA is the information that the cell uses to make proteins.

The sequence of monomers in DNA determines the proteins that are made in a cell. Each group of three monomers represents a specific amino acid in a protein. The resulting proteins that are made determine all of the activities and characteristics of the cell.

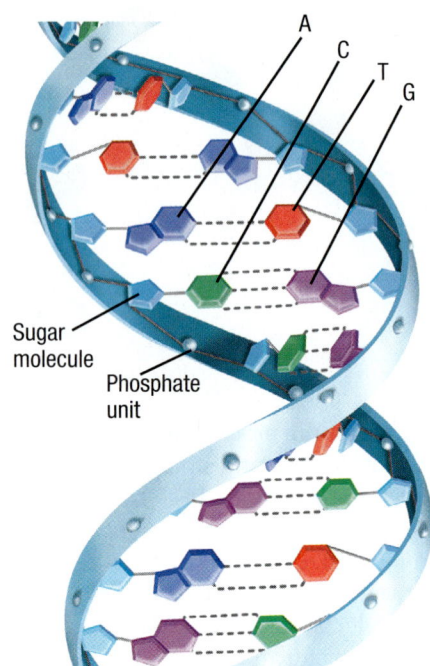

Figure 10 In DNA, cytosine, C, always pairs with guanine, G. Adenine, A, always pairs with thymine, T.

Section 4 Review

KEY IDEAS

1. **Identify** which compound is an alkane: CH_2O, C_6H_{14}, or C_3H_4. Explain your reasoning.
2. **Determine** how many hydrogen atoms a compound has if it is a hydrocarbon and its carbon atom skeleton is C=C–C=C.
3. **Identify** the following compounds as alkanes, alkenes, or alcohols based on their names:
   a. 2-methylpentane
   b. 3-methyloctane
   c. 1-nonene
   d. 2-butanol
   e. 3-heptene
   f. cyclohexanol
4. **Compare** the structures and properties of carbohydrates with those of proteins.

CRITICAL THINKING

5. **Analyzing Information** Why can there be no such compound as CBr_5? Give an acceptable chemical formula for a compound that is made of only carbon and bromine.
6. **Predicting Patterns** *Alkynes* are hydrocarbons that have carbon-carbon triple covalent bonds, or C≡C bonds. Draw the structure of the alkyne that has the chemical formula C_3H_4. Guess the name of this compound.

Why It Matters

DNA Fingerprinting

FORENSICS

For over a century, detectives have solved crimes using fingerprint identification. But more recently, detectives have used DNA analysis to identify traces of evidence that contain human cells.

1 Detectives at a crime scene can often find items that have come into contact with a suspect's skin or hair. Every cell in a person's body has a complete set of that person's DNA, so it takes just a single cell left at a crime scene to get DNA evidence.

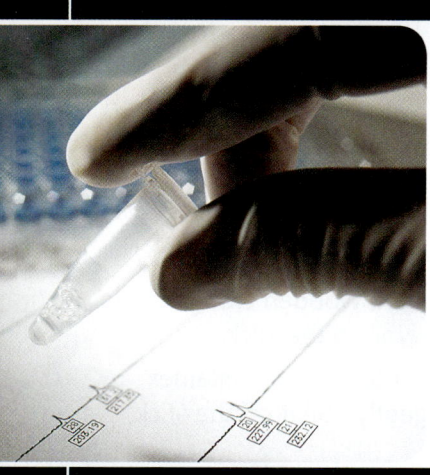

2 The DNA is isolated. Then, large numbers of copies of the DNA are made so that the DNA is easier to work with. Certain highly variable regions of DNA are analyzed and made into a *DNA profile* that has patterns that are distinctive to each individual.

3 DNA evidence is matched to an individual by comparing it to a DNA sample known to be from that individual. The chances that any two people's DNA profile will match is extremely small. However, the chances of laboratory error are much higher and may result in failure to match DNA profiles. However, matching DNA profiles are a very reliable indication that they came from the same person.

SCLINKS
www.scilinks.org
Topic: DNA Fingerprinting
Code: **HK80419**

YOUR TURN

CRITICAL THINKING

1. Imagine a scenario in which a guilty person was not convicted because of failure to match DNA profiles. What could have caused this?

Application Lab

⏱ 50 min

Comparing Polymers

You work in the research and development lab of a toys and novelties company. The company wants to manufacture bouncy toy balls. Such toy balls are made of polymers that bounce back after they are stretched, bent, or compressed. Your job is to review the bounce heights of the polymers and to make a recommendation about which of two polymers to use for the toy balls.

What You'll Do

- **Synthesize** two different polymers, shape each into a ball, and measure how high each ball bounces.
- **Draw conclusions** about which polymer would make a better toy ball.

What You'll Need

acetic acid solution (vinegar), 5%
container, 2 L
craft sticks, wooden (2)
cups, paper, medium-sized (2)
ethanol solution, 50%
graduated cylinder, 10 mL
graduated cylinder, 25 mL (2)
latex, liquid
meterstick
paper towels
sodium silicate solution
water, deionized

Safety

Procedure

1. Prepare a data table like the sample data table shown.

Making Latex Rubber

CAUTION: Wear goggles, gloves, and an apron. If you get a chemical on your skin or clothing, wash it off with lukewarm water while calling to your teacher. If you get a chemical in your eyes, flush it out immediately at the eyewash station and alert your teacher.

2. Pour 1 L of deionized water into a 2 L container.
3. Use a 25 mL graduated cylinder to pour 10 mL of liquid latex into one of the paper cups.
4. Clean the graduated cylinder thoroughly with soap and water. Then, rinse it with deionized water, and use it to add 10 mL of deionized water to the cup of liquid latex.
5. Use the same graduated cylinder to add 10 mL of acetic acid solution to the mixture of liquid latex and water.
6. Immediately begin stirring the mixture with a wooden craft stick. As you stir, a lump of the polymer will form around the stick.
7. Transfer the stick and the attached polymer to the 2 L container. While keeping the polymer underwater, gently pull it off the stick with your gloved hands.
8. Squeeze the polymer underwater to remove any unreacted chemicals, shape it into a ball, and remove the ball from the water.
9. Make the ball smooth by rolling it between your gloved hands. Set the ball on a paper towel to dry while you continue the lab.
10. Wash your gloved hands with soap and water, and then dispose of the gloves. Wash your hands again with soap and water.

Sample Data Table: Bounce Heights of Polymers

Polymer	Bounce height (cm)					
	Trial 1	Trial 2	Trial 3	Trial 4	Trial 5	Average
Latex rubber						
Ethanol-silicate			DO NOT WRITE IN BOOK			

206 Chapter 6 The Structure of Matter

Making an Ethanol-Silicate Polymer

CAUTION: Put on a new pair of disposable gloves. Ethanol is flammable, so make sure there are no flames or other heat sources anywhere in the laboratory.

11. Use a clean 25 mL graduated cylinder to pour 12 mL of sodium silicate solution into the clean paper cup.
12. Use a 10 mL graduated cylinder to add 3 mL of the ethanol solution to the sodium silicate solution.
13. Immediately begin stirring the mixture with a clean, wooden craft stick until a solid polymer forms.
14. Remove the polymer with your gloved hands, and gently press it between your palms until you form a ball that does not crumble. This activity may take some time. Dripping some tap water on the polymer might be helpful.
15. When the ball no longer crumbles, dry it very gently with a paper towel.
16. Repeat step 10, and put on a new pair of disposable gloves.
17. Examine both polymers closely. Record in your lab report how the two polymers are alike and how they are different.
18. Use a meterstick to measure the highest bounce height of each ball when each is dropped from a height of 1 m. Drop each ball five times, and record the highest bounce height each time in your data table.

Analysis

1. **Analyzing Data** Calculate the average bounce height for each ball by adding the five bounce heights and dividing by 5. Record the averages in your data table.

Communicating Your Results

2. **Evaluating Methods** What was the purpose of measuring the bounce heights of each polymer in five trials? If you had only measured the bounce height of each polymer once, how would the validity of your results compare with the validity of your results after several trials?
3. **Drawing Conclusions** On average, which polymer bounced higher?
4. **Applying Concepts** What chemical difference between the two polymers might cause the difference in bounce heights?

Application

Based on only their bounce heights, which polymer would make a better toy ball?

Understanding Symbols

Science › Skills

Technology
Math
▸ Scientific Methods
Graphing

Scientific symbols are a kind of shorthand that makes expressing scientific ideas easier. The meaning of a symbol depends on the context in which it is used. These tips will help you understand some of the most common kinds of scientific symbols.

❶ **Chemical symbols** represent chemical elements. The symbols stand alone when representing elements, but chemical symbols are combined in chemical formulas. To form a chemical equation, we combine chemical symbols and formulas with plus signs and an arrow (a yields sign).

- The symbol for each element can be found in the periodic table. There is a different symbol for each element. Each symbol starts with a capital letter.
- When chemical symbols are used in chemical formulas, subscripts are used to tell you how many atoms of that element are in one unit of the compound. If there is no subscript after an element symbol, that substance contains only one atom of the element per unit.
- The charge on an ion is given by a superscript after the chemical symbol or chemical formula.
- Subscripts and superscripts **before** an element's symbol tell you about a specific isotope of that element. The subscript is the atomic number (Z, the number of protons), and the superscript is the mass number (A, the number of protons + neutrons).

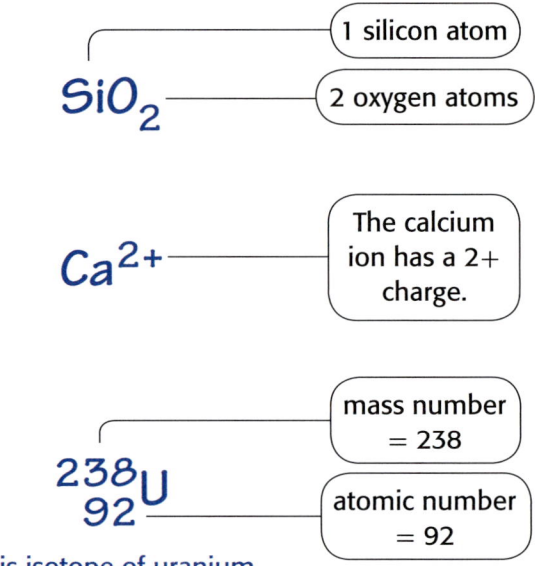

❷ **Physical symbols** are used to represent certain kinds of physical quantities. Equations are used to show the mathematical relationships between physical quantities.

- Physical quantities that are variable are represented by italic letters. When you learn about a physical quantity, take note of the symbol used to represent the quantity.
- Subscripts usually distinguish one variable from another variable of the same kind.
- Superscripts are powers of multiplication, just as in any mathematical equation.

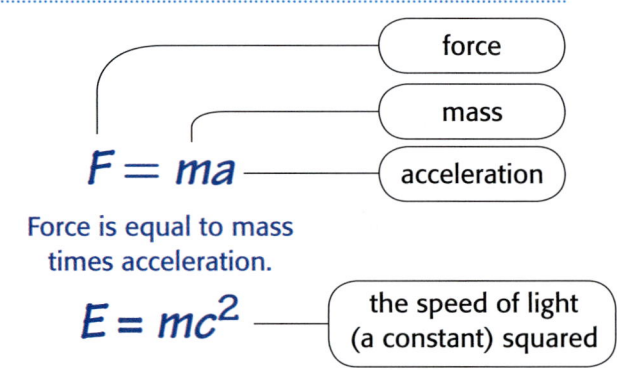

Practice

1. Consider the following: BrO^-
   a. Is this a chemical symbol, a chemical formula, or a chemical equation?
   b. How many elements are represented? What are they? How many atoms are represented?

2. Consider the following: $KE = \frac{1}{2}mv^2$
   a. Is this a physical quantity, a physical equation, or a unit of measurement?
   b. What does the superscript 2 tell you?

CHAPTER 6 Summary

Key Ideas

Section 1 Compounds and Molecules

> **Chemical Bonds** The forces that hold atoms or ions together in a compound are called *chemical bonds*. (p. 177)

> **Chemical Structure** The structure of chemical compounds can be shown by various models. (p. 178)

> **How Does Structure Affect Properties** The chemical structure of a compound determines the properties of that compound. (p. 180)

Section 2 Ionic and Covalent Bonding

> **Why Do Chemical Bonds Form?** Atoms join to form bonds so that each atom has a stable electron configuration. (p. 183)

> **Ionic, Covalent, and Metallic Bonds** Ionic bonds form between oppositely charged ions. (p. 184) Atoms joined by covalent bonds share electrons. (p. 186) Electrons in metal atoms have freedom of movement. (p. 188)

> **Polyatomic Ions** A polyatomic ion acts as a single unit in a compound. (p. 189)

Section 3 Compound Names and Formulas

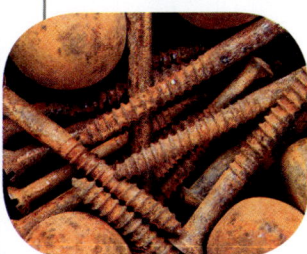

> **Naming Ionic and Covalent Compounds** The names of ionic compounds consist of the names of the ions of which the compounds are made. (p. 191) Numerical prefixes tell how many atoms of each element are in a covalent compound. (p. 194)

> **Empirical Formulas** An empirical formula tells us the smallest whole-number ratio of atoms that are in a compound. (p. 194)

Section 4 Organic and Biochemical Compounds

> **Organic Compounds** An organic compound is a covalent compound that contains carbon. (p. 197)

> **Polymers** A polymer is a molecule that is a long chain made of smaller molecules. (p. 201)

> **Biochemical Compounds** Biochemicals include carbohydrates, proteins, and DNA. (p. 202)

Key Terms

chemical bond, p. 177
chemical structure, p. 178
bond length, p. 178
bond angle, p. 178

ionic bond, p. 184
covalent bond, p. 186
metallic bond, p. 188
polyatomic ion, p. 189

empirical formula, p. 194
molecular formula, p. 195

organic compound, p. 197
polymer, p. 201
carbohydrate, p. 202
protein, p. 203
amino acid, p. 203

The Structure of Matter

CHAPTER 6 Review

1. **Suffixes** Refer to the word parts table that you made for the words in Section 2 containing the suffix -ic. Use each of the words in a sentence.

USING KEY TERMS

2. Explain why *proteins* and *carbohydrates* are *polymers*. What makes up these polymers?

3. List two differences between *ionic bonds* and *covalent bonds*.

4. What does an *organic compound* contain? List several organic compounds that can be found in your body or used in your daily life.

5. What is a *hydroxyl group*? What organic compound contains a hydroxyl group?

6. What makes up a *hydrocarbon*? Name the simplest hydrocarbon.

UNDERSTANDING KEY IDEAS

7. Compounds that are made of molecules
   a. never exist as liquids.
   b. never exist as solids.
   c. never exist as gases.
   d. tend not to have high melting points.

8. A chemical bond can be defined as a force that
   a. holds the parts of an atom together.
   b. joins atoms in a compound.
   c. causes electric repulsion.
   d. blends nuclei together.

9. A compound is different from a mixture because
   a. a compound is held together by chemical bonds.
   b. each substance in a compound maintains its own properties.
   c. each original substance in a compound remains chemically unchanged.
   d. a mixture is held together by chemical bonds.

10. Ionic solids
    a. are formed by networks of ions that have the same charge.
    b. melt at very low temperatures.
    c. have very regular structures.
    d. are sometimes found as gases at room temperature.

11. Crystals of table salt, sodium chloride, are
    a. made of molecules.
    b. made of a network of ions.
    c. chemically similar to sugar crystals.
    d. weak solids.

12. The compound _____ is an example of an ionic compound.
    a. H_2O
    b. CO_2
    c. KCl
    d. PCl_3

13. The chemical formula for calcium chloride is
    a. CaCl.
    b. $CaCl_2$.
    c. Ca_2Cl.
    d. Ca_2Cl_2.

14. All organic compounds
    a. come only from living organisms.
    b. contain only carbon and hydrogen.
    c. are biochemical compounds.
    d. have atoms connected by covalent bonds.

EXPLAINING KEY IDEAS

15. Compare the chemical structure of oxygen difluoride with that of carbon dioxide. Which compound has the larger bond angle?

Carbon dioxide

Oxygen difluoride

16. The figure below shows how atoms are bonded in a molecule of vitamin C. Which elements make up vitamin C? What is its molecular formula?

17. Name the following covalent compounds:
  a. SF_4
  b. N_2O
  c. PCl_3
  d. P_2O_5

CRITICAL THINKING

18. Recognizing Relationships Noble gases, such as helium and neon, have full, stable, outer-level electron configurations. How does this fact explain why atoms of noble gases usually do not form chemical bonds?

19. Analyzing Data A certain compound is a solid at room temperature. It is unable to conduct electricity as a solid but can conduct electricity as a liquid. This compound melts at 755 °C. What type of bonds would you expect this compound to have: ionic, metallic, or covalent bonds?

20. Applying Concepts Dodecane is a combustible organic compound that is used in research on jet fuel. It is an *n*-alkane made of 12 carbon atoms. How many hydrogen atoms does dodecane have? Draw the structural formula for dodecane.

21. Evaluating Assumptions A classmate claims that sodium gains a positive charge when it becomes an ion because it gains a proton. Explain what is wrong with the student's claim.

22. Predicting Outcomes Consider two atoms that form a chemical bond. One atom has a much stronger attraction for electrons than the other atom does. What kind of chemical bond is likely to form between the atoms? Explain.

Graphing Skills

23. The melting points of ionic compounds with cations in the same group follow a pattern. To see this, plot the melting point of each of the ionic compounds in the table below on the *y*-axis and the atomic number of the element from which the cation is made on the *x*-axis.
  a. What trend do you notice in the melting points as you move down Group 2?
  b. The compound $BeCl_2$ has a melting point of 405 °C. Is this likely to be an ionic compound? Explain. (**Hint:** Locate beryllium in the periodic table.)
  c. Predict the melting point of the ionic compound $RaCl_2$. (**Hint:** Check the periodic table, and compare radium's location with the location of magnesium, calcium, strontium, and barium.)

Melting Points of Some Ionic Compounds

Compound	Melting Point (°C)
$MgCl_2$	714
$CaCl_2$	782
$SrCl_2$	875
$BaCl_2$	963

Math Skills

24. Writing Ionic Formulas Determine the chemical formula for each of the following ionic compounds:
  a. strontium nitrate, an ingredient in some fireworks, signal flares, and matches
  b. sodium cyanide, a compound used in electroplating and treating metals
  c. chromium(III) hydroxide, a compound used to tan and dye substances

25. Finding Empirical Formulas A sample of a compound contains 111.7 g of iron and 64.1 g of sulfur. What is the compound's empirical formula?

Standardized Test Prep

Understanding Concepts

Directions (1–4): **For each question, write on a sheet of paper the letter of the correct answer.**

1. What causes atoms to form chemical bonds with other atoms?
   - **A.** Atoms are more stable when they give away electrons.
   - **B.** When two atoms get close together, they merge into one.
   - **C.** The interaction of valence electrons forms a more stable configuration.
   - **D.** The attraction of the nuclei for one another causes atoms to share electrons.

2. How many atoms of oxygen are in one formula unit of aluminum sulfate, $Al_2(SO_4)_3$?
   - **F.** 3
   - **G.** 4
   - **H.** 8
   - **I.** 12

3. A nitride anion, N^{3-}, has a charge of 3–. What is the charge of a titanium cation in the compound Ti_3N_2?
   - **A.** 2+
   - **B.** 2–
   - **C.** 3+
   - **D.** 3–

4. What is the condensed structural formula for the *n*-alkane heptane, which has a molecular formula of C_7H_{16}?
   - **F.** C_7H_{16}
   - **G.** $(CH_2)_6CH_4$
   - **H.** $C_3H_4(CH_3)_4$
   - **I.** $CH_3(CH_2)_5CH_3$

Directions (5): **For each question, write a short response.**

5. The difference between the three types of chemical bonds—covalent, ionic, and metallic—is what happens to valence electrons that are part of the bond. Compare the three types of bonds based on valence electrons.

Reading Skills

Directions (6–8): **Read the passage below. Then, answer the questions that follow.**

SPIDER SILK

Spider silk is one of the strongest known fibers. It is strong enough to support the spider and has enough elasticity to absorb the energy of the collision of a flying insect. The strength comes from the covalent bonds between units of the amino acid polymer of which spider silk, a protein, is made. The elasticity is the result of interactions between different parts of the molecule. Coils or folds in the protein expand on impact.

Spiders can make at least seven kinds of silk for different purposes by varying the amino acids that make up the silk. Scientists studying the structure of silk have identified some of the structures that account for silk's properties. They have even found ways to mimic the properties of spider silk in synthetic fibers. However, there is still much for scientists to learn from the amazing natural properties of spider silk.

6. How do the various kinds of spider silk differ based on their protein structures?

7. Which of the following describes the properties of spider silk?
   - **A.** heavy and strong
   - **B.** light and flimsy
   - **C.** strong and elastic
   - **D.** rigid and heavy

8. Which of the following best describes what scientists have learned about spider silk?
   - **F.** All of its properties have been explained.
   - **G.** Scientists have made synthetic fibers with properties similar to spider silk.
   - **H.** All spider silk has the same chemical structure.
   - **I.** The unique properties of spider silk remain a mystery.

Interpreting Graphics

The illustration below models how water molecules are arranged in the liquid state. Use this illustration to answer question 9.

INTERACTION OF WATER MOLECULES IN THE LIQUID STATE

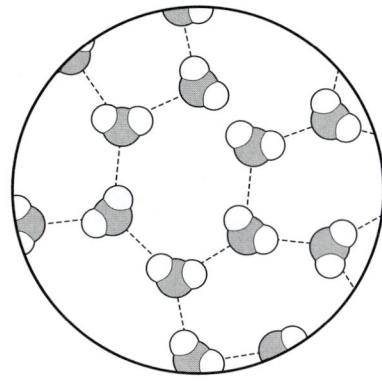

9. Compare the forces of attraction between the atoms of a water molecule to the forces of attraction between two water molecules.

The following graphic shows a model of one molecular unit of the amino acid alanine, which has a structural formula of CH_3CHNH_2COOH. Use this graphic to answer questions 10–11.

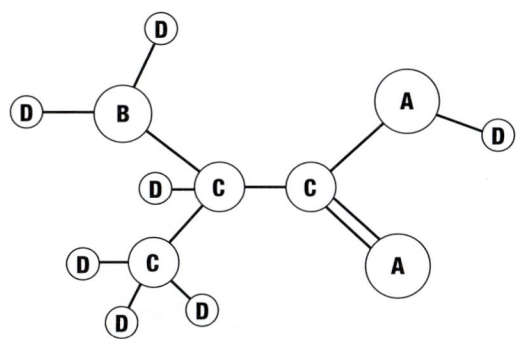

10. What letter represents carbon in the model?
    - **A.** A
    - **B.** B
    - **C.** C
    - **D.** D

11. Atoms of which two elements share a double covalent bond in alanine?

Test Tip

When possible, use the text in multiple-choice questions to help you "jump start" your thinking.

Why It Matters
Careers Using Chemistry

When you think of a chemist, you may think of a lab-coated scientist surrounded by test tubes. But people use chemistry in hundreds of careers, not all of which require work in a lab. Whether designing fuel cells, preserving art, or investigating a crime scene, people use chemistry to get the job done. The careers listed here are examples of careers that use chemistry.

Medical Practitioner

Medical practitioners care for people who suffer from injuries or disease. Medical students study chemistry in order to understand the chemical properties of human body systems. For example, a doctor may have a patient's blood chemically analyzed. Chemical blood tests can detect the presence of compounds such as sugar and specific proteins, which can indicate the cause of illness. Medical practitioners must know the chemical properties of medications to avoid prescribing medicines that have harmful drug interactions.

Arson Investigator

Arson investigators help detectives interpret evidence at crime scenes that involve fire. Arson investigators examine the fire debris and try to determine how a fire was started, how it spread, and whether there are clues that might help identify suspects. The presence of an accelerant is an important indicator that a fire was set intentionally. The most common accelerants are hydrocarbon-based fuels, such as gasoline. Arson investigators use a technique called *gas chromatography-mass spectrometry* (GC-MS) to detect accelerants in fire debris.

Ethnobotanist

Ethnobotanists study how cultures use plants for specific purposes. Sometimes, the compounds that scientists find in plants can be used as medicines or other products. For example, ethnobotanist Paul Cox researched a tea made from a rain-forest tree in Samoa. Local healers used this tea to treat viral hepatitis, a disease of the liver. Chemical analysis showed that the plant contains the virus-fighting chemical prostratin, which is a potential treatment for AIDS.

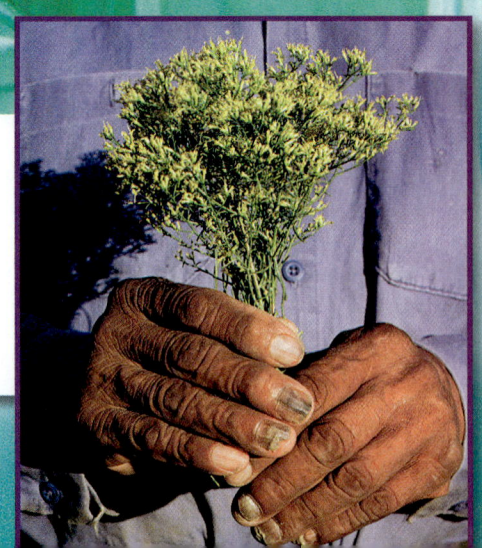

Conservator

Conservators restore and preserve historical artifacts, such as coins, art, documents, and film. To be a conservator, you must understand how factors such as time, use, and humidity affect chemical reactions that damage artifacts. For example, many historic documents were written with iron gall ink. The ink was made by mixing ferrous sulfate with gallic acid extracted from oak trees that had parasitic infections, or galls. Over time, iron gall ink releases sulfuric acid, which destroys the paper on which the ink was printed. Conservators store historic documents in low-temperature, low-humidity environments to limit the rate of this reaction.

Perfumer

The recent discovery of a 4,000-year-old perfume factory in Cyprus suggests that human societies have valued perfumes for a very long time. Modern-day perfumers use analytic, synthetic, and organic chemistry to develop fragrances for everything from soaps and perfumes to food products and new cars. A perfumer must understand chemical properties, such as how gases diffuse, and must understand the chemical reactions that occur between various organic compounds. Perfumers must also understand how the human body detects and perceives fragrances. For example, simple changes in a compound's molecular structure can determine whether the compound has a wonderful smell or an offensive one.

Chef

Cooking—from grilling a steak to baking a cake—involves chemical reactions. Because they must know how to control these reactions, chefs and bakers find a knowledge of chemistry useful. For example, Louis Maillard, a chemist, discovered why all foods brown at temperatures higher than 154 °F (68 °C). He found that a chemical reaction, now called the *Maillard reaction,* occurs when sugars and amino acids are heated together. This reaction makes foods brown and produces many of the flavors and aromas of cooked foods. Understanding chemistry can make cooking more fun.

YOUR TURN

UNDERSTANDING CONCEPTS
1. Describe how understanding chemistry plays an important role in two of the careers described on these pages.

CRITICAL THINKING
2. How can ethnobotanical research benefit indigenous communities?

www.scilinks.org
Topic: Careers in Chemistry
Code: HK81689

Careers Using Chemistry

CHAPTER 7
Chemical Reactions

Chapter Outline

1 The Nature of Chemical Reactions
Chemical Reactions
Energy and Reactions

2 Chemical Equations
Describing Reactions
Balanced Equations and Mole Ratios

3 Reaction Types
Classifying Reactions
Electrons and Chemical Reactions

4 Reaction Rates and Equilibrium
Factors Affecting Reaction Rates
Catalysts
Equilibrium Systems

Tennessee Course Level Expectations (Physical Science)

CLE.3202.1.9 Apply the Laws of Conservation of Mass/Energy to balance chemical equations; **CLE.3202.Inq.1** Recognize that science is a progressive endeavor that reevaluates and extends what is already accepted; **CLE.3202.Inq.2** Design and conduct scientific investigations to explore new phenomena, verify previous results, test how well a theory predicts, and compare opposing theories; **CLE.3202.Inq.3** Use appropriate tools and technology to collect precise and accurate data; **CLE.3202.Inq.4** Apply qualitative and quantitative measures to analyze data and draw conclusions that are free of bias; **CLE.3202.Inq.6** Communicate and defend scientific findings.

Why It Matters

Chemical reactions are everywhere. They are especially important to living things. This sea anemone is an animal that produces its own light by special chemical reactions in its cells.

Inquiry Lab
20 min

Matter and Chemical Reactions

Place about **5 g (1 tsp) of baking soda** into a **sealable plastic bag**. Place about **5 mL (1 tsp) of vinegar** into a **plastic film canister.** Secure the lid. Place the canister into the bag. Squeeze the air out of the bag, and tightly seal the bag.

Use a **balance** to determine the total mass of the bag and its contents. Make a note of this value. Open the canister without opening the bag, and allow the vinegar and baking soda to mix. When the reaction has stopped, measure and record the total mass of the bag and its contents.

Questions to Get You Started

1. What evidence shows that a chemical reaction has taken place?
2. Compare the masses of the bag and its contents before and after the reaction. What does this result demonstrate about chemical reactions?

READING TOOLBOX

These reading tools can help you learn the material in this chapter. For more information on how to use these and other tools, see **Appendix A.**

Word Parts

Prefixes Many scientific words are made up of word parts that come from other languages. These word parts can be prefixes, suffixes, or word roots. Understanding the meanings of these word parts can help you understand new scientific terms.

The prefix *endo-* means "within" or "inside," while the prefix *exo-* means "external" or "outside." If these prefixes are used before a vowel, they can be shortened to *end-* and *ex-*.

Your Turn The table below lists four words for describing chemical reactions based on changes in energy. After you have read Section 1, finish filling out a similar table. Look up the words in a dictionary to find out what the word parts mean.

TABLE OF WORD PARTS

WORD	PREFIX	ROOT	DEFINITION
Exothermic		therm (heat)	releasing energy as heat
Endothermic	endo-		
Exergonic	ex-	erg (energy)	
Endergonic			requiring or absorbing energy

Reading Equations

Chemical Equations Chemical equations are used to represent chemical reactions. Chemical equations are similar to mathematical equations in certain ways:

- The atoms in the substances on the left side are the same as the atoms in the substances on the right side but are rearranged.
- Instead of using an "equals" sign, a chemical equation uses an arrow that means "yields," or "gives." For example, the balanced chemical equation for a reaction between methane and oxygen is as follows:

$$CH_4 + 2O_2 \rightarrow CO_2 + 2H_2O$$

This equation means "The reaction of one methane molecule and two oxygen molecules yields one carbon dioxide molecule and two water molecules." The formulas of the molecules can be read out loud. For example, to read CH_4 aloud, say the letters *C* and *H* and the number 4 (SEE AYCH FAWR).

Your Turn As you read chemical equations in this chapter, practice writing them in words and saying them aloud.

FoldNotes

Table Fold FoldNotes are a fun way to help you learn ideas as you read. FoldNotes help you to organize concepts and to see the "big picture."

Your Turn Follow the instructions in **Appendix A** for making a table fold. As you read Section 3, fill in each section of the table with notes about a type of chemical reaction. Use the FoldNote to review the chapter.

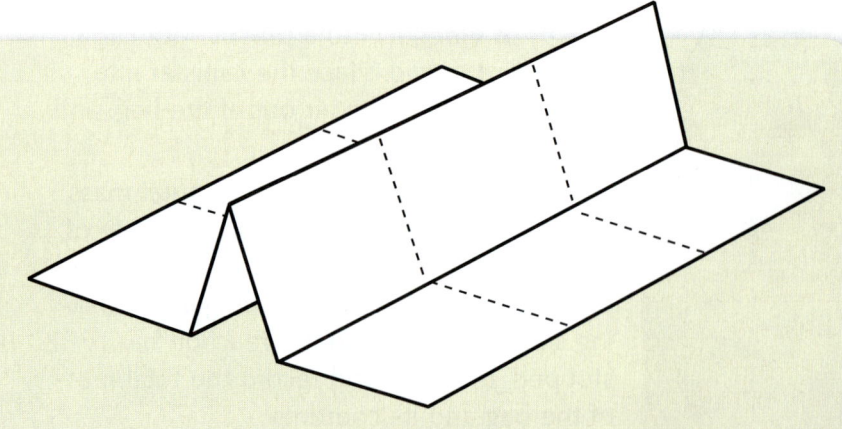

SECTION 1
The Nature of Chemical Reactions

Key Ideas
> When do chemical reactions take place?
> What is the role of energy in chemical reactions?

Key Terms
reactant
product
chemical energy
exothermic reaction
endothermic reaction

Why It Matters
Many of the processes that you see every day—such as the starting of a car, the lighting of a match, or the ripening of a piece of fruit—are chemical reactions.

If you hear the words *chemical reaction,* you might think about scientists doing experiments in laboratories. But words such as *grow, ripen, decay,* and *burn* describe chemical reactions that you see every day. Many different chemical reactions take place inside your body all of the time. The food you eat and the oxygen you breathe change form during reactions inside your body. You breathe out the carbon dioxide that is formed in these reactions into the air.

Tennessee Course Level Expectations (Physical Science)

CLE.3202.1.9; CLE.3202.Inq.1; CLE.3202.Inq.2; CLE.3202.Inq.3; CU.3202.1.24; CU.3202.Inq.3; SPI.3202.1.16; SPI.3202.Inq.3

Chemical Reactions

When sugar, water, and yeast are mixed into flour to make bread dough, a chemical reaction takes place. The yeast acts on the sugar to form new substances, including carbon dioxide and lactic acid. You know that a chemical reaction has happened because lactic acid and carbon dioxide differ from sugar. > **Chemical reactions occur when substances go through chemical changes to form new substances.** Often, you can tell that a chemical reaction is happening because you are able to see changes, such as the ones in **Figure 1.**

Figure 1 Easily visible signs of a chemical reaction include formation of a gas, formation of a solid, and release of energy.

Formation of a gas

Formation of a solid

Release of energy

READING TOOLBOX

Table Fold
Make a table fold, and write some of the key terms about chemical reactions along the top row. Fill in the columns with the important ideas about each term.

Chemical reactions rearrange atoms.

When gasoline burns in the engine of a car or boat, several reactions happen. In one of these reactions, two reactants—isooctane, C_8H_{18}, and oxygen, O_2—react to form two products—carbon dioxide, CO_2, and water, H_2O. A **reactant** is a substance that participates in a chemical reaction. A **product** is a substance that forms in a chemical reaction.

The products and reactants of a chemical reaction contain the same types of atoms. The reaction does not create the atoms of the products or destroy the atoms of the reactants. Instead, the reaction rearranges the bonds between the atoms. In all chemical reactions, mass remains the same.

Energy and Reactions

If isooctane and oxygen reacted whenever they were put in the same place, filling a car's tank with gasoline would be very dangerous. Like most chemical reactions, the isooctane-oxygen reaction needs energy to get started. A small spark gives enough energy to start this reaction. Therefore, having any spark or open flame near a gas pump is not allowed.
❯ **Chemical reactions always involve changes in energy.**

Energy must be added to break bonds.

In each isooctane molecule, such as the one shown in **Figure 2**, all of the bonds to carbon atoms are covalent. In an oxygen molecule, covalent bonds hold the two oxygen atoms together. For the atoms in isooctane and oxygen to react, all of these bonds must be broken. This process takes energy.

Many forms of energy can be used to break bonds. Sometimes, the energy is transferred as heat, as is the case when a spark starts the isooctane-oxygen reaction. Energy also can be transferred as electricity, sound, or light. When molecules collide and enough energy is transferred to separate the atoms, bonds can break.

Figure 2 Gasoline is a mixture of many different compounds, each of which contains 5 to 12 carbon atoms. Isooctane, C_8H_{18}, is one of the compounds of this mixture.

Figure 3 The formation of carbon dioxide and water from isooctane and oxygen produces the energy used to power the engines in cars.

Forming bonds releases energy.

When enough energy is added to start the isooctane-oxygen reaction, new bonds form to make the products, as **Figure 3** shows. Each carbon dioxide molecule consists of two oxygen atoms connected to one carbon atom by a double bond. A water molecule is made when two hydrogen atoms each form a single bond with an oxygen atom.

When new bonds form, chemical energy is released. When gasoline burns, energy in the form of heat and light is released as the products of the reaction form. Other chemical reactions can produce electrical energy.

Energy is conserved in chemical reactions.

Energy may not appear to be conserved in the isooctane-oxygen reaction. After all, a tiny spark can set off an explosion. This fact may suggest that a small amount of energy turns into a large amount of energy. However, the energy in that explosion comes from the bonds between atoms in the reactants.

Energy that is stored in the form of chemical bonds is called **chemical energy.** Molecules of isooctane and oxygen carry stored chemical energy. During the isooctane-oxygen reaction, the chemical energy changes form. But the total amount of energy of the reactants must always equal the total amount of energy of the products and their surroundings. Energy in a chemical reaction can change form, energy is never created or destroyed.

Reading Check Where does the chemical energy released in a chemical reaction come from? (See Appendix E for answers to Reading Checks.)

reactant (ree AK tuhnt) a substance or molecule that participates in a chemical reaction

product (PRAHD uhkt) a substance that forms in a chemical reaction

chemical energy (KEM i kuhl EN uhr jee) the energy released when a chemical compound reacts to produce new compounds

Section 1 The Nature of Chemical Reactions 221

Figure 4 The hump in the middle of each graph represents the energy required to start the reaction. **For each type of reaction, how does the chemical energy of the products versus the energy of the reactants differ?**

In an exothermic reaction, chemical energy is released, often as heat.

In an endothermic reaction, energy is absorbed by the reactants and stored in the products as chemical energy.

exothermic reaction (EK soh THUHR mik ree AK shuhn) a chemical reaction in which energy is released to the surroundings as heat

endothermic reaction (EN doh THUHR mik ree AK shuhn) a chemical reaction that requires energy input

Reactions that release energy are exothermic.

In the reaction between isooctane and oxygen, the amount of energy released as the products form is greater than the amount of energy absorbed to break the bonds in the reactants. This reaction is an **exothermic reaction,** a chemical reaction in which energy is released to the surroundings as heat. The released energy comes from the chemical energy of the reactants. All combustion reactions are exothermic.

Figure 4 shows an energy diagram for an exothermic reaction. This diagram shows what happens to the chemical energy in an exothermic reaction. In all exothermic reactions, the products have less energy than the reactants.

Reactions that absorb energy are endothermic.

If you put hydrated barium hydroxide and ammonium nitrate in a flask, the reaction between them takes so much energy from the surroundings that water in the air will condense and then freeze on the surface of the flask. This reaction is an **endothermic reaction,** a chemical reaction in which more energy is needed to break the bonds in the reactants than is given off by forming bonds in the products.

When an endothermic reaction happens, you may be able to notice a drop in temperature. Sometimes, endothermic reactions need more energy than they can get from their surroundings. In those cases, energy must be added as heat to cause the reaction to take place. The changes in chemical energy for an endothermic reaction are shown in an energy diagram in **Figure 4.**

Reading Check What is the difference between an exothermic reaction and an endothermic reaction?

QuickLab

10 min

An Endothermic Reaction

1. Fill a **plastic cup** halfway with **calcium chloride solution,** and use a **thermometer** to measure the temperature of the solution.
2. Carefully add **5 g (1 tsp) of baking soda** to the cup. Record your observations.
3. When the reaction has stopped, record the temperature of the solution.
4. What evidence of an endothermic reaction did you see?

Weird Science

Why It Matters
Bioluminescence

Fireflies are not the only organisms that can make their own light. The fish shown in this photograph, as well as some kinds of bacteria, fungi, squid, and jellyfish, also give off light. This process, called *bioluminescence*, depends on a chemical reaction made possible by the enzyme *luciferase*. Scientists can use bacteria that contain luciferase to track the spread of infection in the human body.

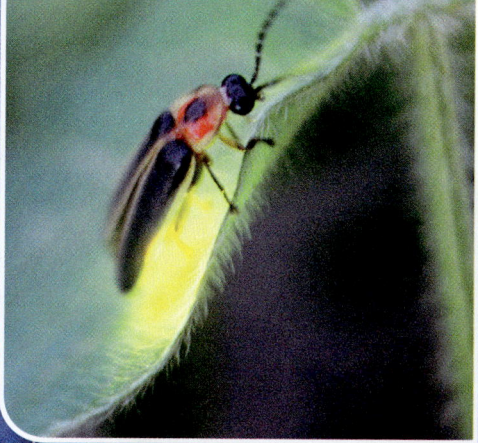

Some living things, such as this firefly, produce light through a chemical process called *bioluminescence*.

The comb jelly (*Mnemiopsis leidyi*) is about 10 cm wide and is native to the Atlantic coast.

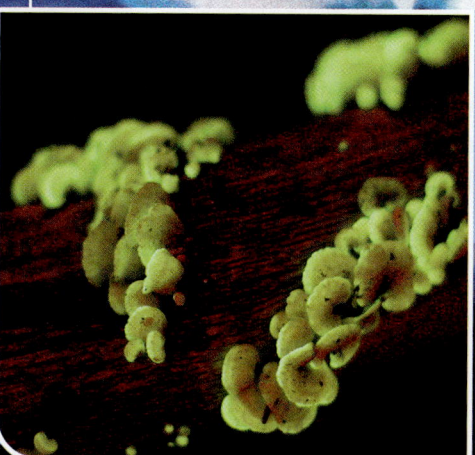

Some kinds of fungi, such as these members of the genus *Armillaria* that are growing on decaying wood, give off bioluminescence.

YOUR TURN

ONLINE RESEARCH

1. Find out more about the chemical process of bioluminescence. Describe one major way in which it differs from most artificial means of light production.

SCILINKS.
www.scilinks.org
Topic: Bioluminescence
Code: HK80156

Photosynthesis is an endothermic reaction.

Photosynthesis, like many reactions in living things, is endothermic. During photosynthesis, plants use energy from light to convert carbon dioxide and water into glucose and oxygen, as **Figure 5** shows. The energy from light is used to form the high-energy bonds that make sugars, from which the plant gets the energy that its cells need. You also get this energy, which originally came from the sun, when you eat fruits or vegetables. Another product of photosynthesis is oxygen, which plants release into the air. You make use of this product of photosynthesis every time you breathe!

Figure 5 Plant cells absorb light energy by photosynthesis and store the energy in the form of sugars.

Section 1 Review

KEY IDEAS

1. **List** three signs that could indicate that a chemical reaction is taking place.
2. **Identify** whether each of the following is a chemical reaction:
   a. melting ice
   b. burning a candle
   c. rusting iron
3. **Predict** which atoms will be found in the products of the following reactions:
   a. Mercury(II) oxide, HgO, is heated and decomposes.
   b. Limestone, $CaCO_3$, reacts with hydrochloric acid, HCl.
   c. Table sugar, $C_{12}H_{22}O_{11}$, burns in air to form caramel.
4. **List** four forms of energy that may be absorbed or released during a chemical reaction.
5. **Classify** each of the following reactions as exothermic or endothermic:
   a. paper burning with a bright flame
   b. plastics becoming brittle after being left in the sun
   c. a firecracker exploding

CRITICAL THINKING

6. **Applying Concepts** Calcium oxide, CaO, is used in cement mixes. When water is added, energy is released as CaO forms calcium hydroxide, $Ca(OH)_2$. What signs indicate a chemical reaction? Draw an energy diagram to represent this reaction. Which has more chemical energy: the reactants or the products?

SECTION 2
Chemical Equations

Key Ideas
› What is a chemical equation?
› What can a balanced chemical equation tell you?

Key Terms
chemical equation
mole ratio

Why It Matters
Chemical reactions are more effective for making the desired products, such as medicines, if the reactants are combined in the correct ratios.

When natural gas burns, methane reacts with oxygen gas to form carbon dioxide and water. Energy is also released as heat and light. You have seen this reaction at home if your kitchen has a gas stove.

Tennessee Course Level Expectations (Physical Science)

CLE.3202.1.9; CLE.3202.Inq.1; CLE.3202.Inq.2; CLE.3202.Inq.3

Describing Reactions

You can describe the reaction between methane and oxygen in many ways, as **Figure 1** shows. One way is to write a word equation. A word equation shows the names of the products and reactants. Another way is to use molecular models, which can be used to show how the atoms are rearranged during the reaction. The clearest way is to write a chemical equation. › **A chemical equation uses symbols to represent a chemical reaction and shows the relationship between the reactants and products of a reaction.**

chemical equation (KEM i kuhl ee KWAY zhuhn) a representation of a chemical reaction that uses symbols to show the relationship between the reactants and the products

Word equation

methane   and   oxygen   yield   carbon dioxide   and   water

Molecular model

 + → +

Chemical equation

CH_4 + $2O_2$ → CO_2 + $2H_2O$

Figure 1 The natural gas that stoves burn is mostly made of the compound methane. Methane burns with oxygen gas to make carbon dioxide and water.

Section 2 Chemical Equations **225**

Chemical equations show products and reactants.

Look at the chemical equation below. The reactants, which are on the left side of the arrow, form the products, which are on the right side of the arrow. In a chemical equation, an arrow pointing to the right (⟶) means "yield," or "give." Chemical equations give chemists all over the world a common way to express chemical reactions, as **Figure 2** shows.

Figure 2 This student is giving a talk on reactions that use copper. You can read the chemical equations even if you cannot read Japanese.

▶ **Chemical equation** | $CH_4 + O_2$ ⟶ $CO_2 + H_2O$
reactants "yield" products

Balanced chemical equations account for the conservation of mass.

As written, the chemical equation above just tells you what compounds are involved in the reaction. When the number of atoms of each element on the right side of the equation matches the number of atoms of each element on the left side, the chemical equation is said to be *balanced*. By accounting for each atom that reacts, a balanced equation follows the law of conservation of mass.

For some of the elements in the equation above, the numbers of atoms on each side do not match. Carbon is balanced because each side of the equation contains one carbon atom. But four hydrogen atoms are on the left, and only two are on the right. Also, two oxygen atoms are on the left, and three are on the right. This cannot be correct, because atoms cannot be created or destroyed in a chemical reaction.

A chemical equation is balanced by adding coefficients in front of one or more of the formulas. A *coefficient* is a number that shows the relative amount of a compound in a reaction. Placing a coefficient of 2 in front of the formula for water means that for each methane molecule that reacted, two water molecules were formed. Thus, all four hydrogen atoms from each methane molecule reacted. Likewise, one must place a 2 in front of the formula for oxygen, one of the reactants.

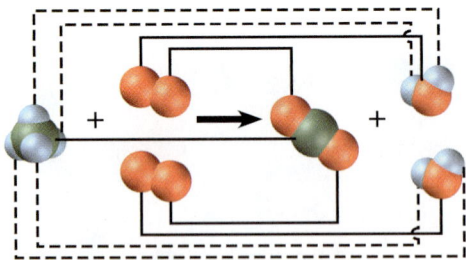

Figure 3 This diagram represents the balanced chemical equation discussed in the text. It shows how the atoms of each element balance. **How many atoms of each element are on each side of the equation?**

▶ **Balanced chemical equation** | $CH_4 + 2O_2 \longrightarrow CO_2 + 2H_2O$

Now, for each element, the number of atoms on one side matches the number of atoms on the other side, so the equation is balanced. **Figure 3** shows how each atom is accounted for on both sides of the above balanced chemical equation.

✓ **Reading Check** Why should chemical equations be balanced?

Math Skills: Balancing Chemical Equations

Write the balanced chemical equation that describes the burning of magnesium in air to form magnesium oxide.

Identify
List the given and unknown values.

Given:
Magnesium and oxygen gas are the reactants that form magnesium oxide, the product.
Unknown:
balanced chemical equation

Plan
Write a word equation for the reaction.

Write the chemical equation by using formulas for the elements and compounds in the word equation.

magnesium + oxygen ⟶ magnesium oxide

Remember that some gaseous elements, such as oxygen, come in molecules of two atoms each. Oxygen in air is O_2.

$Mg + O_2 \longrightarrow MgO$

Solve
Balance the equation one element at a time.

1. **Count the atoms** of each element on each side. There are fewer oxygen atoms in the products than there are in the reactants.

Reactants	Products
$Mg + O_2 \longrightarrow$	MgO
$Mg = 1$ $O = 2$	$Mg = 1$ $O = 1$

2. **To balance the oxygen atoms,** place the coefficient 2 in front of MgO. But now too few magnesium atoms are in the reactants.

Reactants	Products
$Mg + O_2 \longrightarrow$	$2MgO$
$Mg = 1$ $O = 2$	$Mg = 2$ $O = 2$

3. **To balance the magnesium atoms,** place the coefficient 2 in front of Mg. Now, for each element, the number of atoms on each side is the same.

Reactants	Products
$2Mg + O_2 \longrightarrow$	$2MgO$
$Mg = 2$ $O = 2$	$Mg = 2$ $O = 2$

Practice

1. Hydrogen peroxide, H_2O_2, decomposes to give water and oxygen. Write a balanced equation for the decomposition reaction.
2. In a double-displacement reaction, sodium sulfide, Na_2S, reacts with silver nitrate, $AgNO_3$, to form sodium nitrate, $NaNO_3$, and silver sulfide, Ag_2S. Balance this equation.

For more practice, visit **go.hrw.com** and enter keyword **HK8MP**.

Practice Hint

› You cannot balance a chemical equation by changing the subscripts within a chemical formula. Changing a formula would indicate that a different substance participates in the reaction. An equation can be balanced only by putting coefficients in front of the chemical formulas.

› Sometimes, changing the coefficients to balance one element may cause another element in the equation to become unbalanced. So, check your work to ensure that all elements are balanced.

QuickLab: Balancing Chemical Equations

Procedure

1. Use **toothpicks** and **gumdrops of at least three different colors** (representing atoms of different elements) to make models of the reactants in each of the following chemical equations:
   a. $H_2 + Cl_2 \longrightarrow HCl$
   b. $Ca + H_2O \longrightarrow Ca(OH)_2 + H_2$
   c. $C_2H_6 + O_2 \longrightarrow CO_2 + H_2O$

2. Rearrange the "atoms" of the reactants to form the products. (You may need different proportions of some of the reactant compounds.)

Analysis

1. On the basis of your experiment with the gumdrops and toothpicks, balance each of the chemical equations shown in step 1 of the Procedure.

Balanced Equations and Mole Ratios

Other ways of looking at the amounts in a chemical reaction are shown in **Figure 4**. Notice that the numbers of magnesium and oxygen atoms in the product equal the numbers of magnesium and oxygen atoms in the reactants.

▶ **A balanced equation tells you the mole ratio, or proportion of reactants and products, in a chemical reaction.** The balanced equation tells you that for every 2 mol of magnesium, 1 mol of oxygen is needed. So, if you want 4 mol of magnesium to react, you will need 2 mol of oxygen. No matter how much magnesium and oxygen are combined or how the magnesium oxide is made, the balanced equation does not change. This follows *the law of definite proportions*.

READING TOOLBOX

Table Fold
Make a Table Fold, and write the names for the parts of a chemical equation along the top row. Fill in the columns with the information that is given by each part of a chemical equation.

▶ Law of definite proportions	A compound always contains the same elements in the same proportions regardless of how the compound is made or how much of the compound is formed.

Figure 4 Information from a Balanced Equation

Equation:	2Mg	+	O_2	→	2MgO
Amount (mol)	2		1	→	2
Molar mass (g/mol)	24.3		32.0	→	40.3
Mass calculation	24.3 g/mol × 2 mol		32.0 g/mol × 1 mol	→	40.3 g/mol × 2 mol
Mass (g)	48.6		32.0	→	80.6
Model					

Mole ratios tell you the relative amounts of reactants and products.

The mole ratio of magnesium to oxygen in the reaction shown in **Figure 4** is 2:1. Thus, for every 2 mol of magnesium that reacts, 1 mol of oxygen will also react. If 4 mol of magnesium is present, 2 mol of oxygen is needed to react. This is a ratio of 4:2, which is the same as 2:1.

In the following equation for the electrolysis of water, the mole ratio for $H_2O:H_2:O_2$, according to the coefficients from the balanced equation, is 2:2:1.

$$2H_2O \longrightarrow 2H_2 + O_2$$

There are twice as many molecules of hydrogen gas produced in this reaction as there are molecules of oxygen gas. Thus, as **Figure 5** shows, the hydrogen gas produced in this reaction takes up twice as much space as the oxygen gas does.

Mole ratios can be converted to masses.

If you know the mole ratios of the substances in a reaction, you can determine the relative masses of the substances needed to react completely. Simply multiply the molecular mass of each substance by the mole ratio from the balanced equation.

For example, for the reaction shown in **Figure 4**, the molar mass of magnesium, 24.3 g/mol, is multiplied by 2 mol to get a total mass of 48.6 g for the magnesium. The molar mass of molecular oxygen, 32.0 g/mol, is multiplied by 1 mol. So, for the magnesium to react completely with oxygen, there must be 32.0 g of oxygen available for every 48.6 g of magnesium.

mole ratio (MOHL RAY shee OH) the relative number of moles of the substances required to produce a given amount of product in a chemical reaction

Figure 5 Electrical energy causes water to decompose into oxygen (in the test tube on the left) and hydrogen (on the right).

Section 2 Review

KEY IDEAS

1. **Identify** which of the following is a complete and balanced chemical equation:
   a. $H_2O \longrightarrow H_2 + O_2$
   b. $NaCl + H_2O$
   c. $Fe + S \longrightarrow FeS$
   d. $CaCO_3$

2. **Determine** balanced chemical equations for the following chemical reactions:
   a. $KOH + HCl \longrightarrow KCl + H_2O$
   b. $NaHCO_3 \longrightarrow H_2O + CO_2 + Na_2CO_3$
   c. $Pb(NO_3)_2 + KI \longrightarrow KNO_3 + PbI_2$

3. **Explain** why balancing an equation requires changing the coefficients in front of chemical formulas rather than the subscripts within chemical formulas.

4. **Describe** the information needed to calculate the mass of a reactant or product for the following balanced equation:

$$FeS + 2HCl \longrightarrow H_2S + FeCl_2$$

CRITICAL THINKING

5. **Applying Concepts** Chlorine gas is produced by the electrolysis of sodium chloride in water in the following reaction:

$$2NaCl + 2H_2O \longrightarrow Cl_2 + H_2 + 2NaOH$$

What mass of sodium chloride is needed to make 71 g of chlorine gas?

SECTION 3
Reaction Types

Key Ideas

> How does learning about reaction types help in understanding chemical reactions?

> In which kinds of chemical reactions do the numbers of electrons in atoms change?

Key Terms

synthesis reaction
decomposition reaction
combustion reaction
single-displacement reaction
double-displacement reaction
free radical
oxidation-reduction reaction

Why It Matters

Chemical reactions can create ozone (sometimes where ozone is not healthy) and can destroy ozone (sometimes where ozone is needed).

Tennessee Course Level Expectations (Physical Science)
CLE.3202.Inq.1; CLE.3202.Inq.2; CLE.3202.Inq.3

In the last section, you saw what a chemical equation is and what it can tell you. Now that you are familiar with chemical equations, you will learn about the kinds of reactions that can be expressed by a chemical equation.

Classifying Reactions

Even though there are millions of unique substances and millions of possible reactions, there are only a few general kinds of reactions. You have learned how to follow patterns to name compounds. ❯ **You also can use patterns to identify kinds of chemical reactions and to predict the products of the chemical reactions.** For example, look at the long molecule shown in **Figure 1**. A certain kind of reaction joins many small molecules to form a much larger molecule. Recognizing this kind of reaction can help you predict the products that the reaction will form.

Figure 1 Polyethene is used to make many kinds of plastics. A molecule of polyethene is made up of as many as 3,500 units of ethene.

Synthesis reactions combine substances.

Polyethene, shown in **Figure 1**, is a plastic that is often used to make trash bags and soda bottles. It is produced by polymerization, one kind of synthesis reaction. A **synthesis reaction** is a reaction in which multiple substances combine to form a new compound. In polymerization reactions, many small molecules join together in chains to make larger structures called *polymers*. Polyethene is a polymer made up of repeating ethene molecules.

Hydrogen gas reacts with oxygen gas to form water. In a synthesis reaction, at least two reactants join to form a product. Synthesis reactions have the following general form.

▶ **Synthesis reaction** $A + B \longrightarrow AB$

In the synthesis reaction below, the metal sodium reacts with chlorine gas to form sodium chloride, or table salt.

$$2Na + Cl_2 \longrightarrow 2NaCl$$

Because a synthesis reaction joins substances, the product of such a reaction is a compound that is more complex than the reactants.

Decomposition reactions break substances apart.

Digestion is a series of reactions that break down complex foods into simple fuels that the body can use. A kind of reaction known as *cracking* is similar to digestion. In cracking, large molecules made of carbon and hydrogen within crude oil are broken down to make gasoline and other products, such as the ones shown in **Figure 2**. Digestion and cracking oil are **decomposition reactions**, reactions in which substances are broken apart. The general form for decomposition reactions is as follows.

▶ **Decomposition reaction** $AB \longrightarrow A + B$

The following shows the decomposition of water.

$$2H_2O \longrightarrow 2H_2 + O_2$$

The *electrolysis* of water is a simple decomposition reaction. Water breaks down into hydrogen gas and oxygen gas when there is an electric current in the water.

✓ **Reading Check** How do decomposition reactions compare with synthesis reactions?

www.scilinks.org
Topic: Types of Reactions
Code: HK81570

synthesis reaction (SIN thuh sis ree AK shuhn) reaction in which two or more substances combine to form a new compound

decomposition reaction (DEE kahm puh ZISH uhn ree AK shuhn) a reaction in which a single compound breaks down to form two or more simpler substances

Figure 2 Crude oil is broken down in decomposition reactions to form plastics, which can be made into many kinds of products.

www.scilinks.org
Topic: Combustion
Code: HK80315

Academic Vocabulary
undergo (UHN duhr GOH) to go through

Combustion reactions use oxygen as a reactant.

Methane forms carbon dioxide and water during combustion. Oxygen is a reactant in every **combustion reaction,** so at least one product of such a reaction will contain atoms of oxygen. Water is a common product of combustion reactions.

$$CH_4 + 2O_2 \longrightarrow CO_2 + 2H_2O$$

Other carbon compounds, such as those in gasoline and wax, undergo combustion reactions similar to the one above.

When there is not enough oxygen during a combustion reaction, not all fuels are converted completely into carbon dioxide. In that case, some carbon monoxide may form. Carbon monoxide, CO, is a poisonous gas that lowers the ability of the blood to carry oxygen. Carbon monoxide has no color or odor, so you cannot tell when it is present. In some combustion reactions, you can tell if the air supply is limited because the excess carbon is given off as small particles that make a dark, sooty smoke.

Why It Matters

How Are Fires Extinguished?

REAL WORLD

A fire is a combustion reaction in progress that is sped up by high temperatures. Three things are needed for a combustion reaction to occur: a fuel, some oxygen, and an ignition source. If any of these items is absent, combustion cannot occur. So, the goal of firefighting is to remove one or more of these items. Fire extinguishers are effective in firefighting because they separate the fuel from the surrounding air, which is the source of the fire's oxygen supply.

A fire is classified by the type of fuel that combusts to produce the fire. The type of fire extinguisher that is needed depends on the class of fire. Most fire extinguishers are of the "ABC" type, which can put out any of three classes of fires. Type A fires involve solid fuels; type B fires, flammable liquids; and type C fires, "live" electric circuits.

YOUR TURN

UNDERSTANDING CONCEPTS
1. How does a fire extinguisher stop a combustion reaction?

ONLINE RESEARCH
2. What classes of fire extinguishers other than the ones mentioned here are used in the United States? What kinds of fires are they designed to put out?

In single-displacement reactions, elements trade places.

Copper(II) chloride dissolves in water to make a bright blue solution. If you add a piece of aluminum foil to the solution, the color goes away and clumps of reddish brown material form. The reddish brown clumps are copper metal. Aluminum replaces copper in the copper(II) chloride to form aluminum chloride. Aluminum chloride does not make a colored solution, so the blue color goes away as the amount of blue copper(II) chloride decreases, as shown in **Figure 3.**

The copper(II) ions, as part of copper(II) chloride, become neutral copper metal. The aluminum metal atoms become aluminum ions. The chloride ions remain the same. Because the atoms of one element appear to move into a compound and atoms of the other element appear to move out, this reaction is called a **single-displacement reaction.** Single-displacement reactions have the following general form.

> **Single-displacement reaction** $AX + B \longrightarrow BX + A$

The equation for the single-displacement reaction between copper(II) chloride and aluminum is as follows.

$$3CuCl_2 + 2Al \longrightarrow 2AlCl_3 + 3Cu$$

In general, a more reactive element will take the place of a less reactive one in a single-displacement reaction.

Reading Check What do all single-displacement reactions have in common?

READING TOOLBOX

Reading Equations
Pick out some of the chemical equations given in this section, and practice saying them aloud and writing them in the form of sentences.

combustion reaction (kuhm BUHS chuhn ree AK shuhn) the oxidation reaction of an organic compound, in which heat is released

single-displacement reaction (SING guhl dis PLAYS muhnt ree AK shuhn) a reaction in which one element or radical takes the place of another element or radical in a compound

Figure 3 Aluminum undergoes a single-displacement reaction with copper(II) chloride to form copper and aluminum chloride.

$$3CuCl_2 + 2Al \longrightarrow 2AlCl_3 + 3Cu$$

Copper ion, Cu^{2+}

Aluminum atom

Water molecule

Chloride ion, Cl^-

Aluminum ion, Al^{3+}

Copper atom

Section 3 Reaction Types **233**

Potassium 2K · Water 2H₂O · Potassium hydroxide 2KOH · Hydrogen H₂

Figure 4 Potassium reacts with water in a single-displacement reaction. **Which atoms of the reactants trade places to form the products?**

Keyword: HK8REAF4

Alkali metals undergo single-displacement reactions.

Potassium metal is so reactive that it undergoes a single-displacement reaction with water, as **Figure 4** shows. The potassium and water reaction is so exothermic that the H_2 that is produced may explode and burn instantly. All alkali metals and some other metals undergo similar single-displacement reactions with water. All such reactions form hydrogen gas, metal ions, and hydroxide ions.

In double-displacement reactions, ions appear to be exchanged between compounds.

The yellow lines painted on roads are colored with lead chromate, $PbCrO_4$. This compound can be formed by mixing solutions of lead nitrate, $Pb(NO_3)_2$, and potassium chromate, K_2CrO_4. In solution, these compounds form the ions Pb^{2+}, NO_3^-, K^+, and CrO_4^{2-}. The lead ions and chromate ions are more attracted to one another than they are to the water molecules around them. Therefore, when the solutions are mixed, a yellow lead chromate compound forms, and settles to the bottom of the container. This reaction is a **double-displacement reaction,** a reaction in which two compounds appear to exchange ions. The general form of a double-displacement reaction appears below.

> **Double-displacement reaction** : $AX + BY \longrightarrow AY + BX$

The double-displacement reaction that forms lead chromate is as follows.

$$Pb(NO_3)_2 + K_2CrO_4 \longrightarrow PbCrO_4 + 2KNO_3$$

The lead and chromate ions form a compound. Potassium and nitrate ions are soluble together in water, so they do not form a compound. Instead, they stay in solution just as the lead and nitrate ions were before the reaction.

InquiryLab

Determining the Products of a Reaction

⏱ 20 min

Procedure

CAUTION: Wear safety goggles and an apron. Silver nitrate will stain your skin and clothes.

1. With a **wax pencil,** label **three test tubes** "NaCl," "KBr," and "KI."

2. Using a **10 mL graduated cylinder,** measure **5 mL each of sodium chloride, potassium bromide,** and **potassium iodide solutions** into the appropriate test tubes. Rinse the graduated cylinder between each use.

3. Add **1 mL of silver nitrate** solution to each of the test tubes. Record your observations.

Analysis

1. What sign of a reaction did you observe?
2. Identify the reactants and products for each reaction.
3. Write the balanced equation for each reaction.
4. Which ion(s) produced a solid with silver nitrate?
5. Does this test let you identify all the ions? Why or why not?

Electrons and Chemical Reactions

The general classes of reactions described earlier in this section were used by early chemists, who knew nothing about the parts of the atom. After chemists learned about the presence of electrons in atoms, they developed another way to classify reactions. ❯ **Free-radical reactions and redox reactions can be understood as changes in the numbers of electrons that atoms have.**

Free radicals have electrons available for bonding.

Many synthetic fibers, as well as plastic bags and wraps, are made by polymerization reactions, which were discussed earlier. Often, these reactions involve free radicals. A **free radical** is an atom or a group of atoms that has one unpaired electron.

Sometimes, a covalent bond is broken such that an unpaired electron is left on each fragment of the molecule. These fragments are free radicals. Because an uncharged hydrogen atom has one electron available for bonding, it is a free radical. Electrons tend to form pairs with other electrons. So, free radicals react quickly to form covalent bonds with other substances. As a result, new compounds are made. Some free-radical reactions are very important in the environment.

✓ **Reading Check** Why are free radicals so reactive?

---

double-displacement reaction (DUHB uhl dis PLAYS muhnt ree AK shuhn) a reaction in which a gas, a solid precipitate, or a molecular compound forms from the apparent exchange of atoms or ions between two compounds

free radical (FREE RAD i kuhl) an atom or a group of atoms that has one unpaired electron

Why It Matters

Ozone

Ozone is a form of oxygen, but it consists of molecules of O_3 rather than O_2, the oxygen we breathe. When the sun's radiation strikes oxygen molecules in the upper atmosphere, some of them break apart into free radicals. The oxygen radicals react with other oxygen molecules to form the *ozone layer* in the upper atmosphere. Because of its unique properties, ozone is able to absorb much of the sun's radiation and protect Earth's surface. But ozone in the lower atmosphere, created by incomplete combustion, contributes to smog.

EYE ON THE ENVIRONMENT

These diagrams show the ozone layer at different times. Certain chemical byproducts, especially chlorofluorocarbons (CFCs), can destroy large amounts of the ozone layer. Such chemicals play a major role in the gradual depletion of the ozone layer that is shown below. CFCs were banned by most countries many years ago, but CFCs can continue to destroy ozone for a long time after they enter the atmosphere.

YOUR TURN

UNDERSTANDING CONCEPTS

1. Explain how ozone is helpful in the upper atmosphere but harmful in the lower atmosphere.

Electrons are transferred in redox reactions.

A very common type of reaction involves the transfer of electrons. The formation of rust is an example of such a reaction. In the presence of water, atoms of iron metal, Fe, react with oxygen molecules, O_2, to form rust, Fe_2O_3. Each iron atom loses three electrons to form Fe^{3+} ions, and each oxygen atom gains two electrons to form O^{2-} ions.

Substances that accept electrons are said to be *reduced*. Substances that give up electrons are said to be *oxidized*. One way to remember which term is which is that the gain of electrons reduces the positive charge on an ion or makes an uncharged atom become a negative ion. Whenever reduction happens, oxidation happens, too. The reverse is also true. Reactions in which one substance loses electrons and another substance gains electrons are called **oxidation-reduction reactions.** These reactions are called *redox reactions* for short.

Some redox reactions do not involve ions. In these reactions, oxidation is a gain of oxygen or a loss of hydrogen, and reduction is the loss of oxygen or the gain of hydrogen. Respiration and combustion are redox reactions because oxygen gas reacts with carbon compounds to form carbon dioxide. Carbon atoms in CO_2 are oxidized, and oxygen atoms in O_2 are reduced. Scientists knew about redox reactions before they knew about electrons. They now know that oxidation does not necessarily require oxygen. But they still use the name *oxidation* to describe any reaction in which an atom loses electrons.

oxidation-reduction reaction (AHKS i DAY shuhn ri DUHK shuhn ree AK shuhn) any chemical change in which one species is oxidized (loses electrons) and another species is reduced (gains electrons); also called *redox reaction*

Integrating Fine Arts

Redox Reactions and the Statue of Liberty Metal sculptures often corrode because of redox reactions. The Statue of Liberty, which is covered with 200,000 pounds of copper, was as bright as a new penny when it was first built. However, after more than 100 years, the statue had turned green. The copper reacted with the damp air of New York harbor. More important, oxidation reactions between the damp, salty air and the internal iron supports made the structure dangerously weak. The statue was closed for several years in the 1980s while the supports were cleaned and repaired.

Section 3 Review

KEY IDEAS

1. **Classify** each of the following reactions by type:
   a. $S_8 + 8O_2 \rightarrow 8SO_2 + $ energy
   b. $6CO_2 + 6H_2O \rightarrow C_6H_{12}O_6 + 6O_2$
   c. $2NaHCO_3 \rightarrow Na_2CO_3 + H_2O + CO_2$
   d. $Zn + 2HCl \rightarrow ZnCl_2 + H_2$
2. **List** three possible results of a double-displacement reaction.
3. **Define** *free radical*.
4. **Identify** which element is oxidized and which element is reduced in the following reaction:
$$Zn + CuSO_4 \rightarrow ZnSO_4 + Cu$$

CRITICAL THINKING

5. **Predicting Consequences** Explain why charcoal grills or charcoal fires should not be used to heat the inside of a house. (Hint: When it is cold, doors and windows are closed, so there is little fresh air.)
6. **Compare and Contrast** Compare and contrast single-displacement and double-displacement reactions based on the number of reactants. Use the terms *compound*, *atom* or *element*, and *ion*.
7. **Analyzing Ideas** Describe how a polymer is made, and explain how this process is an example of a synthesis reaction.
8. **Analyzing Processes** Explain why a reduction must take place whenever oxidation occurs.

SECTION 4
Reaction Rates and Equilibrium

Key Ideas

› What kinds of things speed up a reaction?
› What does a catalyst do?
› What happens when a reaction goes backward as well as forward?

Key Terms

catalyst
enzyme
substrate
chemical equilibrium

Why It Matters

By raising some reaction rates in the body, a fever can help a person recover from an illness.

> **Tennessee Course Level Expectations (Physical Science)**
> CLE.3202.1.9; CLE.3202.Inq.1; CLE.3202.Inq.2; CLE.3202.Inq.3; CLE.3202.Inq.4; CLE.3202.Inq.6

Chemical reactions can occur at different rates, or speeds. Some reactions, such as the explosion of nitroglycerin, shown in **Figure 1**, are very fast. Other reactions, such as the burning of carbon in charcoal, are much slower. But what happens if you slow down the nitroglycerin reaction to make it safer? What happens if you speed up the reaction by which yeast makes carbon dioxide in order to make bread rise in less time? If you think carefully, you may realize that you already know some ways to change reaction rates. In fact, you may use the factors that affect reaction rates every day.

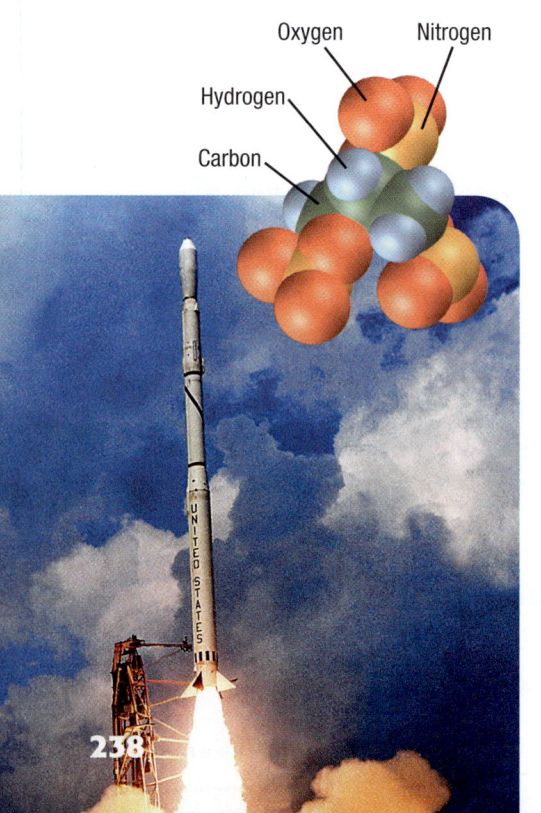

Figure 1 Nitroglycerin, which is used as a rocket fuel, reacts very quickly.

Factors Affecting Reaction Rates

Think about the following observations:

- A potato slice takes 5 minutes to cook at 200 °C but takes 10 minutes to cook at 100 °C. Therefore, potatoes cook faster at higher temperatures.

- Potato slices take 10 minutes to cook, but whole potatoes take about 30 minutes to cook. Therefore, potatoes cut into smaller pieces cook faster.

These observations have to do with the speed of chemical reactions. In each situation in which the potatoes cooked faster, the contact between particles was greater, so the cooking reaction went faster. This relationship reflects a general principle. ›**Anything that increases contact between particles will increase the rate of a reaction.** Factors that affect the rate of a reaction include temperature, surface area, concentration, and pressure.

Most reactions go faster at higher temperatures.

Heating food starts the chemical reactions that happen in cooking. Cooking at higher temperatures cooks food faster. Cooling food slows down the chemical reactions that result in spoiling, as shown in **Figure 2**. Particles move faster at higher temperatures. Faster-moving particles collide more often, so there are more chances for the particles to react. Therefore, reactions are faster at higher temperatures.

A large surface area speeds up reactions.

When a whole potato is placed in boiling water, only its surface touches the boiling water. The energy from the water has to go all the way through the potato. Cutting a potato into pieces exposes inner parts of the potato. Increasing the *surface area* of a reactant in this way speeds up a reaction.

Higher concentrations of reactants react faster.

Imagine building a bonfire. As you read above, a high temperature will get a reaction going. In this case, the energy released in the reaction also keeps the fire going. Small pieces of wood burn faster than thick logs because small pieces have more surface area. Increasing the concentration of the reactants also speeds up a reaction. So, another thing you can do to get a fire blazing is to put plenty of wood on it!

✓ **Reading Check** Why are reactions at high temperatures faster than at low temperatures?

Figure 2 Mold will grow on bread stored at room temperature. Bread stored in the freezer for the same length of time will be free of mold when you take the bread out of the freezer.

Bread stored at room temperature

Bread stored in the freezer

Inquiry Lab

What Affects the Rates of Chemical Reactions?

⏱ 30 min

Procedure

1. Using **tongs**, hold a **paper clip** in the hottest part of a **burner** flame for 30 s. Repeat with a **ball of steel wool**. Record your observations.

2. Label **three test tubes** "A," "B," and "C." Put **10 mL of vinegar** into test tube A, **5 mL of vinegar** and **5 mL of water** into test tube B, and **2.5 mL of vinegar** and **7.5 mL of water** into test tube C. Add a piece of **magnesium ribbon** to each test tube. Record your observations.

3. Label **three more test tubes** "1," "2," and "3." Put **5 mL of vinegar** and **5 mL of water** into each test tube. Submerge the solution in test tube 1 in a **small beaker of ice-cold water.** Submerge the solution in test tube 3 in a **small beaker of hot water.** Add a piece of **magnesium ribbon** to the test tubes. Record your observations.

Analysis

1. Describe and interpret your results. For each step, list the factor(s) that influenced the rate of reaction.

Section 4 Reaction Rates and Equilibrium

Topic: Catalysts
Code: HK80231

catalyst (KAT uh LIST) a substance that changes the rate of a chemical reaction without being consumed or changed significantly

enzyme (EN ZIEM) a molecule, either protein or RNA, that acts as a catalyst in biochemical reactions

substrate (SUHB STRAYT) the reactant in reactions catalyzed by enzymes

Reactions are faster at higher pressure.

The *concentration* of a gas is the number of particles in a certain volume. A gas at high pressure has a higher concentration than the same amount of the gas at a low pressure. The reason is that the gas at high pressure has been squeezed into a smaller space. Gases react faster at higher pressures. When the particles of a gas have less space in which to move, they have more collisions and thus more reactions.

Massive, bulky molecules react more slowly.

The mass of the reactant molecules affects the rate of the reaction. According to the kinetic theory of matter, massive molecules move more slowly than less massive molecules at the same temperature. So, for equal numbers of molecules whose masses differ but whose sizes are similar, the molecules that have more mass collide less often with other molecules.

The size and shape of reactant molecules also affect how fast the molecules react. Large, bulky molecules usually must be in a certain position relative to other molecules to react with the other molecules. Because of their size and their number of branching or bulky parts, large and bulky molecules may not reach the right position. Thus, these molecules tend not to react as readily as small and simple ones.

Catalysts

Why would one add a substance to a reaction if that substance may not react? One reason is to increase the rate of the reaction. A substance that changes the rate of a reaction is called a **catalyst**. ▶ **A catalyst speeds up or slows down a reaction but is not changed by the reaction.** Substances that slow reactions are also called *inhibitors*. Catalysts are used in various industries. For example, they are used to help make ammonia, to process crude oil, and to make plastics. Catalysts can be expensive yet profitable to use because they can be cleaned or renewed and reused. Sometimes, the presence of a catalyst is shown by writing the name of the catalyst over the reaction arrow of a chemical equation.

Catalysts work in various ways. Most solid catalysts, such as the ones in car exhaust systems, speed up reactions by providing a surface where the reactants can collect and react. Then, the reactants can form new bonds to make the products. Most solid catalysts are more effective if they have a large surface area, such as the area of the honeycomb-like metal surface of the catalytic converter in **Figure 3**.

Figure 3 An automobile's catalytic converter reduces pollution by helping pollutant molecules react to form harmless substances.

A metal surface, such as platinum or palladium, can act as a catalyst.

Enzymes are biological catalysts.

Enzymes are catalysts for chemical reactions in living things. Enzymes have very specific purposes. Each enzyme controls one reaction or one set of similar reactions. **Figure 4** lists some common enzymes and the reactions that they control. Most enzymes are fragile. If kept too cold or too warm, they tend to fall apart. Most stop working above about 45 °C.

Catalase, an enzyme in the cells of humans and most other living organisms, breaks down hydrogen peroxide. Hydrogen peroxide is the substrate for catalase. A **substrate** is the reactant that is catalyzed, or acted upon, by an enzyme.

$$2H_2O_2 \longrightarrow 2H_2O + O_2$$

For an enzyme to catalyze a reaction, the substrate and the enzyme must fit like a key in a lock. The location on the enzyme where the substrate fits is called the *active site*, as shown in **Figure 4.** The active site of an enzyme is suited for the particular shape of the substrate and the catalyzed reaction.

Enzymes are very efficient. In 1 min, one molecule of catalase can catalyze the decomposition of 6 million molecules of hydrogen peroxide. Without the enzyme, the reaction would go much more slowly.

Reading Check What does an enzyme do?

QuickLab 20 min

Catalysts in Action

1. Pour **2% hydrogen peroxide** into a **test tube** to a depth of 2 cm.
2. Pour **water** into **another test tube** to a depth of 2 cm.
3. Drop a **small piece of raw liver** into each test tube.
4. Liver contains the enzyme catalase. Watch carefully, and describe what happens. Explain your observations.
5. Using **a piece of liver that has been boiled for 3 min,** repeat steps 1–4. Explain your result.
6. Using **iron filings** instead of liver, repeat steps 1–4 one more time. What happens?
7. Describe some principles of catalysts that you observed in this experiment.

Common Enzymes and Their Uses

Enzyme	Substrate	Role of the enzyme
Amylase	starch	to break down starch into smaller molecules
Cellulase	cellulose	to break down long cellulose molecules into sugars
DNA polymerase	nucleic acid	to build up DNA chains in cell nuclei
Lipase	fat	to break down fat into smaller molecules
Protease	protein	to break down proteins into amino acids

Figure 4 Each enzymes has a specific fit with its substrate. The substrate fits into the enzyme's active site, and then undergoes a particular reaction.

Enzymes have an active site that fits a particular substrate.

The enzyme catalyzes a reaction that the substrate undergoes.

The substrate then leaves the active site, and another substrate takes its place.

Why It Matters

What Kinds of Chemical Reactions Happen in the Human Body?

Chemical reactions happen everywhere in the human body. *Metabolism* is the sum of all of the chemical reactions that occur within an organism. Metabolic reactions are classified into two types. *Catabolic reactions* break down complex molecules into simpler ones and yield energy. *Anabolic reactions* use the energy to build complex molecules from simpler ones.

❶ During digestion, a number of chemical reactions occur. First, decomposition reactions, many of which are catalyzed by enzymes, break down food into smaller molecules. Hydrochloric acid in the stomach breaks down proteins into amino acids. In the small intestine, enzymes from the pancreas break down carbohydrates and fats. Carbohydrates break down into simple sugars, such as glucose. Bile from the liver helps break down fats.

REAL WORLD

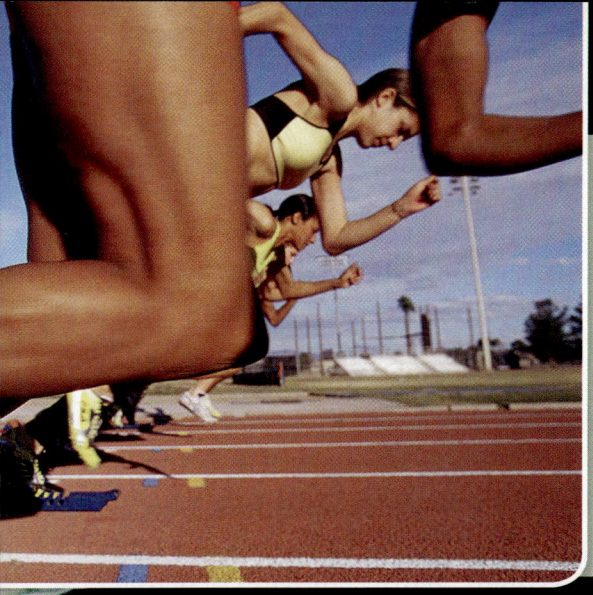

❸ A molecule called *ATP* provides energy for your cells. For example, your muscle cells need ATP to make your muscles move. *Cellular respiration* refers to the various synthesis reactions that make ATP in your cells. One way of making ATP requires the breakdown of simple sugars that come from the food that you eat. But most ATP is made by a redox reaction that uses the oxygen that you breathe.

❷ There are 20 kinds of amino acids that your body needs. Some amino acids come from proteins broken down in the food you eat. Others are made by your body. Using synthesis reactions, your cells combine amino acids into polymers to create the more than 40,000 kinds of proteins that your body needs. The proteins are used to catalyze chemical reactions in cells and to control cellular processes. For example, the protein hemoglobin, which is found in red blood cells, carries oxygen in your blood to your cells.

YOUR TURN

UNDERSTANDING CONCEPTS

1. Give two examples of decomposition reactions that take place in your body. Then, give two examples of synthesis reactions that take place in your body.

www.scilinks.org
Topic: Chemical Reactions in the Human Body
Code: **HK81696**

Prefixes
Make a table of word parts that includes three of the unfamiliar words in this section, such as *catalyst, enzyme, substrate,* and *equilibrium.*

Equilibrium Systems

Reactions may happen slowly or quickly, but still go in the same direction. ❯ **Some processes, however, may go in both directions, which results in an equilibrium system.** *Equilibrium* can be described as a balance that is reached by two opposing processes.

Some changes are reversible.

Some processes do not reach completion each time they occur. Some are reversible. A reversible physical process is shown in **Figure 5.** Carbonated drinks contain carbon dioxide. These drinks are made by dissolving carbon dioxide in water under pressure. While it is under pressure, carbon dioxide is constantly coming both into and out of solution.

Opening the bottle releases the pressurized air, which makes a hissing sound as it escapes. At this point, the process begins to go in only one direction. The carbon dioxide starts to come out of solution, and a stream of carbon dioxide bubbles appears.

$$CO_2 \text{ (gas above liquid)} \underset{\text{increase pressure}}{\overset{\text{decrease pressure}}{\rightleftarrows}} CO_2 \text{ (gas dissolved in liquid)}$$

This change is reversible, as indicated by the ⇆ sign in the chemical equation. The arrow usually seen in chemical reactions, →, indicates a change that goes in one direction.

✓ **Reading Check** When you open a soda bottle, what change occurs that allows the dissolved carbon dioxide in the soda to come out of solution?

Figure 5 Equilibrium of Gas Dissolved in a Soda Bottle

A bottle of carbonated water with the top on is at equilibrium.

When the top is removed, the carbonated water is no longer at equilibrium.

Equilibrium results when rates balance.

When a carbonated drink is in a closed bottle, you cannot see any changes. The system is in equilibrium—a balanced state. But if you could see individual molecules in the bottle, you would see continuous change. Molecules of CO_2 not only are coming out of solution constantly but also are dissolving back into the liquid at the same rate.

The result is that the amount of dissolved and undissolved CO_2 does not change even though individual CO_2 molecules are moving in and out of the solution. This situation is like the situation in which the number of players on a football field is constant. Although different players can be on the field, there are 11 players from each team on the field at any given time.

Systems in equilibrium respond to minimize change.

Chemical equilibrium is a state in which a reversible chemical reaction is proceeding in both directions equally. No net change happens, but if products or reactants are added or removed, the reaction will start going in one direction more than the other.

The conversion of limestone, $CaCO_3$, to lime, CaO, is a chemical reaction that can lead to equilibrium. Limestone and seashells, which are also made of $CaCO_3$, were used to make lime more than 2,000 years ago. Limestone was heated in an open pot, and the lime produced was used to make cement. The ancient buildings in Greece and Rome, such as the one shown in **Figure 6,** were built with cement that was probably made by the following reaction:

$$CaCO_3 + energy \longrightarrow CaO + CO_2$$

Because the CO_2 gas can escape from an open pot, the reaction continues until all of the limestone reacts. However, if some limestone is sealed in a closed container and heated, the result is different. As soon as some CO_2 builds up in the container, the reverse reaction starts. Once the concentrations of the $CaCO_3$, CaO, and CO_2 stabilize, equilibrium is reached.

$$CaCO_3 \leftrightarrows CaO + CO_2$$

If the pressure or temperature does not change, the forward and reverse reactions take place at the same rate. As in the case of the carbonated drink, this equilibrium is reached because the products are not allowed to escape. Once some CO_2 is allowed to escape, the forward reaction goes faster until the forward and reverse reactions are happening at the same rate again. So, a system in equilibrium responds to change by doing whatever is required to go back to an equilibrium state.

Academic Vocabulary

continuous (kuhn TIN yoo uhs) going on without stopping

chemical equilibrium (KEM i kuhl EE kwi LIB ree uhm) a state of balance in which the rate of a forward reaction equals the rate of the reverse reaction and the concentrations of products and reactants remain unchanged

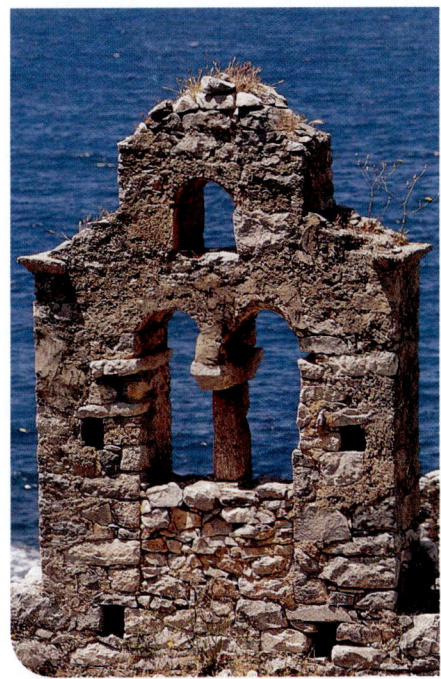

Figure 6 Cement in ancient buildings, such as this one in Limeni, Greece, contains lime that came from seashells.

Figure 7 The Effects of Change on Equilibrium

Condition	Effect
Temperature	Increasing temperature favors the reaction that absorbs energy.
Pressure	Increasing pressure favors the reaction that produces fewer molecules of gas.
Concentration	Increasing the concentration of one substance favors the reaction that produces less of that substance.

Integrating Biology

The Nitrogen Cycle All living things need nitrogen, which cycles through the environment. Nitrogen gas, N_2, is changed to ammonia by bacteria in the soil. Different bacteria in the soil change the ammonia to nitrites and nitrates. Plants need nitrogen in the form of nitrates to grow. Animals eat the plants and deposit nitrogen compounds back in the soil. When plants or animals die, nitrogen compounds are also returned to the soil. Additional bacteria change the nitrogen compounds back to nitrogen gas, and the cycle can start again.

Le Châtelier's principle predicts changes in equilibrium.

Le Châtelier's principle is a general rule that describes how equilibrium systems respond to change.

> **Le Châtelier's principle** If a change is made to a system in chemical equilibrium, the equilibrium shifts to oppose the change until a new equilibrium is reached.

The effects of various changes on an equilibrium system are listed in **Figure 7.**

Ammonia is a chemical building block used to make products such as fertilizers, dyes, plastics, cosmetics, cleaning products, and fire retardants, such as the ones being used in **Figure 8.** The Haber process, which is used to make ammonia industrially, is shown below.

$$\text{nitrogen and hydrogen} \rightleftarrows \text{ammonia and energy}$$
$$N_2(\text{gas}) + 3H_2(\text{gas}) \rightleftarrows 2NH_3(\text{gas}) + \text{energy}$$

At an ammonia-manufacturing plant, chemists must choose the conditions that favor the highest yield of ammonia gas, NH_3. In other words, the conditions of the chemical reaction need to be engineered such that the equilibrium favors the production of NH_3.

Figure 8 Ammonium sulfate and ammonium phosphate are being dropped from the airplane as fire retardants. The red dye that is used for identification fades away after a few days.

Ammonium sulfate, $(NH_4)_2SO_4$

Le Châtelier's principle can be used to control reactions.

A manufacturing plant that uses the Haber process to make ammonia is shown in **Figure 9**. The Haber process is one of the most important industrial reactions. Its invention about 100 years ago led to the ability to produce large amounts of artificial fertilizer, which is made from ammonia. A large percentage of the world's population today is fed by food grown with such artificial fertilizer. Many other important products are made from ammonia. It is estimated that 1% of the entire world's energy output is used to make ammonia by the Haber process!

The Haber process is a good example of balancing equilibrium conditions to make the most product. If you raise the temperature during the Haber process, Le Châtelier's principle predicts that the equilibrium will shift to the left, the process in which energy is absorbed and less ammonia is made. If you raise the pressure, the equilibrium will move to reduce the pressure, according to Le Châtelier's principle. One way to reduce the pressure is to decrease the number of gas molecules. As a result, the equilibrium moves to the right—more ammonia—because fewer gas molecules are on the right. So, getting the most ammonia requires running the reaction at a high pressure and a low temperature.

Figure 9 The Haber process is used to make ammonia in huge quantities in plants like this one.

Section 4 Review

KEY IDEAS

1. **State** one thing that must be done to particles in a chemical reaction to increase the reaction rate.
2. **List** five factors that may affect the rate of a chemical reaction.
3. **Compare** a catalyst and an inhibitor.
4. **Determine** which way an increase in pressure will shift the following equilibrium system: $2C_2H_6(gas) + 7O_2(gas) \leftrightarrows 6H_2O(liquid) + 4CO_2(gas)$.
5. **Describe** the effect of the changes below on the system in which the following reversible reaction is taking place: $4HCl(gas) + O_2(gas) \leftrightarrows 2Cl_2(gas) + 2H_2O(gas)$ + energy.
   a. The pressure of the system increases.
   b. The pressure of the system decreases.
   c. The concentration of O_2 decreases.
   d. The temperature of the system increases.

CRITICAL THINKING

6. **Applying Concepts** All organisms need a certain amount of heat, which may be obtained from outside the body or generated by the body itself. In terms of chemical reactions, explain why.
7. **Evaluating Assumptions** A person claims that a reaction must have stopped because the overall amounts of reactants and products have not changed. Indicate what might be wrong with this person's reasoning.
8. **Analyzing Processes** Consider the decomposition of solid calcium carbonate to solid calcium oxide and carbon dioxide gas.

   $CaCO_3$ + energy $\leftrightarrows$ $CaO + CO_2(gas)$

   What conditions of temperature and pressure would result in the most decomposition of $CaCO_3$? Explain your answer.

Inquiry Lab

 50 min

Rate and Temperature of a Chemical Reaction

Many factors can influence the rate of a chemical reaction. In this lab, you will investigate how the rate of a chemical reaction varies with temperature.

Asking a Question

How does the rate of a chemical reaction vary with temperature?

Observing the Reaction Between Zinc and Hydrochloric Acid

CAUTION: Wear a lab apron, gloves, and safety goggles for this lab. Do not allow zinc to come in contact with your skin. If the zinc comes in contact with your skin, flush thoroughly with water. Hydrochloric acid can cause severe burns. If you get acid on your skin or clothing, wash it off at the sink while calling to your teacher. If you get acid in your eyes, immediately flush it out at the eyewash station while calling to your teacher. Continue rinsing for at least 15 min or until help arrives.

1. On a blank sheet of paper, prepare a data table like the one shown in this lab activity.

2. Fill a 10 mL graduated cylinder with water. Taking care to keep the cylinder full, turn the cylinder upside down in a beaker of water. Place one end of the rubber tubing under the spout of the graduated cylinder. Attach the other end of the tubing to the arm of one of the flasks. Place the flask in a water bath at room temperature. Record the initial gas volume of the cylinder and the temperature of the water bath in your data table.

3. Collect and weigh about 0.2 g of mossy zinc. If necessary, break up larger pieces. Place the zinc in the sidearm flask that is in the water bath.

4. Measure 25 mL of hydrochloric acid in a graduated cylinder.

5. Carefully pour the acid from the graduated cylinder into the flask with the zinc. Start the stopwatch as you begin to pour. Stopper the flask as soon as the acid is transferred.

6. Hydrogen gas should begin to be given off by the reaction, which will cause gas to flow through the tube and into the inverted graduated cylinder. Record the volume of gas in the graduated cylinder every minute for five minutes.

What You'll Do

> **Measure** the volume of gas produced to determine the average rate of the reaction between zinc and hydrochloric acid.

> **Determine** how the rate of this reaction depends on the temperature of the reactants.

What You'll Need

balance
beaker to hold a 10 mL graduated cylinder
flasks, sidearm, with rubber stoppers (2)
graduated cylinder, 10 mL
graduated cylinder, 25 mL
hydrochloric acid, 1.0 M (25 mL)
ice
metric ruler
rubber tubing
scissors, heavy-duty
stopwatch
thermometer
water bath to hold a sidearm flask
zinc, mossy, about 0.5 g

Safety

248 Chapter 7 Chemical Reactions

Forming and Testing a Hypothesis

7 Form a hypothesis about how the reaction that you just observed will differ if it is carried out at a different temperature.

Designing Your Experiment

8 With your lab partners, decide how you will test your hypothesis. By completing steps 1–6, you have half of the data needed to answer the question. How will you collect the rest of the data?

9 In your lab report, list each step that you will perform in your experiment. Because temperature is the variable that you are testing, the other variables in your experiment should be the same as they were in steps 1–6.

Performing Your Experiment

10 Have your teacher approve your plan, and carry out your experiment. Record your results in another similar data table.

Analysis

1. **Describing Events** How did the results of the two reactions differ?
2. **Interpreting Data** Plot the results of volume over time for both reactions on a graph. Which reaction was more rapid?
3. **Analyzing Data** For each time measurement in each experiment, calculate the amount of gas evolved for each time interval. For each experiment, did the reaction rate change over time? How can you tell?
4. **Analyzing Data** Calculate the rate of each reaction, expressed as milliliters of gas produced per minute.
5. **Analyzing Data** Divide the faster rate by the slower rate, and express the reaction rates as a ratio.

Communicating Your Results

6. **Drawing Conclusions** According to your results, how does changing the temperature affect the rate of a chemical reaction?

Extension

How would you design an experiment to test the effect of surface area on this reaction? How would your results be expressed?

Sample Data Table: Measuring Reaction Rate

Initial gas volume (mL)	
Temperature (°C)	
Mass of zinc (g)	
Gas volume at 1 min	DO NOT WRITE IN BOOK
Gas volume at 2 min	
Gas volume at 3 min	
Gas volume at 4 min	
Gas volume at 5 min	

Using Mole Ratios to Calculate Mass

Science Skills

Technology
● Math
Scientific Methods
Graphing

Problem

Determine the mass of hydrogen gas, H_2, and oxygen gas, O_2, produced by 4 mol of water, H_2O, in the following chemical reaction:

$2H_2O \rightarrow 2H_2 + O_2$

Solution

Identify

Write the mole ratio for the balanced equation. Multiply the ratio by the factor that gives the number of moles of H_2O that are present.

There are 4 mol H_2O, so multiply each number in the ratio by 2.

Equation	$2H_2O$	$\rightarrow$	$2H_2$	+	O_2
Mole ratio	2	:	2	:	1
Amount (mol)	4		4		2

Plan

Determine the molar mass of each substance.

Look up the molar mass of each element. There are two hydrogen atoms and one oxygen atom in each molecule of H_2O, so the molar mass of H_2O is 2×1 g/mol + 16 g/mol = 18 g/mol. Similarly, the molar mass of H_2 is 2 g/mol, and the molar mass of O_2 is 32 g/mol.

Solve

Multiply the number of moles of each substance by the molar mass of that substance.

The total mass of the reactants should match the total mass of the products.

Equation	$2H_2O$	$\rightarrow$	$2H_2$	+	O_2
Mole ratio	2	:	2	:	1
Amount (mol)	4		4		2
Molar mass (g/mol)	18		2		32
Mass calculation	18 g/mol × 4 mol	=	2 g/mol × 4 mol	+	32 g/mol × 2 mol
Total mass (g)	72	=	8	+	64

Four moles (72 g) of water, H_2O, will produce 8 g H_2 and 64 g O_2.

Practice

1. Determine the mass of H_2SO_4 produced when 1 mol H_2O reacts with 1 mol SO_3 in the following reaction:
   $H_2O + SO_3 \rightarrow H_2SO_4$

2. Determine the mass of $ZnSO_4$ produced in the following reaction if 2 mol Zn reacts with 2 mol $CuSO_4$.
   $Zn + CuSO_4 \rightarrow ZnSO_4 + Cu$

CHAPTER 7 Summary

go.hrw.com
SUPER SUMMARY
KEYWORD: HK8REAS

Key Ideas	Key Terms
## Section 1 The Nature of Chemical Reactions **› Chemical Reactions** Chemical reactions occur when substances undergo chemical changes to form new substances. (p. 219) **› Energy and Reactions** Chemical reactions involve changes in energy. (p. 220)	**reactant,** p. 220 **product,** p. 220 **chemical energy,** p. 221 **exothermic reaction,** p. 222 **endothermic reaction,** p. 222
## Section 2 Chemical Equations **› Describing Reactions** A chemical equation uses symbols to represent a chemical reaction. (p. 225) **› Balanced Equations and Mole Ratios** A balanced equation tells you the mole ratio, or proportion of reactants and products, in a chemical reaction. (p. 228)	**chemical equation,** p. 225 **mole ratio,** p. 228
## Section 3 Reaction Types **› Classifying Reactions** You can use patterns to identify kinds of chemical reactions and to predict the products of the chemical reactions. (p. 230) **› Electrons and Chemical Reactions** Free-radical reactions and redox reactions can be understood as changes in the numbers of electrons that atoms have. (p. 235)	**synthesis reaction,** p. 231 **decomposition reaction,** p. 231 **combustion reaction,** p. 232 **single-displacement reaction,** p. 233 **double-displacement reaction,** p. 234 **free radical,** p. 235 **oxidation-reduction reaction,** p. 237
## Section 4 Reaction Rates and Equilibrium **› Factors Affecting Reaction Rates** Anything that increases contact between particles will increase the rate of a reaction. (p. 238) **› Catalysts** A catalyst speeds up or slows down a reaction but is not changed by the reaction. (p. 240) **› Equilibrium Systems** Processes that can go in both directions may result in equilibrium. (p. 244)	**catalyst,** p. 240 **enzyme,** p. 241 **substrate,** p. 241 **chemical equilibrium,** p. 245

CHAPTER 7 Review

READING TOOLBOX

1. **Reading Equations** Equations for reversible chemical reactions use a double arrow instead of a single arrow. Such equations can be read as two separate equations. One goes from left to right, and the other goes from right to left. Write out in words the two separate equations for the Haber process, shown below.

$$N_2 + 3H_2 \rightleftarrows 2NH_3 + \text{energy}$$

USING KEY TERMS

2. When wood is burned, energy is released in the form of heat and light. Describe the reaction, and explain why this reaction does not violate the law of conservation of energy. Use the terms *combustion, exothermic,* and *chemical energy.*

3. Translate the following chemical equation into a sentence.

$$CH_4 + 2O_2 \rightarrow CO_2 + 2H_2O$$

4. How does a *combustion reaction* differ from other types of chemical reactions?

5. What is an *oxidation-reduction reaction*?

6. Explain what it means when a system in *chemical equilibrium* shifts to favor the products.

UNDERSTANDING KEY IDEAS

7. When a chemical reaction occurs, atoms are never
   a. ionized.
   b. rearranged.
   c. destroyed.
   d. vaporized.

8. What happens during an exothermic reaction?
   a. Energy is lost.
   b. Energy is created.
   c. Energy is released.
   d. Energy is absorbed.

9. Which of the following statements about free radicals is true?
   a. Free radicals form ionic bonds with other ions.
   b. Free radicals result from broken covalent bonds.
   c. Free radicals usually break apart to form smaller components.
   d. Free radicals bind molecules together.

10. Hydrogen peroxide, H_2O_2, decomposes to produce water and oxygen gas. What is the balanced equation for this reaction?
    a. $H_2O_2 \rightarrow H_2O + O_2$
    b. $2H_2O_2 \rightarrow 2H_2O + O_2$
    c. $2H_2O_2 \rightarrow H_2O + 2O_2$
    d. $2H_2O_2 \rightarrow 2H_2O + 2O_2$

11. Most reactions speed up when
    a. the temperature decreases.
    b. equilibrium is achieved.
    c. the concentration of the products increases.
    d. the reactant is in small pieces.

12. A system in chemical equilibrium
    a. responds to oppose change.
    b. has particles that do not move.
    c. is undergoing visible change.
    d. is stable only when all of the reactants have been used.

EXPLAINING KEY IDEAS

13. Classify each of the following reactions as a synthesis reaction, a decomposition reaction, a single-displacement reaction, a double-displacement reaction, or a combustion reaction:
    a. $N_2 + 3H_2 \rightarrow 2NH_3$
    b. $2Li + 2H_2O \rightarrow 2LiOH + H_2$
    c. $2NaNO_3 \rightarrow 2NaNO_2 + O_2$
    d. $2C_6H_{14} + 19O_2 \rightarrow 12CO_2 + 14H_2O$
    e. $NH_4Cl \rightarrow NH_3 + HCl$
    f. $BaO + H_2O \rightarrow Ba(OH)_2$
    g. $AgNO_3 + NaCl \rightarrow AgCl + NaNO_3$

14. Molecular models of some chemical reactions are pictured below. Copy the drawings, and add coefficients to reflect balanced equations.

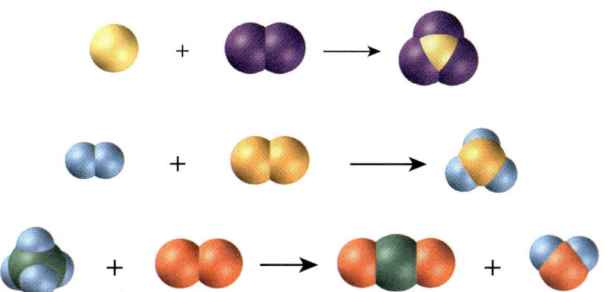

15. For each of the following changes to the equilibrium system below, predict which reaction will be favored—forward (to the right), reverse (to the left), or neither.

$$H_2(gas) + Cl_2(gas) \rightleftarrows 2HCl(gas) + energy$$

   a. addition of Cl_2
   b. removal of HCl
   c. increase in pressure
   d. decrease in temperature
   e. removal of H_2

CRITICAL THINKING

16. Designing Experiments Paper consists mainly of cellulose, a complex compound made up of simple sugars. Suggest a method for turning old newspapers into sugars by using an enzyme. What problems would there be? What precautions would need to be taken?

17. Analyzing Processes Explain why hydrogen gas is given off when a reactive metal undergoes a single-displacement reaction with water.

18. Applying Concepts Sulfur burns in air to form sulfur dioxide in the following reaction:

$$S + O_2 \rightarrow SO_2$$

   a. What mass of SO_2 forms from 64 g of sulfur?
   b. What mass of sulfur is necessary to form 256 g of sulfur dioxide?

Graphing Skills

19. Interpreting Graphs A chemist carried out an experiment to study the effect of temperature on a certain reaction. Her results are shown in the graph below.

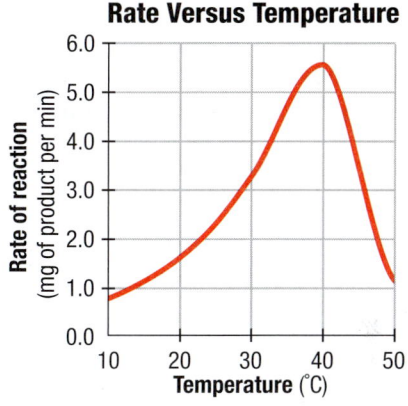

   a. Between which temperatures does the rate of the reaction rise?
   b. Between which temperatures does the rate of the reaction slow down?
   c. At what temperature is the rate of the reaction the fastest?

Math Skills

20. Balancing Chemical Equations In 1774, Joseph Priestley discovered oxygen when he heated solid mercury(II) oxide, HgO, and produced the element mercury and oxygen gas. Write and balance this equation.

21. Balancing Chemical Equations Write the balanced chemical equation for the reaction in which methane, CH_4, reacts with oxygen gas to produce water and carbon dioxide.

22. Balancing Chemical Equations Sucrose, $C_{12}H_{22}O_{11}$, is a sugar that is used to sweeten many foods. Inside the body, it is broken down to produce H_2O and CO_2.

$$C_{12}H_{22}O_{11} + 12O_2 \rightarrow 12CO_2 + 11H_2O$$

List all of the mole ratios that can be determined from this equation.

Standardized Test Prep

Understanding Concepts

Directions (1–4): **For each question, write on a sheet of paper the letter of the correct answer.**

1. What type of reaction is $Pb(NO_3)_2 + 2KI \rightarrow PbI_2 + 2KNO_3$?
   - **A.** a synthesis reaction
   - **B.** a combustion reaction
   - **C.** a decomposition reaction
   - **D.** a double-displacement reaction

2. Which of the following describes an endothermic chemical reaction?
   - **F.** the explosion of fireworks in the sky
   - **G.** photosynthesis in plant cells
   - **H.** respiration in animal cells
   - **I.** the burning of wood in a fireplace

3. Which of the following changes will always increase the rate of a chemical reaction?
   - **A.** lowering the temperature
   - **B.** adding an inhibitor to the reaction mixture
   - **C.** increasing the concentration of the reactants
   - **D.** decreasing the surface area of the reactants

4. The equation $PCl_3 + Cl_2 \leftrightarrows PCl_5 + energy$ describes an equilibrium system. How would raising the temperature affect the system?
   - **F.** The equilibrium would move to the right to create more PCl_3 and Cl_2.
   - **G.** The equilibrium would move to the left to create more PCl_3 and Cl_2.
   - **H.** The equilibrium would move to the right to create more PCl_5.
   - **I.** The equilibrium would move to the left to create more PCl_5.

Directions (5): **For this question, write a short response.**

5. In the redox reaction $H_2 + F_2 \rightarrow 2HF$, which element is reduced, and which is oxidized?

Reading Skills

Directions (6–7): **Read the passage below. Then, answer the questions that follow.**

NITROGEN FIXATION

The element nitrogen makes up about 78% of Earth's atmosphere. It is also an essential component of many of the chemical compounds that are vital to all living things. However, atmospheric nitrogen is not directly accessible to living things; it is primarily in the form of N_2, a molecule composed of two atoms of nitrogen linked by a triple bond. Because of the strength of this bond, large amounts of energy are required to free up the nitrogen atoms so that they can become part of the organic molecules of life.

When sufficient energy is added to N_2 and hydrogen is present in the form of H_2, the result is the compound ammonia, NH_3. The nitrogen in ammonia is much more reactive than that in N_2 and thus is much more readily available to living systems. The process of combining nitrogen and hydrogen into ammonia is an oxidation-reduction reaction known as *nitrogen fixation*. Nitrogen fixation is accomplished by certain microorganisms, which then feed nitrogen-rich compounds into the rest of the ecosystem. Nitrogen fixation is also done artificially at chemical plants where ammonia is made.

6. In addition to being an oxidation-reduction reaction, what type of reaction is nitrogen fixation of N_2 and H_2 into NH_3?
   - **A.** a synthesis reaction
   - **B.** a decomposition reaction
   - **C.** a single-displacement reaction
   - **D.** a double-displacement reaction

7. Write the balanced chemical equation for nitrogen fixation.

Interpreting Graphics

The graphics below plot energy changes during two types of chemical reactions. Use these graphics to answer question 8.

ENERGY CHANGES DURING CHEMICAL REACTIONS

 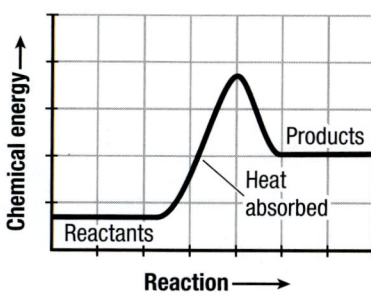

8. In each of these reactions, the chemical energy increases and then decreases during the course of the reaction. What does the height of the "hill" on each graph represent?
   - **A.** energy that must be added to start the reaction
   - **B.** energy released as reactant molecules approach one another
   - **C.** the potential energy of the chemical bonds in the molecules of the reactants
   - **D.** the change in total chemical energy between the reactants and the products

In hydrogen fuel cells, a catalyzed reaction between hydrogen and oxygen gases forms water. One of the diagrams below represents the balanced chemical equation for this reaction. Use these diagrams to answer question 9.

9. Which of the diagrams represents the balanced equation for the reaction?
   - **A.** A
   - **B.** B
   - **C.** C
   - **D.** D

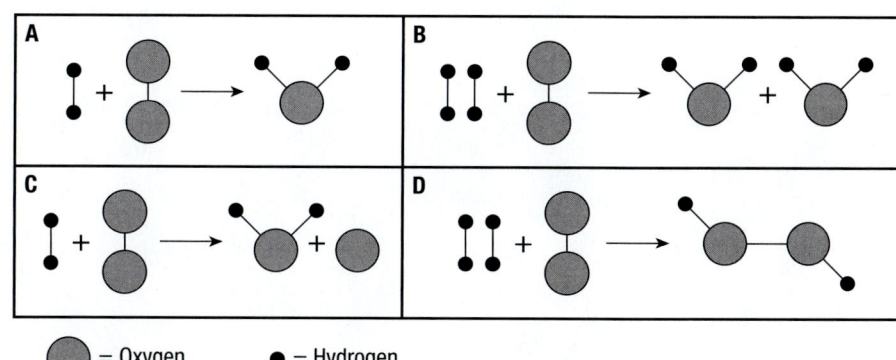

Test Tip

When using a diagram to answer a question, look in the image for evidence that supports your potential answer.

CHAPTER 8 Solutions

Chapter Outline

1 Solutions and Other Mixtures
Heterogeneous Mixtures
Homogeneous Mixtures

2 How Substances Dissolve
Water: A Common Solvent
The Dissolving Process

3 Solubility and Concentration
Solubility in Water
Saturated Solutions
Concentration of Solutions

Tennessee Course Level Expectations (Physical Science)

CLE. 3202.1.8 Investigate relationships among the pressure, temperature, and volume of gases and liquids; **CLE.3202.TE.3** Explain the relationship between the properties of a material and the use of the material in the application of a technology; **CLE.3202.1.5** Evaluate pure substances and mixtures; **CLE.3202.1.6** Distinguish between common ionic and covalent compounds; **CLE.3202.Inq.1** Recognize that science is a progressive endeavor that reevaluates and extends what is already accepted; **CLE.3202.Inq.2** Design and conduct scientific investigations to explore new phenomena, verify previous results, test how well a theory predicts, and compare opposing theories; **CLE.3202.Inq.3** Use appropriate tools and technology to collect precise and accurate data; **CLE.3202.Inq.4** Apply qualitative and quantitative measures to analyze data and draw conclusions that are free of bias; **CLE.3202.Inq.6** Communicate and defend scientific findings; **CLE.3202.TE.4** Describe the dynamic interplay among science, technology, and engineering within living, earth-space, and physical systems.

Why It Matters

Most of Earth's water is a solution of salts in water. This woman is floating easily on the surface of the Dead Sea because so much salt is dissolved in the water of the sea.

Inquiry Lab
⏱ 20 min

Dissolving Salt and Sugar

Fill a **clear plastic cup** with **water**. After the water settles, add **table salt** one **teaspoon** at a time to the water. Stir after you add each spoonful until all of the salt disappears. Continue adding salt and stirring until no more salt dissolves. Repeat this activity using sugar instead of salt.

Questions to Get You Started

1. How much salt are you able to add before it stops dissolving and settles to the bottom of the cup?
2. Does the same amount of sugar dissolve? If not, what might explain the difference?

READING TOOLBOX

These reading tools can help you learn the material in this chapter. For more information on how to use these and other tools, see **Appendix A.**

FoldNotes

Key-Term Fold The key-term fold can help you learn the key terms from this chapter.

Your Turn Create a key-term fold as described in **Appendix A.**

1. Write the key terms from the Chapter Summary on the front of each tab.
2. As you read the chapter, write the definitions under the tabs for each term.
3. Use this FoldNote to study the key terms.

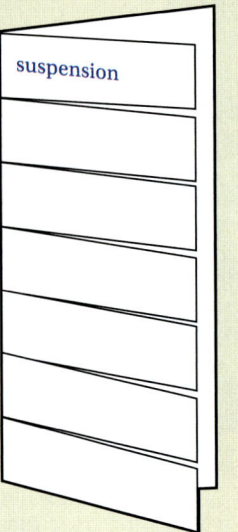

suspension

Finding Examples

Examples of Mixtures Examples can help you picture an idea or concept. Certain words or phrases can serve as signals that an example is about to be introduced. Such signals include

- *for example*
- *such as*
- *for instance*

Your Turn As you read Section 1, make a list like the one started below to organize the examples of heterogeneous mixtures. Some examples may not be signaled by a word or phrase.

HETEROGENEOUS MIXTURES	
EXAMPLE	SIGNAL
1. fruit salad	"just as"
2. garden dirt	no signal

Note Taking

Summarizing Ideas Summarizing the content of each paragraph or set of paragraphs under a heading is a simple way to take notes. A few tips on summarizing are listed below.

1. Summary statements should be short but should fully express the idea.
2. Use the blue subheadings for guidance in forming summary statements.
3. Many paragraphs start or end with a sentence that summarizes the main idea of the paragraph.

Your Turn Use summarizing to take notes for Section 1. You may add structure to your notes by also writing the section titles and red headings in the appropriate places. The example below for Section 1 can help you get started.

Section 1—Solutions and Other Mixtures
- All matter is either a pure substance or a mixture of pure substances.

Heterogeneous Mixtures
- In heterogeneous mixtures, the amount of each substance varies.

SECTION 1
Solutions and Other Mixtures

Key Ideas
> What is a heterogeneous mixture?
> What is a homogeneous mixture?

Key Terms
suspension
colloid
emulsion
solution
solute
solvent
alloy

Why It Matters
During oil refining, the components of a mixture called *crude oil* are separated to form gasoline and other products that we use on a daily basis.

Any sample of matter is either a pure substance or a mixture of pure substances. You can easily tell that fruit salad is a mixture because you can see the various kinds of fruit. But some mixtures look like they are pure substances. For example, a mixture of salt dissolved in water looks the same as pure water. Air is a mixture of several gases, but you cannot see the gases that make up air.

> Tennessee Course Level Expectations (Physical Science)
> CLE.3202.1.5; CLE.3202.Inq.1; CLE.3202.Inq.2; CLE.3202.Inq.3

Heterogeneous Mixtures

> **A heterogeneous mixture does not have a fixed composition.** The amount of each substance in different samples of a heterogeneous mixture varies, just as the amount of each kind of fruit varies in each spoonful of fruit salad, as **Figure 1** shows. If you compare two shovelfuls of dirt from a garden, they will not be exactly the same. The amounts of rock, sand, clay, and decayed matter in each shovelful vary.

Another naturally occurring heterogeneous mixture is granite, a type of igneous rock. Granite is a mixture of crystals of the minerals quartz, mica, and feldspar. Samples of granite from different locations can vary greatly in appearance because the samples have different proportions of minerals.

Figure 1 Fruit salad is a heterogeneous mixture. The composition of each spoonful of fruit varies because the fruits are not distributed evenly throughout the salad.

Figure 2 Orange Juice: A Heterogeneous Mixture

The pulp in the orange juice is spread throughout the mixture right after the orange juice is shaken.

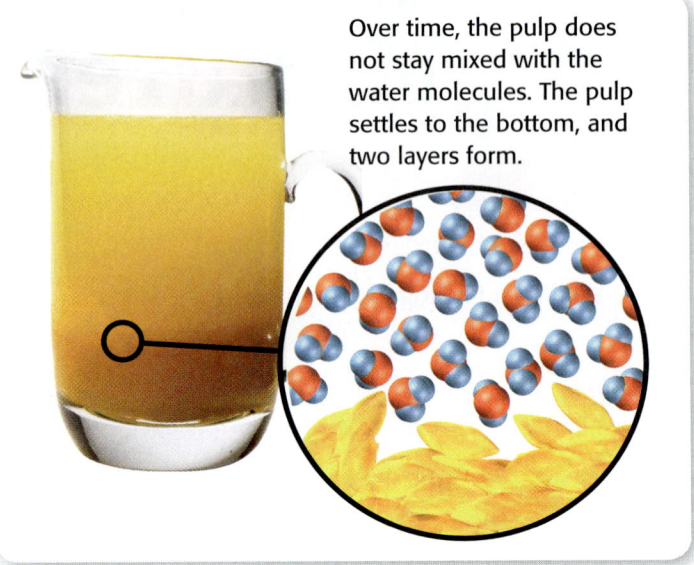

Over time, the pulp does not stay mixed with the water molecules. The pulp settles to the bottom, and two layers form.

suspension (suh SPEN shuhn) a mixture in which particles of a material are more or less evenly dispersed throughout a liquid or gas

colloid (KAHL oyd) a mixture consisting of tiny particles that are intermediate in size between those in solutions and those in suspensions and that are suspended in a liquid, solid, or gas

Particles in a suspension are large and settle out.

Have you ever forgotten to shake the orange juice carton before pouring yourself a glass of juice? The juice was probably thin and watery. Natural orange juice is a suspension of orange pulp in a clear liquid that is mostly water, as **Figure 2** shows. A property of a **suspension** is that the particles settle out when the mixture is allowed to stand. When the orange juice carton is not shaken, the top layer of the juice in the carton is mostly water because all of the pulp has settled to the bottom.

You can see that orange juice is a heterogeneous mixture. After the juice settles, the mixture near the top of the container differs from the mixture near the bottom. Shaking the container mixes the pulp and water, but the pulp pieces are large enough that they will eventually settle out again.

✓ **Reading Check** Over time, what happens to the particles in a suspension? (See Appendix E for answers to Reading Checks.)

Particles in a suspension may be filtered out.

Particles in suspensions are usually about the size of a bacterial cell, which has a diameter of about 1,000 nm. Particles of this size are large enough to be filtered out of the mixture. For example, you can use a filter made of porous paper to catch the suspended pulp in orange juice. That is, the pulp stays in the filter, and smaller particles, such as water molecules, pass through the filter easily. You can classify a mixture as a suspension if the particles settle out or can be filtered out.

Some mixtures of two liquids will separate.

Oil, vinegar, and flavorings can be shaken together to make salad dressing. But the dressing is a heterogeneous mixture. When the dressing stands for a few minutes, two layers form, as **Figure 3** shows. The two liquids separate because they are *immiscible,* which means that they do not mix. Eventually, the oil, which is less dense, rises and floats on the vinegar, which is denser.

One way to separate two immiscible liquids is to carefully pour the less dense liquid off the top. Some cooks use this technique to separate melted fat from meat juices. The cook removes the fat by pouring or spooning it off the meat juices, which are denser than the fat. The process of pouring a less dense liquid off a denser liquid is called *decanting*.

Particles in a colloid are too small to settle out.

Latex paint is an example of another kind of heterogeneous mixture, a **colloid.** The color in latex paint comes from solid particles of colored pigments that are dispersed in water. Other substances in the paint make the pigment stick to a surface. The difference between colloids and suspensions is that the particles in colloids are smaller than those in suspensions. Particles in colloids range from only 1 to 1,000 nm in diameter. Because the particles in colloids are so small, they pass through most filters and stay spread throughout the mixture. Even though the colloid may look like clear water, the particles are large enough to scatter light that passes through the colloid, as **Figure 4** shows. This scattering of light is called the *Tyndall effect*.

Figure 3 Some salad dressings are made with oil and vinegar, which form a suspension when shaken. Because oil-and-vinegar mixtures are heterogeneous, they separate after standing for a few minutes.

Academic Vocabulary

disperse (di SPUHRS) to spread through evenly

www.scilinks.org
Topic: Colloids
Code: **HK80312**

Figure 4 The liquid in the jar on the right is a colloid. Colloids exhibit the Tyndall effect, in which light is scattered by the invisible particles.

QuickLab Making Butter

10 min

Procedure
1. Pour **250 mL (about 1/2 pint) of heavy cream** into an empty **500 mL container.**
2. Add a clean **marble,** and then seal the container tightly so that it will not leak.
3. Take turns shaking the container. When the cream becomes very thick, you will no longer hear the marble moving.
4. Record your observations of the substance that formed.

Analysis
1. Cream is an emulsion of fats in water. If joined fat droplets make up butter, what must make up most of the remaining liquid?
2. Why does butter form when you shake the cream?

Figure 5 Cream may look like a pure substance, but when cream is magnified, you can see that it is an emulsion of droplets of fats, or lipids, dispersed in water.

Other familiar materials are also colloids.

Although the particles in most colloids are made up of many atoms, ions, or molecules, individual protein molecules are also large enough to form colloids. Gelatin, egg whites, and blood plasma are all protein colloids. They consist of protein molecules dispersed in a liquid.

Whipped cream is a colloid that is made by dispersing a gas in a liquid, and marshmallows are made by dispersing a gas in a solid. Fog is made of small droplets of water spread in air, and smoke contains small solid particles dispersed in air.

Some immiscible liquids can form colloids.

Mayonnaise is a colloid made up of tiny droplets of oil suspended in vinegar. Vinegar-and-oil salad dressings separate into two layers, but the egg yolk in mayonnaise keeps the oil and vinegar from separating. Egg yolk coats the oil droplets so that they do not join together and form a separate layer. Mayonnaise is an **emulsion,** a colloid in which liquids that usually do not mix are spread throughout each other. Emulsions are also found in your body. In the small intestine, bile salts cause fats to form an emulsion. Then, enzymes can break down the smaller fat particles more quickly.

Like other colloids, an emulsion has particles so small that it may appear to be uniform, but it is not. For example, cream does not form separate layers, so it looks like a pure substance. But cream is really a mixture of oily fats, proteins, and carbohydrates dispersed in water. The lipid droplets are coated with a protein that acts as an emulsifier. The protein keeps the lipid droplets dispersed in the water so that they can spread throughout the entire mixture, as **Figure 5** shows.

Homogeneous Mixtures

Homogeneous mixtures, such as salt water, are uniform. When you stir aquarium salt—pure sodium chloride—and water, the mixture soon looks like pure water. ❯ **A homogeneous mixture looks uniform even when you examine it under a microscope because the individual components of the mixture are too small to be seen.** In the saltwater mixture, water molecules surround sodium ions and chloride ions, as **Figure 6** shows. The mixture is homogeneous because the number of ions is the same everywhere in the salt water.

Salt and water do not react when mixed. So, the two substances can be separated by evaporating the water. Salt crystals, like those that originally dissolved, form as the water evaporates. Only salt is left after the water has evaporated.

Homogeneous mixtures are solutions.

Mixtures are homogeneous when the smallest particles of one substance are uniformly spread among similar particles of another substance. This description is also true for **solutions,** so all homogeneous mixtures are also solutions. When you add salt to water and stir, the solid seems to disappear. The salt has *dissolved* in water to form a solution. In the saltwater solution, the salt (sodium chloride) is the substance that dissolves, the **solute.** Water is the substance in which the solute dissolves, so water is the **solvent.** When a solute dissolves in a solvent, the solute separates into the smallest particles of the substance—atoms, ions, or molecules.

✓ **Reading Check** What types of solute particles are present in a solution?

> **READING TOOLBOX**
>
> **Examples of Mixtures**
> Create a list of the examples of solutions that you find as you read about homogeneous mixtures.

> **emulsion** (ee MUHL shuhn) any mixture of two or more immiscible liquids in which one liquid is dispersed in the other
>
> **solution** (suh LOO shuhn) a homogeneous mixture throughout which two or more substances are uniformly dispersed
>
> **solute** (SAHL yoot) in a solution, the substance that dissolves in the solvent
>
> **solvent** (SAHL vuhnt) in a solution, the substance in which the solute dissolves

Figure 6 Pure Water and Salt Water

Plain water is homogeneous because it is a single substance.

Salt water is also homogeneous because it is a uniform mixture of water molecules, sodium ions, and chloride ions.

Figure 7 Window cleaner, rubbing alcohol, and gasoline are all mixtures of liquids.

Miscible liquids mix to form solutions.

Two or more liquids that form a single layer when mixed are *miscible*. Liquids can be mixed to form useful solutions, such as those shown in **Figure 7.** For example, water mixed with isopropanol makes a solution called *rubbing alcohol*, which is used to disinfect cuts and scrapes.

Chemists often have to separate miscible liquids when purifying substances. Because miscible liquids do not separate into layers, they are not as easy to separate as immiscible liquids are. One way to separate miscible liquids is by the process of *distillation*. Distillation separates miscible liquids that have different boiling points. For example, a mixture of methanol and water can be separated by distillation because methanol boils at 64.5 °C and water boils at 100.0 °C. When this mixture is heated in a distillation apparatus, the methanol boils away first, and most of the water remains.

Liquid solutions sometimes contain no water.

Many kinds of solutions that are made up of liquids mixed in another liquid do not contain water. For example, some fingernail-polish removers and paint strippers are mixtures of liquids that contain no water. Fuels such as gasoline, diesel, and kerosene are homogeneous mixtures of several liquid carbon compounds. These fuels are made from substances distilled from a mixture known as *petroleum*. Plastics are also made from some of the hydrocarbons that are obtained when petroleum is distilled.

Other states of matter can also form solutions.

Like the water in a saltwater aquarium, many common solutions are solids dissolved in liquids. However, solutes and solvents can be in any state. Vinegar is a solution that is made of two liquids—acetic acid dissolved in water. The air that you breathe is a solution of nitrogen, oxygen, argon, and other gases. Gases can also dissolve in liquids. For example, a soft drink contains carbon dioxide gas dissolved in liquid water. Air fresheners slowly give off fragrant vapor molecules that form a solution with air. The element mercury, a liquid at room temperature, dissolves in solid silver to form a solution called an *amalgam*, which can be used to fill cavities in teeth. In all of these solutions, the substance that there is the most amount of is the solvent and the substance that there is the least amount of is the solute.

Reading Check What states of matter can be mixed with a liquid to form a solution?

Integrating Engineering

Types of Ink Ink is a complicated mixture of substances. Some inks, such as those used in printing books and magazines, contain *pigments* that give the ink most of its color. Pigments are added to a liquid as finely ground, solid particles to form a suspension. A printing press is used to apply the ink to the paper. Then, the ink is allowed to dry.

The ink used in some ballpoint pens is different from ink used in printing. The ink in pens contains a dissolved iron salt, such as ferrous sulfate, and an organic substance called *tannic acid*. When tannic acid and the iron salt are mixed, they form a dark blue solution. This solution gives the ink its blue-black color.

Why It Matters

How Is Crude Oil Turned into Gasoline?

The petroleum that comes out of an oil well is a complex mixture of gases, liquids, and solids. The liquid part of this mixture is known as *crude oil*. Only certain carbon compounds in crude oil can be made into gasoline, and these compounds must first be separated from the rest of the components in the oil. Distillation is a key part of the separation process.

Crude oil is heated and pumped into a large column, which has various sections. The temperature decreases in each section as the gases rise in the column. When the boiling point of a compound in the solution is greater than the temperature in a section of the column, the compound condenses and the liquid can be separated from the gases.

SCLINKS
www.scilinks.org
Topic: Fossil Fuels
Code: HK80614

YOUR TURN

UNDERSTANDING CONCEPTS
1. Why are liquids that have lower boiling points collected at the top of the distillation column?

ONLINE RESEARCH
2. Research two other products that are obtained from crude oil. Are their boiling points higher or lower than those of the compounds that are used to make gasoline?

Figure 8 Many musical wind instruments are made of the alloy brass, which is a solid solution. **Why could it be better for a musical instrument to be made from an alloy than from a pure metal?**

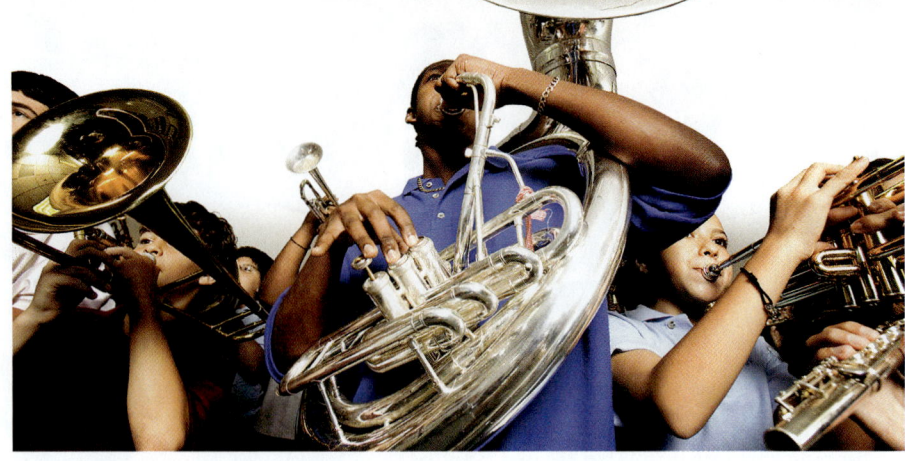

alloy (AL oy) a solid or liquid mixture of two or more metals

Solids can dissolve in other solids.

Many musical instruments, such as the ones shown in **Figure 8,** are made of brass. Brass is a solution of zinc metal dissolved in copper metal. Brass is an **alloy,** a homogeneous mixture that is usually composed of two or more metals. The metals are melted to liquids and mixed. A solid solution of one metal dispersed in another metal forms when the mixture cools.

Alloys are important because they have properties that the individual metals do not have. Pure copper cannot be used to make a sturdy musical instrument because copper is too soft and bends too easily. When zinc is dissolved in copper, the resulting brass is harder than copper but can be easily shaped. Bronze, an alloy of tin in copper, resists corrosion. Many bronze sculptures made in ancient times still exist today. Not all alloys contain only metals. Some types of steel are alloys that contain the nonmetal element carbon.

Section 1 Review

KEY IDEAS

1. **Classify** the following mixtures as heterogeneous or homogeneous.
   a. orange juice without pulp
   b. sweat
   c. cinnamon sugar
   d. concrete
2. **Explain** how a suspension differs from a colloid.
3. **List** three examples of solutions that are not liquids.

CRITICAL THINKING

4. **Evaluating Hypotheses** You suspect that a clear liquid is actually a colloid. How would you test to see if the liquid is a colloid?
5. **Understanding Relationships** Arrange the following mixtures in order of increasing particle size: muddy water, sugar water, and egg white.
6. **Applying Concepts** Identify the solvent and solute in a solution made by dissolving a small quantity of baking soda in water.
7. **Explaining Events** A small child watches you as you stir a spoonful of sugar into a glass of clear lemon-flavored drink. The child says that she believes that the sugar went away because it seemed to disappear. How would you explain to the child what happened to the sugar, and how could you show her that you can get the sugar back?

SECTION 2
How Substances Dissolve

Key Ideas
- Why is water called the universal solvent?
- Why do substances dissolve?

Key Terms
- polar
- hydrogen bond
- nonpolar

Why It Matters
Many substances, including essential minerals and oxygen, are dissolved in your blood.

Suppose that you and a friend are drinking iced tea. You add one spoonful of loose sugar to your glass of tea and stir, and all of the sugar dissolves quickly. Your friend adds a sugar cube to her tea and finds that she must stir longer than you did to dissolve all of the sugar. Why does the sugar cube take longer to dissolve? Why does sugar dissolve in water at all?

Water: A Common Solvent

Two-thirds of Earth's surface is water. The liquids that you drink are mostly water, and three-fourths of your body weight is water. ▶ **Water is called the *universal solvent* because many substances can dissolve in water.**

Water can dissolve ionic compounds.

Water is such a good solvent because of its structure. A water molecule is made up of two hydrogen atoms that are covalently bonded to one oxygen atom. Electrons are not evenly distributed in a water molecule because oxygen atoms strongly attract electrons. The oxygen atom pulls electrons away from the hydrogen atoms and gives the hydrogen atoms a partial positive charge. The electrons are closer to the oxygen atom, so it has a partial negative charge. This uneven distribution of electrons, combined with a water molecule's bent shape, means that water molecules are **polar.** A polar molecule has partially charged positive and negative areas, which are indicated by δ+ and δ− in **Figure 1.** Water dissolves many ionic compounds because the negative side of the water molecule attracts the positive ions and the positive side of the water molecules attracts the negative ions.

> **Tennessee Course Level Expectations (Physical Science)**
> CLE.3202.1.6; CLE.3202.Inq.1; CLE.3202.Inq.2; CLE.3202.Inq.3

polar (POH luhr) describes a molecule in which the positive and negative charges are separated

Figure 1 Water is a polar molecule because the oxygen atom strongly attracts electrons, which leaves the hydrogen atoms slightly positive.

Figure 2 Water breaks apart sodium chloride crystals because water molecules pull the ions away from the crystal. Notice that the partially negative parts of the water molecules are attracted to the positive sodium ions and that the partially positive parts are attracted to the negative chloride ions.

go.hrw.com
interact online
Keyword: HK8SOLF2

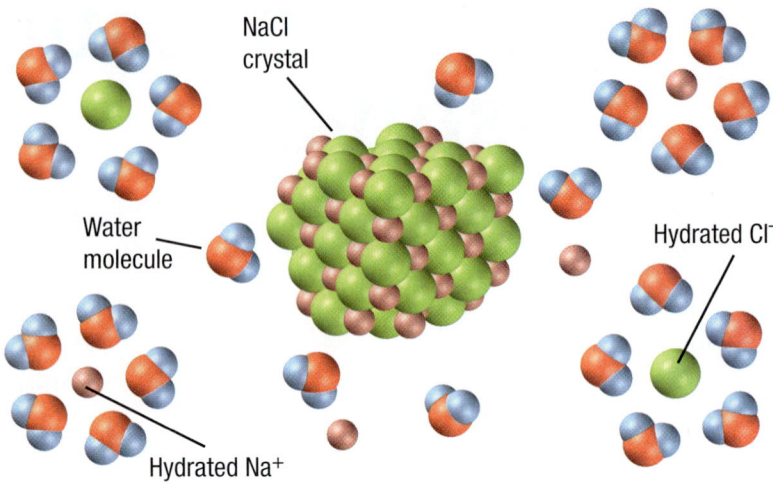

Integrating Biology

Cellular Diffusion Cells rely on *diffusion* to move molecules. When the concentration of a solute is greater inside a cell than outside a cell, the solute moves out of the cell through the cell membrane. But not all substances can diffuse across a cell membrane. Sodium ions and potassium ions move into and out of cells through structures called *sodium-potassium pumps*. These ions give many cells an electric charge. Nerve cells need an electric charge to send signals throughout the body.

Polar water molecules pull ionic crystals apart.

Sodium chloride, NaCl, crystals dissolve in water, as **Figure 2** shows. The partially negative oxygen atoms of water molecules attract the positively charged sodium ions at the surface of the NaCl crystal. The partially positive hydrogen atoms of water molecules attract the negatively charged chloride ions. As more water molecules attract the ions, the amount of attraction between the ions and the water molecules increases. Finally, the attraction between the ions and water molecules becomes stronger than the attraction between the sodium ions and chloride ions in the crystal. So, water molecules pull the ions away from the crystal and surround them. The entire crystal dissolves when all of the ions in the crystal are pulled into water solution.

Dissolving depends on forces between particles.

Water dissolves baking soda and many other ionic compounds in exactly the same way that water dissolves sodium chloride. The attraction of water molecules pulls the crystals apart into individual ions. But many other ionic compounds, such as silver chloride, do not dissolve in water.

The forces of attraction explain why one ionic compound dissolves in water but another one does not. An ionic compound will dissolve in water if the attraction between water molecules and the ions in the crystal is stronger than the attraction between the ions in the crystal. This explanation is true for any solvent and any solute. To dissolve a substance, the force between the solvent molecules and the particles of the substance must be greater than the force between the particles in the crystal.

Water dissolves many molecular compounds.

Water has a low molecular mass. But water is a fairly dense liquid that has a high boiling point. Water has these properties because bonding occurs between water molecules. Recall that in a water molecule, the oxygen atom pulls electrons away from the hydrogen atoms. As a result, a hydrogen atom of one water molecule and the oxygen atom of another water molecule are strongly attracted to each other. This attraction forms a **hydrogen bond.** Hydrogen bonds pull the water molecules close together.

Water dissolves many molecular compounds, such as ethanol, vitamin C, and table sugar, as **Figure 3** shows. These compounds are polar because, like water, they have hydrogen atoms bonded to oxygen. For example, the hydroxyl, –OH, group in ethanol, CH_3CH_2OH, is polar. So, the negative oxygen atom of a water molecule attracts the positive hydrogen atom of an ethanol molecule. And the positive hydrogen atom of a water molecule attracts the negative oxygen atom of an ethanol molecule. The force of attraction of these hydrogen bonds helps pull an ethanol molecule into water solution.

Hydrogen bonding is important in the dissolving of other polar molecular compounds, such as sucrose, $C_{12}H_{22}O_{11}$, as **Figure 4** shows. Water molecules form hydrogen bonds with the –OH groups in the sucrose molecule and pull the sucrose molecules away from the sugar crystal and into solution.

Reading Check Hydrogen bonding occurs between which atoms in water molecules?

Figure 3 As water slowly dissolves the sugar cube, streams of denser sugar solution move downward. Table sugar, or sucrose, is a molecular compound.

hydrogen bond (HIE druh juhn BAHND) the intermolecular force occurring when a hydrogen atom that is bonded to a highly electronegative atom of one molecule is attracted to two unshared electrons of another molecule

Figure 4 Hydrogen bonds form between sucrose and water. Water molecules form many hydrogen bonds with the –OH groups of a sucrose molecule. These forces pull the sucrose molecule away from the sugar crystal and into solution. **Do individual sucrose molecules break apart when they dissolve?**

Section 2   How Substances Dissolve

Figure 5 Nonpolar substances, such as oil-based paint, must be dissolved by a similar solvent. For this reason, a nonpolar solvent must be used.

Like dissolves like.

A rule in chemistry is that "like dissolves like." This rule means that a solvent will dissolve substances that have molecular structures that are like the solvent's structure. For example, water is a polar molecule—it has a partially positive end and a partially negative end. So, water dissolves ions, which have charges, and other polar molecules.

Nonpolar compounds usually will not dissolve in water. Nonpolar molecules do not have partially negative and positive parts because the electrons are <u>distributed</u> evenly over the whole molecule. For example, olive oil, which is a mixture of nonpolar compounds, will not dissolve in water. The attraction between water and nonpolar molecules is less than the attraction between the nonpolar molecules. Nonpolar solvents must be used to dissolve nonpolar materials, as **Figure 5** shows. Nonpolar solvents are often distilled from petroleum.

nonpolar (nahn POH luhr) describes a molecule in which the centers of positive and negative charges are not separated

Academic Vocabulary
distribute (di STRIB yoot) to spread out

Inquiry Lab — What Will Dissolve a Nonpolar Substance?

 10 min

Procedure

1. Dip a **cotton swab** in **tincture of iodine**, and make two small spots on the palm of your hand. Let the spots dry. The spots that remain are iodine.
2. Dip a **second cotton swab** in **water**, and wash one of the iodine spots with it. What happens to the iodine spot?
3. Dip a **third cotton swab** in **ethanol**, and wash the other iodine spot with it. What happens to the iodine spot?

Analysis

1. Did water or did ethanol dissolve the iodine spot better?
2. Is water more polar or less polar than ethanol? Explain your reasoning.

270 Chapter 8 Solutions

The Dissolving Process

The kinetic theory of matter states that molecules are always moving. When sugar is poured into a glass of water, water molecules collide with and transfer energy to the sugar molecules at the surface of the sugar crystal. ❯ **The energy transferred from the solvent to the solute, as well as the attractive forces between the solvent and solute molecules, causes molecules at the surface of the crystal to dissolve.**

Every time that sugar molecules break away from the surface of the crystal, the sugar molecules in the layer below are exposed to the solvent. Sugar molecules keep breaking away from the surface until the crystal completely dissolves.

Solutes with a larger surface area dissolve faster.

Small pieces of a solid dissolve faster than large pieces of the same substance. Smaller pieces have more surface area that is in contact with the solute molecules. As a result, there are more collisions between the solvent and solute molecules. So, the solid dissolves faster.

As **Figure 6** shows, breaking a solid into many smaller pieces increases the total exposed surface area. If a cube is 1 cm on each edge, each face of the cube has an area of 1 cm^2. A cube has six surfaces, so the total surface area is 6 cm^2. If the large cube is cut into 1,000 cubes that are 0.1 cm on each edge, the face of each small cube has an area of 0.1 cm × 0.1 cm = 0.01 cm^2. So, each cube has a surface area of 0.06 cm^2. The total surface area of all the small cubes is 1,000 × 0.06 cm^2 = 60 cm^2, which is 10 times the surface area of the large cube.

✔ **Reading Check** Why does increasing the surface area of a solid help it dissolve faster?

READING TOOLBOX

Summarizing Ideas
As you read about the dissolving process, summarize the ways in which you can make a solute dissolve faster.

This salt crystal has a much smaller surface area than its total volume.

Surface area = 6 cm^2
1 cm
0.1 cm
Surface area = 60 cm^2

Figure 6 When the salt crystal is crushed into small pieces, more of the salt can be exposed to a solute. So, the crushed salt dissolves faster.

Section 2 How Substances Dissolve **271**

Stirring or shaking helps solids dissolve faster.

If you pour table sugar into a glass of water and let the glass sit, the sugar will take a long time to dissolve completely. The solid sugar is at the bottom of the glass surrounded by dissolved sugar molecules, as **Figure 7** shows. Because the dissolved sugar molecules are always moving, they will slowly *diffuse*, or spread out, throughout the solution. Until they diffuse, the dissolved sugar molecules will be near the surface of the crystal. These dissolved molecules keep water molecules from reaching the undissolved sugar. So, the molecules still in crystal will dissolve slowly.

Stirring or shaking the solution moves the dissolved sugar away from the sugar crystals. So, more water molecules can interact with the solid, also shown in **Figure 7,** and the sugar crystals dissolve faster.

Solids dissolve faster when the solvent is hot.

Solid solutes dissolve faster in a hot solvent than in a cold solvent. The kinetic theory states that when matter is heated, its particles move faster. As a result of heating, particles of solvent run into undissolved solute more often. These collisions also transfer more energy than collisions that occur when the solvent is cold. The greater frequency and energy of the collisions help "knock" undissolved solute particles away from each other and spread them throughout the solution. **Figure 8** shows the three ways to make solids dissolve faster.

www.scilinks.org
Topic: Diffusion
Code: **HK80406**

Figure 7 Effect of Stirring on the Dissolving Process

If the solution is not stirred, crystals of sugar become surrounded by dissolved sugar molecules, which prevent water molecules from reaching the undissolved sugar.

Stirring moves the dissolved sugar molecules away from the undissolved sugar, and more water molecules can reach the undissolved sugar.

Crushing the solute

Mixing the solution

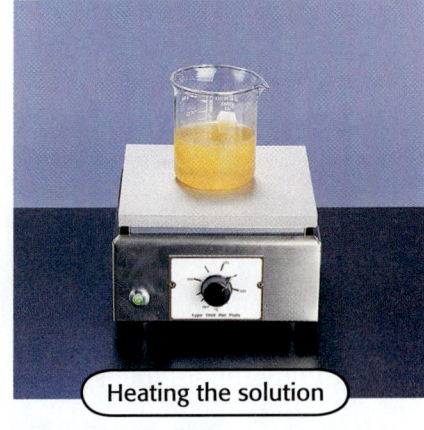
Heating the solution

Figure 8 Crushing the solute, mixing the solution, or heating the solution will speed up the dissolving process.

Solutes affect the physical properties of a solution.

The boiling point of pure water is 100 °C and the freezing point is 0 °C. But if you dissolve 12 g of sodium chloride in 100 mL of water, you will find that the boiling point of the solution is increased to about 102 °C. Also, the freezing point of the solution will be lowered to about −8 °C. Many solutes increase the boiling point of a solution above that of the pure solvent. These same solutes also lower the freezing point of the solution below that of the pure solvent. The amount that the boiling point increases or the freezing point decreases depends on how many solute particles are in the solution.

The effect of a solute on freezing point and boiling point can be useful. For example, a car's cooling system often contains a mixture that is 50% water and 50% ethylene glycol, a type of alcohol. This solution acts as antifreeze in cold weather because its freezing point is about −30 °C. The solution also helps prevent boiling in hot weather because its boiling point is about 109 °C.

Section 2 Review

KEY IDEAS

1. **Explain** why water can dissolve some ionic compounds, such as ammonium chloride, NH_4Cl, as well as some molecular compounds, such as methanol.
2. **Describe** three methods that you could use to make a spoonful of salt dissolve faster in water.

CRITICAL THINKING

3. **Recognizing Relationships** Describe the relationship of attractive forces between molecules and the ability of a solvent to dissolve a substance.
4. **Predicting Outcomes** Use the rule of "like dissolves like" to predict whether the polar molecular compound glycerol is soluble in water.
5. **Applying Ideas** Explain why large crystals of coarse sea salt take longer than crystals of fine table salt to dissolve in water.
6. **Explaining Events** You make strawberry-flavored drink from water, sugar, and drink mix. You decide to freeze the mixture into ice cubes. You place an ice-cube tray filled with the drink and another tray of plain water in the freezer. Two hours later, you find that the water has frozen but the fruit drink has not. How can you explain this result?

Why It Matters

Blood Substitutes

When patients lose a lot of blood, doctors give them a *blood transfusion,* or an infusion of replacement blood. This replacement blood comes from either the patient or a blood donor. Blood donation has declined in recent years, so many communities have severe blood shortages. For several years, sick or injured dogs have received transfusions of a new blood substitute. Someday, blood substitutes could save human lives by easing blood shortages. They could also help people who have rare blood types and other conditions that make traditional blood transfusions difficult.

When an animal or human is injured and loses blood, the number of red blood cells in the body drops. Because red blood cells are responsible for transporting oxygen in the body, a shortage of red blood cells can cause the body's tissues to be starved for oxygen. The artificial blood now available for injured dogs replaces the animals' natural hemoglobin, the protein in red blood cells that carries oxygen throughout the body. The artificial blood given to dogs is made from hemoglobin recycled from slaughtered cows. Because this hemoglobin lacks the complex, natural covering normally present in red blood cells, the hemoglobin is often absorbed by the dog's body in less than a day.

Donated blood is screened, tracked, and stored for transfusions. Donated blood lasts only a few weeks in storage. Artificial blood can last for a year. Artificial blood based on free-floating hemoglobin is being tested for use in human trauma patients.

WEIRD SCIENCE

Scientists are also developing human blood substitutes that do not contain hemoglobin at all. *Perfluorocarbons* (PFCs), compounds made of fluorine and carbon, are used to make synthetic blood. Perfluorocarbons are oily substances, so they do not mix with water. But they can be mixed with other chemicals that allow them to form an emulsion with a water-based saline solution. PFCs can carry twice as much oxygen as human hemoglobin can. This mouse is "breathing" comfortably, thanks to the oxygen-carrying PFCs in this solution.

PFCs have a major advantage over real blood because PFCs do not have to match the patient's blood type. And unlike donated human blood, which must be thrown out after six weeks, artificial blood made from PFCs can be stored for up to two years. However, all artificial blood does have one major limitation—it lacks white blood cells and platelets, a critical part of the body's defense and healing systems. For this reason, artificial blood is not meant to be a permanent replacement for real blood. If approved for humans, blood substitutes will most likely be used for short-term needs (such as during surgery) until matching human blood can be found.

SCLINKS
www.scilinks.org
Topic: Artificial Blood
Code: **HK80100**

YOUR TURN

UNDERSTANDING CONCEPTS
1. If perfluorocarbons are more efficient than natural blood at carrying oxygen through the body, why don't doctors expect to use PFCs as a permanent blood replacement?

CRITICAL THINKING
2. Do you think that the ability of artificial blood to be stored for long periods of time will help reduce blood shortages? Why or why not?

Section 2 How Substances Dissolve **275**

SECTION 3
Solubility and Concentration

Key Ideas
- What is solubility?
- What happens when you add more solute to a saturated solution?
- How do you describe how much of a solute is in a solution?

Key Terms
- solubility
- concentration
- saturated solution
- unsaturated solution
- supersaturated solution
- molarity

Why It Matters
The concentrations of many substances in your water supply need to be under a certain limit. For example, a small amount of fluoride in drinking water can be beneficial, but a larger amount can be harmful.

Tennessee Course Level Expectations (Physical Science)

CLE.3202.1.8; CLE.3202.1.5;
CLE.3202.1.6; CLE.3202.Inq.1;
CLE.3202.Inq.2; CLE.3202.Inq.3;
CLE.3202.Inq.4; CLE.3202.Inq.6;
CLE.3202.TE.3; CLE.3202.TE.4

Figure 1 Olive oil and water form two layers when they are mixed. Olive oil is *insoluble* in water.

How much would you have to shake, stir, or heat the mixture of olive oil and water shown in **Figure 1** to dissolve the oil in the water? The answer is that the oil will not dissolve in the water no matter what you do. Some substances are *insoluble* in water—they do not dissolve. Other substances, such as sugar and baking soda, are *soluble* in water—they dissolve easily in water.

Solubility in Water

There is often a limit to how much of a substance will dissolve. Have you ever mixed a large amount of salt in a glass of water? You may have observed that some of the salt did not dissolve, no matter how much you stirred. Salt is soluble in water, but the amount of salt that will dissolve is limited. The maximum amount of salt that can be dissolved in 100 g of water at room temperature is 36 g, or about two tablespoons.
▶ **The solubility of a substance is the maximum mass of a solute that can dissolve in 100 g of solvent at a certain temperature and standard atmospheric pressure.**

Some substances, such as acetic acid, methanol, ethanol, glycerol, and ethylene glycol, are completely soluble in water. Any amount of these substances will mix with water to form a solution. Some ionic compounds, such as silver chloride, AgCl, are almost completely insoluble in water. Only 0.00019 g of AgCl will dissolve in 100 g of water at 20 °C.

Different substances have different solubilities.

The solubilities of closely related compounds can vary greatly. Compare the solubilities of the ionic compounds in **Figure 2.** Notice that all of the compounds that contain sodium also contain one other element. But sodium iodide is much more soluble than either sodium chloride or sodium fluoride.

The solubility of any substance in water depends on the strength of the forces acting between the solute particles and the strength of the forces acting between water molecules and solute particles. So, in a highly soluble substance, the forces between the solute particles are weaker than the forces between the water molecules and the solute particles. In sodium iodide, the forces between the sodium ions and iodide ions in the sodium iodide crystals are much weaker than the forces between the water molecules and the sodium and iodide ions. So, sodium iodide is more soluble than many other compounds that also contain sodium.

Figure 2 Solubilities of Some Ionic Compounds in Water

Substance	Formula	Solubility in g/100 g H$_2$O at 20 °C
Calcium chloride	CaCl$_2$	75
Calcium fluoride	CaF$_2$	0.0015
Calcium sulfate	CaSO$_4$	0.32
Iron(II) sulfide	FeS	0.0006
Silver chloride	AgCl	0.000 19
Silver nitrate	AgNO$_3$	216
Sodium chloride	NaCl	35.9
Sodium fluoride	NaF	4.06
Sodium iodide	NaI	178
Sodium sulfide	Na$_2$S	26.3

Reading Check Why is sodium iodide so soluble?

How much of a substance is in a solution?

Not all solutions have all of the solute that can be dissolved. How would you compare a solution made with one teaspoon of salt with one made with one tablespoon of salt?

Because the amount of a substance that is dissolved in solution can vary greatly, the amount of solute that is dissolved in a given solution must be specified. A solution may be described as *weak* if only a small amount of solute is dissolved or as *strong* if a large amount of solute is dissolved. However, *weak* and *strong* do not mean the same thing to everyone. For example, the sulfuric acid solution found in automobile batteries can injure the skin. So, most people would describe the solution as strong. But a chemist knows that much stronger solutions of sulfuric acid can be prepared.

The concentration of a solution is not given by the terms *weak* and *strong*. **Concentration** is the quantity of solute that is dissolved in a given volume of solution. A chemist would describe battery acid as having a specific concentration value. A *concentrated* solution has a large amount of solute. A *dilute* solution has only a small amount of solute. However, because the terms *concentrated* and *dilute* are not quantitative, they do not give any information about the actual amount of solute in a solution.

solubility (SAHL yoo BIL uh tee) the ability of one substance to dissolve in another at a given temperature and pressure

concentration (KAHN suhn TRAY shuhn) the amount of a particular substance in a given quantity of a mixture, solution, or ore

www.scilinks.org
Topic: Solubility
Code: HK81421

Academic Vocabulary

maximum (MAKS i muhm) the greatest quantity possible

saturated solution (SACH uh RAYT id suh LOO shuhn) a solution that cannot dissolve any more solute under the given conditions

unsaturated solution (uhn SACH uh RAYT id suh LOO shuhn) a solution that contains less solute than a saturated solution does and that is able to dissolve additional solute

supersaturated solution (SOO puhr SACH uh RAYT id suh LOO shuhn) a solution that holds more dissolved solute than is required to reach equilibrium at a given temperature

Saturated Solutions

The solubility of a substance is how much of that substance will dissolve in a given amount of water at a certain temperature and pressure. When you have added the maximum amount of solute that will dissolve in a solution, you have made a **saturated solution.** No more solute will dissolve. ▶ **In a saturated solution, the dissolved solute is in equilibrium with undissolved solute. So, if you add more solute, it just settles to the bottom of the container.** To be in equilibrium means that the dissolved solute settles out of solution at the same rate that the undissolved solute dissolves.

Unsaturated solutions can become saturated.

Compare the two solutions shown in **Figure 3.** One has a white solid at the bottom, and one does not. The **unsaturated solution** of sodium acetate contains less than the maximum amount of solute that will dissolve in the solvent. If you keep adding sodium acetate to the solution, the compound dissolves until the solution becomes saturated. So, the solution will not have solid at the bottom. A solution is unsaturated as long as more solute can dissolve in it. The saturated solution in **Figure 3** has solid sodium acetate at the bottom of the beaker. No matter how much you stir, no more sodium acetate will dissolve in this saturated solution. The undissolved solid particles will sink to the bottom of the solution.

✓ **Reading Check** What happens when you add more solute to a saturated solution?

Figure 3 Concentration and the Dissolving Process

Unsaturated Solution When more sodium acetate is added to this unsaturated solution, it can dissolve.

Saturated Solution No more sodium acetate will dissolve in this saturated solution. Any additional sodium acetate that is dissolved causes an equal amount to settle out of the solution.

Heating a saturated solution can dissolve more solute.

The solubility of most solutes increases as the temperature of the solution increases. If you heat a saturated solution of sodium acetate, more sodium acetate can dissolve until the solution becomes saturated at the higher temperature.

When the temperature of the sodium acetate solution decreases, sodium acetate crystals do not re-form. The excess solute needs a surface on which to crystallize. This solution now holds more solute than it normally would at the cooler temperature, so it is a **supersaturated solution.** Adding a small crystal of sodium acetate causes the solute to crystallize until the solution is once again saturated, as **Figure 4** shows.

Temperature and pressure affect the solubility of gases.

Soda contains carbon dioxide gas dissolved in water. Unlike solids, gases are less soluble in warmer water. So, warm soda goes flat more quickly than cold soda.

The solubility of gases also depends on pressure, as shown in **Figure 5.** Carbon dioxide is dissolved in the soda under high pressure when the bottle is sealed. When the bottle is opened, the gas pressure decreases to atmospheric pressure and the soda fizzes as the carbon dioxide comes out of solution.

Gas solubility affects scuba divers. Increased pressure underwater causes more nitrogen gas to dissolve in the blood. If the diver returns to the surface too quickly, nitrogen comes out of solution and forms bubbles in blood vessels. This condition, called the *bends*, is very painful and dangerous.

Figure 4 Adding a single crystal of sodium acetate to a supersaturated solution causes the excess sodium acetate to quickly crystallize out of the solution.

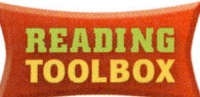

Summarizing Ideas
Make notes about saturated solutions by summarizing the content under the red and blue headings on these two pages.

Figure 5 Effect of Gas Pressure on Gas Solubility in Water

Higher Pressure The pressure inside this bottle is higher than the pressure outside the bottle. Carbon dioxide gas is dissolved in water in this unopened bottle of soda.

Lower Pressure When the bottle is opened, the pressure inside the bottle decreases. Carbon dioxide gas then forms bubbles as it comes out of solution. **Will more bubbles come out of a warm soda or a cold soda?**

Concentration of Solutions

The terms *concentrated*, *dilute*, *saturated*, and *unsaturated* do not reveal the quantity of dissolved solute. For example, 0.173 g of calcium hydroxide will dissolve in 100 g of water. This solution is saturated but is still dilute because so little solute is present. Scientists express the quantity of solute in a solution in several ways. ❯ **One of the most common ways of expressing the concentration of a solution is molarity.** Molarity is expressed as moles of solute per liter of solution.

$$molarity = \frac{moles\ of\ solute}{liters\ of\ solution}, \text{ or } M = \frac{mol}{L}$$

A 1.0 M, which is read as "one molar," solution of NaCl contains 1.0 mol of dissolved NaCl in every 1.0 L of solution.

molarity (moh LA ruh tee) a concentration unit of a solution expressed in moles of solute dissolved per liter of solution

Math Skills — Molarity

Calculate the molarity of sucrose, $C_{12}H_{22}O_{11}$, in a solution of 124 g of solute in 0.500 L of solution.

Identify
List the given and unknown values.

Given:
 mass of sucrose = 124 g
 volume of solution = 0.500 L
Unknown:
 molarity, amount of $C_{12}H_{22}O_{11}$ in 1 L of solution

Plan
Write the equation for moles $C_{12}H_{22}O_{11}$ and molarity.

$$moles\ C_{12}H_{22}O_{11} = \frac{mass\ C_{12}H_{22}O_{11}}{molar\ mass\ C_{12}H_{22}O_{11}}$$

$$molarity = \frac{moles\ C_{12}H_{22}O_{11}}{liters\ of\ solution}$$

Solve
Find the number of moles of $C_{12}H_{22}O_{11}$, and calculate molarity.

molar mass $C_{12}H_{22}O_{11}$ = 342 g

$$moles\ C_{12}H_{22}O_{11} = \frac{124\ g}{342\ g/mol} = 0.362\ mol$$

molarity of solution =
$$\frac{0.362\ mole\ C_{12}H_{22}O_{11}}{0.500\ L\ solution} = 0.724\ M$$

Practice Hint

❯ When calculating molarity, remember that molarity is moles of solute per liter of solution, not moles per liter of solvent.

❯ Problem 2: If volume is given in milliliters, you must multiply by 1 L/1,000 mL to change milliliters to liters.

Practice

1. What is the molarity of 2 mol of calcium chloride, $CaCl_2$, dissolved in 1 L of solution?
2. What is the molarity of 525 g of lead(II) nitrate, $Pb(NO_3)_2$, dissolved in 1,250 mL of solution?

For more practice, visit **go.hrw.com** and enter keyword **HK8MP**.

Why It Matters
Fluoride in Water

SCIENCE & SOCIETY

Fluoride ions occur naturally in drinking water. In proper concentration, these ions strengthen tooth enamel and reduce tooth decay. However, prolonged exposure to too much fluoride damages tooth enamel. The concentration of fluoride in drinking water is very small and is measured in parts per million (ppm). The amount of fluoride in most drinking water is about 1.0 ppm, or 1.0 g of fluoride per 1,000,000 g water. So, 1.0 L of water contains about 1 mg of fluoride.

Fluoride Concentration and Water Source

A limited range of fluoride concentration—0.7 ppm to 1.2 ppm—is best for helping prevent cavities. In many places where the fluoride concentration is below 0.7 ppm, fluoride is added to the water supply.

YOUR TURN

ONLINE RESEARCH
1. Find out if fluoride is added to your water supply and what the concentration of fluoride in your drinking water is.

Section 3 Review

KEY IDEAS

1. **Compare** the solubility of olive oil and acetic acid in water. Why is one substance more soluble than the other?
2. **Describe** how a saturated solution can become supersaturated.
3. **Express** the molarity of a solution that contains 0.5 mol of calcium acetate per 1.0 L of solution.

CRITICAL THINKING

4. **Understanding Relationships** Explain how a solution can be both saturated and dilute at the same time. Use an example from **Figure 2**.
5. **Drawing Conclusions** Determine whether sweat would evaporate more quickly if the humidity were 92% or 37%. (Hint: When the humidity is 100%, the air is saturated with dissolved water vapor.)
6. **Designing Experiments** Propose a way to determine whether a saltwater solution is unsaturated, saturated, or supersaturated.
7. **Applying Ideas** When you fill a glass with cold water from a faucet and then let the glass sit undisturbed for two hours, you will see small bubbles sticking to the glass. What are the bubbles? Why did they form?

Math Skills

8. Calculate the molarity of a solution that contains 35.0 g of barium chloride, $BaCl_2$, dissolved in 450.0 mL of solution.

Application Lab

  50 min

How Temperature Affects Gas Solubility

The management at a soft-drink bottling plant wants to see if turning up the thermostat on the plant's air-conditioning system will save money. The bottling machinery was calibrated at the colder temperature. If the solubility of carbon dioxide decreases when the temperature is raised, the beverage may lose some carbonation in the bottling process. You, the lead engineer, must find out what the effect of increasing the temperature will be. To do so, you will determine the effects of temperature on the solubility of carbon dioxide, a gaseous solute, in a soft drink.

What You'll Do

- **Compare** the volume of carbon dioxide released from a warm soft drink with that released from a cold soft drink.
- **Draw conclusions** to relate carbon dioxide's solubility in each soft drink to the temperature of each soft drink.

What You'll Need

bags, plastic, small (2)
beaker, 1 L
ice, crushed
paper towels
soft drinks, carbonated, in plastic bottles (2)
stopwatch
tape measure, flexible, metric
thermometer
twist ties (4)

Safety

Procedure

Preparing for Your Experiment

1. Prepare a data table in your lab report similar to the one below.

Sample Data Table: Soft-Drink Data

	Temperature (°C)	Circumference of bag (cm)	Radius of bag (cm)	Volume of bag (cm³)
Room-temp soft drink				
Chilled soft drink		DO NOT WRITE IN BOOK		

Testing the Solubility of Carbon Dioxide in a Warm Soft Drink

2. Obtain a bottle of carbonated soft drink that has been stored at room temperature, and carry it to your lab table. Try not to disturb the liquid, and do not open the bottle.

3. Use a thermometer to measure the temperature in the laboratory. Record this temperature in your data table.

4. Remove the bottle's cap, and quickly place the open end of a deflated plastic bag over the bottle's opening. Seal the bag tightly around the bottle's neck with a twist tie. Begin timing with a stopwatch.

5. When the bag is almost fully inflated, stop the stopwatch. Very carefully remove the plastic bag from the bottle. Be sure to keep the bag sealed so that the carbon dioxide inside does not escape. Seal the bag tightly with another twist tie.

6. Gently mold the bag into the shape of a sphere. Measure the bag's circumference in centimeters by wrapping the tape measure around the largest part of the bag. Record the circumference in your data table.

Testing the Solubility of Carbon Dioxide in a Cold Soft Drink

7. Obtain a second bottle of carbonated soft drink that has been chilled. Place the bottle in a 1 L beaker, and pack crushed ice around the bottle. Use paper towels to dry any water on the outside of the beaker, and then carefully move the beaker to your lab table.

8. Repeat step 4. Let the second plastic bag inflate for the same length of time that the first bag was allowed to inflate. Very carefully remove the bag from the bottle as you did before. Seal the plastic bag tightly with a twist tie.

9. Wait for the bag to warm to room temperature. While you are waiting, use the thermometer to measure the temperature of the cold soft drink. Record the temperature in your data table.

10. When the bag has warmed to room temperature, repeat step 6.

Analysis

1. **Analyzing Data** Calculate the radius in centimeters of each inflated plastic bag by using the following equation. Record the results in your data table.

$$radius \text{ (in cm)} = \frac{circumference \text{ (in cm)}}{2\pi}$$

2. **Analyzing Data** Calculate the volume in cubic centimeters of each inflated bag by using the following equation. Record the results in your data table.

$$volume \text{ (in cm}^3\text{)} = \frac{4}{3}\pi \times [radius \text{ (in cm)}]^3$$

Communicating Your Results

3. **Drawing Conclusions** Compare the volume of carbon dioxide released from the two soft drinks. Use your data to explain how the solubility of carbon dioxide in a soft drink is affected by temperature.

4. **Designing Experiments** Suppose that someone tells you that your conclusion is not valid because a soft drink contains many other solutes besides carbon dioxide. How could you verify that your conclusion is correct?

Application

What would be your recommendation to the bottling-plant management, and how would you justify it?

Making Pie Graphs

Science Skills

Technology
Math
Scientific Methods
▶ Graphing

Problem

Often used in jewelry, 14-karat gold is an alloy that contains 58% gold by weight. The table below gives the composition of a 14-karat yellow gold alloy. Show these data in a pie graph.

Solution

① Make sure that all of the parts are given. Calculate percentages if necessary.

The data are already in percentages, and the numbers add up to 100%.

② Draw a circle that is large enough that you can see each section of the pie graph.

Silver is the smallest section. A circle about 3 cm in diameter should be large enough.

③ Determine the size of each pie wedge. Multiply the percentage of each metal by 360°.

The size for the gold section is 360° × 0.58 = 210°. Sizes for the other sections are silver = 14°; copper = 110°; and zinc = 26°.

④ Use a protractor to draw the sections in the circle. Color in each section with a different color.

Draw a line from the center to the edge of the circle. Measure the first section as an angle from that line (210° for gold). Repeat for each section.

⑤ Label each section with the name of the category and the percentage.

The labels in the gold section are "Gold" and "58%."

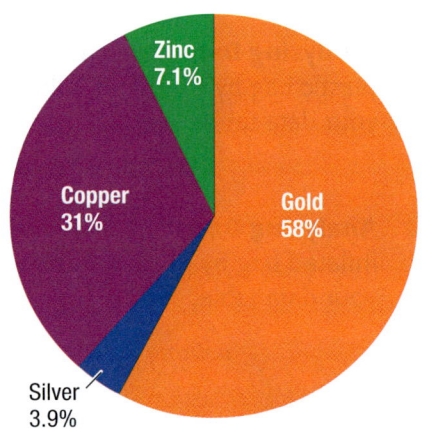

Percentage Composition by Weight of a 14-Karat Yellow Gold Alloy

Metal	Weight (%)
Gold	58
Copper	31
Zinc	7.1
Silver	3.9

Practice

Use the graph above to answer question 1.

1. What is the second most abundant metal by weight in the 14-karat gold alloy?

Use the table below to answer questions 2–5.

Percentage Composition by Weight of a 9-Karat White Gold Alloy

Metal	Weight (%)
Copper	40
Gold	38
Nickel	12
Zinc	10

2. The 9-karat gold is less expensive than the 14-karat gold. Create a pie graph that shows the composition of a 9-karat white gold alloy.

3. How does the amount of gold in the 9-karat white gold alloy compare to the amount of gold in the 14-karat yellow gold alloy?

4. What is the most abundant metal by weight in the 9-karat white gold alloy?

5. Which metal in the yellow gold is not in the white gold? Which metal in the white gold is not in the yellow gold?

CHAPTER 8 Summary

Key Ideas

Section 1 Solutions and Other Mixtures

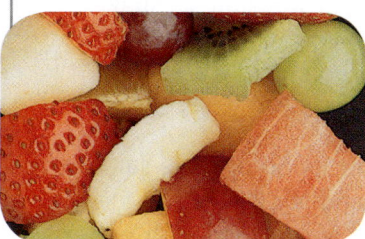

> **Heterogeneous Mixtures** A heterogeneous mixture does not have a fixed composition. The amount of each substance in a heterogeneous mixture varies from sample to sample. (p. 259)

> **Homogeneous Mixtures** A homogeneous mixture looks uniform, even when you examine it under a microscope, because the individual components are too small to be seen. (p. 263)

Section 2 How Substances Dissolve

> **Water: A Common Solvent** Water is called the *universal solvent* because many substances can dissolve in water. Water is a polar compound. (p. 267)

> **The Dissolving Process** The energy transferred from the solvent to the solute, as well as the attractive forces between the solvent and solute molecules, causes molecules at the surface of the crystal to dissolve. (p. 271)

Section 3 Solubility and Concentration

> **Solubility in Water** The solubility of a substance is the maximum mass of a solute that can dissolve in 100 g of solvent at a certain temperature and standard atmospheric pressure. (p. 276)

> **Saturated Solutions** In a saturated solution, the dissolved solute is in equilibrium with the undissolved solute. So, if you add more solute, it just settles to the bottom of the container. (p. 278)

> **Concentration of Solutions** One of the most common ways of expressing the concentration of a solution is molarity. *Molarity* is moles of solute per liter of solution. (p. 280)

Key Terms

suspension, p. 260
colloid, p. 261
emulsion, p. 262
solution, p. 263
solute, p. 263
solvent, p. 263
alloy, p. 266

polar, p. 267
hydrogen bond, p. 269
nonpolar, p. 270

solubility, p. 276
concentration, p. 277
saturated solution, p. 278
unsaturated solution, p. 278
supersaturated solution, p. 279
molarity, p. 280

Solutions **285**

CHAPTER 8 Review

READING TOOLBOX

1. **Finding Examples** List at least two examples of substances that contain nonpolar compounds given in Section 2. If a word or phrase was used to signal the example in the text, write that word or phrase next to the example in your list.

USING KEY TERMS

2. A small amount of *solute* is added to two *solutions.* In the figures below, which solution is *unsaturated*? Which solution is *saturated*? Explain your answer.

   a.   b.

3. Explain why an *alloy* is a type of solution. Why are alloys sometimes used instead of pure metals?

4. Classify the following items as either a *suspension*, a *colloid*, an *emulsion*, or a *solution*: muddy water, salt water, mayonnaise, vinegar, fog, dry air, and cream.

5. Explain why water and ethanol are *polar* or *nonpolar* compounds.

6. The *concentration* of a sodium chloride solution is 0.01 M. How many moles of sodium chloride are in 1 L of this solution?

UNDERSTANDING KEY IDEAS

7. Which of the following mixtures is homogeneous?
   a. tossed salad
   b. soil
   c. salt water
   d. vegetable soup

8. The label on a bottle of medicine states, "Shake well before using." The medicine is probably a
   a. solution.
   b. suspension.
   c. colloid.
   d. gel.

9. Suppose that you add a teaspoon of table salt to a cool saltwater solution and stir until all of the salt dissolves. The solution you started with was
   a. unsaturated.
   b. supersaturated.
   c. saturated.
   d. concentrated.

10. Which of the following materials is an example of a solid dissolved in another solid?
    a. smoke
    b. bronze
    c. mayonnaise
    d. ice

11. The dispersed particles of a suspension are _____ than the particles of a colloid.
    a. larger
    b. smaller
    c. lighter
    d. less dense

12. To dissolve a substance, a solvent must attract particles of the substance more strongly than the _____ attract each other.
    a. solvent particles
    b. water molecules
    c. ions
    d. solute particles

13. The boiling point of a solution of sugar in water is _____ the boiling point of water.
    a. higher than
    b. lower than
    c. the same as
    d. not related to

14. To increase the solubility of a solid substance in a solvent, you could
    a. add more solute.
    b. heat the solution.
    c. stir the solution.
    d. lower the pressure.

15. A _____ solution contains as much dissolved solute as it can hold under certain conditions.
    a. saturated
    b. dilute
    c. supersaturated
    d. concentrated

16. Gases are more soluble in liquids when the pressure is _____ and the temperature is _____.
    a. high, high
    b. high, low
    c. low, high
    d. low, low

286 Chapter 8 Solutions

EXPLAINING KEY IDEAS

17. Why does stirring a solution help the solute dissolve faster?

18. Explain why water dissolves many ionic compounds.

INTERPRETING GRAPHICS The graph below shows how the solubilities of cadmium selenate, $CdSeO_4$, and cobalt(II) chloride, $CoCl_2$, vary with temperature. Use the graph to answer questions 19 and 20.

19. At what temperature is the solubility of $CdSeO_4$ equal to 40 g $CdSeO_4$/100 g H_2O?

20. Which substance has an unusual solubility trend? How is the trend unusual?

CRITICAL THINKING

21. Designing Experiments Sea water is a solution that contains many types of dissolved ions. What is the simplest way to get a clear sea-water solution from a mixture that also contains mud and sand? Explain your answer.

22. Drawing Conclusions Use the observations in the table below to decide whether each mixture is a solution, a suspension, or a colloid.

Sample	Clarity	Settles out	Scatters light
1	clear	no	yes
2	clear	no	no
3	cloudy	yes	yes
4	cloudy	no	yes

Graphing Skills

23. Constructing Graphs The solubility of silver nitrate, $AgNO_3$, in water at various temperatures is given in the table below.

Temperature (°C)	Solubility of $AgNO_3$ in g $AgNO_3$/100 g H_2O
0	122
20	216
40	311
60	440
80	585

Make a graph of the solubility of $AgNO_3$. Plot temperature on the x-axis, and plot solubility on the y-axis. Answer the following questions.

a. How does the solubility of $AgNO_3$ vary with the temperature of water?

b. Estimate the solubility of $AgNO_3$ at 35 °C, at 55 °C, and at 75 °C.

c. At what temperature would the solubility of $AgNO_3$ be 512 g per 100 g H_2O?

d. Is a solution that contains 100 g $AgNO_3$ dissolved in 100 g H_2O at 10 °C saturated?

Math Skills

24. Molarity How many moles of lithium chloride, LiCl, are dissolved in 3.00 L of a 0.200 M solution of lithium chloride?

25. Molarity What is the molarity of 250 mL of a solution that contains 12.5 g of zinc bromide, $ZnBr_2$?

26. Solubility The solubility of sodium fluoride, NaF, is 4.06 g NaF/100 g H_2O at 20 °C. What mass of NaF would you have to dissolve in 1,000 g H_2O to make a saturated solution?

27. Solubility The solubility of copper(II) chloride, $CuCl_2$, at 20 °C is 73 g/100 g H_2O. Suppose that you add 50 g $CuCl_2$ to 50 g of water at 20 °C and stir until no more $CuCl_2$ dissolves. What mass of $CuCl_2$ remains undissolved at 20 °C?

Standardized Test Prep

Understanding Concepts

Directions (1–3): For each question, write on a sheet of paper the letter of the correct answer.

1. An industrial chemist stirs some crystals into water. The resulting liquid appears completely uniform under a microscope. What is the liquid?
   - **A.** a colloid
   - **B.** a solution
   - **C.** a suspension
   - **D.** a heterogeneous mixture

2. After the lungs take in oxygen during respiration, oxygen gas is dissolved in the bloodstream. Under what conditions can the most oxygen be dissolved in the blood?
   - **F.** high blood pressure and high body temperature
   - **G.** low blood pressure and low body temperature
   - **H.** low blood pressure and high body temperature
   - **I.** high blood pressure and low body temperature

3. Potassium sulfate, K_2SO_4, has a molar mass of 174 g. If potassium sulfate is the solute in 2 L of a solution that has a concentration of 0.25 M, how many grams of potassium sulfate are in the solution?
   - **A.** 1,392 g
   - **B.** 348 g
   - **C.** 87 g
   - **D.** 43.5 g

Directions (4): For each question, write a short response.

4. The molecules of compound A have unevenly distributed electric charge. The molecules of compound B have evenly distributed electric charge. Which compound is more likely to dissolve easily in water? Explain your reasoning.

Reading Skills

Directions (5–6): Read the passage below. Then, answer the questions that follow.

SUPERCRITICAL DECAFFEINATION
One of the most common ways to remove caffeine from coffee and to preserve the flavor of the beverage is to use a solvent that dissolves the caffeine but leaves the rest of the plant material undissolved. One of the main difficulties with removing caffeine is that caffeine is a nonpolar compound. Therefore, a nonpolar solvent is required to dissolve caffeine. But most effective nonpolar solvents are poisonous to humans. Although carbon dioxide, CO_2, is a safe nonpolar compound, it is a gas under normal conditions and cannot act as a solvent for caffeine.

When both the pressure and temperature of a fluid are increased beyond a specific (or *critical*) point, a fluid has some properties of liquids and some properties of gases. Fluids under these conditions are called *supercritical fluids*. In the 1960s, coffee companies began using supercritical CO_2 to extract caffeine. The gaslike behavior of CO_2 allows its molecules to penetrate into the plant material. The liquid aspects of CO_2 allow it to dissolve caffeine molecules.

5. Once the caffeine is removed from the plant materials, how might the caffeine be recovered from the supercritical CO_2?
   - **F.** by forcing the CO_2 back through the plant materials
   - **G.** by lowering the temperature and pressure of the CO_2
   - **H.** by changing the polarity of the caffeine molecules
   - **I.** by using a harsher solvent

6. Why can't water be used to dissolve the caffeine found in coffee and tea?

Interpreting Graphics

The graphic below represents three beakers that contain 500 g of water with different amounts of sugar. One is unsaturated, one is saturated, and one is supersaturated. Use this graphic to answer questions 7–8.

7. How many grams of sugar are there altogether in the three cylinders?
   - **A.** 2,670 g
   - **B.** 1,602 g
   - **C.** 534 g
   - **D.** 267 g

8. Which solution would show the most dramatic results if an additional crystal of sugar were dropped into it? What would those results be?

The graph below shows how the solubility of a mystery solid in water depends on temperature. Use this graph to answer questions 9–10.

9. The solubility of the solid is 88 g/100 g H_2O at 20 °C. What is the solubility of the substance at 60 °C?
   - **F.** 88 g/100 g H_2O
   - **G.** 100 g/100 g H_2O
   - **H.** 122 g/100 g H_2O
   - **I.** 264 g/100 g H_2O

10. Water normally boils at 100 °C. The scientists performing this experiment were able to measure the solubility at 100 °C because the solution was not boiling. Why was the solution not boiling at 100 °C?

Test Tip

To develop a short-response or extended-response answer, jot down your key ideas on a piece of scratch paper first.

CHAPTER 9
Acids, Bases, and Salts

Chapter Outline

1 Acids, Bases, and pH
  Acids
  Bases
  pH

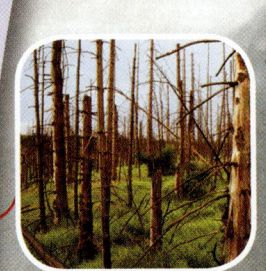

2 Reactions of Acids with Bases
  Acid-Base Reactions
  Salts

3 Acids, Bases, and Salts in the Home
  Cleaning Products
  Personal-Care and Food Products

Tennessee Course Level Expectations (Physical Science)

CLE.3202.TE.3 Explain the relationship between the properties of a material and the use of the material in the application of a technology; **CLE.3202.1.10** Distinguish among acids, bases, and neutral substances; **CLE.3202.Inq.1** Recognize that science is a progressive endeavor that reevaluates and extends what is already accepted; **CLE.3202.Inq.2** Design and conduct scientific investigations to explore new phenomena, verify previous results, test how well a theory predicts, and compare opposing theories; **CLE.3202.Inq.3** Use appropriate tools and technology to collect precise and accurate data; **CLE.3202.Inq.4** Apply qualitative and quantitative measures to analyze data and draw conclusions that are free of bias; **CLE.3202.Inq.6** Communicate and defend scientific findings.

Why It Matters

Carbon dioxide dissolves in water to form an acid. This acid can then react to make a salt. This salt, calcium carbonate, will precipitate out of the water and, over millions of years, form limestone structures, such as these ice-covered rock terraces in Yellowstone National Park.

Inquiry Lab
⏱ 10 min

Acid-Base Reaction

Squeeze the juice from **half of a lemon** into a **clean dish** to get about a teaspoon of juice. Add **one teaspoon of water** to the lemon juice, and stir with your finger. With a clean, dry **spoon,** add **1/2 teaspoon of baking soda,** a basic substance, to the diluted lemon juice.

Questions to Get You Started

1. Do you think that lemon juice is acidic or basic? Give reasons for your decision.
2. What happens when baking soda is added to the lemon juice?
3. What evidence do you see that a chemical reaction takes place?

READING TOOLBOX These reading tools can help you learn the material in this chapter. For more information on how to use these and other tools, see **Appendix A**.

Science Terms

Everyday Words Used in Science Many words used in science are familiar words from everyday speech. However, the meanings of these everyday words are often different from their meanings in scientific contexts.

Your Turn Before you read this chapter, write down an informal definition of what the word *base* means to you. As you come across this word in the chapter, write the scientific definitions next to your informal definition. For each definition, write a sentence that uses the word *base* correctly.

Classification

Classifying Acids and Bases
Classification is a tool for organizing objects and ideas by grouping them into categories. Groups are classified by defining characteristics. For example, the table below shows how acids can be classified by their strength.

CLASS	DEFINING CHARACTERISTIC
strong acids	ionize completely in water
weak acids	do not ionize completely

Your Turn As you read the chapter, create a table like the one shown here for the following classes of substance: strong bases, weak bases, soaps, detergents, and disinfectants.

Graphic Organizers

Cause-and-Effect Maps You can use cause-and-effect maps to show visually how the relationships in physical processes depend on one another. To make a cause-and-effect map, follow these steps:

1. Draw a box, and write a cause inside the box. You can have as many cause boxes as you want.
2. Draw another box to represent an effect of the cause. You can have as many effect boxes as you want.
3. Connect each cause box to an effect box or boxes with an arrow.
4. If an effect is also the cause of another effect(s), you may connect the effect box to another effect box or boxes.

Your Turn As you read Section 1, complete on a separate sheet of paper the cause-and-effect map started below. Add at least two more effects.

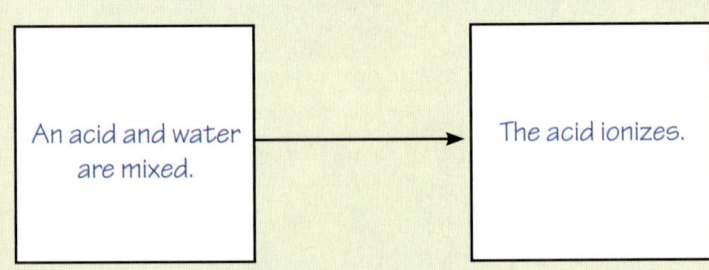

292 Chapter 9 Acids, Bases, and Salts

SECTION 1
Acids, Bases, and pH

Key Ideas
- What are the properties of acids?
- What are the properties of bases?
- How is pH related to the concentration of hydronium ions and hydroxide ions in solution?

Key Terms
- acid
- indicator
- electrolyte
- base
- pH

Why It Matters
Acid rain is a type of pollution that can have harmful effects on many parts of the environment, including animals, plants, and buildings.

Does the thought of eating a lemon cause your mouth to pucker? You expect that sour taste of a lemon. Eating a lime or a dill pickle may cause you to have a similar response.

Acids

Each of the foods shown in **Figure 1** tastes sour because it contains an acid. Citrus fruits, such as grapefruits, lemons, limes, and oranges, contain citric acid. Apples contain malic acid, and grapes contain tartaric acid.

When acids dissolve in water, they *ionize*, which means that they form ions. When **acids** ionize, they form hydrogen ions, H^+, which attach to water molecules to make hydronium ions, H_3O^+. These hydronium ions give acids their properties.
▶ **Acids taste sour, cause indicators to change color, and conduct electric current. They are also corrosive and can damage materials, including your skin.** Blue litmus paper contains an indicator that turns red in the presence of an acid, as **Figure 1** shows. Indicators can help you determine if a substance is acidic.

> **TN** Tennessee Course Level Expectations (Physical Science)
> CLE.3202.1.10; CLE.3202.Inq.1; CLE.3202.Inq.2; CLE.3202.Inq.3

> **acid** (AS id) any compound that increases the number of hydronium ions when dissolved in water
> **indicator** (IN di KAYT uhr) a compound that can reversibly change color depending on conditions such as pH

Figure 1 Many fruits, such as lemons, taste sour because they contain acids. Acids, such as the citric acid in orange juice, turn blue litmus paper red.

Strong acids ionize completely.

All acids ionize when they are dissolved in water. The ionization process shown below occurs when nitric acid is added to water. The single arrow pointing to the right shows that nitric acid ionizes completely in water.

$$HNO_3 + H_2O \longrightarrow H_3O^+ + NO_3^-$$

When nitric acid ionizes, it forms hydronium ions and nitrate ions. These charged ions are able to move around in the solution and conduct electricity, as you see in **Figure 2.** A substance that conducts electricity when the substance is dissolved in water is an **electrolyte.**

Solutions of some acids, such as nitric acid, conduct electricity well. Nitric acid, HNO_3, is a *strong acid* because all of the molecules that are dissolved in water ionize. Other strong acids behave similarly to nitric acid when dissolved in water. A solution of sulfuric acid in water, for example, conducts electric current in car batteries. Strong acids are strong electrolytes because solutions of these acids contain as many hydronium ions as the acid can possibly form.

Figure 2 Nitric acid, HNO_3, is a strong electrolyte and a strong acid because it ionizes completely in water to form hydronium ions, H_3O^+, and nitrate ions, NO_3^-.

Weak acids do not ionize completely.

Solutions of *weak acids*, such as acetic acid, CH_3COOH, do not conduct electricity as well as nitric acid does. When acetic acid is added to water, the equilibrium represented by the reaction below is reached.

$$CH_3COOH + H_2O \rightleftharpoons H_3O^+ + CH_3COO^-$$

When acetic acid is dissolved in water, some molecules of acetic acid combine with water molecules to form ions. Many of the ions then recombine to form molecules of acetic acid. Because there are few charged ions in a solution of acetic acid, the solution does not conduct electricity very well, as **Figure 3** shows. Weak acids, such as acetic acid, are weak electrolytes.

Figure 3 Acetic acid, CH_3COOH, is a weak acid and a weak electrolyte because only a few of the molecules that are dissolved in water ionize to form hydronium ions, H_3O^+, and acetate ions, CH_3COO^-.

Figure 4 Some Common Acids

Acid	Formula	Strength	Uses
Hydrochloric acid	HCl	strong	cleaning masonry; treating metal before plating or painting; adjusting the pH of swimming pools
Sulfuric acid	H_2SO_4	strong	manufacturing fertilizer and chemicals; most-used industrial chemical; the electrolyte in car batteries
Nitric acid	HNO_3	strong	manufacturing fertilizers and explosives
Acetic acid	CH_3COOH	weak	manufacturing chemicals, plastics, and pharmaceuticals; the acid in vinegar
Formic acid	HCOOH	weak	dyeing textiles; the acid in stinging ants
Citric acid	$H_3C_6H_5O_7$	weak	manufacturing flavorings and soft drinks; the acid in citrus fruits (oranges, lemons, and limes)

All of the acids used in familiar products produce hydronium ions when in water solution.

Concentrated acid can be dangerous.

Some examples of common strong and weak acids and their uses are listed in **Figure 4**. Acids are used in many manufacturing processes and are necessary to many organisms. However, strong acids are corrosive and can damage living tissue. For example, your stomach normally contains a dilute solution of hydrochloric acid that helps you digest food, but concentrated hydrochloric acid can burn your skin.

Even weak acids are not always safe to handle. Most vinegar is a 5% solution of acetic acid in water, but concentrated acetic acid can damage the skin. The vapors are harmful to the eyes, mouth, and lungs. To be safe, always wear safety goggles, gloves, and a laboratory apron when working with acids. Never taste a chemical to determine if it is an acid.

Reading Check What precautions should you take when working with acids? (See Appendix E for answers to Reading Checks.)

Academic Vocabulary

process (PRAH ses) a set of steps, events, or changes

electrolyte (ee LEK troh LIET) a substance that dissolves in water to give a solution that conducts an electric current

base (BAYS) any compound that increases the number of hydroxide ions when dissolved in water

Bases

Many common household substances contain bases. Like acids, bases share common properties. **Bases have a bitter taste, and solutions of bases feel slippery. Solutions of bases also conduct electric current, cause indicators to change color, and can damage the skin.** When **bases** dissolve in water, they form hydroxide ions, OH^-. Some basic compounds contain hydroxide ions, but others do not. Bases that do not contain hydroxide ions react with water molecules to form hydroxide ions. The hydroxide ions cause the indicator in red litmus paper to turn blue.

Section 1   Acids, Bases, and pH

Inquiry Lab

Which Household Products Are Acidic, and Which Are Basic?

 20 min

Procedure

1. Prepare a sample of **each substance** that you will test. If the substance is a liquid, pour about 5 mL of it into a **small beaker**. If the substance is a solid, place a small amount of it in a beaker and add about **5 mL of water.** Label each beaker clearly with the name of the substance that is in the beaker.

2. Use a **disposable plastic pipet** to transfer a drop of liquid from one of the samples to **red litmus paper.** Then, transfer another drop of liquid from the same sample to **blue litmus paper.**

3. Record your observations.

4. Repeat steps 2 and 3 for each sample. Be sure to use a clean pipet to transfer each sample.

Analysis

1. Which substances are acidic? Which are basic? How did you make your determinations?
2. Which substances are not acids or bases? How did you make your determinations?

Cause-and-Effect Map
Draw a cause-and-effect map that shows why a solution of sodium hydroxide dissolved in water is basic.

Many common bases contain hydroxide ions.

Like strong acids, *strong bases* produce as many ions as possible when they dissolve. Strong bases are ionic compounds that contain a metal ion and a hydroxide ion. These strong bases are also known as *metal hydroxides*. When a metal hydroxide is dissolved in water, the metal ions and the hydroxide ions *dissociate*, or separate.

Sodium hydroxide, NaOH, is an example of a metal hydroxide. It is found in some drain cleaners. When sodium hydroxide dissolves, it dissociates completely. Solutions of sodium hydroxide conduct electricity well. So, like all strong bases, sodium hydroxide is a strong electrolyte. The dissociation of sodium hydroxide in water is shown below.

$$NaOH \rightarrow Na^+ + OH^-$$

Some metal hydroxides, such as calcium hydroxide and magnesium hydroxide, are not very soluble in water. However, they are still strong bases because all of the ions that do dissolve do separate. The strength of an acid or of a base does not depend on the concentration of the solution. Calcium hydroxide is used to treat soil that is too acidic. **Figure 5** lists other useful bases and shows some bases that you might find around your home.

 Reading Check Why are metal hydroxides strong bases?

Some bases ionize in water to form hydroxide ions.

Even though molecules of ammonia, NH_3, do not contain hydroxide ions, ammonia is still a base. It forms hydroxide ions when it dissolves in water through an ionization process, which is shown below. In this process, water donates a hydrogen ion to ammonia to form an ammonium ion, NH_4^+, and leaves a hydroxide ion, OH^-, behind.

$NH_3 \quad + \quad H_2O \quad \rightleftharpoons \quad NH_4^+ \quad + \quad OH^-$

A solution of ammonia in water is a poor conductor of electricity. Only some of the ammonia molecules actually become ammonium ions when ammonia dissolves. So, an ammonia solution consists mostly of water and dissolved ammonia molecules, along with a few ammonium ions and hydroxide ions. Ammonia is a much weaker base than the metal hydroxides, which dissociate completely. Weak bases, such as ammonia, are also weak electrolytes.

Bases can be very dangerous in concentrated form. Strong bases, such as sodium hydroxide and potassium hydroxide, can be dangerous even in fairly dilute form. Bases attack living tissue very rapidly. To protect yourself when working with bases, always wear safety goggles, gloves, and a laboratory apron. If possible, work only with very dilute bases.

Figure 5 Some Common Bases

Base	Formula	Strength	Uses
Potassium hydroxide (potash)	KOH	strong	manufacturing soap; absorbing carbon dioxide from flue gases; dyeing products
Sodium hydroxide (lye)	NaOH	strong	manufacturing soap; refining petroleum; cleaning drains; manufacturing synthetic fibers
Calcium hydroxide	$Ca(OH)_2$	strong	treating acidic soil; treating lakes polluted by acid precipitation; making mortar, plaster, and cement
Ammonia	NH_3	weak	fertilizing soil; manufacturing other fertilizers; manufacturing nitric acid; making cleaning solutions
Methylamine	CH_3NH_2	weak	manufacturing dyes and medicines; tanning leather
Aniline	$C_6H_5NH_2$	weak	manufacturing dyes and varnishes; used as a solvent

These household items contain bases, so they turn red litmus paper blue.

pH (PEE AYCH) a value that is used to express the acidity or basicity (alkalinity) of a system; each whole number on the scale indicates a tenfold change in acidity

pH

You can tell if a solution is acidic or basic by using an indicator, such as litmus paper. But to know exactly how acidic or basic a solution is, you must measure the concentration of hydronium ions, H_3O^+. ❱ **The pH of a solution indicates its concentration of H_3O^+ ions. In solutions, the concentration of hydronium ions is related to the concentration of hydroxide ions, OH^-. The pH of a solution also indicates the concentration of OH^- ions.**

A pH value corresponds to the concentration of hydronium ions.

The acidity or basicity of a solution is often critical. For example, enzymes in your body will not work if your blood is too acidic or too basic. A pH value can tell you how acidic or basic a solution is. A pH value can even tell you if a solution is *neutral*—that is, neither an acid nor a base.

Typically, the pH values of solutions range from 0 to 14, as **Figure 6** shows. In neutral solutions, or in substances such as pure water, the pH is 7. In neutral solutions, the concentration of hydronium ions is equal to the concentration of hydroxide ions. Acidic solutions have a pH of less than 7. In acidic solutions, such as apple juice, the concentration of hydronium ions is greater than the concentration of hydroxide ions. Basic solutions have a pH of greater than 7. In basic solutions, the concentration of hydroxide ions is greater than the concentration of hydronium ions.

Reading Check What does the pH of a solution tell you?

Figure 6 The pH of a solution is easily measured by moistening a piece of pH paper with the solution and then comparing the color of the pH paper with the color scale on the dispenser of the pH paper.

298 Chapter 9 Acids, Bases, and Salts

You can find pH from the concentration of a strong acid.

The concentration of a substance in a solution is often described by *molarity* (M), or the number of moles of the substance per liter of solution. The hydronium ion concentration of pure water at 25 °C is 0.0000001 mol/L, or 1×10^{-7} M.

Writing the H_3O^+ concentration of a solution as a power of 10 will help you determine the pH. The pH is the negative of the power of 10 that is used to describe the concentration of H_3O^+ ions. So, the pH of pure water is 7. The pH of apple juice is about 3, so the concentration of H_3O^+ ions is 1×10^{-3} M.

You can use the concentration of a strong acid in solution to calculate the pH of the solution. In a solution, strong acids such as HCl and HNO_3 produce one hydronium ion for each particle of acid that dissolves. So, the concentration of hydronium ions in a solution of strong acid is the same as the concentration of the acid itself.

www.scilinks.org
Topic: pH
Code: HK81129

Math Skills — Determining pH

Determine the pH of a 0.0001 M solution of the strong acid HCl.

Identify
List the given and unknown values.

Given:
concentration of HCl in solution = 0.0001 M
Unknown:
pH

Plan
Write the molar concentration of hydroxide ions in scientific notation.

HCl is completely ionized into H_3O^+ and Cl^- ions.
concentration of H_3O^+ ions in solution = concentration of HCl in solution = 0.0001 M = 1×10^{-4} M

Solve
The pH is the negative of the power of 10 in the H_3O^+ concentration.

concentration of H_3O^+ ions = 1×10^{-4} M
pH = −(−4) = 4

Practice Hint

> If a solution contains a base, you should expect the pH to be greater than 7. If the solution contains an acid, the pH will be less than 7.

> To find the concentration of a solution of strong acid from its pH, multiply the pH value by −1. Then, use the result as a power of 10. The result is the concentration of the acid in moles per liter (mol/L).

Practice

1. Calculate the pH of a 1×10^{-4} M solution of HBr, a strong acid.
2. Determine the pH of a 0.01 M solution of HNO_3, a strong acid.
3. Nitric acid, HNO_3, is a strong acid. The pH of a solution of HNO_3 is 3. What is the concentration of the solution?

For more practice, visit **go.hrw.com** and enter keyword **HK8MP**.

Small differences in pH mean large differences in acidity.

Because pH is the negative of the power of 10 of hydronium ion concentration, small differences in pH mean large differences in the hydronium ion concentration. For example, the pH of apple juice is about 3, and the pH of coffee is about 5. This difference of two pH units means that apple juice is 10^2, or 100 times, as acidic as coffee. When antacid tablets are dissolved in water, they form a basic solution with a pH of about 8. So, coffee is about 10^3, or 1,000 times, as acidic as a solution of antacid tablets.

There is more than one way to measure pH.

There are several indicators in pH paper that change color at different pH values. A pH meter may also be used to measure pH, as **Figure 7** shows. Because ions in a solution have an electric charge, a pH meter can measure pH by determining the electric current created by the movement of the ions in the solution. If you use a pH meter properly, you can determine the pH of a solution more precisely than is possible if you use pH paper.

Figure 7 A pH meter can measure the H_3O^+ concentration precisely. **Is the tomato mixture acidic or basic?**

Section 1 Review

KEY IDEAS

1. **Explain** how a strong acid and a weak acid behave differently when each is dissolved in water.
2. **List** three properties of bases.
3. **Arrange** the following substances in order of increasing acidity: vinegar (pH = 2.8), gastric juices from inside your stomach (pH = 2.0), and a soft drink (pH = 3.4).

CRITICAL THINKING

4. **Compare and Contrast** What happens when a weak acid and a weak base ionize in water?
5. **Designing Experiments** Using litmus paper as an example, describe how you would use an indicator to find out if a solution is acidic, basic, or neutral.
6. **Forming Models** Pure water ionizes to produce hydronium ions and hydroxide ions. Write a chemical equation that shows how two water molecules can react to make these ions.
7. **Drawing Conclusions** A solution of an acid in water has a pH of 4, which is slightly acidic. Is this solution a weak acid? Explain your answer.
8. **Applying Ideas** Classify the following solutions as acidic, basic, or neutral.
   a. a soap solution, pH = 9
   b. a sour liquid, pH = 5
   c. a solution that has 4 times as many hydronium ions as hydroxide ions
   d. pure water

Math Skills

9. What is the pH of a 0.01 M solution of the strong acid $HClO_4$, perchloric acid?
10. A basic solution has a pH of 11. What is the hydronium ion concentration in this solution?

300 Chapter 9 Acids, Bases, and Salts

Why It Matters

Acid Rain

EYE ON THE ENVIRONMENT

Normal rain has a pH of about 5.6, so it is slightly acidic. Acid rain is a type of pollution in which the precipitation has a pH that is less than 5.0. Acid rain results from emissions of sulfur dioxide, SO_2, and nitric oxide, NO, which are gases from coal-burning power plants and automobiles. The gases react with compounds in the air to form sulfuric acid, H_2SO_4, and nitric acid, HNO_3.

Most acid rain in the United States has a pH of about 4.3. Not only does acid rain increase the acidity of lakes, streams, and soil, it also changes their chemical composition.

Acid rain has an adverse effect on plants and wildlife. It can reduce fish populations. When there are fewer fish, animals who eat the fish, such as the loon, may not find enough food to feed themselves and their young.

Acid rain can also damage human-made structures. Over time, acid rain reacts with minerals in limestone and marble, so the stone erodes.

SCLINKS
www.scilinks.org
Topic: Acid Precipitation
Code: HK81690

YOUR TURN

UNDERSTANDING CONCEPTS
1. What causes acid rain?

ONLINE RESEARCH
2. Find out how acid rain affects forests, and create a poster that explains what you find.

SECTION 2
Reactions of Acids with Bases

Key Ideas
- What is a neutralization reaction?
- To a chemist, what exactly is a salt?

Key Terms
neutralization reaction
salt

Why It Matters
A household water softener uses a salt to remove ions from water.

> Tennessee Course Level Expectations (Physical Science)
> CLE.3202.1.10

Have you ever used an antacid to feel better when you have an upset stomach or heartburn? Heartburn has nothing to do with your heart. You get heartburn when your stomach's solution of hydrochloric acid, HCl, irritates the lining of your esophagus. The base in antacids reacts with the acid to reduce the acidity of the solution in your stomach.

Acid-Base Reactions

> **A neutralization reaction is the reaction between an acid and a base.** When hydrochloric acid and the base magnesium hydroxide (in an antacid, for example) are mixed, a neutralization reaction happens. As **Figure 1** shows, these types of reactions have many uses.

Neutralization is a reaction between ions.

A solution of a strong acid, such as hydrochloric acid, ionizes completely, as the following equation shows.

$$HCl + H_2O \rightarrow H_3O^+ + Cl^-$$

A solution of a strong base, such as sodium hydroxide, dissociates completely, as the following equation shows.

$$NaOH \rightarrow Na^+ + OH^-$$

If the two solutions are mixed together, the following neutralization reaction takes place.

$$H_3O^+ + Cl^- + Na^+ + OH^- \rightarrow Na^+ + Cl^- + 2H_2O$$

The Na^+ and Cl^- ions are called *spectator ions* because they are like spectators watching on the sidelines. These ions do not change during the reaction between H_3O^+ and OH^- ions. If equal concentrations and equal volumes of a strong acid and a strong base are mixed, all of the H_3O^+ and OH^- ions react to form water. So, the resulting solution is neutral.

Figure 1 Garden lime, calcium carbonate, is basic and is added to the acidic soil to increase the pH.

Strong acids and bases react to form water and a salt.

If you do not include the spectator ions, the equation for the neutralization reaction can be written as follows.

$$H_3O^+ + OH^- \rightarrow 2H_2O$$

When an acid reacts with a base, hydronium ions react with hydroxide ions to form water. The other ions—positive ions from the base and negative ions from the acid—form an ionic compound called a **salt.** When this salt is soluble in water, such as the sodium chloride shown in **Figure 2,** the ions stay separated in solution until the water evaporates.

Neutral solutions are not always formed.

Reactions between acids and bases do not always produce neutral solutions. The pH of the final solution depends on the amounts of acid and base that are combined and on the strength of the acid and the base.

If a strong acid reacts with an equal amount of a weak base of the same concentration, the resulting solution will be acidic. Similarly, when a weak acid reacts with an equal amount of a strong base of the same concentration, the resulting solution will be basic.

Reading Check What forms when a weak base and a strong acid react?

Figure 2 When a solution of HCl reacts with a solution of NaOH, the reaction produces water and leaves sodium ions and chloride ions in solution. When the water evaporates, the sodium ions and chloride ions crystallize to form pure sodium chloride.

Keyword: HK8ABSF2

neutralization reaction (NOO truh li ZAY shuhn ree AK shuhn) the reaction of the ions that characterize acids and the ions that characterize bases to form water molecules and a salt

salt (SAWLT) an ionic compound that forms when a metal atom or a positive radical replaces the hydrogen of an acid

Figure 3 Bromthymol blue is an indicator that changes from yellow to blue between a pH of 6.0 and 7.6. It is an ideal indicator for a titration involving a strong acid and a strong base. **Which solution is basic?**

Titrations are used to determine concentration.

The resulting solution of a neutralization reaction will be acidic if there are more H_3O^+ ions than OH^- ions. The solution will be basic if there are more OH^- ions. If you know the concentration of one of the starting solutions in a neutralization reaction, you can use a titration to find the concentration of the other solution. A *titration* is the process of adding carefully measured amounts of one solution to another solution.

In a titration, an indicator is often used that changes color when the original amount of the base in solution is equal to the amount of the acid added to the solution. The indicator *bromthymol blue* changes from yellow in acids to dark blue in bases at a pH of about 7, as **Figure 3** shows.

If the number of hydronium ions is equal to the number of hydroxide ions in a solution, the solution will be neutral. The *equivalence point* in a titration is reached when the original amount of the acid equals the amount of the base added. For the titration of a strong acid with a strong base, the equivalence point occurs at a pH of 7. For a titration of a weak base with a strong acid, the equivalence point is less than a pH of 7. The equivalence point is greater than a pH of 7 when a weak acid is titrated with a strong base.

Graphing Skills: Interpreting Titration Curves

Hydrochloric acid, HCl, was titrated with potassium hydroxide, KOH. How many moles of KOH were added to reach the equivalence point?

1 Locate the equivalence point on the graph.

A strong acid was titrated with a strong base. The *y*-axis indicates the pH, so the equivalence point on the titration curve has a *y*-value of 7.

2 Read the moles of KOH from the graph.

The *x*-axis indicates how many moles of KOH were added. At pH = 7, 0.4 mol of KOH was added.

Practice

1. Does the solution's acidity increase or decrease as potassium hydroxide is added to the solution? Explain your answer.
2. What was the pH of the initial HCl solution?

Salts

When you hear the word *salt*, you probably think of white crystals that you sprinkle on food. ❯ **To a chemist, a salt can be almost any combination of cations and anions, except hydroxides and oxides, which are bases.**

Salts have many uses.

Common table salt contains the ionic compound sodium chloride, NaCl. Most of the sodium in your diet comes from NaCl. It is widely used to season and preserve food.

As **Figure 4** shows, sodium chloride is not the only salt. Baking soda, sodium hydrogen carbonate, is another salt that you can find in your kitchen. Salts have a variety of uses, including cleaning and highway de-icing. Ceramic glazes, home water softeners, and fire extinguishers all contain salts. The chalk that is used in your classroom is one form of the salt calcium carbonate, $CaCO_3$. The walls in your house may be made of gypsum, which is calcium sulfate, $CaSO_4$. Photographic film contains the light-sensitive salts silver bromide, AgBr, and silver iodide, AgI. **Figure 5** shows how the salt barium sulfate, $BaSO_4$ is used in medical diagnosis.

Salts are rarely manufactured by neutralization reactions. Many salts, such as NaCl and $CaCO_3$, are found in mineral deposits. Underground deposits that were left when ancient seas dried up are the source of most NaCl in the United States. Other salts are produced by other chemical processes.

Reading Check What are three ways that salts are used?

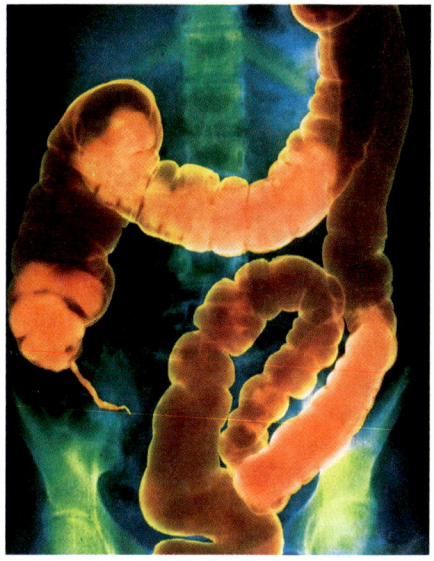

Figure 5 Barium sulfate, $BaSO_4$, is a highly insoluble salt. It can be used to block X rays. After barium sulfate coats the large intestine, the form of the intestine shows up on an X-ray image.

READING TOOLBOX

Everyday Words Used in Science
Before reading about salts, write a list of how you would use salts every day. After reading, write a new list. Compare the lists.

Figure 4 Some Common Salts

Salt	Formula	Uses
Aluminum sulfate	$Al_2(SO_4)_3$	purifying water; used in antiperspirants
Ammonium sulfate	$(NH_4)_2SO_4$	flameproofing fabric; used as fertilizer
Calcium chloride	$CaCl_2$	de-icing streets and highways; used in some kinds of concrete
Potassium chloride	KCl	treating potassium deficiency; used as table-salt substitute
Sodium carbonate	Na_2CO_3	manufacturing glass; added to wash to soften water
Sodium hydrogen carbonate	$NaHCO_3$	treating upset stomach; ingredient in baking powder; used in fire extinguishers
Sodium stearate	$NaO_2C_{18}H_{35}$	typical example of a soap; used in deodorant
Sodium lauryl sulfonate	$NaSO_3C_{12}H_{25}$	typical example of a detergent

Figure 6 Animals need salts in their diet. These butterflies can obtain salt from the dried sweat on an old sneaker. These moose can get salt by licking the salt that was used to de-ice the road.

Salts are important in the body.

You often hear that a healthful diet should include potassium, sodium, calcium, magnesium, iron, phosphorus, and iodine. However, ingesting these nutrients in their elemental form, as metals, is not common and can be harmful. Instead, you get ions of these elements from minerals. Minerals contain the salts of elements that are needed by your body. All animals, including those shown in **Figure 6,** need minerals.

You probably already know that calcium ions, Ca^{2+}, are needed for strong bones and teeth, but calcium ions are also used in other parts of the body. Nerves and muscles need calcium ions to work properly. The correct proportion of potassium ions, K^+, and sodium ions, Na^+, is needed for nerve impulses to work. These ions also control how much water that your cells keep inside. Chloride ions, Cl^-, help balance the charge of these positive ions. Phosphorus, in the form of phosphate ions, PO_4^{3-}, is needed for many processes in living cells, from transportation of energy to reproduction of the genetic code.

www.scilinks.org
Topic: Salts
Code: HK81347

Section 2 Review

KEY IDEAS

1. **Identify** the spectator ions in the neutralization of lithium hydroxide, LiOH, with hydrobromic acid, HBr.
2. **Identify** the two types of compounds produced by a neutralization reaction.
3. **Explain** why your body needs salts.

CRITICAL THINKING

4. **Forming Models** Write the chemical equation for the neutralization of nitric acid, HNO_3, with magnesium hydroxide, $Mg(OH)_2$, first with spectator ions and then without spectator ions.
5. **Applying Ideas** Which acid and which base could react to form the salt aluminum sulfate, $Al_2(SO_4)_3$?
6. **Drawing Conclusions** Predict whether the reaction of equal amounts of each of the following acids and bases will yield an acidic, a basic, or a neutral solution. Explain your answer for each.
   a. sulfuric acid, H_2SO_4, and ammonia, NH_3
   b. formic acid, HCOOH, and potassium hydroxide, KOH
   c. nitric acid, HNO_3, and calcium hydroxide, $Ca(OH)_2$
7. **Communicating Ideas** A classmate observes a neutralization reaction between an acid and a base. After the reaction is complete, your classmate is surprised that the resulting solution has a pH of 4 and is not neutral. What can you tell your classmate to help him understand what happened?

SECTION 3
Acids, Bases, and Salts in the Home

Key Ideas
- Why are cleaning products added to water?
- What are some household products that contain acids, bases, and salts?

Key Terms
- soap
- detergent
- disinfectant
- bleach
- antacid

Why It Matters
Without soaps and detergents, water would not remove grease or oils when you wash dishes or your face.

As you have seen, you do not find acids, bases, and salts only in a laboratory. Many items in your own home, such as soaps, detergents, shampoos, antacids, vitamins, sodas, and juices, are examples of household products that contain acids, bases, and salts.

> **Tennessee Course Level Expectations (Physical Science)**
> CLE.3202.1.10; CLE.3202.Inq.1;
> CLE.3202.Inq.2; CLE.3202.Inq.3;
> CLE.3202.Inq.4; CLE.3202.Inq.6;
> CLE.3202.TE.3

Cleaning Products

If you work on an oily bicycle chain or eat potato chips, water alone will not remove the greasy film from your hands. ▶ **Water does not mix with grease or oil. Cleaning products improve water's ability to clean because they help water mix with oily substances.**

Soaps allow oil and water to mix.

Soap improves water's ability to clean because soap can dissolve in both oil and in water. This property of soap allows oil and water to form an emulsion that can be washed away by rinsing. For example, when you are washing your face with soap, as the girl in **Figure 1** is doing, the oil on your face is emulsified by the soapy water. When you rinse your face, the water carries away both the soap and unwanted oil to leave your face clean.

Soaps are salts of sodium or potassium and fatty acids, which have long hydrocarbon chains. The hydrocarbon chains of the soap molecules are nonpolar, so they can mix with oils. The ionic parts of the soap molecules can mix with water. Animal fats or vegetable oils react with sodium hydroxide or potassium hydroxide to make soap. The products of the reaction are soap and an alcohol called *glycerol*.

soap (SOHP) a substance that is used as a cleaner and that dissolves in water

Figure 1 When you wash with soap, you create an emulsion of oil droplets spread throughout water.

Section 3 Acids, Bases, and Salts in the Home **307**

Why It Matters

How Does Soap Remove Grease?

Soap is able to remove grease and oil because the cations and the negatively charged ends of the chains (–COO⁻) dissolve in water and the hydrocarbon chains dissolve in oil. Soap molecules surround oil droplets and form an emulsion with water. When you wash your hands with soap, you probably rub them together. Rubbing your hands together actually helps clean them. This action lifts most of the emulsion of grease and water into the lather, which can be rinsed into the sink.

REAL WORLD

SCILINKS.
www.scilinks.org
Topic: Surfactants
Code: HK81699

Nonpolar tail
Polar head

1 Soap is an ionic compound. Its negative ion is a long hydrocarbon chain with a carboxylate group (–COO⁻) at one end. A positive sodium or potassium ion balances the charge of the negative ion.

2 Soap acts as an emulsifier by surrounding droplets of oil. The hydrocarbon chains are nonpolar, so they mix with the oil.

3 The charged ends of the soap mix with the polar water. As a result, the droplets of oil surrounded by soap molecules stay suspended in water.

YOUR TURN

UNDERSTANDING CONCEPTS
1. Why do the hydrocarbon ends of the soap molecules mix with oils?

CRITICAL THINKING
2. Could molecules without an ionic part still work as soap does to remove oils?

Figure 3 Stomach acid has about the same concentration of HCl as the solution in the flask in the photograph on the left. When an antacid tablet reacts with the acid, the pH increases to a less acidic level, as shown in the photograph on the right. **Why is the solution in one flask pink and the solution in the other flask orange?**

Many healthcare products are acids or bases.

In the morning before school, you may drink a glass of orange juice that contains vitamin C. Ascorbic acid is the chemical name for vitamin C, which your body needs to grow and repair bone and cartilage. Both sodium hydrogen carbonate and magnesium hydroxide (milk of magnesia) can be used as antacids. **Antacids** are basic substances that you swallow to neutralize stomach acid when you have an upset stomach. The acidic solution shown in **Figure 3** contains an indicator. When the antacid tablet is added to the acidic solution, a neutralization reaction happens. Because there are fewer hydronium ions, the pH of the solution changes. So, the color of the indicator changes from pink to orange.

Shampoos are adjusted for an ideal pH.

Shampoos can be made from soap. But if you use a soap-based shampoo and live in an area with hard water, a sticky soap scum may be left on your hair. Most shampoos are made from detergents, so they are able to remove dirt as well as most of the oil from your hair without leaving soap scum, even when they are used with hard water. Shampoo is not meant to remove all of the oil from your hair. Some oil is needed to give your hair shine and to keep it from becoming dry and brittle.

The appearance of your hair is greatly affected by the pH of the shampoo that you use. Hair looks best when it is kept at either a slightly acidic pH or very close to neutral. Hair strands are made of a protein called *keratin*. A shampoo that is too basic can cause strands of hair to swell, which gives them a dull, lifeless appearance. Shampoos are usually pH balanced—that is, they are made to be in a specific pH range. The pH of most shampoos is between 5 and 8. Shampoos that have higher pH values are better at cleaning oil from your hair. Shampoos that have lower pH values protect dry hair.

disinfectant (DIS in FEK tuhnt) a chemical substance that kills harmful bacteria or viruses

bleach (BLEECH) a chemical compound used to whiten or make lighter, such as hydrogen peroxide or sodium hypochlorite

antacid (ANT AS id) a weak base that neutralizes stomach acid

Academic Vocabulary
specific (spuh SIF ik) special to; exact

InquiryLab: What Does an Antacid Do?

⏱ 20 min

Procedure

1. Pour **100 mL of water** into **one beaker**. Add **vinegar** one drop at a time while stirring. Test the solution with **litmus paper** after each drop is added. Record the number of drops that you add for the solution to turn blue litmus paper bright red.

2. Use the back of a **spoon** to crush an **antacid tablet** to a fine powder on a piece of **wax paper**. Pour **100 mL of water** into a **second beaker**, add the powdered tablet, and stir until a suspension forms.

3. Use litmus paper to find out whether the mixture is acidic, basic, or neutral. Record your results.

4. Now, add vinegar to the antacid mixture. Record the number of drops that you add to cause a reaction with the antacid and turn the blue litmus paper bright red. Compare this solution with the solution that has only vinegar and water. Compare the brand of antacid that you tested with the brands of other groups.

Analysis

1. How does an antacid work to relieve the pain caused by excess stomach acid?
2. Of the brands that were tested, which brand worked best? Explain your reasoning.

Cause-and-Effect Map
Create a cause-and-effect map that shows why a cut apple turns brown and what happens when lemon juice is added to the apple.

Acids can be used as antioxidants.

Some cut fruits, such as the apple shown in **Figure 4,** slowly turn brown when they are exposed to air. The reason is that certain molecules in the apple react with oxygen to form brown compounds. Why does half of the apple look freshly cut? That part was coated with lemon juice shortly after the apple was cut. The citric acid in lemon juice acts as an *antioxidant* and prevents oxygen from reacting with the molecules in the apple that form the brown substances. Vitamin C, ascorbic acid, is another example of a natural antioxidant. Antioxidants work in various ways. Citric acid and vitamin C inhibit the enzyme involved in the reaction. Vitamin C also reacts with oxygen molecules before they can react with other molecules.

Figure 4 The right side of the cut apple was coated with lemon juice. Citric acid in the lemon juice kept the surface of the apple looking fresh.

Detergents have replaced soap in many uses.

As useful as soap is for cleaning, it does not work well in hard water. Hard water contains dissolved Mg^{2+}, Ca^{2+}, and Fe^{3+} ions. These cations combine with the fatty-acid anions of soap to form an insoluble salt called *soap scum*. This soap scum settles out on clothing, dishes, your skin, and your hair. The scum also makes a ring around the bathtub or sink. You can prevent this problem by using detergents instead of soap to wash clothes and dishes. Most shampoos, liquid hand soaps, and body washes contain detergents, not soap.

Detergents are salts of sodium, potassium, and sometimes ammonium. Like anions in soaps, the anions in detergents are composed of long hydrocarbon chains that have negatively charged ends. But the charged end of a detergent is a sulfonate group ($-SO_3^-$), not a carboxylate group ($-CO_2^-$). These sulfonate ions do not form insoluble salts with the ions in hard water. The hydrocarbon chains in detergents come from petroleum products rather than animal fats or plant oils.

Soaps and detergents act in the same way. The long hydrocarbon chains are soluble in oil or grease. The charged ends are soluble in water. Water molecules attract the charged sulfonate group in detergent molecules and keep the oil droplet suspended among the water molecules.

Reading Check Why are detergents often used for cleaning instead of soaps?

Integrating Social Studies

Ancient Soap People have used soap for thousands of years. Ancient Egyptians took baths regularly with soap made from animal fats or vegetable oils and basic solutions of alkali-metal compounds. According to Roman legend, people discovered that the water in the Tiber River near Mount Sapo was good for washing. Mount Sapo was used for elaborate animal-sacrifice rituals, and the combination of animal fat and the basic ash that washed down the mountain made the river soapy.

detergent (dee TUHR juhnt) a water-soluble cleaner that can emulsify dirt and oil

QuickLab

Detergents

⏱ 10 min

Procedure
1. Lay some **wax paper** on a flat surface, and put a drop of **water** on it.
2. Gently touch the drop of water with the tip of a **toothpick**.
3. Now, dip the tip of the toothpick in **liquid detergent**.
4. Gently touch the drop of water with the tip of the toothpick after it has been dipped in detergent.

Analysis
1. Does the water wet the surface of the wax paper? How can you tell?
2. What happened to the drop of water when you touched it with the toothpick?
3. What happened to the drop of water when you touched it with the toothpick that had been dipped in detergent?
4. Based on your results, what is one way that detergents help water clean away dirt?

Figure 2 Basic solutions of ammonia can be used to clean away light grease smears, so ammonia solutions are used to clean windows.

www.scilinks.org
Topic: Acids and Bases at Home
Code: HK80014

Many household cleaners contain ammonia.

Ammonia solutions are also good cleaners. Household ammonia is a solution of ammonia gas in water. Ammonia is a weak base because it ionizes only slightly in water to form ammonium ions and hydroxide ions, as shown in the reaction below. The hydroxide ions make the ammonia solution basic.

$$NH_3 + H_2O \rightleftharpoons NH_4^+ + OH^-$$

The concentration of ions is relatively low in an ammonia solution but is enough to remove fingerprints and oily smears. Many ammonia cleaners also contain alcohols, detergents, and other cleaning agents. These cleaners can be used to clean windows, such as those shown in **Figure 2**.

Bleach can eliminate stains.

A **disinfectant** is a substance that kills viruses and bacteria. Household **bleach,** a very strong disinfectant, is a basic solution of sodium hypochlorite, NaOCl. As you probably know, bleach can remove colors and stains.

Unlike soaps and detergents, bleach does not remove the substance causing the stain. Instead, bleach changes the substance to a colorless form. When mixed with water, the hypochlorite ion, ClO^-, reacts to release an oxygen atom. The oxygen atom reacts with the colored molecule and bleaches it.

If an acid is added to a bleach solution, the acid reacts with the hypochlorite ions and deadly chlorine gas is produced. For this reason, you should never mix bleach with an acid, such as vinegar. Also, ammonia and bleach should not be mixed because toxic chloramine gas, NH_2Cl, is formed.

Reading Check What would happen if you were to mix vinegar with bleach?

Personal-Care and Food Products

You may not have noticed all of the substances in your home that contain acids and bases. For example, many of the clothes in your closet get their color from acidic dyes. These dyes are sodium salts of organic compounds that contain the sulfonic acid group ($-SO_3H$) or the carboxylic acid group ($-CO_2H$). If you have ever had an upset stomach because of excess stomach acid, you may have taken an antacid tablet to feel better. The antacid made you feel better because it neutralized the excess stomach acid. ▶ **Many healthcare, beauty, and food products in your home, in addition to cleaners, contain acids, bases, or salts.**

Acids, bases, and salts are used in the kitchen.

Acids have many uses in the kitchen. Vinegar or citrus juices are used make acidic marinades that can tenderize meats. The acids cause the protein molecules in the meat to unravel. As a result, the meat becomes more tender.

Milk curdles if you add an acid, such as vinegar, to it. This reaction may seem undesirable, but a similar reaction occurs when yogurt is being made. Bacteria change lactose, a sugar in milk, into lactic acid. The lactic acid changes the shape of the protein casein, causing the milk to become a thick gel.

You use salts other than table salt for baking. Baking soda, or sodium hydrogen carbonate, is a salt that forms carbon dioxide gas at high temperatures. Baking soda is added to cookies so that they rise when baked. Baking powder is also used to make baked goods rise, as **Figure 5** shows. Baking powder contains baking soda and an acidic substance. When mixed in water, these compounds react to release CO_2, which makes cake batter light and fluffy and helps biscuits rise.

Bases are also used in the kitchen. Many drain cleaners contain sodium hydroxide. This strong base breaks down the grease and other organic materials that cause clogs.

Figure 5 The carbon dioxide gas released by baking powder during baking causes biscuits to rise.

Section 3 Review

KEY IDEAS

1. **Describe** how soap can dissolve in both oil and water. How does soap work with water to remove oily dirt?
2. **Explain** why soap scum might form in hard water that contains Mg^{2+} ions when soap is used instead of detergent to wash dishes.
3. **Explain** how milk of magnesia, an antacid, can reduce acidity in stomach acid.
4. **List** three acidic household substances and three basic household substances. How are the substances most often used?

CRITICAL THINKING

5. **Applying Ideas** Why does the agitation of a washing machine help a detergent clean your clothes? (Hint: Compare this motion to rubbing your hands together when you wash them.)
6. **Drawing Conclusions** Why it is not necessary for bleach to actually remove the substance that causes a stain?
7. **Analyzing Methods** Crayon companies recommend treating wax stains on clothes by spraying the stains with an oily lubricant, applying dish-washing liquid, and then washing the clothes. Explain why this treatment would remove the stain.

Section 3   Acids, Bases, and Salts in the Home

Skills Practice Lab

⏰ 50 min

Quantities in an Acid-Base Reaction

Acids and bases neutralize each other to form a salt and water. Phenolphthalein is a good indicator to use in the neutralization of a strong acid by a strong base. Phenolphthalein is a good indicator because it changes color at a pH only slightly higher than neutral. The extra amount of a base that is needed to change the color is usually too small to measure.

Procedure

Neutralizing HCl with NaOH

CAUTION: Wear an apron or lab coat to protect your clothing when working with chemicals. If a spill gets on your skin or clothing, rinse it off immediately with water for at least 5 min. Wear safety goggles and gloves when handling chemicals. If any substance gets in your eyes, immediately flush your eyes with running water for at least 15 min and notify your instructor. Always use caution when working with chemicals. Always add the base to the acid; never add the acid to the base.

1. Use the marker to write "HCl" on the bulb of one pipet. This pipet should be used only for hydrochloric acid solution. Mark a second pipet "NaOH." This pipet should be used only for sodium hydroxide solution.
2. Make a data table like the one shown.
3. Add 40 drops of 0.1 M HCl solution to a clean test tube at a steady rate. Do not let the tip of the pipet touch the sides of the test tube. Hold the long tube of the pipet with the other hand, if necessary.
4. Add 2 drops of phenolphthalein indicator to the test tube. Gently swirl the test tube to mix the liquid in the tube. Be careful not to spill or splash the liquid.
5. Note the concentrations of the HCl and NaOH solutions. Predict how many drops of NaOH solution will be required to neutralize the 40 drops of HCl. Record your prediction in the data table.
6. Add 25 drops of 0.1 M NaOH solution to the test tube. You will probably see a pink color—the color of phenolphthalein in a basic solution—develop temporarily. Remember this color. Gently swirl the test tube to mix the liquid. The pink color should disappear.

Sample Data Table: Neutralization

	Number of drops	Drops NaOH needed (predicted)	Drops NaOH needed (measured)
HCl			
H_2SO_4		DO NOT WRITE IN BOOK	

What You'll Do

- **Determine** the volume of a basic solution needed to neutralize a given volume of an acidic solution.
- **Analyze** the results to compare the volume of basic solution needed to neutralize a given volume of HCl solution with the volume needed to neutralize the same volume of H_2SO_4 solution.

What You'll Need

HCl solution, 0.1 M
H_2SO_4 solution, 0.1 M
NaOH solution, 0.1 M
marker
phenolphthalein indicator solution
pipets, plastic, disposable (3)
test-tube rack
test tubes (2)

Safety

7 Add more NaOH solution to the test tube 2 drops at a time, and mix the liquids after each addition. As the pink color starts to disappear more slowly when you mix the liquids, start adding the NaOH solution 1 drop at a time, and mix the solution with each addition. When the mixture remains slightly pink after the addition of a drop and does not change within 10 s, you have reached the end of the neutralization reaction. Record in the data table the total number of drops of NaOH solution that you added.

Neutralizing H_2SO_4 with NaOH

8 Use the marker to label a third pipet "H_2SO_4." Use this pipet only for sulfuric acid solution.

9 Repeat steps 3–7, but start with 40 drops of 0.1 M H_2SO_4 solution instead of 40 drops of HCl solution. Make and record your prediction as you did in step 5.

Analysis

1. **Describing Events** Write a complete nonionic chemical equation for the reaction of HCl and NaOH. Then, write the ionic equation for the reaction without spectator ions.

2. **Describing Events** Write a complete nonionic chemical equation for the reaction of H_2SO_4 and NaOH. Then, write the ionic equation for the reaction without spectator ions.

Communicating Your Results

3. **Drawing Conclusions** In the neutralization of HCl with NaOH, how close was your predicted number of drops to the actual number of drops of NaOH solution needed? If there is a large difference, explain the reasoning that led to your prediction.

4. **Drawing Conclusions** In the neutralization of H_2SO_4 with NaOH, how close was your predicted number of drops to the actual number of drops of NaOH solution needed? If there is a large difference, explain the reasoning that led to your prediction.

Extension

Suppose that someone tries to explain your results by saying that H_2SO_4 is twice as strong an acid as HCl. How could you explain that this person's reasoning is incorrect?

Science Skills

Finding Reputable Sources

Technology
Math
Scientific Methods
Graphing

Anyone can post ideas and information on the Internet. So, you should not believe everything that you read. Below are some tips to help you determine whether or not a Web site is a reputable source.

① **Examine the Web Address** Gather information from the site's Web address (URL).
- The domain name may tell you if a reputable business, agency, or institution created the site.
- Is the top-level domain (.com, .org, .edu, or .gov) appropriate for the information that you are seeking?
- Look for clues that indicate a personal Web site (person's name; an apparent username; or a tilde, "~"). Be cautious with the information on such sites.

Address: http://www.collegename.edu
(Domain name) (Top-level domain)

② **Evaluate Authority** Look for evidence that the author has the authority to present reliable information on the topic.
- What are the credentials of the author or institution?
- Do other cited authors or Web sites seem reputable?
- Does the site have few spelling and grammar errors?

③ **Evaluate Objectivity** Some companies, organizations, and people may benefit from making you think a particular way.
- Ask yourself what reason the author of the page may have to want you to believe the information.
- Does the language on the site have an objective tone?
- Are there links to sites that might contain other views?

Where to look	Information
About page	who runs the Web site; mission statement (what the person's or organization's goals are)
Links; related sites	other Web sites that they would like you to visit; may or may not contain relevant information
FAQ page	frequently asked questions
publications	often a list of scholarly articles produced by the person or organization

④ **Check for Accuracy** Be critical of the information on a site.
- How does the information compare with what you already know?
- Is the information consistent with that on other Web sites, in books, or other publications on the topic?
- Are sources that support the information listed?

Use the following resources to check Web Site information:
- encyclopedias
- science textbooks
- science journals and magazines

Practice

Suppose that you are researching the toxicity of various household products. For each of the following Web sites, discuss why you think that the source is likely or not likely to be reputable.

1. Kenny's eighth-grade science project about household products: www.austinisd.org/~kennyken/sciproject
2. Dr. Hazard's toxicity research page: www.med.unc.edu/toxicology/faculty/hazard/toxicity
3. The Web site for a manufacturer of household chemical products: www.cloroxcompany.com
4. The Web site for the U.S. government's Occupational Safety and Health Administration: www.osha.gov

CHAPTER 9 Summary

go.hrw.com
SUPER SUMMARY
KEYWORD: HK8ABSS

Key Ideas

Section 1 Acids, Bases, and pH

> **Acids** Acids taste sour, cause indicators to change color, and conduct electric current. They are also corrosive and can damage materials, including your skin. (p. 293)

> **Bases** Bases have a bitter taste, and solutions of bases feel slippery. Solutions of bases also conduct electric current, cause indicators to change color, and can damage the skin. (p. 295)

> **pH** The pH of a solution indicates its concentration of H_3O^+ ions. In solutions, the concentration of hydronium ions is related to the concentration of hydroxide ions, OH^-. The pH of a solution also indicates the concentration of OH^- ions. (p. 298)

Section 2 Reactions of Acids with Bases

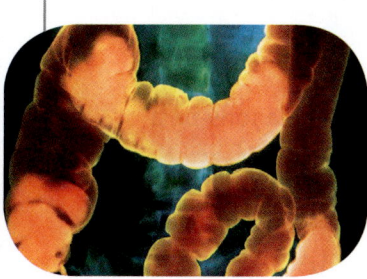

> **Acid-Base Reactions** A neutralization reaction is the reaction between an acid and a base. (p. 302)

> **Salts** To a chemist, a salt can be almost any combination of cations and anions, except hydroxides and oxides, which are bases. (p. 305)

Section 3 Acids, Bases, and Salts in the Home

> **Cleaning Products** Water does not mix with grease or oil. Cleaning products improve water's ability to clean because they help water mix with oily substances. (p. 307)

> **Personal-Care and Food Products** Many healthcare, beauty, and food products in your home, in addition to cleaners, contain acids, bases, or salts. (p. 310).

Key Terms

acid, p. 293
indicator, p. 293
electrolyte, p. 294
base, p. 295
pH, p. 298

neutralization reaction, p. 302
salt, p. 303

soap, p. 307
detergent, p. 309
disinfectant, p. 310
bleach, p. 310
antacid, p. 311

Acids, Bases, and Salts

CHAPTER 9 Review

READING TOOLBOX

1. **Everyday Words Used in Science** In everyday living, we sometimes use the word *soap* to refer to detergents. Identify each of the following as either a soap or a detergent: dish-washing soap, laundry detergent, shampoo, liquid hand soap, and olive oil bar soap.

USING KEY TERMS

2. Explain how you can use the *indicator* litmus, in the form of litmus paper, to determine whether a solution is acidic, basic, or neutral.

3. Explain how the molecular structure of *soaps* and *detergents* causes these substances to help water wash away oil and grease.

4. What is the active substance in *bleach*? How does this substance work to remove stains?

5. Why are most shampoos made from *detergents* rather than *soaps*?

6. Why do microbiologists often disinfect work areas before working with bacterial cultures? What might they use as a *disinfectant*?

7. Explain why a *strong acid* is also a strong *electrolyte* in solution.

8. What is a *neutralization reaction*? How might the product of a neutralization reaction have a *pH* that is less than 7?

9. How can you use the *pH* of a solution to determine how *basic* the solution is?

10. What are two ways that your body uses *salts*?

UNDERSTANDING KEY IDEAS

11. An acid produces _____ ions in solution.
    a. oxygen   c. hydroxide
    b. hydronium   d. sulfur

12. A base produces _____ ions in solution.
    a. oxygen   c. hydroxide
    b. hydronium   d. sulfur

13. What is the formula of the salt formed when a solution of nitric acid is added to a solution of calcium hydroxide?
    a. $Ca(NO_3)_2$ c. H_2O
    b. $Ca(OH)_2$ d. CaH

14. An antacid relieves an overly acidic stomach because antacids are
    a. acidic.   c. basic.
    b. neutral.   d. dilute.

15. Detergents have replaced soap in many uses because detergents
    a. are made from animal fat.
    b. do not form insoluble substances.
    c. are milder than soap.
    d. contain ammonia.

16. Which of the following ionic equations best represents a neutralization reaction?
    a. $Na + H_2O \rightarrow Na^+ + OH^- + H_2$
    b. $HNO_3 + H_2O \rightarrow H_3O^+ + NO_3^-$
    c. $2OH^- + NH_4Cl \rightarrow Cl^- + H_2O + NH_3$
    d. $OH^- + H_3O^+ \rightarrow 2H_2O$

17. An increase in the hydronium ion concentration of a solution _____ the pH.
    a. raises   c. does not affect
    b. lowers   d. doubles

18. Bleach removes stains by
    a. changing the color of the stain.
    b. covering the stain.
    c. removing the stain-causing substances.
    d. disinfecting the stain.

19. Which one of these materials found in the kitchen is not acidic?
    a. baking soda   c. vinegar
    b. lemon juice   d. vitamin C

318 Chapter 9 Acids, Bases, and Salts

EXPLAINING KEY IDEAS

20. Explain how the ionization of a strong acid differs from the ionization of a weak acid in a solution. Give an example of a strong acid and a weak acid. Write an equation that shows which ions form when each acid is dissolved in water.

21. If you wish to change the pH of a solution very slightly, should you add a strong acid or a weak acid? Explain your answer.

CRITICAL THINKING

22. Forming Hypotheses Baking soda, sodium hydrogen carbonate, is useful in the kitchen for baking and for absorbing odors in the refrigerator. Baking soda can also be sprinkled on a grease fire to extinguish it. How can baking soda extinguish fires?

23. Applying Ideas Insect bites hurt because the insect injects a toxin into the victim. When certain kinds of ants bite, they inject a small amount of highly irritating formic acid. Suggest a treatment that might stop an ant bite from itching or hurting.

24. Designing Experiments Suppose that your measurement of the pH of a clear solution is 3. You are asked to find out whether the solution is a very dilute solution of a strong acid or a more concentrated solution of a weak acid. Propose a method to answer the question.

25. Applying Ideas You need several grams of the solid ammonium bromide, NH_4Br, for an experiment, but you do not have any. You do, however, have a solution of hydrobromic acid, HBr, and a solution of ammonia. Suggest a way to use an acid-base reaction to make a small quantity of NH_4Br.

26. Drawing Conclusions Pure water is a poor conductor of electricity. But having any sort of plugged-in appliances near the bathtub or shower is still dangerous. Why does this danger exist? Explain your reasoning by discussing the composition of tap water.

Graphing Skills

27. Line Graphs The graph below shows how the pH of a solution changes during the course of a titration of an acid with a base. Use the graph to answer the following questions.

a. What is the equivalence point?
b. What is the pH at the equivalence point?
c. What is the approximate pH of the solution after 25 mL of base is added? Is the solution acidic or basic at this point?
d. Classify both the acid and the base in this neutralization reaction as either weak or strong. Explain your answer.

Math Skills

28. Determining pH What is the pH of a 0.001 M solution of hydrobromic acid, HBr, a strong acid?

29. Determining pH What is the pH of a solution that contains 0.10 mol of HCl in a volume of 100.0 L?

30. Using pH What is the molar concentration of hydronium ions in a solution with a pH of 6?

31. Determining pH The concentration of hydronium ions in a certain acid solution is 100 times the concentration of hydronium ions in a second acid solution. If the second solution has a pH of 5, what is the pH of the first solution?

Standardized Test Prep

Understanding Concepts

Directions (1–4): For each question, write on a sheet of paper the letter of the correct answer.

1. When an acid dissolves in water, which type of ion is among the products formed?
   - **A.** hydronium
   - **B.** electrolyte
   - **C.** hydroxide
   - **D.** antacid

2. A mystery substance is found to be a very strong base. What will its pH most likely be?
   - **F.** 0
   - **G.** 4
   - **H.** 8
   - **I.** 12

3. A batch of apple cider is found to have a pH of 3. How many moles of H_3O^+ are there in 10 L of the cider?
   - **A.** 30 mol
   - **B.** 1×10^{-30} mol
   - **C.** 1×10^{-4} mol
   - **D.** 1×10^{-2} mol

4. Two acidic solutions are tested for conductivity. If solution A conducts electric current much better than solution B does, what can be concluded about the two solutions?
   - **F.** Solution A has a higher concentration of hydronium ions than solution B does.
   - **G.** Solution A has a higher concentration of hydroxide ions than solution B does.
   - **H.** More acid was dissolved in solution A than in solution B.
   - **I.** The pH of solution A is higher than the pH of solution B.

Directions (5-6): For each question, write a short response.

5. How does the number of hydronium ions in 1 L of a substance with a pH of 6 compare mathematically with the number of hydronium ions in 1 L of a substance with a pH of 2?

6. Write the chemical equation that represents the reaction that takes place in every neutralization reaction.

Reading Skills

Directions (7-9): Read the passage below. Then, answer the questions that follow.

ACID RAIN

In the 1800s, the Industrial Revolution introduced large-scale manufacturing. It also introduced the widespread burning of fossil fuels. One of the negative consequences of this burning was acid rain, which remains an environmental issue to this day.

Acid rain is usually defined as any precipitation that is more acidic than normal. Ordinary precipitation tends to be slightly acidic; it ranges from a pH of about 5.6 to a pH of about 5.0. A drop in the pH of precipitation to below 5.0 usually means that pollution has entered the atmosphere and combined with other substances in the atmosphere. The resulting compounds increase the acidity of the precipitation that falls to the ground.

Coal is a fossil fuel that gives off pollutants, such as sulfur dioxide and nitrogen oxides, when burned. Other fossil fuels, such as gasoline and oil, release similar pollutants. Sulfur dioxide and nitrogen oxides dissolve very easily in water and can be carried very far by the wind. All of these compounds can increase the acidity of precipitation.

7. What is a likely pH reading for acid rain?
   - **A.** 4
   - **B.** 6
   - **C.** 7
   - **D.** 9

8. Which pollutants contribute to acid rain?
   - **F.** sulfur dioxide and nitrogen oxides
   - **G.** nitrogen and hydrogen dioxide
   - **H.** sulfur and oxygen
   - **I.** nitrogen oxides

9. What can individuals do to reduce the acidity of precipitation?

Interpreting Graphics

The graphics below each show an acid being titrated with a base. Use these graphics to answer questions 10–11.

TITRATION CURVE

10. What type of reaction is occurring?
    - **A.** decomposition reaction
    - **B.** neutralization reaction
    - **C.** combustion reaction
    - **D.** synthesis reaction

11. Which of the graphs describes a titration in which the base is stronger than the acid? How do you know?

The graphic below shows the pH of several mystery substances. Use this graphic to answer questions 12–13.

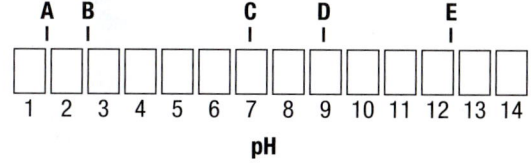

12. Which letters represent the following substances (in order): water, ammonia, battery acid, and lemon juice?
    - **F.** A, B, C, D
    - **G.** B, C, D, E
    - **H.** C, E, A, B
    - **I.** D, B, A, C

13. Which letter shows the pH of the substance that is the most basic?

Test Tip

Sometimes, only a portion of a graph or table is needed to answer a question. Focus only on the necessary information to avoid confusion.

Why It Matters
Chemistry Connections

Science, technology, and society are closely linked. The web below shows just of a few of the connections in the history of chemistry.

1789 Antoine Lavoisier publishes *Elementary Treatise on Chemistry* and describes the composition of many organic compounds.

1803 John Dalton proposes his atomic theory.

1869 Dimitri Mendeleev compiles the first periodic table.

1896 J.J. Thomson discovers electrons.

1909 Earnest Rutherford's gold foil experiment leads to orbital model of atoms.

1954 Linus Pauling awarded the Nobel Prize for his theory of chemical bonding.

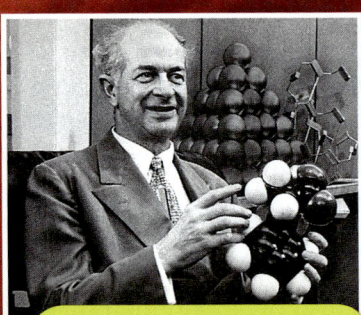

1965 Stephanie Kwolek invents the polymer Kevlar®.

1985 Scientists discover large molecules made entirely of carbon that are shaped like soccer balls or like tubes. These materials are called *fullerenes*, after Buckminster Fuller.

2005 NASA tests solar sails that are made of a polymer film that is 100 times thinner than paper. The next generation of solar sails may be made of materials containing carbon nanotubes.

2005 Sporting goods are made of materials that contain carbon nanotubes.

HISTORY IN SCIENCE

1918 Fritz Haber awarded Nobel Prize for the first industrial fixation of atmospheric nitrogen.

1940s Advances in chemistry lead to the development of synthetic fertilizers and pesticides.

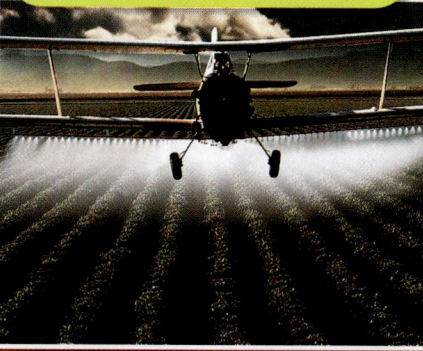

1962 Rachel Carson publishes *Silent Spring,* which draws public attention to the environmental effects of pesticides.

1925 Hermann Staudinger proposes that molecules can form chainlike polymers.

1953 Francis Crick, James Watson, Rosalind Franklin, and Maurice Wilkins publish papers about the structure of DNA.

1973 The first genetically modified organism is created.

1996 Genetically engineered corn is marketed to reduce the use of pesticides.

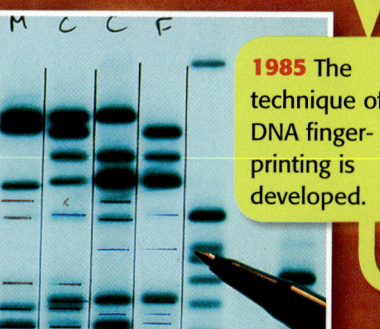

1985 The technique of DNA fingerprinting is developed.

2003 The Human Genome Project completes the sequencing of the human genome. Knowledge of the genome sequence makes finding cures for genetic diseases easier.

YOUR TURN

UNDERSTANDING CONCEPTS
1. Which discoveries contributed to Pauling's theory of chemical bonding?

CRITICAL THINKING
2. Explain the relationship between the development of synthetic pesticides and the publication of *Silent Spring*.

Chemistry Connections **323**

CHAPTER 10
Nuclear Changes

Chapter Outline

❶ What Is Radioactivity?
Nuclear Radiation
Nuclear Decay
Radioactive Decay Rates

❷ Nuclear Fission and Fusion
Nuclear Forces
Nuclear Fission
Nuclear Fusion

❸ Nuclear Radiation Today
Where Is Radiation?
Beneficial Uses of Nuclear Radiation
Risks from Nuclear Radiation
Nuclear Power

TN Tennessee Course Level Expectations (Physical Science)

CLE.3202.TE.1 Explore the impact of technology on social, political, and economic systems; **CLE.3202.TE.3** Explain the relationship between the properties of a material and the use of the material in the application of a technology; **CLE.3202.2.5** Distinguish between nuclear fission and nuclear fusion; **CLE.3202.Inq.1** Recognize that science is a progressive endeavor that reevaluates and extends what is already accepted; **CLE.3202.Inq.2** Design and conduct scientific investigations to explore new phenomena, verify previous results, test how well a theory predicts, and compare opposing theories; **CLE.3202.Inq.3** Use appropriate tools and technology to collect precise and accurate data; **CLE.3202.Inq.4** Apply qualitative and quantitative measures to analyze data and draw conclusions that are free of bias; **CLE.3202.Inq.6** Communicate and defend scientific findings; **CLE.3202.Math.1** Understand the mathematical principles behind the science of physics; **CLE.3202.Math.2** Utilize appropriate mathematical equations and processes to solve basic physics problems; **CLE.3202.TE.4** Describe the dynamic interplay among science, technology, and engineering within living, earth-space, and physical systems.

Why It Matters

This laser-induced fusion test reactor is located at Sandia National Laboratories in New Mexico. This experiment may lead to a new source of energy for our homes and businesses.

InquiryLab

⏱ 30 min

Radiation and Film

Obtain a sheet of **unexposed photographic film** and a new household **smoke detector** that contains a radioactive sample. Remove the detector's casing. In a **dark room,** place the film next to the smoke detector in a **cardboard box.** Close the box. On the next day, open the box in a darkened room. Place the film in a **thick envelope.** Have the film processed, and study the image on the film.

Questions to Get You Started

1. How does the image on the exposed film differ from the rest of the film?
2. How can you tell that the image is related to the radioactive source?

READING TOOLBOX

These reading tools can help you learn the material in this chapter. For more information on how to use these and other tools, see **Appendix A**.

Word Origins

Alpha, Beta, and Gamma Knowing the origins of science terms can give you insight into the history surrounding certain scientific discoveries. The term *radioactivity* was coined by Pierre and Marie Curie. The word was a combination of two Latin root words: *radius*, which means "beam of light," and *activus*, which means "active."

Your Turn As you learn about nuclear radiation, complete a chart like this one about the origin of the name of each type of radiation. (Some entries may need to be researched by using other sources.)

TYPE OF RADIATION	NAMED BY, WHEN NAMED	ORIGIN OF NAME
X ray	Becquerel, 1896	unknown source of radiation
Alpha particle	Rutherford, 1899	first letter of the Greek alphabet
Beta particle		
Gamma ray		
Neutron		

Comparisons

Analyzing Comparisons When you are comparing two things, you describe how they are similar and how they are different. Such comparisons are signaled in language by the use of a few key words or structures. The words *like* or *unlike* can signal that a comparison is being made and can tell you whether the comparison is focused on similarities or differences. Comparative words can be formed by using the suffixes *-er* or *-est*. Comparative phrases can be formed by using the words *more* or *less*.

Your Turn As you read this chapter, fill out a table of comparisons like the one below. In the first two columns, list the two things being compared. In the third column, describe the similarity or difference that the comparison reveals. In the last column, note any words or phrases that signal the comparison. The sample entry below is for the sentence "Like alpha particles, beta particles can easily ionize other atoms."

FIRST THING	SECOND THING	SIMILARITY OR DIFFERENCE	SIGNALING WORD OR PHRASE
alpha particles	beta particles	Both can easily ionize other atoms.	like

FoldNotes

Four-Corner Fold A four-corner fold is useful when you want to compare the characteristics of four topics.

Your Turn Make a four-corner fold by using the instructions in **Appendix A**.

1. Label the four outer flaps with the names of the four primary kinds of nuclear radiation: alpha particles, beta particles, gamma rays, and neutrons.
2. Underneath each flap, take notes about that kind of nuclear radiation.

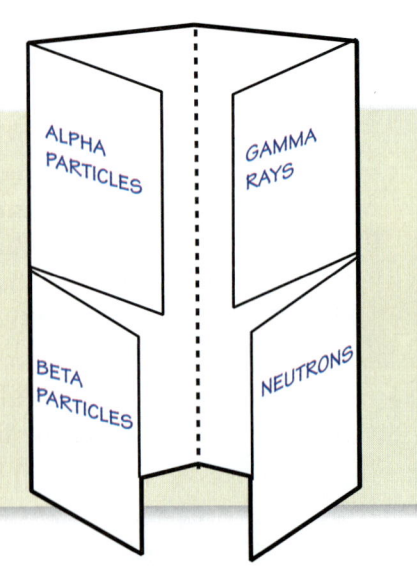

SECTION 1 What Is Radioactivity?

Key Ideas

> What happens when an element undergoes radioactive decay?

> How does radiation affect the nucleus of an unstable isotope?

> How do scientists predict when an atom will undergo radioactive decay?

Key Terms

radioactive decay
nuclear radiation
alpha particle
beta particle
gamma ray
half-life

Why It Matters

Nuclear radiation surrounds us on Earth, but scientists did not identify nuclear radiation until a little more than 100 years ago.

Our lives are affected by radioactivity in many ways. Technology using radioactivity has helped humans detect disease, kill cancer cells, generate electricity, and design smoke detectors. However, there are also risks associated with too much nuclear radiation, so we must know where it may exist and how we can counteract it. But first, what exactly is radioactivity?

Tennessee Course Level Expectations (Physical Science)

CLE.3202.TE.1; CLE.3202.Inq.1; CLE.3202.Inq.2; CLE.3202.Inq.3; CLE.3202.TE.4

Nuclear Radiation

Certain isotopes of many elements undergo a process called radioactive decay. During **radioactive decay,** the unstable nuclei of these isotopes emit particles, or release energy, to become stable isotopes, as **Figure 1** shows. > **After radioactive decay, the element changes into a different isotope of the same element or into an entirely different element.** Recall that isotopes of an element are atoms that have the same number of protons but different numbers of neutrons in their nuclei. Different elements are distinguished by having different numbers of protons.

The released energy and matter are collectively called **nuclear radiation.** Just as materials that undergo radioactive decay are changed, materials that are bombarded with nuclear radiation are also affected. These effects depend on the type of radiation and on the properties of the materials that nuclear radiation encounters. (Note that the term *radiation* can refer to light or to energy transfer. To avoid confusion, the term *nuclear radiation* will be used to describe radiation associated with nuclear changes.)

radioactive decay (RAY dee oh AK tiv dee KAY) the disintegration of an unstable atomic nucleus into one or more different nuclides

nuclear radiation (NOO klee uhr RAY dee AY shuhn) the particles that are released from the nucleus during radioactive decay

Figure 1 During radioactive decay, an unstable nucleus emits one or more particles of high-energy electromagnetic radiation.

www.scilinks.org
Topic: Types of Radiation
Code: HK81569

Figure 2 Types of Nuclear Radiation

Radiation type	Symbol	Mass (kg)	Charge	Graphic
Alpha particle	$^{4}_{2}He$	6.646×10^{-27}	+2	
Beta particle	$^{0}_{-1}e$	9.109×10^{-31}	−1, (+1)	
Gamma ray	γ	none	0	
Neutron	$^{1}_{0}n$	1.675×10^{-27}	0	

There are different types of nuclear radiation.

Essentially, there are four types of nuclear radiation. Nuclear radiation can contain alpha particles, beta particles, gamma rays, or neutrons. Some of the properties of these types are listed in **Figure 2.** When a radioactive nucleus decays, the nuclear radiation leaves the nucleus. This nuclear radiation interacts with nearby matter. This interaction depends in part on the properties of nuclear radiation, such as charge, mass, and energy.

Alpha particles consist of protons and neutrons.

Uranium is a radioactive element that naturally occurs as three isotopes. One of its isotopes, uranium-238, undergoes nuclear decay by emitting positively charged particles. Ernest Rutherford, noted for discovering the nucleus, named this radiation *alpha* (α) *rays* after the first letter of the Greek alphabet. Later, he discovered that alpha rays were actually particles, each made of two protons and two neutrons—the same as helium nuclei. **Alpha particles** are positively charged and more massive than any other type of nuclear radiation.

Alpha particles do not travel far through materials. In fact, they barely pass through a sheet of paper. One factor that limits an alpha particle's ability to pass through matter is that it is massive compared to other subatomic particles. Because alpha particles are charged, they remove electrons from—or ionize—matter as they pass through it. This ionization causes the alpha particle to lose energy and slow further.

Reading Check To which element is an alpha particle related? (See Appendix E for answers to Reading Checks.)

alpha particle (AL fuh PAHRT i kuhl) a positively charged particle that consists of two protons and two neutrons and that is emitted from a nucleus during radioactive decay

beta particle (BAYT uh PAHRT i kuhl) an electron or positron that is emitted from a nucleus during radioactive decay

gamma ray (GAM uh RAY) the high-energy photon emitted by a nucleus during fission and radioactive decay

Beta particles are produced from neutron decay.

Some nuclei emit a type of nuclear radiation that travels farther through matter than alpha particles do. This nuclear radiation is composed of beta particles, named after the second Greek letter, *beta* (β). **Beta particles** are often fast-moving electrons but may also be positively charged particles called *positrons*. Positrons have the same mass as electrons.

Negative particles coming from the positively charged nucleus puzzled scientists for years. However, in the 1930s, another discovery helped clear up the mystery. Neutrons, which are not charged, decay to form a proton and an electron. The electron, which has a very small mass, is then ejected at a high speed from the nucleus as a beta particle.

As **Figure 3** shows, beta particles pass through a piece of paper, but most are stopped by 3 mm of aluminum or 10 mm of wood. This greater penetration occurs because beta particles are not as massive as alpha particles. But like alpha particles, beta particles can easily ionize other atoms. As they ionize atoms, beta particles lose energy. This property prevents them from penetrating matter very deeply.

Gamma rays are high-energy electromagnetic radiation.

Unlike alpha or beta particles, gamma rays are not made of matter and do not have an electric charge. Instead, **gamma rays,** named for the third Greek letter, *gamma* (γ), are a form of electromagnetic energy. Like visible light and X rays, gamma rays consist of energy packets called *photons*. Gamma rays, however, have more energy than light or X rays do.

Although gamma rays have no electric charge, they can easily ionize matter. High-energy gamma rays can cause damage in matter. They can penetrate up to 60 cm of aluminum or 7 cm of lead. They are not easily stopped by clothing or most building materials and therefore pose a greater danger to health than either alpha or beta particles do.

Neutron radioactivity occurs in an unstable nucleus.

Like alpha and beta radiation, *neutron emission* consists of matter that is emitted from an unstable nucleus. In fact, scientists first discovered the neutron as a result of this emission.

Neutrons have no charge, and therefore they do not ionize matter as alpha and beta particles do. Because neutrons do not use their energy to ionize matter, they are able to travel farther through matter than either alpha or beta particles do. A block of lead about 15 cm thick is required to stop most fast neutrons emitted during radioactive decay.

READING TOOLBOX

Analyzing Comparisons As you read about the different kinds of nuclear radiation, look for comparisons among them. Create a table of their similarities and differences.

Figure 3 Different kinds of nuclear radiation penetrate different materials. **Why must both the thickness and material be specified?**

Alpha particles can be blocked by a thick sheet of paper. — Alpha particles

Beta particles can be blocked by about 3 mm of aluminum. — Beta particles

Gamma rays can be blocked by 7 cm or more of lead. — Gamma rays

Nuclear Decay

Nuclear decay causes changes in the nucleus of an atom. ▶ **Anytime that an unstable nucleus emits alpha or beta particles, the number of protons and neutrons changes.** An example is radium-226 (an isotope of radium with the mass number 226), which changes to radon-222 by emitting an alpha particle.

Nuclear-decay equations are similar to those used for chemical reactions. The nucleus before decay is like a reactant and is placed on the left side of the equation. The products are placed on the right side.

Gamma decay changes the energy of the nucleus.

When an atom undergoes nuclear decay and emits gamma rays, there is no change in the atomic number or the atomic mass of the element. The reason is that the number of protons and neutrons does not change. After gamma decay, the energy content of the nucleus is lower because some of its energy was taken away by the energy in the gamma ray.

The atomic number changes during beta decay.

A beta particle is not an atom and does not have an atomic number, which is the number of positive charges in a nucleus. For the sake of convenience, because an electron has a single negative charge, an electron is given an atomic number of –1 in a nuclear-decay equation. Similarly, the electron's mass is so much less than the mass of a proton or a neutron that the electron can be regarded as having a mass number of 0. The beta particle symbol, with the right mass and atomic numbers, is $_{-1}^{0}e$.

A beta-decay process occurs when carbon-14 decays to nitrogen-14 by emitting a beta particle, as **Figure 4** shows. This process can be written as follows.

$$^{14}_{6}\text{C} \rightarrow\ ^{14}_{7}\text{N} +\ ^{0}_{-1}e \qquad \begin{array}{l} 14 = 14 + 0 \\ 6 = 7 + (-1) \end{array}$$

In all cases of beta decay, the mass number before and after the decay does not change. The atomic number of the product nucleus, however, increases by 1, so the atom changes to a different element. During carbon-14 beta decay, a neutron changes into a proton. As a result, the positive charge of the nucleus increases by 1, and an atom of nitrogen forms.

✅ **Reading Check** How do the mass number and the atomic number change during beta decay?

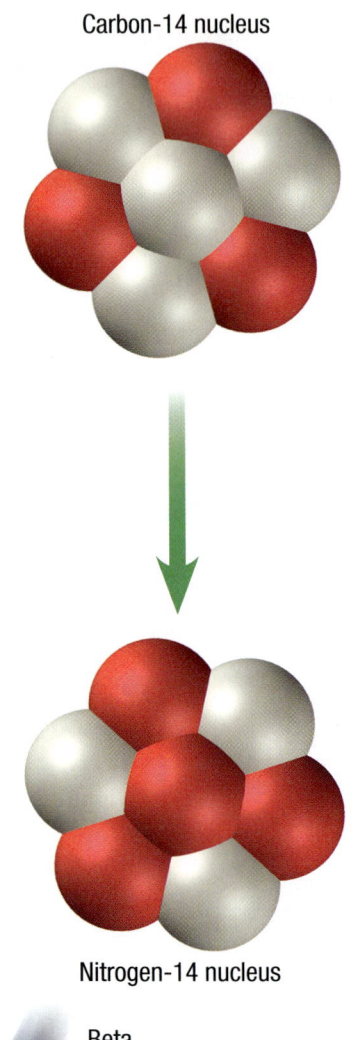

Figure 4 A nucleus that undergoes beta decay has nearly the same atomic mass afterward, but it has one more proton and one less neutron.

Both atomic mass and number change in alpha decay.

In alpha decay, the form of the decay equation is the same except that the symbol for an alpha particle is used. The alpha decay of radium-226 is written as follows.

$$^{226}_{88}Ra \rightarrow \, ^{222}_{86}Rn + \, ^{4}_{2}He \qquad \begin{aligned} 226 &= 222 + 4 \\ 88 &= 86 + 2 \end{aligned}$$

The mass number of the atom before decay is 226. The mass number equals the sum of the mass numbers of the products, 222 and 4. The atomic numbers follow the same principle. The 88 protons in radium before the nuclear decay equal the 86 protons in the radon-222 nucleus and 2 protons in the alpha particle.

Academic Vocabulary
principle (PRIN suh puhl) basic law, rule, or belief

Math Skills — Nuclear Decay

Actinium-217 decays by releasing an alpha particle. Write the equation for this decay process, and determine which element is formed.

Identify
Write the equation with the original element on the left side and the products on the right side.

$^{217}_{89}Ac \rightarrow \, ^{A}_{Z}X + \, ^{4}_{2}He$

X = unknown product
A = unknown mass
Z = unknown atomic number

Plan
Write math equations for the atomic and mass numbers. Rearrange the equations.

$217 = A + 4 \qquad 89 = Z + 2$
$A = 217 - 4 \qquad Z = 89 - 2$

Solve
Solve for the unknown values, and rewrite the equation with all nuclei represented.

$A = 213 \qquad Z = 87$

According to the periodic table, francium has an atomic number of 87. The unknown element is therefore $^{213}_{87}Fr$.

$^{217}_{89}Ac \rightarrow \, ^{213}_{87}Fr + \, ^{4}_{2}He$

Practice Hint

› In all nuclear-decay problems, the atomic number of the new atom is the key to identifying the new atom.

› After determining the new atomic number, use the periodic table to find out the name of the new element.

Practice

Complete the following radioactive-decay equations. Identify the isotope X. Indicate whether alpha or beta decay takes place.

1. $^{12}_{5}B \rightarrow \, ^{12}_{6}C + \, ^{A}_{Z}X$
2. $^{225}_{89}Ac \rightarrow \, ^{221}_{87}Fr + \, ^{A}_{Z}X$
3. $^{63}_{28}Ni \rightarrow \, ^{A}_{Z}X + \, ^{0}_{-1}e$
4. $^{212}_{83}Bi \rightarrow \, ^{A}_{Z}X + \, ^{4}_{2}He$

For more practice, visit **go.hrw.com** and enter keyword **HK8MP**.

Why It Matters

Discovering Nuclear Radiation

HISTORY IN SCIENCE

In 1898, Marie Curie and her husband, Pierre, discovered two previously unknown elements, both of which were radioactive. They named one element *polonium,* after Marie's homeland of Poland. They named the second element *radium,* from the Latin word for "ray." In 1903, Marie Curie completed her doctoral thesis and was the first woman in France to receive a doctorate. Later that year, Marie and Pierre Curie were awarded the Nobel Prize in physics for their studies of radioactive substances. In 1911, Marie also won the Nobel Prize in chemistry for the discovery of these new elements.

Marie Curie used this *ionization chamber* in her studies of radioactivity. It consists of a tube from which some of the air has been removed. When ionizing radiation—alpha particles, beta particles, or gamma rays—passes through the chamber, some of the remaining atoms are ionized. Applying a voltage across the ends of the chamber creates a current in the chamber. The Curies used that current to detect the presence of radioactive substances.

Marie and Pierre Curie used this glass flask to hold solutions of radioactive elements. Radiation clouded and changed the color of the glass. Like most scientists of her day, Marie did not realize the danger of ionizing radiation and often walked around with uranium ore in her pockets.

www.scilinks.org
Topic: Radium
Code: HK81262

YOUR TURN

WRITING IN SCIENCE
1. Research and write about how the Curies isolated radium.

ONLINE RESEARCH
2. What other scientists have won Nobel Prizes in physics or chemistry? Have any other scientists won both prizes?

Radioactive Decay Rates

If you were asked to determine the age of a rock, you would probably not be able to do so. After all, old rocks do not look much different from new rocks. How, then, would you go about finding the rock's age? Likewise, how would a scientist find out the age of a piece of cloth found at the site of an ancient village?

One way to find the age involves radioactive decay. ❯ **It is impossible to predict the moment when any particular nucleus will decay, but it is possible to predict the time required for half of the nuclei in a given radioactive sample to decay.** The time in which half of a radioactive substance decays is called the substance's **half-life.**

Half-life is a measure of how quickly a substance decays.

Different radioactive isotopes have different half-lives, as indicated in the table in **Figure 5.** Half-lives can last from nanoseconds to billions of years, depending on the stability of the isotope's nucleus.

Doctors use isotopes with short half-lives, such as iodine-131, to help diagnose medical problems. A detector follows the element as it moves through the patient's body.

Scientists can also use half-life to predict how old an object is. Geologists calculate the age of rocks by using the half-lives of long-lasting isotopes, such as potassium-40. Potassium-40 decays to argon-40, so the ratio of potassium-40 to argon-40 is smaller for older rocks than it is for younger rocks.

Integrating Earth Science

Internal Furnace Earth's interior is extremely hot. One reason is that uranium and the radioactive elements produced by its decay are present in amounts of about 3 parts per million beneath the surface of Earth and their nuclear decay produces energy that escapes into the surroundings.

The long half-lives of uranium isotopes allow the radioactive decay to heat Earth for billions of years. The very large distance that this energy must travel to reach Earth's surface keeps the interior of Earth much hotter than its surface.

half-life (HAF LIEF) the time required for half of a sample of a radioactive isotope to break down by radioactive decay to form a daughter isotope

Figure 5 Half-Lives of Selected Isotopes

Isotope	Half-life	Nuclear radiation emitted
Thorium-219	1.05×10^{-6} s	α
Hafnium-156	2.5×10^{-2} s	α
Radon-222	3.82 days	α, γ
Iodine-131	8.1 days	β, γ
Radium-226	1,599 years	α, γ
Carbon-14	5,715 years	β
Plutonium-239	2.412×10^4 years	α, γ
Uranium-235	7.04×10^8 years	α, γ
Potassium-40	1.28×10^9 years	β, γ
Uranium-238	4.47×10^9 years	α, γ

Math Skills: Half-Life

Radium-226 has a half-life of 1,599 years. How long will seven-eighths of a sample of radium-226 take to decay?

Identify
List the given and unknown values.

Given:
half-life = 1,599 years
fraction of sample decayed = $\frac{7}{8}$

Unknown:
fraction of sample remaining = ?
total time of decay = ?

Plan
Subtract the fraction decayed from 1 to find how much of the sample is remaining.

Determine how much of the sample is remaining after each half-life.

fraction of sample remaining =
1 − fraction decayed =
$1 - \frac{7}{8} = \frac{1}{8}$

amount of sample remaining after one half-life = $\frac{1}{2}$

amount of sample remaining after two half-lives = $\frac{1}{2} \times \frac{1}{2} = \frac{1}{4}$

amount of sample remaining after three half-lives = $\frac{1}{2} \times \frac{1}{2} \times \frac{1}{2} = \frac{1}{8}$

Solve
Multiply the number of half-lives by the time for each half-life to calculate the total time required for the radioactive decay.

Each half-life lasts 1,599 years.
total time of decay =

$3 \text{ half-lives} \times \frac{1,599 \text{ y}}{\text{half-life}} = 4,797 \text{ y}$

Practice Hint

> Make a diagram that shows how much of the original sample is left:
>
> 1 → 1/2 → 1/4 → 1/8 → 1/16 → . . .
>
> Each arrow represents one half-life.

> Problems 4 and 5: You will need to work backward from the final answer to get to the time when one-half of the original sample remains.

Practice

1. The half-life of iodine-131 is 8.1 days. How long will three-fourths of a sample of iodine-131 take to decay?
2. Radon-222 is a radioactive gas with a half-life of 3.82 days. How long will fifteen-sixteenths of a sample of radon-222 take to decay?
3. Uranium-238 decays very slowly. Its half-life is 4.47 billion years. What percentage of a sample of uranium-238 will remain after 13.4 billion years?
4. A sample of strontium-90 is found to have decayed to one-eighth of its original amount after 87.3 years. What is the half-life of strontium-90?

For more practice, visit **go.hrw.com** and enter keyword **HK8MP**.

QuickLab: Modeling Decay and Half-Life

  20 min

Procedure

1. Place **128 pennies** in a **jar**, and place the **lid** on the jar. Shake the jar, and then pour the pennies onto a **flat work surface**.

2. Separate pennies that are heads up from those that are tails up. Count and record the number of heads-up pennies, and set these pennies aside. Place the tails-up pennies back in the jar.

3. Repeat the process until all of the pennies have been set aside.

Analysis

1. For each trial, divide the number of heads-up pennies set aside by the total number of pennies used in the trial. Are these ratios nearly equal to each other? What fraction are they closest to?

2. How well does this experiment model radioactive half-life?

Radioactive decay is exponential decay.

The definition of *half-life* tells us that after the first half-life of a radioactive sample has passed, half of the sample remains unchanged. After the next half-life, half of the remaining half decays, so only a quarter of the original element remains. Of that quarter, half will decay in the next half-life. Only one-eighth will then remain unchanged. This relationship is called an *exponential decay*.

A *decay curve* is a graph of the number of radioactive parent nuclei remaining in a sample as a function of time. The relationship between the fraction of carbon-14 versus time is graphed in **Figure 6**. Notice that the total number of nuclei remains constant and the number of carbon atoms continually decreases over time. As the number of carbon-14 atoms decreases, the number of nitrogen-14 atoms increases.

Figure 6 With each successive half-life, half of the remaining sample decays to form another element. **How much of the original element will remain after four half-lives?**

Keyword: HK8NUCF6

Section 1 What Is Radioactivity? **335**

Figure 7 Carbon-14 dating is used to date the remains of living things, such as this mummy of Petamenophis.

www.scilinks.org
Topic: Carbon Dating
Code: HK80218

Carbon-14 is used to date materials.

Archaeologists use the half-life of radioactive carbon-14 to date more-recent materials, such as fibers from ancient clothing, and animal or human remains, such as the mummy shown in **Figure 7**. All of these materials came from organisms that were once alive. When plants absorb carbon dioxide during photosynthesis, a tiny fraction of the CO_2 molecules contains carbon-14 rather than the more common carbon-12. While the plant, or an animal that eats plants, is alive, the ratio of the carbon isotopes remains constant.

When a plant or animal dies, it no longer takes in carbon. The amount of carbon-14 decreases through beta decay, while the amount of carbon-12 remains constant. Thus, the ratio of carbon-14 to carbon-12 decreases with time. By measuring this ratio and comparing it with the ratio in a living plant or animal, scientists can estimate how long ago the once-living organism died.

Section 1 Review

KEY IDEAS

1. **Identify** which of the four common types of nuclear radiation correspond to the following descriptions.
   a. an electron
   b. uncharged particle
   c. particle that can be stopped by a piece of paper
   d. high-energy electromagnetic radiation
2. **Describe** what happens when beta decay occurs.
3. **Explain** why charged particles do not penetrate matter deeply.

CRITICAL THINKING

4. **Analyzing Methods** An archaeologist finds an old piece of wood whose carbon-14 to carbon-12 ratio is one-sixteenth the ratio measured in a newly fallen tree. How old does the wood seem to be?

Math Skills

5. Determine the product denoted by X in the following alpha decay.

   $$^{212}_{86}Rn \rightarrow {}^{A}_{Z}X + {}^{4}_{2}He$$

6. Determine the isotope produced in the beta decay of iodine-131, an isotope used to check thyroid-gland function.

   $$^{131}_{53}I \rightarrow {}^{A}_{Z}X + {}^{0}_{-1}e$$

7. Calculate the time required for three-fourths of a sample of cesium-138 to decay, given that its half-life is 32.2 min.

8. Calculate the half-life of cesium-135 if seven-eighths of a sample decays in 6×10^6 years.

SECTION 2
Nuclear Fission and Fusion

Key Ideas

> What holds the nuclei of atoms together?
> What is released when the nucleus of a heavy atom is split?
> What happens when the nuclei of small atoms are joined?

Key Terms

fission
nuclear chain reaction
critical mass
fusion

Why It Matters

Nuclear fission can be controlled and used to generate electricity.

In 1939, German scientists Otto Hahn and Fritz Strassman conducted experiments in the hope of forming heavy nuclei. Hahn and Strassman bombarded uranium samples with neutrons and expected that a few nuclei would capture one or more neutrons. The new elements that formed had chemical properties that the scientists could not explain.

An explanation for these results came only after the scientists' former colleague Lise Meitner and her nephew Otto Frisch read the results of the experiments. Meitner and Frisch believed that instead of making heavier elements, the uranium nuclei had split into smaller elements.

In the early 1940s, Enrico Fermi and other scientists at the University of Chicago built stacks of graphite and uranium blocks, similar to the one shown in **Figure 1.** This *nuclear pile* was used to create the first controlled nuclear fission chain reaction and to launch the Manhattan Project, which led to the creation of nuclear weapons.

Tennessee Course Level Expectations (Physical Science)

CLE.3202.TE.1; CLE.3202.2.5;
CLE.3202.Inq.1; CLE.3202.Inq.2;
CLE.3202.Inq.3; CLE.3202.Math.1;
CLE.3202.Math.2; CLE.3202.TE.3;
CLE.3202.TE.4

Figure 1 This nuclear pile was used in the late 1940s and early 1950s to better understand controlled nuclear fission.

Nuclear Forces

Protons and neutrons are tightly packed in the tiny nucleus of an atom. As explained in Section 1, certain nuclei are unstable and undergo decay by emitting nuclear radiation. Also, an element can have both stable and unstable isotopes. For example, carbon-12 is a stable isotope, but carbon-14 is unstable and radioactive. > **The stability of a nucleus depends on the nuclear forces that hold the nucleus together. These forces act between the protons and the neutrons.**

Like charges repel, so how can so many positively charged protons fit into an atomic nucleus without flying apart?

Nuclei are held together by a special force.

The neutrons and protons are able to exist together in the nuclei of atoms because of the *strong nuclear force*. This force causes protons and neutrons in the nucleus to attract one another. The attraction is much stronger than the electric repulsion between protons. However, the attraction due to the strong nuclear force occurs over a very short distance, less than 3×10^{-15} m, or about the width of three protons.

Neutrons contribute to nuclear stability.

Because of the strong nuclear force, neutrons and protons in a nucleus attract other protons and neutrons. Because neutrons have no charge, they do not repel one another or the protons. However, the protons in a nucleus both repel and attract one another, as **Figure 2** shows. In stable nuclei, the attractive forces are stronger than the repulsive forces, and the element does not undergo nuclear decay.

Too many neutrons or protons can cause a nucleus to become unstable and decay.

Although a greater number of neutrons can help hold a nucleus together, there is a limit to how many neutrons that a nucleus can have. Nuclei with too many or too few neutrons are unstable and undergo decay.

Nuclei with more than 83 protons are always unstable, no matter how many neutrons that the nuclei have. These nuclei will always decay and, in the process, release large amounts of energy and nuclear radiation. Some of this released energy is transferred to the various particles ejected from the nucleus. As a result, the least massive of these particles move very fast. The rest of the energy is emitted in the form of gamma rays. The radioactive decay that takes place results in a more stable nucleus.

Reading Check What is the maximum number of protons that can be found in a stable nucleus?

READING TOOLBOX

Word Origins
Research how the strong nuclear force was discovered. What is the origin of its name? Is there another nuclear force that is "not strong"?

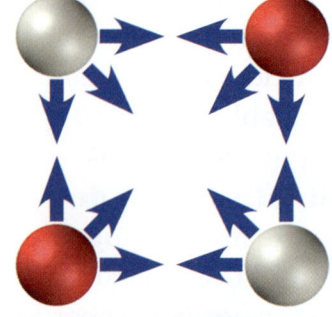

Strong nuclear force
(acts on protons and neutrons)

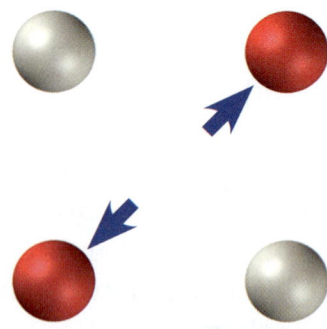

Electric repulsion
(acts on protons)

Figure 2 The nucleus is held together by the attractions among protons and neutrons. These forces are greater than the electric repulsion among the protons alone.

Nuclear Fission

The process of splitting heavier nuclei into lighter nuclei, which Hahn and Strassman observed, is called **fission.** In their experiment, uranium-235 was bombarded by neutrons. One set of products for this type of fission reaction includes two lighter nuclei, barium-140 and krypton-93, together with neutrons and energy.

$$^{235}_{92}U + ^{1}_{0}n \rightarrow ^{140}_{56}Ba + ^{93}_{36}Kr + 3^{1}_{0}n + \text{energy}$$

Notice that the products include three neutrons plus energy. Uranium-235 can also undergo fission by producing different pairs of lighter nuclei. An alternative fission of the isotope uranium-235, for example, produces strontium-90, xenon-143, and three neutrons. ❯ **In the fission process, when the nucleus splits, both neutrons and energy are released.**

> **fission** (FISH uhn) the process by which a nucleus splits into two or more fragments and releases neutrons and energy

Energy is released during nuclear fission.

During fission, as **Figure 3** shows, the nucleus breaks into smaller nuclei. The reaction also releases large amounts of energy. Each dividing nucleus releases about 3.2×10^{-11} J of energy. In comparison, the chemical reaction of one molecule of the explosive trinitrotoluene (TNT) releases 4.8×10^{-18} J.

In their experiment, Hahn and Strassman determined the masses of all of the nuclei and particles before and after the reaction. They found that the overall mass had decreased after the reaction. The missing mass must have been changed into energy.

The equivalence of mass and energy observed in nature is explained by the special theory of relativity, which Albert Einstein presented in 1905. This equivalence means that matter can be converted into energy, and energy into matter, and is given by the following equation.

> ❯ **Mass-energy equation**   energy = mass × (speed of light)^2
> $E = mc^2$

The constant, c, is equal to 3.0×10^8 m/s. So, the energy associated with even a small mass is very large. The mass-equivalent energy of 1 kg of matter is 9×10^{16} J, which is more than the chemical energy of 22 million tons of TNT.

Obviously, if objects around us changed into their equivalent energies, the results would be devastating. Under ordinary conditions of pressure and temperature, matter is very stable. Objects, such as chairs and tables, never spontaneously change into energy.

Figure 3 When the uranium-235 nucleus is bombarded by a neutron, the nucleus breaks apart. It forms smaller nuclei, such as xenon-143 and strontium-90, and releases energy through fast neutrons.

www.scilinks.org
Topic: Fission
Code: HK80580

Energy is released when nuclei form.

When the total mass of any nucleus is measured, the mass is less than the individual masses of the neutrons and protons that make up the nucleus. This missing mass is referred to as the *mass defect*. What happens to the missing mass? Einstein's equation provides an explanation—the mass changes into energy. However, the mass defect of a nucleus is very small.

Another way to think about mass defect is to imagine constructing a nucleus by bringing individual protons and neutrons together. During this process, a small amount of mass changes into energy, as described by $E = mc^2$.

Neutrons released by fission can start a chain reaction.

Have you ever played marbles with a lot of marbles in the ring? When one marble is shot into the ring, the resulting collisions cause some of the marbles to scatter. Some nuclear reactions are similar—one reaction <u>triggers</u> another.

A nucleus that splits when it is struck by a neutron forms smaller product nuclei. These smaller nuclei need fewer neutrons to be held together. Therefore, excess neutrons are emitted. One of these neutrons can collide with another large nucleus, triggering another nuclear reaction that releases more neutrons. This process starts a **nuclear chain reaction,** which is a continuous series of nuclear fission reactions.

When Hahn and Strassman continued experimenting, they discovered that each dividing uranium nucleus, on average, produced between two and three additional neutrons. Therefore, two or three new fission reactions could be started from the neutrons that were ejected from one reaction.

If each of these 3 new reactions produces 3 additional neutrons, a total of 9 neutrons become available to trigger 9 additional fission reactions. From these 9 reactions, a total of 27 neutrons are produced, which set off 27 new reactions, and so on. You can probably see from **Figure 4** how the reaction of uranium-235 nuclei would very quickly result in an uncontrolled nuclear chain reaction. Therefore, the ability to create a chain reaction partly depends on the number of neutrons released during each fission reaction.

Academic Vocabulary
trigger (TRIG uhr) to begin or cause something to start

Figure 4 A nuclear chain reaction may be triggered by a single neutron.

Reading Check What causes a nuclear chain reaction?

QuickLab: Modeling Chain Reactions

  10 min

Procedure

1. To model a fission chain reaction, you will need a **small wooden building block** and a **set of dominoes**.
2. Place the building block on a **table or counter**. Stand one domino upright in front of the block and parallel to one of its sides. Stand two more dominoes vertically, parallel, and symmetrical to the first domino.
3. Continue this process until you have used all of the dominoes and have created a triangular shape, as shown here.
4. Gently push the first domino away from the block so that it falls and hits the second group. Note that more dominoes fall with each step.

Analysis

1. Use Newton's first law of motion to explain your results.

Chain reactions can be controlled.

Energy produced in a controlled chain reaction can be used to generate electricity. Particles released by the splitting of the atom strike other uranium atoms and split them. The particles that are given off split still other atoms. A chain reaction is begun, which gives off energy that is used to heat water. The superheated water then transfers energy into a heat exchanger filled with water that is used to make steam. The steam then rotates a turbine to generate electricity. Energy released by the chain reaction changes the atomic energy into thermal energy, which ends up as electrical energy.

The chain-reaction principle is also used in making a nuclear bomb. Two or more masses of uranium-235 are contained in the bomb. These masses are surrounded by a powerful chemical explosive. When the explosive is detonated, all of the uranium is pushed together to create a *critical mass*. The **critical mass** refers to the minimum amount of a substance that can undergo a fission reaction and can also sustain a chain reaction. If the amount of fissionable substance is less than the critical mass, a chain reaction will not continue. Fortunately, the concentration of uranium-235 in nature is too low to start a chain reaction naturally. Almost all of the escaping neutrons are absorbed by the more common and more stable isotope uranium-238.

In nuclear power plants, control rods are used to regulate fission by slowing the chain reaction. In nuclear bombs, reactions are not controlled, and almost pure pieces of the element uranium-235 or plutonium of a precise mass and shape must be brought together and held together with great force. These conditions are not present in a nuclear reactor.

nuclear chain reaction (NOO klee uhr CHAYN ree AK shuhn) a continuous series of nuclear fission reactions

critical mass (KRIT i kuhl MAS) the minimum mass of a fissionable isotope that provides the number of neutrons needed to sustain a chain reaction

Section 2 Nuclear Fission and Fusion

Nuclear Fusion

Obtaining energy from the fission of heavy nuclei is not the only nuclear process that produces energy. ❯ **Energy can be obtained when very light nuclei are combined to form heavier nuclei.** This type of nuclear process is called **fusion.**

In stars, including the sun, energy is produced primarily when hydrogen nuclei combine, or fuse together, and release tremendous amounts of energy. However, a large amount of energy is needed to start a fusion reaction. The reason is that all nuclei are positively charged and repel one another with the electric force. Energy is required to bring the hydrogen nuclei close enough to one another that the repulsive electric force is overcome by the attractive strong nuclear force. In stars, the extreme temperatures provide the energy needed to bring hydrogen nuclei together.

Four hydrogen atoms combine in the sun to make a helium atom and high-energy gamma rays. This nuclear fusion of hydrogen happens in a three step process that involves two isotopes of hydrogen: ordinary hydrogen, ^1_1H, and deuterium, ^2_1H, as **Figure 5** shows.

fusion (FYOO zhuhn) the process in which light nuclei combine at extremely high temperatures, forming heavier nuclei and releasing energy

www.scilinks.org
Topic: Fusion
Code: HK80629

$^1_1H + ^1_1H \rightarrow ^2_1H +$ other particles

$^2_1H + ^1_1H \rightarrow ^3_2He + ^0_0\gamma$

$^3_2He + ^3_2He \rightarrow ^4_2He + ^1_1H + ^1_1H$

Figure 5 The nuclear fusion of hydrogen takes place in a three-step process that releases large amounts of energy.

Section 2 Review

KEY IDEAS

1. **Explain** why most isotopes of elements that have a high atomic number are radioactive.

2. **Indicate** whether the following are fission or fusion reactions.
   a. $^1_1H + ^2_1H \rightarrow ^3_2He + \gamma$
   b. $^1_0n + ^{235}_{92}U \rightarrow ^{146}_{57}La + ^{87}_{35}Br + 3^1_0n$
   c. $^{21}_{10}Ne + ^4_2He \rightarrow ^{24}_{12}Mg + ^1_0n$
   d. $^{208}_{82}Pb + ^{58}_{26}Fe \rightarrow ^{265}_{108}Hs + ^1_0n$

3. **Predict** whether the total mass of a nucleus of an atom of $^{56}_{26}Fe$ is greater than, less than, or equal to the combined mass of the 26 protons and 30 neutrons that make up the nucleus. If the masses are not equal, explain why.

CRITICAL THINKING

4. **Predicting Outcomes** Suppose that a nucleus captures two neutrons and decays to produce one neutron. Is this process likely to produce a chain reaction? Explain your reasoning.

Why It Matters

The Power of Fission

The United States receives about 20% of its electric power from power plants that use nuclear fission as an energy source. Today, there are more than 1,100 nuclear reactors in use around the world. This number includes 440 large reactors that generate electricity, more than 400 reactors that power ships and submarines, and about 280 small reactors that are used for research and for the creation of isotopes for medicine and energy. The country that currently receives the greatest percentage of its electric power from fission is France. France receives more than 75% of its electricity from nuclear power.

1 Energy released by the nuclear reaction heats water in the high-pressure first circuit to a very high temperature.

3 Steam is directed against a turbine and sets it in motion. The turbine sets the generator in motion to generate electricity.

2 The superheated water is pumped into a heat exchanger, which transfers the heat of the first circuit to the second circuit. Water in the second circuit flashes into high-pressure steam.

4 A third circuit cools the steam from the turbine. The waste heat is released from the cooling tower in the form of steam.

SCILINKS
www.scilinks.org
Topic: Nuclear Energy
Code: HK81047

YOUR TURN

UNDERSTANDING CONCEPTS
1. What do nuclear power plants and other electric power plants have in common?

CRITICAL THINKING
2. How would using three circuits help the environment?

SECTION 3
Nuclear Radiation Today

Key Ideas
> Where are we exposed to radiation?
> What are some beneficial uses of nuclear radiation?
> What factors determine the risks of nuclear radiation?
> How is the energy produced by nuclear fission used?

Key Terms
background radiation
rem
radioactive tracer

Why It Matters
Radioactive tracer elements are used in medical diagnostic procedures such as positron emission tomography.

Tennessee Course Level Expectations (Physical Science)
CLE.3202.TE.1; CLE 3202.2.5;
CLE.3202.Inq.1; CLE.3202.Inq.2;
CLE.3202.Inq.3; CLE.3202.Inq.4;
CLE.3202.Inq.6; CLE.3202.TE.4

You may be surprised to learn that you are exposed to some form of nuclear radiation every day. Some forms of nuclear radiation are beneficial. Others present some risks. This section will discuss both the benefits and the possible risks of nuclear radiation.

Where Is Radiation?

Nuclear radiation is all around you. The form of nuclear radiation that arises naturally is called **background radiation.** > **We are continually exposed to radiation from natural sources, such as the sun, soil, rocks, and plants.** More than 80% of the radiation that we are exposed to comes from natural sources, such as those shown in **Figure 1.** The living tissues of most organisms are adapted to survive these low levels of natural nuclear radiation. Human-made sources, such as computer monitors, smoke detectors, and X rays, account for at least 20% of our everyday exposure.

background radiation (BAK GROWND RAY dee AY shuhn) the nuclear radiation that arises naturally from cosmic rays and from radioactive isotopes in the soil and air

rem (REM) the quantity of ionizing radiation that does as much damage to human tissue as 1 roentgen of high-voltage X rays does

Figure 1 Sources of background radiation, both natural and artificial, are all around us.

Figure 2 Dental X rays expose a patient to about 1 millirem of radiation.

Radiation is measured in units of rems.

Levels of radiation absorbed by the human body are measured in **rems** or millirems (1 rem = 1,000 millirems). Typical exposure for an X ray at the dentist's office, shown in **Figure 2,** is about 1 millirem.

In the United States, many people work in occupations that involve nuclear radiation. Nuclear engineering, health physics, radiology, radiochemistry, X-ray technology, and other nuclear medical technology all involve nuclear radiation. A safe limit for these workers has been set at 5,000 millirems per year, in addition to natural background exposures.

Exposure varies from one location to another.

People in the United States receive varying amounts of natural radiation. Those at higher elevations receive more exposure to nuclear radiation from space than people do at lower elevations. People in areas with many rocks have higher nuclear radiation exposure than people do in areas without many rocks. Because of large differences both in elevation and background radiation sources, exposure varies greatly from one location to another, as **Figure 3** illustrates.

Some activities add to the amount of nuclear radiation exposure.

Another factor that affects levels of exposure is participation in certain activities. **Figure 4** shows actual exposure to nuclear radiation for just a few activities. Other activities besides those listed in this table also add to the amount of nuclear radiation exposure. All activities that add nuclear radiation to the air will affect everyone in the area around these activities.

Figure 3 Radiation Exposure per Location

Location	Radiation exposure (millirems/year)
Tampa, FL	63.7
Richmond, VA	64.1
Las Vegas, NV	69.5
Los Angeles, CA	73.6
Portland, OR	86.7
Rochester, NY	88.1
Wheeling, WV	111.9
Denver, CO	164.6

Figure 4 Radiation Exposure per Activity

Activity	Radiation exposure (millirems/year)
Smoking 1 1/2 packs of cigarettes per day	8,000
Flying for 720 hours (airline crew)	267
Inhaling radon from the environment	360
Giving or receiving medical X rays	100

Section 3 Nuclear Radiation Today

Figure 5 In a smoke alarm, a small amount of alpha-emitting isotope detects smoke particles in the air.

radioactive tracer (RAY dee oh AK tiv TRAYS uhr) a radioactive material that is added to a substance so that its distribution can be detected later

Figure 6 Research farms use radioactive tracers to reveal water movement and other biochemical processes.

Beneficial Uses of Nuclear Radiation

Radioactive substances have a wide range of applications. In these applications, nuclear radiation is used in a controlled way to take advantage of its effects on other materials. ❯ **Some common applications of nuclear radiation include medical diagnosis and treatment, smoke detectors, manufacturing, and agriculture.**

Smoke detectors help save lives.

Small radioactive sources are present in smoke alarms, such as the one shown in **Figure 5**. These sources release alpha particles, which are charged, to produce an electric current. Smoke particles in the air reduce the flow of the current. The drop in current sets off the alarm when even small levels of smoke are present.

Nuclear radiation is used to detect diseases.

The digital computer, ultrasound scanning, CT scanning, PET, and magnetic resonance imaging (MRI) have combined to create a variety of diagnostic imaging techniques. Using these procedures, doctors can view images of parts of the organs and can detect dysfunction or disease.

Radioactive tracers are short-lived isotopes that tend to concentrate in affected cells and are used to locate tumors. Tracers are widely used in medicine.

Nuclear radiation therapy is used to treat cancer.

Radiotherapy is treatment that uses controlled doses of nuclear radiation for treating diseases such as cancer. For example, certain brain tumors can be targeted with small beams of gamma rays.

Radiotherapy treats thyroid cancer by using an iodine isotope. Treatment of leukemia also uses radiotherapy. The defective bone marrow is first killed with a massive dose of nuclear radiation and then replaced with healthy bone marrow from a donor.

Agriculture uses radioactive tracers and radioisotopes.

On research farms, such as the one shown in **Figure 6**, radioactive tracers in flowing water can show how fast water moves through the soil or through stems and leaves of crops. Tracers help us understand biochemical processes in plants. Radioisotopes are chemically identical with other isotopes of the same element. Because of that similarity, they can be substituted in chemical reactions. Radioactive forms of the element are then easily located with sensors.

Why It Matters

How Do PET Scans Work?

REAL WORLD

Positron emission tomography (PET) is a medical procedure that can be used to study how a patient's body is functioning. PET scans can help doctors detect medical problems, such as cancer and heart disease. These scans can show changes in biological processes earlier than changes in anatomy are visible by using other procedures, such as CAT scans and MRIs.

1. Patients receiving a PET scan are injected with a radioactive tracer that is attached to a natural body compound, such as glucose.

2. After 30 to 45 minutes, patients are taken to the PET scanner. They must lie very still while the detectors record the emission of energy from the injected radioactive materials.

3. Because living tissues use glucose for energy, different colors on the computer screen correspond to the different levels of function in the body.

Researchers use PET imaging to understand brain function, both for disease detection and for research. In these scans, a research subject's brain was scanned with different sets of stimuli. Scientists can use this information to learn which areas of the brain are used to process different sensations.

SCILINKS
www.scilinks.org
Topic: Radioactive Tracers
Code: HK81257

YOUR TURN

CRITICAL THINKING
1. Name some advantages and disadvantages of PET scans for medical diagnosis.

WRITING IN SCIENCE
2. Research other medical diagnostic techniques. How do they compare to PET scans?

READING TOOLBOX

Word Origins
What are the origins of the words *ionization* and *dosimeter*? Do these words have root words from other languages? If so, what are the meanings of those root words?

Figure 7 A dosimeter contains a piece of film that detects radiation in the environment. Dosimeters help indicate exposure to ionizing radiation.

Risks from Nuclear Radiation

Although nuclear radiation has many benefits, there are also risks, because nuclear radiation interacts with living tissue. Alpha and beta particles, as well as gamma rays and X rays, can change the number of electrons in the molecules of living materials. This process is known as *ionization*. Ionized molecules may form substances that are harmful to life.

❯ **The risk of damage from nuclear radiation depends on both the type and the amount of radiation exposure.** The effects of low levels of nuclear radiation on living cells are so small that they may not be detected. However, studies have shown a relationship between exposure to high levels of nuclear radiation and cancer. Cancers associated with high-dose exposure include leukemia and breast, lung, and stomach cancers.

The ability to penetrate matter differs among different types of nuclear radiation. A layer of clothing or an inch of air can stop alpha particles. Beta particles are lighter and faster than alpha particles. Beta particles can penetrate a fraction of an inch in solids and liquids and can travel several feet in air. Several feet of material may be required to protect you from high-energy gamma rays.

High levels of nuclear radiation can cause radiation sickness.

Radiation sickness is an illness that results from excessive exposure to nuclear radiation. This sickness may occur from a single massive exposure, such as a nuclear explosion, or repeated exposures to very high nuclear radiation levels. Individuals who work with nuclear radiation must protect themselves with shields and special clothing. People who work in radioactive areas wear *dosimeters*, devices for measuring the amount of nuclear radiation exposure. **Figure 7** shows one example of a dosimeter.

High concentrations of radon gas can be hazardous.

Colorless and inert, *radon gas* is produced by the radioactive decay of the uranium-238 present in soil and rock. Radon gas emits alpha and beta particles and gamma rays. Tests have shown a correlation between lung cancer and high levels of exposure to radon gas, especially for smokers. Some areas have higher radon levels than others do. Tests for radon gas in buildings are widely available.

High concentrations of radon-222 in homes or offices can be eliminated by sealing cracks in foundations or by installing vents that draw air out of the building.

Figure 8 Nuclear reactors such as this one are used over much of the world to generate electricity. **What are some advantages to nuclear power?**

Nuclear Power

Nuclear reactors, such as the one shown in **Figure 8,** are used in dozens of countries to generate electricity. ❯ **Energy produced from fission is used to provide electrical energy to millions of homes and businesses.** There are many advantages to this source of energy. There are also disadvantages.

Nuclear fission has both advantages and disadvantages.

One advantage of nuclear fission is that it does not produce gaseous pollutants. Also, there is much more energy in the known uranium reserves than in the known reserves of coal and oil.

In nuclear fission reactors, energy is produced when a controlled fission reaction is triggered in uranium-235. However, the products of fission reactions are often radioactive isotopes. Therefore, serious safety concerns must be addressed. Radioactive products of fission must be handled carefully so that they do not escape into the environment and release nuclear radiation.

Another safety issue involves the safe operation of the nuclear reactors in which the controlled fission reaction is carried out. A nuclear reactor must be equipped with many safety features. The reactor requires considerable shielding and must meet very strict safety requirements. Thus, nuclear power plants are expensive to build.

Reading Check How do energy reserves for uranium compare to those of coal and oil?

www.scilinks.org
Topic: Nuclear Power
Code: HK81052

Academic Vocabulary
issue (ISH oo) a point of debate

Section 3 Nuclear Radiation Today **349**

Figure 9 Storage facilities for nuclear waste must be designed to contain radioactive materials safely for thousands of years.

Nuclear waste must be safely stored.

Besides the expense that occurs during the life of a nuclear power plant is the expense of storing radioactive materials, such as the fuel rods used in the reactors. After their use, they must be placed in safe facilities that are well shielded, as **Figure 9** shows. These precautions are necessary to keep nuclear radiation from leaking out and harming living things. The facilities must also keep nuclear radiation from contacting groundwater.

Ideal places for such facilities are sparsely populated areas that have little water on the surface or underground. These areas must also be free from earthquakes.

Nuclear fusion releases large quantities of energy.

The sun uses the nuclear fusion of hydrogen atoms; this fusion results in larger helium atoms. Solar energy can be captured by solar panels or other means to provide energy for homes and businesses. Another option that holds some promise as an energy source is controlled nuclear fusion.

Some scientists estimate that 1 kg of hydrogen in a fusion reactor could release as much energy as 16 million kg of burning coal. The fusion reaction itself releases very little waste or pollution.

Because fusion requires that the electric repulsion between protons be overcome, these reactions are difficult to produce in the laboratory. However, scientists are conducting many experiments in the United States, Japan, and Europe to learn how people can exploit fusion to create a clean source of power that uses fuels extracted from ordinary water.

Integrating Space Science

Element Factory All heavy elements, from cobalt to uranium, are made when massive stars explode. The pressure that is produced in the explosion causes nearby nuclei to fuse, in some cases, more than once.

The explosion carries the newly created elements into space. These elements later become parts of new stars and planets. The elements of Earth are believed to have formed in the outer layers of an exploding star.

Nuclear fusion also has advantages and disadvantages.

The most attractive feature of fusion is that the fuel for fusion is abundant. Hydrogen is the most common element in the universe, and it is plentiful in many compounds on Earth, such as water. Earth's oceans could provide enough hydrogen to meet current world energy demands for millions of years.

Practical fusion-based power, illustrated by the concept drawing in **Figure 10,** is far from being a reality. Fusion reactions have some drawbacks. They can produce fast neutrons, a highly energetic and potentially dangerous form of nuclear radiation. Because shielding material in the reactor would have to be replaced periodically, the expense of operating a fusion power plant would still be high. Lithium can be used to slow down these neutrons, but lithium is chemically reactive and rare, so its use is impractical.

Research on nuclear fusion is still in its infancy. Successful experiments are just beginning. Who can say what the future may hold? Perhaps future scientists will find the answers to the nagging questions that plague the government today concerning the perfect fuel for U.S. citizens.

Figure 10 The ITER experimental nuclear fusion research reactor will be built in France.

Section 3 Review

KEY IDEAS

1. **List** three sources of background radiation.
2. **Identify** three activities that add to background radiation under normal circumstances.
3. **Describe** how smoke detectors use alpha particles and what sets off the alarm.
4. **Explain** how radioactive tracers help locate tumors.
5. **Describe** three factors that contribute to how much damage is done to living tissue by radiation.
6. **Identify** some of the advantages and disadvantages of using nuclear energy.

CRITICAL THINKING

7. **Compare and Contrast** What are the benefits and risks of radiation therapy?
8. **Inferring Conclusions** Explain why it is important to use low levels of nuclear radiation for detection and treatment of disease.
9. **Drawing Conclusions** Why is the testing of buildings for radon gas levels important?
10. **Making Predictions** Suppose that uranium-238 could undergo fission as easily as uranium-235 does. Predict how that situation would change the advantages and disadvantages of fission reactors.

Skills Practice Lab

Simulating Nuclear Decay Reactions

50 min

What You'll Do
- **Simulate** the decay of radioactive isotopes by throwing a set of dice, and observe the results.
- **Graph** the results to identify patterns in the amounts of isotopes present.

What You'll Need
cup, paper, large, with plastic lid
dice (10)
pencil
tape, masking

In this lab, you will simulate the decay of lead-210 into its isotope lead-206. This decay of lead-210 into lead-206 occurs in a multistep process. Lead-210, $^{210}_{82}Pb$, first decays into bismuth-210, $^{210}_{83}Bi$, which then decays into polonium-210, $^{210}_{84}Po$, which finally decays into the isotope lead-206, $^{206}_{82}Pb$.

Procedure

Modeling Isotope Decay

1. On a sheet of paper, prepare a data table as shown below. Leave room to add extra rows at the bottom, if necessary.

Sample Data Table: Dice Rolls Modeling Isotope Decay

Throw #	Number of dice representing each isotope			
	$^{210}_{82}Pb$	$^{210}_{83}Bi$	$^{210}_{84}Po$	$^{206}_{82}Pb$
0 (start)	10	0	0	0
1				
2				
3				
4				

DO NOT WRITE IN BOOK

2. Place all 10 dice in the cup. Each die represents an atom of $^{210}_{82}Pb$, a radioactive isotope.

3. Put the lid on the cup, and shake the cup a few times. Then, remove the lid, and spill the dice. In this simulation, each throw represents a *half-life*.

4. All of the dice that land with *1*, *2*, or *3* up represent atoms of $^{210}_{82}Pb$ that have decayed into $^{210}_{83}Bi$. The remaining dice still represent $^{210}_{82}Pb$ atoms. Separate the two sets of dice. Count the dice, and record the results in your data table.

5. To keep track of the dice representing the decayed atoms, you will make a small mark on them. On a die, the faces with *1*, *2*, and *3* share a corner. With a pencil, draw a small circle or loop around this shared corner. This die represents the $^{210}_{83}Bi$ atoms.

6. Put all the dice back in the cup, shake them, and roll them again. In a decay process, there are two possibilities: some atoms decay, and some do not. See the table "Guide to Isotope Decay" to help track your results.

352 Chapter 10 Nuclear Changes

Guide to Isotope Decay

Isotope type	Decays into	Signs of decay	Identifying the atoms in column 2
$^{210}_{82}Pb$	$^{210}_{83}Bi$	Unmarked dice land on *1*, *2*, or *3*.	Mark $^{210}_{83}Bi$ by drawing a circle around the corner where faces *1*, *2*, and *3* meet.
$^{210}_{83}Bi$	$^{210}_{84}Po$	Dice with one loop land on *1*, *2*, or *3*.	Draw a circle around the corner where faces *4*, *5*, and *6* meet.
$^{210}_{84}Po$	$^{206}_{82}Pb$	Dice with two loops land on *1*, *2*, or *3*.	Put a small piece of masking tape over the two circles.
$^{206}_{82}Pb$	Decay ends		

Sorting the Isotopes That Decayed

7 After the second throw, you have three types of atoms. Sort the dice into three sets.

  a. The first set consists of dice with a circle drawn on them that landed with *1*, *2*, or *3* facing up. These dice represent $^{210}_{83}Bi$ atoms that have decayed into $^{210}_{84}Po$.

  b. The second set consists of two types of dice: the dice with one circle that did not land on *1*, *2*, or *3* (undecayed $^{210}_{83}Bi$) and the unmarked dice that landed with *1*, *2*, or *3* facing up (representing the decay of original $^{210}_{82}Pb$ into $^{210}_{83}Bi$).

  c. The third set includes unmarked dice that did not land with *1*, *2*, or *3* facing up. These dice represent the undecayed $^{210}_{82}Pb$ atoms.

8 For your third throw, put all of the dice back into the cup. After the third throw, some of the $^{210}_{84}Po$ will decay into the stable isotope $^{206}_{82}Pb$. After this and each additional throw, do the following: separate the different types of atoms in groups, count the atoms in each group, record your data in your table, and mark the dice to identify each isotope. Use the table above as a guide.

9 Continue throwing the dice until all of the dice have indicated decay into $^{206}_{82}Pb$, which is a stable isotope.

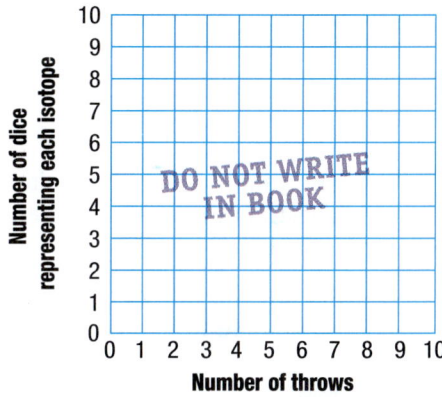

Analysis

1. **Describing Events** Write nuclear-decay equations for the nuclear reactions modeled in this lab.
2. **Graphing Data** In your lab report, prepare a graph like the one shown here. Using a different color or symbol for each atom, plot the data for all four atoms on the same graph.

Communicating Your Results

3. **Drawing Conclusions** What do your results suggest about how the amounts of $^{210}_{82}Pb$ and $^{206}_{82}Pb$ on Earth are changing over time?

Extension

$^{210}_{82}Pb$ is continually produced through a series of nuclear decays that begin with $^{238}_{92}U$. Does this information cause you to modify your answer to item 3? Explain.

Counting Nuclear Decay

Science > Skills

Technology
> Math
Scientific Methods
Graphing

Problem

In a sample of francium-223, 93.75% of the sample has undergone radioactive decay. Francium-223 has a half-life of 22 min.

a. What fraction of francium-223 remains in the sample?
b. How many half-lives did it take for the sample to decay?
c. How long did the sample take to decay?

Solution

Identify

List all given and unknown values.

Given:
percentage of sample decayed = 93.75%
half-life = 22 min

Unknown:
a. fraction of sample remaining
b. n = number of half-lives
c. time of decay

Plan

a. Subtract the fraction decayed from 1 to find the amount of sample remaining.
b. Determine how many multiples of 1/2 are in the fraction of sample remaining.
c. Multiply the number of half-lives by the half-life to find the time of decay.

a. fraction of sample remaining =
$1 - $ fraction of sample decayed =
$$1 - \frac{\text{percentage of sample decayed}}{100}$$

b. $\left(\frac{1}{2}\right)^n = $ fraction of sample remaining

c. time of decay = $n \times$ half-life

Solve

Substitute the given values into the equation, calculate the unknown quantities, and solve.

a. fraction of sample remaining =
$$1 - \frac{93.75}{100} = 1 - 0.9375 = 0.0625 = \frac{1}{16}$$

b. $\frac{1}{16} = \left(\frac{1}{2}\right) \times \left(\frac{1}{2}\right) \times \left(\frac{1}{2}\right) \times \left(\frac{1}{2}\right) = \left(\frac{1}{2}\right)^4$

number of half-lives = $n = 4$

c. time of decay = 4×22 min = 88 min

Practice

1. What fraction of iodine-132 remains if 87.5% has undergone radioactive decay?
2. How many half-lives are required for the sample to decay?
3. Iodine-132 has a half-life of 2.3 h. How long does the sample take to decay completely?

Chapter 10   Nuclear Changes

CHAPTER 10 Summary

go.hrw.com
SUPER SUMMARY
KEYWORD: HK8NUCS

Key Ideas

Section 1 What Is Radioactivity?

› **Nuclear Radiation** After radioactive decay, elements change into different isotopes of the same element or into entirely different elements. (p. 327)

› **Nuclear Decay** Anytime an unstable nucleus emits alpha or beta particles, the number of protons and neutrons changes. (p. 330)

› **Radioactive Decay Rates** The time required for half of a sample of radioactive material to decay is its half-life. (p. 333)

Section 2 Nuclear Fission and Fusion

› **Nuclear Forces** The stability of a nucleus depends on the nuclear forces that hold the nucleus together. These forces act between the protons and the neutrons. (p. 337)

› **Nuclear Fission** Nuclear fission takes place when a large nucleus divides into smaller nuclei. Energy is released in the process. (p. 339)

› **Nuclear Fusion** Energy is released when light nuclei are combined to form heavier nuclei. (p. 342)

Section 3 Nuclear Radiation Today

› **Where Is Radiation?** We are continually exposed to radiation from natural sources, such as the sun, soil, rocks, and plants. (p. 344)

› **Beneficial Uses of Nuclear Radiation** Applications of nuclear radiation include medical diagnosis and treatment, smoke detectors, and agriculture. (p. 346)

› **Risks from Nuclear Radiation** The risk of damage from nuclear radiation depends on both the type and the amount of radiation exposure. (p. 348)

› **Nuclear Power** Energy produced from fission is used to provide electrical energy to millions of homes and businesses. (p. 349)

Key Terms

radioactive decay, p. 327
nuclear radiation, p. 327
alpha particle, p. 328
beta particle, p. 329
gamma ray, p. 329
half-life, p. 333

fission, p. 339
nuclear chain reaction, p. 340
critical mass, p. 341
fusion, p. 342

background radiation, p. 344
rem, p. 345
radioactive tracer, p. 346

CHAPTER 10 Review

1. **Four-Corner Fold** Create a four-corner fold as described in Appendix A. Under two of the flaps, describe (1) nuclear fission and (2) nuclear fusion. Under the other two flaps, describe (3) some beneficial uses of nuclear radiation and (4) some risks of nuclear radiation.

USING KEY TERMS

2. Describe the main differences between the four principal types of nuclear radiation: *alpha particles, beta particles, gamma rays,* and *neutron emission.*

3. Where do *beta particles* come from?

4. Why do *gamma rays* have no mass at all?

5. Would a substance with a one-second *half-life* be effective as a *radioactive tracer*?

6. For the nuclear *fission* process, how is *critical mass* important in a *nuclear chain reaction*?

7. What is *background radiation*, and what are its sources?

8. How does nuclear *fusion* account for the energy produced in stars?

UNDERSTANDING KEY IDEAS

9. When a heavy nucleus decays, it may emit any of the following except
   a. alpha particles.
   b. beta particles.
   c. gamma rays.
   d. X rays.

10. A neutron decays to form a proton and a(n)
    a. alpha particle.
    b. beta particle.
    c. gamma ray.
    d. emitted neutron.

11. After three half-lives, _____ of a radioactive sample remains.
    a. all
    b. one-half
    c. one-third
    d. one-eighth

12. Carbon dating can be used to measure the age of each of the following except
    a. a 7,000-year-old human body.
    b. a 1,200-year-old wooden statue.
    c. a 2,600-year-old iron sword.
    d. a 3,500-year-old piece of fabric.

13. The strong nuclear force
    a. attracts protons to electrons.
    b. holds molecules together.
    c. holds the atomic nucleus together.
    d. attracts electrons to neutrons.

14. The process in which a heavy nucleus splits into two lighter nuclei is called
    a. fission.
    b. fusion.
    c. alpha decay.
    d. a chain reaction.

15. The amount of energy produced during nuclear fission is related to
    a. the temperature in the atmosphere during nuclear fission.
    b. the masses of the original nuclei and the particles released.
    c. the volume of the nuclear reactor.
    d. the square of the speed of sound.

16. Which condition is *not* necessary for a chain reaction to occur?
    a. The radioactive sample must have a short half-life.
    b. The neutrons from one split nucleus must cause other nuclei to divide.
    c. The radioactive sample must be at critical mass.
    d. Not too many neutrons must be allowed to leave the radioactive sample.

17. Which of the following is *not* a use for radioactive isotopes?
    a. as tracers for diagnosing disease
    b. as an additive to paints to increase durability
    c. as a way to treat forms of cancer
    d. as a way to study biochemical processes in plants

356 Chapter 10 Nuclear Changes

EXPLAINING KEY IDEAS

18. How does nuclear decay affect the atomic number and mass number of a nucleus that changes after undergoing decay?

19. What are two factors that cause alpha particles to lose energy and travel less distance than neutrons travel?

20. The nuclei of atoms are made of protons and neutrons. Every atomic nucleus larger than that of hydrogen has as least two positively charged protons. Why do the nuclei remain intact instead of being broken apart by the repulsion of their electric charges?

21. The amount of nuclear radiation exposure absorbed by the human body is measured in rems. How does the amount of exposure in rems per year in Denver, Colorado, compare with the amount that has been set as a safe limit for workers in occupations with relatively high radiation exposure? Explain your answer.

22. How can a radioactive tracer be used to locate tumors?

CRITICAL THINKING

23. **Compare and Contrast** Describe the similarities and differences between atomic electrons and beta particles.

24. **Identifying Functions** Why do people working around radioactive waste in a radioactive storage facility wear badges that contain strips of photographic film?

25. **Drawing Conclusions** Why would carbon-14 not be a good choice to use in household smoke detectors?

26. **Predicting Outcomes** Would an emitter of alpha particles be useful in measuring the thickness of a brick? Explain your answer.

Graphing Skills

27. **Graphing Data** The first 20 elements on the periodic table have stable nuclei composed of equal numbers of protons and neutrons. Create a graph on which you plot these elements based on the number of protons (x-axis) and neutrons (y-axis) they contain.

28. **Graphing Data** Extend your graph of the first 20 elements to include the other elements on the periodic table. What happens to the graph? What does this indicate about the stability of a nucleus?

29. **Interpreting Graphics** Using a graphing calculator or computer graphing program, create a graph for the decay of iodine-131, which has a half-life of 8.1 days. Use the graph to answer the following questions.
    a. Approximately what percentage of the iodine-131 has decayed after 4 days?
    b. Approximately what percentage of the iodine-131 has decayed after 12.1 days?
    c. What fraction of iodine-131 has decayed after 2.5 half-lives have elapsed?

Math Skills

30. **Nuclear Decay** Bismuth-212 undergoes a combination of alpha and beta decays to form lead-208. Depending on which decay process occurs first, different isotopes are temporarily formed during the process. Identify these isotopes by completing the equations given below.

    a. $^{212}_{83}\text{Bi} \rightarrow {}^{A}_{Z}X + {}^{4}_{2}\text{He}$
       $^{A}_{Z}X \rightarrow {}^{208}_{82}\text{Pb} + {}^{0}_{-1}e$

    b. $^{212}_{83}\text{Bi} \rightarrow {}^{A}_{Z}X + {}^{0}_{-1}e$
       $^{A}_{Z}X \rightarrow {}^{208}_{82}\text{Pb} + {}^{4}_{2}\text{He}$

31. **Half-Life** Health officials are concerned about radon levels in homes. The half-life of radon-222 is 3.82 days. If a sample of gas contains 4.38 μg of radon-222, how much will remain in the sample after 15.2 days?

Standardized Test Prep

Understanding Concepts

Directions (1-3): For each question, write on a sheet of paper the letter of the correct answer.

1. The beta-decay equation for the decay of cesium-137 into an isotope of barium is

$$^{137}_{55}\text{Cs} \rightarrow {}^{X}_{Y}\text{Ba} + {}^{Z}_{-1}\text{e}$$

    What are the correct values for *X, Y* and *Z*?
    - A. 136, 55, 1
    - B. 137, 56, 0
    - C. 68, 56, 69
    - D. 69, 54, 68

2. The half-life of a particular radioactive isotope is 10 years. If you begin with 100 g of the substance, how much will be left after 40 years?
    - F. 6.25 g
    - G. 12.5 g
    - H. 25 g
    - I. 60 g

3. What happens to an atom's mass number and atomic number after the atom emits a beta particle?
    - A. Both the mass number and the atomic number increase by 1.
    - B. The atomic number does not change, but the mass number decreases by 1.
    - C. The mass number does not change, but the atomic number increases by 1.
    - D. Both the mass number and the atomic number decrease by 1.

Directions (4-5): For each question, write a short response.

4. In a particular case of alpha decay, an isotope of uranium, U, with a mass number of 238 and an atomic number of 92 emits an alpha particle and transforms into thorium, Th, which has an atomic number of 90. Write the equation for this decay process.

5. Why doesn't a nucleus full of protons fly apart because of electric repulsion?

Reading Skills

Directions (6-7): Read the passage below. Then, answer the questions that follow.

POSITRON

Like an electron, a positron has very little mass; however, an electron has an electric charge of –1, and a positron has an electric charge of +1. Scientists theorize that for every kind of particle, there is an antiparticle, which has the same mass but an opposite electric charge.

There are at least two ways in which positrons can be generated. One way is beta decay. In the most common form of beta decay, a neutron in the nucleus of an isotope is converted to a proton, and a beta particle is emitted in the form of an electron. This form of beta decay is properly called *beta minus decay*. In certain isotopes, however, the mirror image of this process, called *beta plus decay*, takes place: a proton is converted to a neutron, and a beta particle with a positive charge is emitted. This beta particle is a positron.

Another way that positrons can be created is for a photon to collide with a charged particle (such as an alpha particle) with a great amount of energy. The collision can result in the simultaneous creation of an electron and a positron from the energy of the photon, in a process called *pair production*.

6. What are the two types of beta particles?
    - F. protons and electrons
    - G. positrons and photons
    - H. electrons and photons
    - I. positrons and electrons

7. Which has greater mass, a positron or a photon? Explain.

Interpreting Graphics

The graphic below shows the radioactive decay of carbon-14. Use this graphic to answer questions 8–10.

RADIOACTIVE DECAY OF CARBON-14

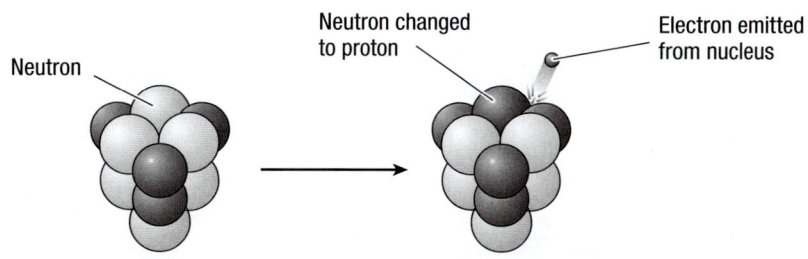

8. What type of nuclear reaction is depicted in the diagram?
   A. alpha decay
   B. beta decay
   C. fission
   D. fusion

9. What isotope is created by this process?
   F. carbon-14
   G. carbon-12
   H. nitrogen-14
   I. nitrogen-13

10. Write the equation that describes this process.

One way to measure how much of a radioactive isotope is present is to make a count of how many times per second a particle of radiation is emitted. This count is called an *activity count*. The graphic below shows the change in the activity count for a particular isotope over a period of 24 days. Use this graphic to answer questions 11–12.

11. What is the half-life of the isotope?
    A. 40 days
    B. 24 days
    C. 12 days
    D. 6 days

12. Assuming that this quantity of isotope had been decaying at the same rate that is shown in the graph for weeks before the measuring began, what would the activity count have been 12 days before day 0?

Test Tip

Try to figure out the answer to a question before you look at the choices. Then, compare your answer with each answer choice. Choose the answer that most closely matches your own.

Physics

Chapter 11 Motion 362
Chapter 12 Forces 394
Chapter 13 Work and Energy 428
Chapter 14 Heat and Temperature 470
Chapter 15 Waves 502
Chapter 16 Sound and Light 540
Chapter 17 Electricity 582
Chapter 18 Magnetism 616

CHAPTER 11 Motion

Chapter Outline

1 Measuring Motion
Observing Motion
Speed and Velocity
Calculating Speed
Graphing Motion

2 Acceleration
Acceleration and Motion
Calculating Acceleration
Graphing Accelerated Motion

3 Motion and Force
Fundamental Forces
Balanced and Unbalanced Forces
The Force of Friction
Friction and Motion

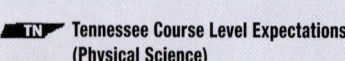

Tennessee Course Level Expectations (Physical Science)

CLE.3202.3.1 Investigate the relationships among speed, position, time, velocity, and acceleration; **CLE.3202.Inq.1** Recognize that science is a progressive endeavor that reevaluates and extends what is already accepted; **CLE.3202.Inq.2** Design and conduct scientific investigations to explore new phenomena, verify previous results, test how well a theory predicts, and compare opposing theories; **CLE.3202.Inq.3** Use appropriate tools and technology to collect precise and accurate data; **CLE.3202.Inq.4** Apply qualitative and quantitative measures to analyze data and draw conclusions that are free of bias; **CLE.3202.Inq.6** Communicate and defend scientific findings.

Why It Matters

This multiple-exposure photograph of a gymnast shows her motion as she moves with respect to the balance beam. We can use our understanding of motion to describe the many activities in our lives.

Inquiry Lab

 20 min

Motion on Motion

Choose a **windup** or **battery-operated toy.** You will also need a **meterstick,** a **stopwatch, paper,** and a **pencil.** Set the toy in motion. Measure the time, distance, direction, and any pattern of the toy's motion. Record your findings. Next, set the moving toy on a **toy truck** or **train.** Then, put that toy truck or train in motion. Measure and record the distance traveled by the toy on the moving truck or train and the corresponding time interval. Repeat this activity several times, and record all of your findings.

Questions to Get You Started

1. What are different ways that you could use to describe the toy's motion?
2. How does your description of the toy's motion change after you place the toy on a moving platform?

READING TOOLBOX

These reading tools can help you learn the material in this chapter. For more information on how to use these and other tools, see **Appendix A.**

Science Terms

Everyday Words Used in Science Many words used in science are familiar words from everyday speech. However, when these words are used in science, their meanings are often different from or are more precise than the everyday meanings. You should pay attention to the definitions of these words so that you use them correctly in scientific contexts.

Your Turn As you read this chapter, complete the table below.

WORD	EVERYDAY MEANING	SCIENTIFIC MEANING
speed	the act of moving fast	the distance an object travels divided by the time interval over which the motion occurs
velocity	speed	
acceleration	an increase in speed	

Describing Space and Time

Words and Phrases Describing the motion of objects involves describing changes in both space and time. Paying attention to language that describes space and time can help you recognize when and what kind of motion is described.

For example, if a bicycle is moving at 15 m/s, the bicycle will move a certain distance in space (15 m) in a given amount of time (1 s).

Your Turn As you read this chapter, make a two-column list like the one below on a separate sheet of paper. Add words or phrases that describe space and time.

SPACE (POSITION, SHAPE, DIRECTIONS)	TIME
in a straight line	one day
north	

FoldNotes

Tri-Fold FoldNotes are a fun way to help you learn and remember ideas that you read. FoldNotes help you organize concepts and see the "big picture." Tri-folds can help you remember the definitions or equations that go with the terms that you learn.

Your Turn Make a tri-fold, following the instructions in **Appendix A.**

1. Label the first column "Term/Quantity," the second column "Definition/Equation," and the third column "Notes."
2. Add new terms or new physical quantities to the first column.
3. Write the definition and the equation in the second column.
4. Write additional notes, such as the units, in the third column.

364 Chapter 11 Motion

SECTION 1
Measuring Motion

Key Ideas
> How is a frame of reference used to describe motion?
> What is the difference between speed and velocity?
> What do you need to know to find the speed of an object?
> How can you study speed by using graphs?

Key Terms
motion
frame of reference
displacement
speed
velocity

Why It Matters
Rescue workers can use the last-known velocity of a lost airplane to determine where to look for survivors.

We are surrounded by moving things. From a car moving in a straight line to a satellite traveling in a circle around Earth, objects move in many ways. In everyday life, motion is so common that it seems very simple. But describing motion scientifically calls for careful use of definitions.

Observing Motion

You may think that the **motion** of an object is easy to detect—just look at the object. But you really must observe the object in relation to other objects that stay in place, called *reference points*. A **frame of reference** is used to describe the motion of an object relative to these reference points. The trees in the background in **Figure 1** can be used as a frame of reference to describe the motion of the snowboarder.

> **When an object changes position with respect to a frame of reference, the object is in motion.** You can describe the direction of an object's motion with a reference direction, such as north, south, east, west, up, or down.

Distance measures the path taken.

In addition to knowing direction, you need to know how far an object moves if you want to correctly describe its motion. To measure distance, you measure the length of the path that the object took. For example, if you start at your home and drift around your neighborhood, changing directions a few times, a string that follows your path would be as long as the distance you traveled.

Tennessee Course Level Expectations (Physical Science)
CLE.3202.3.1; CLE.3202.Inq.1; CLE.3202.Inq.2; CLE.3202.Inq.3

motion–(MOH SHUHN)–an object's change in position relative to a reference point

frame of reference–(FRAYM UHV REF uhr uhns)–a system for specifying the precise location of objects in space and time

Figure 1 In this multiple-exposure photograph, the trees can provide a frame of reference.

Section 1 Measuring Motion **365**

Figure 2 A student runs around the outside of a soccer field. The yellow line shows the path traveled, or distance, that he ran. The black arrow shows the displacement that he traveled.

Displacement is the change of an object's position.

Suppose that a student runs around the outside of a soccer field, as shown in **Figure 2**. The distance traveled is found by measuring the whole path, shown by the yellow line. The line from the starting point directly to the ending point, shown as a black arrow, is called the **displacement**.

Distance measures how far an object moves along a path. Displacement measures how far it is between the starting and ending points. Displacement is often shorter than the distance traveled, unless the motion is all in a straight line.

The direction of a displacement must also be given. The distance between your home and school may be 12 blocks, but that information does not tell whether you are going toward or away from school. Displacement must always indicate the direction, such as 12 blocks *toward school*.

✓ **Reading Check** What is the difference between distance and displacement? (See Appendix E for answers to Reading Checks.)

Figure 3 We encounter a wide range of speeds in our everyday life.

Person walking
1.4 m/s

Wheelchair racer
7.3 m/s

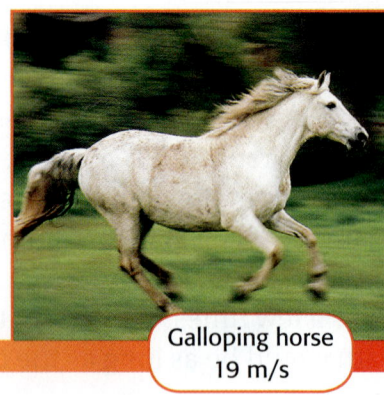

Galloping horse
19 m/s

366 Chapter 11 Motion

Speed and Velocity

You know from experience that some objects move faster than others. **Speed** describes how fast an object moves. The speed for some everyday objects is shown in **Figure 3,** and the distance versus time of the objects is graphed in **Figure 4.**

Sometimes, you may need to know the direction in which an object is moving. In 1997, a 200 kg lion escaped from a zoo in Florida. A helicopter crew was able to guide searchers on the ground by reporting the lion's **velocity,** which is its speed and direction of motion. The lion's velocity may have been reported as 4.5 m/s to the north or 2.0 km/h toward the highway. Without knowing the direction of the lion's motion, searchers could not have predicted its position. ❯ **Speed tells us how fast an object moves, and velocity tells us both the speed and the direction that the object moves.**

Velocity is described relative to a reference point.

The direction of motion can be described in different ways, such as east, west, south, or north of a fixed point. Or it can be an angle from a fixed line. Direction is described as positive or negative along the line of motion. So, if a body is moving in one direction, it has positive velocity. If it is moving in the opposite direction, it has negative velocity. By convention, up and right are usually positive, and left and down are negative.

Combined velocities determine the resultant velocity.

If you are riding in a bus traveling east at 15 m/s, you and all the other passengers are traveling at a velocity of 15 m/s east relative to the street. But suppose that you stand up and walk at 1 m/s toward the back of the bus. Are you still moving at the same velocity as the bus relative to the street? No, but your new velocity can be easily calculated. Your new velocity is equal to 15 m/s east + (–1 m/s east) = 14 m/s east.

> **displacement** (dis PLAYS muhnt) the change in position of an object
>
> **speed** (SPEED) the distance traveled divided by the time interval during which the motion occurred
>
> **velocity** (vuh LAHS uh tee) the speed of an object in a particular direction

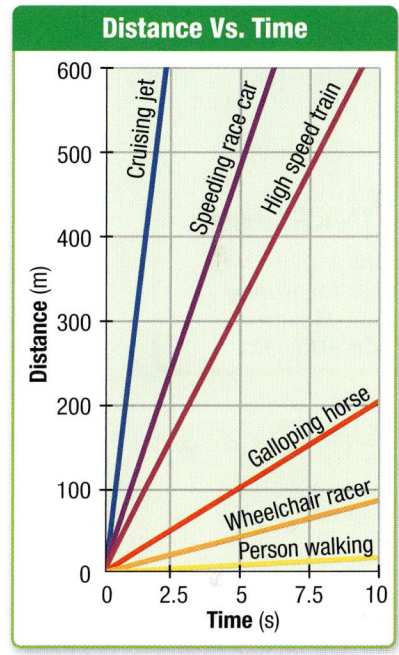

Figure 4 When an object's motion is graphed by plotting distance on the y-axis and time on the x-axis, the slope of the graph is speed.

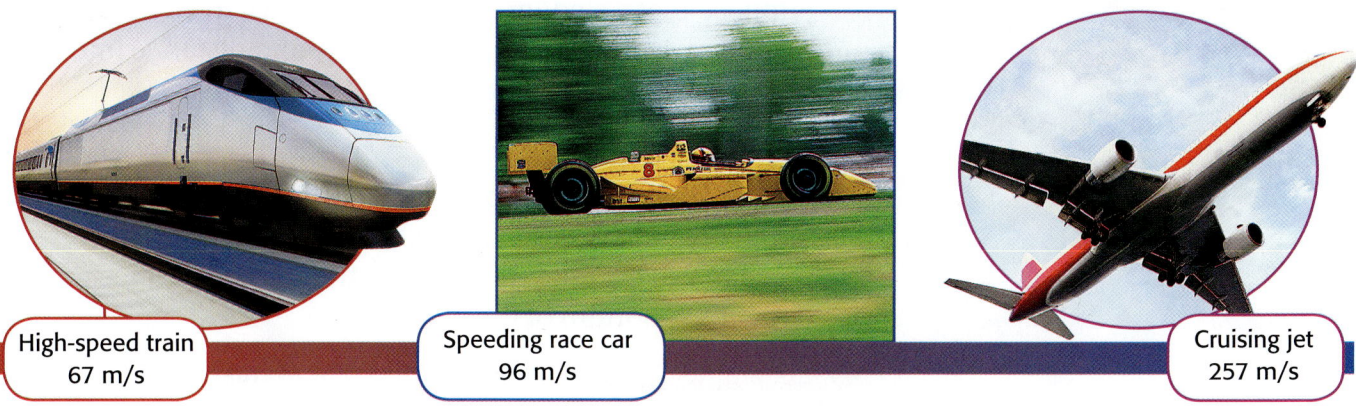

High-speed train
67 m/s

Speeding race car
96 m/s

Cruising jet
257 m/s

Section 1 Measuring Motion **367**

QuickLab

Measuring Speed

⏱ 10 min

Procedure

1. Stand up **25 dominoes** in a straight line. Try to keep equal spacing between the dominoes.
2. Use a **meterstick** to measure the total length of your row of dominoes, and record the length.
3. Tip over the first domino. Use a **stopwatch** to time how long it takes for all of the dominoes to fall.
4. Repeat steps 1–3 several times using smaller and larger distances between the dominoes.

Analysis

1. To calculate the average speed for each trial, divide the total distance by the time that it takes the dominoes to fall.
2. How did the spacing between dominoes affect the average speed? Is this the result that you expected?

www.scilinks.org
Topic: Measuring Motion
Code: HK80927

Figure 5 A sledder's average speed can be determined by timing the rider on a set course.

Calculating Speed

Speed describes distance traveled over a specified time. **▶ To calculate speed, you must measure two quantities: the distance traveled and the time it took to travel that distance.** The SI unit for speed is meters per second (m/s).

When an object covers equal distances in equal amounts of time, it is moving at a *constant speed.* For example, if a train has a constant speed of 67 m/s, the train moves a length of 67 m every second.

Average speed is calculated as distance divided by time.

Most objects do not move at a constant speed but change speed from one instant to another. One way to make it easier to describe the motion of an object is to use *average speed.* Average speed is the distance traveled by an object divided by the time the object takes to travel that distance.

▶ **Average speed**
$$\text{speed} = \frac{\text{distance}}{\text{time}} \qquad v = \frac{d}{t}$$

Suppose that a sledder, such as one shown in **Figure 5**, moves 132 m in 18 s. By putting the time and distance into the formula above, you can calculate her average speed.

$$v = \frac{d}{t} = \frac{132 \text{ m}}{18 \text{ s}} = 7.3 \text{ m/s}$$

The sledder's average speed over the length is 7.3 m/s. But she probably did not travel at this speed for the whole race. Her pace may have been slower near the start of the race and faster near the bottom of the hill.

✓ **Reading Check** How do you calculate average speed?

Instantaneous speed is the speed at a given time.

You could find the sledder's speed at any given point in time by measuring the distance traveled in a shorter time interval. The smaller the time interval, the more accurate the measurement of speed will be. Speed measured in an infinitely small time interval is called *instantaneous speed*. Although it is impossible to measure an infinitely small time interval, some devices measure speed over very small time intervals. Practically speaking, a car's speedometer gives the instantaneous speed of the car.

Academic Vocabulary
interval (IN tuhr vuhl) a space between objects, units, points, or states

Math Skills — Velocity

Metal stakes are sometimes placed in a glacier to help measure the glacier's movement. For several days in 1936, Alaska's Black Rapids glacier surged as swiftly as 89 m per day down the valley. Find the glacier's velocity in m/s. Remember to include direction.

Identify
List the given and the unknown values.

Given:
time, $t = 1$ day
distance, $d = 89$ m down the valley
Unknown:
velocity, $v = ?$ (m/s and direction)

Plan
a. Perform any necessary conversions.
b. Write the equation for speed.

To find the velocity in meters per second, convert the time to seconds.

$t = 1 \text{ day} = 24 \text{ h} \times \frac{60 \text{ min}}{1 \text{ h}} \times \frac{60 \text{ s}}{1 \text{ min}}$

$t = 86{,}400 \text{ s} = 8.64 \times 10^4 \text{ s}$

$speed = \frac{distance}{time} = \frac{d}{t}$

Solve
Insert the known values into the equation, and solve.

$v = \frac{d}{t} = \frac{89 \text{ m}}{8.64 \times 10^4 \text{ s}}$
(For velocity, include direction.)
$v = 1.0 \times 10^{-3}$ m/s down the valley

Practice

1. Find the velocity in meters per second of a swimmer who swims 110 m toward the shore in 72 s.
2. Find the velocity in meters per second of a baseball thrown 38 m from third base to first base in 1.7 s.
3. Calculate the displacement in meters that a cyclist would travel in 5.00 h at an average velocity of 12.0 km/h to the southwest. Remember to include direction.

For more practice, visit **go.hrw.com** and enter the keyword **HK8MP**.

Practice Hint

> When a problem requires you to calculate velocity, you can use the speed equation. Remember to specify direction.

> Problem 3: The speed equation can be rearranged to isolate distance on the left side of the equation. First, multiply both sides by *t*.

$$v = \frac{d}{t}$$
$$v \times t = \frac{d}{t} \times t$$
$$vt = d$$
$$d = vt$$

Be sure to rearrange the equation before you substitute numbers for *v*, *d*, or *t*.

> You can use the distance form of the equation to find displacement. Remember to specify direction when you solve for displacement.

Graphing Motion

You can investigate the relationship between distance and time in many ways. You can use mathematical equations and calculations. ❱ **You can plot a graph showing distance on the vertical axis and time on the horizontal axis.** Whichever method you use, you measure either distance or, if you know the direction, displacement and the time interval during which the distances or displacements take place.

Motion can be studied using a distance vs. time graph.

In a distance vs. time graph, the distance covered by an object is noted at equal intervals of time. As a rule, line graphs are made with the *x*-axis (horizontal axis) representing the independent variable and the *y*-axis (vertical axis) representing the dependent variable. Time is the independent variable because time will pass whether the object moves or not. Distance is the dependent variable because the distance depends upon the amount of time that the object is moving.

> **READING TOOLBOX**
>
> **Everyday Words Used in Science**
> The words *independent* and *dependent* are used to describe variables in equations. What do these words mean in everyday speech? What do they mean in a scientific context?

Distance Vs. Time

horizontal change = 3 s
vertical change = 6 m

Graphing Skills — Calculating Slope

The slope of a straight line equals the vertical change divided by the horizontal change. Determine the slope of the blue line shown in the top distance vs. time graph.

❶ Choose two points that you will use to calculate the slope.

Point 1:
  time, $t = 1$ s and
  distance, $d = 6$ m
Point 2:
  $t = 4$ s and $d = 12$ m

❷ Calculate the vertical change and the horizontal change.

vertical change = 12 m − 6 m = 6 m
horizontal change = 4 s − 1 s = 3 s

❸ Divide the vertical change by the horizontal change.

$slope = \frac{6 \text{ m}}{3 \text{ s}} = 2 \text{ m/s}$

Distance Vs. Time

Practice

1. Visually compare the red line with the blue line in the bottom distance vs. time graph. Which line has a larger slope? Calculate the slope of the red line.

2. Which of the three lines on the bottom graph has the smallest slope? What are the relative speeds of the objects represented by the three lines?

Figure 6 When an object's motion is graphed by plotting distance on the *y*-axis and time on the *x*-axis, the slope of the graph is speed. **What is the average speed of each car?**

The slope of a distance vs. time graph equals speed.

For a car moving at a constant speed, the distance vs. time graph is a straight line. **Figure 6** shows three cars moving at different speeds. The speed of each car can be found by calculating the slope of the line. The slope of any distance vs. time graph gives the speed of the object. Notice that the distance vs. time graph for the fast-moving car is steeper than the graph for the slow-moving car.

A car stopped at a stop sign has a speed of 0 m/s. Its position does not change as time goes by. So, the distance vs. time graph of a resting object is a flat line with a slope of zero. The third graph in **Figure 6** shows a car with changing speed. Between 2 s and 3 s, the car is stopped and the graph is flat.

Section 1 Review

KEY IDEAS

1. **Explain** the relationship between motion and frame of reference.
2. **Identify** the following measurements as speed or velocity.
   a. 88 km/h
   b. 9 m/s to the west
   c. 18 m/s down
   d. 10 m/s
3. **Describe** the measurements necessary to find the average speed of a high school track athlete.
4. **Determine** the unit of a caterpillar's speed if you measure the distance in centimeters (cm) and the time it takes to travel that distance in minutes (min). How would you graph the data?

CRITICAL THINKING

5. **Identifying Relationships** Imagine that you could ride a baseball that is hit hard enough for a home run. If the baseball is your frame of reference, what does the Earth appear to do?

Math Skills

6. How much time does it take for a student running at an average speed of 5.00 m/s to cover a distance of 2.00 km?

SECTION 2 Acceleration

Key Ideas
> What changes when an object accelerates?
> How do you calculate the acceleration of an object moving in a straight line?
> How can a graph be used to find acceleration?

Key Terms
acceleration

Why It Matters
Acceleration is calculated by reconstructionists investigating automobile accidents.

Tennessee Course Level Expectations (Physical Science)
CLE.3202.3.1

Imagine that you are a race-car driver. You push on the accelerator. The car goes forward, moving faster and faster. As you come up to a curve in the track, you remove your foot from the accelerator to make the turn. In both situations, your velocity changes. When you increase speed, your velocity changes. Your velocity also changes if you decrease speed or if your motion changes direction.

Acceleration and Motion

Recall that velocity has both a speed and a direction. Like velocity, *acceleration* has a value and a direction. > **When an object undergoes acceleration, its velocity changes.** Positive acceleration is in the same direction as the motion and increases velocity.

acceleration (ak SEL uhr AY shuhn) the rate at which velocity changes over time; an object accelerates if its speed, direction, or both change

Acceleration can be a change in speed.

Suppose you start moving south on your bicycle and speed up as you go, as shown in **Figure 1.** Every second, your velocity increases by 1 m/s. After 1 s, your velocity is 1 m/s south. After 2 s, your velocity is 2 m/s south. Your velocity after 5 s is 5 m/s south. Your acceleration can be stated as an increase of one meter per second per second (1 m/s/s) or 1 m/s^2 south.

Figure 1 You are accelerating whenever your speed changes. This cyclist's speed increases by 1 m/s every second. **How much does his speed change in 5 s?**

Figure 2 These skaters accelerate when changing direction, even if their speed does not change.

Acceleration can also be a change in direction.

Besides being a change in speed, acceleration can be a change in direction. The skaters in **Figure 2** are accelerating because they are changing direction. Why is changing direction considered to be an acceleration? Acceleration is defined as the rate at which velocity changes with time. Velocity includes both speed and direction, so an object accelerates if its speed, direction, or both change. This idea leads to the strange but correct conclusion that you can constantly accelerate while never speeding up or slowing down.

Uniform circular motion has centripetal acceleration.

If you move at a constant speed in a circle, even though your speed is never changing, your direction is always changing. So, you are always accelerating. The moon is constantly accelerating in its orbit around Earth. A motorcyclist who rides around the inside of a large barrel is constantly accelerating. When you ride a Ferris wheel at an amusement park, you are accelerating. All these examples have one thing in common—change in direction as the cause of acceleration.

Are you surprised to find out that as you stand still on Earth's surface, you are accelerating? You are not changing speed, but you are moving in a circle as Earth revolves. An object moving in a circular motion is always changing its direction. As a result, its velocity is always changing, even if its speed does not change. The acceleration that occurs in circular motion is known as *centripetal acceleration*. Another example of centripetal acceleration is shown in **Figure 3**.

✓ **Reading Check** Describe the motion of a person who is standing still on Earth's surface.

www.scilinks.org
Topic: Acceleration
Code: **HK80007**

Figure 3 The blades of these windmills are constantly changing direction as they travel in a circle, so centripetal acceleration is occurring.

Section 2   Acceleration   **373**

Integrating Mathematics

In the 17th century, both Sir Isaac Newton and Gottfried Leibniz studied acceleration and other rates of change. Independently, each created *calculus*, a branch of mathematics that allows for describing rates of change of a quantity such as velocity.

Calculating Acceleration

To find the acceleration of an object moving in a straight line, you need to measure the object's velocity at different times. ▶ **The average acceleration over a given time interval can be calculated by dividing the change in the object's velocity by the time over which the change occurs.** The change in an object's velocity is symbolized by Δv.

> **Average acceleration (for straight-line motion)**
> $$acceleration = \frac{final\ velocity - initial\ velocity}{time}$$
> $$a = \frac{\Delta v}{t}$$

If the acceleration is small, the velocity is increasing very gradually. If the acceleration is large, the velocity is increasing more rapidly. A person can accelerate at about 2 m/s^2, whereas a sports car can accelerate at 7.2 m/s^2.

In this book, for straight-line motion, a positive acceleration always means that the object's velocity is increasing—the object is speeding up. Negative acceleration means that the object's velocity is decreasing—the object is slowing down.

Acceleration is the rate at which velocity changes.

The person in **Figure 4** is slowing down on a bicycle. He starts at a speed of 5.5 m/s and slows to 1.0 m/s over a time of 3.0 s. The change in speed, Δv, is 1.0 m/s − 5.5 m/s = −4.5 m/s. The change in speed is negative because he is slowing down. The equation above can be used to find average acceleration:

$$a = \frac{1.0\ m/s - 5.5\ m/s}{3.0\ s} = -1.5\ m/s^2$$

In science, acceleration describes any change in velocity, not just "speeding up." When you slow down, your acceleration is negative because it is opposite the direction of motion.

✓ **Reading Check** How can you tell if an object is speeding up or slowing down?

Figure 4 Average acceleration can be calculated when you know the initial speed, final speed, and the time over which the acceleration takes place.

Acceleration is negative when slowing down.

When the driver pushes on the gas pedal in a car, the car speeds up. The acceleration is in the direction of the motion and therefore is positive. When the driver pushes on the brake pedal, the acceleration is opposite the direction of motion. The car slows down, and its acceleration is negative. When the driver turns the steering wheel, the velocity changes because the car is changing direction.

Math Skills Acceleration

A flowerpot falls off a second-story windowsill. The flowerpot starts from rest and hits the sidewalk 1.5 s later with a velocity of 14.7 m/s. Find the average acceleration of the flowerpot.

Identify
List the given and unknown values.

Given:
time, $t = 1.5$ s
initial velocity, $v_i = 0$ m/s
final velocity, $v_f = 14.7$ m/s down
Unknown:
acceleration, $a = ?$ m/s^2 (and direction)

Plan
Write the equation for acceleration.

$$acceleration = \frac{final\ velocity - initial\ velocity}{time}$$
$$a = \frac{v_f - v_i}{t}$$

Solve
Insert the known values into the equation, and solve.

$$a = \frac{v_f - v_i}{t} = \frac{14.7\ m/s - 0\ m/s}{1.5\ s}$$
$$a = \frac{14.7\ m/s}{1.5\ s} = 9.8\ m/s^2\ down$$

Practice

1. Natalie accelerates her skateboard along a straight path from 0 m/s to 4.0 m/s in 2.5 s. Find her average acceleration.
2. A turtle swimming in a straight line toward shore has a speed of 0.50 m/s. After 4.0 s, its speed is 0.80 m/s. What is the turtle's average acceleration?
3. Find the average acceleration of a northbound subway train that slows down from 12 m/s to 9.6 m/s in 0.8 s.
4. Mai's car accelerates at an average rate of 2.6 m/s^2. How long will it take her car to speed up from 24.6 m/s to 26.8 m/s?
5. A cyclist travels at a constant velocity of 4.5 m/s westward and then speeds up with a steady acceleration of 2.3 m/s^2. Calculate the cyclist's speed after accelerating for 5.0 s.

For more practice, visit **go.hrw.com** and enter keyword **HK8MP**.

Practice Hint

> When a problem asks you to calculate acceleration, you can use the acceleration equation.
$$a = \frac{\Delta v}{t}$$
To solve for other variables, rearrange it as follows.

> Problem 4: To isolate t, first multiply both sides by t.
$$a \times t = \frac{\Delta v}{t} \times t$$
$$\Delta v = at$$
Next, divide both sides by a.
$$\frac{\Delta v}{a} = \frac{at}{a}$$
$$t = \frac{\Delta v}{a}$$

> Problem 5: Rearrange the acceleration equation to isolate final velocity.
$$v_f = v_i + at$$

READING TOOLBOX

Describing Space and Time
Words are not the only way to describe space and time. Redraw one of the graphs in this section to show how the graph is used to describe space and time.

Academic Vocabulary
constant (KAHN stuhnt) a quantity whose value does not change

Graphing Accelerated Motion

You have learned that an object's speed can be determined from a distance vs. time graph of its motion. You can also find acceleration by making a speed vs. time graph. Plot speed on the vertical axis and time on the horizontal axis.

A straight line on a speed vs. time graph means that the speed changes by the same amount over each time interval. This is called <u>constant</u> acceleration. ❯ **The slope of a straight line on a speed vs. time graph is equal to the acceleration.**

You can look at a speed vs. time graph and easily see if an object is speeding up or slowing down. A line with a positive slope represents an object that is speeding up. A line with a negative slope represents an object that is slowing down.

Graphing Skills: Graphing Acceleration

A bus traveling on a straight road at 20 m/s uniformly slows to a stop over 20 s. The bus remains stopped for 20 s, then accelerates at a rate of 1.5 m/s² for 10 s, and then continues at a constant speed. Graph speed vs. time for 60 s. What is the bus's final speed?

❶ Determine the *x*-axis and the *y*-axis of your graph.	The *x*-axis will indicate time, *t*, measured in s. The *y*-axis will indicate speed, *v*, measured in m/s.
❷ Starting from the origin, graph each section of the motion.	**A.** The bus begins at $t = 0$ s and $v = 20$ m/s. The next point is $t = 20$ s and $v = 0$ m/s. Connect these points. **B.** Draw a horizontal line from $t = 20$ s to $t = 40$ s at $v = 0$ m/s. **C.** Starting at $t = 40$ s and $v = 0$ m/s, draw a line with a slope of 1.5 m/s². **D.** Draw a horizontal line from $t = 50$ s to $t = 60$ s at $v = 15$ m/s.
❸ Read the graph to find the final speed.	At time, $t = 60$ s, the speed is 15 m/s.

Speed Vs. Time

Practice

1. A car accelerates from a stop at a rate of 2 m/s² for 20 s, then continues at a constant speed for 40 s. Graph the speed vs. time of the car. What is the car's speed at 10 s? What is its final speed?

2. A train traveling at 30 m/s takes 60 s to slow to a complete stop. Assume that the train's acceleration is constant as it moves down the track. Graph the speed vs. time of the train for 80 s. What is the slope of the graph at 30 s?

Figure 5 The rate of velocity change is acceleration, which is positive when speeding up and negative when slowing down.

Acceleration can be seen on a distance vs. time graph.

Imagine that one of the riders in **Figure 5** is slowing uniformly from 10.0 m/s to a complete stop over a period of 5.0 s. A speed vs. time graph of this motion is a straight line with a negative slope. This straight line indicates that the acceleration is constant. You can find the acceleration by calculating the slope of the line.

$$a = \frac{0.0 \text{ m/s} - 10.0 \text{ m/s}}{5.0 \text{ s}} = -2.0 \text{ m/s}^2$$

Thus, the rider's speed decreases by 2.0 m/s each second.

The distance vs. time graph, also shown in **Figure 5,** is not a straight line when the rider's velocity is not constant. This curved line indicates that the object is under acceleration.

www.scilinks.org
Topic: Graphing Speed, Velocity, Acceleration
Code: HK80687

Section 2 Review

KEY IDEAS

1. **Explain** why circular motion includes continuous acceleration even when the speed does not change.
2. **Identify** the straight-line accelerations below as either speeding up or slowing down.
   a. 5.7 m/s^2
   b. −29.8 m/s^2
   c. −2.43 m/s^2
   d. 9.8 m/s^2
3. **Graph** the velocity vs. time from 0 s to 10 s of a car that accelerates from a standstill at a constant rate of 1.5 m/s^2.

CRITICAL THINKING

4. **Interpreting Data** Joshua skates in a straight line at a constant speed for 1 min, then begins going in circles at the same rate of speed, and finally begins to increase speed. When is he accelerating? Explain your answer.

Math Skills

5. What is the final speed of a skater who accelerates at a rate of 2.0 m/s^2 from rest for 3.5 s?
6. Graph the velocity of a car accelerating at a uniform rate from 7.0 m/s to 12.0 m/s in 2.0 s. Calculate the acceleration.

Why It Matters

Accident Reconstruction

Evidence collected from the scene of an accident can be used to learn about the accident. Accident investigators apply physics formulas to find out important information, such as the speed of a vehicle at the time the brakes were applied. A good accident investigator combines information from many sources, including skid marks, vehicle damage, and witness statements. The investigator must come up with a theory that matches all of the evidence.

1 Accident investigators measure the skid distance at the accident or determine it from accident photographs.

Using Skid Marks
Skid marks occur when a vehicle is moving but the tires are not rolling. The marks are created from the heat between the tires and the road that is caused by friction. Skid marks can be used to find the change in speed from the time the brakes were applied.

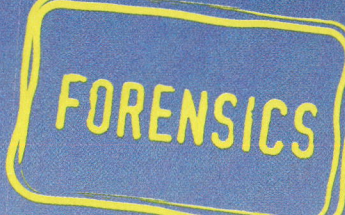

FORENSICS

Accelerometers

Investigators use a device called an *accelerometer* to measure acceleration. The investigator sets up conditions like those during the accident, using a similar vehicle and road surface. The coefficient of friction depends on many factors, such as the weight of the vehicle, the type of tires, and the condition of the road—whether wet, dry, or icy. The accelerometer results are used to estimate the coefficient of friction between the road surface and the tires.

2 Investigators calculate the coefficient of friction between the road surface and the tires. This coefficient depends on the type of tire and road conditions.

Event Data Recorders

Some auto makers are now installing devices called *Event Data Recorders* (EDRs) in cars. EDRs in automobiles are similar to the "black boxes" in airplanes. EDRs measure the change in speed over time during a crash. In other words, they measure acceleration. EDRs are especially useful in situations in which the change in speed is hard to estimate with traditional techniques.

3 The skid distance and the coefficient of friction are then used to calculate the speed of the car at the time of the wreck.

YOUR TURN

UNDERSTANDING CONCEPTS

1. As soon as the brakes are applied, a car begins to slow down. Although the car's speed is decreasing, this is still an example of acceleration. Explain why.

CRITICAL THINKING

2. Why is it important to collect forensic evidence and witness accounts as soon as possible after an accident?

SECTION 3
Motion and Force

Key Ideas
- What do scientists identify as the fundamental forces of nature?
- What happens when there is a net force acting on an object?
- What force always opposes motion?
- Why is friction sometimes necessary?

Key Terms
force
friction
static friction
kinetic friction

Why It Matters
The force of friction is essential to making automobile brakes work properly—and essential to making a car move forward.

Tennessee Course Level Expectations (Physical Science)
CLE.3202.3.1; CLE.3202.Inq.1; CLE.3202.Inq.2; CLE.3202.Inq.3; CLE.3202.Inq.4; CLE.3202.Inq.6

You often hear the word *force* used in everyday conversation: "Our basketball team is an awesome force!" But what exactly is a force? In science, **force** is defined as any action that can change the state of motion of an object.

Fundamental Forces

Scientists identify four *fundamental forces* in nature. ❯ **These forces are the force of gravity, the electromagnetic force, the strong nuclear force, and the weak nuclear force.** The strong and weak nuclear forces act only over a short distance, so you do not experience them directly in everyday life. The force of gravity, as shown in **Figure 1,** is a force that you feel every day. Other everyday forces, such as friction, are a result of the electromagnetic force.

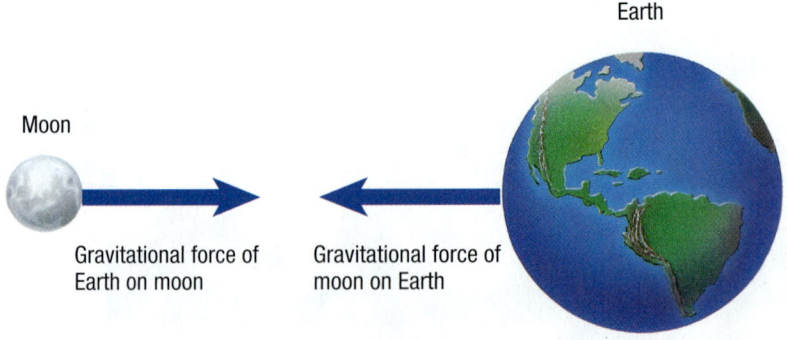

Figure 1 The force of gravity is one of the four fundamental forces in the universe. **On what objects does the force of gravity act?**

Fundamental forces vary in strength.

The fundamental forces vary widely in strength and the distance over which they act. The strong nuclear force holds together the protons and neutrons in the nuclei of atoms and is the strongest of all the forces. However, it is negligible over distances greater than the size of an atomic nucleus. The gravitational and electromagnetic forces act over longer distances. The electromagnetic force is about 1/100 the strength of the strong force. The gravitational force is very much weaker than the electromagnetic force. Consider a proton and an electron in an atom. The electromagnetic force is about 10^{40} times as great as the gravitational force between them!

Forces can act through contact or at a distance.

If you push a cart, the cart moves. When you catch a ball, it stops moving. These pushes and pulls are examples of *contact forces.* There is another class of forces—called *field forces*—that do not require that the objects touch each other. The attraction of gravity or the repulsion between two north poles of a magnet are examples of field forces. Both contact and field forces can cause an object to move or to stop moving.

Academic Vocabulary
fundamental (FUHN duh MENT'l) basic

force (FAWRS) an action exerted on a body in order to change the body's state of rest or motion; force has magnitude and direction

Balanced and Unbalanced Forces

Suppose that you and your friends need to move a heavy sofa, as shown in **Figure 2.** Will you push from opposite sides of the sofa, or will you both push in the same direction? The *net force,* the combination of all of the forces acting on the sofa, determines if the sofa will change its motion. ▶ **Whenever there is a net force acting on an object, the object accelerates in the direction of the net force.** An object will not accelerate if the net force acting on it is zero.

Figure 2 When two forces acting on the same object are unequal, the forces are unbalanced. A change in motion occurs in the direction of the greater force.

Reading Toolbox

Tri-Fold
Create a tri-fold. Write "balanced forces" and "unbalanced forces" in the first column. In the second column, define these terms. In the third column, create a sketch that illustrates each concept.

Balanced forces do not change motion.

When the forces applied to an object produce a net force of zero, the forces are balanced. Balanced forces do not cause an object at rest to start moving. Furthermore, balanced forces do not cause a change in the motion of a moving object.

Many objects have only balanced forces acting on them. For example, a light hanging from the ceiling does not move up or down, because the force due to tension in the cord pulls the light up and balances the force of gravity pulling the light down. A hat resting on your head is also an example of balanced forces.

Unbalanced forces do not cancel completely.

Suppose that two students push against an object on one side and only one student pushes against the object on the other side. If the students are all pushing with the same force, there is an unbalanced force: two students pushing against one student. Because the net force on the object is greater than zero, the object will accelerate in the direction of the greater force.

What happens if forces act in different directions that are not opposite to each other? In this situation, the combination of forces acts like a single force on the object and causes acceleration in a direction that combines the directions of the applied forces. If you push a box to the east and your friend pushes the box to the north, the box will accelerate in a northeasterly direction.

Reading Check What happens when an unbalanced force acts on an object?

The Force of Friction

Imagine a car that is rolling along a flat, evenly paved street. Experience tells you that the car will keep slowing down until it finally stops. This steady change in the car's speed gives you a hint that a force must be acting on the car. The unbalanced force that acts against the car's direction of motion is **friction.** ▶ **The force of friction always opposes the motion.**

Friction occurs because the surface of any object is rough. The rubbing together of two rough surfaces creates heat. The heat from friction causes the match in **Figure 3** to strike. Surfaces that look or feel very smooth are really covered with microscopic hills and valleys. When two surfaces are touching, the hills and valleys of one surface stick to the hills and valleys of the other surface.

Figure 3 Energy provided by friction causes this match to ignite.

Static friction is greater than kinetic friction.

The friction between surfaces that are stationary is called **static friction.** The friction between moving surfaces is called **kinetic friction.** Because of forces between the molecules on the two surfaces, the force required to make a stationary object start moving is usually greater than the force necessary to keep it moving. In other words, static friction is usually greater than kinetic friction.

Not all kinetic friction is the same.

There are different kinds of kinetic friction. The type of friction depends on the motion and the nature of the objects. For example, when objects slide past each other, the friction that occurs is called *sliding friction*. If a rounded object rolls over a flat surface, the friction that occurs is called *rolling friction*. Rolling friction is usually less than sliding friction.

> **friction** (FRIK shuhn) a force that opposes motion between two surfaces that are in contact
>
> **static friction** (STAT ik FRIK shuhn) the force that resists the initiation of sliding motion between two surfaces that are in contact and at rest
>
> **kinetic friction** (ki NET ik FRIK shuhn) the force that opposes the movement of two surfaces that are in contact and are moving over each other

Why It Matters
How Do Brakes Work?

Automobile brakes rely on the force of friction to slow down a moving car and bring it to a stop. Two common types of brakes are typically found in modern cars: *disc brakes* and *drum brakes*. Disc brakes are frequently used to stop the front wheels of a car. To make brakes work properly, the system requires *leverage, hydraulic force,* and *friction.*

❶ *Leverage* is provided by the driver's foot pressing on the brake pedal.

❷ The brake pedal is connected using a *hydraulic* system that multiplies and transfers the force applied by the foot to the rotor and brake pads.

❸ The caliper assembly transfers the hydraulic force to the brake pads. *Friction* between the brake pads and rotor stop the car. The rotor is attached to the car's wheels through the hub/bearing assembly. Because of friction, brake pads wear down and must be replaced periodically.

YOUR TURN

UNDERSTANDING CONCEPTS
1. Why would friction cause brake pads to wear down?

ONLINE RESEARCH
2. Research drum brakes. How do disc brakes and drum brakes differ? How are they alike?

QuickLab

Friction

⏲ 20 min

Procedure

1. Make a holder for **50 marbles** with a **plastic cup** and **string.** Screw a **hook** into a **block of wood.**
2. Place the wood on top of a sheet of **waxed paper** lying on a **table.** Hook the string on the block, and hang the empty cup over the edge.
3. Add marbles to the cup until the block of wood begins to move.
4. Repeat the process using different surfaces, such as **sandpaper, notebook paper,** and the bare table.

Analysis

1. Is the number of marbles needed to start moving the block the same for each type of surface?
2. Relate the number of marbles used in each trial to the roughness of the surface.

SCiLINKS
www.scilinks.org
Topic: Force and Friction
Code: HK80601

Friction and Motion

Without friction, the tires of a car would not be able to push against the ground and move the car forward, the brakes would not be able to stop the car, and you would not even be able to grip the steering wheel to turn it. Without friction, a car is useless. Friction between your pencil and your paper is necessary for the pencil to leave a mark. Without friction, you would slip and fall whenever you tried to walk. ❯ **Friction is necessary for many everyday tasks to work correctly.**

Unwanted friction can be lowered.

It is sometimes desirable to lower unwanted friction. One way to lower friction is to use low-friction materials, such as nonstick coatings on cooking pans, as shown in **Figure 4**.

Another way to reduce friction is to use *lubricants,* substances that are applied to surfaces to lower the friction between them. Some examples of common lubricants are motor oil, wax, and grease. The air that comes out of the tiny holes of an air-hockey table also acts as a lubricant.

Helpful friction can be increased.

Helpful friction is increased by making surfaces rougher. For example, sand scattered on icy roads keeps cars from skidding. Baseball players sometimes wear textured batting gloves to increase the friction between their hands and the bat so that the bat does not slide or fly out of their hands.

Friction is also greater if the force pushing the surfaces together is increased. Your homework will not blow away if you put a heavy rock on top of it. The added mass of the rock increases friction between the paper and the ground.

Figure 4 A nonstick skillet has a coating that lowers the friction between the pan and the food.

Cars could not move without friction.

What causes a car to move? As a car's wheels turn, they push against the road. As a reaction, the road pushes forward on the car. Without friction between the tires and the road, the tires would not be able to push against the road and the car would not move forward.

The force pushing the car forward must be greater than the force of friction that opposes the car's motion, as shown in **Figure 5.** Because of friction, a constant force must be applied to a car just to keep it moving at the same speed. Friction also affects objects that are not moving. When a truck is parked on a hill and its brakes are set, friction opposes the force of gravity down the hill and stops the truck from sliding.

Figure 5 Frictional Forces and Acceleration

When a car moves at constant speed, the force moving the car forward exactly balances the friction.

When a car accelerates, the force moving the car forward is greater than the opposing force of friction.

This truck does not slide because the friction between the wheels and the ground balances the force of gravity.

Balanced forces: constant speed **Unbalanced forces: acceleration** **Balanced forces: no motion**

Section 3 Review

KEY IDEAS

1. **List** the fundamental forces of nature.
2. **Describe** a situation in which unbalanced forces are acting on an object. What is the net force on the object, and how does the net force change the motion of the object?
3. **Identify** the type of friction in each situation described below.
   a. Two students are pushing a box that is at rest.
   b. The box pushed by the students is now sliding.
   c. The students put rollers under the box and push it forward.
4. **Explain** why driving on a road requires friction. How could you increase friction on an icy road?

CRITICAL THINKING

5. **Understanding Relationships** Describe three ways to decrease the force of friction between two surfaces that are moving past each other.
6. **Analyzing Ideas** When you wrap a sandwich in plastic food wrap to protect it, you must first unroll the plastic wrap from the container and then wrap the plastic around the sandwich. In both steps, you encounter friction. In each step, is friction helpful or not? Explain your answer.
7. **Interpreting Data** The force pulling a truck downhill is 2,000 N. What is the amount of static friction acting on the truck if the truck does not move?

Application Lab

⏱ 50 min

Static, Sliding, and Rolling Friction

Current car brakes make use of static friction. As an engineer in the research and development department of a car manufacturing company, you have been asked to find out if a different approach to brakes might work better. To do so, you will investigate the circumstances under which friction is maximized.

What You'll Do

> **Predict** which type of friction force—static, sliding, or rolling—will be greatest and which will be smallest.

> **Measure** the static, sliding, and rolling friction when pulling a textbook across a table.

> **Apply** your results by describing how friction affects objects being pulled across a surface.

What You'll Need

rods, wooden (or metal) (4)
scissors
spring scale
string
textbook

Safety

Procedure

Preparing for Your Experiment

1. Which type of friction do you think is the largest force: static, sliding, or rolling? Which is the smallest?

2. Form a hypothesis by writing a short paragraph that answers the question above. Explain your reasoning.

3. Prepare a data table like the one shown below. **CAUTION:** Secure loose clothing, and remove dangling jewelry. Do not wear open-toed shoes or sandals in the lab.

Sample Data Table: Friction Measurements

	Static friction (N)	Sliding friction (N)	Rolling friction (N)
Trial 1			
Trial 2			
Trial 3			
Average			

DO NOT WRITE IN BOOK

Collecting Data and Testing the Hypothesis

4. Cut a piece of string, and tie it in a loop that fits inside a textbook. Hook the string to the spring scale as shown.

5. To measure the static friction between the book and the table, pull the spring scale very slowly. Gradually increase the force with which you pull on the spring scale until the book starts to slide across the table. Pull very gently. If you pull too hard, the book will start lurching and you will not get accurate results.

6. Practice pulling the book as in step 5 several times until you can pull back smoothly. On a smooth trial, note the largest force that appears on the scale before the book starts to move. Record this result in your data table as static friction in Trial 1.

7. Repeat step 6 two more times, and record the results in your data table as Trials 2 and 3.

386 Chapter 11 Motion

8. After the textbook begins to move, you can determine the sliding friction. Start pulling the book as in step 5. Once the book starts to slide, continue applying just enough force to keep the book sliding at a slow, constant speed. Practice this several times. On a smooth trial, note the force that appears on the scale as the book is sliding at a slow, constant speed. Record this force in your data table as sliding friction in Trial 1.

9. Repeat step 8 two times, and record the results as Trials 2 and 3 in your data table.

10. Place two or three rods under the textbook to act as rollers. Make sure the rods are evenly spaced. Place another rod in front of the book so that the book will roll onto it. Pull the spring scale slowly so that the book rolls across the rods at a slow, constant speed. Practice this several times, repositioning the rods each time. On a smooth trial, note the force that appears on the scale as the book is moving at a slow, constant speed. Record this force in your data table as rolling friction.

11. Repeat step 10 two times, and record the results in your data table.

Analysis

1. **Organizing Data** For each type of friction, add the results of the three trials and divide by 3 to get an average. Record these averages in your data table.

2. **Analyzing Data** Which of the three types of friction was the largest force, on average?

3. **Analyzing Data** Which of the three types of friction was the smallest force, on average?

Communicating Your Results

4. **Drawing Conclusions** Did your answers to Analysis questions 2 and 3 agree with the hypotheses you made before collecting data? If not, explain how your results differed from what you predicted.

5. **Evaluating Methods** In each trial, the force that you measured was actually the force that you were exerting on the spring scale. This force was, in turn, exerted on the book. Why could you assume that this force was equal to the force of friction in each case?

Application

If the car manufacturer that you work for wants to develop an innovative braking system, should it be based on a kind of friction different from that used in existing braking systems? Explain.

Graphing Motion

Science Skills

Technology
Math
Scientific Methods
▶ Graphing

Problem

The graph shown here contains data about a runner. What information is being graphed? What can be determined from the graph about the runner's speed? Is the speed constant during the run? Explain.

Solution

1 Examine the graph. Determine what the *x*-axis and *y*-axis are to find out what is being graphed.

The *x*-axis is time, measured in seconds. The *y*-axis is distance, measured in meters. This is a graph of the runner's distance from some arbitrary starting point as a function of time.

2 Speed is equal to the slope of a distance vs. time graph.

The runner's average speed at various times can be determined from the graph.

3 A horizontal line indicates zero speed and acceleration. A straight line has a constant speed and zero acceleration.

The slope of the graph is different at different times. The runner's speed is not constant but varies from time to time.

Practice

Use the graph above to answer questions 1–5.

1. Does the graph indicate an increase or decrease in distance during different time intervals? Explain.
2. Identify the independent and dependent variables. What is the relationship between the two variables?
3. What is the runner's maximum speed? During what time interval does the runner reach this speed? What is the runner's minimum speed?
4. What is the total distance traveled by the runner? What trend suggests that this is the total distance run even though the graph continues?
5. How is this graph similar to any graph showing distance traveled in a single direction over a given time interval?

Use the table below to make a graph. Use the graph to answer questions 6–8.

Time (s)	Speed of A (m/s)	Speed of B (m/s)	Speed of C (m/s)
0	0.0	0.0	22.5
5	12.5	16.5	22.5
10	25.0	33.0	22.5

6. For each object (A, B, C), does the graph indicate an increase, decrease, or no change in speed?
7. Which object has the greatest acceleration? Which object is not accelerating?
8. Could you graph the same data on a distance vs. time graph? Explain.

388 Chapter 11 Motion

CHAPTER 11 Summary

Key Ideas

Section 1 Measuring Motion

› **Observing Motion** When an object continuously changes position in comparison to a reference point, the object is in motion. (p. 365)

› **Speed and Velocity** Speed tells us how fast an object moves, and velocity tells us both the speed and the direction that the object moves. (p. 367)

› **Calculating Speed** Average speed is calculated as distance divided by time. (p. 368)

› **Graphing Motion** A distance vs. time graph of an object moving at constant speed is a straight line. The slope of the line is the object's speed. (p. 370)

Section 2 Acceleration

› **Acceleration and Motion** Acceleration is a change in an object's velocity. Accelerating means speeding up, slowing down, or changing direction. (p. 372)

› **Calculating Acceleration** The average acceleration can be calculated by dividing the change in the object's velocity by the time over which the change occurs. (p. 374)

› **Graphing Accelerated Motion** The slope of a line on a velocity vs. time graph gives you the value of the acceleration. (p. 376)

Section 3 Motion and Force

› **Fundamental Forces** Scientists describe four fundamental forces in nature: the force of gravity, the electromagnetic force, the strong nuclear force, and the weak nuclear force. (p. 380)

› **Balanced and Unbalanced Forces** If there is a net force acting on an object, the object accelerates in the direction of the net force. (p. 381)

› **The Force of Friction** Friction is a force that opposes motion between the surfaces of objects. (p. 382)

› **Friction and Motion** Friction is necessary for many everyday tasks to work correctly. (p. 384)

Key Terms

motion, p. 365
frame of reference, p. 365
displacement, p. 366
speed, p. 367
velocity, p. 367

acceleration, p. 372

force, p. 380
friction, p. 382
static friction, p. 383
kinetic friction, p. 383

CHAPTER 11 Review

READING TOOLBOX

1. **Everyday Words Used in Science** The word *friction* can be used metaphorically in a nonscientific context. For example, *friction* can mean "conflict," as between two people. Write two sentences, one using the scientific meaning of *friction* and another using the word in a nonscientific way.

USING KEY TERMS

2. State whether 30 m/s westward represents a *speed*, a *velocity*, or both.

3. Why is identifying the *frame of reference* important in describing motion?

4. What is the difference between *distance* and *displacement*?

5. What is *uniform circular motion*?

6. How do *static friction* and *kinetic friction* differ from each other?

UNDERSTANDING KEY IDEAS

7. If you jog for 1 h and travel 10 km, 10 km/h describes your
   a. momentum.
   b. average speed.
   c. displacement.
   d. acceleration.

8. An object's speed is a measure of
   a. how fast the object is moving.
   b. the object's direction.
   c. the object's displacement per unit of time.
   d. All of the above

9. Which of the quantities below represents a velocity?
   a. 25 m/s
   b. 10 km/min
   c. 15 mi/h eastward
   d. 3 mi/h

10. A car travels a distance of 210 mi in exactly 4 h. The driver calculates that he traveled 52.5 mi/h. Which of the following terms most nearly describes his calculation?
    a. average speed
    b. instantaneous speed
    c. instantaneous acceleration
    d. displacement

11. Which of the following is *not* accelerated motion?
    a. a ball being juggled
    b. a woman walking at 2.5 m/s along a straight road
    c. a satellite circling Earth
    d. a braking cyclist

INTERPRETING GRAPHICS Use the graphs below to answer questions 12–14.

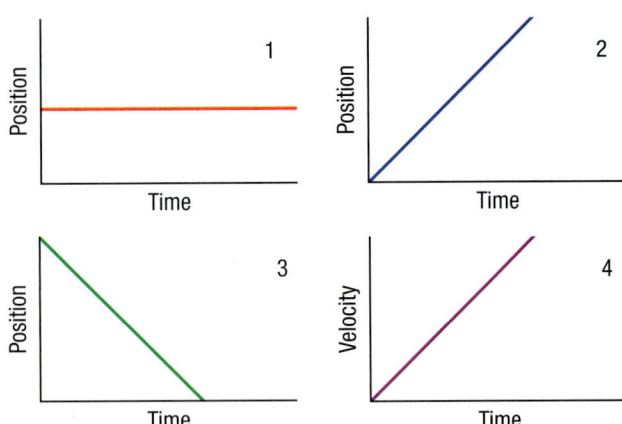

12. Which graph represents an object moving with a constant positive velocity?
    a. 1   c. 3
    b. 2   d. 4

13. Which graph represents an object at rest?
    a. 1   c. 3
    b. 2   d. 4

14. Which graph represents an object moving with constant positive acceleration?
    a. 1   c. 3
    b. 2   d. 4

EXPLAINING KEY IDEAS

15. At the end of a game, a basketball player on the winning team throws the basketball straight up as high as he can throw it. What is the basketball's velocity at the top of its path?

16. A book is sitting still on your desk. Are the forces acting on the book balanced or unbalanced? Explain.

17. Bob straps on his in-line skates and pushes himself down a hill. At the bottom of the hill, he slowly rolls to a stop. When is he accelerating?

CRITICAL THINKING

18. Interpreting Data A baseball is hit straight up at an initial velocity of 30 m/s. If the ball has a negative acceleration of about 10 m/s^2, how long does the ball take to reach the top of its path?

19. Understanding Relationships What can you conclude about the forces acting on an object traveling in uniform circular motion?

20. Interpreting Data When you drive, you will sometimes have to decide in a brief moment whether to stop for a yellow light. Discuss the variables that you must consider in making your decision. Use the concepts of force, acceleration, and velocity in your discussion.

21. Identifying Relationships What are some of the ways that competitive swimmers can decrease the amount of friction or drag between themselves and the water through which they are swimming? How does each method work to decrease friction?

Math Skills

22. Velocity Simpson drives his car with an average velocity of 85 km/h eastward. How long will it take him to drive 560 km on a perfectly straight highway?

23. Acceleration A driver is traveling eastward on a dirt road when she spots a pothole ahead. She slows her car from 14.0 m/s to 5.5 m/s in 6.0 s. What is the car's acceleration?

24. Acceleration How long will it take a cyclist with an acceleration of −2.50 m/s^2 to bring a bicycle with an initial forward velocity of 13.5 m/s to a complete stop?

Graphing Skills

25. The graphs below describe the motion of four different balls—a, b, c, and d. Use the graphs to determine whether each ball is accelerating, sitting still, or moving at a constant velocity.

26. A rock is dropped from a bridge, and the distance it travels and the speed at which it is falling are measured every second until it hits the water. The data are shown in the chart below. Make two graphs of the data: a distance vs. time graph and a velocity vs. time graph. Use your graphs to answer the following questions.
a. What shape is the distance vs. time graph? Explain.
b. What shape is the velocity vs. time graph? Explain.
c. Use the velocity vs. time graph to determine the rock's acceleration.

Time	Distance traveled	Downward speed
0 s	0 m	0 m/s
1 s	5 m	10 m/s
2 s	20 m	20 m/s
3 s	45 m	30 m/s

Standardized Test Prep

Understanding Concepts

Directions (1–3): **For each question, write on a sheet of paper the letter of the correct answer.**

1. A meteorologist describes a tropical storm as traveling northwest at 50 mi/h. Which attribute of the storm's motion has the meteorologist described?
   - **A.** force
   - **B.** acceleration
   - **C.** velocity
   - **D.** displacement

2. Which of the following must be applied to move an object at rest, such as a large rock?
   - **F.** static friction
   - **G.** kinetic friction
   - **H.** balanced forces
   - **I.** unbalanced forces

3. A fish swimming at a constant speed of 0.5 m/s suddenly notices a shark appear behind it. Five seconds later, the fish is swimming in the same direction at a speed of 2.5 m/s. What was the fish's average acceleration?
   - **A.** 0.4 m/s^2
   - **B.** 0.6 m/s^2
   - **C.** 1.7 m/s^2
   - **D.** 2.5 m/s^2

Directions (4–5): **For each question, write a short response.**

4. Bowling lanes are made as smooth as possible in order to minimize kinetic friction. Why is this desirable in a bowling lane?

5. Two amateur entomologists are observing the movement of a beetle traveling in a straight line across a driveway. Every 10 s, they measure the distance that the beetle has traveled. Afterward, they create a graph of the beetle's motion, with distance on the *y*-axis and time on the *x*-axis. What does the slope of their graph represent?

Reading Skills

Directions (6–7): **Read the passage below. Then, answer the questions that follow.**

MOVING BY FRICTION

Friction is usually thought of as interfering with motion, but there are many sorts of movement that depend on friction. When any two surfaces move against each other, friction exerts force in a direction opposite to the direction of push. Runners use the energy in their leg muscles to push backward on the ground with one foot. The ground forces their body forward. If not for the friction between the running shoes and the ground, their feet would slip backward against the ground instead.

The friction between two surfaces before they move is called static friction. After the two surfaces begin moving against each other, the frictional force lessens; the force is then called kinetic friction. Once a runner's foot begins to slip, the frictional force decreases, as does the force exerted on the runner in the opposite direction—toward the finish line! Runners need friction to move forward.

6. When a runner's shoe slips against the ground, what is the effect on the net force affecting the runner?
   - **F.** The net force pushing the runner forward increases.
   - **G.** The net force pushing the runner forward decreases.
   - **H.** The net force pushing the runner toward the ground increases.
   - **I.** The net force pushing the runner toward the ground decreases.

7. A runner decides to get new running shoes because the old ones are slipping too much against the ground. What should the runner look for in a new pair of shoes?

Interpreting Graphics

The graphic below shows four motorcycle racers on the last 800 m of a track. Use this graphic to answer questions 8 and 9.

SPEED AND LOCATION OF FOUR MOTORCYCLES

8. Assuming that each motorcycle continues to travel toward the finish line at the given constant velocity above, which event will occur first?
   - **A.** Cycle A passes Cycle B.
   - **B.** Cycle B passes Cycle C.
   - **C.** Cycle B crosses the finish line.
   - **D.** Cycle D crosses the finish line.

9. From Cycle A's frame of reference, which cycle or cycles are moving toward Cycle A the fastest?
   - **F.** Cycle B appears to be moving the fastest.
   - **G.** Cycle D appears to be moving the fastest.
   - **H.** Cycles B and D appear to be moving at the same speed.
   - **I.** All three cycles appear to be moving at the same speed.

The graph below shows how long it took for two vehicles to stop from a speed of 30 m/s. Use the graph below to answer questions 10 and 11.

SPEED VS. TIME FOR TWO VEHICLES

10. What can we conclude from the graph about the car and the truck?
    - **A.** The truck's final velocity is greater than the car's.
    - **B.** The car's final velocity is greater than the truck's.
    - **C.** The truck's acceleration has greater absolute value than the car's.
    - **D.** The car's acceleration has greater absolute value than the truck's.

11. If the slope of the two lines remained the same, how long would it take each vehicle to coast to a stop from an initial velocity of 100 mph?

Test Tip

When several questions refer to the same graph or table, answer the questions that you are most sure of first.

CHAPTER 12 Forces

Chapter Outline

① Newton's First and Second Laws
Newton's First Law
Newton's Second Law

② Gravity
Weight and Mass
Law of Universal Gravitation
Free Fall
Projectile Motion

③ Newton's Third Law
Action and Reaction Forces
Momentum
Conservation of Momentum

Tennessee Course Level Expectations (Physical Science)

CLE.3202.TE.3 Explain the relationship between the properties of a material and the use of the material in the application of a technology; **CLE.3202.3.2** Investigate and apply Newton's three laws of motion; **CLE.3202.3.3** Examine the Law of Conservation of Momentum in real world situations; **CLE.3202.4.1** Explore the difference between mass and weight; **CLE.3202.4.2** Relate gravitational force to mass; **CLE.3202.Inq.1** Recognize that science is a progressive endeavor that reevaluates and extends what is already accepted; **CLE.3202.Inq.2** Design and conduct scientific investigations to explore new phenomena, verify previous results, test how well a theory predicts, and compare opposing theories; **CLE.3202.Inq.3** Use appropriate tools and technology to collect precise and accurate data; **CLE.3202.Inq.4** Apply qualitative and quantitative measures to analyze data and draw conclusions that are free of bias; **CLE.3202.Inq.6** Communicate and defend scientific findings; **CLE.3202.Math.1** Understand the mathematical principles behind the science of physics; **CLE.3202.Math.2** Utilize appropriate mathematical equations and processes to solve basic physics problems; **CLE.3202.TE.2** Differentiate among elements of the engineering design cycle: design constraints, model building, testing, evaluating, modifying, and retesting.

Why It Matters

Force is an important aspect of activities such as soccer, baseball, and bike riding. Forces produce change in motion. Once this bicycle and rider leave the ground, for example, the only force acting on them is gravity.

Inquiry Lab
10 min

Earth's Attraction

You can investigate Earth's pull on objects by using a **stopwatch**, a **board**, and **two balls** of different masses. Set one end of the board on a stack of books and the other end on the floor. Mark a point on the floor across the room to be the finish line. Time each ball as it rolls down the board to the finish line. Then, several more times, roll both balls down the board at different angles. Adjust the angle by changing the number of books under the end of the board.

Questions to Get You Started

1. Does the heavier ball move faster, move more slowly, or move at the same speed as the lighter one?
2. What factors do you think may have affected the motion of the two balls?

READING TOOLBOX

These reading tools can help you learn the material in this chapter. For more information on how to use these and other tools, see **Appendix A**.

FoldNotes

Key-Term Fold The key-term fold can help you learn the key terms from this chapter.

Your Turn Create a key-term fold, as described in **Appendix A**.

1. Write one key term from the Summary page on the front of each tab.
2. As you read the chapter, write the definition for each term under its tab.
3. Use this FoldNote to study the key terms.

Tabs:
- inertia
- weight
- free fall
- terminal velocity
- projectile motion
- momentum

Cause and Effect

Signal Words Certain words or phrases can serve as signals of cause and effect relationships. Such signals are called *cause and effect markers*.

CAUSE MARKERS	EFFECT MARKERS
cause	therefore
affect	thus
produce	as a result
as a result of	is an effect of
due to	results from
because	consequently

Your Turn Complete the table of cause and effect markers that are in this chapter.

CAUSE	EFFECT	MARKER(S)
Inertia	You appear to slide toward the side of a car	Because

Note Taking

Two-Column Notes Two-column notes can help you learn the Key Ideas from each section.

- The Key Ideas are in the left column.
- In your own words, write detailed notes and examples in the right column.

Your Turn Complete the two-column notes for Section 1, adding another row for each Key Idea.

KEY IDEA #1: What makes an object speed up, slow down, or change directions?	• Objects change their state of motion only when a net force is applied. • When there is no net force, an object does not change its state of motion. • For example, if there were no friction, a bowling ball would keep rolling forever. It would not stop.

396 Chapter 12 Forces

SECTION 1
Newton's First and Second Laws

Key Ideas
› What makes an object speed up, slow down, or change directions?
› What determines how much an object speeds up or slows down?

Key Terms
inertia

Why It Matters
Newton's second law of motion helps explain how air bags have saved lives.

Every change in motion that you observe or feel is caused by a force. Sir Isaac Newton (1642–1727), a British scientist, described the relationship between motion and force in three laws that we now call *Newton's laws of motion*. Newton's laws apply to a wide range of motion—a caterpillar crawling on a leaf, a person riding a bicycle, or a rocket moving in space.

Tennessee Course Level Expectations (Physical Science)
CLE.3202.3.2; CLE.3202.Inq.1;
CLE.3202.Inq.2; CLE.3202.Inq.3;
CLE.3202.Math.1; CLE.3202.Math.2;
CLE.3202.TE.3

Newton's First Law

If you start your book sliding across a rough surface, such as carpet, the book soon comes to rest. On a smooth surface, such as ice, the book will slide much farther. Because there is less frictional force between the ice and the book, the smaller force must act over a longer time before the book stops. Without friction, the book would keep sliding. This is an example of Newton's first law, which is stated as follows.

| Newton's first law | An object at rest remains at rest and an object in motion maintains its velocity unless it experiences a net force. |

› **Objects change their state of motion only when a net force is applied.** A book sliding on carpet comes to rest because friction acts on the book. If no net force acted on the book, the book would continue moving with the same velocity.

Objects tend to maintain their state of motion.

If you have ever bowled, you know that a bowling ball, such as the one shown in **Figure 1,** will continue moving down the alley until it comes in contact with the bowling pins. In fact, if the alley were infinitely long and frictionless, the ball would keep rolling on and on! In the real world, friction (an outside force) will eventually cause the ball to stop.

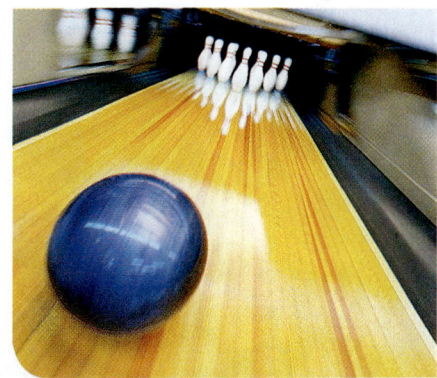

Figure 1 A bowling ball in motion tends to remain in motion unless acted on by an outside force. **Why is it difficult to start a bowling ball moving?**

Academic Vocabulary
infinite (IN fuh nit) without limits

Section 1 Newton's First and Second Laws 397

QuickLab

Newton's First Law

 10 min

Procedure

1. Set an **index card** over a **glass**. Put a **coin** on top of the card.
2. With your thumb and forefinger, quickly flick the card sideways off the glass. Observe what happens to the coin. Does the coin move with the index card?
3. Repeat step 1. This time, slowly pull the card sideways, and observe what happens to the coin.

Analysis

1. Use Newton's first law of motion to explain your results.

---

inertia (in UHR shuh) the tendency of an object to resist a change in motion unless an outside force acts on the object

Inertia is related to an object's mass.

Inertia is the tendency of an object at rest to remain at rest or, if moving, to continue moving at a constant velocity. All objects resist changes in motion, so all objects have inertia. An object that has a small mass, such as a baseball, can be accelerated by a small force. But accelerating an object whose mass is larger, such as a car, requires a much larger force. Thus, mass is a measure of inertia. An object whose mass is small has less inertia than an object whose mass is large does.

Newton's first law of motion is often summed up as follows: Matter resists any change in motion. Because this property of matter is called *inertia,* Newton's first law is sometimes called the *law of inertia.*

Reading Check How is inertia related to mass? (See Appendix E for answers to Reading Checks.)

Seat belts and car seats provide protection.

Because of inertia, you appear to slide toward the side of a car when the driver makes a sharp turn. You continue in the same direction while the car makes the turn. Inertia is also the reason that a plane, car, or bicycle cannot stop instantaneously. There is always a time lag between the moment the brakes are applied and the moment the car comes to rest.

When the car that you are riding in comes to a stop, your seat belt and the friction between you and the seat stop your forward motion. They provide the unbalanced backward force that is needed to bring you to a stop as the car stops.

Babies are placed in backward-facing car seats, as shown in **Figure 2.** When this kind of car seat is used, the force that is needed to bring the baby to a stop is safely spread out over the baby's whole body.

Figure 2 This backward-facing car seat stops the forward motion of the baby and distributes the force of the stop over the baby's whole body.

Why It Matters
How Do Air Bags Work?

REAL WORLD

Air bags are standard equipment in every new automobile sold in the United States. In a collision, air bags explode from a compartment to cushion the passenger's head. By decreasing the acceleration of a passenger's head and body during a crash, an air bag reduces the force acting on the passenger and makes injuries less likely. Air bags are credited with saving more than 5,000 lives between 1986 and 2000.

Labels (left diagram): Steering wheel, Air bag, Inflator, Crash sensor

Labels (right diagram): Nitrogen gas, Air bag, Steering wheel, Inflator, Crash sensor

❶ When a car comes to an abrupt stop, sensors in the car detect the sudden change in speed and trigger a chemical reaction inside the air bags.

❷ This reaction very quickly produces nitrogen gas, which causes the bags to inflate and explode out of their storage compartments in a fraction of a second.

❸ The inflated air bags cushion the head and upper body of the driver and the passenger in the front seat, who keep moving forward at the time of impact because of their inertia.

SCLINKS.
www.scilinks.org
Topic: Newton's First Law
Code: HK81027

YOUR TURN

UNDERSTANDING CONCEPTS
1. Are air bags useful if a car is struck from behind by another vehicle?

CRITICAL THINKING
2. If a car has air bags, do the passengers need to wear seat belts? Explain why or why not.

Section 1 Newton's First and Second Laws

READING TOOLBOX

Two-Column Notes
Create two-column notes for Newton's second law. Put the Key Idea in the left column, and add details and examples in your own words in the right column.

Newton's Second Law

Newton's first law describes what happens when no net force is acting on an object: the object either remains at rest or keeps moving at a constant velocity. What happens when the net force is not zero?

When the net force is not zero, Newton's second law applies. Newton's second law describes the effect of an unbalanced force on the motion of an object. This law can be stated as follows.

| **Newton's second law** | The unbalanced force acting on an object equals the object's mass times its acceleration. |

❯ **Net force is equal to mass times acceleration. The unbalanced force on an object determines how much an object speeds up or slows down.** Newton's second law can also be written as a mathematical equation.

| ▷ **Newton's second law** | net force = mass × acceleration
$F = ma$ |

For equal forces, a larger mass accelerates less.

Consider the difference between the two photos shown in **Figure 3.** The students on the left are pushing a sled with nobody on it. In contrast, the students on the right are pushing a sled with three people on it. If the students push with the same force in each case, the first sled will have a greater acceleration because its mass is smaller than the mass of the second sled. This is an example of Newton's second law.

Figure 3 Because the left sled has a smaller mass than the right sled does, the same force gives the left sled a greater acceleration. **How would the acceleration of the right sled change if the force were larger?**

400   Chapter 12   Forces

Force is measured in newtons.

Newton's second law can be used to derive the SI unit of force, the newton (N). One newton is the force that gives a mass of one kilogram an acceleration of one meter per second squared:

$$1 \text{ N} = 1 \text{ kg} \times 1 \text{ m/s}^2$$

The pound (lb) is sometimes used as a unit of force. One newton is equal to 0.225 lb. Conversely, 1 lb equals 4.45 N.

✓ **Reading Check** Name two units of force.

Math Skills — Newton's Second Law

Zoo keepers lift a stretcher that holds a sedated lion. The total mass of the lion and stretcher is 175 kg, and the upward acceleration of the lion and stretcher is 0.657 m/s². What force is needed to produce this acceleration of the lion and the stretcher?

Identify
List the given and unknown values.

Given:
mass, $m = 175$ kg
acceleration, $a = 0.657$ m/s²
Unknown:
force, $F = ?$ N

Plan
Write the equation for Newton's second law.

net force = mass × acceleration
$F = ma$

Solve
Insert the known values into the equation, and solve.

$F = 175 \text{ kg} \times 0.657 \text{ m/s}^2$
$F = 115 \text{ kg} \times \text{m/s}^2 = 115$ N

Practice

1. What net force is needed to accelerate a 1.6×10^3 kg automobile forward at 2.0 m/s²?
2. A baseball accelerates downward at 9.8 m/s². If the gravitational force is the only force acting on the baseball and is 1.4 N, what is the baseball's mass?
3. A sailboat and its crew have a combined mass of 655 kg. If a net force of 895 N is pushing the sailboat forward, what is the sailboat's acceleration?
4. The net forward force on the propeller of a 3.2 kg model airplane is 7.0 N. What is the acceleration of the airplane?

For more practice, visit **go.hrw.com** and enter keyword **HK8MP**.

Practice Hint

▶ When a problem requires you to calculate the unbalanced force on an object, you can use Newton's second law ($F = ma$).

▶ Problem 2: The equation for Newton's second law can be rearranged to isolate mass on the left side as follows.

$$F = ma$$

Divide both sides by a.

$$\frac{F}{a} = \frac{ma}{a}$$
$$m = \frac{F}{a}$$

▶ Problem 3: To isolate acceleration on the left, you need to rearrange the equation. Be sure to rearrange the equation before substituting numeric values for F and a.

Figure 4 For a given mass, a larger force causes a greater acceleration.

Acceleration depends on force and mass.

So far, we have talked about Newton's second law in terms of force. The second law can also be given in terms of acceleration:

| Newton's second law | The acceleration of an object is directly proportional to the net force on the object and inversely proportional to the object's mass. |

The mathematical version of this form of the law is as follows.

| ▶ Newton's second law | $acceleration = \frac{net\ force}{mass}$
 $a = \frac{F}{m}$ |

For example, the mass of the car shown in **Figure 4** is the same in both photos. When the masses are the same, a greater force causes a greater acceleration.

Section 1 Review

KEY IDEAS

1. **State** Newton's first law of motion in your own words. Give an example that illustrates the law.
2. **List** two examples of Newton's second law of motion.

CRITICAL THINKING

3. **Applying Ideas** Explain how the law of inertia relates to seat belt safety.
4. **Drawing Conclusions** Determine whether each example below is a case of Newton's first law or Newton's second law.
   a. a skydiver accelerating toward the ground
   b. a skydiver falling with constant velocity
   c. a skydiver on the ground at rest
5. **Making Predictions** Predict what will happen in the following situations. (Hint: Use Newton's laws.)
   a. A car traveling on an icy road comes to a sharp bend.
   b. A car traveling on an icy road has to stop quickly.

Math Skills

6. What is the acceleration of a boy on a skateboard if the net force on the boy is 15 N? The total mass of the boy and the skateboard is 58 kg.
7. What is the mass of an object if a force of 34 N produces an acceleration of 4.0 m/s^2?

SECTION 2
Gravity

Key Ideas
› How are weight and mass related?
› Why do objects fall to the ground when dropped?
› What is the relationship between free-fall acceleration and mass?
› Why does a projectile follow a curved path?

Key Terms
weight
free fall
terminal velocity
projectile motion

Why It Matters
Even though we can't see black holes, we know where they might be by measuring how they attract mass nearby.

Have you ever seen a movie about the Apollo astronauts walking on the moon? When they tried to walk on the lunar surface, they bounced all over the place! Why does the astronaut wearing a massive spacesuit in **Figure 1** bounce around so easily on the moon? The answer is that gravity is not as strong on the moon as it is on Earth.

> **Tennessee Course Level Expectations (Physical Science)**
> CLE.3202.4.1; CLE.3202.4.2;
> CLE.3202.Math.1; CLE.3202.Math.2

Weight and Mass

The force on an object due to gravity is called **weight.** On Earth, your weight is simply the amount of gravitational force exerted on you by Earth. The *free-fall acceleration* near a massive object is a constant acceleration that all masses near that object experience. Near Earth's surface, the free-fall acceleration, *g*, is about 9.8 m/s². You can use $F = ma$ (Newton's second law) to calculate a body's weight. › **Thus, weight is equal to mass times free-fall acceleration.** Mathematically, this relationship is as follows:

weight (WAYT) a measure of the gravitational force exerted on an object

Figure 1 Because gravity on the moon is less than gravity on Earth, the Apollo astronauts bounced as they walked on the moon's surface.

› **Weight** weight = mass × free-fall acceleration
$w = mg$

Weight is measured in newtons.

Because weight is a force, the SI unit of weight is the newton (N). A small apple weighs about 1 N on Earth. A typical textbook, which has a mass of about 2,250 g, has a weight of 2.25 kg × 9.8 m/s² = 22 N on Earth.

403

Integrating Space Science

Planets in our solar system have different masses and different diameters. Therefore, each planet has its own unique value for g. Find the weight of a 58 kg person on the following planets:

 Earth, where $g = 9.8$ m/s^2

 Venus, where $g = 8.9$ m/s^2

 Mars, where $g = 3.7$ m/s^2

 Neptune, where $g = 11.0$ m/s^2

Weight is different from mass.

Mass and weight are easy to confuse. Although mass and weight are directly proportional to one another, they are not the same. Mass is a measure of the amount of matter in an object. Weight is the gravitational force that an object experiences because of its mass.

The weight of an object depends on the gravitational force at the location, so moving an object may change its weight. For example, a 66 kg astronaut weighs 66 kg × 9.8 m/s^2 = 650 N (about 150 lb) on Earth. On the moon's surface, where g is only 1.6 m/s^2, the astronaut would weigh 66 kg × 1.6 m/s^2, which equals only 110 N (about 24 lb). The astronaut's mass remains the same everywhere, but his or her weight changes as the gravitational force acting on the astronaut changes in each place.

Reading Check What is the difference between weight and mass?

Weight influences shape.

Gravitational force affects the shapes of living things. On land, large animals need strong skeletons to support their mass against the force of gravity. Tall trees need rigid trunks to support their mass. **Figure 2** shows the difference between the legs of a very heavy land animal and those of a much smaller bird. The more massive elephant has a much larger skeleton to support it larger weight. In contrast, the bird has a much smaller mass and can support its weight on long, thin legs.

Figure 2 Elephants and flamingos have quite different legs because one animal weighs much more than the other. **How has their weight affected the shape of the animals' legs?**

Figure 3 The force of gravity acts between all objects in the universe. For example, the moon is affected by the gravity of both Earth and the sun. (The force arrows shown here are not drawn to scale.)

Law of Universal Gravitation

For thousands of years, two of the most puzzling questions were "Why do objects fall toward Earth?" and "What keeps the planets in motion in the sky?" Newton understood that these two questions have the same answer.

› All objects in the universe attract each other through the force of gravity. The same force that causes objects to fall to Earth controls the motion of planets in the sky.

Newton stated his observations on gravity in a law known as the *law of universal gravitation*, given by the following equation.

> **Universal gravitation equation**
> $$F = G \frac{m_1 m_2}{d^2}$$

This equation says that gravitational force increases as one or both masses increase. It also says that gravitational force decreases as the distance between two masses increases. The symbol G in the equation is a constant.

All matter is affected by gravity.

Whether two objects are very large or very small, there is a gravitational force between them. When one object is very massive, as Earth is, the force is easy to detect. The force exerted by something that has a small mass, such as a paper clip, however, is not noticeable. Yet no matter how small or how large an object is, it exerts this force on every other object, as shown in the Earth-moon-sun system in **Figure 3.** The force of gravity between two masses is easier to understand if you consider it in two parts: (1) the size of the masses and (2) the distance between the masses.

Integrating Biology

Blood Pressure Gravity plays a role in your body. Blood pressure, for example, is affected by gravity. Therefore, when you are standing, your blood pressure will be greater in the lower part of your body than in the upper part. Doctors and nurses take your blood pressure on your arm at the level of your heart to see what your blood pressure is likely to be at your heart.

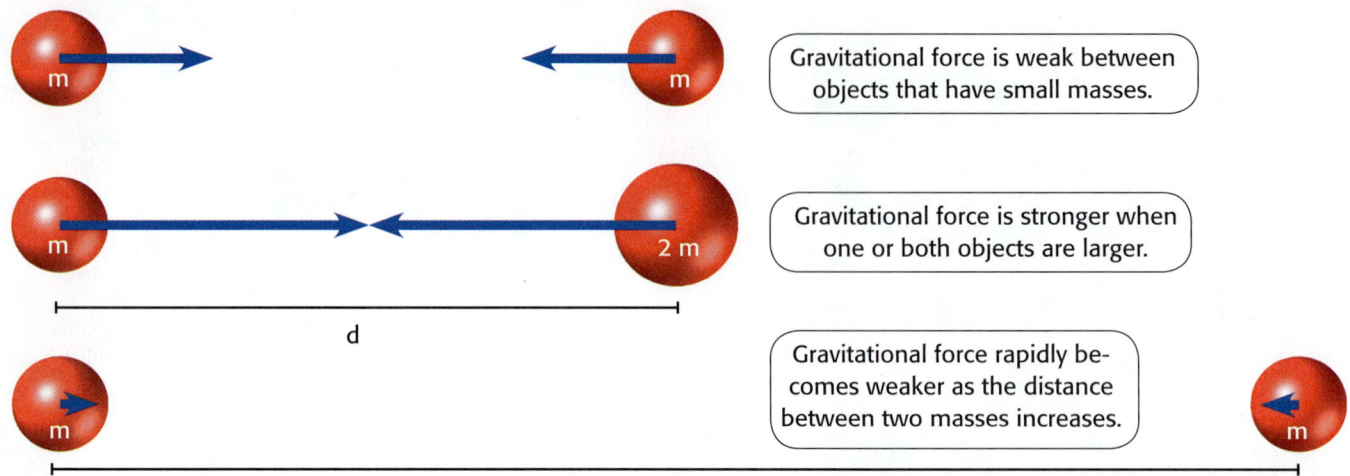

Figure 4 Arrows indicate the gravitational force between objects. The length of an arrow indicates the strength of the force.

READING TOOLBOX

Signal Words Locate the signal words on this page that indicate a cause and effect relationship. Use a table with 3 columns to record causes, effects, and their markers.

Gravitational force increases as mass increases.

Gravity is the reason that an apple falls from a tree. When an apple's stem breaks, the apple falls down because the gravitational force between Earth and the apple is much greater than the gravitational force between the apple and the tree. The relationship between mass and gravitational force is shown in **Figure 4.**

Imagine an elephant and a cat. Because the elephant has a larger mass than the cat does, the gravitational force between the elephant and Earth is greater than the gravitational force between the cat and Earth. Thus, picking up a cat is much easier than picking up an elephant! Gravitational force also exists between the cat and the elephant, but it is very weak because the cat's mass and the elephant's mass are so much smaller than Earth's mass.

Reading Check How does mass affect gravitational force?

Gravitational force decreases as distance increases.

Gravitational force depends on the distance between two objects. When calculating the gravitational force between two large objects, use the distance between the objects' centers. As **Figure 4** shows, if the distance between the two balls is doubled, the gravitational force between them decreases to one-fourth its original value. If the distance is tripled, the gravitational force decreases to one-ninth its original value.

Gravitational force is weaker than other types of forces because the gravitational constant, G, is a very small number. When the masses are very large, however, the gravitational force will be strong enough to hold the planets, stars, and galaxies together.

Free Fall

When Earth's gravity is the only force acting on an object, the object is said to be in **free fall.** Free-fall acceleration is directed toward the center of Earth. ❯ **In the absence of air resistance, all objects falling near Earth's surface accelerate at the same rate regardless of their mass.**

Why do all objects have the same free-fall acceleration? Newton's second law states that acceleration depends on both force and mass. A heavy object has a greater gravitational force than a light object does. However, it is harder to accelerate a heavy object than a light object because the heavy object has more mass.

Free-fall acceleration is constant because of the law of universal gravitation.

Let's look again at the universal gravitation equation. The constant G does not change at any location. Near the surface of Earth, two other values are nearly constant. The distance, d, is about equal to the radius of Earth at or near the surface of Earth. The first mass, m_1, is the mass of Earth. Using these values, we can calculate the free-fall acceleration of an object.

Near the surface of Earth, the only variable in the gravity equation is m_2, the mass of the object near Earth. Thus, we can calculate the weight of an object by using Newton's gravitation equation.

Air resistance can balance weight.

Both air resistance and gravity act on objects moving through Earth's atmosphere. A falling object stops accelerating when the force of air resistance becomes equal to the gravitational force on the object (the weight of the object), as **Figure 5** shows. The reason is that the air resistance acts in the opposite direction to the weight. When air resistance and weight are equal, the object stops accelerating and reaches its maximum velocity, which is called **terminal velocity.**

When sky divers start a jump, their parachutes are closed and they are accelerated toward Earth by the force of gravity. As their velocity increases, the force that they experience increases because of air resistance. When air resistance and the force of gravity are equal, sky divers reach a terminal velocity of about 320 km/h (200 mi/h). But when they open their parachutes, the increased air resistance slows them down. Eventually, they reach a new terminal velocity of several kilometers per hour, which allows them to land safely.

free fall (FREE FAWL) the motion of a body when only the force of gravity is acting on the body

terminal velocity (TUHR muh nuhl vuh LAHS uh tee) the constant velocity of a falling object when the force of air resistance is equal in magnitude and opposite in direction to the force of gravity

Figure 5 When a sky diver reaches terminal velocity, the force of gravity is balanced by air resistance.

Figure 6 In the orbiting space shuttle, which is in free fall, astronauts experience apparent weightlessness.

Astronauts in orbit are in free fall.

Why do astronauts appear to float inside a space shuttle? Are they "weightless" in space? You may have heard that objects are weightless in space, but this statement is not true. Very far from any galaxies or other massive objects, gravitational force is very weak. But one cannot be truly weightless anywhere in the universe.

Astronauts in orbit are actually quite near Earth and are certainly not weightless. However, astronauts in orbit experience *apparent weightlessness* because they are in free fall. The astronauts and the vehicle in which they are traveling are falling toward Earth with the same acceleration.

Reading Check Why do astronauts in orbit seem weightless?

Projectile Motion

The orbit of the space shuttle around Earth is an example of *projectile motion*. **Projectile motion** is the curved path followed by an object that is thrown, launched, or otherwise projected near the surface of Earth. The motions of leaping frogs, thrown balls, and arrows shot from a bow are examples of projectile motion. ❯ **Projectile motion has two components—horizontal and vertical. When the two motions are combined, they form a curved path.**

The two components of projectile motion are independent; that is, they do not affect each other. In other words, the downward acceleration due to gravity does not change a projectile's horizontal motion, and the horizontal motion does not affect the downward motion.

Figure 7 Two motions combine to form projectile motion.

go.hrw.com
interact online
Keyword: HK8FORF7

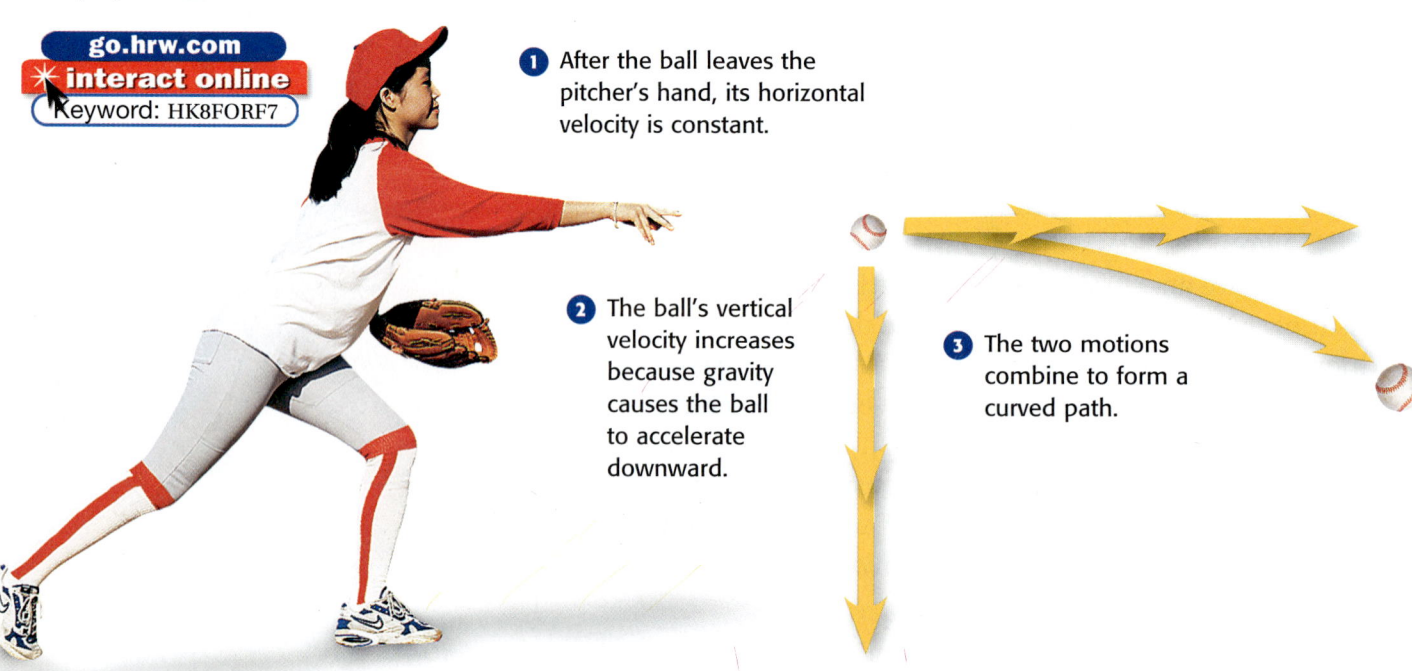

① After the ball leaves the pitcher's hand, its horizontal velocity is constant.

② The ball's vertical velocity increases because gravity causes the ball to accelerate downward.

③ The two motions combine to form a curved path.

Projectile motion has a horizontal component.

As **Figure 7** shows, when you throw a ball, your hand and arm exert a force on the ball that makes the ball move forward. This force gives the ball its horizontal motion. Horizontal motion is motion that is perpendicular, or at a 90° angle, to Earth's gravitational force.

After you have thrown a ball, no horizontal forces are acting on the ball (if air resistance is ignored). So, the horizontal component of velocity of the ball is constant after the ball leaves your hand. Ignoring air resistance, when it is small, allows one to simplify projectile motion.

Projectile motion also has a vertical component.

The movement of a ball is affected not only by horizontal motion but also by vertical motion. If not affected by gravitational acceleration, the ball would continue moving in a straight line and never fall. When you throw a ball, gravity pulls it downward, which gives the ball vertical motion.

In the absence of air resistance, gravity on Earth pulls objects that are in projectile motion downward with an acceleration of 9.8 m/s^2, just as it pulls down all falling objects. **Figure 8** shows that the downward accelerations of a thrown object and a falling object are identical.

Because objects in projectile motion accelerate downward, you should aim above a target if you want to hit the target with a thrown or propelled object. For example, if you aim an arrow directly at a bull's-eye, the arrow will strike below the center of the target rather than the middle.

Academic Vocabulary

component (kuhm POH nuhnt) a part of something

projectile motion (proh JEK tuhl MOH shuhn) the curved path that an object follows when thrown, launched, or otherwise projected near the surface of Earth

The yellow ball was given a horizontal push off the ledge. It follows a projectile-motion path.

The red ball was dropped without a horizontal push.

Figure 8 The red ball and the yellow ball have the same downward acceleration. The horizontal motion of the yellow ball does not affect the vertical motion of the ball.

Orbiting is projectile motion.

An object is said to be orbiting when it is traveling in a circular or nearly circular path around another object. When a spaceship orbits Earth, it is moving forward but it is also in free fall toward Earth. **Figure 9** shows how these two motions combine to cause orbiting. Because of free fall, the moon stays in orbit around Earth, and the planets stay in orbit around the sun.

Figure 9 Forward motion and free-fall motion combine to form an orbit around Earth or another massive body.

❶ The shuttle moves forward at a constant speed. Its path would be straight if Earth did not exert a gravitational pull.

❷ The shuttle is in free fall because gravity pulls it toward Earth. Its path would be straight down if it were not traveling forward.

❸ When the forward motion combines with free fall, the shuttle follows the curve of Earth's surface. Following this curve is known as *orbiting*.

Section 2 Review

KEY IDEAS

1. **Explain** why your weight would be less on the moon than on Earth even though your mass would not change.
2. **State** the law of universal gravitation, and use examples to explain how changes in mass and changes in distance affect gravitational force.
3. **Explain** why free-fall acceleration near Earth's surface is constant.
4. **Name** the two components that make up orbital motion, and explain why objects stay in orbit.

CRITICAL THINKING

5. **Making Inferences** Explain why the gravitational acceleration of any object near Earth is the same no matter what the mass of the object is.

Math Skills

6. The force between a planet and a spacecraft is 1 million newtons. If the spacecraft moves to half of its original distance from the center of the planet, what will the force be?

Why It Matters

Black Holes

A black hole is an object in space that has a huge amount of mass packed into a relatively small volume. For example, a black hole 10 times as massive as the sun would have a radius of only 30 km.

Because of its great mass, a black hole has a very strong gravitational force. In fact, this force is so powerful that it crushes any matter that falls into the black hole to the point that the matter has almost no volume. Objects that enter a black hole can never get out. Not even light can escape from a black hole.

How Black Holes Form

Scientists think that black holes form from dying stars. The death of a star is a massive explosion called a *supernova*. The remaining mass of the star contracts under its own gravity into a dense core.

WEIRD SCIENCE

Sagittarius A* is a supermassive black hole at the center of our galaxy. Scientists suspect that there is a black hole at the center of every galaxy in the universe.

This artist's conception shows a disk of material orbiting a black hole. Such disks provide indirect evidence of black holes within our own galaxy.

SCILINKS
www.scilinks.org
Topic: Black Holes
Code: HK80174

YOUR TURN

UNDERSTANDING CONCEPTS
1. How does mass relate to the powerful gravitational force of a black hole? (Hint: Think of Newton's law of gravitation.)

CRITICAL THINKING
2. How might scientists detect and locate black holes?

SECTION 3
Newton's Third Law

Key Ideas
› What happens when an object exerts a force on another object?
› How do you calculate the momentum of an object?
› What is the total momentum after objects collide?

Key Terms
momentum

Why It Matters
Newton's third law explains how rockets lift off the ground and maintain acceleration in space.

Tennessee Course Level Expectations (Physical Science)
CLE.3202.3.2; CLE.3202.3.3;
CLE.3202.4.1; CLE.3202.4.2;
CLE.3202.Inq.1; CLE.3202.Inq.2;
CLE.3202.Inq.3; CLE.3202.Inq.4;
CLE.3202.Inq.6; CLE.3202.Math.1;
CLE.3202.Math.2; CLE.3202.TE.2

When you kick a soccer ball, as shown in **Figure 1,** you notice the effect of the force exerted by your foot on the ball. The ball experiences a change in motion. Is the force that moves the ball the only force present? Do you feel a force acting on your foot?

Action and Reaction Forces

The moment that you kick the ball, the ball exerts an equal and opposite force on your foot. The force exerted on the ball by your foot is called the *action force,* and the force exerted on your foot by the ball is called the *reaction force.* This pair of forces gives an example of Newton's third law of motion, also called the *law of action and reaction.*

| **Newton's third law** | For every action force, there is an equal and opposite reaction force. |

› **When one object exerts a force on a second object, the second object exerts a force equal in size and opposite in direction on the first object.**

Forces always occur in pairs.

Action and reaction forces are applied to different objects. These forces are equal and opposite. The action force acts on the ball, and the reaction force acts on the foot. Action and reaction force pairs are present even when there is no motion. For example, when you sit on a chair, your weight pushes down on the chair. The force of your weight is the action force. The chair pushing back up with a force equal to your weight is the reaction force.

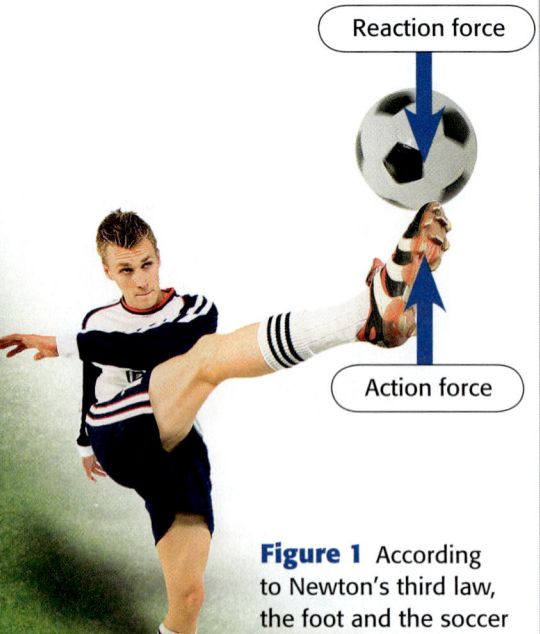

Figure 1 According to Newton's third law, the foot and the soccer ball exert equal and opposite forces on each other.

412 Chapter 12 Forces

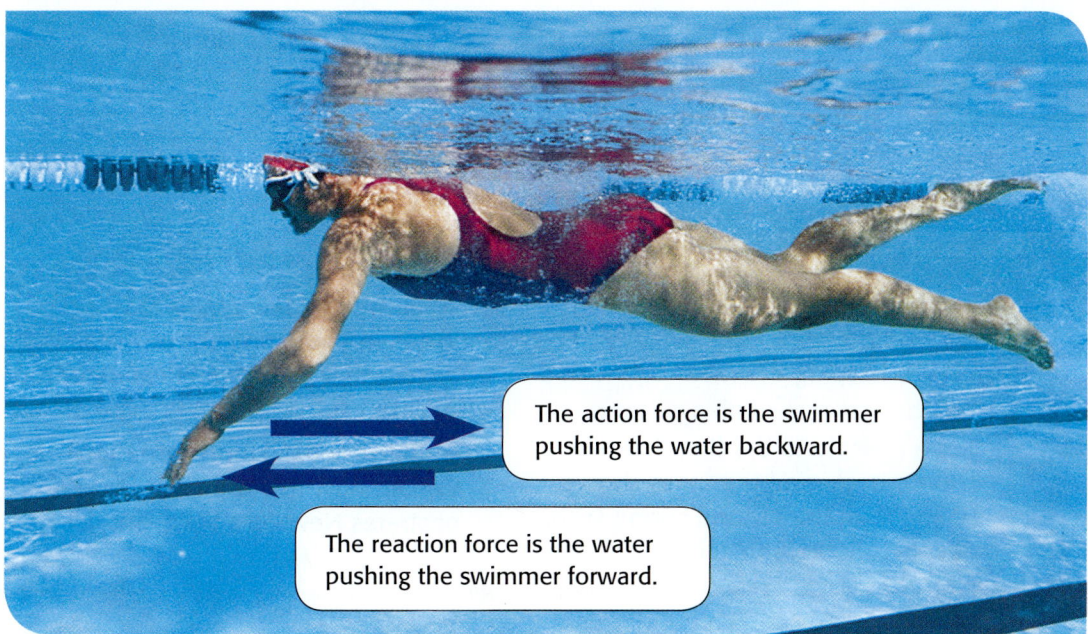

The action force is the swimmer pushing the water backward.

The reaction force is the water pushing the swimmer forward.

Forces in a force pair do not act on the same object.

Newton's third law states that forces happen in pairs. In other words, every force is part of a force pair made up of an action force and a reaction force. Although the forces are equal and opposite, they do not cancel each other because they act on different objects. In the example shown in **Figure 2,** the swimmer's hands and feet exert the action force on the water. The water exerts the reaction force on the swimmer's hands and feet. Note that action and reaction forces occur at the same time. But the action and reaction forces never act on the same object.

Reading Check Why don't the forces in a force pair cancel each other?

Equal forces don't always have equal effects.

Another example of an action-reaction force pair is shown in **Figure 3.** If you drop a ball, the force of gravity pulls the ball toward Earth. This force is the action force exerted by Earth on the ball. But the same force of gravity also pulls Earth toward the ball. That force is the reaction force exerted by the ball on Earth.

It is easy to see the effect of the action force—the ball falls to Earth. Why don't you notice the effect of the reaction force—Earth is pulled upward? Remember Newton's second law: an object's acceleration is equal to the force applied to the object divided by the object's mass. The force applied to Earth is equal to the force applied to the ball. However, Earth's mass is much larger than the ball's mass. Thus, compared with the ball's acceleration, Earth's acceleration is almost undetectable.

Figure 2 The two forces in a force pair act on different objects. In this example, the action force acts on the water, and the reaction force acts on the swimmer.

Figure 3 Earth accelerates toward the ball as the ball accelerates toward Earth. (The acceleration arrows are not drawn to scale.) **Why is Earth's acceleration so much smaller than the ball's?**

Section 3 Newton's Third Law **413**

QuickLab — Action and Reaction Forces

  10 min

Procedure
1. Hang a **2 kg mass** from a **spring scale**.
2. Observe and record the reading on the spring scale.
3. While keeping the mass connected to the first scale, link a **second spring scale** to the first. The first spring scale and the mass should hang from the second spring scale, as the photograph shows.
4. Observe and record the readings on each spring scale.

Analysis
1. What are the action and reaction forces in the spring scale–mass system that you have constructed?
2. How did the readings on the two spring scales in step 4 compare? Explain how this experiment demonstrates Newton's third law.

momentum (moh MEN tuhm) a quantity defined as the product of the mass and velocity of an object

READING TOOLBOX

Two-Column Notes After reading this page and the next, take two-column notes on the key idea of momentum. Write down the key idea in the first column, and add detailed notes and examples in the second column.

Momentum

If a small car and a large truck are moving with the same velocity and the same braking force is applied to each vehicle, the truck takes more time to stop than the car does. Likewise, a fast-moving car takes more time to stop than a slow-moving car of the same mass does. The large truck and the fast-moving car have more **momentum** than the small car and the slow-moving car do. Momentum is a property of all moving objects. ▸ **For movement along a straight line, momentum is calculated by multiplying an object's mass and velocity.**

 Momentum equation
$$momentum = mass \times velocity$$
$$p = mv$$

In the SI, momentum is expressed in kilograms times meters per second (kg•m/s). Like velocity, momentum has direction. An object's momentum and velocity are in the same direction.

Momentum increases as mass and velocity increase.

The momentum equation states that for a given velocity, the greater the mass of an object, the greater the momentum of the object. A tractor-trailer truck has much more momentum than a sports car moving at the same speed does. The momentum equation also states that the faster an object is moving, the greater the momentum of the object. If an object is not moving, its momentum is zero.

Reading Check To what two quantities is momentum proportional?

414 Chapter 12 Forces

Force is related to change in momentum.

To catch a baseball, you must apply a force on the ball to make the ball stop moving. When you force an object to change its motion, you force it to change its momentum. In fact, you are changing the momentum of the ball over a period of time.

As the period of time of the momentum's change becomes longer, the force needed to cause this change in momentum becomes smaller. So, if you pull your glove back while you are catching a ball, as shown in **Figure 4,** you increase the time for changing the ball's momentum. Increasing the time causes the ball to put less force on your hand. As a result, the sting to your hand is less than it would be otherwise.

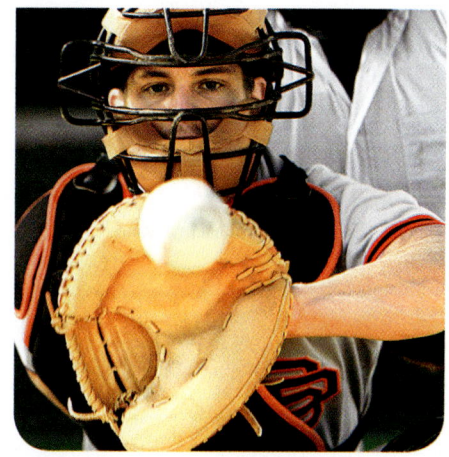

Figure 4 Moving the glove back during the catch increases the time of the momentum's change. **How does this movement change the force?**

Math Skills — Momentum

Calculate the momentum of a 6.00 kg bowling ball moving at 10.0 m/s down the alley toward the pins.

Identify
List the given and unknown values.

Given:
  mass, $m = 6.00$ kg
  velocity, $v = 10.0$ m/s
Unknown:
  momentum, $p = ?$ kg • m/s (and direction)

Plan
Write the equation for momentum.

momentum = mass × velocity
$p = mv$

Solve
Insert the known values into the equation, and solve.

$p = mv = 6.00$ kg × 10.0 m/s
$p = 60.0$ kg • m/s (toward the pins)

www.scilinks.org
Topic: Momentum
Code: HK80988

Practice

1. Calculate the momentum of the following objects:
   a. a 75 kg speed skater moving forward at 16 m/s
   b. a 135 kg ostrich running north at 16.2 m/s
   c. a 5.0 kg baby on a train moving eastward at 72 m/s
   d. a 48.5 kg passenger seated on a train that is stopped
2. Calculate the velocity of a 0.8 kg kitten with a forward momentum of 5 kg • m/s.

For more practice, visit **go.hrw.com** and enter keyword **HK8MP**.

Practice Hint

› When a problem requires that you calculate velocity when you know momentum and mass, you can use the momentum equation.

› Problem 2: You may rearrange the momentum equation to isolate velocity on the left side:

$$v = \frac{p}{m}$$

Section 3 Newton's Third Law

Academic Vocabulary

predict (pree DIKT) to tell in advance

Conservation of Momentum

Imagine that two cars of different masses moving with different velocities collide head on. The momentum of the cars after the collision can be predicted. This prediction can be made because momentum is always conserved, or, in other words, always remains constant. Some momentum may be transferred from one car to the other, but the total momentum remains the same. This principle is known as the *law of conservation of momentum*.

| Law of conservation of momentum | The total amount of momentum in an isolated system is conserved. |

❯ **The total momentum of two or more objects after a collision is the same as it was before the collision.** In some cases, cars bounce off each other and move in opposite directions. If the cars stick together after a collision, they will move in the direction of the car that had the greater momentum initially.

Why It Matters

How Do Rockets Work?

REAL WORLD

Rockets are made in various sizes and designs, but the basic principle of each rocket is the same. The outward push of the hot gases through the nozzle is matched by an equal push in the opposite direction on the combustion chamber. This push accelerates the rocket forward.

Gases push the rocket forward.

The rocket pushes the gases backward.

Conservation of Momentum

Together, the rocket and fuel form a system. The change in the fuel's momentum as it exits must be matched by an equal change in the rocket's momentum in the opposite direction. Thus, the total momentum of the system stays the same.

Newton's Third Law

The upward push on the rocket equals the downward push on the exhaust gases. These two forces form an action-reaction pair.

YOUR TURN

WRITING IN SCIENCE

1. Some people think that rockets work because flowing hot gases push against the atmosphere. If this were true, rockets could not travel through space. Write a paragraph to explain why.

Figure 5 Some of the cue ball's momentum is transferred to the billiard ball during a collision.

Momentum is conserved in collisions.

When a moving object hits a second object, some or all of the momentum of the first object is transferred to the second object. Imagine hitting a billiard ball with a cue ball such that the billiard ball starts moving, as **Figure 5** shows. During a collision with a billiard ball, the cue ball transfers some of its momentum to the billiard ball. Anytime two or more objects interact, they may exchange momentum, but the total momentum of the system always stays the same.

Newton's third law explains conservation of momentum. In a game of pool, the cue ball hits the billiard ball with a force—the action force. The equal but opposite force exerted by the billiard ball on the cue ball is the reaction force.

Section 3 Review

KEY IDEAS

1. **State** Newton's third law of motion, and give an example that shows how this law works.
2. **Describe** how momentum is calculated.
3. **Explain** what the law of conservation of momentum means, and give an example.

CRITICAL THINKING

4. **Evaluating Models** Which of the following models explains why the action and reaction forces don't cancel each other when a soccer ball is kicked?
   a. The force of the player's foot on the ball is greater than the force of the ball on the player's foot.
   b. The forces do not act on the same object.
   c. The reaction force happens after the action force.

5. **Identifying Examples** List the action and reaction forces in three force pairs. Do not use examples from the chapter.

6. **Applying Ideas** The forces exerted by Earth and a skier become an action-reaction force pair when the skier pushes the ski poles against Earth. Explain why the skier accelerates while Earth does not seem to move at all. (Hint: Think about the math equation for Newton's second law of motion for each of the forces.)

Math Skills

7. Calculate the momentum of a 1 kg ball that is moving eastward at 12 m/s.

Inquiry Lab

⏱ 50 min

Building a Catapult

Catapults have been used for centuries to throw objects great distances. According to Newton's third law of motion (whenever one object exerts a force on a second object, the second object exerts an equal and opposite force on the first), when an object is launched, something must also happen to the catapult. In this activity, you will build a simple catapult that will allow you to observe the effects of Newton's third law of motion and the law of conservation of momentum.

What You'll Do

> **Construct** a simple catapult.
> **Predict** how Newton's third law of motion will affect a catapult and an object shot from the catapult.

What You'll Need

cardboard rectangles, 10 cm × 15 cm (3)
glue
marble
meterstick
pushpins (3)
rubber band
scale
scissors
straws, plastic (6)
string

Safety

Asking a Question

According to Newton's third law of motion, how will the motion of an object shot from a catapult compare with the motion of the catapult?

Building the Catapult

1. Glue the cardboard rectangles together to make a stack of three. Let the glue dry for 5–10 min.

2. Push two of the pushpins into the cardboard stack near the corners at one end, as shown below. These pushpins will be the anchors for the rubber band.

3. Make a small loop of string.

4. Put the rubber band through the loop of string, and then place the rubber band over the two pushpin anchors. The rubber band should be stretched between the two anchors with the string loop in the middle.

5. Pull the string loop toward the end of the cardboard stack opposite the end with the anchors, and fasten the loop in place with the third pushpin.

418 Chapter 12 Forces

Forming and Testing a Hypothesis

6 Weigh and record the mass of the catapult and the marble. Consider the operation of the catapult in light of Newton's third law of motion, and form a hypothesis about how the motion of a marble shot from the catapult will compare with the motion of the catapult.

Designing Your Experiment

7 With your lab partner(s), decide how you will test your hypothesis.

8 In your lab report, list each step you will perform in your experiment. (Hint: Use the scissors to cut the string as well as the straws to lay your catapult on.)

Performing Your Experiment

9 Have your teacher approve your plan, and carry out your experiment.

Analysis

1. **Identifying Relationships** Which has more mass, the marble or the catapult?
2. **Describing Events** What happened to the catapult when the marble was launched?
3. **Describing Events** How far did the marble fly before it landed? Did the catapult move as far as the marble did?

Communicating Your Results

4. **Drawing Conclusions** Explain, in terms of Newton's third law of motion, why the marble and the catapult moved as they did.
5. **Explaining Events** If the forces that made the marble and the catapult move apart are equal, why didn't the marble and the catapult move apart the same distance? Suggest two contributing factors.
6. **Applying Concepts** Using the law of conservation of momentum, explain why the marble and the catapult moved in opposite directions after the launch.

Extension

How would you modify the catapult if you wanted to keep it from moving backward as far as it did, while still having it rest on straws? Using items that you can find in the classroom, design a catapult that will move backward less than the one originally designed.

Rearranging Equations

Science Skills: Technology, **Math**, Scientific Methods, Graphing

Problem

A car's engine exerts a force of 1.5×10^4 N in the forward direction, while friction exerts an opposing force of 9.0×10^3 N. If the car's mass is 1.5×10^3 kg, what is the magnitude of the car's net acceleration?

Solution

Identify

List all given and unknown values.

Given:

forward force, $F_1 = 1.5 \times 10^4$ N
opposing force, $F_2 = 9.0 \times 10^3$ N
mass, $m = 1.5 \times 10^3$ kg

Unknown:

acceleration, $a = ?$ m/s^2

Diagram:

Plan

a. Use Newton's second law, and rearrange for acceleration.
b. Because the given forces act in different directions, subtract to find the net force, F.
c. Combine the two equations.

a. $F = ma$

$a = \dfrac{F}{m}$

b. $F = F_1 - F_2$

c. $a = \dfrac{F}{m} = \dfrac{F_1 - F_2}{m}$

Solve

Substitute the given values into the equation, and solve.

$$a = \dfrac{F_1 - F_2}{m} = \dfrac{(1.5 \times 10^4 \text{ N}) - (9.0 \times 10^3 \text{ N})}{1.5 \times 10^3 \text{ kg}}$$

$$a = \dfrac{6.0 \times 10^3 \text{ N}}{1.5 \times 10^3 \text{ kg}} = \dfrac{6.0 \times 10^3 \text{ kg} \cdot \text{m/s}^2}{1.5 \times 10^3 \text{ kg}} = 4.0 \text{ m/s}^2$$

Practice

1. A car has a mass of 1.50×10^3 kg. If the net force acting on the car is 6.75×10^3 N to the east, what is the car's acceleration?

2. A bicyclist slows with a force of 3.5×10^2 N. If the bicyclist and bicycle have a total mass of 1.0×10^2 kg, what is the acceleration?

3. Roberto and Laura study across from each other at a wide table. Laura pushes a 2.2 kg book toward Roberto with a force of 11.0 N straight ahead. If the force of friction opposing the movement is 8.4 N, what is the magnitude and direction of the book's acceleration?

CHAPTER 12 Summary

go.hrw.com
SUPER SUMMARY
KEYWORD: HK8FORS

Key Ideas

Key Terms

Section 1 Newton's First and Second Laws

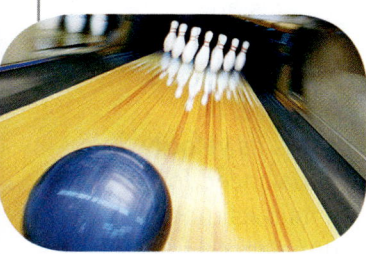

> **Newton's First Law** Objects change their state of motion only when a net force is applied. (p. 397)

> **Newton's Second Law** The unbalanced force acting on an object determines how much an object speeds up or slows down. It equals the object's mass times its acceleration, or $F = ma$. (p. 400)

inertia, p. 398

Section 2 Gravity

> **Weight and Mass** Weight is equal to the force of gravity on an object and is proportional to an object's mass. Mathematically: $w = mg$. (p. 403)

> **Law of Universal Gravitation** Objects fall to the ground when dropped because all objects in the universe attract each other through the force of gravity. (p. 405)

> **Free Fall** In the absence of air resistance, all objects near Earth's surface accelerate at the same rate, regardless of their mass. (p. 407)

> **Projectile Motion** Projectile motion has two components—horizontal and vertical. When the two motions are combined, they form a curved path. (p. 408)

weight, p. 403
free fall, p. 407
terminal velocity, p. 407
projectile motion, p. 408

Section 3 Newton's Third Law

> **Action and Reaction Forces** When one object exerts a force on a second object, the second object exerts a force equal in size and opposite in direction on the first object. (p. 412)

> **Momentum** For movement along a straight line, momentum is calculated by multiplying an object's mass by its speed. (p. 414)

> **Conservation of Momentum** The total momentum of two or more objects after they collide is the same as it was before the collision. (p. 416)

momentum, p. 414

Forces **421**

CHAPTER 12 Review

READING TOOLBOX

1. **Key-Term Fold** Use the FoldNote that you made at the beginning of the chapter to study the key terms for this chapter. See if you know all of the definitions. When you have reviewed the terms, use each term in a sentence.

USING KEY TERMS

2. What is *inertia,* and why is it important in the laws of motion?

3. A wrestler weighs in for the first match on the moon. Will the athlete weigh more or less on the moon than he does on Earth? Explain your answer by using the terms *weight, mass, force,* and *gravity.*

4. Describe a skydiver's jump from the airplane to the ground. In your answer, use the terms *air resistance, gravity,* and *terminal velocity.*

INTERPRETING GRAPHICS The photo below shows part of a Newton's cradle. Study the photo and use it to answer question 5.

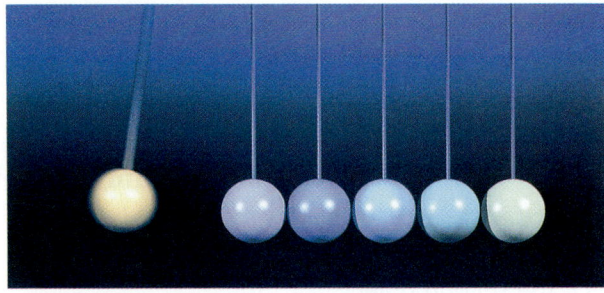

5. What will happen next? Explain by using the terms *collision* and *conservtion of momentum.*

UNDERSTANDING KEY IDEAS

6. The first law of motion applies to
   a. only objects that are moving.
   b. only objects that are not moving.
   c. all objects, whether moving or not.
   d. no object, whether moving or not.

7. Newton's first law of motion states any of the following except
   a. an object at rest remains at rest unless it experiences an unbalanced force.
   b. an object in motion maintains its velocity unless it experiences an unbalanced force.
   c. an object will tend to maintain its motion unless it experiences an unbalanced force.
   d. an object will tend to maintain its motion unless it experiences a balanced force.

8. A measure of inertia is an object's
   a. mass.   c. velocity.
   b. weight.   d. acceleration.

9. Automobile seat belts are necessary for safety because of a passenger's
   a. weight.   c. speed.
   b. inertia.   d. gravity.

10. Suppose you are pushing a car with a certain net force. If you then push with twice the net force, the car's acceleration
    a. becomes four times as much.
    b. becomes two times as much.
    c. stays the same.
    d. becomes half as much.

11. Any change in an object's velocity is caused by
    a. the object's mass.
    b. the object's direction.
    c. a balanced force.
    d. an unbalanced force.

12. An object's acceleration is never
    a. directly proportional to the net force.
    b. inversely proportional to the object's mass.
    c. in the same direction as the net force.
    d. in the opposite direction as the net force.

13. Gravitational force between two masses _____ as the masses increase and rapidly _____ as the distance between the masses increases.
    a. increases, increases
    b. decreases, decreases
    c. decreases, increases
    d. increases, decreases

422   Chapter 12   Forces

EXPLAINING KEY IDEAS

14. What is the difference between free fall and weightlessness?

INTERPRETING GRAPHICS The graph below shows the velocity of a bicycle over time. Use the graph below to answer questions 15 and 16.

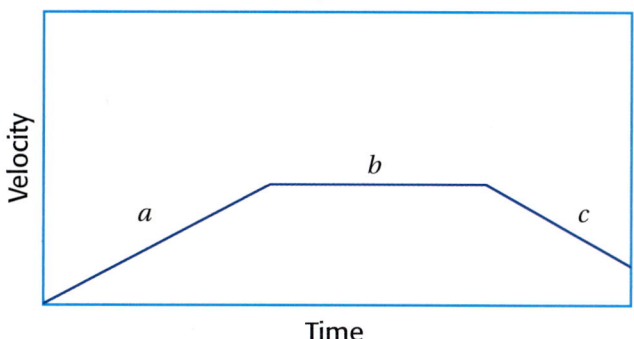

Velocity Vs. Time

15. Determine whether the acceleration is positive, negative, or zero for each segment.

16. Where is the net force on the bicycle zero?

CRITICAL THINKING

17. Applying Concepts What happens to the gravitational force between two objects if their masses do not change but the distance between them becomes four times as much?

18. Analyzing Ideas There is no gravity in outer space. Write a paragraph explaining whether this statement is true or false.

19. Making Predictions How will acceleration change if the mass being accelerated is multiplied by three but the net force is reduced to half?

20. Applying Knowledge For each pair, determine whether the objects have the same momentum. If the objects have different momentums, determine which object has more momentum.
a. a car and train that have the same velocity
b. a moving ball and a still bat
c. two identical balls moving at the same speed in opposite directions

Math Skills

21. Newton's Second Law A student tests the second law of motion by accelerating a block of ice at a rate of 3.5 m/s². If the ice has a mass of 12.5 kg, what force must the student apply to the ice?

22. Weight A bag of sugar has a mass of 2.26 kg. What is its weight in newtons on the moon, where the acceleration due to gravity is one-sixth of that on Earth? (Hint: On Earth, $g = 9.8$ m/s².)

23. Momentum Calculate the momentum of the following objects:
a. a 65 kg skateboarder moving forward at the rate of 3 m/s
b. a 20 kg toddler in a car traveling west at the rate of 22 m/s
c. a 16 kg penguin at rest

Graphing Skills

24. Line Graphs An experiment is done using a lab cart. Varying forces are applied to the cart and measured while the cart is accelerating. Each force is applied in the same direction as the movement of the cart. The following data are obtained from the experiment.

Trial	Acceleration (m/s²)	Applied force (N)
1	0.70	0.35
2	1.70	0.85
3	2.70	1.35
4	3.70	1.85
5	4.70	2.35

a. Graph the data in the table. Place acceleration on the x-axis and applied force on the y-axis.
b. Recall that $F = ma$. What does the line on the graph represent?
c. Use your graph to determine the mass of the lab cart.

Chapter Review

Standardized Test Prep

Understanding Concepts

Directions (1–4): **For each question, write on a sheet of paper the letter of the correct answer.**

1. After a bank customer cashes a check, some of the money received accidentally slips from the customer's hands. What force causes the bills to hit the ground later than the coins do?
    A. static friction
    B. gravity
    C. air resistance
    D. magnetism

2. If the nickel and iron at the Earth's core were suddenly replaced with cotton candy, what would happen to the mass and weight of the objects on the Earth's surface?
    F. Their mass and weight both increase.
    G. Their mass would stay the same and their weight would decrease.
    H. Their mass would decrease and their weight would increase.
    I. Neither their mass nor weight change.

3. A truck with a mass of 2,000 kg is traveling at a constant velocity of 40 m/s. What is the net force acting upon the truck?
    A. 0.0 N
    B. 0.02 N
    C. 50 N
    D. 800 N

4. A high-altitude balloonist at an altitude of 15,000 m drops an instrument package. When does the package reach terminal velocity?
    F. as it begins to fall
    G. as it matches the speed of the plane
    H. as it stops accelerating from air resistance
    I. as it impacts the Earth's surface

Directions (5–6): **For each question, write a short response.**

5. Explain why the moon does not fly off into space in a straight line nor plummet directly toward the Earth's surface.

6. A racing motorcycle with a mass of 300 kg accelerates from 0 to 60 m/s in 5 seconds. How much force is acting on the motorcycle?

Reading Skills

Directions (7–8): **Read the passage below. Then, answer the questions that follow.**

A REGULAR VISITOR

A microgravity environment is one in which the apparent weight of an object is much less than its weight on Earth. The term *microgravity* is used instead of weightlessness because every object has some weight, though that weight may be so minuscule as to be undetectable. Because every object in the universe exerts a gravitational pull on every other object, every object possesses weight.

Microgravity occurs whenever an object is in free fall. Scientists achieve microgravity environments in a number of ways. Drop towers and research aircraft provide it for up to 20 s. The Shuttle and the International Space Station can provide it for months.

A rocket ship that is accelerating by firing its rockets cannot provide microgravity. Even if the rocket is accelerating uniformly, force is applied to the rocket by the gas escaping out the back. This force must be transferred to each part of the ship through either pressure or tension, and thus weightlessness is not experienced.

7. When the Shuttle is orbiting, it is in constant motion around the Earth. Why isn't this motion experienced as weight?
    A. There is no net force acting on the Shuttle.
    B. The Shuttle's mass is not large enough to exert a measurable gravitational pull.
    C. The Earth is exerting the same pull on both the Shuttle and its passengers.
    D. The Earth is too far away to have a measurable gravitational effect.

8. Why can the Shuttle provide microgravity only after it achieves orbit?

Interpreting Graphics

The following graph charts the speeds of three objects in motion. Use this graph to answer questions 9 and 10.

SPEED VS. TIME FOR FALLING OBJECTS

9. At the 1 s mark, which objects have equal momentum?
   A. the bicycle and the rock
   B. the rock and the bowling ball
   C. the bowling ball and the bicycle
   D. All three objects have the same momentum.

10. At the 3 s mark, which object or objects have a net force acting on them?
    F. the bicycle
    G. the rock
    H. the bowling ball
    I. the bicycle and the bowling ball

The following graphic shows a long jumper making a jump from west to east. Use this graphic to answer questions 11 and 12.

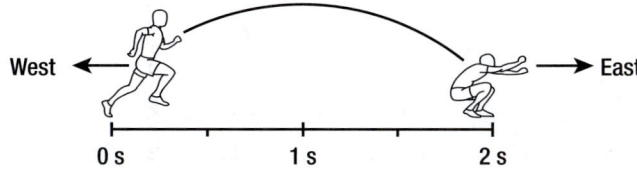

11. In what direction or directions is the net force acting on the jumper between 0.5 s and 2 s?
    A. first up and to the east, then down and to the west
    B. first up and to the east, then down and to the east
    C. up and to the east
    D. down and to the west

12. When the long jumper jumps, Earth exerts a force that moves him up and to the east. Since there is a reaction force exerted on Earth, why doesn't Earth move the same distance down and to the west?

Test Tip

Pay attention to your time limit. If you begin to run short on time, quickly read the remaining questions and answer those that are the easiest for you.

Why It Matters

Careers Using Physics

When you think of a physicist, you might think of a scientist who studies subatomic particles or neutron stars. Actually, there are hundreds of careers in which people use physics. Whether designing buildings, engineering movie stunts, or lighting up a rock show, people use physics to get the job done. The careers discussed here are just a few examples of careers that use physics.

Lighting Designer

Lighting designers apply their knowledge of light and optics to light up architectural displays, movie sets, theater productions, and concerts. Lights such as lasers, strobes, and high-intensity projectors are used at concerts. Lighting designers also filter white light sources and combine the resulting colors of light to match a particular song. The movement of the filters and the lights is controlled precisely by motors. Because timing is essential, computers are used to control the light changes. The next time you see a light display or concert, think of how physics helped light up the show!

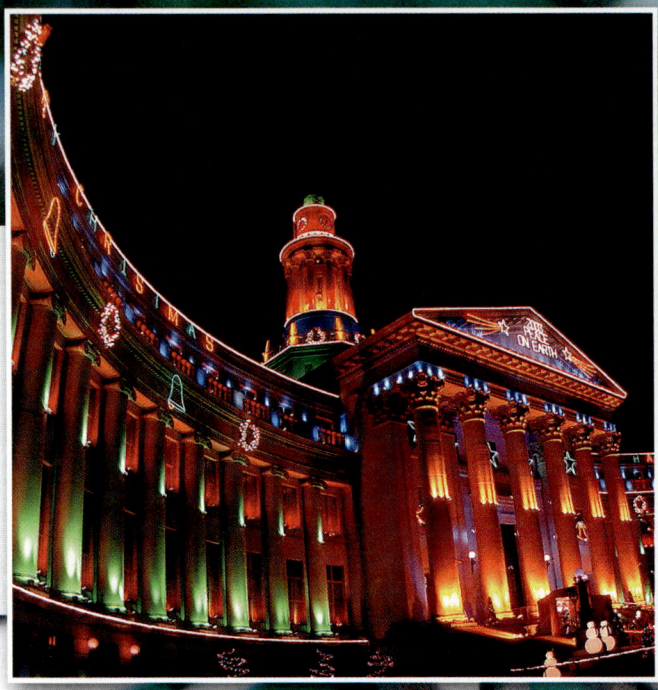

Architect

To design buildings, architects must understand many aspects of physical science. For example, architects must know how to calculate the weight and stress that a building's walls can bear. To make such calculations, architects often use computer-modeling programs that incorporate data about the weight and strength of various materials. Architects must understand the physics of heat transfer to be able to design houses that are comfortable to live in. For example, architects use the thickness and thermal conductivity of a building material to calculate the material's thermal resistance.

Fab Technician

Have you ever thought about all of the steps that are needed to make a computer chip? Manufacturing computer chips requires knowledge of physics and a high degree of precision. Building a computer chip is similar to printing a series of extremely detailed photographs on a silicon wafer. Fab technicians need to know how to use specialized equipment to create the circuit patterns on the chips, to measure the tiny dimensions of the pattern, and to test the circuits to make sure that they work properly.

Robotics Engineer

The introduction of the first commercially successful housecleaning robot in 2002 demonstrated that robots are becoming parts of our lives. Robotics engineers work in a wide variety of fields. They may invent assistive devices for the disabled or develop rovers to explore the surface of Mars. Robotics engineers must design reliable, efficient machines that accomplish specific tasks. Knowledge of the mechanics of movement and of electrical circuits, motors, and simple machines are essential to designing robots that can move, sense, and respond to their environment.

Windsmith

Wind turbines are as tall as a football field is long, and their blades can be larger than the wings of a 747 jet. Wind turbines are the fastest growing source of renewable energy in the world, and each one requires regular maintenance. Windsmiths are people who operate and maintain the wind turbines on a wind farm. Wind turbines convert the work done by moving air into electrical energy, and in some places, they spin almost continuously throughout the year. Therefore, a wind turbine's moving parts can wear quickly. To ensure that wind turbines are operating at peak efficiency, windsmiths use knowledge of physical science to maintain the mechanical, electrical, and hydraulic systems that enable wind turbines to produce electricity.

Video Game Programmer

Imagine that your job was to crash cars, blow things up, and help people dive off the tops of buildings—in the virtual world of video games! Increasingly, video games are programmed using the principles of Newtonian physics. To simulate the behavior of objects in the natural world, programmers must calculate inertia, friction, velocity, and wind resistance. Integrating principles of physical science into video games makes virtual car races and flight simulators more realistic. Physics is so important to video games that dedicated physics processing chips, which perform millions of calculations per second, are built into video game consoles.

YOUR TURN

UNDERSTANDING CONCEPTS
1. Describe how understanding physics plays an important role in two of the careers described on these pages.

CRITICAL THINKING
2. Why would an architect calculate a material's thermal resistivity?

SCILINKS.
www.scilinks.org
Topic: Careers in Physics
Code: HK81246

CHAPTER 13
Work and Energy

Chapter Outline

❶ Work, Power, and Machines
What Is Work?
Power
Machines and Mechanical Advantage

❷ Simple Machines
What Are Simple Machines?
The Lever Family
The Inclined Plane Family
Compound Machines

❸ What Is Energy?
Energy and Work
Potential Energy
Kinetic Energy
Other Forms of Energy

❹ Conservation of Energy
Energy Transformations
The Law of Conservation of Energy
Efficiency of Machines

Tennessee Course Level Expectations (Physical Science)

CLE.3202.TE.3 Explain the relationship between the properties of a material and the use of the material in the application of a technology; **CLE.3202.2.1** Investigate the properties and behaviors of mechanical and electromagnetic waves; **CLE.3202.2.6** Investigate the Law of Conservation of Energy; **CLE.3202.4.3** Demonstrate the relationships among work, power, and machines; **CLE.3202.Inq.1** Recognize that science is a progressive endeavor that reevaluates and extends what is already accepted.

Why It Matters
This whimsical sculpture created by artist George Rhoads is called an *audiokinetic sculpture*. Kinetic, potential, and sonic energy are in constant interplay in this piece of art.

Inquiry Lab

⏱ 10 min

Kitchen Tools

Study some common kitchen tools, such as a **bottle opener,** a **cork screw,** a **nut cracker,** and an **eggbeater.** How does each tool help the person using it? Consider where force is applied to each tool and how the tool applies force to another object.

Questions to Get You Started

1. Is the applied force transferred to another part of the tool? Which part of the tool does the work?
2. Is the force that the tool exerts on an object greater or lesser than the force exerted on the tool? Explain.

READING TOOLBOX

These reading tools can help you learn the material in this chapter. For more information on how to use these and other tools, see **Appendix A.**

Science Terms

Everyday Words Used in Science
Many words used in science are familiar from everyday speech. However, when these words are used in science, their meanings are often different from or more precise than the everyday meanings. Pay special attention to the definitions of such words so that you use the words correctly in scientific contexts.

Your Turn As you read this chapter, complete a table like the one below.

WORD	EVERYDAY MEANING	SCIENTIFIC MEANING
work	a job; to do labor	the transfer of energy to a body when a force causes the body to move
power	physical strength	
efficiency		

Word Problems

Mathematical Language Word problems describe science or math problems in words. To solve a word problem, you need to translate the language of words to the language of equations, mathematical symbols, variables, and numbers.

Your Turn Complete a table like the one below for the following word problem.
A crane uses an average force of 5,200 N to lift a girder 25 m. How much work does the crane do on the girder?

PHRASE	VARIABLE	VALUE
uses an average force of 5,200 N	force, F	
	distance, d	25 m
How much work		unknown

Graphic Organizers

Concept Maps A concept map is a diagram that helps you see relationships between the key ideas and categories of a topic. To construct a concept map, do the following:

1. Select a main concept for the map.
2. List all of the other related concepts.
3. Build the map by arranging the concepts according to their importance under the main concept. Add linking words to give meaning to the arrangement of concepts.

Your Turn Make a concept map for Section 2 using this as a start.

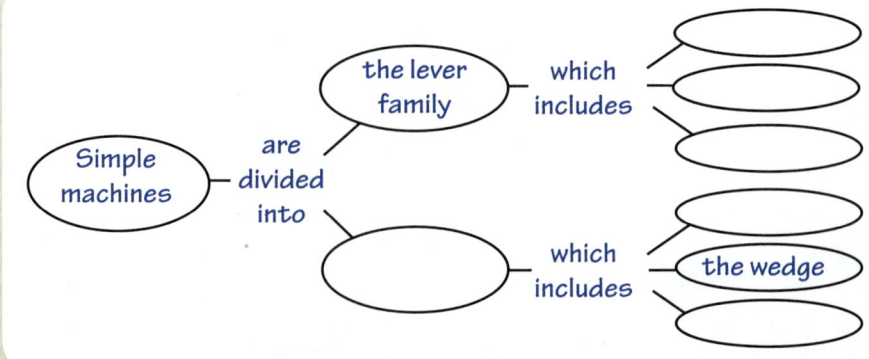

430   Chapter 13   Work and Energy

SECTION 1
Work, Power, and Machines

Key Ideas
- How is work calculated?
- What is the relationship between work and power?
- How do machines make work easier?

Key Terms
- work
- power
- mechanical advantage

Why It Matters
We use many types of simple machines to repair other machines, such as bikes and cars.

If you needed to change a flat tire, you would use a car jack to lift the car. Machines—from complex ones such as cars to relatively simple ones such as car jacks, hammers, and ramps—help people to get things done every day.

> **Tennessee Course Level Expectations (Physical Science)**
> CLE.3202.4.3; CLE.3202.Inq.1; CLE.3202.Inq.2; CLE.3202.Inq.3; CLE.3202.Math.1; CLE.3202.Math.2; CLE.3202.TE.3

What Is Work?

Imagine trying to lift the front of a car without using a jack. You could exert a lot of force without moving the car at all. Exerting all that force may seem like hard work. In science, however, the word *work* has a very specific meaning.

Work is done only when force is applied to an object and the object moves in the same direction as the applied force. **Work is calculated by multiplying the force by the distance over which the force is applied.** The force used to calculate work must be applied in the direction of the object's motion.

work (WUHRK) the transfer of energy to an object by the application of a force that causes the object to move in the direction of the force

> **Work equation**
> work = force × distance
> $W = Fd$

Work is zero when an object is not moving.

If you are trying to lift a car, you might apply a large force, but if the distance that the car moves is equal to zero, the work done on the car is also equal to zero. However, once the car moves even a small amount, you have done some work on it. You could calculate how much by multiplying the force that you have applied by the distance that the car moves. The weightlifter in **Figure 1** is applying a force to the barbell as she holds the barbell over her head, but the barbell is not moving. Is she doing any work on the barbell?

Figure 1 This weightlifter is holding a barbell over her head. **Is she doing any work on the barbell?**

READING TOOLBOX

Word Problems As you read through the practice problems on this page, create a table showing the variable to which each phrase corresponds and the value given for each variable.

Work is measured in joules.

Because work is calculated as force times distance, it is expressed in newtons times meters (N • m). This combination of SI units is also called *joules* (J). One joule is equal to one kilogram times meter squared per second squared:

$$1 \text{ N} \cdot \text{m} = 1 \text{ J} = 1 \text{ kg} \cdot \text{m}^2/\text{s}^2$$

Because all of these units are equivalent, when solving a particular problem, you can choose which unit to use. Substituting equivalent units will often help you cancel out other units in a problem.

You do about 1 J of work when you lift an apple, which weighs about 1 N, from your arm's length down at your side to the top of your head, a distance of about 1 m.

Math Skills — Work

Imagine a father playing with his daughter by lifting her repeatedly in the air. How much work does he do with each lift if he lifts her 2.0 m and exerts an average force of 190 N?

Identify
List the given and unknown values.

Given:
 force, $F = 190$ N
 distance, $d = 2.0$ m
Unknown:
 work, $W = ?$ J

Plan
Write the equation for work.

work = force × distance
$W = Fd$

Solve
Insert the known values into the equation, and solve.

$W = 190 \text{ N} \times 2.0 \text{ m} = 380 \text{ N} \cdot \text{m} = 380 \text{ J}$

Practice Hint

> **Problem 4:** To use the work equation, you must use units of newtons for force and units of meters for distance. To convert from mass to force (weight), use the definition of weight:
>
> $$w = mg$$
>
> where m is the mass in kilograms and $g = 9.8$ m/s². The force in the work equation is equal to the value of the weight.

Practice

1. A crane uses an average force of 5,200 N to lift a girder 25 m. How much work does the crane do on the girder?
2. An apple weighing 1 N falls a distance of 1 m. How much work is done on the apple by the force of gravity?
3. A bicycle's brakes apply 125 N of frictional force to the wheels as the bike moves 14.0 m. How much work do the brakes do?
4. A mechanic uses a hydraulic lift to raise a 1,200 kg car 0.50 m off the ground. How much work does the lift do on the car?

For more practice, visit **go.hrw.com** and enter keyword **HK8MP**.

QuickLab

Power Output

 20 min

Procedure

1. Use a **scale** to determine your weight in newtons. If your scale measures in pounds, multiply your weight by 4.45 N/lb.

2. With a classmate, use a **stopwatch** to time how long each of you takes to walk quickly up the **stairs**. Record your results.

3. Use a **meterstick** to measure the height of one step in meters. Multiply by the number of steps to calculate the height of the stairway.

4. Multiply your weight in newtons by the height of the stairs in meters to find the work that you did in joules.

5. To express your power in watts, divide the work done in joules by the time in seconds that you took to climb the stairs.

Analysis

1. How would your power output change if you walked up the stairs faster?
2. What would your power output be if you climbed the stairs in the same amount of time while carrying a stack of books weighing 20 N?
3. Why did you use your weight as the force in the work equation?

Power

Running up a flight of stairs does not require more work than walking up slowly does, but running is more exhausting than walking. The amount of time that a given amount of work takes is an important factor when you consider work and machines. The quantity that measures work in relation to time is **power.** ▶ **Power is the rate at which work is done, or how much work is done in a given amount of time.**

 Power equation $\quad power = \dfrac{work}{time} \quad\quad P = \dfrac{W}{t}$

Running a given distance takes less time than walking the same distance does. How does reducing the time in the power equation change the power if the work done stays the same?

Power is measured in watts.

The SI unit used to express power is the watt (W). One watt is the amount of power needed to do one joule of work in one second. It is about equal to the power needed to lift an apple over your head in 1 s. Do not confuse the symbol for work, *W*, which is italic, with the symbol for the watt, W. You can tell which one is meant from the context and by the use of italics.

✓ **Reading Check** What is the SI unit for power? (See Appendix E for answers to Reading Checks.)

---

power (POW uhr) a quantity that measures the rate at which work is done or energy is transformed

Academic Vocabulary

factor (FAK tuhr) a condition or event that brings about a result

Section 1   Work, Power, and Machines   **433**

Math Skills Power

Lifting an elevator 18 m takes 100 kJ. If doing so takes 20 s, what is the average power of the elevator during the process?

Identify
List the given and unknown values.

Given:
  work, $W = 100$ kJ $= 1 \times 10^5$ J
  time, $t = 20$ s
  Distance is not needed.
Unknown:
  power, $P = ?$ W

Plan
Write the equation for power.

$$power = \frac{work}{time}$$

$$P = \frac{W}{t}$$

Solve
Insert the known values into the equation, and solve.

$$P = \frac{1 \times 10^5 \text{J}}{20 \text{ s}} = 5 \times 10^3 \text{ J/s}$$

$$P = 5 \times 10^3 \text{ W}$$

$$P = 5 \text{ kW}$$

Practice Hint

> Problem 2: To calculate power, first use the work equation to calculate the work done in each case.

Practice

1. While rowing across the lake during a race, John does 3,960 J of work on the oars in 60.0 s. What is his power output in watts?
2. Anna walks up the stairs on her way to class. She weighs 565 N, and the stairs go up 3.25 m vertically.
   a. If Anna climbs the stairs in 12.6 s, what is her power output?
   b. What is her power output if she climbs the stairs in 10.5 s?

For more practice, visit **go.hrw.com** and enter keyword **HK8MP**.

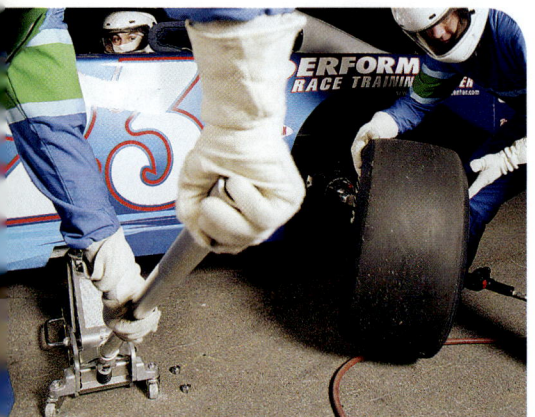

Figure 2 A jack makes lifting a car easy by multiplying the input force. How does a jack spread out the work over a large distance?

Machines and Mechanical Advantage

Which is easier, lifting a car by hand or lifting the car with a jack? Obviously, using a jack, shown in **Figure 2**, takes less effort. But you may be surprised to learn that both methods require the same amount of work. The jack makes the work easier by allowing you to apply less force at any given moment. ❭ **Machines help do work by changing the size of an input force, the direction of the force, or both.** Machines redistribute the work that we put into them and can change the direction of an input force. Machines can also make the force greater by decreasing the distance over which the force is applied. This process is often called *multiplying the force*.

Reading Check How do machines make work easier?

Why It Matters

What Machines Are Used on Bicycles?

REAL WORLD

Bicycles consist of many mechanical components. Many tools, each of which is some kind of machine, are used to maintain and repair bicycles. Each tool provides a mechanical advantage—by multiplying or changing the direction of the applied force—and makes working on bicycles much easier than it would be otherwise.

Tire lever

A tire lever is used to pry the tire from its rim.

Air pump

An air pump compresses air to increase the pressure in the tires.

Allen wrenches

A wrench changes the direction of an applied force.

This bicyclist can use several simple machines to attach the back wheel to the bicycle. He is using a wrench to change the direction of the force from his hand to turn a nut onto a bolt.

YOUR TURN

SUMMARIZING INFORMATION
1. What other tools are used to work on a bicycle? What is each tool used to do?

APPLYING CONCEPTS
2. When climbing a steep hill, would you want a larger or a smaller bicycle gear?

435

mechanical advantage (muh KAN i kuhl ad VANT ij) a quantity that expresses how much a machine multiplies force or distance

www.scilinks.org
Topic: Mechanical Advantage
Code: HK80928

Mechanical advantage is an important ratio.

A ramp makes doing work easier by multiplying the force that is applied. Scientists and engineers use a number that describes how much the force or distance is multiplied by a machine. This number, called the **mechanical advantage,** is defined as the ratio between the output force and the input force. It is also equal to the ratio between the input distance and the output distance if friction is ignored.

Mechanical advantage equation
$$\text{mechanical advantage} = \frac{\text{output force}}{\text{input force}} = \frac{\text{input distance}}{\text{output distance}}$$

A machine that has a mechanical advantage greater than one multiplies the input force. Such a machine can help you move or lift a heavy object, such as a car or a box of books. A machine that has a mechanical advantage of less than one does not multiply force but increases distance and speed.

Math Skills — Mechanical Advantage

Calculate the mechanical advantage of a ramp that is 5.0 m long and 1.5 m high.

Identify
List the given and unknown values.

Given:
  input distance = 5.0 m
  output distance = 1.5 m
Unknown:
  mechanical advantage = ?

Plan
Write the equation for mechanical advantage.

We need only the distance part of the full equation:
$$\text{mechanical advantage} = \frac{\text{input distance}}{\text{output distance}}$$

Solve
Insert the known values, and solve.

$$\text{mechanical advantage} = \frac{5.0 \text{ m}}{1.5 \text{ m}} = 3.3$$

Practice Hint

▸ The mechanical advantage equation can be rearranged to isolate any of the variables on the left.
▸ Problem 2: Rearrange the equation to isolate output force on the left.
▸ When rearranging, use only the part of the full equation that you need.

Practice

1. Find the mechanical advantage of a ramp that is 6.0 m long and 1.5 m tall.
2. Alex pulls on the handle of a claw hammer with a force of 15 N. If the hammer has a mechanical advantage of 5.2, how much force is exerted on the nail in the claw?

For more practice, visit **go.hrw.com** and enter keyword **HK8MP.**

When lifting a box straight up, a mover applies a large force over a short distance.

When using a ramp to lift the box, the mover applies a smaller force over a longer distance.

Figure 3 Lifting a box directly onto a truck and pushing the box up a ramp require the same amount of work.

Different forces can do the same amount of work.

Compare the amount of work required to lift a box onto the bed of a truck with the amount of work required to push the same box up a ramp. When the mover shown in **Figure 3** lifts the box straight up, he applies 225 N of force over a short distance. Using the ramp, he applies a smaller force over a longer distance. But the work done is the same in both cases.

Both a car jack and a loading ramp make doing work easier by increasing the distance over which force is applied. Both allow the same amount of work to be done by decreasing the force while increasing the distance.

Section 1 Review

KEY IDEAS

1. **Define** *work* and *power*. How are work and power related?
2. **Determine** if work is being done in the following situations:
   a. lifting a spoonful of soup to your mouth
   b. holding a large stack of books motionless over your head
   c. letting a pencil fall to the ground
3. **Describe** how a ramp can make lifting a box easy without changing the amount of work being done.

CRITICAL THINKING

4. **Applying Concepts** Both a short ramp and a long ramp reach a height of 1 m. Which ramp has a greater mechanical advantage?

Math Skills

5. How much work is done by a person who uses a horizontal force of 25 N to move a desk 3.0 m?
6. A bus driver applies a force of 55.0 N to the steering wheel, which in turn applies 132 N of force to the steering column. What is the mechanical advantage of the steering wheel?
7. A 400 N student climbs up a 3.0 m ladder in 4.0 s.
   a. How much work does the student do?
   b. What is the student's power output?
8. An outboard engine on a boat can do 1.0×10^6 J of work in 50.0 s. Calculate its power in watts. Convert your answer to horsepower (1 hp = 746 W).

SECTION 2
Simple Machines

Key Ideas

> What are the six types of simple machines?
> What are the two principal parts of all levers?
> How does using an inclined plane change the force required to do work?
> What simple machines make up a pair of scissors?

Key Terms

simple machine
compound machine

Why It Matters

A simple machine, such as a ramp, makes work easier by reducing the force required to do work.

Tennessee Course Level Expectations (Physical Science)
CLE.3202.4.3; CLE.3202.Inq.1; CLE.3202.Inq.2; CLE.3202.Inq.3

simple machine (SIM puhl muh SHEEN) one of the six basic types of machines, which are the basis for all other forms of machines

Can you pop the cap off of a bottle of soda by using just your fingers? You probably can't, especially if the bottle doesn't have a screw cap! Instead, you use a bottle opener. Similarly, you don't use the palm of your hand to drive a nail into a block of wood. Instead, you use a hammer. These simple machines make doing work easier.

What Are Simple Machines?

The most basic machines are called **simple machines.** Other machines are either modifications of simple machines or combinations of several simple machines. **Figure 1** shows examples of the six kinds of simple machines. > **The six types of simple machines are the simple lever, the pulley, the wheel and axle, the simple inclined plane, the wedge, and the screw.** Simple machines are divided into two families: the *lever family* and the *inclined plane family*.

Figure 1 The Six Simple Machines

The lever family: Simple lever, Pulley, Wheel and axle

The inclined plane family: Simple inclined plane, Wedge, Screw

Figure 2 The Three Classes of Levers

A **first-class lever** has a fulcrum located between the points of application of the input and output forces.

In a **second-class lever**, the fulcrum is at one end of the arm, and the input force is applied to the other end. The wheel of a wheelbarrow is a fulcrum.

Third-class levers multiply distance rather than force. As a result, they have a mechanical advantage of less than one. The human body contains many third-class levers.

The Lever Family

Imagine using a claw hammer to pull out a nail. As you pull on the handle of the hammer, the head of the hammer turns around the point where the hammer meets the wood. The force applied to the handle is transferred to the claw on the other end of the hammer. The claw hammer is a lever. ❯ **All levers have a rigid *arm* that turns around a point called the *fulcrum*.** The input force is multiplied or redirected into an output force.

Levers are divided into three classes.

Levers are divided into three classes depending on the locations of the fulcrum, the input force, and the output force, as **Figure 2** shows. First-class levers, such as the claw hammer, are the most common kind of lever. A pair of pliers is made of two first-class levers joined together.

Wheelbarrows, nutcrackers, and hinged doors are examples of second-class levers. A person's forearm is an example of a third-class lever. The biceps muscle, which is attached to the bone near the elbow, contracts a short distance to move the hand a large distance.

Concept Maps
Using *levers* for the main concept, create a simple concept map. Include the words *fulcrum, input force,* and *output force* in the map.

Section 2 Simple Machines **439**

Figure 3 The Mechanical Advantage of Pulleys

When a 150 N weight is lifted by using a single, fixed pulley, the weight must be fully supported by the rope on each side of the pulley. This kind of pulley has a mechanical advantage of one.

When a moving pulley is used, the load is shared by two sections of rope pulling upward. The input force supports only half of the weight. This pulley system has a mechanical advantage of two.

In this arrangement of multiple pulleys, all of the sections of rope are pulling up against the downward force of the weight. This arrangement gives an even higher mechanical advantage.

Figure 4 A wheel and axle is in the lever family of simple machines. **How does a wheel and axle differ from a pulley?**

Pulleys are modified levers.

A pulley is another kind of simple machine in the lever family. You may have used a pulley to lift things, such as a flag on a flagpole or a sail on a boat.

Figure 3 shows how a pulley is like a lever. The point in the middle of a pulley is like the fulcrum of a lever. The rest of the pulley behaves like the rigid arm of a first-class lever. Because the length from the fulcrum is the same on both sides of a fixed pulley, this kind of pulley has a mechanical advantage of one—it simply changes the direction of the force.

Using moving pulleys or more than one pulley at a time can increase the mechanical advantage, as **Figure 3** also shows. Multiple pulleys are sometimes combined into a single unit called a *block and tackle*.

✓ **Reading Check** What is the mechanical advantage of a single, fixed pulley?

A wheel and axle is a lever connected to a shaft.

The steering wheel of a car is another kind of simple machine: a wheel and axle. A wheel and axle is made of a lever or a pulley (the wheel) connected to a shaft (the axle), as shown in **Figure 4.** When the wheel is turned, the axle also turns. When a small input force is applied to the steering wheel, the force is multiplied to become a large output force applied to the steering column, which turns the front wheels of the car. Screwdrivers and cranks are other everyday wheel-and-axle machines.

440 Chapter 13 Work and Energy

QuickLab

A Simple Inclined Plane

⏱ 10 min

Procedure

1. Make an inclined plane out of a **board** and a stack of **books**.
2. Tie a **string** to an object that is heavy but has low friction, such as a metal **toy car** or a **roll of wire**. Use the string to pull the object up the plane.
3. Still using the string, try to lift the object straight up through the same distance.

Analysis

1. Which action required more force?
2. Which action required more work?

The Inclined Plane Family

Imagine that you need to load a piano into a moving van. Which will require more force: lifting the piano directly into the van or rolling the piano up a ramp? A ramp, such as the one in **Figure 5**, is an inclined plane, another kind of simple machine. ▶ **Pushing an object up an inclined plane requires less input force than lifting the same object does.**

The same amount of work must be done whether you lift something straight up or push it up a ramp. When you push an object up a ramp, you apply a force in the direction parallel to the ramp over the length of the ramp. When you lift something straight up, the force applied is perpendicular to the ground.

Pushing an object up a long, gradual ramp takes less force than pushing the object up a short, steep ramp. The mechanical advantage of an inclined plane is equal to the length of the inclined plane divided by the height to which the load is lifted.

Academic Vocabulary

require (ri KWIER) to need

Figure 5 An inclined plane reduces the force needed to lift an object by applying the force over a longer distance.

Section 2 Simple Machines **441**

Figure 6 A wedge turns a downward force into two forces directed out to the sides.

Integrating Social Studies

The ancient Egyptians built dozens of large stone pyramids as tombs for the bodies of kings and queens. The largest one is the pyramid of Khufu at Giza, or the Great Pyramid. It is made of more than 2 million blocks of stone. These blocks have an average weight of 2.5 tons, and the largest blocks weigh 15 tons. These blocks were lifted by using long inclined planes.

A wedge is a modified inclined plane.

When an ax blade or a splitting wedge hits a piece of wood, it pushes through and breaks apart the wood, as shown in **Figure 6.** An ax blade is an example of a wedge, another kind of simple machine in the inclined plane family. A wedge is formed of two inclined planes placed back to back. Using a wedge is like pushing a ramp instead of pushing something up a ramp. A wedge turns a single downward force into two forces directed out to the sides. Some kinds of wedges, such as nails, are used as fasteners.

A screw is an inclined plane wrapped around a cylinder.

A kind of simple machine that you probably use often is a screw. The threads on a screw look like a spiral inclined plane. In fact, a screw is an inclined plane wrapped around a cylinder. Like pushing something up a ramp, tightening a screw with gently sloping threads requires a small force to act over a long distance. Tightening a screw with steeper threads requires more force over less distance. A drill bit, such as the one shown in **Figure 7,** is another example of a screw. Jar lids are screws that people use every day. Spiral staircases are also everyday screws.

Reading Check What are two examples of a modified inclined plane?

Figure 7 If you could unwind a screw, you would see that it is an inclined plane wrapped around a cylinder. **How is a drill bit like a screw?**

442   Chapter 13   Work and Energy

Compound Machines

Many devices that you use every day are made of more than one simple machine. A **compound machine** is a machine that combines two or more simple machines. ▶ **A pair of scissors, for example, uses two first-class levers joined at a common fulcrum; each lever arm has a wedge that cuts into the paper.** Most car jacks use a lever in combination with a large screw.

Bicycles and cars are compound machines. How many simple machines can you identify in the bicycle shown in **Figure 8?** How many can you identify in a car?

compound machine (KAHM POWND muh SHEEN) a machine made of more than one simple machine

Figure 8 A bicycle is made of many simple machines.

Section 2 Review

KEY IDEAS

1. **List** the six types of simple machines.
2. **Identify** the kind of simple machine represented by each of the following examples:
   a. a drill bit
   b. a skateboard ramp
   c. a boat oar
3. **Describe** how a lever can increase the force applied without changing the amount of work being done.
4. **Explain** why pulleys are in the lever family.

CRITICAL THINKING

5. **Making Predictions** Can an inclined plane have a mechanical advantage of less than one? Explain.

6. **Interpreting Graphics** Study the lever drawn here. To which class of levers does this lever belong? Where is the output force?

7. **Applying Concepts** Explain why it is easier to open a door by pushing near the knob than to open a door by pushing near the hinges. To which class of levers does a door belong?

8. **Identifying Functions** Think of a compound machine that you use every day, and identify the simple machines that make it up.

Section 2   Simple Machines   **443**

SECTION 3
What Is Energy?

Key Ideas
> What is the relationship between energy and work?
> Why is potential energy called *energy of position*?
> What factors does kinetic energy depend on?
> What is nonmechanical energy?

Key Terms
energy
potential energy
kinetic energy
mechanical energy

Why It Matters
Some of the energy that reaches Earth from the sun is stored in plants. This energy is converted to work by the animals that consume plants.

The world around us is full of energy. Energy exists in many forms. A lightning bolt has electrical energy. A flashlight battery has chemical energy. A moving bicycle has mechanical energy. A rock sitting still on top of a mountain also has mechanical energy, simply because it could move downhill! We harness various forms of energy to power tools and machines, from flashlights to submarines.

Energy and Work

A moving object has **energy** associated with its motion. The mallet that the person in **Figure 1** is swinging has energy. When the mallet hits the lever, the mallet's energy is transferred to the puck, the puck rises to strike the bell, and the bell releases energy into the air as sound. Work has been done. > **Whenever work is done, energy is transformed or is transferred from one system to another system.** In fact, one definition of *energy* is "the ability to do work."

Energy is measured in joules.

Although work is done only when an object experiences a change in its position or its motion, energy can be present in an object or a system that is at rest. The energy in an object can be calculated whether the object is in motion or at rest. The transfer of energy from one object or system to another, such as the transfer of energy from the puck to the bell in **Figure 1,** can be measured by how much work is done on the receiving object. Because energy is the ability to do work, measurements of energy and work are expressed in the same units—joules.

Figure 1 The moving mallet has energy and can do work on the puck. The transfer of energy causes the puck to rise against gravity and ring the bell.

Potential Energy

When you stretch a rubber band, you do work. The energy used to stretch the rubber band is stored until you release the rubber band. When you release the rubber band, it flies from your hand. But where is the energy between the time you stretch the rubber band and the time you release the rubber band?

A stretched rubber band stores energy in a form called **potential energy.** **Potential energy (*PE*) is sometimes called *energy of position* because it results from the relative positions of objects in a system.** Any object that is stretched or compressed to increase or decrease the distance between its parts has potential energy that is called *elastic potential energy*. Stretched bungee cords and compressed springs have elastic potential energy.

Imagine that you are at the top of the first hill of the roller coaster shown in **Figure 2**. Your position above the ground gives you energy that could potentially do work as you move toward the ground. Any system of two or more objects separated by a vertical distance has potential energy that results from the gravitational attraction between the objects. This kind of stored energy is called *gravitational potential energy*.

Reading Check What kind of energy does a stretched rubber band have?

Figure 2 This roller coaster car has gravitational potential energy. This energy results from the gravitational attraction between the car and Earth.

energy (EN uhr jee) the capacity to do work

potential energy (poh TEN shuhl EN uhr jee) the energy that an object has because of the position, shape, or condition of the object

Gravitational potential energy depends on both mass and height.

An apple at the top of a tree has more gravitational potential energy with respect to the Earth than an apple of the same size on a lower branch does. But if two apples of different masses are at the same height, the heavier apple has more gravitational potential energy than the lighter one does.

Because it is caused by the force of gravity, gravitational potential energy near Earth depends on both the mass of the object and the height of the object relative to Earth's surface.

▶ **Gravitational potential energy equation**

grav. $PE = mass \times free\text{-}fall\ acceleration \times height$
$PE = mgh$

Notice that mg is the weight of the object in newtons, which is equal to the force on the object due to gravity. So, like work, gravitational potential energy is calculated by multiplying force and distance.

www.scilinks.org
Topic: Potential Energy
Code: HK81197

Height is relative.

The value for h in the equation for gravitational potential energy is often measured from the ground. But in some cases, a different height may be more important. For example, if an apple were about to fall into a bird's nest on a branch below the apple, the apple's height above the nest would be used to calculate the apple's potential energy with respect to the nest.

Math Skills: Potential Energy

A 65 kg rock climber ascends a cliff. What is the climber's gravitational potential energy at a point 35 m above the base of the cliff?

Identify
List the given and unknown values.

Given:
- mass, $m = 65$ kg
- height, $h = 35$ m
- free-fall acceleration, $g = 9.8$ m/s^2

Unknown:
- gravitational potential energy, $PE = ?$ J

Plan
Write the equation for gravitational potential energy.

grav. PE = mass × free-fall acceleration × height

$PE = mgh$

Solve
Insert the known values into the equation, and solve.

$PE = (65 \text{ kg})(9.8 \text{ m/s}^2)(35 \text{ m})$
$PE = 2.2 \times 10^4 \text{ kg} \cdot \text{m}^2/\text{s}^2 = 2.2 \times 10^4 \text{ J}$

Practice Hint

▶ Problem 2: The gravitational potential energy equation can be rearranged to isolate height on the left.

$mgh = PE$

Divide both sides by mg, and cancel.

$\frac{mgh}{mg} = \frac{PE}{mg}$

$h = \frac{PE}{mg}$

▶ Problem 3: Rearrange the equation to isolate mass on the left.

▶ When solving all of these problems, use $g = 9.8$ m/s^2.

Practice

1. Calculate the gravitational potential energy of the following:
   a. a 1,200 kg car at the top of a hill that is 42 m high
   b. a 65 kg climber on top of Mount Everest (8,800 m high)
   c. a 0.52 kg bird flying at an altitude of 550 m

2. A science student holds a 55 g egg out a window. Just before the student releases the egg, the egg has 8.0 J of gravitational potential energy with respect to the ground. How high is the student's arm above the ground, in meters? (Hint: Convert the mass to kilograms before solving.)

3. A diver has 3,400 J of gravitational potential energy after climbing up onto a diving platform that is 6.0 m above the water. What is the diver's mass in kilograms?

For more practice, visit go.hrw.com and enter keyword **HK8MP**.

Kinetic Energy

Once an object begins to move, it has the ability to do work. Consider an apple that falls from a tree. The apple can do work when it hits the ground or lands on someone's head. The energy that an object has because it is moving is called **kinetic energy.**

The kinetic energy (*KE*) of an object depends on the object's mass. A bowling ball can do more work than a table-tennis ball if both balls are moving at the same speed. The kinetic energy of the object also depends on the object's rate of acceleration. An apple that is falling at 10 m/s can do more work than an apple that is falling at 1 m/s. In fact, the kinetic energy of a moving object depends on the square of the object's speed. ❯ **Kinetic energy depends on both the mass and the speed of an object.**

kinetic energy (ki NET ik EN uhr jee) the energy of an object due to the object's motion

> **Kinetic energy equation**
>
> $\text{kinetic energy} = \frac{1}{2} \times \text{mass} \times \text{speed squared}$
>
> $KE = \frac{1}{2}mv^2$

Figure 3 shows a graph of kinetic energy versus speed for a snowboarding student who has a mass of 50 kg. Notice that kinetic energy is expressed in joules. Because kinetic energy is calculated by using mass and speed squared, kinetic energy is expressed in kilograms times meter squared per second squared (kg • m²/s²), which is equivalent to joules.

READING TOOLBOX

Mathematical Language Mathematical language is often used to describe physical quantities. What is meant by the phrase *speed squared*? Can you find other examples of mathematical language in this section?

✓ **Reading Check** What are the SI units for kinetic energy?

Figure 3 A small increase in speed causes a large increase in kinetic energy. Kinetic energy varies as the speed squared. **How would the kinetic energy of this snow boarder change if he were wearing a heavy backpack?**

Section 3 What Is Energy? **447**

www.scilinks.org
Topic: Kinetic Energy
Code: HK80833

Kinetic energy depends on speed more than it depends on mass.

You may have heard that car crashes are more dangerous at speeds above the speed limit than at the speed limit. The kinetic energy equation provides a scientific reason. In the kinetic energy equation, speed is squared, so a small change in speed causes a large change in kinetic energy. Because a car has much more kinetic energy at high speeds, it can do much more work—and thus much more damage—in a collision.

Atoms and molecules have kinetic energy.

Atoms and molecules are always moving. Therefore, these tiny particles have kinetic energy. The motion of particles is related to temperature. The higher the kinetic energy of the atoms and molecules in an object is, the higher the object's temperature is.

Math Skills Kinetic Energy

What is the kinetic energy of a 44 kg cheetah running at 31 m/s?

Identify
List the given and unknown values.

Given:
mass, $m = 44$ kg
speed, $v = 31$ m/s
Unknown:
kinetic energy, $KE = ?$ J

Plan
Write the equation for kinetic energy.

kinetic energy $= \frac{1}{2} \times$ mass $\times$ speed squared
$KE = \frac{1}{2} mv^2$

Solve
Insert the known values into the equation, and solve.

$KE = \frac{1}{2}(44 \text{ kg})(31 \text{ m/s})^2$
$KE = 2.1 \times 10^4$ kg • m²/s² $= 2.1 \times 10^4$ J

Practice Hint

> **Problem 2:** Rearrange the kinetic energy equation to isolate speed on the left. First, write the equation for kinetic energy.
> $$\frac{1}{2} mv^2 = KE$$
> Multiply both sides by $\frac{2}{m}$.
> $$\left(\frac{2}{m}\right) \times \frac{1}{2} mv^2 = \left(\frac{2}{m}\right) \times KE$$
> $$v^2 = \frac{2KE}{m}$$
> Take the square root of each side.
> $$\sqrt{v^2} = \sqrt{\frac{2KE}{m}}$$
> $$v = \sqrt{\frac{2KE}{m}}$$
>
> **Problem 3:** Rearrange the kinetic energy equation to isolate mass on the left:
> $$m = \frac{2KE}{v^2}$$

Practice

1. Calculate the kinetic energy in joules of a 1,500 kg car that is moving at a speed of 42 km/h. (Hint: Convert the speed to meters per second before substituting into the equation.)
2. A 35 kg child has 190 J of kinetic energy after he sleds down a hill. What is the child's speed at the bottom of the hill?
3. A bowling ball traveling 2.0 m/s has 16 J of kinetic energy. What is the mass of the bowling ball in kilograms?

For more practice, visit **go.hrw.com** and enter keyword **HK8MP**.

Other Forms of Energy

An apple that is falling from a tree has both kinetic and potential energy. The sum of the kinetic energy and the potential energy in a system is called **mechanical energy.** Mechanical energy can also be thought of as the amount of work that something can do because of its kinetic and potential energies.

An apple can give you energy when you eat it. What form of energy is that? In almost every system, there are hidden forms of energy that are related to the arrangement of atoms that make up the objects in the system.

▶ **Energy that lies at the level of the atom is sometimes called *nonmechanical energy*.** However, a close look at the different forms of energy in a system reveals that in most cases, nonmechanical forms of energy are just special forms of either kinetic or potential energy.

mechanical energy (muh KAN i kuhl EN uhr jee) the amount of work an object can do because of the object's kinetic and potential energies

Chemical reactions involve potential energy.

Chemical energy is a kind of potential energy. In a chemical reaction, bonds between atoms break apart. When the atoms form new bonds, a different substance is formed. Both the formation of bonds and the breaking of bonds involve changes in energy. The amount of *chemical energy* in a substance depends in part on the relative positions of the atoms in the substance.

Reactions that release energy decrease the potential energy in a substance. For example, when a match is struck, as shown in **Figure 4,** the release of stored energy from the match head produces light and a small explosion of hot gas.

Reading Check What does chemical energy depend on?

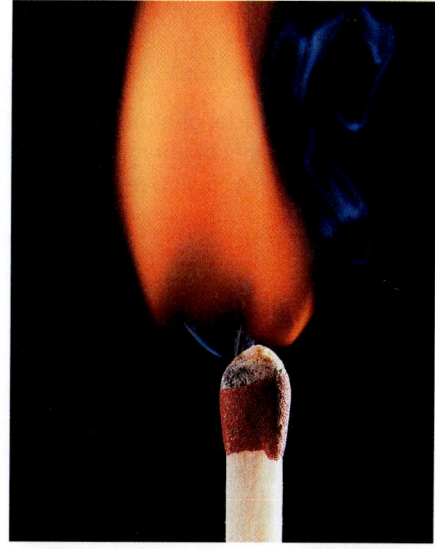

Figure 4 When a match is struck, the chemical energy stored inside the head of the match is released as light and heat.

Living things get energy from the sun.

Where does the lightning bug shown in **Figure 5** get the energy to glow? Where do you get the energy you need to live? The energy comes from food. When you eat a meal, you eat plants, animals, or both. Animals also eat plants, other animals, or both. Plants and algae do not need to eat, because they get their energy directly from sunlight.

Plants use *photosynthesis* to turn the energy in sunlight into chemical energy. This energy is stored in sugars and other organic molecules that make up cells in living tissue. Thus, when you eat a meal, you are really eating stored energy. When your body needs energy, some organic molecules are broken down through respiration. Respiration releases the energy your body needs in order to live and do work.

Figure 5 A lightning bug produces light through an efficient chemical reaction in its abdomen. Over 95% of the chemical energy is converted to light. **What other plants and animals produce light?**

Section 3 What Is Energy? **449**

The sun gets energy from nuclear reactions.

The sun, shown in **Figure 6,** not only gives energy to living things but also keeps our whole planet warm and bright. And the energy that reaches Earth from the sun is only a small portion of the sun's total energy output. How does the sun produce so much energy?

The sun's energy comes from nuclear fusion, a kind of reaction in which light atomic nuclei combine to form a heavier nucleus. This nuclear energy is a kind of potential energy stored by the forces holding subatomic particles together in the nuclei of atoms.

Nuclear power plants use a different process, called *nuclear fission,* to release nuclear energy. In fission, a single large nucleus is split into two or more smaller nuclei. In both fusion and fission, small quantities of mass are converted into large quantities of energy.

Energy can be stored in fields.

The lights and appliances in your home are powered by another form of energy, electrical energy. Electrical energy results from the location of charged particles in an *electric field.* An electric field is similar to a gravitational field. Certain places have high *electric potential,* while others have low electric potential. When electrons move from an area of higher electric potential to an area of lower electric potential, they gain energy. Moving electrons also create magnetic fields, which can do work to power a motor. Electrons moving through the air between the ground and a cloud cause the lightning shown in **Figure 7.**

Figure 6 The nuclei of atoms contain enormous amounts of energy. The sun is fueled by nuclear fusion reactions in its core.

Figure 7 Electrical energy is derived from the flow of charged particles, as in a bolt of lightning or in a wire. We can harness electricity to power appliances in our homes.

Why It Matters

Energy Stored in Plants

REAL WORLD

The sun floods Earth with a large amount of energy in the form of *electromagnetic radiation*. Nature has a unique way to store this energy from the sun. Green plants, algae, and some kinds of bacteria convert solar energy into chemical potential energy through the process of *photosynthesis*. Photosynthesis is a set of chemical reactions that use solar energy, carbon dioxide, and water to produce carbohydrates and oxygen. Chemical reactions in the bodies of animals and humans on Earth convert carbohydrates into work and thermal energy.

An average of 340 W/m² of energy from the sun reaches the surface of Earth. Some of that energy is stored as chemical energy in plants, and some of that energy is converted to thermal energy through the *greenhouse effect*.

The *Calorie* (or *kilocalorie*) is the most common measurement of food energy. One kilocalorie equals 4,186 J. A typical ear of corn has about 108 kcal, or 452 kJ, of energy.

When a plant is burned, the chemical energy that is stored in its cells is converted to thermal energy and light. Plants can also be converted to biofuels, such as ethanol or methane, and used as an energy source.

YOUR TURN

UNDERSTANDING CONCEPTS
1. How can you convert Calories to joules?

EVALUATING IDEAS
2. What are some of the advantages and disadvantages of using biofuels, such as ethanol and methane?

Figure 8 Electromagnetic waves carry energy from the sun to Earth. **Why is it cooler in the shade than in the sun?**

Light can carry energy across empty space.

Consider a bright summer day at a beach such as the one shown in **Figure 8.** Is it hotter where light is shining directly on the sand or under the shade of the umbrella? You might guess, correctly, that a seat in the direct sunlight is hotter. The reason is that light carries energy.

Light energy travels from the sun to Earth across empty space in the form of *electromagnetic waves.* Electromagnetic waves are made of electric and *magnetic fields,* so light energy is another example of energy stored in a field. You will learn more about light and waves in another chapter.

Section 3 Review

KEY IDEAS

1. **List** three forms of energy.
2. **Explain** how energy differs from work.
3. **Explain** the difference between potential energy and kinetic energy.
4. **Determine** what form or forms of energy apply to each of the following situations, and specify whether each form is mechanical or nonmechanical:
   a. a flying disk moving through the air
   b. a hot cup of soup
   c. a wound clock spring
   d. sunlight
   e. a boulder sitting at the top of a cliff

CRITICAL THINKING

5. **Applying Concepts** Water storage tanks are usually built on towers or placed on hilltops. Why?

6. **Analyzing Ideas** Name one situation in which gravitational potential energy might be useful, and name one situation in which it might be dangerous.

Math Skills

7. Calculate the gravitational potential energy of a 93.0 kg sky diver who is 550 m above the ground.
8. What is the kinetic energy of a 0.02 kg bullet that is traveling 300 m/s? Express your answer in joules.
9. Calculate the kinetic or potential energy in joules for each of the following situations:
   a. A 2.5 kg book is held 2.0 m above the ground.
   b. A 15 g snowball is moving through the air at 3.5 m/s.
   c. A 35 kg child is sitting at the top of a slide that is 3.5 m above the ground.
   d. An 8,500 kg airplane is flying at 220 km/h.

SECTION 4
Conservation of Energy

Key Ideas
- How does energy change?
- What is the law of conservation of energy?
- How much of the work done by a machine is actually useful work?

Key Terms
efficiency

Why It Matters
Hydroelectric power plants use conservation of energy to generate the electricity that you use every day.

Imagine that you are sitting in the front car of a roller coaster, such as the one shown in **Figure 1.** A conveyor belt pulls the car slowly up the first hill. When you reach the crest of the hill, you are barely moving. Then, you go over the edge and start to race down the hill. You speed faster and faster until you reach the bottom of the hill. The wheels are roaring along the track. You continue to move up, down, and around through smaller humps, twists, and turns. Finally, you climb another hill almost as big as the first, drop down again, and coast to the end of the ride.

Energy Transformations

In the course of a roller coaster ride, energy changes form many times. You may not have noticed the conveyor belt at the beginning, but in terms of energy input, the conveyor belt is the most important part of the ride. All of the energy required for the whole ride comes from work done by the conveyor belt as it lifts the cars and the passengers up the first hill.

The energy from that initial work is stored as gravitational potential energy at the top of the first hill. After that point, most of the energy goes through a series of transformations, or changes, turning into kinetic energy and then back into potential energy.

A small quantity of the stored energy is transferred to the wheels as heat and to the air as vibrations that make a roaring sound. ❯**Energy readily changes from one form to another.** But whatever forms the energy takes during a transformation, the total amount of energy always remains the same.

> Tennessee Course Level Expectations (Physical Science)
> CLE.3202.2.6; CLE.3202.4.3;
> CLE.3202.Inq.1; CLE.3202.Inq.2;
> CLE.3202.Inq.3; CLE.3202.Inq.4;
> CLE.3202.Inq.6; CLE.3202.Math.1;
> CLE.3202.Math.2; CLE.3202.TE.4

Figure 1 The Kingda Ka roller coaster, located in New Jersey, takes riders up 139 m and allows them to drop at near free-fall acceleration. **What forms of energy propel a roller coaster car?**

Section 4 Conservation of Energy **453**

Figure 2 The energy of a roller coaster car changes from potential energy to kinetic energy and back again many times during a ride.

Potential energy can become kinetic energy.

Compare the energy of a roller coaster car at the top of a hill with the car's energy at the bottom of a hill. As **Figure 2** shows, almost all of the energy of the roller coaster car is potential energy at the top of a tall hill. The potential energy slowly changes to kinetic energy as the car accelerates down the hill. At the bottom of the lowest hill, the car has the most kinetic energy and the least potential energy.

Notice that the system has the same total amount of energy whether the car is at the top or the bottom of the hill. All of the gravitational potential energy at the top changes to kinetic energy as the car goes down the hill. When the car reaches the lowest point, the system has no potential energy left. If all of the energy were to remain as mechanical energy, then the increase in kinetic energy would exactly equal the decrease in potential energy.

Reading Check Where on a roller coaster is the potential energy the least?

Kinetic energy can become potential energy.

When the car is at the lowest point on the roller coaster, its energy is almost all kinetic. This kinetic energy can do the work to carry the car up another hill. As the car climbs the hill, the car slows down and its kinetic energy decreases. Where does that energy go? Most of it turns back into potential energy.

At the top of a smaller hill, the car will still have some kinetic energy, along with some potential energy. The kinetic energy will carry the car forward over the top of the next hill. Of course, the roller coaster car cannot climb a hill that is taller than the first hill without an extra boost. The car does not have enough energy.

QuickLab

10 min

Energy Transfer

1. Flex a piece of **thick wire** or part of a **coat hanger** back and forth about 10 times with your hands.
2. After flexing the wire, cautiously touch the part of the wire where you bent it.
3. How does the wire feel? What happened to the energy you put into it? Did you do work?

454 Chapter 13 Work and Energy

Mechanical energy can change to other forms of energy.

If changes from potential energy to kinetic energy and back again were always complete, then balls would always bounce back to the same height from which they were dropped and cars on roller coasters could keep gliding forever. When a ball bounces on the ground, not all of its kinetic energy changes to elastic potential energy. Some of the kinetic energy compresses the air around the ball, which makes a sound, and some of the kinetic energy makes the ball, the air, and the ground a little warmer. As **Figure 3** shows, each time the ball bounces, it loses some mechanical energy.

Likewise, a moving roller coaster car loses mechanical energy as it rolls, because of friction and air resistance. This energy does not just disappear, though. Some of it increases the temperature of the track, the car's wheels, and the air. Some of the energy compresses the air and causes a roaring sound. Often, when energy seems to disappear, it is really just changing to a nonmechanical form.

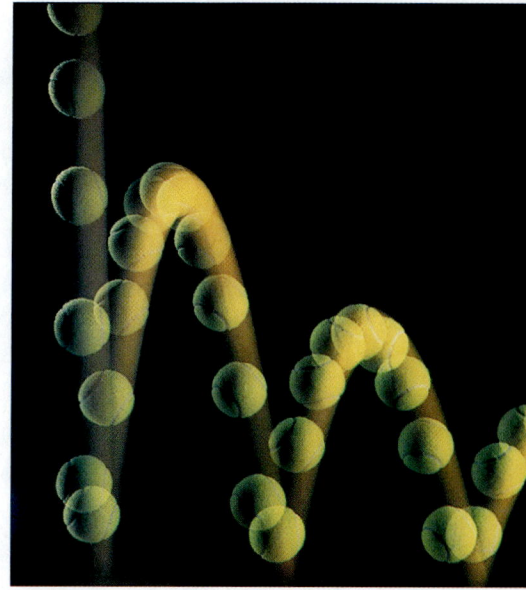

Figure 3 Each time a tennis ball bounces, some of its mechanical energy changes to nonmechanical energy.

Graphing Skills: Graphing Mechanical Energy

The bar graph shown here presents data about a roller coaster car. What variables are plotted? Identify the dependent and independent variables. What does the legend tell you about this graph?

Identify
Study the axes and legend to determine the variables.

Location is the variable on the *x*-axis. Two variables are plotted on the *y*-axis: kinetic and potential energy.

Plan
Consider the relationship between the variables.

The independent variable is location, because the car's kinetic energy and potential energy change with location.

Solve
Examine the legend and how it relates to the graph.

The legend indicates that the car's mechanical energy consists of both kinetic energy and potential energy.

Practice

1. At which location does the car have the greatest potential energy? At which location does the car have the least potential energy?
2. Given the data in this graph, can you calculate the car's speed?
3. What does this graph show about the relationship between potential energy and kinetic energy?

www.scilinks.org
Topic: Energy Transformations
Code: HK80517

When fireworks explode, potential energy is converted to many other forms of energy: kinetic energy, sound, light, and heat.

Midway through its path, the rocket has both potential and kinetic energy.

Figure 4 When it is on the ground, the fireworks rocket has chemical potential energy.

The Law of Conservation of Energy

In our study of machines, we saw that the work done on a machine is equal to the work that it can do. Similarly, in our study of the roller coaster, we found that the energy present at the beginning of the ride is present throughout the ride and at the end of the ride even though the energy changes form.

These simple observations are based on one of the most important principles in science—the law of conservation of energy. Here is the law in its simplest form.

| **Law of conservation of energy** | Energy cannot be created or destroyed. |

❯ **In other words, the total amount of energy in the universe never changes, although energy may change from one form to another.** Energy never disappears, but it does change form.

Energy does not appear or disappear.

Energy cannot be created from nothing. Imagine a girl jumping on a trampoline. If her second bounce is higher than her first bounce, we must conclude that she added energy to her bounce by doing work with her legs. Whenever the total energy in a system increases, the increase must be due to energy that enters the system.

Mechanical energy can change to nonmechanical energy through chemical reactions, air resistance, and other factors. Some of the energy in a system may leak out into the surrounding environment. When fireworks explode in a burst of heat, light, and sound, as shown in **Figure 4,** the conversion of energy is spectacular!

Thermodynamics describes energy conservation.

Energy can be transferred as work or as heat. For example, when you lift a ball, you give the ball potential energy. When you sand wood, the wood gets warm and energy is transferred as heat. ❯ **For any system, the net change in energy equals the energy transferred as work and as heat.** When no energy is transferred as heat or as work, mechanical energy is conserved. This form of the law of energy conservation is called the *first law of thermodynamics.*

Energy has many forms and can be found almost everywhere. Accounting for all of the energy in a given case can be complicated. To make studying a case easier, scientists often limit their view to a small area or a small number of objects. These boundaries define a system.

Systems may be open, closed or isolated.

A system in which energy and matter are exchanged with the surroundings is an *open* system. If energy, but not matter, is exchanged, the system is *closed*. An *isolated* system is one in which neither energy nor matter is exchanged. Imagine a beaker of water over a burner. If you considered only the flow of energy as the water was heated, it might seem like a closed system. But matter in the form of water vapor leaves the beaker, especially if the water is boiling. Thus, it is an open system.

Very few real-world systems are isolated systems. Most systems are open. Earth itself might be considered a closed system because its limited exchange of matter with outer space could be ignored. However, Earth receives energy from the sun that is reradiated to space. So Earth is not an isolated system.

Academic Vocabulary
ignore (ig NAWR) to refuse to notice

Reading Check What is the difference between an open system and a closed system?

Inquiry Lab: Is energy conserved by a pendulum? 30 min

Procedure

1. Hang a **pendulum bob** from a **string** in front of a **chalkboard** or a **white board.** On the board, draw the diagram shown in the photograph below. Use a **meterstick** and a **level** to make sure the horizontal line is parallel to the ground.

2. Pull the pendulum ball back to the "X." Make sure that everyone is out of the way. Release the pendulum. Mark how high the pendulum swings on the other side in the first swing.

3. Let the pendulum swing back and forth several times. How many swings does the pendulum make before the ball noticeably fails to reach its original height?

4. Stop the pendulum, and hold it again at the "X." Get another student to place the eraser end of a **pencil** on the intersection of the horizontal and vertical lines. Again, make sure that everyone, especially your helper, is out of the way.

5. Release the pendulum again. This time, its motion will be altered halfway through the swing as the string hits the pencil. How high does the pendulum swing now? Why?

6. Place the pencil at different heights along the vertical line. How is the motion of the pendulum affected? If you put the pencil down close enough to the arc of the pendulum, the pendulum will do a loop around the pencil. Explain why.?

Analysis

1. Use the law of conservation of energy to explain your observations in steps 2–6.

2. If you let the pendulum swing long enough, it will start to slow down and will not rise to the line anymore. Has the system lost energy? Where did the energy go?

Section 4 Conservation of Energy

Why It Matters

How Do Engineers Use Conservation of Energy?

REAL WORLD

Engineers take advantage of water that flows from higher to lower elevations to convert gravitational potential energy to electrical energy. Today, 11% of the electricity in the United States comes from hydroelectric power plants. At a hydroelectric plant, massive dams hold back running water and channel the water through large turbines attached to generators within the plant.

A generator is a machine that converts mechanical energy to electrical energy. Generators consist of conducting loops that move through a magnetic field. When a loop moves through a magnetic field, the law of conservation of energy guarantees that there will be an electric current.

❶ A water supply flows down the penstock from a reservoir that is held back by a dam.

❷ Flowing water turns the turbine, which then turns an electric generator.

❸ Water is discharged back into the river below the dam.

YOUR TURN

SUMMARIZING INFORMATION
1. Explain how electrical energy is generated from running water.

PREDICTING OUTCOMES
2. Does the discharged water have the same kinetic energy that it had going into the hydroelectric power plant?

Efficiency of Machines

If you use a pulley to raise a sail on a sailboat like the one in **Figure 5,** you have to do work against the force of friction in the pulley. You also must lift the added weight of the rope and the hook connected to the sail. As a result, only some of the energy that you transfer to the pulley is available to raise the sail. ❯ **Only a portion of the work done by any machine is *useful* work— that is, work that the machine is designed or intended to do.**

Not all of the work done by a machine is useful work.

Because of friction and other factors, only some of the work done by a machine is applied to the task at hand. The machine also does some incidental work that does not serve any intended purpose. There is a difference between the total work and the useful work done by a machine.

Even though all of the work done on a machine has some effect on the output work that the machine does, the output work may not be in the form that you expect. For example, because of friction, some of the energy applied to the pulley to lift the sail is transferred as heat that warms the pulley. This warming is not a desired effect. The amount of useful work might decrease slightly more if the pulley squeaks, because some energy is "lost" as it dissipates into forces that vibrate the pulley and the air to produce the squeaking sound.

✓ **Reading Check** What are some of the ways that energy is "lost" in machines?

Efficiency is the ratio of useful work out to work in.

The **efficiency** of a machine is a measure of how much useful work a machine can do. Efficiency is defined as the ratio of useful work output to total work input.

❯ **Efficiency equation**
$$\text{efficiency} = \frac{\text{useful work output}}{\text{work input}}$$

Efficiency is usually expressed as a percentage. To change an answer found by using the efficiency equation into a percentage, multiply the answer by 100 and then add the percent sign (%).

A machine that is 100% efficient would produce exactly as much useful work as the work done on the machine. Because every machine has some friction, no machine is 100% efficient. The useful work output of a machine never equals—and certainly cannot exceed—the work input.

Figure 5 The pulleys on a sailboat, like all machines, are less than 100% efficient.

efficiency (e FISH uhn see) a quantity, usually expressed as a percentage, that measures the ratio of useful work output to work input

Perpetual motion machines are impossible.

A machine designed to keep going forever without any input of energy is shown in **Figure 6.** Such a theoretical machine is called a *perpetual motion machine*. Many clever inventors have devoted a lot of time and effort to designing such a machine. But a perpetual motion machine could work only in the absence of friction and air resistance, a condition not found in this world.

Figure 6 Theoretically, a perpetual motion machine could keep going forever without any energy loss or energy input. **Why is a perpetual motion machine impossible?**

Math Skills Efficiency

A sailor uses a rope and an old, squeaky pulley to raise a sail that weighs 140 N. He finds that he must do 180 J of work on the rope to raise the sail by 1 m. (He does 140 J of work on the sail.) What is the efficiency of the pulley? Express your answer as a percentage.

Identify
List the given and unknown values.

Given:
work input = 180 J
useful work output = 140 J
Unknown:
efficiency = ? %

Plan
Write the equation for efficiency.

$$\text{efficiency} = \frac{\text{useful work output}}{\text{work input}}$$

Solve
Insert the known values into the equation, and solve.

$$\text{efficiency} = \frac{140 \text{ J}}{180 \text{ J}} = 0.78$$

To express this number as a percentage, multiply by 100 and add the percent sign (%).
$$\text{efficiency} = 0.78 \times 100 = 78\%$$

Practice Hint

> The efficiency equation can be rearranged to isolate any of the variables on the left.
> Problem 2: Rearrange the efficiency equation to isolate work input on the left side.
> Problem 3: Rearrange the efficiency equation to isolate useful work output.
> When using these rearranged forms to solve the problems, you will have to plug in values for efficiency. When doing so, do not use a percentage. Instead, convert the percentage to a decimal by dropping the percent sign and dividing by 100.

Practice

1. Alice and Jim calculate that they must do 1,800 J of work to push a piano up a ramp. However, because they must also overcome friction, they actually must do 2,400 J of work. What is the efficiency of the ramp?
2. It takes 1,200 J of work to lift a car high enough to change a tire. How much work must be done by the person operating the jack if the jack is 25% efficient?
3. A windmill has an efficiency of 37.5%. If a gust of wind does 125 J of work on the blades of the windmill, how much output work can the windmill do as a result of the gust?

For more practice, visit **go.hrw.com** and enter keyword **HK8MP**.

Machines need energy input.

Because energy always leaks out of a system, a machine such as the solar car in **Figure 7** needs at least a small amount of energy input to keep going. But new technologies, from magnetic trains to high-speed microprocessors, reduce the amount of energy that leaks from systems so that energy can be used as efficiently as possible.

Figure 7 This solar electric car converts solar energy to electrical energy and converts electrical energy to mechanical energy and work.

Section 4 Review

KEY IDEAS

1. **List** three cases in which potential energy becomes kinetic energy and three cases in which kinetic energy becomes potential energy.
2. **State** the law of conservation of energy in your own words. Give an example of a situation that you have either encountered or know about in which the law of conservation of energy is demonstrated.
3. **Explain** why machines are never 100% efficient.
4. **Describe** the rise and fall of a thrown basketball by using the concepts of kinetic energy and potential energy.

CRITICAL THINKING

5. **Creative Thinking** Using what you have learned about energy transformations, explain why the driver of a car has to continuously apply pressure to the gas pedal in order to keep the car cruising at a steady speed, even on a flat road. Does this situation violate the law of conservation of energy? Explain.

6. **Applying Knowledge** Use the concepts of kinetic energy and potential energy to describe the motion of a child on a swing. Why does the child need a push from time to time?

Math Skills

7. When you do 100 J of work on the handle of a bicycle pump, the pump does 40 J of work pushing the air into the tire. What is the efficiency of the pump?
8. A river does 6,500 J of work on a water wheel every second. The wheel's efficiency is 12%.
   a. How much work in joules can the axle of the wheel do?
   b. What is the power output of the wheel in 1 s?
9. John is using a pulley to lift the sail on his sailboat. The sail weighs 150 N, and he must lift it 4.0 m.
   a. How much work must be done on the sail?
   b. If the pulley is 50% efficient, how much work must John do on the rope to lift the sail?

Skills Practice Lab

Energy of a Rolling Ball

Raised objects have gravitational potential energy. Moving objects have kinetic energy. In this lab, you will find out how these two kinds of energy are related in a system in which a ball rolls down a ramp.

⏱ 50 min

Objectives
- **Measure** the height, distance traveled, and time interval for a ball rolling down a ramp.
- **Calculate** the ball's potential energy at the top of the ramp and its kinetic energy at the bottom of the ramp.
- **Analyze** the results to find the relationship between potential energy and kinetic energy.

Materials
balance
board, at least 90 cm (3 ft) long
box
golf ball, racquet ball, or handball
masking tape
meterstick
stack of books, at least 45 cm high
stopwatch

Procedure

Preparing for Your Experiment

1. On a blank sheet of paper, prepare a table like the one shown below.

Sample Data Table: Potential Energy and Kinetic Energy

	Height 1	Height 2	Height 3
Mass of ball (kg)			
Length of ramp (m)			
Height of ramp (m)			
Time ball traveled, first trial (s)			
Time ball traveled, second trial (s)			
Time ball traveled, third trial (s)			
Average time ball traveled (s)			
Average speed of ball (m/s)			
Final speed of ball (m/s)			
Final kinetic energy of ball (J)			
Initial potential energy of ball (J)			
Initial PE − Final KE (J)			

DO NOT WRITE IN BOOK

2. Measure the mass of the ball, and record it in your table.
3. Place a strip of masking tape across the board close to one end, and measure the distance from the tape to the opposite end of the board. Record this distance in the row labeled "Length of ramp."
4. Make a catch box by cutting out one side of a box.
5. Make a stack of books approximately 15 cm high. Build a ramp like the one shown in the photograph by setting the taped end of the board on top of the books. Place the other end of the board in the catch box. Measure the vertical height of the ramp at the tape, and record this value in your table in the row labeled "Height of ramp."

Making Time Measurements

6 Place the ball on the ramp at the tape. Release the ball, and use a stopwatch to measure how long the ball takes to travel to the bottom of the ramp. Record the time in your table.

7 Repeat step 6 two times, and record the results in your table. After three trials, calculate the average travel time, and record it in your table.

8 Using a stack of books that is approximately 30 cm high, repeat steps 5–7. Using a stack that is approximately 45 cm high, repeat the steps again.

Analysis

1. **Analyzing Data** Calculate the average speed of the ball by using the following equation:

$$\text{average speed} = \frac{\text{length of ramp}}{\text{average time ball traveled}}$$

Multiply the average speed by 2 to obtain the final speed of the ball, and record the final speed.

2. **Analyzing Data** Calculate the final kinetic energy of the ball by using the equation below. Record this value in your table.

$$KE = \frac{1}{2} \times \text{mass of ball} \times (\text{final speed})^2$$

$$KE = \frac{1}{2} mv^2$$

3. **Analyzing Data** Calculate and record the initial potential energy of the ball by using the following equation:

$$\text{grav. } PE = \text{mass of ball} \times (9.8 \text{ m/s}^2) \times \text{height of ramp}$$

$$PE = mgh$$

Communicating Your Results

4. **Making Comparisons** For each of the three heights, compare the ball's potential energy at the top of the ramp with the ball's kinetic energy at the bottom of the ramp.

5. **Drawing Conclusions** How did the values for the ball's potential and kinetic energy change as the height of the ramp was increased?

Extension

Suppose that you perform this experiment and find that the values for kinetic energy are always just a little less than the values for potential energy. Did you do the experiment wrong? Why or why not?

Making Measurements and Observations

Science > Skills

Technology
Math
▶ **Scientific Methods**
Graphing

Observations and measurements are at the heart of science. We get *qualitative* information about the physical world with observations, and we gather *quantitative* information with measurements.

❶ Start with General Observations
Science starts with observations. Observations help you to form questions and hypotheses that you can test. Write down all your observations and measurements in a notebook. Detailed records help you to remember what you did and saw and help others to reproduce the work.

- Observation: Mom fills up the tank of her pickup truck more often than Dad fills up his compact car.
- Observation: Both Mom and Dad drive about the same amount.
- Hypothesis: Dad's car has better gas mileage than Mom's truck.

❷ Plan Measurements and Choose Instruments
Decide what measurements are necessary to test your hypothesis. Choose the instruments you will need for the measurements. You should also plan for any calculations you will need to make. It is often useful to create a data table to record your measurements.

- Measurements: distance traveled and fuel used
- Instruments: odometers of vehicles; meters on gas pumps
- Calculations:
  $$\text{mileage} = \frac{\text{distance traveled}}{\text{fuel used}}$$

❸ Make Multiple Measurements
If possible, make multiple measurements, and then calculate an average.

- Record 10 fills for each vehicle.
- Add all 10 mileage values for each vehicle, then divide by the total gas used.

❹ Avoid Measurement Pitfalls
Try to keep all variables constant except for those you are testing. Be careful to avoid errors when reading instruments. Read any available instructions on calibrating and reading instruments properly.

- Use the same grade of gasoline in both cars.
- Always fill the tank until the pump stops itself.
- If possible, use the same gas pump every time.

Practice

1. Suppose you want to find out how long it takes you to accelerate from rest to a speed of 30 miles per hour on your bicycle. Work through the steps above to plan this measurement.

2. Suppose you want to compare the cycling speeds of your little brother and your little sister. You want to know which one can ride a distance of one block in the shortest time. Would you do this with measurements or with observations? Explain.

CHAPTER 13 Summary

Key Ideas

Key Terms

Section 1 Work, Power, and Machines

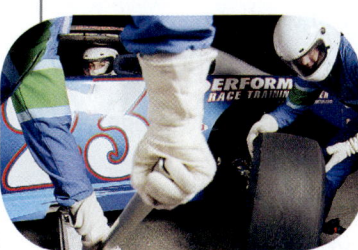

- **What Is Work?** Work is done when a force causes an object to change its motion or position. (p. 431)
- **Power** Power is the rate that work is done. (p. 433)
- **Machines and Mechanical Advantage** Machines change the size and/or direction of forces. (p. 434)

work, p. 431
power, p. 433
mechanical advantage, p. 436

Section 2 Simple Machines

- **What Are Simple Machines?** The lever, pulley, wheel and axle, inclined plane, wedge, and screw are simple machines. (p. 438)
- **The Lever Family** Levers have a rigid arm. (p. 439)
- **The Inclined Plane Family** Inclined planes turn a small input force into a large output force. (p. 441)
- **Compound Machines** Compound machines are made of two or more simple machines. (p. 443)

simple machine, p. 438
compound machine, p. 443

Section 3 What Is Energy?

- **Energy and Work** Whenever work is done, energy is transformed or transferred. (p. 444)
- **Potential Energy** Potential energy results from the relative positions of objects in a system. (p. 445)
- **Kinetic Energy** Kinetic energy depends on both mass and speed. (p. 447)
- **Other Forms of Energy** Nonmechanical energy occurs on the level of atoms. (p. 449)

energy, p. 444
potential energy, p. 445
kinetic energy, p. 447
mechanical energy, p. 449

Section 4 Conservation of Energy

- **Energy Transformations** Energy readily changes from one form to another. (p. 453)
- **The Law of Conservation of Energy** Energy can never be created or destroyed. (p. 456)
- **Efficiency of Machines** A machine can't do more work than the work required to operate it. (p. 459)

efficiency, p. 459

CHAPTER 13 Review

READING TOOLBOX

1. Write one sentence using the word *work* in the scientific sense, and write another sentence using the word in a nonscientific sense. Explain the difference in the meaning of *work* in the two sentences.

USING KEY TERMS

2. For each of the following, state whether the system contains primarily *kinetic energy* or *potential energy*:
   a. a stone in a stretched slingshot
   b. a speeding race car
   c. water above a hydroelectric dam

3. How is *energy* related to *work, force,* and *power*?

4. List several examples that show how *electrical energy* and *light energy* are useful to you.

5. Name three *simple machines* that make up a can opener, which is a *compound machine*.

UNDERSTANDING KEY IDEAS

6. _____ is defined as force times distance.
   a. Power   c. Work
   b. Energy   d. Potential energy

7. The quantity that measures how much a machine multiplies force is called
   a. mechanical advantage.
   b. leverage.
   c. efficiency.
   d. power.

8. The unit that represents 1 J of work done each second is the
   a. power.   c. watt.
   b. newton.   d. mechanical advantage.

9. Which of the following phrases describes a situation in which potential energy is *not* changed into kinetic energy?
   a. an apple falling from a tree
   b. a dart being shot from a spring-loaded gun
   c. the string of a bow being pulled back
   d. a creek flowing downstream

10. _____ is determined by both mass and velocity.
    a. Work   c. Potential energy
    b. Power   d. Kinetic energy

11. Energy that does not involve the large-scale motion or the position of objects in a system is called
    a. potential energy.
    b. mechanical energy.
    c. nonmechanical energy.
    d. conserved energy.

12. A machine cannot
    a. change the direction of a force.
    b. multiply or increase a force.
    c. redistribute work.
    d. increase the total amount of work done.

13. A machine that has a mechanical advantage of less than one
    a. increases speed and distance.
    b. multiplies force.
    c. increases output force.
    d. reduces distance and speed.

14. Which of these statements describes the law of conservation of energy?
    a. No machine is 100% efficient.
    b. Energy is neither created nor destroyed.
    c. The energy resources of Earth are limited.
    d. The energy of a system is always decreasing.

466 Chapter 13 Work and Energy

EXPLAINING KEY IDEAS

15. Use the law of conservation of energy to explain why the work output of a machine can never exceed the work input.

16. If a machine cannot multiply the amount of work, what is the advantage of using a machine?

17. You are trying to pry the lid off a paint can by using a screwdriver, but the lid will not budge. Should you try using a shorter screwdriver or a longer screwdriver? Explain.

18. Many fuels come from fossilized plant and animal matter. How is energy stored in these fuels? How do you think that energy got into the fuels in the first place?

CRITICAL THINKING

19. **Analyzing Information** If a bumper car triples its speed, how much more work can it do on a bumper car at rest? (Hint: Use the equation for kinetic energy.)

20. **Drawing Conclusions** You are attempting to move a large rock by using a long lever. Will the work you do on the lever be greater than, the same as, or less than the work the lever does on the rock? Explain your answer.

21. **Predicting Outcomes** You are designing a roller coaster ride in which a car will be pulled to the top of a hill and then will be released to roll freely down the hill and up again toward the top of the next hill. The next hill is twice as high. Will your design be successful? Explain.

22. **Applying Knowledge** In two or three sentences, explain the force-distance trade-off that occurs when a machine is used to make work easier. Use the lever as an example of one type of trade-off.

Graphing Skills

23. **Interpreting Graphics** The diagram below shows five points on a roller coaster.

a. List the points in order from the point where the car has the greatest potential energy to the point where the car has the least potential energy.
b. Now, list the points in order from the point where the car has the greatest kinetic energy to the point where the car has the least kinetic energy.
c. How do your two lists relate to each other?

Math Skills

24. You and two friends apply a force of 425 N to push a piano up a 2.0 m long ramp.
   a. **Work** How much work, in joules, has been done when you reach the top of the ramp?
   b. **Power** If you make it to the top in 5.0 s, what is your power output in watts?
   c. **Mechanical Advantage** If lifting the piano straight up requires 1,700 N of force, what is the mechanical advantage of the ramp?

25. A crane uses a block and tackle to lift a 2,200 N flagstone to a height of 25 m.
   a. **Work** How much work is done on the flagstone?
   b. **Efficiency** The crane's hydraulic motor does 110 kJ of work on the cable in the block and tackle. What is the efficiency of the block and tackle?
   c. **Potential Energy** When the flagstone is 25 m above the ground, what is its potential energy?

Standardized Test Prep

Understanding Concepts

Directions (1–4): *For each question, write on a sheet of paper the letter of the correct answer.*

1. What type of simple machine turns a downward force into two forces directed out to the sides?
   - **A.** lever
   - **B.** screw
   - **C.** wedge
   - **D.** pulley

2. The mass of a penny is 2.5 g. If the penny is held out a window on one of the upper floors of the Empire State Building, 350 m off the ground, what is the gravitational potential energy of the penny with respect to the ground?
   - **F.** 0.875 J
   - **G.** 8.575 J
   - **H.** 140 J
   - **I.** 875 J

3. What type of potential energy is stored within food and used by the consumer of the food?
   - **A.** elastic energy
   - **B.** chemical energy
   - **C.** mechanical energy
   - **D.** gravitational energy

4. A veterinarian picks up a small dog from the floor and places it on the operating table. If the dog weighs 80 N and the operating table is 1.25 m high, how much work does the veterinarian do?
   - **F.** 64 W
   - **G.** 64 J
   - **H.** 100 W
   - **I.** 100 J

Directions (5-6): *For each question, write a short response.*

5. If a motorcycle with a mass of 250 kg has a kinetic energy of 200,000 J, what is the motorcycle's speed in m/s?

6. The pull of gravity (g) on Mars is 3.7 m/s². If an astronaut on Mars lifts a 10 kg rock 1 m off the ground, just to see what's under it, how much work has the astronaut performed?

Reading Skills

Directions (7-9): **Read the passage below. Then, answer the questions that follow.**

PYRAMID POWER

One of the most ancient and amazing architectural creations in the world is the Great Pyramid of Egypt. This structure consists of several million rectangular blocks, each weighing an average of 2.5 tons.

The pyramid was assembled by using simple machines. Ramps made of wood, rock, and mud were most likely used to raise the blocks. Although the slope of a single ramp would be too steep to move such heavy objects, the workers may have used a series of smaller ramps.

Another possibility is that the gigantic blocks were moved by using a pulley connected to a counterweight set on a sloping ramp on the other side of the Pyramid. When the counterweight was set, it would be attached to a heavy block and released. The lowering of the counterweight would raise the massive block.

7. What two simple machines may have been used to construct the Great Pyramid?
   - **A.** lever and pulley
   - **B.** lever and inclined plane
   - **C.** pulley and wedge
   - **D.** pulley and inclined plane

8. 100 workers pull a 3 ton block to 100 m high using a ramp with a mechanical advantage of 4. With each heave, each worker does 50 J of net work. How many heaves will it take for the workers to pull the block all the way up the ramp? (Note: 1 ton = 8,896 newtons.)
   - **F.** 14 heaves
   - **G.** 134 heaves
   - **H.** 1,335 heaves
   - **I.** 13,344 heaves

9. Why would a long series of gradual ramps be better than one short, steep ramp for moving heavy blocks of stone?

Interpreting Graphics

The following diagram shows the complete arc of one swing of a pendulum. Use this diagram to answer questions 10–11.

ARC OF A PENDULUM

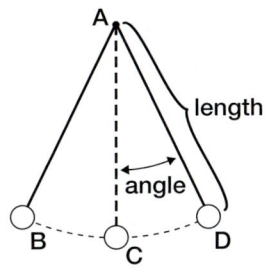

10. Where does the pendulum weight have the greatest gravitational potential energy?
   A. A
   B. A and C
   C. C
   D. B and D

11. Where does the pendulum weight have the greatest kinetic energy?
   F. A
   G. A and C
   H. C
   I. B and D

On a distant planet, an extraterrestrial fruit falls from a tree. We know the gravitational potential energy of the alien fruit at point A and its velocity at point B. Use this graphic to answer questions 12–13.

FREE FALL ON AN ALIEN PLANET

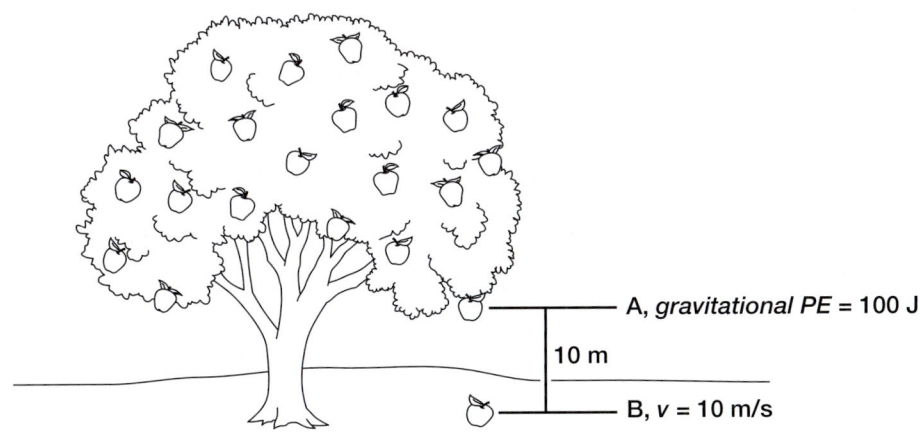

12. What is the mass of the alien fruit?
   A. 1 kg
   B. 2 kg
   C. 5 kg
   D. 10 kg

13. What is the free-fall acceleration of the alien planet?

> **Test Tip**
>
> Test questions may not be arranged in order of increasing difficulty. If you are unable to answer a question, mark it and move on to another question.

Standardized Test Prep **469**

CHAPTER 14
Heat and Temperature

Chapter Outline

1 Temperature
Temperature and Energy
Temperature Scales
Relating Temperature to Energy Transfer

2 Energy Transfer
Methods of Energy Transfer
Conductors and Insulators
Specific Heat

3 Using Heat
Laws of Thermodynamics
Heat Engines

Tennessee Course Level Expectations (Physical Science)

CLE.3202.TE.1 Explore the impact of technology on social, political, and economic systems; **CLE.3202.TE.3** Explain the relationship between the properties of a material and the use of the material in the application of a technology; **CLE.3202.2.1** Investigate the properties and behaviors of mechanical and electromagnetic waves; **CLE.3202.2.3** Examine the applications and effects of heat energy; **CLE.3202.Inq.1** Recognize that science is a progressive endeavor that reevaluates and extends what is already accepted; **CLE.3202.Inq.2** Design and conduct scientific investigations to explore new phenomena, verify previous results, test how well a theory predicts, and compare opposing theories; **CLE.3202.Inq.3** Use appropriate tools and technology to collect precise and accurate data; **CLE.3202.Inq.4** Apply qualitative and quantitative measures to analyze data and draw conclusions that are free of bias; **CLE.3202.Inq.6** Communicate and defend scientific findings; **CLE.3202.Math.1** Understand the mathematical principles behind the science of physics; **CLE.3202.Math.2** Utilize appropriate mathematical equations and processes to solve basic physics problems; **CLE.3202.TE.2** Differentiate among elements of the engineering design cycle: design constraints, model building, testing, evaluating, modifying, and retesting; **CLE.3202.TE.4** Describe the dynamic interplay among science, technology, and engineering within living, earth-space, and physical systems.

Why It Matters
We want to keep our houses at a comfortable temperature and to do so as cheaply as possible. The white and red areas on this thermogram show where energy, as heat, is escaping from a house. These areas show where the house needs to be better insulated so that heating energy is not wasted.

Inquiry Lab
⏱ 20 min

Color and Temperature

Use a **prism** to separate a beam of sunlight into its component colors, and project these colors onto a **sheet of paper**. Use a **thermometer** to record the temperature of the air in the room, and then place the thermometer bulb in each colored band for 3 min. Record the final temperature of each colored band. Place the thermometer bulb for 3 min on the dark side of the red band, where infrared radiation is found.

Questions to Get You Started

1. What patterns do you notice in the differences in the final temperature readings among the bands?
2. What do your results suggest about why infrared radiation is associated with hot objects?

READING TOOLBOX

These reading tools can help you learn the material in this chapter. For more information on how to use these and other tools, see **Appendix A**.

Word Families

Prefixes and Suffixes What do you think of when you hear the word *thermal*? You may think of the word *thermos* or perhaps the phrase *thermal blanket*. The noun *thermal* means "a current of warm air." What do these words or phrases have in common? They are related to heat or temperature. These words or phrases have a common root, *thermo-*, which means "heat" or "hot."

Your Turn On a separate sheet of paper, start a table like the one below. As you read the chapter, find words that contain the root *thermo-* and make entries in the table for them.

WORD	ROOT	PREFIX OR SUFFIX	DEFINITION
thermometer	thermo-	-meter	a device that measures temperature

Comparisons

Comparison Table When you are comparing two things, you can describe how they are similar or how they are different.

- Often, a comparison describes one thing as *greater than* or *less than* another thing in some way.
- A single comparative word can also be used to make comparisons. Comparative words use the suffixes *-er* or *-est*.
- Comparative phrases may use the words *more* or *less*.

Your Turn As you read this chapter, fill out a comparison table like the one below. Each row of the table should list the things being compared and the word or phrase that indicates a comparison.

FIRST THING	COMPARISON WORD OR PHRASE	SECOND THING
air near the equator	hotter than	air near the poles

Graphic Organizers

Flow Chart Graphic Organizers are drawings that you can make to help you organize the concepts that you learn. A flow chart is a Graphic Organizer that shows the order and direction of the steps in a process.

Your Turn As you read Section 3, create your own flow chart for the cycle of an internal-combustion engine. At right is an example to get you started.

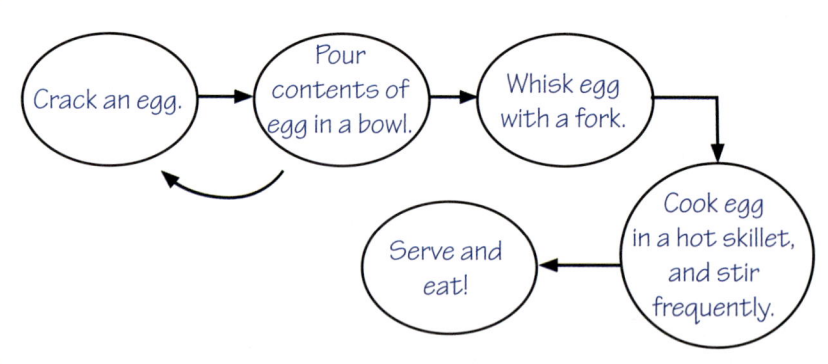

SECTION 1 Temperature

Key Ideas

> What does temperature have to do with energy?
> What three temperature scales are commonly used?
> What makes things feel hot or cold?

Key Terms

temperature
thermometer
absolute zero
heat

Why It Matters

We control temperatures for many reasons, such as keeping ourselves comfortable.

When you touch the hood of an automobile, you sense how hot or cold the car is. In everyday life, we sometimes call this feeling of hot or cold the *temperature* of an object. However, the words *hot* and *cold* serve only as rough indicators of temperature. Temperature itself is closely related to energy.

Temperature and Energy

People use **temperature** readings, such as the ones shown in **Figure 1,** to make many kinds of decisions every day. You check the temperature of the air outside to decide what to wear. To find out if a roasting turkey is done, a cook checks its temperature. You take your temperature to find out if you are ill. In all these cases, what is actually being measured is kinetic energy. > **The temperature of a substance is proportional to the average kinetic energy of the substance's particles.**

Tennessee Course Level Expectations (Physical Science)

CLE.3202.Inq.1; CLE.3202.Inq.2; CLE.3202.Inq.3; CLE.3202.Math.1; CLE.3202.Math.2

temperature (TEM puhr uh chuhr) a measure of how hot (or cold) something is; specifically, a measure of the average kinetic energy of the particles in an object

Figure 1 Many decisions are made based on temperature.

QuickLab

Sensing Hot and Cold

 20 min

Procedure

1. Gather small pieces of the following materials: **metal, wood, plastic foam, rock, plastic,** and **cardboard.** Allow the materials to sit untouched on a table for a few minutes.

2. For each of the materials, put the palms of your hands on the material until you can tell how cool or warm it feels. List the materials in order from coolest to warmest.

3. Place a **thermometer strip** on the surface of each material. Record the temperature of each material.

Analysis

1. Which material felt the warmest to your hands? Which material had the highest temperature?

2. Why do you think some materials felt warmer than others? Was your hand a good thermometer? Explain.

All particles have kinetic energy.

All particles in a substance are constantly moving. Like all moving objects, each particle has kinetic energy. Temperature is related to the kinetic energy of particles.

As the average kinetic energy of the particles in an object increases, the object's temperature increases. The particles in a hot car hood move faster than particles in a cool car hood because the hot particles have more kinetic energy. But how do we measure the temperature of an object? It is impossible to find the kinetic energy of every particle in an object and calculate their average energy. Actually, there is a very simple way to measure temperature directly.

✓ **Reading Check** How is the temperature of a substance related to the kinetic energy of the particles in the substance? (See Appendix E for answers to Reading Checks.)

Common thermometers rely on expansion.

To measure temperature, we use a simple physical property of substances: Most substances expand when their temperatures increase. **Thermometers,** such as the one shown in **Figure 2,** use the expansion of liquids such as mercury or colored alcohol to measure temperature. These liquids expand as their temperature increases and contract as their temperature falls.

As the temperature rises, the particles in the liquid inside a thermometer gain kinetic energy and move faster. With this increased motion, the particles in the liquid move farther apart. So, the liquid expands and rises up the narrow tube.

---

thermometer
(thuhr MAHM uht uhr) an instrument that measures and indicates temperature

Figure 2 This thermometer uses the expansion of a liquid, colored alcohol in this case, to indicate changes in temperature.

Thermostats rely on the expansion of different metals.

Most metals also expand when heated and contract when cooled. This turns out to be a useful property in making thermometers that are part of household appliances.

The thermometer inside a thermostat is based on the expansion of metal, as shown in **Figure 3.** The thermometer contains a coil made from two different metal strips pressed together. Both strips expand and contract at different rates as the temperature changes. As the temperature falls, the coil unwinds and moves the pointer to the new temperature mark. As the temperature rises, the coil winds up and moves the pointer in the opposite direction.

Figure 3 Inside a thermostat, a coil made of two different metal strips expands and contracts in response to the temperature.

Temperature Scales

Suppose you hear someone say that it is 37 degrees outside. How do you know whether to wear a sweater or a T-shirt? On the Fahrenheit temperature scale, 37 degrees is just above freezing. But on the Celsius scale, this temperature would mean that it is very hot outside! ▶ **The Fahrenheit, Celsius, and Kelvin temperature scales are commonly used for different applications in different parts of the world.**

The Fahrenheit and Celsius scales are two different temperature scales.

The units on the Fahrenheit scale are called *degrees Fahrenheit* (°F). On the Fahrenheit scale, water freezes at 32 °F and boils at 212 °F.

Most countries other than the United States use the Celsius scale. This scale is also the one that is widely used in science. The Celsius scale gives a value of 0 °C to the freezing point of water and a value of 100 °C to the boiling point of water at standard atmospheric pressure. The difference between these two points is divided into 100 equal parts, called *degrees Celsius* (°C).

One degree Celsius is equal to 1.8 degrees Fahrenheit. Also, the temperature at which water freezes differs for the two scales by 32 degrees. To convert from one scale to the other, use one of the following formulas.

READING TOOLBOX

Word Families
The word *thermostat* begins with the root *therm-*. What do you think the root *stat-* means, based on what the root *therm-* means and what a thermostat does?

▶ **Fahrenheit-Celsius conversion equations**

Fahrenheit temperature = (1.8 × Celsius temperature) + 32.0

$$T_F = 1.8 T_C + 32.0$$

Celsius temperature = $\dfrac{\text{Fahrenheit temperature} - 32.0}{1.8}$

$$T_C = \dfrac{T_F - 32.0}{1.8}$$

The Kelvin scale is based on absolute zero.

You have probably heard of negative temperatures, such as those reported on very cold winter days in the northern United States and Canada. Remember that temperature is a measure of the average kinetic energy of the particles in an object. Even far below 0 °C, these particles are still moving, so they have some kinetic energy. But how low can the temperature fall? The theoretically lowest temperature is –273.15 °C and is called **absolute zero.** At a temperature of absolute zero, the kinetic energy of an object would be zero.

Some recent experiments have reached temperatures that are very close to absolute zero. Matter behaves very differently at these extremely low temperatures. Absolute zero can never be reached, however, because particles never completely stop moving.

Figure 4 Temperature can be converted from one of the three temperature scales—Fahrenheit, Celsius, and Kelvin—to another. **How does the Kelvin scale differ from the other two temperature scales?**

Absolute zero is the basis for the Kelvin temperature scale. On this scale, 0 kelvin, or 0 K, is absolute zero. Because the theoretically lowest temperature is given a value of zero, there are no negative temperature values on the Kelvin scale. The Kelvin scale is used in many fields of science, especially those involving low temperatures. The three temperature scales are compared in **Figure 4.**

One kelvin is equal to one degree on the Celsius scale. The only difference between the two scales is the way that *zero* is defined. To approximate any temperature in kelvins, just add 273 to the same temperature in degrees Celsius. The equation for this conversion is given below.

absolute zero (AB suh LOOT ZIR oh) the temperature at which molecular energy is at a minimum (0 K on the Kelvin scale or –273.15 °C on the Celsius scale)

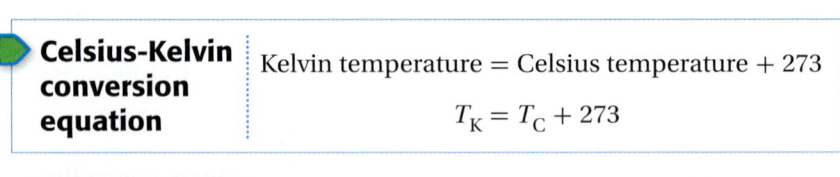

Celsius-Kelvin conversion equation

Kelvin temperature = Celsius temperature + 273

$$T_K = T_C + 273$$

Reading Check What is the difference between the Celsius and Kelvin temperature scales?

Math Skills: Temperature-Scale Conversion

The highest temperature ever recorded in Earth's atmosphere was 57.8 °C at Al-Aziziyah, Libya, in 1922. Express this temperature in degrees Fahrenheit and in kelvins.

Identify
List the given and unknown values.

Given:
$T_C = 57.8\,°C$
Unknown:
$T_F = ?\,°F,\ T_K = ?\,K$

Plan
Write down the equations for temperature conversions.

$T_F = 1.8 T_C + 32.0$
$T_K = T_C + 273$

Solve
Insert the known values into the equations, and solve.

$T_F = (1.8 \times 57.8) + 32.0$
$ = 104 + 32.0 = 136\,°F$
$T_K = 57.8 + 273 = 331\,K$

Integrating Space Science

Temperatures in Space
Astronomers measure a wide range of temperatures in the universe, from the cold of deep space to the heat of stars. All objects produce different types of electromagnetic waves depending on their temperature. By identifying the distribution of wavelengths that an object radiates, astronomers can estimate the object's temperature. The sun gives off electromagnetic radiations at many wavelengths. Light received from the sun indicates that the temperature of the sun's surface is 6,000 K. And the temperature at the center of the sun is 15,000,000 K!

Practice

1. Express these temperatures in degrees Fahrenheit and in kelvins.
   a. the boiling point of liquid hydrogen (−252.87 °C)
   b. the temperature of a winter day at the North Pole (−40.0 °C)
   c. the melting point of gold (1,064 °C)

2. Make the necessary conversions to complete the table below.

Example	Temp. (°C)	Temp. (°F)	Temp. (K)
Air in a typical living room	21	?	?
Metal in a running car engine	?	?	388
Liquid nitrogen	−196	?	?
Air on a summer day in the desert	?	110	?

3. Use **Figure 4** to determine which of the following is a likely temperature for ice cubes in a freezer.
   a. 20 °C
   b. −4 °F
   c. 20 K
   d. 100 K

4. Use **Figure 4** to determine which of the following values is closest to the normal temperature of the human body.
   a. 50 °C
   b. 75 °F
   c. 98 °C
   d. 310 K

For more practice, visit **go.hrw.com** and enter keyword **HK8MP**.

SCLINKS.
www.scilinks.org
Topic: Temperature Scales
Code: HK81506

Relating Temperature to Energy Transfer

When you touch a piece of ice, it feels very cold. When you step into a hot bath, the water feels very hot. Clasping your hands together usually produces neither sensation. These three cases can be explained by comparing the temperatures of the two objects that are making contact with each other. When two objects that are at different temperatures are touching, energy will be <u>transferred</u> from one to the other. ❯ **The feeling associated with temperature difference results from energy transfer.** Imagine that you are holding a piece of ice. The temperature of ice is lower than the temperature of your hand. Therefore, the molecules in the ice move slower than the molecules in your hand. As the molecules on the surface of your hand collide with those on the surface of the ice, energy is transferred from your hand to the ice. As a result, the molecules in the ice speed up, and their kinetic energy increases. This process causes the ice to melt.

Academic Vocabulary
transfer (TRANS fuhr) to carry or cause to pass from one thing to another

Inquiry Lab — Temperature and Energy

⏱ 30 min

Procedure

1. Tie **10 metal washers** on one piece of **string** and **30 identical washers** on another piece of string.
2. Fill a **beaker** two-thirds full with **water.** Lower the washers into the beaker. (Let enough string hang out such that you can safely remove the washers later.) Set the beaker on a **hot plate.**
3. Heat the water to boiling.
4. Put **50 mL of cool water** in **two plastic-foam cups.** Use a **thermometer** to measure and record the initial temperature of the water in each cup.
5. When the water in the beaker has boiled for about 3 min, remove the group of 30 washers.
6. Gently shake any water off the washers, and quickly place them into one of the plastic-foam cups. Observe the change in temperature of the cup's water. Record the highest temperature reached.
7. Repeat steps 5 and 6, this time removing the 10 washers and placing them in the other cup.

Analysis

1. Which cup's water reached the higher temperature?
2. Both cups had the same starting temperature. Both sets of washers started at 100 °C. Why did one cup reach a higher final temperature?
3. What general principle does this result illustrate about the relationship between temperature changes and energy changes?

478 Chapter 14 Heat and Temperature

Temperature changes indicate an energy transfer.

The energy transferred between the particles of two objects, because of a temperature difference between the two objects, is called **heat**. This transfer of energy is always from something at a higher temperature to something at a lower temperature. As **Figure 5** shows, if you hold a glass of ice water in your hands, energy will be transferred as heat from your hand to the glass. But if you hold a cup of hot tea, energy will be transferred as heat from the cup to your hand.

Because temperature is a measure of the average kinetic energy of internal particles, you can use temperature to predict the direction in which energy will be transferred. Internal kinetic energy will be transferred as heat from the warmer object to the cooler object. The reason is that rapidly moving particles will always transfer the energy of their motion to particles that are not moving as rapidly. So, when energy is transferred from the hot water in the cup to your skin, the temperature of the water falls while the temperature of your skin rises.

When two materials that are at very different temperatures touch, the energy transfer between them happens quickly at first. The greater the difference in the temperatures of the two objects, the faster the energy will be transferred as heat. But when both your skin and the cup in your hand approach the same temperature, energy is transferred more slowly from the cup to your skin.

heat (HEET) the energy transferred between objects that are at different temperatures

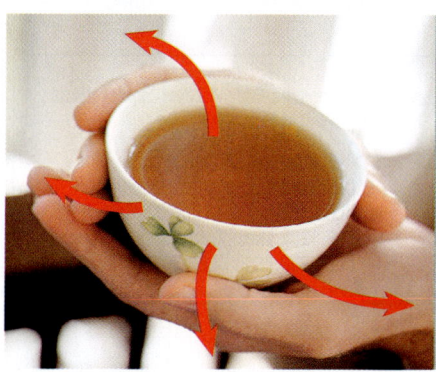

Figure 5 The direction in which energy is transferred between your hand and whatever it is touching determines whether your hand feels hot or cold.

Section 1 Review

KEY IDEAS

1. **Define** *absolute zero* in terms of the kinetic energy of particles.
2. **Predict** which molecules will move faster on average: water molecules in hot soup or water molecules in iced lemonade.
3. **Describe** the relationship between temperature and energy.
4. **Predict** whether a greater amount of energy will be transferred as heat between 1 kg of water at 10 °C and a freezer at −15 °C or between 1 kg of water at 60 °C and an oven at 65 °C.

CRITICAL THINKING

5. **Applying Concepts** Consider two samples of water: Lake Michigan and a cup of boiling water. Which has a higher average kinetic energy? Which has a higher total kinetic energy?

Math Skills

6. Convert the temperature of the air in a room air-conditioned to 20.0 °C to equivalent temperatures on the Fahrenheit and Kelvin scales.
7. The coldest outdoor temperature ever recorded was −128.6 °F in Vostok, Antarctica. Convert this temperature to degrees Celsius and kelvins.

SECTION 2
Energy Transfer

Key Ideas

> How does energy transfer happen?
> What do conductors and insulators do?
> What makes something a good conductor of heat?

Key Terms

thermal conduction
convection
convection current
radiation
specific heat

Why It Matters

Energy transfer is a crucial factor that governs global wind patterns, which mariners use to navigate safely.

Tennessee Course Level Expectations (Physical Science)

CLE.3202.2.1; CLE.3202.2.3;
CLE.3202.Inq.1; CLE.3202.Inq.2;
CLE.3202.Inq.3; CLE.3202.Math.1;
CLE.3202.Math.2; CLE.3202.TE.2;
CLE.3202.TE.3; CLE.3202.TE.4

While water is being heated for your morning shower, your breakfast food is cooking. In the freezer, water in ice trays becomes solid after the freezer cools the water to 0 °C. Outside, the morning dew evaporates soon after light from the rising sun strikes it. These examples are ways that energy transfers from one object to another.

Methods of Energy Transfer

> **Heat energy can be transferred in three ways: conduction, convection, and radiation.** Roasting marshmallows around a campfire, as **Figure 1** shows, provides an opportunity to experience each of these three ways.

Figure 1 Ways of Transferring Energy

Conduction transfers energy as heat along the wire and into the hand.

Electromagnetic waves emitted by the hot campfire transfer energy by radiation.

Sparks swirl upward in the convection currents that are created as warmed air above the fire rises.

480 Chapter 14 Heat and Temperature

Figure 2 Conduction

Before conduction takes place, the average kinetic energy of the particles in the metal wire is the same throughout.

During conduction, the rapidly moving particles in the wire transfer some of their energy to slowly moving particles nearby.

Conduction occurs between objects in direct contact.

Imagine that you place a marshmallow on one end of a wire made from a metal coat hanger. Then, you hold the other end of the wire while letting the marshmallow cook over the campfire flame. Soon, the end of the wire that you are holding gets warmer. This transfer of energy as heat through the wire is an example of **thermal conduction.**

Conduction takes place when objects that are in direct contact are at unequal temperatures. It also takes place between particles within an object. The energy transferred from the fire to the atoms in the wire causes the atoms to vibrate rapidly. As **Figure 2** shows, when these rapidly vibrating atoms collide with slowly vibrating atoms, energy is transferred as heat all along the wire and to your hand.

Convection results from the movement of warm fluids.

While roasting your marshmallow, you may notice that sparks from the fire rise and begin to swirl. They are following the movement of air away from the fire. The air close to the fire becomes hot and expands, so the space between the air particles increases. As a result, the air becomes less dense and moves upward, carrying its extra energy with it, as **Figure 3** shows. The rising warm air is forced upward by cooler, denser air. The cooler air then expands and rises as it is heated by the fire. Eventually, the rising hot air cools, contracts, becomes denser, and sinks. Energy transfer resulting from the movement of warm fluids is **convection.**

Convection is possible only in fluids. Most fluids are liquids or gases. The cycle of a heated fluid that rises and then cools and falls is called a **convection current.** The heating and cooling of a room involves convection currents. Warm air expands and rises from vents near the floor. It cools and contracts near the ceiling and then sinks back to the floor. In this way, all of the air in the room gets heated.

thermal conduction (THUHR muhl kuhn DUHK shuhn) the transfer of energy as heat through a material

convection (kuhn VEK shuhn) the movement of matter due to differences in density that are caused by temperature variations

convection current (kuhn VEK shuhn KUHR uhnt) any movement of matter that results from differences in density; may be vertical, circular, or cyclical

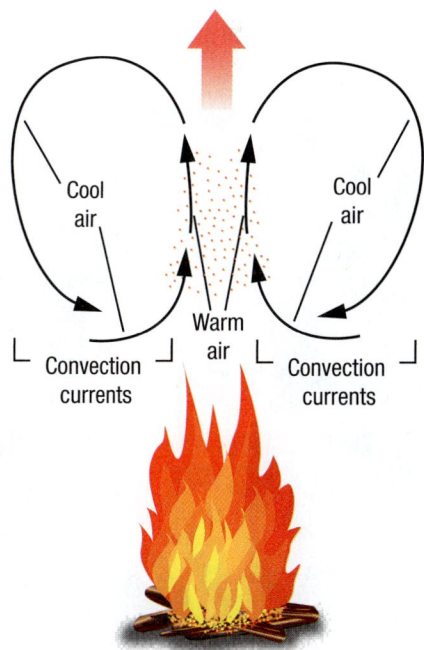

Figure 3 During convection, energy is carried away by a heated fluid that expands and rises above cooler, denser fluids.

Section 2 Energy Transfer

InquiryLab Absorption of Radiated Heat 30 min

Procedure

1. Obtain **two empty soup cans,** and remove the labels. Paint the inside and outside of one soup can with **black paint.**
2. Pour **50 mL of cool water** into each can.
3. Place a **thermometer** in each can, and record the temperature of the water in each can at the start. Leave the thermometers in the cans. Aim a bright **lamp** at the cans, or place them in sunlight.
4. Record the temperature of the water in each can every 3 min for at least 15 min.

Analysis

1. Prepare a graph. Label the *x*-axis "Time" and the *y*-axis "Temperature." Plot your data for each can of water.
2. The water in which can absorbed more radiation?
3. Which variables in the lab were controlled (unchanged throughout the experiment)? How did the controlled variables help you obtain valid results?
4. Use your results to explain why panels used for solar heating are often painted black.
5. Based on your results, what color would you want your car to be in the winter? in the summer? Justify your answer.

radiation (RAY dee AY shuhn) the energy that is transferred as electromagnetic waves, such as visible light and infrared waves

Figure 4 Heat as infrared radiation is visible in this thermogram. The warmest parts of the dog are white, and the coolest parts are dark blue.

Radiation does not require physical contact between objects.

As you stand close to a campfire, you can feel its warmth. This warmth can be felt even when you are not in the path of a convection current. The fire emits energy in the form of *electromagnetic waves,* which include infrared radiation, visible light, and ultraviolet rays. Energy that is transferred as electromagnetic waves is called **radiation.** When the molecules in your skin absorb this energy, the average kinetic energy of these molecules—and thus the temperature of your skin—increases.

All hot objects give off infrared radiation, which is electromagnetic waves at a frequency lower than that of visible light. The warmer an object is, the more infrared radiation it gives off. The image of the dog in **Figure 4** shows the areas of the dog that are warmer (white and red) and the areas that are cooler (black and blue).

Radiation differs from conduction and convection in that it does not involve the movement of matter across space. Only electromagnetic waves carry radiation. Radiation is therefore the only way that energy can be transferred through a vacuum, such as outer space. Much of the energy that we receive from the sun is transferred by radiation.

Reading Check How does radiation differ from conduction and convection?

Why It Matters

Why Does the Wind Blow?

REAL WORLD

As Earth rotates, the sun's rays heat up the part of Earth facing the sun. This differential heating causes convection, in which cooler air or water moves to replace warmer air or water. Convection affects global wind and ocean-current patterns. Mariners have known about and taken advantage of these patterns for centuries.

Convection currents over Earth's surface are partly responsible for the global wind patterns shown here.

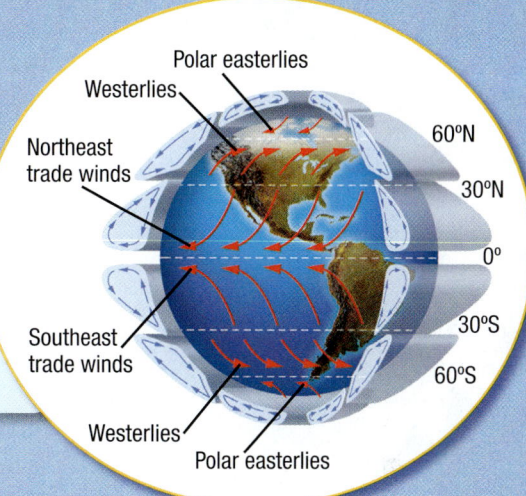

Seagoing navigators can take advantage of prevailing winds and ocean currents in planning routes.

Convection of ocean water causes ocean currents, such as the ones shown here in the Atlantic Ocean.

SCLINKS
www.scilinks.org
Topic: Convection Within the Atmosphere
Code: HK80353

YOUR TURN

UNDERSTANDING CONCEPTS
1. How do convection patterns determine global wind and ocean-current patterns?

CRITICAL THINKING
2. How would Earth's convection patterns be different if the sun's radiation reached every part of Earth equally?

Section 2 Energy Transfer 483

Conductors and Insulators

When you are cooking, the pan must conduct energy to heat the food, but the handle must be insulated from the heat so that you can hold the handle. If you are using conduction to increase the temperature of a substance, you must use materials through which energy can be quickly transferred as heat. Cooking pans are usually made of metal because energy passes quickly between the particles in most metals.

▶ **A *conductor* is a material through which energy can be easily transferred as heat.**

Many people avoid wasting energy. Energy is most often wasted by its transfer through the roof or walls of a house. Using an insulator can reduce energy transfer. ▶ **An *insulator*, or insulation, is a material that transfers energy poorly.** Insulation in the attic or walls of a house helps keep energy from escaping. Insulation in warm clothing, such as that shown in **Figure 5,** keeps energy as heat from leaving the body.

Heat energy is transferred through particle collisions.

Gases are very poor heat conductors because their particles are so far apart. Much less energy per volume can be transferred through a gas than through a solid or a liquid, whose particles are much closer together. Denser materials usually conduct energy better than less dense materials do. Metals tend to conduct energy very well, and plastics conduct energy poorly. For this reason, metal pots and pans often have plastic handles. Energy as heat moves through the plastic slower than it moves through the metal.

Reading Check What makes a material a good conductor?

Figure 5 A well-insulated coat can keep in body heat even in cold temperatures.

Academic Vocabulary

conduct (kuhn DUHKT) to be able to carry

QuickLab — Conductors and Insulators ⏱ 10 min

Procedure

❶ For this activity, you will need **several flatware utensils.** Each one should be made of a different material, such as **stainless steel, aluminum,** and **plastic.** You will also need a **bowl** and **ice cubes.**

❷ Place the ice cubes in the bowl. Place an equal length of each utensil under the ice.

Analysis

1. After the utensils have been in the ice for 30 s, briefly touch each utensil at the same distance from the ice. Which utensil feels coldest? Which differences between the utensils might account for the different results? Explain.

Specific Heat

You have probably noticed that a metal spoon, such as the one shown in **Figure 6**, becomes hot when placed in a cup of hot liquid. And you may have noticed that a spoon made of a different material, such as plastic, does not become hot as quickly. The difference between the final temperatures of the two spoons depends on whether the spoons are good conductors or good insulators. ❯ **What makes a substance a good or poor conductor depends in part on how much energy is required to change the temperature of the substance by a certain amount.**

Figure 6 The spoon's temperature increases rapidly because of the spoon's low specific heat.

Specific heat describes how much energy is required to raise an object's temperature.

Not all substances behave the same way when they absorb energy. For example, a metal spoon left in a metal pot becomes hot seconds after the pot is placed on a hot stovetop burner. The reason is that a small amount of energy is enough to raise the spoon's temperature by a lot. However, if you place a wooden spoon that has the same mass as the metal spoon in the same pot, that same amount of energy produces a much smaller temperature change in the wooden spoon.

For all substances, specific heat is a characteristic physical property, which is represented by c. In this book, the **specific heat** of any substance is the amount of energy required to raise the temperature of 1 kg of that substance by 1 K.

Some values for specific heat are given in **Figure 7**. These values are in units of joules per kilogram times kelvin (J/kg•K). Thus, each value is the amount of energy in joules needed to raise the temperature of 1 kg of the substance by exactly 1 K.

READING TOOLBOX

Comparison Table
To help you understand specific heat, make a comparison table. Compare the amount of heat it takes to raise the temperature of some of the substances listed on this page.

specific heat (spuh SIF ik HEET) the quantity of heat required to raise a unit mass of homogenous material 1 K or 1 °C in a specified way given constant pressure and volume

Figure 7 Values of Specific Heat at 25 °C

Substance	c (J/kg•K)	Substance	c (J/kg•K)
Water (liquid)	4,186	Copper	385
Ethanol (liquid)	2,440	Iron	449
Ammonia (gas)	2,060	Silver	234
Steam	1,870	Mercury	140
Aluminum	897	Gold	129
Carbon (graphite)	709	Lead	129

Integrating Earth Science

Specific Heat and Sea Breezes
Sea breezes result from convection currents in the coastal air and from differences in the specific heats of water and land. During the day, the temperature of the land increases more than that of the ocean water, which has a larger specific heat. Thus, the temperature of the air over land increases more than the temperature of air over the ocean. As a result, the warm air over the land rises, and the cool ocean air moves inland to replace the rising warm air. At night, the temperature of the land drops below that of the ocean, and the breezes reverse direction.

Specific heat can be used to figure out how much energy it takes to raise an object's temperature.

Because specific heat is a ratio, it can be used to predict the effects of temperature changes for masses other than 1 kg. For example, if 4,186 J is required to raise the temperature of 1 kg of water by 1 K, twice as much energy, 8,372 J, will raise the temperature of 2 kg of water by 1 K. About 25,120 J will be required to raise the temperature of the 2 kg of water by 3 K. This relationship is described by the equation below.

> **Specific heat equation**
> energy = specific heat × mass × temperature change
> energy = $cm\Delta T$

The specific heat of a substance can change slightly with changes in pressure and volume. However, the problems in this chapter will assume that specific heat does not change.

Math Skills — Specific Heat

How much energy must be transferred as heat to 200 kg of water in a bathtub to raise the water's temperature from 25 °C to 37 °C?

Identify
List the given and unknown values.

Given:
$\Delta T = 37\,°C - 25\,°C = 12\,°C = 12\,K$
$\Delta T = 12\,K$
$m = 200\,kg$
$c = 4,186\,J/kg \cdot K$

Unknown:
energy = ? J

Plan
Write down the specific heat equation from this page.

energy = $cm\Delta T$

Solve
Substitute values of specific heat, mass, and temperature change, and solve.

$energy = \left(\dfrac{4{,}186\,J}{kg \cdot K}\right) \times (200\,kg) \times (12\,K)$

$energy = 10{,}000{,}000\,J = 1.0 \times 10^4\,kJ$

Practice

1. How much energy is needed to increase the temperature of 755 g of iron from 283 K to 403 K?
2. How much energy must a refrigerator absorb from 225 g of water to decrease the temperature of the water from 35 °C to 5 °C?

For more practice, visit **go.hrw.com** and enter keyword **HK8MP**.

Heat raises an object's temperature or changes the object's state.

The graph in **Figure 8** represents what happens to water over a range of temperatures as energy is added. At 0 °C, the water is at first in the solid state (ice). A certain amount of energy per kilogram is required to melt the ice. While the ice is melting, the temperature does not change. The same is true when water is at 100 °C and is boiling. Energy is required to pull liquid molecules apart. While the water is boiling, energy added to the water is used in changing the water to a gas. While water is changing to a gas, the temperature does not change. For any substance, added energy either raises its temperature or changes its state, not both at the same time.

Figure 8 Energy put into a substance either raises the substance's temperature or changes the substance's state. **As energy is added to water, what is happening during the times that temperature does not change?**

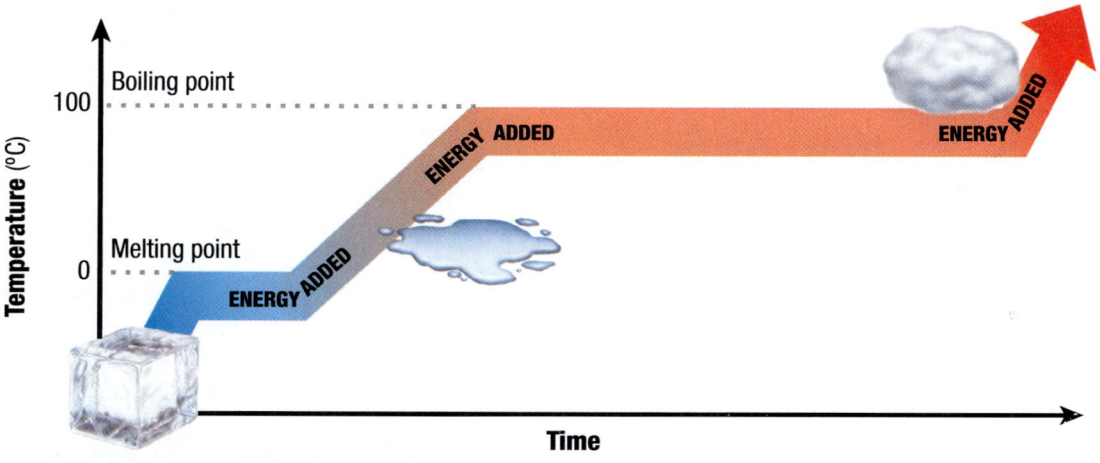

Section 2 Review

KEY IDEAS

1. **Describe** how energy is transferred by conduction, convection, and radiation.
2. **Predict** whether the hottest part of a room will be near the ceiling, in the center, or near the floor, given that there is a hot-air vent near the floor. Explain your reasoning.
3. **Explain** why there are temperature differences on the moon's surface even though there is no atmosphere present.

CRITICAL THINKING

4. **Applying Concepts** Explain why cookies baked near the turned-up edges of a cookie sheet receive more energy than those baked near the center do.

Math Skills

5. How much energy would be absorbed by 550 g of copper that is heated from 24 °C to 45 °C? (Hint: Refer to **Figure 7**.)
6. A 144 kg park bench made of iron sits in the sun, and its temperature increases from 25 °C to 35 °C. How many kilojoules of energy does the bench absorb? (Hint: Refer to **Figure 7**.)
7. Suppose that a car's radiator contains 2.0 kg of water. The water absorbs energy from the car engine. In the process, the water's temperature increases from 298 K to 355 K. How much energy did the water absorb?

Why It Matters

How Are Homes Heated and Cooled?

People tend to be most comfortable when the temperature of the air around them is in the range of 21 °C to 25° C (70 °F to 77 °F). To raise the indoor temperature on colder days, one must use a heating system to transfer energy into a room's air. Most heating systems use a source of energy to raise the temperature of a substance such as air or water. In cooling systems, energy is transferred as heat from one substance to another, which leaves the first substance at a lower temperature. Cooled or heated air circulates throughout a home by convection currents. For the temperature of a home to be effectively regulated, heating and cooling units must be designed to make the best use of the flow of heat energy by convection.

An active solar-heating system moves solar-heated water through pipes and a heat exchanger.

Hot-water, steam, and hot-air systems heat buildings by circulating heated fluids through each room.

SCILINKS.
www.scilinks.org
Topic: Heating and Cooling Systems
Code: HK80732

REAL WORLD

① A substance that easily evaporates and condenses is used in air conditioners to transfer energy from a room to the air outside.

② When the liquid evaporates, it absorbs energy from the surrounding air, which cools the air.

③ Outside, the air conditioner condenses the gas, which releases energy.

① Liquid refrigerant flowing through the pipes inside a refrigerator cools the compartment by evaporation.

② Energy is removed by the outside coils as the warmed refrigerant vapor cools and condenses back into a liquid.

YOUR TURN

UNDERSTANDING CONCEPTS

1. Name one type of home heating system, and describe how it transfers energy to warm the air inside the rooms.

2. Why does an air conditioner heat up while it is operating?

Section 2 Energy Transfer **489**

SECTION 3 Using Heat

Key Ideas
> What happens to heat energy when it is transferred?
> What do heat engines do?

Key Terms
entropy
heat engine

Why It Matters
Heat engines are used to do important work, such as running automobiles.

> **Tennessee Course Level Expectations (Physical Science)**
> CLE.3202.TE.1; CLE.3202.2.3;
> CLE.3202.Inq.1; CLE.3202.Inq.2;
> CLE.3202.Inq.3; CLE.3202.Inq.4;
> CLE.3202.Inq.6; CLE.3202.Math.1;
> CLE.3202.Math.2

Heating a house in the winter, cooling an office building in the summer, or preserving food throughout the year is possible because of machines that transfer energy as heat from one place to another. An air conditioner does work to remove energy as heat from the warm air inside a room and then transfers the energy to the warmer air outside the room.

Laws of Thermodynamics

Two principles about the conservation of energy explain how an air conditioner can transfer energy and make a room cooler. The two principles are the first and second laws of thermodynamics. > **The *first law of thermodynamics* states that the total energy used in any process is conserved, whether that energy is transferred as a result of work, heat, or both.** The *second law of thermodynamics* states that the energy transferred as heat always moves from an object at a higher temperature to an object at a lower temperature.

Work can increase average kinetic energy.

When you rub your hands together, they become warmer. This process is an example of *work*, a transfer of energy. The energy that you transfer to your hands by work is transferred to the molecules of your hands, and the temperature of your hands increases. Processes in which energy is transferred by work are called *mechanical processes*.

Transfer of kinetic energy can be used to start a fire, as shown in **Figure 1**. Rubbing two sticks together requires work, because there is friction between the sticks. The friction turns the work into kinetic energy. If there is enough kinetic energy, the sticks will heat up enough to catch fire.

Figure 1 Kinetic energy can be used to start a fire.

The disorder of a system tends to increase.

According to the second law of thermodynamics, a system left to itself tends to move from a state of higher energy to a state of lower energy. Many highly ordered states, such as the state of the house of cards shown in **Figure 2,** are high-energy states. This means that you have to put a lot of energy into the cards to get them to that state. A high-energy state can very easily become a lower-energy state. For this reason, just a nudge will cause a house of cards to crash to the floor. In the science of thermodynamics, the measure of the disorder of a system is called **entropy.** Over time, in any given system left to itself, the entropy of that system will tend to increase.

You can do work on a system to decrease its entropy. But the second law of thermodynamics states that if you do work on a system, the total entropy of a larger system will increase. For example, the sun's energy enables plants to make sugars from smaller molecules. The result is an increase in order and therefore a decrease in entropy. But the total energy that the sun gives off represents a huge increase in entropy. So, the entropy of the larger system increases.

Reading Check What does the second law of thermodynamics state about the energy state of a system left to itself?

Usable energy decreases in all energy transfers.

When energy can be easily transformed and transferred to do work, such as heating a room, we say that the energy is in a usable form. After this transfer, the same amount of energy exists, according to the law of conservation of energy. But because of an increase in entropy, less of this energy is in a form that can be used.

The energy used to increase the temperature of the water in the tank of a hot-water heater should ideally stay in the hot water. However, keeping some energy from being transferred as heat to parts of the tank and its surroundings is impossible. The amount of usable energy decreases even in the most efficient heating systems.

Because of conduction and radiation, some energy is lost to the tank's surroundings, such as the air and nearby walls. Cold water in the pipes that feed into the hot-water heater also draws energy from some of the hot water in the tank. When energy from electricity is used to heat water in the tank, some of the energy is used to increase the temperature of the water heater itself. In general, the amount of usable energy always decreases whenever energy is transferred or transformed.

Figure 2 A house of cards falling is an example of an increase in entropy. **How can you tell that the cards in the first picture are in a high-energy state?**

entropy (EN truh pee) a measure of the randomness or disorder of a system

heat engine (HEET EN juhn) a machine that transforms heat into mechanical energy, or work

Academic Vocabulary

internal (in TUHR nuhl) taking place inside

Flow Chart
Create a flow chart that outlines the steps that an automobile cylinder goes through in a complete cycle.

Heat Engines

▶ **In a heat engine, chemical energy is converted to mechanical energy through the process of combustion.** Internal-combustion engines and external-combustion engines are the two main types of heat engines. They are named for the place where combustion occurs—inside the engine or outside the engine. Engines in cars and trucks are internal-combustion engines. A steam engine is an external-combustion engine.

Internal-combustion engines burn fuel inside the engine.

In an internal-combustion engine, fuel burns in cylinders within the engine. There are pistons inside the cylinders, as shown in **Figure 3**. Up-and-down movements, or strokes, of the pistons cause the crankshaft to turn. The motion of the crankshaft is transferred to the wheels of the car or truck.

Most automobile engines are four-stroke engines. In these engines, four strokes take place for each cycle of the piston. The four strokes are called *intake, compression, power,* and *exhaust* strokes. In the power stroke, a spark plug ignites the fuel.

Diesel engines are also internal-combustion engines, but they work differently. A diesel engine has no spark plugs. Instead, the fuel-air mixture is compressed so much that it becomes hot enough to ignite without a spark.

Internal-combustion engines always generate heat.

In an internal-combustion engine, only part of the chemical energy is converted to mechanical energy. As engine parts move, friction and other forces cause much of the energy to be lost to the atmosphere as heat. An internal-combustion engine becomes so hot that a cooling system must be used to cool the engine.

Figure 3 The pistons move within the cylinders of the four-stroke engine to turn the crankshaft, which transfers motion to the wheels of the car or truck.

Automobile engines use carburetors or fuel injectors.

The four-stroke cycle of an engine with a carburetor is illustrated in **Figure 4.** A *carburetor* is another part of the engine, in which liquid gasoline becomes vaporized.

Some engines have fuel injectors instead of carburetors. In some fuel-injected engines, only air enters the cylinder during the intake stroke. During the compression stroke, fuel vapor is injected directly into the compressed air in the cylinder. The other steps are the same as in an engine with a carburetor.

Figure 4 The Four Strokes of an Automobile Cylinder

In the *intake* stroke, a mixture of fuel vapor and air is brought into the cylinder from the carburetor as the piston moves downward.

In the *compression* stroke, the piston moves up and compresses the fuel-air mixture.

In the *power* stroke, the spark plug ignites the mixture, which expands quickly and moves the piston down to turn the crankshaft.

The *exhaust* stroke takes place when the piston moves up again and forces the waste products to move out of the exhaust valve.

Section 3 Review

KEY IDEAS

1. **Restate** the first two laws of thermodynamics in your own words.
2. **Describe** what happens over time to the disorder of a system left to itself.
3. **Define** the term *entropy* in your own words.
4. **Name** the two types of heat engines.
5. **Relate** the output of energy from a heat engine to the energy put into the heat engine, considering the second law of thermodynamics.

CRITICAL THINKING

6. **Applying Concepts** Give an example of work that you can do to transfer kinetic energy. Explain, in terms of the first two laws of thermodynamics, what happens to that energy.
7. **Explaining Events** Describe each of the strokes of an automobile engine. Explain how the spark-plug ignition of compressed gas results in work done by the engine.
8. **Analyzing Processes** If you clean up your room, its order increases. According to the second law of thermodynamics, what else must happen?

Inquiry Lab

 50 min

Conduction of Heat by Metals

Metals are typically very good conductors of energy. In this lab, you will test wires of different thicknesses to see whether the thickness of a metal wire affects the wire's ability to conduct energy as heat.

Asking a Question

How does the thickness of a metal wire affect the wire's ability to conduct energy as heat?

Investigating Conduction in Wires

1. Obtain three wires of different thicknesses. Clip a clothespin on one end of one of the wires. Lay the wire and attached clothespin on the lab table. Spread some newspaper or other covering below the wire to catch any extra hot wax.

2. Light the candle. **CAUTION:** Tie back long hair, and confine loose clothing. Never reach across an open flame. To avoid burning yourself, always use the clothespin to hold the wire as you heat and move the wire. Remember that the wires will be hot for some time after they are removed from the flame.

3. Hold the lighted candle above the middle of the wire, and tilt the candle slightly so that some of the melted wax drips onto the middle of the wire.

4. Wait a couple of minutes for the wire and dripped wax to cool completely. The dripped wax will harden and form a small ball. Using the clothespin to hold the wire, place the other end of the wire in the candle's flame. When the ball of wax melts, remove the wire from the flame and place it on the lab table.

Forming and Testing a Hypothesis

5. Think about what caused the wax on the wire to melt. Form a hypothesis about whether a thick wire will conduct energy more quickly or more slowly than a thin wire.

Designing Your Experiment

6. With your lab partner(s), decide how you will use the materials available in this lab activity to compare the speed of conduction in three wires of different thicknesses.

7. In your lab report, list each step that you will perform in your experiment.

8. Have your teacher approve your plan before you carry out your experiment.

What You'll Do

- **Develop** a plan to measure how quickly energy is transferred as heat through a metal wire.
- **Compare** the speed of energy conduction in metal wires of different thicknesses.

What You'll Need

caliper or metric ruler
candle
clothespin
lighter or matches
newspaper or other covering to catch hot wax
stopwatch
wires, metal, of various thicknesses, each about 30 cm long (3)

Safety

Performing Your Experiment

9. After your teacher approves your plan, you can carry out your experiment.

10. Prepare a data table that is similar to the sample data table.

11. Record in your table how many seconds the ball of wax on each wire takes to melt. Perform three trials for each wire. Allow the wires to cool to room temperature between trials.

Sample Data Table: Conductivity

Wire	Wire diameter (mm)	Time to melt wax (s)		
		Trial 1	Trial 2	Trial 3
Wire 1				
Wire 2				
Wire 3				

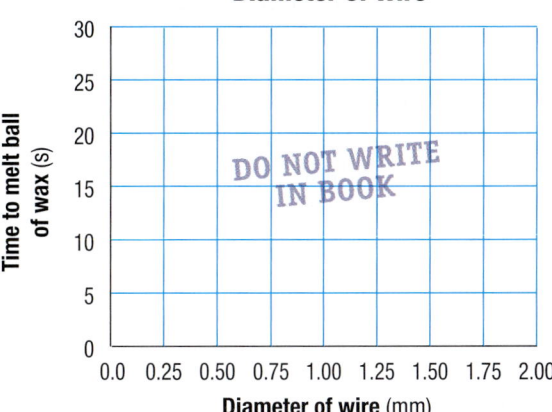

Time to Melt Wax Versus Diameter of Wire

DO NOT WRITE IN BOOK

Analysis

1. **Analyzing Data** Measure the diameter of each wire that you tested. If the diameter is listed in inches, convert it to millimeters by multiplying by 25.4. If the diameter is listed in mils, convert it to millimeters by multiplying by 0.0254. In your data table, record the diameter of each wire in millimeters.

2. **Analyzing Data** Calculate the average time required to melt the ball of wax for each wire. Record your answers in your data table.

3. **Graphing Data** Plot the data in your lab report in the form of a graph like the one shown. On your graph, draw the line or smooth curve that best fits the points.

Communicating Your Results

4. **Drawing Conclusions** Based on your graph, which conducts energy more quickly: a thick wire or a thin wire?

5. **Justifying Conclusions** Suppose that someone tells you that your conclusion is valid only for the particular metal that you tested. Without doing further experiments, how can you argue that your conclusion is valid for other metals, too?

Extension

When roasting a large cut of meat, some cooks insert a metal skewer into the meat to make the inside cook more quickly. What difference would the thickness of the skewer make in this case? Explain.

Solving Problems

Science Skills

Technology
Math
Scientific Methods
Graphing

Problem

A dinner plate that has a temperature of 95.0 °C is placed in a container of water whose temperature is 26.0 °C. The final temperature reached by the plate and water is 28.2 °C. The mass of the plate is 1.5 kg, and the mass of the water is 3.0 kg. What is the plate's specific heat? First calculate the energy transferred as heat to the water, which is the same as the energy transferred from the plate. Then rearrange the equation to calculate the plate's specific heat.

Solution

Identify

List all the given and unknown values. Note that a change of temperature is the same whether expressed in degrees Celsius or kelvins.

The first step for this type of problem is to calculate the temperature changes.

Given:

temperature change of plate (ΔT_{plate}) =
95.0 °C − 28.2 °C = 66.8 °C = 66.8 K

temperature change of water (ΔT_{water}) =
28.2 °C − 26.0 °C = 2.2 °C = 2.2 K

mass of plate (m_{plate}) = 1.5 kg

mass of water (m_{water}) = 3.0 kg

specific heat of water (c_{water}) = 4,186 J/kg•K

Unknown:

specific heat of plate (c_{plate}) in J/kg•K

Plan

Write down the specific heat equation, and then rearrange it to calculate the specific heat of the plate.

$$energy = cm\Delta T = c_{water} m_{water} \Delta T_{water}$$
$$= c_{plate} m_{plate} \Delta T_{plate}$$

$$c_{plate} = \frac{energy}{m_{plate} \Delta T_{plate}}$$

Solve

Find the energy transferred, and then calculate the specific heat of the plate.

$$energy = \left(\frac{4,186 \text{ J}}{\text{kg•K}}\right) \times (3.0 \text{ kg}) \times (2.2 \text{ K}) = 2.8 \times 10^4 \text{ J}$$

$$c_{plate} = \frac{2.8 \times 10^4 \text{ J}}{1.5 \text{ kg} \times 66.8 \text{ K}} = \frac{2.8 \times 10^4 \text{ J}}{1.0 \times 10^2 \text{ kg•K}} = 280 \text{ J/kg•K}$$

Practice

1. Suppose that in the example problem, the final temperature of the plate and water was 27.1 °C. Calculate what the specific heat of the plate would have been in that case.

2. Suppose that in the example problem, the water's initial temperature was 29.0 °C and the final temperature of the plate and water was 35.0 °C. If the plate is the same, what is the water's mass?

CHAPTER 14 Summary

go.hrw.com
SUPER SUMMARY
KEYWORD: HK8HTMS

Key Ideas

Section 1 Temperature

› **Temperature and Energy** The temperature of a substance is proportional to the average kinetic energy of the substance's particles. (p. 473)

› **Temperature Scales** The Fahrenheit, Celsius, and Kelvin temperature scales are commonly used for different applications in different parts of the world. (p. 475)

› **Relating Temperature to Energy Transfer** The feeling associated with temperature difference results from energy transfer. (p. 478)

Section 2 Energy Transfer

› **Methods of Energy Transfer** Energy can be transferred in three ways: conduction, convection, and radiation. (p. 480)

› **Conductors and Insulators** A conductor is a material through which energy can be easily transferred. An insulator is a material that transfers energy poorly. (p. 484)

› **Specific Heat** What makes a substance a good or poor conductor depends in part on how much energy is required to change the temperature of the substance by a certain amount. (p. 485)

Section 3 Using Heat

› **Laws of Thermodynamics** The first law of thermodynamics states that the total energy used in any process is conserved, whether that energy is transferred as a result of work, heat, or both. (p. 491)

› **Heat Engines** In a heat engine, chemical energy is converted to mechanical energy through the process of combustion. (p. 492)

Key Terms

temperature, p. 473
thermometer, p. 474
absolute zero, p. 476
heat, p. 479

thermal conduction, p. 481
convection, p. 481
convection current, p. 481
radiation, p. 482
specific heat, p. 485

entropy, p. 491
heat engine, p. 492

Heat and Temperature **497**

CHAPTER 14 Review

READING TOOLBOX

1. **Comparison Table** Make a comparison table that gives three ways in which insulators differ, or are likely to differ, from conductors.

USING KEY TERMS

2. How would a *thermometer* that measures temperatures on the Kelvin scale differ from one that measures temperatures on the Celsius scale?

3. Explain how *convection currents* form downdrafts in deserts near tall mountain ranges, as shown in the figure below.

4. Use the differences between a *conductor* and an *insulator* and the concept of *specific heat* to explain whether you would rather drink a hot beverage from a metal cup or from a china cup.

5. If you wear dark clothing on a sunny day, the clothing will become hot after a while. Explain why by using the concept of *radiation*.

6. Describe how the amount of *entropy* compares between the books on a library shelf and books in a pile in a library return bin.

UNDERSTANDING KEY IDEAS

7. The temperature at which the particles of a substance would have no kinetic energy is
   a. 2,273 K.
   b. 0 K.
   c. 0 °C.
   d. 273 K.

8. Temperature is proportional to the average kinetic energy of particles in an object. Thus, an increase in temperature results in a(n)
   a. increase in mass.
   b. decrease in average kinetic energy.
   c. increase in average kinetic energy.
   d. decrease in mass.

9. The type of energy transfer that takes place between objects in direct contact is
   a. conduction.
   b. convection.
   c. contraction.
   d. radiation.

10. A type of energy transfer that can occur in empty space is
    a. convection.
    b. contraction.
    c. conduction.
    d. radiation.

11. A material made of _____ would be a very good conductor of energy.
    a. air
    b. liquid
    c. wood
    d. metal

12. Of the following substances, which is the poorest conductor of energy?
    a. air
    b. liquid
    c. wood
    d. metal

13. The amount of usable energy decreases
    a. only when systems are used for heating.
    b. only when systems are used for cooling.
    c. only if a heating or cooling system is poorly designed.
    d. whenever energy is transferred.

EXPLAINING KEY IDEAS

14. Explain how the common thermometer works by expansion. What expands, and how does that expansion indicate the temperature?

15. If two objects that have different temperatures come into contact, what will happen to their temperatures after several minutes?

16. If you bite into a piece of hot apple pie, the pie filling might burn your mouth but the crust, at the same temperature, will not. Explain why.

CRITICAL THINKING

17. Applying Concepts Why do the metal shades of desk lamps have small holes at the top?

18. Analyzing Processes Glass can conduct some energy. Double-pane windows consist of two plates of glass separated by a small layer of insulating air. Explain why a double-pane window prevents more energy from escaping from a house than a single-pane window does.

19. Applying Concepts Explain why the back part of window-unit air conditioners always hangs outside. Why can't the entire air conditioner be in the room?

20. Identifying Patterns In one southern state, the projected yearly costs for heating a home are $463 if a heat pump is used, $508 if a natural-gas furnace is used, and $1,220 if electric radiators are used. Find out from your local utility company what the projected yearly costs for the three heating systems are in your area. Make a table that compares the costs of the three systems.

21. Inferring Relationships Considering specific heat only, indicate which would make a better coolant for car engines: water (c = 4,186 J/kg·K) or ethanol (c = 2,440 J/kg·K). Explain why.

Graphing Skills

22. Interpreting Graphics The graph shown here gives the monthly cost of heating a certain house over the course of one year. What seasonal patterns are represented in the graph? Explain the patterns in the graph based on the first law of thermodynamics.

Math Skills

23. Temperature-Scale Conversion A piece of dry ice, solid CO_2, has a temperature of −78 °C. What is its temperature in kelvins and in degrees Fahrenheit?

24. Temperature-Scale Conversion The temperature in deep space is thought to be about 3 K. What is 3 K in degrees Celsius and in degrees Fahrenheit?

25. Specific Heat It takes 3,190 J to increase the temperature of a 0.400 kg sample of glass from 273 K to 308 K. What is the specific heat for this type of glass?

26. Specific Heat A vanadium bolt gives up 1,124 J of energy as its temperature drops 25 K. If its mass is 93 g, what is its specific heat?

27. Specific Heat An aluminum baking sheet (c = 897 J/kg·K) whose mass is 225 g absorbs 2.4×10^4 J from an oven. If its temperature was initially 25 °C, what will its temperature be after it is heated in the oven?

Standardized Test Prep

Understanding Concepts

Directions (1–3): **For each question, write on a sheet of paper the letter of the correct answer.**

1. What method of transferring energy carries energy from the sun to Earth?
    - **A.** conduction
    - **B.** convection
    - **C.** insulation
    - **D.** radiation

2. A certain amount of energy is added to an iron bar. Afterward, the iron bar glows white-hot and gives off energy both as light and heat. What does this energy release indicate about the particles of iron in the bar?
    - **F.** They have high kinetic energy.
    - **G.** They have low kinetic energy.
    - **H.** They are being emitted from the bar.
    - **I.** They are changing phase.

3. What happens to the energy that is not used when an engine is less than 100% efficient?
    - **A.** It is destroyed during combustion.
    - **B.** It is used to decrease entropy.
    - **C.** It is converted to heat.
    - **D.** It is converted to matter.

Directions (4–5): **For each question, write a short response.**

4. Mercury has a specific heat of 140 J/kg·K. How much energy is required to raise the temperature of 2 kg of mercury by 1 °C?

5. If the rate of expansion of mercury increased as it was heated, in what way would mercury thermometers have to be different so that the same temperature range could be accurately read from them?

Reading Skills

Directions (6–7): **Read the passage below. Then, answer the questions that follow.**

CLIMATE IS ALL ABOUT THE OCEANS

The high specific heat of the ocean plays a central role in shaping Earth's climate. Earth's atmosphere cannot store as much energy as the oceans can. The heat energy that can be stored in the entire atmosphere can be stored in a layer of the ocean just 3.2 m deep.

The specific heat of dry land is less than 25% that of sea water. The land surface also has a low conductivity. As a result, only the top 2 m or so of the land typically plays an active role in energy storage and release. Therefore, land plays a much smaller role in the storage of energy than the ocean does.

Major ice sheets, such as those over Antarctica and Greenland, have a large mass. Ice has a higher heat conductivity than land does, but as on land, the transfer of energy as heat occurs primarily through conduction. The key difference between ice and water is that energy as heat can transfer through water by convection because water is a fluid. Convection can occur faster than conduction, so ice sheets and glaciers do not play a major role in energy storage and transfer.

6. Which characteristic makes the ocean play such a major role in shaping Earth's climate?
    - **F.** the mass of the ocean
    - **G.** the area of the ocean
    - **H.** the specific heat of the ocean
    - **I.** the conductivity of the ocean

7. Summarize how energy as heat is transferred through different parts of Earth's surface by conduction and convection.

Interpreting Graphics

The graphic below shows energy transfer above a campfire. Use this graphic to answer questions 8–10.

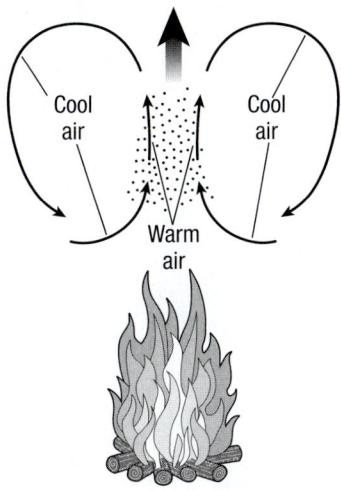

8. What form of energy transfer is represented by this illustration?
   A. conduction
   B. convection
   C. insulation
   D. radiation

9. In what form of energy transfer other than the form represented by this illustration does the fire participate?
   F. conduction
   G. convection
   H. insulation
   I. radiation

10. Which of the following principles of energy transfer causes the flow of air shown in the illustration to be circular?
    A. Warmer air descends.
    B. Cooler air descends.
    C. Warm air and cool air are attracted to each other.
    D. Warm air and cool air tend to repel each other.

Test Tip

If you find a particular question difficult, put a light pencil mark beside it and keep working. (Do not write in this book.) As you answer other questions, you may find information that helps you answer the difficult question.

CHAPTER 15 Waves

Chapter Outline

1 Types of Waves
What Is a Wave?
Vibrations and Waves
Transverse and Longitudinal Waves
Surface Waves

2 Characteristics of Waves
Wave Properties
Wave Speed
The Doppler Effect

3 Wave Interactions
Reflection, Diffraction, and Refraction
Interference
Standing Waves

Tennessee Course Level Expectations (Physical Science)

CLE.3202.TE.1 Explore the impact of technology on social, political, and economic systems; **CLE.3202.2.1** Investigate the properties and behaviors of mechanical and electromagnetic waves; **CLE.3202.Inq.1** Recognize that science is a progressive endeavor that reevaluates and extends what is already accepted; **CLE.3202.Inq.2** Design and conduct scientific investigations to explore new phenomena, verify previous results, test how well a theory predicts, and compare opposing theories; **CLE.3202. Inq.3** Use appropriate tools and technology to collect precise and accurate data; **CLE.3202.Inq.4** Apply qualitative and quantitative measures to analyze data and draw conclusions that are free of bias; **CLE.3202.Inq.6** Communicate and defend scientific findings; **CLE.3202.Math.1** Understand the mathematical principles behind the science of physics; **CLE.3202.Math.2** Utilize appropriate mathematical equations and processes to solve basic physics problems.

Why It Matters

This award-winning photo—shown here upside down—was taken by a high school student. Reflected light waves create a mirror image of the landscape in the lake.

Inquiry Lab

⏲ 20 min

Making Waves

Fill a **long, rectangular pan** with **water.** Experiment with making waves in different ways. Try making waves by sticking the end of a **pencil** into the water, by moving a **wide stick or board** back and forth, and by striking the side of the pan. Place **wooden blocks or other obstacles** in the pan, and observe how the waves change when they encounter the obstacles.

Questions to Get You Started

1. How do the waves created by the pencil compare to waves created by the wide stick?
2. What happens when the waves encounter an obstacle?
3. What happens when two waves meet?

503

READING TOOLBOX These reading tools can help you learn the material in this chapter. For more information on how to use these and other tools, see **Appendix A.**

Word Parts

Root Words Many scientific words are made up of word parts derived from Latin and Greek. You can unlock the meaning of an unfamiliar science term by analyzing its word parts. **Appendix A** contains a list of many word parts and their meanings. A root word from two key terms in this chapter is shown below.

ROOT	SOURCE	MEANING
fract	Latin verb frangere	"to break"

Your Turn

1. After you have read Section 3, write out the definitions of *diffraction* and *refraction*. Explain why it is appropriate that these terms contain a root meaning "to break."
2. Make a list of other words that contain the same root, then write the definitions of those words. Use a dictionary if you need to.

Classification

Types of Waves Classification is a logical tool for organizing the many things and ideas in our world. Classification involves grouping things into categories.

> **Example:** In the classification of states of matter, *liquids* are defined as substances that can easily change shape but have a fixed volume.

Your Turn In Section 1, you will learn about different kinds of waves. As you learn about these wave types, make a table with three columns. In the first column, list the wave types. In the second column, describe the basis for classification for each wave type. In the third column, list examples of each wave type.

Note Taking

Outlining Taking notes in outline form can help you see how information is organized in a chapter. You can use your outline notes to review the chapter before a test.

Your Turn As you read through this chapter, make notes about the chapter in outline form. An example from Section 1 is shown on the right to help you get started. You can find more information about outlines in **Appendix A.**

> I. TYPES OF WAVES
>   A. What Is a Wave?
>   1. A wave is a disturbance that carries energy through matter or space.
>   2. Most waves travel through a medium.
>   a. Waves that require a medium are called mechanical waves.
>   b. Sound waves are mechanical waves. Air is a common medium for sound waves.

SECTION 1
Types of Waves

Key Ideas

› What does a wave carry?
› How are waves generated?
› What is the difference between a transverse wave and a longitudinal wave?
› How do the particles in ocean waves move?

Key Terms

medium
mechanical wave
electromagnetic wave
transverse wave
longitudinal wave
crest
trough

Why It Matters

Shock absorbers in mountain bikes minimize vibrations to help the biker stay in control. Vibrations are closely related to waves.

When you throw a stone into a pond, ripples form on the surface of the water. Ripples are a type of *wave*. In this section, you will learn about different types of waves.

Tennessee Course Level Expectations (Physical Science)
CLE.3202.2.1; CLE.3202.Inq.1; CLE.3202.Inq.2; CLE.3202.Inq.3

What Is a Wave?

A leaf floating on water, such as the one shown in **Figure 1**, will bob up as a wave passes by. After the wave passes, the leaf will drop back close to its original position. Likewise, individual drops of water are lifted up when a wave passes and then drop back close to their resting places. They do not travel with the wave. If leaves and drops of water do not move along with a wave as the wave passes, then what does move along with the wave? Energy does. › **A wave is a disturbance that carries energy through matter or space.**

Figure 1 This leaf moves up and down as the wave passes by. **What does the wave carry?**

Topic: Waves
Code: HK81641

medium (MEE dee uhm) a physical environment in which phenomena occur

mechanical wave (muh KAN i kuhl WAYV) a wave that requires a medium through which to travel

electromagnetic wave (ee LEK troh mag NET ik WAYV) a wave that consists of oscillating electric and magnetic fields, which radiate outward at the speed of light

Most waves travel through a medium.

Ripples in a pond, such as the ones shown in **Figure 2,** are disturbances that travel through water. The sound you hear from your stereo is a disturbance that travels in waves through air. Earthquakes are disturbances that travel in *seismic waves,* waves that travel through Earth.

In each of these examples, waves involve the movement of some kind of matter. The matter through which a wave travels is called the **medium**. For waves on a pond, water is the medium. For sound from a stereo, air is the medium. And for earthquakes, Earth itself is the medium.

Waves that require a medium are called **mechanical waves.** Most waves are mechanical waves. The only waves that do not require a medium are electromagnetic waves.

Electromagnetic waves do not require a medium.

The laser lights shown in **Figure 2** are an example of electromagnetic waves. **Electromagnetic waves** consist of changing electric and magnetic fields in space. Electromagnetic waves do not require a medium. For instance, light can travel from the sun to Earth across empty space.

Visible light waves are just one type of electromagnetic wave. Radio waves, such as those that carry signals to your radio or television, are also electromagnetic waves. Other kinds of electromagnetic waves will be introduced in later chapters.

✓ **Reading Check** Are light waves mechanical waves? (See Appendix E for answers to Reading Checks.)

Figure 2 Mechanical waves require a medium, but electromagnetic waves do not.

Mechanical waves

Electromagnetic waves

Figure 3 This image of a tsunami was created by the Japanese artist Hokusai in 1830.

Waves transfer energy.

Energy is the ability to exert a force over a certain distance, or to do *work*. We know that waves carry energy because they can do work. For example, water waves can do work on a leaf or on a boat. Sound waves can do work on your eardrum.

The bigger the wave is, the more energy it carries. A wave caused by dropping a stone in a pond may carry enough energy to move a leaf up and down several centimeters. A cruise ship moving through the ocean may create waves big enough to move a fishing boat up and down a few meters.

Figure 3 shows a woodblock print of a *tsunami,* a huge ocean wave that is caused by an earthquake. A tsunami may be as high as 30 m—taller than a 10-story building—when it reaches shore. Such a wave carries enough energy to cause a lot of damage to coastal towns. Normal ocean waves do work on the shore, too; their energy breaks up rocks into tiny pieces to form sandy beaches.

Energy may spread out as a wave travels.

If you stand next to the speakers at a rock concert, the sound waves may damage your ears. But if you stand 100 m away, the sound of the rock band is harmless. Why?

Think about the waves created when a stone falls into a pond. The waves spread out in circles that get bigger as the waves move farther from the center. Each of these circles, called a *wave front,* carries the same amount of energy. But in the larger circles, the energy is spread out over a larger area. When sound waves travel in air, the waves spread out in spheres. As the waves travel outward, the spherical wave fronts get bigger, so the energy spreads out over a larger volume.

READING TOOLBOX

Classification
Waves are classified in different ways. As you read this section, list two ways in which waves are classified, and give examples of each type of wave.

Academic Vocabulary

sphere (SFIR) a three-dimensional surface whose points are equally distant from the center; a globe

SC_INKS.
www.scilinks.org
Topic: Vibrations and Waves
Code: HK81604

Vibrations and Waves

When a singer sings a note, vocal cords in the singer's throat move back and forth. That motion makes the air in the throat vibrate, which creates sound waves that eventually reach your ears. The vibration of the air in your ears causes your eardrums to vibrate. The motion of the eardrum triggers a series of electrical pulses to your brain, and your brain interprets these electrical pulses as sounds.

Waves are related to vibrations. **Most waves are caused by vibrating objects.** The sound waves produced by a singer are caused by vibrating vocal cords. Electromagnetic waves may be caused by vibrating charged particles. In the case of a mechanical wave, the particles in the medium through which the wave passes vibrate, too.

Reading Check What is the source of most waves?

The mechanical energy of a vibrating mass-spring system changes form.

A mass hanging on a spring is shown in **Figure 4.** If the mass is pulled down slightly and released, it will begin to move up and down around its original resting position.

When the mass is pulled away from its resting place, the mass-spring system gains elastic potential energy. The spring exerts a force that pulls the mass back toward its original position. **Figure 4** shows the changes in energy that occur as the spring moves up and down. Although the form of the energy changes, the total amount of mechanical energy does not change (if losses due to friction are ignored).

Whenever the spring is expanded or compressed, it exerts a force that moves the mass back to the original resting position. Thus, the mass bounces up and down, or vibrates. This type of vibration is called *simple harmonic motion*.

Figure 4 When a mass hanging on a spring is disturbed from rest, it starts to vibrate up and down about its original position. **Does the total amount of mechanical energy change?**

Figure 5 A wave can pass through a series of masses on springs. The masses act like the particles in a medium.

A wave can pass through a series of vibrating objects.

Imagine a series of masses and springs tied together in a row, such as the series shown in **Figure 5.** If you pull down on a mass at the end of the row, that mass will begin to vibrate. As the mass vibrates, it pulls on the mass next to it and causes that mass to vibrate. The energy in the vibration of the first mass, which is a combination of kinetic energy and elastic potential energy, is transferred to the second mass-spring system. In this way, the disturbance that started with the first mass travels down the row. This disturbance is a wave that carries energy from one end of the row to the other.

If the first mass were not connected to the other masses, it would keep vibrating on its own. However, because it transfers its energy to the second mass, it slows down and returns to its resting position sooner than it would if it were free. A vibration that fades out as energy is transferred from one object to another is called *damped harmonic motion.*

QuickLab

Particle Motion in a Wave

 20 min

Procedure

1. Ask a partner to hold one end of a **spring.** Take the other end, and stretch it out along a smooth floor.

2. Have another person tie a small piece of **colored ribbon** to a coil near the middle of the spring. The ribbon will help you compare particle motion with wave motion.

3. Swing your end of the spring from side to side to start a wave traveling along the spring. Observe the motion of the ribbon as the wave passes by.

4. Take a section of the spring, and bunch it together. Release the spring to create a different kind of wave traveling along the spring. Observe the motion of the ribbon as this wave passes by.

Analysis

1. How would you describe the motion of the ribbon in step 3? How would you describe the motion of the ribbon in step 4?

2. How can you tell that energy is passing along the spring? Where does that energy come from?

Section 1   Types of Waves   **509**

Why It Matters

How does mountain-bike suspension work?

Mountain bikers often ride over rough terrain. Good suspension systems keep bikers from being jolted by every bump in the road and smooth their landings when they jump. Many of today's mountain bikes have suspension systems in both the front and the rear. The diagrams below show how a rear suspension system works.

1 A suspension system has two parts, the spring and the damper. Together, these parts form a shock absorber. The spring compresses when the bike hits a bump.

2 The damper is an oil-filled device that dissipates the energy in the spring. Without a damper, the spring would continue vibrating in simple harmonic motion. Instead, the spring quickly returns to its rest position.

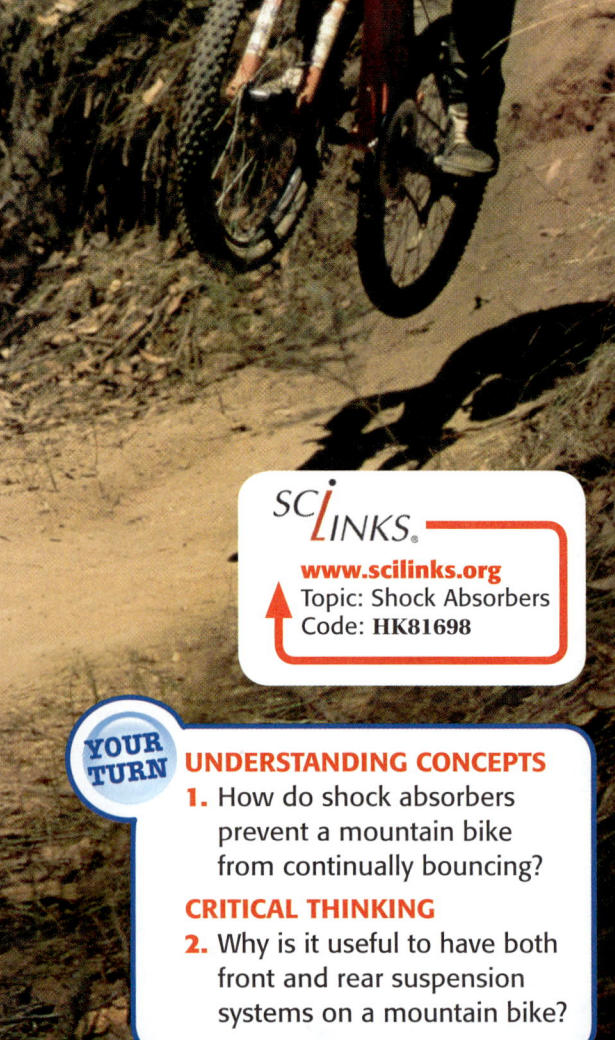

www.scilinks.org
Topic: Shock Absorbers
Code: HK81698

YOUR TURN

UNDERSTANDING CONCEPTS
1. How do shock absorbers prevent a mountain bike from continually bouncing?

CRITICAL THINKING
2. Why is it useful to have both front and rear suspension systems on a mountain bike?

Wave particles move like masses on springs.

If you tie one end of a rope to a doorknob, pull the rope straight, and then rapidly move your hand up and down once, you will generate a single wave, as **Figure 6** shows. As the wave moves along the rope, each ribbon moves up, down, and back to its starting point. The motion of each part of the rope is like the vibrating motion of a mass hanging on a spring. As one part of the rope moves, it pulls on the part next to it. In this way, a wave passes along the length of the rope.

Transverse and Longitudinal Waves

Particles in a medium can vibrate either up and down or back and forth. Waves are often classified according to the direction in which the particles in the medium move as a wave passes by. ▶ **A transverse wave is a wave in which the wave motion is perpendicular to the particle motion. A longitudinal wave is a wave in which the wave motion is parallel to the particle motion.**

Transverse waves have perpendicular motion.

When a crowd does "the wave" at a sporting event, people stand up and raise their arms as the wave reaches their part of the stadium. The wave travels around the stadium, but the individual people move straight up and down. This wave motion is similar to the wave motion in the rope in **Figure 6.** In these cases, the motion of the "particles"—the people in the crowd or the points on the rope—is perpendicular to the motion of the wave as a whole. Waves in which the motion of the particles is perpendicular to the motion of the wave are called **transverse waves.**

Electromagnetic waves are another example of transverse waves. The changing electric and magnetic fields that make up an electromagnetic wave are perpendicular to each other and to the direction in which the wave travels.

Reading Check What is one example of a transverse wave?

QuickLab 10 min

Polarization

1. Polarizing filters block all light waves except for those waves that vibrate in a certain direction. Look through **two polarizing filters** at once, and note your observations.
2. Now, rotate one filter by 90°, and look again. What do you observe this time?
3. Do your observations support the idea that light is a transverse wave? Explain your answer.

---

transverse wave (TRANS VUHRS WAYV) a wave in which the particles of the medium move perpendicularly to the direction the wave is traveling

---

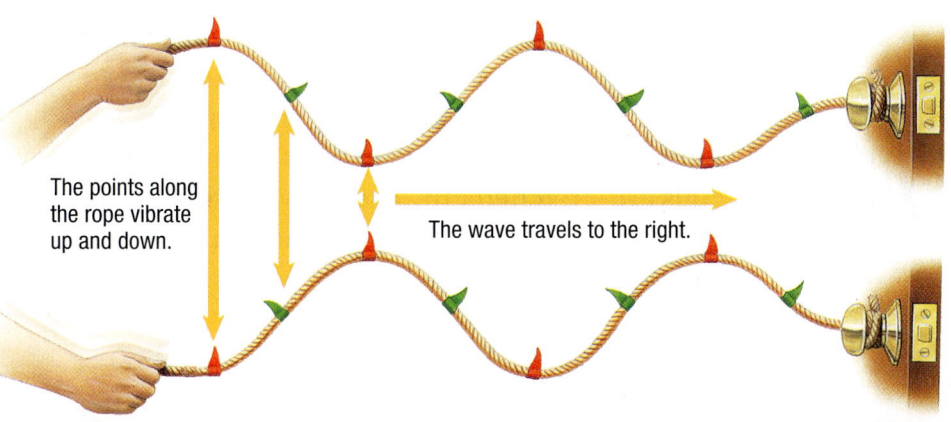

The points along the rope vibrate up and down.

The wave travels to the right.

Figure 6 As a wave passes along this rope, the ribbons move up and down as the wave moves to the right. **Why is this situation an example of a transverse wave?**

Keyword: HK8WAVF6

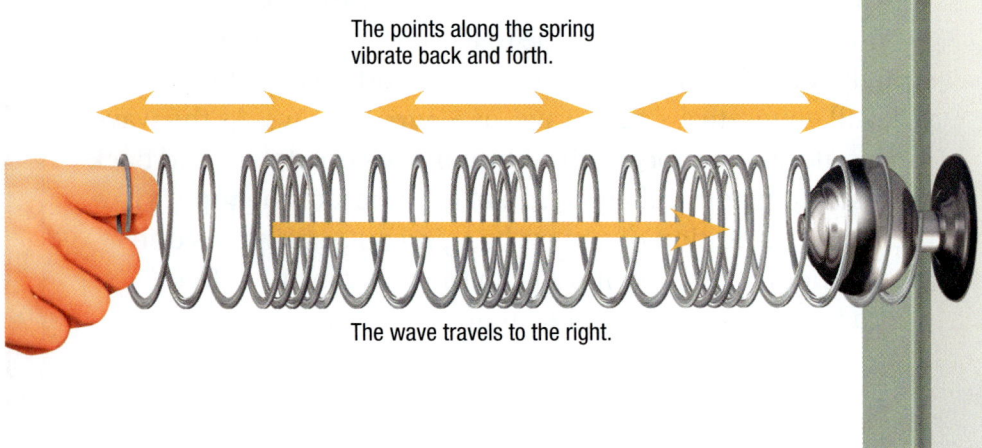

Figure 7 As a longitudinal wave passes along this spring, the coils move back and forth, parallel to the direction of the wave.

longitudinal wave (LAHN juh TOOD'n uhl WAYV) a wave in which the particles of the medium vibrate parallel to the direction of wave motion

crest (KREST) the highest point of a wave

trough (TRAWF) the lowest point of a wave

Figure 8 Transverse waves have crests and troughs, while longitudinal waves have compressions and rarefactions.

Longitudinal waves have parallel motion.

Suppose you attach a long, flexible spring to a doorknob, grab one end, and move your hand back and forth. You will see a wave travel along the spring, as shown in **Figure 7.** As the wave passes along the spring, a ribbon tied to one of the spring's coils would move back and forth, parallel to the direction in which the wave travels. Waves that cause the particles in a medium to vibrate parallel to the direction of wave motion are called **longitudinal waves.**

Sound waves are an example of longitudinal waves that we encounter every day. Sound waves traveling in air compress and expand the air in bands. Molecules in the air move backward and forward, parallel to the direction in which the sound waves travel.

Reading Check What is the difference between a transverse wave and a longitudinal wave?

Waves have crests and troughs or compressions and rarefactions.

Look at the transverse wave in **Figure 8.** The high points of a transverse wave are called **crests.** The low points of a transverse wave are called **troughs.** Now look at the longitudinal wave in **Figure 8.** This wave does not have crests and troughs because the particles move back and forth instead of up and down. If you look closely at a longitudinal wave in a spring, you will see a moving pattern of areas where the coils are bunched up alternating with areas where the coils are stretched out. The crowded areas are called *compressions*. The stretched-out areas are called *rarefactions*.

512 Chapter 15 Waves

Surface Waves

Unlike the examples of waves discussed so far, waves on the ocean or in a swimming pool are not simply transverse waves or longitudinal waves. Water waves are an example of *surface waves.*
❯ **The particles in a surface wave move both perpendicularly and parallel to the direction in which the wave travels.** Surface waves occur at the boundary between two different mediums, such as water and air.

Follow the motion of the beach ball shown in **Figure 9** as a wave passes by. The wave is traveling from left to right. At first, the ball is in a trough. As the crest approaches, the ball moves to the left (parallel to the wave) and upward (perpendicularly to the wave). When the ball is near the crest, it starts to move to the right. Once the crest has passed, the ball starts to fall back downward and then to the left. The up-and-down motions combine with the side-to-side motions to produce a circular motion overall.

Particles in surface waves move, as the beach ball does, in an ellipse. (A circle is a special case of an ellipse.) The motion of the beach ball helps make visible the motion of the particles (water molecules) in a surface wave.

Figure 9 Ocean waves are surface waves at the boundary between air and water.

Section 1 Review

KEY IDEAS

1. **Identify** the mediums for the following waves:
   a. ripples on a pond
   b. the sound waves from a stereo speaker
   c. seismic waves
   d. waves on a spring
   e. ocean waves
2. **Name** the one kind of wave that does not require a medium.
3. **Describe** the motion of a mass vibrating on a spring. How does this motion relate to wave motion? What is the source of the wave?
4. **Explain** the difference between transverse waves and longitudinal waves. Give an example of each type of wave.
5. **Draw** a transverse wave and a longitudinal wave. Label a crest, a trough, a compression, and a rarefaction.
6. **Describe** the motion of a water molecule on the surface of the ocean as a wave passes by.

CRITICAL THINKING

7. **Applying Concepts** Describe a situation that demonstrates that water waves carry energy.
8. **Making Inferences** Sometimes, people at a sports event do "the wave" across a stadium. Is "the wave" really an example of a wave? Why or why not?
9. **Drawing Conclusions** Why can supernova explosions in space be seen but not heard on Earth?

SECTION 2
Characteristics of Waves

Key Ideas
- What are some ways to measure and compare waves?
- How can you calculate the speed of a wave?
- Why does the pitch of an ambulance siren change as the ambulance rushes past you?

Key Terms
amplitude
wavelength
period
frequency
Doppler effect

Why It Matters
Surfers observe characteristics of ocean waves to determine when and where the conditions are best for surfing.

Tennessee Course Level Expectations (Physical Science)
CLE.3202.2.1; CLE.3202.Inq.1; CLE.3202.Inq.2; CLE.3202.Inq.3; CLE.3202.Math.1; CLE.3202.Math.22

If you have spent any time at the beach or on a boat, you have probably observed many properties of waves. Sometimes the waves are very large; other times they are smaller. Sometimes they are close together, and sometimes they are farther apart. How can these differences be described and measured in more detail?

Wave Properties

In this section, you will learn about several wave properties, including amplitude, wavelength, period, and frequency. ❯ **Amplitude and wavelength are measurements of distance. Period and frequency are measurements based on time.** These four properties are useful for describing and comparing waves.

Amplitude measures the amount of particle vibration.

The greatest distance that particles are displaced from their normal resting positions is called the **amplitude** of the wave. In a transverse wave, the amplitude is the distance from the rest position to a crest or to a trough. The amplitude of a transverse wave is illustrated in **Figure 1**.

The simplest transverse waves have similar shapes no matter how big they are or what medium they travel through. An ideal transverse wave has the shape of a *sine curve*. A sine curve looks like an *S* lying on its side. Waves that have the shape of a sine curve are called *sine waves*. The wave illustrated in **Figure 1** is an example of a sine wave. Although many waves are not perfect sine waves, their shapes can be approximated by the graph of a sine curve.

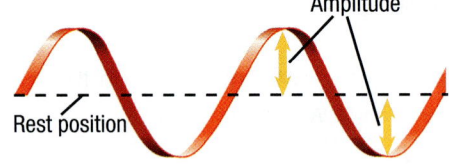

Figure 1 The amplitude of a transverse wave is measured from the rest position to the crest or the trough.

Transverse wave

Longitudinal wave

Figure 2 Wavelength is the distance between two identical points on a wave. **Does the distance between crests equal the distance between troughs?**

Wavelength is the distance between two equivalent parts of a wave.

The crests of ocean waves at a beach may be separated by several meters, while ripples in a pond may be separated by only a few centimeters. The distance from one crest to the next crest, or from one trough to the next trough, is called the <mark>wavelength.</mark> In a longitudinal wave, the wavelength is the distance between two compressions or between two rarefactions. More generally, the wavelength is the distance between any two successive identical parts of a wave. **Figure 2** shows the wavelengths of a transverse wave and a longitudinal wave.

Not all waves have a single wavelength that is easy to measure. For instance, most sound waves have a complicated shape, so the wavelength can be difficult to determine. When used in equations, wavelength is represented by the Greek letter lambda, λ. Because wavelength is a distance measurement, it is expressed in the SI unit, meters.

Reading Check How is the wavelength of a longitudinal wave measured?

Amplitude and wavelength tell you about energy.

Earthquake waves can cause serious damage, as **Figure 3** shows. The larger the amplitude of a wave is, the more energy it carries. The waves of destructive earthquakes have greater amplitudes, and therefore more energy, than the waves of minor earthquakes. The wavelength of a wave is also related to the wave's energy: The shorter the wavelength of a wave is, the more energy it carries.

amplitude (AM pluh TOOD) the maximum distance that the particles of a wave's medium vibrate from their rest position

wavelength (WAYV LENGKTH) the distance from any point on a wave to an identical point on the next wave

Figure 3 In 1989, portions of the Cypress Freeway in Oakland, California collapsed during a major earthquake.

Section 2 Characteristics of Waves

Academic Vocabulary

successive (suhk SES iv) following one after the other; consecutive

period (PIR ee uhd) in physics, the time that it takes a complete cycle or wave oscillation to occur

frequency (FREE kwuhn see) the number of cycles or vibrations per unit of time; also the number of waves produced in a given amount of time

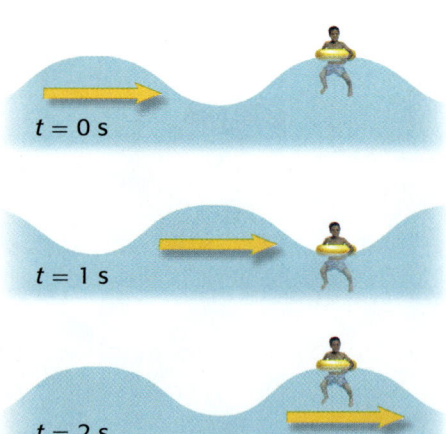

Figure 4 A person floating in an inner tube can determine the period and frequency of the waves by counting the number of seconds that pass between wave crests.

The period is a measurement of the time it takes for a wave to pass a given point.

If you swim out into the ocean until your feet can no longer touch the bottom, your body will be free to move up and down as waves come into shore. As your body rises and falls, you can count the number of seconds between two successive wave crests.

The time required for one complete vibration of a particle in a medium—or of one rise and fall of a swimmer in the ocean—is called the **period** of the wave. The period is also the time required for one full wavelength of a wave to pass a certain point. In equations, the period is represented by the symbol *T*. Because the period is a time measurement, it is expressed in the SI unit, seconds.

Frequency is a measurement of the vibration rate.

If you were floating in an inner tube, like the person shown in **Figure 4**, you could count the number of crests that passed by in a certain time, say, in one minute. The number of wavelengths that pass a point in a given time interval is called the **frequency** of a wave. Frequency also refers to how rapidly vibrations occur in the medium, at the source of the wave, or both.

The symbol for frequency is *f*. The SI unit for frequency is hertz (Hz). (This unit is named after Heinrich Hertz, the scientist who experimentally demonstrated, in 1888, the existence of electromagnetic waves.) Hertz units measure the number of vibrations per second. One vibration per second is 1 Hz, two vibrations per second is 2 Hz, and so on. You can hear sounds with frequencies as low as 20 Hz and as high as 20,000 Hz. At 20,000 Hz, there are 20,000 compressions hitting your ear every second.

The frequency and the period of a wave are related.

The more vibrations that are made in a second, the less time each vibration takes. In other words, the frequency is the inverse of the period.

> **Frequency-Period equation**
> $$\text{frequency} = \frac{1}{\text{period}}$$
> $$f = \frac{1}{T}$$

In **Figure 4**, a wave crest passes the inner tube every 2 s, so the period is 2 s. The frequency can be found by using the frequency-period equation above: $f = 1/T = 1/2 \text{ s} = 0.5 \text{ Hz}$.

Reading Check How are frequency and period related?

Why It Matters

How Are Good Surfing Waves Formed?

Storms on the ocean usually create large waves. Often, the waves die out at sea. But if a storm is strong enough, the waves may crash into each other, and combine their energies. The resulting waves can travel all the way to shore and provide enjoyment for surfers.

REAL WORLD

Three main factors affect the magnitude of surfing waves: the speed of the wind (*wind velocity*), the surface area of the ocean affected by the wind (*fetch*), and the time that the wind blows over the area (*duration*). Surfers check weather forecasts—and sometimes even satellite data—to see which storms will create good surfing opportunities.

YOUR TURN

CRITICAL THINKING
1. What vertical forces act on a surfer?
2. If a surfer accelerates forward while riding a wave, are the horizontal forces balanced?

SCLINKS
www.scilinks.org
Topic: Ocean Waves
Code: HK81066

Figure 5 By observing the frequency and wavelength of waves passing a pier, you can calculate the speed of the waves.

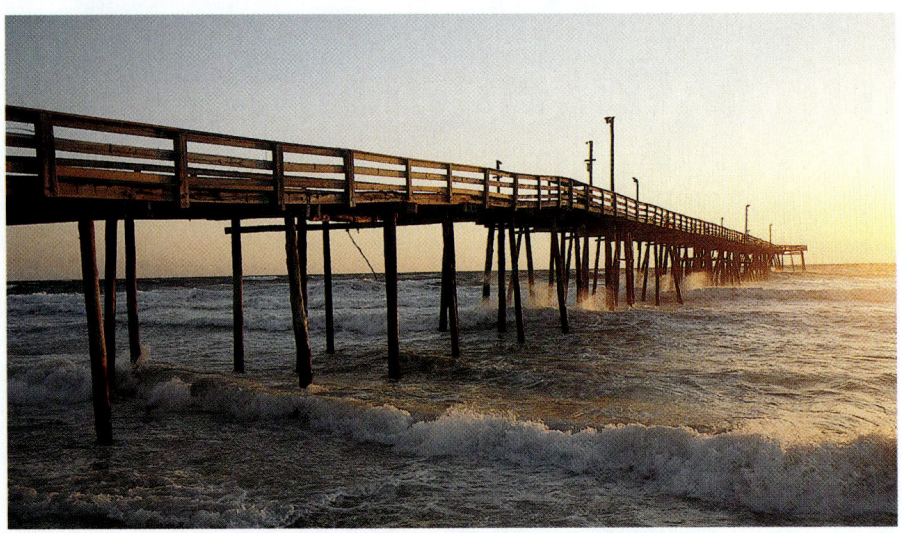

Integrating Earth Science

Seismic Waves Earthquakes create waves, called *seismic waves,* that travel through Earth. There are two main types of seismic waves, *P waves* (primary waves) and *S waves* (secondary waves). P waves are longitudinal waves that can travel through solids and liquids. S waves are transverse waves that can travel only through solids. P waves travel faster than S waves, so they always move ahead of S waves. S waves move more slowly, but they carry more energy than P waves.

Wave Speed

Imagine watching water waves as they move past a post of a pier such as the one in **Figure 5.** If you count the number of crests passing the post for 10 s, you can determine the frequency of the waves. If you measure the distance between crests, you can find the wavelength of the waves. But how can you know the speed of the waves? ▸ **The speed of a wave is equal to wavelength divided by period, or to frequency multiplied by wavelength.**

✓ **Reading Check** What are two ways to calculate wave speed?

Wave speed equals wavelength divided by period.

The speed of a moving object is found by dividing the distance the object travels by the time it takes the object to travel that distance. This calculation is shown in the following equation:

$$speed = \frac{distance}{time} \qquad v = \frac{d}{t}$$

If SI units are used for distance and time, speed is expressed as meters per second (m/s). The *wave speed* is simply how fast a wave moves, or, more precisely, how far the wave travels in a certain amount of time. To calculate wave speed, use the wavelength as the distance traveled, and the period as the amount of time it takes the wave to travel a distance of one wavelength.

▸ **Wave speed equation** $\qquad wave\ speed = \frac{wavelength}{period} \qquad v = \frac{\lambda}{T}$

Wave speed equals frequency times wavelength.

Because period is the inverse of frequency, dividing by the period is equivalent to multiplying by the frequency. Therefore, the speed of a wave can also be calculated by multiplying the wavelength by the frequency.

> **Wave speed equation**
> wave speed = frequency × wavelength
> $v = f \times \lambda$

For example, suppose waves passing by a post of a pier have a frequency of 0.4 Hz and a wavelength of 10 m. The waves in this case have a wave speed of 0.4 Hz × 10 m = 4 m/s.

Math Skills — Wave Speed

The string of a piano that produces the note middle C vibrates with a frequency of 262 Hz. If the sound waves produced by this string have a wavelength in air of 1.30 m, what is the speed of the sound waves?

Identify
List the given and unknown values.

Given:
frequency, $f = 262$ Hz
wavelength, $\lambda = 1.30$ m
Unknown:
wave speed, $v = ?$ m/s

Plan
Write the equation for wave speed.

$v = f \times \lambda$

Solve
Insert the known values into the equation, and solve.

$v = 262$ Hz $\times 1.30$ m
$v = 341$ m/s

Practice

1. The average wavelength in a series of ocean waves is 15.0 m. A wave crest arrives at the shore on average every 10.0 s, so the frequency is 0.100 Hz. What is the average speed of the waves?
2. Green light has a wavelength of 5.20×10^{-7} m. The speed of light is 3.00×10^8 m/s. Calculate the frequency of green light waves with this wavelength.
3. The speed of sound in air is about 340 m/s. What is the wavelength of a sound wave with a frequency of 220 Hz (on a piano, the A below middle C)?

For more practice, visit **go.hrw.com** and enter keyword **HK8MP**.

Practice Hint

> Problem 2: The wave speed equation can be rearranged to isolate frequency in the following way:
> $$v = f \times \lambda$$
> Divide both sides by λ.
> $$\frac{v}{\lambda} = \frac{f \times \cancel{\lambda}}{\cancel{\lambda}}$$
> $$f = \frac{v}{\lambda}$$

> Problem 3: In this problem, you will need to rearrange the equation to isolate wavelength.

Section 2 **Characteristics of Waves**

QuickLab — Wave Speed

  10 min

Procedure

1. Place a **rectangular pan** on a level surface, and fill the pan with **water** to a depth of about 2 cm.
2. Cut a **wooden dowel** (3 cm or more in diameter) to a length slightly less than the width of the pan, and place the dowel in one end of the pan.
3. Move or roll the dowel back and forth slowly, and observe the length of the wave generated.
4. Now move the dowel back and forth faster (to increase frequency), and observe the wavelength.

Analysis

1. Do the waves always travel at the same speed in the pan?

The speed of a wave depends on the medium.

Sound waves can travel through air. If they couldn't, you would not be able to have a conversation with a friend or hear music from a radio across the room. Because sound travels very fast in air (about 340 m/s), you don't notice a time delay in most situations.

Sound waves travel three to four times faster in water than they do in air. If you swim with your head underwater, you may hear certain sounds very clearly. Dolphins, such as those shown in **Figure 6,** use sound waves to communicate with one another over long distances underwater.

Sound waves travel even faster in solids than they do in air or in water. Sound waves have speeds 15 to 20 times as fast in rock or metal as in air. If someone strikes a long steel rail with a hammer at one end, you might hear two bangs at the other end. The first sound, which has traveled through the steel rail itself, reaches you shortly before the second sound, which has traveled through the air.

The speed of a wave depends on the medium. In a given medium, though, the speed of waves is constant; it does not depend on the frequency of the wave. No matter how fast you shake your hand up and down to create waves on a rope, the waves will travel at the same speed. Shaking your hand faster just increases the frequency and decreases the wavelength.

Figure 6 Dolphins use sound waves to communicate with one another. **Does sound in water travel faster or slower than sound in air?**

Kinetic theory explains differences in wave speed.

The arrangement of particles in a medium determines how well waves travel through it. Solids, liquids, and gases have different degrees of organization at the particle level.

In gases, the molecules are far apart and move around randomly. A molecule must travel through a lot of empty space before it bumps into another molecule. Waves don't travel as fast in gases as they do in solids and liquids.

In liquids, such as water, the molecules are much closer together than they are in gases, and they are free to slide past one another. Molecules in a liquid can be compared to vibrating masses on springs that are so close together that the masses rub against each other. In the case of masses on springs, vibrations are transferred easily from one mass to the next. In the case of a liquid, vibrations are transferred easily from one molecule to another. As a result, waves travel faster in liquids than they do in gases. For example, sound waves travel faster through water than they do through air.

In solids, molecules are closer yet, and are bound tightly to each other. Molecules in a solid can be compared to vibrating masses that are glued together. When one mass starts to vibrate, all the others also start to vibrate almost immediately. As a result, waves travel very quickly through most solids.

Reading Check Why does sound travel faster in solids than it does in liquids or in gases?

Light has a finite speed.

When you flip a light switch, light seems to fill the room instantly. However, light does take time to travel from place to place. All electromagnetic waves in empty space travel at the same speed, known as the *speed of light*. The speed of light in empty space is 3.00×10^8 m/s (186,000 mi/s). This value is a constant that is often represented by the symbol c. Light travels more slowly when it has to pass through a medium such as air or water.

Our eyes can detect light with frequencies ranging from about 4.3×10^{14} Hz to 7.5×10^{14} Hz. Light in this range is called *visible light*. The differences in frequency in visible light account for the differences in color that we see in **Figure 7**. Electromagnetic waves also exist in a range of frequencies that we cannot see directly. The full range of light at different frequencies and wavelengths is called the *electromagnetic spectrum*. Because the speed of light is constant, you can use the wave speed equation ($f \times \lambda = c$) to find frequency if you know wavelength, or vice versa.

Figure 7 The part of the electromagnetic spectrum that we can see is called visible light. **How does frequency change as wavelength increases?**

The Doppler Effect

Imagine that you are standing on a corner as an ambulance rushes by. As the ambulance passes, the sound of the siren changes from a high pitch to a lower pitch. Why? ❯ **Motion between the source of waves and the observer creates a change in observed frequency.** In the case of sound waves, motion creates a change in pitch.

Pitch is determined by the frequency of sound waves.

The *pitch* of a sound, how high or low it is, is determined by the frequency at which sound waves strike the eardrum in your ear. A high-pitched sound is caused by sound waves of high frequency. As you know from the wave speed equation, frequency and wavelength are also related to the speed of a wave.

Suppose you could see the sound waves from the ambulance siren when the ambulance is at rest. You would see the sound waves traveling out from the siren in spherical wave fronts, as shown in **Figure 8.** The distance between two successive wave fronts represents the wavelength of the sound waves. When the sound waves reach your ears, they have a frequency equal to the number of wave fronts that strike your eardrum each second. That frequency determines the pitch of the sound that you hear.

READING TOOLBOX

Outlining
Create an outline using the main ideas from this section. Include all key ideas, key terms, and red and blue topic headings. Use the outline to review the material.

Figure 8 The Doppler Effect

When an ambulance is not moving, the sound waves produced by the siren spread out in spheres. The frequency of the waves is the same at all locations.

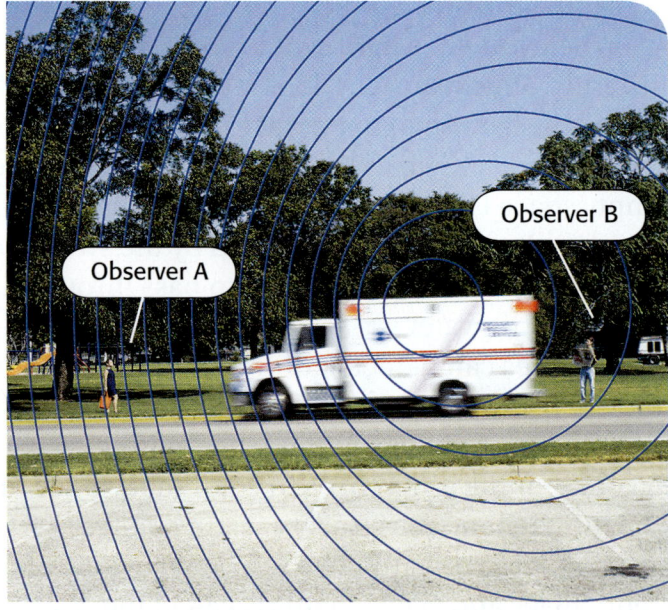

When an ambulance is moving, the sound waves produced by the siren are closer together in front and farther apart behind. Observer A hears a higher-pitched sound than Observer B hears.

Frequency changes when the source of waves is moving.

If an ambulance is moving toward you, the sound waves from the siren are compressed in the direction of motion, as shown in **Figure 8.** Between the time that one sound wave and the next sound wave are emitted, the ambulance moves forward. The distance between wave fronts is shortened, though the wave speed remains the same. As a result, the sound waves reach your ear at a higher frequency; they sound higher-pitched than they would if the ambulance were at rest.

Conversely, if an ambulance is moving away from you, the frequency at which the waves reach your ear is less, and you hear the sound of the siren at a lower pitch than you would if the ambulance were at rest. This change in the observed frequency of a wave is called the **Doppler effect.** This effect can result from the motion of the source or the observer or both. The Doppler effect occurs for light waves and for other types of waves as well. The Doppler effect can be used to track storms, as **Figure 9** shows.

Figure 9 This Doppler radar dome receives radio waves that have been sent out and then reflected back by rain, snow, and hail. The observed frequency shifts help meteorologists track storms.

www.scilinks.org
Topic: Doppler Effect
Code: HK80424

Doppler effect (DAHP luhr e FEKT) an observed change in the frequency of a wave when the source or observer is moving

Section 2 Review

KEY IDEAS

1. **Draw** a sine curve, and label a crest, a trough, and the amplitude.
2. **Describe** how the frequency and period of a wave are related.
3. **Explain** why sound waves travel faster in liquids or solids than in air.
4. **Describe** the Doppler effect, and explain why it occurs.

CRITICAL THINKING

5. **Identifying Relationships** What happens to the wavelength of a wave when the frequency of the wave is doubled but the wave speed stays the same?

6. **Applying Concepts** Imagine you are waiting for a train to pass at a railroad crossing. Will the train whistle have a higher pitch as the train approaches you or after it has passed you by?

Math Skills

7. A wave along a guitar string has a frequency of 440 Hz and a wavelength of 1.5 m. What is the speed of the wave?
8. The speed of sound in air is about 340 m/s. What is the wavelength of sound waves produced by a guitar string vibrating at 440 Hz?
9. The speed of light is 3×10^8 m/s. What is the frequency of microwaves with a wavelength of 1 cm?

SECTION 3 Wave Interactions

Key Ideas

> How do waves behave when they hit a boundary, when they pass around an edge or opening, and when they pass from one medium to another?

> What happens when two or more waves are in the same location?

> How does a standing wave affect the medium in which it travels?

Key Terms

reflection
diffraction
refraction
interference
constructive interference
destructive interference
standing wave

Why It Matters

Wave interactions make it possible to see your reflection in a mirror, to hear sounds from a nearby room, and to see colorful patterns on soap bubbles.

Tennessee Course Level Expectations (Physical Science)

CLE.3202.TE.1; CLE.3202.2.1;
CLE.3202.Inq.1; CLE.3202.Inq.2;
CLE.3202.Inq.3; CLE.3202.Inq.4;
CLE.3202.Inq.6; CLE.3202.Math.1;
CLE.3202.Math.2

Have you ever seen a landscape reflected in a still lake? This reflection occurs because of the way waves interact with their environment and with other waves. You will learn about wave interactions in this section.

Reflection, Diffraction, and Refraction

When waves are moving through a continuous medium or through space, they may move in straight lines like waves on the ocean, spread out in circles like ripples on a pond, or spread out in spheres like sound waves in air. But what happens when a wave meets an object? And what happens when a wave passes into another medium? **› When a wave meets a surface or a boundary, the wave bounces back. When a wave passes the edge of an object or passes through an opening, the wave bends. A wave also bends when it passes from one medium to another at an angle.**

Reflection occurs when a wave meets a boundary.

When light waves strike a shiny surface, they reflect off the surface. **Reflection** is simply the bouncing back of a wave when it meets a surface or boundary. The reflection of light waves can create a mirror image of a landscape when they hit the surface of a lake. Other types of waves reflect, too. When water waves hit the side of a boat, they are reflected. **Figure 1** shows another example of the reflection of water waves.

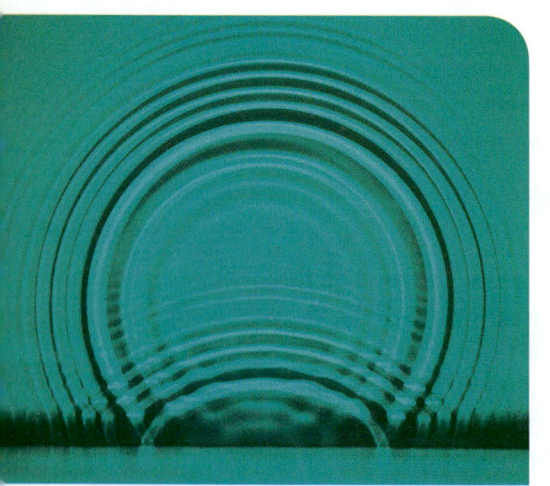

Figure 1 These water waves bounce back when they hit the surface. **What wave behavior does this illustrate?**

Figure 2 Diffraction

Waves bend when they pass the edge of an obstacle.

When they pass through an opening, waves bend around both edges.

Diffraction is the bending of waves around an edge.

If you stand outside the doorway of a classroom, you may be able to hear the sound of voices inside the room. But if the sound waves cannot travel in a straight line to your ear, how are you able to hear the voices?

When waves pass the edge of an object, they spread out as if a new wave were created there. The same effect occurs when waves pass through an opening, such as an open window or a door. In effect, the waves bend around an object or opening. This bending of waves as they pass an edge is called **diffraction.** The amount of diffraction of a wave depends on its wavelength and on the size of the barrier or opening. Diffraction is the reason that shadows never have perfectly sharp edges.

The photograph on the left in **Figure 2** shows waves passing around a block in a tank of water. Before they reach the block, the waves travel in a straight line. After they pass the block, the waves near the edge bend and spread out into the space behind the block. This is an example of diffraction.

The photograph on the right in **Figure 2** shows two blocks placed end to end with a small gap between them. Water waves bend around the two edges and spread out as they pass through the opening. Sound waves passing through a door behave in the same way. Because sound waves spread out into the space beyond the door, a person who is near the door on the outside can hear sounds from inside the room.

Reading Check What is one example of diffraction?

www.scilinks.org
Topic: Reflection, Refraction, Diffraction
Code: HK81284

reflection (ri FLEK shuhn) the bouncing back of a ray of light, sound, or heat when the ray hits a surface that it does not go through

diffraction (di FRAK shuhn) a change in the direction of a wave when the wave finds an obstacle or an edge, such as an opening

Figure 3 Because light waves bend when they pass from one medium to another, this spoon looks like it is in two pieces. **What is this phenomenon called?**

Waves can also bend by refraction.

Why does the spoon in **Figure 3** look as though it is broken into two pieces? This strange appearance results from the bending of light waves. The bending of waves when they pass from one medium into another is called **refraction**. All waves are refracted when they pass from one medium to another at an angle.

Light waves which reflect from the top of the spoon handle pass straight through the glass and the air to your eyes. But the light waves which reflect from the bottom part of the spoon start out in the water, then pass through the glass, then pass through the air to your eyes. Each time the waves enter a new medium, they bend slightly because of a change in wave speed. The waves reflected from the bottom part of the spoon reach your eyes from a different angle than the waves reflected from the top of the spoon handle. Because one set of light waves is reaching your eyes from one direction, and another set of light waves is reaching your eyes from a different direction, the spoon appears to be broken.

Reading Check How is refraction different from diffraction?

Interference

What would happen if you and another person tried to walk through the exact same space at the same time? You would run into each other. Material objects, such as human bodies, cannot share space with other material objects. Waves, however, can share space with other waves. ▶ **When several waves are in the same location, they combine to produce a single, new wave that is different from the original waves.** This interaction is called **interference. Figure 4** shows interference occurring as water waves pass through each other. Once the waves have passed through each other and moved on, they will return to their original shapes.

---

refraction (ri FRAK shuhn) the bending of a wave front as the wave front passes between two substances in which the speed of the wave differs

interference (IN tuhr FIR uhns) the combination of two or more waves that results in a single wave

constructive interference (kuhn STRUHK tiv IN tuhr FIR uhns) a superposition of two or more waves that produces an intensity equal to the sum of the intensities of the individual waves

destructive interference (di STRUHK tiv IN tuhr FIR uhns) a superposition of two or more waves that produces an intensity equal to the difference of the intensities of the individual waves

---

Figure 4 Interference patterns form when water waves pass through each other.

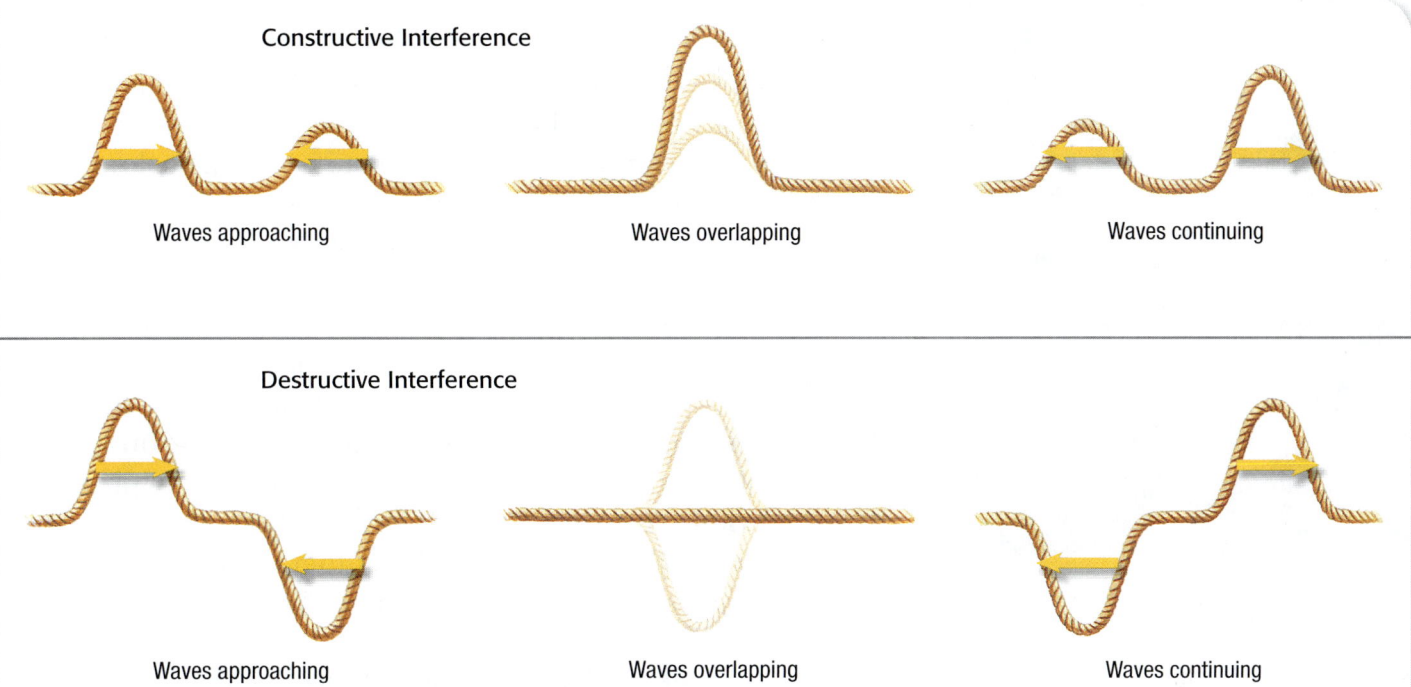

Figure 5 Waves can interfere constructively or destructively. **What condition is required for complete destructive interference?**

Constructive interference increases amplitude.

When the crest of one wave overlaps the crest of another wave, the waves reinforce each other, as the top image in **Figure 5** shows. Think about what happens at the particle level. Suppose the crest of one wave moves a particle up 4 cm from its original position, and the crest of another wave moves the particle up 3 cm.

When these waves overlap, the result is a wave whose amplitude is the sum of the amplitudes of the two individual waves. The particle moves up 4 cm because of one wave and 3 cm because of the other, for a total displacement of 7 cm. This phenomenon is called **constructive interference.**

Destructive interference decreases amplitude.

When the crest of one wave meets the trough of another wave, the resulting wave has a smaller amplitude than the larger of the two waves. This phenomenon is called **destructive interference.**

To understand how destructive interference works, imagine the following scenario between two waves. Suppose the crest of one wave has an amplitude of 4 cm, and the trough of the other wave has an amplitude of 3 cm. If the crest and trough overlap, a new wave will be formed with an amplitude of just 1 cm. When destructive interference occurs between two waves that have the same amplitude, the waves may completely cancel each other out, as the lower image in **Figure 5** shows.

Integrating Architecture

Dead Spots You might have experienced destructive interference in an auditorium or a concert hall. As sound waves reflect from the walls, there are places, known as *dead spots*, where the waves interfere destructively and cancel each other out. Dead spots are produced by the interaction of sound waves coming directly from the stage with waves reflected off the walls. To prevent dead spots, architects design concert halls so that the dimensions are not simple multiples of each other. They also try to avoid smooth, parallel walls in the design. Irregularities in the wall and ceiling tend to reduce the direct reflections of waves and the resulting interference.

Section 3 Wave Interactions

Figure 6 The colorful swirls on a bubble result from the constructive interference of some light waves and the destructive interference of other light waves.

Outlining
Create an outline that covers the material in this section. Be sure to include all of the key ideas. Also include supporting ideas, examples, and key terms.

Interference of light waves creates colorful displays.

You can see a rainbow of colors when oil is spilled onto a watery surface. Soap bubbles, like the ones shown in **Figure 6**, have reds, blues, and yellows on their surfaces. The colors are due to interference patterns between light waves.

When light waves strike a soap bubble, some waves bounce off the outside of the bubble and travel directly to your eye. Other light waves travel into the thin shell of the bubble, bounce off the inner side of the bubble's shell, then travel back through the shell, into the air, and to your eye. These waves travel farther than the waves reflected directly off the outside of the bubble. At times the two sets of waves are out of phase with each other. They interfere constructively at some frequencies (colors) and destructively at other frequencies (colors). The result is a swirling rainbow effect.

Interference of sound waves produces beats.

The sound waves from two tuning forks of slightly different frequencies will interfere with each other as shown in **Figure 7**. The compressions and rarefactions of their respective sound waves will arrive at your ear at different rates.

When compressions from the two tuning forks arrive at your ear at the same time, constructive interference occurs, and the sound is louder. A short time later, a compression from one and a rarefaction from the other arrive together. Destructive interference occurs, and a softer sound is heard. Within the overall sound, you hear a pattern of alternating loud and soft sounds, called *beats*.

Piano tuners listen for beats between a tuning fork of known frequency and a string on a piano. By adjusting the tension in the string, the tuner can change the pitch (frequency) of the string's vibration. When no beats are heard, the string is vibrating at the same frequency as the tuning fork.

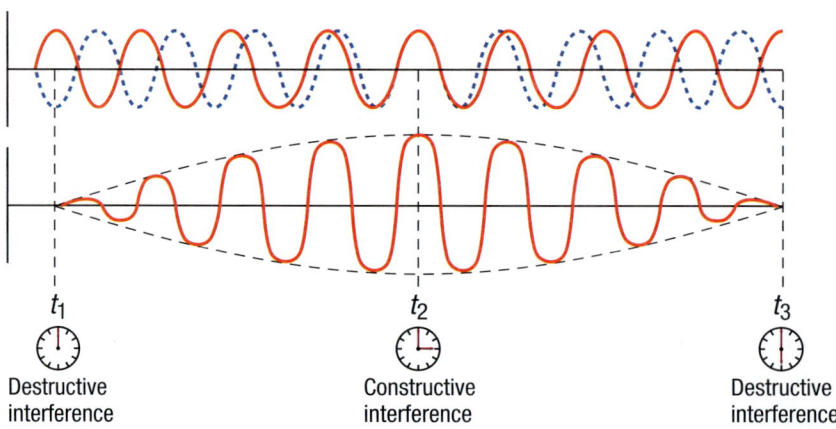

Figure 7
When two waves of slightly different frequencies interfere with each other, they produce beats.
When is the amplitude of the resultant wave greatest?

Standing Waves

Suppose you send a wave through a rope tied to a wall at the other end. The wave is reflected from the wall and travels back along the rope. If you continue to send waves down the rope, the waves that you make will interfere with those waves that reflect off the wall and travel back toward you, to form *standing waves*.

A **standing wave** results from interference between a wave and its reflected wave. **▶ A standing wave causes the medium to vibrate in a stationary pattern that resembles a loop or a series of loops.** Although it appears as if one wave is standing still, in reality two waves are traveling in opposite directions. **Figure 8** shows standing waves that were captured with strobe photography.

Standing waves have nodes and antinodes.

Each loop of a standing wave is separated from the next loop by points that have no vibration, called *nodes*. Nodes lie at the points where the crests of the original waves meet the troughs of the reflected waves. Nodes are points of complete destructive interference. The top wave in **Figure 8** has a node at each end.

Midway between the nodes lie points of maximum vibration, called *antinodes*. Antinodes form where the crests of the original waves line up with the crests of the reflected waves so that complete constructive interference occurs. The top wave in **Figure 8** has a single antinode in the middle.

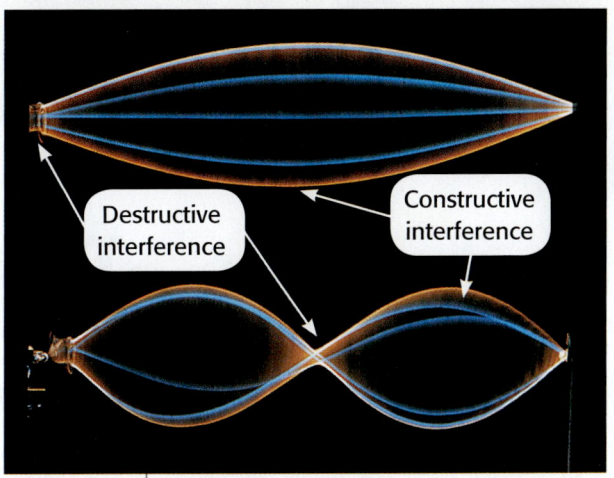

Figure 8 These photos of standing waves were captured using a strobe light that flashes different colors at different times. **How many nodes and antinodes does each wave have?**

standing wave (STAN ding WAYV) a pattern of vibration that simulates a wave that is standing still

Section 3 Review

KEY IDEAS

1. **Describe** what may happen when ripples on a pond encounter a large rock in the water.
2. **Explain** why you can hear two people talking even after they walk around a corner.
3. **Name** the conditions required for two waves to interfere constructively.
4. **Name** the conditions required for two waves on a rope to interfere completely destructively.
5. **Explain** why colors appear on the surface of a soap bubble.
6. **Draw** a standing wave, and label the nodes and antinodes.

CRITICAL THINKING

7. **Applying Concepts** Imagine that you and a friend are trying to tune the lowest strings on two different guitars to the same pitch. Explain how you could use beats to determine if the strings are tuned to the same frequency.
8. **Drawing Conclusions** Determine the longest possible wavelength of a standing wave on a string that is 2 m long.

Skills Practice Lab

 50 min

Transverse Waves

You can model transverse waves by making a pendulum out of a cup that drops colored sand onto paper. In this lab, you will investigate variations in wave characteristics by making variations in the pendulum.

Procedure

Making Sine Curves with a Sand Pendulum

1 Review the discussion in Section 2 of this chapter on the use of sine curves to represent transverse waves.

2 On a blank sheet of paper, prepare a table like the one below.

Sample Data Table: Characteristics of Transverse Waves

Length along paper = 1 m	Time (s)	Average wavelength (m)	Average amplitude (m)
Curve 1			
Curve 2		DO NOT WRITE IN BOOK	
Curve 3			

3 Use a small nail to poke a small hole in the bottom of a paper or plastic-foam cup. Also punch two holes on opposite sides of the cup near the rim. Tie strings of equal length through the upper holes. Make a pendulum by tying the strings from the cup to a ring stand or other support. Clamp the stand down at the end of a table. Cover the bottom hole with a large piece of tape, then fill the cup with sand.

4 Unroll some of the paper, and mark off a length of 1 m using a dotted line at each end. Then roll the paper back up, and position the paper under the pendulum.

5 Remove the tape over the hole. Start the pendulum swinging as your lab partner pulls the paper perpendicular to the cup's swing. Another lab partner should loosely hold the paper roll. Try to pull the paper in a straight line with a constant speed. The sand should trace an approximation of a sine curve, as shown in the photograph.

6 As your partner pulls the paper under the pendulum, start the stopwatch when the sand trace reaches the first dotted line. When the sand trace reaches the second dotted line (marking the length of 1 m), stop the watch. Record the time in your table.

7 When you are finished making the curve, stop the pendulum and cover the hole in the bottom of the cup. (You may want to temporarily move the sand to another container before retaping the cup.) Be careful not to jostle the paper; if you do, your trace may be erased. You may want to tape the paper down.

What You'll Do

› **Create** sine curves by pulling paper under a sand pendulum.

› **Measure** the amplitude, wavelength, and period of transverse waves using sine curves as models.

› **Form a hypothesis** about how changes to the experiment may change the amplitude and wavelength of the sine curve.

› **Calculate** frequency and wave speed using your measurements.

What You'll Need

cup, paper or plastic-foam
meterstick
small nail
ring stand or other support
sand, colored
stopwatch
string and scissors
tape, masking
white paper, about 30-cm-wide rolls

Safety

530 Chapter 15 Waves

⑧ For the part of the curve between the dotted lines, measure the distance from the first crest to the last crest, then divide that distance by the total number of crests. Record your answer in the table under "Average wavelength."

⑨ For the same part of the curve, measure the vertical distance between the first crest and the first trough, between the second crest and the second trough, and so on. Add the distances together, and divide by two. Then, divide by the number of distances you measured. Record your answer in the table under "Average amplitude."

Designing Your Experiment

⑩ With your lab partners, form a hypothesis about how to make two additional sine curve traces: one with an average wavelength different from that of the first trace, and one with an average amplitude different from that of the first trace.

⑪ In your lab report, write down your plan for changing these two factors. Before you carry out your experiment, your teacher must approve your plan.

Performing Your Experiment

⑫ After your teacher approves your plan, carry out your experiment. For each curve, measure and record the time, the average wavelength, and the average amplitude.

⑬ After each trace, return the sand to the cup and roll the paper back up.

Analysis

1. **Analyzing Data** For each of your three curves, calculate the average speed at which the paper was pulled by dividing the length of 1 m by the time measurement. This is equivalent to the speed of the wave that the curve models or represents.

2. **Analyzing Data** For each curve, use the wave speed equation to calculate average frequency.

$$\text{average frequency} = \frac{\text{average wave speed}}{\text{average wavelength}}$$

$$f = \frac{v}{\lambda}$$

Communicating Your Results

3. **Drawing Conclusions** What factor did you change to alter the average wavelength of the curve? Did your plan work? If so, did the wavelength increase or decrease?

4. **Drawing Conclusions** What factor did you change to alter the average amplitude? Did your plan work?

Extension

To determine the period of each of the wave traces you made, divide the time by the number of wavelengths in one meter. Then determine the frequency of each wave. **Hint:** What is the relationship between period and frequency?

Graphing Waves

Science Skills

Problem

The graphs below show the behavior of a single transverse wave. Study the graphs, and answer the following questions.

Technology
Math
Scientific Methods
▶ Graphing

Practice

Use the graphs to answer questions 1–6.

1. What type of graph are the graphs shown here?
2. What variable is described in the *x*-axis of the first graph? What variable is described in the *x*-axis of the second graph?
3. What information about the wave is indicated by the first graph? What information is indicated by the second graph?
4. Determine from the graphs the period, the amplitude, and the wavelength of the wave.
5. Using the frequency-period equation, calculate the frequency of the wave. Use the wave speed equation to calculate the speed of the wave.
6. Why are both graphs needed to provide complete information about the wave?

Use the data table to complete question 7.

7. Plot the data given in the table shown here. From the graph, calculate the wavelength and the amplitude of the wave.

x-axis (cm)	y-axis (cm)
0	0.93
0.25	2.43
0.50	3.00
0.75	2.43
1.00	0.93
1.25	−0.93
1.50	−2.43
1.75	−3.00
2.00	−2.43
2.25	−0.93
2.50	0.93
2.75	2.43
3.00	3.00

CHAPTER 15 Summary

go.hrw.com
SUPER SUMMARY
KEYWORD: HK8WAVS

Key Ideas

Section 1 Types of Waves

- **What Is a Wave?** A wave is a disturbance that carries energy through matter or space. (p. 505)
- **Vibrations and Waves** Most waves are caused by vibrating objects. (p. 508)
- **Transverse and Longitudinal Waves** A transverse wave is a wave in which the wave motion is perpendicular to the particle motion. A longitudinal wave is a wave in which the wave motion is parallel to the particle motion. (p. 511)
- **Surface Waves** The particles in a surface wave move both perpendicularly and parallel to the direction in which the wave travels. (p. 513)

Section 2 Characteristics of Waves

- **Waves Properties** Wave properties include amplitude, wavelength (λ), period (T), and frequency (f). (p. 514)
- **Wave Speed** The speed of a wave is equal to wavelength divided by period, or to frequency multiplied by wavelength: $v = \lambda/T = f \times \lambda$. (p. 518)
- **The Doppler Effect** Motion between the source of waves and the observer creates a change in observed frequency. (p. 522)

Section 3 Wave Interactions

- **Reflection, Diffraction, and Refraction** When a wave meets a surface or a boundary, the wave bounces back. When a wave passes the edge of an object or passes through an opening, the wave bends. A wave also bends when it passes from one medium to another at an angle. (p. 524)
- **Interference** When several waves are in the same location, they combine to produce a single wave that is different from the original waves. (p. 526)
- **Standing Waves** A standing wave causes the medium to vibrate in a stationary pattern that resembles a loop or a series of loops. (p. 529)

Key Terms

medium, p. 506
mechanical wave, p. 506
electromagnetic wave, p. 506
transverse wave, p. 511
longitudinal wave, p. 512
crest, p. 512
trough, p. 512

amplitude, p. 514
wavelength, p. 515
period, p. 516
frequency, p. 516
Doppler effect, p. 523

reflection, p. 524
diffraction, p. 525
refraction, p. 526
interference, p. 526
constructive interference, p. 527
destructive interference, p. 527
standing wave, p. 529

CHAPTER 15 Review

1. **Root Words** The word *reflection* contains the root *flect*. Use a dictionary to find the origin and meaning of this root, and explain why it is appropriate that the word *reflection* contains this root. Then, list at least three other words that contain the root.

USING KEY TERMS

2. How would you describe the *amplitude* of a wave using the words *crest* and *trough*?

3. Explain the difference between waves bending due to *refraction* and *diffraction*.

4. How do beats help determine whether two sound waves are of the same *frequency*? Use the terms *constructive interference* and *destructive interference* in your answer.

5. How is an *electromagnetic wave* different from a *mechanical wave*?

6. You have a long metal rod and a hammer. How would you hit the metal rod to create a *longitudinal wave*? How would you hit it to create a *transverse wave*?

7. Draw a picture of a *standing wave*, and label a *node* and an *antinode*.

UNDERSTANDING KEY IDEAS

8. A wave is a disturbance that transmits
   a. matter.
   b. particles.
   c. energy.
   d. a medium.

9. The speed of a wave depends on the
   a. medium.
   b. frequency.
   c. amplitude.
   d. wavelength.

10. Most waves are caused by
    a. velocity.
    b. amplitude.
    c. a vibration.
    d. earthquakes.

11. A sound wave is an example of
    a. an electromagnetic wave.
    b. a transverse wave.
    c. a longitudinal wave.
    d. a surface wave.

12. In an ocean wave, the molecules of water
    a. move perpendicularly to the direction of wave travel.
    b. move parallel to the direction of wave travel.
    c. move in ellipses.
    d. don't move at all.

13. Half the vertical distance between the crest and the trough of a wave is called the
    a. frequency.
    b. crest.
    c. wavelength.
    d. amplitude.

14. The number of waves passing a given point per unit of time is called the
    a. frequency.
    b. wave speed.
    c. wavelength.
    d. amplitude.

15. The combining of waves as they meet is known as
    a. a crest.
    b. noise.
    c. interference.
    d. the Doppler effect.

16. The Greek letter λ is often used to represent a wave's
    a. period.
    b. wavelength.
    c. frequency.
    d. amplitude.

EXPLAINING KEY IDEAS

17. Imagine you are shaking the end of a rope to create a series of waves. What will you observe if you begin shaking the rope more quickly?

18. Describe the changes in *elastic potential energy* and *kinetic energy* that occur when a mass vibrates on a spring.

19. Use the kinetic theory to explain the difference in wave speed in solids, liquids, and gases.

CRITICAL THINKING

20. Making Inferences A friend standing 2 m away strikes two tuning forks—one at a frequency of 256 Hz and the other at 240 Hz—at the same time. Which sound will reach your ear first? Explain your answer.

21. Analyzing Relationships When you are watching a baseball game, you may hear the crack of the bat a short time after you see the batter hit the ball. Why does this happen? (**Hint:** Consider the relationship between the speed of sound and the speed of light.)

22. Applying Concepts You are standing on a street corner, and you hear a fire truck approaching. As the fire truck gets closer to you, does the pitch of the siren increase, decrease, or stay constant? Explain.

23. Drawing Conclusions If you yell or clap your hands while standing at the edge of a large rock canyon, you may hear an echo a few seconds later. Explain why this happens.

24. Applying Concepts A piano tuner listens to a tuning fork vibrating at 440 Hz to tune a string of a piano. He hears beats between the tuning fork and the piano string. Is the string in tune? Explain your answer.

25. Making Observations Describe how you interact with waves during a typical school day. Document the types of waves you encounter. Document also how often you interact with each type of wave. Decide whether some types of waves are more important in your life than others.

26. Evaluating Information A new car is advertised as having antinoise technology. The manufacturer claims that inside the car any sounds are negated. Evaluate the possibility of such a claim. What would have to be created to cause destructive interference with any sound in the car? Do you believe that the manufacturer's claim is correct?

Graphing Skills

27. Making Graphs Draw a sine curve, and label its crest, trough, and amplitude.

28. Interpreting Graphs The wave shown in the figure below has a frequency of 25.0 Hz. Find the following values for this wave:
 a. amplitude c. speed
 b. wavelength d. period

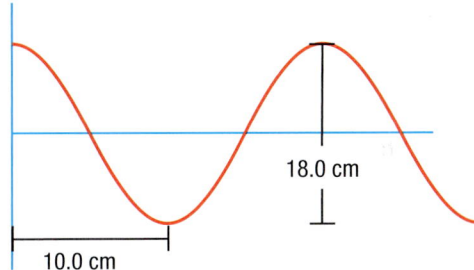

29. Interpreting Graphs For each image below, draw the wave that results from interference between the two waves.

a. b.

Math Skills

30. Wave Speed Ocean waves are hitting a beach at a rate of 2.0 Hz. The distance between wave crests is 1.5 m. Calculate the speed of the waves.

31. Wavelength The frequencies of radio waves range from approximately 3.00×10^5 Hz to 3.00×10^7 Hz. What is the range of wavelengths of these waves? Use 3.00×10^8 m/s as the speed of electromagnetic waves.

32. Frequency The note A above middle C on a piano emits a sound wave with wavelength 0.7750 m. What is the frequency of the wave? Use 341.0 m/s as the speed of sound in air.

Standardized Test Prep

Understanding Concepts

Directions (1–3): **For each question, write on a sheet of paper the letter of the correct answer.**

1. A wave pool at a water amusement park has a machine at one end that generates regular waves that are 7.5 m long. At the other end, waves crest over the side every 5 s. How fast are the waves traveling?
    - **A.** 0.2 m/s
    - **B.** 0.67 m/s
    - **C.** 1.5 m/s
    - **D.** 37.5 m/s

2. Two waves that have exactly the same wavelength, frequency, and amplitude are occupying the same space. If the second wave follows exactly half a wavelength behind the first, what is true of the resulting wave?
    - **F.** The resulting wave has zero amplitude.
    - **G.** The resulting wave has twice the amplitude of the original waves.
    - **H.** The resulting wave has zero wavelength.
    - **I.** The resulting wave has a wavelength twice as long as the original waves.

3. A sine wave measures 12 cm from the top of the crest to the bottom of the trough, and 30 cm from the top of one crest to the top of the next. What is the amplitude of the wave?
    - **A.** 2.5 cm
    - **B.** 6 cm
    - **C.** 15 cm
    - **D.** 18 cm

Directions (4–6): **For each question, write a short response.**

4. Many home computers have a frequency of over 1 GHz, meaning 1×10^9 cycles per second. What is the period of a 1 GHz computer?

5. A motorcyclist approaches an outdoor concert. How does the pitch that the motorcyclist hears from the concert differ from the pitch that a stationary listener at the concert hears?

6. Why do waves tend to travel faster through a solid medium than through a liquid or a gas?

Reading Skills

Directions (7–8): **Read the passage below. Then answer the questions that follow.**

THE DOPPLER EFFECT IN SPACE
The Doppler effect is defined as a change in the wavelength (or frequency) of waves, as a result of motion of either the source or the receiver of the waves. If the source of the waves and the receiver are approaching each other (because of the motion of either or both), the frequency of the waves will increase and the wavelength will be shortened. As a result, sounds will become higher pitched and light will appear bluer. If the sender and receiver are moving apart, sounds will become lower pitched and light will appear redder.

In astronomy, the Doppler effect is used to measure the velocity and rotation of stars and galaxies. Both blue shifts and red shifts are observed for various objects, indicating relative motion both toward and away from Earth. The Doppler effect also explains the red shifts of distant galaxies. These shifts indicate that distant galaxies are moving away from us and from each other.

7. If light from a celestial object is observed to shift towards the blue end of the spectrum, what conclusion can be drawn?
    - **F.** The object is moving toward Earth.
    - **G.** The object is reflecting radio waves emanating from the Earth.
    - **H.** The velocity of the object is increasing.
    - **I.** The velocity of the light emanating from the object is decreasing.

8. If two trains are moving down the same track, in the same direction and at the same speed, and the train in front blows its whistle, will the passengers in the rear of the second train experience the Doppler effect? Why or why not?

Interpreting Graphics

The following two graphs each describe two waves and the resultant wave that occurs when the original two waves interfere with each other. Use these graphs to answer questions 9–11.

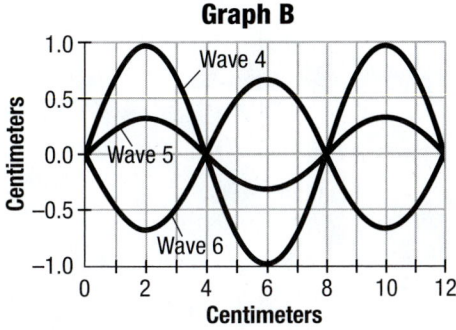

9. In Graph A, "Wave 1" is the resultant wave. What type of interference is shown in Graph A?
   - **A.** constructive
   - **B.** partial destructive
   - **C.** complete destructive
   - **D.** constructive and destructive

10. In Graph B, which wave is the resultant wave?
    - **F.** Wave 4
    - **G.** Wave 5
    - **H.** Wave 6
    - **I.** This cannot be determined.

11. What characteristic do all six of these waves have in common?

The following graph describes two waves. Use this graph to answer questions 12–13.

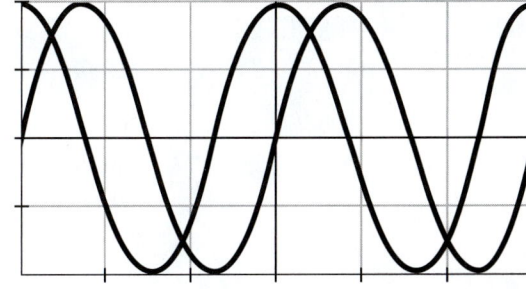

12. If these waves interfere with each other, what will result?
    - **A.** constructive interference
    - **B.** destructive interference
    - **C.** constructive interference in some places and destructive interference in others
    - **D.** neither constructive nor destructive interference

13. The two waves have identical amplitudes. What else would they have in common if the *x*-axis were in units of time? What else would they have in common if the *x*-axis were in units of distance?

Test Tip

Take a few minutes at the end of the test period to review your answers.

Why It Matters
Physics Connections

Science, technology, and society are closely linked. The web below shows just a few of the connections in the history of physics.

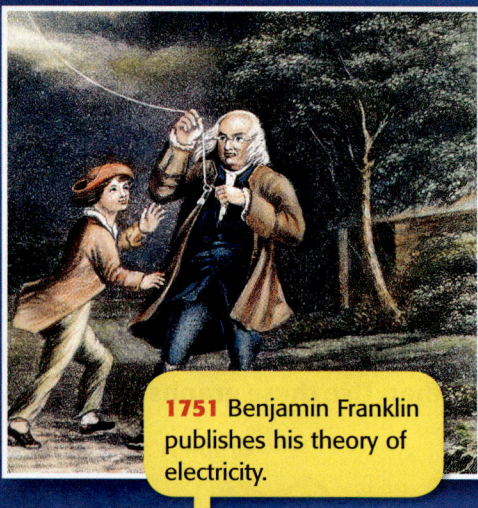

1751 Benjamin Franklin publishes his theory of electricity.

1785 Charles-Augustin de Coulomb identifies a law that describes the force between two electrical charges.

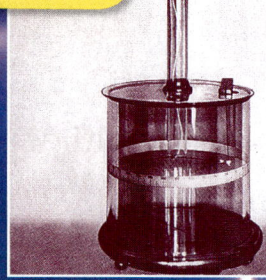

1880s "The War of the Currents"—a fight between Thomas Edison and Nikola Tesla over AC versus DC—results in AC being the source of power for electrical devices in the United States.

1831 Michael Faraday discovers electromagnetic induction and builds an electric dynamo.

1991 Rechargeable lithium-ion batteries are commercially introduced.

1947 The first transistor is invented.

1959 Integrated circuits are developed.

2001 The iPod® is introduced, and MP3 players become popular.

HISTORY IN SCIENCE

1859 The first oil well leads to a boom in oil production.

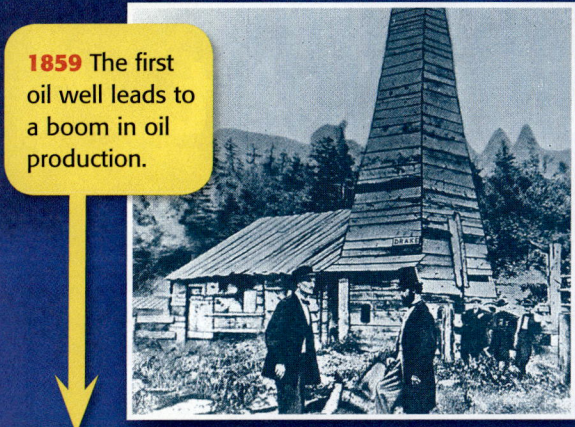

1769 To pump water out of mine shafts, Watts develops the modern steam engine.

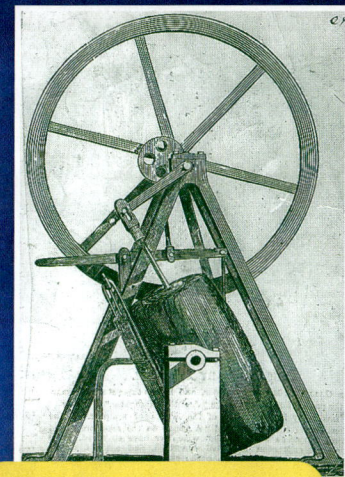

1885 Gottlieb Daimler develops the first automobile.

1908 Ford Motor Company introduces the Model T.

1958 Ford Motor Company introduces the Nucleon, a concept car designed to be powered by a nuclear reactor in the trunk.

1970s An oil crisis promotes research into alternative fuels and more-efficient batteries.

1950s President Eisenhower greatly expands the U. S. highway system.

2006 Gas-electric hybrid cars become commercially popular.

YOUR TURN

UNDERSTANDING CONCEPTS
1. What was the significance of "The War of the Currents?"

CRITICAL THINKING
2. Why did the oil crisis in the 1970s lead to the development of new technologies?

CHAPTER 16
Sound and Light

Chapter Outline

❶ Sound
Properties of Sound
Musical Instruments
Hearing and the Ear
Ultrasound and Sonar

❷ The Nature of Light
Waves and Particles
The Electromagnetic Spectrum

❸ Reflection and Color
Reflection of Light
Mirrors
Seeing Colors

❹ Refraction, Lenses, and Prisms
Refraction of Light
Lenses
Dispersion and Prisms

TN Tennessee Course Level Expectations (Physical Science)

CLE.3202.TE.3 Explain the relationship between the properties of a material and the use of the material in the application of a technology; **CLE.3202.2.1** Investigate the properties and behaviors of mechanical and electromagnetic waves; **CLE.3202.2.2** Explore and explain the nature of sound and light energy; **CLE.3202.Inq.1** Recognize that science is a progressive endeavor that reevaluates and extends what is already accepted; **CLE.3202.Inq.2** Design and conduct scientific investigations to explore new phenomena, verify previous results, test how well a theory predicts, and compare opposing theories; **CLE.3202.Inq.3** Use appropriate tools and technology to collect precise and accurate data; **CLE.3202.Inq.4** Apply qualitative and quantitative measures to analyze data and draw conclusions that are free of bias.

Why It Matters
The properties of sound and light waves affect how we experience our surroundings. The properties of light can explain both the colors of the car lights and the colors of the road signs on this busy highway system.

Inquiry Lab ⏱ 20 min

Colors in White Light

Your teacher will give you a **spectroscope** or instructions for making one. Turn on an **incandescent light bulb.** Look at the light bulb through your spectroscope. Write a description of what you see. Then, repeat the procedure with a **fluorescent light bulb.** Again, describe what you see.

Questions to Get You Started

1. Compare your observations of the incandescent light bulb and your observations of the fluorescent light bulb.
2. Both kinds of bulbs produce white light. What did you learn about white light by using the spectroscope?
3. Light from a flame is yellowish but is similar to white light. What do you think you would see if you used a spectroscope to look at light from a flame?

READING TOOLBOX These reading tools can help you learn the material in this chapter. For more information on how to use these and other tools, see **Appendix A**.

Word Parts

Prefixes Analyzing the parts of a science term can help you figure out the meaning of the word. Some word parts and their meanings are listed in **Appendix A**.

Prefixes are used in front of word roots to modify the meaning of the word root. Two prefixes that are used in this chapter are listed below.

- *ultra-* means "beyond" or "extremely"
- *infra-* means "below"

Your Turn As you read this chapter, make a table like the one started below that lists each word that contains the prefix *ultra-* or *infra-*, the root of the word, and the word's definition.

WORDS WITH THE PREFIX *ULTRA-* OR *INFRA-*		
WORD	ROOT	DEFINITION
infrasound	sound	sound below the range of human hearing (below 20 Hz)
ultrasound		

Mnemonics

Colors of the Spectrum A mnemonic device can help you remember related words. Although the electromagnetic spectrum is continuous, the colors in the visible part can be divided into six main colors—red, orange, yellow, green, blue, and violet. One way to remember these colors and their order is by using a made-up name, such as the one below, as a mnemonic device.

> **ROY G BiV**

Note that the letter "i" is added so that you can pronounce the last name.

Your Turn Practice saying the name above to help yourself learn and remember the colors of the visible spectrum and the order of the colors. Make up a sentence with words that start with these letters to create another type of mnemonic device.

FoldNotes

Booklet FoldNotes can help you remember ideas that you learn as you read. You can use a booklet to organize the details of a main topic in the chapter.

Your Turn Make a booklet by following the instructions in **Appendix A**.

1. Label the front of the booklet "Sound."
2. Label each of the pages of the booklet with one of the red headings from Section 1.
3. Take notes from Section 1 on the appropriate page of the booklet.

542 Chapter 16 Sound and Light

SECTION 1
Sound

Key Ideas

› What are the characteristics of sound waves?
› How do musical instruments make sound?
› How do ears help humans hear sound waves?
› How are the reflections of sound waves used?

Key Terms

sound wave
pitch
infrasound
ultrasound
resonance
sonar

Why It Matters

Sound waves are responsible for much more than the sounds we hear. They are used to create images of the human body that are used in medicine.

When you listen to your favorite musical group, you hear a variety of sounds. Although these sounds come from different sources, they are all longitudinal waves that are produced by vibrating objects. Musical instruments and stereo speakers make sound waves in the air.

Tennessee Course Level Expectations (Physical Science)
CLE.3202.2.2; CLE.3202.Inq.1; CLE.3202.Inq.2; CLE.3202.Inq.3; CLE.3202.Math.1; CLE.3202.Math.2

Properties of Sound

The head of a drum vibrates up and down when a drummer hits it. Each time the drumhead moves upward, it compresses the air above it. When the head moves back down, it leaves a small region of air that has a lower pressure. A series of compressions and rarefactions is created in the air as the drumhead moves up and down repeatedly, as **Figure 1** shows.

Sound waves, such as those created by a drum, are longitudinal waves caused by vibrations. The particles of air in these waves vibrate in the same direction the waves travel. › **Sound waves are caused by vibrations and carry energy through a medium.** All sound waves are made by vibrating objects that cause the surrounding medium to move. In air, the waves spread out in all directions away from the source. When sound waves from the drum reach your ears, the waves cause your eardrums to vibrate.

sound wave (SOWND WAYV) a longitudinal wave that is caused by vibrations and that travels through a material medium

Figure 1 Vibrations create sound waves.

① The head of a drum vibrates up and down when it is struck by the drummer's hand.

② The vibrations of the drumhead create sound waves in the air.

QuickLab: Sound in Different Mediums

⏱ 10 min

Procedure
1. Tie a **spoon** or other utensil to the middle of a 1 to 2 m length of **string**.
2. Wrap the loose ends of the string around your index fingers, and place your fingers against your ears.
3. Swing the spoon so that it strikes a **tabletop**.

Analysis
1. Compare the volume and quality of the sound received through the string with the volume and quality of the sound received through the air.
2. Does sound travel better through the string or through the air? Explain.
3. Explain your results.

Academic Vocabulary

transmit (trans MIT) to send from one place to another

www.scilinks.org
Topic: Properties of Sound
Code: HK81233

The speed of sound depends on the medium.

If you stand near a drummer, you may think that you hear the sound from the drum at the same time that the drummer's hand strikes the drum head. Sound waves travel very fast. The speed of sound in air at room temperature is about 346 m/s.

The speed of a sound wave depends on the temperature and the material through which the wave travels, as **Figure 2** shows. The speed of sound in a medium depends on how quickly the particles transmit the motion of the sound waves. The molecules in a gaseous medium, such as air, are farther apart than the particles in a solid or liquid are, so sound waves travel slower in air. Gas molecules move faster and collide more frequently at high temperatures than at low temperatures, so sound waves travel faster at high temperatures.

In a liquid or solid, the particles are much closer together than in a gas, so the vibrations are transferred more rapidly from one particle to the next. However, some solids, such as rubber, dampen vibrations so that sound does not travel well. Materials like rubber can be used for soundproofing.

Figure 2 Speed of Sound in Various Mediums

Medium	Speed of sound (m/s)	Medium	Speed of sound (m/s)
Gases		**Liquids at 25 °C**	
Air (0 °C)	331	Water	1,490
Air (25 °C)	346	Sea water	1,530
Air (100 °C)	386	**Solids**	
Helium (0 °C)	972	Copper	3,813
Hydrogen (0 °C)	1,290	Iron	5,000
Oxygen (0 °C)	317	Rubber	54

Loudness is determined by intensity.

How do the sound waves change when you increase the volume on your stereo or television? The *loudness* of a sound depends partly on the energy contained in the sound waves. The *intensity* of a sound wave describes the rate at which a sound wave transmits energy through a given area of a medium. Intensity depends on the amplitude of the sound wave and your distance from the source of the sound. The greater the intensity of a sound is, the louder the sound will seem.

However, a sound that has twice the intensity of another sound does not seem twice as loud. Humans perceive loudness on a logarithmic scale. So, a sound seems twice as loud when its intensity is 10 times the intensity of another sound.

The quietest sound a human can hear is the threshold of hearing. The *relative intensity* of a sound is found by comparing the intensity of a sound with the intensity at the threshold of hearing. Intensity is measured in units called *decibels*, dB. An increase in intensity of 10 dB means a sound seems about twice as loud. A few common sounds and their decibel levels are shown in **Figure 3**.

The quietest sound a human can hear is 0 dB. A sound of 120 dB is at the threshold of pain, so sounds louder than this can hurt your ears and give you headaches. Extensive exposure to sounds above 120 dB can cause permanent deafness.

Reading Check What determines the intensity of a sound wave? (See Appendix E for answers to Reading Checks.)

Figure 3 Sound intensity is measured on a logarithmic scale of decibels. **How many times louder than a cat purring will a normal conversation seem?**

pitch (PICH) a measure of how high or low a sound is perceived to be, depending on the frequency of the sound wave

infrasound (IN fruh SOWND) slow vibrations of frequencies lower than 20 Hz

ultrasound (UHL truh SOWND) any sound wave with frequencies higher than 20,000 Hz

Pitch is determined by frequency.

Pitch is a measure of how high or low a sound is and depends on the sound wave's frequency. A high-pitched sound is made by something vibrating rapidly, such as a violin string or air in a flute. A low-pitched sound is made by something vibrating slowly, such as a cello string or the air in a tuba.

In other words, high-pitched sounds have high frequencies, and low-pitched sounds have low frequencies. Trained musicians are capable of detecting subtle differences in frequency, even a change as slight as 2 Hz.

Humans hear sound waves in a limited frequency range.

The human ear can hear sounds from sources that vibrate as slowly as 20 vibrations per second (20 Hz) and as rapidly as 20,000 Hz. Any sound that has a frequency below the range of human hearing is **infrasound.** Any sound that has a frequency above the range of human hearing is **ultrasound.** Many animals can hear frequencies of sound outside the range of human hearing, as **Figure 4** shows.

Reading Check What are the upper limit and the lower limit of frequencies that humans can hear?

Figure 4 Humans can hear sounds that have frequencies of 20 Hz to about 20,000 Hz, but many other animals can hear sounds into the infrasound and ultrasound ranges.

Musical Instruments

Musical instruments, from deep-sounding tubas to twangy banjos, come in a wide variety of shapes and sizes and produce a wide variety of sounds. But musical instruments can be grouped into a small number of categories based on how they make sound. ❱ **Most instruments produce sound through the vibration of strings, air columns, or membranes.**

Musical instruments rely on standing waves.

When you pluck the string of a guitar, as **Figure 5** shows, particles in the string vibrate. Sound waves travel out to the ends of the string and then reflect back toward the middle. These vibrations cause a standing wave on the string. The two ends of the string are called *nodes,* and the middle of the string is called an *antinode.*

You can change the pitch by placing your finger on the string anywhere on the guitar's neck. A shorter length of string vibrates more rapidly, and the standing wave has a higher frequency. The resulting sound has a high pitch.

Standing waves can exist only at certain wavelengths on a string. The primary standing wave on a vibrating string has a wavelength that is twice the length of the string. The frequency of this wave, which is also the frequency of the string's vibrations, is called the *fundamental frequency*.

All musical instruments use standing waves to produce sound. The standing waves that form on the head of a drum are shown in **Figure 5.** In a flute, standing waves form in the column of air inside the flute. Opening or closing holes in the flute body changes the length of the air column, which changes the wavelength and frequency of the standing waves.

QuickLab 10 min

Frequency and Pitch

1. Hold one end of a **flexible metal or plastic ruler** on a **desk** with about half of the ruler hanging off the edge. Bend the free end of the ruler, and then release it. Can you hear a sound?

2. Try changing the position of the ruler so that less hangs over the edge. How does the change in position change the sound produced?

Figure 5 Musical instruments produce standing waves, which in turn produce sound waves in the air.

Vibrations on a guitar string produce standing waves on the string.

Vibrations on a drum head produce standing waves on the head.

InquiryLab

How Can You Amplify the Sound of a Tuning Fork?

 20 min

Procedure

1. Activate a **tuning fork** by striking the tongs of the fork against a **rubber block**.
2. Touch the base of the tuning fork to various **wood or metal objects**. Listen for any changes in the sound of the tuning fork.
3. Activate the fork again. Then, try touching the base of the tuning fork to the bases of other tuning forks. Make sure that the tines of the forks are free to vibrate and are not touching anything.
4. If you find two tuning forks that resonate with each other, try activating one and holding it near the tines of the other one.

Analysis

1. What are some characteristics of the objects that helped to amplify the sound of the tuning fork in step 2?
2. In step 3, could you make another tuning fork start vibrating by touching it with the base of your tuning fork?
3. In step 4, could you make another tuning fork vibrate without touching it with your tuning fork?
4. What is the relationship between the frequencies of the tuning forks that resonate with each other in steps 3 and 4?

resonance (REZ uh nuhns) a phenomenon that occurs when two objects naturally vibrate at the same frequency

Instruments use resonance to amplify sound.

When you pluck a guitar string, you can feel that the bridge and the body of the guitar vibrate. These vibrations, which are a response to the vibrating string, are called *forced vibrations*. The body of the guitar has *natural frequencies,* which are the specific frequencies at which it is most likely to vibrate.

The sound produced by the guitar will be loudest when the forced vibrations cause the body of the guitar to vibrate at a natural frequency. This effect is called resonance. When **resonance** occurs, both the string and the guitar body are vibrating at the same frequency, which amplifies the sound. The guitar body has a larger area than the string and is in contact with more molecules in the air. So, the guitar body is better at transferring the vibrations to the air than the string is.

The natural frequency of an object depends on the object's shape, size, mass, and the material from which the object is made. Complex objects such as guitars have many natural frequencies, so they resonate well at many pitches. However, some musical instruments, such as an electric guitar, do not resonate well and must be amplified electronically.

✓ **Reading Check** Why does resonance amplify a sound?

Hearing and the Ear

How do you hear waves and interpret them as different sounds? ❯ **The human ear is a sensitive organ that senses vibrations in the air, amplifies them, and then transmits signals to the brain.** In some ways, the process of hearing is the reverse of the process by which a drum head makes a sound. In the ear, sound waves cause membranes to vibrate.

Vibrations pass through three regions in the ear.

Your ear is divided into three regions—outer, middle, and inner—as **Figure 6** shows. Sound waves travel through the fleshy part of your outer ear and down the ear canal. The ear canal ends at the eardrum, a thin, flat piece of tissue. The vibrations pass from the eardrum through the three small bones of the middle ear—the hammer, the anvil, and the stirrup. The vibrations cause the stirrup to strike a membrane at the opening of the inner ear, which sends waves through the spiral-shaped cochlea.

Resonance occurs in the inner ear.

The cochlea contains a long, flexible membrane called the *basilar membrane*. Different parts of this membrane vibrate at different natural frequencies. So, a wave of a particular frequency causes a specific part of the basilar membrane to vibrate. Hair cells near that part of the membrane then stimulate nerve fibers that send an impulse to the brain. The brain interprets this impulse as a sound that has a specific frequency and intensity.

READING TOOLBOX

Mnemonics
Create a sentence to help you remember the parts of the ear (eardrum, anvil, hammer, stirrup, and cochlea). The words in the sentence should begin with the letters *E, A, H, S,* and *C.*

SCLINKS.
www.scilinks.org
Topic: The Ear
Code: **HK80440**

Figure 6 Sound waves are transmitted as vibrations through the ear.

Keyword: HK8SALF6

❶ In the outer ear, sound waves cause the eardrum to vibrate.

❷ In the middle ear, vibrations cause the stirrup bone to strike the outer membrane of the inner ear.

❸ In the inner ear, the basilar membrane vibrates. The movement of this membrane causes a signal to be sent to the brain.

Ultrasound and Sonar

If you shout over the edge of a rock canyon, the sound may be reflected by the rock walls. If the reflected sound reaches your ears, you will hear an echo. ❯ **Reflected sound waves are used to determine distances and to create images.**

Some ultrasound waves are reflected at boundaries.

Ultrasound waves have frequencies greater than 20,000 Hz. At high frequencies, ultrasound waves can travel through most materials. But some sound waves are reflected when they pass from one type of material into another. The number of waves reflected depends on the density of the materials at each boundary. The reflected waves from different boundary surfaces can be made into a computer image called a *sonogram*.

Ultrasound is used to see inside the human body because it does not harm living cells. For one to see the details in a sonogram, the wavelengths of the ultrasound must be slightly smaller than the smallest parts of the object being viewed. The higher the frequency of a wave is, the shorter the wave's wavelength is. Sound waves that have a frequency of 15,000,000 Hz have a wavelength of less than 1 mm when they pass through soft tissue. So, in a sonogram, you would be able to see details that are about 1 mm in size.

Why It Matters

What are sonograms?

Ultrasound imaging is used in medicine. The echoes of high frequency ultrasound waves between 1,000,000 Hz and 15,000,000 Hz are used to produce computerized images called *sonograms*. Using sonograms, doctors can safely view organs inside the body without having to perform surgery. Sonograms can be used to diagnose problems and to guide surgical procedures.

Sonograms are often used to view unborn fetuses. Because ultrasound does not harm the mother or fetus, it is a common way to check the progress of a pregnancy.

REAL WORLD

YOUR TURN

WRITING IN SCIENCE
1. Research one way, other than fetal ultrasound, that ultrasound is used in medicine. Write a one-page report that explains how ultrasound is used for this application.

Sonar is used to locate objects underwater.

How can a person on a ship measure the distance to the ocean floor, which may be thousands of meters from the water's surface? **Sonar** is a system that uses reflected sound waves for measurement and can measure large distances.

Using sonar, distance can be determined by measuring the time it takes for sound waves to be reflected from a surface. A sonar device on a ship sends a pulse of sound downward and measures the time, t, that it takes for the sound to be reflected back to the device from the ocean floor. The distance, d, can be calculated by using a form of the speed equation that solves for distance, using the average speed of sound in water, v.

$$d = vt$$

Because the sound waves travel to a surface and back to the device, the measured time must be divided by two to obtain the distance from the device to the surface. Fisherman and researchers can use sonar to detect fish. If a school of fish passes under the ship, the sound pulse will be reflected back much sooner than the sound from the ocean floor. Submarines can also be detected using sonar.

Ultrasound works very well in sonar systems because the waves can be focused into narrow beams and can be directed more easily than other sound waves. Bats use reflected ultrasound to navigate in flight and to locate insects for food.

QuickLab

Echoes and Distance

1. Stand outside in front of a **large wall,** and clap your hands. Do you hear an echo?
2. Use a **stopwatch** to measure the time that passes between the time you clap your hands and the time you hear the echo.
3. The speed of sound in air is about 340 m/s. Use the approximate time from step 2 and the speed equation to estimate the distance to the wall.

sonar (SOH NAHR) **so**und **n**avigation **a**nd **r**anging, a system that uses acoustic signals and echoes to determine the location of objects or to communicate

Section 1 Review

KEY IDEAS

1. **Identify** two factors that affect the speed of sound.
2. **Explain** why sound travels slower in air than in water.
3. **Distinguish** between infrasound and ultrasound.
4. **Determine** which two properties of a sound wave change when pitch gets higher.
5. **Determine** which two properties of a sound wave change when a sound gets louder.

CRITICAL THINKING

6. **Analyzing Information** Your friend tells you that a clap of thunder has a sound intensity of about 130 dB, so it is almost twice as loud as a vacuum cleaner. Explain whether or not your friend is correct.

7. **Applying Ideas** Why does an acoustic guitar generally sound louder than an electric guitar without an electronic amplifier sounds?
8. **Inferring Relationships** On a piano keyboard, the C5 key has a frequency that is twice the frequency of the middle C key. Is the string that vibrates to make the sound waves for the C5 key shorter or longer than the middle C string? Explain your reasoning.
9. **Describing Events** You hear a phone ring. Describe the process that occurs in your ear that results in sound waves from the phone being translated into nerve impulses that are sent to the brain.
10. **Analyzing Methods** To create sonograms, why are ultrasound waves used instead of audible sound waves?

SECTION 2
The Nature of Light

Key Ideas
- How do scientific models describe light?
- What does the electromagnetic spectrum consist of?

Key Terms
photon
intensity
radar

Why It Matters
Cell phones use radio waves, not sound waves, to send signals.

> **Tennessee Course Level Expectations (Physical Science)**
> CLE.3202.2.1; CLE.3202.2.2;
> CLE.3202.Math.1; CLE.3202.Math.2;
> CLE.3202.TE.3; CLE.3202.TE.4

Most of us see and feel light almost every moment of our lives. We even feel the warmth of the sun on our skin, which is an effect of infrared light. We are very familiar with light, but how much do we understand about what light really is?

Waves and Particles

It is difficult to describe all of the properties of light with a single scientific model. ❯ **The two most common models describe light either as a wave or as a stream of particles.**

Light produces interference patterns as water waves do.

In 1801, the English scientist Thomas Young devised an experiment to test the nature of light. He passed a beam of light through two narrow openings and then onto a screen on the other side of the openings. He found that the light produced a striped pattern on the screen, like the pattern in **Figure 1.** This striped pattern is an interference pattern that is formed when waves interfere with each other.

Figure 1 Light can produce an interference pattern.

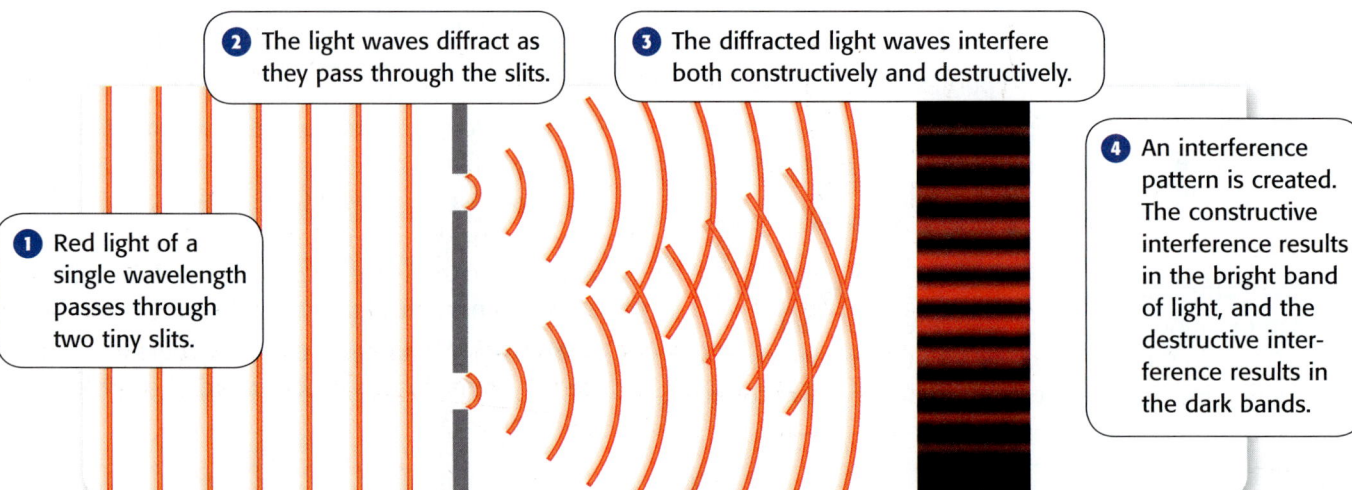

❶ Red light of a single wavelength passes through two tiny slits.

❷ The light waves diffract as they pass through the slits.

❸ The diffracted light waves interfere both constructively and destructively.

❹ An interference pattern is created. The constructive interference results in the bright band of light, and the destructive interference results in the dark bands.

Light can be modeled as a wave.

Because the light in Young's experiment produced interference patterns, Young concluded that light consists of waves. The model of light as a wave is still used today to explain many of the basic properties of light and light's behavior.

This model describes light as transverse waves that do not require a medium in which to travel. Light waves are also called *electromagnetic waves* because they consist of changing electric and magnetic fields. The transverse waves produced by these fields can be described by their amplitude, wavelength, and frequency.

The wave model of light explains how light waves interfere with one another. It also explains why light waves may reflect when they meet a mirror, refract when they pass through a lens, and diffract when they pass through a narrow opening.

The wave model cannot explain some observations.

In the early part of the 20th century, physicists began to realize that some observations could not be explained by the wave model of light. For example, when light strikes a piece of metal, electrons may fly off the metal's surface. Experiments show that in some cases, dim, blue light may knock some electrons off a metal plate, while very bright, red light cannot knock off any electrons, as **Figure 2** shows.

According to the wave model, very bright, red light has more energy than dim, blue light has because the waves in bright light have greater amplitude than the waves in dim light. But this energy difference does not explain how blue light can knock electrons off the plate while red light cannot.

Light can be modeled as a stream of particles.

One way to explain the effects of light striking a metal plate is to assume that the energy of the light is contained in small packets. A packet of blue light carries enough energy to knock an electron off the plate, but a packet of red light does not. Bright, red light contains many packets, but no single packet has enough energy to knock an electron off the plate.

In the particle model of light, these packets, or units of light, are called **photons**. A beam of light is a stream of photons. Photons are considered particles, but they are not like ordinary particles of matter. Photons do not have mass. They are like little bundles of energy. Unlike the energy in a wave, the energy in a photon is located in a specific area.

✓ **Reading Check** What can the particle model of light explain that the wave model cannot explain?

Figure 2 The particle model of light can explain some effects that the wave model cannot explain.

Bright, red light cannot knock electrons off this metal plate.

Dim, blue light can knock electrons off the plate. The wave model of light cannot explain this effect, but the particle model can.

photon (FOH TAHN) a unit or quantum of light

Topic: Properties of Light
Code: HK81227

READING TOOLBOX

Booklet
Create a booklet, and label the cover "Models of light." Label half of pages inside the booklet "Wave model" and the other half of the pages "Particle model." Write details about each model on the appropriate pages of your booklet.

The model of light used depends on the situation.

Light can be modeled as either waves or particles. Which model is correct? The success of any scientific theory depends on how well the theory can explain various observations. Some effects, such as the interference of light, are more easily explained with the wave model. Other effects, such as light knocking electrons off a metal plate, are better explained by the particle model. The particle model also easily explains how light can travel across empty space without a medium.

Most scientists currently accept both the wave model and the particle model of light. The model they use depends on the situation that they are studying. Some scientists think that light has a *dual nature*, which means that light can behave both as waves and as particles. In many cases, using either the wave model or the particle model of light gives good results.

The energy of light is proportional to frequency.

Whether modeled as a particle or as a wave, light is also a form of energy. Each photon of light can be thought of as carrying a small amount of energy. The amount of this energy is proportional to the frequency of the corresponding electromagnetic wave, as **Figure 3** shows.

A photon of red light, for example, carries an amount of energy that corresponds to the frequency of waves in red light, 4.5×10^{14} Hz. Ultraviolet photons have about twice as much energy as red light photons. So, the frequency of ultraviolet waves is about twice the frequency of red light waves. Likewise, a photon that has half the energy of red light, a photon of infrared light, corresponds to a wave that has half the frequency of a wave of red light.

Figure 3 The energy of photons of light is related to the frequency of electromagnetic waves. **What happens to the frequency of the waves as the energy increases?**

Type of wave	Wavelength	Wave frequency	Photon energy
Infrared	1.33×10^{-6} m	2.25×10^{14} Hz	1.5×10^{-19} J
Visible light	6.67×10^{-7} m	4.5×10^{14} Hz	3.0×10^{-19} J
Ultraviolet	3.33×10^{-7} m	9.0×10^{14} Hz	6.0×10^{-19} J

The speed of light depends on the medium.

In a vacuum, all light travels at the same speed and is represented by the variable *c*. The speed of light is very fast, about 3×10^8 m/s (about 186,000 mi/s). There is no known entity in the universe that is faster than light.

Light travels through transparent media, such as air, water, and glass. When light passes through a medium, however, the light travels slower than it does in a vacuum. **Figure 4** shows the speed of light in several mediums.

The brightness of light depends on intensity.

Reading near a lamp that has a 100 W bulb is easier than reading near a lamp that has a 60 W bulb. A 100 W bulb is brighter than a 60 W bulb and helps you see. The quantity that measures the amount of light illuminating a surface is **intensity.** Intensity depends on the number of photons per second, or power, that pass through a certain area of space.

The intensity of light decreases as distance from the light source increases because the light spreads out in spherical wave fronts. Imagine a series of spheres centered on a source of light, as **Figure 5** shows. As light spreads out from the source, the number of photons or the power passing through a given area on a sphere decreases. So, the light is dimmer for an observer farther from the light source than for an observer closer to the light source.

Reading Check What does the intensity of light depend on?

Figure 4 Speed of Light in Various Mediums

Medium	Speed of light ($\times 10^8$ m/s)
Vacuum	2.997925
Air	2.997047
Ice	2.29
Water	2.25
Quartz	2.05
Glass	1.97
Diamond	1.24

intensity (in TEN suh tee) the rate at which energy flows through a given area of space

Figure 5 Less light falls on each unit square as the distance from the source increases.

1 m   2 m   3 m

The Electromagnetic Spectrum

Light fills the air and space around us. Our eyes can detect light waves that have wavelengths of 400 nm (violet light) to 700 nm (red light). But the visible spectrum is only a small part of the electromagnetic spectrum, as **Figure 6** shows. We live in a sea of electromagnetic waves that range from radio waves given off by TV stations to the sun's ultraviolet waves.

▶ **The electromagnetic spectrum consists of waves at all possible energies, frequencies, and wavelengths.** Although all electromagnetic waves are similar in certain ways, each part of the electromagnetic spectrum has unique properties. Many modern technologies, including radar guns and cancer treatments, use electromagnetic waves.

Radio waves are used in communications and radar.

Radio waves are the longest waves in the electromagnetic spectrum and have wavelengths from tenths of a meter to thousands of meters. This part of the electromagnetic spectrum includes TV signals, and AM and FM radio signals.

Air traffic control towers at airports use radar to find the locations of aircraft. **Radar** is a system that uses radio waves to find the locations of objects. Antennas at the control tower emit radio waves. The radio waves bounce off the aircraft and return to a receiver at the tower. Many airplanes are equipped with special radios called *transponders*. These radios receive a signal from the tower and send a new signal back to the tower. This signal gives the plane's location and elevation. Radar is also used by police to monitor the speed of vehicles.

SCILINKS
www.scilinks.org
Topic: Electromagnetic Spectrum
Code: HK80482

radar (RAY DAHR) **ra**dio **d**etection **a**nd **r**anging, a system that uses reflected radio waves to determine the velocity and location of objects

Figure 6 The Electromagnetic Spectrum

Wavelength (m): 10^6, 10^5, 10^4, 10^3, 10^2, 10^1, 1, 10^{-1}, 10^{-2}, 10^{-3}, 10^{-4}

Radio waves are used in radar systems to monitor air traffic.

Microwaves are used to send phone signals long distances.

Infrared waves are used by special cameras to image the temperature differences in an object.

Microwaves are used in cooking and communication.

Electromagnetic waves that have wavelengths in the range of centimeters are known as *microwaves*. Microwaves are used to carry telecommunication signals over long distances. Space probes use microwaves to transmit signals back to Earth.

Microwaves are reflected by metals and are easily transmitted through air, glass, paper, and plastic. However, the water, fat, and sugar molecules in food all absorb microwaves. The absorbed microwaves can cook food. Microwaves can travel about 3 to 5 cm into most foods. They are absorbed as they go deeper into food. The energy from the absorbed waves causes water and other molecules to rotate. The energy of these rotations spreads throughout the food and warms it.

Infrared light can be felt as warmth.

Electromagnetic waves that have wavelengths slightly longer than wavelengths of red visible light are in the *infrared* (IR) part of the spectrum. Infrared light from the sun warms you. Infrared light from heat lamps is used to keep food warm.

Devices and photographic film that are sensitive to infrared light can reveal images of objects. An infrared sensor can measure the heat energy that objects radiate. These data can then be used to create images that show temperature variations. Remote infrared sensors on weather satellites can record temperature changes in the atmosphere and track the movement of clouds. Many computers can <u>detect</u> infrared signals from external devices, such as a computer mouse.

Academic Vocabulary

detect (dee TEKT) to discover the presence of something

✓ **Reading Check** Name three devices that use infrared light.

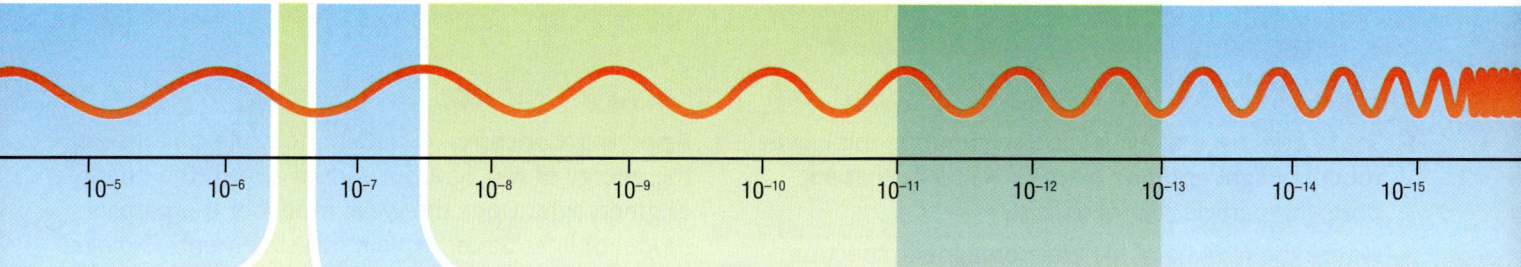

10^{-5} 10^{-6} 10^{-7} 10^{-8} 10^{-9} 10^{-10} 10^{-11} 10^{-12} 10^{-13} 10^{-14} 10^{-15}

Visible light, the colors that we can see, is a small part of the electromagnetic spectrum.

Ultraviolet light is emitted by the sun and has more energy than visible light does.

X rays are absorbed by bones and make bright areas in X-ray images.

Gamma rays, such as those produced by nuclear reactions, have the highest energy of any waves in the electromagnetic spectrum.

Figure 7 We cannot see ultraviolet light, but it can still damage the skin. Sunscreens protect skin by absorbing or blocking ultraviolet light before it reaches the skin.

Sunlight contains ultraviolet light.

The invisible light that lies just beyond violet light falls into the *ultraviolet* (UV) part of the spectrum. Ultraviolet light has higher energy and shorter wavelengths than visible light does. Although humans cannot see UV light, many insects can see it.

Nine percent of the energy emitted by the sun is ultraviolet light. Earth's atmosphere, in particular the *ozone layer,* absorbs much of this UV light. The UV light that makes it through the ozone layer has enough energy that some of the energy can pass through thin layers of clouds. As a result, you can get a sunburn, as **Figure 7** shows, on overcast days.

X rays and gamma rays are used in medicine.

Beyond the ultraviolet part of the spectrum are waves called *X rays*, which have higher energy and shorter wavelengths than ultraviolet waves do. X rays have wavelengths less than 10^{-8} m. *Gamma rays* are the electromagnetic waves with the highest energy and have wavelengths shorter than 10^{-10} m.

An X-ray image of bones is made by passing X rays through the body. Most of them pass right through, but a few are absorbed by bones and other tissues. The X rays that pass through the body to a photographic plate produce an image.

X rays are useful tools for doctors, but they can also be dangerous. Both X rays and gamma rays have very high energies, so they may kill living cells or turn them into cancer cells. However, gamma rays can also be used to treat cancer by killing the diseased cells.

Section 2 Review

KEY IDEAS

1. **State** one piece of evidence that supports the wave model of light and one piece of evidence that supports the particle model of light.
2. **Name** the regions of the electromagnetic spectrum from the shortest wavelengths to the longest wavelengths.
3. **Determine** which photons have more energy, those associated with microwaves or those associated with visible light.
4. **Determine** which band of the electromagnetic spectrum has the following:
    a. the lowest frequency
    b. the shortest wavelength
    c. the most energy
    d. the least energy

CRITICAL THINKING

5. **Applying Concepts** A certain molecule can absorb the energy of red light but cannot absorb the energy of green light. Does the wave model or the particle model of light better explain this statement? Explain.
6. **Applying Ideas** You and a friend are looking at the stars, and you notice two stars close together, one bright and one fairly dim. Your friend comments that the bright star emits much more light than the dimmer star. Is your friend correct? Explain your answer.
7. **Evaluating Conclusions** You and a friend decide to go hiking on a cloudy day. Your friend claims that she does not need any sunscreen because the sun is not shining. What is wrong with her reasoning?

SECTION 3
Reflection and Color

Key Ideas
- How do objects interact with incoming light?
- How can you see an image in a mirror?
- Why do we see colors?

Key Terms
light ray
virtual image
real image

Why It Matters
An object's color comes from the light that is reflected by the object.

Tennessee Course Level Expectations (Physical Science)
CLE.3202.2.2; CLE.3202.Inq.1; CLE.3202.Inq.2; CLE.3202.Inq.3; CLE.3202.Math.1

You may be used to thinking about light bulbs, candles, and the sun as objects that send light to your eyes. But all of the other objects that you see, including this book, also send light to your eyes. Otherwise, you would not be able to see them.

Light from the sun differs from light from a book. The sun emits its own light. The light from a book is light that is given off by the sun or a lamp and that then bounces off the book.

Reflection of Light

Mirrors, such as those on the solar collector shown in **Figure 1**, reflect almost all incoming light. ▶ **Every object reflects some light and absorbs some light.** The way light is reflected depends on the surface of the object. Because of the way mirrors reflect light, you can see an image of yourself in a mirror.

Light can be modeled as a ray.

It is useful to use another model for light, the light ray, to describe reflection, refraction, and many other ways light behaves. A **light ray** is an imaginary line running in the direction that the light travels. The direction of the light ray is the same as the direction of wave travel in the wave model of light or as the path of photons in the particle model of light.

Light rays do not represent a full picture of the complex nature of light but are good for showing how light will behave in many cases. The study of light in cases in which light behaves like a ray is called *geometrical optics*. Using light rays, one can trace the path of light in geometrical drawings called *ray diagrams*.

light ray (LIET RAY) a line in space that matches the direction of the flow of radiant energy

✓ **Reading Check** What are two behaviors of light that light rays are used to model?

Figure 1 This solar collector in the French Pyrenees uses mirrors to reflect and focus light. **Where is the light focused?**

560 Chapter 16 Sound and Light

Rough surfaces reflect light rays in many directions.

Many of the surfaces that we see every day, such as paper, wood, cloth, and skin, reflect light but do not appear shiny. When a beam of light is reflected, the path of each light ray in the beam changes from its initial direction to another direction. If a surface is rough, light striking the surface will be reflected at all angles, as **Figure 2** shows. This reflection of light into random directions is called *diffuse reflection*.

Smooth surfaces reflect light rays in one direction.

When light hits a smooth surface, such as a polished mirror, the light does not reflect diffusely. Instead, all of the light hitting a mirror from one direction is reflected together into a single, new direction, as the bottom of **Figure 2** shows.

The new direction of the light rays is related to the old direction in a definite way. The angle of the light rays reflecting off the surface, called the *angle of reflection,* is the same as the angle of the light rays striking the surface, called the *angle of incidence*. This equality of angles is the *law of reflection*.

Law of reflection : The angle of incidence equals the angle of reflection.

Both of these angles are measured from a line that is perpendicular to the surface at the point where the light hits the surface. This line is called the *normal*. **Figure 3** shows a ray diagram that illustrates how the law of reflection works.

Figure 2 Surfaces affect how light is reflected.

Light rays that are reflected from a rough surface are reflected in many directions.

Light rays that are reflected from a smooth surface are reflected in the same direction.

Figure 3 When light hits a surface, the angle of incidence (θ) equals the angle of reflection (θ').

READING TOOLBOX

Prefixes The word *reflection* contains the prefix *re-*. What is the meaning of this prefix? How can it help you understand the word *reflection*?

virtual image (VUHR choo uhl IM ij) an image from which light rays appear to diverge, even though they are not actually focused there; a virtual image cannot be projected on a screen

real image (REE uhl IM ij) an image that is formed by the intersection of light rays; a real image can be projected on a screen

Mirrors

When you look into a flat mirror, you see an image of yourself that appears to be behind the mirror. You see a twin or copy of yourself standing on the other side of the glass, but your image is flipped from left to right. You also see a whole room, a whole world of space beyond the mirror. ❱ **Mirrors reflect light as described by the law of reflection, and this light reaches your eyes. The type of image you perceive depends on the type of mirror.**

Flat mirrors form virtual images by reflection.

The ray diagram in **Figure 4** shows the path of light rays striking a flat mirror. When a light ray is reflected by a flat mirror, the angle at which it is reflected is equal to the angle of incidence, as described by the law of reflection.

When the reflected rays reach your eyes, your eyes sense light coming from certain directions. Your brain interprets the light as if it traveled in straight lines from an object to your eyes. So, you perceive an image of yourself behind the mirror.

Of course, there is not actually a copy of you behind the mirror. The image that you see, called a **virtual image,** results from the apparent path of the light rays, not an actual path. The virtual image appears to be as far behind the mirror as you are in front of the mirror.

Reading Check Why is the image that a flat mirror creates called a *virtual image*?

Figure 4 Flat mirrors create virtual images.

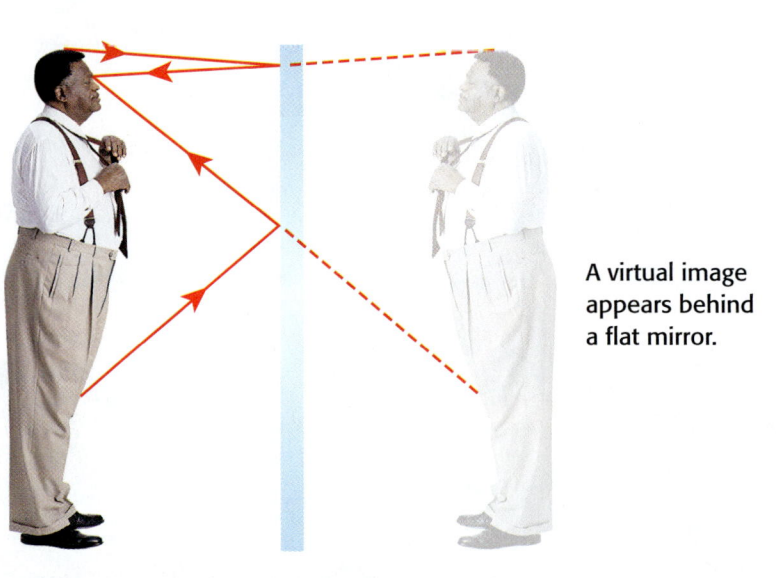

A virtual image appears behind a flat mirror.

A ray diagram shows where the light actually travels as well as where you perceive that it has come from.

QuickLab

Curved Mirror

 10 min

Procedure

1. Observe the reflection of a **short pencil** in the inner part of a **large, stainless steel spoon.**
2. Slowly move the spoon closer to the pencil. Note any changes in the appearance of the pencil's reflection.
3. Repeat steps 1 and 2 by using the other side of the spoon as the mirror.

Analysis

1. Which side of the spoon is a concave mirror? Which side is a convex mirror?
2. What differences in the reflected images did you observe?
3. How does distance affect an object's image in concave and convex mirrors?

Curved mirrors can distort images.

If you have ever looked into the passenger's side mirror on a car or a dressing table mirror, you have used a curved mirror. The images created by these mirrors are distorted so that they are smaller or larger than the real object.

Curved mirrors create images by reflecting light according to the law of reflection. But because the surface is not flat, the line perpendicular to the mirror (the normal) points in different directions for different parts of the mirror.

Mirrors that bulge out are called *convex mirrors*. Convex mirrors, such as that on the passenger's side of the car shown in **Figure 5,** make images appear smaller than they actually are. Indented mirrors are called *concave mirrors*. Some concave mirrors magnify objects so that the image created is larger than the object.

Concave mirrors can create real images.

Concave mirrors are used to focus reflected light. A concave mirror can form one of two kinds of images. It may form a virtual image behind the mirror or a real image in front of the mirror. When light rays from an object are focused onto a small area, a **real image** forms.

If a piece of paper is placed at the point where the light rays come together, the real image appears on the paper. If you placed a piece of paper behind a mirror where the virtual image seemed to appear, you would not see the image on the paper. This example shows the primary difference between a real and a virtual image. Light rays exist at the point where the real image appears. A virtual image appears to exist in a certain place, but no light rays exist there.

Academic Vocabulary

distort (di STAWRT) to change the natural appearance of something

Figure 5 Images formed by a convex mirror are smaller than the original object.

Section 3 Reflection and Color **563**

QuickLab

20 min

Filtering Light

1. Look through one of **four colored filters**—red, blue, yellow, or green—at an object across the room. Describe the object's color.

2. Repeat step 1 with each one of the filters.

3. Look at the same object through two filters placed together. Describe the object's color. Why does the object's color differ from the color when one filter is used?

4. Place the red, blue, and yellow filters together, and look at the same object. Describe what you see. Why do you see this?

Figure 6 A Rose in White and Red Light

Seeing Colors

› **The colors that you perceive depend on the wavelengths of visible light that reach your eyes.** When you see light that has a wavelength of about 550 nm, your brain interprets the light as *green*. If the light comes from the direction of a leaf, then you will think that the leaf is green.

A leaf does not emit light. And in the darkness of night, you may not be able to see the leaf at all. The leaf reflects green light from another light source.

Objects have the color of the wavelengths they reflect.

If you pass the light from the sun through a prism, the prism separates the light into a rainbow of colors. White light from the sun actually contains light that has all of the wavelengths in the visible region of the electromagnetic spectrum.

When white light strikes a leaf, as **Figure 6** shows, the leaf reflects light that has a wavelength of about 550 nm, which corresponds to the color green. The leaf absorbs light at other wavelengths, so those wavelengths are not reflected. When the light reflected from the leaf enters your eyes, your brain interprets the light as *green*. When you look through a transparent object, such as a color filter, you see the color of the light that passes through the filter. A green filter transmits green light and absorbs other colors of light.

Likewise, the petals of a red rose reflect red light and absorb other colors. So, the petals appear to be red. If you view a rose and its leaves under red light, as **Figure 6** shows, the petals will appear red but the leaves will appear black.

Under white light, the petals of a rose reflect red light, while the leaves reflect green light.

Under red light, the petals still look red, but the leaves look black because there is no green light for them to reflect.

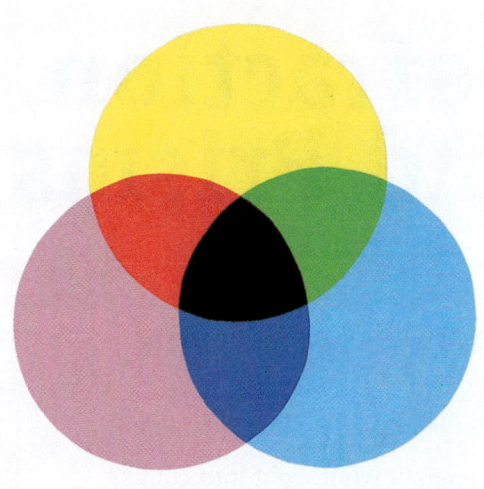

Red, green, and blue lights can combine to produce yellow, magenta, cyan, or white lights.

Yellow, magenta, and cyan filters can be combined to produce red, green, blue, or black.

Mixtures of colors produce other colors.

Most of the colors that we see are not pure colors. They are mixtures of primary colors. Televisions and computer monitors display many colors by combining light of the *additive primary colors*—red, green, and blue. Mixing light of two of these colors can produce the secondary colors yellow, cyan, and magenta, as shown on the left of **Figure 7.** Mixing light of the three additive primary colors makes white light.

Because pigments and filters absorb light, the opposite effect happens when they are mixed. The *subtractive primary colors*—yellow, cyan, and magenta—can be combined to create red, green, and blue, as shown in the right of **Figure 7.** If filters or pigments of all three colors are combined in equal proportions, all visible light is absorbed. No light gets to your eyes, so you see black. Black is not a color. It is the absence of color.

Figure 7 Colors combine to produce other colors. **Why is the center of the lights white and the center of the filters black?**

Section 3 Review

KEY IDEAS

1. **List** three examples of the diffuse reflection of light.
2. **Describe** the law of reflection in your own words.
3. **Draw** a ray diagram that represents a light reflecting off of a flat surface to illustrate the law of reflection.
4. **Discuss** how reflection from objects that appear blue differs from objects that appear yellow.
5. **Explain** why a plant may look green in sunlight but black under red light.

CRITICAL THINKING

6. **Analyzing Information** A friend says that only mirrors and other shiny surfaces reflect light. Explain what is wrong with this reasoning.
7. **Applying ideas** How does a flat mirror form a virtual image?
8. **Forming Models** A convex mirror can be used to see around the corner of a hallway. Draw a simple ray diagram that illustrates how this works.

SECTION 4
Refraction, Lenses, and Prisms

Key Ideas
- What happens to light when it passes from one medium to another medium?
- What happens when light passes through a lens?
- How can a prism separate white light into colors?

Key Terms
lens
magnification
prism
dispersion

Why It Matters
Your eyes contain lenses that bend and focus light to allow you to see objects around you.

Tennessee Course Level Expectations (Physical Science)
CLE.3202.2.1; CLE.3202.2.2; CLE.3202.Inq.1; CLE.3202.Inq.2; CLE.3202.Inq.3; CLE.3202.Inq.4; CLE.3202.Inq.6; CLE.3202.Math.1; CLE.3202.Math.2; CLE.3202.TE.3

Light travels in straight lines through empty space. But we also see light that passes through various media, such as air, water, or glass. The direction of a light wave may change when the light passes from one medium into another.

Refraction of Light

>**Light waves bend, or refract, when they pass from one transparent medium to another.** Light bends when it changes mediums because the speed of light differs in each medium. If light meets the boundary of two mediums at an angle to the normal, as in **Figure 1,** the light changes direction.

When light moves from a material in which its speed is high to a material in which its speed is lower, such as from air to glass, the ray is bent toward the normal. If light moves from a material in which its speed is low to one in which its speed is higher, the ray is bent away from the normal.

Figure 1 Light waves can change direction.

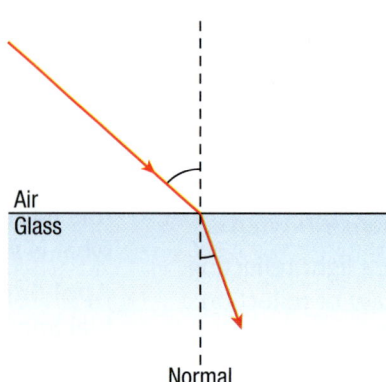

The path of a light ray bends toward the normal when the light ray moves from air into glass.

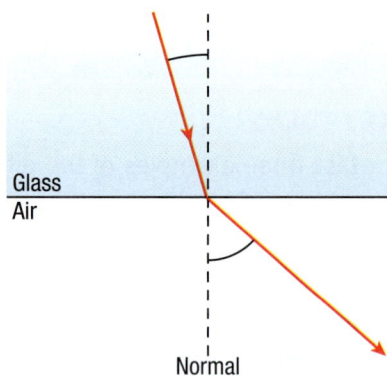

The path of a light ray is bent away from the normal when the ray passes from glass into air.

Refraction makes objects appear to be in different positions.

When a cat looks at a fish underwater, the cat perceives the fish as closer than it actually is, as the ray diagram in the top of **Figure 2** shows. On the other hand, when the fish looks at the cat above the surface, the fish perceives the cat as farther than it really is, as **Figure 2** also shows.

The images that the cat and the fish see are virtual images like the images that form behind a mirror. The light rays that pass from the fish to the cat bend away from the normal when they pass from water to air. But the cat's brain interprets the light as if it traveled in a straight line, and thus the cat sees a virtual image. Similarly, the light from the cat to the fish bends toward the normal as it passes from the air into water, which causes the fish to see a virtual image.

Reading Check Why does the fish seem closer than it is?

Refraction in the atmosphere creates mirages.

Have you ever seen what looks like water on the road on a hot, dry summer day? If so, then you may have seen a *mirage* like the one shown in **Figure 3**. A mirage is a virtual image that is caused by refraction of light in the atmosphere.

The air temperature affects the speed at which light travels. When light from the sky passes into the layer of hot air just above the asphalt on a road, the light refracts and bends upward away from the road. This refraction creates a virtual image of the sky coming from the direction of the road. Your mind may assume that a reflection was caused by water.

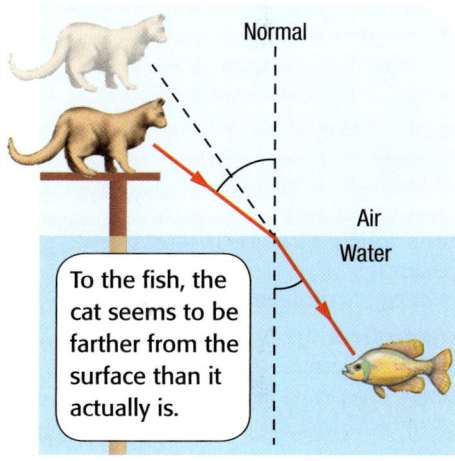

Figure 2 Refraction creates virtual images.

To the cat on the pier, the fish appears to be closer than it actually is.

To the fish, the cat seems to be farther from the surface than it actually is.

Figure 3 A mirage is produced when light bends as it passes through air at different temperatures.

Section 4 Refraction, Lenses, and Prisms

Converging Lens When light rays pass through a lens that is thicker at the middle, the rays are bent inward.

Diverging Lens When light rays pass through a lens that is thicker at the ends, the rays are bent outward.

Figure 4 The way the surface of a lens curves affects how light rays bend as the rays pass through the lens.

Lenses

You may not realize that you use the refraction of light every day. Human eyes, as well as cameras, contact lenses, eyeglasses, and microscopes, contain parts that bend light.

Light traveling at an angle through a thin, flat medium is refracted twice—once when it enters the medium and again when it reenters the air. So, the position of a light ray that exits the medium is shifted, but the light ray is still parallel to the original light ray. However, if the medium has a curved surface, the exiting rays will not be parallel to the original ray.

▶ **When light passes through a medium that has a curved surface, a lens, the light rays change direction.** Each light ray strikes the surface of the curved surface at a slightly different angle, so angles at which the rays are bent differ. The effects of a *converging lens* and a *diverging lens* on light rays are shown in **Figure 4**. A converging lens bends light inward. This type of lens can create either a virtual image or a real image, depending on the distance from the lens to the object. A diverging lens bends light outward and can create only a virtual image.

Reading Check Which type of lens can create a real image?

lens (LENZ) a transparent object that refracts light waves such that they converge or diverge to create an image

magnification (MAG nuh fi KAY shuhn) the increase of an object's apparent size by using lenses or mirrors

Lenses can magnify images.

A magnifying glass is a familiar example of a converging lens. A magnifying glass reveals details that you would not usually be able to see, such as the small parts of the flower in **Figure 5**. The large image that you see through the lens is a virtual image. **Magnification** is any change in the size of an image compared with the size of the object. Magnification can produce an image that is larger than the object.

If you hold a magnifying glass over a piece of paper in bright sunlight, you can see a real image of the sun on the paper. By adjusting the height of the lens above the paper, you can focus the light rays together into a small area, called the *focal point*. At the focal point, the image of the sun may contain enough energy to eventually set the paper on fire.

Figure 5 A magnifying glass makes a large virtual image of a small object.

Microscopes use multiple lenses.

A compound light microscope, shown in **Figure 6,** uses multiple lenses to provide greater magnification than a single magnifying glass can. The objective lens is closest to the object and forms a large, real image of the object. The eyepiece then acts like a magnifying glass and creates a larger virtual image that you see when you look through the microscope.

The eye depends on refraction and lenses.

Without refraction of light, you would not be able to see at all. The way a human eye bends light, which is shown in **Figure 7,** is similar to the way a simple camera operates. Light enters a camera through a large lens, which focuses the light into an image on the film at the back of the camera.

Light first enters the eye through a transparent tissue called the *cornea.* The cornea is responsible for 70% of the refraction of light in the eye. After the cornea, light passes through the *pupil.* Then, light travels through the *lens,* which is composed of fibers. The curvature of the lens determines how much the lens refracts light. Muscles can adjust the curvature of the lens until an image is focused on the *retina.*

The retina is composed of tiny, light-sensitive structures called *rods* and *cones.* When light strikes the rods and cones, signals are sent to the brain where they are interpreted as images. Most cones are in the center of the retina, and most rods are on the outer edges. The cones are responsible for color vision, but they respond only to bright light. Therefore, you cannot see color in very dim light. The rods are more sensitive to dim light but cannot resolve details well. So, you can glimpse faint movements from the corners of your eyes.

Figure 6 A compound light microscope uses several lenses to produce a highly magnified image.

Figure 7 Eyes focus light.

❶ The cornea is a transparent membrane that covers the eye and refracts light.

❷ Light passes through a hole in the colorful iris known as the pupil.

❸ Light is refracted again by the lens, which is made up of transparent fibers.

❹ The refracted light is focused onto the back surface of the eye, the retina.

❺ The light is detected by rods and cones in the retina.

❻ The optic nerve carries signals to the brain.

Section 4 Refraction, Lenses, and Prisms

QuickLab

10 min

Water Prism

1. Fill a **shallow dish** with about 3 cm of **water**.
2. Place a **flat mirror** in the tray so that about half of the mirror is under the water. The mirror should be placed at an angle and should lean against the side of the dish.
3. Use a **white piece of paper** to capture the **sunlight** that is reflected by the mirror. Change the distance of the paper from the mirror and the angle of the paper until you see colors in the reflection. What colors do you see?
4. Why are the colors of the reflected sunlight separated by the water?

prism (PRIZ uhm) in optics, a system that consists of two or more plane surfaces of a transparent solid at an angle with each other

dispersion (di SPUHR zhuhn) in optics, the process of separating a wave (such as white light) of different frequencies into its individual component waves (the different colors)

www.scilinks.org
Topic: Refraction
Code: HK81285

Dispersion and Prisms

A **prism**, such as the one in **Figure 8**, can separate white light into its component colors. Water droplets in the air can also separate the color in white light to produce a rainbow. ❯ **A prism can separate the colors of light because the speeds of light waves traveling through the medium depend on the wavelengths of light.**

Different colors of light are refracted by different amounts.

Light waves of all wavelengths travel at the same speed (3.0×10^8 m/s) in a vacuum. But when a light wave travels through a medium, the speed of the light wave depends on the light wave's wavelength. The colors in the visible spectrum, in order of longest to shortest wavelength, are red, orange, yellow, green, blue, and violet. In the visible spectrum, violet light has the shortest wavelength and travels the slowest. Red light has the longest wavelength and travels the fastest.

Because violet light travels slower than red light, violet light bends more than red light when it passes from one medium to another. When white light passes from air to the glass in the prism, violet bends the most and red bends the least. When the light exits the prism, the light is separated into the colors in the visible spectrum. This effect in which light separates into different colors because of differences in wave speed is called **dispersion.**

Figure 8 A prism separates white light into its component colors.

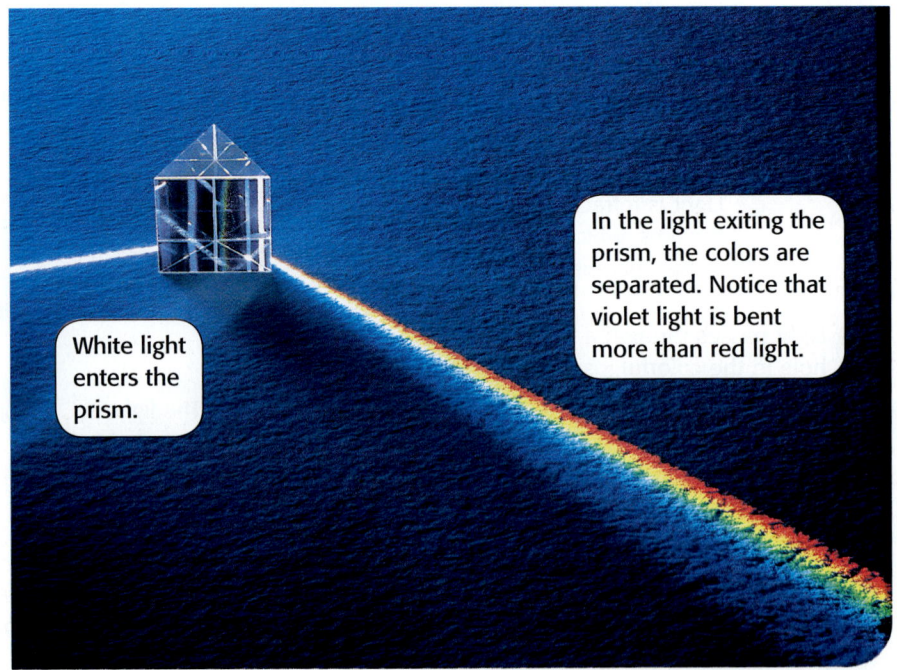

White light enters the prism.

In the light exiting the prism, the colors are separated. Notice that violet light is bent more than red light.

Figure 9 Sunlight is dispersed and reflected by water droplets to form a rainbow.

Rainbows are caused by dispersion and reflection.

Rainbows, such as the one in **Figure 9,** may form any time that water droplets are in the air. When sunlight strikes a droplet of water, the light is dispersed into different colors as it passes from the air into the water. If the angle at which the refracted light rays meet the back surface of the water droplet is small enough, the rays can be reflected. Some of the light will reflect back through the droplet. The light disperses further when it passes out of the water back into the air.

When light finally leaves the droplet, violet light emerges at an angle of 40°, red light emerges at 42°, and the other colors are in between these angles. We see light from many droplets as arcs of color, which form a rainbow. Only the red light from droplets higher in the air and only the violet light from lower droplets reaches your eyes. So, the colors of a rainbow are separated in space.

READING TOOLBOX

Booklet
Create a booklet you can use to compare mirrors, lenses, and prisms. Label the cover "Mirror, Lenses, and Prisms." Label the first two pages "Mirrors," the next two pages "Lenses," and the last two pages "Prisms."

Section 4 Review

KEY IDEAS

1. **Draw** a ray diagram that shows the path of light when the light travels from air into glass.
2. **Describe** how a mirage is formed.
3. **Explain** how a simple magnifying glass works.
4. **Explain** why light is dispersed by a prism.

CRITICAL THINKING

5. **Explaining Events** How does your eye focus light on the retina?
6. **Applying Ideas** A spoon partially immersed in a glass of water may appear to be bent. Is the image of the spoon in the water a real image or a virtual image?
7. **Forming Conclusions** In the dispersed light that exits a glass prism, green light is closer to violet light than yellow light is. Does green light or yellow light travel faster through the glass prism?
8. **Applying Ideas** If light traveled at the same speed in raindrops as it does in air, could rainbows exist? Explain your reasoning.

Section 4 Refraction, Lenses, and Prisms

Why It Matters

Detecting Counterfeit Money

You might think that high-quality photocopiers, scanners, and printers would make it easy to print fake money. However, newer 10, 20, and 50 dollar bills have security features that cannot be duplicated by an ink-jet printer. The United States Treasury introduced a redesigned 10 dollar bill in 2006. This bill, along with 20 and 50 dollar bills, was updated to include security features that make counterfeit money harder to make and easier to detect. Several of the security features depend on how light interacts with the paper and inks used to make money. These features include a security thread, a watermark, and features that are printed using color-shifting ink.

A plastic strip known as a security thread is embedded in the paper. If you hold the bill up to the light and look to the right of the portrait of Alexander Hamilton, you will be able to see the words *USA TEN* printed on the thread. This strip glows orange when the bill is held under ultraviolet light.

It may be obvious that more colors are used in the new bills. But if you look closely at a bill, you will notice that the patterns are made by very fine lines. The colors appear darker where the lines are more closely spaced. The bills even include text, called *microprinting*, that you cannot read without a magnifying lens. The fine patterns and microprinting make it hard for counterfeiters to reproduce the quality of the printing on real money.

Have you ever left a dollar bill in your pocket and found that it is still in one piece after it has been through the washing machine? If money were printed on regular paper, it would have fallen apart. All paper money is printed on special paper made from linen and cotton, which is known as rag paper. This paper is very thin and does not feel like other papers. Counterfeiters cannot buy this paper. It is made only for the U.S. government.

FORENSICS

Color-shifting ink is used to print the number 10 in the lower right of the bill. This ink contains metal particles that reflect light. Only certain wavelengths make it out of the ink to produce the color you see. The other light waves destructively interfere with one another. The light waves that you see also depend on the angle of the light. When you tilt the bill, you see a different color. The color on the new bills shifts from copper to green.

If you hold the bill up to the light and look in the white oval, you will see another image of Alexander Hamilton. This image is a watermark. The image is not created with ink. It is part of the paper. The thickness of the paper is varied to make a watermark. Less light comes through the thicker parts of the paper, which creates an image that is darker than the surrounding area. The watermark can be seen through both sides of the paper.

YOUR TURN

UNDERSTANDIING CONCEPTS

1. If you tilt a 10 dollar bill, what should you see change?

CRITICAL THINKING

2. Suppose counterfeiters use paper that is similar to the paper that the government uses to print money. Do you think that they would be able to successfully make fake money? Explain your reasoning.

www.scilinks.org
Topic: Printing Processes
Code: HK81700

Application Lab

⏱ 50 min

Lenses and Images

As an optical engineer for a camera company, you have been given a lens for which your job is to figure out the focal length. Based on the specifications you obtain by doing an experiment, a new model of camera will be designed that uses that lens.

What You'll Do

▸ **Observe** images formed by a convex lens.

▸ **Measure** the distance of objects and images from the lens.

▸ **Analyze** your results to determine the focal length of the lens.

What You'll Need

cardboard screen, 10 cm × 20 cm
convex lens, 10 cm to 15 cm focal length
lens holder
light box with light bulb
meterstick
ruler, metric
screen holder
supports for meterstick

Safety

Procedure

Preparing for Your Experiment

❶ The shape of a lens determines the size, position, and types of images that it may form. When parallel rays of light from a distant object pass through a converging lens, they come together to form an image at a point called the *focal point*. The distance from this point to the lens is called the *focal length*. In this experiment, you will find the focal length of a lens. Then, verify this value by forming images, measuring distances, and using the lens formula below.

$$\frac{1}{d_o} + \frac{1}{d_i} = \frac{1}{f}$$

where d_o = object distance,

d_i = image distance, and

f = focal length

❷ On a clean sheet of paper, make a data table like the one shown.

❸ Set up the equipment as illustrated in the figure below. Make sure the lens and screen are securely fastened to the meterstick.

Determining Focal Length

❹ Stand about 1 m from a window, and point the meterstick at a tree, parked car, or similar object. Slide the screen holder along the meterstick until a clear image of the distant object forms on the screen. Measure the distance between the lens and the screen in centimeters. This distance is very close to the focal length of the lens that you are using. Record this value at the top of your data table.

574 Chapter 16 Sound and Light

Sample Data Table: Objects, Lenses, and Images

Focal length of lens, f: _____ cm	Object distance, d_o (cm)	Image distance, d_i (cm)	$\frac{1}{d_o}$	$\frac{1}{d_i}$	$\frac{1}{d_o} + \frac{1}{d_i}$	$\frac{1}{f}$	Size of object (mm)	Size of image (mm)
Trial 1								
Trial 2			DO NOT WRITE IN BOOK					
Trial 3								

Forming Images

5 Set up the equipment as illustrated in the figure. Place the lens more than twice the focal length from the light box.

6 Move the screen along the meterstick until a clear image forms. Record the distance from the light to the lens, d_o, and the distance from the lens to the screen, d_i, in centimeters as Trial 1 in your data table. Also, record the height of the object and of the image in millimeters. The object in this case may be either the filament of the light bulb or a cut-out shape in the light box.

7 For Trial 2, place the lens exactly twice the focal length from the object. Slide the screen along the stick until a clear image is formed, as in step 6. Record the distances from the screen and the sizes of the object and image as you did in step 6.

8 For Trial 3, place the lens at a distance from the object that is greater than the focal length but less than twice the focal length. Adjust the screen, and record the measurements as you did in step 7.

Analysis

1. **Analyzing Data** Perform the necessary calculations to complete your data table.
2. **Analyzing Data** How does $\frac{1}{d_o} + \frac{1}{d_i}$ compare with $\frac{1}{f}$ in each of the three trials?

Communicating Results

3. **Drawing Conclusions** If the object distance is greater than the image distance, how will the size of the image compare with the size of the object?

Application

Does the lens that you tested conform to the lens equations for image formation? If a camera that contained this lens was made, what would the minimum length of the camera have to be? Explain your answer.

Using Fractions

Science Skills

Technology
Math
Scientific Methods
Graphing

Problem

The intensity of light at a distance, r, from a source with power output, P, is described by the following equation:

$$\text{intensity} = \frac{power}{4\pi \, (distance)^2} = \frac{P}{4\pi r^2}$$

What is the intensity of a 100.0 W light bulb at a distance of 5.00 m from the light bulb?

Solution

Identify

List all given and unknown values.

Given:
$power \, (P) = 100.0 \text{ W}$
$distance \, (r) = 5.00 \text{ m}$

Unknown:
$intensity \, (\text{W/m}^2)$

Plan

Write down the equation for intensity.

Given:
$$intensity = \frac{P}{4\pi r^2}$$

Solve

Solve for intensity.

a. To evaluate an equation that is written as a fraction, first evaluate the top and the bottom parts of the fraction separately.

b. Then, divide the top number by the bottom number to get the final answer.

a. $intensity = \dfrac{100.0 \text{ W}}{4 \times \pi \times (5.00 \text{ m})^2}$

$intensity = \dfrac{100.0 \text{ W}}{4 \times 3.14 \times 25 \text{ m}^2}$

b. $intensity = \dfrac{100.0 \text{ W}}{314 \text{ m}^2} = 0.318 \text{ W/m}^2$

Because a watt (W) is the amount of power required to do 1 joule (J) of work in 1 s, 0.318 J of energy pass through each square meter of area at a distance of 5.00 m from the light bulb each second.

Practice

1. What is the intensity of the 100.0 W light bulb at a distance of 1.00 m from the light bulb? How many times greater is the intensity at 1.00 m than the intensity at 5.00 m?

2. The total power output of the sun is equal to 3.85×10^{26} W. What is the intensity of sunlight at a distance of 1.50×10^{11} m (the average distance of Earth from the sun) from the sun?

3. When the sun is directly above the clouds that form the surface of Saturn, the intensity of sunlight on the surface is 15.0 W/m². What is the distance from the sun to Saturn? How many times larger is the distance between the sun and Saturn than the distance between the sun and Earth?

CHAPTER 16 Summary

Key Ideas

Section 1 Sound

- **Properties of Sound** Sound waves are caused by vibrations and carry energy through a medium. (p. 543)
- **Musical Instruments** Most instruments produce sound through the vibrations of strings, air columns, or membranes. (p. 547)
- **Hearing and the Ear** The human ear is a sensitive organ that senses vibrations in the air and amplifies them. (p. 549)
- **Ultrasound and Sonar** Reflected sound waves are used to determine distances and to create images. (p. 550)

Section 2 The Nature of Light

- **Waves and Particles** The two most common models describe light either as a wave or as a stream of particles. (p. 552)
- **The Electromagnetic Spectrum** The electromagnetic spectrum consists of waves at all possible energies, frequencies, and wavelengths. (p. 556)

Section 3 Reflection and Color

- **Reflection of Light** Every object reflects some light and absorbs some light. (p. 560)
- **Mirrors** Mirrors reflect light as described by the law of reflection, and this light reaches your eyes. The type of image you perceive depends on the type of mirror. (p. 562)
- **Seeing Colors** The colors that you perceive depend on the wavelengths of visible light that reach your eyes. (p. 564)

Section 4 Refraction, Lenses, and Prisms

- **Refraction of Light** Light waves bend, or refract, when they pass from one transparent medium to another. (p. 566)
- **Lenses** When light passes through a medium with a curved surface, a lens, the light rays change direction. (p. 568)
- **Dispersion and Prisms** A prism can separate the colors of light because the speeds of light waves traveling through the medium depend on the wavelengths of light. (p. 570)

Key Terms

sound wave, p. 543
pitch, p. 546
infrasound, p. 546
ultrasound, p. 546
resonance, p. 548
sonar, p. 551

photon, p. 553
intensity, p. 555
radar, p. 556

light ray, p. 560
virtual image, p. 562
real image, p. 563

lens, p. 568
magnification, p. 568
prism, p. 570
dispersion, p. 570

CHAPTER 16 Review

1. **Word Roots** The word root *son* or *sono* means "sound," and the root *phot* or *photo* means "light." For each of the roots, list two words that contain the root. Define the words in your list.

USING KEY TERMS

2. How is the loudness of a sound related to *amplitude* and *intensity*?

3. How is the *pitch* of a sound related to the sound's *frequency*?

4. Explain how a guitar produces sound by using the terms *standing waves* and *resonance*.

5. Explain why you would not expect a clarinet to have the same *fundamental frequency* as a saxophone.

6. Describe *infrasound* and *ultrasound*, and explain why humans cannot hear these waves.

7. Define *sonar* and *radar*. State their differences and their similarities, and describe a situation in which each system would be useful.

8. Explain how a *virtual image* differs from a *real image*. Give an example of each type of image.

9. Explain why a leaf may appear green in white light but black in red light. Use the following terms in your answer: *wavelength* and *reflection*.

10. What happens to light after it passes through a *converging lens* and after is passes through a *diverging lens*?

UNDERSTANDING KEY IDEAS

11. Relative intensity of sound is measured in units that have the symbol
    a. dB.
    b. Hz.
    c. J.
    d. V.

12. Sound waves travel faster through liquid water than through air because
    a. water is hotter than air.
    b. water is less dense than air.
    c. the particles of the liquid transfer energy better than the particles in a gas.
    d. the particles in the liquid vibrate more than the particles in a gas.

13. A flat mirror forms an image that is
    a. smaller than the object.
    b. larger than the object.
    c. virtual.
    d. real.

14. Microwaves are higher in energy than
    a. radio waves.   c. gamma rays.
    b. visible light.   d. X rays.

15. Light can be modeled as
    a. reflection and refraction.
    b. a stream of particles called *photons*.
    c. rays that travel in a curved path.
    d. sound waves.

16. In the eye, most of the refraction of light is done by the
    a. lens.   c. rods and cones.
    b. pupil.   d. cornea.

17. The energy of a photon is proportional to
    a. the amplitude of a wave.
    b. the wavelength of a wave.
    c. the frequency of a wave.
    d. the speed of light.

18. When white light passes through a prism, the light is separated into the colors in the visible spectrum because
    a. the prism reflects the light.
    b. the prism filters the light.
    c. the wavelengths of light travel at different speeds in the prism.
    d. the wavelengths of light increase in the prism.

578 Chapter 16 Sound and Light

EXPLAINING KEY IDEAS

19. Describe the anatomy of the human ear, and explain how the ear senses vibrations.

20. Draw a figure that illustrates what happens when light rays hit a rough surface and what happens when they hit a smooth surface. Explain how your illustration demonstrates diffuse reflection and the law of reflection.

21. How can an object appear bigger under a magnifying glass?

22. Describe how you can make red, green, blue, and black paint with a paint set that contains only yellow, magenta, and cyan paint.

CRITICAL THINKING

23. **Applying Ideas** A guitar has six strings, each tuned to a different pitch. What, other than the length of the strings, determines the pitch of the strings? (**Hint:** Think about what will affect the frequency at which the string vibrates.)

24. **Drawing Conclusions** By listening to an orchestra, how can you determine that the speed of sound is the same for all frequencies?

25. **Analyzing Methods** Sonar devices on ships use a narrow ultrasonic beam for determining depth. Why would a wider beam be used to locate fish?

26. **Predicting Outcomes** Imagine laying this page flat on a table and then standing a mirror upright at the top of the page. Using the law of reflection, draw the image of each of the following letters of the alphabet in the mirror.

    A B C F W T

27. **Forming Hypotheses** Why is white light not dispersed into a spectrum when it passes through a flat pane of glass such as a window?

28. **Understanding Relationships** People who are *colorblind* are unable to see at least one of the primary colors. What part of the eye do you think is not working in colorblind people?

Graphing Skills

29. **Line Graphs** As a ship travels across a lake, a sonar device on the ship sends out downward pulses of ultrasound and detects the reflected pulses. The table below gives the ship's distance from the shore and the time for each pulse to return to the ship.

Distance from shore (m)	Time to receive pulse ($\times 10^{-2}$ s)
100	1.7
120	2.0
140	2.6
150	3.1
170	3.2
200	4.1
220	3.7
250	4.4
270	5.0
300	4.6

a. Use the speed of sound in water to calculate the depth of the lake at each distance from shore.

b. Construct a graph of the depth of the lake as a function of distance from the shore. Mark the maximum and minimum depth.

Math Skills

30. **Sonar** Calculate the distance to the bottom of a lake when a ship using sonar receives the reflection of a pulse in 0.055 s.

31. **Electromagnetic Waves** Using the speed of light, calculate the wavelength of radio waves from an AM radio station that is broadcasting at 1,200 kHz. (**Hint:** The wave speed equation is $v = f \times \lambda$.)

32. **Electromagnetic Waves** Waves that make up green light have a wavelength of about 550 nm. Use the wave speed equation and the speed of light to find their frequency.

Standardized Test Prep

Understanding Concepts

Directions (1-4): For each question, write on a sheet of paper the letter of the correct answer.

1. A family notices that the garbage disposal in the sink sounds twice as loud as the vacuum cleaner does. If the sound of the garbage disposal is 80 dB, about how loud is the vacuum cleaner?
   - A. 40 dB
   - B. 70 dB
   - C. 90 dB
   - D. 160 dB

2. A medical student is examining a model of the ear. Where should the student look to find the hammer, anvil, and stirrup?
   - F. in the outer ear
   - G. in the ear canal
   - H. in the middle ear
   - I. in the cochlea

3. What sounds can an ultrasound system, such as sonar, detect that the human ear cannot?
   - A. sounds greater than 150 dB
   - B. sounds greater than 20,000 Hz
   - C. sounds traveling faster than 400 m/s
   - D. sounds traveling through a medium that is denser than air

4. Light striking a pane of glass passes through the glass, but the angle of the light changes while inside the pane of glass. What is this change called?
   - F. refraction
   - G. reflection
   - H. incidence
   - I. diffusion

Directions (5-7): For each question, write a short response.

5. A surface reflects all colors of light except for green. A light filter that allows only green light to pass through is placed between a light source and the surface. What color or colors will the surface appear to be under the filter?

6. How are radar and sonar alike? How are they different?

7. Is sound likely to travel faster through the air on a very cold day or on a very hot day? Why?

Reading Skills

Directions (8-9): Read the passage below. Then, answer the questions that follow.

STIMULATING EMISSIONS

Today, there is an astonishing variety of uses for lasers, from CD players to surgery. Lasers are beams of focused and concentrated light. The word *laser* began as an acronym for *Light Amplification by the Stimulated Emission of Radiation*.

Laser light is created by first adding energy to a chamber that contains certain types of atoms. Elements in the noble gas family work well for lasers. This addition of energy is the stimulation. The energy is absorbed by electrons in the atoms, which causes the electrons to jump to a higher energy level. At this point, the atoms are in an excited state. They can return to their original energy level by losing the energy they gained. When the electrons return to their original energy level, the lost energy is emitted as photons. This energy is the radiation referred to in the acronym.

The emitted photons can then strike other atoms that are in an excited state and cause them to emit photons in turn. The new photons are aimed in the same direction as the original photons. When mirrors are placed in certain positions within the chamber, the photons bounce back and forth many times and multiply, or amplify, the intensity of the photon emissions.

8. What optical effect is responsible for the amplification referred to in the acronym *laser*?
   - A. refraction
   - B. reflection
   - C. dispersion
   - D. diffusion

9. What happens when a photon strikes an atom that is in an excited state?

Interpreting Graphics

The diagram below shows the electromagnetic spectrum, and various ranges of the spectrum are labeled. Use the diagram to answer questions 10–12.

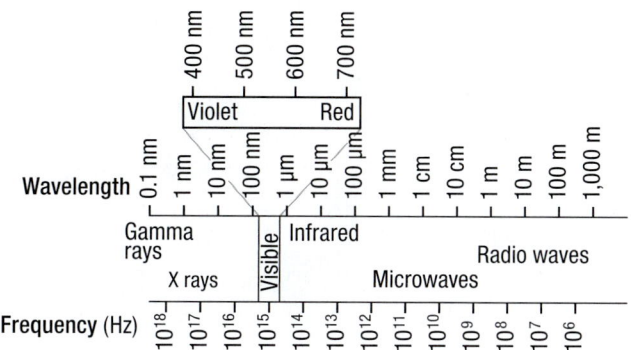

10. What is the wavelength of red light?
  F. about 7 m
  G. about 70 nm
  H. about 5 μm
  I. about 700 nm

11. Which of the following statements about gamma rays is true?
  A. They have a frequency of 10^{16} Hz.
  B. They have less energy than X rays have.
  C. They have more energy than X rays have.
  D. They have wavelengths that are greater than 10 nm.

12. As the wavelengths of electromagnetic waves increase, what happens to the frequency of the waves?

The diagram below shows a ray of light being reflected by two mirrors, which are aligned in parallel. Use this diagram to answer questions 13–14.

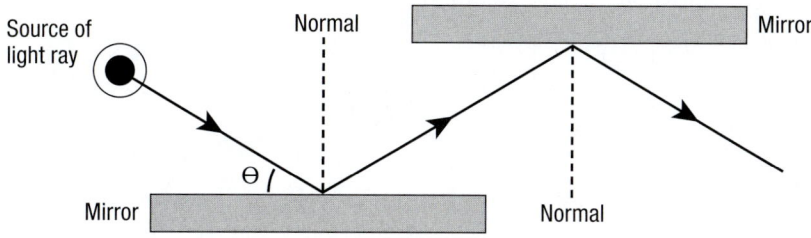

13. If angle θ is 40°, what is the angle of reflection on the second mirror?
  F. 40°
  G. 50°
  H. 90°
  I. 130°

14. Are either the first or second reflections diffuse reflections? Explain.

Test Tip

Carefully read the instructions, the question, and the answer options before choosing the answer.

CHAPTER 17 Electricity

Chapter Outline

1 Electric Charge and Force
Electric Charge
Transfer of Electric Charge
Electric Force

2 Current
Voltage and Current
Electrical Resistance

3 Circuits
What Are Circuits?
Series and Parallel Circuits
Electrical Energy and Electric Power
Fuses and Circuit Breakers

Tennessee Course Level Expectations (Physical Science)

CLE.3202.TE.3 Explain the relationship between the properties of a material and the use of the material in the application of a technology; **CLE.3202.2.4** Probe the fundamental principles and applications of electricity; **CLE.3202.Inq.1** Recognize that science is a progressive endeavor that reevaluates and extends what is already accepted; **CLE.3202.Inq.2** Design and conduct scientific investigations to explore new phenomena, verify previous results, test how well a theory predicts, and compare opposing theories; **CLE.3202.Inq.3** Use appropriate tools and technology to collect precise and accurate data; **CLE.3202.Inq.6** Communicate and defend scientific findings; **CLE.3202.Math.1** Understand the mathematical principles behind the science of physics; **CLE.3202.Math.2** Utilize appropriate mathematical equations and processes to solve basic physics problems; **CLE.3202.TE.2** Differentiate among elements of the engineering design cycle: design constraints, model building, testing, evaluating, modifying, and retesting; **CLE.3202.TE.4** Describe the dynamic interplay among science, technology, and engineering within living, earth-space, and physical systems.

Why It Matters
A Tesla coil creates a very large voltage that can be discharged as an impressive electrical arc. Nicola Tesla used his invention to study the electrical nature of Earth and its atmosphere.

Inquiry Lab
⏱ 20 min

A Simple Circuit

You can investigate electricity by using the parts of a simple **flashlight**. Use the **bulb** and **battery** from a flashlight and some **wire** or **aluminum foil** to make the bulb light. Try connecting the light bulb to the battery in several different ways.

Questions to Get You Started

1. Which method caused the bulb to light? Why did that method work?
2. Which method did not cause the bulb to light? Why didn't that method work?

READING TOOLBOX

These reading tools can help you learn the material in this chapter. For more information on how to use these and other tools, see **Appendix A**.

Word Families

Electric You will soon learn many new terms containing the words *electric* or *electrical*. These new terms use *electric* in the same way—meaning "pertaining to electricity." Here are some familiar words that you will see again in this chapter.

TERM	DEFINITION
energy	the capacity to do work
power	the rate at which work is done
field	a region of space in which a force operates
circuit	a closed loop

Your Turn Combine each of the words in the chart with *electric* or *electrical*, and write your own definition of the new term. Here is an example to get you started:

electrical energy: the capacity to do work using electricity

Analogies

Comparisons Analogies compare two things that may seem quite different. Analogies can make an unfamiliar idea easier to understand by linking it to something more familiar. Certain phrases help us spot analogies.

WORD OR PHRASE	HOW IT IS USED
just as	Turning a corner is acceleration, just as speeding up is.
is similar/equal to	Force is equal to mass times acceleration.
act like/is like	A screw is like an inclined plane wrapped around a cylinder.

Your Turn Complete a table that is similar to this one as you come across analogies in this chapter.

ANALOGY PHRASE	ITEM 1	ITEM 2
just as	a ball will roll downhill	a negative charge will move away from another negative charge

FoldNotes

Tri-Fold KWL notes can help you start thinking about the subject matter before you read. KWL stands for "what I **K**now, what I **W**ant to know, and what I **L**earned." KWL notes also help you relate new ideas to those you already know. This can help make new ideas easier to understand.

Your Turn Create a tri-fold FoldNote. In the left column, labeled "Know," write what you know about electricity. In the center column, labeled "Want to know," write what you want to know. As you read the chapter, write in the final column, labeled "Learned," what you learn about electricity.

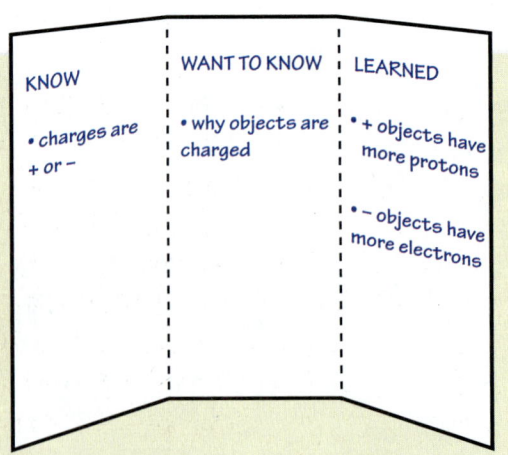

584 Chapter 17 Electricity

SECTION 1
Electric Charge and Force

Key Ideas
> What are the different kinds of electric charge?
> How do materials become charged when rubbed together?
> What force is responsible for most everyday forces?

Key Terms
electric charge
electrical conductor
electrical insulator
electric force
electric field

Why It Matters
We consider electrons to be *negative* because of a guess made by Benjamin Franklin. Almost all of the technology that you use is based on controlling the flow of electrons.

When you speak into a telephone, the microphone in the handset changes your sound waves into electrical signals. Light shines in your room when you flip a switch. And if you step on a pin with bare feet, your nerves send messages back and forth between your brain and your muscles so that you react quickly. Electric pulses moving through your nerve cells carry these messages.

Tennessee Course Level Expectations (Physical Science)
CLE.3202.2.4; CLE.3202.Inq.1;
CLE.3202.Inq.2; CLE.3202.Inq.3;
CLE.3202.TE.3; CLE.3202.TE.4

Electric Charge

You have probably noticed that after running a plastic comb through your hair on a dry day, the comb attracts strands of your hair. It might even attract small bits of paper. Maybe you have reached for a doorknob after walking across a rug and received a shock, as **Figure 1** shows. You receive a shock because your body picks up electric charge as your shoes move across the carpet. Although you may not notice these charges when they are spread throughout your body, you notice them as they pass from your finger to the metal doorknob. You experience this movement of charges as a little tingle or perhaps a sharp snap.

Electric charge is an electrical property of matter. > **An object can have a *negative* charge, a *positive* charge, or no charge at all.** Positive and negative electric charges are said to be opposite, because an object with an equal amount of positive and negative charge has no net charge. Like energy, electric charge is never created or destroyed. Conservation of charge is one of the fundamental laws of nature.

electric charge (ee LEK trik CHAHRJ) an electrical property of matter that creates electric and magnetic forces and interactions

Figure 1 Electric charge can jump from your body to a doorknob. **What kind of floor is likely to cause the buildup of electric charge?**

Figure 2 If you rub a balloon across your hair on a dry day, both the balloon and your hair become electrically charged.

The balloon and hair are oppositely charged and attract each other.

These two charged balloons have the same charge and repel each other.

www.scilinks.org
Topic: Static Electricity
Code: HK81451

Like charges repel, and opposite charges attract.

One way to observe charge is to rub a balloon back and forth across your hair. You may find that the balloon is attracted to your hair, as **Figure 2** shows. If you rub two balloons across your hair and then gently bring them near each other, also shown in **Figure 2,** the balloons will push away from, or repel, each other.

After this rubbing, the balloons and your hair have some kind of charge on them. Your hair is attracted to the balloon, yet the two balloons are repelled by each other. This demonstration shows that there are different kinds of charges—the kind on the balloons and the kind on your hair.

The two balloons must have the same kind of charge because each became charged in the same way. Because the two charged balloons repel each other, we see that like charges repel each other. However, the balloon and your hair did not become charged in the same way, and they are attracted to each other. The reason is that unlike charges attract one another.

Reading Check How do electric charges affect each other? (See Appendix E for answers to Reading Checks.)

Electric charge depends on an imbalance of protons and electrons.

All matter, including you, is made of atoms. Atoms, in turn, are made up of even smaller building blocks—electrons, protons, and neutrons. Electrons are negatively charged, protons are positively charged, and neutrons have no charge.

Objects are made up of an enormous number of neutrons, protons, and electrons. Whenever there is an imbalance in the number of protons and electrons in an atom, molecule, or other object, the object has a net electric charge. The difference in the numbers of protons and electrons determines an object's electric charge. Negatively charged objects have more electrons than protons. Positively charged objects have fewer electrons than protons.

The SI unit of electric charge is the *coulomb* (C). The electron and the proton have exactly the same amount of charge, 1.6×10^{-19} C. Electrons and protons are oppositely charged—a proton has a charge of $+1.6 \times 10^{-19}$ C, and an electron has a charge of -1.6×10^{-19} C. An object with a charge of -1.0 C has 6.25×10^{18} excess electrons. Because the amount of electric charge on an object depends on the number of protons and electrons, the net electric charge of a charged object is always an exact multiple of 1.6×10^{-19} C.

Why It Matters
Benjamin Franklin

HISTORY IN SCIENCE

Benjamin Franklin (1706–1790) first suggested the terms *positive* and *negative* for the two types of charge. At the age of 40, Franklin was a successful printer and journalist. He saw some experiments on electricity and was so fascinated by them that he began to devote much of his time to experimenting. Franklin was the first person to realize that lightning is a huge electric discharge, or spark. He invented the first lightning rod, for which he became famous. He also flew a kite into thunderclouds—at great risk to his life—to collect charge from them. During and after the Revolutionary War, Franklin gained fame as a politician and statesman.

Benjamin Franklin used a kite to gather charges from a cloud during a thunderstorm. In a very dangerous experiment, he was able to gather charges on a key tied to the kite string and let the charges jump to his knuckles.

After convincing himself that lightning was indeed a form of electricity, Franklin used that knowledge to design the lightning rod, a simple conducting rod used to direct lightning strikes away from homes and buildings to the ground.

SCLINKS
www.scilinks.org
Topic: Benjamin Franklin
Code: HK80159

YOUR TURN

WRITING IN SCIENCE
1. Franklin is credited with much work in addition to his groundbreaking electricity experiments. Prepare a presentation in the form of a skit, story, or computer program about his work on fire departments, public libraries, or post offices.

WRITING IN SCIENCE
2. One of Franklin's other technological achievements was the invention of the Franklin stove. Research this stove, and write a brochure explaining the benefits of this stove to prospective customers of Franklin's time.

Section 1   Electric Charge and Force

Transfer of Electric Charge

Protons and neutrons are relatively fixed in the nucleus of the atom, but the outermost electrons can easily move from one atom to another. ❯ **When different materials are rubbed together, electrons can be transferred from one material to the other.** The direction in which the electrons are transferred depends on the materials.

Conductors allow charges to flow; insulators do not.

Have you ever noticed that the electrical cords attached to appliances, such as the toaster shown in **Figure 3,** are plastic? These cords are not plastic all the way through, however. The center of an electrical cord is made of thin copper wires. Cords are layered in this way because of the electrical properties of each material.

Materials such as the copper in cords are called **electrical conductors.** Conductors allow electric charges to move freely. The plastic in the cord, however, does not allow the electric charges to move freely. Materials that do not transfer charge easily are called **electrical insulators.** Cardboard, glass, silk, and plastic are insulators. Charges in the electrical cord attached to an appliance can move through the conducting center but cannot escape through the surrounding insulator.

Charges can move within uncharged objects.

The charges in a neutral conductor can be redistributed without actually changing the overall charge of the object. **Figure 4** shows a negatively charged rubber rod brought close to, but not touching, a metal doorknob. The electrons in the doorknob are repelled by the rod and move away. As a result, the part of the doorknob closest to the rod is positively charged. The part of the doorknob farthest from the rod is negatively charged. The total charge on the doorknob will still be zero, but the opposite sides will have an *induced* charge.

Figure 3 Appliance cords are made of metal wire surrounded by plastic insulation. **How does this insulation make the appliance safer to use?**

electrical conductor (ee LEK tri kuhl kuhn DUHK tuhr) a material in which charges can move freely

electrical insulator (ee LEK tri kuhl IN suh LAYT uhr) a material in which charges cannot move freely

Figure 4 A negatively charged rod brought near a metal doorknob induces a positive charge on the side of the doorknob closest to the rod and a negative charge on the side farthest from the rod.

Figure 5 Electric Charging by Contact

① When a negative rod touches a neutral doorknob, electrons move from the rod to the doorknob.

② The transfer of electrons to the metal doorknob gives the doorknob a net negative charge.

Objects can be charged by contact.

The transfer of electrons from one object to another can charge objects. For example, when a negatively charged rubber rod touches a neutral object, such as the doorknob shown in **Figure 5**, some electrons move from the rod to the doorknob. The doorknob then has a net negative charge. The rubber rod still has a negative charge, but its charge becomes smaller. Objects charged by touching a charged object to a neutral object are said to be charged by *contact*.

If a positively charged rod were to touch a neutral doorknob, electrons would move from the doorknob into the positively charged rod. The doorknob would then have a net positive charge, and the net charge on the rod would again be decreased.

Objects can be charged by friction.

When you slide across a fabric car seat, some electrons are transferred between your clothes and the car seat. Depending on the types of materials involved, the electrons can be transferred from your clothes to the seat or from the seat to your clothes. One material gains electrons and becomes negatively charged, and the other loses electrons and becomes positively charged. This is an example of *charging by friction*.

Have you ever pulled clothes out of the dryer and had them stick together? They stick together because of *static electricity*. Your clothes are charged by friction as they rub against each other inside the dryer, and the electric charge builds up on the clothes. Static electricity can damage sensitive electronics when it discharges quickly through them.

Reading Check What causes static electricity?

Integrating Biology

Charges and Living Organisms
Atoms or molecules with a net electric charge are known as *ions*. All living cells contain ions. Most cells also need to be bathed in solutions of ions to stay alive. As a result, most living things are fairly good conductors.

Dry skin can be a good insulator. But if your skin gets wet, it becomes a conductor and charge can move through your body more easily. So, there is a greatly increased risk of electrocution when your skin is wet.

QuickLab

Charging Objects

 20 min

Procedure

1. Tear a **sheet of tissue paper** into small pieces, and pile the pieces on a table.
2. Use a **plastic comb** to vigorously comb your hair.
3. Use the comb to pick up the pieces of tissue.

Analysis

1. Are the plastic comb and tissue paper conductors or insulators?
2. What happens to the charges in the comb, tissue, and your hair?
3. What would happen if you held the comb near your hair?

A surface charge can be induced on insulators.

How can a negatively charged comb pick up pieces of neutral tissue paper? The electrons in tissue paper cannot move about freely because the paper is an insulator. But when a charged object is brought near an insulator, the positions of the electrons within the individual molecules of the insulator change slightly. One side of a molecule will be slightly more positive or negative than the other side. This *polarization* of the atoms or molecules of an insulator produces an induced charge on the surface of the insulator. Molecules of water are polarized and respond easily to charged objects, such as the balloon shown in **Figure 6**.

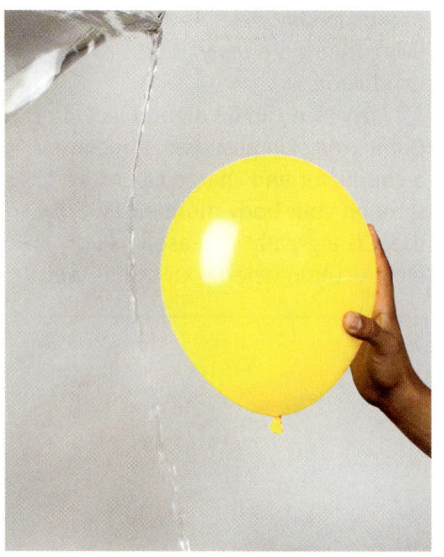

Figure 6 Rubbing a balloon with wool induces a negative charge on the balloon. The balloon can then deflect a stream of water. **What property of water causes this movement to occur?**

Electric Force

The attraction of tissue paper to a negatively charged comb and the repulsion of two similarly charged balloons are examples of **electric force.** Such pushes and pulls between charges are all around you. For example, a table feels solid, even though its atoms contain mostly empty space. The electric force between the electrons in the table's atoms and your hand is strong enough to prevent your hand from going through the table. ❯ **The electric force at the atomic and molecular levels is responsible for most of the everyday forces that we observe, such as the force of a spring and the force of friction.**

The electric force is also responsible for effects that we cannot see. It is part of what holds atoms together. The bonding of atoms to form molecules is also due to the electric force. The electric force plays a part in the interactions among molecules, such as the proteins and other building blocks of our bodies. Without the electric force, life itself would be impossible.

Electric force depends on charge and distance.

The electric force between two charged objects varies depending on the amount of charge on each object and the distance between them. The electric force between two objects is proportional to the product of the charges on the objects. If the charge on one object is doubled, the electric force between the objects will also be doubled, as long as the distance between the objects remains the same.

The electric force is also inversely proportional to the square of the distance between two objects. For example, if the distance between two charges is doubled, the electric force between them decreases to one-fourth its original value. If the distance between two small charges is quadrupled, the electric force between them decreases to one-sixteenth its original value.

Reading Check On what factors does electric force depend?

Electric force acts through a field.

As described earlier, electric force does not require that objects touch. How do charges interact over a distance? One way to model this property of charges is with the concept of an electric field. An **electric field** always exists in the space around a charged particle. Any other charged particle in that field will experience an electric force. This force is due to the electric field associated with the first charged particle.

One way to show an electric field is by drawing *electric field lines*. Electric field lines point in the direction of the electric force on a positive charge. Electric field lines near isolated charges are shown in **Figure 7**. Because two positive charges repel each other, the electric field lines around a positive charge point outward. In contrast, the electric field lines around a negative charge point inward.

electric force (ee LEK trik FAWRS) the force of attraction or repulsion on a charged particle that is due to an electric field

electric field (ee LEK trik FEELD) the space around a charged object in which another charged object experiences an electric force

READING TOOLBOX

Word Families
Go back to the definitions that you created earlier for terms containing the word *electric*. How do they compare to the formal definitions found on this page?

Figure 7 Electric Field Lines near an Isolated Charge

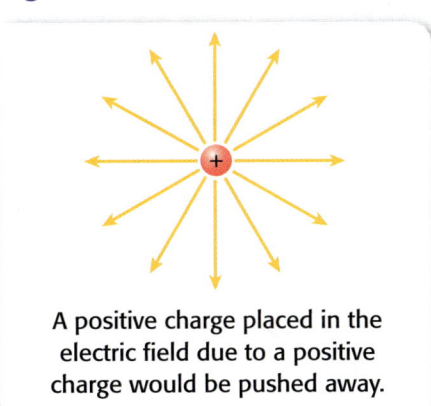

A positive charge placed in the electric field due to a positive charge would be pushed away.

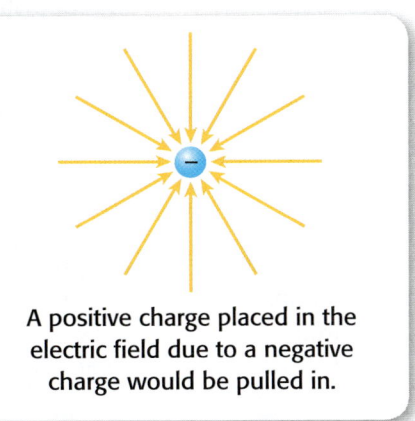

A positive charge placed in the electric field due to a negative charge would be pulled in.

Figure 8 Electric Field Lines near Two Charges

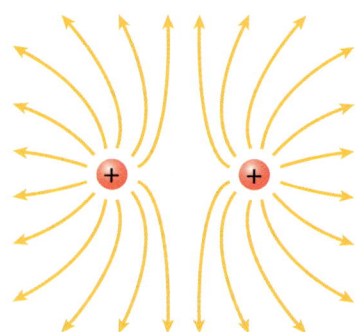

The electric field lines for two positive charges located near each other show the repulsion between the charges.

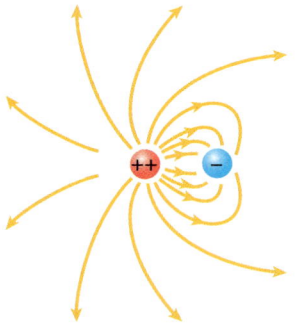

Half of the field lines starting on the positive charge end on the negative charge because the positive charge is twice as large as the negative charge.

Electric field lines never cross one another.
You can see from **Figure 8** that the electric field near two charges can also be drawn. The field lines near two positive charges point away from each other, and show that the positive charges repel each other. At a great distance from the charges, the electric field looks like that of a single charge with a charge of +2.

Field lines can show both the direction of an electric field and the relative strength of each charge. The electric field lines near two charges—one positive charge and one negative charge—will show a different pattern. When the positive charge is two times as large as the negative charge, only half of the electric field lines that leave the positive charge end at the negative charge.

Section 1 Review

KEY IDEAS

1. **Describe** the interaction between two like charges. Is the interaction the same between two unlike charges?
2. **Categorize** the following objects as conductors or insulators:
   a. copper wire
   b. your body when your skin is wet
   c. a plastic comb
3. **Explain** how the electric force between two positive charges changes under the following conditions:
   a. the distance between the charges is tripled
   b. the amount of one charge is doubled

CRITICAL THINKING

4. **Classifying** Identify the electric charge of each of the following atomic particles: a proton, a neutron, and an electron.
5. **Using Graphics** Diagram what will happen if a positively charged rod is brought near the following:
   a. a metal washer
   b. a plastic disk
6. **Interpreting Graphics** What missing electric charge would produce the electric field shown in this diagram?

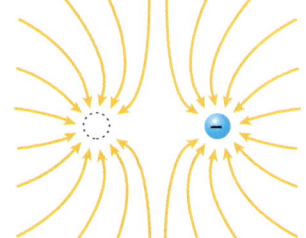

592 Chapter 17 Electricity

SECTION 2
Current

Key Ideas
- How are electrical potential energy and gravitational potential energy similar?
- What causes electrical resistance?

Key Terms
electrical potential energy
potential difference
cell
electric current
resistance

Why It Matters
Once started, current will flow forever in a loop of superconducting material. Modern MRI machines, which help identify health problems, contain superconducting magnets.

When you wake up in the morning, you reach up and turn on the light switch. The light bulb is powered by moving charges. How do charges move through a light bulb? What causes the charges to move?

Voltage and Current

Gravitational potential energy of a ball depends on the relative position of the ball, as **Figure 1** shows. A ball rolling downhill moves from a position of higher gravitational potential energy to one of lower gravitational potential energy. An electric charge also has potential energy—**electrical potential energy**—that depends on its position in an electric field.

❯ **Just as a ball will roll downhill, a negative charge will move away from another negative charge.** The movement is the result of the first negative charge's electric field. The electrical potential energy of the moving charge decreases because the electric field does work on the charge.

You can do work on a ball to move it uphill. As a result, the ball's gravitational potential energy increases. In the same way, a force can push a charge in the opposite direction of the electric force. As a result, the electrical potential energy associated with the charge's relative position increases.

Figure 1 The gravitational potential energy of a ball decreases as the ball rolls downhill. Similarly, the electrical potential energy between two like charges decreases as the distance between the charges increases.

Tennessee Course Level Expectations (Physical Science)

CLE.3202.2.4; CLE.3202.Inq.1;
CLE.3202.Inq.2; CLE.3202.Inq.3;
CLE.3202.Math.1; CLE.3202.Math.2

electrical potential energy (ee LEK tri kuhl poh TEN shuhl EN uhr jee) the ability to move an electric charge from one point to another

Figure 2 Electrical Potential Energy and Relative Position

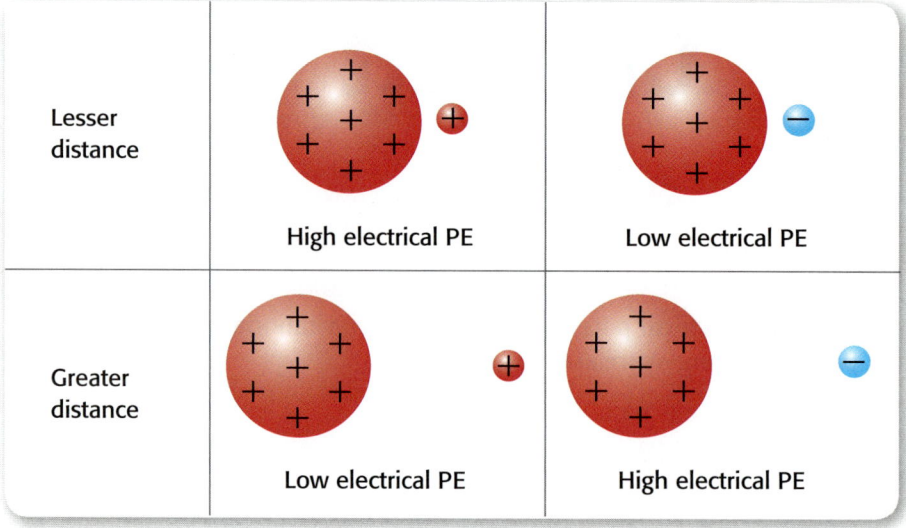

Potential difference is measured in volts.

The electrical potential energy (PE) changes with distance between two charges, as **Figure 2** shows. For a repulsive force—that between two like charges—electrical potential energy increases as the charges move closer to each other. The opposite holds for the attractive force between unlike charges.

Usually, it is more practical to consider potential difference than electrical potential energy. **Potential difference** is the change in the electrical potential energy of a charged particle divided by its charge. This change occurs as a charge moves from one place to another in an electric field.

The SI unit for potential difference is the *volt* (V), which is equivalent to one joule per coulomb (1 J/C). For this reason, potential difference is often called *voltage*.

✓ **Reading Check** What is another common name for potential difference?

There is a voltage across the terminals of a battery.

The potential difference, or voltage, across the two ends, or *terminals*, of a battery ranges from about 1.5 V for a small battery to about 12 V for a car battery, such as the one shown in **Figure 3**. Most batteries are *electrochemical* **cells**—or groups of connected cells—that convert chemical energy into electrical energy. A common cell has a potential difference of 1.5 V between the positive and negative terminals.

Electrochemical cells contain an *electrolyte*, a solution that conducts electricity, and two *electrodes*, each a different conducting material. These cells can be dry cells or wet cells. Dry cells, such as those used in flashlights, contain a pastelike electrolyte. Wet cells, such as those used in almost all car batteries, contain a liquid electrolyte.

Academic Vocabulary

convert (kuhn VUHRT) to change from one form to another

Figure 3 A typical car battery has a voltage of 12 V between the positive and negative terminals. **What is the voltage across a flashlight battery?**

A voltage sets charges in motion.

When a flashlight is switched on, the terminals of the battery are connected through the light bulb. This connection creates a voltage across the filament of the light bulb. This voltage makes the charges move from the side with a higher electrical potential energy to the side with a lower electrical potential energy. In other words, charges begin to move. This movement is similar to an object falling from a region of higher to lower gravitational potential energy.

Current is the rate of charge movement.

The **electric current** is the rate at which the charges move through the wire. The SI unit of current is the *ampere* (A). One ampere equals 1 C of charge moving past a point in 1 s.

A battery is a *direct current* source because the charges always move from one terminal to the other in the same direction. Current can be made up of positive, negative, or a combination of both positive and negative charges. In metals, moving electrons make up the current. In gases and many chemical solutions, current is the result of both positive and negative charges in motion.

A negative charge moving in one direction has the same effect as a positive charge moving in the opposite direction. *Conventional current* is the current made of positive charge that would have the same effect as the actual motion of charge in the material. So, the direction of current is *opposite* to the direction that electrons move.

> **potential difference** (poh TEN shuhl DIF uhr uhns) the voltage difference in potential between two points in a circuit
>
> **cell** (SEL) a device that produces an electric current by converting chemical or radiant energy into electrical energy
>
> **electric current** (ee LEK trik KUHR uhnt) the rate at which charges pass through a given point

Analogies
As you read about electric current, look for analogies. Create a table or appropriate FoldNote. Record the analogy phrase and the two items that are compared.

QuickLab — Using a Lemon as a Cell

 20 min

Procedure

1. Using a **knife,** make two parallel cuts 6 cm apart along the middle of a **juicy lemon.** Insert a **copper strip** into one of the cuts and a **zinc strip** of the same size into the other.

2. Cut two equal lengths of **insulated copper wire.** Use **wire strippers** to remove the insulation from both ends of each wire. Connect one end of each wire to one of the terminals of a **galvanometer.**

3. Touch the free end of one wire to the copper strip in the lemon. Touch the free end of the other wire to the zinc strip. Record the galvanometer reading for the zinc-copper cell.

4. Replace the strips of copper and zinc with equally sized **strips of different metals.** Record the galvanometer readings for each pair of electrodes.

Analysis

1. Which pair of electrodes resulted in the largest current?
2. Construct a table of your results.

Electrical Resistance

Electrical appliances that you plug into a standard outlet are designed for the same voltage: 120 V. But different appliances have different power ratings. For example, light bulbs may be dim 40 W bulbs or bright 100 W bulbs. These bulbs use different amounts of power because they have different currents in them. The difference in current between these bulbs is due to their resistance. ▶ **Resistance is caused by internal friction, which slows the movement of charges through a conducting material.** Because measuring the internal friction directly is difficult, resistance is defined by a relationship between the voltage across a conductor and the current through it.

The resistance of the *filament* of a light bulb, such as the one shown in **Figure 4,** determines how bright the bulb will be. The filament of a 40 W light bulb has a higher resistance than the filament of a 100 W light bulb.

Resistance can be calculated if current and voltage are known.

You have probably noticed that electrical devices such as televisions or stereos become warm after they have been on for a while. As moving electrons collide with the atoms of the material, some of the *kinetic energy* of the electrons is transferred to the atoms. This energy transfer causes the atoms to vibrate, and the material warms up. In most materials, some of the kinetic energy of electrons is lost as heat.

A conductor's resistance indicates how much the motion of charges within it is resisted because of collisions. Resistance is found by dividing the voltage across the conductor by the current.

resistance (ri ZIS tuhns) the opposition presented to the current by a material or device

Figure 4 When current flows in the tungsten filament of a light bulb, the bulb converts electrical energy to heat and light.

> **Resistance equation**
>
> $$\text{resistance} = \frac{\text{voltage}}{\text{current}} \qquad R = \frac{V}{I}$$

This equation is also commonly called *Ohm's law.* The SI unit of resistance is the ohm (Ω), which is equal to one volt per ampere. If a voltage of 1 V across a conductor produces a current of 1 A, then the resistance of the conductor is 1 Ω.

A *resistor* is a special type of conductor used to control current. Every resistor is designed to have a specific resistance. For example, for any applied voltage, the current in a 10 Ω resistor is half the current in a 5 Ω resistor.

Reading Check What is another name for the resistance equation?

Math Skills: Resistance

The headlights of a typical car are powered by a 12 V battery. What is the resistance of the headlights if they draw 3.0 A of current when they are turned on?

Identify
List the given and unknown values.

Given:
current, $I = 3.0$ A
voltage, $V = 12$ V
Unknown:
resistance, $R = ?$ Ω

Plan
Write the equation for resistance.

$$\text{resistance} = \frac{\text{voltage}}{\text{current}}$$
$$R = \frac{V}{I}$$

Solve
Insert the known values into the equation, and solve.

$$R = \frac{V}{I} = \frac{12 \text{ V}}{3.0 \text{ A}}$$
$$R = 4.0 \text{ Ω}$$

Practice

1. Find the resistance of a portable lantern that uses a 24 V power supply and draws a current of 0.80 A.
2. The current in a resistor is 0.50 A when connected across a voltage of 120 V. What is the resistance of the resistor?
3. The current in a video game is 0.50 A. If the resistance of the game's circuitry is 12 Ω, what is the voltage of the battery?
4. A 1.5 V battery is connected to a small light bulb that has a resistance of 3.5 Ω. What is the current in the bulb?

For more practice, visit **go.hrw.com** and enter keyword **HK8MP**.

Practice Hint

› When a problem requires you to calculate the resistance of an object, you can use the resistance equation $R = V/I$.

› Problem 3: The resistance equation can be rearranged to isolate voltage on the left in the following way:
$$R = \frac{V}{I}$$
Multiply both sides by I.
$$IR = \frac{V\cancel{I}}{\cancel{I}}$$
$$V = IR$$

› Problem 4: You will need to rearrange the equation to isolate current on the left.

Conductors have low resistance.

Whether or not charges will move in a material depends partly on how tightly electrons are held in the atoms of the material. A good conductor is any material in which electrons can flow easily under the influence of an electric field. Metals, such as the copper found in wires, are some of the best conductors because electrons can move freely throughout them. Certain metals, conducting alloys, or carbon can be used in resistors. When you flip the switch on a flashlight, the light seems to come on immediately. But the electrons do not travel that rapidly. The electric field, however, is directed through the conductor at almost the speed of light when a voltage source is connected to the conductor.

Inquiry Lab: How Can Materials Be Classified by Resistance?

⏱ 30 min

Procedure

1. Construct a conductivity tester. First, screw **two metal hooks** into a **block of wood**.
2. Create a circuit using **three wire leads** with **alligator clips**, a **6 V battery**, and a **flashlight bulb** in a **base holder**, as the diagram shows.
3. Collect some or all of the following materials to test: a **glass stirring rod**, an **iron nail**, a **wooden dowel**, a **copper wire**, a **piece of chalk**, a **strip of cardboard**, a **plastic spoon**, an **aluminum nail**, a **brass key**, and a **strip of cork**.
4. Test the conductivity of the materials by laying each object, one at a time, across the hooks of the conductivity tester.

Analysis

1. What happens to the conductivity tester if the material is a good conductor?
2. Which materials were good conductors? Which materials were poor conductors?
3. Explain your results in terms of resistance.

Insulators have high resistance.

Insulators have a high resistance to charge movement. For this reason, insulating materials are used to prevent electric current from flowing in directions other than the desired direction. The plastic coating around the copper wire of an electrical cord is an example of an insulator. This coating keeps the current from escaping into the floor or into your body.

Most electrical sockets are wired with three connections: two current-carrying wires and a *ground* wire. The ground wire is literally connected to the ground. The ground wire conducts any excess charge to Earth, where it spreads safely over the planet.

Semiconductors conduct under certain conditions.

Semiconductors belong to a third class of materials that have electrical properties between those of insulators and conductors. In their pure state, semiconductors are insulators. The controlled addition of specific atoms of other materials as impurities greatly increases a semiconductor's ability to conduct electric charge.

Silicon and germanium are two common semiconductors. Electronic devices, such as the computer board shown in **Figure 5,** are usually made of conductors, insulators, and semiconductors.

www.scilinks.org
Topic: Semiconductors and Insulators
Code: HK81377

Figure 5 Most electronic devices contain conductors, insulators, and semiconductors.

Some materials can become superconductors.

Some metals and compounds have zero resistance when their temperature falls below a *critical temperature*. These types of materials are called *superconductors*. Metals such as niobium, tin, and mercury and some metal compounds containing barium, copper, and oxygen become superconductors below their respective critical temperatures. The critical temperature depends on the material and ranges from less than –272 °C (–458 °F) to as high as –123 °C (–189 °F). The search continues for a material that is superconducting at room temperature.

Once a current is established in a superconductor, the current continues even if the applied voltage is removed. In fact, steady currents in superconducting loops have been observed to continue for many years without any signs of stopping. This feature makes such materials useful for a wide variety of applications.

One useful application of these materials is in superconducting magnets. These magnets are strong enough to levitate commuter trains, such as the one shown in **Figure 6**, above the tracks. As a result, the friction that would exist between the tracks and a normal train is eliminated. These magnets are also being studied for storing energy.

Figure 6 This train uses superconducting magnets to float above the tracks.

Section 2 Review

KEY IDEAS

1. **Describe** the motion of charges from one terminal of a battery to the other through a flashlight.
2. **Identify** which of the following could produce a current:
   a. a wire connected across a battery's terminals
   b. two electrodes in a solution of positive and negative ions
   c. a salt crystal whose ions cannot move
   d. a sugar-water mixture

CRITICAL THINKING

3. **Making Predictions** Predict which way a positive charge will move between two positions of different electrical potential energy, one high and one low.
   a. from low to high
   b. from high to low
   c. back and forth between high and low
4. **Identifying Variables** What quantities are needed to calculate an object's resistance?
5. **Classifying** Classify the following materials as conductors or insulators: wood, paper clip, glass, air, paper, plastic, steel nail, and rubber.
6. **Inferring Conclusions** Recent discoveries have led some scientists to hope that a material will be found that is superconducting at room temperature. Why would such a material be useful?

Math Skills

7. If the current in a certain resistor is 6.2 A and the voltage across the resistor is 110 V, what is the resistance of the resistor?
8. If the voltage across a flashlight bulb is 3 V and the bulb's resistance is 6 Ω, what is the current through the bulb?

SECTION 3
Circuits

Key Ideas
> What is a closed circuit?
> What are the two ways that devices can be connected in a circuit?
> What happens to the energy that charges have in a circuit?
> Why is an overloaded circuit dangerous?

Key Terms
electric circuit
schematic diagram
series circuit
parallel circuit
electric power
fuse
circuit breaker

Why It Matters
The electric circuits used to make computers have changed and have become much smaller over the years. The first computers took up large rooms, but computers today can be held in the palm of your hand.

Tennessee Course Level Expectations (Physical Science)
CLE.3202.2.4; CLE.3202.Inq.1; CLE.3202.Inq.2; CLE.3202.Inq.3; CLE.3202.Inq.6; CLE.3202.Math.1; CLE.3202.Math.2; CLE.3202.TE.2; CLE.3202.TE.3; CLE.3202.TE.4

Think about how you get a flashlight bulb to light. Would the bulb light if it were not fully screwed into its socket? Would it light if it were connected to only one side of a battery? What elements are necessary to make the bulb light?

What Are Circuits?

When plug and wires connect an electrical outlet to a string of light bulbs, as **Figure 1** shows, electric charges have a complete path to follow. Together, the bulb, electrical outlet, and wires form an **electric circuit.** In this circuit, the outlet is the source of voltage. Because of the voltage of the outlet, charges move through the wires and bulbs from one side of the outlet to the other.

In other words, there is a closed-loop path for electrons to follow. Because charges are moving, there is a current in the circuit. > **The conducting path produced when a load, such as a string of light bulbs, is connected across a source of voltage is called a *closed circuit*.** Without a complete path and a source of voltage, there is no charge flow and therefore no current. When there is no complete path, the circuit is called an *open circuit*.

If a bulb is connected to a battery, the inside of the battery is part of the closed path of current through the circuit. The voltage source, whether a battery or an outlet, is always part of the conducting path of a closed circuit.

Figure 1 When a string of light bulbs is plugged into an electrical outlet, the voltage across the plug prongs generates a current that lights the bulbs.

Switches interrupt the flow of charges in a circuit.

A device called a *switch* can be added to a circuit, as **Figure 2** shows. You use a switch to open and close a circuit, as you have probably done many times. The switches on your walls at home are used to turn lights on and off. When you flip a light switch, you either close or open the circuit to turn a light on or off.

The switch shown in **Figure 2** is a *knife switch*. The metal bar is a *conductor*. When the bar is touching both sides of the switch, the circuit is closed. Electrons can move through the bar to reach the other side of the switch and light the bulb. If the metal bar on the switch is lifted, the circuit is open. Then, there is no current, and the bulb does not glow.

Figure 2 When added to the circuit, a switch can be used to open and close the circuit. **Is this switch open or closed?**

✅ **Reading Check** What is the purpose of a switch in a circuit?

Schematic diagrams are used to represent circuits.

Suppose that you want to describe to someone the contents and connections in the light bulb and battery shown in **Figure 3**. How might you draw each element? Could you use the same representations of the elements to draw a more complex circuit?

A diagram that depicts the construction of an electric circuit or apparatus is called a **schematic diagram. Figure 3** shows how the battery, wires, and light bulb can be drawn as a schematic diagram. The symbols that are used in this figure can be used to describe any other circuit that has a battery and one or more bulbs. All electrical devices, from toasters to computers, can be described by schematic diagrams.

> **electric circuit** (ee LEK trik SUHR kit) a set of electrical components connected such that they provide one or more complete paths for the movement of charges
>
> **schematic diagram** (skee MAT ik DIE uh GRAM) a graphical representation of a circuit that uses lines to represent wires and different symbols to represent components

Figure 3 The connections between the light bulb and battery can be represented by symbols. This type of illustration is called a *schematic diagram*.

Section 3 Circuits **601**

www.scilinks.org
Topic: Electric Circuits
Code: HK80471

Schematic diagrams use standard symbols.

As **Figure 4** shows, each element used in a piece of electrical equipment is represented by a symbol that reflects the element's construction or function. For example, the symbol in the schematic diagram that represents an open switch resembles the knife switch shown in the corresponding photograph. Any circuit can be drawn by using a combination of these and other, more complex schematic-diagram symbols.

Reading Check What are used to draw schematic diagrams?

Figure 4 Schematic-Diagram Symbols

Component	Symbol used in this book	Explanation
Wire or conductor		Wires that connect elements are conductors.
Resistor		Resistors are shown as wires with multiple bends. These bends indicate resistance to a straight path.
Light bulb		The winding of the filament indirectly indicates that the light bulb is a resistor, something that impedes the movement of electrons or the flow of charge.
Battery or other direct current source		The difference in line height indicates a voltage between positive and negative terminals of the battery. The taller line represents the positive terminal of the battery.
Switch (Open / Closed)	Open / Closed	The small circles indicate the two places where the switch makes contact with the wires. Most switches work by breaking only one of the contacts, not both.

602 Chapter 17 Electricity

Series and Parallel Circuits

Most circuits in everyday use contain more than one element. Usually, two or more devices—such as appliances or light bulbs—are connected in a circuit. ❯ **Electrical devices can be connected as a series circuit so that the voltage is divided among the devices. They can also be connected as a parallel circuit so that the voltage is the same across each device.** A more complex circuit will contain combinations of both series and parallel components.

series circuit (SIR eez SUHR kit) a circuit in which the parts are joined one after another such that the current in each part is the same

parallel circuit (PAR uh LEL SUHR kit) a circuit in which the parts are joined in branches such that the potential difference across each part is the same

Series circuits have a single path for current.

When appliances or other devices are connected in a series circuit, as **Figure 5** shows, they form a single pathway for charges to flow. Charges cannot build up or disappear at a point in a circuit. For this reason, the amount of charge that enters one device in a given time interval equals the amount of charge that exits that device in the same amount of time. Because there is only one path for a charge to follow when devices are connected in series, the current in each device is the same. Even though the current in each device is the same, the resistances may be different. Therefore, the voltage across each device in a series circuit can be different.

If one element along the path in a series circuit is removed, the circuit will not work. For example, if either of the light bulbs in **Figure 5** were removed, the other one would not glow. The series circuit would be open. Several kinds of breaks may interrupt a series circuit. An open switch, a burned-out light bulb, a cut wire, or any other interruption can cause the whole circuit to fail.

Figure 5 When light bulbs are connected in series, charges must pass through both light bulbs to complete the circuit.

Parallel circuits have multiple paths for current.

When devices are connected in parallel rather than in series, the voltage across each device is the same. The current in each device does not have to be the same. Instead, the sum of the currents in all of the devices equals the total current. **Figure 6** shows a simple parallel circuit. The two lights are connected to the same points. The electrons leaving one end of the battery can pass through either bulb before returning to the other terminal. If one bulb has less resistance, more charge moves through that bulb because the bulb offers less opposition to the movement of charges.

Even if one of the bulbs in the circuit shown in **Figure 6** were removed, charges would still move through the other loop. Thus, a break in any one path in a parallel circuit does not interrupt the flow of electric charge in the other paths.

Figure 6 When light bulbs are connected in parallel, charges have more than one path to follow. The circuit can be complete even if one light bulb burns out.

Why It Matters
Miniaturization of Circuits

SCIENCE & SOCIETY

The first electronic computer, the Electronic Numerical Integrator and Computer (ENIAC), was developed during World War II. ENIAC was as big as a house and weighed 30 tons. This machine consumed 200 kW of electric power and had about 18,000 vacuum tubes, which frequently burned out and made ENIAC very unreliable. As computers became smaller, faster, and cheaper, their use in offices and homes quickly increased. Today, computers are so common that we hardly notice them.

The integrated circuit, developed in 1958, greatly reduced the size and power use of computers. By the late 1960s, computers were becoming common in businesses and universities.

Today, handheld graphing calculators are commonly used by students in high school science and math classes. Can you imagine taking the ENIAC to class?

The first personal computer (PC) system was introduced to the market in early 1981. A modern PC easily fits on a desk and computes hundreds of thousands of times as fast as the ENIAC.

SCLINKS
www.scilinks.org
Topic: Computer Technology
Code: HK80334

YOUR TURN

UNDERSTANDING CONCEPTS
1. How are modern computers different from ENIAC?

ONLINE RESEARCH
2. Research the history of the integrated circuit.

Electrical Energy and Electric Power

Many of the devices that you use on a daily basis, such as a flashlight or a toaster, require *electrical energy* to run. The energy for these devices may come from a battery or from a power plant miles away.

When a charge moves in a circuit, the charge loses energy. ❯ **Some of this energy is transformed into useful *work*, such as the turning of a motor, and some is lost as heat.** The rate at which electrical energy is changed to other forms of energy is called **electric power**. Electric power is calculated by multiplying the total current, I, by the voltage, V, in a circuit.

> **Electric power equation**
> $$\text{power} = \text{current} \times \text{voltage}$$
> $$P = IV$$

electric power (ee LEK trik POW uhr) the rate at which electrical energy is converted into other forms of energy

Academic Vocabulary
transform (trans FAWRM) to change form

If you combine the electric power equation with the resistance equation, $V = IR$, you can calculate the power lost, or *dissipated*, by a resistor.

$$P = I(IR) = I^2 R = \frac{V^2}{R}$$

Earlier in this text, you learned that *power* is the rate at which work is done. The same is true for electric power; electric power is the rate at which electrical work is done.

The SI unit for power is the watt.

Most light bulbs are labeled in terms of watts (W). The amount of heat and light given off by a bulb is related to the power rating. For example, a typical desk lamp uses a 60 W bulb. A typical hair dryer is rated at about 1,800 W.

In terms of energy, 1 W is equal to 1 J/s. A watt is also equal to 1 A × 1 V. Another common unit of power is the kilowatt (kW). One kilowatt is equal to 1,000 W.

READING TOOLBOX

Tri-Fold
Create a tri-fold FoldNote. Label the columns "Current," "Voltage," and "Resistance." Describe in words and equations how power depends on each quantity.

Electric companies measure energy in kilowatt-hours.

Power companies charge for energy, not power, used in the home. The unit of energy that power companies use to track consumption of energy is the kilowatt-hour (kW•h). One kilowatt-hour is the energy delivered in 1 h at the rate of 1 kW. In SI units, 1 kW•h = 3.6 × 10⁶ J.

Depending on where you live, the cost of energy ranges from 5 to 20 cents per kilowatt-hour. Power companies use electric meters, such as the one shown in **Figure 7**, to determine how much electrical energy is consumed over a certain time interval.

Figure 7 An electric meter records the amount of energy consumed.

Math Skills: Electric Power

When a hair dryer is plugged into a 120 V outlet, the hair dryer has a 9.1 A current in it. What is the hair dryer's power rating?

Identify
List the given and unknown values.

Given:
voltage, $V = 120$ V
current, $I = 9.1$ A
Unknown:
electric power, $P = ?$ W

Plan
Write the equation for electric power.

power = current × voltage
$P = IV$

Solve
Insert the known values into the equation, and solve.

$P = (9.1 \text{ A})(120 \text{ V})$
$P = 1.1 \times 10^3$ W

Practice Hint

> Problem 3: The electric power equation can also be rearranged to isolate current on the left in the following way:
>
> $P = IV$
>
> Divide both sides by V.
>
> $\dfrac{P}{V} = \dfrac{I\cancel{V}}{\cancel{V}}$
>
> $I = \dfrac{P}{V}$

> Problem 4: You will need to rearrange the equation to isolate voltage on the left.

Practice

1. An electric space heater draws 29 A of current when plugged into a 120 V outlet. What is the power rating of the heater?
2. A graphing calculator uses a 6.0 V battery and draws 2.6×10^{-3} A of current. What is the power rating of the calculator?
3. A color television has a power rating of 320 W. How much current is in the television when it is connected across 120 V?
4. The current in the heating element of an iron is 5.0 A. If the iron dissipates 590 W of power, what is the voltage across the iron?

For more practice, visit **go.hrw.com** and enter keyword **HK8MP**.

Figure 8 These fuses are typical for modern electronic devices. The one on the left has been overloaded and is "blown."

Fuses and Circuit Breakers

If many devices are connected across an electrical outlet, the overall resistance of the circuit is lowered. As a result, the electrical wires carry more than a safe level of current, and the circuit is said to be *overloaded*. ❯ **The high currents in overloaded circuits can cause fires.**

Worn insulation on wires can also be a fire hazard. If a wire's insulation wears down, two wires may touch and create an alternative pathway for current, or a *short circuit*. The lower resistance greatly increases the current in the circuit. Short circuits can be very dangerous. Fuses, such as the ones shown in **Figure 8,** and circuit breakers can reduce the danger and the threat to sensitive electronic devices.

Fuses melt to prevent circuit overloads.

To prevent overloading in circuits, fuses are connected in series along the supply path. A **fuse** is a ribbon of wire that has a low melting point. If the current in the line becomes too large, the fuse melts and the circuit is opened.

Fuses "blow out" when the current in the circuit reaches a certain level. For example, a 20 A fuse will melt if the current in the circuit exceeds 20 A. A blown fuse is a sign that a short circuit or a circuit overload may exist somewhere in your home. It is wise to find out what made a fuse blow out before replacing it.

Circuit breakers open circuits with high current.

Many homes are equipped with circuit breakers, such as those shown in **Figure 9**, instead of fuses. A **circuit breaker** uses a magnet or *bimetallic strip*, a strip with two different metals welded together, that responds to current overload by opening the circuit. The circuit breaker acts as a switch. As you would for blown fuses, you should determine why the circuit breaker opened the circuit. Unlike fuses, circuit breakers can be reset by turning the switch back on.

A *ground fault circuit interrupter* (GFCI) is a special kind of electrical outlet that acts as a small circuit breaker. These special outlets are often found in bathrooms and kitchens, where water is used near electricity.

Figure 9 Many homes have a panel of circuit breakers such as these. **Are the circuits on each switch wired in series or in parallel? Why?**

fuse (FYOOZ) an electrical device that contains a metal strip that melts when current in the circuit becomes too great

circuit breaker (SUHR kit BRAYK uhr) a switch that opens a circuit automatically when the current exceeds a certain value

Section 3 Review

KEY IDEAS

1. **Identify** the number of and types of elements in this schematic diagram.
2. **Describe** the advantage of using a parallel arrangement of decorative lights rather than a series arrangement.
3. **Demonstrate** how to calculate power if you are given the voltage and resistance in a circuit.
4. **Contrast** how a fuse and a circuit breaker work to prevent overloading in circuits.

CRITICAL THINKING

5. **Making Predictions** Predict whether a fuse will work successfully if it is connected in parallel with the device it is supposed to protect.

6. **Applying Ideas** Draw a schematic diagram with four lights in parallel.
7. **Predicting Outcomes** Draw a schematic diagram of a circuit with two light bulbs in which you could turn off either light and still have a complete circuit. (Hint: You will need to use two switches.)

Math Skills

8. When a VCR is connected across a 120 V outlet, the VCR has a 0.33 A current in it. What is the power rating of the VCR?
9. A 40 W light bulb and a 75 W light bulb are in parallel across a 120 V outlet. Which bulb has the greater current in it?

Skills Practice Lab

Constructing Electric Circuits

🕐 50 min

The current that flows through an electric circuit depends on voltage and resistance. All these factors are dependent on one another. In this lab, you will make circuits using different configurations of resistors and batteries to see how the voltage and current depend on them.

What You'll Do
> **Construct** parallel and series circuits.
> **Predict** voltage and current by using the resistance law.
> **Measure** voltage, current, and resistance.

What You'll Need
battery, dry-cell
battery holder
multimeter
resistors (2)
tape, masking
wires, connecting (5)

Safety

Procedure

Preparing for Your Experiment

1 In this laboratory exercise, you will use an instrument called a *multimeter* to measure voltage, current, and resistance. Your teacher will demonstrate how to use the multimeter to make each type of measurement.

2 As you read the steps listed below, refer to the diagrams for help making the measurements. Write down your predictions and measurements in your lab notebook. **CAUTION:** Handle the wires only where they are insulated.

Circuits with a Single Resistor

3 Using the multimeter, measure the resistance in ohms of one of the resistors. Write the resistance on a small piece of masking tape, and tape it to the resistor. Repeat for the other resistor.

4 Use the resistance equation, $R = V/I$, to predict the current in amps that will be in a circuit consisting of one of the resistors and one battery. (Hint: You must rearrange the equation to solve for current.)

5 Test your prediction by building the circuit. Do the same for the other resistor.

Circuits with Two Resistors in Series

6 Measure the total resistance across both resistors when they are connected in series.

7. Using the total resistance that you measured, predict the current that will be in a circuit consisting of one battery and both resistors in series. Test your prediction.

8. Using the current that you measured, predict the voltage across each resistor in the circuit that you just built. Test your prediction.

Circuits with Two Resistors in Parallel

9. Measure the total resistance across both resistors when they are connected in parallel.

10. Using the total resistance that you measured, predict the total current that will be in an entire circuit consisting of one battery and both resistors in parallel. Test your prediction.

11. Predict the current that will be in each resistor individually in the circuit that you just built. Test your prediction.

Analysis

1. **Describing Events** If you have a circuit consisting of one battery and one resistor, what happens to the current if you double the resistance?

2. **Describing Events** What happens to the current if you add a second, identical battery in series with the first battery?

3. **Describing Events** What happens to the current if you add a second resistor in parallel with the first resistor?

Communicating Your Results

4. **Drawing Conclusions** Suppose that you have a circuit consisting of one battery plus a 10 Ω resistor and a 5 Ω resistor in series. Which resistor will have the greater voltage across it?

5. **Drawing Conclusions** Suppose that you have a circuit consisting of one battery plus a 10 Ω resistor and a 5 Ω resistor in parallel. Which resistor will have more current in it?

Extension

Suppose that someone tells you that you can make the battery in a circuit last longer by adding more resistors in parallel. Is this statement correct? Explain your reasoning.

Chapter Lab

Learning Internet Terminology

Science > Skills

Technology
Math
Scientific Methods
Graphing

Knowing the basic terms associated with the Internet and its use can help you understand how the Internet works and how you can use it more effectively.

Term	Definition
Internet	a worldwide, decentralized network of computers that can communicate with one another
World Wide Web (www or "the Web")	part of the Internet consisting of linked documents that allow the combined presentation of text, graphics, sounds, and other media
TCP/IP (Transmission Control Protocol/Internet Protocol)	the primary communications protocol used by computers on the Internet
URL (Uniform Resource Locator)	a unique address for every file on the Web; for example, http://go.hrw.com/gopages/index.html
domain name	the part of a URL that tells the logical or sometimes geographical location of a computer on the Internet (in the example URL, go.hrw.com is the domain name)
HTML (Hypertext Markup Language)	the language behind all documents on the Web; allows areas of text or images to be hyperlinks to other files
hyperlink (or link)	a URL embedded in an HTML document; clicking on that part of the document allows you to connect to that URL; often appears as underlined text
Web page	a single HTML document
Web site	a group of linked documents under a single domain name
Web browser (or browser)	software that allows you to view HTML and other documents on the World Wide Web
plug-in	a program that allows a browser to handle files other than HTML files
search engine	a Web site used to search for files on the Web
keyword	a word used in a search by a search engine
bookmark or favorite	a URL stored in a browser so that you can return to it later
cookie	text put on your computer by a Web site; contains information that the Web site can use when you return to that site
spam	unwanted e-mail messages, usually in mass mailings
instant messaging or chat	interactive communication in which users send short messages back and forth in real time (with little delay)

Practice

1. In what language are most files on the World Wide Web written?
2. What kind of program is used for viewing files on the Web?
3. Name three kinds of elements that could appear on a Web page.
4. What is the difference between a Web page and a Web site?

CHAPTER 17 Summary

Key Ideas

Key Terms

Section 1 Electric Charge and Force

> **Electric Charge** An object can have a negative charge, a positive charge, or no charge at all. Like charges repel; unlike charges attract. (p. 585)

> **Transfer of Electric Charge** When different materials are rubbed together, electrons can be transferred from one material to the other. (p. 588)

> **Electric Force** The electric force at the atomic and molecular levels is responsible for most of the everyday forces that we observe, such as the force of a spring and the force of friction. (p. 590)

electric charge, p. 585
electrical conductor, p. 588
electrical insulator, p. 588
electric force, p. 590
electric field, p. 591

Section 2 Current

> **Voltage and Current** Just as a ball will roll downhill, a negative charge will move away from another negative charge. (p. 593)

> **Electrical Resistance** Resistance is caused by internal friction, which slows the movement of charges through a conducting material. (p. 596)

electrical potential energy, p. 593
potential difference, p. 594
cell, p. 594
electric current, p. 595
resistance, p. 596

Section 3 Circuits

> **What Are Circuits?** The conducting path produced when a load, such as a string of light bulbs, is connected across a source of voltage is called a *closed circuit*. (p. 600)

> **Series and Parallel Circuits** Electrical devices can be connected either as a series circuit, so that the voltage is divided among the devices, or as a parallel circuit, so that the voltage is the same across each device. (p. 603)

> **Electrical Energy and Electric Power** Electrical energy is transformed into useful work, such as the turning of a motor, and some is lost as heat. (p. 605)

> **Fuses and Circuit Breakers** The high currents in overloaded circuits can cause fires. (p. 606)

electric circuit, p. 600
schematic diagram, p. 601
series circuit, p. 603
parallel circuit, p. 603
electric power, p. 605
fuse, p. 607
circuit breaker, p. 607

Electricity

CHAPTER 17 Review

READING TOOLBOX

1. **Comparisons** Electrical resistance is sometimes explained by saying that it is like friction for electric current. Describe how resistance and friction are alike and how they may be different.

USING KEY TERMS

2. Explain the energy changes involved when a positive charge moves because of a nearby, negatively charged object. Use the terms *electrical potential energy, work,* and *kinetic energy* in your answer.

3. What causes *resistance* in an electric circuit? How is resistance measured?

4. How do charges move through an insulated wire connected across a battery? Use the terms *potential difference, electric current, electrical conductor,* and *electrical insulator* in your answer.

5. How would you *ground* an electrical appliance?

6. Contrast the movement of charges in a *series circuit* and in a *parallel circuit*. Use a diagram to aid in your explanation.

7. If a string of lights goes out when one of the bulbs is removed, are the lights probably connected in a *series circuit* or a *parallel circuit*? Explain your answer.

8. Explain the difference between a *fuse* and a *circuit breaker*. If you were designing a circuit for a reading lamp, would you include a fuse, a circuit breaker, or neither? Explain your answer.

UNDERSTANDING KEY IDEAS

9. If two charges attract each other,
   a. both charges must be positive.
   b. both charges must be negative.
   c. the charges must be different.
   d. the charges must be the same.

10. The electric force between two objects depends on all of the following *except*
    a. the distance between the objects.
    b. the electric charge of the first object.
    c. the way that the two objects became electrically charged.
    d. the electric charge of the second object.

11. In the figure below,
    a. the positive charge is greater than the negative charge.
    b. the negative charge is greater than the positive charge.
    c. both charges are positive.
    d. both charges are negative.

12. In order to produce a current in a cell, the terminals must
    a. have a potential difference.
    b. be exposed to light.
    c. be in a liquid.
    d. be at two different temperatures.

13. An electric current does *not* exist in
    a. a closed circuit.
    b. a series circuit.
    c. a parallel circuit.
    d. an open circuit.

14. Which of the following can help prevent a circuit from overloading?
    a. a resistor
    b. a switch
    c. a galvanometer
    d. a fuse

EXPLAINING KEY IDEAS

INTERPRETING GRAPHICS The schematic diagrams below represent four different circuits. Use the diagrams to answer question 15.

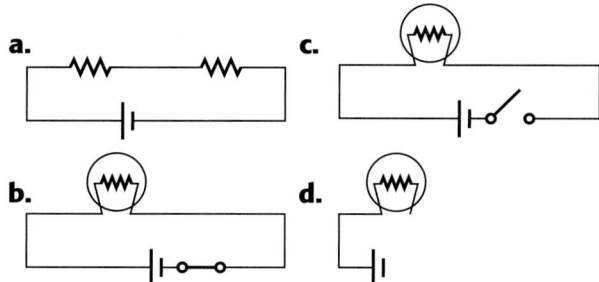

15. Which of the diagrams represent circuits that cannot have current in them as drawn?

16. Describe the characteristics of the electric field due to a single positive charge. How does the electric field of a negative charge differ?

17. Compare and contrast conductors, superconductors, semiconductors, and insulators.

18. Explain how fuses and circuit breakers are used to prevent circuit overload.

CRITICAL THINKING

19. Making Comparisons The gravitational force is always attractive, and the electric force is both attractive and repulsive. What accounts for this difference?

20. Understanding Relationships Why is charge usually transferred by electrons? Which materials transfer electrons most easily? In what situations can positive charge move?

21. Designing Systems How many ways can you connect three light bulbs and a battery in a circuit? Draw a schematic diagram of each circuit.

22. Applying Knowledge At a given voltage, which light bulb has the greater resistance, a 200 W light bulb or a 75 W light bulb? Explain.

Graphing Skills

23. The graph below shows how electrical potential energy changes as the distance between two charges changes. Is the second charge positive or negative? Explain.

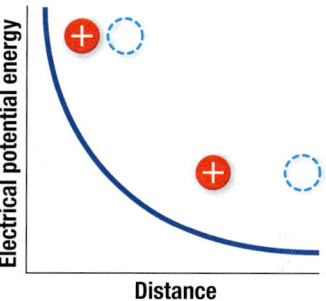

Math Skills

24. Electric Force Electric force is directly proportional to the product of the charges and inversely proportional to the square of the distance between them. If q_1 and q_2 are the charges on two objects and d is the distance between them, which of the following represents the electric force, F, between them?

a. $F \alpha \dfrac{q_1 q_2}{d}$

b. $F \alpha \dfrac{q_1 q_2}{d^2}$

c. $F \alpha \dfrac{d^2}{q_1 q_2}$

d. $F \alpha \dfrac{(q_1 q_2)^2}{d}$

25. Resistance A potential difference of 12 V produces a current of 0.30 A in a piece of copper wire. What is the resistance of the wire?

26. Resistance What is the voltage across a 75 Ω resistor with 1.6 A of current?

27. Electric Power A portable cassette player uses 3.0 V (two 1.5 V batteries in series) and has 0.33 A of current. What is its power rating?

28. Electric Power Find the current in a 2.4 W flashlight bulb powered by a 1.5 V battery.

Chapter Review **613**

Standardized Test Prep

Understanding Concepts

Directions (1–3): For each question, write on a sheet of paper the letter of the correct answer.

1. Over a period of 5 min, 7,500 C is found to have traveled past a particular point in a circuit. How much current must have been flowing through the circuit?
   - **A.** 25 A
   - **B.** 1,500 V
   - **C.** 7,500 V
   - **D.** 37,500 A

2. If 0.5 A is flowing through a household light bulb and the bulb is plugged into a 120 V outlet, what is the bulb's power output?
   - **F.** 0.5 Ω
   - **G.** 60 W
   - **H.** 120 Ω
   - **I.** 240 W

3. To cool a microprocessor, an engineer designs a circuit with a battery and four tiny fans. If the voltage across each fan must be identical, how should the circuit be designed?
   - **A.** The circuit should resemble a circle made of a single wire, with the battery and two fans in a series.
   - **B.** There should be at least one fuse or circuit breaker for each fan.
   - **C.** The fans should be connected in parallel in the circuit.
   - **D.** Each fan must offer the same amount of resistance.

Directions (4–6): For each question, write a short response.

4. Before the adoption of SI units, the power output of some engines was measured in horsepower. One horsepower is equal to approximately 746 W. If a 5.0 horsepower engine is putting out 17 A of current, what is the voltage of the circuit?

5. Why are circuit breakers preferable to fuses?

6. Why aren't resistors made from copper?

Reading Skills

Directions (7–8): Read the passage below. Then, answer the questions that follow.

TURNING LIGHT INTO ELECTRICITY
On a clear day, sunlight strikes Earth's surface with an intensity of approximately 1,000 W/m^2. If all of that energy could be collected and transformed into electricity, there would be more than enough to run all the homes and businesses on the planet. At this point, the most efficient solar cells in existence capture only about 15% of the energy of sunlight, or approximately 150 W/m^2.

Solar cells can be constructed in a variety of shapes and sizes. Individual cells, regardless of their size, always produce a voltage of about 0.5 V. However, larger cells produce more current, and therefore more power (measured in W), because power is current times voltage. When multiple solar cells are connected in series, their voltages are added, but the current remains the same. When solar cells are connected in parallel, their current is added, but the voltage remains the same. Solar panels consist of a grid of cells, some connected in series and some in parallel, so that both voltage and current can be raised to useful levels.

7. A particular solar panel has a potential difference of 48 V. What is the minimum number of solar cells the panel could have?
   - **A.** 12
   - **B.** 24
   - **C.** 48
   - **D.** 96

8. A solar panel measuring 15 m by 10 m is operating at the maximum efficiency currently possible. If the panel has a potential difference of 225 V, how much current is the panel producing?
   - **F.** 100 W
   - **G.** 100 A
   - **H.** 150 W
   - **I.** 150 A

Interpreting Graphics

The schematic diagram below depicts an electrical circuit. Use this schematic to answer questions 9–11.

LIGHT BULB CIRCUIT

9. Which bulb burning out would mean that no current could flow through the circuit?
   A. bulb A
   B. bulb B
   C. bulb C
   D. bulb D

10. Which bulbs are connected in parallel with each other?
    F. Bulb A is connected in parallel with bulb C.
    G. Bulb B is connected in parallel with bulb D.
    H. Bulb A is connected in parallel with bulbs B and D.
    I. Bulb C is connected in parallel with bulbs B and D.

11. What must change in the circuit for the bulbs to light?

The following graphic displays the resistance graphs of two thermistors. Use this graphic to answer questions 12–13.

RESISTANCE VS. TEMPERATURE

12. At approximately what temperature do the two thermistors experience the same resistance?
    A. 0 °C
    B. 50 °C
    C. 100 °C
    D. The two thermistors never experience the same resistance.

13. Which of the two thermistors is more likely to be made of platinum wire? Which is more likely to be made of manganese oxide?

> **Test Tip**
>
> If using a graph to answer a question, read the graph's title and the labels on the axes. For graphs that show a change in some variable over time, keep in mind that the steepness and direction of a curve indicate the relative rate of change at a given point in time.

CHAPTER 18: Magnetism

Chapter Outline

1 Magnets and Magnetic Fields
Magnets
Magnetic Fields
Earth's Magnetic Field

2 Magnetism from Electric Currents
Electromagnetism
Electromagnetic Devices

3 Electric Currents from Magnetism
Electromagnetic Induction
The Electromagnetic Force
Transformers

Tennessee Course Level Expectations (Physical Science)

CLE.3202.TE.3 Explain the relationship between the properties of a material and the use of the material in the application of a technology; **CLE.3202.2.1** Investigate the properties and behaviors of mechanical and electromagnetic waves; **CLE.3202.Inq.1** Recognize that science is a progressive endeavor that reevaluates and extends what is already accepted; **CLE.3202.Inq.2** Design and conduct scientific investigations to explore new phenomena, verify previous results, test how well a theory predicts, and compare opposing theories; **CLE.3202.Inq.3** Use appropriate tools and technology to collect precise and accurate data; **CLE.3202.Inq.4** Apply qualitative and quantitative measures to analyze data and draw conclusions that are free of bias; **CLE.3202.Inq.6** Communicate and defend scientific findings; **CLE.3202.Math.1** Understand the mathematical principles behind the science of physics; **CLE.3202.Math.2** Utilize appropriate mathematical equations and processes to solve basic physics problems; **CLE.3202.TE.2** Differentiate among elements of the engineering design cycle: design constraints, model building, testing, evaluating, modifying, and retesting; **CLE.3202.TE.4** Describe the dynamic interplay among science, technology, and engineering within living, earth-space, and physical systems.

Why It Matters

In the far north and far south of our planet, the night sky sometimes glows with beautiful lights called *auroras*. These lights occur because Earth's magnetic field directs tiny particles from the sun toward the poles, where the particles collide with atoms in Earth's atmosphere.

Inquiry Lab 20 min

Magnetic Levitation

You can use **two ring-shaped magnets** and a **pencil** to see levitation in action. First, use a **scale** to find the mass of each magnet. Record the masses. Drop one of the magnets over the end of the pencil so that the magnet rests on your hand. Now, drop the other magnet over the end of the pencil. If the magnets are oriented correctly, the second magnet will levitate above the first. If the magnets attract, remove the second magnet, flip it over, and drop it over the end of the pencil.

Questions to Get You Started

1. How much magnetic force is necessary to levitate the magnet?
2. How does the force between the magnets change when you flip one of the magnets over?

READING TOOLBOX These reading tools can help you learn the material in this chapter. For more information on how to use these and other tools, see **Appendix A.**

Word Parts

Suffixes The word *meter* often refers to an instrument used for measuring, such as a *parking meter*. The word *meter* is also used as a suffix. An instrument's name is often a root plus *–meter*. The root identifies what the instrument measures. For example, an *altimeter* measures altitude. If the root ends in a consonant, an *o* can be added. So, the suffix becomes *–ometer,* as in *speedometer.*

Your Turn As you read this chapter, note words that use the suffix *–meter*. Use words from this chapter to continue a table like the one shown here. Many of the root words are derived from the names of scientists. Note the connection that each scientist has to what is being measured.

WORD	ROOT	WHAT IT MEASURES
altimeter	alti	altitude
speedometer	speed	speed

Cause and Effect

Signal Words Certain words or phrases can signal cause-and-effect relationships. Words and phrases that signal causes include
- *produce*
- *as a result of*
- *because*

Words and phrases that signal effects include
- *therefore*
- *results from*
- *consequently*

Sentences can also express cause-and-effect relationships without using explicit markers.

Your Turn In Sections 2 and 3 of this chapter, you will read about cause-and-effect relationships between electricity and magnetism. Complete a table like this one of cause-and-effect pairs.

CAUSE	EFFECT	MARKER(S)
bolt of lightning	the direction of a compass needle changes	(none)

FoldNotes

Double-Door Fold FoldNotes are a fun way to help you learn and remember ideas that you encounter as you read. FoldNotes help you organize concepts and see the "big picture."

Your Turn Following the instructions in **Appendix A,** make a double-door fold. Label the first door "Magnetism from Electric Currents" and the second door "Electric Currents from Magnetism." Take notes about Section 2 behind the first door, and take notes about Section 3 behind the second door.

618 Chapter 18 Magnetism

SECTION 1
Magnets and Magnetic Fields

Key Ideas
- What happens when the poles of two magnets are brought close together?
- What causes a magnet to attract or repel another magnet?
- How is Earth's magnetic field oriented?

Key Terms
magnetic pole
magnetic field

Why It Matters
Earth's magnetic field has reversed direction in its geologic history and may reverse again in the future, which will affect all compasses on Earth.

Magnets are often used to attach papers or photos to a refrigerator door. But magnets are also used in many devices, such as motors, VCRs, and medical-imaging machines. Some home alarm systems use the simple magnetic attraction between a piece of iron and a magnet to alert homeowners that a window or door has been opened.

> Tennessee Course Level Expectations (Physical Science)
> CLE.3202.Inq.1; CLE.3202.Inq.2; CLE.3202.Inq.3

Magnets

Magnets got their name from a region of Magnesia, which is now part of present-day Greece. The first lodestones, which are naturally occurring magnetic rocks, were found in this region almost 3,000 years ago. A lodestone, shown in **Figure 1,** is composed of an iron-based mineral called *magnetite*.

You know that like electric charges repel each other and that the attraction between two opposite charges gets stronger as those charges are brought closer together. A similar situation exists for **magnetic poles,** points that have opposing magnetic properties.

All magnets have at least one pair of poles, a *north pole* and a *south pole*. The poles of magnets exert a force on each other. ▶ **Two like poles repel each other. Two unlike poles attract each other.** Thus, the north pole of one magnet will repel the north pole of another magnet. But the north pole of one magnet will attract the south pole of another magnet.

It is impossible to isolate a magnet's south pole from the magnet's north pole. If a magnet is cut into two or more pieces, each piece will still have two poles. No matter how small the pieces of a magnet are, each piece still has both a north pole and a south pole.

magnetic pole (mag NET ik POHL) one of two points, such as the ends of a magnet, that have opposing magnetic qualities

Figure 1 A naturally occurring magnetic rock, called a lodestone, will attract a variety of iron objects.

Section 1 Magnets and Magnetic Fields **619**

Topic: Properties of Magnets
Code: HK81229

Some materials can be made into permanent magnets.

Some substances, such as lodestones, are magnetic all of the time. These magnets are called *permanent magnets*. You can change any piece of iron, such as a nail, into a magnet by stroking the iron several times with a magnet. Placing a piece of iron near a strong magnet will also change the iron into a magnet. After a time, the iron becomes magnetic and remains that way even if the strong magnet is removed.

Although a magnetized piece of iron is called a *permanent* magnet, its magnetism can be weakened or even removed. Heating or hammering a magnetic object can reduce its magnetic properties.

Some materials retain their magnetism better than others do. Scientists classify materials as either magnetically *hard* or magnetically *soft*. Iron is a soft magnetic material. A piece of iron is easily magnetized, but it also tends to lose its magnetic properties easily. Hard magnetic materials, such as cobalt and nickel, are difficult to magnetize. However, these materials do not lose their magnetism easily.

Reading Check What can you do to decrease the magnetism of a soft magnetic material? (See Appendix E for answers to Reading Checks.)

Magnets exert magnetic forces on each other.

As **Figure 2** shows, a magnet that is dipped into a bucket of nails will often pick up several nails. As soon as a nail touches the magnet, the nail itself acts as a magnet and attracts other nails. More than one nail is lifted because each nail in the chain becomes temporarily magnetized and exerts a *magnetic force* on the nail below.

The iron nails are a soft magnetic material. So, the temporary magnetism disappears when the chain of nails is no longer touching the magnet. Sometimes, the nails remain slightly magnetized after the chain is no longer in contact with the permanent magnet. However, the nails will eventually return to their unmagnetized state.

The length of the chain of nails is limited. The length depends on the ability of the nails to become magnetized and on the strength of the magnet. The greater the distance between a nail and the magnet, the weaker the nail's magnetic force. Eventually, the magnetic force between the two lowest nails is not strong enough to overcome the force of gravity. In other words, the bottom nail weighs too much to stay attached, so it falls.

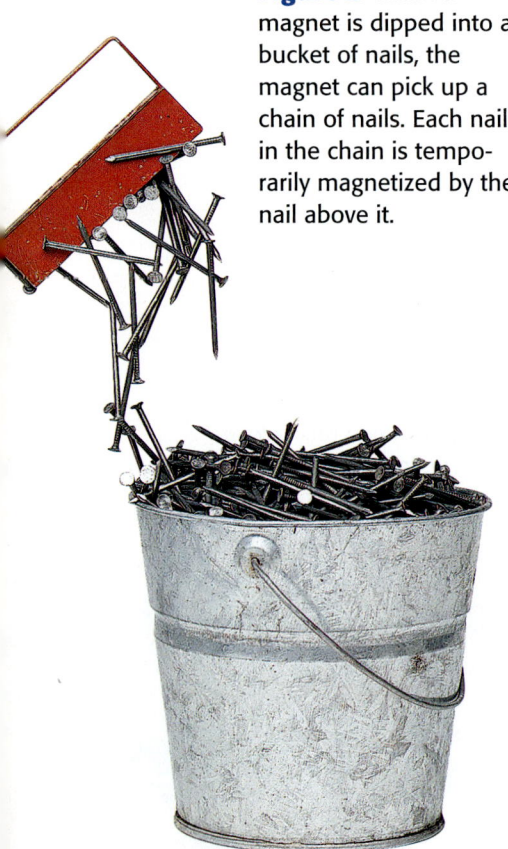

Figure 2 When a magnet is dipped into a bucket of nails, the magnet can pick up a chain of nails. Each nail in the chain is temporarily magnetized by the nail above it.

QuickLab

Magnetic Poles

⏱ 10 min

Procedure

1. Use **strips of tape** to cover the pole markings at both ends of a **bar magnet**.
2. Tie a **piece of string** to the center of the magnet, and suspend the magnet from a **support stand**.
3. Use another **bar magnet** to determine the north pole and the south pole of the hanging magnet.

Analysis

1. What happens when you bring one pole of your magnet near each end of the hanging magnet?
2. After you have decided the identity of each pole, remove the tape to check. Could you have determined the north pole and the south pole of the hanging magnet if you had covered the poles of both magnets?

Magnetic Fields

Try holding a magnet and moving its south pole toward the south pole of a magnet that can move freely. Do not let the magnets touch. The magnet that you are not holding moves away from the other one. A force is being exerted on the freely moving magnet even though the magnets never touch.

Because it acts at a distance, a magnetic force is a field force. You should already be familiar with other forces that act at a distance. For example, gravitational forces and the force between electric charges act at a distance. A **magnetic field** is a region where a magnetic force can be detected. ❯ **Magnets repel or attract each other because of the interaction of their magnetic fields.**

Magnets are sources of magnetic fields.

A magnetic field surrounds any magnetized material. Some magnetic fields are stronger than others. The strength of a magnetic field depends on the material the magnet is made of and on how much the material has been magnetized.

Moving charges create magnetic fields. An atom has magnetic properties because of the movement of the electrons within the atom. In most materials, such as copper and aluminum, the magnetic fields of the individual atoms cancel each other out. These materials are not magnetic.

In materials such as iron, nickel, and cobalt, groups of atoms tend to create larger groups of atoms called *magnetic domains*. These groups of atoms all line up the same way and form small, magnetized regions within the material. When an external magnetic field is applied near this material, the small regions align and increase the magnetic field of the material.

magnetic field (mag NET ik FEELD) a region where a magnetic force can be detected

Integrating Social Studies

Finding North With the invention of iron ships and steel ships in the late 1800s, it became necessary to develop a nonmagnetic compass. The *gyrocompass*, a device containing a spinning loop, was the solution. Because of inertia, the gyrocompass always points toward Earth's geographic North Pole, regardless of which way the ship turns.

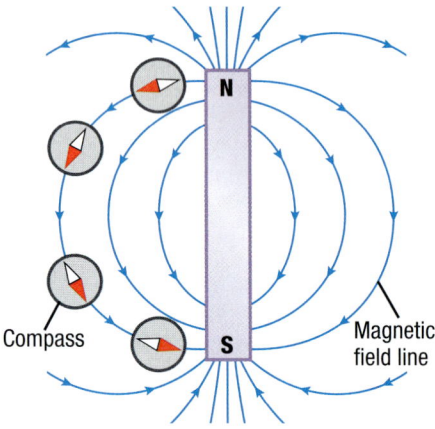

Figure 3 The magnetic field of a bar magnet can be traced with a compass. **In which direction do magnetic field lines seem to travel?**

www.scilinks.org
Topic: Magnetism
Code: HK80900

Magnetic field lines can be used to represent magnetic fields.

Electric field lines are often used to represent an electric field. Similarly, magnetic field lines can be used to represent the magnetic field of a bar magnet. These field lines always form closed loops.

In the photograph of the magnet in **Figure 3,** small pieces of iron are used to show the field around the bar magnet. The field also exists within the magnet and continues farther away from the magnet. The greater the distance between the magnetic field and the magnet, the weaker the magnetic field is. As is the case with electric field lines, magnetic field lines that are close together indicate a strong magnetic field. Field lines that are farther apart indicate a weaker field. So, you can tell from **Figure 3** that a magnet's field is strongest near its poles.

Magnetic field lines always form closed loops.

As the drawing in **Figure 3** shows, a compass can be used to analyze the direction of a magnetic field. A compass is a magnet suspended on top of a pivot so that the magnet can rotate freely. You can make a simple compass by using a piece of string to hang a bar magnet from a support. Simply tie the string to the magnet's midpoint and the support.

By convention, magnetic field lines begin at the north pole of a magnet and end at the south pole of the magnet. However, magnetic field lines do not really have a beginning or end. They always form closed loops. In a permanent magnet, the field lines actually continue within the magnet itself to form the loops. (Note: These lines are not shown in the illustration.)

Reading Check In a bar magnet, where do magnetic field lines begin and where do they end?

Compasses align with Earth's magnetic field.

If it is not near another strong magnet, a compass will align with Earth's magnetic field like iron filings aligning with a bar magnet's field. The compass points in the direction that lies along, or is *tangent* to, the magnetic field line at a given point.

Sailors used lodestones to make the first compasses. The sailors would place a lodestone on a small plank of wood that was floating in calm water. Then, they would watch the wood as it turned and pointed toward the north star. Thus, sailors could gauge their direction even during the day, when stars are not visible. Later, sailors found that a steel or iron needle rubbed with lodestone acted in the same manner. By convention, the pole of a magnet that points north is painted red.

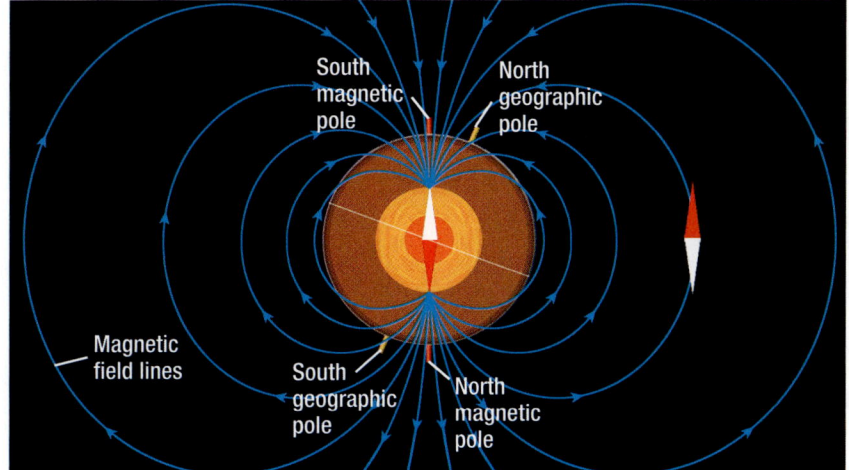

Figure 4 Earth's Geographic and Magnetic Poles

Earth's Magnetic Field

Earth's magnetic poles are not in the same place as its geographic poles, as **Figure 4** shows. ❯ **Earth's magnetic field lines run from geographic south to geographic north.** The pole in Antarctica is actually a magnetic north pole, and the pole in northern Canada is a magnetic south pole. For historical reasons, the poles of magnets are named for the geographic pole to which they point. Thus, the end labeled *N* is the "north-seeking" pole of the magnet, and the end labeled *S* is the "south-seeking" pole of the magnet.

Earth's magnetic field has both direction and strength. If you were to move northward along Earth's surface and you had a compass whose needle could point up and down, the needle of the compass would slowly tilt forward. At a point in northeastern Canada, the needle would point straight down. This point is one of Earth's magnetic poles. There is an opposite magnetic pole in Antarctica.

READING TOOLBOX

Double-Door FoldNote
Create a double-door FoldNote. Label the first door "Earth's North Pole" and the second door "Earth's South Pole." Take notes about these topics behind each door.

QuickLab

Magnetic Field of a File Cabinet

 10 min

Procedure

1. Stand in front of a **metal file cabinet**, and hold a **compass** face up and parallel to the ground.

2. Move the compass from the top of the cabinet to the bottom to see if the direction in which the compass needle points changes. If the direction in which the needle points changes, the cabinet is magnetized.

Analysis

1. Can you explain what might have caused the file cabinet to become magnetized? Remember that Earth's magnetic field lines run not only horizontally to Earth's surface but also up and down.

2. Can you find other objects in your classroom that have become magnetized by Earth's magnetic field?

Section 1   Magnets and Magnetic Fields

Figure 5 Birds may use Earth's magnetic field to guide them during migration.

The source of Earth's magnetism is not yet fully understood.

The source of Earth's magnetism is a topic of scientific debate. Although Earth's core is made mostly of iron, the iron in the core is too hot to retain any magnetic properties. Instead, many researchers believe that the circulation of ions or electrons in the liquid layer of Earth's core may be the source of the magnetism. Others believe Earth's magnetism is due to a combination of several factors.

The sun also has a magnetic field and ejects charged particles into space. Earth's magnetic field deflects most of these particles so that the charged particles enter Earth's atmosphere only near the magnetic poles. Collisions between these particles and atoms in Earth's atmosphere cause the Northern and Southern lights.

For years, scientists have speculated that some birds, such as the geese in **Figure 5,** use Earth's magnetic field to guide their migrations. Magnetic particles that seem to have a navigational role have been found in the tissues of migrating animals, such as birds, bees, and fish.

Section 1 Review

KEY IDEAS

1. **Determine** whether the magnets will attract or repel each other in each of the following cases.

2. **Illustrate** the magnetic field around a permanent magnet.

3. **Describe** the direction in which a compass needle points in Australia.

CRITICAL THINKING

4. **Interpreting Graphics** Which orientation of the compass needles in the figure below correctly describes the direction of the bar magnet's magnetic field at the given location?

   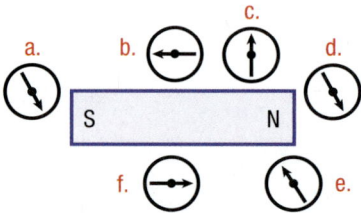

5. **Applying Concepts** The north pole of a magnet points toward the geographic North Pole, yet like poles repel. Explain this seeming discrepancy.

624 Chapter 18 Magnetism

Why It Matters

Earth's Changing Magnetic Field

Earth's magnetic field has decreased in strength by about 10% in the past 150 years. This change suggests that Earth's magnetic field may be heading toward a magnetic field reversal—a 180° change in direction. Earth's magnetic field has changed direction throughout geologic time. Evidence of more than 20 reversals in the last 5 million years is preserved in the magnetization of ocean-floor rocks. To explain how this change is possible, some scientists propose that a *geodynamo* may be the source of Earth's magnetic field.

WEIRD SCIENCE

This computer simulation of a geodynamo represents one possible model of Earth's magnetic field. The orange field lines point outward (as does a magnetic north pole), and the blue field lines point inward.

After running the geodynamo model for a long time, the computer simulation shows that the field undergoes a magnetic field reversal. Computer models such as this one help scientists understand the behavior of Earth's magnetic field.

A history of Earth's magnetic field is recorded in the volcanic rocks on the floor of Earth's oceans. Scientists collect samples using a core sampler, such as the one shown here, at a number of locations on the ocean floor near mid-ocean ridges.

YOUR TURN

UNDERSTANDING CONCEPTS
1. What evidence suggests that Earth is heading toward a magnetic field reversal?

ONLINE RESEARCH
2. Research the mid-ocean ridges. What do their magnetic patterns say about the history of Earth's continents?

SCILINKS.
www.scilinks.org
Topic: Earth's Magnetic Field
Code: HK80448

SECTION 2
Magnetism from Electric Currents

Key Ideas
- What happens to a compass near a wire that is carrying a current?
- Why are electric motors useful?

Key Terms
solenoid
electromagnet
electric motor
galvanometer

Why It Matters
Because magnetic fields are created by electric currents, metal detectors used by airport security guards are able to detect metal.

During the 18th century, people noticed that lightning could momentarily change the direction of a compass needle. They also noticed that iron pans sometimes became magnetized during lightning storms. These observations suggested a relationship between electricity and magnetism, but the relationship was not understood until 1820.

Electromagnetism

In 1820, Hans Christian Oersted, a Danish science teacher, first experimented with the effects of an electric current on the needle of a compass. He found that moving electric charges produce magnetism. After class, Oersted showed some of his students that when a compass is brought near a wire carrying a current, the compass needle is deflected from its usual north-south orientation.

The apparatus shown in **Figure 1** uses compasses to reveal the magnetic field near a current-carrying wire. When no current is in the wire, all of the needles will point in the same direction—that of Earth's magnetic field. ▶ **When the wire carries a strong, steady current, all of the compass needles move to align with the magnetic field created by the electric current.** If the current is reversed, each needle will point in the opposite direction.

The direction that the compass needles are pointing in **Figure 1** suggests that the magnetic field around a current-carrying wire forms a circle around the wire. Each needle points in a direction tangent to a circle centered at the wire.

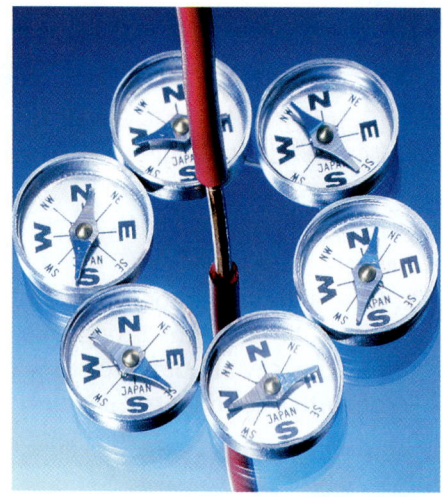

Figure 1 When a wire carries a current, the magnetic field induced by the current forms concentric circles around the wire.

The right-hand rule is used to find the direction of the magnetic field produced by a current.

Is the direction of a wire's magnetic field clockwise or counterclockwise? Repeated measurements have suggested an easy way to predict the direction of a field. This method is summarized by the *right-hand rule*.

| **Right-hand rule** | If you hold a wire in your right hand and point your thumb in the direction of the positive current, the direction that your fingers curl is the direction of the magnetic field. |

The right-hand rule is illustrated in **Figure 2**. The right hand grasps the wire while the thumb points in the direction of the current. The fingers encircle the wire, and the fingertips point in the direction of the magnetic field—counterclockwise when viewed from the top. If the direction of the current were from the top to the bottom of the page, the thumb would point downward, and the magnetic field would run clockwise. *Remember: Never grasp or touch an uninsulated wire connected to a power source. You could be electrocuted.*

Reading Check When using the right-hand rule, you should point your thumb in which direction?

Solenoids and bar magnets have similar magnetic fields.

As you have learned, the magnetic field of a current-carrying wire exerts a force on a compass needle. This force causes the needle to turn in the direction of the wire's magnetic field. However, this force is very weak for a small current. Increasing the current in the wire is one way to increase the force, but large currents can be fire hazards. Wrapping the wire into a coil is a safer way to create a stronger magnetic field, as **Figure 3** shows. This device is called a **solenoid.**

In a solenoid, the magnetic field of each loop of wire adds to the strength of the magnetic field of any neighboring loops. The result is a strong magnetic field similar to the magnetic field produced by a bar magnet. Like a magnet, a solenoid has a north and south pole.

Figure 2 You can use the right-hand rule to find the direction of the magnetic field near a wire that is carrying a current.

solenoid (SOH luh NOYD) a coil of wire with an electric current in it

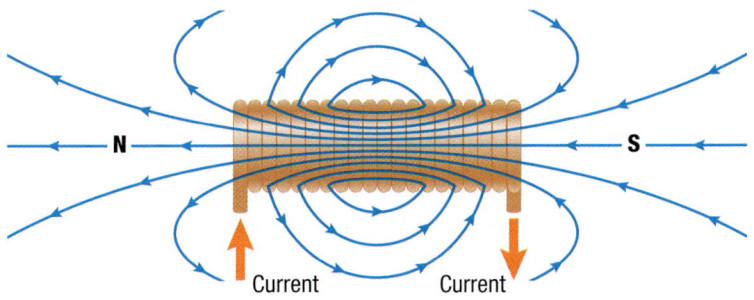

Figure 3 The magnetic field of a solenoid resembles the magnetic field of a bar magnet.

Section 2 Magnetism from Electric Currents

QuickLab

Electromagnet

  20 min

Procedure

1. Wind **1 m of insulated wire** around a **large iron or steel nail**.
2. Remove the insulation from the ends of the wire. Hold the insulated wire so that the ends touch the terminals of a **6 V lantern battery**.
3. Move a **compass** toward the nail.
4. Flip the battery around so that the current is reversed. Bring the compass near the same part of the nail.

Analysis

1. What type of device have you produced? Explain your answer.
2. What happened to the compass needle after you reversed the direction of the current? Explain your observation?
3. After you detach the coil from the cell, what can you do to make the nail nonmagnetic?

---

electromagnet (ee LEK troh MAG nit) a coil that has a soft iron core and that acts as a magnet when an electric current is in the coil

Academic Vocabulary

device (di VIES) a piece of equipment made for a specific use

The strength of a solenoid can be increased.

The strength of the magnetic field of a solenoid depends on the number of loops of wire and the amount of current in the wire. In particular, more loops or more current can create a stronger magnetic field.

The strength of a solenoid's magnetic field can also be increased by inserting a rod made of a magnetic metal, such as iron, through the center of the coils. The resulting device is called an **electromagnet.** The magnetic field of the solenoid causes the rod to become a magnet as well. Then, the magnetic field of the rod adds to the coil's field and thus creates a magnet that is stronger than the solenoid alone.

Reading Check What relationship does the number of loops of wire in a solenoid have to the strength of a solenoid?

Moving charges cause magnetism.

The movement of charges is the cause of all magnetism. But what charges are moving in a bar magnet? Negatively charged electrons moving around the nuclei of atoms make magnetic fields. Atomic nuclei also have magnetic fields because protons move within the nuclei. Each electron has a property called *electron spin,* which also produces a tiny magnetic field.

In most cases, the various sources of magnetic fields in an element cancel out and leave the atom essentially nonmagnetic. However, not all of the fields cancel in some materials, such as iron, nickel, and cobalt. Thus, the magnetism of the uncanceled fields in these materials combines to make the materials magnetic overall.

Why It Matters
Airport Security

Before traveling on an airplane, you are required to pass through a metal detector on your way to the gate. You may also be asked to submit to a sweep with a hand-held metal detector. Metal detectors make use of electromagnetism. Most airport metal detectors use a system called *pulse induction* (PI). These systems consist of a power supply, a sensor circuit, and a coil of metal through which a current can pass.

① Short pulses of current are passed through the coil at a rate of about 100 pulses per second. Each pulse creates a short-lived magnetic field that quickly collapses.

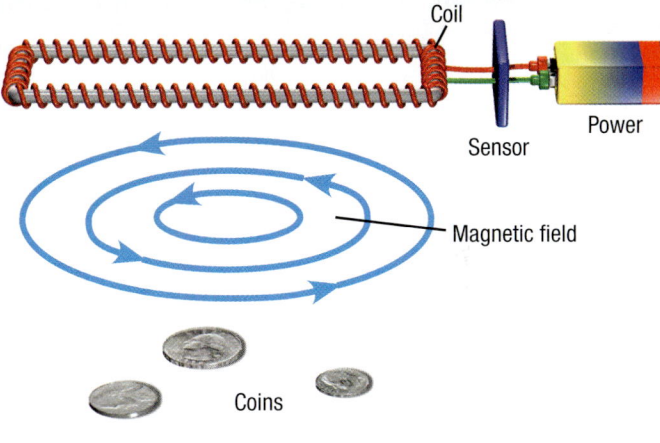

② When a metal object passes through the metal detector or a hand-held detector passes near a metal object, an opposite magnetic field is induced in the metal object.

③ When it detects the opposing magnetic field, the sensor activates a light or sound that signals the operator of the metal detector.

UNDERSTANDING CONCEPTS
1. Does the field induced in the metal object increase or decrease the pulsed field?

WRITING IN SCIENCE
2. Choose another device used in airport security, and describe how this device works.

629

Figure 4 A blow-dryer is one example of an everyday device that uses an electric motor.

Electromagnetic Devices

Many modern devices, such as blow-dryers and stereo speakers, make use of the magnetic field produced by coils of current-carrying wire. Devices such as the blow-dryer shown in **Figure 4,** are able to function because the coils inside the devices work as motors.

Electric motors are machines that convert electrical energy into mechanical energy. ❱ **A motor can perform mechanical work when it is attached to an external device.** Electric motors are used in many devices around your home, including many toys. Larger motors are found in washing machines and clothes dryers, and simple motors can be found in common household fans.

Galvanometers detect current.

Galvanometers are devices that are used to measure current. The basic construction of a galvanometer is shown in **Figure 5.** In all cases, a galvanometer detects current, or the movement of charges in a circuit.

A galvanometer consists of a coil of insulated wire wrapped around an iron core that can rotate between the poles of a permanent magnet. When the galvanometer is attached to a circuit, a current exists in the coil of wire. The coil and iron core act as an electromagnet and produce a magnetic field. This magnetic field interacts with the magnetic field of the surrounding permanent magnet. The resulting forces turn the core, which moves a needle along a scale.

A galvanometer can be used with other circuit elements to function as an *ammeter,* which measures current, or as a *voltmeter,* which measures voltage.

electric motor (ee LEK trik MOHT uhr) a device that converts electrical energy into mechanical energy

galvanometer (GAL vuh NAHM uht uhr) an instrument that detects, measures, and determines the direction of a small electric current

www.scilinks.org
Topic: Electromagnets
Code: **HK80484**

Figure 5 When there is current in the coil of a galvanometer, magnetic repulsion between the coil and the magnet causes the coil to twist. **How does the direction of the motion change if the current is reversed?**

Figure 6 In an electric motor, the current in the coil produces a magnetic field that interacts with the magnetic field of the surrounding magnet and thus causes the coil to turn.

Motors use a commutator to spin in one direction.

The arrow in **Figure 6** shows how the coil of wire in a motor turns when a current is in the wire. Unlike the coil in a galvanometer, the coil in an electric motor keeps spinning. A device called *commutator* is used to make the current change direction every time the flat coil makes a half revolution. This commutator is two half rings of metal. Devices called *brushes* connect the commutator to the wires from the battery. Because of the slits in the commutator, charges must move through the coil of wire to reach the opposite half of the ring.

So, the magnetic field of the coil changes direction as the coil spins. In this way, the coil is repelled by both the north and south poles of the magnet surrounding it. Because the current keeps reversing, the loop rotates in one direction. If the current did not keep changing direction, the loop would simply bounce back and forth in the magnetic field until the force of friction caused the loop to come to rest.

READING TOOLBOX

Cause and Effect
Many factors influence how a motor works. As you read this page and the previous page, look for multiple causes and multiple effects that enable a motor to turn.

Section 2 Review

KEY IDEAS

1. **Describe** the shape of a magnetic field produced by a straight wire that is carrying a current.
2. **Determine** the direction in which a compass needle will point when the compass is held above a wire carrying positive charges that are moving west.
3. **Explain** how galvanometers and electric motors function.

CRITICAL THINKING

4. **Predicting Outcomes** Predict whether a solenoid suspended by a string could be used as a compass.
5. **Analyzing Ideas** A friend claims to have built a motor by attaching a shaft to the core of a galvanometer and removing the spring. Can this motor rotate through a full rotation? Explain your answer.

SECTION 3
Electric Currents from Magnetism

Key Ideas

> What happens when a magnet is moved into or out of a coil of wire?
> How are electricity and magnetism related?
> What are the basic components of a transformer?

Key Terms

electromagnetic induction
generator
alternating current
transformer

Why It Matters

Many common devices, such as electric guitars and speakers, rely on electromagnetic induction to function.

Tennessee Course Level Expectations (Physical Science)
CLE.3202.2.1; CLE.3202.Inq.1;
CLE.3202.Inq.2; CLE.3202.Inq.3;
CLE.3202.Inq.4; CLE.3202.Inq.6;
CLE.3202.Math.1; CLE.3202.Math.2;
CLE.3202.TE.2; CLE.3202.TE.3;
CLE.3202.TE.4

Electric power plants convert mechanical energy—usually the movement of water or steam—into electrical energy. How can electrical energy be generated from mechanical energy?

Electromagnetic Induction

In 1831, Michael Faraday discovered that a current can be produced by pushing a magnet through a coil of wire. This happens without a battery or other source of voltage. **> Moving a magnet into and out of a coil of wire causes charges in the wire to move.** The process of creating a current in a circuit by changing a magnetic field is called **electromagnetic induction.** Electromagnetic induction is so fundamental that it has become one of the laws of physics—*Faraday's law.*

| Faraday's law | An electric current can be produced in a circuit by changing the magnetic field crossing the circuit. |

Consider the loop of wire moving between the two magnetic poles in **Figure 1.** As the loop moves into and out of the magnetic field of the magnet, a current is *induced* in the circuit. As long as the wire continues to move into or out of the field in a direction that is not parallel to the field, an induced current will exist in the circuit.

Rotating the circuit or changing the strength of the magnetic field will also induce a current in the circuit. In each case, a changing magnetic field is passing through the loop. You can use the concept of magnetic field lines to predict whether a current will be induced. A current will be induced if the number of field lines that pass through the loop changes.

Figure 1 When the loop moves into or out of the magnetic field, a current is induced in the wire. **What happens if the loop is rotated between the magnets?**

Electromagnetic induction obeys conservation of energy.

Although electromagnetic induction may seem to create energy from nothing, it does not. Electromagnetic induction does not violate the law of conservation of energy. Pushing a loop through a magnetic field requires work. The greater the magnetic field, the stronger the force required to push the loop through the field. The energy required for this work comes from an outside source, such as your muscles pushing the loop through the magnetic field. So, electromagnetic induction produces electrical energy, but energy is required for electromangetic induction to occur.

The magnetic force acts on moving electric charges.

A charged particle moving in a magnetic field will experience a force in a direction that is at right angles to the direction of the magnetic field lines. This magnetic force is zero when the charge moves in the same direction as the magnetic field lines. The force is at its maximum value when the charge moves perpendicularly to the field. As the angle between the charge's direction and the direction of the magnetic field decreases, the force on the charge also decreases. This force also acts on a wire that is carrying a current.

Academic Vocabulary

violate (VIE uh LAYT) to fail to keep

electromagnetic induction (ee LEK troh mag NET ik in DUHK shuhn) the process of creating a current in a circuit by changing a magnetic field

InquiryLab

Can You Demonstrate Electromagnetic Induction?

 30 min

Procedure

1. Connect each end of a **hollow-core wire coil,** or **solenoid,** to a **galvanometer,** as shown in the photo.
2. Any current induced in the solenoid will pass through the galvanometer. For each of the following motions, record the direction in which the galvanometer needle points and the amount by which it moves.
3. Insert the north pole of a **bar magnet** into the solenoid.
4. Pull the magnet out of the solenoid.
5. Turn the magnet around, and move the south pole into and out of the solenoid.
6. Vary the speed of your motion.
7. Use **two magnets,** and hold them alongside each other so that like poles are touching.

Analysis

1. What evidence indicates that a changing magnetic field induces a current? What happens if you do not move the magnet at all?
2. Compare the current induced by a south pole with the current induced by a north pole.
3. What two observations show that more current is induced if the magnetic field changes rapidly?
4. How does the amount of current induced depend on the strength of the magnetic field?

Section 3 Electric Currents from Magnetism **633**

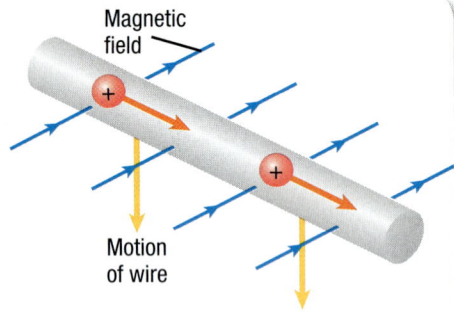

When the wire in a circuit moves perpendicularly to the magnetic field, the current induced in the wire is at a maximum.

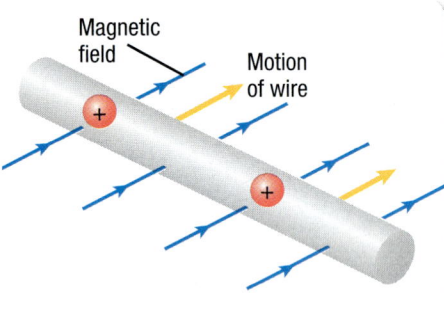

When the wire moves parallel to the magnetic field, no current is induced in the wire.

Figure 2 A current is induced in a closed circuit when the circuit moves through a magnetic field.

generator (JEN uhr AYT uhr) a machine that converts mechanical energy into electrical energy

alternating current (AWL tuhr NAYT ing KUHR uhnt) an electric current that changes direction at regular intervals (abbreviation, AC)

The magnetic force acts on wires carrying a current.

When studying electromagnetic induction, you may find it helpful to imagine the individual charges in a wire. Imagine that the wire in a circuit is a tube full of charges, as illustrated in **Figure 2.** When the wire is moving perpendicularly to a magnetic field, the force on the charges is at a maximum. In this case, a current is in the wire and circuit. When the wire is moving parallel to the field, no current is induced in the wire. Because the charges are moving parallel to the field, they experience no magnetic force.

Generators convert mechanical energy into electrical energy.

Generators are similar to motors but convert mechanical energy into electrical energy. If you expend energy to do work on a simple generator, such as the one in **Figure 3,** the loop of wire inside turns within a magnetic field and thus produces a current. For each half rotation of the loop, the current produced by the generator reverses direction. A current that changes direction at regular intervals is called an **alternating current** (AC).

The generators that produce the electrical energy that you use at home are alternating-current generators. The current supplied by the outlets in your home and in most of the world is alternating current. The glowing light bulb in **Figure 3** indicates that the coil turning in the magnetic field of the magnet creates a current. The magnitude and direction of the current that results from the coil's rotation vary depending on the orientation of the loop in the field.

Reading Check What must be done to produce a current using a generator?

Figure 3 In an alternating-current generator, the mechanical energy of the loop's rotation is converted into electrical energy when a current is induced in the wire. The current lights the light bulb.

Why It Matters

How Do Electric Guitars Work?

The word *pickup* refers to a device that "picks up" the sound of an instrument and turns that sound into an electrical signal. The most common type of electric guitar pickup uses electromagnetic induction to convert string vibrations into electrical energy. Conversely, a speaker converts an electrical signal back into sound.

Electric guitar pickups come in many styles, and a single electric guitar often has two or three kinds of pickups. One kind of pickup, the humbucker, is designed to reduce the noise, or hum, that simpler pickups make because of alternating current.

Magnetic guitar pickups contain a permanent magnet that is wrapped with a coil of wire. The pole of the magnet is directly under the guitar strings. The guitar strings are made of a magnetic material—usually steel, nickel, or both. As a string vibrates, it induces a current in the pickup coil, and the vibration is converted into an electrical signal.

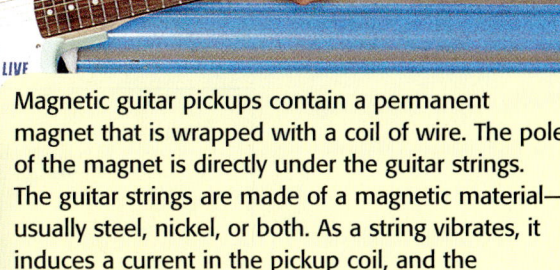

Speakers contain a permanent magnet and a coil of wire attached to a flexible paper cone. Current in the coil induces a magnetic field, which causes the paper cone to move. Varying the current changes how much and how fast the cone vibrates. These vibrations produce sound waves.

www.scilinks.org
Topic: Electromagnetic Induction
Code: **HK80481**

YOUR TURN

UNDERSTANDING CONCEPTS
1. How are vibrations in a paper cone related to sound?

CRITICAL THINKING
2. Explain why a magnetic pickup does not work with nylon guitar strings.

Figure 4 Induced Current in a Generator

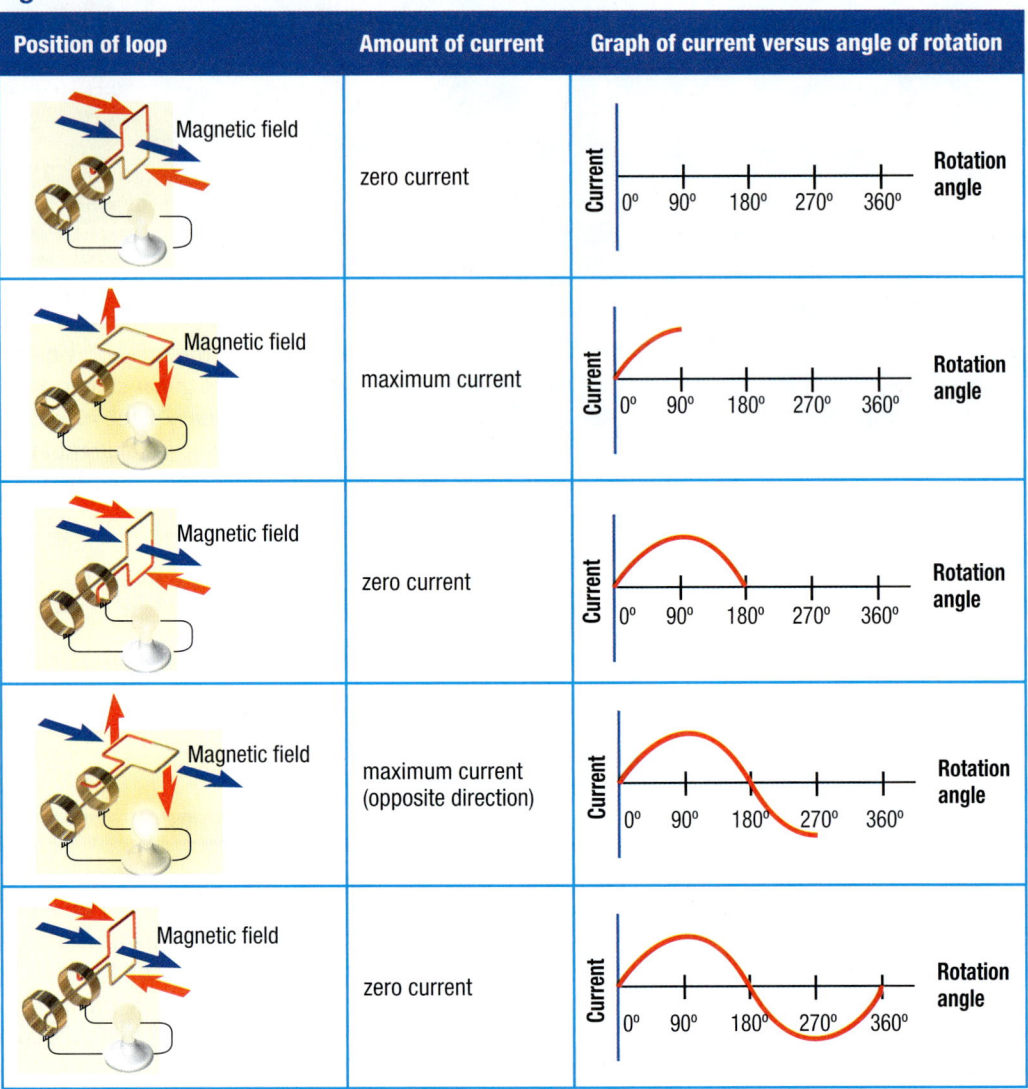

The amount of current produced by an AC generator changes with time.

Study the diagrams in **Figure 4.** When the loop is perpendicular to the field, the current is zero. Recall that a charge moving parallel to a magnetic field experiences no magnetic force. This is the case here. The charges in the wire experience no magnetic force, so no current is induced in the wire.

As the loop turns, the current increases until it reaches a maximum. When the loop is parallel to the field, charges on either side of the wire move perpendicularly to the magnetic field. Thus, the charges experience the maximum magnetic force, and the current is large. Current decreases as the loop rotates. When the loop is perpendicular to the magnetic field again, the current once again reaches zero. As the loop continues to rotate, the direction of the current reverses.

Cause and Effect
As you read this page, look for cause-and-effect markers. Make a two-column table or appropriate FoldNote, and label the columns "Cause" and "Effect." Fill the table with information that you learn about induced current.

Generators produce the electrical energy that you use in your home.

Large power plants use generators to convert mechanical energy into electrical energy. The mechanical energy used in a commercial power plant comes from a variety of sources. One of the most common sources is running water. Dams are built to harness the kinetic energy of falling water. Water is forced through small channels at the top of a dam. As the water falls to the base of the dam, it turns the blades of large turbines. The turbines are attached to a core wrapped with many loops of wire that rotate within a strong magnetic field. The end result is electrical energy.

Coal power plants use the energy from burning coal to make steam that eventually turns the blades of turbines. Other sources of energy are nuclear power (fission), wind power, geothermal power, and solar power.

Some mechanical energy is always lost as waste heat, and resistance in the wires of the generator reduces the electrical energy that is available. Many power plants are not very efficient. Methods of producing energy that are more efficient and safer are constantly being sought.

Reading Check What are three sources of mechanical energy used by power plants to produce electrical energy?

The Electromagnetic Force

So far, you have learned that moving charges produce magnetic fields and that changing magnetic fields cause electric charges to move. ❯ **Electricity and magnetism are two aspects of a single force, the electromagnetic force.**

The energy that results from the electromagnetic force is electromagnetic energy. Light is a form of electromagnetic energy. Visible light travels as electromagnetic waves, or *EM waves,* as do other forms of radiation, such as radio signals and X rays. As **Figure 5** shows, EM waves are made up of oscillating electric and magnetic fields that are perpendicular to each other. This is true of any type of EM wave regardless of the frequency.

Both the electric and magnetic fields in an EM wave are perpendicular to the direction in which the wave travels. So, EM waves are transverse waves. As an EM wave moves along, the changing electric field generates the magnetic field. The changing magnetic field generates the electric field. Because each field regenerates the other, EM waves are able to travel through empty space.

Integrating Biology

Biomagnets Many types of bacteria contain magnetic particles of iron oxide and iron sulfide. Encased in a membrane within the cell, these particles form a magnetosome. The magnetosomes in a bacterium spread out in a line and align with Earth's magnetic field. As the cell uses its flagella to swim, it travels along a north-south axis. Recently, magnetite crystals have been found in human brain cells, but the role that these particles play remains uncertain.

www.scilinks.org
Topic: Generators
Code: HK80643

Figure 5 An electromagnetic wave consists of electric and magnetic field waves that are at right angles.

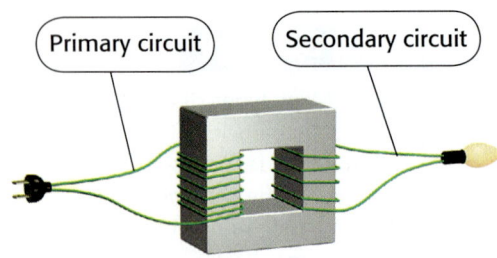

Figure 6 A transformer uses the alternating current in the primary circuit to induce an alternating current in the secondary circuit.

transformer (trans FAWRM uhr) a device that increases or decreases the voltage of alternating current

Transformers

You may have seen metal cylinders on power line poles in your neighborhood. These cylinders hold devices called **transformers**, devices that increase or decrease the voltage of alternating current. ❯ **In its simplest form, a transformer consists of two coils of wire wrapped around opposite sides of a closed iron loop.** In the transformer shown in **Figure 6,** one wire is attached to a source of alternating current, such as a power outlet, and is called the *primary circuit*. The other wire is attached to an appliance, such as a lamp, and is called the *secondary circuit*.

When there is current in the primary circuit, this current creates a changing magnetic field in the primary coil that magnetizes the iron core. The changing magnetic field of the iron core then induces a current in the secondary coil. The direction of the current in the secondary coil changes every time the direction of the current in the primary coil changes.

Transformers can increase or decrease voltage.

The voltage induced in the secondary circuit of a transformer depends on the number of loops, or *turns*, in the coil, as shown in **Figure 7.** In *step-up transformers,* the primary coil has fewer turns than the secondary coil does. In this case, the voltage across the secondary coil is greater than the voltage across the primary coil. In *step-down transformers,* the secondary coil has fewer loops than the primary coil does. The voltage across the secondary circuit is lower than the voltage across the primary circuit.

Figure 7 How Transformers Change Voltage

In a step-up transformer, the primary coil has fewer loops than the secondary coil does. The voltage in the secondary coil must be higher than the voltage in the primary coil.

In a step-down transformer, the primary coil has more loops than the secondary coil does. The voltage in the secondary coil must be lower than the voltage in the primary coil.

Transformers must obey the law of conservation of energy.

Transformers may seem to provide something—more voltage—for nothing. But they do not. The power output of the secondary coil is, at best, equal to the power input to the primary coil. One cannot get more electrical energy per unit of time, or power, out of the transformer than one puts into it. For this reason, the current in the secondary coil of a step-up transformer is always less than the current in the primary coil.

Real transformers are not perfectly efficient. Some of the energy that is put into a transformer is lost as heat because of resistance in the coils. The power lost increases quickly as current increases. To decrease loss and maximize the energy that is delivered, power companies use a high voltage and a low current when transferring power over long distances.

Transformers are used in the transfer of electrical energy.

Step-up and step-down transformers are used in the transmission of electrical energy from power plants to homes and businesses. A step-up transformer is used at or near a power plant to increase the voltage to about 120,000 V. This high voltage limits the loss of energy that the resistance of the transmission wires causes. Then, step-down transformers like the ones in **Figure 8** are used near homes to reduce the voltage to about 120 V. This low voltage is much safer to use in homes.

Figure 8 Step-down transformers like the ones shown here are used to reduce the voltage across power lines. **What is the advantage of using a lower voltage within homes?**

Section 3 Review

KEY IDEAS

1. **Identify** which of the following will not increase the current induced in a wire loop moving through a magnetic field.
   a. increasing the strength of the magnetic field
   b. increasing the speed of the wire
   c. rotating the loop until it is perpendicular to the field

2. **Explain** how hydroelectric power plants use moving water to produce electricity.

3. **Explain** how electricity and magnetism are related to one another.

4. **Determine** whether the following statement describes a step-up transformer or a step-down transformer: The primary coil has 7,000 turns, and the secondary coil has 500 turns.

CRITICAL THINKING

5. **Making Predictions** For each of the following actions, predict the movement of the needle of a galvanometer attached to a coil of wire. Assume that the north pole of a bar magnet has been inserted into the coil, which causes the needle to deflect to the right.
   a. pulling the magnet out of the coil
   b. letting the magnet rest in the coil
   c. thrusting the south pole of the magnet into the coil

6. **Determining Cause and Effect** A spacecraft orbiting Earth contains a coil of wire. An astronaut measures a small current in the coil even though the coil is not connected to a battery and the spacecraft does not contain any magnets. What is causing the current?

Inquiry Lab

⏱ 50 min

Making a Better Electromagnet

In a Quick Lab earlier in this chapter, you made an electromagnet by using batteries and a wire coil. In this lab, you will experiment with the characteristics that make an electromagnet stronger.

Asking a Question

What combination of various batteries, wires, and metal rods will make the strongest electromagnet?

Building an Electromagnet

1. Review the basic steps in making an electromagnet by looking at the Quick Lab in Section 2.
2. On a blank sheet of paper, prepare a data table like the one shown in this activity.
3. Wind the thin wire around the thickest metal core. Carefully pull the core out of the center of the thin wire coil. Using the thick wire, repeat the steps above. You now have two wire coils that can be used to make electromagnets. **CAUTION:** Handle the wires only where they are insulated.

Forming and Testing a Hypothesis

4. Think about the following, and predict the features that the strongest electromagnet would have.
   a. Which metal rod would make the best core?
   b. Which of the two wires would make a stronger electromagnet?
   c. How many coils should the electromagnet have?
   d. Should the batteries be connected in series or in parallel?

What You'll Do

> **Build** several electromagnets.
> **Determine** how many paper clips each electromagnet can lift.
> **Analyze** your results to identify the features of a strong electromagnet.

What You'll Need

batteries, D-cell (2)
battery holders (2)
electrical tape
metal rods (1 iron, 1 tin, 1 aluminum, and 1 nickel)
paper clips, small (1 box)
wire, extra-insulated
wire, insulated, thick, 1 m long
wire, insulated, thin, 1 m long
wire stripper

Safety

Sample Data Table: Differences in Electromagnets

Electromagnet number	Wire (thick or thin)	No. of coils	Core (iron, tin, alum., or nickel)	Batteries (series or parallel)	No. of paper clips lifted
1					
2					
3		DO NOT WRITE IN BOOK			
4					
5					
6					

Designing Your Experiment

5 With your lab partners, decide how you will determine the features that combine to make a strong electromagnet.

6 In your lab report, list each step you will perform in your experiment.

Performing Your Experiment

7 After your teacher approves your plan, carry out your experiment. You should test all four metal rods, both thicknesses of wire, and both battery connections (series and parallel). Count the number of coils of wire in each electromagnet that you build.

8 Record your results in your data table.

Analysis

1. **Explaining Events** Which wire made a stronger electromagnet: the thick wire or the thin wire? How can you explain this result?

2. **Explaining Events** Which metal cores made the strongest electromagnets? Why?

3. **Explaining Events** Could your electromagnet pick up more paper clips when the batteries were connected in series or when they were connected in parallel? Explain why.

Communicating Your Results

4. **Drawing Conclusions** What combination of wire, metal core, and battery connection made the strongest electromagnet?

Extension

Suppose someone tells you that your conclusion is invalid because each time you tested a magnet on the paper clips, the paper clips became more and more magnetized. How could you show that your conclusion is valid?

Making Predictions

Science Skills

One of the main goals of science is to explain the nature of the world around us. Another important goal is to allow us to predict—with a reasonable degree of confidence and accuracy—what will happen in the future. Predictions based on hypotheses help scientists design experiments. Predictions based on established scientific laws or theories help scientists apply science to solve real-world problems.

- Technology
- Math
- ▶ Scientific Methods
- Graphing

1 Predictions Based on Hypotheses

- A hypothesis is formed from observations that you have made or data that you have collected.
- After you have a hypothesis, you should make two kinds of predictions: one that states what will happen if the hypothesis is true and one that states what will happen if the hypothesis is not true.
- These predictions can help you plan how to test the hypothesis.

> - Observations: Magnets stick to a metal refrigerator door, but not to a door made of wood or plastic.
> - Hypothesis: Magnets are attracted to any kind of metal, but not to anything else.
> - Predictions if hypothesis is true: (1) I will not be able to find a metal to which a magnet will not stick and (2) I will not be able to find a nonmetal to which a magnet will stick.
> - Predictions if hypothesis is NOT true: (1) I will be able to find a metal to which a magnet will not stick and (2) I will be able to find a nonmetal to which a magnet will stick.

2 Predictions Based on Established Theories

- After a hypothesis has been tested and confirmed repeatedly by many scientists, the hypothesis can be accepted as a scientific law or as part of a theory. You can then use this theory to make further predictions.
- You can use equations to make precise, quantitative predictions.
- You can extrapolate, or continue the trend suggested by past known data, using graphs to obtain quantitative predictions.

> - Established scientific law: Observations of sunspots (dark patches on the surface of the sun) have shown that the spots grow and fade in an 11-year cycle.
> - Fact: The last time the sunspot cycle was at a maximum was in 2001.
> - Prediction: The next time the cycle will be at a maximum will be around 2012.

Practice

1. Suppose that you want to test the hypothesis that Earth's North Pole is like the south pole of a bar magnet. Predict how a compass will behave around a bar magnet if (a) the hypothesis is true and (b) the hypothesis is not true.

2. The "sunspot number" is an index that is used to measure the amount of sunspot activity on a given day. Use the Internet to research the sunspot cycle for the sun. Predict what the peak sunspot number will be in 2023.

CHAPTER 18 Summary

go.hrw.com
SUPER SUMMARY
KEYWORD: HK8MAGS

Key Ideas

Key Terms

Section 1 Magnets and Magnetic Fields

- **Magnets** All magnets have two poles that cannot be isolated. Like poles repel each other, and unlike poles attract each other. (p. 619)
- **Magnetic Fields** Magnets repel or attract each other because of the interaction of their magnetic fields. (p. 621)
- **Earth's Magnetic Field** Earth's magnetic field lines run from geographic south to geographic north. The magnetic north pole is in Antarctica, and the magnetic south pole is in northern Canada. (p. 623)

magnetic pole, p. 619
magnetic field, p. 621

Section 2 Magnetism from Electric Currents

- **Electromagnetism** When a wire carries a strong, steady current, the needles of any compasses nearby move to align with the magnetic field created by the electric current. (p. 626)
- **Electromagnetic Devices** A motor can perform mechanical work when it is attached to an external device. Electric motors convert electrical energy into mechanical energy. (p. 630)

solenoid, p. 627
electromagnet, p. 628
electric motor, p. 630
galvanometer, p. 630

Section 3 Electric Currents from Magnetism

- **Electromagnetic Induction** Moving a magnet into and out of a coil of wire causes charges in the wire to move. A current is produced in a circuit by a changing magnetic field. (p. 632)
- **The Electromagnetic Force** Electricity and magnetism are two aspects of a single force, the electromagnetic force. Electromagnetic waves consist of magnetic and electric fields oscillating at right angles to each other. (p. 637)
- **Transformers** A transformer consists of two coils or wire wrapped around opposite sides of a closed iron loop. In a transformer, the magnetic field produced by a primary coil induces a current in a secondary coil. (p. 638)

electromagnetic induction, p. 632
generator, p. 634
alternating current, p. 634
transformer, p. 638

Magnetism **643**

CHAPTER 18 Review

READING TOOLBOX

1. **Suffixes** The magnetometer was first designed in 1833 by Carl Friedrich Gauss, a German mathematician and scientist. A magnetometer is also sometimes called a *gaussmeter*. A gauss is also a unit for measuring the strength of magnetic fields. Given this information, what do you think a magnetometer is?

USING KEY TERMS

2. Use the terms *magnetic pole* and *magnetic field* to explain why the north pole of a compass needle points toward northern Canada.

3. Write a paragraph explaining the advantages and disadvantages of using a magnetic compass to determine direction. Use the terms *magnetic pole* and *magnetic field* in your answer.

4. How does a *galvanometer* measure electric current? How is it similar to and different from an *electric motor*?

5. What is the purpose of a *commutator* in an *electric motor*?

6. Use the terms *generator* and *electromagnetic induction* to explain how *kinetic energy* of falling water is used to generate *electrical energy*.

UNDERSTANDING KEY IDEAS

7. If the poles of two magnets repel each other,
   a. both poles must be south poles.
   b. both poles must be north poles.
   c. one pole is south and the other is north.
   d. the poles are the same type.

8. The part of a magnet where the magnetic field and forces are strongest is called a magnetic
   a. field.
   b. pole.
   c. attraction.
   d. repulsion.

9. A compass held directly below a current-carrying wire in which positive charges are moving north will point

   a. Current 　　c. Current

   b. Current 　　d. Current

10. An electric motor uses an electromagnet to change
    a. mechanical energy into electrical energy.
    b. magnetic fields in the motor.
    c. magnetic poles in the motor.
    d. electrical energy into mechanical energy.

11. An electric generator is a device that can convert
    a. nuclear energy into electrical energy.
    b. wind energy into electrical energy.
    c. energy from burning coal into electrical energy.
    d. All of the above

12. The process of producing an electric current by moving a magnet into and out of a coil of wire is called
    a. magnetic deduction.
    b. electromagnetic induction.
    c. magnetic reduction.
    d. electromagnetic production.

13. In a transformer, the voltage of a current will increase if the secondary circuit
    a. has more turns than the primary circuit does.
    b. has fewer turns than the primary circuit does.
    c. has the same number of turns that the primary circuit does.
    d. is parallel to the primary circuit.

EXPLAINING KEY IDEAS

14. How could you use a compass that has a magnetized needle to determine if a steel nail is magnetized?

15. What happens to the magnetic domains in a material when the material is placed in a strong magnetic field?

INTERPRETING GRAPHICS The diagram below shows a wire wrapped around a magnetic compass. Use the diagram to answer question 16.

16. Which of the following might be the purpose of the device shown here?
   a. to measure the amount of voltage across the wire
   b. to determine the direction of the current in the wire
   c. to find the resistance of the wire

17. Transformers are usually used to raise or lower the voltage across an alternating-current circuit. Can a transformer be used in a direct-current circuit? Can a transformer be used if the direct current is pulsating (turning on and off)?

CRITICAL THINKING

18. Understanding Systems Fire doors are doors that, when closed, can slow the spread of fire from room to room. In some buildings, fire doors are held open by electromagnets. Explain why electromagnets rather than permanent magnets are used.

19. Making Decisions You have two iron bars and a ball of string. One bar is magnetized, and the other is not magnetized. How can you determine which bar is magnetized?

20. Applying Technology Use your imagination and your knowledge of electromagnetism to invent a useful electromagnetic device. Use a computer-drawing program to make sketches of your invention, and write a description of how it works.

21. Applying Knowledge What do adaptors do to voltage and current? Examine the input/output information on several electrical adapters to find out. Do they contain step-up or step-down transformers?

22. Relating Concepts Research how electromagnetism is used in containing nuclear fusion reactions. Write a report on your findings.

Graphing Skills

23. Induced Current The figure below is a graph of current versus rotation angle for the output of an alternating-current generator.
   a. At what point(s) does the generator produce no current?
   b. Is the current produced at point B less than or more than the current at points C and E?
   c. Is the current produced at point D less than or more than the current at points C and E?
   d. What does the negative value for the current at point D signify?

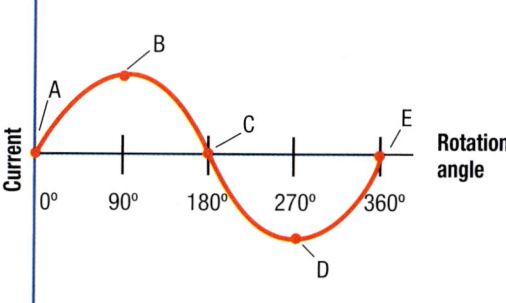

Standardized Test Prep

Understanding Concepts

Directions (1–4): For each question, write on a sheet of paper the letter of the correct answer.

1. A straight vertical wire is carrying an electric current. Positive charges are flowing straight down. What is the direction of the magnetic field generated by the wire as viewed from above?
    - **A.** straight up
    - **B.** straight down
    - **C.** clockwise
    - **D.** counterclockwise

2. What type of device is used to measure the current in an electromagnet?
    - **F.** an electric motor
    - **G.** a galvanometer
    - **H.** a generator
    - **I.** a solenoid

3. A charged particle is moving through a magnetic field. In which direction is the particle moving when the magnetic force acting on the particle is at its greatest?
    - **A.** in the same direction as the magnetic field lines
    - **B.** in the opposite direction from the magnetic field lines
    - **C.** at right angles to the magnetic field lines
    - **D.** clockwise around the magnetic field lines

4. In an AC generator, a loop of wire rotates between two magnetic poles. At what angle(s) of rotation relative to the magnet does the loop generate the most current?
    - **F.** 0° and 180°
    - **G.** 90° and 270°
    - **H.** 180°
    - **I.** 360°

Directions (5–6): For each question, write a short response.

5. How would a compass located precisely at the Earth's geographic north pole behave?

6. What is the difference between a solenoid and an electromagnet?

Reading Skills

Directions (7–10): Read the passage below. Then, answer the questions that follow.

GETTING IT ON TAPE

Magnetic tape consists of a thin plastic strip bonded to a coating of ferric oxide powder. The ferric oxide, Fe_2O_3, makes the tape magnetizable. Early tape recorders were first developed in Germany and Britain. The first tape recorder used by the British Broadcasting Corporation in 1932 was a huge machine. It used steel razor tape that was 3 mm wide and 0.08 mm thick. The tape had to be run at 90 m/min, so the length of tape required for a half-hour program was nearly 3 km long, and a full reel had a mass of 25 kg. Furthermore, the quality of the sound experienced considerable degradation in the recording and playback process.

Higher-quality sound recording was developed in Germany during the late 1930s. During World War II, the Allies became aware of German radio broadcasts that seemed to be recorded. However, the audio quality and duration of the recordings were far greater than Allied technology would allow. At the end of the war, the Allies captured a number of German Magnetophon recorders from Radio Luxembourg, and commercial-quality magnetic recording entered the English-speaking world.

7. How is a tape coated with Fe_2O_3 similar to a steel wire?

8. Was the sound of a British recording during World War II better or worse after the recording was played?

9. The Allies captured recording devices called *magnetophons*. Why is this name appropriate?

10. Why would bringing audiotape near a powerful magnet be a bad idea?

Interpreting Graphics

The diagram below shows an electric circuit that includes a solenoid. Use this diagram to answer questions 11–12.

ELECTRIC CIRCUIT WITH SOLENOID

11. What is the direction of the magnetic field at point X due to the current in section EF?
    - **A.** into the page
    - **B.** out of the page
    - **C.** to the left
    - **D.** to the right

12. To which point is the north pole of the solenoid the closest?
    - **F.** A
    - **G.** B
    - **H.** C
    - **I.** D

The following graphic shows four bar magnets and the magnetic fields that they generate. Use this graphic to answer questions 13–14.

MAGNETIC FIELD OF TWO PAIRS OF BAR MAGNETS

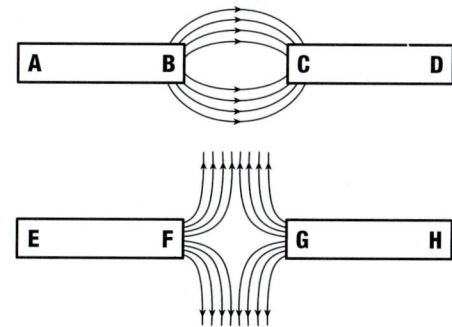

13. Suppose that A and E are the north poles of their magnets. What other points have a north polarity?
    - **A.** B and G
    - **B.** C and H
    - **C.** D and G
    - **D.** D and H

14. Which two magnets could combine their magnetic fields into one long magnet without being rotated? What would happen to their poles?

Test Tip

When using an illustration that has labels to answer a question, read the labels carefully, and then check that the answer you choose matches your interpretation of the labels.

Earth and Space Science

Chapter 19 The Solar System 650
Chapter 20 The Universe 690
Chapter 21 Planet Earth 726
Chapter 22 The Atmosphere 770
Chapter 23 Using Natural Resources 804

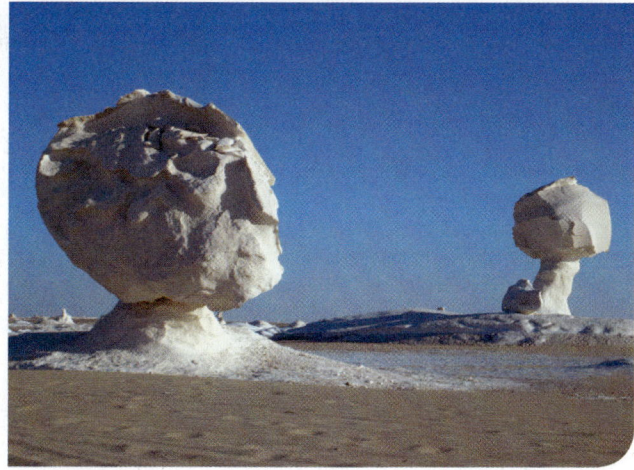

CHAPTER 19
The Solar System

Chapter Outline

1 Sun, Earth, and Moon
The View from Earth
A Family of Planets
The Moon

2 The Inner and Outer Planets
The Inner Planets
The Gas Giants
Beyond the Gas Giants

3 Formation of the Solar System
Early Astronomy
The Nebular Hypothesis
Rocks in Space
How the Moon Formed
Do Other Stars Have Planets?

TN Tennessee Course Level Expectations (Physical Science)

CLE.3202.TE.3 Explain the relationship between the properties of a material and the use of the material in the application of a technology; **CLE.3202.Inq.1** Recognize that science is a progressive endeavor that reevaluates and extends what is already accepted; **CLE.3202.Inq.2** Design and conduct scientific investigations to explore new phenomena, verify previous results, test how well a theory predicts, and compare opposing theories; **CLE.3202.Inq.3** Use appropriate tools and technology to collect precise and accurate data; **CLE.3202.Inq.4** Apply qualitative and quantitative measures to analyze data and draw conclusions that are free of bias; **CLE.3202.Inq.6** Communicate and defend scientific findings; **CLE.3202.Math.1** Understand the mathematical principles behind the science of physics; **CLE.3202.Math.2** Utilize appropriate mathematical equations and processes to solve basic physics problems; **CLE.3202.TE.4** Describe the dynamic interplay among science, technology, and engineering within living, earth-space, and physical systems

Why It Matters

The Mars Expedition Rovers *Spirit* and *Opportunity* (shown here) were meant to study Mars for about 90 days but sent back information for several years. Even the scientists who built the Rovers were surprised. In this chapter, you will learn more about our solar system and how scientists study it.

Inquiry Lab   20 min

Observing Stars

Go outside on a clear evening at dusk, and look up at the sky. Spend 20 min counting stars as they become visible.

Questions to Get You Started

1. How many stars did you count in 20 min?
2. Do you see any lights in the sky that might not be stars? What do you think they might be, and how would you find out what they are?

READING TOOLBOX

These reading tools can help you learn the material in this chapter. For more information on how to use these and other tools, see **Appendix A**.

Word Origins

Names of the Planets The ancient Romans named the five planets that they could see moving in the night sky after gods from Roman mythology: Mercury, Venus, Mars, Jupiter, and Saturn. When Uranus and Neptune were discovered, they were also named for Roman gods.

Your Turn Each planet was named for the god in mythology that has something in common with the planet. As you learn about the planets, complete the list of connections between the planets and the Roman gods for which they are named.

PLANET	CHARACTERISTIC OF PLANET	CHARACTERISTIC OF ROMAN GOD
Mercury	fastest-moving planet	fast messenger of the gods
Jupiter	largest planet	king of the Roman gods

Mnemonics

Order of the Planets A mnemonic is a sentence or phrase that you can create to help you remember specific information. For example, the order of the planets from the sun outward is Mercury, Venus, Earth, Mars, Jupiter, Saturn, Uranus, and Neptune. You can use a mnemonic to help you remember this order.

> **M**y **V**ery **E**mpathetic **M**other **J**ust **S**erved **U**s **N**achos.

Notice that the first letter of each word is the same as the first letter of the corresponding planet in the order.

Your Turn Practice saying this mnemonic to help you learn and remember the order of the planets. Make up a new mnemonic that you could use to remember the order of the planets.

Graphic Organizers

Chain-of-Events Chart Use a chain-of-events chart when you need to remember the steps of a process.

Your Turn As you read Section 3, complete the chain-of-events chart that outlines the formation of the solar system.

1. The first step of the process is written in the first box.
2. The next step of the process is written in the second box, and an arrow shows the order of the process.
3. Continue adding boxes and arrows until the process for the formation of the solar system is complete.

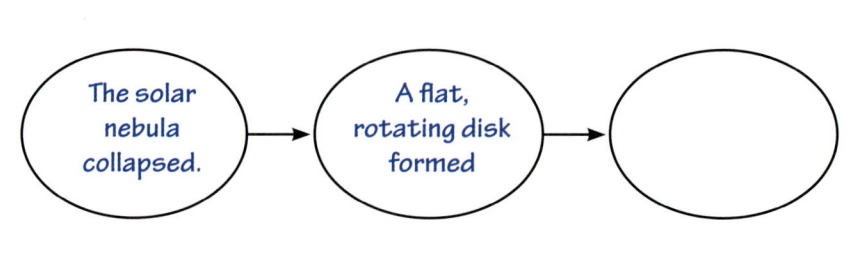

SECTION 1
Sun, Earth, and Moon

Key Ideas
- Why does the night sky look the way it does from Earth?
- What objects make up the solar system?
- How does the moon affect Earth?

Key Terms
- planet
- solar system
- satellite
- phase
- eclipse

Why It Matters
Studying the solar system and its various planets can help us understand our own planet better.

The sun, moon, and stars appear to rise and set each day because Earth spins on its axis. The stars that are visible at night change throughout the year as Earth orbits the sun. These two motions affect our view of the sky.

The View from Earth

If you go out and look at the sky tonight and then look at it again in six months, it will look different. In fact, you can see some star groups move across the sky in just a few hours! ❯ **The positions of objects in the sky change over time because Earth, and everything else in the universe, is constantly moving.** Earth's spinning on its axis and orbiting the sun create apparent movement in the sky. Many distant objects, such as stars, move slowly and appear to move together. Closer objects, such as planets and comets, move across this background of stars. A **planet** is a celestial body that orbits the sun, is round because of its own gravity, and has cleared the area around its orbital path.

The sun is the closest star to Earth.

It took thousands of years for people to realize that the sun is a star. The sun is the brightest object in the sky because it is so close to us. Our atmosphere scatters the sun's light and makes the daytime sky so bright that we cannot see the other stars. But the sun is an average star. It is not particularly hot or cool and is of average size. Its diameter is 1.4 million kilometers. As **Figure 1** shows, the sun's diameter is much larger than Earth's. The sun has a mass that is about 330,000 times the mass of Earth.

> **Tennessee Course Level Expectations (Physical Science)**
> CLE.3202.Inq.1; CLE.3202.Inq.2; CLE.3202.Inq.3; CLE.3202.TE.4

planet (PLAN it) a celestial body that orbits the sun, is round because of its own gravity, and has cleared the neighborhood around its orbital path

Figure 1 The sun looks small to us only because it is so far away. If it were next to Earth, the sun would look many times larger.

 Earth

Sun

Nature uses the sun to set daily cycles.

The sun is the major external source of heat and light for Earth. As Earth turns on its axis every 24 h, we see the sun rise and set. Many patterns of animal and human life, such as rising in the morning, eating meals at certain times, and sleeping at night, follow the sun's cycle.

As each year progresses, you can watch the growing seasons of plants change. Some plants, such as the tulips shown in **Figure 2,** are very sensitive to sunlight. They open during the day and close at night.

Energy from the sun is also a main cause of weather patterns and ocean currents on Earth.

Reading Check Name two ways in which the sun affects life on Earth. (See Appendix E for answers to Reading Checks.)

Planets and distant stars are visible in the night sky.

When we pick out the shapes of *constellations,* or groups of stars organized in recognizable patterns, we use some of the same patterns that ancient Greek scholars saw and named. These scholars also watched the five bright planets wander in regular paths among the stars. **Figure 3** shows Saturn wandering slowly through the constellation Leo. By watching the sky for many years, the ancient Greeks calculated that the stars were more distant than the planets were. More than a thousand years later, after the invention of the telescope, people found other objects in the night sky, including many faint stars; two more planets, Uranus and Neptune; and several other large celestial bodies, such as Ceres and Pluto.

Figure 2 These tulips open to the sun's rays during the day and close at night. **What are some other plants or animals that behave differently during the day and night?**

Figure 3 The planet Saturn moves against the background of stars in the constellation Leo, named for its lionlike shape.

A Family of Planets

A football game consists of a ball, players, referees, and coaches, which all interact according to a set of rules. The solar system also has its objects and its own set of rules. ❯ **The solar system is the sun and all of the objects that orbit it.** The sun is the most important part of our system and makes up nearly 99% of the total mass of the solar system. The eight planets and their moons make up most of the remaining 1%. The solar system also contains many other smaller objects, such as dwarf planets, asteroids, comets, dust, and gas.

solar system (SOH luhr SIS tuhm) the sun and all of the planets and other bodies that travel around it

Gravity holds the solar system together.

Every object in the solar system pulls on every other object. The force of gravity between two objects depends upon their masses and the distance between them. The greater the mass is, the larger the gravitational force an object exerts on another object. The closer two objects are to each other, the stronger the gravitational pull is between them. The sun exerts the largest force in the solar system because its mass is so large. The pull of the sun keeps Earth in its orbit, as shown in **Figure 4.** Imagine swinging a ball on a string. If you let go of the string, the ball will fly off in a straight line. Without the sun's pull, Earth and all the other planets would similarly shoot off into space. **Figure 5** shows the orbits of the planets in order of distance from the sun. Even at great distances, the sun keeps the planets in their orbits.

Gravity is also the force that keeps moons orbiting around planets. You experience gravity as the force that keeps you on Earth. Even though Jupiter is far more massive than Earth, you do not notice its pull on you because it is too far away.

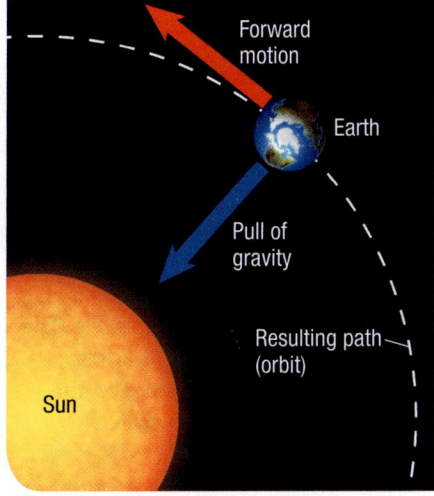

Figure 4 The pull of gravity causes Earth to fall toward the sun and changes what would be a straight line into a curve.

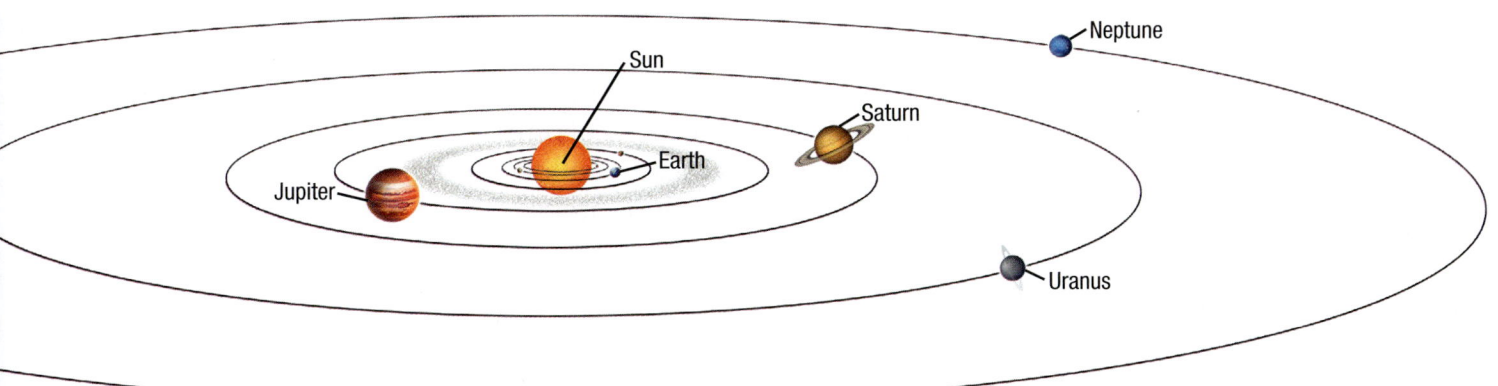

Figure 5 The sun's gravitational force holds the planets in almost circular orbits.

Section 1 Sun, Earth, and Moon

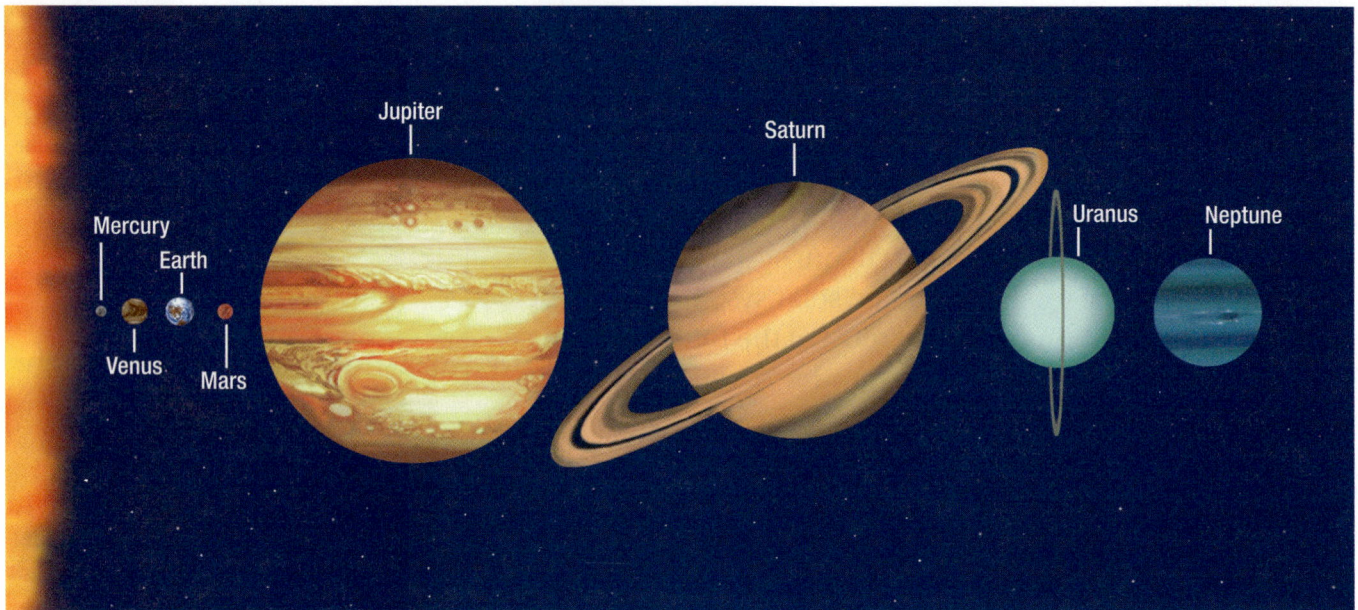

Figure 6 The planets in the solar system are shown in relative scale. The sun's diameter is almost 10 times Jupiter's. The distances between the planets are not shown to scale.

READING TOOLBOX

Word Origins
Mars was named for the Roman god of war. Its moons, Phobos and Deimos, were named for Mars's sons. Look up the names of moons of other planets, and see how they relate to the name of the planet they orbit.

Eight planets orbit the sun.

Planets can be seen because their surfaces or atmospheres reflect sunlight. A planet's distance from the sun determines how long it takes to orbit the sun. Mercury, the closest, takes only 88 days to orbit the sun. Earth takes one year, or 365.25 days. Neptune, the most distant planet, takes 165 years, or more than 60,225 days. The relative diameters of the planets are shown in **Figure 6.** The diameters of large planets, such as Jupiter and Saturn, are still only a fraction of the sun's diameter.

Satellites orbit objects that have a larger mass.

A **satellite** is an object in orbit around a body that has a larger mass. The moon is Earth's satellite because Earth has the larger mass. The four planets closest to the sun are small and rocky and have few or no satellites. The next four planets are large and gaseous and have many satellites.

All of the planets in our solar system except Mercury and Venus have moons. Currently, we know of more than 135 natural satellites, or moons, orbiting the planets in our solar system. In 1970, we knew of only 33. Space missions have discovered many small satellites, and more could be found in the future. The smallest satellites are less than 3 km in diameter. The largest moons in the solar system, including Jupiter's Ganymede and Saturn's Titan, are larger than the planet Mercury. All moons are held in their orbits by the gravitational forces of their planets. Like planets, satellites can be seen because of the sunlight they reflect.

Reading Check What force keeps a satellite in orbit around a planet?

656 Chapter 19 The Solar System

The Moon

The moon does not orbit the sun directly; it orbits Earth at a distance of about 384,000 km. The moon's surface is covered with craters, mostly caused by collisions with smaller bodies early in the history of the solar system. The *maria*, or large, dark patches on the moon, shown in **Figure 7,** are areas of lava that flowed out of the moon's interior, filled the impact craters, and cooled to solid rock. ❯ **Like the sun, the moon affects life on Earth through its movements and gravitational influence.**

The moon has phases because it revolves around Earth.

The moon appears to have different shapes throughout the month that are called **phases.** The relative positions of Earth, the moon, and the sun determine the phases of the moon, as shown in **Figure 8.** At any given time, the sun illuminates half the moon's surface, just as at any given time, it is day on one half of Earth and night on the other half. As the moon revolves around Earth, the illuminated portion of the moon that faces Earth changes. When the moon is full, the half that is lit is facing you. When the moon is new, the side that is dark is facing you, so you cannot see it. The time from one full moon to the next is 29.5 days, or one calendar month. In fact, many calendars have been based on the movement of the moon.

Figure 7 The moon has dark maria and light highlands and craters.

satellite (SAT'l iet) a natural or artificial body that revolves around a celestial body that is greater in mass

phase (FAYZ) the change in the illuminated area of one celestial body as seen from another celestial body; phases of the moon are caused by the positions of Earth, the sun, and the moon

Figure 8 Although the sun always lights half of the moon (red circle), the moon's appearance from Earth (boxes) changes over time.

Keyword: HK8SYSF8

www.scilinks.org
Topic: Moons of Other Planets
Code: HK80993

Section 1 Sun, Earth, and Moon **657**

QuickLab — Modeling Eclipses

 10 min

Procedure

1. Make two balls from **modeling clay,** one about 4 cm in diameter and one about 1 cm in diameter.
2. Using a **metric ruler,** position the balls about 15 cm apart on a **sheet of paper.**
3. Turn off nearby lights. Place a **penlight** about 15 cm in front of and almost level with the larger ball. Shine the light on the larger ball. Sketch your model, and note the effect of the beam of light.
4. Repeat step 3, but reverse the positions of the two balls. You may need to raise the small ball slightly so that its shadow is centered on the larger ball.

Analysis

1. Which planetary bodies do the larger clay ball, the small clay ball, and the penlight represent?
2. As viewed from Earth, what event did your model in step 3 represent? What event did step 4 represent?

eclipse (i KLIPS) an event in which the shadow of one celestial body falls on another

Figure 9 Depending on the alignment of Earth, the sun, and the moon, an eclipse may be called *solar* or *lunar*. The distance between Earth and the moon is not shown to scale.

Eclipses are caused by bodies casting shadows.

When Earth, the sun, and the moon are in a straight line, observers on Earth may witness an event known as an **eclipse.** An eclipse occurs when one object moves into the shadow cast by another object.

During a new moon, the moon may cast a shadow onto Earth. Observers within that small shadow on Earth see the sky turn dark as the moon blocks out the sun. This event is called a *solar eclipse*. When the moon is full, it may pass into the shadow of Earth. All the observers on the nightside of Earth can see the full moon darken as the moon passes through Earth's shadow. This event is called a *lunar eclipse*. Both of these eclipses are shown in **Figure 9.**

Reading Check What causes a lunar eclipse?

658 Chapter 19 The Solar System

Why It Matters

A Return to the Moon

NASA's Apollo program first landed a man on the moon in 1969, but the program was shut down in 1972. No human has been back to the moon since. However, after nearly 40 years, NASA has turned its attention to the idea of another moon landing. New spacecraft are currently being planned with the goal of landing humans on the moon again by 2020.

SCIENCE & SOCIETY

① NASA's current plan is to build a new Crew Exploration Vehicle (CEV) that will land our astronauts safely on the moon.

② Once on the moon, astronauts will look for resources and building sites for more permanent moon bases. The landing vehicle itself will carry the living quarters.

③ Returning to the moon will make it easier to get to Mars. We can test life-support technologies and launch spacecraft from the moon.

www.scilinks.org
Topic: History of NASA
Code: **HK80745**

YOUR TURN

UNDERSTANDING CONCEPTS
1. Why might we want to use the moon as a launch pad for landing humans on Mars?

CRITICAL THINKING
2. What are some possible benefits of humans returning to the moon?

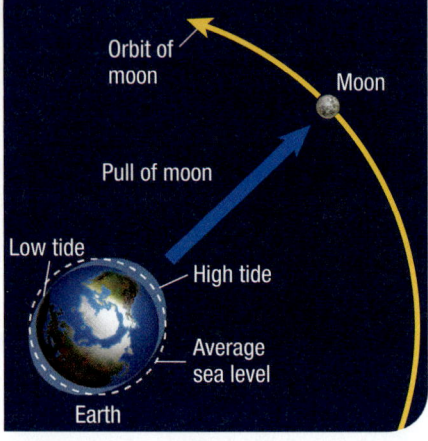

Figure 10 The gravitational pull of the moon is the main cause of tides on Earth.

The moon affects Earth's tides.

Most coastal areas on Earth, such as the one shown in **Figure 10,** have two high tides and two low tides each day. Even though tides are affected by Earth's landscape, tides are mainly a result of the gravitational influence of the moon. The moon's gravitational pull is strongest on the side of Earth nearest the moon. On this side, the ocean is pulled toward the moon, so a slight bulge is created. The solid Earth also moves slightly under the moon's gravity, but the movement of water is more noticeable because water is a liquid.

Because Earth rotates, one area on Earth will have two maximum, or high, tides and two minimum, or low, tides in a period of 24 h 50 min. Because the moon is also orbiting Earth, the times of these tides change throughout the month.

The sun also has an effect on tides, although it is minor. When the sun is on the same side of Earth as the moon, the gravitational forces are at their strongest and tides are at their highest for the month.

Section 1 Review

KEY IDEAS

1. **Explain** why objects in the sky appear to move.
2. **Describe** the star that is closest to Earth.
3. **Describe** the basic structure of the solar system.
4. **Explain** how gravity keeps planets in orbit around the sun.
5. **Predict** which satellite experiences the larger gravitational force if two satellites have the same mass but one is twice as far away from the planet.
6. **Describe** two features of the moon, and explain how they formed.
7. **Explain** what happens during a lunar eclipse and what phase the moon is in during a lunar eclipse.
8. **State** the moon's role in the formation of tides.

CRITICAL THINKING

9. **Making Inferences** How might the patterns of plants and animals change if the sun were not visible to them?
10. **Analyzing Conclusions** The Greeks thought that there were five planets visible with the unaided eye: Mercury, Venus, Mars, Jupiter, and Saturn. What other planet is visible with the unaided eye?
11. **Applying Concepts** At what phase of the moon will tides be the highest? Explain.

SECTION 2
The Inner and Outer Planets

Key Ideas
- How are the inner planets similar to one another?
- What are gas giants?
- What type of bodies lie beyond the gas giants?

Key Terms
terrestrial planet
hydrosphere
asteroid
dwarf planet
gas giant

Why It Matters
Since 1959, scientists from many countries have launched probes to study the planets and other objects in our solar system.

The solar system has inner planets close to the sun and more-distant outer planets. It also has several regions full of debris in the form of asteroids and other small bodies. The inner planets receive more of the sun's energy and have higher temperatures than the outer planets do.

> Tennessee Course Level Expectations (Physical Science)
> CLE.3202.Inq.1; CLE.3202.Inq.2; CLE.3202.Inq.3; CLE.3202.Math.1; CLE.3202.Math.2; CLE.3202.TE.4

The Inner Planets

The orbits of the **terrestrial planets**—Mercury, Venus, Earth, and Mars—are shown in **Figure 1**. **These terrestrial planets are relatively small and have solid, rocky surfaces.** Using telescopes, satellites, and surface probes, scientists can study the geologic features of these planets.

The inner planets have similar compositions and share many similar surface features. The inner planets have metallic cores and rocky surfaces with some of the same terrain features as Earth, including mountains, canyons, and craters.

terrestrial planet (tuh RES tree uhl PLAN it) one of the highly dense planets nearest to the sun; Mercury, Venus, Earth, and Mars

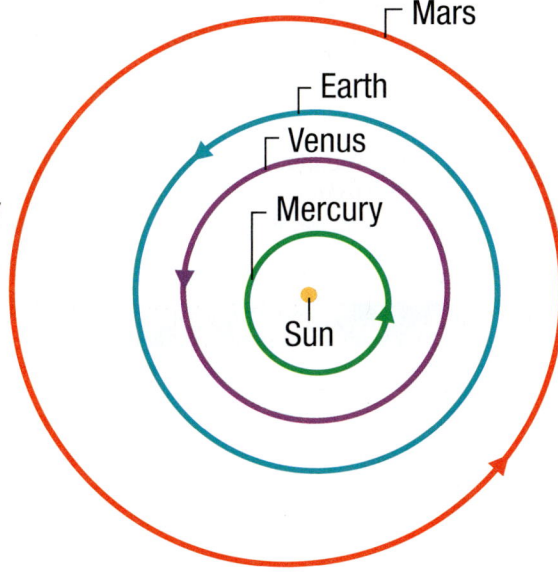

Figure 1 Notice that gravity keeps the orbits of the four terrestrial planets in nearly circular paths around the sun.

661

Mercury has extreme temperatures.

Until we sent space probes, such as *Mariner 10*, to investigate Mercury, we did not know much about it. The photograph in **Figure 2** shows that Mercury, much like Earth's moon, is covered with craters. Because Mercury has such a small orbit around the sun, it is never very far from the sun.

Distances in the solar system are often measured in terms of the distance from Earth to the sun, which is one astronomical unit (AU), or 150 million kilometers. Mercury is 0.4 AU from the sun. Mercury's surface temperature can reach more than 720 K. The temperature on Mercury's nightside drops to 103 K, which is far below the freezing point of water. A day on Mercury, or the time it takes to rotate once on its axis, lasts nearly 59 Earth days. But a year on Mercury, the time it takes to orbit the sun, is only 88 Earth days long, or 0.24 Earth years. Mercury has almost no atmosphere and no water.

Thick clouds on Venus cause a greenhouse effect.

Venus, shown in **Figure 3,** is 0.7 AU from the sun. It can be seen near sunrise or sunset and is called the *morning* or *evening star*. The surface of Venus has numerous mountains and plains. Venus spins very slowly in a direction opposite that of most other planets and the sun. One day on Venus is 243 Earth days long, and a year on Venus is 0.6 Earth years long, or 225 Earth days. So, Venus's day is longer than its year!

Venus does not provide an environment that can support life as we know it. Venus is hot, and its atmosphere contains large amounts of sulfuric acid. In addition, the atmospheric pressure at the surface is more than 90 times the pressure on Earth. Venus's thick atmosphere, made up mostly of carbon dioxide, absorbs the radiation emitted by the sun-warmed planet. The result is a "runaway" greenhouse effect that raises atmosphere temperatures and keeps the surface temperature greater than 700 K. A greenhouse effect occurs when infrared radiation is absorbed and heat builds up.

Mercury	
Diameter	38% of Earth's
Density	98% of Earth's
Surface gravity	38% of Earth's

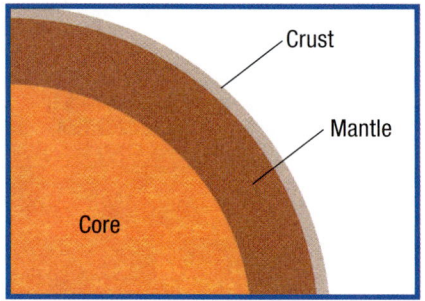

Figure 2 Mercury, the planet closest to the sun, is pocked with craters.

Figure 3 The *Magellan* spacecraft used radar to map the surface below Venus's thick clouds.

Venus	
Diameter	95% of Earth's
Density	89% of Earth's
Surface gravity	91% of Earth's

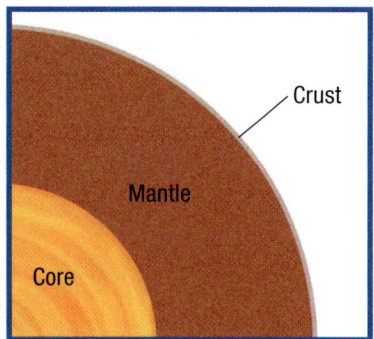

Earth has ideal conditions for living creatures.

Earth, our home, is the third planet from the sun. We measure other planets in the solar system in relation to Earth. Earth rotates on its axis in 1 Earth day. It revolves around the sun at a distance of 1 AU in 1 Earth year. It has a mass of 1 Earth mass.

Earth is the only planet we know that sustains life. It is also the only planet that has large amounts of liquid water on its surface. All the water on Earth's surface, both liquid and frozen, is called the **hydrosphere.** Because water takes a relatively long time to heat or cool, the hydrosphere helps moderate the temperature of Earth.

> **Reading Check** Name two ways that Earth is different from the other planets.

Academic Vocabulary
sustain (suh STAYN) to support

hydrosphere (HIE droh SFIR) the portion of Earth that is water

The atmosphere protects Earth from radiation.

Earth, shown in **Figure 4,** has an atmosphere composed of 78% nitrogen, 21% oxygen, and 1% argon, carbon dioxide, and other gases. The atmosphere helps moderate temperatures between day and night. Because of the greenhouse effect, the atmosphere absorbs energy radiated by the sun, so Earth's surface does not freeze at night.

Earth's atmosphere protects us from some harmful ultraviolet radiation and high-energy particles from the sun. The radiation and particles are blocked in our upper atmosphere before they can cause damage to life on Earth. The atmosphere also protects us from space debris, formed of leftover portions of artificial satellites or small rocks from space. As they speed through the atmosphere toward Earth's surface, these objects heat up and vaporize or shatter. Only very large objects can survive the trip through Earth's atmosphere.

Earth's original atmosphere changed over time as gases were released from microbes and, later, by plants during photosynthesis. Earth's early atmosphere contained more carbon dioxide than it does now, as well as other gases such as methane and ammonia.

Figure 4 An image of Earth taken from space shows clouds, oceans, and land.

Earth	
Diameter	12,756 km
Density	5.515 g/cm^3
Surface gravity	9.8 m/s^2

Section 2 The Inner and Outer Planets

Figure 5 This artist's rendition shows a Mars Exploration Rover. Two of these robots, named *Spirit* and *Opportunity*, landed on Mars in January 2004.

Many missions have explored the planet Mars.

Although humans have yet to visit Mars, many probes have landed on its surface. *Viking 1* and *Viking 2* each sent a lander to the surface in 1976. In 2004, two Mars Exploration Rovers, similar to the one shown in **Figure 5,** landed on Mars.

White regions at the poles of Mars can be seen in **Figure 6.** These are polar icecaps made of frozen carbon dioxide and may also contain small amounts of frozen water. Features on other parts of the planet suggest that water once flowed across the surface as a liquid. Mars has a very thin atmosphere, composed mostly of carbon dioxide. Mars is 1.5 AU from the sun and has two small satellites, Phobos and Deimos. The mass of Mars is 11% of Earth's mass. Mars orbits the sun in 1.9 Earth years, and its day is 24.7 Earth hours. Mars is very cold; its surface temperature ranges from 144 K to 300 K.

Mars has many extreme landforms.

Orbiting space missions have detected some unique features on Mars. The Martian volcano Olympus Mons is the largest mountain in the solar system. It is almost 3 times the height of Mount Everest. Because Mars has no plate tectonics, the volcanic lava flows remain in the same location, and volcanoes can grow very large.

Like Earth's moon, Mars has many impact craters. Its thin atmosphere does not burn up objects from space, so they often impact the surface. Also, the lack of liquid water slows down the weathering of these craters.

The surface of Mars is red from iron oxide in its soil. Mars has frequent dust storms that are stronger than those in the Sahara. These dust storms form large, red dunes.

Reading Check What compound causes the surface of Mars to appear red?

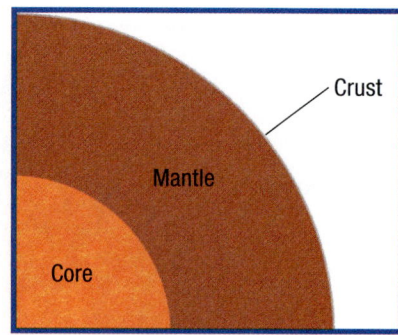

Figure 6 The *Hubble Space Telescope* captured this striking image of Mars.

Mars	
Diameter	53% of Earth's
Density	71% of Earth's
Surface gravity	38% of Earth's

Why It Matters
Exploring Planets

Because we cannot send people to other planets yet, scientists use robots instead. These robots are explorers, geologists, journalists, and ambassadors that venture into the unknown. They record what they find so that we can learn from it. Scientists have been launching spacecraft for only about 50 years, but we have already learned a lot of new information from the data they have collected and sent back to Earth.

HISTORY IN SCIENCE

Phoenix The Mars lander *Phoenix* was designed to drill into the Martian soil and search for water.
2007

Selected planetary missions

1959

Luna The Russian probe *Luna 2* was the first probe to reach the lunar surface, making the trip from Earth in about 33.5 hours.

1972

Pioneer *Pioneer 10* explored Jupiter and became the first human-made craft to venture into the Kuiper-Belt region.

1977

Voyager The probe *Voyager 2* explored Jupiter, Saturn, Uranus, and Neptune, along with many of their moons.

1997

Cassini-Huygens This probe team was designed to study Saturn. The *Huygens* probe landed on the moon Titan. *Cassini* continued to orbit Saturn and its moons.

SCLINKS
www.scilinks.org
Topic: Space Probes
Code: HK81432

YOUR TURN
CRITICAL THINKING
1. Why might scientists want to send robotic probes instead of humans to planets such as Venus and Saturn?

Figure 7 At 58 km long, Ida is large enough to have captured its own small satellite, named *Dactyl*.

Academic Vocabulary

attribute (uh TRIB yoot) to indicate as the cause of

asteroid (AS tuhr OYD) a small, rocky object that orbits the sun; most asteroids are located in a band between the orbits of Mars and Jupiter

dwarf planet (DWAWRF PLAN it) a celestial body that orbits the sun, is round because of its own gravity, but has not cleared its orbital path

gas giant (GAS JIE uhnt) a planet that has a deep, massive atmosphere, such as Jupiter, Saturn, Uranus, or Neptune

An asteroid belt lies beyond the orbit of Mars.

Between Mars and Jupiter lie hundreds of smaller, rocky objects that range in diameter from 3 km to 700 km. These objects are called **asteroids,** or small solar system bodies. The asteroid Ida, photographed in 1993, is shown in **Figure 7.** Most asteroids remain in orbit between Mars and Jupiter, but some wander away from this region and may cross Earth's orbit. The odds of a large asteroid hitting Earth are very small, but many research programs are tracking asteroids. Mass extinctions on Earth have been attributed to past collisions with an asteroid.

The largest celestial body in the asteroid belt is Ceres, which has a diameter of 940 km. Initially, many scientists thought that Ceres was a planet because of its size and location. It was later classified as an asteroid. In addition to being an asteroid, Ceres is also considered to be a **dwarf planet,** a celestial body that orbits the sun, is round because of its own gravity, but has not cleared its orbital path.

The Gas Giants

The orbits of the planets most distant from the sun—Jupiter, Saturn, Uranus, and Neptune—are shown in **Figure 8.** ❯ **The outer planets are much larger than the inner planets and have thick, gaseous atmospheres, many satellites, and rings.** These large planets are called the **gas giants.**

Because the gas giants have no solid surface, a spacecraft cannot land on them. However, the Pioneer missions, launched in 1972 and 1973; the *Voyager 1* and *Voyager 2* missions, launched in 1977; and the *Galileo* mission, launched in 1989, investigated the large outer planets. The *Cassini-Huygens* probe reached Saturn in 2004.

Reading Check Name three ways in which the gas giants differ from the inner planets.

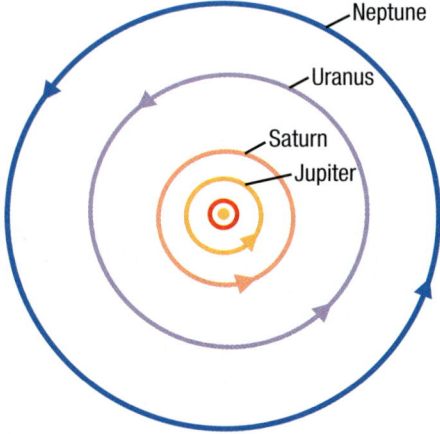

Figure 8 Jupiter, Saturn, Uranus, and Neptune—the gas giants—are the most distant planets known in the solar system.

Figure 9 The storm known as the *Great Red Spot* can be seen in the lower portion of this photograph of Jupiter.

Jupiter	
Diameter	11 times Earth's
Density	24% of Earth's
Surface gravity	2.54 times Earth's

All the gas giants have rings and satellites.

Although the vast rings of Saturn were recognized in 1659, it took modern technology to discover the thin, faint rings around the other gas giants. Uranus's rings were not discovered until 1977. Most of the known satellites in the solar system were discovered through space missions. Jupiter has more than 60, Saturn has more than 40, Uranus has at least 27, and Neptune has at least 13. Most are cratered, and some have thin atmospheres.

Jupiter is the largest planet in the solar system.

Jupiter, shown in **Figure 9,** is the first planet beyond the asteroid belt and the largest planet that orbits the sun. Jupiter is 1,300 times the size of Earth. If it were 80 times as massive as it is, it could have become a star. At a distance of 5 AU, Jupiter takes about 12 Earth years to orbit the sun; however, a day on Jupiter is less than 10 Earth hours long. Images of Jupiter's atmosphere show swirling clouds of hydrogen, helium, methane, and ammonia. Complex features in Jupiter's atmosphere appear to be jet streams and enormous storms. One of these storms, the Great Red Spot, is a huge hurricane that measures more than twice the diameter of Earth. The Great Red Spot has existed for hundreds of years.

In 1610, Galileo discovered Jupiter's four largest satellites, which he named Ganymede, Callisto, Io, and Europa. Using binoculars or a small telescope, you can see them near Jupiter. Io has a thin atmosphere and active volcanoes. Europa may have liquid water under its icy surface.

READING TOOLBOX

Mnemonic
Create a mnemonic to remember the moons of Jupiter that Galileo discovered. They are listed in the text from largest to smallest.

www.scilinks.org
Topic: Planets
Code: HK81152

QuickLab 20 min

Planetary Distances

1. Using a large open space, such as a football field, have one classmate stand at one end of the space. This person represents the sun.
2. Have another person, representing Earth, stand 1 m away from the first person.
3. Other classmates should calculate where they would stand if they were the other planets.
4. Research other bodies in the solar system, such as Kuiper Belt objects. Have classmates stand where these objects would be. What is the farthest distance that two people stood from each other? What objects in the solar system did they represent?

Saturn has the most extensive ring system.

Saturn is 95 times the mass of Earth and takes more than 29 years to orbit the sun. However, despite its large size, a day on Saturn is only 10.7 h long. Like Jupiter, it is a gas giant and rotates fastest at the equator and slower near the poles. In addition to its many satellites, Saturn has a spectacular system of rings, as shown in **Figure 10**.

These rings are narrow bands of tiny particles of dust, rock, and ice. The particles range in size from a few millimeters to several meters. Most are probably the size of a large snowball on Earth. Competing gravitational forces from Saturn and its many satellites hold the particles in place around the planet. The rings are rather thin in comparison to their diameter. Many are only 10 or 20 m thick and stretch around the entire planet. Scientists are not sure exactly how the rings formed. Some think that they came from a smashed satellite. Others think that the rings formed from leftover material when Saturn and its satellites formed long ago.

Saturn may still be forming.

Saturn radiates 3 times as much energy as it receives from the sun. Scientists think that helium in Saturn's outer layers is condensing and falling inward. As the helium nears the central core, the gas heats up. Think about pumping air into a bicycle tire. As you pump, the air inside the tire compresses, which causes the tire to heat up. Eventually, for both the tire and Saturn, the extra energy is radiated away. When Saturn uses up its atmospheric helium, this process will stop and Saturn will reach a state of equilibrium. Until then, Saturn is considered to still be forming.

Figure 10 You can see the shadow of the rings on Saturn's surface if you look closely.

Saturn	
Diameter	9.4 times Earth's
Density	13% of Earth's
Surface gravity	1.07 times Earth's

Uranus and Neptune are blue gas giants.

Beyond Saturn lie the planets Uranus and Neptune, which are shown in **Figure 11** and **Figure 12**, respectively. These two gas giants are similar to each other in size and color. Although they are smaller than Saturn and Jupiter, they are still large enough to hold thick, gaseous atmospheres composed of hydrogen, helium, and methane. The methane gives both planets a bluish color.

William Herschel discovered Uranus in 1781. He wanted to name it after King George III, but another astronomer suggested that it be given a name from mythology, as had the other planets. Uranus is about 14 Earth masses, and it takes approximately 84 years to orbit the sun at its distance of 19 AU.

After Uranus was discovered, astronomers used what they knew about gravity to guide their search for other planets. Because every mass attracts every other mass, changes in the expected orbit of Uranus could be used to predict the existence and position of other planets. Because of these changes in Uranus's orbit, Neptune was discovered in 1846 by Johann Galle. It is 17 Earth masses and takes approximately 165 years to orbit the sun at a distance of 30 AU.

The gas in the upper atmospheres of Uranus and Neptune is very cold, about 58 K. A day on Uranus is about 17.25 h, but its pole is tilted on its side at a 98° angle. Because of this tilt, Uranus has the most extreme seasons in the solar system. The few clouds in the atmosphere of Uranus show wind speeds of 200 to 700 km/h. A day on Neptune is 16 h. Neptune also has storm systems similar to Jupiter's. Winds on Neptune may reach speeds of 1,100 km/h.

Reading Check How did astronomers predict the existence of the planet Neptune before discovering it?

Uranus	
Diameter	4 times Earth's
Density	24% of Earth's
Surface gravity	91% of Earth's

Figure 11 Methane in the atmosphere of Uranus gives the planet a blue color.

Figure 12 Neptune is similar in composition and appearance to Uranus.

Neptune	
Diameter	3.9 times Earth's
Density	32% of Earth's
Surface gravity	1.2 times Earth's

Beyond the Gas Giants

▶ **Beyond the gas giants are numerous small bodies composed of ice and rock.** While many of these bodies are relatively small, some are rather large. One of these larger bodies, Pluto, was even considered to be a planet until 2006.

Not all large objects in the solar system are planets.

Until 2006, the word *planet* never had a clear scientific definition. But as technology allowed new bodies beyond Neptune to be discovered, astronomers knew that a clear definition of *planet* was needed. The International Astronomical Union (IAU) met in 2006 and voted on a definition for *planet*. Because Pluto has not cleared the area around its orbital path of debris, it does not meet the full requirements of the definition. It was reclassified as a *dwarf planet*.

Pluto, shown in **Figure 13** with its satellites, has only a thin, gaseous atmosphere and a solid, icy surface. It orbits the sun in a long ellipse. It is half as large as Mercury, and its mass is only 0.002 Earth's mass. Pluto's average distance from the sun is almost 40 AU. It takes 248 Earth years to complete one orbit.

There are many objects beyond Neptune.

Beyond Neptune lies the Kuiper Belt (KIE puhr BELT). This region is populated by many small bodies made of ice and rock, including Pluto. Scientists think that these bodies are the remnants of the material that formed the early solar system. In recent years, astronomers have found several large bodies in this region. One of these, named Eris, is larger than Pluto and is also considered a dwarf planet. It orbits the sun at distances reaching more than 90 AU. Astronomers are actively exploring this region of space.

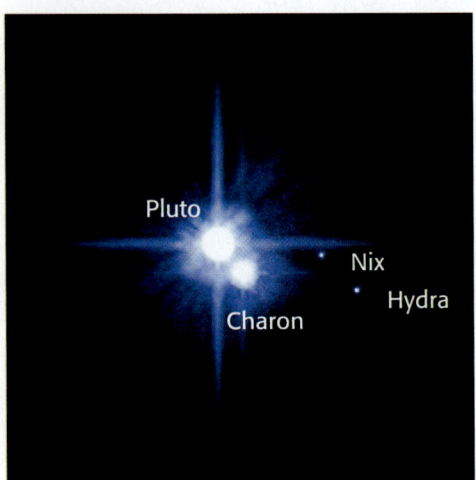

Figure 13 Pluto's main satellite, Charon, has a diameter almost half Pluto's diameter. Pluto was discovered in 1930, and Charon was discovered in 1978. Two satellites, Hydra and Nix, were discovered in 2005.

Section 2 Review

KEY IDEAS

1. **List** three ways in which the four terrestrial planets are similar to one another.
2. **Identify** the only terrestrial planet that supports life.
3. **Explain** why the surface of Venus is so hot.
4. **Describe** the features that distinguish a gas giant from a terrestrial planet.
5. **Explain** why Saturn is thought to still be forming.
6. **Describe** the types of objects that are found in the Kuiper Belt.

CRITICAL THINKING

7. **Applying Concepts** Why are space missions and robotic probes necessary for scientists to learn about other planets?
8. **Making Inferences** Why might the gas giants have so many more moons than the terrestrial planets do?
9. **Evaluating Ideas** Why might it have been important for scientists to develop a clear definition for the word *planet*?

SECTION 3
Formation of the Solar System

Key Ideas
> How did early astronomers understand and describe the solar system?
> Why is the solar system organized like it is?
> What else is in the solar system besides planets?
> How did Earth's moon form?
> How do astronomers find planets around other stars?

Key Terms
nebular hypothesis
nebula
comet
exoplanet

Why It Matters
By understanding how our own solar system formed, astronomers will know what to look for around other stars when they look for new planets.

The oldest record of human interest in astronomy was found in Nabta, Egypt. Scientists and historians think that a group of stones were specially arranged 6,000 to 7,000 years ago to line up with the sun on the summer solstice.

Tennessee Course Level Expectations (Physical Science)
CLE.3202.Inq.1; CLE.3202.Inq.2;
CLE.3202.Inq.3; CLE.3202.Inq.4;
CLE.3202.Inq.6; CLE.3202.Math.1;
CLE.3202.Math.2; CLE.3202.TE.3

Early Astronomy

Many ancient peoples watched for changes in the sky. Stonehenge, shown in **Figure 1,** was probably used for keeping time. Its stones are aligned with the seasonal solstices.

Ancient peoples used myths to explain star movements that they did not understand. > **Eventually, mathematical tools began to be used to make more accurate models of observed astronomical objects.** Ancient questions about how the universe worked and how it was organized helped develop science and the scientific method.

Figure 1 Stonehenge, located in England, is one of the world's oldest observatories.

QuickLab

Estimating 4.6 Billion

1. Find a **small box,** and measure its length, width, and height
2. To find the volume of the box, multiply the height by the width by the length.
3. Fill the box halfway with **popcorn kernels.**
4. Count the number of kernels in the box, and multiply that number by 2.
5. Divide 4,600,000,000 by the total number from step 4.
6. How big would your box need to be to hold 4.6 billion popcorn kernels?
7. If you have time, estimate the weight of 4.6 billion kernels.

Figure 2 Before scientists were able to prove that Earth revolved around the sun, most people believed that Earth was in the center of the universe.

Medieval art of the solar system

The first model put Earth at the center.

Like many people who came before them, the ancient Greeks observed the sky to keep track of time. But they took a new approach in trying to understand Earth's place in the universe. They used logic and mathematics, especially geometry. The Greek philosopher Aristotle explained the phases of the moon and eclipses by using a model of the solar system with Earth at the center. His *geocentric,* or "Earth-centered," model is shown in **Figure 2.**

This model was expanded by Ptolemy in 140 CE. Ptolemy thought that the sun, moon, and planets orbited Earth in perfect circles. His theory described what we see in day-to-day life, including motions of the sun and planets. Because it predicted many astronomical events well, Ptolemy's model was used for more than a thousand years.

Copernicus's model put the sun at the center.

In 1543, Nicolaus Copernicus proposed a *heliocentric,* or "sun-centered," model. He realized that many adjustments used to make Ptolemy's model work would not be needed in a model in which the sun was at the center. In this new model, Earth and the other planets orbit the sun in perfect circles. Although Copernicus's model was not perfect, it explained the motion of the planets more simply than Ptolemy's model did. In 1605, Johannes Kepler further improved the model by proposing that the orbits around the sun are ellipses, or ovals, rather than circles.

Reading Check Name the main way in which the heliocentric model differs from the geocentric model?

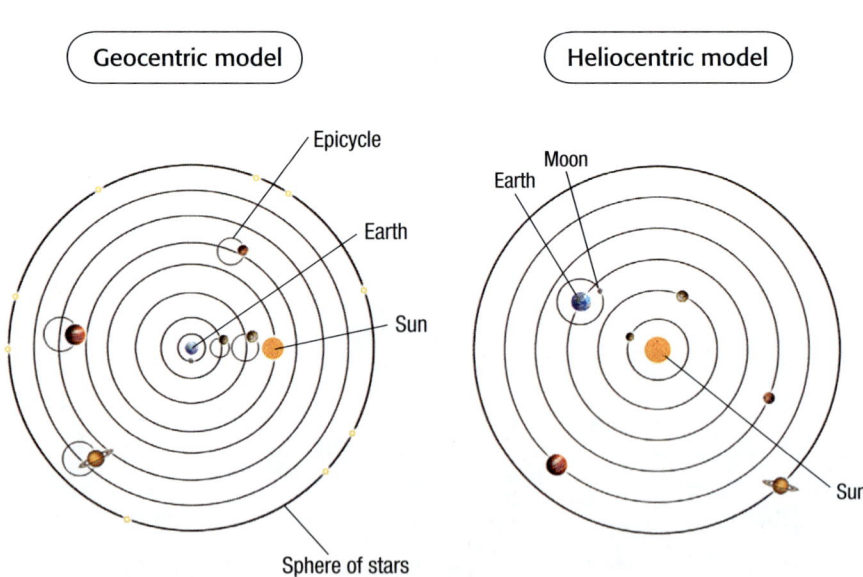

Geocentric model

Heliocentric model

Newton explained it all.

No one could explain why planets orbited the sun in elliptical orbits until 1687. Isaac Newton was the first to explain that gravity keeps the planets in orbit around the sun and satellites in orbit around planets. His theory states that every object in the universe exerts a gravitational force on every other object. Newton was the first to propose that everything in the universe follows the same rules and acts in a predictable way. All of classical physics, including much of astronomy, is built on this assumption.

The Nebular Hypothesis

From their dating of rocks, scientists estimate that the solar system is approximately 4.6 billion years old. Scientists trying to build a good model to explain how the solar system formed started by asking questions: Why are the planets almost in the same plane? Why are their orbits nearly circular? A good model would also have to explain the presence and behavior of objects such as satellites, comets, and asteroids.

Scientists developed the **nebular hypothesis,** which is shown in **Figure 3** on the next page, to explain how our solar system formed. A **nebula** is a large cloud of dust and gas in space. ▶ **This hypothesis explains why objects that form from a disk will lie in the same plane, have almost circular orbits, and orbit in the same direction.**

Planets formed by the accretion of matter in the disk.

The nebular hypothesis states that planets formed mostly through the process by which small particles collide and stick together, called *accretion.* The nebular hypothesis also explains why the terrestrial planets are different in composition from the gas giants. Warm temperatures near the sun prevented light gases from remaining in the atmospheres of the terrestrial planets. Colder gas and dust in the outer part of the disk became the gas giants. These planets were large enough and cold enough to hold light nebular gases, such as hydrogen, in their atmospheres.

The nebular hypothesis explains smaller rocks in space.

Satellites may have formed around gas giants through the process of accretion. Another possibility is that particles that might have formed planets were captured by the gravitational pull of the gas giants. Some smaller satellites may have broken off from larger ones. Most satellites orbit planets in the same direction that the planets orbit the sun.

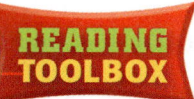

Chain-of-Events Chart
Create a chain-of-events chart to describe the formation of the solar system and the concept of the nebular model.

Academic Vocabulary
approximate (uh PRAHK suh mit) almost; about

nebular hypothesis (NEB yu luhr hie PAHTH uh sis) a model for the formation of the solar system in which the sun and planets condense from a cloud (or nebula) of gas and dust

nebula (NEB yu luh) a large cloud of dust and gas in interstellar space; a region in space where stars are born

Figure 3 The Nebular Hypothesis

1 According to the nebular hypothesis, the sun, like every star, formed from a cloud of gas and dust that collapsed because of gravity. In our solar system, this process began almost 5 billion years ago.

2 As the cloud collapsed, it formed into a rotating disk. In the center, where the material became denser and hotter, a star began to form. As the cloud continued to collapse, it spun faster and faster.

3 The spinning motion of the disk caused it to flatten. Planetesimals, or particles that become planets, began to form in the disk. Their formation caused more changes in the disk.

4 As the planetesimals grew, their gravitational pull increased. The largest planetesimals began to collect more of the gas and dust of the nebula.

5 Small planetesimals collided with larger ones, and the planets began to grow larger and more stable. The warmer, inner planets were rocky, and the colder, outer planets accumulated lightweight gases in their atmospheres.

6 Because each planet swept up the material in its region, the planetary orbits are separate from each other. Asteroids and other small rocks are most likely leftover debris from solar system formation.

Rocks in Space

▸ **There are many types of small bodies in our solar system, including satellites, comets, asteroids, and meteoroids.** Satellites orbit planets, and **comets** are probably composed of material left over from the formation of the solar system. Most asteroids in our solar system can be found between Mars and Jupiter. Meteoroids are small pieces of rock that enter Earth's atmosphere. Most meteoroids that strike Earth burn up in the atmosphere, and we see them as meteors streaking through the night sky. If a meteoroid does not completely burn up in the atmosphere and hits the ground, it is called *a meteorite*.

Comets may give clues to the origin of the solar system.

By studying comets, scientists have gained important information about the material that made the solar system. Comets are composed of dust and of ice made from methane, ammonia, carbon dioxide, and water. In 1994, pieces of the comet Shoemaker-Levy 9 collided with Jupiter, as shown in **Figure 4.** Analysis of the impacts revealed that the comet also contained silicon, magnesium, and iron. Because of their composition, comets are sometimes called *dirty snowballs*.

Figure 4 The many pieces of the comet Shoemaker-Levy 9 hit Jupiter.

comet (KAHM it) a small body of ice, rock, and cosmic dust that follows an elliptical orbit and that gives off gas and dust in the form of a tail as it passes close to the sun

Comets have long tails and icy centers.

When a comet passes near the sun, the comet gives off gases in the form of a long tail. Some comets, such as the one shown in **Figure 5,** have two tails—an ion tail made of charged particles that is blown by the solar wind and a dust tail that follows the comet's orbit.

A comet's orbit is usually very long. When its tail eventually disappears, a comet becomes more difficult to see. It will brighten only when it passes by the sun again.

Reading Check Why is it easier to see a comet when it is near the sun?

Figure 5 In this photograph, you can see the two tails of the comet Hale-Bopp. The blue streak is the ion tail, and the white streak is the dust tail.

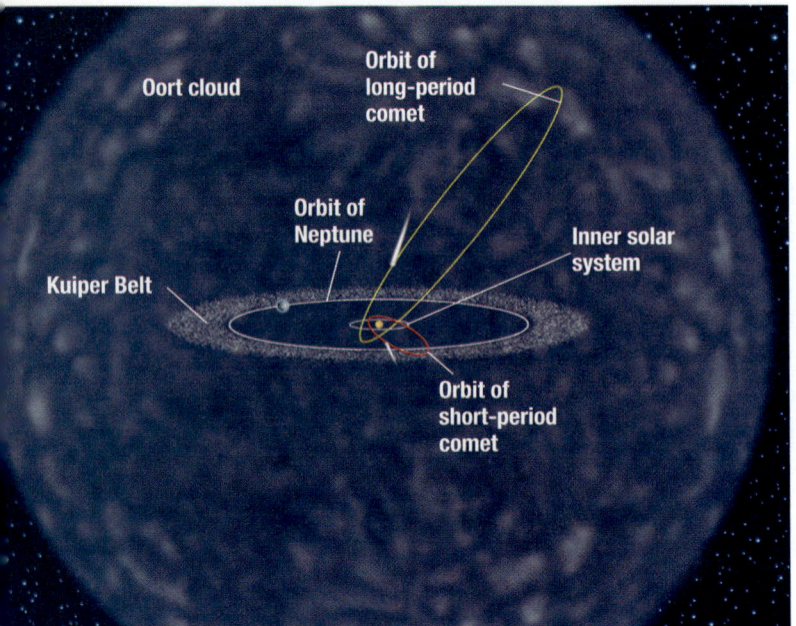

Figure 6 Comets come from the Oort cloud, a spherical region in the outer solar system beyond the Kuiper Belt, a disk-shaped region beyond the orbit of Neptune.

Where do comets come from?

During the formation of our solar system, some small planetesimals did not combine with other planetesimals. These leftovers strayed far from the sun and developed very long orbital periods. These far-flung pieces make up the Oort cloud of comets, shown in **Figure 6.** The Oort cloud may be up to 100,000 AU wide and extend in all directions. Planetesimals that remained in the nebular disk formed the Kuiper Belt beyond the orbit of Neptune. Most of these small bodies are rocky and covered by ice. Most comets come from this region of the solar system.

Halley's comet is one of the most famous comets. It travels in a highly elliptical orbit that takes it out into the Kuiper Belt. It appears in Earth's sky once every 76 years. In contrast to the other bodies in the solar system, Halley's comet orbits backward. Its orbit was probably greatly altered by a planet's gravity.

✓ **Reading Check** Describe the type of objects that make up the Kuiper Belt.

Meteorites can be made of many elements.

We can study asteroids by studying meteorites. Many of the larger rocks that make it through Earth's atmosphere come directly from asteroids. As shown in **Figure 7,** there are three major types of meteorites. Stony meteorites include carbon-rich specimens that contain organic materials and water. Iron meteorites are made mostly of iron and nickel. Stony-iron meteorites are a combination of the two types. Most meteorites that have been collected are stony and have compositions like those of Earth and the moon.

Figure 7 There are three major types of meteorites.

Stony Rocky material

Iron Iron and nickel

Stony-iron Rocky, iron and nickel

Meteoroids sometimes strike Earth.

Most meteoroids were once part of asteroids, although a few came from Mars or from our moon. These rocks were probably thrown off Mars or the moon when they were hit by a smaller body. Objects less than 10 m across usually burn up in Earth's atmosphere. **Figure 8** shows Barringer Crater, which was formed by the impact of a meteoroid that probably weighed 200,000 metric tons (200,000,000 kg). Barringer Crater is more than 1 km wide and 175 m deep. Twenty-five metric tons (25,000 kg) of iron meteorite fragments have been found at the site. The rest vaporized on impact or were scattered, broken by weathering, or buried. Earth has nearly 100 craters larger than 0.1 km in diameter.

Many scientists think that an asteroid or comet 10 to 15 km wide struck Earth about 65 million years ago and caused the extinction of the dinosaurs. The energy released was probably as much as the energy of 10 million hydrogen bombs. Large amounts of dust may have swirled into Earth's atmosphere and darkened the sky for years. Plants—and the dinosaurs that depended on plants for food—died. Today, scientists use telescopes to track asteroids that pass near Earth.

Figure 8 Barringer Crater in Arizona was formed from an impact that happened about 50,000 years ago.

Why It Matters
Where Are Earth's Craters?

Although Earth has been hit by many meteoroids in its past, there are few easily visible craters. The reason is that processes common on Earth, such as erosion and volcanic activity, can erase traces of the craters over time. New technologies, including satellite photographs, can help locate these ancient impact sites. Kara-Kul, shown here, is a lake in the country of Tajikistan. This lake is located in the remains of an impact site that is nearly 25 million years old!

YOUR TURN

COMPARING PROCESSES
1. Do craters erode as fast on other planets as they do on Earth? Explain.

APPLYING INFORMATION
2. Why is it easier to see the remains of a crater from the sky than from the ground?

How the Moon Formed

Before the moon's composition was known, scientists had several theories for how the moon formed. Some thought that a separate body was captured by Earth's gravity. If this theory were true, the moon's composition should be different from Earth's. Others thought that the moon formed from the same material as Earth, so its composition would be identical to Earth's. When the moon's composition was found to be similar to Earth's, but not identical, a third theory emerged. ❯ **The current theory is that the moon resulted from a collision between Earth and another large body.**

Figure 9 How the Moon Formed

Earth collided with a large body.

About 4.4 billion years ago, when Earth was still forming, it was molten, or heated to an almost liquid state. Heavy material slowly sank to the center of the new planet to form the core. Lighter material rose toward the surface to form the mantle and crust. Then, a Mars-sized body struck Earth at an angle and was deflected, as shown in **Figure 9a.** At impact, a large part of Earth's mantle was blasted into space.

The ejected material clumped together.

The debris began to clump together to form the moon, as shown in **Figure 9b.** The debris consisted of iron core and mantle material from the impacting body as well as mantle material from Earth. The iron core became the core of the moon. This theory explains why moon rocks brought back to Earth from the Apollo mission share some characteristics of Earth's mantle.

The moon began to orbit Earth.

Figure 9c shows the material that formed the moon revolving around Earth as the result of Earth's gravitational pull. After the moon cooled, impacts by comets and asteroids created basins on the surface. Lava flooded the basins to make the maria. Smaller impacts made craters on the lunar surface.

Some scientists doubt this theory because it involves a *unique* event, one that has happened only once. But the moon itself is a unique celestial body in our solar system. It is the only large satellite of a terrestrial planet, and it is the largest moon relative to its planet.

Figure 10 The Keck telescopes and others like them help astronomers find exoplanets that exist around stars other than our sun.

Do Other Stars Have Planets?

An **exoplanet** is a planetlike body that orbits a star other than the sun. An exoplanet orbiting its star causes the star to wobble back and forth. ▶ **Astronomers have discovered more than 200 exoplanets by measuring the small gravitational effects that they have on their parent stars.** Because exoplanets are smaller than the stars that they orbit, the wobble they produce is very slight.

Because exoplanets shine by reflected starlight, they are too faint to be seen by our current optical telescopes. In order to determine whether an exoplanet is present, astronomers use special techniques and powerful technology, such as the Keck telescope shown in **Figure 10,** to observe the movements of the parent star over time.

Almost all of the newly discovered exoplanets have masses similar to the mass of Jupiter or Saturn. Many of them have noncircular orbits that bring them within a few million kilometers of their star. Only a few are in systems that have more than one detected exoplanet. Modern detection methods favor finding large exoplanets, although scientists are working on many innovative ways to detect smaller exoplanets.

exoplanet (EK soh PLAN it) a planetlike body that orbits a star other than the sun

Section 3 Review

KEY IDEAS

1. **Explain** how our current model of the solar system differs from Ptolemy's model.
2. **State** the approximate age of the solar system.
3. **Summarize** the main steps of the nebular hypothesis.
4. **Describe** how comets change when they near the sun.
5. **List** the three types of meteorites.
6. **Contrast** the theory of how our moon formed with how the satellites of gas giants may have formed.
7. **Explain** why it is difficult to detect an exoplanet orbiting a distant star.

CRITICAL THINKING

8. **Forming Reasoned Opinions** Do you think that the government should spend money on programs to search for asteroids that may strike Earth? Explain why you think that this is a good or bad idea.
9. **Making Predictions** Do you think that planets like Earth exist around other stars? Do you think that they may contain life? Explain.

Skills Practice Lab

⏱ 50 min

The Size and Power Output of the Sun

The sun is 1.496×10^{11} m from Earth. How can you use this distance and a few simple measurements to find the size and power output of the sun?

What You'll Do

› **Construct** devices for indirectly observing and measuring the sun.

› **Analyze** the results by calculating the size of the sun and the power output of the sun.

What You'll Need

aluminum foil
clay, modeling
index card
jar, glass, with a hole in the lid
lamp with 100 W bulb
meterstick
paint or magic marker, black
pin, straight
scissors
shoe box
tape, masking
thermometer, Celsius

Safety

Procedure

Constructing a Solar Viewer and a Solar Collector

1 Construct a solar viewer in the following way.
   a. Cut a round hole in one end of the shoe box.
   b. Tape a piece of aluminum foil over the hole. Use the pin to make a tiny hole in the center of the foil.
   c. Tape the index card inside the shoe box on the end opposite the hole.

2 Construct a solar collector in the following way.
   a. Cut an 8 cm × 64 cm piece of aluminum foil. Fold it in half lengthwise 5 times to make a 2 cm × 8 cm strip. Wrap the strip snugly around at least half of the bulb of the thermometer, and tape the back of the foil onto the thermometer. Bend the edges out so that they form "wings," as shown in the photo. Paint the wings black. **CAUTION:** Thermometers are fragile. Do not squeeze the bulb of the thermometer or let the thermometer strike any solid objects.
   b. Slide the top of the thermometer through the hole in the lid of the jar. Use modeling clay and masking tape to hold the thermometer in place.
   c. Place the lid on the jar. Adjust the thermometer so that the wings of the foil directly face the lamp.

3 Place the lamp on one end of a table that is not in direct sunlight. Remove any shade or reflector from the lamp.

Taking Measurements with the Solar Collector

4 Stand in direct sunlight, with your back to the sun, and position the solar viewer so that an image of the sun appears on the index card. **CAUTION:** Never look directly at the sun. Permanent eye damage or even blindness may result.

5 Carefully measure and record the diameter of the image of the sun. Also, measure and record the distance from the image to the pinhole.

6 Place the solar collector in sunlight. Tilt the jar so that the sun shines directly on the metal wings. Watch the temperature reading rise until it reaches a maximum value. Record that value. Place the collector in the shade to cool.

680 Chapter 19 The Solar System

7 Now, place the solar collector about 30 cm from the lamp on the table. Tilt the jar so that the light shines directly on the metal wings. Watch the temperature reading rise until it reaches a stable value.

8 Move the collector toward the lamp in 2 cm increments. At each position, let the collector sit until the temperature reading stabilizes. When you find a point at which the reading on the thermometer matches the reading you observed in step 6, measure and record the distance from the solar collector to the light bulb.

Analysis

1. **Analyzing Data** The ratio of the sun's actual diameter to its distance from Earth is the same as the ratio of the diameter of the sun's image to the distance beetween the pinhole and the image.

$$\frac{\text{diameter of the Sun (S)}}{\text{Earth-to-sun distance}} = \frac{\text{diameter of image, }i}{\text{pinhole-to-image distance, }d}$$

Solving for the sun's diameter, S, gives the following equation.

$$S = \frac{D}{d} \times i$$

Substitute your measured values and $D = 1.5 \times 10^{11}$ m into this equation to calculate the value of S. Remember to convert all distance measurements to meters.

2. **Analyzing Data** The ratio of the power output of the sun to the sun's distance from Earth squared is the same as the ratio of the power output of the light bulb to the solar collector's distance from the bulb squared.

$$\frac{\text{power of sun, }P}{(\text{Earth-to-sun distance, }D)^2} = \frac{\text{power of light bulb, }b}{(\text{bulb-to-collector distance, }d)^2}$$

Solving for the sun's power output, P, gives the following equation.

$$P = \frac{D^2}{d^2} \times b$$

Substitute your measured distance for d, the known wattage of the bulb for b, and $D = 1.5 \times 10^{11}$ m into this equation to calculate the value of P in watts. Remember to convert all distance measurements to units of meters.

Communicating Your Results

3. **Making Comparisons** How does your value for S compare with the accepted diameter of the sun, 1.39×10^9 m? How does your value for P compare with the accepted power output of the sun, 3.86×10^{26} W?

4. **Analyzing Methods** What factors may have caused error in your measurements? If you did the experiment again, how could you minimize such errors?

Extension

The average amount of the sun's power that reaches Earth's surface is about 1,000 W/m². What percentage of the sun's power output per square meter of the sun's surface does this average represent? (Hint: Use the equation $A = 4\pi r^2$, where A is the surface area of a sphere and r is its radius.)

Using Search Engines

Science Skills

▸ **Technology**
Math
Scientific Methods
Graphing

Search engines are tools for sorting through the huge amounts of information on the World Wide Web so that you can find the specific information you need. Here are some tips to help you use search engines effectively.

① Determine in advance what kind of information you are looking for. Many search sites use a keyword search by default, but they also have a subject index, or directory.
- To find information about a broad subject, do a directory search.
- To find information on a specific topic, do a keyword, or Web, search.

② Pay attention to spelling and formatting in your search query.
- Be sure to spell all words correctly and to include spaces where appropriate.
- For most searches, use all lowercase letters. Some search engines, however, are case sensitive and you must combine capital and lowercase letters.
- Use the form of words (such as singular or plural, present or past tense) that is most likely to be on the pages you are looking for.

③ If you receive too many irrelevant results, try refining your search in one or more of the following ways.
- Add words or phrases that you would expect to be on the pages you are looking for. Try to use words that will rule out irrelevant pages.
- Add words that are synonyms of other words in your query.
- Specify exact phrases by grouping words within quotes. The search engine will then look for those words only in the exact combination that you have specified.
- Exclude pages that contain certain words by adding those words to the query with a minus sign in front.

Practice

1. Write a search query for finding information about the Galileo mission to the large outer planets—but *not* about the scientist and mathematician Galileo Galilei.

2. Write a search query for finding information about planets around stars in the constellation Virgo—but *not* about Virgo as an astrological sign.

682 Chapter 19 The Solar System

CHAPTER 19 Summary

Key Ideas

Section 1 Sun, Earth, and Moon

> **The View from Earth** The position of objects in the sky appears to change because Earth, and everything else in the universe, is constantly moving. (p. 653)

> **A Family of Planets** The solar system is the sun and all of the objects that orbit it. (p. 655)

> **The Moon** The moon affects life on Earth through its movements and gravitational influence. (p. 657)

Section 2 The Inner and Outer Planets

> **The Inner Planets** The terrestrial planets are reletively small and have solid, rocky surfaces. (p. 661)

> **The Gas Giants** The outer planets are much larger than the inner planets and have thick, gaseous atmospheres, many satellites, and rings. (p. 666)

> **Beyond the Gas Giants** Beyond the gas giants are numerous small bodies composed of ice and rock. (p. 670)

Section 3 Formation of the Solar System

> **Early Astronomy** Mathematical tools are used to make more accurate models of observed astronomical objects. (p. 671)

> **The Nebular Hypothesis** The nebular hypothesis explains why objects that form from a disk will lie in the same plane, have almost circular orbits, and orbit in the same direction. (p. 673)

> **Rocks in Space** There are many types of small bodies in the solar system, including satellites, comets, asteroids, and meteoroids. (p. 675)

> **How the Moon Formed** Current theory states that the moon resulted from a collision between Earth and another large body. (p. 678)

> **Do Other Stars Have Planets?** Astronomers have discovered many exoplanets by measuring their gravitational effects on their parent star. (p. 679)

Key Terms

planet, p. 653
solar system, p. 655
satellite, p. 656
phase, p. 657
eclipse, p. 658

terrestrial planet, p. 661
hydrosphere, p. 663
asteroid, p. 666
dwarf planet, p. 666
gas giant, p. 666

nebular hypothesis, p. 673
nebula, p. 673
comet, p. 675
exoplanet, p. 679

CHAPTER 19 Review

READING TOOLBOX

1. **Word Origins** The word *planet* comes from a Greek word meaning "wanderer." Why is "wanderer" an appropriate word for describing a planet?

USING KEY TERMS

2. Arrange the following from the largest to smallest in mass: *terrestrial planet, gas giant, meteorite,* and *solar system*.

3. List the names of the four largest *satellites* of the planet Jupiter.

4. Write a paragraph explaining the origin of the solar system according to the nebular theory. Use the following terms: *planet, accretion, nebula,* and *nebular hypothesis*.

5. Describe the arrangement of the sun, the moon, and Earth during a *solar eclipse* and a *lunar eclipse*.

6. Describe how the *phases* of the moon change over the course of a month.

7. List the names of the *terrestrial planets* in order of distance from the sun.

8. List the names of the *gas giants* in the order of their mass from largest to smallest.

UNDERSTANDING KEY IDEAS

9. Which outer planet is the largest gas giant?
   a. Uranus   c. Saturn
   b. Neptune   d. Jupiter

10. Earth is gravitationally attracted to
    a. Mercury.   c. the sun.
    b. the moon.   d. All of the above

11. How many gas giants are in our solar system?
    a. one   c. four
    b. three   d. nine

12. Meteors occur when
    a. meteoroids enter Earth's atmosphere.
    b. a large asteroid comes near Earth.
    c. Earth enters the asteroid belt.
    d. Earth enters the Oort cloud.

13. The current accepted theory states that our moon formed when
    a. a Jupiter-sized object collided with Earth.
    b. a Mars-sized object collided with Earth.
    c. planetesimals came together in a disk around Earth.
    d. Earth's gravity captured a stray object in space, and it began to orbit Earth.

14. The planet Jupiter has a day that is
    a. twice as long as 1 Earth day.
    b. shorter than 1 Earth day.
    c. equal to 1 Earth day.
    d. equal to 1 Jupiter year.

15. The hypothesis that the sun and planets formed out of the same cloud of gas and dust is called the _____ hypothesis.
    a. big bang   c. nebular
    b. planetary   d. nuclear

16. The solar system is about _____ years old.
    a. 0.5 million c. 0.5 billion
    b. 4.6 million d. 4.6 billion

17. Which of the planets shown below is an example of a gas giant?

a.

c.

b.

d.

EXPLAINING KEY IDEAS

18. Describe the ways in which the heliocentric model of the solar system differs from the geocentric model of the solar system.

19. List two ways in which the moon affects life on Earth.

20. Describe the ways in which the terrestrial planets differ from the gas giants.

21. Explain how astronomers are able to detect the exoplanets of distant stars.

22. Name three objects in the solar system besides the sun and the planets.

23. Summarize the theory stating that Earth's moon was formed as the result of a collision.

CRITICAL THINKING

24. Understanding Relationships Imagine that you are an astronaut on Mars. You look into the sky and see Deimos directly overhead. It is in full phase. What time is it on Mars?

25. Analyzing Conclusions The moon rotates at the same rate as it revolves, so one side never faces Earth. This portion of the moon is known as the *far side* of the moon. Is the far side of the moon always dark? Explain your answer.

26. Drawing Conclusions The moon and Earth both orbit at an average of 1 AU from the sun. The moon's surface is covered with craters. Earth has very few craters visible on its surface. Explain what causes this difference.

27. Predicting Patterns If the nebular hypothesis is correct and planetary systems around other stars formed in the same manner, how might those planetary systems be similar to our own?

28. Analyzing Information The dwarf planet Pluto rotates on its axis every 6.387 Earth days. Charon, Pluto's moon, orbits Pluto in 6.387 Earth days. Explain how Charon would look from the surface of Pluto.

Graphing Skills

29. Graphing Data The table shows the average distance from the sun for each planet and its orbital period. Plot the data in a graph with distance on the *x*-axis and period on the *y*-axis.

Planet	Distance (AU)	Period (year)
Mercury	0.4	0.2
Venus	0.7	0.6
Earth	1.0	1
Mars	1.5	2
Jupiter	5.2	12
Saturn	9.5	29
Uranus	19.2	84
Neptune	30	164

30. Interpreting Graphs The dwarf planet Ceres has an average distance of 2.8 AU from the sun. Using your graph from item 29, estimate how long Ceres will take to orbit the sun.

31. Identifying Patterns Halley's comet has a period of 76 years. Using your graph from item 29, determine Halley comet's average distance from the sun.

32. Graphing Data The table below gives the density and mass for selected planets. Using the data in the table, make two kinds of graphs to show the information. Which of your graphs best displays the information? Explain.

Planet	Mass (Earth mass)	Density (gm/cm^3)
Mercury	0.055	5.43
Earth	1.00	5.52
Mars	0.11	3.94
Jupiter	318	1.33
Saturn	95.2	0.70

Standardized Test Prep

Understanding Concepts

Directions (1–4): **For each question, write on a sheet of paper the letter of the correct answer.**

1. Earth's tides are most influenced by the gravitational pull of what celestial body?
   - **A.** the sun
   - **B.** Venus
   - **C.** the moon
   - **D.** Jupiter

2. On what planet can we see an enormous atmospheric storm called the Great Red Spot?
   - **F.** Mars
   - **G.** Jupiter
   - **H.** Saturn
   - **I.** Mercury

3. Between the orbits of Mars and Jupiter is an orbital ring consisting of what?
   - **A.** asteroids
   - **B.** comets
   - **C.** meteors
   - **D.** nebulae

4. According to Newton, what fundamental force holds the solar system together and is responsible for the orbits of the planets?
   - **F.** electromagnetism
   - **G.** gravity
   - **H.** weak nuclear force
   - **I.** strong nuclear force

Directions (5-7): **For each question, write a short response.**

5. Before Copernicus proposed that the sun lay at the center of the solar system, many people believed in a geocentric model of the universe. Describe the geocentric model.

6. Pieces of Earth's moon brought back by astronauts show a composition similar to that of Earth's mantle. What theory of the origin of the moon explains this fact?

7. Which four planets are known as the gas giants?

Reading Skills

Directions (8-10): **Read the passage below. Then, answer the questions that follow.**

A REGULAR VISITOR

In 1682, a bright comet appeared in the night sky. An astronomer named Edmond G. Halley noticed that the comet matched the descriptions given of previous comets seen in 1531 and 1607. Halley theorized that this was the very same comet, in a 76-year orbit around the sun, and he predicted that the comet would return in 1758. Due to the gravitational pull of Jupiter and Saturn, the comet was a bit later than predicted, but it arrived in March 1759. Since then, the comet has returned in 1835, 1910, and 1986.

Halley's comet is not expected to visit Earth again until 2061, but comet fans can see bits and pieces of the comet each year during the annual Orionids meteor shower. This meteor shower occurs when Earth crosses the comet's orbital path, which is made of tiny debris particles of rock and ice, usually no bigger than grains of sand. Although they are very small, these tiny meteors make brilliant shooting stars when they strike Earth's atmosphere, because they travel at nearly 145,000 km/h.

8. For Halley's comet, what lasts approximately 76 Earth years?
   - **A.** one day
   - **B.** one month
   - **C.** one year
   - **D.** one century

9. After its 2061 appearance, when is Halley's comet likely to be seen next?
   - **F.** 2076 CE
   - **G.** 2137 CE
   - **H.** 2161 CE
   - **I.** 2821 CE

10. How does Halley's discovery illustrate the importance of keeping accurate records of observations in science?

Interpreting Graphics

Directions (11–12): **The graphic below shows two kinds of eclipses. Use the graphic to answer questions 11–12. (Diagrams are not to scale.)**

HOW AN ECLIPSE IS PRODUCED

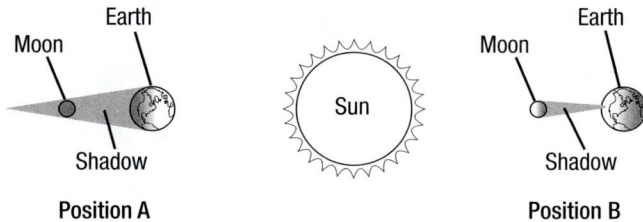

11. What type of eclipse is each of the eclipses shown above?
    A. Eclipse A is a solar eclipse, and eclipse B is a lunar eclipse.
    B. Eclipse A is a lunar eclipse, and eclipse B is a solar eclipse.
    C. They are both solar eclipses.
    D. They are both lunar eclipses.

12. Which phase of the moon is shown in each of the diagrams above?

Use the graphic below to answer questions 13–14.

THE SUN, THE MOON, AND TIDES

Neap Tides

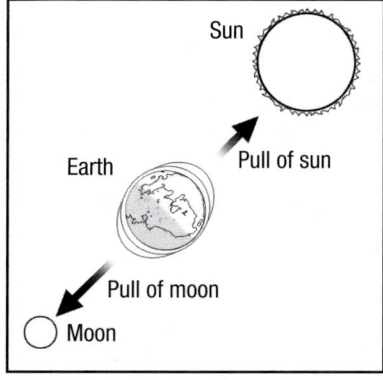
Spring Tides

13. During which phases of the moon will the tides be most extreme?
    F. full moon and new moon
    G. first quarter and third quarter
    H. waxing and waning gibbous
    I. waxing crescent and waxing gibbous

14. Why are tides weakest when Earth, the sun, and the moon are not aligned?

> **Test Tip**
>
> If you are unsure of the correct answer to a multiple-choice question, start by crossing out answers that you know are wrong.

Why It Matters
Careers Using Earth Science

When you think of an Earth scientist, you may think of a person who works for a petroleum company, or of a scientist who generates complex computer models of Earth's climate. People use Earth science in hundreds of careers. Whether protecting the environment, chasing hurricanes, or examining gemstones, people use Earth science to get the job done. The careers discussed here are examples of careers that use Earth science.

Volcanologist

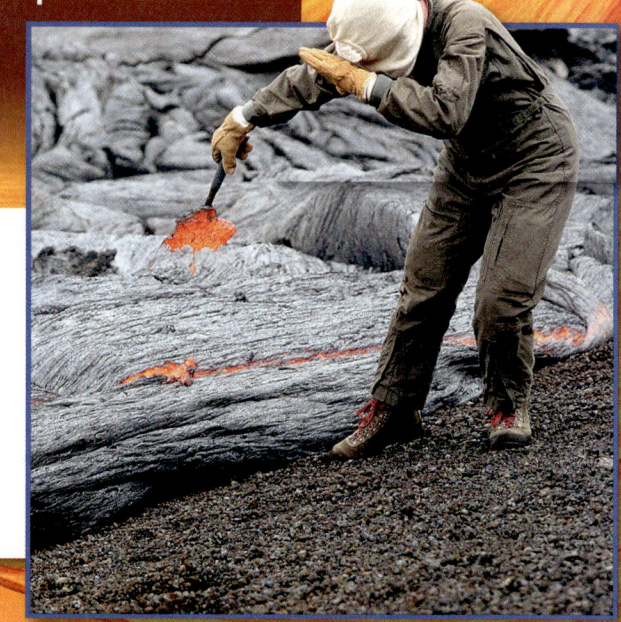

At this moment, about 20 volcanic eruptions are happening somewhere on Earth, and it is estimated that 9% of the world's population lives within 100 km of a historically active volcano. Volcanologists study volcanoes to learn more about Earth's processes and to help protect populations from volcanic eruptions. However, forecasting the timing, size, and characteristics of a volcanic eruption is very difficult. Volcanologists monitor volcanoes by using seismometers and by studying the composition of gases and lava released by volcanoes.

Astronaut

Ever since Apollo astronaut Harrison Schmitt became the first geologist in space, NASA has included Earth scientists, such as geologists and geophysicists, on space missions. There are many ways that these missions help scientists understand the dynamics of Earth systems. For example, some space missions carry satellites in which there is remote sensing equipment that is used to study Earth from space. NASA's Earth Observing System (EOS) is a network of satellites that collect long-term observations of Earth's oceans, atmosphere, biosphere, and land surface.

Metallurgist

A feature that cars, bicycles, space probes, airplanes, and cooking pots share is that they contain metal parts. Metallurgists specialize in the production of metals. The mining industry employs many metallurgists who work to develop processes for extracting metals from mineral ores. Metallurgists also develop alloys. By combining metals and other substances, a metallurgist can change a metal's characteristics, such as its weight, strength, hardness, ductility, or corrosion resistance.

Hurricane Hunter

Most people try to avoid hurricanes and extreme weather. However, some scientists, known as *hurricane hunters,* fly airplanes directly into these deadly storms. Hurricane hunters fly into storms because satellite data are not accurate enough to measure the size and strength of a hurricane. On a typical mission, hurricane hunters may fly repeatedly through the violent storms that circle the eye of a hurricane. Each time that they pass through the hurricane, the scientists release instruments that record weather data such as temperature, pressure, humidity, and wind speed. These data help scientists estimate a hurricane's size, strength, and future path.

Gemologist

Can you tell the difference between a diamond and a piece of cubic zirconia? Gemologists use their knowledge about the properties of minerals to evaluate gems and minerals. Their knowledge enables gemologists to detect impurities or imperfections that affect the value of gemstones. To study gemstones, gemologists use a variety of techniques, such as X-ray diffraction, spectrophotometry, and gamma spectroscopy. Gemologists most often use binocular microscopes to observe gemstones closely and detect impurities. By using such microscopes, gemologists can tell the difference between a valuable gem and a well-designed fake.

Environmental Engineer

Environmental engineers use science and engineering principles to prevent, control, and remediate environmental hazards. Environmental engineers help protect natural resources in many ways. For example, an environmental engineer may design wastewater treatment facilities, help conserve wetlands, or act as a consultant on a project to clean up a toxic waste site. Many industries employ environmental engineers who work to reduce pollution and conserve resources. Environmental engineers must understand hydrology, soil formation, and the carbon, nitrogen, and water cycles. Environmental engineers use chemistry to analyze soil, water, and air.

YOUR TURN

UNDERSTANDING CONCEPTS
1. Explain how understanding Earth science plays an important role in two of the careers described on these pages.

CRITICAL THINKING
2. Why do hurricane hunters need to fly airplanes into the path of hurricanes?

www.scilinks.org
Topic: Careers in Earth Science
Code: **HK80222**

CHAPTER 20
The Universe

Chapter Outline

❶ The Life and Death of Stars
What Are Stars?
Studying Stars
The Life Cycle of Stars

❷ The Milky Way and Other Galaxies
Galaxies
Types of Galaxies
How Galaxies Change Over Time

❸ Origin of the Universe
What Is the Universe?
What Happened at the Beginning?
Predicting the Future of the Universe

Tennessee Course Level Expectations (Physical Science)

CLE.3202.2.1 Investigate the properties and behaviors of mechanical and electromagnetic waves; **CLE.3202.2.5** Distinguish between nuclear fission and nuclear fusion; **CLE.3202.Inq.1** Recognize that science is a progressive endeavor that reevaluates and extends what is already accepted; **CLE.3202.Inq.2** Design and conduct scientific investigations to explore new phenomena, verify previous results, test how well a theory predicts, and compare opposing theories; **CLE.3202.Inq.3** Use appropriate tools and technology to collect precise and accurate data; **CLE.3202.Inq.4** Apply qualitative and quantitative measures to analyze data and draw conclusions that are free of bias; **CLE.3202.Inq.6** Communicate and defend scientific findings; **CLE.3202.Math.1** Understand the mathematical principles behind the science of physics; **CLE.3202.Math.2** Utilize appropriate mathematical equations and processes to solve basic physics problems; **CLE.3202.TE.4** Describe the dynamic interplay among science, technology, and engineering within living, earth-space, and physical systems.

Inquiry Lab
⏱ 20 min

Constellation Names

Turn to Appendix C, and locate the sky maps. Pick a constellation, and brainstorm with a classmate on how and why it might have been given its name. You may need to look up the name in a dictionary or online to find out what the name means in its language of origin. Write a few paragraphs that explain your hypothesis.

Questions To Get You Started

1. Planets and their moons are named for ancient mythological figures. What factors may have led to the naming of constellations?
2. Why might people want to name constellations?

Why It Matters

This large cloud of dust and gas in space is known as the Horsehead Nebula because of the distinctive dark spot that looks like a horse's head. Scientists study regions of space such as this one to learn more about how stars form and how the universe works.

READING TOOLBOX

These reading tools can help you learn the material in this chapter. For more information on how to use these and other tools, see **Appendix A.**

Science Terms

Everyday Words Used in Science Many of the words used in science are familiar words taken from everyday speech. Scientists sometimes choose familiar words to describe things that are new, unfamiliar, or difficult to understand.

One example of a term that you may have studied is *absolute zero*. Absolute zero is the lowest possible temperature. Because the word *absolute* means "complete" or "without exception," this word works well to describe the lowest possible temperature at zero kelvins.

Your Turn You will learn about stars called *white dwarfs* and *red giants*. Based on the terms alone, explain what you would expect a white dwarf and a red giant star to be. After reading Section 1, write the scientific definitions of these terms. How do the scientific definitions compare with what you expected the meanings of the terms to be?

	WHAT I THINK IT MEANS	SCIENTIFIC DEFINITION
White dwarf		
Red giant		

Describing Space

Using Spatial Language Spatial language is used to describe space and the universe. It can include language that describes:
- the shape of objects
- the location of objects
- distance
- orientation
- direction of motion

Your Turn As you read this chapter, complete a table like the one below. Add words or phrases that describe something by using spatial language.

SHAPE	LOCATION	DISTANCE	ORIENTATION	DIRECTION
sphere	in the core		vertical	outward
spiral		light-year	vertical	outward
irregular				

FoldNotes

Tri-Fold FoldNotes are a fun way to help you learn and remember ideas that you read. FoldNotes help you to organize concepts and see the overall idea. Tri-folds are a great way to organize information that comes in threes.

Your Turn As you read Section 2, make a tri-fold, as described in **Appendix A,** to organize your notes about the three types of galaxies. Label the columns "Spiral galaxy," "Elliptical galaxy," and "Irregular galaxy."

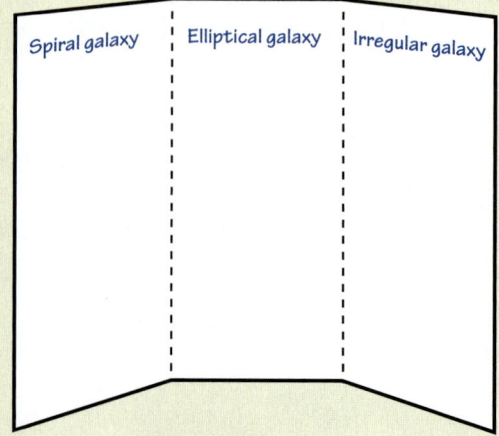

692 Chapter 20 The Universe

SECTION 1
The Life and Death of Stars

Key Ideas

> How are stars formed?
> How can we learn about stars if they are so far away?
> What natural cycles do stars go through?

Key Terms

star
light-year
red giant
white dwarf
supernova
black hole

Why It Matters

Stars have influenced cultures for thousands of years by helping people mark the passage of time and by providing markers for navigation in the night sky.

Only about 6,000 stars can be seen from Earth with the naked eye. People have observed stars for thousands of years, but only in the last 100 years have we begun to understand the life cycle of stars.

Tennessee Course Level Expectations (Physical Science)

CLE.3202.2.1; CLE.3202.2.5;
CLE.3202.Inq.1; CLE.3202.Inq.2;
CLE.3202.Inq.3; CLE.3202.TE.4

What Are Stars?

From Earth, most stars look like tiny dots of light, which is not how stars appear up close. **Stars** are huge spheres of very hot gas that emit light and other radiation. Although people do not usually think of the sun as a star, it is actually the star that is nearest to Earth. ▶ **Stars are formed from clouds of dust and gas, or nebulas, and go through different stages as they age.** Figure 1 shows the birth and death of different stars.

Stars are located at various distances from Earth. We use the light-year (ly) to describe the distance from Earth to faraway objects such as stars and galaxies. A **light-year** is the distance that light travels in one year, or about 9.5×10^{12} km.

star (STAHR) a large celestial body that is composed of gas and that emits light

light-year (LIET YIR) the distance that light travels in one year; about 9.46 trillion kilometers

Figure 1 Stars are born in a nebula (left). After billions of years, most stars become old and lose their outer layers of gas. As a star begins to die, it may become a planetary nebula (right).

Stars are powered by nuclear fusion reactions.

A star is a huge sphere of very hot hydrogen and helium gas that emits light. A star is held together by the enormous gravitational forces that result from its own mass. Inside the core of a star, the pressure is more than a billion times the atmospheric pressure on Earth. The temperature in this incredibly dense core is hotter than 15 million kelvins.

Stars get their energy from nuclear fusion, which takes place in the core. Fusion combines the nuclei of hydrogen atoms into helium nuclei. When hydrogen nuclei collide, they fuse to form *deuterons*, which have one proton and one neutron. Another proton collides with a deuteron to form a helium isotope, helium-3. Next, two helium-3 isotopes collide to form the nucleus of a helium-4 atom, releasing two hydrogen nuclei. Each time that two particles fuse, energy is released.

Energy moves slowly through the layers of a star.

The layers of the sun are shown in **Figure 2.** Other stars have similar structures, but the temperatures and depths of the layers may vary. Energy moves slowly through the layers of a star by a combination of radiation and convection. During convection, hot gas moves away from the star's core. During radiation, energy is transferred to individual atoms. The atoms absorb the energy and transfer it to other atoms in random directions. Atoms near the surface radiate energy into space.

Energy from a nuclear fusion reaction in the core may take tens of thousands of years to reach a star's surface. When the energy reaches the surface, the energy is released into space as electromagnetic radiation.

www.scilinks.org
Topic: Nuclear Fusion in the Sun
Code: HK81051

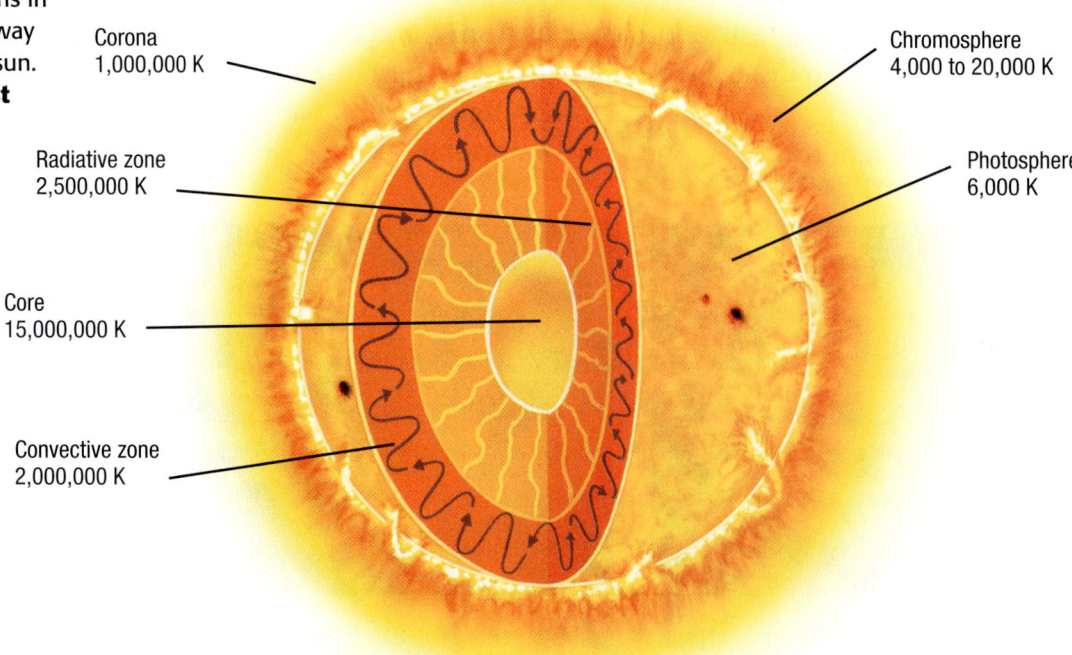

Figure 2 Energy that is released by fusion reactions in the core slowly works its way through the layers of the sun. **What layer is the hottest part of the sun?**

Corona 1,000,000 K
Chromosphere 4,000 to 20,000 K
Radiative zone 2,500,000 K
Photosphere 6,000 K
Core 15,000,000 K
Convective zone 2,000,000 K

QuickLab

Modeling Fusion

⏱ 10 min

Procedure

1. Mark **six coins** using a **marker** or **piece of paper.** Put a P for "proton" on the head side and an N for "neutron" on the tail side.

2. Place the coins P-side up. These coins represent hydrogen's simplest isotope, H. Place two H isotopes so that their edges touch. Flip one of them to be N-side up. This flip represents the proton becoming a neutron during fusion. The resulting nucleus represents the isotope hydrogen-2, or ^{2}H.

3. To model the next step, place a third coin, P-side up, against the ^{2}H nucleus. This step forms the isotope helium-3, or ^{3}He.

4. Repeat steps 2 and 3.

5. Move the two ^{3}He nuclei so that their edges touch. Move two of the protons away from the other four particles. These four particles form a new nucleus: helium-4, or ^{4}He.

Analysis

1. How many energy-producing reactions did your model show?

Studying Stars

Although the ancient Greeks noticed that stars had color and divided stars by their apparent brightness, astronomers did not really begin to learn about the nature of stars until the optical telescope was invented. ❯ **The telescope allowed astronomers to study stars in more detail for the first time.** As science and technology have improved, telescopes have become more powerful and have thus allowed us to see more.

Some stars appear brighter than others.

The brightness of a star depends on the star's temperature, size, and distance from Earth. The brightest star in the night sky is Sirius in the constellation Canis Major. Sirius appears so bright because it is close to Earth, only about 8.7 light-years away. The surface temperature of Sirius is about 10,000 K. The sun's surface is only 6,000 K, but the sun is so close to Earth that it prevents us from seeing other stars during the day.

We learn about stars by studying energy.

Stars produce wavelengths of electromagnetic radiation other than visible light. These wavelengths range from high-energy X rays to low-energy radio waves. Scientists use optical telescopes to study visible light and radio telescopes to study radio waves emitted from astronomical objects. Earth's atmosphere blocks other wavelengths, so telescopes in space are used to study a wider range of the electromagnetic spectrum than telescopes on the ground are.

✓ **Reading Check** Why do scientists put telescopes in space? (See Appendix E for answers to Reading Checks.)

Academic Vocabulary

apparent (uh PER uhnt) readily observed; visible

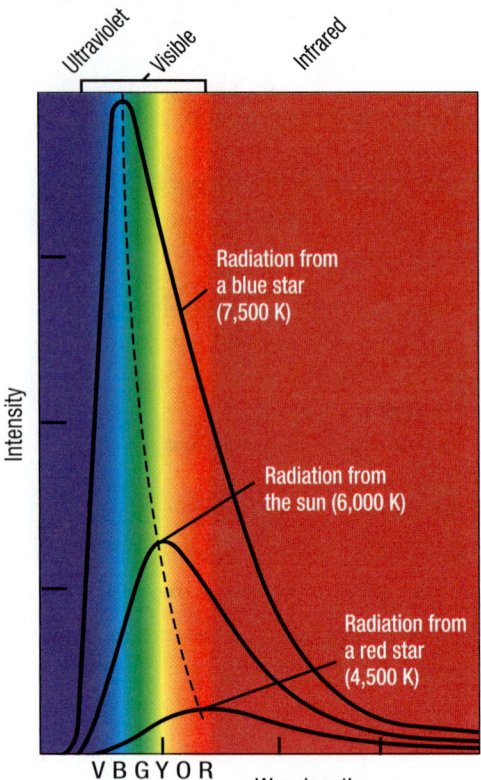

Figure 3 This graph shows the intensity of light at different wavelengths for the sun and for two other stars.

A star's color is related to its temperature.

When light from a glowing, hot object passes through a prism, the result is a spectrum of many colors. This spectrum changes based on temperature: hotter objects glow with light that is more intense and that has shorter wavelengths (closer to the blue end of the spectrum). The light from cooler objects has less intensity and longer wavelengths (closer to red).

Although the light from a glowing object contains many colors, the color that we see when we look directly at a hot object is determined mainly by the wavelength at which the object emits the most light. A graph that shows the intensity, or brightness, of light at different wavelengths for three stars is shown in **Figure 3**. The sun appears yellow because the peak wavelength of the sun's energy is near yellow on the spectrum. Yellow also corresponds to a temperature near 6,000 K. Hot stars emit more energy at every wavelength than cool stars do. Hot stars emit the most energy at blue wavelengths.

Spectral lines reveal the composition of stars.

Light can be separated into a spectrum by passing it through a spectrograph, as **Figure 4** shows. The spectra of most stars contain dark lines. These dark lines are caused by gases in the outer layers of the stars that absorb the light at these wavelengths. The gases composing these outer layers determine which spectral lines are produced. Because each element produces a unique pattern of lines, astronomers can match the dark lines in starlight to the known lines of elements found on Earth to determine what elements make up a star. Astronomers have analyzed more than 20,000 lines in the sun's spectrum to find the makeup of the sun's atmosphere.

Reading Check How does the spectrum of a star tell us what makes up the star?

Figure 4 A continuous spectrum (left) shows all colors while an absorption spectrum (right) absorbs some colors. Black lines appear in the spectrum where light at specific wavelengths is absorbed by the gas.

Why It Matters

Constellations

Many ancient cultures organized the stars into patterns to make it easier for them to identify specific star groups. These patterns are called *constellations*, and we still use many of the patterns identified by the ancient Greeks today. Astronomers use 88 official constellations to divide up the sky.

Although a constellation looks like a single group of stars to observers on Earth, each star may be a different distance from Earth. Orion, the constellation shown here, is made up of stars that range from 200 ly away to more than 1,400 ly away.

Farmers used the positions of constellations in the sky to mark the changes in season and to know when to plant or harvest their crops.

Ancient cultures used stars and constellations for navigation. The sextant helped sailors align stars while at sea.

YOUR TURN

UNDERSTANDING CONCEPTS
1. Why do stars that are different distances from Earth look like they are part of a single grouping?

CRITICAL THINKING
2. How might we be able to use constellations in today's world?

The Life Cycle of Stars

Stars may appear different from one another because they are at different stages in their life cycles, as **Figure 5** shows. ❯ **In a way that is similar to other natural cycles, stars are born, go through stages of development, and eventually die.** About 90% of all stars in our galaxy, including the sun, are in midlife, or converting hydrogen into helium in their interiors.

Figure 5 Stars change in many ways over their life cycle. They are born in giant nebulas of dust and gas and often end up as white dwarfs billions of years later. The images in this life cycle are not shown to scale. **Why might astronomers use the term *life cycle* to refer to the changes a star goes through over time?**

The sun formed from a cloud of gas and dust.

About 5 billion years ago, a thin cloud of gas and dust, or nebula, collapsed inward as it was pulled by the force of its own gravity. As the nebula collapsed, it began to spin. This small, spinning cloud formed a *protostar*. About 30 million years after the nebula started to collapse, the center of the nebula reached a temperature of 15 million kelvins.

Electrons were stripped from hydrogen atoms to leave hydrogen nuclei, which are protons. At very high pressures, protons may get as close to each other as 10^{-15} m. At such a small distance, the strong nuclear force overpowers electrical repulsion and the protons fuse. The protons combine to form helium through this process of nuclear fusion. The onset of fusion marks the birth of a star. Once this process started in the core of the nebula, the star that we call the sun was born.

The sun has a balance of inward and outward forces.

Fusion reactions in the sun's core generate energy that produces an outward pressure that balances the inward force due to gravity, as **Figure 6** shows. Because of these balanced forces, the sun has maintained a stable size for 5 billion years.

The sun is currently converting hydrogen into helium. Over time, the percentage of the core that is helium becomes larger. Eventually, the core will exhaust about 25% of its hydrogen, and the number of fusion reactions will decrease. When this happens, the sun will begin to die. Scientists estimate, however, that the sun will exist for another 5 billion years.

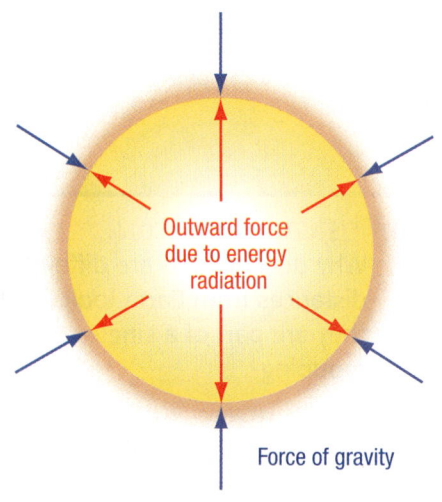

Figure 6 A balance between the inward force of gravity and the outward force of energy radiation keeps the sun at a stable size.

The sun will become a red giant before it dies.

As the number of fusion reactions decreases, the pressure from the release of energy in the core of the sun drops, and the core will contract under the weight of its outer layers. This contraction will cause the temperature in the core to rise. The sun's outer layers will expand, and the sun will become a **red giant,** a large, reddish star late in its life cycle. The star is red because its surface is relatively cool. But the core is hot enough to convert helium into carbon and oxygen.

When the core of a red giant sun depletes most of its helium, it will contract further, which will cause the outer layers to expand again. At this point, the temperature at the core is not high enough to fuse heavier elements. The outer layers will expand out from the core and will eventually leave the star. The remnants will become a **white dwarf,** a small, dim, and very dense star about the size of Earth. White dwarfs no longer fuse elements, so they slowly cool. All stars that have a mass of 1.4 solar masses or smaller, or a mass of less than 1.4 times the mass of our sun, will have a similar life cycle. In fact, most stars in our galaxy will end as white dwarfs.

Reading Check What type of star will the sun end up as?

Supergiant stars explode in supernovas.

Massive stars evolve faster than smaller stars do. They also develop hotter cores that create heavier elements through fusion. The formation of an iron core signals the beginning of a supergiant star's death because, unlike fusing lighter elements, fusing iron atoms to make heavier elements requires adding energy rather than releasing it. When fusion requires more energy than it can produce, there is no longer any outward pressure to balance the gravitational force. The core collapses because of its own gravity and then rebounds with a shock wave that violently blows the star's outer layers away from the core. The resulting huge, bright explosion is called a **supernova,** an example of which is shown in **Figure 7.**

---

red giant (RED JIE uhnt) a large, reddish star late in its life cycle

white dwarf (WIET DWAWRF) a small, hot, dim star that is the leftover center of an old star

supernova (soo puhr NOH vuh) a gigantic explosion in which a massive star collapses and throws its outer layers into space

Figure 7 Supernova 1987A, a Type II supernova, was the first supernova visible to the unaided eye in 400 years. The first image shows what the original star looked like before the explosion.

READING TOOLBOX

Using Everyday Words
Make a list of the key terms from this chapter. Describe what each term makes you think of. Compare your descriptions with what the terms actually mean.

black hole (BLAK HOHL) an object so massive and dense that not even light can escape its gravity

Figure 8 The Crab Nebula is the remains of a supernova that was seen by Chinese observers in the year 1054.

Some supernovas form neutron stars and black holes.

The nebular remnant of a supernova is shown in **Figure 8.** If the core that remains after such a supernova has occurred has a mass of 1.4 to 3 solar masses, the remnant can become a *neutron star*. Neutron stars are only a few dozen kilometers in diameter, but they are very massive. A neutron star is as dense as matter in the nucleus of an atom, about 10^{17} kg/m^3. Just a teaspoon of matter from a neutron star would weigh more than 100 million tons on Earth. Neutron stars can be detected as *pulsars*, or spinning neutron stars that are sources of pulsating radio waves.

If the leftover core has a mass that is greater than 3 solar masses, it will collapse to form something else—a **black hole,** which consists of matter so massive and compressed that nothing, not even light, can escape its gravitational pull. Because no light can escape a black hole, black holes cannot be seen directly. Black holes can, however, be detected indirectly by observing the radiation of light and X rays from objects that revolve rapidly around them.

✓ **Reading Check** How can scientists detect a black hole even though it does not emit or reflect any light?

The H-R diagram shows how stars evolve.

In 1911, Ejnar Hertzsprung, a Danish astronomer, compared the temperature and absolute magnitude of stars and carefully plotted his data on a graph. Absolute magnitude tells us how bright stars would be if they were all the same distance from Earth. In 1913, American astronomer Henry Norris Russell made similar graphs. Together, the two graphs form the Hertzsprung-Russell diagram, or H-R diagram, shown in **Figure 9.** The vertical axis shows the luminosity (the total energy output at every wavelength) or the brightness of stars. The horizontal axis shows the surface temperature of the stars, with hotter temperatures on the left side of the diagram.

Once a star is stable—fusing hydrogen into helium in its core—it appears on a diagonal line in the H-R diagram called the *main sequence.* Most stars are main-sequence stars. The position of a star on the main sequence depends on the initial mass of the star. As stars age and pass through different stages in their life cycles, their positions on the H-R diagram change. Because most stars spend most of their lives in midlife, more stars appear on the main sequence than on other parts of the H-R diagram. Red giant stars are both cool and bright, so they appear in the upper right. White dwarf stars are both faint and hot, so they appear in the lower left.

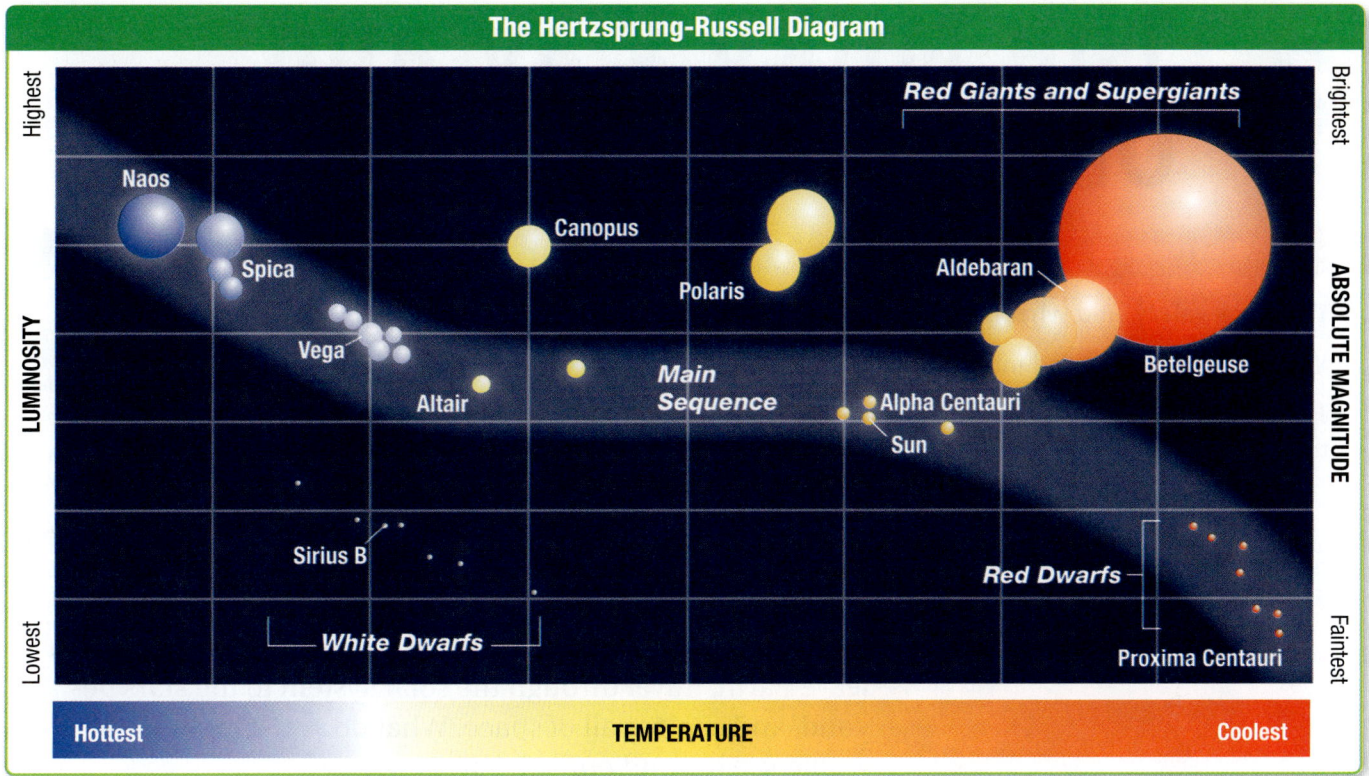

Figure 9 The H-R diagram is a tool that astronomers use to help them understand how stars change over time.

The sun is currently a main-sequence star.

Our sun changed from a protostar to a main-sequence star over the course of tens of millions of years. It will stay on the main sequence for about 10 billion years. As it becomes a red giant, it will become brighter, cooler, and redder; it will move up and to the right on the H-R diagram. The sun will stay in this location on the diagram for about 100 million years. Eventually, the sun will become a white dwarf, and it will move to the lower left on the H-R diagram, where the other white dwarfs are located.

Section 1 Review

KEY IDEAS

1. **Define** the term *star*, and name the star that is closest to Earth.
2. **Compare** the two ways that energy is transferred through the layers of a star.
3. **Explain** how scientists can use a star's light to determine what makes up a star.
4. **Describe** the life cycle of a sunlike star.
5. **List** the types of objects that may result from a supernova.

CRITICAL THINKING

6. **Making Predictions** Which of the following elements is not likely to be formed in the sun at some time during its life cycle? Why not?
   a. helium
   b. carbon
   c. oxygen
   d. iron
7. **Communicating Ideas** You and a friend are looking at the stars, and your friend says, "Stars must be shrinking because gravity is constantly pulling their particles together." Explain what is wrong with your friend's reasoning.

SECTION 2
The Milky Way and Other Galaxies

Key Ideas
- What is a galaxy, and what is it made of?
- Why are galaxies divided into three major types?
- How do scientists know that galaxies change over time?

Key Terms
- galaxy
- cluster
- interstellar matter
- quasar

Why It Matters
By learning how the universe is structured, scientists can make better predictions about where new objects can be found.

Imagine that you are in a special spaceship that allows you to leave Earth, travel through the solar system to the stars beyond, and explore all of space. What do you imagine you would see beyond our solar system?

Galaxies

While the nearest stars are a few light-years away from Earth, the nearest galaxy to our own is millions of light-years from Earth. ❯ **A galaxy is a collection of millions to billions of stars.** The deeper scientists look into space, the more galaxies they find. There may be more than 100 billion galaxies. If you counted 1,000 galaxies per night, it would take 275,000 years to count all of them.

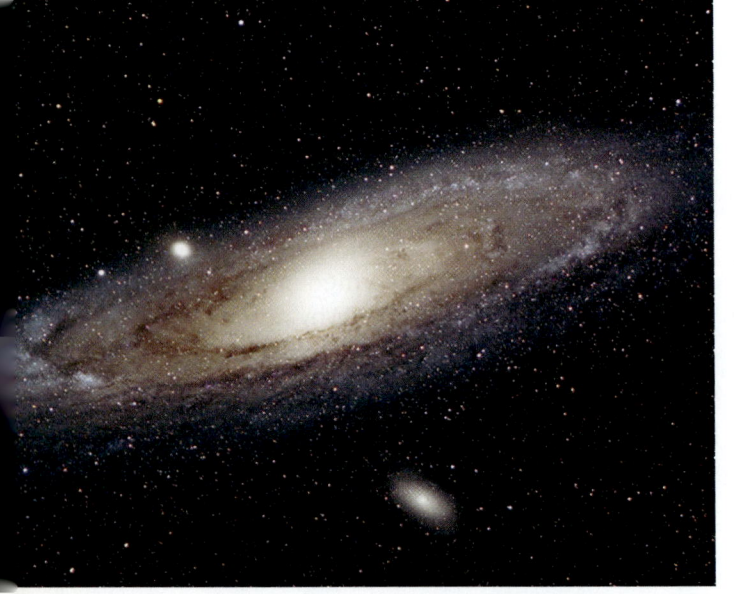

Figure 1 The Andromeda galaxy is 2.2 million light-years from Earth. From a dark location, this galaxy is visible to the unaided eye as a faint blur.

Galaxies contain millions or billions of stars.

Galaxies, such as the Andromeda galaxy, which is shown in **Figure 1**, contain millions to billions of stars bound together by gravity. A galaxy may contain many types of stars. Evidence indicates that young stars are often found near the nebular gas and dust where they were born, while older stars may be found throughout the galaxy or in regions that contain no gas and dust. Although galaxies contain many stars, scientists do not expect to be able to observe planetary systems within other galaxies. The distances to other galaxies are so large that searches for other planets focus on nearby stars in our own galaxy. Luckily, we can search among the billions of stars within our own galaxy.

702 Chapter 20 The Universe

Figure 2 The *Hubble Space Telescope* orbits above Earth. It is named after the astronomer Edwin Hubble, shown in the early 1920s in the inset.

Gravity holds galaxies together.

Without gravity, everything in space might be a veil of gas spread out through space. But because of gravity, clouds of gas come together and collapse to form stars. As the first stars in a galaxy age, they throw off gas and dust or become supernovas. New stars then form. The gas, dust, and stars form galaxies because of gravity.

Just as Earth revolves around the sun because of gravity, the solar system revolves around the center of the galaxy because of gravity. It takes our solar system about 226 million years to complete one orbit of our galaxy.

Reading Check What might space look like if the force of gravity did not cause gas and dust to clump together?

galaxy (GAL uhk see) a collection of stars, dust, and gas bound together by gravity

cluster (KLUHS tuhr) a group of stars or galaxies bound by gravity

Galaxies are often found together in clusters.

Galaxies are not spread out evenly through space. Galaxies are grouped together and bound by gravity in **clusters** like the cluster shown in **Figure 3.** The Milky Way galaxy and the Andromeda galaxy are two of the largest members of the Local Group, a cluster of more than 30 galaxies. New members of the Local Group are being discovered as more telescopes, such as the *Hubble Space Telescope* that is shown in **Figure 2,** become available.

Clusters of galaxies can form even larger groups called *superclusters.* A typical supercluster contains thousands of galaxies that contain trillions of stars in individual clusters. Superclusters can be as large as 100 million light-years across. They are the largest known structures in the universe.

Figure 3 This small cluster of galaxies, known as Stephan's Quintet, is about 270 million light-years from Earth.

Section 2 The Milky Way and Other Galaxies

Types of Galaxies

Galaxies can be divided into three major types: spiral, elliptical, and irregular. ❯ **The three types of galaxies have many stars, but differ in structure.** Spiral galaxies have spiral arms that are made of gas, dust, and stars. Elliptical galaxies have little gas or dust and a round shape. Irregular galaxies do not have a particular shape.

We live in the Milky Way galaxy.

If you live away from bright outdoor lights, you may be able to see the Milky Way, a faint, narrow band of light and dark patches in the sky. This band, shown in **Figure 4**, consists of stars, gas, and dust in our galaxy, the Milky Way galaxy.

Most of the objects you see in the night sky are part of the Milky Way galaxy. Because our solar system is inside the Milky Way galaxy, we cannot see all of our galaxy at once. But scientists can use astronomical data to piece together a picture of the Milky Way galaxy, such as the artistic representation shown in **Figure 5**. Our solar system is located within a spiral arm, about 26,000 light-years from the center of the galaxy, or about half of the distance to the edge.

The Milky Way is a spiral galaxy.

Our galaxy is a huge spiraling disk of stars, gas, and dust. Like most spiral galaxies, the Milky Way has a huge bulge in the center. The nucleus of the galaxy is very dense and has many old stars. The gas and dust have been used up to form stars. Many astronomers think that a large black hole is at the center of our galaxy. The spiral arms of these galaxies have gas and dust between the stars. This gas and dust is called **interstellar matter**. Clouds of interstellar matter provide materials that allow new stars to form. Because the spiral arms appear blue, scientists assume that the arms are composed of young stars. Hot stars that emit more energy at blue wavelengths should burn out quickly. So if they are visible, they must be young. The center bulge contains primarily red stars that use energy more slowly and thus would be older stars.

Figure 4 When we see the band of light called the *Milky Way*, we are looking along the plane of our galaxy, the Milky Way galaxy.

interstellar matter (IN tuhr STEL uhr MAT uhr) the gas and dust located between the stars in a galaxy

Figure 5 An artistic representation of what our own Milky Way galaxy might look like from the outside can be pieced together from astronomical data. **Why can't astronomers take a picture of our own galaxy?**

Figure 6 The Three Types of Galaxies

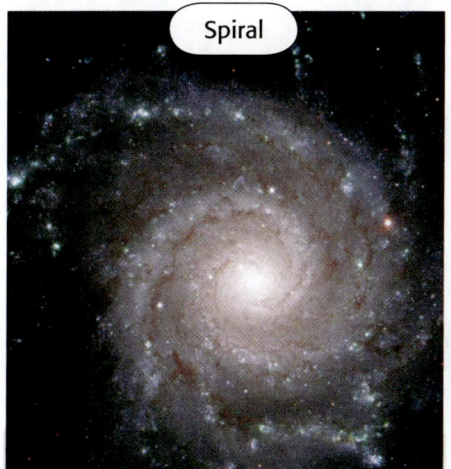
Spiral

Seen from above, the Milky Way galaxy might look similar to this spiral galaxy named Messier 74.

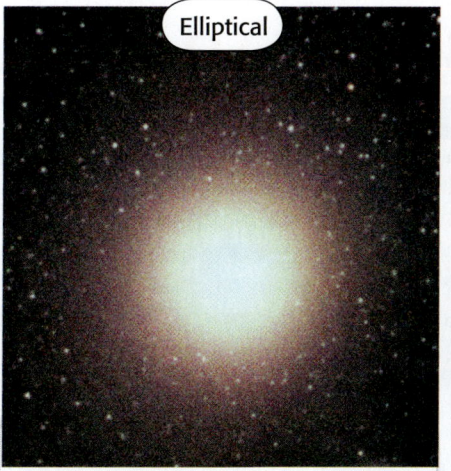
Elliptical

Unlike the Milky Way galaxy, elliptical galaxies, such as Messier 87, do not have spiral arms.

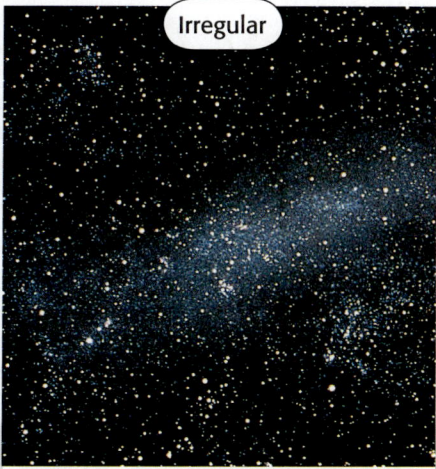
Irregular

The Large Magellanic Cloud is an irregular galaxy that is easily seen from the Southern Hemisphere.

Elliptical galaxies have no spiral arms.

Elliptical galaxies have no spiral arms and are spherical or egg shaped. Elliptical galaxies, such as Messier 87 (M87) shown in **Figure 6,** often have a reddish color. Because elliptical galaxies commonly appear red, astronomers assume that they contain mostly older stars and have little interstellar matter. Elliptical galaxies are found in a wide range of sizes. Giant elliptical galaxies contain trillions of stars and can have diameters of up to 200,000 light-years. Dwarf elliptical galaxies contain a few million stars and are much smaller.

Because an elliptical galaxy has no regular features, such as the arms of a spiral galaxy, astronomers have trouble knowing the orientation of an elliptical galaxy in relation to Earth.

✓ **Reading Check** How does an elliptical galaxy differ from a spiral galaxy?

All other galaxies are irregular galaxies.

Edwin Hubble named the third category of galaxies *irregular galaxies* because they lack regular shapes and do not have a well-defined structure. Some irregular galaxies contain little interstellar matter, while others have large amounts and contain mostly young blue stars. **Figure 6** shows the large irregular galaxy that is nearest to the Milky Way, the Large Magellanic Cloud. This galaxy is a part of the Local Group.

There are many more dwarf irregular galaxies than giant galaxies. Dwarf galaxies are often found near larger galaxies. Some irregular galaxies may be oddly shaped because the gravitational pull of nearby galaxies distorts their shape.

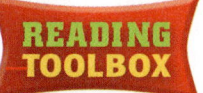

READING TOOLBOX

Using Spatial Language
Make a chart that shows the spatial language that is used to describe the different types of galaxies.

Why It Matters
Any Aliens Out There?

In 1977, a radio astronomer picked up a powerful signal. Thinking it might be a sign of an intelligent source, he marked it with a "Wow" and alerted other astronomers. The signal, however, was never heard again.

In 1984, the SETI Institute (Search for Extraterrestrial Intelligence Institute) was founded. SETI is dedicated to searching for evidence of extraterrestrial life and signs of alien intelligence. But SETI is not humanity's first attempt to contact alien civilizations. The Voyager probes, launched in 1977, each carry a golden disc with information about Earth and human beings.

YOUR TURN

WRITING IN SCIENCE
1. Write a short story describing what you think alien life might look and act like.

How Galaxies Change Over Time

When scientists observe distant galaxies, they are looking back in time. When astronomers observe a galaxy that is 1 billion light-years away, they are observing light that left the galaxy 1 billion years ago. ❯ **Scientists do not know what such a galaxy looks like now, but by studying closer galaxies that might be similar to ancient ones, they can slowly piece together the puzzle of how galaxies evolve.**

Like the stars that make up a galaxy, galaxies themselves change over time. Because galaxies change over billions of years, astronomers have never seen the whole process, but they have theories about how galaxies change over time.

Quasars may be infant galaxies.

When astronomers first detected radio waves in space, they had difficulty finding stars that could produce some of the signals. In 1960, a faint object was finally matched with a strong radio signal. This object—the first identified **quasar,** or quasi-stellar object—was so named for its starlike appearance. On further study, scientists discovered that quasars are the most distant and most radiant objects in space. One explanation for the strong radiation is that quasars are enormous black holes that are surrounded by large disks of gas and dust. Friction in these disks releases energy at many wavelengths, especially radio waves. Quasars may be the central parts of distant galaxies, seen as they were when very young.

Galaxies change over time.

The gas, dust, and stars that make up galaxies is in constant motion. As galaxies consume their gas and dust, they become unable to make stars. Many galaxies in the Hubble Deep Field image, shown in **Figure 7,** are blue, which indicates that we are viewing them when they were young, before they have used up their stores of gas and dust by making stars.

Galaxies also change as a result of collisions. As galaxies approach each other, the gravitational attraction changes their shapes. While individual stars rarely hit one another, the collision of gas and dust sets off rapid bursts of new star formation. Scientists are trying to find out why elliptical galaxies do not have young stars and how they used up their gas and dust. One possibility is that gas and dust were stripped away in collisions that also stripped away many of the younger stars.

Figure 7 The Hubble Deep Field project discovered many faint and very distant galaxies.

quasar (KWAY ZAHR) a very luminous object that produces energy at a high rate; quasars are thought to be the most distant objects in the universe

Section 2 Review

KEY IDEAS

1. **Describe** what a galaxy is, and tell how many galaxies may exist according to astronomers.
2. **Define** the terms *cluster* and *supercluster*.
3. **List** the types of galaxies, and describe each one in terms of shape and the types of stars and other interstellar material that it contains.
4. **Draw** a sketch of the Milky Way galaxy. Label the nucleus and the central bulge, and indicate the position of our solar system.
5. **Explain** why the Milky Way galaxy appears as a narrow band of light in the night sky.
6. **Describe** how quasars got their name.
7. **Explain** how galaxies may change through collisions with other galaxies.

CRITICAL THINKING

8. **Analyzing Information** Why might scientists conclude that we are living in a spiral galaxy and not in an elliptical or irregular galaxy?
9. **Recognizing Patterns** Why do galaxies clump together in clusters and superclusters?
10. **Evaluating Ideas** Why do stars rarely collide during galactic collisions?

SECTION 3 Origin of the Universe

Key Ideas
- What makes up the universe?
- How did the universe begin?
- How do scientists make predictions about the future of the universe?

Key Terms
universe
Doppler effect
big bang theory

Why It Matters
Understanding the origins of the universe helps us understand our solar system's place in the universe.

Tennessee Course Level Expectations (Physical Science)
CLE.3202.Inq.1; CLE.3202.Inq.2; CLE.3202.Inq.3; CLE.3202.Inq.4; CLE.3202.Inq.6; CLE.3202.Math.1; CLE.3202.Math.2

Just imagine the following: colliding galaxies that rip stars away from each other, a dead star so dense that one teaspoon of its matter would weigh more than 100 million tons on Earth, and a volcano that is nearly three times taller than Mount Everest and that has a base larger than Louisiana. All of these things are part of the universe.

What Is the Universe?

The **universe** is everything physical that exists in space and time. ▶ **The universe consists of all space, matter, and energy that exists—now, in the past, or in the future.** Objects in the universe can be very tiny or extremely large. The relative sizes of some objects are shown in **Figure 1**.

Figure 1 Scale and Distance

The average baseball player is between 1.5 m and 2.0 m tall.

At 1,000 m, or 1 km, away, you could see an entire baseball stadium.

At 100 km away, you could get a good view of the entire city in which the stadium is located.

Everything is part of the universe.

You are part of the universe, as is Earth and everything on it. With the naked eye, and a very dark sky, we can see about 6,000 stars, five of the planets, our moon, and several nebulas, star clusters, and galaxies. As **Figure 1** shows, huge distances are a part of studying the universe. Perhaps you can imagine the size of a baseball field, your city, your country, or even Earth, but the comparisons become difficult as we imagine objects on scales beyond Earth, such as the solar system. The solar system is only a small part of our galaxy, which is just one of many galaxies in one of many clusters of galaxies.

We see the universe now as it was in the past.

Astronomers need large units of measure to express distances. A light-year, which is approximately 9.5×10^{12} km, is so long that driving a light-year in a car moving at highway speeds would take more than 10 million years. Remember that while a year is a unit of time, a light-year is a unit of distance.

It takes time for light to travel in space. The farther an object is, the older the light that we get from that object is. When we say the sun is 8 light-minutes away, we are expressing not only its distance from Earth, but also that we see the sun as it was 8 min ago. We never see it as it is in the present. The same is true for stars, planets, and galaxies. For example, Pluto is more than 5 light-hours away. When we see distant objects, we see them as they were when they were younger. Astronomers can compare how galaxies age by looking at many galaxies at various distances and thus at different ages.

Reading Check Why can't we see distant objects as they currently appear?

www.scilinks.org
Topic: Structure of the Universe
Code: HK81469

universe (YOON uh VUHRS) the sum of all space, matter, and energy that exist, that have existed in the past, and that will exist in the future

If you were about 5 light-hours away, you could see the planets in orbit around the sun.

At 150 light-days away, you could see the solar system surrounded by a cloud of icy comets.

By the time you were 10 light-years away, the sun would resemble any other star in space.

Section 3   Origin of the Universe

Figure 2 Astronaut Bruce McCandless maneuvers through space in a suit specifically designed to protect him. **Why do humans need special suits to survive in space?**

Figure 3 The arrows show how the direction a star is moving relative to Earth affects the way we see the light, shifted toward the blue or red end of the spectrum.

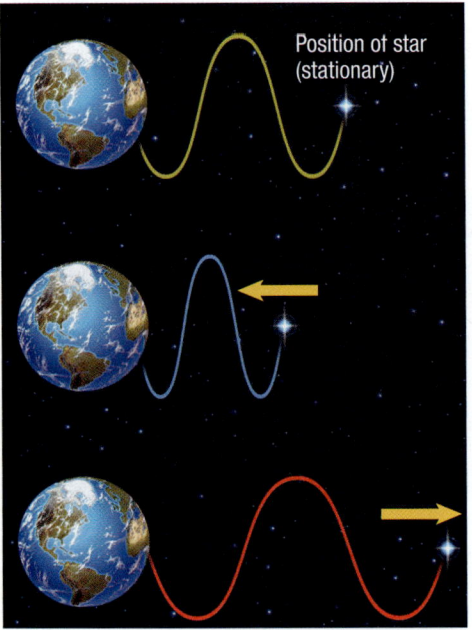

Most of the universe is empty space.

Despite the variety of objects in the universe, such as planets, stars, and galaxies, there is almost nothing between objects. **Figure 2** shows an astronaut in a suit designed to help a person survive in space. The side facing the sun is extremely hot, and the side facing away from the sun is very cold. Space is a vacuum with no air and no air pressure. The suit provides the insulation, breathable air, and air pressure that the human body needs to survive. Within our solar system, tiny particles stream out from the sun, but between stars, there is so little matter that the space can truly be called empty.

What Happened at the Beginning?

From the beginning of human history, people have wondered where the universe came from. Ancient cultures had myths to explain the origin of the universe. Today, scientists use new tools and new techniques to study stars and galaxies for clues. Scientists who are interested in the early history of our universe use powerful telescopes to study the most distant objects, whose light was emitted billions of years ago. ❱ **By studying this ancient light and looking at other evidence, scientists have been able to theorize that the universe formed during a cataclysmic event known as the big bang.**

The universe is expanding.

In 1929, American astronomer Edwin Hubble announced that the universe is expanding. He based his conclusion on observations of spectral lines in the light from other galaxies. He found that these lines were almost always shifted toward the red end of the spectrum. This effect, called *red shift,* can be explained by the Doppler effect. The **Doppler effect** is a change in the observed frequency of electromagnetic radiation when an object or observer is moving. Thus, as **Figure 3** shows, light waves emitted from an object that is moving away would be stretched out. The faster a light source moves away, the more the light stretches to longer wavelengths and the more it shifts toward the red end of the spectrum.

When an object is approaching us, however, the shift is toward shorter wavelengths at the spectrum's blue end and is called *blue shift.* Hubble found that most galaxies have red shifts and that galaxies that are farther away have greater red shifts. Hubble explained this by proposing that almost every galaxy is moving away from Earth. Therefore, galaxies are also moving away from each other, and the universe is expanding.

QuickLab

An Expanding Universe Model ⏱ 10 min

Procedure

1. Inflate a round **balloon** to about half full, and then pinch it closed to keep the air inside.
2. Use a **marker** to draw several dots close together on the balloon. Mark one of the dots with an M to indicate the Milky Way galaxy. Mark the other dots with other letters.
3. Blow the balloon up until taut, and pinch the end. Take a measurement of the distances between the dot labeled M and the other dots.
4. Continue inflating the balloon. Measure the distance between the dot labeled M and the other dots on the balloon.

Analysis

1. How do the dots move relative to one another as the balloon expands?
2. How is this inflating balloon a good model for the expanding universe?
3. In what ways might this balloon not be a good model for the expanding universe?

Expansion implies that the universe was once smaller.

Although galaxies that are close to each other are attracted to each other by gravity, most galaxies are moving away from each other. Imagine time running backward like a movie being rewound. If every galaxy normally moves away from every other galaxy, then as time goes backward, the galaxies move closer together. Long ago, the entire universe might have been contained in an extremely small space.

If time moves forward from that point, all of the matter in the universe appears to expand rapidly outward like a gigantic explosion. A lump of raisin bread dough can be used to model this concept. **Figure 4** shows that as the dough between the raisins rises and spreads, all of the raisins move away from one another. If you were standing on any given raisin, nearly all of the other raisins would appear to be moving away from you.

✅ **Reading Check** What evidence supports the concept that the universe was once contained in an extremely small space?

> **Doppler effect** (DAHP luhr e FEKT) an observed change in the frequency of a wave when the source or observer is moving

Figure 4 As the raisin bread rises, all of the raisins move away from one another.

go.hrw.com
✴ interact online
Keyword: HK8UNVF4

Section 3 Origin of the Universe

big bang theory (BIG BANG THEE uh ree) the theory that all matter and energy in the universe was compressed into an extremely small volume that 13 billion to 15 billion years ago exploded and began expanding in all directions

Tri-Fold Note
As you read through this section on the evolution of the universe, make a Tri-Fold Note that describes the three possible futures for the universe.

Did the universe start with a big bang?

Although scientists have proposed several different theories to explain the expansion of the universe, the most complete and widely accepted is the big bang theory. The **big bang theory** states that the universe began with a gigantic explosion 13 billion to 15 billion years ago. Based on recent data from the NASA's WMAP project, scientists estimate that the universe is about 13.7 billion years old.

According to this theory, nothing existed before the big bang. There was no time and no space. But out of this nothingness came the vast system of space, time, matter, and energy that now makes up the universe. The explosion released all of the matter and energy that still exist in the universe today.

Cosmic background radiation supports the big bang theory.

In 1965, scientists Arno Penzias and Robert Wilson were making adjustments to a new radio antenna that they had built. They could not explain a steady but very dim signal from all over the sky in the form of radiation at microwave wavelengths. They finally realized that the signal was the *cosmic background radiation* predicted by the big bang theory.

Imagine the changes in color that occur as the burner on an electric stove cools. First, the hot burner glows yellow or white. As the burner cools, it becomes dimmer and glows red. It may still be rather hot when it finally looks black. The color that you see corresponds to the wavelength at which the burner radiates the most light. In outer space, the burner would cool until it reached the temperature of space.

According to the accepted theory of cosmic origins, the microwaves detected by Penzias and Wilson are dim remnants of the radiation produced during the big bang. Using maps of cosmic background radiation, such as the map shown in **Figure 5,** astronomers have found that the universe has an overall temperature of about 2.7 K.

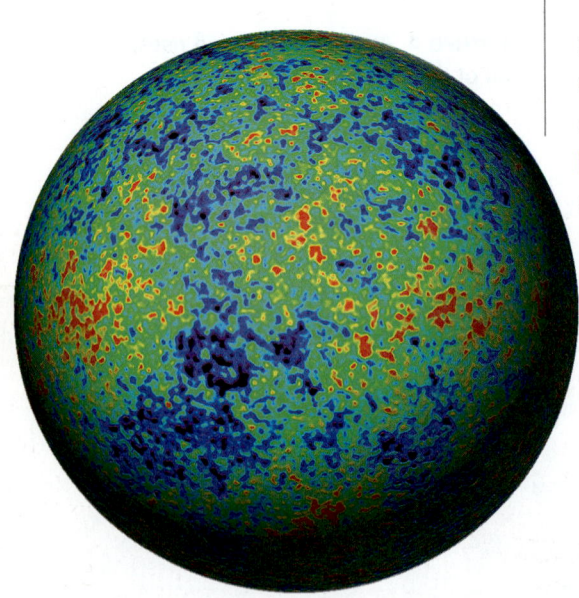

Figure 5 The colors in this computerized map of cosmic background radiation across the entire sky represent slight differences in temperature above and below 2.7 K.

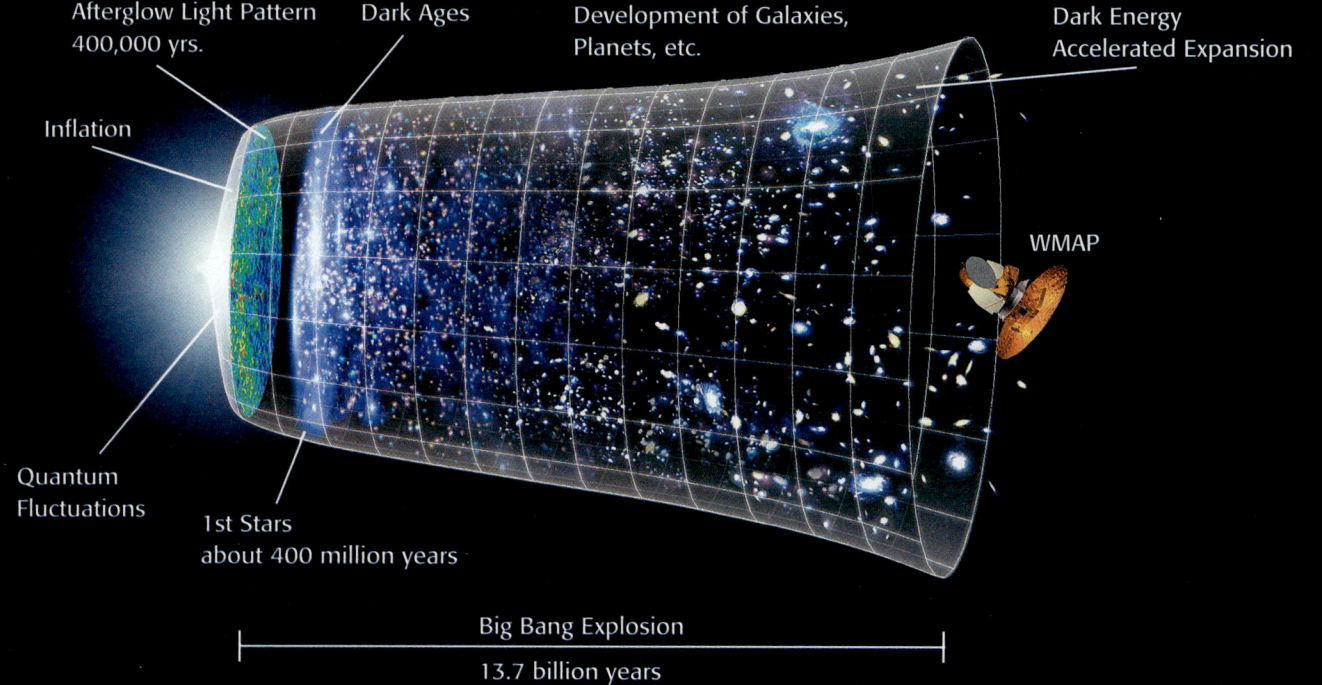

Figure 6 This model was built based on data collected by NASA's WMAP mission. Notice how the universe expanded extremely rapidly at first and has expanded at a gradual rate for most of its history.

Radiation dominated the early universe.

According to the big bang theory, immediately after the big bang, the universe was extremely hot and made up of pure energy. There was a period of rapid expansion that caused the energy to cool and allowed sub-atomic particles, such as protons, electrons, and neutrons, to form. Hydrogen nuclei began forming about one second after the big bang, but the temperature was still too high for atoms to form and remain stable. Electrons did not combine with atomic nuclei to form atoms until about 380,000 years after the big bang. The first stars were born about 400 million years after the big bang. **Figure 6** shows a model of the expansion of the universe.

The big bang theory is constantly being tested.

Like any scientific theory, the big bang theory is continually tested against each new discovery about the universe. As new information emerges, the big bang theory may be refined and revised, or a new theory may become more widely accepted by astronomers.

During the past 100 years, other theories for the origin of the universe have been proposed. A few are still being studied, but the big bang theory is the one that is best supported by the current evidence including the cosmic background radiation and observations of the movement of distant galaxies.

Reading Check Why do scientists feel that the big bang is the best theory to explain the origin of the universe?

Why It Matters

We're All Stars!

WEIRD SCIENCE

All elements other than hydrogen and helium formed in stars. Nuclear fusion in stars produces most of the helium and all other elements up to the atomic number of iron. Heavier elements form during supernovas, or star explosions. Even the elements that make up Earth and all of the things on it were originally created in a star or star explosion. So, the metal in your silverware, the tree outside your window, the shirt on your back—even you!—are made of the remains of stars that have been dead for a long time.

You may find elements like potassium in vitamins, but they originally came from a star.

Iron is the heaviest element that can be made through fusion in stars.

Stars convert hydrogen into the helium used in these balloons through fusion.

All of the elements that are in your body came from a star or star explosion.

YOUR TURN

CRITICAL THINKING

1. How might the objects found in the early universe differ from the objects found in the universe now?
2. What will eventually happen to the elements that are currently being created in our sun?

Predicting the Future of the Universe

▶ **Scientists use their increasing knowledge of the universe to hypothesize what might happen to the universe in the future.** They depend on a mixture of theories and precise observations of very faint and distant objects. These observations depend on technology, such as the telescopes shown in **Figure 7.** New space telescopes that collect infrared radiation and X rays are being built and launched. Data in these regions of the electromagnetic spectrum may provide important clues about the beginning and future of the universe.

The future of the universe is uncertain.

The universe is still expanding, but it may not do so forever. The combined gravity of all of the mass in the universe is also pulling the universe inward, in the direction opposite to the expansion. The competition between these two forces leaves three possible outcomes for the universe:

1. The universe will keep expanding forever.
2. The expansion of the universe will gradually slow down, and the universe will approach a limit in size.
3. The universe will stop expanding and start to fall back on itself.

The future of the universe depends on mass.

The possible futures of the universe are shown in **Figure 8.** The future of the universe depends on the amount of matter in the universe. If there is not enough mass, the gravitational force will be too weak to stop the expansion, so the universe will keep expanding forever. If there is just the right amount of mass, the expansion will continue to slow down but will never stop completely. If there is too much mass, then gravity will eventually overcome the expansion and the universe will start to contract. Eventually, a contracting universe could collapse back to a single point in what is called the *big crunch*. As things came closer to each other, galaxies and stars would collide. The universe would become extremely hot and very small. At this point, the universe may end, or another big bang could start the cycle again.

It is hard to predict what will happen in this very distant future because much of the mass in the universe is very difficult to detect. Astronomers refine their predictions with each new discovery.

✓ **Reading Check** How does the amount of mass affect the future of the universe?

Figure 7 Modern telescopes use advanced technologies to improve their capabilities. Here, a laser is used to create a false star in the sky. Astronomers can use this false star to help them guide their telescope and take clear pictures of dim objects.

Figure 8 Astronomers try to predict the future of the universe by collecting data on amount of matter it contains.

Figure 9 The *Chandra X-Ray Observatory* (top) collects information from matter at very high temperatures, such as the Crab Nebula (bottom).

www.scilinks.org
Topic: Dark Matter
Code: **HK80377**

New technology helps scientists test theories.

Predictions about the future of the universe rest on theories about the past universe. Scientists test theories by making observations to see whether the theories make accurate predictions. If observations do not agree with the theory, new theories are needed. To make these observations, scientists need sensitive equipment, such as powerful telescopes.

One example of new, more sensitive technology is the *Chandra X-Ray Observatory,* which was launched into orbit around Earth in 1999. This observatory can take photographs in the X-ray part of the electromagnetic spectrum. The presence of X rays indicates matter at temperatures of more than one million degrees. The Crab Nebula emits radiation at many wavelengths, including X rays, as **Figure 9** shows. Observations at various wavelengths give us information about the Crab Nebula and about other supernovas of similar kind.

There is debate about dark matter.

Astronomers estimate the mass of the universe by measuring stars, galaxies, and matter in the interstellar medium. But observations of gravitational interactions between galaxies, such as the interaction shown in **Figure 10,** show that there is more matter than what is visible. Astronomers call this matter that is not visible *dark matter.* Dark matter may consist of planets, black holes, or brown dwarfs. Brown dwarfs are starlike objects that lack enough mass to begin fusion and thus do not emit light. Dark matter could also consist of strange atomic particles that no one knows how to observe. Although astronomers think that the universe has more dark matter than visible matter, what dark matter is and where it is located remain a mystery.

Figure 10 The collision of NCG 2207 and IC 2163 may point to the presence of dark matter. The amount of distortion indicates that there may be more matter present than we can see.

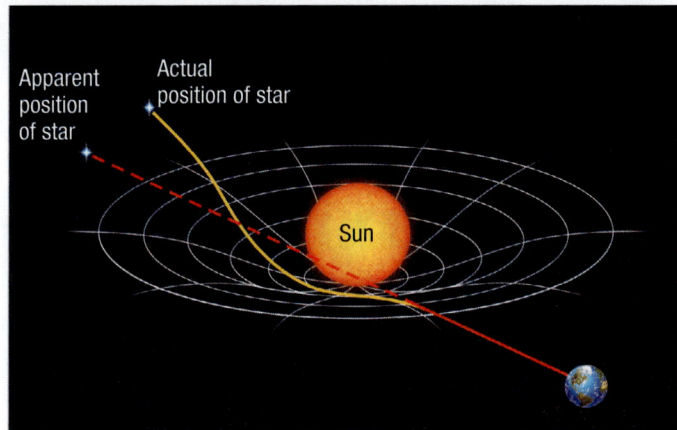

Figure 11 According to Einstein's theory of relativity, the mass of the sun curves the space near the sun.

Scientists use mathematics to build better models.

We easily accept Isaac Newton's theory of gravity because it corresponds to our experiences of the world around us. Newton wrote his theory in a mathematical form that can be applied to many circumstances on Earth and in space. In 1916, Albert Einstein expanded on Newton's theories by developing the general theory of relativity, which he also expressed in mathematical form.

According to Einstein's theory, mass curves space, much in the same way that your body curves a mattress when you sit on it. In 1919, observations of a total solar eclipse showed that Einstein was correct. In the direction of the sun, stars that could be seen only during the eclipse were in slightly different positions than expected. The mass of the sun had curved space and made the light appear to come from a slightly different location, as **Figure 11** shows. Larger masses, such as galaxies, will distort space even more than stars do. In this way, a mathematical model of relativity was tested and supported by observation.

Section 3 Review

KEY IDEAS

1. **Define** the word *universe*.
2. **Describe** the current evidence that shows that the universe is expanding.
3. **Describe** what would happen to the universe in terms of size and temperature if you were able to go back in time.
4. **List** three possible futures for the universe.
5. **Explain** the effect that a massive object, such as a galaxy, has on space according to Einstein's general theory of relativity.

CRITICAL THINKING

6. **Applying Ideas** Why didn't the first stars that formed in the early universe have solar systems with Earthlike planets and satellites?
7. **Evaluating Theories** Scientists crafted the big bang theory after studying numerous galaxies and finding that most of them had red shifts. Describe what kind of theory scientists might have crafted if most of the galaxies they studied had blue shifts.
8. **Making Inferences** Why is it unlikely that dark matter is made up mostly of stars?

Skills Practice Lab

Types of Galaxies

Galaxies occur in many sizes and types. Our own galaxy has a spiral shape. How can you tell the difference between galaxies by taking simple measurements of their images?

⏱ 50 min

What You'll Do

▸ **Recognize** the orientation of galaxies.
▸ **Classify** galaxies according to type.
▸ **Measure** the diameters of galaxies.
▸ **Analyze** the results by calculating the ratio of spiral galaxies to elliptical galaxies within a cluster.

What You'll Need

magnifying glass
photograph of a galaxy cluster
ruler, metric, clear plastic

Procedure

Preparing for Your Experiment

① Examine the images of galaxies in this chapter. Make sketches of what each galaxy might look like if you rotated it from a view from above to a view from the side.

② Examine the large image of the Hercules Cluster of galaxies in this lab activity. Your teacher may also provide you with a larger version of the image. The image also contains stars that are between our galaxy and the galaxies within the cluster. Write your criteria for distinguishing between a nearby star and a galaxy.

Classifying Galaxies

③ Set up a classification system that divides galaxies into categories. Ignore the individual identity of stars. You should divde the galaxies into at least three types. Discuss in your group what types you will use and what characteristics define each type.

④ Find at least one example of each type of galaxy in the image, and write down the coordinates of each example by using the letters and numbers on the grid. Compare your examples with the examples of others in your group.

⑤ Classify each galaxy that you see in the image, and note the coordinates of each galaxy. If necessary, use a magnifying glass to view the image more clearly. If you can identify something as a galaxy but are unclear of its type, classify it as "uncertain galaxy."

Measuring Galaxies

⑥ Locate the largest and smallest galaxy for each type of galaxy.

⑦ Measure the sizes of these galaxies in millimeters. This process may be easier if you use a magnifying glass and a clear ruler.

The Hercules Cluster

Analysis

1. **Analyzing Data** Count the number of each type of galaxy that you have observed. Calculate the total number of galaxies observed.
2. **Analyzing Data** Calculate the ratio of each type of galaxy to the other types by dividing the number of one type by the total number of galaxies observed. For example, if you have 33 of type A and 100 total galaxies, the ratio would be about 33/100, or 1/3.

Communicating Your Results

3. **Organizing Data** Make a table that shows the types of galaxies, the total number of each type, and the calculated ratios.
4. **Drawing Conclusions** What type of galaxy is most common in the Hercules Cluster?
5. **Analyzing Results** Which type of galaxy is usually the largest?
6. **Analyzing Methods** Do you think that there may be smaller galaxies that you overlooked? Explain.
7. **Analyzing Methods** Which type of galaxy is easiest to confuse with foreground stars?

Extension

Assume that all of the galaxies in a cluster are about the same distance from Earth. Thus, differences in cluster size are due to differences in the sizes of the galaxies. If the largest spiral galaxy you measured was the same size as the Milky Way galaxy, estimate the total diameter of this cluster of galaxies.

Chapter Lab

Making Bar Graphs

Science › Skills

Technology
Math
Scientific Methods
▶ Graphing

Problem

The colors of stars depend on the stars' masses and ages. The data table shows the color distribution of the 100 stars that are nearest to Earth. Show these data in a bar graph.

Solution

① Determine the x axis and the y axis. One axis is a numerical axis, and the other is a category axis.	Make the category axis—the star color—the y axis, and make the numerical axis—the number of stars—the x axis.
② Determine the range of the numerical axis, and add tick marks that are equally spaced. Label the numerical axis.	The data for the number of stars range from 2 to 57. Extend the horizontal axis from 0 to 60. Add a number for every 10. Label the axis "Number of stars."
③ Label the categories on the category axis, and then label the axis.	Write the star colors along the vertical axis. Label the axis "Star color."
④ Draw a different color bar for each category. Extend the bars according to the numerical data.	For example, the bar for the blue-white colored stars should extend from zero to 2.
⑤ Add a title.	Above the bar graph, add the title "Color Distribution of Nearest 100 Stars."

Color Distribution of the 100 Stars Nearest Earth

Star Color	Number of Stars
Blue-white	2
White	3
Yellow-white	3
Yellow	9
Orange	26
Red	57

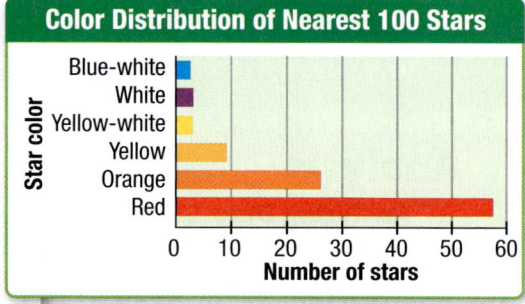

Practice

Use the graph above to answer questions 1–2.

1. What is the most common color for stars near Earth? What is the least common color for stars near Earth?

2. Most stars are main-sequence stars. The more massive a main-sequence star is, the greater its temperature and brightness. Based on this information and the data in the graph, answer the following questions: a) Which are more common, hot stars or cool stars? b) Which are more common, low-mass stars or high-mass stars? c) Which are more common, bright or dim stars?

Use the table below to answer question 3.

Color Distribution of the 100 Brightest Stars (as seen from Earth)

Star color	Number of stars
Blue-white	38
Yellow-white	26
Yellow	8
Orange	21
Red	7

3. The data above are for the 100 brightest stars as seen from Earth. Show these data in a bar graph.

720 Chapter 20 The Universe

CHAPTER 20 Summary

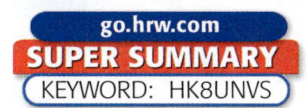

go.hrw.com
SUPER SUMMARY
KEYWORD: HK8UNVS

Key Ideas

Section 1 The Life and Death of Stars

› **What Are Stars?** Stars are huge spheres of very hot gas that emit light and other radiation. Stars are formed from clouds of dust and gas, or nebulas, and go through different stages as they age. (p. 693)

› **Studying Stars** The telescope allowed astronomers to accurately study stars for the first time. (p. 695)

› **The Life Cycle of Stars** In a way that is similar to other natural cycles, stars are born, go through stages of development, and eventually die. (p. 698)

Section 2 The Milky Way and Other Galaxies

› **Galaxies** A galaxy is a collection of millions to billions of stars bound together by gravity. (p. 702)

› **Types of Galaxies** There are three types of galaxies that differ in structure. They are named for their general shape: spiral, elliptical, and irregular. (p. 704)

› **How Galaxies Change Over Time** By studying closer galaxies that might be similar to ancient ones, scientists can slowly piece together the puzzle of how galaxies evolve. (p. 706)

Section 3 Origin of the Universe

› **What Is the Universe?** The universe consists of all space, matter, and energy that exists—now, in the past, or in the future. (p. 708)

› **What Happened at the Beginning?** Scientists theorize that the universe formed during a cataclysmic event known as the big bang. (p. 710)

› **Predicting the Future of the Universe** Scientists use their increasing knowledge of the universe to hypothesize what might happen to the universe in the future. (p. 715)

Key Terms

star, p. 693
light-year, p. 693
red giant, p. 699
white dwarf, p. 699
supernova, p. 699
black hole, p. 700

galaxy, p. 702
cluster, p. 703
interstellar matter, p. 704
quasar, p. 707

universe, p. 708
Doppler effect, p. 710
big bang theory, p. 712

The Universe

CHAPTER 20 Review

READING TOOLBOX

1. **Everyday Words Used in Science** Describe what the word *bang* means in everyday speech. Then, explain why you think this is or is not an appropriate word to use in the scientific term *big bang theory*.

USING KEY TERMS

2. Arrange the following from largest to smallest: *white dwarf, spiral galaxy, red giant,* and *supercluster.*

3. Describe *nuclear fusion,* and identify the part of a star in which nuclear fusion takes place. Describe how it is taking place in the sun.

4. Describe the arrangement of the components of the Milky Way galaxy. Use the terms *interstellar matter, stars, bulge,* and *spiral arms.*

5. Explain the current theory of what a *quasar* is and where quasars can be found.

6. Write a paragraph that describes how the mass of a star determines the death of the star. Include the terms *star, white dwarf, supernova, neutron star,* and *black hole.*

7. Describe the difference between *blue shift* and *red shift.*

UNDERSTANDING KEY IDEAS

8. What are the three major types of galaxies?
    a. spiral, elliptical, and irregular
    b. closed, elliptical, and open
    c. spiral, quasar, and pulsar
    d. irregular, giant, and cluster

9. The diagonal line of stars in the H-R diagram is known as the
    a. galaxy.
    b. supercluster.
    c. Milky Way.
    d. main sequence.

INTERPRETING GRAPHICS Use the diagram below to answer questions 10 and 11.

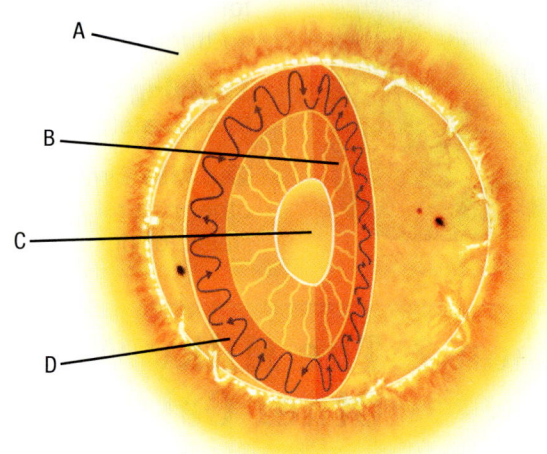

10. In which layer of the sun does fusion take place?
    a. layer A   c. layer C
    b. layer B   d. layer D

11. In which layer of the sun is energy transferred through a process known as convection?
    a. layer A   c. layer C
    b. layer B   d. layer D

12. A main-sequence star generates energy by fusing
    a. nitrogen into iron.
    b. helium into carbon.
    c. nitrogen into carbon.
    d. hydrogen into helium.

13. Which of the following is a possible age of the universe, according to the big bang theory?
    a. 4.6 million years   c. 4.6 billion years
    b. 13.7 million years   d. 13.7 billion years

14. The heaviest element formed in a star's core is
    a. helium.   c. carbon.
    b. iron.   d. nitrogen.

15. According to Einstein's general theory of relativity, space is curved by
    a. mass.   c. a vacuum.
    b. energy.   d. light.

722 Chapter 20 The Universe

EXPLAINING KEY IDEAS

16. Describe what stars are made of and how they produce energy as light and heat.

17. Describe how astronomers are able to use the light from a distant star to determine what elements make up the stars.

18. List the three major types of galaxies, and describe how each one is different in shape from the other types.

19. Explain how we can tell that many of the galaxies that we see in the Hubble Deep Field are young.

20. Explain what it means when we say that the sun is 8 light-minutes away. What does it mean when we say a star is 1,000 light-years away?

21. Explain the big bang theory in terms of what it states about how the universe began, how the universe has changed over time, and how long the universe has existed.

22. List the types of evidence that support the big bang theory.

CRITICAL THINKING

23. **Critical Thinking** What can we infer from knowing that most of the stars that we see in the center of the Milky Way galaxy are red? Explain your answer?

24. **Understanding Systems** What keeps a star from collapsing under its own weight?

25. **Applying Knowledge** If the universe were to slow down its expansion and begin to contract, what changes in our observations of other galaxies might take place? Explain your answer.

26. **Critical Thinking** Where in a galaxy would a black hole most likely be found?

27. **Applying Knowledge** Could a black hole consume an entire galaxy? Explain your answer in a paragraph. Use concepts that you learned in the chapter.

Graphing Skills

28. **Graphing** Graph the data from the table below. These data show the distance to several galaxies and each galaxy's velocity in relation to Earth. Put distance on the horizontal axis, and put velocity in relation to Earth on the vertical axis.

Object	Distance (light-years)	Velocity (km/s)
Andromeda galaxy	224,000	−10
Centaurus A	2,116,000	251
M66	3,680,000	593
M49	6,746,000	822
Fornax A	9,200,000	1,713

29. **Understanding Relationships** Estimate the distance between Earth and a galaxy whose velocity is 2,000 km/s.

30. **Predicting Patterns** What is the approximate velocity for a galaxy that is 5,000,000 light-years from Earth?

31. **Analyzing Information** Note that the closest galaxy in the table, the Andromeda galaxy, falls below the zero on the velocity axis. What does this position mean for the motion of the galaxy in relation to Earth?

32. **Building Models** The graph shown here is based on Edwin Hubble's actual data from observations that he made in 1929. The graph shows the relationship between a galaxy's velocity and the galaxy's distance from Earth. How do these data support Hubble's conclusion that the universe is expanding?

Standardized Test Prep

Understanding Concepts

Directions (1-5): For each question, write on a sheet of paper the letter of the correct answer.

1. Inside a star's core, hydrogen nuclei fuse to form deuterons, which consist of one proton and one neutron. When deuterons fuse with hydrogen nuclei, what do they form?
   - A. plasma
   - B. hydrogen atoms
   - C. hydrogen nuclei
   - D. helium nuclei

2. The hottest stars appear to be which color?
   - F. blue
   - G. green
   - H. red
   - I. yellow

3. What is the final stage in the life cycle of most stars in our galaxy?
   - A. red giant
   - B. white dwarf
   - C. nebula
   - D. supernova

4. What objects are thought to be the most distant objects in the universe?
   - F. spiral galaxies
   - G. elliptical galaxies
   - H. quasars
   - I. nebulas

5. About how long does it take light from the sun to reach Earth?
   - A. 8 seconds
   - B. 8 minutes
   - C. 8 days
   - D. 8 years

Directions (6-8): For each question, write a short response.

6. Why is the light from distant galaxies almost always shifted toward the red end of the spectrum?

7. What is the name for the process in which atoms combine to form larger atoms, and where does it take place?

8. If the Milky Way galaxy has a spiral shape, why do we see it as a streak across the sky?

Reading Skills

Directions (9-10): Read the passage below. Then, answer the questions that follow.

AFTER THE BANG

Astronomers and physicists generally agree that the universe began about 13 billion to 15 billion years ago in the big bang. For some time after the big bang occurred, the universe was much hotter and denser than it is today. In fact, it was so hot and dense that there were no individual atoms; instead, subatomic particles, including protons, neutrons, and photons (particles of pure energy) made a dense fluid called *plasma*. Every time that a proton and an electron combined, drawn together by their opposite charges, a photon collided with them and ripped them apart again. After a few hundred thousand years, the average temperature of the plasma was low enough that the protons could hold onto their electrons to form neutral atoms, and photons could escape without being absorbed.

9. Why couldn't stable atoms form before the cooling of the superheated plasma?
   - F. Protons and electrons were moving too fast to combine.
   - G. Before the plasma cooled, subatomic particles carried no charge and therefore were not attracted to one another.
   - H. Colliding with photons caused immediate destruction of any atom that formed.
   - I. Cosmic background radiation prevented the atoms from forming.

10. Telescopes show images based on the photons they receive, in the form of light, radio waves, or other radiation. They show us events of the past, because photons take time to travel to us from those events. Why would it be difficult for telescopes to observe events that took place before the cooling of the superheated plasma?

Interpreting Graphics

The following chart shows the fusion reactions in a large-mass star, which create elements that are heavier than those found in stars like the sun. Use this diagram to answer questions 11–12.

FUSION REACTIONS IN A LARGE-MASS STAR

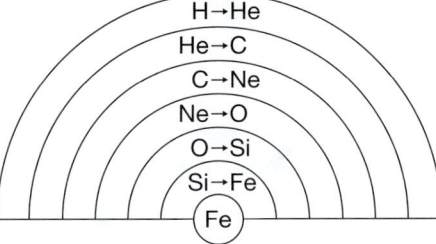

11. Which element fuses to become oxygen?
- **A.** carbon
- **B.** neon
- **C.** silicon
- **D.** iron

12. Do the elements that are produced by fusion get heavier or lighter as they get closer to the center of the large-mass star? Why?

Astronomers have determined that black holes, with masses from a few million to a billion times greater than the mass of our sun, reside in the centers of nearby galaxies. The graphic below shows the relationship between black-hole mass and the size of the bulge of stars at the center of these galaxies. Use the graphic to answer questions 13–14.

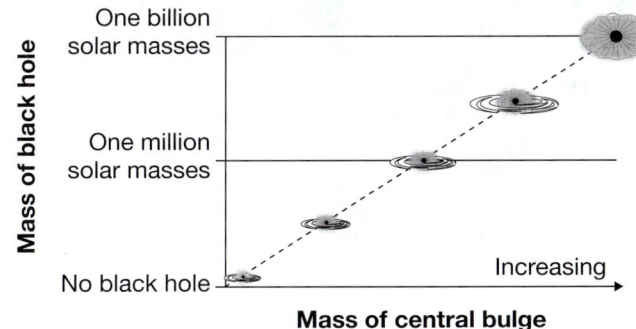

13. How does the mass of the black hole at the center of a galaxy relate to the mass of the bulge of stars that surrounds the black hole?
- **F.** The two masses are always equal.
- **G** The two masses are directly proportional.
- **H.** The two masses are inversely proportional.
- **I.** The two masses are unrelated to one another.

14. Why would a black hole be surrounded by a bulge of stars?

> **Test Tip**
>
> When using a diagram to answer questions, carefully study each part of the diagram as well as any lines or labels used to indicate parts of the figure.

CHAPTER 21
Planet Earth

Chapter Outline

❶ Earth's Interior and Plate Tectonics
What Is Earth's Interior Like?
Plate Tectonics
Plate Boundaries

❷ Earthquakes and Volcanoes
What Are Earthquakes?
Measuring Earthquakes
Volcanoes

❸ Minerals and Rocks
Structure and Origins of Rocks
How Old Are Rocks?

❹ Weathering and Erosion
Physical Weathering
Chemical Weathering
Erosion

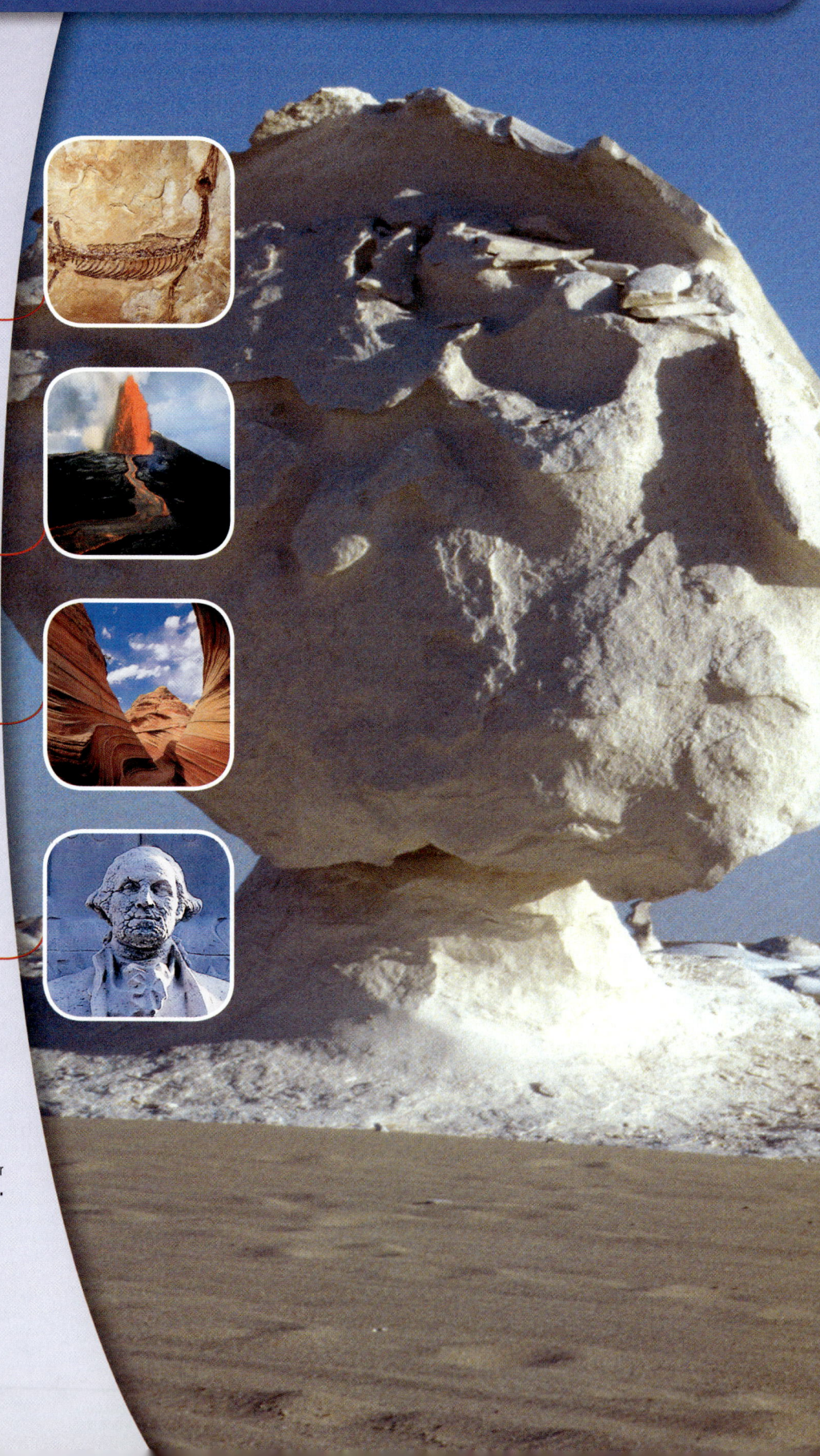

Tennessee Course Level Expectations (Physical Science)

CLE.3202.Inq.1 Recognize that science is a progressive endeavor that reevaluates and extends what is already accepted; **CLE.3202.Inq.2** Design and conduct scientific investigations to explore new phenomena, verify previous results, test how well a theory predicts, and compare opposing theories; **CLE.3202.Inq.3** Use appropriate tools and technology to collect precise and accurate data; **CLE.3202.Inq.4** Apply qualitative and quantitative measures to analyze data and draw conclusions that are free of bias; **CLE.3202.Inq.6** Communicate and defend scientific findings.

Inquiry Lab

⏱ 30 min

Observing Changes in Rocks

Collect a **handful of rocks** of different sizes. Use a **magnifying glass** to examine them, and make notes about each rock's shape and texture. Place the rocks in a **plastic container,** add enough **water** to cover the rocks, and close the container. Shake the container 100 times, and drain the water into a **second plastic container.** Examine the rocks and the water carefully.

Questions to Get You Started

1. What changes occurred in the rocks and water as a result of being shaken?
2. What natural forces does this activity mimic?

Why It Matters

The forces of weathering and erosion are constantly shaping the world around us. These formations, found in Egypt, are made of chalk and were shaped by the weathering effects of windblown sand particles.

READING TOOLBOX

These reading tools can help you learn the material in this chapter. For more information on how to use these and other tools, see **Appendix A**.

Word Parts

Root Words Many scientific words are made up of word parts such as prefixes, suffixes, or word roots. You can unlock the meaning of an unfamiliar science term by analyzing its word parts.

Your Turn The word *tectonics* in the term *plate tectonics* contains the root word *tect*. *Tect* comes from the Greek word *tektonikos*, which means "having to do with construction." A closely related root is *tech*, which means "having to do with art or skill." On a sheet of paper, complete a table like the one shown below by adding related words that contain these roots.

WORD	ROOT	DEFINITION
plate tectonics	tect	
	tech	

Fact, Hypothesis, or Theory?

Recognizing Facts, Hypotheses, and Theories A *fact* is a statement about the world that is more or less undisputed. A *hypothesis* is a possible explanation or answer to a question that can be tested. A *scientific theory* is an established model or explanation that ties together many hypotheses and observations.

Your Turn Make a table, and list statements of fact, hypotheses, and theories from Section 1 in the first column. In the second column, identify whether each is a fact, hypothesis, or theory. In the third column, write any language from the text that signals which type of statement each is.

STATEMENT	FACT, HYPOTHESIS, OR THEORY	KEY WORDS
	hypothesis	"scientists believe …"
	fact	"scientists know …"
	theory	"according to the _____ theory"

Graphic Organizers

Concept Maps A concept map is a visual road map that presents key ideas, meanings, and relationships. Here is what you do:

1. Select a main concept for the map.
2. List all of the important concepts.
3. Build the map by placing the concepts according to their importance after the main concept. Add linking words to give meaning to the arrangement of concepts.

Your Turn Complete this concept map as you read Section 2.

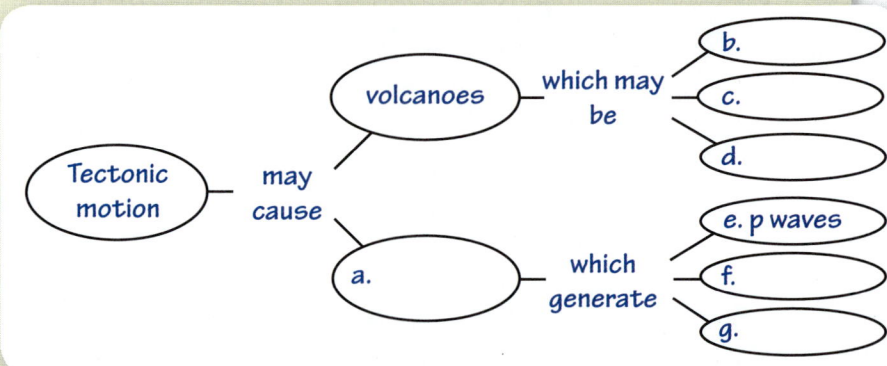

728   Chapter 21   Planet Earth

SECTION 1 Earth's Interior and Plate Tectonics

Key Ideas
- How is Earth's interior structured?
- How has the appearance of Earth changed over time?
- What geologic features are common near tectonic plate boundaries?

Key Terms
crust
mantle
core
lithosphere
plate tectonics
subduction
fault

Why It Matters
Scientists can identify locations where events such as earthquakes may take place by studying how Earth's tectonic plates interact. This information can be used to make preparations and save lives.

You know from experience that Earth's surface is solid. You walk on it every day. You may have even dug into it and found that it is often more solid once you dig down through the loose dirt and reach rock. However, Earth is not solid all the way to the center.

> **Tennessee Course Level Expectations (Physical Science)**
> CLE.3202.Inq.1; CLE.3202.Inq.2; CLE.3202.Inq.3

What Is Earth's Interior Like?

▶ **Earth's interior is made up of several distinct compositional layers.** We live on the topmost layer of Earth—the **crust.** The crust is cooler than the interior of Earth and is made up of hard, solid rock. The crust is relatively thin and makes up only 1% of Earth's mass. The crust beneath the ocean is called *oceanic crust* and has an average thickness of 5 to 8 km (3.1 to 4.9 mi). Continental crust is thicker and less dense than oceanic crust. Continental crust has an average thickness of 20 to 40 km (12 to 25 mi). It is deepest beneath high mountains, where it reaches depths of 70 km or more.

Beneath the crust lies a layer of rock that is denser than the crust, the **mantle,** which is shown in **Figure 1.** Almost 2,900 km (1,800 mi) thick, the mantle makes up about 80% of Earth's total volume. Because humans have never drilled all the way to the mantle, we do not know for sure what it is like. However, scientists can infer what the mantle's consistency is like from geologic events, such as earthquakes and volcanoes. Scientists hope that new technologies and drilling methods will one day allow them to see the mantle directly.

crust (KRUHST) the thin and solid outermost layer of Earth above the mantle

mantle (MANTLE) the layer of rock between Earth's crust and core

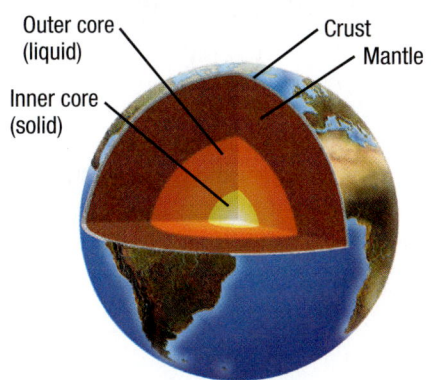

Figure 1 Earth is composed of a crust, mantle, outer core, and inner core.

Section 1 Earth's Interior and Plate Tectonics **729**

core (KAWR) the center part of Earth below the mantle

Earth's interior gets warmer with depth.

If you have ever been in a cave, you may have noticed that the temperature in the cave was cool. The reason is that the air and rocks beneath Earth's surface are shielded from the warming effects of the sun. However, if you were to travel far beneath the surface, such as into a deep mine, you would find that the temperature becomes uncomfortably hot. South African gold mines, for example, reach depths of up to 3 km (2 mi), and their temperatures approach 50 °C (120 °F). The high temperatures in these deep mines are not caused by the sun but by energy that comes from Earth's interior.

Geologists believe that Earth's mantle is much thicker and hotter than the crust, as **Figure 2** illustrates. The composition of the mantle is thought to be mostly solid. The outermost part of the mantle is rigid, as the crust is. Deeper than a few hundred kilometers, however, the mantle is extremely hot and under incredible pressure. Geologists believe that this inner portion of the mantle is *plastic*—soft and easily deformed, like a piece of gum.

Earth's core is nearly as hot as the surface of the sun.

Geologists believe that the center of Earth, the **core,** is composed mainly of iron and nickel. The core has two layers. The inner core, which is thought to be solid metal, is surrounded by a liquid metal outer core.

On Earth's surface, the metals contained in the core would boil at the temperatures shown in **Figure 2.** Iron boils at 2,750 °C (4,982 °F), and nickel boils at 2,732 °C (4,950 °F). But in the outer core, these metals remain liquid because the pressure due to the weight of the mantle and crust is so great that the substances in the outer core are prevented from changing to their gaseous form. Similarly, pressure in the inner core is so great that the atoms are forced together as a solid despite the intense heat.

Reading Check Why don't the metals in the liquid outer core turn to gases? (See Appendix E for answers to Reading Checks.)

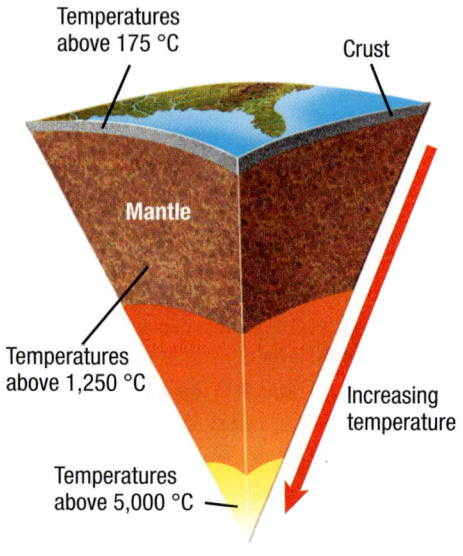

Figure 2 Temperatures in Earth's interior increase with depth. Temperatures near the center of the core are thought to be as hot as the surface of the sun.

Radioactivity contributes to high internal temperatures.

Earth's interior contains radioactive isotopes. Their nuclei decay and release energy as they become more stable. These radioactive isotopes (mainly uranium, thorium, and potassium) are quite rare. Because Earth is so large, however, it contains enough atoms of these elements to produce a huge quantity of energy as heat. This energy is one of the major factors contributing to Earth's high internal temperature.

Figure 3 This map shows Pangaea as it might have looked almost 200 million years ago.

Plate Tectonics

While some scientists were trying to figure out what Earth looked like on the inside, others were looking at Earth's surface. In the early 1900s, a German scientist named Alfred Wegener noticed that the eastern coast of South America and the western coast of Africa appeared to fit together like pieces of a puzzle. Wegener found that several other continents' coastlines also seemed to fit together. ❯ **Wegener hypothesized that all of the continents might have been part of one landmass in the past before they drifted apart.** He pieced all the continents together to form a supercontinent that he called *Pangaea* (pan JEE uh), shown in **Figure 3**.

Using fossil evidence, Wegener showed that 200 million years ago, the same kinds of animals lived on continents that are now oceans apart. He argued that the animals could not have evolved on separate continents. **Figure 4** shows the fossil of a *Mesosaurus* found in Brazil. Fossils of the same species were found in western Africa. These fossils give scientists strong evidence for a past connection between the continents.

Evidence for Wegener's ideas came later.

The evidence for *continental drift,* or the theory that Earth's surface is made up of large moving plates, was compelling. However, Wegener's theory was largely ignored until the mid-1960s, when structures discovered on the ocean floor gave evidence of a mechanism for continental drift.

This evidence was discovered in the middle of the oceans and helped explain how the massive continents were able to move across Earth's surface. New technology provided images of "bands" of rock on the ocean floor that have alternating magnetic polarities. These bands differ from one another in the magnetic alignment of the rocks that they contain.

Figure 4 These *Mesosaurus* bones were discovered in São Paulo, Brazil.

Section 1 Earth's Interior and Plate Tectonics

Figure 5 Hydrothermal vents are one result of the eruption of fresh lava on the sea floor.

lithosphere (LITH oh SFIR) the solid, outer layer of Earth that consists of the crust and the rigid upper part of the mantle

plate tectonics (PLAYT tek TAHN iks) the theory that explains how large pieces of the lithosphere, called *plates*, move and change shape

Alignment of oceanic rocks supports the theory of moving plates.

Molten rock pouring out onto the ocean floor creates new rock and hydrothermal vents, as shown in **Figure 5**. Iron minerals, such as magnetite, in the magma align with Earth's magnetic field. After the rocks cool to about 550 °C (1,020 °F), the alignment of the magnetic regions in the iron minerals becomes fixed. The result is a permanent record of Earth's magnetic field as it was just before the rock cooled.

Scientists conclude from these bands of rock that Earth's magnetic field has reversed direction many times during its history—that is, the north magnetic pole becomes the south magnetic pole. This process is recorded in the rocks as bands, as **Figure 6** shows, and occurs once every 200,000 years, on average. These magnetic bands are symmetrical on either side of the Mid-Atlantic Ridge. The rocks are youngest near the center of the ridge. The farther away from the ridge that you go, the older the rocks are, which suggests that the crust was moving away from the plate boundary in both directions.

Earth has plates that move over the mantle.

The **lithosphere** is approximately 100 km (60 mi) thick and is made up of the crust and the upper portion of the mantle. The lithosphere is made up of about seven large pieces (and several smaller pieces) called *tectonic plates*. The word *tectonic* refers to the structure of the crust of a planet. The continents are embedded into these plates, which move in relation to one another. The theory describing the movement of plates is called **plate tectonics.**

Tectonic plates move at speeds ranging from 1 to 10 cm (0.4 to 4 in) per year. Although this speed may seem slow, tectonic plates have moved a considerable distance because they have been moving for hundreds of millions of years.

Reading Check What is the plate tectonics theory?

Figure 6 The stripes, or bands, illustrate Earth's alternating magnetic field. The dark stripes represent times when Earth's polarity was the same as it is today, and the lighter stripes show reversed polarity.

QuickLab

Convection and Plate Tectonics

⏱ 20 min

Procedure

1. Fill a **shallow pan** with **water** until the water is 3 cm from the top.
2. Use a **hot plate** or **Bunsen burner** to heat the water for 30 s over low heat. Add a few drops of **food coloring** and turn off the heat.
3. Place **five cardboard pieces** as close together as possible in the center of the pan.
4. Turn on the heat, and sketch the movement of the cardboard pieces.

Analysis

1. How was the movement in step 4 like continental drift? How could you make a more accurate model of plate tectonics?

Scientists do not understand exactly what makes tectonic plates move.

The boundaries of Earth's tectonic plates are shown in **Figure 7.** These boundaries do not always coincide with continental boundaries. The arrows indicate the direction of plate movement. Some plates move toward each other, some move away from each other, and others move alongside each other.

One hypothesis suggests that plate movement results from convection currents in the *asthenosphere,* the hot, plastic portion of the mantle. The plates of the lithosphere "float" on top of the asthenosphere. The soft rock in the asthenosphere circulates by convection, similar to the way that thick oatmeal circulates as it boils. This slow movement of rock might push the plates of the lithosphere along.

Other scientists believe that the forces generated by these convection currents are not sufficient to move the plates. Some scientists propose that the plates are driven by the force of gravity acting on their own massive weight.

Academic Vocabulary

coincide (KOH in SIED) to agree or align exactly

Figure 7 Some continents are on one plate, and other continents are formed by several colliding plates. **On what major plate is most of the United States located?**

Figure 8 An earthquake that occurred in 1999 damaged this running track in Taiwan.

subduction (suhb DUHK shuhn) the process by which one lithospheric plate moves beneath another as a result of tectonic forces

Figure 9 Where tectonic plates move apart at divergent boundaries, rift valleys form. The photograph shows an above-water portion of the Mid-Atlantic Ridge that runs through Iceland.

Plate Boundaries

The theory of plate tectonics helps scientists study and predict volcanic eruptions and has provided information on earthquakes. The damage caused by one of these earthquakes can be seen in **Figure 8.** ❯ **Volcanoes and earthquakes most often occur where tectonic plates come together. At plate boundaries, many other dramatic geologic features, such as mountains and rift valleys, can also occur.**

Mid-oceanic ridges result from divergent boundaries.

A *divergent boundary* occurs where two plates move apart and create a gap between them. Then, hot rock rises from the asthenosphere and cools to form new lithospheric rock. The two diverging plates then pull the newly formed lithosphere away from the gap. The drop in pressure also causes the rising asthenosphere to partially melt and form *magma,* which then forms new oceanic crust.

Mid-oceanic ridges are mountain ranges at divergent boundaries in oceanic crust. Unlike most mountains on land, which are formed by the bending and folding of continental crust, mid-oceanic ridges are mountain ranges created by magma rising to Earth's surface and cooling. Along the center of a mid-ocean ridge is a *rift valley,* a narrow valley that forms where plates separate. The most-studied mid-oceanic ridge is the Mid-Atlantic Ridge. Although most of the ridge is underwater, it can be seen above sea level in Iceland, as **Figure 9** shows. This ridge runs roughly down the center of the Atlantic Ocean from the Arctic Ocean to an area off the southern tip of South America.

734 Chapter 21 Planet Earth

Oceanic plates dive beneath continental plates at convergent boundaries.

While new lithosphere is formed at divergent boundaries, older lithosphere is destroyed at *convergent boundaries*. The Andes Mountains formed along a convergent boundary between an oceanic plate and the South American continental plate. The lithosphere of the oceanic plate, which is denser than the lithosphere of the continental plate, sinks into the mantle and drags the oceanic crust along with it. This process is called **subduction.** As shown in **Figure 10,** ocean trenches, mountains, and volcanoes are formed at *subduction zones*.

Ocean trenches form along the boundary between two oceanic plates or between an oceanic plate and a continental plate. These trenches can be very deep. The deepest is the Mariana Trench, located off the coast of Asia in the Pacific Ocean. The deepest point in the trench is more than 11 km (6.8 mi) beneath the ocean surface.

 Why does oceanic lithosphere sink beneath continental lithosphere at a subduction zone?

Subduction of ocean crust generates volcanoes.

Chains of volcanic mountains often form on the overriding plate at subduction zones. As the water-bearing rocks and sediments of the subducting oceanic lithosphere are heated by surrounding mantle, they release water into the overlying mantle. Water is very effective at lowering the melting point of rock at high pressure, so magma forms and rises into the crust. The magma cools, and the accumulation of low-density rock over millions of years forms a chain of high mountains and plateaus.

Concept Map
Create a concept map that shows the different types of plate boundaries and the types of landforms that occur at each.

Figure 10 The Andes Mountains, shown in the photograph, formed near the boundary where oceanic and continental plates collide.

QuickLab: Tectonic-Plate Boundaries

  20 min

Procedure

1. Use a **ruler** to draw two 10 cm × 20 cm rectangles on a piece of **paper**, and cut them out.
2. Use a **rolling pin** to flatten two pieces of **clay** until they are each about 1 cm thick. Place a paper rectangle on each piece of clay. Using a **plastic knife**, trim each piece of clay along the edges to match the shape of the paper.
3. Flip the two clay rectangles so that the paper is at the bottom, and place them side by side on a flat surface. Slowly push the models toward each other until the edges of the clay begin to buckle and rise off the table.
4. Turn the models around so that the unbuckled edges are touching. Place one hand on each. Slide one piece of clay toward you and the other away from you. Apply only slight pressure toward the seam where the two pieces of clay touch.

Analysis

1. What type of plate boundary are you demonstrating with the model in step 3?
2. What type of plate boundary are you demonstrating in step 4?
3. Compare the appearances of the facing edges of the models in each of the two processes. How might similar processes affect Earth's surface?

Islands may form where two oceanic plates meet.

Sometimes, a convergent boundary occurs when two plates that are made of oceanic lithosphere collide. The denser of the two plates will sink beneath the less dense plate. This process forms a deep-ocean trench. Fluids released from the subducted plate cause mantle rock to melt and form magma. The magma rises to the surface to form an *island arc,* which is a chain of volcanic islands. The islands of Japan are perhaps the best-known example of an island arc. These islands formed as a result of the subduction of the Pacific plate.

Colliding tectonic plates create mountains.

The mountains of the Himalayas, the tallest mountain range in the world, are shown in **Figure 11.** They began forming during the collision between the Indian continental plate and the Eurasian continental plate. They are growing in both width and height as the two plates continue to collide. However, because the plates move so slowly, the mountains grow by only several centimeters a year. Mount Everest, the tallest mountain in the world, with a peak 8,850 m (29,035 ft) above sea level, is part of this range.

Reading Check Why are the mountains of the Himalayas considered to still be forming?

Figure 11 The Himalayas are still growing today as the tectonic plate containing Asia and the plate containing India continue to collide.

Transform fault boundaries can crack Earth.

Plate movement can cause breaks in the lithosphere. Once a break occurs, rock in the lithosphere continues to move and scrapes past nearby rock. The crack where rock moves in this manner is called a **fault**. Faults can occur in any area where forces are great enough to break rock. When rock moves horizontally at faults along plate boundaries, the boundary is called a *transform fault boundary*.

Plate movement at transform fault boundaries is one cause of earthquakes. You may have heard of earthquakes along the San Andreas fault, which is shown in **Figure 12**. The fault runs from Mexico through California and out to sea north of San Francisco. Transform fault boundaries occur in many places across Earth, including the ocean floor.

fault (FAWLT) a break in a body of rock along which one block slides relative to another

Figure 12 The change in the course of the river results from plate movement along the fault. The San Andreas fault system is more than 500 km long.

Section 1 Review

KEY IDEAS

1. **List** the major compositional layers of Earth.
2. **Explain** why the inner core remains a solid even though it is very hot.
3. **Summarize** the plate tectonics theory.
4. **Describe** how the gap is filled when two tectonic plates move away from each other.
5. **Determine** whether each of the following is likely to occur at convergent or divergent boundaries:
   a. rift valley
   b. continental mountains
   c. mid-oceanic ridge
   d. ocean trench
6. **Predict** what type of plate boundary would be found along the coastline near Japan's volcanic mountain ranges.

CRITICAL THINKING

7. **Understanding Relationships** Why would a mine that is more than 1500 m deep be much hotter than a mine that is only 150 m deep?
8. **Analyzing Information** The oldest continental rocks are 4 billion years old, whereas the oldest sea-floor rocks are 200 million years old. Explain why these ages differ.

Section 1 Earth's Interior and Plate Tectonics

SECTION 2
Earthquakes and Volcanoes

Key Ideas
- Where do most earthquakes occur?
- How do scientists learn about earthquakes and the Earth's interior?
- What is a volcano?

Key Terms
focus
epicenter
surface wave
seismology
Richter scale
vent

Why It Matters
By learning how to more accurately predict earthquakes, scientists can figure out ways to warn people before an earthquake strikes.

TN Tennessee Course Level Expectations (Physical Science)
CLE.3202.Inq.1; CLE.3202.Inq.2; CLE.3202.Inq.3

www.scilinks.org
Topic: Earthquakes
Code: HK80453

Imagine rubbing two rough-sided rocks back and forth against each other. The movement will not be smooth. Instead, the rocks will scrape and jump and create a vibration that is transferred to your hands. Similar vibrations happen when rocks slide past one another at a fault. The resulting vibrations are called *earthquakes*.

What Are Earthquakes?

Compare the occurrence of earthquakes, shown as red dots in **Figure 1,** with the plate boundaries, marked by thin, black lines. Each red dot marks the occurrence of an earthquake over a 10-year period. ❯ **You can see that earthquakes occur mostly at the boundaries of tectonic plates, where the plates move with respect to each other.**

Figure 1 Each red dot marks the occurrence of a moderate to large earthquake sometime between 1985 and 1995.

738 Chapter 21 Planet Earth

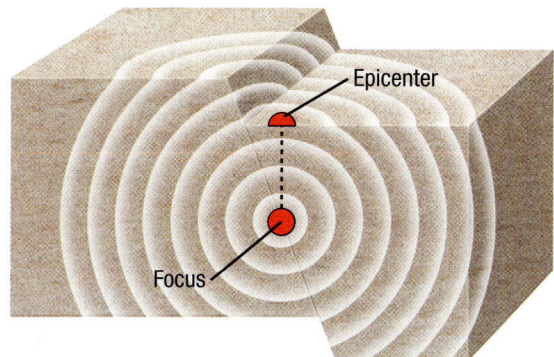

Figure 2 The epicenter of an earthquake is the point on the surface directly above the focus.

Earthquakes occur at plate boundaries.

As plates move, their edges experience stress. If the plates cannot move freely, energy from stress on the rocks will build up. Eventually, the stress becomes so great that it breaks rock along a fault line. Energy is released as *seismic waves*. As the seismic waves travel through Earth and along its surface, they create the shaking that we experience during an earthquake.

The exact point inside Earth where an earthquake originates is the **focus.** Seismic waves travel in all directions from the focus, which is often located far below Earth's surface. The point on the surface directly above the focus is the **epicenter,** as **Figure 2** shows. Because the epicenter is the point on Earth's surface that is closest to the focus, the damage there is usually greatest, although damage can occur many kilometers from the epicenter.

Reading Check On a flat map, are an earthquake's focus and its epicenter in the same place? Explain.

Energy from earthquakes is transferred by waves.

The energy released by an earthquake is measured as shock waves. Earthquakes generate three types of shock waves. *Longitudinal waves* originate from an earthquake's focus. Longitudinal waves move faster through rock than other waves do and are the first waves to reach recording stations. For this reason, longitudinal waves are also called *primary*, or *P waves.*

A longitudinal wave travels by compressing Earth's crust in front of it and stretching the crust in back of it. You can simulate longitudinal waves by compressing a portion of a spring and then releasing it. Energy will travel through the coil as a longitudinal wave.

The second type of wave is a *transverse wave*. Transverse waves move more slowly than longitudinal waves. Thus, these slower waves are called *secondary*, or *S waves*. The motion of a transverse wave is similar to that of the wave created when a rope is shaken up and down.

focus (FOH kuhs) the location within Earth along a fault at which the first motion of an earthquake occurs

epicenter (EP i SENT uhr) the point on Earth's surface directly above an earthquake's starting point, or focus

QuickLab 10 min

Seismic Waves

1. Stretch a **spring toy** lengthwise on a table.
2. Hold one end of the spring while a partner holds the other end. Push your end toward your partner's end, and observe what happens.
3. Repeat step 2, but this time, shake the spring from side to side.
4. Which type of seismic wave is represented in step 2? in step 3?

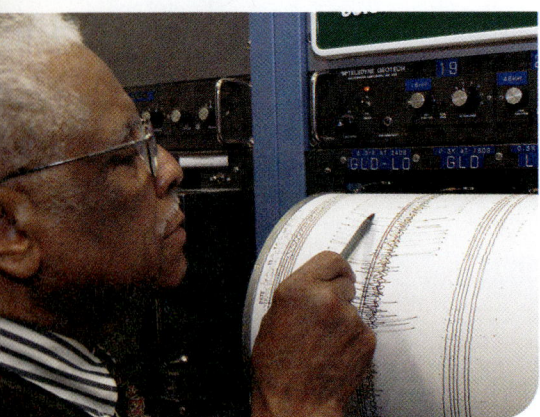

Figure 3 A seismologist points out a surface wave that was measured during a large earthquake.

surface wave (SUHR fis WAYV) a seismic wave that travels along the surface of a medium and has a stronger effect near the surface of the medium than it has in the interior

seismology (siez MAHL uh jee) the study of earthquakes including their origin, propagation, energy, and prediction

Waves move through Earth and along its surface.

Both P waves and S waves spread out from the focus in all directions, as light from a light bulb does. In contrast, the third type of seismic wave, a **surface wave,** moves only across Earth's surface. These waves are the result of Earth's entire mass shaking like a bell that has been rung. Earth's surface bends and reshapes as it shakes. The resulting rolling motion of Earth's surface is a combination of up-and-down motion and back-and-forth motion. In this type of wave, points on Earth's surface have a circular motion, like the movement of ocean waves far from shore.

Surface waves cause more destruction than either P waves or S waves. P waves and S waves shake buildings back and forth or up and down at relatively high frequencies. But the rolling action of surface waves, combined with their longer wavelengths, can cause buildings to collapse.

Measuring Earthquakes

❯ **Because energy from earthquakes is transferred by waves, scientists can measure the waves to learn about earthquakes and about the interior of Earth through which the waves travel.** Scientists measure the power of each earthquake and the amount of damage that the earthquake causes. To measure earthquakes, scientists have developed highly sensitive tools.

Seismologists detect and measure earthquakes.

Seismology is the study of earthquakes. Seismologists use sensitive machines called *seismographs,* shown in **Figure 3,** to record data about earthquakes. These data include information about the power and time intervals between P waves, S waves, and surface waves. Seismographs use an inertial mass to measure ground motion during an earthquake.

Examine the seismograph in **Figure 4.** A stationary pendulum with a pen at its tip hangs from a support fastened to bedrock. A drum of paper turns beneath the pendulum. Most of the time, the seismograph records an almost straight line. If the ground shakes, the base of the seismograph moves. The pendulum, however, is slower to respond because of the inertia of the weight.

The pendulum draws zigzag lines to indicate that an earthquake has occurred. Records of seismic activity are called *seismograms.* Fast-moving P waves are the first waves to be recorded, followed by slower S waves and surface waves.

Figure 4 When the ground shakes, the pendulum remains still while a rotating drum of paper records Earth's movement.

740 Chapter 21 Planet Earth

Three seismograph stations are needed to locate the epicenter of an earthquake.

There are more than 1,000 seismograph stations across the world. At each station, three seismographs are used to measure different motions: north to south, east to west, and up and down. P waves, the first waves to be recorded by seismographs, make a series of small, zigzag lines. S waves arrive later and appear as larger, more ragged lines. Surface waves arrive last and make the largest lines.

The difference in time between the arrival of P waves and the arrival of S waves enables seismologists to calculate the distance between the seismograph station and the earthquake's epicenter. When the distances from three seismograph stations are calculated, three circles can be drawn on a map, as **Figure 5** shows. Each circle has the geographic location of a seismograph station as its center, and the radius of the circle is the distance to the epicenter. The epicenter is the location where all three circles intersect.

Figure 5 The point where the three circles intersect is the epicenter of the earthquake.

Reading Check How can scientists use the data from three seismograph stations to find the epicenter of an earthquake?

Geologists use seismographs to study Earth's interior.

Seismologists have found that S waves do not reach seismographs on the side of Earth's core opposite the focus, as **Figure 6** shows. This discovery leads scientists to believe that part of the core is liquid because S waves, which are transverse waves, cannot travel through a liquid.

By comparing seismograms recorded during earthquakes, seismologists have noticed that the velocity of seismic waves varies depending on where the waves are measured. Waves change speed and direction whenever the density and rigidity of the material they are traveling through changes. The differences in velocity suggest that Earth's interior consists of layers of different densities. By comparing data, scientists have constructed a model of Earth's interior. Though this structure has never been directly seen, this model is the best fit for the current evidence. This model is constantly refined as new data are collected.

Figure 6 No direct S waves can be detected more than 105° from the focus. No direct P waves can be detected between 105° and 140° from the focus.

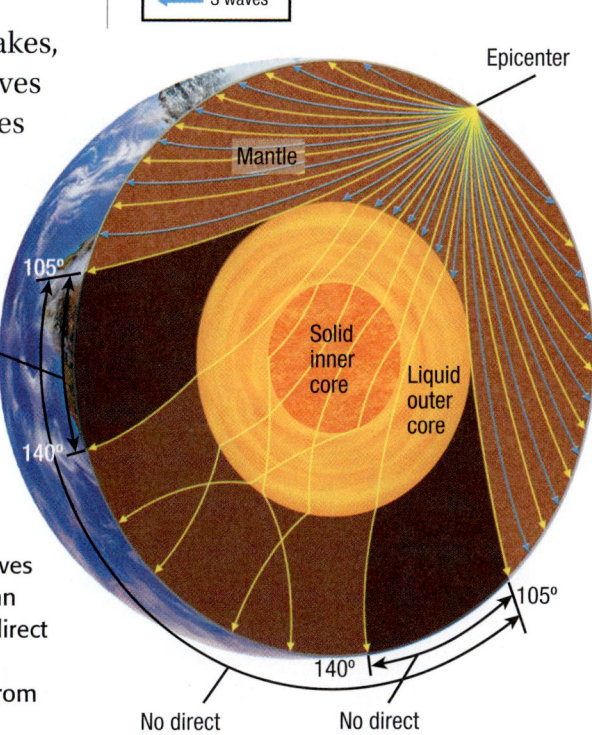

Section 2   Earthquakes and Volcanoes   **741**

Figure 7 Earthquake Magnitude, Effects, and Frequency

Magnitude (Richter scale)	Characteristic effects of shallow earthquakes	Estimated number of earthquakes recorded each year
2.0 to 3.4	not felt but recorded	more than 150,000
3.5 to 4.2	felt by a few people in the affected area	30,000
4.3 to 4.8	felt by most people in the affected area	4,800
4.9 to 5.4	felt by everyone in the affected area	1,400
5.5 to 6.1	moderate to slight damage	500
6.2 to 6.9	widespread damage to most structures	100
7.0 to 7.3	serious damage	15
7.4 to 7.9	great damage	4
8.0 to 8.9	very great damage	occur infrequently
9.0 to 9.9	would be felt in most parts of Earth	very rare
10.0	would be felt all over Earth	possible but never recorded

Richter scale (RIK tuhr SKAYL) a scale that expresses the magnitude of an earthquake

vent (VENT) an opening at the surface of Earth through which volcanic material passes

The Richter scale is used to measure earthquakes.

The **Richter scale** is one way that scientists measure the energy released by an earthquake. Each step on the Richter scale represents a 30-fold increase in the energy released. So, an earthquake of magnitude 8 releases 30^4, or 810,000, times as much energy as one of magnitude 4. **Figure 7** summarizes the effects and number of earthquakes with various magnitudes. Although the Richter scale was the most popular scale for much of the 20th century, scientists today more often use other scales, such as the moment-magnitude scale.

Reading Check What is the energy difference between each step on the Richter scale?

Magnitude scales alone cannot predict how severe an earthquake will be.

The amount of damage caused by an earthquake depends on several factors, such as the distance between populated areas and the epicenter, the depth of the focus, and the type of soil and construction found in the area.

The Armenian earthquake of 1988 and the San Francisco earthquake of 1989 both had a magnitude of 7 on the Richter scale. In Armenia, there was a lot of property damage, and more than 25,000 people died. Fewer than 70 people died in San Francisco. However, the focus in San Francisco was also nearly 4 times as deep as the focus of the Armenian quake.

Scientists are trying to predict earthquakes.

In the past, people tried to predict earthquakes by watching animals for strange behavior. Today, scientists are trying to measure changes in Earth's crust that can signal an earthquake. By learning to observe rock for signs of stress and strain, scientists might someday be able to warn people of an impending earthquake and save lives. The random nature of earthquakes makes prediction extremely difficult, but finding a reliable system could save tens of thousands of lives.

Volcanoes

A volcano is any opening in Earth's crust through which magma has reached Earth's surface. These openings are called **vents.** Volcanoes often form hills or mountains as materials pour or explode from the vent, as **Figure 8** shows. Volcanoes release molten rock, small rock and mineral particles called *ash,* and a variety of gases that result from the melting of rocks in the mantle or in the crust.

Volcanoes generally have one central vent, but they can also have several smaller vents. Magma from inside a volcano can reach Earth's surface through any of these vents. When magma reaches the surface, the magma begins to cool and releases trapped gases. The molten rock is then called *lava.*

Shield volcanoes have mild eruptions.

Magma rich in iron and magnesium is very fluid and forms lava that tends to flow great distances. The eruptions are usually not very explosive and can occur several times. The buildup of this kind of lava produces a gently sloping mountain, or *shield volcano.* Shield volcanoes are some of the largest volcanoes. Mauna Loa in Hawaii is a shield volcano. Mauna Loa's summit is more than 4,000 m (13,000 ft) above sea level and more than 9,020 m (29,500 ft) above the sea floor.

Composite volcanoes have trapped gas.

Composite volcanoes are made of alternating layers of ash, cinders, and lava. The magma in a composite volcano is thick and rich in silica. Gases are also trapped in the magma. As a result, eruptions in these volcanos alternate between lava flows and explosive activity that produces cinders and ash. Composite volcanoes are typically thousands of meters high and have much steeper slopes than shield volcanoes. Japan's Mount Fuji is a composite volcano. Mount Hood, Mount Rainier, Mount St. Helens, and Mount Shasta, all in the western United States, are also composite volcanoes.

Academic Vocabulary

predict (pree DIKT) to say ahead of time

Concept Map
As you read through the section on volcanoes, make a concept map that shows how each type of volcano forms and how the types are different from one another.

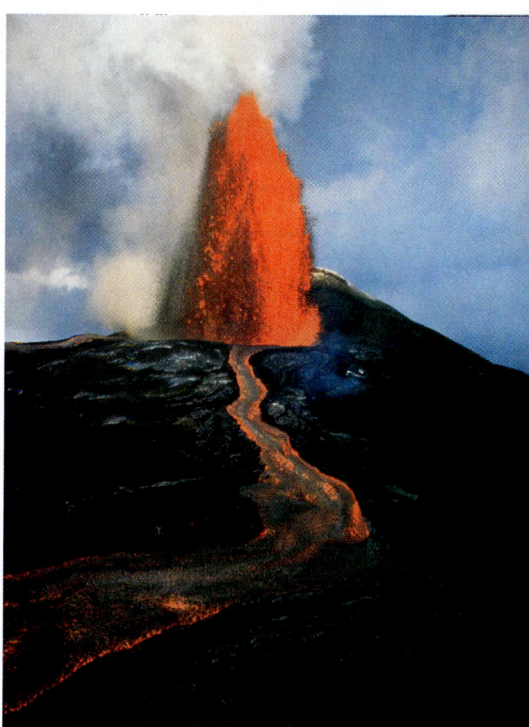

Figure 8 Volcanoes build up into hills or mountains as lava and ash explode from vents, or openings in Earth.

Cinder cones are the most abundant volcanoes.

Cinder cones are the smallest and most abundant volcanoes. When large amounts of gas are trapped in magma, violent eruptions occur—vast quantities of hot ash and lava are thrown from the vent. These particles then fall to the ground around the vent and form the cone. Cinder cones tend to be active for only a short time and then become dormant. As **Figure 9** shows, Paricutín (pah ree koo TEEN), a volcano in Mexico, is a cinder cone. Paricutín erupted in 1943. After just two years, the volcano's cone had grown to a height of 450 m (1,480 ft). The eruptions finally ended in 1952. Volcanoes form not only on land but also under the oceans. In shallow water, volcanoes can erupt violently. As a result, clouds of ash and steam form. An underwater volcano is called a *seamount* and looks like a composite volcano.

Figure 9 The type of volcano that forms depends largely on the chemical composition of the magma. Differences in the fluidity of the magma determine the type of eruption that occurs. These models are not shown to relative scale.

744 Chapter 21 Planet Earth

Figure 10 Seventy-five percent of the active volcanoes on Earth occur in the area known as the *Ring of Fire*. **Where do most volcanoes in the United States occur?**

Most volcanoes occur at convergent plate boundaries.

Like earthquakes, volcanoes are linked to plate motion. Volcanoes are common around the edges of the Pacific Ocean, where oceanic tectonic plates subduct beneath continental plates. This area, seen in **Figure 10,** is known as the *Ring of Fire* because of the number of volcanoes found there. In fact, 75% of the active volcanoes on Earth are located in the Ring of Fire.

A plate sinking at a convergent boundary causes melting in the mantle, and magma rises to the surface. The volcanoes that result form the edges of the Ring of Fire. These volcanoes tend to erupt cooler, less-fluid lava and clouds of ash and gases. The gases cannot easily escape the high-viscosity lava. Gas pressure builds up, and explosive eruptions result.

✓ **Reading Check** Why do most volcanoes form at convergent boundaries where one plate sinks beneath another plate?

Underwater volcanoes occur at divergent plate boundaries.

As plates move apart at divergent boundaries, magma rises to fill in the gap. This magma creates the volcanic mountains that form the ridges around a central rift valley.

The volcanic island of Iceland, located in the North Atlantic Ocean, is on the Mid-Atlantic Ridge. The island is continuously expanding from its center; the eastern and western sides of the island are growing outward in opposite directions. As a result, a great deal of geologic activity, such as volcanoes and hot springs, occurs on the island.

Section 2 Earthquakes and Volcanoes **745**

Figure 11 Tropical plants often grow on the fertile ground that results from volcanoes.

Volcanoes also occur at hot spots.

Some volcanoes occur in the middle of plates. Volcanoes occur because mushroom-shaped trails of hot rock, called *mantle plumes*, rise from deep inside the mantle, melt as they rise, and erupt from volcanoes at *hot spots* at the surface.

When mantle plumes break through oceanic plates, lava and ash build up on the ocean floor. If the resulting volcanoes grow large enough, they break through the water's surface and become islands. As the oceanic plate continues moving, however, the mantle plume does not move along with it. The plume continues to rise under the moving oceanic plate, and a new volcano is formed at a different point. A chain of extinct volcanic islands is left behind.

The Hawaiian Islands lie in a line that roughly corresponds to the motion of the Pacific plate. The island of Hawaii is the most recently formed in the chain and contains the active volcanoes situated over the mantle plume. Volcanic activity produces ash and rock, which become fertile soil for tropical plants, such as those shown in **Figure 11.**

Section 2 Review

KEY IDEAS

1. **Identify** the areas where most earthquakes occur.
2. **Differentiate** between the focus and the epicenter of an earthquake.
3. **Explain** what the numbers on the Richter scale mean and how much increase in energy is represented by each step.
4. **Describe** why three seismologic stations are necessary to determine the epicenter of an earthquake.
5. **Identify** the three main types of volcanic cones and the composition of each.

CRITICAL THINKING

6. **Understanding Relationships** Why might surface waves cause the greatest damage during an earthquake?
7. **Identifying Patterns** If a seismograph station measures P waves but no S waves from an earthquake, what can a seismologist conclude about the earthquake's location?
8. **Drawing Conclusions** Why might a sudden increase in the number of earthquakes around a volcano indicate a possible eruption?

Why It Matters
Volcanoes and Humans

Volcanoes have influenced and affected human culture for thousands of years. Sometimes, that relationship can be destructive—an erupting volcano threatens human life. However, volcanoes can also be beneficial, even beautiful. For example, images of Japan's Mount Fuji, shown here, have been a focal point in Japanese art dating back hundreds of years.

HISTORY IN SCIENCE

1 In 79 CE, Mount Vesuvius in Italy erupted and buried the nearby town of Pompeii in lava, ash, and soot. The eruption caught many people by surprise.

2 The effects of the Krakatau eruption in 1883 could be seen all over the world. The skies from New York to northern Europe were tinted by the eruption's debris.

3 The Hawaiian Islands were formed by an undersea hot spot and are still being formed. The shape of the island chain is caused by the movement of Hawaii's tectonic plate.

www.scilinks.org
Topic: Volcanic Effects
Code: HK81615

YOUR TURN
CRITICAL THINKING
1. What effects might a massive eruption, such as the one caused by Krakatau, have on wildlife and people a thousand kilometers away?

SECTION 3 Minerals and Rocks

Key Ideas
> What materials make up rocks?
> How are scientists able to tell how old a rock is?

Key Terms
mineral
igneous rock
weathering
sedimentary rock
metamorphic rock

Why It Matters
Craftspeople use the elements and minerals found in rocks to produce useful items, such as computer parts, kitchen utensils, and jewelry.

Tennessee Course Level Expectations (Physical Science)
CLE.3202.Inq.1; CLE.3202.Inq.2; CLE.3202.Inq.3

Devils Tower in Wyoming, shown in **Figure 1**, rises 264 m (867 ft) above its base. According to an American Indian legend, the tower's jagged columns were formed by a giant bear scraping its claws across the rock. The tower was actually formed by molten rock that solidified underground. Over millions of years, the surrounding softer rock layers were worn away by wind and rain, so the formation was finally exposed.

Structure and Origins of Rocks

> **All rocks are composed of minerals. Minerals** have a definite crystal structure, a regular, repeating internal alignment of atoms and molecules. Quartz, for example, is a single mineral made of silicon dioxide, SiO_2. Quartz, like all minerals, forms crystals. Granite is not a mineral; it is a rock that is made up of different minerals.

There are more than 4,000 known minerals in Earth's crust. However, only about 20 of these minerals are commonly found in rocks. Together, these 20 minerals make up more than 95% of all of the rocks in Earth's crust. Some of the most common of these rock-forming minerals are feldspar, pyroxene, mica, olivine, dolomite, quartz, amphibole, and calcite.

Each combination of rock-forming minerals results in a rock with a unique set of properties. Rocks may be porous, granular, or smooth. They may also be soft or hard and have different densities or colors. The appearance and characteristics of a rock reflect both the manner in which it formed and its mineral composition. Rocks may be formed in several ways. The manner in which a rock forms is crucial to determining the physical and chemical properties of that rock.

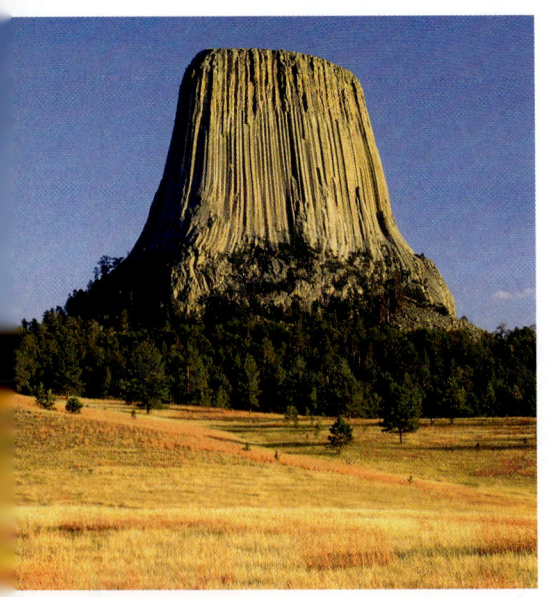

Figure 1 Devils Tower in northeastern Wyoming was formed by the cooling of magma beneath Earth's surface.

748 Chapter 21 Planet Earth

Figure 2 Igneous Rocks

Notice the coarse-grained texture of this sample of granite, an intrusive igneous rock.

Obsidian, an extrusive igneous rock, cools much more quickly than granite.

Molten rock cools to form igneous rock.

When molten rock cools and solidifies, it forms **igneous rock.** Nearly all igneous rocks are made of crystals of various minerals, such as those shown in the granite in **Figure 2.** As the rock cools, the minerals crystallize and grow. In general, the more quickly the rock cools, the less time there is for the crystals to grow. For example, obsidian, a smooth igneous rock used by early American Indians to make tools, is similar to granite in composition but cools much more quickly. As a result, obsidian has either very small crystals or no crystals at all and is mostly glass. **Figure 2** shows a piece of obsidian.

Igneous rock can be extrusive or intrusive.

Obsidian is categorized as an *extrusive* igneous rock because it cools on Earth's surface. *Basalt*, a fine-grained, dark-colored rock, is the most common extrusive igneous rock. Rocks that form from the magma that is released during a volcanic eruption are extrusive igneous rocks. Granite, in contrast, is an *intrusive* igneous rock because it forms from magma that cools while trapped beneath Earth's surface. Because the magma is insulated by the surrounding rocks, it takes a very long time to cool—sometimes as long as millions of years. Because of this long cooling period, the crystals in intrusive igneous rocks are larger than those in extrusive igneous rocks. The minerals of granite, for example, are easy to see with the naked eye. They are much lighter in color than those of basalt. Basalt crystals are also smaller than those in granite.

Reading Check What is the difference in the formation of an extrusive igneous rock and an intrusive igneous rock?

mineral (MIN uhr uhl) a natural, usually inorganic solid that has a characteristic chemical composition, an orderly internal structure, and a characteristic set of physical properties

igneous rock (IG nee uhs RAHK) rock that forms when magma cools and solidifies

Integrating Social Studies

Exploring History Throughout history, humans have used rocks and minerals to fashion tools. During the Stone Age, the Bronze Age, and the Iron Age, people used stone, bronze, and iron, respectively, to make tools and weapons. The Industrial Revolution began when humans learned to burn coal to run machinery. After humans learned to extract oil from Earth's crust, gasoline-powered vehicles were invented, and we entered the automobile age.

Figure 3 Sedimentary rock can have many distinct layers, as shown here in the Vermilion Cliffs of Arizona.

The remains of older rocks form sedimentary rocks.

Even very hard rock with large crystals will break down over thousands of years. The process by which rocks are broken down is called **weathering.** Pieces of rock fall down hillsides because of gravity or get washed down by wind and rain. Rivers then carry the pieces into deltas, lakes, or the sea. Chemical processes also serve to slowly break rocks apart. The action of physical and chemical weathering eventually breaks the pieces into pebbles, sand, mud, and dissolved chemicals.

As pieces of rock accumulate, they can form another type of rock—**sedimentary rock.** Think of sedimentary rocks, such as those shown in **Figure 3,** as recycled rocks. The sediment they are made of contains fragments of older rocks and, in some cases, fossils that have been compacted and cemented together with the dissolved chemicals.

Loose sediment forms rock in two ways.

There are two ways that sediment can become rock. Layers of sediment can be compressed from weight above them and form rock. Or minerals dissolved in water seep between bits of sediment and "glue" them together. Both processes are generally involved in most sedimentary rock formation.

Sedimentary rocks are named according to the size of the fragments that they contain. A rock made of pebbles is called a *conglomerate*. In **Figure 4,** the bits of rock in the conglomerate are cemented together with material that contains mostly quartz. A rock made of sand is called *sandstone*. A rock made of fine mud is usually called *mudstone,* but if it is flaky and breaks easily into layers, it is called *shale. Limestone,* another kind of sedimentary rock, is often made of the fossils of organisms that lived in the water, shown in **Figure 4.** Sometimes, the fossilized skeletons are so small or are broken up into such small fragments that they cannot be seen with the unaided eye. Places where limestone is found were once beneath water.

Figure 4 Sedimentary Rocks

Conglomerate rock is composed of rounded, pebble-sized fragments of weathered rock.

This limestone is made mostly of fossils of the shells of sea creatures.

Rocks that change because of pressure and heating without melting form metamorphic rock.

Metamorphic rocks form when heat and pressure within Earth cause changes in the texture and mineral content of rock. The word *metamorphic* comes from the Greek word *metamorphosis*, which means "to change form."

Limestone, a type of sedimentary rock, will turn into marble, a metamorphic rock, under the effects of heat and pressure. Marble is a stone that is often used in the construction of buildings and monuments. Notice the swirling, colored bands in the stairs shown in **Figure 5.** These bands are the result of different chemicals that existed in the limestone before it was transformed into marble. Although marble is very strong, its chemical composition makes it highly susceptible to the effects of acid precipitation.

Metamorphic rocks may be changed in two ways.

Rocks may be changed, or *metamorphosed*, in two ways: by heat alone or, more commonly, by a combination of heat and pressure. In both cases, the solid rock undergoes a chemical change over millions of years but does not melt. As a result, new minerals and crystals form in the rocks. The texture of the rocks is also changed, and any fossils in sedimentary rocks are transformed and destroyed.

The most common types of metamorphic rock are formed by heat and pressure deep in the crust. *Slate* is a rock that forms in this way. It metamorphoses from mudstone or shale, as **Figure 6** shows. Slate is a hard rock that can be split very easily along planes in the rock to create large, flat surfaces.

Reading Check What are the two ways in which a rock may change, or undergo metamorphosis?

Figure 5 This marble staircase shows the attractive, swirling bands of color that are often associated with marble.

weathering (WETH uhr ing) the natural process by which atmospheric and environmental agents, such as wind, rain, and temperature changes, disintegrate and decompose rocks

sedimentary rock (SED uh MEN tuhr ee RAHK) a rock that forms from compressed or cemented layers of sediment

metamorphic rock (MET uh MAWR fik RAHK) a rock that forms from other rocks as a result of intense heat, pressure, or chemical processes

Figure 6 Metamorphosis

Mudstone is made of silt- or clay-sized particles. Its characteristics can sometimes still be seen after metamorphosis.

Slate is a metamorphic rock that is transformed under heat and pressure from sedimentary rocks, such as mudstone or shale.

Old rocks in the rock cycle form new rocks.

So far, you have seen some examples of one type of rock becoming another. For example, limestone exposed to heat and pressure becomes marble. When exposed rocks are weathered, they form sediments. These sediments may be cemented together to make sedimentary rock. The various types of rock are all part of one rock system. The sequence of events in which rocks can be weathered, melted, altered, and formed is described by the *rock cycle.*

Figure 7 illustrates the stages of the rock cycle. With the exception of volcanic eruptions, which allow magma to cool and form new rocks in hours or days, rock formation occurs very slowly, often over thousands to millions of years.

Magma cooling underground forms igneous rock, such as granite. If the granite is heated and put under pressure, it may become metamorphic rock. Granite exposed at the surface of Earth may be weathered and become sand. The sand may be transported, deposited, and cemented to become the sedimentary rock sandstone. As more time passes, more layers of sediment are deposited above the sandstone. With enough heat and pressure, the sandstone becomes a metamorphic rock. This metamorphic rock may then be forced deep within Earth, where it melts and forms magma.

Reading Check What forces at the surface of Earth break down rocks into sediment?

> **READING TOOLBOX**
>
> **Concept Map**
> Create a concept map that shows how rocks change from one form to another in the rock cycle.

Figure 7 The rock cycle illustrates the changes that sedimentary, igneous, and metamorphic rocks undergo. **How does a sedimentary rock become an igneous rock?**

QuickLab

Rock Formation

 20 min

Procedure

1. Gather a pile of **candy chips** made of different colors. Separate them into different piles based on color.
2. Using a **pair of scissors,** carefully shave each pile of chips into smaller pieces, and keep the piles separate.
3. Sprinkle different types of chip shavings on a piece of **wax paper** to form a 4 cm square.
4. Place a second piece of wax paper on top of this square, and place a heavy **book** on top for 10 s.

Analysis

1. What did the whole chips represent in your model? What do the scissors represent? the chip shavings?
2. What kind of rock formation does your model represent?

How Old Are Rocks?

Because rocks form and change over millions of years, it can be difficult to know the exact time when a particular rock formed. ❯ **Scientists have developed several methods to determine the age of rocks on a geologic time scale.**

The position of a rock can show its relative age.

Think about a hamper of dirty clothes. If you do not disturb the clothes in the hamper, you can tell the relative time that the clothes were placed in the hamper. In other words, you may not know how long ago a particular red shirt was placed in the hamper, but you can tell that the clothes above the red shirt were placed there more recently. In a similar manner, the *relative age* of rocks can be determined by using the *principle of superposition,* which states:

| **Principle of superposition** | If there has been no disturbance in the position of the rock layers, the oldest will be on the bottom, and the youngest will be on top. |

The principle of superposition is useful in many ways. For example, the cliff side shown in **Figure 8** is composed of several sedimentary layers. According to the principle, the layers on the bottom would be older than the layers above them.

Although the various layers of sedimentary rock are most visible in cliff sides and canyon walls, you would find layering if you dug down anywhere that there is sedimentary rock. By applying the principle of superposition, scientists know that fossils in the upper layers are the remains of animals that lived more recently than the animals fossilized in lower layers.

Figure 8 According to the principle of superposition, the layers of sedimentary rock on top are the most recent layers if the rocks have not been disturbed.

Section 3   Minerals and Rocks   **753**

www.scilinks.org
Topic: Radiometric Dating
Code: HK81261

Radiometric dating gives the absolute age of rocks.

Atoms of the same element that have different numbers of neutrons are called *isotopes*. As the nuclei of some isotopes decay, the nuclei emit energy at a fairly constant rate. These isotopes are said to be *radioactive*. The radioactive elements that make up minerals in rocks decay at different rates. Physicists have determined the rates at which these elements decay. Geologists can use the data to determine the age of rocks. Although some elements decay very quickly, scientists use isotopes that decay over periods of billions of years to make accurate, long-term measurements of a rock's age.

Whereas the principle of superposition gives only the relative age of a rock, radiometric dating gives the *absolute age* of a rock. Scientists measure the amount of the original radioactive material left undecayed in the rock, or *parent isotope*, and the amount of the product of the radioactive material's decay, or *daughter isotope*. Part of this process is shown in **Figure 9.** Using the known decay rate for each type of isotope, scientists compare the proportions of the parent and daughter isotopes to determine the absolute age of the rock.

Many isotopes can be analyzed when rocks are dated. Some of the most reliable are isotopes of potassium, which decays to become argon; rubidium, which decays to become strontium; and uranium, which decays to become lead. Most of these methods can be used to date rocks found on Earth that are as old as 4.6 billion years.

Figure 9 A scientist examines a device that is used to measure the amount of isotopes of different elements present in a rock sample.

Section 3 Review

KEY IDEAS

1. **Explain** what a mineral is, and give three examples of minerals found in Earth's crust.
2. **List** the three different types of rock.
3. **Determine** the type of rock that will form in each of the following situations:
   a. Lava pours onto the ocean floor and cools.
   b. Minerals cement small pieces of sand together.
   c. Mudstone is subjected to great heat and pressure over a long period of time.
4. **Describe** the role of weathering and erosion in the rock cycle.
5. **Explain** how scientists can use the principle of superposition to determine the age of a rock layer.
6. **Summarize** the distinction between relative dating and absolute dating.

CRITICAL THINKING

7. **Applying Ideas** If you wanted to create in a laboratory a rock that has large crystals, what conditions would you have to control? Explain your answer.
8. **Identifying Relationships** How could a scientist use a sedimentary rock to provide evidence that the rock cycle is a valid scientific model?
9. **Analyzing Information** A paleontologist who is researching extinctions notices that certain fossils are never found above a layer of sediment that contains a lava flow. Should the paleontologist use relative dating, absolute dating, or a combination of the two to determine when these animals became extinct? Explain your answer.

Why It Matters
What Are Rocks Good For?

Looking at a rock on the ground may seem uninteresting, but humans use rocks in a variety of ways. Some rocks, when polished and cut, may be used as gemstones in jewelry. Other rocks are melted down through the process of refining and are used to make many of the objects common in everyday life. Some metals found in rocks, such as iron, are more common than other metals, such as silver or gold.

❶ First, miners dig up ore. *Ore* is any type of natural material that contains a valuable mineral. Ore may not look like the metal it contains.

❷ The ore is melted down, and the valuable minerals are separated out through smelting and refining.

❸ The metal that is obtained can be molded into useful items, such as car frames, utensils, building materials, jewelry, cookware, or paper clips.

YOUR TURN

UNDERSTANDING CONCEPTS
1. Look at the student in the photograph. What items are being used that may have come from refined ore?

CRITICAL THINKING
2. Why are some forms of metal more expensive than others?

SECTION 4: Weathering and Erosion

Key Ideas
- How does physical weathering affect rocks?
- How are rocks affected by chemical weathering?
- What is erosion, and what causes it to happen?

Key Terms
acid precipitation
erosion
deposition

Why It Matters
Many parks, such as the Grand Canyon National Park, are devoted to spectacular examples of large-scale erosion.

Tennessee Course Level Expectations (Physical Science)
CLE.3202.Inq.1; CLE.3202.Inq.2; CLE.3202.Inq.3; CLE.3202.Inq.4; CLE.3202.Inq.6

Compared to the power of an earthquake, the force exerted by a river may seem small. But over time, the forces exerted by wind and water can make vast changes in the landscape. Parunuweap Canyon, shown in **Figure 1,** is one of the most magnificent examples of how water can shape Earth's surface.

Physical Weathering

There are two types of weathering processes: physical and chemical. ▶ **Physical, or mechanical, weathering breaks rocks into smaller pieces but does not alter their chemical compositions.** *Abrasion* caused by particles suspended in wind or water is an example of *physical weathering.* The weathering process occurs at different rates depending on local climate and the type of rock.

Ice can break rocks.

Ice can play a part in the physical or mechanical weathering of rock. A common kind of mechanical weathering, *frost wedging*, occurs when water seeps into cracks in rock and then freezes. When the water freezes, its volume increases by about 10%, so the rock is pushed apart. Each time that the ice thaws and refreezes, it wedges farther into the rock, and the crack in the rock widens and deepens. This process eventually breaks off pieces of the rock or splits the rock apart.

Plants can also break rocks.

The roots of plants can also act as wedges as the roots grow into cracks in the rocks. As the plant grows, the roots exert a constant pressure on the rock. The crack continues to deepen and widen. Eventually, a piece of the rock breaks off.

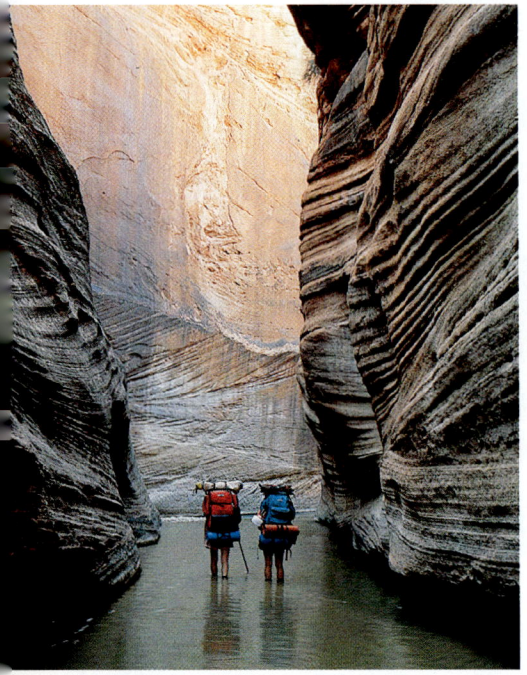
Figure 1 Parunuweap Canyon in Zion National Park, Utah, is a striking example of the effect of water on Earth's surface.

756 Chapter 21 Planet Earth

Chemical Weathering

The sedimentary layers in Badlands National Park, shown in **Figure 2,** appear red because they contain hematite, an iron oxide. Hematite is formed as iron reacts with oxygen in an oxidation reaction. When elements react with oxygen and become oxides, their properties change. When these elements are in minerals, oxidation can cause the mineral to decompose or form new minerals. In this process of *chemical weathering*, a rock is broken down because of chemical reactions with the environment. ❯ **Chemical weathering can cause rocks to weaken, decompose, or dissolve, and it can affect the chemical composition of a rock.** Over millions of years, chemical weathering can have a great affect on the landscape.

Figure 2 Red sedimentary layers in Badlands National Park in South Dakota show the evidence of chemical changes due to oxidation.

Carbon dioxide can cause chemical weathering.

Another common type of chemical weathering occurs when carbon dioxide from the air dissolves in rainwater. The result is water that contains carbonic acid, H_2CO_3. Although carbonic acid is a weak acid, it does react slowly with some minerals. The slightly acidic water seeping into the ground can weather rock underground.

For example, calcite, the major mineral in limestone, reacts with carbonic acid to form calcium bicarbonate. Because the calcium bicarbonate dissolves in water, the decomposed rock is carried away in the water and underground pockets form. The cave shown in **Figure 3** resulted from the weathering action of carbonic acid in layers of limestone.

Academic Vocabulary

react (ree AKT) to act in return; to respond

✓ **Reading Check** What is the formula for carbonic acid?

Figure 3 Carbonic acid dissolved the calcite in the sedimentary rock limestone to produce this underground cavern.

Figure 4 This statue of George Washington has been severely damaged since the 1930s, when the photograph on the left was taken.

www.scilinks.org
Topic: Weathering
Code: HK81648

Water plays a key role in chemical weathering.

Almost all chemical weathering reactions take place in the presence of water. These reactions change the physical properties of minerals. The change in the composition of minerals when they react chemically with water is called *hydrolysis*. Minerals that are affected by hydrolysis often dissolve in water and are carried away. These minerals may be transported to lower layers of rock in a process called *leaching*. Ores used to make aluminum are often formed in this way.

Acid precipitation can slowly dissolve minerals.

Rain and other forms of precipitation naturally have a slightly acidic pH (about 5.7) because they contain carbonic acid. When fossil fuels are burned, sulfur dioxide and nitrogen oxides are released and may react with water in clouds to form sulfuric acid and nitric acid. These clouds form precipitation that falls to Earth as **acid precipitation.**

Acid precipitation causes damage to both living organisms and inorganic matter. Acid precipitation can erode metal and rock, such as the statue shown in **Figure 4**. Marble and limestone dissolve relatively rapidly even with dilute acid.

To help reduce the amount of acid precipitation, governments sometimes pass laws. The Clean Air Act, initially passed in 1970, has been amended several times through the years. In 1990, the Acid Rain Control Program was added to the Clean Air Act. These regulations were designed to help reduce the acidity of rain by limiting the pollution output of factories and power plants. The occurrence of acid rain in some areas has been greatly reduced because power plants have installed scrubbers that remove much of the sulfur dioxide before it can be released into the air.

Reading Check Name two places where you might see evidence of acid precipitation.

---

acid precipitation (AS id pree SIP uh TAY shuhn) precipitation, such as rain, sleet, or snow, that contains a high concentration of acids, often because of pollution of the atmosphere

erosion (ee ROH zhuhn) a process in which the materials of the Earth's surface are loosened, dissolved, or worn away and transported from one place to another by a natural agent, such as wind, water, ice, or gravity

deposition (DEP uh ZISH uhn) the process in which material is laid down

Erosion

Erosion is another process that changes the appearance of landscapes. ❯**Erosion is the removal and transportation of weathered and nonweathered materials by gravity, running water, wind, waves, ice, and underground water.**

Water erosion shapes Earth's surface.

Water is the most effective physical weathering agent. It is also the most effective agent of erosion. Muddy rivers carry sediment in their water. As sediment moves along with the water, the sediment scrapes the riverbanks and the river bottom. The water continues to scour the surface and carries the new sediment away.

The oceans also have a dramatic effect on Earth's landscape. On seashores, the waves crashing onto land create tall cliffs and jagged coastlines. The Cliffs of Moher in western Ireland, shown in **Figure 5,** reach heights of 204 m (669 ft) above the water. The cliffs were formed partially by the force of the Atlantic Ocean as waves eroded the rocky shale and sandstone coast by washing particles of the rock out to sea.

Figure 5 The action of waves slowly tearing away at the rocky coast formed the Cliffs of Moher.

Deposition occurs if a stream has too much sediment.

There is a direct relationship between the velocity of the water and the size and amount of sediment that the water can carry. Quick moving rivers can carry away a lot of sediment and create extraordinary canyons.

As a river becomes wider or deepens, it flows more slowly and cannot carry as much sediment. As a result, sediment is left on the floor of these calmer portions of the stream. The process in which sediment moves by erosion, is dropped, and comes to rest is called **deposition.** Rivers eventually flow into large bodies of water, such as oceans, where the sediment is deposited along the continental shores. As rivers slow at the continental boundary, large, fertile deposits called *deltas,* such as the one shown in **Figure 6,** are laid down.

Figure 6 Deltas, such as this one in Alaska's Prince William Sound, are formed by deposition.

Figure 7 Tustumena Glacier, on the left, slowly pushes its way through the Kenai Mountains of Alaska. Glaciers can carve out large U-shaped valleys, such as that shown on the right.

Glaciers erode mountains.

Large masses of ice can exert tremendous forces on rocks. A constantly moving ice mass carves the surface that it rests on and often creates U-shaped valleys, such as the one shown in **Figure 7**. The weight of the ice and the forward movement of the glacier cause the mass to act like a huge scouring pad. Immense boulders that are carried by the ice scrape across other rocks and grind them to a fine powder. Streams of glacial meltwater then erode the fine sediment that the glacier has weathered. The meltwater streams carry the sediment to the banks and bottoms of streams or to the bottom of glacier-formed lakes. Some debris is caught in the glacial ice and moved slowly over long periods of time.

Glacial erosion is a long, powerful process. Some glaciers may move only a few centimeters over the course of a year. So, a single glacier may erode a landscape over thousands of years, depositing debris as it slowly melts.

Wind can also shape the landscape.

Just as water or glaciers can carry rocks and sediment as they move, wind can erode Earth's surface by blowing fine particles through the air. Have you ever been in a dust storm and felt your skin "burn" from the swirling dust? You feel the burn because fast-moving wind can carry sediment. Wind that carries sediment creates a sandblasting effect, which increases the weathering and eroding of the landscape.

The sandstone arches of Arches National Park are formed partly by wind erosion. The sandblasting effect of the wind weathers the formation shown in **Figure 8** through abrasion. The wind then erodes the loose particles and carries them away from the arch to deposit them in a new location. Over time, the wind will destroy the arches that it helped create.

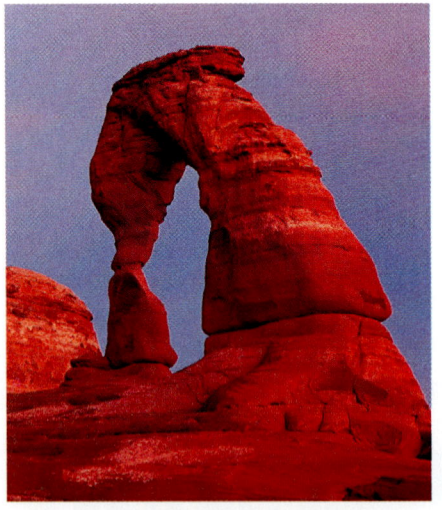

Figure 8 This sandstone arch in Arches National Park in Utah was created as high-speed winds weathered the terrain.

Reading Check How is wind like water and ice in the way that it erodes the landscape?

Gravity moves weathered materials downhill.

Gravity causes rock fragments to move down inclines. This movement of rock fragments down a slope is known as *mass movement*. There are many types of mass movement. Masses of loose rock and soil suddenly falling down a slope create a *landslide*. *Mudflows*, another type of mass movement, occur when large amounts of mud rapidly move downhill, usually after a heavy rain.

Some forms of mass movement are fairly slow. The slow, downhill movement of weathered rock is called *creep*. Soil creep moves more soil than other types of mass movement. But soil creep is so slow that it may go unnoticed unless some other surface object, such as a house, moves along with it.

Humans can also cause erosion.

Humans often create conditions that speed up erosion. Whenever we destroy too many plants, whose strong root systems prevent soil from eroding, we put the terrain at risk. *Deforestation* is the clearing of trees from an area without replacing them. Deforestation, shown in **Figure 9**, creates conditions that accelerate erosion and lead to mass movements of soil and rock. Plants are also destroyed when livestock are allowed to overgraze a piece of land. When animals overgraze, too many plants are eaten or trampled and too few plants are left to prevent the soil from eroding.

As we build cities and extract resources from our natural environment, we must be careful not to create conditions that cause undue harm to the environment through erosion.

Figure 9 Most of the trees on this hillside have been cut down. As the trees are cut down, the roots die and cannot hold the soil in place. **Can you think of any other human activities that cause erosion?**

Section 4 Review

KEY IDEAS

1. **List** two agents of physical weathering that might occur in a mountainous region.
2. **Distinguish** between physical weathering and chemical weathering.
3. **Describe** how acid precipitation forms.
4. **Contrast** erosion and deposition.
5. **Predict** which will experience more weathering, a rock in the Sonoran Desert in southern Arizona or the same rock on a beach in North Carolina.
6. **List** two ways in which humans may cause land to erode faster than it would naturally.

CRITICAL THINKING

7. **Making Predictions** Suppose that one day, you see a crack on a sidewalk. That night is very cold. The next day, you notice that the crack is filled with ice. What might happen to the crack over the course of the winter months?
8. **Understanding Relationships** Automobile exhaust contains nitrogen oxides. How might these pollutants affect chemical weathering processes?
9. **Making Decisions** On many coastlines, weathering and erosion are wearing the beach away and threatening to destroy homes. How would you prevent this destruction?

Application Lab

Finding the Epicenter of an Earthquake

⏱ 50 min

You are part of a student project working with the National Earthquake Information Center. An earthquake has just occurred somewhere in the United States, and several schools have recorded the event. Your job is to analyze seismic waves detected at three different schools in order to figure out the epicenter of the earthquake.

What You'll Do
> **Calculate** the distance from surrounding seismometers to an earthquake's epicenter.
> **Find** the location of the earthquake's epicenter.
> **Explain** the relationship between seismic waves and the location of an earthquake's epicenter.

What You'll Need
calculator
compass, drawing
paper, tracing
ruler

Procedure

Preparing for Your Activity

1. You will examine seismograms showing two kinds of seismic waves: primary waves (P waves) and secondary waves (S waves).

2. P waves have an average speed of 6.1 km/s. S waves have an average speed of 4.1 km/s.
   a. How long does it take P waves to travel 100 km?
   b. How long does it take S waves to travel 100 km?

   (Hint: You will need to use the equation for velocity and rearrange it to solve for time.)

3. Because S waves travel more slowly than P waves, S waves will reach a seismograph after P waves arrive. This difference in arrival times is known as the *lag time*.

4. Use the time intervals found in step 2 to calculate the lag time that you would expect from a seismograph located exactly 100 km from the epicenter of an earthquake.

Measuring the Lag Time from Seismographic Records

5. On a blank sheet of paper, prepare a table like the one below.

Sample Data Table: Distance of Three Cities from Epicenter

City	Lag time (s)	Distance to epicenter
Austin, TX		
Bismarck, ND	DO NOT WRITE	
Portland, OR	IN BOOK	

6. The sample seismograms here show the records produced by seismographs in three cities following an earthquake.

7. Using the time scale at the bottom of the seismograms, measure the lag time for each city. Be sure to measure from the start of the P wave to the start of the S wave. Enter your measurements in your data table.

8. Using the lag time that you found in step 4 and the formula below, calculate the distance from each city to the epicenter of the earthquake. Enter your results in your data table.

   distance = (measured lag time ÷ lag time for 100 km) × 100 km

Analysis

1. **Analyzing Data** Trace the map shown here on a blank sheet of paper. Using the scale below your map, adjust the drawing compass so that it will draw a circle whose radius equals the distance from the epicenter of the earthquake to Austin. Then, put the point of the compass on Austin, and draw a circle on your map. How is the location of the epicenter related to the circle?

2. **Analyzing Data** Repeat the process in item 1 by using the distance from Portland to the epicenter. This time, put the point of the compass on Portland, and draw the circle. The epicenter is one of the two sites where the circles intersect. Repeat the process once more for Bismarck, and find that city's distance from the epicenter.

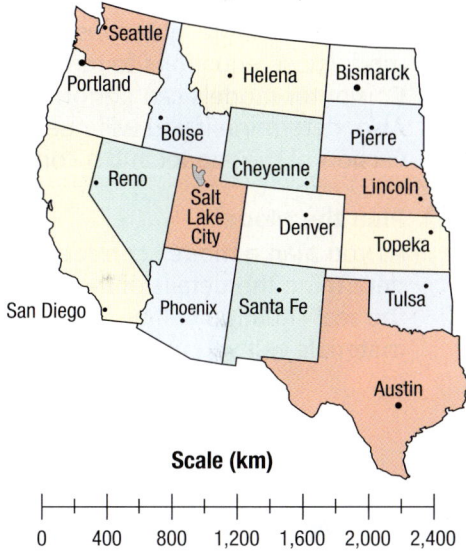

Communicating Your Results

3. **Analyzing Methods** Why is it necessary to use seismographs in three different locations to find the epicenter of an earthquake in this manner?

4. **Analyzing Methods** Would it be possible to use this method for locating an earthquake's epicenter if earthquakes produced only one kind of seismic wave? Explain your answer.

5. **Evaluating Ideas** Someone tells you that the best way to determine the epicenter is to find a seismograph where the P waves and S waves occur at the same time. What is wrong with this reasoning?

Application

The epicenter is located at the site where all three circles intersect. Which city is closest to that site?

Making Models

Science › Skills

Models are simplified representations of reality. By using models in experiments, you can focus on only the variables you are interested in and remove other factors that may be unimportant. In many cases, using models is also much more practical than doing experiments directly on the real systems that you are studying.

Technology
Math
▸ Scientific Methods
Graphing

1. Determine the Model's Purpose
Suppose that you have formed a hypothesis that plants reduce the rate of erosion along the edges of rivers. It is not always practical to manipulate the environment around a real river in order to test your hypothesis. In this case, using a model makes more sense.

- The purpose of this model is to test the hypothesis that plants reduce the erosion of soil along the edges of rivers.

2. Choose the Type of Model
There are many kinds of models. Physical models are physical representations of reality. Mathematical models use equations to represent a real system. Computer models can perform complex calculations. Also, determine if you will need both an experimental version of the model and a control version.

- To test the erosion hypothesis, I will construct physical models.
- There will be two versions of the model: an experimental model and a control model.

3. Plan the Model
As you plan a model, consider questions that will determine the details of the model. What aspects of the real situation will be included in the model? What materials will you use?

- Both models will be 1 m long and tilted 2 degrees. Water will enter at the top. The amount of soil and the rate of water flow will be the same. The experimental tray will have plants, and the control tray will have no plants.

4. Build and Use the Model
After you build a model, you should check to see if it compares favorably to the real system that it models. After you have used the model in an experiment, remember to translate your results to the real-world situation that you are modeling.

- The trench is significantly narrower in the tray with the plants. This result supports the hypothesis that plants help to reduce erosion along the edges of rivers.

Practice

1. For each of the following situations, choose the best type of model to use: a physical model, a mathematical model, or a computer model.
   a. You want to model the flow of lava on the sides of an asymmetrical volcano.
   b. You want to model weather patterns and predict precipitation in your hometown.

2. You are developing a sealant for statues and buildings that you hope will reduce weathering due to acid precipitation. You have three versions of the sealant, and you want to test which one is most effective. Describe the model or models that you could use to do this test.

CHAPTER 21 Summary

go.hrw.com
SUPER SUMMARY
KEYWORD: HK8PEAS

Key Ideas

Section 1 Earth's Interior and Plate Tectonics

› **What Is Earth's Interior Like?** Earth's interior is made up of several distinct layers. (p. 729)

› **Plate Tectonics** Earth's outer layer is broken into several tectonic plates, which ride on top of the mantle beneath. (p. 731)

› **Plate Boundaries** Volcanoes and earthquakes are common at tectonic plate boundaries. (p. 734)

Section 2 Earthquakes and Volcanoes

› **What Are Earthquakes?** Most earthquakes occur along tectonic plate boundaries as a result of sudden movement within Earth's lithosphere. (p. 738)

› **Measuring Earthquakes** Scientists measure the energy released to learn about earthquakes. (p. 740)

› **Volcanoes** Volcanoes are formed when magma rises and penetrates the surface of Earth. (p. 743)

Section 3 Minerals and Rocks

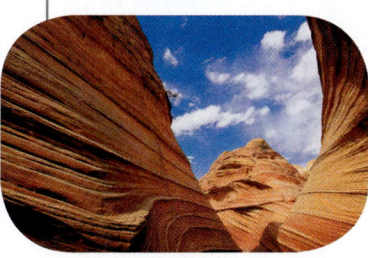

› **Structure and Origins of Rocks** All rocks are made of one or more types of minerals. (p. 748)

› **How Old Are Rocks?** Scientists have developed techniques to learn both the relative age and the absolute age of rock. (p. 753)

Section 4 Weathering and Erosion

› **Physical Weathering** Physical weathering breaks rock apart but does not alter the physical composition of the rock. (p. 756)

› **Chemical Weathering** In chemical weathering, a rock's composition is altered as minerals in the rock react chemically. (p. 757)

› **Erosion** Wind, water, ice, and gravity help remove and transport weathered and nonweathered materials in a process known as *erosion*. (p. 759)

Key Terms

crust, p. 729
mantle, p. 729
core, p. 730
lithosphere, p. 732
plate tectonics, p. 732
subduction, p. 735
fault, p. 737

focus, p. 739
epicenter, p. 739
surface wave, p. 740
seismology, p. 740
Richter scale, p. 742
vent, p. 743

mineral, p. 748
igneous rock, p. 749
weathering, p. 750
sedimentary rock, p. 750
metamorphic rock, p. 751

acid precipitation, p. 758
erosion, p. 759
deposition, p. 759

Planet Earth

CHAPTER 21 Review

READING TOOLBOX

1. **Recognizing Facts, Hypotheses, and Theories** Make a chart that shows which ideas and evidence concerning the plate tectonics theory are facts and which are hypotheses.

USING KEY TERMS

2. Using the terms *crust, mantle,* and *core,* describe Earth's internal structure.

3. Explain the difference between the *relative age* and the *absolute age* of a rock.

4. Use the terms *focus, epicenter, P waves, S waves,* and *surface waves* to describe what happens during an earthquake.

5. In which type of rock—*igneous, sedimentary,* or *metamorphic*—are you most likely to find a fossil?

6. What is the name of the process of breaking down rock?

7. Describe how wind can weather rock and shape Earth's surface, and list two other agents that can cause *weathering*.

8. Describe the difference between a *divergent* and a *convergent* plate boundary. Name the geologic features found near each type of boundary.

UNDERSTANDING KEY IDEAS

9. Vibrations in Earth caused by sudden movements of rock are called
   a. epicenters.　　c. faults.
   b. earthquakes.　d. volcanoes.

10. Using the difference in the time recorded for P waves and S waves to arrive at three different seismograph stations, seismologists can find an earthquake's
    a. epicenter.　　c. fault zone.
    b. surface waves.　d. intensity.

11. The type of volcano shown here is known as a
    a. cinder cone.　　c. shield volcano.
    b. hot spot.　　　d. composite volcano.

12. Magnitude expresses an earthquake's release of
    a. damage.　c. duration.
    b. location.　d. energy.

13. High pressure and high temperature can cause igneous rocks to change and become
    a. sedimentary rocks.
    b. limestone.
    c. metamorphic rocks.
    d. clay.

14. Almost all forms of chemical weathering take place in the presence of
    a. magma.　　c. water.
    b. hematite.　d. seismic waves.

15. _____ rock is formed from magma.
    a. Igneous　　c. Sedimentary
    b. Metamorphic　d. Schist

16. Underground caves in limestone can be formed by a reaction that includes
    a. iron.　　c. ice crystals.
    b. hematite.　d. carbonic acid.

17. Which of the following rocks is an example of an igneous rock?

    a. 　　c.

    b.　　　　　　　　d.

766 Chapter 21　Planet Earth

EXPLAINING KEY IDEAS

18. Describe the major layers of Earth in terms of their composition and temperature.

19. List three geologic features that may form where tectonic plates meet.

20. Explain how seismic waves help scientists learn about Earth's interior.

21. List the three types of volcanoes, and describe their composition.

22. Identify the three main types of rocks.

23. Explain how radiometric dating is used to estimate the absolute age of a rock.

24. Differentiate between physical weathering and chemical weathering.

25. List four agents of erosion.

CRITICAL THINKING

26. **Evaluating models** Why are mathematics and theory the only practical ways to determine the temperature of Earth's core?

27. **Applying Concepts** Is a tall building more likely to be damaged by an earthquake if the building is on a mountain of granite or in a valley of loose sediment? Explain.

28. **Analyzing Data** Imagine that you find two sets of dinosaur bones entwined as if the dinosaurs were engaged in battle. You know that one of the dinosaurs lived 180 million to 120 million years ago and the other lived 130 million to 115 million years ago. What can you say about the age of the rock in which the dinosaur fossils were found?

29. **Explaining Events** Explain how metamorphic rock can change into either of the other two types of rock through the rock cycle.

30. **Analyzing Methods** Explain why scientists would have difficulty locating the epicenter of an earthquake if they had seismic-wave information from only two locations.

Graphing Skills

31. **Graphing** The graph below shows the arrival times of a P wave and an S wave at a seismograph station. Use this graph to answer the questions that follow.

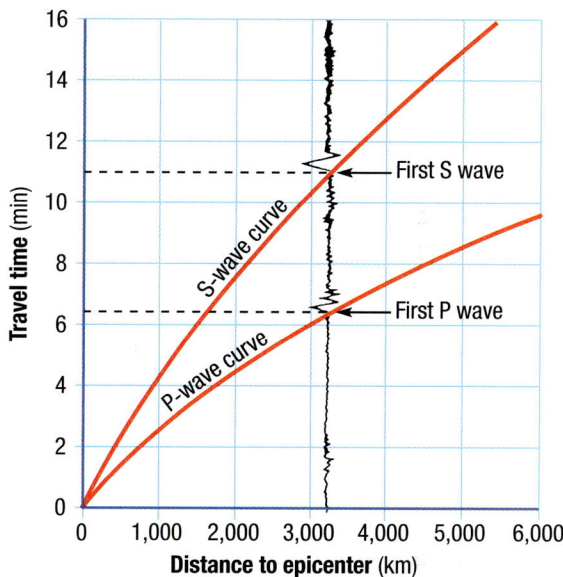

Arrival Time of P Waves and S Waves

a. Approximately how far, in kilometers, was the epicenter of the earthquake from the seismograph that recorded this seismogram?
b. How long did it take the P wave to reach the seismograph station?
c. How long did it take the S wave to reach the seismograph station?
d. What is the difference in travel time between the two waves?

Math Skills

32. **Making Calculations** The gram formula weight (weight of one mole) of the mineral quartz is 60.1 g. The gram formula weight of magnetite is 231.5 g. If you have 4 moles of magnetite, how many moles of quartz would be equal to the weight of the magnetite?

33. **Making Calculations** How much more energy is released by a magnitude 7 earthquake than a magnitude 4 earthquake?

Chapter Review

Standardized Test Prep

Understanding Concepts

Directions (1-4): **For each question, write on a sheet of paper the letter of the correct answer.**

1. If a geologist dug a shaft down to the bottom of the lithosphere, how deep into Earth would the shaft go?
   - **A.** to the bottom of the crust
   - **B.** through the crust and partway into the mantle
   - **C.** to the bottom of the mantle
   - **D.** through the mantle and into Earth's core

2. Which type of wave coming from an earthquake's epicenter travels the fastest and reaches detection stations first?
   - **F.** longitudinal wave
   - **G.** transverse wave
   - **H.** standing wave
   - **I.** surface wave

3. In the Mississippi Delta, minerals eroded from riverbanks upstream are deposited in the soil of a wide floodplain. What type of rock does this process create?
   - **A.** sedimentary rock
   - **B.** igneous rock
   - **C.** metamorphic rock
   - **D.** progressive rock

4. An earthquake with a magnitude of 6 on the Richter scale releases how many times more energy than one that has a magnitude of 3?
   - **F.** 3
   - **G.** 30
   - **H.** 900
   - **I.** 27,000

Directions (5-6): **For each question, write a short response.**

5. What is the difference between lava and magma?

6. What do mid-oceanic ridges, rift valleys, volcanoes, and mountain ranges have in common?

Reading Skills

Directions (7): **Read the passage below. Then, answer the question that follows.**

GAZING INTO THE DEEP

The deepest valley ever discovered is an undersea trench called the *Mariana Trench*. It is located in the Pacific Ocean, north of Indonesia and south of Japan.

The Mariana Trench is located at the boundary of two tectonic plates. As the tectonic plates slowly grind into each other, the Pacific plate flexes and slips underneath the Philippine plate. This movement creates a deep valley at the plate boundary.

Nearby the Mariana Trench are the Mariana Islands, a ridge of volcanic islands created by the same subduction forces. As the Philippine plate is thrust upward, its crust buckles and magma comes up through the cracks. This process creates the volcanic islands. Although there are only 15 volcanic summits above sea level in the Mariana Islands, they are just the southernmost tip of a submerged mountain range. The range extends more than 2,500 km from Guam to near Japan and parallels the border between the tectonic plates.

7. What can you tell about the lithosphere containing the Pacific plate from the information in the passage?
   - **A.** The Pacific plate is larger than the Philippine plate.
   - **B.** The lithosphere of the Pacific plate is denser than the lithosphere of the Philippine plate.
   - **C.** The lithosphere of the Pacific plate is moving away from the lithosphere of the Philippine plate.
   - **D.** The boundary between the Pacific plate and the Philippine plate is a transform fault boundary.

Interpreting Graphics

The graphic below shows the steps of the rock cycle. Use this graphic to answer questions 8–9.

THE ROCK CYCLE

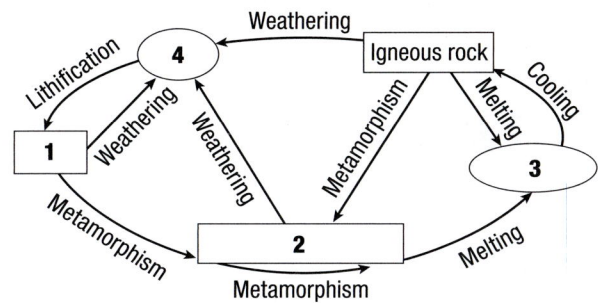

8. Which of the processes on the flow chart takes place only under conditions of great heat and pressure?
   - **F.** metamorphism
   - **G.** lithification
   - **H.** weathering
   - **I.** melting

9. Which of the processes named in the flow chart can take place above the surface of Earth?

The graphic below displays the paths taken by primary (P) waves and secondary (S) waves. Use this graphic to answer questions 10–11.

LAYERS OF THE EARTH

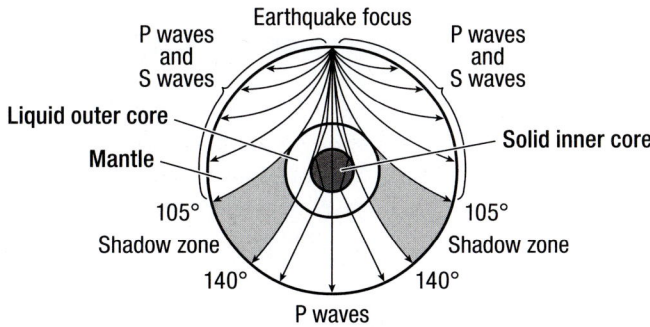

10. Through which layer of Earth can both P waves and S waves travel?
   - **A.** the shadow zone
   - **B.** the mantle
   - **C.** the outer core
   - **D.** the inner core

11. How would knowing the wave patterns shown in the graphic help locate the epicenter of an earthquake?

> **Test Tip**
>
> When possible, highlight or underline numbers or words critical to the understanding of a question.

CHAPTER 22: The Atmosphere

Chapter Outline

1. Characteristics of the Atmosphere
Layers of the Atmosphere
Changes in Earth's Atmosphere

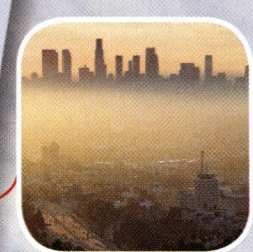

2. Water and Wind
The Water Cycle
Air Pressure
Wind

3. Weather and Climate
Fronts and Severe Weather
Climate

Tennessee Course Level Expectations (Physical Science)

CLE.3202.TE.3 Explain the relationship between the properties of a material and the use of the material in the application of a technology; **CLE.3202.Inq.1** Recognize that science is a progressive endeavor that reevaluates and extends what is already accepted; **CLE.3202.Inq.2** Design and conduct scientific investigations to explore new phenomena, verify previous results, test how well a theory predicts, and compare opposing theories; **CLE.3202.Inq.3** Use appropriate tools and technology to collect precise and accurate data; **CLE.3202.Inq.4** Apply qualitative and quantitative measures to analyze data and draw conclusions that are free of bias; **CLE.3202.Inq.5** Compare experimental evidence and conclusions with those drawn by others about the same testable question; **CLE.3202.Inq.6** Communicate and defend scientific findings; **CLE.3202.TE.4** Describe the dynamic interplay among science, technology, and engineering within living, earth-space, and physical systems.

Why It Matters

Severe weather involves changes in temperature and water content of the atmosphere. Understanding these relationships helps us predict the weather so that we can prepare for severe storms, such as the one shown in the photograph.

Inquiry Lab   10 min

Making a Rainbow

Rainbows result from interactions of sunlight with water droplets in the atmosphere. Light that hits water droplets will refract, or split, into its component colors. You can make a rainbow outside by using a water hose, as you may have done before. On a warm, clear day when the sun is overhead, turn on a **water hose** and make a fine spray into the sunlight.

Questions to Get You Started

1. Move the water spray up and down while the rainbow is visible. Does the rainbow move when you move the position of the spray? Describe what you see.

READING TOOLBOX

These reading tools can help you learn the material in this chapter. For more information on how to use these and other tools, see **Appendix A**.

Word Parts

Prefixes Many scientific words are made up of word parts that come from Latin and Greek. These word parts can be prefixes, suffixes, or word roots. You can figure out the meaning of unfamiliar science terms by looking at their word parts. **Appendix A** contains a list of many word parts and their meanings.

The word *atmosphere* is formed by combining the prefix *atmos-* with the root *sphere*. *Atmos-* comes from the Greek word for "vapor" and means "air." The root *sphere* is used because the atmosphere is shaped like a sphere around Earth.

Your Turn As you read Section 1, make a table like the one started below. It should list each layer of the atmosphere, the prefix for that layer, and your guess at the meaning of the prefix. After you have finished, look up the prefixes in a dictionary and correct your table as necessary.

LAYER	PREFIX	MEANING
troposphere	tropo-	
stratosphere		

Predictions

The Language of Prediction Scientific theories can be used to explain things that happened in the past. They can also be used to make predictions about what will happen in the future.

To recognize a statement of prediction, look for words such as these:

- the word *will* before a verb
- words such as *might* or *likely*
- the word *if* followed by a condition and the word *then* followed by a result

Your Turn As you read this chapter, make a list of statements of prediction. In each statement, underline the key words that tell you that the statement is a prediction. Some examples are given below.

Prediction Statements
- If the humidity is high and the temperature is low, rain is <u>likely</u>.
- If the barometric pressure decreases, the mercury level in a barometer <u>will</u> drop.

FoldNotes

Three-Panel Flip Chart FoldNotes are a fun way to help you learn and remember ideas that you encounter as you read. FoldNotes help you organize concepts and see the "big picture."

Your Turn Follow the instructions in **Appendix A** for making a three-panel flip chart. Label the first panel "Warm front," the second "Cold front," and the third "Stationary front." Open the appropriate flap to take notes about and draw sketches of each of the three kinds of fronts discussed in Section 3.

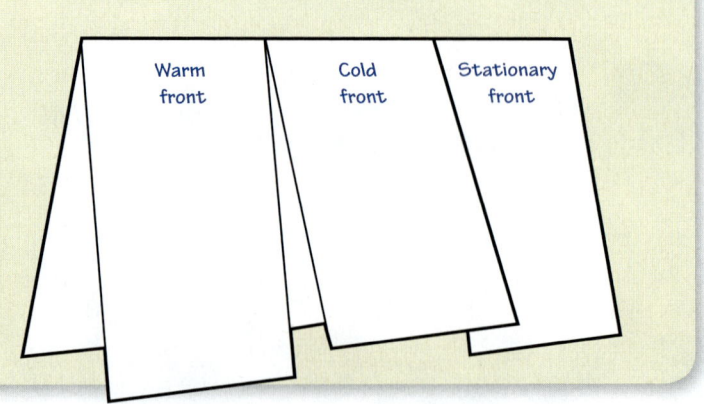

SECTION 1
Characteristics of the Atmosphere

Key Ideas
- What are the parts of Earth's atmosphere?
- Where did Earth's atmosphere come from?

Key Terms
troposphere
stratosphere
mesosphere
thermosphere
greenhouse effect

Why It Matters
If it were not for the top layer of Earth's atmosphere, the radio waves that carry your favorite radio station would not travel nearly as far.

You probably take the air you breathe for granted. Likewise, you may not think much about the clouds that you see in the sky. If you were to see Earth's atmosphere from space, though, it would look like just a thin, blue halo of light around Earth. This fragile envelope provides the air that we breathe, regulates global temperature, and filters out dangerous solar radiation. The atmosphere has a complex structure with many parts and layers.

Tennessee Course Level Expectations (Physical Science)
CLE.3202.Inq.1; CLE.3202.Inq.2; CLE.3202.Inq.3

Layers of the Atmosphere

Without the atmosphere, you would have no oxygen to breathe. Oxygen, however, is not the only gas in the atmosphere. Earth's atmosphere consists of a variety of gases. The two main gases in the atmosphere are nitrogen (about 78%) and oxygen (about 21%). The remaining gases exist only in very small amounts and are called *trace gases*. ❯ **The atmosphere has several layers. These layers differ in temperature, in density, and in the relative amounts of the different gases that are present.** Figure 1 shows the position and relative thicknesses of Earth's atmospheric layers.

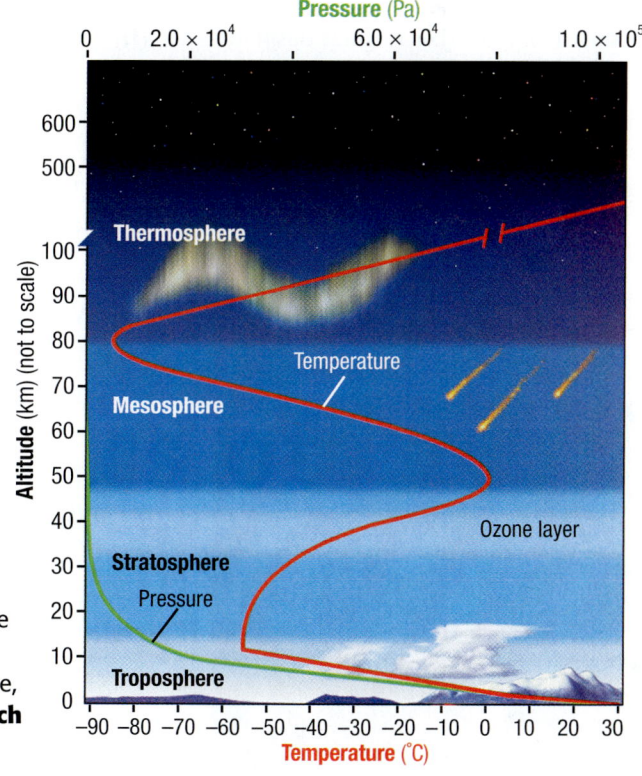

Figure 1 The layers of the atmosphere are marked by differences in temperature and pressure. The red line indicates temperature, and the green line indicates pressure. **Which part of the atmosphere do we live in?**

READING TOOLBOX

Three-Panel Flip Chart
Make a three-panel flip chart, and label the first panel "Troposphere," the second panel "Stratosphere," and the third panel "Mesosphere and thermosphere." Inside each panel, write key ideas about the corresponding layers of the atmosphere.

troposphere (TROH poh SFIR) the lowest layer of the atmosphere, in which temperature drops at a constant rate as altitude increases

stratosphere (STRAT uh SFIR) the layer of the atmosphere that lies between the troposphere and the mesosphere and in which temperature increases as altitude increases; contains the ozone layer

Figure 2 Temperature inversions trap polluted air in the Los Angeles Basin in California.

Almost all weather occurs in the troposphere.

You live in the **troposphere**, the layer of the atmosphere that is closest to Earth's surface. Clouds, wind, rain, and snow happen mainly in the troposphere.

The troposphere is the densest of the atmospheric layers. Consider the weight of all of the gases above pressing down on the gases in the troposphere. The weight makes the gas molecules squeeze together into a smaller volume. The result is a greater density than that of the higher layers of the atmosphere.

The troposphere gets cooler with increasing altitude.

If you were to climb a mountain, you would notice that the air is much colder at the top of the mountain than it is at the base. The lower air is warmed by the ground and oceans, which absorb solar energy during the day and heat the atmosphere by radiation and conduction. Air at higher altitudes is less dense and is not as close to those sources of energy. As you travel higher into the troposphere, the temperature decreases by about 6 °C for every kilometer of altitude.

At the top of the troposphere, the temperature stops decreasing. This boundary where this occurs is called the *tropopause*. The low temperature (−55 °C) at the tropopause keeps the water vapor in the troposphere. For this reason, clouds, rain, and snow are usually found in the troposphere. The tropopause acts like a lid on the water and water vapor in the troposphere. The altitude of the tropopause is different at different places on Earth. At the poles, its altitude is about 8 km (5 mi). Near the equator, it is as high as 18 km (11 mi).

Cool air can become trapped beneath warm air.

Although the troposphere is generally warmer close to Earth's surface, cool air sometimes gets trapped beneath the warm air. This condition is called a *temperature inversion*.

When a temperature inversion occurs, cooler air cannot rise and the air can become thick with pollution. Mountains can also prevent the polluted air from escaping. For example, the Los Angeles Basin in California is often filled with a brown haze, as **Figure 2** shows. Cool air from the Pacific Ocean blows into the basin, becomes trapped by the overriding warm air, and fills with pollutants.

As long as a temperature inversion remains, trapped pollutants cannot escape. When this happens, it is not healthy to exercise outside, because you will inhale a greater amount of pollutants as you breathe heavily.

Figure 3 A heated cabin in this aircraft allows its pilot to do high-altitude atmospheric research, such as collecting air and particle samples after a volcanic eruption.

The stratosphere gets *warmer* with increasing altitude.

In 1892, balloons were made that could record temperatures in the **stratosphere,** the layer above the tropopause. Later, humans further explored this cold, low-pressure layer by using airplanes with enclosed, heated cabins, such as the WB-57F shown in **Figure 3.** These explorers found that the temperature in the lower stratosphere remains fairly constant. From near the tropopause up to an altitude of about 25 km (about 16 mi), the temperature stays about –55 °C (–67 °F). At 25 km, however, the temperature begins to increase with altitude until it reaches about 0 °C (32 °F).

The stratosphere goes up to about 50 km (31 mi). In addition to getting warmer instead of cooler, the stratosphere differs from the troposphere in composition, weather, and density. Unlike the troposphere, the stratosphere has little water vapor, the gaseous form of water, because water vapor cannot get through the cold tropopause. Because of this lack of water vapor, the stratosphere contains few clouds and no storms.

The increase in temperature in the upper stratosphere occurs in the atmospheric layer known as the *ozone layer*. The ozone layer is warmer because it contains a form of oxygen called *ozone* that absorbs solar radiation. As **Figure 4** shows, molecules of the oxygen that we breathe have two oxygen atoms, whereas ozone molecules have three oxygen atoms. Ozone is important because it absorbs much of the sun's ultraviolet (UV) radiation. The ozone layer shields living things on Earth's surface from ultraviolet-radiation damage.

Reading Check Why does the stratosphere get warmer with increasing altitude? (See Appendix E for answers to Reading Checks.)

Figure 4 An Oxygen Molecule and an Ozone Molecule

Oxygen molecules have two atoms of oxygen.

Ozone molecules have three atoms of oxygen.

Section 1 Characteristics of the Atmosphere **775**

The mesosphere and thermosphere exhibit extremes of temperature.

In the **mesosphere,** 50 to 80 km (31 to 50 mi) above Earth's surface, the temperature begins to fall again as you go up. As in the troposphere, temperatures in the mesosphere decrease with increasing altitude. Near the top of this layer, temperatures fall to below −80 °C (−112 °F), the coldest temperatures in Earth's atmosphere.

Beyond the mesosphere, temperatures begin to rise again. This layer, at an altitude of about 80 to 480 km (50 to 298 mi), is called the **thermosphere.** The main gases are still nitrogen and oxygen, but the molecules are very far apart. For this reason, you may think that the thermosphere is very cold, but it is actually very hot. Temperatures in this layer average about 980 °C (1,796 °F) because the small amount of molecular oxygen in the thermosphere heats up as it absorbs intense solar radiation.

The outermost part of the thermosphere, at about 480 km, is known as the *exosphere*. In the exosphere, some gases escape from the gravitational pull of Earth and exit into space. Also, some gases in space are captured by Earth's gravity and added to Earth's atmosphere.

The ionosphere is important to radio communication.

When solar energy is absorbed in the lower thermosphere and upper mesosphere, electrically charged ions are formed. The area of the atmosphere where these ions form is sometimes called the *ionosphere*.

Electrons in the ionosphere reflect radio waves, as **Figure 5** shows, so the radio waves can be received over long distances. Without the ionosphere, most radio signals would travel directly into space, and only locations very close to a transmitter could receive the signals.

Because these ions form as a result of solar radiation, there are fewer of them at night in the lower layers of the ionosphere. So, the radio waves can travel higher into the atmosphere before being reflected. As a result, the radio waves return to Earth's surface farther from their source than they do in the daytime, as **Figure 5** shows.

Reading Check Why does the ionosphere allow radio signals to travel farther at night?

> **mesosphere** (MES oh SFIR) the coldest layer of the atmosphere, between the stratosphere and the thermosphere, in which temperature decreases as altitude decreases
>
> **thermosphere** (THUHR moh SFIR) the uppermost layer of the atmosphere, in which temperature increases as altitude increases

Figure 5 Radio waves can be received far from their source because they are reflected by the ionosphere. At night, when ion density decreases in the lower atmosphere, transmissions can be received even farther away.

Figure 6 Auroras, such as this one seen above mountains in Alaska, occur in the ionosphere.

Auroras take place in the ionosphere.

Colorful light displays called *auroras* can be seen encircling Earth's magnetic poles. Auroras take place in the ionosphere. They form when ions from the sun hit atoms and molecules in the ionosphere, causing photons to be emitted. The *aurora borealis*, shown in **Figure 6,** appears in the skies of the Northern Hemisphere. A similar phenomenon, the *aurora australis*, is observed in the south, above Antarctica.

Changes in Earth's Atmosphere

▶ **When Earth began to solidify about 4.4 billion years ago, volcanic eruptions released a variety of gases.** This process, called *outgassing*, created an atmosphere of many gases, some of which would be poisonous to us. As **Figure 7** shows, these gases included hydrogen, H_2; water vapor, H_2O; ammonia, NH_3; methane, CH_4; carbon monoxide, CO; carbon dioxide, CO_2; and nitrogen, N_2; but not oxygen, O_2.

Photosynthetic plants contribute oxygen to the atmosphere.

The first life-forms that evolved were able to live in this early atmosphere. Bacteria and other single-celled organisms lived in the oceans. About 2.5 billion years ago, some cells evolved *photosynthesis,* a method of capturing energy from the sun. This process also produced oxygen as a byproduct. These organisms needed only sunlight, water, and carbon dioxide for their survival, so they thrived and multiplied in this environment. Gradually, the oxygen content of the atmosphere increased to about 20%. **Figure 7** shows the difference between the ancient Earth's atmosphere and the atmosphere today. About 350 million years ago, the concentration of oxygen reached a level similar to what it is today.

Figure 7 Earth's Atmosphere Billions of Years Ago and Now

Early in Earth's history, the atmosphere contained mostly water vapor, carbon dioxide, nitrogen, and a few other trace gases.

As Earth and life changed, so did the balance of gases in the atmosphere.

Section 1 Characteristics of the Atmosphere

SCILINKS
www.scilinks.org
Topic: Carbon Cycle
Code: HK80216

Animals produce carbon dioxide necessary for photosynthesis.

As *aerobic*, or oxygen-breathing, organisms evolved, they joined plants in a balance that led to our present atmosphere. The steps of the oxygen–carbon dioxide cycle describe this balance, as **Figure 8** shows. Plants need carbon dioxide, CO_2, for food production by photosynthesis. Oxygen, O_2, is then released as a waste product of photosynthesis. Animals breathe oxygen and release carbon dioxide as waste. The carbon dioxide that they exhale is then used by plants and other photosynthetic organisms, and the process repeats.

Human-made chemicals can deplete the ozone layer.

Recall that the stratosphere contains a layer of ozone molecules. Ozone forms when the sun's ultraviolet rays strike molecules of O_2, which break apart. The single atoms of oxygen bond with O_2 molecules to make ozone, O_3. These O_3 molecules, in turn, absorb much of the sun's damaging ultraviolet radiation. If the ozone layer were not present, ultraviolet rays would cause serious damage to the cells of living things. So, scientists were concerned when they found low concentrations of ozone in the stratosphere in the 1980s.

Ozone destruction is caused mainly by chemicals known as *chlorofluorocarbons*, or CFCs. CFCs were widely used through much of the 20th century as refrigerants and in spray cans. Persuaded by evidence of a connection between CFCs and ozone destruction, most countries have passed laws that ban the manufacture of CFCs. As a result, the amount of CFCs entering the stratosphere has greatly decreased.

Reading Check How does life on Earth benefit from ozone in the upper atmosphere?

Academic Vocabulary
evidence (EV uh duhns) information showing whether an idea or belief is true or valid

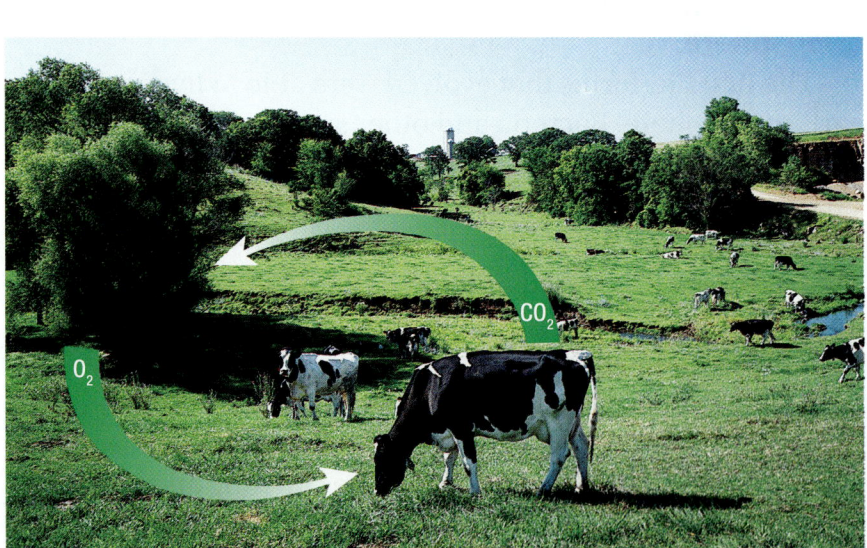

Figure 8 In the oxygen–carbon dioxide cycle, plants produce oxygen, which is used by animals for respiration. Animals produce carbon dioxide, which is used by plants for photosynthesis.

QuickLab

The Greenhouse Effect

⏱ 20 min

Procedure

1. Pour **100 mL of water** into **two identical glass jars.**
2. Add **five ice cubes** and a **thermometer** to each jar, and wrap one jar in a **resealable plastic bag.**
3. Put both jars in the sun or under identical **lamps.**
4. Record the temperature of the water in each jar every 5 min, and record your observations.

Analysis

1. Make a line graph of your results.
2. Which jar warmed up more quickly? Explain why.

The greenhouse effect keeps Earth warm.

Have you ever opened a car on a sunny day? It is surprisingly warm inside. Much of that warmth results from the sun's energy entering and becoming trapped inside. The same is true of the glass walls of a greenhouse used to grow plants.

Earth's atmosphere does not have solid walls as a greenhouse does, so Earth does not trap the sun's energy in the same way. But certain atmospheric gases keep Earth much warmer than it would be without an atmosphere. As **Figure 9** shows, energy released from the sun as radiation is absorbed by Earth's surface. Then, some of this energy is transferred back toward space as radiation. Carbon dioxide, water vapor, and other gases absorb some of this energy, so the atmosphere becomes warmer. The warm atmosphere releases some of this energy in the form of radiation, some of which warms Earth's surface. This effect is known as the **greenhouse effect.**

✓ **Reading Check** How does the greenhouse effect work?

greenhouse effect (GREEN HOWS e FEKT) the warming of the surface and lower atmosphere of Earth that occurs when carbon dioxide, water vapor, and other gases in the air absorb and reradiate infrared radiation

Figure 9 The Greenhouse Effect in Earth's Atmosphere

Solar radiation warms Earth's surface. Then, energy is radiated back into the atmosphere as heat radiation.

Greenhouse gases, such as CO_2 and H_2O, receive this radiation, which warms the atmosphere. Energy from the atmosphere is radiated to Earth's surface.

CO_2 is added to the air in the burning of fossil fuels and in forest fires.

Figure 10 The average yearly temperature on Earth has been rising during the past several years.

Too much carbon dioxide may cause global warming.

Without the greenhouse effect, Earth would be much colder. But if too much energy is absorbed by the atmosphere, global temperatures will rise. This *global warming* could cause problems such as rising ocean levels, because of melting polar icecaps, and droughts. The average temperature during the past few decades has been rising somewhat, as the graph in **Figure 10** shows. Thus, some global warming appears to be happening. Combustion of coal, oil, and gas in the 19th and 20th centuries has added more carbon dioxide, a greenhouse gas, to the air. Many scientists now think that this increase in carbon dioxide is a major reason that temperatures in the troposphere have risen above the normal average.

Section 1 Review

KEY IDEAS

1. **Identify** the two atmospheric layers that contain air as warm as 25 °C.
2. **Identify** which of these characteristics is true of the ionosphere.
   a. It gets warmer with altitude.
   b. It is the layer where weather takes place.
   c. It is the layer where auroras take place.
   d. It exhibits extremes in temperature.
3. **Identify** which of the following gases is most abundant in Earth's atmosphere today.
   a. argon
   b. nitrogen
   c. oxygen
   d. carbon dioxide
4. **Compare** Earth's early atmosphere with its present atmosphere.
5. **Describe** the role that plants play in the oxygen–carbon dioxide cycle.

CRITICAL THINKING

6. **Evaluating Arguments** Explain why the following statement is incorrect: "Global warming could cause oceans to rise, so the greenhouse effect must be eliminated completely."
7. **Predicting Consequences** In 1982, Larry Walters rose to an altitude of approximately 4,900 m on a lawn chair attached to 45 helium-filled weather balloons. Give two reasons why Walters's efforts were dangerous.

SECTION 2
Water and Wind

Key Ideas
- What happens to water in the troposphere?
- What is air pressure, and by what terms is it also known?
- What causes wind?

Key Terms
water cycle
transpiration
precipitation
humidity
dew point
Coriolis effect

Why It Matters
Temperature and movements of water and air in the atmosphere determine whether the air feels cool, warm, dry, or moist when you step outside in the morning.

You come in contact with water throughout every day, not just when you drink it or when you shower or wash your hands. Water, in the form of a gas, is in the air. It is also in the air as a liquid, in droplets suspended in the atmosphere as clouds or fog or falling as rain or snow. All of this water in the atmosphere affects the weather on Earth.

The Water Cycle

> **Water is continuously being moved through the troposphere.** This process, called the **water cycle,** is shown in **Figure 1**.

The major part of the water cycle happens between the oceans and the continents. The sun's energy striking the ocean water makes water molecules escape from the liquid and rise as gaseous water vapor. This process is known as *evaporation*.

Tennessee Course Level Expectations (Physical Science)
CLE.3202.Inq.1; CLE.3202.Inq.2; CLE.3202.Inq.3; CLE.3202.Inq.5; CLE.3202.TE.3; CLE.3202.TE.4

water cycle (WAWT uhr SIE kuhl) the continuous movement of water between the atmosphere, the land, and the oceans

Figure 1 Evaporation, transpiration, condensation, and precipitation make up the continuous process called the *water cycle*.

781

Evaporated water vapor condenses to form precipitation.

Evaporation also takes place when sunlight strikes water in lakes, rivers, and the soil. Additional water comes into the air through transpiration. During **transpiration,** plants lose moisture through small pores in their leaves. You may not think that this moisture makes much difference. But transpiration adds a lot of water vapor to the atmosphere. For example, a 1 km^2 cornfield may transpire 3,400,000 L (900,000 gal) of water per day.

In the atmosphere, water vapor rises until the air is cool enough to condense the vapor into tiny droplets of water. We can see these droplets as clouds. As clouds cool and condense more vapor, they often release their moisture in the form of **precipitation.** Most precipitation falls as rain, snow, hail, or sleet. Precipitation can happen over land or water. Precipitation that falls on land stays on the surface until it evaporates, flows into a larger body of water, or is absorbed into the ground to become groundwater.

Air contains varying amounts of water vapor.

You have probably noticed that air feels different from day to day. Sometimes, it feels thick and moist; and at other times, it feels crisp and dry. The air around you contains varying amounts of water vapor, and you experience the effects of changing **humidity,** or the amount of moisture in the atmosphere. Some animals, such as the frog shown in **Figure 2,** need a certain amount of humidity.

In weather forecasts, you may hear the relative humidity given. *Relative humidity* is the ratio between the water vapor pressure in the air and the maximum water vapor pressure for air at that temperature and pressure. Relative humidity is usually given as a percentage. Air that has a relative humidity of 100% is said to be *saturated*.

Warmer temperatures evaporate more water.

Water in the atmosphere is constantly either *condensing,* (changing state from a gas to a liquid), or *evaporating* (changing state from a liquid to a gas). The temperature of the air determines the rate of evaporation. At warm temperatures, molecules move very quickly and are farther apart. Thus, the water is more likely to exist as a gas. As the temperature decreases, the rate of evaporation decreases and the rate of condensation increases. Therefore, at lower temperatures, water is more likely to be liquid and therefore fall as rain.

Figure 2 This frog depends on the humidity in its environment.

transpiration (TRAN spuh RAY shuhn) the process by which plants release water vapor into the air through stomata

precipitation (pree SIP uh TAY shuhn) any form of water that falls to Earth's surface from the clouds

humidity (hyoo MID uh tee) the amount of water vapor in the air

dew point (DOO POYNT) at constant pressure and water vapor content, the temperature at which the rate of condensation equals the rate of evaporation

Water vapor becomes liquid at the dew point.

The temperature at which the rate of condensation equals the rate of evaporation for water vapor in the atmosphere is called the **dew point.** The graph in **Figure 3** represents the dew point over a range of temperatures. When the humidity is high, there is more water vapor in the air, so the water vapor can more easily condense into liquid water. So, the higher the humidity is, the higher the dew point is.

You may have seen condensation, or drops of water, on a glass of ice water. The cold surface of the glass provides a place where the dew point is reached. The rate of condensation is greater than the rate of evaporation, so water vapor in the air becomes liquid.

Clouds form as warm, moist air rises.

You may know from walking through fog—a low-lying cloud—that clouds are wet. Clouds are formed when warm air rises and water vapor condenses into tiny droplets of liquid as it cools. This process happens only in the troposphere. Clouds are made up of tiny droplets of liquid water and, at higher altitudes, small ice crystals. Depending on where clouds form, they can have different shapes and characteristics.

Reading Check What are clouds made of?

Figure 3 Warm air can contain more water vapor than cold air can. **About how much water vapor can there be in air that is at 20 °C?**

Cloud names describe their shape and the altitude at which they form.

The different kinds of clouds that can form in different parts of the atmosphere are shown in **Figure 4.** Cloud names describe both their appearance and the altitude at which they are found. Clouds are named using combinations of the root words *cirrus, stratus,* and *cumulus.*

Cirrus clouds are thin and wispy and occur at high altitudes—between 6 km and 11 km (between 3.7 mi and 6.8 mi) above Earth. Stratus clouds are layered and look like sheets. These clouds typically form at lower altitudes—less than 6 km (3.8 mi). Cumulus clouds are white and fluffy with somewhat flat bottoms. The flat base is the place where rising air reaches the dew point. Cumulus clouds can form anywhere from about 500 m to about 12 km (7.5 mi) above Earth.

Figure 4 Clouds are classified by their form and the altitude at which they occur.

QuickLab 10 min
Measuring Rainfall

1. Set an **empty soup can** outside in the open, away from any source of water runoff. At the same time each day, use a **metric ruler** to measure the amount of rain or other precipitation that has accumulated in the can.

2. Record your measurements. Keep a record of the precipitation in your area for a week.

3. Listen to or read local weather reports to see if your measurements are close to those given in the reports.

Cloud names reflect combined characteristics.

Cloud names reflect the combined characteristics of each cloud type. *Cirrostratus* clouds are high, layered clouds that form a thin, white veil over the sky. *Altostratus* and *altocumulus* clouds are simply stratus and cumulus clouds that occur at middle altitudes. When a cloud name includes the root *nimbo* or *nimbus*, the cloud is a type that produces precipitation. Cumulonimbus clouds are towering rain clouds that often produce thunderstorms. Nimbostratus clouds are large, gray clouds that often produce steady precipitation.

You may have seen a halo around the sun or moon. This halo results from the refraction of light as it passes through ice crystals in cirrostratus clouds. Sometimes, the presence of a halo is the only way to tell that a very thin, transparent layer of cirrostratus clouds is present.

Air Pressure

Barometers are instruments that are used to measure air pressure. *Barometric pressure* is a term that is sometimes used in weather reports in the newspaper and on television. Changes in barometric pressure often accompany changes in the weather. ▶ **The barometric pressure, also called *atmospheric pressure* or *air pressure*, is the pressure that results from the weight of a column of air extending from the top of the thermosphere to the point of measurement.** Falling pressure may mean that a large air mass is leaving the area, and rising pressure can mean that an air mass is moving in.

Mercury barometers indicate air pressure by a column of mercury.

Figure 5 shows a simple mercury barometer. The mercury barometer contains a long tube that is open at one end and closed at the other. The tube is filled with mercury and then inverted into a small container of mercury. Some, but not all, of the mercury flows out of the tube and into the container. The atmospheric pressure holds the mercury in the tube to a height above the mercury in the container. Any change in the height of the column of mercury means that the atmosphere's pressure has changed.

At sea level, the barometric pressure of air at 0 °C is about 760 mm of mercury. This amount of pressure is defined as 1 atmosphere (1 atm) of pressure. The SI unit for pressure is the pascal (Pa), which is equal to 1 newton per square meter.

✅ **Reading Check** What does the height of a mercury barometer indicate?

Figure 5 The height of the mercury in the tube of a mercury barometer indicates the barometric pressure in millimeters.

Figure 6 An aneroid barometer consists of a sealed chamber of air that expands and contracts according to the pressure, which moves a lever that is attached to a pointer.

Aneroid barometers do not contain liquid.

Figure 6 shows an aneroid barometer. *Aneroid barometers* indicate the pressure based on the volume of a sealed chamber of air. They are more portable than mercury barometers, but mercury barometers are more accurate.

Academic Vocabulary
indicate (IN di KAYT) to be or give a sign of; to show

Wind

Have you ever seen a movie in which an airplane window breaks? When the window breaks, all of the loose objects in the plane are pushed out the window. Something like this might actually happen if an airplane window were to break. ❯ **The reason is that differences in pressure create winds.**

Pressure gradients cause air to move.

Commercial airplanes fly very high in the troposphere, between 10 km and 13 km above Earth. At this altitude, the atmospheric pressure is very low. However, the air inside the airplane is at a pressure similar to that at Earth's surface.

If an airplane window were to break, the dense air in the plane's cabin would spread out into the less dense air outside the cabin. The flow of air produced in this situation would push loose objects out the window.

Just as a difference in air pressure would create a flow of air from inside the airplane to the outside, differences in pressure in the atmosphere can cause wind. A difference in air pressure from one place to another is called a *pressure gradient*. The air in a pressure gradient moves from areas of high pressure to areas of low pressure, just as an object placed on the side of a hill will tend to roll downhill. This movement of air from a high-pressure area to a low-pressure area is called *wind*.

READING TOOLBOX

Prefixes
Make a table of prefixes that lists the names of types of clouds. Note the meanings of the prefixes in common between them.

Section 2 Water and Wind **785**

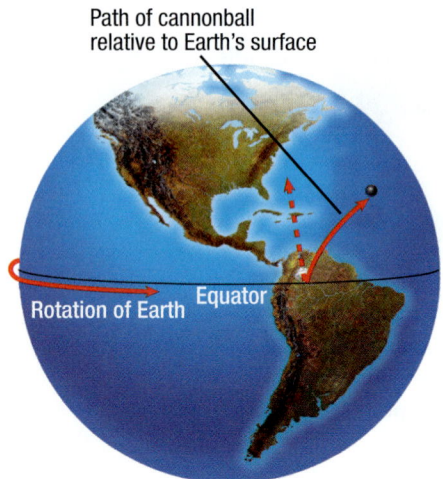

Figure 7 Because of Earth's rotation, a cannonball fired directly north from the equator will curve to the east relative to Earth's surface.

Coriolis effect (KAWR ee OH lis e FEKT) the curving of the path of a moving object from an otherwise straight path due to Earth's rotation

Earth's rotation affects the direction of winds.

Earth's rotation influences the direction in which wind moves. The effect of Earth's rotation on the direction of wind is described by the **Coriolis effect.** To understand how the Coriolis effect works, you must first understand that points at different latitudes on Earth move at different speeds as Earth rotates.

Consider two houses at different latitudes. A house located on the equator travels faster than a house located near one of the poles. Can you see why this statement must be true? Earth goes through one full rotation in 24 hours. During this time, the house at the equator must travel the distance of Earth's circumference. A circle of latitude that is closer to the poles is smaller than the circle of latitude on the equator. Therefore, the house closer to the pole moves through a shorter distance in the same amount of time. Thus, this house moves more slowly.

Imagine a cannonball in a cannon at the equator. The cannonball is moving along with Earth as it rotates. The cannonball's speed at this time is a little greater than 1,610 km/h (1,000 mi/h) to the east—the speed at which all points on the equator move because of Earth's rotation. When the cannonball is fired to the north, it continues to move east at about 1,610 km/h. As the cannonball moves farther north, however, the portion of Earth beneath the cannonball is moving more slowly. The result is a flight path like the one shown in **Figure 7,** in which the cannonball's path curves eastward.

Predictable air circulation forms wind patterns.

The path of a cannonball northward is affected by Earth's rotation. Winds moving north or south are affected in a similar way. When winds move north in the Northern Hemisphere, they curve to the right. When winds move south in the Southern Hemisphere, they curve to the left. Now, consider air moving south from the North Pole. The wind lags behind the rotation of Earth and travels west—to the left, as **Figure 8** shows—because the wind has a slower speed than the spinning Earth. Similarly, wind moving north from the South Pole travels west because of its slower speed.

In summary, *winds in the Northern Hemisphere curve clockwise, and winds in the Southern Hemisphere curve counterclockwise.* The resulting circulation patterns are so regular that meteorologists have named them, as **Figure 8** shows.

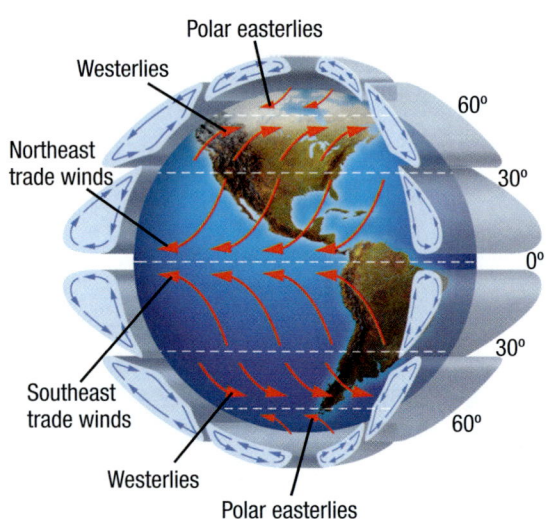

Figure 8 Both the Northern Hemisphere and the Southern Hemisphere have three wind belts.

Figure 9 Global wind patterns can be harnessed by sailors and even by ballooners.

Global wind patterns form circulation cells.

Global wind patterns are predictable enough that people can use them to travel all the way around the planet, as one person has in the balloon shown in **Figure 9.** Note in **Figure 8** that there are also wind patterns that form a loop at about every 30° of latitude.

In each of Earth's two hemispheres, much of the air moving toward the pole sinks at about 30° latitude, so a high-pressure area forms near Earth's surface. Flowing from a high-pressure area to a low-pressure area, air flows both north and south in a large loop. At about 60° latitude, air flowing along the surface from the high-pressure bands at the pole and at 30° meet. Air rises as these air masses meet, so a low-pressure belt forms. Thus, air in each of the hemispheres completes three loops, called *cells*.

Section 2 Review

KEY IDEAS

1. **Identify** which one of the following processes is *not* a step in the water cycle.
   a. evaporation
   b. condensation
   c. photosynthesis
   d. precipitation

2. **Determine** whether wind moving north from the equator will curve eastward or westward because of the Coriolis effect.

3. **Distinguish** between humidity and relative humidity.

4. **Select** which one of the following describes a cumulus cloud.
   a. sheetlike
   b. fluffy, white, and flat bottomed
   c. wispy and feathery
   d. high altitude

5. **Identify** which one of the following statements describes a mercury barometer.
   a. It is less accurate than an aneroid barometer.
   b. It has a chamber that contains a lot of water.
   c. It indicates barometric pressure by the height of the mercury in the tube.
   d. It is more commonly used than an aneroid barometer.

6. **Predict** which of the following areas would be more humid: the Sahara on a cold night or the Florida coast on a warm day.

CRITICAL THINKING

7. **Applying Concepts** Which has a lower pressure, the air in your lungs as you inhale or the air outside your body?

Why It Matters

Harnessing the Wind

Only in relatively recent times have people been able to explain what causes wind. Yet for thousands of years, people have found ways to harness, or make use of, the wind. Wind energy is free and reliable, and the possibilities in using it are limited only by human ingenuity.

SCIENCE & SOCIETY

Wind power is harnessed by sailing vessels. This Chinese junk is a type of sailing vessel that has been used in some form for more than 2,000 years.

Before electricity began to be used, wind power was used to grind grain in windmills. Many windmills like this one are still standing in Holland.

Today, wind power is used to generate electricity in "wind farms," such as this one, that have dozens of turbines. Wind power is a clean energy source.

About the end of the 18th century, people began to construct large hot-air balloons that would go wherever the wind carried them.

YOUR TURN

ONLINE RESEARCH
1. Find a method of harnessing wind power that is not shown on this page. Compare it with one of the methods shown on this page.

CRITICAL THINKING
2. What limitations to using wind energy can you think of?

SECTION 3
Weather and Climate

Key Ideas
› How do fronts affect the weather?
› How is climate different from weather?

Key Terms
air mass
front
climate
topography

Why It Matters
Weather processes include natural disasters that are powerful enough to destroy your home.

How is a weather forecast made? *Meteorologists,* people who study weather, gather data about weather conditions in different areas. By using weather maps, meteorologists can try to predict weather by tracking the movement of large bodies of air called **air masses.** Interactions between air masses have predictable effects on the weather in a given location.

Tennessee Course Level Expectations (Physical Science)
CLE.3202.Inq.1; CLE.3202.Inq.2;
CLE.3202.Inq.3; CLE.3202.Inq.4;
CLE.3202.Inq.6

Fronts and Severe Weather

You have probably heard about *cold fronts* and *warm fronts.* A **front** is the place where a cold air mass and a warm air mass meet. Look at the weather map in **Figure 1.** A cold front is shown as a blue line with blue triangles. A warm front is shown as a red line with red semicircles. Clouds, rain, and sometimes snow can occur at fronts. › **When fronts move through an area, the result is usually precipitation and a change in wind direction and temperature.**

air mass (ER MAS) a large body of air throughout which temperature and moisture content are similar

front (FRUHNT) the boundary between air masses of different densities and usually different temperatures

Figure 1 Weather maps show the location of fronts and areas of different pressure. They also show a large-scale view of the weather.

789

Figure 2 Warm Fronts and Cold Fronts

At a warm front, a warm air mass moves above a slower cold air mass.

At a cold front, a cold air mass moves quickly under a warm air mass. The warm air then rises rapidly.

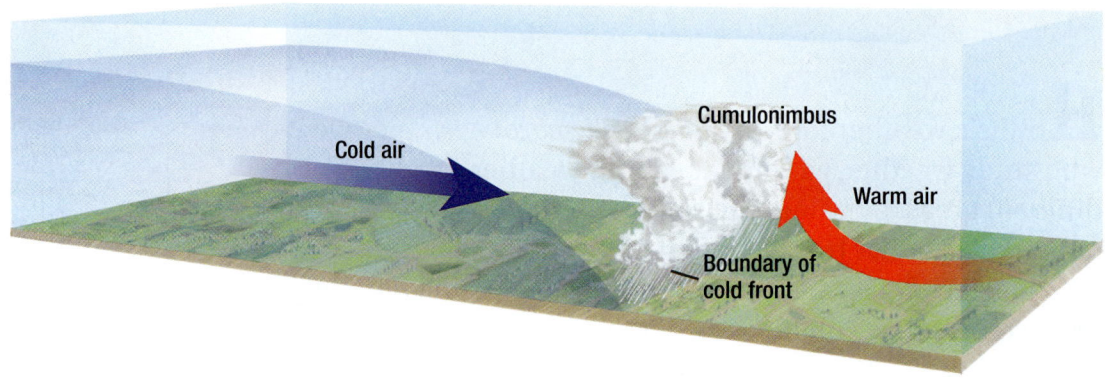

SCLINKS.
www.scilinks.org
Topic: Air Masses and Fronts
Code: HK80032

Front types include warm, cold, and stationary fronts.

There are three main types of fronts: warm, cold, and stationary fronts. At a warm front, a mass of warm air moves toward and over a slower, denser mass of cold air, as **Figure 2** shows. The warm air, as it is pushed up over the cool air, cools and forms clouds. Cirrus and cirrostratus clouds can be seen high in the sky as a warm front approaches. As time passes, lower-lying clouds move overhead. Often, nimbostratus clouds release steady rain or snow for one to two days.

At a cold front, the forward edge of a mass of cold air moves under a slower mass of warm air and pushes it up, as **Figure 2** shows. Note that the front edge of the cold front is steeper than the edge of the warm front. Because of this steep edge, warm air rises quickly and forms cumulonimbus clouds. High winds, thunderstorms, and sometimes tornadoes accompany this type of front.

A *stationary front* occurs when two air masses meet but neither is displaced. Instead, the air masses move side by side along the front. The weather conditions near a stationary front are similar to those near a warm front.

Reading Check What kind of weather typically results from a cold front?

790 Chapter 22 The Atmosphere

Lightning is a discharge of electrical energy.

Water droplets and ice crystals in thunderclouds build up electric charges. When charge builds up in one place, lightning may result. Lightning is a big spark that jumps between clouds, or between a cloud and Earth's surface, to equalize the charge. Lightning instantly heats the air around it so much that the air expands faster than the speed of sound. The shock wave created is thunder.

Tornadoes are funnels of high-speed wind.

Tornadoes, such as the one shown in **Figure 3,** are high-speed, rotating winds. Tornadic winds are the most violent winds on Earth. Winds in a tornado may reach speeds as high as 500 km/h (about 310 mi/h). Tornadoes happen most commonly in the United States, especially in the Midwest. Most of them form in spring and early summer, typically along a front between cool, dry air and warm, humid air.

Typically, a tornado begins as a column of water droplets, called a *funnel cloud*, that descends from dark storm clouds. The air inside the funnel has very low pressure. As the funnel reaches the ground, higher-pressure air rushes into the low-pressure area. The result is high-speed winds, which cause the damage associated with tornadoes. The rotating winds on the outer edge of a tornado can tear apart homes and trees. Tornadoes are too fast and unpredictable for you to attempt to outrun, even if you are in a car. If you see a tornado, move to a storm cellar or basement or lie flat under a table at the center of a room with few windows. If you are outside, lie in a ditch or low-lying area and cover your head with your hands.

QuickLab

Thunder and Lightning

1. Have a **stopwatch or watch, calculator,** and **pencil** and **paper** handy for the next time that a thunderstorm is in your area.

2. When you see a flash of lightning, start the stopwatch or note the seconds indicated on the watch. When you hear the thunder, stop the stopwatch or note the seconds indicated on the watch.

3. The speed of sound in air is about 340 m/s. Based on the time lag between the lightning and the thunder, how far away was the lightning strike?

Figure 3 A tornado is a rapidly spinning funnel cloud.

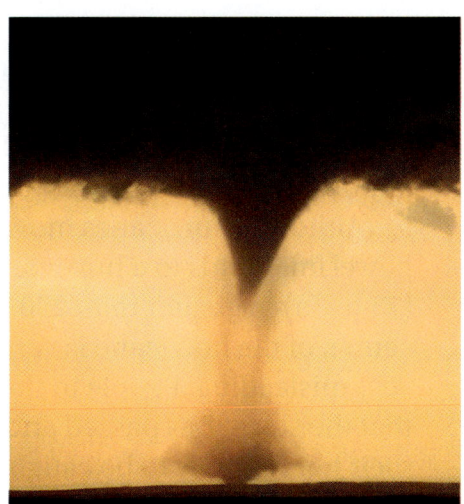

A tornado begins when rotating air in a thundercloud begins to descend.

The lowering column becomes a funnel, and winds increase on the ground.

The visible funnel can cause major damage when it reaches the ground.

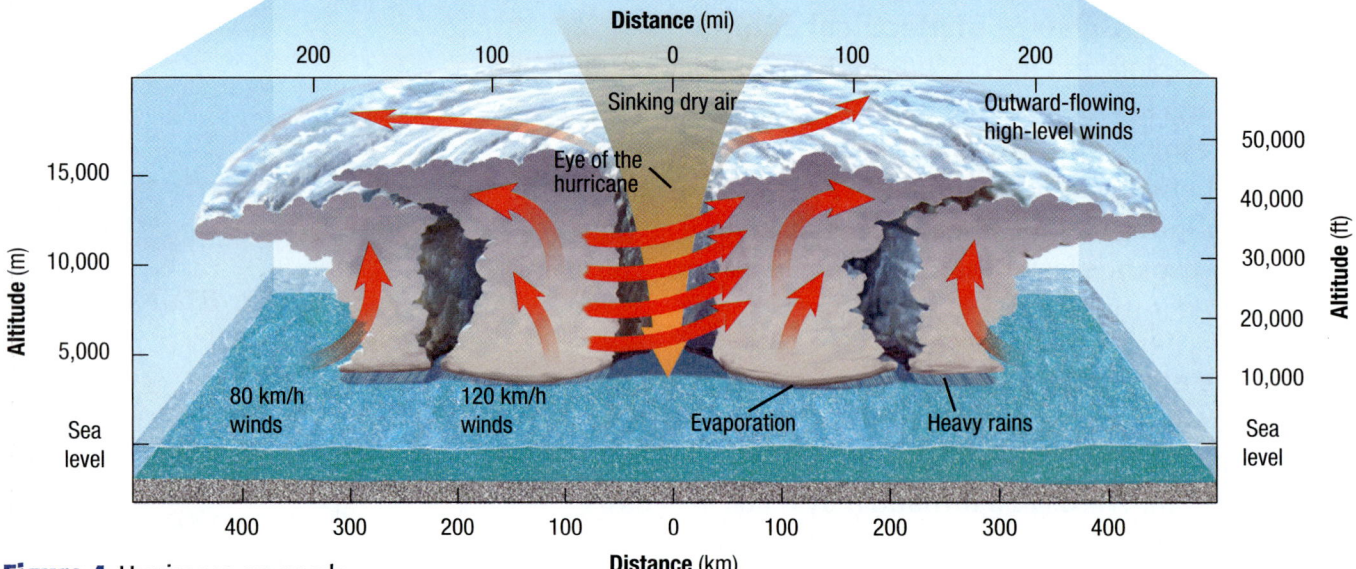

Figure 4 Hurricanes are nearly circular in shape and rotate around a center called the *eye*, as this cross section shows.

READING TOOLBOX

The Language of Prediction
In your own words, rephrase in the form of statements of prediction the explanation on this page of how hurricanes form.

Hurricanes are large, rotating tropical storm systems.

Hurricanes are unique storm systems that occur over warm ocean water. These storms are called *hurricanes* in North America and the Caribbean, *cyclones* in the Indian Ocean, and *typhoons* in the western Pacific. Hurricanes occur in late summer and early fall, when the oceans are warmest. As the warm water evaporates and the water vapor rises, intense low-pressure areas called *tropical depressions* form. These tropical depressions can build strength and become hurricanes. As **Figure 4** shows, hurricanes are large, circulating masses of clouds, wind, and rain, with diameters that can be more than 600 km (373 mi).

Hurricanes are powered by the energy released as water vapor condenses to form clouds. As the water vapor condenses, it releases energy as heat into the air, the air heats up and expands, and the pressure inside the clouds decreases. Warm, moist air continues to rise and condense, so more energy is released. This rising air creates fierce winds, shown by the red arrows in **Figure 4.** The storm gradually weakens as it moves over land or cool water.

Although hurricanes move fairly slowly, they are extremely powerful. Winds in a hurricane reach speeds from 118 km/h (73 mi/h) to greater than 250 km/h (155 mi/h). The *eye*, or center, of the hurricane is very calm. This calmness can be very misleading. People in the eye of a hurricane often believe that the storm has passed and leave the protective cover of their homes, only to be caught in the storm again.

Reading Check What is the source of the tremendous amount of energy released in a hurricane?

Why It **Matters**

Surviving Natural Disasters

Natural disasters can threaten lives. But you can lessen the danger to yourself by taking steps to prepare beforehand. A major disaster, such as a flood, hurricane, or earthquake, can cause loss of electricity and water and make traveling difficult or impossible. So, the key to disaster preparedness is to keep a survival kit in case you are not able to leave your house for several days. Other tips are listed here for your reference.

SOME WAYS TO PREPARE FOR A NATURAL DISASTER
1. Keep aware of weather reports so that you know where and when a disaster may occur.
2. Have your family plan to meet in a designated place in case you get separated.
3. Keep a survival kit with water, nonperishable food, a flashlight, and a battery-powered radio.

A hurricane on a populated coastline can be a very destructive natural disaster. These pictures show a part of the Gulf Coast in Mississippi before and after Hurricane Katrina hit in 2005.

As you make a survival kit to prepare for any natural disaster that may occur, think about items that you may need if you are stranded for several days without water or electricity.

YOUR TURN

UNDERSTANDING CONCEPTS
1. Because you may not have access to some items during a natural disaster, what items should you include when preparing a survival kit?

www.scilinks.org
Topic: Natural Disasters
Code: **HK81014**

Climate

▶ **Weather** changes from day to day, but climate does not change as quickly. **Climate** is the average weather of a region and is measured over many years.

Temperatures tend to be higher close to the equator.

Sunlight strikes Earth at different angles. This fact is illustrated in **Figure 5.** Rays striking farther from the equator spread out over a greater surface area and are less concentrated than rays that strike at the equator. At the poles, rays pass nearly parallel to Earth's surface and do not warm the atmosphere as much. For this reason, the poles are very cold. Earth is not always oriented so that the equator is perpendicular to incoming solar radiation. But throughout the year, the surface of the Earth near the equator is almost perpendicular to the sunlight. As a result, areas close to the equator have warm climates.

Figure 5 Solar energy is more concentrated at the equator than at the poles because Earth's surface is curved.

Earth's tilt and rotation account for our seasons.

In the Northern Hemisphere, there is more daylight in summer and less daylight in winter. What causes these yearly patterns? Earth's orbit is an ellipse, and you might expect that summer occurs when Earth is closest to the sun. This is not true, however. In fact, Earth is farthest from the sun on July 4 and closest to the sun about January 3. Earth's seasons are actually caused by the tilt of Earth on its axis. Because of the tilt of Earth's axis, as **Figure 6** shows, different portions of Earth receive more direct sunlight in different seasons.

When the North Pole is tilted toward the sun, as in position A in **Figure 6,** the sun rises higher in the Northern Hemisphere than when the North Pole is pointed away from the sun. There is more daylight, and the temperature increases. So, the season is summer in the Northern Hemisphere and winter in the Southern Hemisphere. When the South Pole is tilted toward the sun, as in position C, the sun rises higher in the Southern Hemisphere. So, the season is summer in the Southern Hemisphere and winter in the Northern Hemisphere.

Figure 6 This illustration (not to scale) shows that Earth's axis is tilted 23.5° from the perpendicular to the orbital plane. **At which position and season does Earth's Northern Hemisphere receive the least amount of sunlight?**

go.hrw.com
interact online
Keyword: HK8ATMF6

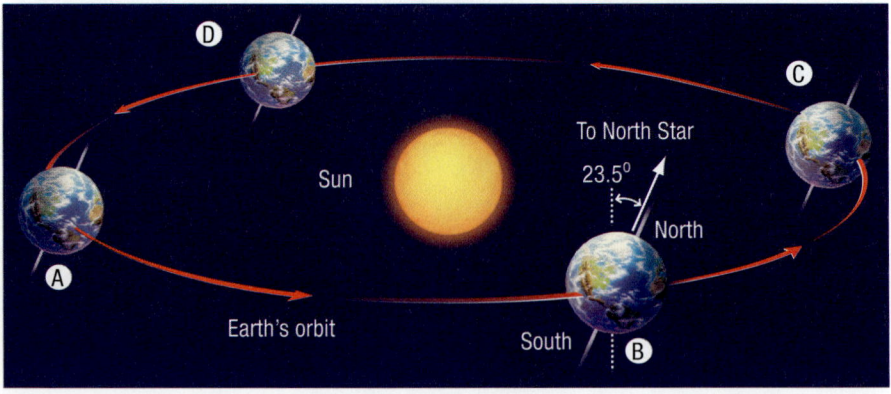

794

Earth's surface features affect climate.

The rise and fall of a land surface is called **topography**. The topography of a region affects its climate. Mountains can have an especially important effect on the climate of an area. As air rises over a mountain, the air cools and clouds form. When mountains are near oceans, as **Figure 7** shows, the air is so humid that condensation of water vapor happens easily, so the ocean side of the mountain gets a lot of rain.

On the other side of the mountain, cool, dry air warms as it descends. Deserts often form on this dry side of the mountain. Areas such as these are said to be in a *rain shadow,* because clouds have released all of their moisture by the time that they reach the dry side of the mountain.

Broad, flat surfaces, such as the Great Plains, have unique weather patterns. Plains do not stop wind flow. Winds can come from far off and merge on the plains. This mixing of wind produces thunderstorms and even tornadoes.

Global climate changes over long periods of time.

Earth's climate has varied greatly over time. Many factors contribute to these changes. These factors include eruptions of volcanoes, shift of the continents, and changes in Earth's tilt over very long periods of time. All of these factors will cause Earth's climate to continue to change naturally over the millennia to come.

As discussed in the previous section, much shorter-term climate change also seems to be happening. Many scientists think that increases in human-made greenhouse gases have caused the recent increase in global average temperature. The long-term effects of these changes remain to be seen.

climate (KLIE muht) the average weather conditions in an area over a long period of time

topography (tuh PAHG ruh fee) the size and shape of the land surface features of a region, including its relief

Figure 7 Air passing over a mountain loses moisture as it rises and cools. This dry air warms as it descends on the other side of the mountain.

Section 3 Review

KEY IDEAS

1. **Determine** whether each of the following statements describes a warm front or a cold front.
   a. A warm air mass moves above a slower-moving cold air mass.
   b. Thunderstorms and high winds characterize this type of front.
   c. A cold air mass moves quickly under a slower-moving warm air mass.
   d. It is characterized by steady rain.
2. **Determine** whether a tornado is more likely to form along a cold front or a warm front.
3. **Distinguish** between lightning and thunder.
4. **Identify** which of the following would not have an effect on the climate of a nearby region.
   a. a mountain range
   b. the equator
   c. a thunderstorm

CRITICAL THINKING

5. **Applying Concepts** Grapes grow well in areas where the climate is generally mild. Would you recommend planting grapes in California or on the plains of North Dakota? Explain your answer.

Effects of Temperature on the Buoyancy of Air

Air rises or sinks in Earth's atmosphere because of differences in buoyancy. These differences relate to changes in the density of air that are caused by differences in temperature.

What You'll Do

- **Measure** the volume of a constant mass of air at different temperatures.
- **Draw conclusions** by inferring changes in buoyancy and density from changes in volume.

What You'll Need

container, wide-mouth
glycerin
ice
petroleum jelly
syringe, disposable, 60 mL
thermometer
water, tap, hot and cold

Safety

Asking a Question

What is the effect of temperature on the buoyancy of air?

Preparing for Your Experiment

① On a blank sheet of paper, prepare a table like the one shown.

Sample Data Table: Temperature and Volume

Temperature (°C)	Pull volume (mL)	Push volume (mL)	Average volume (mL)

② Measure and record the air temperature in the room.

③ Remove the cap from the tip of the syringe, and move the plunger. If the plunger does not move smoothly and easily, lubricate the inside wall of the syringe with a few drops of glycerin.

④ Adjust the position of the plunger until the syringe is about two-thirds full of air. Add a dab of petroleum jelly to the tip of the syringe, and replace the cap.

Measuring the Volume of Air

⑤ Gently pull on the plunger, and then release it. When the plunger stops, read the volume of air inside the syringe. Record the volume in your data table in the column labeled "Pull volume."

⑥ With your finger on the cap, gently push on the plunger and then release it. When the plunger stops, read the volume of air inside the syringe. Record the volume in your data table in the column labeled "Push volume."

Forming and Testing a Hypothesis

⑦ Form a hypothesis about how different temperatures might affect the results you get in the procedure you just carried out.

796 Chapter 22   The Atmosphere

Designing Your Experiment

8. Design an experiment in which you test at least two temperatures below room temperature and two temperatures above room temperature. It is important that the mass of air inside the syringe does not change during your experiment. How can you ensure that the mass of air remains constant?

9. In your lab report, list each step that you will perform in your experiment.

10. Before you carry out your experiment, your teacher must approve your plan.

Performing Your Experiment

11. After your teacher approves your plan, carry out your experiment.

12. Record your results in your data table.

Analysis

1. **Analyzing Data** At each temperature that you tested, calculate the average volume by adding the pull volume and push volume and dividing the sum by 2. Record the result in your data table in the column labeled "Average volume."

2. **Analyzing Data** Plot your data in your lab report in the form of a graph set up like the one shown. Draw a straight line on the graph that best fits the data points.

Communicating Your Results

3. **Drawing Conclusions** How does the volume of a constant mass of air change as the temperature of the air increases? For the mass of air that you used in your experiment, how much would the volume change if the temperature increased from 10 °C to 60 °C?

4. **Drawing Conclusions** Recall that the density of a substance equals the substance's mass divided by its volume. Do your results indicate that the density of air increases or decreases as the temperature of the air increases? Explain.

5. **Reaching Conclusions** Based on your results, would a body of air become more or less buoyant as it becomes colder than the surrounding air?

Extension

Suppose that someone tells you that your conclusions are invalid because some of your data points lie above or below the best-fit line that you drew. How could you argue that your results are valid?

Finding Percentages

Science > Skills

Technology

▸ Math

Scientific Methods

Graphing

Problem

Relative humidity is the water-vapor pressure in the air divided by the maximum water-vapor pressure for air at the same temperature. Relative humidity is usually expressed as a percentage. It can be calculated as the amount of water vapor in a certain amount of air divided by the maximum amount of water vapor that can exist in air at that temperature. If 40.0 g/m³ of water vapor can be in air at 35 °C, what is the amount of water vapor actually present if the relative humidity is 65%?

Solution

Identify

List all given and unknown values.

Given:
relative humidity, 65%
maximum amount of water vapor in air, 40.0 g/m³

Unknown:
actual amount of water vapor in air (g/m³)

Plan

Write down the equation for relative humidity. Rearrange it so that you can calculate the actual amount of water in the air.

$$\text{relative humidity} = \frac{\text{actual water in air}}{\text{maximum water in air}} \times 100$$

$$\text{actual water in air} = \frac{\text{relative humidity} \times \text{maximum water in air}}{100}$$

Solve

Solve for the actual amount of water in the air.

$$\text{actual water in air} = \frac{65 \times 40.0 \text{ g/m}^3}{100} = 26 \text{ g/m}^3$$

Therefore, 26 g of water vapor is actually present in each cubic meter of air at a temperature of 35 °C.

Practice

1. If the maximum amount of water vapor in air at 15 °C is 12.5 g/m³, what is the actual amount of water vapor in the air if the relative humidity is 85%?

2. If at a relative humidity of 60%, the actual amount of water vapor in air at 30 °C is 18.0 g/m³, what is the maximum amount of water vapor in the air?

3. If the maximum amount of water vapor in air at 20.0 °C is 17.0 g/m³ and the actual amount of water vapor in the air is 14.0 g/m³, what is the relative humidity?

4. If the maximum amount of water vapor in air at 30 °C is 30.0 g/m³ and the actual amount of water vapor in the air is 14.0 g/m³, what is the relative humidity?

CHAPTER 22 Summary

go.hrw.com
SUPER SUMMARY
KEYWORD: HK8ATMS

Key Ideas

Section 1 Characteristics of the Atmosphere

- **Layers of the Atmosphere** The atmosphere has several layers, which differ in temperature, in density, and in the relative amounts of the different gases that are present. (p. 773)
- **Changes in Earth's Atmosphere** About 4.4 billion years ago, volcanic eruptions released a variety of gases, which formed the atmosphere of early Earth. (p. 777)

Section 2 Water and Wind

- **Water Cycle** Water is continuously being moved through the troposphere. (p. 781)
- **Air Pressure** Atmospheric pressure is the pressure that results from the weight of a column of air extending from the top of the thermosphere to the point of measurement. (p. 784)
- **Wind** Differences in atmospheric pressure create winds. (p. 785)

Section 3 Weather and Climate

- **Fronts and Severe Weather** When fronts move through an area, the result is usually precipitation and a change in wind direction and temperature. (p. 789)
- **Climate** Weather changes from day to day, but climate does not change as quickly. (p. 794)

Key Terms

troposphere, p. 774
stratosphere, p. 775
mesosphere, p. 776
thermosphere, p. 776
greenhouse effect, p. 779

water cycle, p. 781
transpiration, p. 782
precipitation, p. 782
humidity, p. 782
dew point, p. 783
Coriolis effect, p. 786

air mass, p. 789
front, p. 789
climate, p. 794
topography, p. 795

CHAPTER 22 Review

READING TOOLBOX

1. **Prefixes** The prefix *bar-* means "pressure." Identify a word from this chapter that has the prefix *bar-*, and give the word's definition.

USING KEY TERMS

2. Explain how carbon dioxide in the atmosphere relates to the *greenhouse effect*.

3. How is *ozone* formed?

4. Describe the *water cycle* by using the terms *precipitation, condensation, transpiration,* and *evaporation*.

5. Describe the formation of a *warm front*.

6. Explain the difference between *weather* and *climate*.

7. Describe the relationship between air temperature and *humidity*.

8. Use the terms *hurricane, tropical depression,* and *winds* to explain how a storm becomes a hurricane.

UNDERSTANDING KEY IDEAS

9. Almost all of the water vapor in the atmosphere is in the
   a. exosphere.
   b. ionosphere.
   c. stratosphere.
   d. troposphere.

10. Clouds form when water vapor in the air condenses as
    a. the air is heated.
    b. the air is cooled.
    c. snow falls.
    d. snow forms.

11. CFCs, chemicals that are used as refrigerants and as propellants in spray cans, are partly to blame for the reduction of stratospheric
    a. carbon dioxide.
    b. oxygen.
    c. ozone.
    d. clouds.

12. Winds in the Northern Hemisphere curve clockwise because of
    a. CO_2.
    b. climate.
    c. the Coriolis effect.
    d. CFCs.

13. Cumulonimbus and nimbostratus clouds both
    a. appear white and fluffy.
    b. produce precipitation.
    c. occur at high altitudes.
    d. look thin and wispy.

14. When a moving warm air mass encounters a mountain range, the air mass
    a. stops moving.
    b. slows and sinks.
    c. rises and cools.
    d. reverses direction.

EXPLAINING KEY IDEAS

15. What is a temperature inversion?

16. Explain the differences in seasons between the Northern Hemisphere and the Southern Hemisphere.

17. Explain, in terms of the concept of dew point, why you might find small droplets of water on grass early in the morning.

18. What conditions are necessary for the formation of a tornado?

19. Describe the two common types of barometer.

CRITICAL THINKING

20. Applying Concepts The temperature in the troposphere decreases by 6 °C/km as you go up. Based only on the altitude, how much colder would you expect the temperature to be at the top of Mount Everest, which is almost 9 km above sea level, than at the coastline of India?

21. Predicting Consequences Imagine that average global temperatures increase by several degrees. Name two ways, other than feeling warmer, that this change would affect your life.

22. Relating Concepts What evidence do scientists have that Earth's climate has changed over time? How can this evidence help scientists study changes that our climate is now undergoing?

23. Identifying Relationships One body of air has a relative humidity of 97%. Another has a relative humidity of 44%. At the same temperature, which body of air is closer to its dew point? Explain your answer.

24. Evaluating Methods Which areas of Earth should meteorologists monitor to detect developing hurricanes? Explain your answer.

25. Analyzing Processes Explain why precipitation is likely to happen when the temperature drops.

26. Analyzing Processes Why does thunder always accompany lightning?

27. Making Decisions Would you be safe in a car on the road during a tornado? Explain.

Graphing Skills

28. Constructing Graphs Research the average rainfall in your city, area, or state for each month of the year. Using this data, create two kinds of graphs. Decide which graph is better for clearly representing the information. Include both of your graphs with a short paragraph that explains which graph you would use in a presentation.

29. Interpreting Graphics Use the weather map shown below to name three states that have a cold front moving through them. Predict what kind of weather people there can expect.

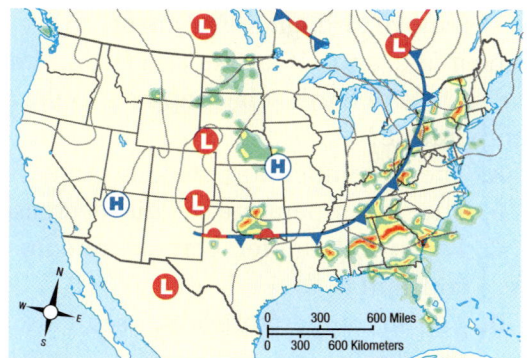

30. Interpreting Graphics Visual aids called *climatographs* are used to display information about the climate of a specific region. Using the climatograph for Moscow, Idaho, in the figure below, answer the following questions:

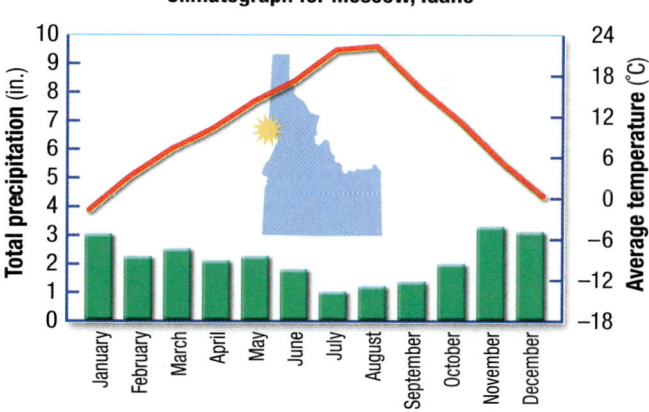

a. What was the average temperature in Moscow during August?

b. What was the total precipitation in the Moscow area for the month of January?

c. What was the approximate total precipitation for the year?

Standardized Test Prep

Understanding Concepts

Directions (1–3): For each question, write on a sheet of paper the letter of the correct answer.

1. As you move through the layers of the atmosphere and get farther and farther from the surface of Earth, what happens to the air temperature?
    A. The air temperature steadily increases.
    B. The air temperature steadily decreases.
    C. The average air temperature remains constant.
    D. The air temperature falls, rises, falls, and rises again.

2. Without the evolution of photosynthesis, which element would still be missing from Earth's atmosphere?
    F. oxygen
    G. nitrogen
    H. hydrogen
    I. chlorophyll

3. Which type of cloud formation is a good indication that a thunderstorm might be approaching?
    A. cirrostratus
    B. cirrocumulus
    C. stratocumulus
    D. cumulonimbus

Directions (4–5): For each question, write a short response.

4. In which level of the atmosphere could the temperature reach 980 °C (1,796 °F)?

5. What happens to the dew point as humidity increases? Will water condense more or less easily as the humidity increases?

Reading Skills

Directions (6–7): Read the passage below. Then, answer the questions that follow.

LIGHTNING

The first stage in the process of lightning formation happens when an electric field builds up in a tall cloud. This electric field is the result of ions separating within the cloud and forming layers with different polarities. Positive ions tend to come together near the top of the cloud, and negative ions come together near the bottom.

As a result of the electric field, free electrons in the cloud begin to move very quickly. They begin to collide with particles and knock loose more electrons, which then begin accelerating as well. The result is a chain reaction, known as an *electron avalanche*. This chain reaction creates a path of positively charged ions, called a *step leader,* which extends down toward Earth.

When the positive charge is great enough, a lightning strike occurs. Charges nearest the ground cause a *return stroke* of negative charge to spread upward toward the cloud. The return stroke sends out photons and shows us the brilliant displays of lightning that we see in a stormy sky. The return stroke also causes the shock wave that we hear as thunder.

6. Which part of the lightning bolt connects first with particles from the ground?
    F. the step leader
    G. the return stroke
    H. the electron avalanche
    I. the negative cloud layer

7. How does the electric field form that causes lightning?

Interpreting Graphics

The graphic below shows the amount of ozone, O_3, that is found at different levels of the atmosphere. Use this graphic to answer questions 8–11.

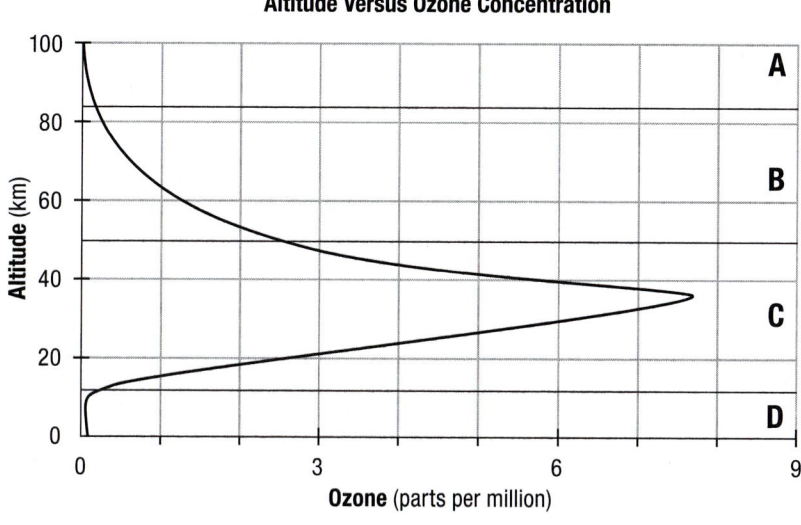

8. Which layer of the atmosphere does B represent?
   A. the mesosphere
   B. the stratosphere
   C. the thermosphere
   D. the troposphere

9. The point in the atmosphere with the highest concentration of ozone is the ozone layer. Within which atmospheric layer is the ozone layer located?
   F. the ionosphere
   G. the stratosphere
   H. the thermosphere
   I. the troposphere

10. Which area of the graph indicates the part of the atmosphere that contains the air that you breathe?
    A. area A
    B. area B
    C. area C
    D. area D

11. As you move upward from the surface of Earth, what happens to the concentration of ozone in the atmosphere as you pass the tropopause?

> **Test Tip**
>
> Slow, deep breathing may help you relax. If you suffer from test anxiety, focus on your breathing to calm down.

CHAPTER 23
Using Natural Resources

Chapter Outline

❶ Organisms and Their Environment
What Is an Ecosystem?
Stability in Ecosystems
Evaluating Changes in Ecosystems

❷ Energy and Resources
The Search for Resources
Alternative Sources of Energy
The Efficiency of Energy Conversion

❸ Pollution and Recycling
What Causes Pollution?
Air Pollution
Water Pollution
Pollution on Land
Reducing Pollution

Tennessee Course Level Expectations (Physical Science)

CLE.3202.TE.1 Explore the impact of technology on social, political, and economic systems; **CLE.3202.TE.3** Explain the relationship between the properties of a material and the use of the material in the application of a technology; **CLE.3202.Inq.1** Recognize that science is a progressive endeavor that reevaluates and extends what is already accepted; **CLE.3202.Inq.2** Design and conduct scientific investigations to explore new phenomena, verify previous results, test how well a theory predicts, and compare opposing theories; **CLE.3202.Inq.3** Use appropriate tools and technology to collect precise and accurate data; **CLE.3202.Inq.4** Apply qualitative and quantitative measures to analyze data and draw conclusions that are free of bias; **CLE.3202.Inq.6** Communicate and defend scientific findings; **CLE.3202.TE.2** Differentiate among elements of the engineering design cycle: design constraints, model building, testing, evaluating, modifying, and retesting; **CLE.3202.TE.4** Describe the dynamic interplay among science, technology, and engineering within living, earth-space, and physical systems.

Why It Matters

All societies use natural resources for power, food, and other needs. In California, a giant array of solar cells collects energy directly from sunlight and converts the energy into electricity that is used to power homes and businesses.

Inquiry Lab
⏱ 20 min

Using Energy at Home

Make a list of the sources of energy that you have at home. Find out from your parents the average monthly cost of electrical energy in your home. Make a pie chart showing your results. Then, call your local power company to find out what natural resource is used to generate electrical energy in your area.

Questions To Get You Started

1. How many sources of energy did you find in your home?
2. How many sources of energy are being used in your classroom?

READING TOOLBOX These reading tools can help you learn the material in this chapter. For more information on how to use these and other tools, see **Appendix A.**

FoldNotes

Key-Term Fold A key-term FoldNote can help you learn the key terms in this chapter.

Your Turn Create a key-term fold, as described in **Appendix A.**

1. Write one key term from the Summary page on the front of each tab.
2. As you read the chapter, write the definition for each term under its tab.
3. Use this FoldNote to study the key terms.

Tabs: ecosystem, community, succession, fossil fuel, pollution, recycling

Describing Time

Temporal Language *Temporal language* is language that is used to describe time. Paying careful attention to temporal language can help you understand the nature of events and processes in the environment.

Your Turn As you read this chapter, make a two-column table. In the first column, write words or phrases you encounter in the text that refer to time. In the second column, write whether the word or phrase describes a specific time, duration, frequency, or a sequence of events.

TEMPORAL WORDS	DESCRIBES...
in the 1990's	specific time
gradually	duration

Graphic Organizers

Venn Diagrams A Venn diagram is a graphic representation of the relationships between similar things or ideas. Here are instructions for making a Venn diagram.

Your Turn As you read Section 3, complete the Venn diagram that represents the relationships between different kinds of pollution.

1. Draw three overlapping circles, as shown at the right.
2. Label one circle "Air Pollution," another circle "Water Pollution" and the third circle "Land Pollution."
3. Write the terms for various pollutants and sources of pollution in the appropriate circles. If a pollutant or source fits in more than one category, write it in the area in which those categories overlap.

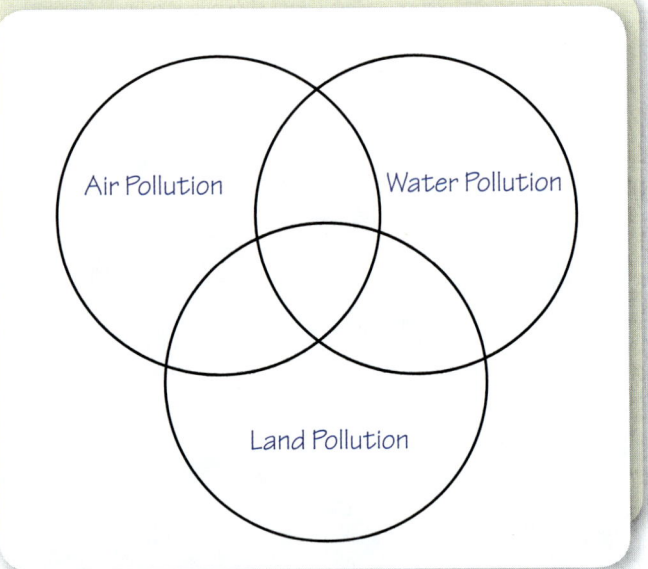

806 Chapter 23 Using Natural Resources

SECTION 1
Organisms and Their Environment

Key Ideas
- What makes up an ecosystem?
- How does an ecosystem maintain stability?
- How long does it take for changes in an ecosystem to be reversed?

Key Terms
ecosystem
community
succession

Why It Matters
Humans can affect the stability of ecosystems and cause long-term changes, for better or for worse.

Should money be spent drilling for oil in the wilderness of Alaska, or would the money be better spent promoting solar power? Should wetlands be drained to provide parking for a mall in your town, or are the wetlands best left alone? No matter how you feel about these issues, you need to know how they will affect the world around you.

Tennessee Course Level Expectations (Physical Science)

CLE.3202.Inq.1; CLE.3202.Inq.2; CLE.3202.Inq.3

What Is an Ecosystem?

Every action that we take, whether it is turning on a light bulb or draining a swamp, affects all of the other living things in the ecosystem. ▶ **An ecosystem is made up of all organisms living in an area and their physical environment.** Living elements in an ecosystem can include plants and animals, such as the ones shown in **Figure 1.** Nonliving elements include sunlight, air, soil, and water. Cycles of energy and matter are at the base of an ecosystem.

ecosystem (EE koh sis tuhm) a community of organisms and their abiotic environment

Figure 1 Each living and nonliving element in this desert ecosystem directly affects the others.

Topic: Ecosystems
Code: HK80466

community (kuh MYOO nuh tee) a group of various species that live in the same habitat and interact with each other

Ecosystems exist all around us.

To properly evaluate the effects of your decisions on the issues that may change your environment, you must first understand how the many parts of an ecosystem are related to one another. Whether you live in a city or in the countryside, you are part of numerous ecosystems.

Consider a city park as an ecosystem. A squirrel in the park gathers and stores food. It lives in a tree and drinks water from a nearby pond. The soil, trees, sunshine, and water are natural resources found within the park. When you are in the park, you, too, are part of that ecosystem.

Some of the interrelated elements in a desert ecosystem might be cactuses, sagebrush, lizards, snakes, scorpions, and birds. They interact with one another and with their surroundings to make a stable, balanced ecosystem.

Not all ecosystems are the same size.

Ecosystems can be large or small. Our planet is one big ecosystem containing all living and nonliving things on Earth—the land and water, the organisms, and the atmosphere. A shallow forest pool no bigger than a rain puddle is also an ecosystem. This ecosystem is made up of water, mud, bacteria, mosquitoes, air, and insect larvae.

Figure 2 Ecosystems are made up of communities that contain different populations of organisms.

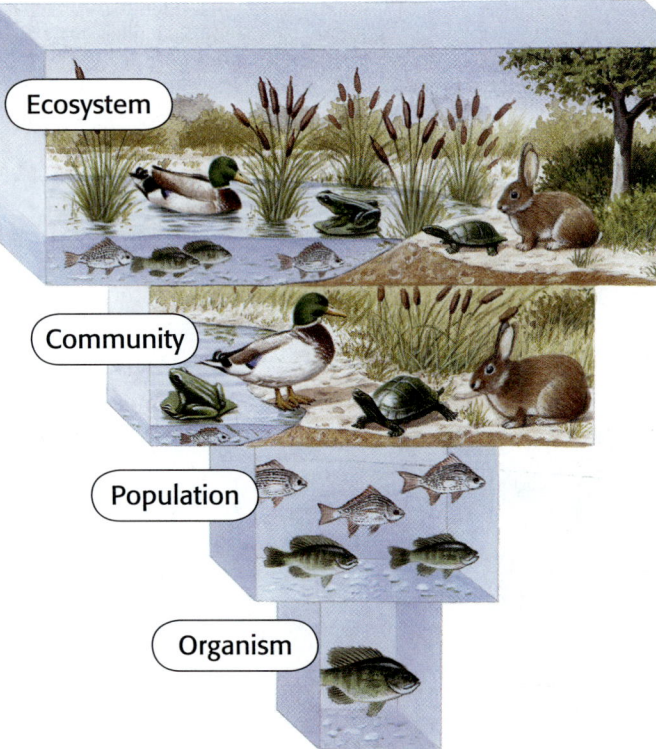

Living things are adapted to their ecosystems.

Living things are found almost everywhere: on land, in the air, and in water. Each organism has adapted to factors in its environment such as temperature, humidity, and other living things. For instance, polar bears are adapted to cold, wet places, and camels are adapted to hot, dry places. Neither animal could survive in the other's environment.

Ecosystems are divided into communities.

All of the interacting animals and plants living in one area within an ecosystem form a **community**. Depending on how the organisms interact, there can be several communities in an ecosystem. The animals and plants of the tundra make up one community. The seals, fish, and algae of the nearby ocean make up another. Polar bears belong to *both* communities. **Figure 2** shows the different divisions within an ecosystem.

Stability in Ecosystems

The elements that make up an ecosystem, such as sunlight, water, air, soil, animals, and plants, are numerous. ❯ **Each element is in balance with the others so that the ecosystem can be maintained over a long period of time.** As long as the elements in an ecosystem are well balanced, the ecosystem will remain stable and healthy.

Look at the aquarium shown in **Figure 3.** The amount of salt in the water and the temperature of the water are at the proper levels. The fish, snails, and plants have sufficient space and food. There are enough resources for every living thing in the aquarium ecosystem. The ecosystem is balanced.

Balanced ecosystems remain stable.

When an ecosystem is balanced, the population sizes of different species do not change much relative to one another. Overall, there is a natural balance between the populations of species that make their own food and the populations of species that use others for food. Factors such as disease and food shortage prevent populations from growing too much.

If the balance within an ecosystem is disturbed, change results. The graph in **Figure 4** is based on a Canadian study of the snowshoe hare and its predator, the lynx. When the prey population decreases, there is less food for the predators. As a result, some of the predators die. If the prey population increases, more predators may move into the area. Factors such as population change can affect the balance in an ecosystem.

✅ **Reading Check** What is required for an ecosystem to remain stable over a long period of time? (See Appendix E for answers to Reading Checks.)

Figure 3 Living and nonliving elements help keep this aquarium ecosystem balanced.

Figure 4 The population of snowshoe hares directly affects the population of lynxes.
What happened to the lynx population when there were fewer snowshoe hares?

Figure 5
Nearly all of Yellowstone National Park's plant communities have burned at one time or another. The following spring, new plant life flourishes in the recovering park. Full recovery of an area can take 25 to 50 years.

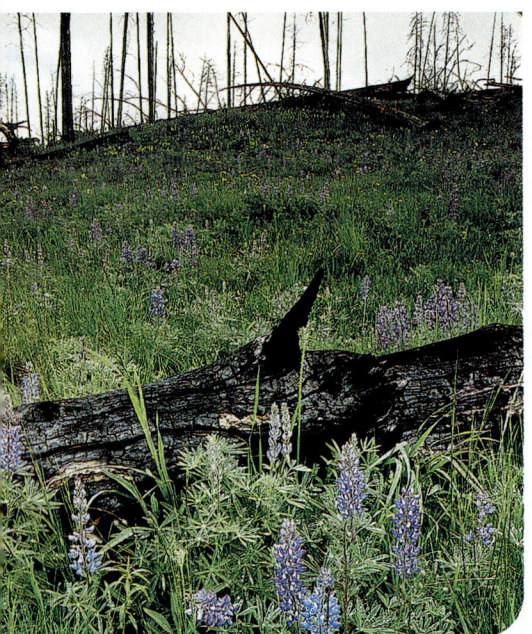

A change in one feature can affect a whole ecosystem.

Throughout the 1990s, researchers kept a close watch on an area in Central America that was once a tropical rain forest. As the trees were logged, a species of wild pig vanished from the forest. Three species of frogs disappeared soon thereafter. Were these two events related? Scientists asked how the loss of the forest affected the wild pigs and how the loss of the pigs might have led to the loss of the frog species.

The pigs disappeared because they no longer had enough food or shelter. The scientists determined that when the pigs wallowed in the mud, they formed puddles that the frogs used for breeding. After the pigs were gone, there were no puddles, and the frogs had to find another place to breed. A change in one factor of an ecosystem can affect all living and nonliving elements within the system.

The key to understanding ecosystems can be summed up in one word: *interrelatedness*. The elements that make up an ecosystem function together to keep the entire system stable.

Ecosystems tend to gradually return to their original conditions.

If one element or factor in an ecosystem changes, time and natural forces often work to return the ecosystem to its previous state. Yellowstone National Park is one of the largest tourist attractions in the United States. The park, located mostly in northwestern Wyoming and southern Montana, covers about 2.2 million acres (8,987 km^2) and is known for its active geysers, hot springs, and large expanses of forest. Wildfire has played a role in the dynamics of this area for thousands of years, since long before it was a park.

During the dry summer of 1988, large areas of the park were burned to the ground by fires, as the upper photo in **Figure 5** shows. The fires, which were started by lightning as well as by careless human activity, spread quickly through the open forest and left nearly a third of the park blackened with ash. Firefighters tried to contain the blazes, but they were unsuccessful in putting out all of the fires. Rain and snow eventually put the fires out.

The following spring, the appearance of the "dead" forest began to change. Large numbers of small, green plants began to flourish in areas that had been covered with fallen trees. Vegetation is gradually returning to the area, as the lower photo in **Figure 5** shows. However, the recovery of the area is slow. The process by which this part of the forest returns to its former state will take several decades.

New ecosystems develop through the process of succession.

A somewhat regular progression of species replacement is called **succession**. After the forest fires in Yellowstone National Park, new plants replaced the burned-down forest through the process of succession. This process is constantly happening all around you. A weed growing up through a crack in a paved lot is an example of the first step in a succession. If the weed is left alone, it will set seed, more plants will appear, and the ecosystem of the lot will change.

The end product of succession is a stable but complicated community where birth, growth, death, and decay take place continuously.

Academic Vocabulary

constantly (KAHN stuhnt lee) continually occurring or recurring

succession (suhk SESH uhn) the replacement of one type of community by another at a single location over a period of time

Evaluating Changes in Ecosystems

Ecosystems undergo both short-term and long-term changes. **Short-term changes are usually easily reversed, but long-term changes can take many years to be reversed and may never be reversed at all.** Most disruptions to an ecosystem occur naturally, but human activity causes many changes in the world around us.

Short-term ecosystem changes include the seasons.

During autumn, many trees and shrubs lose their leaves. In the winter, many birds migrate to warmer places. Some animals hibernate by slowing their metabolism. In spring, the migrating birds return, animals come out of hibernation, buds open, and seeds begin to sprout. As **Figure 7** shows, the same ecosystem can appear quite different during different times of the year.

✓ **Reading Check** Name two ways in which an ecosystem may change from one season to another.

Figure 7 This area of forest looks quite different in the spring than it does in the winter.

QuickLab

Why Do Seasons Occur?

 10 min

Procedure

1. Place a **lamp** on a table, and turn the lamp on.
2. Stand about 2 m from the table, and hold a **globe** at arm's length. Point the globe toward the lamp.
3. Tilt the globe slightly so that the bottom half—the Southern Hemisphere—is illuminated by the lamp.
4. Keeping the axis of Earth's rotation pointing in the same direction, walk the globe halfway around the table.

Analysis

1. What part of the globe is lit by the lamp's light now? What season does this represent in this part of Earth?
2. Would any seasonal changes occur if the Earth's axis were not tilted? Explain your answer.
3. In addition to experiencing short-term seasonal changes, ecosystems experience short-term changes as day changes into night. What movement of Earth causes night and day to occur?

Figure 8 Icy glaciers covered much of North America and parts of Europe and Asia during the last ice age (which reached its maximum approximately 18,000 years ago).

Long-term ecosystem changes result from large-scale changes on the planet.

In your lifetime, the climate where you live probably has not changed much. Some years may be colder than others, but average monthly temperatures do not vary greatly from year to year. Throughout Earth's geologic history, however, there have been periods known as *ice ages,* when glaciers covered much of the continents. During ice ages, temperatures are much colder than average. **Figure 8** shows the extent of the glacier that covered much of North America during the last ice age.

Glacial periods alternate with periods of warmer temperatures. Scientists hypothesize that glacial periods are caused by a variety of factors, including plate tectonics, changes in the tilt of Earth's axis, changes in the shape of Earth's orbit around the sun, and changes in the speed and pattern of the oceans' circulation. The precise effect of each of these changes can be difficult to predict accurately. But global temperature changes always result in long-term changes in ecosystems.

Long-term changes in ecosystems can also be caused by events such as volcanic eruptions, which change both Earth and its atmosphere. Sometimes, many small factors, both natural and human-made, act together to cause change in an ecosystem. In these cases, it may be hard to know how much each factor adds to the change. One such case is global warming, which is a result of the interaction of many factors.

✓ **Reading Check** Name two natural events that may cause long-term changes in an ecosystem.

Changes can be caused by human activity.

Natural events are not the only factors that cause changes in ecosystems. People also alter the environment in a variety of ways, as **Figure 9** shows. Activities such as logging, growing crops, constructing roads and buildings, and driving cars change the environment.

Building dams can improve the environment for human purposes. For instance, the El Chocon Cerros Colorados project brought much-needed flood control to the foothills of the Andes Mountains in Argentina. Formerly, the rivers that flowed down from the mountains flooded twice each year. At other times, the region was too dry to grow crops. A system of dams was built to stop this cycle. Excess water is now stored in large reservoirs and is used for irrigation. As a result, farmers can grow crops year-round. The dam is also used to generate hydroelectric power for Argentina.

Human solutions can cause environmental problems.

Such large dams, however, can also cause problems. Without the floods, rivers no longer deposit naturally nutrient-rich soil, so most farmers use chemical fertilizers on their crops. Runoff from these fertilizers can contaminate groundwater and streams, which makes water supplies unsafe for humans and other living things.

Many of the adverse effects of dams constructed before the 1970s were not foreseen by developers. Today, scientists and engineers have a better understanding of how ecosystems work. Often, a major project such as a dam must undergo an environmental analysis before construction begins. If the project is likely to destroy an entire ecosystem, it may have to be redesigned, relocated, or canceled altogether.

READING TOOLBOX

Venn Diagrams
Make a Venn Diagram that has two circles. In one circle, list natural causes of changes to an ecosystem. In the other circle, list human causes of change. Where the circles overlap, list causes that may be natural or human-made, such as fire.

www.scilinks.org
Topic: Human Impact
Code: HK80771

Figure 9 Clearing trees, driving cars, and farming are just a few human activities that cause changes in ecosystems.

Logging

Driving cars

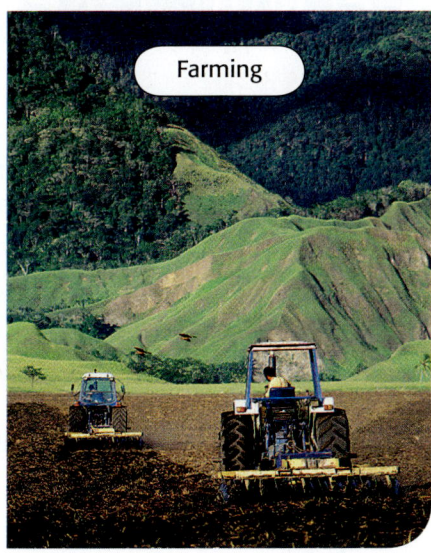

Farming

Nonnative species can cause changes in an ecosystem.

Some species move from one ecosystem to another on their own. Animals may migrate to new areas, and seeds can be carried by wind or water to different places. Humans often influence the spread of species from one ecosystem to another, sometimes accidentally and sometimes on purpose.

Starlings, for instance, were purposely brought to the United States. In the 1800s, a few dozen European starlings were released in New York City. The birds multiplied rapidly, and today there are millions of them across the United States.

Both starlings and native North American bluebirds, shown in **Figure 10,** nest in holes in tree trunks and fence posts. After the starling was introduced, the two species competed for shelter. The bluebirds nearly lost the battle. Concerned citizens launched a multistate effort to build and distribute bird boxes. These boxes, specially designed with small entrances, provide nesting places for bluebirds and keep the larger starlings out.

Nonnative species can be introduced in many ways.

Nonnative organisms may be introduced to an ecosystem accidentally. For instance, insects hidden in crates of fruit and vegetables can be carried across borders.

In its new environment, a nonnative species may have no natural enemies to keep its numbers in check. As a result, its population can increase quickly. The accidentally introduced species will cause a change in the ecosystem and may wipe out a native species.

Figure 10 Starlings (bottom) compete with bluebirds (top) for nesting sites in the holes of tree trunks or fence posts.

Section 1 Review

KEY IDEAS

1. **Explain** how a community relates to an ecosystem.
2. **Analyze** the following statement: An aquarium is a good example of a balanced ecosystem.
3. **List** two factors that help keep populations in an ecosystem stable.
4. **Define** succession.
5. **Compare** the effects of short-term and long-term change in an ecosystem.
6. **Predict** how a thunderstorm could lead to a long-term change in an ecosystem.

CRITICAL THINKING

7. **Recognizing Relationships** If a disease started killing a certain species of tree, how might the tree's ecosystem be affected?
8. **Predicting Consequences** Predators help control the populations in an ecosystem. What might happen to a well-balanced ecosystem if the predators were suddenly removed from that ecosystem?
9. **Forming Reasoned Opinions** Describe a common human activity that can disrupt an ecosystem. Propose a solution to the problem.

SECTION 2
Energy and Resources

Key Ideas

> What kinds of benefits do people get from natural resources?
> Why should energy consumers use alternative energy resources?
> Why is energy conversion never completely efficient?

Key Terms

fossil fuel
nonrenewable resource
renewable resource
geothermal energy

Why It Matters

The sources of energy we use have different effects on our resources and our environment. Some resources cost less but cause pollution; others are more expensive but cleaner.

You probably use more energy than you think you do. Energy is needed to light streets and homes, heat water and buildings, cook food, power vehicles, run appliances, and make the products that you use every day. In fact, energy is needed to do any kind of work—even to read this book. Where does all of this energy come from?

Tennessee Course Level Expectations (Physical Science)

CLE.3202.TE.1; CLE.3202.TE.4

The Search for Resources

We rely on natural resources to meet our basic needs for food and shelter. **› We also depend on natural resources to provide the energy and raw materials needed at home, at work, and for growing food.** The current patterns of energy use in the United States are shown in **Figure 1**.

Plants convert solar energy into chemical energy.

Almost all energy on Earth comes from the sun. The sun sends out energy as radiation of various wavelengths. Plants use some of the sun's energy to change the simple molecules of carbon dioxide and water into oxygen and molecules of simple sugars. This process is called *photosynthesis*. It allows plants to change the sun's energy into stored chemical energy.

Some animals eat plants to obtain energy. Through a series of chemical reactions, the animals are able to convert the sugars in the plants that they eat back to carbon dioxide, water, and energy. This process is known as *cellular respiration*. This process of energy transfer repeats itself continuously in nature.

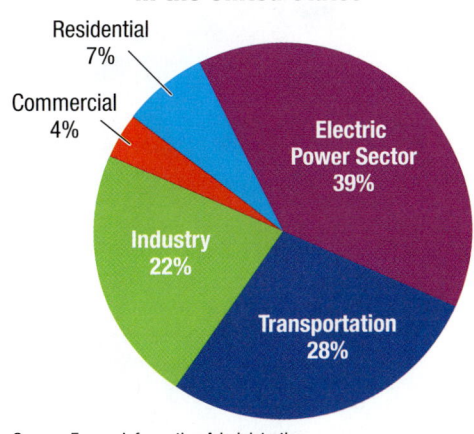

Source: Energy Information Administration, U.S. Department of Energy, 2004.

Figure 1 Energy is used in many ways in the United States.

Section 2   Energy and Resources   **815**

fossil fuel (FAHS uhl FYOO uhl) a nonrenewable energy resource formed from the remains of organisms that lived long ago; examples include oil, coal, and natural gas

nonrenewable resource (NAHN ri NOO uh buhl REE SAWRS) a resource that forms at a rate that is much slower than the rate at which the resource is consumed

Fossil fuels form deep underground.

Even after plants and animals die, they still contain energy. Most of the energy that we use to run cars, planes, and the factories that generate electricity comes from substances known as fossil fuels. A **fossil fuel** is an energy resource that is formed from the remains of plants and animals that lived a long time ago. Examples of fossil fuels are oil, natural gas, and coal. If you rode in a car or bus today, used a plastic utensil, or even sat in a room with electric lights, you probably used some energy from sunlight that warmed Earth millions of years ago.

Most organic material needs oxygen in order to decompose and to release its stored energy. However, microscopic plants and animals that live in the ocean die and are buried under layers of sediment where there is little oxygen. Without oxygen, the organic compounds in the remains of the living organisms cannot change back into carbon dioxide and water. Instead, heat from Earth and pressure from the sedimentary rock above the remains cause a different series of chemical reactions to take place. These reactions turn the organic compounds into substances that contain mainly carbon and hydrogen. This process, shown in **Figure 2,** is very slow; it can take millions of years.

Reading Check What is the source of fossil fuels?

Figure 2 Formation of Oil and Natural Gas

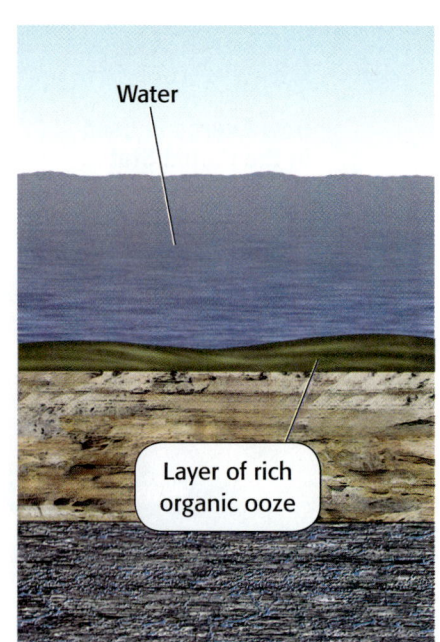

Microscopic plants and animals collect in layers of mud and form a rich organic ooze.

This organic layer is surrounded by sedimentary rock. Heat and pressure "cook" the ooze and transform biological debris into crude oil.

If geologic forces cause the rock layers to bend, the oil is forced out of its original layer. The oil migrates into porous rocks and is trapped.

Figure 3 Oil is used to make fuel for cars and airplanes. **What is another way that you use oil or natural gas in your everyday life?**

Fossil fuels can be solids, liquids, or gases.

Although substances such as natural gas, oil, and coal seem very different, all are made of molecules containing carbon and hydrogen.

Oil is a mixture of many substances. It comes out of the ground as a tarlike black liquid. Before it can be used, however, it must be purified and separated. Refineries separate oil into gasoline, kerosene, diesel fuel, and other products. Oil products are used to power vehicles, as shown in **Figure 3**.

Natural gas is made mostly of methane, a colorless, odorless, and flammable gas. It is often used for heating homes and for cooking. In the United States, natural gas accounts for 25% of the fossil fuels used.

Coal is a solid fossil fuel composed mainly of carbon. It formed in ancient swamps when the remains of large, fernlike plants were buried under layers of sediment.

Some fossil fuels are mixtures of liquids and gases. Liquid oil and natural gas are sometimes contained in porous rocks. Reaching the fossil fuels requires drilling into these rocks.

The supply of fossil fuels is limited.

When fossil fuels are burned, carbon dioxide and water are formed and energy is released. This energy is actually the energy of the sun that was trapped in plants tens or hundreds of millions of years ago. Because fossil fuels take so long to form, they are considered **nonrenewable resources.** They are now being used by humans much faster than natural processes can replace them.

The vast majority of the energy used in the world comes from burning fossil fuels, as **Figure 4** shows. Only 14% of the energy used in the world is supplied by sources other than fossil fuels. If oil and natural gas use continues at current rates, the reserves may run out during your lifetime. The reserves of coal are much larger, but they, too, will run out someday.

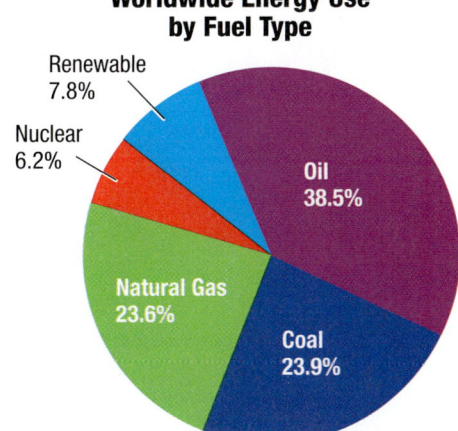

Figure 4 Although 84% of the world's energy is supplied by fossil fuels, oil and natural gas will become expensive as the reserves are depleted in the next 50 years.

Worldwide Energy Use by Fuel Type

- Renewable 7.8%
- Nuclear 6.2%
- Oil 38.5%
- Natural Gas 23.6%
- Coal 23.9%

Source: Energy Information Administration, U.S. Department of Energy, 2003.

renewable resource (ri NOO uh buhl REE sawrs) a natural resource that can be replaced at the same rate at which the resource is consumed

geothermal energy (JEE oh THUHR muhl EN uhr jee) the energy produced by heat within Earth

Figure 5 This roadside telephone is powered by a panel of solar cells. While the sun is out, the phone is charged and power is stored in batteries for when it is dark.

Alternative Sources of Energy

Fossils fuels are not the only source of energy. We can also harness energy from the sun, wind, water, and Earth. We can even obtain energy from atoms. ❯ **The more these alternative sources of energy are used, the less we will rely on fossil fuels.**

An advantage of using alternative sources of energy is that many of them are renewable resources. **Renewable resources** are resources that can be replaced through natural processes in a relatively short amount of time.

Atoms produce nuclear energy.

Atomic reactions can be controlled to produce *nuclear energy.* Chain reactions involving nuclear fission produce a great deal of energy. This energy can be transferred as heat to water in a nuclear reactor. The heated water or steam can then be used to turn a turbine and generate electricity. Unlike the burning of fossil fuels, nuclear fission does not release pollutants into the air, but it does produce highly radioactive wastes and warm water runoff.

Nuclear energy production is limited in the United States. Currently, it provides about 20% of the total energy consumed. Scientists working with nuclear fusion hope that it will be a useful and renewable resource someday. But so far, more energy is needed to sustain a fusion reaction than is produced by the reaction.

Solar power plants and solar cells can make electricity from sunlight.

Every day, Earth receives more energy from the sun than the United States uses in an entire year. But harnessing the sun's energy to supply electricity is not easy. Some parts of Earth do not get as much sunlight as other parts do. Even when there is enough sunlight, tools are needed to convert the sun's energy into useful forms.

In the 1990s, the first solar power plant capable of storing energy as heat was built in the Mojave Desert in California. The solar panels of the power plant store the sun's energy and use this energy to generate electricity.

Another tool used to harness the sun's energy is the solar cell, shown in **Figure 5**. Although the use of solar cells has been limited, the efficiency of solar cells has greatly improved in the last two decades.

✓ **Reading Check** Why is harnessing solar power easier in some parts of the world than it is in others?

The energy in wind can be harnessed by windmills.

Energy from the sun is a contributing factor in the production of another renewable energy resource—wind energy. Wind energy actually comes from the sun. Variations in the amount of sunlight striking different parts of Earth cause variations in temperature. These temperature differences cause the movement of air, known as *wind*.

Wind has been used as a source of renewable energy by humans for thousands of years. It has been used since ancient times to power sailing ships. Like other sources of energy, wind energy has advantages and disadvantages. One disadvantage is that wind can be unreliable. Even in exceptionally windy areas, wind does not blow steadily all of the time. Thus, fluctuations in the amount of power generated can occur.

Windmills have been used for more than 1,000 years. Today, their use is increasing in some areas because of their low cost and nondependence on fossil fuels. Large wind farms, such as the one in **Figure 6,** generate electric power.

Figure 6 The spinning blades of a wind turbine are connected to a generator. When the blades spin faster, the generator converts more energy.

Geothermal energy taps Earth's warmth.

Under Earth's crust, reservoirs of steam or hot water produce **geothermal energy.** These holding pools usually lie near beds of molten magma, which heat the steam or water. When wells are drilled into the reservoirs, the steam or hot water rises to the surface, where it is used to turn turbines to generate electric power.

Geothermal energy is a major source of electricity in volcanically active areas, such as New Zealand, Iceland, and parts of California. Geothermal plants, such as the one shown in **Figure 7,** are common in these places. Geothermal energy is easiest to harness when the beds of molten rock lie very close to Earth's surface. However, not many areas have magma beds close to the surface, so use of this resource is limited.

Figure 7 This geothermal plant in New Zealand produces electricity.

Section 2   Energy and Resources

Figure 8 The incoming water causes the turbines in a dam to turn. The turbines run a generator that produces electricity.

READING TOOLBOX

Key-Term Fold
Make a FoldNote for the various sources of renewable energy. List each type of energy source and three facts about how the source works.

Moving water produces hydroelectric energy.

Falling water releases a lot of energy. This energy, like wind energy, depends ultimately on sunlight. The warmth of the sun causes the water in oceans to evaporate. Water vapor rises into the atmosphere, falls back to Earth later as rain or snow, and flows into creeks and rivers. From there, it flows back to the ocean, and the cycle begins again.

Water power is harnessed by building dams on rivers to create large holding places for water. **Figure 8** shows how the stored water pours through turbines and makes the turbines spin. The turbines are connected to generators that produce hydroelectric power. Because the water cycle keeps the rivers flowing, hydroelectric power is a renewable resource.

There are drawbacks to using water power. Dams can alter a river's flood and erosion patterns. Also, dams have already been built on most of the world's big rivers, so the potential for increasing the energy from this source is limited. However, advances in technology may make energy production at existing dams more efficient.

Reading Check How is the movement of water used to generate electricity?

820 Chapter 23 Using Natural Resources

The Efficiency of Energy Conversion

Energy conversion is not 100% efficient. Often, some converted energy is lost as waste heat. In some cases, this heat can be used as an additional energy source. ❯ **Regardless of which energy resource is used, some energy is lost each time energy is converted from one form to another.**

Energy is wasted when input is greater than output.

In a coal-fired power plant, chemical energy is released as heat when coal combines with oxygen in a combustion reaction. This heat energy is <u>transferred</u> to water, which is converted into steam. Some energy is lost in this conversion. The steam is then heated to increase its pressure. High pressure provides the force to turn huge steam turbines. More energy is lost as the potential energy in the steam is converted into kinetic energy in the turbines.

The turbines are connected to coils of large generators. As the generators spin, they generate a high voltage in the fixed coils surrounding them. These coils carry current and act as large electromagnets. The energy is now in the form of electrical potential energy. The current is carried to local consumers through cables. The diagram in **Figure 9** shows how electricity is produced in a typical power station.

A large power station might be rated at 1,000 megawatts. Thus, it delivers 1 billion joules of electrical energy per second. But 3 billion joules is used to produce that energy, so two-thirds of the energy input is wasted. Most power stations that use fossil fuels for energy are only 30% to 40% efficient. To increase efficiency, newer models recycle waste heat.

Academic Vocabulary
transfer (TRANS fuhr) the carrying or moving of something from one thing or place to another

Figure 9 This power plant converts coal into electrical energy. Most of what looks like smoke in this photo is actually steam that is released during the energy generation process.

Burning fossil fuels, such as coal, releases energy that is used to heat water into steam.

The steam is highly pressurized, often by additional heating, and then directed toward a turbine, which the steam spins.

The steam turbine is connected to a generator that produces an electric current as it spins.

Coal • Combustion chamber • High-pressure steam • Steam turbine • Electric current • Generator

www.scilinks.org
Topic: Alternative Energy Sources
Code: HK80052

Energy waste can be recovered and used.

Some energy is wasted in the production of all types of energy. Nuclear power stations are roughly as efficient, or as inefficient, as fossil-fuel plants are. Both types of power plants produce waste. Even wind-power has some inefficiency.

Waste heat is the major byproduct of an energy conversion. Luckily, some of this waste heat can be put to good use. For example, although the wastewater from power stations is not hot enough to make electricity, it can be used to heat homes. In Germany, most towns have their own small power stations. Instead of dumping wastewater into a river, the power stations pipe the warm water to homes to heat the homes. This recycling of waste heat conserves energy and makes electricity less expensive. Heat recovery units, such as the one in **Figure 10,** capture excess heat and use it to control water and air temperatures.

Energy conversion sometimes produces physical waste.

Most energy production produces material in the form of waste. Nuclear power stations produce toxic radioactive waste that must be kept isolated from the environment. Coal plants produce smoke and air particulates. Thanks to new technologies, energy production is becoming cleaner than it was in the past. Special scrubbers in smoke stacks, for example, can clean many particulates out of power plant exhaust.

Figure 10 This heat recovery unit captures heat energy that is normally wasted and uses it to control the temperature of the air.

Section 2 Review

KEY IDEAS

1. **Describe** the process of energy transfer between organisms. Name the process that plants use to convert energy from the sun into chemical energy.
2. **List** three natural resources that you might use in preparing a hot meal.
3. **Explain** why some resources are considered to be renewable and other resources are considered to be nonrenewable.
4. **Describe** some advantages and some disadvantages of solar energy.
5. **Explain** in a paragraph the energy conversions that occur when a drop of rain falls on a mountain, rolls downhill, passes through a hydroelectric plant, and turns a turbine to generate electricity.
6. **Predict** which of the following will be more efficient in capturing energy. Justify your answer.
   a. burning paper to boil water to make steam to turn a turbine
   b. using wind to turn a turbine

CRITICAL THINKING

7. **Predicting Consequences** Oil and natural gas are nonrenewable fuel supplies. As demand for these supplies increases, what will be the effect on the supply and cost?
8. **Communicating Ideas** Explain how the use of windmills can reduce our dependence on nonrenewable resources, such as coal and natural gas.
9. **Understanding Concepts** A classmate says that geothermal energy is perfectly efficient because it never runs out. What is wrong with this reasoning?

Why It Matters
A Natural Cooler

In order to help the poor, rural citizens of his country, Mohammed Bah Abba, a teacher in Nigeria, invented a system of refrigeration using nothing more than two clay pots, some sand, a bit of water, and his knowledge of science. This simple "pot-in-a-pot" design allows eggplants to stay fresh in the summer heat of the African markets for up to 27 days. Previously, farmers were able to keep eggplants fresh for only 3 days.

Here, the inventor Mohammed Bah Abba teaches local pot makers how to make his pot-in-a-pot design.

When moisture evaporates in dry air, it causes a drop in temperature. As the water in the sand between the two pots evaporates, the water pulls the heat away from the inner pot and keeps the container cool.

Fruits or vegetables
Smaller inner pot
Moist sand
Larger outer pot

YOUR TURN
CRITICAL THINKING
1. What are some of the benefits of using a "natural cooler" to keep foods cool instead of using electricity and large refrigeration units?

SECTION 3
Pollution and Recycling

Key Ideas
- What does pollution look like?
- What is air pollution made of?
- What causes water pollution?
- Where does land pollution come from?
- How can we reduce pollution?

Key Terms
- pollution
- global warming
- eutrophication
- recycling

Why It Matters
Waste materials can make our environment dirty and dangerous, although many waste materials can be reused or recycled to help our environment.

Tennessee Course Level Expectations (Physical Science)
CLE.3202.TE.1; CLE.3202.Inq.1; CLE.3202.Inq.2; CLE.3202.Inq.3; CLE.3202.Inq.4; CLE.3202.Inq.6; CLE.3202.TE.2; CLE.3202.TE.3

pollution (puh LOO shuhn) an undesirable change in the natural environment that is caused by the introduction of substances that are harmful to living organisms or by excessive wastes, heat, noise, or radiation

Think about the objects in your classroom—desks, lights, chalk, paper, pencils, backpacks, books, doors, and windows. Your classroom contains many products, all of which are made from natural resources.

Manufacturing each product required energy. And the making of nearly all of the products caused some kind of pollution. When natural resources generate energy or become products, other products, called *byproducts,* are usually made in the process. If undesirable byproducts are thrown out, they may cause pollution. **Pollution** is the contamination of air, water, or soil. An example of pollution is shown in **Figure 1**.

What Causes Pollution?

When you think of pollution, you may think of litter. Or you may think of smog—the clouds of dust, smoke, and chemicals in the air of many large cities. ▶ **Pollution can be as imperceptible as a colorless, odorless gas or as obvious as bad-smelling trash left by the side of the road.**

Some pollution has natural causes.

Pollution can be caused by natural processes. For example, following an explosive volcanic eruption, dust and ash spreads through the air. This air pollution can make it hard for some people to breathe. When the dust and ash cover leaves of trees and plants, the leaves cannot absorb sunlight.

Animal and human wastes may become pollutants if they are produced faster than they can be assimilated into the environment.

Figure 1 Trash pollutes the waters of a beach in Oahu, Hawaii.

Most pollution is made by humans.

Human activities are responsible for most pollution. We harness chemical reactions to make new materials and to release energy. But most chemical reactions produce two or more products. If the unintended products are not reused properly or recycled, they can add to the pollution problem.

The human activities that result in pollution are usually intended to achieve desirable goals. While electricity and cars help society in many ways, they also produce pollution. Some pesticides, designed to protect farm crops, can leak into water supplies and pollute the water.

Air Pollution

▶ **Air pollution comes in many forms, from individual molecules to particulates, which are clumps of dust and other matter.** Figure 2 shows major air pollutants in the United States. Figure 3 describes these forms of pollution and lists the primary sources for each type of pollutant.

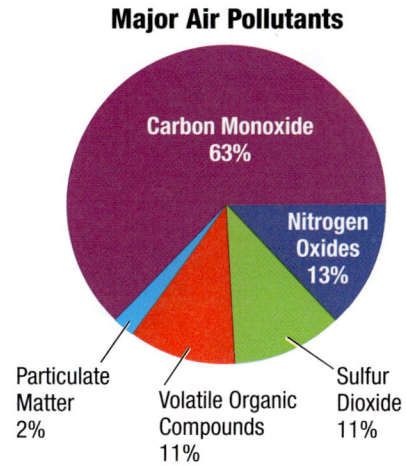

Figure 2 Carbon monoxide, produced by the burning of fossil fuels, is one of the major air pollutants in the United States.

Combustion of fuels produces most air pollution.

As you have learned, most of the energy used to drive cars, to heat and light buildings, and to power machinery comes from the burning of fossil fuels. This burning process is known as *combustion*.

During combustion, the fuel, which contains carbon and hydrogen, reacts with oxygen to release energy. Along with this desirable product, other products, such as carbon monoxide, carbon dioxide, and water vapor, form. These combustion products escape into the air as invisible gases.

www.scilinks.org
Topic: Pollution
Code: HK81179

Figure 3 Air Pollutants

Pollutant	Description	Primary sources
Carbon monoxide, CO	CO is an odorless, colorless, and poisonous gas.	CO is produced by the incomplete burning of fossil fuels in cars, trucks, buses, small engines, and some industrial processes.
Nitrogen oxides, NO_x	Nitrogen and oxygen combine to form nitrogen oxides when combustion (burning) temperatures are greater than 538 °C (1,000 °F).	NO_x compounds come from the burning of fossil fuels in vehicles, power plants, and industrial boilers.
Sulfur dioxide, SO_2	SO_2 is produced by chemical interactions between sulfur and oxygen.	SO_2 comes from the burning of fossil fuels. It is released from refineries, smelters, paper mills, and chemical plants.
Volatile organic compounds (VOCs)	VOCs are organic chemicals that vaporize readily and produce toxic fumes. Gasoline and paint thinner are examples of VOCs.	Cars and gasoline stations are a major source of VOCs. VOCs also come from solvents, paints, glues, and burning fuels.
Particulate matter (particulates or PM)	Particulates are tiny particles of liquid or solid matter. Some examples are smoke, dust, and acid droplets.	Construction, agriculture, forestry, and fires produce particulates. Industrial processes and motor vehicles that burn fossil fuels also produce particulates.

Section 3 Pollution and Recycling **825**

Figure 4 Some gases in the atmosphere prevent energy from escaping back into space.

Energy from the sun is absorbed by Earth's surface and reradiated into the atmosphere as heat, most of which escapes into space.

Greenhouse gases absorb some of the energy from Earth and radiate it back toward the lower atmosphere and Earth's surface.

Solar radiation passes through the atmosphere and warms Earth's surface.

global warming (GLOH buhl WAWRM ing) a gradual increase in the average global temperatures

Figure 5 These trees show the characteristic damage caused by exposure to acidic rain and snow.

Carbon dioxide is a greenhouse gas.

Carbon dioxide is found naturally in Earth's atmosphere. It is one of the greenhouse gases, which help keep average temperatures on Earth above freezing. **Figure 4** shows how the greenhouse effect works. Without the greenhouse effect, temperatures on Earth would be roughly 30 °C lower.

Currently, human activities release about 21 billion tons of carbon dioxide into the air each year. Records indicate that as carbon dioxide pollution in the atmosphere has increased, the average temperature of Earth has increased, too. In the past 100 years, the average temperature in the United States has increased by about 0.7 °C. This **global warming** may not sound like a lot, but it could significantly affect Earth's climate. Weather patterns could change and bring droughts to some areas and floods to others.

Long-term climate changes have occurred in the past without large human contributions to the level of carbon dioxide in the atmosphere. Scientists will continue to study the impact of human-generated carbon dioxide.

Burning fossil fuels can cause acid precipitation.

Burning fossil fuels releases sulfur dioxide and nitrogen dioxide. When these gases react with other atmospheric gases and with water, the result is acid rain, sleet, and snow. Normal precipitation is slightly acidic; it has a pH of roughly 5.6. Acid precipitation is much more acidic; it has a pH of 4.0 to 5.0.

Acid precipitation can harm or even kill aquatic life. It can also leach nutrients from soil and damage forests, as **Figure 5** shows. In addition, it can corrode metals and damage buildings by eroding stonework.

Reading Check Name two effects that acid precipitation may have on the environment.

Air pollution can cause breathing problems.

When nitrogen-oxide compounds in car exhaust react with sunlight, a mixture of chemicals called *photochemical smog* is produced. The result is a brown haze that can make eyes sting and can cause severe headaches and breathing difficulties.

Ozone high in the atmosphere blocks harmful ultraviolet radiation from reaching Earth. Close to Earth's surface, however, ozone is a pollutant. It is one of the harmful chemicals in photochemical smog. Ozone can cause problems for people who suffer from asthma or other throat and lung conditions.

Photochemical smog is most common in sunny, densely populated cities such as Los Angeles and Tokyo. Pollution in Tokyo can get so bad that people wear masks to protect themselves from the polluted air and companies supply fresh-air dispensers to their employees. Smog also damages plants. Scientists think that the ozone found in photochemical smog can harm plants and reduce crop yields in rural areas near large cities. To combat the problem, many cities have made concerted efforts to expand public transportation systems and to encourage people to carpool. These efforts help reduce the number of vehicles on the road, and thus reduce the amount of pollution released into the air.

Water Pollution

All living things need water to survive. In fact, the bodies of most organisms, including humans, consist mostly of water. Unpolluted water is especially important to aquatic organisms, which spend their entire lives in a liquid environment.

Water can be contaminated in many ways. Sometimes, solid trash is dumped in the water, as **Figure 6** shows. This type of pollution may be easy to spot and clean up. Other times, chemical waste is dumped into the water, either intentionally or accidentally. Cleaning up this kind of pollution is very difficult.

▶ **Most water pollution can be traced to industrial waste, agricultural fertilizers, and everyday human activities.** A bucket of dirty, soapy water dumped down a kitchen drain can eventually make its way into the water supply. Flushing toilets, washing cars, and pouring chemicals down drains are actions that can contribute to water pollution.

In many countries, water is cleaned at water purification plants before it is piped to consumers. But because many chemicals dissolve easily in water, it is difficult to remove all of the impurities from the water.

QuickLab 10 min

Observing Air Pollution

Procedure

1. Cut a **piece of cellophane tape** that is about 8 cm long.
2. Place the sticky side of the tape against an outside wall of a building, and press gently.
3. Remove the tape, and hold it against **a sheet of white paper.**
4. Did the tape pick up dust? If so, what might be the source of the dust?
5. Repeat the experiment on other walls in different places, and compare the amounts of dust observed.
6. Why might some walls appear to have more dust than others?

Figure 6 The plastic six-pack ring around the neck of this herring gull is one example of how water pollution can affect the environment.

Figure 7 This algal bloom is the result of an abundance of nitrates in the water.

Fertilizer runoff can pollute water.

Most modern farms use chemical fertilizers. These fertilizers can get washed away by rain and end up in streams, rivers, lakes, or oceans. Many fertilizers contain nitrate ions, which encourage the growth of algae and weeds. The result is an algal bloom, such as the one shown in **Figure 7.**

The process by which additional nutrients lead to excessive plant growth is called **eutrophication.** If hot water from power stations or factories is discharged into the river or lake, the situation worsens. The extra warmth makes the algae multiply even faster. As the algae die and decay, the amount of dissolved oxygen in the water decreases. Aquatic wildlife and fish suffocate in these reduced oxygen environments and die.

✓ **Reading Check** How does eutrophication affect fish?

eutrophication (yoo TRAHF i KAY shuhn) an increase in the amount of nutrients, such as nitrates, in a marine or aquatic ecosystem

Pesticides can affect more than just insects.

Animals on land and in water can be affected by another group of chemicals that eventually make their way into bodies of water. These chemicals, called *pesticides,* are used to control crop-damaging pests. Pesticides can be washed by rain into streams, rivers, and lakes. There, pesticides are ingested by fish and other aquatic animals. As larger animals eat the fish, the chemicals are passed along the food chain.

In the 1970s, a pesticide called *DDT* was widely used to control mosquitoes and led to the eradication of malaria in the United States. DDT in the water was ingested by fish. These fish were then eaten by pelicans. The DDT in the fish caused the eggs of the pelicans to become thin and fragile. With fewer eggs hatching successfully, the pelicans nearly became extinct before the use of DDT was banned in the United States.

Academic Vocabulary

ingest (in JEST) to take into the body or to absorb as food

Pollution on Land

❯ **Land pollution has many sources. Some of these sources are obvious, but others may be hard to pinpoint.** When trash is dumped illegally by a roadside, the source of the pollution is sometimes easy to find. The sources of other land pollutants are less obvious. For example, dirt near many highways contains an unusually high amount of lead. This lead originally came from car exhaust. The lead was part of a compound added to gasoline to help cars run more smoothly. Leaded gasoline was phased out of common use beginning in the mid-1970s, but the soil near busy highways still contains large amounts of lead.

Contaminants in soil are hard to remove.

A common type of land-based pollution occurs when hazardous chemicals soak into the soil. For example, in 1983, the town of Times Beach, Missouri, suffered soil contamination by a toxic chemical compound called *dioxin*.

Exposure to dioxin, a chemical produced in the paper-making process, has been linked to an increased risk of cancer. The soil in the town had become contaminated because the waste oil used to keep down the dust on the town's roads contained small amounts of dioxin. After the roads had been repeatedly sprayed for several years, dioxin levels in the soil became very high. As a result, some livestock and other animals died, and some of the town's residents got sick.

Dioxin, like many land-based pollutants, does not dissolve in water. It does not break down easily. Therefore, removing it from the soil is very difficult. The U.S. Environmental Protection Agency bought the entire town of Times Beach, Missouri because this solution was less expensive than cleaning all of the town's soil.

READING TOOLBOX

Temporal Language
As you read about the various types of pollution, make a table that describes the temporal language that is used.

Inquiry Lab: How Can Oil Spills Be Cleaned Up?

 20 min

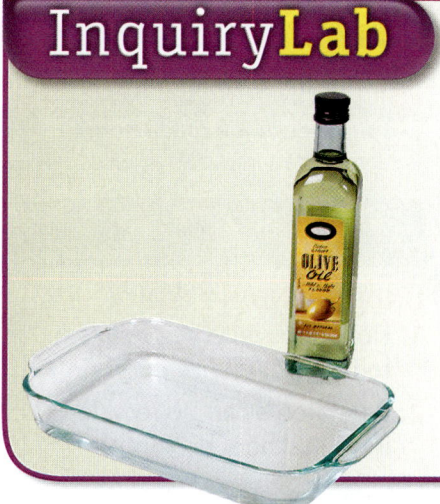

Procedure
1. Fill a **pan** halfway with cold water.
2. Pour a small amount of **cooking oil** into the water.
3. Try to clean up the "oil spill" by using at least four different cleaning materials.

Analysis
1. Evaluate the effectiveness of each material. Which worked best? Explain why.
2. Did any of the materials "pollute" the water with additional particles or residue? How might you clean up this pollution?

SCILINKS
www.scilinks.org
Topic: Recycling
Code: HK81277

Reducing Pollution

In most cases, pollution is a problem that can be prevented. ❯ **Pollution can be reduced through the protection and conservation of resources.** Many federal, state, and local laws encourage the preservation of clean water supplies and discourage the pollution of air, soil, and water. At the international level, countries may work together by drawing up treaties aimed at reducing pollution.

Choosing alternatives often involves trade-offs.

Pollution can be reduced when individuals, communities, and companies make careful choices. Individuals can make a big difference by conserving energy. To reduce the air pollution caused by fossil fuels, individuals and industry can make an effort to use alternative energy sources. However, even nonpolluting sources of energy, such as wind, solar, and hydroelectric power, require large amounts of land and are potentially disruptive to ecosystems.

Small-scale sources of energy, such as disposable batteries, have an environmental impact, too. Batteries contain mercury and other potentially toxic chemicals. When discarded, these toxic chemicals can leak into the ground and pollute water supplies and soil. Using reusable batteries and solar-powered devices can help reduce pollution.

Why It Matters

What Is Recycling?

REAL WORLD

Recycling converts used goods into new goods. Metals, plastics, paper, batteries, and computers are among the common household items that can be recycled. Plastic bottles, for example, can be made into new bottles, construction materials, toys, and other items.

❶ Discarded materials, such as these plastic bottles, are collected and sorted by type and color.

❷ The materials are cleaned and then crushed or shredded to produce small chips.

❸ Useful items such as this park bench are made from processed, recycled plastic.

YOUR TURN

UNDERSTANDING CONCEPTS
1. How does recycling help reduce pollution?
2. What items can be recycled in your school or home?

Reducing the use of energy and products can cut down on pollution.

Many people believe that the best solution to the problem of pollution is to reduce our overall consumption. If less energy is used, less pollution is generated. Turning off lights and lowering thermostats are two simple ways to conserve energy. Carpooling or buying a car with higher-than-average gas mileage is another way to conserve energy.

Some people conserve water by reusing rinse water from dishes and laundry to water gardens and lawns. This way, they use less water, so less energy is required to purify the water and pump the water to their house. In addition, the water they use does not enter the sewer system. Thus, the amount of energy used by the water treatment plant decreases.

Recycling is another way to prevent pollution.

After you have tried to reduce the amount you use and are successfully reusing as much as possible, there is still one more thing you can do. When something is no longer useful, instead of throwing it away, you can try recycling it.

Recycling allows materials to be used again to make other products. **Figure 8** shows part of a recycling plant in New York City. Such plants commonly recycle paper products, such as cardboard and newspapers; metal products, such as copper, aluminum, and tin; and plastics, such as detergent bottles and shopping bags.

Recycling these materials greatly reduces the amount of waste that ends up in a landfill. Paper products alone take up 41% of landfill space in the United States. Yet we currently recycle less than 30% of our paper.

Figure 8 Recycling metal and paper reduces the amount of waste that goes into landfills.

recycling (ree SIE kling) the process of recovering valuable or useful materials from waste or scrap; the process of reusing some items

Section 3 Review

KEY IDEAS

1. **List** one type of invisible pollution and one type of visible pollution in your neighborhood.
2. **Explain** how riding a bike can help reduce photochemical smog.
3. **List** an activity related to home, to work, and to growing food that can lead to water pollution.
4. **Define** *eutrophication*. Explain how it occurs and how it affects aquatic wildlife.
5. **Name** two types of land pollution, and describe the source of each type.
6. **Propose** a plan for increasing recycling in your home. List the resources that are not currently being reused, and describe how they could be.

CRITICAL THINKING

7. **Expressing Opinions** Pesticides and fertilizers can help farmers grow bigger and healthier crops. However, both of these resources may pollute the environment. Do the benefits of these products outweigh the drawbacks? Explain your answer.
8. **Evaluating Viewpoints** Do you think recycling should be mandatory? Explain your reasoning.

Section 3 Pollution and Recycling

Application Lab

Designing a Windmill

Alternative Energy Systems Corporation is accepting design proposals to develop a windmill that can be used to lift window washers to the tops of buildings. Your division of the design engineering team has been asked to develop a working model for such a windmill. Your task is to design and build a model that can lift 30 large paper clips a vertical distance of 50 cm. The job will be given to the team whose model can lift the paper clips the fastest.

⏱ 50 min

What You'll Do

> **Prepare** a detailed sketch of your solution to the design problem.

> **Design and build** a functional windmill that lifts a specific weight as quickly as possible.

What You'll Need

blow-dryer, 1,500 W

dowel or smooth rod

foam board

glue, white

paper clips, large (32)

paper cup, small (1)

paper plates, paper cups, wooden popsicle sticks, and any other lightweight materials out of which to make windmill blades

stopwatch

string (70 cm)

tape, masking

Safety

Procedure

1. With a partner or small group, brainstorm a windmill design which uses only the objects listed in the materials list. Some design ideas are shown in the diagrams. Sketch your design, and write a few sentences about how you think your windmill design will perform.

Performing Your Experiment

2. Have your teacher approve your design before you begin construction. Build the base for your windmill by taking two straightened-out paper clips, making a loop with each one, and sticking the ends into the foam board. Make sure that the loops line up with each other, and pass a dowel rod through them. The dowel should rotate freely. Attach one end of the string securely to the dowel between the two loops.

3. Poke a hole through the middle of the foam board to allow the string to pass through. Place your windmill base between two lab tables or in any area that will allow the string to hang freely. If the string touches the side, friction will result, and reduce efficiency.

4. After you have decided on your final design, attach the windmill blades to the base.

5. Attach the cup to the end of the string. Fill the cup with 30 paper clips. Turn on the blow-dryer, and measure the time it takes for your windmill to lift the cup.

6. If you have time, you may want to try using different materials to construct your windmill blades. Test the various blades to determine whether they improve the original design. You may also want to vary the number and the size of the blades on your windmill.

Analysis

1. **Evaluating Hypotheses** How did you decide on the windmill design(s) that you tested? Did the windmill work as well as you hoped? Explain.

Communicating Your Results

2. **Drawing Conclusions** After you test all of your designs, determine which design lifted the paper clips the fastest. What elements of the design do you think made it the strongest?
3. **Evaluating Methods** Describe how you would change your design to make your windmill work better or faster.

Extension
Adapt your design to make a water wheel. Find designs on the Internet for micro-hydropower water wheels, such as the Pelton wheel, and use the designs as inspiration for your model. You will find that a water wheel can lift much more weight than a windmill can.

Recognizing Bias

Science > Skills

> Technology
> Math
> Scientific Methods
> Graphing

Everything that is written and posted on the Internet has a particular intention. In some cases, the author of a Web site may intend to be objective, but may have an unintentionally biased viewpoint. Here are some tips for recognizing whether or not a Web site is biased.

❶ Consider the source Determine the site's author, owner, or sponsor. Does the person, business, or agency have an interest in getting you to think or feel a particular way?
- Examine the Web address and the headers and footers on the site to find out who has created the site.
- Read pages labeled "About," "Who We Are," "Philosophy," or something similar.

❷ Consider the purpose and intended audience Most Web sites are informational sites, news sites, commercial sites, advocacy sites, or personal sites.
- **Informational sites** (often .edu or .gov) may include scholarly papers, reference sources, or fact sheets.
- **News sites** (usually .com) cover news stories. These sites may contain opinion as well as unbiased news.
- **Commercial sites** (usually .com) sell products and services. Their aim is to promote their own business.
- **Advocacy sites** (often .org) inform people about an issue and may have a political or ideological bias.
- **Personal sites** convey information about a single individual and that individual's interests.

❸ Consider the tone The feeling you get from a Web site's language can tell you a lot about the Web site's intent.
- Does the language on the site have an objective tone?
- Does the author express opinions or show emotion?
- Could the site be an advertisement? Could it be satire?

> **Simple questions you can ask to help you recognize bias:**
>
> - Who is the author of this Web site?
>
> - Is the author expressing personal opinions or citing facts from other, reputable sources?
>
> - If the author is presenting facts, what are his sources and how recent are they?
>
> - Is the author trying to persuade you or simply inform you?
>
> - If the author is attempting to persuade you, does he or she attempt to sway you emotionally or intellectually?
>
> - What do other Web sites or reputable sources say about this Web site?

Practice

1. Suppose you are researching the relationship between the use of fossil fuels and global warming. You find the following sites, both of which seem to contain a lot of information:
   a) A Web site for the Global Warming Fallacy Project, ending in ".com" and sponsored by Acme Oil and Gas.
   b) A Web site run by the Save Our Shale Organization, ending in ".org" and dedicated to protecting the oily rocks of the world.

   Determine which of the five categories of sites described above each of these sites might fit into, and discuss why you think each site might or might not be biased toward a particular viewpoint.

2. Find two examples of sites in each of the five categories described above—one you think is more biased and one you think is less biased. Describe the clues you find that tell you how biased or unbiased each of the sites is.

CHAPTER 23 Summary

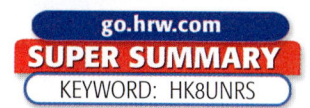

Key Ideas

Section 1 Organisms and Their Environment

- **What Is an Ecosystem?** Living and nonliving elements form an ecosystem. (p. 807)
- **Stability in Ecosystems** If the elements of an ecosystem are balanced then the ecosystem may remain stable for a long period of time. (p. 809)
- **Evaluating Changes in Ecosystems** Ecosystem changes can be short-term or long-term. Some changes may be irreversible. (p. 811)

Section 2 Energy and Resources

- **The Search for Resources** Humans depend on natural resources to provide energy and raw materials for our homes and industry. (p. 815)
- **Alternative Sources of Energy** Using alternative energy sources, such as hydroelectric, solar, geothermal, and wind power, will reduce our reliance on fossil fuels. (p. 818)
- **The Efficiency of Energy Conversion** Energy is lost each time it is converted from one form to another form. (p. 821)

Section 3 Pollution and Recycling

- **What Causes Pollution?** Pollution can invisible or easily seen, depending on its form. (p. 824)
- **Air Pollution** Air pollution takes many forms, including gas, dust, and other particulates. (p. 825)
- **Water Pollution** Most water pollution can be traced to human causes, such as industrial waste and agricultural fertilizers. (p. 827)
- **Pollution on Land** Contaminants responsible for land pollution come from many sources, which may be hard to pinpoint. (p. 829)
- **Reducing Pollution** Pollution can be reduced by conserving energy and resources, by reusing goods, and by recycling. (p. 830)

Key Terms

ecosystem, p. 807
community, p. 808
succession, p. 811

fossil fuel, p. 816
nonrenewable resource, p. 817
renewable resource, p. 818
geothermal energy, p. 819

pollution, p. 824
global warming, p. 826
eutrophication, p. 828
recycling, p. 831

Using Natural Resources

CHAPTER 23 Review

READING TOOLBOX

1. **Key-Term Fold** Make a key-term FoldNote for the various types of pollution. List two sources for each type of pollution, and tell how each form of pollution affects the environment.

USING KEY TERMS

2. Describe how *interrelatedness* is crucial to the concept of *ecosystems*.

3. A forest *ecosystem* is wiped out by disease. Using the concept of *succession*, explain how the forest might recover.

4. Most energy on Earth comes from the sun. Describe how the burning of *fossil fuels* releases stored energy from the sun.

5. Is land a *renewable resource* or a *nonrenewable resource*? Explain your reasoning.

6. Name one of the greenhouse gases, and state its relationship to *global warming*.

7. Describe the process of *eutrophication*. List several sources of nitrates, and name several consequences of *eutrophication*.

UNDERSTANDING KEY IDEAS

8. Choose the list that is ordered from largest to smallest.
   a. population, organism, community, ecosystem
   b. organism, population, ecosystem, community
   c. ecosystem, community, population, organism
   d. ecosystem, population, community, organism

9. When fossil fuels are burned, they form carbon dioxide, energy, and
   a. water.
   b. oxygen.
   c. hydrocarbons.
   d. carbohydrates

10. The major air pollutant in the United States is
    a. sulfur dioxide.
    b. carbon monoxide.
    c. nitrogen oxide.
    d. particulate matter.

11. How much of the energy input in power stations is wasted?
    a. one-third
    b. one-half
    c. two-thirds
    d. all

12. Fossil fuels consist mostly of what elements?
    a. carbon and hydrogen
    b. carbon and calcium
    c. calcium and hydrogen
    d. potassium and chlorine

13. Which of the following statements about recycling is false?
    a. Recycling does not affect the amount of waste that ends up in a landfill.
    b. Recycling reduces litter.
    c. Recycling reduces energy usage.
    d. Recycled materials can be used to make other products.

14. Atomic reactions can produce an alternative source of energy called
    a. fossil fuels.
    b. solar energy.
    c. geothermal energy.
    d. nuclear energy.

15. Usable energy is lost each time energy is
    a. gained.
    b. released.
    c. converted.
    d. trapped.

16. Which type of power is produced by the facility shown in the image below?
    a. hydroelectric
    b. solar
    c. geothermal
    d. nuclear

836 Chapter 23 Using Natural Resources

EXPLAINING KEY IDEAS

17. Describe the concept of stability in an ecosystem, and explain how various factors interrelate to create a stable ecosystem.

18. List three events that may cause a long-term change in an ecosystem.

19. Explain why solar power and wind are considered to be renewable resources.

20. List two sources for each of the following: water pollution, air pollution, and land pollution.

21. Summarize why recycling can be a useful strategy for reducing pollution.

CRITICAL THINKING

22. Applying Knowledge A farm is situated on the bank of a river. A factory is located farther upstream. Researchers are finding dead fish in the river. Describe the steps you would take to determine why fish are dying.

23. Relating Concepts During the 1970s, the production of municipal solid waste decreased. An economic recession was also occurring. In what ways might the reduction of waste have been related to the recession?

24. Creative Thinking In political and environmental circles, *NIMBY* stands for "Not In My Back Yard." Using what you have learned about natural resources and pollution, what do you think this phrase means? Would you apply this sentiment to anything in your life?

25. Acquiring and Evaluating Data The United States has a lot of space in comparison to certain other countries, like Japan. Using a search engine on the Internet, research what countries with small land areas like Switzerland and Japan do instead of using landfills for their garbage.

26. Evaluating Methods Analyze all of the possible polluting steps in the making of a pencil. Write a paragraph describing each step.

Graphing Skills

27. Interpreting Graphs The graph below shows the average use of various energy sources in the United States. British thermal units (Btu) are commonly used to measure energy usage. In what year did oil first become more important than coal as an energy source?

28. Identifying Trends The data for oil and natural gas use are nearly parallel—they rise and fall together. Why do you think this pattern exists?

Math Skills

29. Calculating Each person in the United States produces roughly 2 kg (4.4 lb) of garbage per day. How long would it take each person to fill a dump truck with a 16,000 lb capacity? If each person recycled half of his or her trash, how much less garbage would each person produce in 1 year?

30. Allocating Resources Three people live in the same neighborhood and work at the same office. They work 51 weeks per year. One person spends $20 per week, one spends $25 per week, and one spends $30 per week for gasoline and parking. If the three people formed a car pool, how much could each person save annually? Assume that each person drives for 17 weeks.

Standardized Test Prep

Understanding Concepts

Directions (1–3): For each question, write on a sheet of paper the letter of the correct answer.

1. In a particular ecosystem, hawks prey on bats, which prey on mosquitoes. Suppose the area is sprayed with a pesticide that kills most of the mosquito population. What are the effects on the other two populations likely to be?
   - **A.** The populations of bats and hawks will both increase.
   - **B.** The population of bats will increase and the population of hawks will decrease.
   - **C.** The population of bats will decrease and the population of hawks will increase.
   - **D.** The populations of bats and hawks will both decrease.

2. What source of energy is likely to run out first, assuming use continues at its current rates and no new supplies are discovered?
   - **F.** coal
   - **G.** natural gas
   - **H.** solar power
   - **I.** nuclear power

3. What type of energy source originates in dead plant and animal matter which has not been able to decompose in air?
   - **A** fossil fuels
   - **B.** nuclear energy
   - **C.** geothermal energy
   - **D.** hydroelectric power

Directions (4–5): For each question, write a short response.

4. Name three likely sources of pollution arising from a process whose endpoint is a customer in a store buying vegetables that were grown in another state.

5. How do agricultural pollution and hot-water discharge from power plants combine to create eutrophication? What are the consequences of eutrophication?

Reading Skills

Directions (6–8): Read the passage below. Then answer the questions that follow.

NUCLEAR ENERGY: RISK AND PROMISE
The first self-sustaining nuclear chain reaction was created in the United States in 1942, by a team of scientists led by Enrico Fermi. It was not until 1951 that electricity was first generated by a nuclear reactor, in Arco, Idaho. That first nuclear power station had a power output of only 100 kilowatts. In 1960, Pittsburgh, Pennsylvania became the first nuclear-powered city. The total power output from nuclear power, across the world, was just under 1 gigawatt in 1960; it had risen to 300 gigawatts by the late 1980s. The growth of nuclear energy slowed at that point, after two major accidents at nuclear power plants resulted in a public backlash against nuclear power. Today there is an estimated world power output from nuclear energy of 350 gigawatts. Nuclear power accounts for approximately 18% of electricity generated worldwide, though it varies greatly from country to country; the United States generates approximately 20% of its electricity from nuclear power, whereas France generates 78% of its electricity from nuclear power.

6. Approximately what is the total world electricity output?
   - **F.** 19 gigawatts
   - **G.** 63 gigawatts
   - **H.** 350 gigawatts
   - **I.** 1,900 gigawatts

7. How long was it between the first man-made nuclear chain reaction and the first use of a chain reaction to produce electricity?
   - **A.** 9 years
   - **B.** 12 years
   - **C.** 18 years
   - **D.** 20 years

8. Is it likely that nuclear reactors will be generating more power in 50 years than they do now? Why?

Interpreting Graphics

The graph below shows how much solid waste was produced by a city in the year 2000. Use this graph to answer question 9.

MUNICIPAL SOLID WASTE BY TYPE

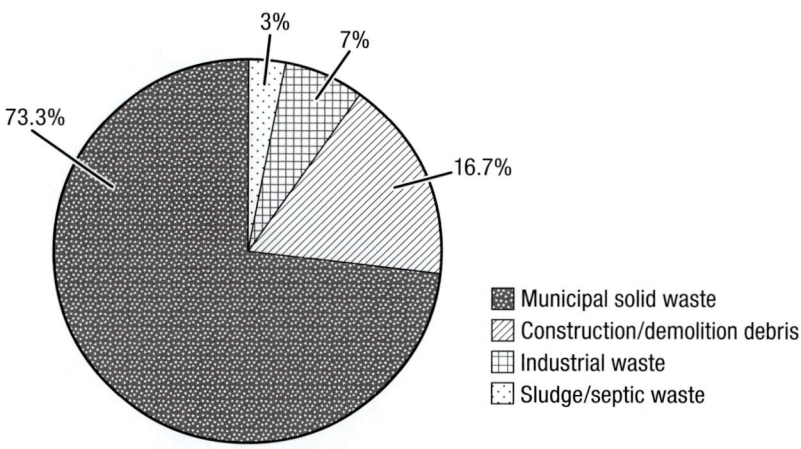

9. If the municipal solid waste amounted to 1.9×10^9 kg, how much total waste did the city produce?
   - **F.** 2.6×10^9 kg
   - **G.** 4.1×10^9 kg
   - **H.** 2.7×10^{10} kg
   - **I.** 7.3×10^{10} kg

The diagram below shows the use of hydroelectric power for every state in the United States. Use this diagram to answer question 10.

HYDROELECTRIC POWER

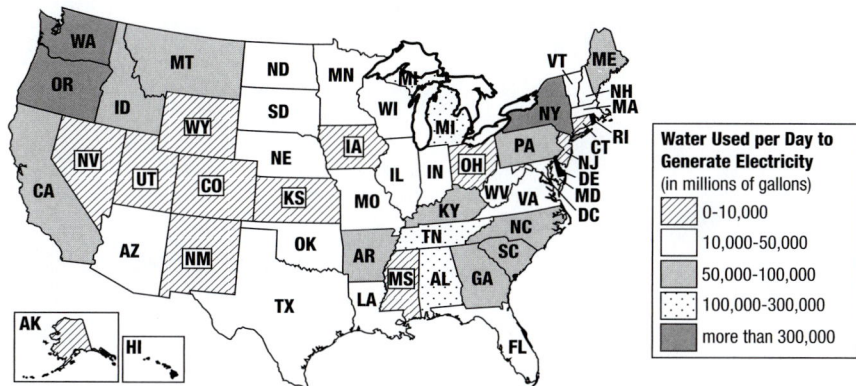

10. How many states use 10,000 million gallons of water per day or less?
    - **A.** 5
    - **B.** 10
    - **C.** 15
    - **D.** 20

Test Tip

Before you answer an extended-response question, make an outline of the points you plan to make.

Reference

Appendix A	Reading ToolBox	**842**
Appendix B	Science Skills	**862**
Appendix C	Useful Data	**880**
Appendix D	Selected Math Answers	**887**
Appendix E	Answers to Reading Checks	**890**
	Glossary	**898**
	Index	**919**

APPENDIX A

Reading Toolbox Overview

Science textbooks can be hard to read because you have to learn new words and new ideas. The Reading Toolbox page at the beginning of each chapter in this book contains tools that can help you get the most out of your reading. Each of the sections on these pages is designed to help you analyze words, language, or ideas.

Analyzing Words

Analyzing Words tools will help you learn and understand specific words or phrases in a chapter.

- **FoldNotes** The key-term fold will help you learn the key terms in the chapter. Instructions for making a key-term fold are on page 848.

- **Science Terms** This tool will help you understand how the common meanings of words can differ from the scientific meanings. A table of everyday words used in science can be found on pages 860–861.

- **Word Parts** If you understand the meanings of the prefixes, suffixes, or word roots, you can understand many science terms. A table of word parts used in science terms is on pages 858–859.

- **Word Origins** Learning the origin of words and phrases used in science can help you remember the word.

- **Word Families** Because similar words can be grouped together into word families, understanding one word can help you understand all of the words in the family.

Analyzing Language

Analyzing Language tools will help you discover connections between ideas and specific kinds of language.

- **Analogies, Comparisons, and Cause and Effect** These tools help you understand the relationship between various words and phrases.

- **Generalizations, Making Predictions, Frequency, and Finding Examples** These tools help you identify language that can key you into when generalizations or predictions are being made, how often something occurs, and when an example is being used.

- **Fact, Hypothesis, or Theory?; Describing Time and Space; Reading Equations; and Word Problems** These tools can help you understand language that is used to describe science concepts and mathematical language.

- **Classification** This tool will help you understand how language is used to organize items.

- **Mnemonics** A mnemonic is a useful study tool to help you remember related words.

Analyzing Ideas

Analyzing Ideas tools will help you organize ideas and create materials that you can use to study.

- **Note Taking** These tools are various methods for taking notes while you read. For details about note-taking methods, see pages 843–847.

- **FoldNotes** There are various types of FoldNotes that you can make to help you learn information. Instructions for making FoldNotes can be found on pages 848–851.

- **Graphic Organizers** These tools are a visual way of showing relationships between ideas. Information on how to create various types of graphic organizers can be found on pages 852–857.

Note Taking

It is important to organize the information that you learn while you are reading a chapter so that you can use those notes to study for your tests. There are many ways to take notes. Each of these note-taking methods is a way to create a clear summary of the key points that you will need to remember for exams.

Comparison Table

A comparison table is useful when you want to compare the characteristics of two or more topics in science. Organizing information in a table helps you compare several topics at one time. In a table, all topics are described in terms of the same list of characteristics, which helps you make a thorough comparison.

1. **Create Table** Draw as many columns and rows as you need to compare the topics of interest, as shown below.

2. **Identify Topics** In the top row, write the topics that you want to compare.

3. **Identify Characteristics** In the left-column, write the general characteristics that you want to compare. As you read the chapter, fill in the characteristics for each topic in the appropriate boxes.

	Solid	Liquid	Gas	Plasma
Definite volume	yes	yes	no	no
Definite shape	yes	no	no	no
Possible changes of state	melting, sublimation	freezing, evaporation	condensation	

Practice

1. Make a comparison table to compare apples, oranges, and broccoli. Compare the following characteristics: color, shape, fruit or vegetable, and vitamins contained.

APPENDIX A

Outlining

Outlining is one of the most widely used methods for taking notes. A well-prepared outline can be an effective tool for understanding, comprehending, and achieving success on tests. Most outlines follow the same structure. This textbook is organized in such a way that you can easily outline the important ideas in a chapter or section.

❶ List Main Ideas List main ideas or topics first. Each topic can be a section title and is listed after a Roman numeral.

❷ Add Major Points Add major points that give you important information about the topic. Each major point will appear in red type in the section. You should add the points to your outline following capitalized letters.

❸ Add Subpoints Add subpoints that describe or explain the major points. The first subpoint should be the key idea that appears in bold after the red heading in the chapter. The blue headings that appear after the red main topic can be used as other subpoints. Subpoints should be added after numerals in your outline.

❹ Include Supporting Details Finally, add supporting details for each subpoint. Pick important details from the text that follow the blue sentences. Add the details to your outline following lower-case letters.

> I. The Nature of Chemical Reactions
>   A. Chemical Reactions
>   1. Chemical reactions occur when substances undergo chemical changes to form new substances.
>   2. Chemical reactions rearrange atoms.
>   a. Products and reactants contain the same types of atoms.
>   b. Mass is always conserved in chemical reactions.

Practice

1. Outline one of the sections in the chapter that you are currently covering in class.

APPENDIX A

Pattern Puzzles

You can use pattern puzzles to help you remember information in the correct order. Pattern puzzles are not just a tool for memorization. They can also help you better understand a variety of scientific processes, from the steps used to solve a mathematical conversion to the procedure used to write a lab report. Pattern puzzles are useful tools to practice and to review before tests. They also work very well in problem solving.

1 Write Steps In your own words, write down the steps of a process on a sheet of paper. Write one step per line, and do not number the steps. You should divide longer steps into two or three shorter steps.

2 Separate Steps Cut the sheet of paper into strips with only one step per strip of paper. Shuffle the strips of paper so that they are out of sequence.

3 Reorganize Steps Place the strips in their proper sequence. Confirm the order of the process by checking your text or your class notes.

How to convert an amount of a substance to mass

- List the given and unknown information.
- Look at the periodic table to determine the molar mass of the substance.
- Write the correct conversion factor to convert moles to grams.
- Multiply the amount of substance by the conversion factor.
- Solve the equation, and check your answer.

- Write the correct conversion factor to convert moles to grams.
- List the given and unknown information.
- Solve the equation, and check your answer.
- Look at the periodic table to determine the molar mass of the substance.
- Multiply the amount of substance by the conversion factor.

Practice

1. Create a pattern puzzle that describes the steps that you take during one of your favorite activities (for example, baking cookies, writing a short story, playing a song on the guitar, or scoring a soccer goal). See if a friend can put the pieces of your puzzle in the correct order.

APPENDIX A

Summarizing

Summarizing is a simple method of taking notes in which you restate what you read in your own words. A summary is simply a brief restatement of a longer passage. Summarizing is a useful way to take notes because it helps you focus on the most important ideas. You can use your notes when you are reviewing for a test so that you can study all of the main points without having to reread the entire chapter.

1 Identify Main Ideas Identify the main idea in a paragraph by reading completely through the paragraph. Sometimes, the first or last sentence of a paragraph states the main idea directly. Key-idea sentences may also be used as the main idea.

2 Create Summary Statement Write a short statement that expresses the main idea. It is best to use complete sentences. You can use abbreviations as long as you will remember later what they mean. You may be able to summarize more than one paragraph in a single statement. In other cases, you may need more than one sentence to summarize a paragraph. Skip a couple of lines, and then repeat these first two steps for each paragraph in the section or chapter that you are reading.

3 Include Additional Notes Add important notes or facts in the lines in between your summary statements. Read the text in Section 2 of Chapter 12 that follows the heading" Weight is different from mass." The heading, "Weight is different from mass," is too simple to be a summary statement because it does not tell you *how* weight and mass are different. On the other hand, you don't need to include any of the information about the astronaut in your summary. A good summary for this text is given below.

> Mass is the amount of matter in an object. Weight is the gravitational force on an object due to its mass.
>
> Mass is the same everywhere, but weight changes with location.

Practice

1. Summarize the first paragraph of this page.

Two-Column Notes

Two-column notes can be used to learn and review definitions of vocabulary terms or details of specific concepts. One strategy for using two-column notes is to organize main ideas and their details. The two-column method of review is great for preparing for quizzes or tests. Cover the information in the right-hand column with a sheet of paper, and after reciting what you know, uncover the notes to check your answers.

1. **Make Table** Divide a blank sheet of paper into two columns. Label the left-hand column "Main idea" and the right-hand column "Detail notes."

2. **Identify Main Ideas** Identify the main ideas. Key ideas are listed at the beginning of each section. However, you should decide which ideas to include in your notes. Key words can include boldface terms as well as any other terms that you may have trouble remembering. Questions may include those that the author has asked or any questions that your teacher may have asked during class.

3. **Add Main Ideas** In the right-hand column, write the main ideas as questions, key words, or a combination of both. The table below shows some of the main ideas from the first section of Chapter 1, "Introduction to Science."

4. **Create Detail Notes** Do not copy ideas from the book or waste time writing in complete sentences. Summarize your ideas using by phrases that are easy to understand and remember. Decide how many details you need for each main idea, and include that number to help you focus on the necessary information.

5. **Include Detail Notes** Write the detail notes in the right-hand column. Be sure to list as many details as you designated in the main-idea column.

Main idea	Detail notes
Branches of science (4 important details)	• natural science—how nature works • three main branches—biological science, physical science, Earth science • physical science—physics and chemistry • branches of science overlap (biochemistry)
Scientific theory (4 important details)	• tested experimentally • possible explanation • explains a natural event • used to predict

Practice

1. Make your own two-column notes using the periodic table. Include in the details the symbol and the atomic number of each of the following elements.
   a. neon
   b. oxygen
   c. copper
   d. calcium
   e. lead
   f. sodium

FoldNotes

FoldNotes are a useful study tool that you can use to organize concepts. One FoldNote focuses on a few main concepts. By using a FoldNote, you can learn how concepts fit together. FoldNotes are designed to make studying concepts easier so that you can remember the ideas for tests.

Key-Term Fold

A key-term fold is useful for studying definitions of key terms in a chapter. Each tab can contain a key term on one side and its definition on the other. Use the key-term fold to quiz yourself on the definitions of the key terms in a chapter.

1. Fold a **sheet of lined notebook paper** in half from left to right.
2. Using **scissors,** cut along every third line from the right edge of the paper to the center fold to make tabs.

Booklet

A booklet is a useful tool for taking notes as you read a chapter. Each page of the booklet can contain a main topic from the chapter. Write details of each main topic on the appropriate page to create an outline of the chapter.

1. Fold a **sheet of paper** in half from left to right. Then, unfold the paper.
2. Fold the sheet of paper in half again from the top to the bottom. Then, unfold the paper.
3. Refold the sheet of paper in half from left to right.
4. Fold the top and bottom edges to the center crease.
5. Completely unfold the paper.
6. Refold the paper from top to bottom.
7. Using **scissors,** cut a slit along the center crease of the sheet from the folded edge to the creases made in step 4. Do not cut the entire sheet in half. Unfold the paper.
8. Fold the sheet of paper in half from left to right. While holding the bottom and top edges of the paper, push the bottom and top edges together so that the center collapses at the center slit. Fold the four flaps to form a four-page book.

Double-Door Fold

A double-door fold is useful when you want to compare the characteristics of two topics. The double-door fold can organize characteristics of the two topics side by side under the flaps. Similarities and differences between the two topics can then be easily identified.

1. Fold a **sheet of paper** in half from the top to the bottom. Then, unfold the paper.
2. Fold the top and bottom edges of the paper to the center crease.

Four-Corner Fold

A four-corner fold is useful when you want to compare the characteristics of four topics. The four-corner fold can organize the characteristics of the four topics side by side under the flaps. Similarities and differences between the four topics can then be easily identified.

1. Fold a **sheet of paper** in half from top to bottom. Then, unfold the paper.
2. Fold the top and bottom of the paper to the crease in the center of the paper.
3. Fold the paper in half from side to side. Then, unfold the paper.
4. Using **scissors,** cut the top flap creases made in step 3 to form four flaps.

FoldNotes

Layered Book

A layered book is a useful tool for taking notes as you read a chapter. The four flaps of the layered book can summarize information into four categories. Write details of each category on the appropriate flap to create a summary of the chapter.

1. Lay one **sheet of paper** on top of **another sheet.** Slide the top sheet up so that 2 cm of the bottom sheet is showing.
2. Holding the two sheets together, fold down the top of the two sheets so that you see four 2 cm tabs along the bottom.
3. Using a **stapler,** staple the top of the FoldNote.

Pyramid

A pyramid provides a unique way for taking notes. The three sides of the pyramid can summarize information into three categories. Use the pyramid as a tool for studying information in a chapter.

1. Place a **sheet of paper** in front of you. Fold the lower left-hand corner of the paper diagonally to the opposite edge of the paper.
2. Cut off the tab of paper created by the fold (at the top).
3. Open the paper so that it is a square. Fold the lower right-hand corner of the paper diagonally to the opposite corner to form a triangle.
4. Open the paper. The creases of the two folds will have created an X.
5. Using **scissors,** cut along one of the creases. Start from any corner, and stop at the center point to create two flaps. Use **tape** or **glue** to attach one of the flaps on top of the other flap.

Table Fold

A table fold is a useful tool for comparing the characteristics of two or three topics. In a table fold, all topics are described in terms of the same characteristics so that you can easily make a thorough comparison.

1. Fold a **piece of paper** in half from the top to the bottom. Then, fold the paper in half again.
2. Fold the paper in thirds from side to side.
3. Unfold the paper completely. Carefully trace the fold lines by using a pen or pencil.

Tri-Fold

A tri-fold is a useful tool that helps you track your progress. By organizing the chapter topic into what you know, what you want to know, and what you learn, you can see how much you have learned after reading a chapter.

1. Fold a piece a paper in thirds from the top to the bottom.
2. Unfold the paper so that you can see the three sections. Then, turn the paper sideways so that the three sections form vertical columns.
3. Trace the fold lines by using a **pen** or **pencil.** Label the columns "Know," "Want," and "Learn."

Three-Panel Flip Chart

A three-panel flip chart is useful when you want to compare the characteristics of three topics. The three-panel flip chart can organize the characteristics of the three topics side by side under the flaps. Similarities and differences between the three topics can then be easily identified.

1. Fold a **piece of paper** in half from the top to the bottom.
2. Fold the paper in thirds from side to side. Then, unfold the paper so that you can see the three sections.
3. From the top of the paper, cut along each of the vertical fold lines to the fold in the middle of the paper. You will now have three flaps.

Two-Panel Flip Chart

A two-panel flip chart is useful when you want to compare the characteristics of two topics. The two-panel flip chart can organize the characteristics of the two topics side by side under the flaps. Similarities and differences between the two topics can then be easily identified.

1. Fold a **piece of paper** in half from the top to the bottom.
2. Fold the paper in half from side to side. Then, unfold the paper so that you can see the two sections.
3. From the top of the paper, cut along the vertical fold line to the fold in the middle of the paper. You will now have two flaps.

Graphic Organizers

Graphic Organizers are a way to draw or map concepts. Graphic Organizers can show simply how concepts are connected, when steps occur in a process, or how events are related. When you outline a concept using Graphic Organizers, you will understand the concept better and have a study tool that you can use later.

Concept Map

Concept maps are useful when you are trying to identify how several ideas are connected to a main concept. Concept maps may be based on vocabulary terms or on main topics from the text. As you read about science, look for terms that can be organized in a concept map.

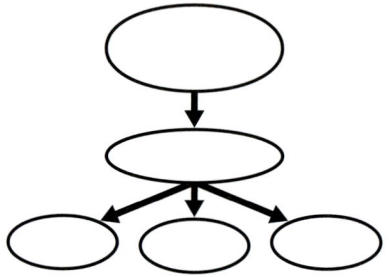

How to Make a Concept Map

1. **Main Ideas** Identify main ideas from the text. Write the ideas as short phrases or single words.

2. **Main Concepts** Select a main concept. Place this concept at the top or center of a piece of paper.

3. **More Ideas** Place other ideas under or around the main concept based on their relationship to the main concept. Draw a circle around each idea.

4. **Connections** Draw lines between the concepts. Add linking words to connect the ideas.

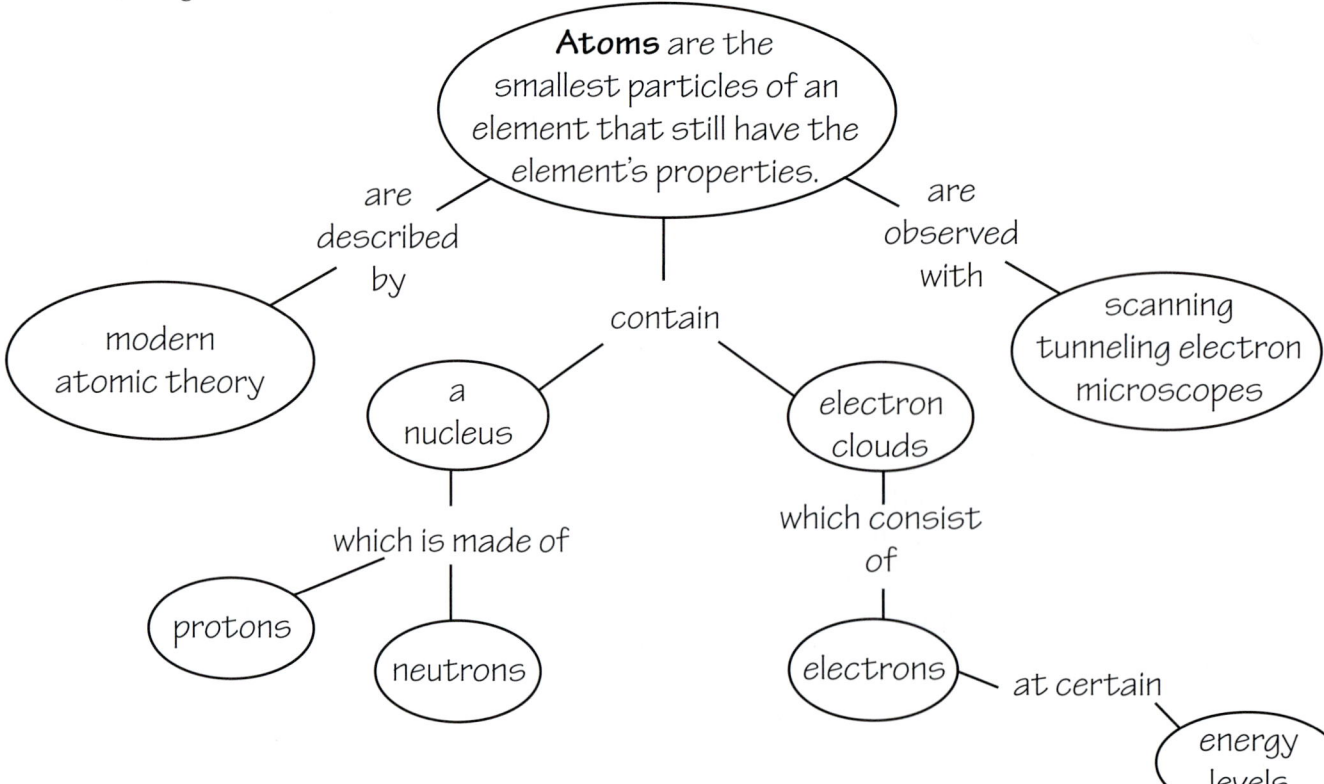

Flow Chart

Science is full of processes. A flow chart shows the steps that a process takes to get from one point to another point. Timelines and cycles are examples of the kinds of information that can be organized well in a flow chart. As you read, look for information that is described in steps or in a sequence, and draw a process chart that shows the progression of the steps or sequence.

How to Make a Flow Chart

① **Box First Step** Draw a box. In the box, write the first step of a process or cycle.

② **Add Next Step** Under the box, draw another box, and draw an arrow to connect the two boxes. In the second box, write the next step of the process.

③ **Add More Steps** Continue adding boxes until each step of the process or cycle is written in a box. For cycles only, draw an arrow to connect the last box and the first box.

Chain-of-Events Chart

When to Use a Chain-of-Events Chart
A chain-of-events chart is similar to a flow chart. A chain-of-events chart shows the order in which steps occur. As you read, look for information that occurs in a sequence, and draw a chain-of-events chart that shows the order of the sequence.

How to Make a Chain-of-Events Chart

1. **Box First Event** Draw a box. In the box, write the first event of a chain of events.

2. **Add Next Event** Draw another box to the right of the first box. Draw an arrow to connect the two boxes. In the second box, write the next event in the timeline.

3. **Add More Events** Continue adding boxes until each step of the chain of events is written in a box.

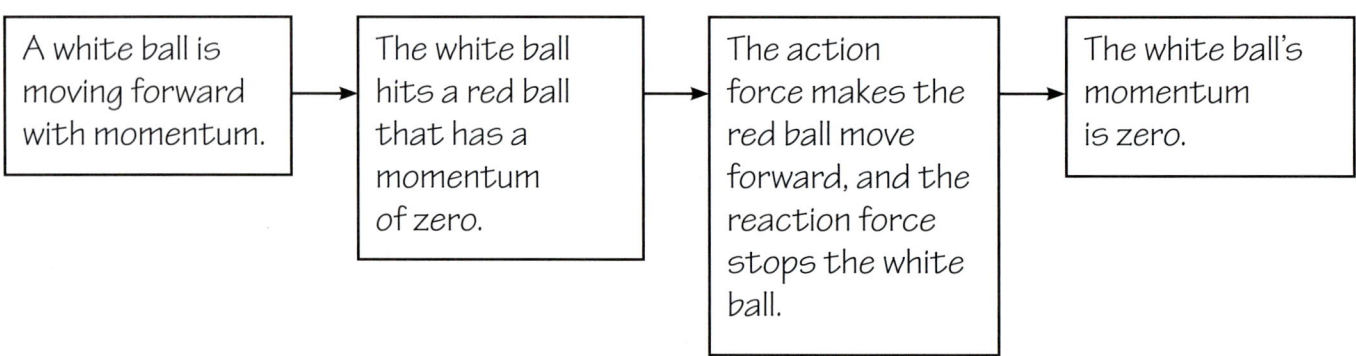

Cause-and-Effect Map

A cause-and-effect map is a useful tool for illustrating a specific type of scientific process. Use a cause-and-effect map when you want to describe how, when, or why one event causes another event. As you read, look for events that are either causes or results of other events, and draw a cause-and-effect map that shows the relationships between the events.

How to Make a Cause-and-Effect Map

1. **Cause Box** Draw a box, and write a cause in the box. You can have as many cause boxes as you want. The diagram shown here is one example of a cause-and-effect map.

2. **Effect Boxes** Draw another box to the right of the cause box to represent an effect. You can have as many effect boxes as you want. Draw arrows from each cause box to the appropriate effect boxes.

3. **Descriptions** In the cause boxes, explain the process that makes up the cause. In the effect boxes, write a description of the effect or details about the effect.

APPENDIX A

Spider Map

A spider map is an effective tool for classifying the details of a specific topic in science. A spider map divides a topic into ideas and details. As you read about a topic, look for the main ideas or characteristics of the topic. Within each idea, look for details. Use a spider map to organize the ideas and details of each topic.

How to Make a Spider Map

1. **Main Topic** Write the main topic in the center of your paper. Draw a circle around the topic.

2. **Main Ideas** From the circle, draw legs to represent the main ideas or characteristics of the topic. Draw as many legs as you want. Write an idea or characteristic along each leg.

3. **Details** From each leg, draw horizontal lines. As you read the chapter, write details about each idea on the idea's horizontal lines. To add more details, make the legs longer and add more horizontal lines.

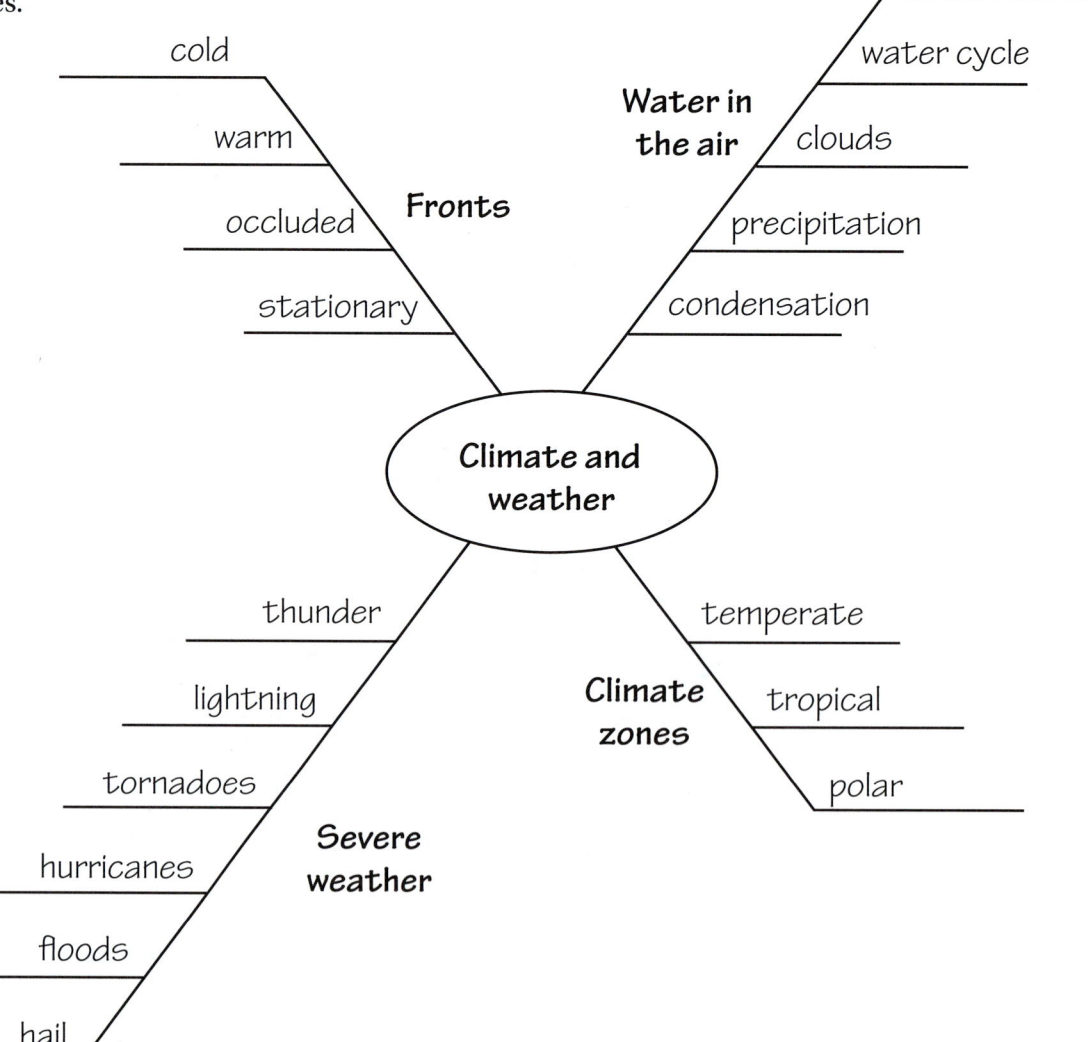

856 Graphic Organizers

APPENDIX A

Venn Diagram

A Venn diagram is a useful tool for comparing two or three topics in science. A Venn diagram shows which characteristics that the topics share and which characteristics are unique to each topic. Venn diagrams are ideal when you want to illustrate relationships in a pair or small group of topics. As you read, look for topics that have both shared and unique characteristics, and draw a Venn diagram that shows how the topics are related.

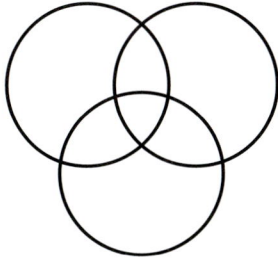

How to Make a Venn Diagram

1. **Circles** Draw overlapping circles. Draw one circle for each topic, and make sure that each circle partially overlaps the other circles.

2. **Main Topics** In each circle, write a topic that you want to compare with the topics in the other circles.

3. **Shared Characteristics** In the areas of the diagram where circles overlap, write the characteristics that the topics in the overlapping circles share.

4. **Unique Characteristics** In the areas of the diagram where circles do not overlap, write the characteristics that are unique to the topic of the particular circle.

Physical properties
- can be observed or measured without changing the identity of a substance
- color, odor, mass, volume, weight, density, strength, flexibility, magnetism, and electrical conductivity

- help describe and define matter
- can be characteristic properties

Chemical properties
- describe matter based on its ability to change into new matter that has different properties
- cannot always be observed
- reactivity, including flammability

Graphic Organizers **857**

Understanding Word Parts

Many scientific words are made up of parts based on the Greek and Latin languages. Understanding the meaning of the parts will help you understand the meaning of the scientific words. The tables here provide definitions and examples of prefixes, roots, and suffixes that you may see in this textbook.

Prefix	Definition	Example
bio-	life	**biochemistry** the study of the matter of living things
co-	with; together	**covalent bond** a bond formed when atoms share one or more pairs of electrons
com-	with; together	**compound** a substance made up of atoms of two or more different elements joined by chemical bonds
counter-	opposite; contrary to	**counterclockwise** in a direction opposite to that in which the hands of a clock move
dis-	away; in different directions	**displace** to move out of place; to move away from
endo-	in; within	**endothermic reaction** a chemical reaction that requires energy input
exo-	outside; external	**exothermic reaction** a chemical reaction in which energy is released to the surroundings as heat
infra-	below; beneath	**infrared** describes electromagnetic radiation with energy that is less than, or just below, the red end of the visible spectrum
ir-	not	**irregular galaxy** a small galaxy that has no identifiable shape and that contains a great amount of dust and gas
iso-	equal	**isotope** an atom that has the same number of protons (or the same atomic number) as other atoms of the same element do but that has a different number of neutrons (and thus a different atomic mass)
non-	not	**nonmetal** an element that conducts heat and electricity poorly and that does not form positive ions in an electrolytic solution; not a metal
retro-	backward	**retrograde rotation** the clockwise, or backward, spin of a planet or moon as seen from above the planet's North Pole
super-	above; over	**supernova** a gigantic, or oversized, explosion in which a massive star collapses and throws its outer layers into space
trans-	across; through	**transmission** the passing of light or another form of energy through matter
ultra-	beyond; exceedingly	**ultraviolet** a band of electromagnetic radiation that has wavelengths that are shorter than the wavelengths of violet light; beyond violet
uni-	one	**universe** the sum of all space, matter, and energy that exist, that have existed in the past, and that will exist in the future; the sum of all things as one unit

Word root	Definition	Example
astr	star	**astronomy** the scientific study of the universe
flamm	to burn; flame	**flammability** the ability of a substance to burn
ject	to throw	**projectile motion** the curved path that an object follows when thrown, launched, or otherwise projected near the surface of Earth
mer	part	**polymer** a large molecule that is formed by more than five monomers, or small units; a molecule made of many parts
phot	light	**photon** a unit or quantum of light
poly	many	**polyatomic ion** an ion made of two or more atoms
solute	to free; to loosen	**solubility** the ability of one substance to dissolve when in contact with another substance at a given temperature and pressure; as the substance dissolves, each of its particles becomes free from the surrounding particles
spec	to look	**spectrum** the band of colors produced when white light passes through a prism
therm	heat	**thermal conduction** the transfer of energy as heat through a material
thesis	proposition	**hypothesis** a testable idea or explanation that leads to scientific investigation
vapor	gaseous form of any substance	**evaporation** the change of state from a liquid to a gas

Suffix	Definition	Example
-cule	little	**molecule** the smallest unit of a substance that can exist by itself and retain all of the substance's chemical properties
-gram	thing written	**schematic diagram** a graphical representation of a circuit that uses lines to represent wires and different symbols to represent components
-ic	pertaining to	**periodic** describes something that occurs or repeats at regular intervals; pertaining to periods
-ion	the act of	**compression** a force that is exerted when matter is pushed or squeezed together; the act of squeezing
-meter	to measure	**thermometer** an instrument that measures and indicates temperature
-nomy	the science of	**astronomy** the scientific study of the universe
-oid	resembling	**metalloids** elements that have properties of both metals and nonmetals; they resemble metals more than nonmetals do
-scope	an instrument for seeing or observing	**telescope** an instrument that collects light from the sky and concentrates it for better observation

Understanding Word Parts

APPENDIX A

Everyday Words Used in Science

Scientific words may have common meanings that you already know. Understanding the difference between everyday meanings and scientific meanings will help you develop a scientific vocabulary. The table here provides common and scientific meanings for words that you will see in this textbook.

Word	Common meaning	Scientific meaning
base	the lowest part	any compound that increases the number of hydroxide ions when dissolved in water
catalyst	something that causes change	a substance that changes the rate of a chemical reaction without being consumed or changed significantly
cell	a small room, as in a prison	in electricity, a device that produces an electric current by converting chemical or radiant energy into electrical energy
concentration	the act of focusing one's attention on something	the amount of a particular substance in a given quantity of a mixture or solution
condensation	the droplets of liquid on the outside of a glass or window	the change of state from a gas to a liquid
conservation	protection of something	conservation of mass—mass cannot be created or destroyed in ordinary chemical or physical changes
element	a fundamental constituent part	a substance that cannot be separated or broken down into simpler substances by chemical means
energy	the ability to be active	the capacity to do work
fluid	smooth; graceful (for example, fluid movement)	a nonsolid state of matter in which the atoms or molecules are free to move past each other, as in a gas or liquid
force	violence used to compel a person or thing	an action exerted on a body in order to change the body's state of rest or motion; force has magnitude and direction
friction	conflict between people who have opposing views	a force that opposes motion between two surfaces that are in contact
gas	short for *gasoline;* a liquid fuel used by vehicles, such as cars and buses	a form of matter that does not have a definite volume or shape
gravity	seriousness (for example, the gravity of the situation)	a force of attraction between objects that is due to their masses and that decreases as the distance between the objects increases
group	a number of people gathered together	a vertical column of elements in the periodic table; elements in a group share chemical properties
inertia	resistance to change	the tendency of an object to resist a change in motion unless an outside force acts on the object
mass	a quantity of material that has an unspecified shape	a measure of the amount of matter in an object

Word	Common meaning	Scientific meaning
matter	a subject of concern or topic of discussion	anything that has mass and takes up space
medium	a measurement that is intermediate between small and large	a physical environment in which phenomena occur
model	a miniature representation of a larger object	a pattern, plan, representation, or description designed to show the structure or workings of an object, system, or concept
mole	a small, brown, permanent mark on the skin; a small mammal that burrows underground	the SI base unit used to measure the amount of a substance whose number of particles is the same as the number of atoms of carbon in exactly 12 g of carbon-12
motion	movement	an object's change in position relative to a reference point
organic	describes an organism or object that is produced without the use of synthetic drugs, fertilizers, or hormones	describes a covalently bonded compound that contains carbon, excluding carbonates
period	a punctuation mark used to indicate the end of a sentence	in chemistry, a horizontal row of elements in the periodic table
phase	a distinguishable stage in a cycle	in astronomy, the change in the illuminated area of one celestial body as seen from another celestial body
pressure	the burden of mental stress	the amount of force exerted per unit area of a surface
product	something available for sale (for example, a computer product)	a substance that forms in a chemical reaction
reaction	a response to a stimulus	the process by which one or more substances change to produce one or more different substances
revolution	the overthrow of one government and the substitution of that government with another (for example, the American Revolution)	the motion of a body that travels around another body in space; one complete trip along an orbit
solution	the answer to a problem	a homogeneous mixture throughout which two or more substances are uniformly dispersed
star	a person who is highly celebrated in a particular field	a large celestial body that is composed of gas and that emits light
table	a piece of furniture that has a flat, horizontal surface	an orderly arrangement of data
theory	an assumption based on limited knowledge	a system of ideas that explains many related observations and is supported by a large body of evidence acquired through scientific investigation
volume	a measure of how loud a sound is	a measure of the size of a body or region in three-dimensional space
work	a job; a task to be done	the transfer of energy to a body by the application of a force that causes the body to move in the direction of the force

Everyday Words Used in Science

Math Skills

Fractions

Fractions represent numbers that are less than 1. In other words, fractions are a way of using numbers to represent a part of a whole. For example, if you have a pizza with 8 slices and you eat 2 of the slices, you have 6 out of the 8 slices, or $\frac{6}{8}$, of the pizza left. The top number in the fraction is called the *numerator*. The bottom number is called the *denominator*.

There are special rules for adding, subtracting, multiplying, and dividing fractions. **Figure 1** summarizes these rules.

Figure 1 Basic Operations for Fractions

	Rule and example
Multiplication	$\left(\frac{a}{b}\right)\left(\frac{c}{d}\right) = \frac{ac}{bd}$ $\left(\frac{2}{3}\right)\left(\frac{4}{5}\right) = \frac{8}{15}$
Division	$\frac{a}{b} \div \frac{c}{d} = \frac{\left(\frac{a}{b}\right)}{\left(\frac{c}{d}\right)} = \frac{ad}{bc}$ $\frac{2}{3} \div \frac{4}{5} = \frac{\left(\frac{2}{3}\right)}{\left(\frac{4}{5}\right)} = \frac{(2)(5)}{(3)(4)} = \frac{10}{12}$
Addition and subtraction	$\frac{a}{b} \pm \frac{c}{d} = \frac{ad \pm bc}{bd}$ $\frac{2}{3} - \frac{4}{5} = \frac{(2)(5) - (3)(4)}{(3)(5)} = -\frac{2}{15}$

Practice

1. Perform the following calculations:
   a. $\frac{7}{8} + \frac{1}{3} =$
   b. $\frac{7}{8} \times \frac{1}{3} =$
   c. $\frac{7}{8} \div \frac{1}{3} =$
   d. $\frac{7}{8} - \frac{1}{3} =$

Percentages

Percentages are the same as other fractions except that in a percentage the whole (or the number in the denominator) is considered to be 100. Any percentage, $x\%$, can be read as x out of 100. For example, if you completed 50% of an assignment, you completed $\frac{50}{100}$, or $\frac{1}{2}$, of the assignment.

Percentages can be calculated by dividing the part by the whole. Your calculator displays a decimal value when it solves a division problem that has an answer that is less than 1. The decimal value can be written as a fraction. For example, 0.45 can be written as the fraction $\frac{45}{100}$.

An easy way to calculate a percentage is to divide the part by the whole and then multiply by 100. This multiplication moves the decimal point two positions to the right and gives you the number that would be over 100 in a fraction. So, $0.45 = 45\%$.

Try this example:

> You scored 73 out of 92 problems on your last exam. What was your percentage score?

First, divide the part by the whole to get a decimal value. The fraction $\frac{73}{92} = 0.7935$, which is equal to $\frac{79.35}{100}$.

Then, multiply by 100 to find the percentage: $0.7935 \times 100 = 79.35\%$.

Practice

1. The molar mass of the oxygen atom in a water molecule is 16.00 g/mol. A water molecule has a total molar mass of 18.01 g/mol. What percentage of the mass of water is made up of oxygen?
2. A candy bar contains 14 g of fat. The total fat contains 3.0 g of saturated fat and 11 g of unsaturated fat. What percentage of the fat is saturated? What percentage is unsaturated?

Exponents

An exponent is a number that is a superscript to the right of another number. The best way to explain how an exponent works is with an example. In the value 5^4, 4 is the exponent on 5. The number with its exponent means that 5 is multiplied by itself 4 times.

$$5^4 = 5 \times 5 \times 5 \times 5 = 625$$

Exponent are powers.

You will frequently hear exponents referred to as *powers*. Using this terminology, one could read the above equation as *five to the fourth power equals 625*. Keep in mind that any number raised to the zero power is equal to 1. Also, any number raised to the first power is equal to itself:

$$5^1 = 5$$

Figure 2 summarizes the rules for dealing with exponents.

Figure 2 Rules for Dealing with Exponents

	Rule	Example
Zero power	$x^0 = 1$	$7^0 = 1$
First power	$x^1 = x$	$6^1 = 6$
Multiplication	$(x^n)(x^m) = x^{(n+m)}$	$(x^2)(x^4) = x^{(2+4)} = x^6$
Division	$\dfrac{x^n}{x^m} = x^{(n-m)}$	$\dfrac{x^8}{x^2} = x^{(8-2)} = x^6$
Exponents that are fractions	$x^{1/n} = \sqrt[n]{x}$	$4^{1/3} = \sqrt[3]{4} = 1.5874$
Exponents raised to a power	$(x^n)^m = x^{nm}$	$(5^2)^3 = 5^6 = 15{,}625$

Roots are the opposite of exponents.

The symbol for a square root is $\sqrt{}$. The value underneath this symbol is equal to a number times itself. It is also possible to have roots other than the square root. For example, $\sqrt[3]{x}$ is a cube root, which means that if you multiply some number, n, by itself 3 times, you will get the number x, or $x = n \times n \times n$.

We can turn our example of $5^4 = 625$ around to solve for the fourth root of 625.

$$\sqrt[4]{625} = 5$$

Taking the *n*th root of a number is the same as raising that number to the power of $1/n$. Therefore, $\sqrt[4]{625} = 625^{1/4}$.

Use a calculator to solve exponents and roots.

You can solve problems involving exponents and roots easily by using a scientific calculator. Many calculators have dedicated keys for squares and square roots. But what do you do if you want to find other powers, such as cubes and cube roots? Most scientific calculators have a key with a caret symbol, (^), that is used to enter exponents. If you type in "5^4" and hit the equals sign or the enter key, the calculator will display the answer 625.

Many scientific calculators have a key with the symbol $\sqrt[x]{}$ that you can use to enter roots. When using this key, enter the root first. To solve the problem of the fourth root of 625, you would type "4 $\sqrt[x]{}$ 625," and the calculator would return the answer 5. If your calculator does not have the root key, you may be able to enter the root as a fraction if your calculator has a key that allows you to enter fractions. In this case you would use the exponent key and the fraction key to enter "625^ $\frac{1}{4}$." If your calculator does not have a fraction key, you can enter the decimal equivalent of the fractional exponent to find the root. Instead of entering $\frac{1}{4}$ as the exponent, enter "625^0.25," because 0.25 is equal to $\frac{1}{4}$.

Practice

1. Perform the following calculations:

   a. $9^1 =$

   b. $(3^3)^5 =$

   c. $\dfrac{2^8}{2^2} =$

   d. $(14^2)(14^3) =$

   e. $11^0 =$

   f. $6^{1/6} =$

APPENDIX B

Order of Operations

Use the following phrase to remember the correct order for long mathematical problems: *Please Excuse My Dear Aunt Sally*. This phrase stands for "Parentheses, Exponents, Multiplication, Division, Addition, Subtraction." **Figure 3** summarizes these rules.

Figure 3 Order of Operations

Step	Operation
1	**Parentheses** Simplify groups inside parentheses. Start with the innermost group, and work out.
2	**Exponents** Simplify all exponents.
3	**Multiplication and Division** Perform multiplication and division in order from left to right.
4	**Addition and Subtraction** Perform addition and subtraction in order from left to right.

Try the following example:

$$4^3 + 2 \times [8 - (3 - 1)] = ?$$

1 Simplify the operations inside parentheses. Begin with the innermost parentheses:

$$(3 - 1) = 2$$
$$4^3 + 2 \times [8 - 2] = ?$$

Move on to the next-outer brackets:

$$[8 - 2] = 6$$
$$4^3 + 2 \times 6 = ?$$

2 Simplify all exponents:

$$4^3 = 64$$
$$64 + 2 \times 6 = ?$$

3 Perform multiplication:

$$2 \times 6 = 12$$
$$64 + 12 = ?$$

4 Solve the addition problem:

$$64 + 12 = 76$$

Practice

1. $2^3 \div 2 + 4 \times (9 - 2^2) =$
2. $\dfrac{2 \times (6 - 3) + 8}{4 \times 2 - 6} =$

Geometry

Shapes are a useful way to model many objects and substances studied in science. For example, many of the properties of a wheel can be understood by using a perfect circle as a model.

Therefore, knowing how to calculate the area or the volume of certain shapes is a useful skill in science. Equations for the area and volume of several geometric shapes are provided in **Figure 4.**

Figure 4 Geometric Areas and Volumes

Geometric shape		Useful equations
Rectangle	▭	$area = lw$
Circle	○	$area = \pi r^2$ $circumference = 2\pi r$
Triangle	△	$area = \dfrac{1}{2}bh$
Sphere	●	$surface\ area = 4\pi r^2$ $volume = \dfrac{4}{3}\pi r^3$
Cylinder	▮	$volume = \pi r^2 h$
Rectangular box	▰	$surface\ area = 2(lh + lw + hw)$ $volume = lwh$

Practice

1. A cylinder has a diameter of 14 cm and a height of 8 cm. What is the cylinder's volume?
2. Calculate the surface area of a 4 cm cube.
3. Will a sphere with a volume of 76 cm^3 fit in a rectangular box that is 7 cm × 4 cm × 10 cm?

Algebraic Rearrangements

Often in science, you will need to determine the value of a variable from an equation written as an algebraic expression.

Algebraic expressions contain constants and variables. *Constants* are numbers that you know and that do not change, such as 2, 3.14, and 100. *Variables* are represented by letters, such as x, y, a, and b. Variables in equations are unspecified quantities and are also called the *unknowns*.

An algebraic expression contains one or more of the four basic mathematical operations: addition, subtraction, multiplication, and division. Constants, variables, or terms made up of both constants and variables can be involved in the basic operations.

Solve for the variable.

To find the value of some variable, you need to simplify the expression by rearranging the equation. Ideally, after you have finished rearranging the equation, you will end up with a simple equation that tells you the value of the variable.

To get from a complicated equation to a simpler one, you need to isolate the variable on one side of the equation. You can do so by performing the same operations on both sides of the equation until the variable is alone. Because both sides of the equation are equal, if you do the same operation on both sides of the equation, the results will still be equal.

Look at the following simple problem:

$$8x = 32$$

In this equation, you need to solve for the variable x. You can add, subtract, multiply, or divide anything to or from one side of an equation as long as you do the same thing to the other side of the equation. In this case, we need to get rid of the 8 so that the x is by itself. If we divide both sides by 8, we have this equation:

$$\frac{8x}{8} = \frac{32}{8}$$

The 8s on the left side of the equation cancel each other out, and the fraction $\frac{32}{8}$ can be reduced to give the whole number 4.

$$x = 4$$

Next, consider the following equation:

$$x + 2 = 8$$

Remember that you can add or subtract the same quantity from each side. To isolate x, you need subtract 2 from each side:

$$x + 2 - 2 = 8 - 2$$
$$x + 0 = 6$$
$$x = 6$$

Now, consider one more equation:

$$-3(x - 2) + 4 = 29$$

One way to solve this more complicated expression is to follow the order of operations in reverse order to isolate x. First, subtract the 4.

$$-3(x - 2) + 4 - 4 = 29 - 4$$
$$-3(x - 2) = 25$$

Now, divide by –3.

$$\frac{-3(x - 2)}{-3} = \frac{25}{-3}$$
$$x - 2 = -8.3$$

Now, only the expression that was inside the parentheses remains on the left side of the equation. You can find the value of x by adding 2 to both sides of the equation.

$$x - 2 + 2 = -8.3 + 2$$
$$x = -6.3$$

Practice

1. Rearrange each of the following equations to give the value of the variable indicated with a letter:
   a. $8x - 32 = 128$
   b. $6 - 5(4a + 3) = 26$
   c. $-2(3m + 5) = 14$
   d. $\left[8 \frac{(8 + 2z)}{32} \right] + 2 = 5$
   e. $\frac{(6b + 3)}{3} - 9 = 2$

APPENDIX B

Scientific Notation

Often, scientists deal with very large or very small quantities. For example, in one second, about 3,000,000,000,000,000,000 electrons' worth of charge pass through a standard light bulb; and the ink required to make the dot over an *i* in this textbook has a mass of about 0.000000001 kg.

Obviously, it is very time-consuming to read and write such large and small numbers. It is also easy to lose track of the zeros and make an error when doing calculations with numbers that have many zeros. Powers of the number 10 are used to keep track of the zeros in large and small numbers. Numbers that are expressed as some power of 10 multiplied by another number with only one digit to the left of the decimal point are said to be written in *scientific notation*.

Use exponents to write large numbers.

Study the positive powers of 10 shown in the chapter entitled "Introduction to Science." The number of zeros corresponds to the exponent to the right of the 10. The number for 10^4 is 10,000; it has 4 zeros.

But how can you use the powers of 10 to simplify large numbers such as the number of electron-sized charges passing through a light bulb? The number 3,000,000,000,000,000,000 can be written as $3 \times 1,000,000,000,000,000,000$. To write the large number as an exponent, count the zeros—there are 18 zeros. Therefore, the exponent is 10^{18}. So, 3,000,000,000,000,000,000 can be expressed as 3×10^{18} in scientific notation.

Use exponents to write small numbers.

Now, you know how to simplify really large numbers, but how do you simplify really small numbers, such as 0.000000001? To simplify numbers that are less than 1, use negative exponents.

Next, study the negative powers of 10. To determine the exponent that you need to use, count the number of decimal places that you must move the decimal point to the right so that only one digit is to the left of the decimal point. To simplify the mass of the ink in the dot on an *i*, 0.000000001 kg, you must move the decimal point 9 decimal places to the right for the numeral 1 to be on the left side of the decimal point. In scientific notation, the mass of the ink is 1×10^{-9} kg.

Use scientific notation to write any number.

Values that have more than one nonzero number can also be written using scientific notation. For example, 5,943,000,000 is 5.943×10^9 when expressed in scientific notation. The number 0.0000832 is 8.32×10^{-5} when expressed in scientific notation.

When you use scientific notation in calculations, follow the rules for using exponents in calculations. When you multiply two numbers expressed in scientific notation, add the exponents, as shown below.

$$(4 \times 10^5) \times (2 \times 10^3) = [(4 \times 2) \times 10^{(5+3)}] = 8 \times 10^8$$

When you divide two numbers expressed in scientific notation, subtract the exponents.

The order of magnitude is the power of 10.

When a number is expressed in scientific notation, you can easily determine the order of magnitude of the number. For numbers less than 5, the order of magnitude is the power of 10 when the number is written in scientific notation. For numbers greater than 5, the order of magnitude is the power of 10 to which the number would be rounded. For example, in the number 5.943×10^9, the order of magnitude is 10^{10}, because 5.943 rounds to another 10, and 10 times 10^9 is 10^{10}.

The order of magnitude can be used to help quickly estimate your answers. Simply perform the operations required, but instead of using numbers, use the orders of magnitude. Your final answer should be within two orders of magnitude of your estimate.

Practice

1. Rewrite the following values using scientific notation:
   a. 12,300,000 m/s
   b. 0.0000000000045 kg
   c. 0.0000653 m
   d. 55,432,000,000,000 s
   e. 273.15 K
   f. 0.00062714 kg

SI

One of the most important parts of scientific research is being able to communicate your findings to other scientists. Today, scientists need to be able to communicate with other scientists all around the world. They need a common language in which to report data. If you do an experiment in which all of your measurements are in pounds and you want to compare your results to those of a French scientist whose measurements are in grams, you will need to convert all of your measurements. For this reason, the *Système International d'Unités*, or SI, was created in 1960.

You are probably accustomed to measuring distance in inches, feet, and miles. Most of the world, however, measures distance in centimeters (cm), meters (m), and kilometers (km). The meter is the official SI unit for measuring distance. **Figure 5** lists the SI units for some common measurements.

Prefixes are used to indicate quantities.

Notice that cent*imeter* and kilo*meter* each contain the word *meter*. When dealing with SI units, you frequently use the base unit, in this case the meter, and add a prefix to indicate that the quantity that you are measuring is a multiple of that unit. Most SI prefixes indicate multiples of 10. For example, the centimeter is 1/100 of a meter. Any SI unit with the prefix *centi-* will be 1/100 of the base unit. A centigram is 1/100 of a gram.

Figure 5 Some SI Units

Quantity	Unit name	Symbol
Length	meter	m
Mass	kilogram	kg
Time	second	s
Temperature	kelvin	K
Amount of substance	mole	mol
Electric current	ampere	A
Pressure	pascal	Pa
Volume	cubic meters	m³

Figure 6 Some SI Prefixes

Prefix	Symbol	Exponential factor
giga-	G	10^9
mega-	M	10^6
kilo-	k	10^3
hecto-	h	10^2
deka-	da	10^1
deci-	d	10^{-1}
centi-	c	10^{-2}
milli-	m	10^{-3}
micro-	μ	10^{-6}
nano-	n	10^{-9}
pico-	p	10^{-12}
femto-	f	10^{-15}

How many meters are in a *kilo*meter? The prefix *kilo-* indicates that the unit is 1,000 times the base unit. A kilometer is equal to 1,000 meters. Multiples of 10 make dealing with SI values much easier than values such as feet or gallons. To convert from feet to miles, you must remember a large conversion factor, 1.893939×10^{-4} miles per foot. To convert from kilometers to meters, you need to look only at the prefix to know that you will multiply by 1,000.

Figure 6 lists possible prefixes and their meanings. When working with a prefix, simply take the unit symbol and add the prefix symbol to the front of the unit symbol. For example, the symbol for *kilometer* is written "km."

Practice

1. Convert each value to the requested units:
   a. 0.035 m to decimeters
   b. 5.24 m³ to cubic centimeters
   c. 13,450 g to kilograms

Math Skills

APPENDIX B

Significant Figures

Significant figures indicate the precision of a value. You can use the rules in the following list to determine the number of significant figures in a reported value. After you have reviewed the rules, use **Figure 7** to check your understanding of the rules. Cover up the second column of the table, and try to determine how many significant figures each number has.

You can use a few rules to determining the number of significant figures in a measurement.

1. All nonzero digits are significant.

   Example 1,246 (four significant figures, shown in red)

2. Any zeros between significant digits are also significant.

   Example 1,206 (four significant figures)

3. If the value does not contain a decimal point, any zeros to the right of a nonzero digit are not significant.

   Example 1,200 (two significant figures)

4. Any zeros to the right of a significant digit and to the left of a decimal point are significant.

   Example 1,200. (four significant figures)

5. If a value has no significant digits to the left of a decimal point, any zeros to the right of the decimal point and to the left of a nonzero digit are not significant.

   Example 0.0012 (two significant figures)

6. If a measurement is reported that ends with zeros to the right of a decimal point, those zeros are significant.

   Example 0.1200 (four significant figures)

If you are adding or subtracting two measurements, your answer can have only as many decimal positions as the value with the least number of decimal places. The final answer in the following problem has five significant figures. It has been rounded to two decimal places because 0.04 g has only two decimal places.

$$\begin{array}{r} 134.050 \text{ g} \\ -0.04 \text{ g} \\ \hline 134.01 \text{ g} \end{array}$$

Figure 7 Significant Figures

Measurement	Number of significant figures	Rule
12,345	5	1
2,400 cm	2	3
305 kg	3	2
2,350. cm	4	4
234.005 K	6	2
12.340	5	6
0.001	1	5
0.002450	4	5 and 6

When you multiply or divide measurements, your final answer can have only as many significant figures as the value with the least number of significant figures. Examine the following multiplication problem.

$$\begin{array}{r} 12.0 \text{ cm}^2 \\ \times 0.04 \text{ cm} \\ \hline 0.5 \text{ cm}^3 \end{array}$$

The final answer has been rounded to one significant figure because 0.04 cm has only one. When performing both types of operations (addition/subtraction and multiplication/division), round the result after you complete each type of operation, and round the final result.

Practice

1. Determine the number of significant figures in each of the following measurements:
   a. 65.04 mL
   b. 564.00 m
   c. 0.007504 kg
   d. 1,210 K

2. Perform each of the following calculations, and report your answer with the correct number of significant figures and units:
   a. 0.004 dm + 0.12508 dm
   b. 340 m ÷ 0.1257 s
   c. 40.1 kg × 0.2453 m^2
   d. 1.03 g − 0.0456 g

Graphing Skills

Line Graphs

Usually, in laboratory experiments, you will control one variable and see how changes in that variable affect another variable. Line graphs can show these relationships clearly. Suppose that you want to determine the rate of a plant's growth by measuring the growth of a plant over time. In this experiment, you would control the time intervals at which the plant height is measured. Thus, time is the *independent variable*. The change in the height of the plant that you measure depends on the time interval that you choose. So, plant height is the *dependent variable*. The table in **Figure 8** shows some sample data from an experiment that measured the rate of plant growth.

When you make a line graph, always plot the independent variable on the *x*-axis. For the plant-height experiment, the axis will be labeled "Time (days)." Remember to include the units in your axis label. Pick a range for your graph that is just large enough to enter all of your data points. From the data in **Figure 8,** you can see that plant height was measured over 35 days. Therefore, the *x*-axis should have a range of 0 days to 35 days.

Plot the dependent variable on the *y*-axis. In this case, the *y*-axis is labeled "Plant height (cm)" and has a range from 0 cm to 5 cm.

When you draw the axes for your graph, you want to use as much of the available space as possible. You should label the grid marks for each axis at intervals that evenly divide up the data range. In the graph in **Figure 9,** the *y*-axis has grid marks at intervals of 1, and the *x*-axis has grid marks at intervals of 5. Notice that the interval of the grid marks on the *x*-axis is not the same interval at which the data were measured.

Think of your graph as a grid with lines running horizontally from the *y*-axis and vertically from the *x*-axis. To plot a point, find the *x*-value for that point on the *x*-axis. Follow the vertical line from the *x*-axis until it intersects the horizontal line from the *y*-axis at the corresponding *y*-value. At the intersection of these two lines, place your point. After you have plotted all of your data points, connect each point with a straight line. **Figure 9** shows a line graph of the data in **Figure 8.**

Figure 8 Data for Plant Growth Versus Time

Time (days)	Plant height (cm)
0	1.43
7	2.16
14	2.67
21	3.25
28	4.04
35	4.67

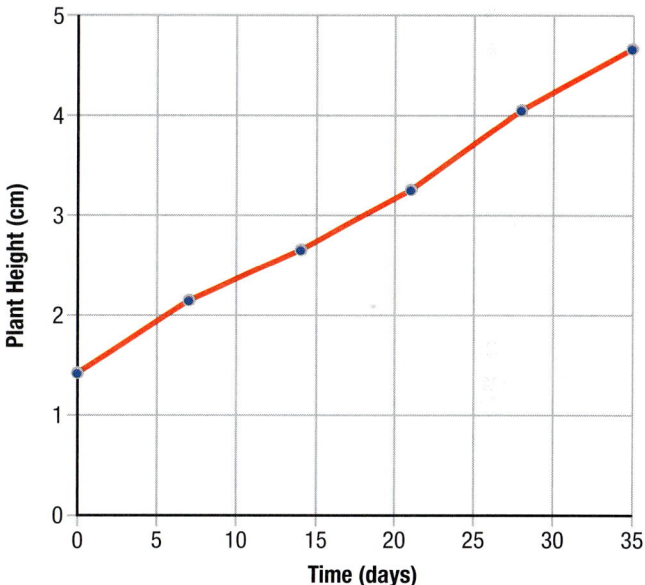

Figure 9 Line Graph for Plant Growth Versus Time

Practice

1. Create a line graph of the data below.

Time (days)	Plant height (cm)
0	1.46
7	2.67
14	3.89
21	4.82

2. Compare the graph you made with **Figure 9.** What can you conclude about the two groups of plants?

APPENDIX B

Scatter Plots

Some groups of data are best represented in a graph called a *scatter plot*. Scatter plots are often used to find trends, or general patterns, in data. A scatter plot is similar to a line graph. The data points are plotted on the graph that has an *x*-axis and a *y*-axis, but each point is not connected with a line. Instead, a straight best-fit line is drawn through the data points to show the overall trend. A best-fit line is a single, smooth line that represents all of the data points without necessarily going through all of them. To find a best-fit line, pick a line that is equidistant from as many data points as possible. Examine the graph in **Figure 10.**

If we connected all of the data points with lines, the lines would create a zigzag pattern. It would be hard to see the general pattern in the data. But if we find a best-fit line, we can see a trend more clearly. The trend in a scatter plot depends on the data. The best-fit line in **Figure 11** shows that magazine subscriptions increased.

If you pick two points on the best-fit line, you can estimate the line's slope. The slope will tell you the average rate of increase in magazine subscriptions. By using the dotted lines in **Figure 11,** you can estimate the data point for 1940 as 18 magazine subscriptions per 1,000 households and for 1960 as 42 magazine subscriptions per 1,000 households. The slope is (42 subscriptions – 18 subscriptions) divided by (1960 – 1940). The slope tells you that there is an increase of 24 subscriptions per 1,000 households every 20 years.

Figure 10

Figure 11

Practice

1. Create a scatter plot, and draw a best-fit line for the data below.

Year	Magazine subscriptions per 1,000 households
1918	17
1931	15
1942	42
1954	36
1967	64
1980	73
1992	60
2008	70

2. What does the best-fit line represent?
3. If these data are from a different city than the data in **Figure 11,** what conclusions could you draw about the two cities?

870 Graphing Skills

Bar Graphs

Bar graphs should be used for noncontinuous data. They make it easy to compare data quickly when you have one value for multiple items. You can see from **Figure 12** that Jupiter has the largest radius and Mercury has the smallest radius. You could easily arrange the planets in order of size.

Figure 12

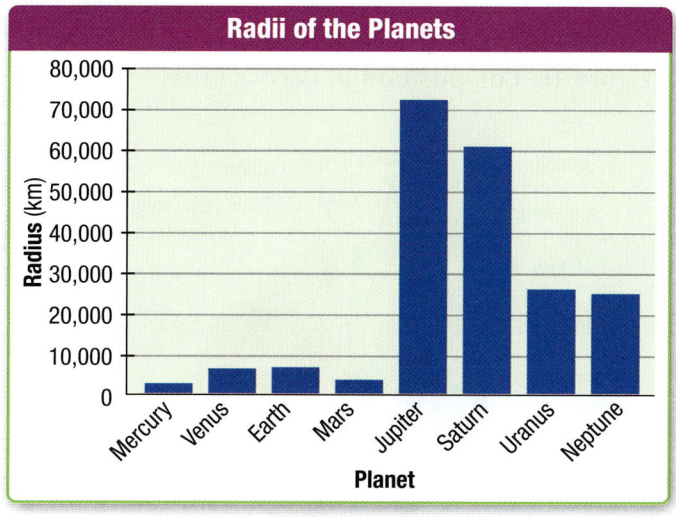

Choosing the scale of a bar graph will make identifying trends in the data easier. Examine **Figure 13** below.

Figure 13

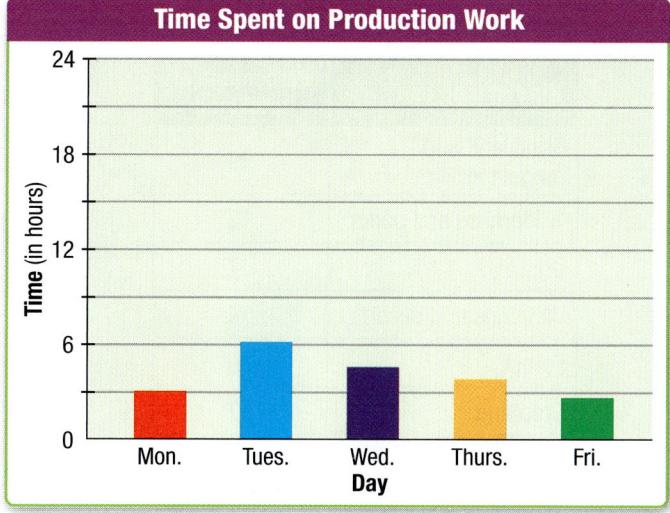

The data are represented accurately in **Figure 13,** but you cannot draw conclusions quickly. Remember that when you create a graph, you want the graph to be as clear as possible. The same data are graphed in **Figure 14,** but the range and scale of the y-axis are smaller than they are in **Figure 13**. The trend in the data is much easier to see in **Figure 14**.

Figure 14

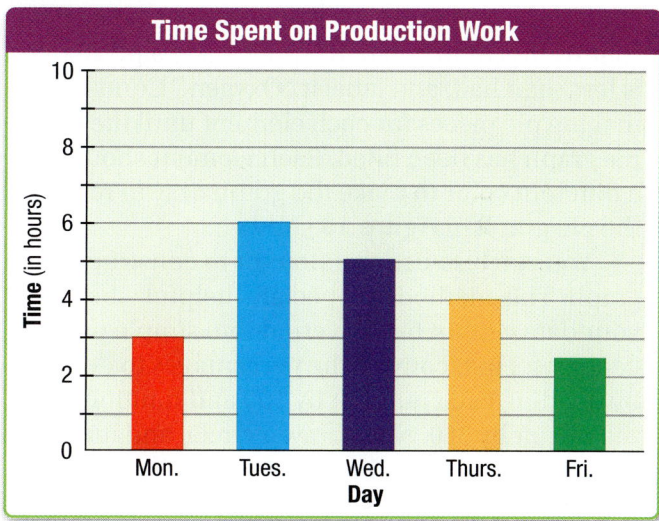

Practice

1. Which day of the week is most productive, according to **Figure 14**?
2. Which day of the week is least productive, according to **Figure 14**?
3. Using the following data, create an easily readable bar graph.

Fiscal period	Money spent (in millions)
First quarter	89
Second quarter	56
Third quarter	72
Fourth quarter	41

Pie Graphs

Pie graphs are an easy way to visualize how parts make up a whole. Often, pie graphs are made from percentage data, such as the data in **Figure 15.**

To create a pie graph, begin by drawing a circle. Because percentages represent parts of 100, imagine dividing the circle into 100 equal parts. Then, you need to figure out how much of the pie each part takes up. It is easiest to start with the largest piece. To graph the data in **Figure 15,** you would start with the data for oxygen. Half of the circle equals 50 parts, so you know that 46% will be slightly less than half of the pie. Shade a piece that is less than half, and label it "Oxygen." Continue making pie pieces for each element until the entire pie graph has been filled. Each element should be a different color to make the graph easy to read as the pie graph in **Figure 16** shows.

You can also use a protractor to construct a pie graph. This method is especially helpful when your data cannot be converted into simple percentages. First, convert the percentages to degrees by dividing each number by 100 and multiplying that result by 360. Next, draw a circle, and make a vertical mark across the top of the circle. Use a protractor to measure the largest angle from your table. Mark this angle along the circumference. For example, 32.9% would be 118° because 32.9/100 = 0.329 and 0.329 × 360 = 118.

To create the next pie piece, measure a second angle from the second mark to make a third mark along the circumference. Continue measuring the angles for each segment until all of your slices are measured. Draw lines from the marks to the center of the circle, and label each slice.

Figure 16 Composition of Earth's Crust

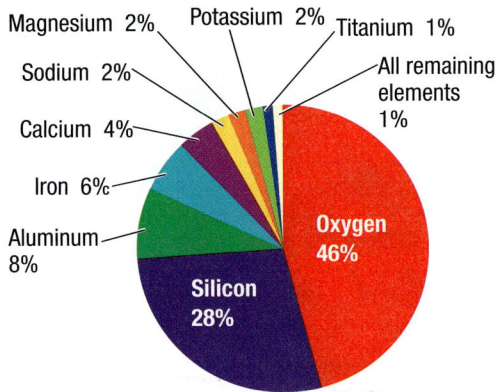

Figure 15 Composition of Earth's Crust

Element	Percentage of Earth's crust
Oxygen	46%
Silicon	28%
Aluminium	8%
Iron	6%
Calcium	4%
Sodium	2%
Magnesium	2%
Potassium	2%
Titanium	1%
All remaining elements	1%

Practice

1. Use the data below to make a pie graph.

Kind of land use	Percentage of total land
Grassland and rangeland	29
Wilderness and parks	13
Urban	7
Wetlands and deserts	4
Forest	30
Cropland	17

2. If humans use half of forests and grasslands, as well as all croplands and urban areas, how much of the total land do humans use?

Technology Skills

Using Search Engines

The World Wide Web is filled with information on almost any topic imaginable. Search engines make it possible to sort through this vast amount of information to find what you need.

A search engine is software that you use to search for Web pages by using keywords. Some search engines let you search huge databases that cover large portions of the Web. Other search engines may search a limited but more focused range of pages, such as the pages on a single Web site or journal articles in a specific subject area.

Although the scope of search engines may differ, most search engines work in a similar way. For example, consider Scirus, a search engine that searches for scientific information. You can access Scirus by entering the Web address *www.scirus.com* into the address bar of your Web browser, as **Figure 17** shows.

Figure 17 Address Bar of Web Browser

Once you are on the Scirus home page, you will see a search box. To find information on a specific topic, type into the search box keywords that you think are most likely to target the web pages about that topic. Then, click on the Search button to start the search. For example, if you are researching black holes, you would type the keywords "black hole." The search engine will return a list of pages containing those keywords. You can then click on the links to visit the pages that seem most promising for your research goals.

Use the help pages to improve your searches.

Although all search engines work in a similar way, they are all slightly different. To make your searches more effective on a particular site, look at the site's help page or advanced search page for helpful tips and advanced search options.

If you search a broad topic, you may get too many Web sites in your search results. The help page or advanced search page can also help you determine the best way to narrow your search so that you will find a more manageable number of Web sites. For example, these pages may allow you to select other keywords to include or exclude from your search, tell you where to look for the keywords on Web pages, and tell you what types of Web sites to include in the search. Suppose that you wanted to find only Web pages that contain information about neutrinos and black holes. You could use the advanced search page to help narrow your results, as **Figure 18** shows.

Figure 18 Advanced Search Page

Check the reliability of Web sites.

When you visit a site to find factual information, remember to check the source of the information. Anyone can post information on the Internet, but the information does not have to be correct. Usually, government and educational institutions are reliable sources of information; personal Web sites may not contain accurate information.

> **Practice**
>
> 1. Use an Internet search engine to find information about gamma rays. List three Web sites, and discuss how reliable each one might be.

APPENDIX B

How Search Engines Work

Most search engines rely on Boolean logic. Boolean logic uses three words—*AND, OR,* and *NOT*—to define the relationships between topics. These three words, known as *Boolean operators,* can be used to make very effective searches.

Use the AND operator to find multiple terms.

When you use the AND operator between two search terms, both of the terms must be present in the results. For example, to find Web pages that contain both the words *work* and *power,* you would enter both search terms, as **Figure 19** shows. The shaded area of the Venn diagram in **Figure 19** represents the results of this search.

Figure 19 Search Results Using AND

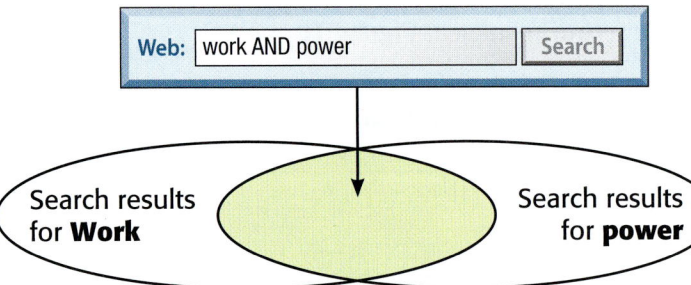

Note that the AND operator is in all capital letters. Some search engines require that you use all capital letters to distinguish the operators from the search terms.

Use the OR operator to find either term.

When you use the OR operator between two search terms, the results should show pages that contain either one or both of the terms. If you use the OR operator, your search result will have more Web pages, as the shaded area in **Figure 20** shows.

Figure 20 Search Results Using OR

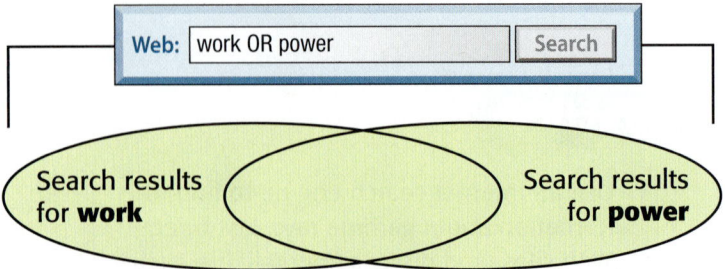

Use the NOT operator to exclude a term.

When you use the NOT operator before a word, your search results should not contain that term. This operator will help you narrow your search by excluding a certain set of Web pages that commonly have the word of the topic that you are looking for. **Figure 21** shows a Venn diagram of the search results for the search "work NOT power."

Figure 21 Search Results Using NOT

Using more than one Boolean operator will make your searches more specific. For example, to find Web sites that contain information about work and power, but not electricity, you would search "work AND power NOT electricity."

Some search engines do not support the direct use of Boolean operators. You may have to go to the advanced search page to do Boolean searches. Many advanced search pages allow you to fill in search fields that are similar to the Boolean operators, as **Figure 22** shows.

Figure 22 Search Fields and Boolean Operators

Advanced search field	Boolean operator
All of the words	AND
Any of the words	OR
None of the words	NOT

Practice

1. Write a Boolean search query to find Web pages that must contain the word *circuit* and either the word *series* or the word *parallel.*

2. Draw a Venn diagram to represent the search query that you wrote in item 1.

APPENDIX B

Technology in the Library

Libraries are one of the best places to find highly reliable reference materials, such as encyclopedias, dictionaries, and nonfiction books. Printed materials are often subject to editing and peer review, unlike much of the information on the Internet. Libraries also have books, magazines, newspapers, and journals that may not be available on the Internet or are expensive to access.

If you do not have a specific source in mind, the best place to start your library research is the library's catalog. Most libraries now have systems for searching their catalogs by computer. So, searching the catalog is similar to using a search engine on the Web. When you are doing a library search, you should specify whether the keywords are for a subject, a title, or an author.

Once you have the results of a catalog search, you will need to know where to find the books that come up in your search results. Most libraries use one of two classification systems—the Library of Congress system or the Dewey decimal system. Whichever system your library uses, you should write down the call numbers for the books that you want to find from your catalog search. Then, use a map or directory of the library to find the books.

Both classification systems organize nonfiction books by subject, as **Figure 23** and **Figure 24** show. Most large libraries use the Library of Congress system, whereas many smaller libraries use the Dewey decimal system.

Figure 24 Library of Congress Classification System

Letter on book binding	Subject
A	General works
B	Philosophy, psychology, and religion
C–F	History
G–H	Geography and social sciences (e.g., anthropology)
J	Political science
K	Law
L	Education
M	Music
N	Fine arts
P	Literature
Q	Science
R	Medicine
S	Agriculture
T	Technology
U–V	Military and naval science
Z	Bibliography and library science

Figure 23 Dewey Decimal System

Number on book binding	Subject
000–099	General works
100–199	Philosophy and psychology
200–299	Religion
300–399	Social studies
400–499	Language
500–599	Pure sciences
600–699	Technology
700–799	Arts
800–899	Literature
900–999	History

Practice

1. What system does your school library use to classify books?
2. List three magazines or journals in your school or local library that could contain current information on scientific research.
3. Name the title and call number for a book on science.

Technology Skills **875**

Scientific Methods

Scientists gain new knowledge and understanding of the natural world by using scientific methods. These methods are sometimes presented in a series of ordered steps. However, there is no single scientific method. The steps may be done in a different order, or certain steps may be repeated in some scientific investigations.

Making Observations Observing objects and events in the natural world is an important step in any scientific method. Observation is usually the starting point of any scientific study. You also make observations when doing experiments. It is important to keep detailed records of observations so that you can accurately remember them.

Asking Questions Careful observations eventually lead to questions. A good question should be specific and should serve as the focus for the entire investigation.

Forming a Hypothesis A hypothesis is a possible explanation or answer to your question. You do not know whether a hypothesis is the right answer until it is tested. You should be able to test your hypothesis to determine whether it is true or false. You should make predictions about what you think will happen if your hypothesis is true and what will happen if your hypothesis is false. These predictions can help you design an experiment to test the hypothesis.

Testing a Hypothesis Once you have a question, a hypothesis, and a set of predictions, you are ready to do an experiment to test the hypothesis. You should design your experiment to be as simple as possible, and you should consider which variables you want to control. Your design should also include plans about what instruments and materials you will use and how you will analyze the data that you collect.

Drawing Conclusions After you finish an experiment, you will determine whether your hypothesis is correct by examining your results. You may evaluate your hypothesis by seeing if your original predictions were correct. If your results do not support your hypothesis, they may lead you to ask more questions. You may need to form a new hypothesis, make new predictions, and perform a new or modified version of your experiment.

Communicating Results If you carry out an investigation that provides new information, you should publish your results. Others who read about your investigation may try to understand how you drew your conclusions. They may try your experiment to see if they get the same results or use your results to form new hypotheses and do new experiments.

Conducting Experiments

Many scientific experiments try to determine a cause-and-effect relationship—"When A happens, B happens." The A and the B in this relationship are variables, or changing quantities. The variable that you change intentionally in an experiment is called the *independent variable* and, in this case, is A. The *dependent variable*, B, changes in response to the changes in the independent variable.

Suppose that your experiment is seeking to answer the following question: "What happens to the speed of a motor when the voltage of the power supply changes?" In this case, voltage would be the independent variable, and the speed of the motor would be the dependent variable. You would change the voltage and then measure the resulting change in speed. When you graph your results, independent variables are represented on the x-axis, and dependent variables are represented on the y-axis.

Make observations in the lab.

You should write down any observations that you make during an experiment, along with any data that you collect. Record the characteristics of the materials that you use, the conditions during your experiment, any changes that occur, and anything that you think might be relevant to the experiment. These observations will help you when you are reporting your results. They can also help you figure out why your experimental results may not be what you expected. Usually, a pen is used to record your observations in a lab notebook because people reading the notes later can be sure that you did not change your notes after the experiment.

Avoid measurement pitfalls.

One common error in taking measurements results from parallax. *Parallax* is an apparent shift in position caused by a change in viewing angle. To avoid parallax errors, always line up your eyes with the part of the measurement scale that you are reading.

Another common measurement error is recording the wrong units of measurement. Always check the instrument to make sure that you know which units it uses, and record those units.

Taking Measurements

It is important to note the limits of the tools that you use to collect data. The exactness of a measurement is called *precision*, and it is determined by the instrument that you use. Precision is reflected in the number of significant figures. When you record measurements, you should use the correct number of significant figures. Usually, instruments with a digital readout give you the correct number of significant figures. So, you can record the measurement exactly as you see it on the instrument. When you need to read the measurement from a scale on an instrument, you should record as many digits as are marked on the scale and estimate one more digit beyond that.

Measure volume with a graduated cylinder.

You should use a graduated cylinder when you need precise measurements of volume.

1. Place the graduated cylinder on a flat, level surface.

2. Make sure that you are at eye level with the surface of the liquid.

3. Read the mark closest to the liquid level. Because most liquids climb slightly up the glass walls of a graduated cylinder, they produce a curved surface called a *meniscus*, shown in **Figure 25.** You should always take volume readings from the bottom of the meniscus.

Tip Holding a piece of white paper behind the graduated cylinder can make the meniscus easier to see.

Figure 25 Meniscus in a Graduated Cylinder

Scientific Methods

APPENDIX B

Measure mass with a balance.

A triple-beam balance, shown in **Figure 26,** can measure mass to a precision of 0.01 g.

1. Make sure that the balance is properly "zeroed." First, make sure that the balance is on a level surface. Then, slide all of the slider weights to zero. Turn the zero adjustment knob until the pointer is in line with the zero at the center of the arrow.

2. Place the object to be measured on the pan. **Caution:** Never place chemicals or hot objects directly on the balance pan.

3. To determine the total mass of the object, add the readings from all three beams.

4. Move the largest slider weight to the right along the beam until the balance tips. Then, move the slider back one notch so that the beam tips back the other way. Repeat this step for the next-largest slider weight. Then, move the smallest slider weight to the right until the pointer points to the zero on the right end.

5. If you are measuring solid chemicals, start by putting a piece of weighing paper on the pan. Record the mass of the weighing paper. Then, place the chemical on the weighing paper. Measure the total mass of the chemical and paper. Then, subtract the mass of the paper to determine the mass of the chemical alone. You may use a similar method for measuring the mass of a liquid in a container.

Tip If you want to use a specified amount of a substance, move the sliders to the right by the amount of mass that you want to obtain. The balance will tip. Slowly add the substance until the balance points to zero.

Measure temperature with a thermometer.

Digital thermometers and bulb thermometers are often used in the lab. Bulb thermometers consist of a column of liquid—either mercury or colored alcohol—in a glass tube, as shown in **Figure 27**. As the liquid heats up, it expands, so the column of liquid rises up the tube.

1. To measure temperature with a digital thermometer, immerse the probe in the liquid or touch it to an object. Wait for the digital readout to stabilize, and then record the temperature. Make sure that the thermometer is set to the desired scale (Celsius or Fahrenheit).

2. To measure temperature with a bulb thermometer, put the thermometer in the liquid to be measured. Wait for the level of colored liquid inside the thermometer to stabilize.

3. With your eyes level with the top of the liquid inside the thermometer, take the reading on the scale next to the column of liquid. Pay attention to the scale on the thermometer. The smallest unit marked on a bulb thermometer is usually 1 °C. These markings are close together, so you can only estimate half a unit between marks, or 0.05 °C.

CAUTION A glass thermometer can break if it hits a solid object or overheats. In addition to producing broken glass, the liquid inside will spill. If a mercury thermometer should ever break, immediately notify your teacher or another adult. Let your teacher clean up the spill. Do not touch the mercury. Because mercury is a hazardous substance, mercury thermometers are rarely used in class laboratories.

Figure 26 Triple-Beam Balance

Figure 27 Alcohol Thermometer

Communicating Scientific Results

Whether you are writing a laboratory report for your teacher or submitting a paper to a scientific journal, you should use a similar structure to report the results of an experiment. Your lab report should contain enough information so that others can use it to reproduce your experiment and compare their results to yours. Laboratory reports should contain the same basic parts.

Start with a title.

Choose a title that clearly conveys the nature of the experiment. The title could describe the subject, the hypothesis, or the result. If you are doing an experiment from a lab manual, this title could be the same as the title of the experiment given in the manual.

Include background information.

The background section should briefly explain why your experiment is important. State the question that your experiment is trying to answer. You could also include a description of the initial observations that led you to the question. Sometimes, the background section includes the basic principles that you will use when you analyze your experiment.

State your hypothesis.

This section should state your hypothesis and your predictions of what will happen if the hypothesis is true and what will happen if the hypothesis if false. Your hypothesis is what you think will happen in the experiment. Often, a hypothesis is written as an "If . . . then" statement. The independent variable, or variable that you will change, should follow the "If" in the statement. The effect on the dependent variable should follow the "then" in the statement. Suppose that you want to find out if adding salt to water changes the boiling temperature of water. You would change the amount of salt that you add to water and measure the temperature at which the water boils. So, the amount of salt would be your independent variable, and the boiling temperature would be your dependent variable. Your hypothesis statement could be "If salt is added to water, the temperature at which water boils will increase."

List your materials before you start your experiment.

To make sure that you have everything that you need for your experiment, list all of the equipment and other supplies that you use in the experiment. For experiments taken from a lab manual, these materials are usually listed in the manual.

Describe the procedure that you used.

Detailed steps that describe exactly how you did your experiment are included in the procedure. Include details about how you set up the equipment, how you took your measurements, and what analysis or calculations you did with your data after collecting it. Your description should be detailed enough that someone else could reproduce the experiment exactly as you did it. If you are doing an experiment from a lab manual, you should write the steps in your own words and note anything that you did that was different from the procedure in the manual.

Record your observations, data, and analysis.

You should list all of the data you collected and show the results of any analysis or calculations that you performed with the data. It is often useful to present data or other results using tables or graphs. Also, include any observations that you made that might be relevant to your conclusions. Some experiments in lab manuals list specific questions that you should answer in your analysis.

End the report with your conclusions.

In your conclusions, you should discuss whether or not your experiment supports your original hypothesis. Remember that your experiment may not support your hypothesis. You can still explain why you think that the experiment did not turn out the way that you expected. You can also present a new or modified hypothesis and briefly describe additional experiments that could be done if you were to continue or expand your investigation. Some experiments in lab manuals list specific questions that you should answer in your conclusions.

APPENDIX C

Figure 1 The Electromagnetic Spectrum

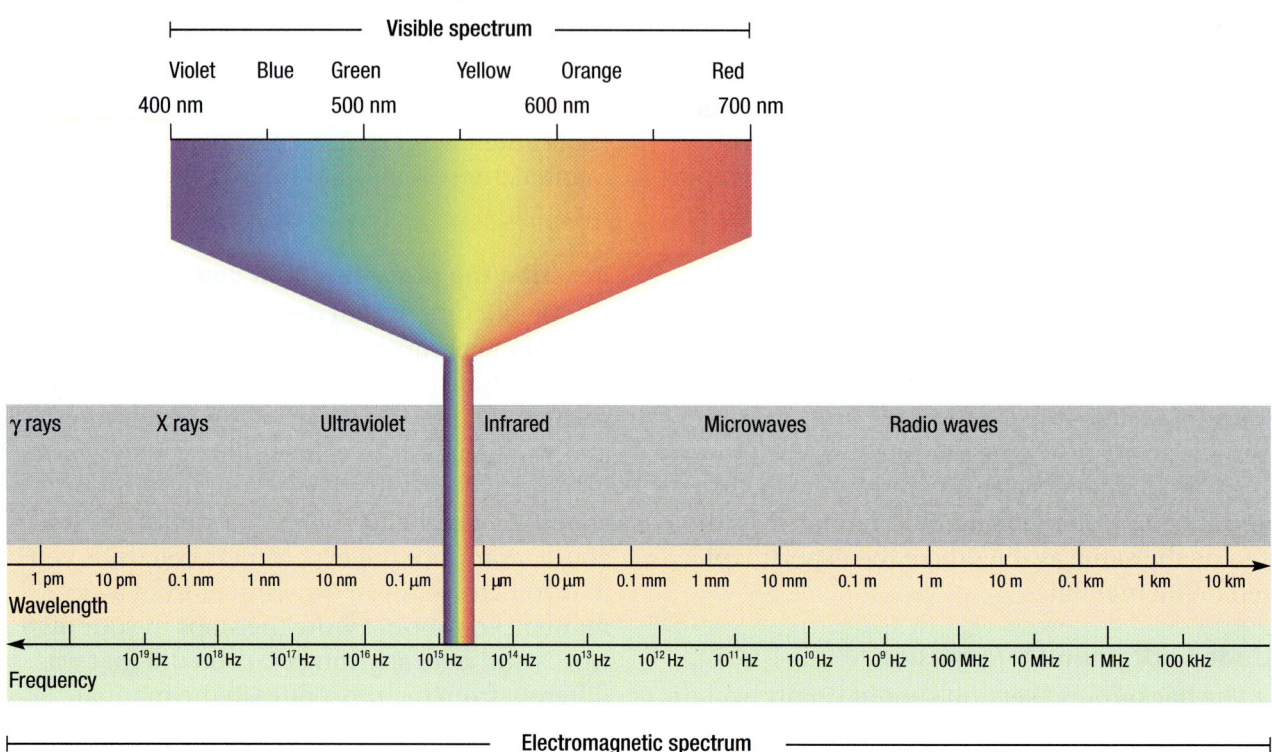

Figure 2 SI Base Units

Quantity	Unit	Symbol
Length	meter	m
Mass	kilogram	kg
Time	second	s
Temperature	kelvin	K
Electric current	ampere	A
Amount of substance	mole	mol
Luminous intensity	candela	cd

Figure 3 Other Commonly Used Units

Quantity	Unit	Symbol	Conversion
Electric charge	coulomb	C	1 A·s
Temperature	degree Celsius	°C	1 K
Frequency	hertz	Hz	1/s
Work and energy	joule	J	$\frac{1 \text{ kg} \cdot \text{m}^2}{\text{s}^2} = 1 \text{ N} \cdot \text{m}$
Force	newton	N	$1 \frac{\text{kg} \cdot \text{m}}{\text{s}^2}$
Pressure	pascal	Pa	$1 \frac{\text{kg}}{\text{m} \cdot \text{s}^2} = 1 \frac{\text{N}}{\text{m}^2}$
Angular displacement	radian	rad	(unitless)
Electric potential difference	volt	V	$1 \frac{\text{kg} \cdot \text{m}^2}{\text{A} \cdot \text{s}^3} = 1 \frac{\text{J}}{\text{C}}$
Power	watt	W	$1 \frac{\text{kg} \cdot \text{m}^2}{\text{s}^3} = 1 \frac{\text{J}}{\text{s}}$
Resistance	ohm	Ω	$1 \frac{\text{kg} \cdot \text{m}^2}{\text{A}^2 \cdot \text{s}^3} = 1 \frac{\text{V}}{\text{A}}$

Figure 4 Densities of Various Materials

Material	Density (g/cm³)
Air, dry	1.293×10^{-3}
Aluminum	2.70
Bone	1.7–2.0
Brick, common	1.9
Butter	0.86–0.87
Carbon (diamond)	3.5155
Carbon (graphite)	2.2670
Copper	8.96
Cork	0.22–0.26
Ethanol	0.783
Gasoline	0.7
Gold	19.3
Helium	1.78×10^{-4}
Iron	7.86
Lead	11.3
Mercury	13.5336
Paper	0.7–1.15
Rock salt	2.18
Silver	10.5
Sodium	0.97
Stainless steel	8.02
Steel	7.8
Sugar	1.59
Water (at 25 °C)	0.99705
Water (ice)	0.917

Figure 5 Specific Heats

Material	c (J/kg·K)
Acetic acid (CH_3COOH)	2,070
Air	1,007
Aluminum (Al)	897
Calcium (Ca)	647
Calcium carbonate ($CaCO_3$)	818
Carbon (C, diamond)	487
Carbon (C, graphite)	709
Carbon dioxide (CO_2)	843
Copper (Cu)	385
Ethanol (CH_3CH_2OH)	2,440
Gold (Au)	129
Helium (He)	5,193
Hematite (Fe_2O_3)	650
Hydrogen (H_2)	14,304
Hydrogen peroxide (H_2O_2)	2,620
Iron (Fe)	449
Lead (Pb)	129
Magnetite (Fe_3O_4)	619
Mercury (Hg)	140
Methane (CH_4)	2,200
Neon (Ne)	1,030
Nickel (Ni)	444
Nitrogen (N_2)	1,040
Oxygen (O_2)	918
Platinum (Pt)	133
Silver (Ag)	234
Sodium (Na)	1,228
Sodium chloride (NaCl)	864
Tin (Sn)	228
Tungsten (W)	132
Water (H_2O)	4,186
Zinc (Zn)	388

Values at 25 °C and 1 atm pressure

APPENDIX C

Figure 6 Properties of the Planets

Planet	Diameter (km)	Average surface temperature (°C)	Number of moons	Atmosphere
Mercury	4,879	350	0	Essentially none
Venus	12,104	460	0	Thick: carbon dioxide, nitrogen
Earth	12,756	20	1	Nitrogen, oxygen
Mars	6,794	−23	2	Thin: carbon dioxide
Jupiter	142,984	−130	63	Hydrogen, helium, ammonia, methane
Saturn	120,536	−180	47	Hydrogen, helium, ammonia, methane
Uranus	51,118	−210	27	Hydrogen, helium, ammonia, methane
Neptune	49,528	−220	13	Hydrogen, helium, methane

Figure 7 International Weather Symbols

Current weather

Hail	△	Light drizzle	9	Light rain	°	Light snow	*
Freezing rain	∽	Steady, light drizzle	9 9	Steady, light rain	° °	Steady, light snow	* *
Smoke	⌒	Intermittent, moderate drizzle	9/9	Intermittent, moderate rain	°/°	Intermittent, moderate snow	*/*
Tornado	)(	Steady, moderate drizzle	9 9,9	Steady, moderate rain	° °,°	Steady, moderate snow	* *,*
Dust storms	⇳	Intermittent, heavy drizzle	9/9/9	Intermittent, heavy rain	°/°/°	Intermittent, heavy snow	*/*/*
Fog	≡	Steady, heavy drizzle	9 9,9 9	Steady, heavy rain	° °,° °	Steady, heavy snow	* *,* *
Thunderstorm	⎡						
Lightning	⟨						
Hurricane	𝕾						

Cloud coverage

Clear	○	Scattered	◔	Four-eighths covered	◑	Seven-eighths covered	◕
One-eighth Coverage	⊘	Three-eighths covered	◔	Five-eighths covered	◕	Overcast	●

Clouds

Low:	Stratus	—	Cumulus	⌒	Cumulonimbus calvus	⌂
	Stratocumulus	⌣	Cumulus congestus	⌂	Cumulonimbus with anvil	⛉
Middle:	Altostratus	∠	Altocumulus	⌒	Altocumulus castellanus	M
High:	Cirrus	⌒	Cirrostratus	2	Cirrocumulus	⌇

Wind speed (in km/h)

Calm	◎	4–13	⌐	24–33	⌐⌐		
1–3	—	14–23	⌐⌐	34–40	⌐⌐⌐		

APPENDIX C

Figure 8 Sky Maps for the Northern Hemisphere

Facing North / **Facing North**

Facing South / **Facing South**

DATE	LOCAL TIME	D.S.T.
January 1	Midnight	1 AM
January 15	11 PM	Midnight
February 1	10 PM	11 PM
February 15	9 PM	10 PM
March 1	8 PM	9 PM
etc.		

MAGNITUDES: -1, 0, 1, 2, 3, 4, 5

- Variable Stars
- Open Star Cluster
- Globular Star Cluster
- Nebula
- Galaxy

Useful Data **883**

APPENDIX C

Figure 9 The World: Physical

APPENDIX C

Useful Data **885**

APPENDIX C

Figure 10 Map of Natural Resources in the United States

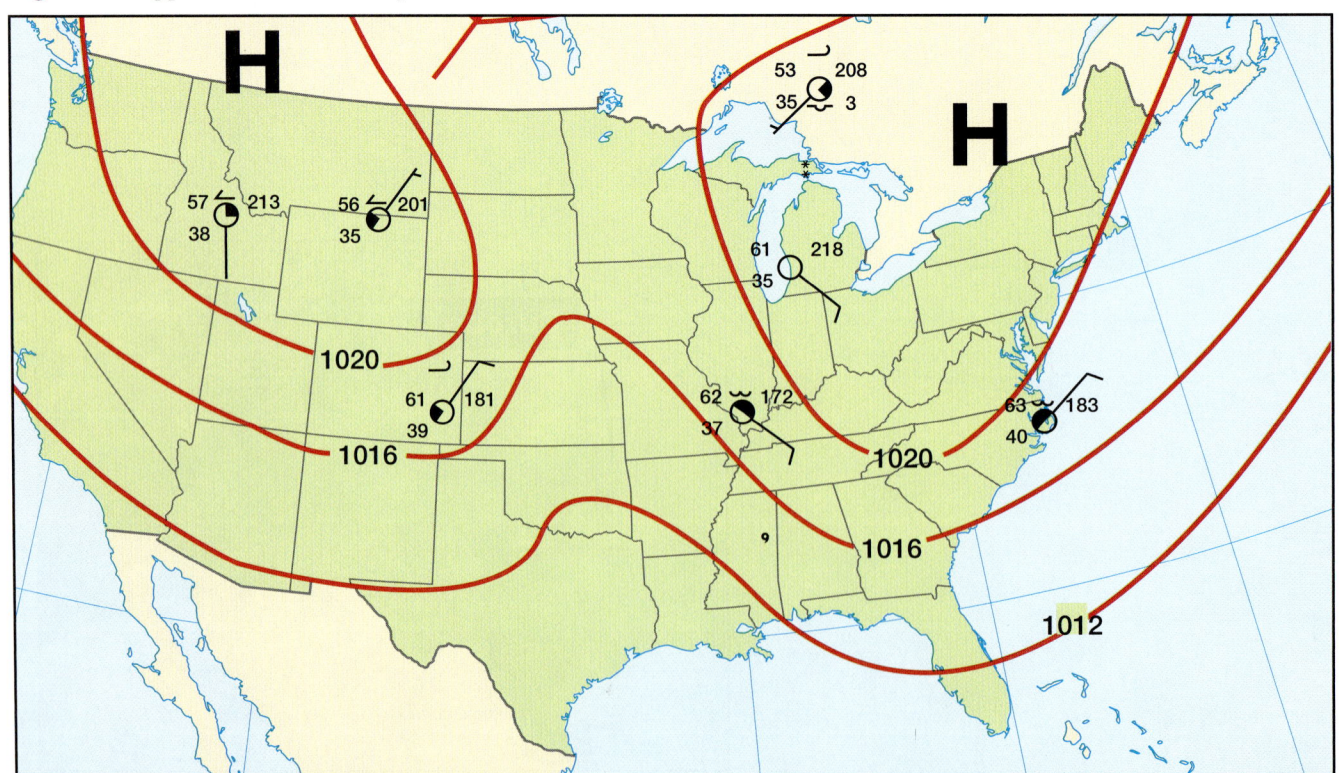

Figure 11 Typical Weather Map

Selected Math Answers

Chapter 1
Introduction to Science

Practice, page 19
2. 1,600 g
4. 6,100 mA

Section 2 Review, page 21
10. 420 m

Practice, page 25
2. a. 4,500 g
   b. 0.0000000199 cm

Practice, page 26
2. a. 5.5×10^5 cm^2
   b. 6.9 g/cm^3

Section 3 Review, page 28
6. a. 9.20×10^7 m^2
   b. 9.66×10^{-5} cm^2

Chapter Review, page 37
28. a. 2.6×10^{14} A•s
    b. 6.42×10^{-7} m^3/s
30. a. 133 m^2
    b. 210 L/min

Chapter 2
Matter

Practice, page 54
2. 3.26 g/cm^3

Section 2 Review, page 58
6. 1.4×10^{-4} g/cm^3

Science Skills Practice, page 68
2. 0.001 g/mm^3
4. greater; 700,000 g/m^3

Chapter Review, page 71
24. 4.5 g/cm^3
26. 61 cm^3

Chapter 3
States of Matter

Section 3 Review, page 94
8. 273 Pa

Practice, page 98
2. 200 mL

Section 4 Review, page 101
10. 3.50×10^3 L

Chapter Review, page 107
26. 5×10^3 N
28. 12 L

Chapter 4
Atoms

Section 2 Review, page 127
14. 620 g Hg
16. 51.3 mol He

Chapter Review, page 139
28. 407 g Al

Chapter 6
The Structure of Matter

Practice, page 193
2. BeCl$_2$

Practice, page 196
2. BH$_3$

Section 3 Review, page 196
6. H$_2$SO$_4$

Chapter Review, page 211
24. a. Sr(NO$_3$)$_2$
    b. NaCN
    c. Cr(OH)$_3$

Chapter 7
Chemical Reactions

Science Skills Practice, page 250
2. 323.0 g ZnSO$_4$

Chapter Review, page 253
20. $2HgO \rightarrow 2Hg + O_2$

Chapter 8
Solutions

Practice, page 280
2. 1.27 M

Section 3 Review, page 281
8. 0.374 M

Chapter Review, page 287
24. 0.600 mol LiCl
26. 40.6 g NaF

Chapter 9
Acids, Bases, and Salts

Practice, page 299
2. pH = 2

Section 1 Review, page 300
10. 1×10^{-11} M

Chapter Review, page 319
28. pH = 3
30. 1×10^{-6} M

APPENDIX D

Chapter 10
Nuclear Changes

Practice, page 331

2. $A = 4$
   $Z = 2$
   $X = $ He
   Alpha decay occurs, and $^{4}_{2}$He is produced.

4. $A = 208$
   $Z = 81$
   $X = $ Tl
   Alpha decay occurs, and $^{208}_{81}$Tl is produced.

Practice, page 334

2. 15.3 days
4. 29.1 years

Section 1 Review, page 336

6. $A = 131$
   $Z = 54$
   $X = $ Xe
   $^{131}_{54}$Xe

8. 2×10^6 years

Science Skills Practice, 354

2. 3 half-lives

Chapter Review, page 357

30. a. $^{212}_{83}\text{Bi} \rightarrow \,^{208}_{81}\text{Tl} + \,^{4}_{2}\text{He}$
    $^{208}_{81}\text{Tl} \rightarrow \,^{208}_{82}\text{Pb} + \,^{0}_{-1}e$
    b. $^{212}_{83}\text{Bi} \rightarrow \,^{212}_{84}\text{Po} + \,^{0}_{-1}e$
    $^{212}_{84}\text{Po} \rightarrow \,^{208}_{82}\text{Pb} + \,^{4}_{2}\text{He}$

Chapter 11
Motion

Practice, page 369

2. 22 m/s toward first base

Section 1 Review, page 371

6. 400 s or 6.67 min

Practice, page 375

2. 0.075 m/s^2 toward the shore
4. 0.85 s

Section 2 Review, page 377

6. acceleration = 2.5 m/s^2

Chapter Review, page 391

22. 6.6 h
24. 5.4 s

Chapter 12
Forces

Practice, page 401

2. 0.14 kg
4. 2.2 m/s^2 forward

Section 1 Review, page 402

6. 0.26 m/s^2 forward

Section 2 Review, page 410

6. 4,000,000 N

Practice, page 415

2. 6 m/s forward

Science Skills Practice, page 420

2. 3.5 m/s^2 in a backward direction (deceleration)

Chapter Review, page 423

22. 3.7 N

Chapter 13
Work and Energy

Practice, page 432

2. 1 J
4. 6,000 J

Practice, page 434

2. a. 146 W
   b. 175 W

Practice, page 436

2. 78 N

Section 1 Review, page 437

6. MA = 2.40
8. 2.0×10^4 W, 27 hp

Practice, page 446

2. 15 m

Practice, page 448

2. 3.3 m/s

Section 3 Review, page 452

8. 900 J

Practice, page 460

2. work input = 4,800 J

Section 4 Review, page 461

8. a. useful work output = 780 J
   b. 780 W

Chapter Review, page 467

24. a. 850 J
    b. 170 W
    c. 4

APPENDIX D

Chapter 14
Heat and Temperature

Practice, page 477
2. Row 1: 70 °F, 294 K
   Row 2: 115 °C, 239 °F
   Row 3: −321 °F, 77 K
   Row 4: 43 °C, 316 K
4. d

Section 1 Review, page 479
6. 68.0 °F, 293 K

Practice, page 486
2. 28,000 J (28 kJ)

Section 2 Review, page 487
6. 550 kJ

Science Skills Practice, page 496
2. 1.0 kg

Chapter Review, page 499
24. −270 °C, −454 °F
26. 480 J/kg•K

Chapter 15
Waves

Practice, page 519
2. 5.77×10^{14} Hz

Section 2 Review, page 523
8. 0.77 m

Chapter Review, page 535
30. 3.0 m/s
32. 440.0 Hz

Chapter 16
Sound and Light

Science Skills Practice, page 576
2. 1.36×10^3 W/m^2

Chapter Review, page 579
30. 41 m
32. 5.5×10^{14} Hz

Chapter 17
Electricity

Practice, page 597
2. 240 Ω
4. 0.43 A

Section 2 Review, page 599
8. 0.5 A

Practice, page 606
2. 1.6×10^{-2} W
4. 120 V

Section 3 Review, page 607
8. 40 W

Chapter Review, page 613
24. b
26. 120 V
28. 1.6 A

Selected Math Answers **889**

APPENDIX E

Answers to Reading Checks

Chapter 1
Introduction to Science

Section 1, page 7
Roentgen repeated his experiment.

Section 1, page 9
A scientific law explains how something works but does not explain why it happens. A scientific theory explains why something happens.

Section 1, page 11
Models can be pictures on paper, real objects, and mental pictures.

Section 2, page 15
No, the sequence of steps in a scientific method can vary depending on the question that you are trying to answer.

Section 2, page 16
Scientists should publish their results so the results can be reviewed by other scientists.

Section 2, page 18
SI units are used to express very small or large measurements, so that you do not have to write many zeros.

Section 3, page 23
I should use a line graph to represent data that changes continuously during an experiment.

Section 3, page 24
I should use scientific notation when working with very large or very small numbers.

Section 3, page 27
The answer should have as many significant figures as the least precise value that I am adding.

Chapter 2
Matter

Section 1, page 46
No, elements cannot be broken down into simpler substances.

Section 1, page 48
Compounds are pure substances because they have fixed compositions and definite properties.

Section 2, page 52
Answers should list five physical properties. Physical properties include shape, color, mass, odor, texture, state, melting point, boiling point, strength, hardness, density, and the ability to conduct electricity, magnetism, or heat.

Section 2, page 54
Water's density is 1.00 g/mL.

Section 2, page 56
Two chemical properties are flammability and reactivity.

Section 3, page 61
Physical changes do not change the identity of a substance, whereas chemical changes do.

Section 3, page 63
Compounds can be broken down only by chemical changes because compounds are made of atoms that are chemically combined. Mixtures can be separated by physical changes because substances in a mixture are not chemically combined.

Chapter 3
States of Matter

Section 1, page 79
Liquids do not change volume, but gases do.

Section 1, page 80
Temperature is a measure of the average kinetic energy of the particles in an object.

Section 2, page 85
Answers may vary. One example of sublimation is dry ice changing into gaseous carbon dioxide.

Section 2, page 86
The freezing and melting points are the same.

Section 3, page 91
A substance that is denser than another substance will sink in that substance, whereas a substance that is less dense will float.

Section 3, page 92
A small force is applied to a small area. This force exerts pressure on a liquid in the device. The pressure is transmitted equally to a larger area, where the pressure creates a larger force.

Section 4, page 97
Boyle's law relates pressure and volume.

Section 4, page 99
The pressure decreases.

Chapter 4
Atoms

Section 1, page 114
Dalton and Democritus both believed that atoms are the fundamental units of matter and that atoms are indivisible.

Section 1, page 117
Rutherford's results were surprising because they did not match his predictions based on Thomson's model of the atom. He expected most of the positive particles to pass straight through, but instead, several were deflected at large angles.

Section 2, page 121
The atomic number defines the element because atoms of each element always have the same number of protons but can have different numbers of neutrons.

Section 2, page 122
The isotope tritium ($A = 3$) has the most mass.

Section 2, page 125
A mole of iron contains 6.022×10^{23} iron atoms.

Section 3, page 129
In earlier atomic models, electrons were considered to be particles. In the electron-wave model, electrons act more like waves than like particles.

Section 3, page 131
An electron jumps to an excited state when it absorbs a photon.

Chapter 5
The Periodic Table

Section 1, page 146
Mendeleev left gaps in his periodic table for the new elements that he predicted would be discovered. These gaps were needed to make the patterns work out correctly.

Section 2, page 153
Group 1 and group 17 elements easily form ions because the addition or removal of a single electron creates a full outer energy level.

Section 2, page 154
The category "metals" contains the most elements, and the category "semiconductors" contains the least elements.

Section 3, page 157
Alkali metals are reactive because each atom has one valence electron that can easily be removed. Thus, they form compounds very easily.

Section 3, page 159
Answers will vary. Transition metals include gold, silver, platinum, and titanium.

Section 3, page 161
The noble gases are unreactive because their s and p orbitals are full of electrons.

Section 3, page 163
Answers will vary but could include chlorophyll, glucose, and isooctane.

Chapter 6
The Structure of Matter

Section 1, page 178
A ball-and-stick model shows bond lengths, and a space-filling model shows relative atom sizes.

Section 1, page 180
The hardness of minerals is explained by the fact that their chemical structure consists of rigid networks of bonded atoms.

Section 2, page 184
In an ionic bond, ions are held together by the attraction between their opposite charges.

Section 2, page 186
Covalently bonded atoms are held together by the sharing of electrons between the atoms.

Section 2, page 189
Parentheses are used in a chemical formula to represent the fact that a polyatomic ion acts as a single unit.

Section 3, page 192
The number of each kind of ion in a compound is determined by whatever number of those ions will give a charge of zero to the compound.

Section 3, page 194
An empirical formula shows the simplest possible ratio of atoms present in a compound.

Section 4, page 199
The shortest carbon chain with more than one possible arrangement is one with four carbon atoms; carbon chains with three or fewer carbon atoms cannot form branched chains.

Section 4, page 201
A polymer is a molecule that is a long chain of smaller molecules called *monomers*.

Section 4, page 202
You need to eat carbohydrates so your body can get the energy that it needs.

Chapter 7
Chemical Reactions

Section 1, page 221
Most of the energy that is released in a chemical reaction comes from the stored energy in chemical bonds.

Section 1, page 222
An exothermic reaction is a reaction that releases energy, and an endothermic reaction is a reaction that absorbs energy.

Section 2, page 226
Chemical equations should be balanced so that they accurately show the conservation of mass in a chemical reaction.

Section 3, page 231
Decomposition reactions are the opposite processes of synthesis reactions.

Section 3, page 233
In all single-displacement reactions, one reactant changes place with part of another reactant.

Section 3, page 235
A free radical, an atom or molecule with an unpaired electron, is very reactive because electrons tend to form pairs with each other.

Section 4, page 239
Reactions are faster at higher temperatures because molecular motion is greater at higher temperatures, so more-frequent collisions between molecules occur.

Section 4, page 241
An enzyme catalyzes biological reactions.

Section 4, page 244
When a soda bottle is opened, the pressure of the gas on top of the soda is released, so the dissolved gas in the soda can come out of solution.

Chapter 8
Solutions

Section 1, page 260
The particles will settle out of a suspension if it is left undisturbed.

Section 1, page 263
Atoms, ions, or molecules of solute are present in a solution.

Section 1, page 264
A solid, liquid, or gas can be mixed with a liquid to form a solution.

Section 2, page 269
Hydrogen bonding occurs between the hydrogen atom of one water molecule and the oxygen atom of another molecule.

Section 2, page 271
Increasing the surface area of a solid exposes more of the molecules in the solid to the solvent. So, there are more collisions between the solute and the solvent molecules, and the solid dissolves faster.

Section 3, page 277
Sodium iodide is soluble because the forces between the water molecules and the sodium ions and the iodide ions are much greater than the forces between the sodium ions and iodide ions in the crystal.

Section 3, page 278
The solute will not dissolve and will sink to the bottom of the solution.

Chapter 9
Acids, Bases, and Salts

Section 1, page 295
I should wear safety goggles, gloves, and a laboratory apron when working with acids.

Section 1, page 296
Metal hydroxides are strong bases because they dissociate completely when they dissolve in water.

Section 1, page 298
The pH of a solution tells me how acidic or basic a solution is by telling me the concentration of hydroxide ions in solution.

Section 2, page 303
Water and a salt form when an acid reacts with a base. When a weak base reacts with a strong acid, the resulting solution will be acidic.

Section 2, page 305
Answers may vary. Sample answer: Salts are used in ceramic glazes, as chalk, and as a highway de-icer.

Section 3, page 309
Detergents do not form soap scum, so they are used instead of soap.

Section 3, page 310
Chlorine gas will be produced if an acid is mixed with bleach.

Chapter 10
Nuclear Changes

Section 1, page 328
An alpha particle is the nucleus of a helium atom.

Section 1, page 330
The mass number does not change, but the atomic number increases by 1.

Section 2, page 338
The maximum number of protons in a stable nucleus is 83.

Section 2, page 340
A nuclear chain reaction is triggered by a single neutron that strikes a nucleus.

Section 3, page 349
There is more energy in the known reserves of uranium than in the known reserves of coal and oil.

Chapter 11
Motion

Section 1, page 366
Distance measures how far an object travels along a path. Displacement measures how far it is between the starting and ending points of the path.

Section 1, page 368
Average speed is calculated by dividing the distance traveled by the time it takes to travel that distance.

Section 2, page 373
Any object standing still on Earth's surface is traveling in a circle (accelerating) as Earth revolves, including people.

Section 2, page 374
A positive velocity means that an object is speeding up, and a negative velocity means that an object is slowing down.

Section 3, page 382
When an unbalanced force acts on an object, the object accelerates in the direction of the combined force.

Chapter 12
Forces

Section 1, page 398
Inertia is directly related to mass; the larger an object's mass is, the greater its inertia will be.

Section 1, page 401
The newton (N) is the SI unit of force. The pound (lb) is also used to measure force.

Section 2, page 404
Mass is a measure of how much matter is in an object; weight is a measure of the gravitational force that acts on an object. Weight depends on the gravitational force at a location, but mass does not depend on an object's location.

Section 2, page 406
Gravitational force increases as mass increases.

Section 2, page 408
Astronauts seem weightless because they are accelerating toward Earth at the same rate as their spacecraft. They are in free fall.

Section 3, page 413
Force pairs do not cancel out each other because the action and reaction forces do not act on the same object.

Section 3, page 414
Momentum is proportional to the mass and velocity of an object.

Chapter 13
Work and Energy

Section 1, page 433
The SI unit for power is the watt, which equals 1 J/s.

Section 1, page 434
Machines make work easier by either multiplying a force or changing the direction of the applied force.

Answers to Reading Checks

APPENDIX E

Section 2, page 440
The mechanical advantage of a single fixed pulley is one.

Section 2, page 442
The wedge and the screw are both modified inclined planes.

Section 3, page 445
A stretched rubber band has elastic potential energy.

Section 3, page 447
The SI unit for kinetic energy is the joule.

Section 3, page 449
Chemical energy depends on the relative positions of the atoms in molecules.

Section 4, page 454
The potential energy on a roller coaster is smallest at the roller coaster's lowest point.

Section 4, page 457
An open system exchanges both energy and matter with the surroundings. A closed system exchanges energy, but not matter, with the surroundings.

Section 4, page 459
Energy may be lost as heat, sound, and vibrations.

Chapter 14
Heat and Temperature

Section 1, page 474
The temperature of a substance is proportional to the kinetic energy of its particles.

Section 1, page 476
The Celsius temperature scale has 0 defined as the freezing point of water, whereas the Kelvin temperature scale has 0 defined as absolute zero.

Section 2, page 482
Radiation differs from conduction and convection because radiation does not involve the movement of matter and therefore can take place in a vacuum.

Section 2, page 484
A material through which energy can be easily transferred as heat is a good conductor.

Section 3, page 491
The second law of thermodynamics states that disorder will always increase in a system left to itself.

Chapter 15
Waves

Section 1, page 506
No, light waves are not mechanical. They are electromagnetic.

Section 1, page 508
Most waves are caused by vibrating objects.

Section 1, page 511
Answers may vary. One example of a transverse wave is an electromagnetic wave.

Section 1, page 512
In a transverse wave, the wave motion and the vibrations are perpendicular. In a longitudinal wave, they are parallel.

Section 2, page 515
The wavelength can be measured from any two identical, consecutive points, such as from crest to crest.

Section 2, page 516
Period and frequency are inversely related.

Section 2, page 518
Wave speed equals wavelength divided by period, or wavelength times frequency.

Section 2, page 521
Sound waves travel faster in solids than in liquids or gases because the particles are closer together and, thus, can transfer vibrations faster.

Section 3, page 525
Answers may vary. One example of diffraction is hearing sounds from inside a room when you are standing outside the room's doorway.

Section 3, page 526
Both involve the bending of waves. Diffraction is the bending of waves around an obstacle, whereas refraction is the bending that occurs when a wave passes into a new medium.

Chapter 16
Sound and Light

Section 1, page 545
The amplitude determines the intensity of a sound wave.

Section 1, page 546
The lowest frequency that humans can hear is 20 Hz, and the highest frequency that humans can hear is 20,000 Hz.

894 Answers to Reading Checks

Section 1, page 548
Resonance amplifies sound because two objects are vibrating at the same frequency.

Section 2, page 553
The particle model of light can be used to explain why blue light can knock electrons out of a metal plate but red light cannot.

Section 2, page 555
The intensity of light depends on the number of photons per second that pass through a certain area of space.

Section 2, page 557
Answers may include heat lamps, weather satellites, and computer mice, all of which use infrared light.

Section 3, page 560
Light rays are used to model reflection and refraction.

Section 3, page 562
A virtual image is the result of the apparent path of the light rays and appears to be behind the mirror.

Section 4, page 567
The fish seems closer because the light rays coming from the fish bend away from the normal when they pass from water to air. The cat sees a virtual image of the fish.

Section 4, page 567
A converging lens can create a real image.

Chapter 17
Electricity

Section 1, page 586
Like charges repel and unlike charges attract each other.

Section 1, page 589
Charging by friction causes static electricity.

Section 1, page 591
Electric force depends on charge and distance.

Section 2, page 594
Potential difference is commonly called *voltage*.

Section 2, page 596
The resistance equation is called *Ohm's law*.

Section 3, page 601
Switches are used to interrupt the electric current in a circuit.

Section 3, page 602
Standardized symbols are used to draw schematic diagrams.

Chapter 18
Magnetism

Section 1, page 620
Heating or hammering a soft magnetic material can reduce its magnetism.

Section 1, page 622
Magnetic field lines have no beginning and no ending. They always form closed loops.

Section 2, page 627
Your thumb points in the direction of the current when using the right-hand rule.

Section 2, page 628
The more loops of wire there are in a solenoid, the stronger the magnetic field is.

Section 3, page 634
You must move a closed loop of wire within a magnetic field to produce a current using a generator.

Section 3, page 637
Answers may include running water, burning coal, nulcear fission, wind, geothermal power, and solar power.

Chapter 19
The Solar System

Section 1, page 654
Some plants respond to the sun's light by opening or closing their petals. Also, many animals develop active and inactive schedules, such as waking and sleeping, in response to the sun.

Section 1, page 656
Gravity is the major force that keeps satellites in orbit around planets.

Section 1, page 658
A lunar eclipse is caused when the moon passes through the shadow of Earth.

Section 2, page 663
Earth has liquid water on its surface and is the only planet known to harbor life.

Section 2, page 664
Mars appears red because of the iron oxide in its soil.

Section 2, page 666
The gas giants are larger than the inner planets; have thick, gaseous atmospheres; and have many more moons than the inner planets.

APPENDIX E

Section 2, page 669
Changes in the orbit of Uranus caused by another gravitational body allowed astronomers to predict the presence of Neptune before seeing it.

Section 3, page 672
The heliocentric model puts the sun at the center of the solar system. The geocentric model puts Earth at the center of the solar system.

Section 3, page 675
When a comet is near the sun, the energy of the sun causes a long tail to form, which makes the comet easier to see.

Section 3, page 676
The Kuiper Belt is made up of planetesimals and small rocky bodies left over from the formation of the solar system.

Chapter 20
The Universe

Section 1, page 695
Telescopes in space can study a wider range of the electromagnetic spectrum than telescopes on the ground can.

Section 1, page 696
Each element produces a unique set of spectral lines, so astronomers can analyze spectral lines to discover the composition of a star.

Section 1, page 699
The sun will eventually become a red giant and then a white dwarf.

Section 1, page 700
Black holes can be located indirectly by observing the radiation from objects that revolve around them.

Section 2, page 703
Space would be a veil of gas spread fairly evenly through space if gravity did not exist.

Section 2, page 705
An elliptical galaxy has no spiral arms, has less dust and gas, and contains mostly older stars than a spiral galaxy contains.

Section 3, page 709
Light takes time to travel through space. We see an object as it looked when light left it, which may have been thousands of years ago.

Section 3, page 711
Observations of the universe indicate that most objects, such as galaxies, are moving away from one another. So, going backward in time, the objects would move toward each other and eventually meet at a single point.

Section 3, page 713
The big bang theory is the theory best supported by the current observational evidence for the shape and movements of the universe.

Section 3, page 715
The amount of mass will determine whether the universe expands forever, reaches stasis, or contracts on itself.

Chapter 21
Planet Earth

Section 1, page 730
The pressure due to the weight of the mantle and crust is so great that the metals cannot turn into gases, despite the high temperatures.

Section 1, page 732
The plate tectonics theory describes the movements of the parts of the lithosphere known as *tectonic plates.*

Section 1, page 735
Oceanic plates are denser than continental plates and therefore sink beneath the continental plates.

Section 1, page 736
The Indian plate is still colliding with the Eurasian plate, albeit very slowly.

Section 2, page 739
The epicenter of an earthquake is located on Earth's surface directly above the focus.

Section 2, page 741
Scientists can use the data from three or more seismograph stations by determining where the radii of the circles intersect.

Section 2, page 742
Each step up on the Richter scale is 30 times as powerful as the preceding number.

Section 2, page 745
The sinking plate melts in the mantle, and the resulting magma rises to the surface.

Section 3, page 749
Intrusive igneous rocks cool while trapped beneath Earth's surface. Extrusive igneous rocks cool on Earth's surface.

Section 3, page 751
Rocks may undergo metamorphosis through the application of heat alone or through the combined application of heat and pressure.

Section 3, page 752
The forces of weathering and erosion break down rocks into sediment.

Section 4, page 757
H_2CO_3

Section 4, page 758
Answers may include objects made of metal or rock, including statues, buildings, or bridges.

Section 4, page 760
Fast-moving wind can carry sediment that erodes rock through abrasion.

Chapter 22
The Atmosphere

Section 1, page 775
The stratosphere gets warmer with increasing altitude because the ozone layer in the stratosphere absorbs solar radiation.

Section 1, page 776
At night, ion density is lower because fewer solar rays pass through the ionosphere. Therefore, at night radio transmissions can go higher in the atmosphere before being bounced back by ionized particles.

Section 1, page 778
The ozone in the upper atmosphere protects living things on Earth from much of the sun's radiation.

Section 1, page 779
Certain atmospheric gases keep Earth warm by absorbing radiation from the sun and returning it to Earth.

Section 2, page 783
Clouds are made of tiny droplets of liquid water.

Section 2, page 785
The height of a mercury barometer indicates the air pressure.

Section 3, page 790
A cold front often causes high winds and thunderstorms.

Section 3, page 792
The energy in a hurricane comes from the condensation of rising moist air.

Chapter 23
Using Natural Resources

Section 1, page 809
Ecosystems are maintained when all of the elements in the ecosystem, both living and nonliving, are balanced with respect to one another.

Section 1, page 811
Answers may mention changes in temperatures; changes in the landscape, such as trees losing their leaves; the migration of animals; and the stage of an organism's life cycle.

Section 1, page 812
Answers may include earthquakes, volcanic eruptions, meteor strikes, catastrophic fires, glacial periods, or any other natural event that may alter the balance of an ecosystem.

Section 2, page 816
Fossil fuels come from the remains of ancient plants and animals that have been altered by heat and pressure for millions of years.

Section 2, page 818
Different areas of the world experience different amounts of sunlight. Some areas receive more direct sunlight than others. Areas that produce a lot of rain or have a lot of cloud cover, for example, are less suited to capturing solar energy than areas such as a desert.

Section 2, page 820
Water pours through turbines, which causes them to spin. The turbines are connected to electric generators. As the generators spin, they produce electricity.

Section 3, page 826
Acidic precipitation can erode metal and rock, contaminate water supplies, leach nutrients from soil, and damage plant life.

Section 3, page 828
Eutrophication reduces the amount of oxygen that is available in the water supply. As a result, fish may not get enough oxygen and die.

GLOSSARY • GLOSARIO

absolute zero (AB suh LOOT ZIR oh) the temperature at which molecular energy is at a minimum (0 K on the Kelvin scale or –273.15 °C on the Celsius scale) (476)

cero absoluto la temperatura a la que la energía molecular es mínima (0 K en la escala de Kelvin ó –273.15 °C en la escala de Celsius) (476)

acceleration (ak SEL uhr AY shuhn) the rate at which velocity changes over time; an object accelerates if its speed, direction, or both change (372)

aceleración la tasa a la que la velocidad cambia con el tiempo; un objeto acelera si su rapidez cambia, si su dirección cambia, o si tanto su rapidez como su dirección cambian (372)

accuracy (AK yur uh see) a description of how close a measurement is to the true value of the quantity measured (27)

exactitud término que describe qué tanto se aproxima una medida al valor verdadero de la cantidad medida (27)

acid (AS id) any compound that increases the number of hydronium ions when dissolved in water; acids turn blue litmus paper red and react with bases and some metals to form salts (293)

ácido cualquier compuesto que aumenta el número de iones de hidrógeno cuando se disuelve en agua; los ácidos cambian el color del papel tornasol a rojo y forman sales al reaccionar con bases y con algunos metales (293)

acid precipitation (AS id pree SIP uh TAY shuhn) precipitation, such as rain, sleet, or snow, that contains a high concentration of acids, often because of the pollution of the atmosphere (758)

precipitación ácida precipitación tal como lluvia, aguanieve o nieve, que contiene una alta concentración de ácidos debido a la contaminación de la atmósfera (758)

air mass (ER MAS) a large body of air throughout which temperature and moisture content are similar (789)

masa de aire un gran volumen de aire, cuya temperatura y cuyo contenido de humedad son similares en toda su extensión (789)

alkali metal (AL kuh LIE MET'l) one of the elements of Group 1 of the periodic table (lithium, sodium, potassium, rubidium, cesium, and francium) (157)

metal alcalino uno de los elementos del Grupo 1 de la tabla periódica (litio, sodio, potasio, rubidio, cesio y francio) (157)

alkaline-earth metal (AL kuh LIEN UHRTH MET'l) one of the elements of Group 2 of the periodic table (beryllium, magnesium, calcium, strontium, barium, and radium) (158)

metal alcalinotérreo uno de los elementos del Grupo 2 de la tabla periódica (berilio, magnesio, calcio, estroncio, bario y radio) (158)

alloy (AL oy) a solid or liquid mixture of two or more metals (266)

aleación una mezcla sólida o líquida de dos o más metales (266)

alpha particle (AL fuh PAHRT i kuhl) a positively charged particle that consists of two protons and two neutrons and that is emitted from a nucleus during radioactive decay; it is identical to the nucleus of a helium atom and has a charge of +2 (328)

partícula alfa una partícula con carga positiva que está formada por dos protones y dos neutrones y que se emite desde el núcleo durante la desintegración radiactiva; es idéntica al núcleo de un átomo de helio y tiene una carga de +2 (328)

alternating current (AWL tuhr NAYT ing KUHR uhnt) an electric current that changes direction at regular intervals (abbreviation, AC) (634)

corriente alterna una corriente eléctrica que cambia de dirección en intervalos regulares (abreviatura: CA) (634)

amino acid (uh MEE noh AS id) a compound of a class of simple organic compounds that contain a carboxyl group and an amino group and that combine to form proteins (203)

aminoácido un compuesto de una clase de compuestos orgánicos simples que contienen un grupo carboxilo y un grupo amino y que al combinarse forman proteínas (203)

amplitude (AM pluh TOOD) the maximum distance that the particles of a wave's medium vibrate from their rest position (514)

amplitud la distancia máxima a la que vibran las partículas del medio de una onda a partir de su posición de reposo (514)

antacid (ANT AS id) a weak base that neutralizes stomach acid (311)

antiácido una base débil que neutraliza el ácido del estómago (311)

asteroid (AS tuhr OYD) a small, rocky object that orbits the sun; most asteroids are located in a band between the orbits of Mars and Jupiter (666)

asteroide un objeto pequeño y rocoso que se encuentra en órbita alrededor del Sol; la mayoría de los asteroides se ubican en una banda entre las órbitas de Marte y Júpiter (666)

atom (AT uhm) the smallest unit of an element that maintains the chemical properties of that element (46)

átomo la unidad más pequeña de un elemento que conserva las propiedades químicas de ese elemento (46)

atomic number (uh TAHM ik NUHM buhr) the number of protons in the nucleus of an atom; the atomic number is the same for all atoms of an element (121)

número atómico el número de protones en el núcleo de un átomo; el número atómico es el mismo para todos los átomos de un elemento (121)

B

background radiation (BAK GROWND RAY dee AY shuhn) the nuclear radiation that arises naturally from cosmic rays and from radioactive isotopes in the soil and air (344)

radiación de fondo la radiación nuclear que surge naturalmente de los rayos cósmicos y de los isótopos radiactivos que están en el suelo y en el aire (344)

base (BAYS) any compound that increases the number of hydroxide ions when dissolved in water; bases turn red litmus paper blue and react with acids to form salts (295)

base cualquier compuesto que aumenta el número de iones de hidróxido cuando se disuelve en agua; las bases cambian el color del papel tornasol a azul y forman sales al reaccionar con ácidos (295)

beta particle (BAYT uh PAHRT i kuhl) an electron or positron that is emitted from a nucleus during radioactive decay (329)

partícula beta un electrón o positrón que se emite desde un núcleo durante la desintegración radiactiva (329)

big bang theory (BIG BANG THEE uh ree) the theory that all matter and energy in the universe was compressed into an extremely small volume that 13 billion to 15 billion years ago exploded and began expanding in all directions (712)

teoría del Big Bang la teoría que establece que toda la materia y la energía del universo estaban comprimidas en un volumen extremadamente pequeño que explotó hace aproximadamente 13 a 15 mil millones de años y empezó a expandirse en todas direcciones (712)

black hole (BLAK HOHL) an object so massive and dense that even light cannot escape its gravity (700)

hoyo negro un objeto tan masivo y denso que ni siquiera la luz puede salir de su campo gravitacional (700)

bleach (BLEECH) a chemical compound used to whiten or make lighter, such as hydrogen peroxide or sodium hypochlorite (310)

blanqueador un compuesto químico que se usa para blanquear o aclarar, tal como el peróxido de hidrógeno o el hipoclorito de sodio (310)

boiling point (BOYL ing POYNT) the temperature and pressure at which a liquid becomes a gas (52)

punto de ebullición la temperatura y presión a la que un líquido se transforma en gas (52)

bond angle (BAHND ANG guhl) the angle formed by two bonds to the same atom (178)

ángulo de enlace el ángulo formado por dos enlaces al mismo átomo (178)

bond length (BAHND LENGKTH) the distance between two bonded atoms at their minimum potential energy; the average distance between the nuclei of two bonded atoms (178)

longitud de enlace la distancia entre dos átomos que están enlazados en el punto en que su energía potencial es mínima; la distancia promedio entre los núcleos de dos átomos enlazados (178)

buoyant force (BOY uhnt FAWRS) the upward force that keeps an object immersed in or floating on a fluid (90)

fuerza boyante la fuerza ascendente que hace que un objeto se mantenga sumergido en un fluido o flotando en él (90)

GLOSSARY • GLOSARIO

carbohydrate (KAHR boh HIE drayt) a class of molecules that includes sugars, starches, and fiber; contains carbon, hydrogen, and oxygen (202)

carbohidrato una clase de moléculas entre las que se incluyen azúcares, almidones y fibra; contiene carbono, hidrógeno y oxígeno (202)

catalyst (KAT uh LIST) a substance that changes the rate of a chemical reaction without being consumed or changed significantly (240)

catalizador una sustancia que cambia la tasa de una reacción química sin ser consumida ni cambiar significativamente (240)

cell (SEL) in electricity, a device that produces an electric current by converting chemical or radiant energy into electrical energy (594)

celda en electricidad, un aparato que produce una corriente eléctrica transformando la energía química o radiante en energía eléctrica (594)

chemical bond (KEM i kuhl BAHND) the attractive force that holds atoms or ions together (177)

enlace químico la fuerza de atracción que mantiene unidos a los átomos o iones (177)

chemical change (KEM i kuhl CHAYNJ) a change that occurs when one or more substances change into entirely new substances with different properties (61)

cambio químico un cambio que ocurre cuando una o más sustancias se transforman en sustancias totalmente nuevas con propiedades diferentes (61)

chemical energy (KEM i kuhl EN uhr jee) the energy released when a chemical compound reacts to produce new compounds (221)

energía química la energía que se libera cuando un compuesto químico reacciona para producir nuevos compuestos (221)

chemical equation (KEM i kuhl ee KWAY zhuhn) a representation of a chemical reaction that uses symbols to show the relationship between the reactants and the products (225)

ecuación química una representación de una reacción química que usa símbolos para mostrar la relación entre los reactivos y los productos (225)

chemical equilibrium (KEM i kuhl EE kwi LIB ree uhm) a state of balance in which the rate of a forward reaction equals the rate of the reverse reaction and the concentrations of products and reactants remain unchanged (245)

equilibrio químico un estado de equilibrio en el que la tasa de la reacción directa es igual a la tasa de la reacción inversa y las concentraciones de los productos y reactivos no sufren cambios (245)

chemical structure (KEM i kuhl STRUHK chuhr) the arrangement of the atoms in a molecule (178)

estructura química la disposición de los átomos en una molécula (178)

circuit breaker (SUHR kit BRAYK uhr) a switch that opens a circuit automatically when the current exceeds a certain value (607)

disyuntor un interruptor que abre un circuito automáticamente cuando la corriente excede un valor determinado (607)

climate (KLIE muht) the average weather conditions in an area over a long period of time (794)

clima las condiciones promedio del tiempo en un área durante un largo período de tiempo (794)

cluster (KLUHS tuhr) a group of stars or galaxies bound by gravity (703)

conglomerado un grupo de estrellas o galaxias unidas por la gravedad (703)

colloid (KAHL OYD) a mixture consisting of tiny particles that are intermediate in size between those in solutions and those in suspensions and that are suspended in a liquid, solid, or gas (261)

coloide una mezcla formada por partículas diminutas que son de tamaño intermedio entre las partículas de las soluciones y las de las suspensiones y que se encuentran suspendidas en un líquido, sólido o gas (261)

combustion reaction (kuhm BUHS chuhn ree AK shuhn) the oxidation reaction of an organic compound, in which heat is released (232)

reacción de combustión la reacción de oxidación de un compuesto orgánico, durante la cual se libera calor (232)

comet (KAHM it) a small body of ice, rock, and cosmic dust that follows an elliptical orbit around the sun and that gives off gas and dust in the form of a tail as it passes close to the sun (675)

cometa un cuerpo pequeño formado por hielo, roca y polvo cósmico que sigue una órbita elíptica alrededor del Sol y que libera gas y polvo, los cuales forman una cola al pasar cerca del Sol (675)

community (kuh MYOO nuh tee) a group of various species that live in the same habitat and interact with each other (808)

comunidad un grupo de varias especies que viven en el mismo hábitat e interactúan unas con otras (808)

compound (KAHM POWND) a substance made up of atoms of two or more different elements joined by chemical bonds (47)

compuesto una sustancia formada por átomos de dos o más elementos diferentes unidos por enlaces químicos (47)

compound machine (KAHM POWND muh SHEEN) a machine made of more than one simple machine (443)

máquina compuesta una máquina hecha de más de una máquina simple (443)

concentration (KAHN suhn TRAY shuhn) the amount of a particular substance in a given quantity of a mixture, solution, or ore (277)

concentración la cantidad de una cierta sustancia en una cantidad determinada de mezcla, solución o mena (277)

condensation (KAHN duhn SAY shuhn) the change of state from a gas to a liquid (86)

condensación el cambio de estado de gas a líquido (86)

constructive interference (kuhn STRUHK tiv IN tuhr FIR uhns) a superposition of two or more waves that produces an intensity equal to the sum of the intensities of the individual waves (527)

interferencia constructiva una superposición de dos o más ondas que produce una intensidad igual a la suma de las intensidades de las ondas individuales (527)

convection (kuhn VEK shuhn) the movement of matter due to differences in density that are caused by temperature variations; can result in the transfer of energy as heat (481)

convección el movimiento de la materia debido a diferencias en la densidad que se producen por variaciones en la temperatura; puede resultar en la transferencia de energía en forma de calor (481)

convection current (kuhn VEK shuhn KUHR uhnt) any movement of matter that results from differences in density; may be vertical, circular, or cyclical (481)

corriente de convección cualquier movimiento de la materia que se produce como resultado de diferencias en la densidad; puede ser vertical, circular o cíclico (481)

core (KAWR) the central part of Earth below the mantle; *also* the center of the sun (730)

núcleo la parte central de la Tierra, debajo del manto; *también*, el centro del Sol (730)

Coriolis effect (KAWR ee OH lis e FEKT) the curving of the path of a moving object from an otherwise straight path due to Earth's rotation (786)

efecto de Coriolis la desviación de la trayectoria recta que experimentan los objetos en movimiento debido a la rotación de la Tierra (786)

covalent bond (koh VAY luhnt BAHND) a bond formed when atoms share one or more pairs of electrons (186)

enlace covalente un enlace formado cuando los átomos comparten uno o más pares de electrones (186)

crest (KREST) the highest point of a wave (512)

cresta el punto más alto de una onda (512)

critical mass (KRIT i kuhl MAS) the minimum mass of a fissionable isotope that provides the number of neutrons needed to sustain a chain reaction (341)

masa crítica la cantidad mínima de masa de un isótopo fisionable que proporciona el número de neutrones que se requieren para sostener una reacción en cadena (341)

critical thinking (KRIT i kuhl THINGK ing) the ability and willingness to assess claims critically and to make judgments on the basis of objective and supported reasons (14)

razonamiento crítico la capacidad y voluntad de evaluar declaraciones críticamente y de hacer juicios basados en razones objetivas y documentadas (14)

crust (KRUHST) the thin and solid outermost layer of Earth above the mantle (729)

corteza la capa externa, delgada y sólida de la Tierra, que se encuentra sobre el manto (729)

decomposition reaction (DEE kahm puh ZISH uhn ree AK shuhn) a reaction in which a single compound breaks down to form two or more simpler substances (231)

reacción de descomposición una reacción en la que un solo compuesto se descompone para formar dos o más sustancias más simples (231)

density (DEN suh tee) the ratio of the mass of a substance to the volume of the substance; commonly expressed as grams per cubic centimeter for solids and liquids and as grams per liter for gases (54)

densidad la relación entre la masa de una sustancia y su volumen; comúnmente se expresa en gramos por centímetro cúbico para los sólidos y líquidos, y como gramos por litro para los gases (54)

deposition (DEP uh ZISH uhn) the process in which material is laid down (759)

deposición el proceso por medio del cual un material se deposita (759)

destructive interference (di STRUHK tiv IN tuhr FIR uhns) a superposition of two or more waves that produces an intensity equal to the difference of the intensities of the individual waves (527)

interferencia destructiva una superposición de dos o más ondas que produce una intensidad igual a la diferencia de las intensidades de las ondas individuales (527)

detergent (dee TUHR juhnt) a water-soluble cleaner that can emulsify dirt and oil (309)

detergente un limpiador no jabonoso, soluble en agua, que emulsiona la suciedad y el aceite (309)

dew point (DOO POYNT) at constant pressure and water vapor content, the temperature at which the rate of condensation equals the rate of evaporation (783)

punto de rocío a presión y contenido de vapor de agua constantes, la temperatura a la que la tasa de condensación es igual a la tasa de evaporación (783)

diffraction (di FRAK shuhn) a change in the direction of a wave when the wave finds an obstacle or an edge, such as an opening (525)

difracción un cambio en la dirección de una onda cuando ésta se encuentra con un obstáculo o un borde, tal como una abertura (525)

disinfectant (DIS in FEK tuhnt) a chemical substance that kills harmful bacteria or viruses (310)

desinfectante una sustancia química que elimina bacterias dañinas o virus (310)

dispersion (di SPUHR zhuhn) in optics, the process of separating a wave (such as white light) of different frequencies into its individual component waves (the different colors) (570)

dispersión en óptica, el proceso de separar una onda que tiene diferentes frecuencias (por ejemplo, la luz blanca) de las ondas individuales que la componen (los distintos colores) (570)

displacement (dis PLAYS muhnt) the change in position of an object (366)

desplazamiento el cambio en la posición de un objeto (366)

Doppler effect (DAHP luhr e FEKT) an observed change in the frequency of a wave when the source or observer is moving (523, 710)

efecto Doppler un cambio que se observa en la frecuencia de una onda cuando la fuente o el observador está en movimiento (523, 710)

double-displacement reaction (DUHB uhl dis PLAYS muhnt ree AK shuhn) a reaction in which a gas, a solid precipitate, or a molecular compound forms from the apparent exchange of atoms or ions between two compounds (234)

reacción de doble desplazamiento una reacción en la que un gas, un precipitado sólido o un compuesto molecular se forma a partir del intercambio aparente de átomos o iones entre dos compuestos (234)

dwarf planet (DWAWRF PLAN it) a celestial body that orbits the sun, is round because of its own gravity, but has not cleared its orbital path (666)

planeta enano un cuerpo celeste que orbita alrededor del Sol, es redondo debido a su propia fuerza de gravedad, pero no ha despejado los alrededores de su trayectoria orbital (666)

eclipse (i KLIPS) an event in which the shadow of one celestial body falls on another (658)

eclipse un suceso en el que la sombra de un cuerpo celeste cubre otro cuerpo celeste (658)

ecosystem (EE koh SIS tuhm) a community of organisms and their abiotic environment (807)

ecosistema una comunidad de organismos y su ambiente abiótico (807)

efficiency (e FISH uhn see) a quantity, usually expressed as a percentage, that measures the ratio of work output to work input (459)

eficiencia una cantidad, generalmente expresada como un porcentaje, que mide la relación entre el trabajo de entrada y el trabajo de salida (459)

electrical conductor (ee LEK tri kuhl kuhn DUHK tuhr) a material in which charges can move freely (588)

conductor eléctrico un material en el que las cargas se mueven libremente (588)

electrical insulator (ee LEK tri kuhl IN suh LAYT uhr) a material in which charges cannot move freely (588)

aislante eléctrico un material en el que las cargas no pueden moverse libremente (588)

electrical potential energy (ee LEK tri kuhl poh TEN shuhl EN uhr jee) the ability to move an electric charge from one point to another (593)

energía potencial eléctrica la capacidad de mover una carga eléctrica de un punto a otro (593)

electric charge (ee LEK trik CHAHRJ) an electrical property of matter that creates electric and magnetic forces and interactions (585)

carga eléctrica una propiedad eléctrica de la materia que crea fuerzas e interacciones eléctricas y magnéticas (585)

electric circuit (ee LEK trik SUHR kit) a set of electrical components connected such that they provide one or more complete paths for the movement of charges (600)

circuito eléctrico un conjunto de componentes eléctricos conectados de modo que proporcionen una o más rutas completas para el movimiento de las cargas (600)

electric current (ee LEK trik KUHR uhnt) the rate at which charges pass through a given point; measured in amperes (595)

corriente eléctrica la tasa a la que las cargas pasan por un punto determinado; se mide en amperes (595)

electric field (ee LEK trik FEELD) the space around a charged object in which another charged object experiences an electric force (591)

campo eléctrico el espacio que se encuentra alrededor de un objeto con carga y en el que otro objeto con carga experimenta una fuerza eléctrica (591)

electric force (ee LEK trik FAWRS) the force of attraction or repulsion on a charged particle that is due to an electric field (590)

fuerza eléctrica la fuerza de atracción o repulsión en una partícula con carga debido a un campo eléctrico (590)

electric motor (ee LEK trik MOHT uhr) a device that converts electrical energy into mechanical energy (630)

motor eléctrico un aparato que transforma la energía eléctrica en energía mecánica (630)

electric power (ee LEK trik POW uhr) the rate at which electrical energy is converted into other forms of energy (605)

potencia eléctrica la tasa a la que la energía eléctrica se transforma en otras formas de energía (605)

electrolyte (ee LEK troh LIET) a substance that dissolves in water to give a solution that conducts an electric current (294)

electrolito una sustancia que se disuelve en agua y crea una solución que conduce la corriente eléctrica (294)

electromagnet (ee LEK troh MAG nit) a coil that has a soft iron core and that acts as a magnet when an electric current is in the coil (628)

electroimán una bobina que tiene un centro de hierro suave y que funciona como un imán cuando hay una corriente eléctrica en la bobina (628)

electromagnetic induction (ee LEK troh mag NET ik in DUHK shuhn) the process of creating a current in a circuit by changing a magnetic field (632)

inducción electromagnética el proceso de crear una corriente en un circuito por medio de un cambio en el campo magnético (632)

GLOSSARY • GLOSARIO

electromagnetic wave (ee LEK troh mag NET ik WAYV) a wave that consists of oscillating electric and magnetic fields, which radiate outward at the speed of light (506)

onda electromagnética una onda que está formada por campos eléctricos y magnéticos oscilantes, que irradia hacia fuera a la velocidad de la luz (506)

electron (ee LEK TRAHN) a subatomic particle that has a negative charge (115)

electrón una partícula subatómica que tiene carga negativa (115)

element (EL uh muhnt) a substance that cannot be separated or broken down into simpler substances by chemical means; all atoms of an element have the same atomic number (46)

elemento una sustancia que no se puede separar o descomponer en sustancias más simples por medio de métodos químicos; todos los átomos de un elemento tienen el mismo número atómico (46)

empirical formula (em PIR i kuhl FAWR myoo luh) a chemical formula that shows the composition of a compound in terms of the relative numbers and kinds of atoms in the simplest ratio (194)

fórmula empírica una fórmula química que muestra la composición de un compuesto en función del número relativo y el tipo de átomos que hay en la proporción más simple (194)

emulsion (ee MUHL shuhn) any mixture of two or more immiscible liquids in which one liquid is dispersed in the other (262)

emulsión cualquier mezcla de dos o más líquidos inmiscibles en la que un líquido se encuentra disperso en el otro (262)

endothermic reaction (EN doh THUHR mik ree AK shuhn) a chemical reaction that requires energy input (222)

reacción endotérmica una reacción química que necesita una entrada de energía (222)

energy (EN uhr jee) the capacity to do work (80, 444)

energía la capacidad de realizar un trabajo (80, 444)

entropy (EN truh pee) a measure of the randomness or disorder of a system (491)

entropía una medida del grado de aleatoriedad o desorden de un sistema (491)

enzyme (EN ziem) a molecule, either protein or RNA, that acts as a catalyst in biochemical reactions (241)

enzima una molécula, ya sea una proteína o ARN, que actúa como catalizador en las reacciones bioquímicas (241)

epicenter (EP i SENT uhr) the point on Earth's surface directly above an earthquake's starting point, or focus (739)

epicentro el punto de la superficie de la Tierra que queda justo arriba del punto de inicio, o foco, de un terremoto (739)

erosion (ee ROH zhuhn) a process in which the materials of Earth's surface are loosened, dissolved, or worn away and transported from one place to another by a natural agent, such as wind, water, ice, or gravity (759)

erosión un proceso por medio del cual los materiales de la superficie de la Tierra se aflojan, disuelven o desgastan y son transportados de un lugar a otro por un agente natural, como el viento, el agua, el hielo o la gravedad (759)

eutrophication (yoo TRAHF i KAY shuhn) an increase in the amount of nutrients, such as nitrates, in a marine or aquatic ecosystem (828)

eutrofización un aumento en la cantidad de nutrientes, tales como nitratos, en un ecosistema marino o acuático (828)

evaporation (ee VAP uh RAY shuhn) the change of state from a liquid to a gas (85)

evaporación el cambio de estado de líquido a gas (85)

exoplanet (EK soh PLAN it) a planetlike body that orbits a star other than the sun (85)

exoplaneta un cuerpo parecido a un planeta que orbita alrededor de una estrella que no es el Sol (85)

exothermic reaction (EK soh THUHR mik ree AK shuhn) a chemical reaction in which energy is released to the surroundings as heat (222)

reacción exotérmica una reacción química en la que se libera energía a los alrededores en forma de calor (222)

fault (FAWLT) a break in a body of rock along which one block slides relative to another; a form of brittle strain (737)

falla una grieta en un cuerpo rocoso a lo largo de la cual un bloque se desliza respecto a otro; una forma de tensión quebradiza (737)

fission (FISH uhn) the process by which a nucleus splits into two or more fragments and releases neutrons and energy (339)

fisión el proceso por medio del cual un núcleo se divide en dos o más fragmentos y libera neutrones y energía (339)

fluid (FLOO id) a nonsolid state of matter in which the atoms or molecules are free to move past each other, as in a gas or liquid (79)

fluido un estado no sólido de la materia en el que los átomos o moléculas tienen libertad de movimiento, como en el caso de un gas o un líquido (79)

focus (FOH kuhs) the location within Earth along a fault at which the first motion of an earthquake occurs (739)

foco el lugar dentro de la Tierra a lo largo de una falla donde ocurre el primer movimiento de un terremoto (739)

force (FAWRS) an action exerted on a body in order to change the body's state of rest or motion; force has magnitude and direction (380)

fuerza una acción que se ejerce en un cuerpo con el fin de cambiar su estado de reposo o movimiento; la fuerza tiene magnitud y dirección (380)

fossil fuel (FAHS uhl FYOO uhl) a nonrenewable energy resource formed from the remains of organisms that lived long ago; examples include oil, coal, and natural gas (816)

combustible fósil un recurso energético no renovable formado a partir de los restos de organismos que vivieron hace mucho tiempo; algunos ejemplos incluyen el petróleo, el carbón y el gas natural (816)

frame of reference (FRAYM UHV REF uhr uhns) a system for specifying the precise location of objects in space and time (365)

marco de referencia un sistema para especificar la ubicación precisa de los objetos en el tiempo y el espacio (365)

free fall (FREE FAWL) the motion of a body when only the force of gravity is acting on the body (407)

caída libre el movimiento de un cuerpo cuando la única fuerza que actúa sobre él es la fuerza de gravedad (407)

free radical (FREE RAD i kuhl) an atom or a group of atoms that has one unpaired electron (235)

radical libre un átomo o un grupo de átomos que tiene un electrón no apareado (235)

frequency (FREE kwuhn see) the number of cycles or vibrations per unit of time; *also* the number of waves produced in a given amount of time (516)

frecuencia el número de ciclos o vibraciones por unidad de tiempo; *también*, el número de ondas producidas en una cantidad de tiempo determinada (516)

friction (FRIK shuhn) a force that opposes motion between two surfaces that are in contact (382)

fricción una fuerza que se opone al movimiento entre dos superficies que están en contacto (382)

front (FRUHNT) the boundary between air masses of different densities and usually different temperatures (789)

frente el límite entre masas de aire de diferentes densidades y, normalmente, diferentes temperaturas (789)

fuse (FYOOZ) an electrical device that contains a metal strip that melts when current in the circuit becomes too great (607)

fusible un aparato eléctrico que contiene una tira de metal que se derrite cuando la corriente en el circuito es demasiado elevada (607)

fusion (FYOO zhuhn) the process in which light nuclei combine at extremely high temperatures, forming heavier nuclei and releasing energy (342)

fusión el proceso por medio del cual núcleos ligeros se combinan a temperaturas extremadamente altas formando núcleos más pesados y liberando energía (342)

galaxy (GAL uhk see) a collection of stars, dust, and gas bound together by gravity (702)

galaxia un conjunto de estrellas, polvo y gas unidos por la gravedad (702)

galvanometer (GAL vuh NAHM uht uhr) an instrument that detects, measures, and determines the direction of a small electric current (630)

galvanómetro un instrumento que detecta, mide y determina la dirección de una corriente eléctrica pequeña (630)

gamma ray (GAM uh RAY) the high-energy photon emitted by a nucleus during fission and radioactive decay (329)

rayo gamma el fotón de alta energía emitido por un núcleo durante la fisión y la desintegración radiactiva (329)

GLOSSARY • GLOSARIO

gas giant (GAS JIE uhnt) a planet that has a deep, massive atmosphere, such as Jupiter, Saturn, Uranus, or Neptune (666)

gigante gaseoso un planeta con una atmósfera masiva y profunda, como por ejemplo, Júpiter, Saturno, Urano o Neptuno (666)

gas laws (GAS LAWZ) the laws that state the mathematical relationships between the volume, temperature, pressure, and quantity of a gas (97)

leyes de los gases las leyes que establecen las relaciones matemáticas entre el volumen, temperatura, presión y cantidad de un gas (97)

generator (JEN uhr AYT uhr) a machine that converts mechanical energy into electrical energy (634)

generador una máquina que transforma la energía mecánica en energía eléctrica (634)

geothermal energy (JEE oh THUHR muhl EN uhr jee) the energy produced by heat within Earth (819)

energía geotérmica la energía producida por el calor del interior de la Tierra (819)

global warming (GLOH buhl WAWRM ing) a gradual increase in average global temperature (826)

calentamiento global un aumento gradual de la temperatura global promedio (826)

greenhouse effect (GREEN HOWS e FEKT) the warming of the surface and lower atmosphere of Earth that occurs when carbon dioxide, water vapor, and other gases in the air absorb and reradiate infrared radiation (779)

efecto invernadero el calentamiento de la superficie terrestre y de la parte más baja de la atmósfera, el cual se produce cuando el dióxido de carbono, el vapor de agua y otros gases del aire absorben radiación infrarroja y la vuelven a irradiar (779)

group (GROOP) a vertical column of elements in the periodic table; elements in a group share chemical properties (150)

grupo una columna vertical de elementos de la tabla periódica; los elementos de un grupo comparten propiedades químicas (150)

half-life (HAF LIEF) the time required for half of a sample of a radioactive isotope to break down by radioactive decay to form a daughter isotope (333)

vida media el tiempo que se requiere para que la mitad de una muestra de un isótopo radiactivo se descomponga por desintegración radiactiva y forme un isótopo hijo (333)

halogen (HAL oh juhn) one of the elements of Group 17 of the periodic table (fluorine, chlorine, bromine, iodine, and astatine); halogens combine with most metals to form salts (162)

halógeno uno de los elementos del Grupo 17 de la tabla periódica (flúor, cloro, bromo, yodo y ástato); los halógenos se combinan con la mayoría de los metales para formar sales (162)

heat (HEET) the energy transferred between objects that are at different temperatures; energy is always transferred from higher-temperature objects to lower-temperature objects until thermal equilibrium is reached (479)

calor la transferencia de energía entre objetos que están a temperaturas diferentes; la energía siempre se transfiere de los objetos que están a la temperatura más alta a los objetos que están a una temperatura más baja, hasta que se llega a un equilibrio térmico (479)

heat engine (HEET EN juhn) a machine that transforms heat into mechanical energy, or work (492)

motor térmico una máquina que transforma el calor en energía mecánica, o trabajo (492)

humidity (hyoo MID uh tee) the amount of water vapor in the air (782)

humedad la cantidad de vapor de agua que hay en el aire (782)

hydrogen bond (HIE druh juhn BAHND) the intermolecular force occurring when a hydrogen atom that is bonded to a highly electronegative atom of one molecule is attracted to two unshared electrons of another molecule (269)

enlace de hidrógeno la fuerza intermolecular producida por un átomo de hidrógeno que está unido a un átomo muy electronegativo de una molécula y que experimenta atracción a dos electrones no compartidos de otra molécula (269)

hydrosphere (HIE droh SFIR) the portion of Earth that is water (663)

hidrosfera la porción de la Tierra que es agua (663)

igneous rock (IG nee uhs RAHK) rock that forms when magma cools and solidifies (749)

roca ígnea una roca que se forma cuando el magma se enfría y se solidifica (749)

indicator (IN di KAYT uhr) a compound that can reversibly change color depending on conditions such as pH (293)

indicador un compuesto que puede cambiar de color de forma reversible dependiendo de condiciones tales como el pH (293)

inertia (in UHR shuh) the tendency of an object to resist a change in motion unless an outside force acts on the object (398)

inercia la tendencia de un objeto a resistir un cambio en el movimiento a menos que actúe una fuerza externa sobre el objeto (398)

infrasound (IN fruh SOWND) slow vibrations of frequencies lower than 20 Hz (546)

infrasonido vibraciones lentas de frecuencias inferiores a 20 Hz (546)

intensity (in TEN suh tee) in physical science, the rate at which energy flows through a given area of space (555)

intensidad en las ciencias físicas, la tasa a la que la energía fluye a través de un área determinada de espacio (555)

interference (IN tuhr FIR uhns) the combination of two or more waves that results in a single wave (526)

interferencia la combinación de dos o más ondas que resulta en una sola onda (526)

interstellar matter (IN tuhr STEL uhr MAT uhr) the gas and dust located between the stars in a galaxy (704)

materia interestelar el gas y polvo que están entre las estrellas de una galaxia (704)

ion (IE AHN) an atom, radical, or molecule that has gained or lost one or more electrons and has a negative or positive charge (153)

ion un átomo, radical o molécula que ha ganado o perdido uno o más electrones y que tiene una carga negativa o positiva (153)

ionic bond (ie AHN ik BAHND) the attractive force between oppositely charged ions, which form when electrons are transferred from one atom to another (184)

enlace iónico la fuerza de atracción entre iones con cargas opuestas, que se forman cuando se transfieren electrones de un átomo a otro (184)

isotope (IE suh TOHP) an atom that has the same number of protons (or the same atomic number) as other atoms of the same element do but that has a different number of neutrons (and thus a different atomic mass) (122)

isótopo un átomo que tiene el mismo número de protones (o el mismo número atómico) que otros átomos del mismo elemento, pero que tiene un número diferente de neutrones (y, por lo tanto, otra masa atómica) (122)

kinetic energy (ki NET ik EN uhr jee) the energy of an object that is due to the object's motion (447)

energía cinética la energía de un objeto debido al movimiento del objeto (447)

kinetic friction (ki NET ik FRIK shuhn) the force that opposes the movement of two surfaces that are in contact and are moving over each other (383)

fricción cinética la fuerza que se opone al movimiento de dos superficies que están en contacto y se mueven una sobre la otra (383)

law (LAW) a descriptive statement or equation that reliably predicts events under certain conditions (9)

ley una ecuación o afirmación descriptiva que predice sucesos de manera confiable en determinadas condiciones (9)

length (LENGKTH) a measure of the straight-line distance between two points (21)

longitud una medida de la distancia en línea recta entre dos puntos (21)

lens (LENZ) a transparent object that refracts light waves such that they converge or diverge to create an image (568)

lente un objeto transparente que refracta las ondas de luz de modo que converjan o diverjan para crear una imagen (568)

light ray (LIET RAY) a line in space that matches the direction of the flow of radiant energy (560)

rayo luz una línea en el espacio que corresponde con la dirección del flujo de energía radiante (560)

light-year (LIET YIR) the distance that light travels in one year; about 9.46 trillion kilometers (693)

año luz la distancia que viaja la luz en un año; aproximadamente 9.46 trillones de kilómetros (693)

lithosphere (LITH oh SFIR) the solid, outer layer of Earth that consists of the crust and the rigid upper part of the mantle (732)

litosfera la capa externa y sólida de la Tierra que está formada por la corteza y la parte superior y rígida del manto (732)

GLOSSARY • GLOSARIO

longitudinal wave (LAHN juh TOOD'n uhl WAYV) a wave in which the particles of the medium vibrate parallel to the direction of wave motion (512)

onda longitudinal una onda en la que las partículas del medio vibran paralelamente a la dirección del movimiento de la onda (512)

magnetic field (mag NET ik FEELD) a region where a magnetic force can be detected (621)

campo magnético una región donde puede detectarse una fuerza magnética (621)

magnetic pole (mag NET ik POHL) one of two points, such as the ends of a magnet, that have opposing magnetic qualities (619)

polo magnético uno de dos puntos, tales como los extremos de un imán, que tienen cualidades magnéticas opuestas (619)

magnification (MAG nuh fi KAY shuhn) the increase of an object's apparent size by using lenses or mirrors (568)

magnificación el aumento del tamaño aparente de un objeto mediante el uso de lentes o espejos (568)

mantle (MAN tuhl) in Earth science, the layer of rock between Earth's crust and core (729)

manto en las ciencias de la Tierra, la capa de roca que se encuentra entre la corteza terrestre y el núcleo (729)

mass (MAS) a measure of the amount of matter in an object; a fundamental property of an object that is not affected by the forces that act on the object, such as the gravitational force (21)

masa una medida de la cantidad de materia que tiene un objeto; una propiedad fundamental de un objeto que no está afectada por las fuerzas que actúan sobre el objeto, como por ejemplo, la fuerza gravitacional (21)

mass number (MAS NUHM buhr) the sum of the numbers of protons and neutrons in the nucleus of an atom (121)

número de masa la suma de los números de protones y neutrones que hay en el núcleo de un átomo (121)

matter (MAT uhr) anything that has mass and takes up space (45)

materia cualquier cosa que tiene masa y ocupa un lugar en el espacio (45)

mechanical advantage (muh KAN i kuhl ad VANT ij) a number that tells how many times a machine multiplies force; it can be calculated by dividing the output force by the input force (436)

ventaja mecánica un número que dice cuántas veces una máquina multiplica una fuerza; se calcula dividiendo la fuerza de salida entre la fuerza de entrada (436)

mechanical energy (muh KAN i kuhl EN uhr jee) the amount of work an object can do because of the object's kinetic and potential energies (449)

energía mecánica la cantidad de trabajo que un objeto realiza debido a las energías cinética y potencial del objeto (449)

mechanical wave (muh KAN i kuhl WAYV) a wave that requires a medium through which to travel (506)

onda mecánica una onda que requiere un medio para desplazarse (506)

medium (MEE dee uhm) a physical environment in which phenomena occur (506)

medio un ambiente físico en el que ocurren fenómenos (506)

melting point (MELT ing POYNT) the temperature and pressure at which a solid becomes a liquid (52)

punto de fusión la temperatura y presión a la cual un sólido se convierte en líquido (52)

mesosphere (MES oh SFIR) the coldest layer of the atmosphere, between the stratosphere and the thermosphere, in which temperature decreases as altitude increases (776)

mesosfera la capa más fría de la atmósfera que se encuentra entre la estratosfera y la termosfera, en la cual la temperatura disminuye al aumentar la altitud (776)

metal (MET'l) an element that is shiny and that conducts heat and electricity well (154)

metal un elemento que es brillante y conduce bien el calor y la electricidad (154)

metallic bond (muh TAL ik BAHND) a bond formed by the attraction between positively charged metal ions and the electrons around them (188)

enlace metálico un enlace formado por la atracción entre iones metálicos cargados positivamente y los electrones que los rodean (188)

metamorphic rock (MET uh MAWR fik RAHK) a rock that forms from other rocks as a result of intense heat, pressure, or chemical processes (751)

roca metamórfica una roca que se forma a partir de otras rocas como resultado de calor intenso, presión o procesos químicos (751)

mineral (MIN uhr uhl) a natural, usually inorganic solid that has a characteristic chemical composition, an orderly internal structure, and a characteristic set of physical properties (748)

mineral un sólido natural, normalmente inorgánico, que tiene una composición química característica, una estructura interna ordenada y propiedades físicas y químicas características (748)

mixture (MIKS chuhr) a combination of two or more substances that are not chemically combined (48)

mezcla una combinación de dos o más sustancias que no están combinadas químicamente (48)

molarity (moh LA ruh tee) a concentration unit of a solution expressed as moles of solute dissolved per liter of solution (280)

molaridad una unidad de concentración de una solución, expresada en moles de soluto disuelto por litro de solución (280)

mole (MOHL) the SI base unit used to measure the amount of a substance whose number of particles is the same as the number of atoms of carbon in exactly 12 g of carbon-12 (125)

mol la unidad fundamental del sistema internacional de unidades que se usa para medir la cantidad de una sustancia cuyo número de partículas es el mismo que el número de átomos de carbono en exactamente 12 g de carbono-12 (125)

molecular formula (moh LEK yoo luhr FAWR myoo luh) a chemical formula that shows the number and kinds of atoms in a molecule, but not the arrangement of the atoms (195)

fórmula molecular una fórmula química que muestra el número y los tipos de átomos que hay en una molécula, pero que no muestra cómo están distribuidos (195)

molecule (MAHL i KYOOL) a group of atoms that are held together by chemical forces; a molecule is the smallest unit of matter that can exist by itself and retain all of a substance's chemical properties (47)

molécula un conjunto de átomos que se mantienen unidos por acción de las fuerzas químicas; una molécula es la unidad más pequeña de la materia capaz de existir en forma independiente y conservar todas las propiedades químicas de una sustancia (47)

mole ratio (MOHL RAY shee OH) the relative number of moles of the substances required to produce a given amount of product in a chemical reaction (228)

razón molar el número relativo de moles de las sustancias que se requieren para producir una cantidad determinada de producto en una reacción química (228)

momentum (moh MEN tuhm) a quantity defined as the product of the mass and velocity of an object (414)

momento una cantidad que se define como el producto de la masa de un objeto por su velocidad (414)

motion (MOH shuhn) an object's change in position relative to a reference point (365)

movimiento el cambio en la posición de un objeto respecto a un punto de referencia (365)

nebula (NEB yu luh) a large cloud of gas and dust in interstellar space; a region in space where stars are born (673)

nebulosa una nube grande de gas y polvo en el espacio interestelar; una región en el espacio donde las estrellas nacen (673)

nebular hypothesis (NEB yu luhr hie PAHTH uh sis) a model for the formation of the solar system in which the sun and planets condense from a cloud (or nebula) of gas and dust (673)

teoría nebular un modelo de la formación del Sistema Solar en el que el Sol y los planetas se condensan a partir de una nube (o nebulosa) de gas y polvo (673)

neutralization reaction (NOO truh li ZAY shuhn ree AK shuhn) the reaction of the ions that characterize acids (hydronium ions) and the ions that characterize bases (hydroxide ions) to form water molecules and a salt (302)

reacción de neutralización la reacción de los iones que caracterizan a los ácidos (iones hidronio) y de los iones que caracterizan a las bases (iones hidróxido) para formar moléculas de agua y una sal (302)

neutron (NOO TRAHN) a subatomic particle that has no charge and that is located in the nucleus of an atom (119)

neutrón una partícula subatómica que no tiene carga y que está ubicada en el núcleo de un átomo (119)

noble gas (NOH buhl GAS) one of the elements of Group 18 of the periodic table (helium, neon, argon, krypton, xenon, and radon); noble gases are unreactive (161)

gas noble uno de los elementos del Grupo 18 de la tabla periódica (helio, neón, argón, criptón, xenón y radón); los gases nobles son no reactivos (161)

nonmetal (nahn MET'l) an element that conducts heat and electricity poorly and that does not form positive ions in an electrolytic solution (154)

no metal un elemento que es mal conductor del calor y la electricidad y que no forma iones positivos en una solución de electrolitos (154)

nonpolar (nahn POH luhr) describes a molecule in which centers of positive and negative charge are not separated (270)

no polar término que describe una molécula en la que los centros de carga positiva y negativa no están separados (270)

nonrenewable resource (NAHN ri NOO uh buhl REE SAWRS) a resource that forms at a rate that is much slower than the rate at which the resource is consumed (817)

recurso no renovable un recurso que se forma a una tasa que es mucho más lenta que la tasa a la que se consume (817)

nuclear chain reaction (NOO klee uhr CHAYN ree AK shuhn) a continuous series of nuclear fission reactions (340)

reacción nuclear en cadena una serie continua de reacciones nucleares de fisión (340)

nuclear radiation (NOO klee uhr RAY dee AY shuhn) the particles that are released from the nucleus during radioactive decay, such as neutrons, electrons, and photons (327)

radiación nuclear las partículas que el núcleo libera durante la desintegración radiactiva, tales como neutrones, electrones y fotones (327)

nucleus (NOO klee uhs) in physical science, an atom's central region, which is made up of protons and neutrons (118)

núcleo en ciencias físicas, la región central de un átomo, la cual está constituida por protones y neutrones (118)

orbital (AWR buh tuhl) a region in an atom where there is a high probability of finding electrons (129)

orbital una región en un átomo donde hay una alta probabilidad de encontrar electrones (129)

organic compound (awr GAN ik KAHM POWND) a covalently bonded compound that contains carbon, excluding carbonates and oxides (197)

compuesto orgánico un compuesto enlazado de manera covalente que contiene carbono, excluyendo a los carbonatos y óxidos (197)

oxidation-reduction reaction (AHKS i DAY shuhn ri DUHK shuhn ree AK shuhn) any chemical change in which one species is oxidized (loses electrons) and another species is reduced (gains electrons); also called *redox reaction* (237)

reacción de óxido-reducción cualquier cambio químico en el que una especie se oxida (pierde electrones) y otra especie se reduce (gana electrones); también se denomina *reacción redox* (237)

parallel circuit (PAR uh LEL SUHR kit) a circuit in which the parts are joined in branches such that the potential difference across each part is the same (603)

circuito paralelo un circuito en el que las partes están unidas en ramas de manera tal que la diferencia de potencial entre cada parte es la misma (603)

pascal (pas KAL) the SI unit of pressure; equal to the force of 1 N exerted over an area of 1 m^2 (symbol, Pa) (89)

pascal la unidad de presión del sistema internacional de unidades; es igual a la fuerza de 1 N ejercida sobre un área de 1 m^2 (símbolo: Pa) (89)

period (PIR ee uhd) in chemistry, a horizontal row of elements in the periodic table (150); in physics, the time that it takes a complete cycle or wave oscillation to occur (516)

período en química, una hilera horizontal de elementos en la tabla periódica (150); en física, el tiempo que se requiere para completar un ciclo o la oscilación de una onda (516)

periodic law (PIR ee AHD ik LAW) the law that states that the repeating chemical and physical properties of elements change periodically with the atomic numbers of the elements (147)

ley periódica la ley que establece que las propiedades químicas y físicas repetitivas de un elemento cambian periódicamente en función del número atómico de los elementos (147)

pH (PEE AYCH) a value that is used to express the acidity or alkalinity (basicity) of a system; each whole number on the scale indicates a tenfold change in acidity; a pH of 7 is neutral, a pH of less than 7 is acidic, and a pH of greater than 7 is basic (298)

pH un valor que expresa la acidez o la alcalinidad (basicidad) de un sistema; cada número entero de la escala indica un cambio de 10 veces en la acidez; un pH de 7 es neutro, un pH de menos de 7 es ácido y un pH de más de 7 es básico (298)

phase (FAYZ) in astronomy, the change in the illuminated area of one celestial body as seen from another celestial body; phases of the moon are caused by the changing positions of Earth, the sun, and the moon (657)

fase en astronomía, el cambio en el área iluminada de un cuerpo celeste según se ve desde otro cuerpo celeste; las fases de la Luna se producen como resultado de los cambios en la posición de la Tierra, el Sol y la Luna (657)

photon (FOH TAHN) a unit or quantum of light; a particle of electromagnetic radiation that has zero rest mass and carries a quantum of energy (131, 553)

fotón una unidad o quantum de luz; una partícula de radiación electromagnética que tiene una masa de reposo de cero y que lleva un quantum de energía (131, 553)

physical change (FIZ i kuhl CHAYNJ) a change of matter from one form to another without a change in chemical properties (59)

cambio físico un cambio de materia de una forma a otra sin que ocurra un cambio en sus propiedades químicas (59)

pitch (PICH) a measure of how high or low a sound is perceived to be, depending on the frequency of the sound wave (546)

altura tonal una medida de qué tan agudo o grave se percibe un sonido, dependiendo de la frecuencia de la onda sonora (546)

planet (PLAN it) a celestial body that orbits the sun, is round because of its own gravity, and has cleared the neighborhood around its orbital path (653)

planeta un cuerpo celeste que orbita alrededor del Sol, es redondo debido a su propia fuerza de gravedad y ha despejado los alrededores de su trayectoria orbital (653)

plasma (PLAZ muh) in physical science, a state of matter that consists of free-moving ions and electrons; a plasma's properties differ from the properties of a solid, liquid, or gas (79)

plasma en ciencias físicas, un estado de la materia que consiste en iones y electrones que se mueven libremente; las propiedades de un plasma son distintas de las propiedades de un sólido, de un líquido o de un gas (79)

plate tectonics (PLAYT tek TAHN iks) the theory that explains how large pieces of the lithosphere, called *plates*, move and change shape (732)

tectónica de placas la teoría que explica cómo las grandes partes de litosfera, denominadas *placas*, se mueven y cambian de forma (732)

polar (POH luhr) describes a molecule in which the positive and negative charges are separated (267)

polar término que describe una molécula en la que las cargas positivas y negativas están separadas (267)

pollution (puh LOO shuhn) an undesirable change in the natural environment that is caused by the introduction of substances that are harmful to living organisms or by excessive wastes, heat, noise, or radiation (824)

contaminación un cambio indeseable en el ambiente natural, producido por la introducción de sustancias que son dañinas para los organismos vivos o por desechos, calor, ruido o radiación excesivos (824)

polyatomic ion (PAHL ee uh TAHM ik IE ahn) an ion made of two or more atoms (189)

ion poliatómico un ion formado por dos o más átomos (189)

polymer (PAHL uh muhr) a large molecule that is formed by more than five monomers, or small units (201)

polímero una molécula grande que está formada por más de cinco monómeros, o unidades pequeñas (201)

potential difference (poh TEN shuhl DIF uhr uhns) the voltage difference in potential between two points in a circuit (594)

diferencia de potencial la diferencia de voltaje en el potencial entre dos puntos de un circuito (594)

potential energy (poh TEN shuhl EN uhr jee) the energy that an object has because of the position, shape, or condition of the object (445)

energía potencial la energía que tiene un objeto debido a su posición, forma o condición (445)

power (POW uhr) a quantity that measures the rate at which work is done or energy is transformed (433)

potencia una cantidad que mide la tasa a la que se realiza un trabajo o a la que se transforma la energía (433)

precipitation (pree SIP uh TAY shuhn) any form of water that falls to Earth's surface from the clouds; includes rain, snow, sleet, and hail (782)

precipitación cualquier forma de agua que cae de las nubes a la superficie de la Tierra; incluye a la lluvia, nieve, aguanieve y granizo (782)

precision (pree SIZH uhn) the exactness of a measurement (26)

precisión la exactitud de una medición (26)

pressure (PRESH uhr) the amount of force exerted per unit area of a surface (89)

presión la cantidad de fuerza ejercida en una superficie por unidad de área (89)

GLOSSARY · GLOSARIO

prism (PRIZ uhm) in optics, a system that consists of two or more plane surfaces of a transparent solid at an angle with each other (570)

prisma en óptica, un sistema formado por dos o más superficies planas de un sólido transparente ubicadas en un ángulo unas respecto a otras (570)

product (PRAHD uhkt) a substance that forms in a chemical reaction (220)

producto una sustancia que se forma en una reacción química (220)

projectile motion (proh JEK tuhl MOH shuhn) the curved path that an object follows when thrown, launched, or otherwise projected near the surface of Earth; the motion of objects that are moving in two dimensions under the influence of gravity (408)

movimiento proyectil la trayectoria curva que sigue un objeto cuando es aventado, lanzado o proyectado de cualquier otra manera cerca de la superficie de la Tierra; el movimiento de objetos que se mueven en dos dimensiones bajo la influencia de la gravedad (408)

protein (PROH teen) an organic compound that is made of one or more chains of amino acids and that is a principal component of all cells (203)

proteína un compuesto orgánico que está hecho de una o más cadenas de aminoácidos y que es el principal componente de todas las células (203)

proton (PROH TAHN) a subatomic particle that has a positive charge and that is located in the nucleus of an atom; the number of protons in the nucleus is the atomic number, which determines the identity of an element (119)

protón una partícula subatómica que tiene una carga positiva y que está ubicada en el núcleo de un átomo; el número de protones que hay en el núcleo es el número atómico, y éste determina la identidad del elemento (119)

pure substance (PYOOR SUHB stuhns) a sample of matter, either a single element or a single compound, that has definite chemical and physical properties (48)

sustancia pura una muestra de materia, ya sea un solo elemento o un solo compuesto, que tiene propiedades químicas y físicas definidas (48)

quasar (KWAY ZAHR) quasi-stellar radio source; a very luminous object that produces energy at a high rate; quasars are thought to be the most distant objects in the universe (707)

cuasar fuente de radio cuasi-estelar; un objeto muy luminoso que produce energía a una gran velocidad; se piensa que los cuasares son los objetos más distantes del universo (707)

radar (RAY DAHR) **ra**dio **d**etection **a**nd **r**anging, a system that uses reflected radio waves to determine the velocity and location of objects (556)

radar detección y exploración a gran distancia por medio de ondas de radio; un sistema que usa ondas de radio reflejadas para determinar la velocidad y ubicación de los objetos (556)

radiation (RAY dee AY shuhn) the energy that is transferred as electromagnetic waves, such as visible light and infrared waves (482)

radiación la energía que se transfiere en forma de ondas electromagnéticas, tales como las ondas de luz y las infrarrojas (482)

radioactive decay (RAY dee oh AK tiv dee KAY) the disintegration of an unstable atomic nucleus into one or more different nuclides, accompanied by the emission of radiation, the nuclear capture or ejection of electrons, or fission (327)

desintegración radiactiva la desintegración de un núcleo atómico inestable para formar uno o más nucleidos diferentes, lo cual va acompañado de la emisión de radiación, la captura o expulsión nuclear de electrones, o fisión (327)

radioactive tracer (RAY dee oh AK tiv TRAYS uhr) a radioactive material that is added to a substance so that its distribution can be detected later (346)

trazador radiactivo un material radiactivo que se añade a una sustancia de modo que su distribución pueda ser detectada posteriormente (346)

reactant (ree AK tuhnt) a substance or molecule that participates in a chemical reaction (220)

reactivo una sustancia o molécula que participa en una reacción química (220)

reactivity (REE ak TIV uh tee) the capacity of a substance to combine chemically with another substance (56)

reactividad la capacidad de una sustancia de combinarse químicamente con otra sustancia (56)

real image (REE uhl IM ij) an image that is formed by the intersection of light rays; a real image can be projected on a screen (563)

imagen real una imagen que se forma por la intersección de rayos de luz; una imagen real se puede proyectar en una pantalla (563)

recycling (ree SIE kling) the process of recovering valuable or useful materials from waste or scrap; the process of reusing some items (831)

reciclar el proceso de recuperar materiales valiosos o útiles de los desechos o de la basura; el proceso de reutilizar algunas cosas (831)

red giant (RED JIE uhnt) a large, reddish star late in its life cycle (699)

gigante roja una estrella grande de color rojizo que se encuentra en una etapa avanzada de su vida (699)

reflection (ri FLEK shuhn) the bouncing back of a ray of light, sound, or heat when the ray hits a surface that it does not go through (524)

reflexión el rebote de un rayo de luz, sonido o calor cuando el rayo golpea una superficie pero no la atraviesa (524)

refraction (ri FRAK shuhn) the bending of a wavefront as the wavefront passes between two substances in which the speed of the wave differs (526)

refracción el curvamiento de un frente de ondas a medida que el frente pasa entre dos sustancias en las que la velocidad de las ondas difiere (526)

rem (REM) the quantity of ionizing radiation that does as much damage to human tissue as 1 roentgen of high-voltage X rays does (345)

rem la cantidad de radiación ionizante que produce el mismo daño a los tejidos humanos que 1 roentgen de rayos X de alto voltaje (345)

renewable resource (ri NOO uh buhl REE SAWRS) a natural resource that can be replaced at the same rate at which the resource is consumed (818)

recurso renovable un recurso natural que puede reemplazarse a la misma tasa a la que se consume (818)

resistance (ri ZIS tuhns) in physical science, the opposition presented to the current by a material or device (596)

resistencia en ciencias físicas, la oposición que un material o aparato presenta a la corriente (596)

resonance (REZ uh nuhns) a phenomenon that occurs when two objects naturally vibrate at the same frequency; the sound produced by one object causes the other object to vibrate (548)

resonancia un fenómeno que ocurre cuando dos objetos vibran naturalmente a la misma frecuencia; el sonido producido por un objeto hace que el otro objeto vibre (548)

Richter scale (RIK tuhr SKAYL) a scale that expresses the magnitude of an earthquake (742)

escala de Richter una escala que expresa la magnitud de un terremoto (742)

salt (SAWLT) an ionic compound that forms when a metal atom or a positive radical replaces the hydrogen of an acid (303)

sal un compuesto iónico que se forma cuando el átomo de un metal o un radical positivo reemplaza el hidrógeno de un ácido (303)

satellite (SAT'l IET) a natural or artificial body that revolves around a celestial body that is greater in mass (656)

satélite un cuerpo natural o artificial que gira alrededor de un cuerpo celeste que tiene mayor masa (656)

saturated solution (SACH uh RAYT id suh LOO shuhn) a solution that cannot dissolve any more solute under the given conditions (278)

solución saturada una solución que no puede disolver más soluto bajo las condiciones dadas (278)

GLOSSARY • GLOSARIO

schematic diagram (skee MAT ik DIE uh GRAM) a graphical representation of a circuit that uses lines to represent wires and different symbols to represent components (601)

diagrama esquemático una representación gráfica de un circuito, la cual usa líneas para representar cables y diferentes símbolos para representar los componentes (601)

science (SIE uhns) the knowledge obtained by observing natural events and conditions in order to discover facts and formulate laws or principles that can be verified or tested (7)

ciencia el conocimiento que se obtiene por medio de la observación natural de acontecimientos y condiciones con el fin de descubrir hechos y formular leyes o principios que puedan ser verificados o probados (7)

scientific methods (SIE uhn TIF ik METH uhdz) a series of steps followed to solve problems, including collecting data, formulating a hypothesis, testing the hypothesis, and stating conclusions (15)

métodos científicos una serie de pasos que se siguen para solucionar problemas, los cuales incluyen recopilar información, formular una hipótesis, comprobar la hipótesis y sacar conclusiones (15)

scientific notation (SIE uhn TIF ik noh TAY shuhn) a method of expressing a quantity as a number multiplied by 10 to the appropriate power (24)

notación científica un método para expresar una cantidad en forma de un número multiplicado por 10 a la potencia adecuada (24)

sedimentary rock (SED uh MEN tuhr ee RAHK) a rock that forms from compressed or cemented layers of sediment (750)

roca sedimentaria una roca que se forma a partir de capas comprimidas o cementadas de sedimento (750)

seismology (siez MAHL uh jee) the study of earthquakes, including their origin, propagation, energy, and prediction (740)

sismología el estudio de los terremotos, incluyendo su origen, propagación, energía y predicción (740)

semiconductor (SEM i kuhn DUK tuhr) an element or compound that conducts electric current better than an insulator does but not as well as a conductor does (154)

semiconductor un elemento o compuesto que conduce la corriente eléctrica mejor que un aislante, pero no tan bien como un conductor (154)

series circuit (SIR eez SUHR kit) a circuit in which the parts are joined one after another such that the current in each part is the same (603)

circuito en serie un circuito en el que las partes están unidas una después de la otra de manera tal que la corriente en cada parte es la misma (603)

significant figure (sig NIF uh kuhnt FIG yuhr) a prescribed decimal place that determines the amount of rounding off to be done based on the precision of the measurement (26)

cifra significativa un lugar decimal prescrito que determina la cantidad de redondeo que se hará con base en la precisión de la medición (26)

simple machine (SIM puhl muh SHEEN) one of the six basic types of machines, which are the basis for all other forms of machines (438)

máquina simple uno de los seis tipos fundamentales de máquinas, las cuales son la base de todas las demás formas de máquinas (438)

single-displacement reaction (SING guhl dis PLAYS muhnt ree AK shuhn) a reaction in which one element or radical takes the place of another element or radical in a compound (233)

reacción de sustitución simple una reacción en la que un elemento o radical toma el lugar de otro elemento o radical en el compuesto (233)

soap (SOHP) a substance that is used as a cleaner and that dissolves in water (307)

jabón una sustancia que se usa como limpiador y que se disuelve en el agua (307)

solar system (SOH luhr SIS tuhm) the sun and all of the planets and other bodies that travel around it (655)

Sistema Sola el Sol y todos los planetas y otros cuerpos que se desplazan alrededor de él (655)

solenoid (SOH luh NOYD) a coil of wire with an electric current in it (627)

solenoide una bobina de alambre que tiene una corriente eléctrica (627)

solubility (SAHL yoo BIL uh tee) the ability of one substance to dissolve in another at a given temperature and pressure; expressed in terms of the amount of solute that will dissolve in a given amount of solvent to produce a saturated solution (276)

solubilidad la capacidad de una sustancia de disolverse en otra a una temperatura y presión dadas; se expresa en términos de la cantidad de soluto que se disolverá en una cantidad determinada de solvente para producir una solución saturada (276)

GLOSSARY • GLOSARIO

solute (SAHL yoot) in a solution, the substance that dissolves in the solvent (263)

soluto en una solución, la sustancia que se disuelve en el solvente (263)

solution (suh LOO shuhn) a homogeneous mixture throughout which two or more substances are uniformly dispersed (263)

solución una mezcla homogénea en la cual dos o más sustancias se dispersan de manera uniforme (263)

solvent (SAHL vuhnt) in a solution, the substance in which the solute dissolves (263)

solvente en una solución, la sustancia en la que se disuelve el soluto (263)

sonar (SOH NAHR) **so**und **n**avigation **a**nd **r**anging, a system that uses acoustic signals and returned echoes to determine the location of objects or to communicate (551)

sonar navegación y exploración por medio del sonido; un sistema que usa señales acústicas y ondas de eco que regresan para determinar la ubicación de los objetos o para comunicarse (551)

sound wave (SOWND WAYV) a longitudinal wave that is caused by vibrations and that travels through a material medium (543)

onda sonora una onda longitudinal que se origina debido a vibraciones y que se desplaza a través de un medio material (543)

specific heat (spuh SIF ik HEET) the quantity of heat required to raise a unit mass of homogeneous material 1 K or 1 °C in a specified way given constant pressure and volume (485)

calor específico la cantidad de calor que se requiere para aumentar una unidad de masa de un material homogéneo 1 K ó 1 °C de una manera especificada, dados un volumen y una presión constantes (485)

speed (SPEED) the distance traveled divided by the time interval during which the motion occurred (367)

rapidez la distancia que un objeto se desplaza dividida entre el intervalo de tiempo durante el cual ocurrió el movimiento (367)

standing wave (STAN ding WAYV) a pattern of vibration that simulates a wave that is standing still (529)

onda estacionaria un patrón de vibración que simula una onda que está parada (529)

star (STAHR) a large celestial body that is composed of gas and that emits light; the sun is a typical star (693)

estrella un cuerpo celeste grande que está compuesto de gas y emite luz; el Sol es una estrella típica (693)

static friction (STAT ik FRIK shuhn) the force that resists the initiation of sliding motion between two surfaces that are in contact and at rest (383)

fricción estática la fuerza que se opone a que se inicie el movimiento de deslizamiento entre dos superficies que están en contacto y en reposo (383)

stratosphere (STRAT uh SFIR) the layer of the atmosphere that lies between the troposphere and the mesosphere and in which temperature increases as altitude increases; contains the ozone layer (775)

estratosfera la capa de la atmósfera que se encuentra entre la troposfera y la mesosfera y en la cual la temperatura aumenta al aumentar la altitud; contiene la capa de ozono (775)

subduction (suhb DUHK shuhn) the process by which one lithospheric plate moves beneath another plate as a result of tectonic forces (735)

subducción el proceso por medio del cual una placa de la litosfera se mueve debajo de otra como resultado de las fuerzas tectónicas (735)

sublimation (SUHB luh MAY shuhn) the process in which a solid changes directly into a gas (the term is sometimes also used for the reverse process) (85)

sublimación el proceso por medio del cual un sólido se transforma directamente en un gas (en ocasiones, este término también se usa para describir el proceso inverso) (85)

substrate (SUHB STRAYT) a part, substance, or element that lies beneath and supports another part, substance, or element; the reactant in reactions catalyzed by enzymes (241)

sustrato una parte, sustancia o elemento que se encuentra debajo de otra parte, sustancia o elemento y lo sostiene; el reactivo en reacciones que son catalizadas por enzimas (241)

succession (suhk SESH uhn) the replacement of one type of community by another at a single location over a period of time (811)

sucesión el reemplazo de un tipo de comunidad por otro en un mismo lugar a lo largo de un período de tiempo (811)

supernova (soo puhr NOH vuh) a gigantic explosion in which a massive star collapses and throws its outer layers into space (699)

supernova una explosión gigantesca en la que una estrella masiva se colapsa y lanza sus capas externas hacia el espacio (699)

supersaturated solution (SOO puhr SACH uh RAYT id suh LOO shuhn) a solution that holds more dissolved solute than is required to reach equilibrium at a given temperature (279)

solución sobresaturada una solución que contiene más soluto disuelto que el que se requiere para llegar al equilibro a una temperatura dada (279)

surface wave (SUHR fis WAYV) in geology, a seismic wave that travels along the surface of a medium and that has a stronger effect near the surface of the medium than it has in the interior (740)

onda superficial en geología, una onda sísmica que se desplaza a lo largo de la superficie de un medio, cuyo efecto es más fuerte cerca de la superficie del medio que en el interior de éste (740)

suspension (suh SPEN shuhn) a mixture in which particles of a material are more or less evenly dispersed throughout a liquid or gas (260)

suspensión una mezcla en la que las partículas de un material se encuentran dispersas de manera más o menos uniforme a través de un líquido o de un gas (260)

synthesis reaction (SIN thuh sis ree AK shuhn) a reaction in which two or more substances combine to form a new compound (231)

reacción de síntesis una reacción en la que dos o más sustancias se combinan para formar un compuesto nuevo (231)

technology (tek NAHL uh jee) the application of science for practical purposes; the use of tools, machines, materials, and processes to meet human needs (8)

tecnología la aplicación de la ciencia con fines prácticos; el uso de herramientas, máquinas, materiales y procesos para satisfacer las necesidades de los seres humanos (8)

temperature (TEM puhr uh chuhr) a measure of how hot (or cold) something is; specifically, a measure of the average kinetic energy of the particles in an object (80, 473)

temperatura una medida de qué tan caliente (o frío) está algo; específicamente, una medida de la energía cinética promedio de las partículas de un objeto (80, 473)

terminal velocity (TUHR muh nuhl vuh LAHS uh tee) the constant velocity of a falling object when the force of air resistance is equal in magnitude and opposite in direction to the force of gravity (407)

velocidad terminal la velocidad constante de un objeto en caída cuando la fuerza de resistencia del aire es igual en magnitud y opuesta en dirección a la fuerza de gravedad (407)

terrestrial planet (tuh RES tree uhl PLAN it) one of the highly dense planets nearest to the sun; Mercury, Venus, Mars, and Earth (661)

planeta terrestre uno de los planetas muy densos que se encuentran más cerca del Sol; Mercurio, Venus, Marte y la Tierra (661)

theory (THEE uh ree) a system of ideas that explains many related observations and is supported by a large body of evidence acquired through scientific investigation (9)

teoría un sistema de ideas que explica muchas observaciones relacionadas y que está respaldado por una gran cantidad de pruebas obtenidas mediante la investigación científica (9)

thermal conduction (THUHR muhl kuhn DUHK shuhn) the transfer of energy as heat through a material (481)

conducción térmica la transferencia de energía en forma de calor a través de un material (481)

thermal energy (THUHR muhl EN uhr jee) the total kinetic energy of a substance's atoms (81)

energía térmica la energía cinética total de los átomos de una sustancia (81)

thermometer (thuhr MAHM uht uhr) an instrument that measures and indicates temperature (474)

termómetro un instrumento que mide e indica la temperatura (474)

thermosphere (THUHR moh SFIR) the uppermost layer of the atmosphere, in which temperature increases as altitude increases; includes the ionosphere (776)

termosfera la capa más alta de la atmósfera, en la cual la temperatura aumenta a medida que la altitud aumenta; incluye la ionosfera (776)

topography (tuh PAHG ruh fee) the size and shape of the land surface features of a region, including its relief (795)

topografía el tamaño y la forma de las características de una superficie de terreno, incluyendo su relieve (795)

transformer (trans FAWRM uhr) a device that increases or decreases the voltage of alternating current (638)

transformador un aparato que aumenta o disminuye el voltaje de la corriente alterna (638)

transition metal (tran ZISH uhn MET'l) one of the metals that can use the inner shell before using the outer shell to bond (159)

metal de transición uno de los metales que tienen la capacidad de usar su orbital interno antes de usar su orbital externo para formar un enlace (159)

transpiration (TRAN spuh RAY shuhn) the process by which plants release water vapor into the air through stomata; *also* the release of water vapor into the air by other organisms (782)

transpiración el proceso por medio del cual las plantas liberan vapor de agua al aire por medio de los estomas; *también*, la liberación de vapor de agua al aire por otros organismos (782)

transverse wave (TRANS VUHRS WAYV) a wave in which the particles of the medium move perpendicularly to the direction the wave is traveling (511)

onda transversal una onda en la que las partículas del medio se mueven perpendicularmente respecto a la dirección en la que se desplaza la onda (511)

troposphere (TROH poh SFIR) the lowest layer of the atmosphere, in which temperature drops at a constant rate as altitude increases; the part of the atmosphere where weather conditions exist (774)

troposfera la capa inferior de la atmósfera, en la que la temperatura disminuye a una tasa constante a medida que la altitud aumenta; la parte de la atmósfera donde se dan las condiciones del tiempo (774)

trough (TRAWF) the lowest point of a wave (512)

seno el punto más bajo de una onda (512)

ultrasound (UHL truh SOWND) any sound wave with frequencies higher than 20,000 Hz (546)

ultrasonido cualquier onda de sonido que tenga frecuencias superiores a los 20,000 Hz (546)

unified atomic mass unit (YOON uh FIED uh TAHM ik MAS YOON it) a unit of mass that describes the mass of an atom or molecule; it is exactly 1/12 of the mass of a carbon atom with mass number 12 (symbol, u) (124)

unidad de masa atómica unificada una unidad de masa que describe la masa de un átomo o molécula; es exactamente 1/12 de la masa de un átomo de carbono con número de masa de 12 (símbolo: u) (124)

universe (YOON uh VUHRS) the sum of all space, matter, and energy that exist, that have existed in the past, and that will exist in the future (708)

universo la suma de todo el espacio, materia y energía que existen, que han existido en el pasado y que existirán en el futuro (708)

unsaturated solution (uhn SACH uh RAYT id suh LOO shuhn) a solution that contains less solute than a saturated solution does and that is able to dissolve additional solute (278)

solución no saturada una solución que contiene menos soluto que una solución saturada, y que tiene la capacidad de disolver más soluto (278)

valence electron (VAY luhns ee LEK TRAHN) an electron that is found in the outermost shell of an atom and that determines the atom's chemical properties (130)

electrón de valencia un electrón que se encuentra en la capa más externa de un átomo y que determina las propiedades químicas del átomo (130)

variable (VER ee uh buhl) a factor that changes in an experiment in order to test a hypothesis (15)

variable un factor que se modifica en un experimento con el fin de probar una hipótesis (15)

velocity (vuh LAHS uh tee) the speed of an object in a particular direction (367)

velocidad la rapidez de un objeto en una dirección dada (367)

vent (VENT) an opening at the surface of the Earth through which volcanic material passes (743)

chimenea una abertura en la superficie de la Tierra a través de la cual pasa material volcánico (743)

virtual image (VUHR choo uhl IM ij) an image from which light rays appear to diverge, even though they are not actually focused there; a virtual image cannot be projected on a screen (562)

imagen virtual una imagen de la que los rayos de luz parecen divergir, aunque no están enfocados allí realmente; una imagen virtual no se puede proyectar en una pantalla (562)

viscosity (vis KAHS uh tee) the resistance of a gas or liquid to flow (94)

viscosidad la resistencia de un gas o un líquido a fluir (94)

volume (VAHL yoom) a measure of the size of a body or region in three-dimensional space (21)

volumen una medida del tamaño de un cuerpo o región en un espacio de tres dimensiones (21)

water cycle (WAWT uhr SIE kuhl) the continuous movement of water between the atmosphere, the land, and the oceans (781)

ciclo del agua el movimiento continuo del agua entre la atmósfera, la tierra y los océanos (781)

wavelength (WAYV LENGKTH) the distance from any point on a wave to an identical point on the next wave (515)

longitud de onda la distancia entre cualquier punto de una onda y un punto idéntico en la onda siguiente (515)

weathering (WETH uhr ing) the natural process by which atmospheric and environmental agents, such as wind, rain, and temperature changes, disintegrate and decompose rocks (750)

meteorización el proceso natural por medio del cual los agentes atmosféricos o ambientales, como el viento, la lluvia y los cambios de temperatura, desintegran y descomponen las rocas (750)

weight (WAYT) a measure of the gravitational force exerted on an object; its value can change with the location of the object in the universe (21, 403)

peso una medida de la fuerza gravitacional ejercida sobre un objeto; su valor puede cambiar en función de la ubicación del objeto en el universo (21, 403)

white dwarf (WIET DWAWRF) a small, hot, dim star that is the leftover center of an old star (699)

enana blanca una estrella pequeña, caliente y tenue que es el centro sobrante de una estrella vieja (699)

work (WUHRK) the transfer of energy to a body by the application of a force that causes the body to move in the direction of the force; it is equal to the product of the magnitude of the component of a force along the direction of displacement and the magnitude of the displacement (431)

trabajo la transferencia de energía a un cuerpo por medio de la aplicación de una fuerza que hace que el cuerpo se mueva en la dirección de la fuerza; es igual al producto de la magnitud del componente de una fuerza aplicada en la dirección del desplazamiento por la magnitud del desplazamiento (431)

INDEX

Note: Page references followed by *f* refer to illustrative material, such as figures and tables.

A

absolute zero, 476
acceleration, 372–377
    in automobile accidents, 378–379
    average, 374, 374*f*, 375
    calculation of, 374–375, 374*f*, 377
    centripetal, 373, 373*f*
    as change in velocity, 372–373, 372*f*, 373*f*
    constant, 376–377, 377*f*
    force and, 381, 382, 400–402, 400*f*, 402*f*
    graphing of, 376–377, 377*f*
    negative, 374–375, 376, 377*f*
accelerators, particle, 17
accelerometers, 379
accident investigators, 378–379
accretion, 673
accuracy, 27, 27*f*, 29
acid-base reactions, 302–304, 302*f*, 303*f*
    with antacids, 311
    labs on, 312, 314–315
acid precipitation, 301, 758, 758*f*, 826, 826*f*
    marble and, 751, 758
acid rain. *See* **acid precipitation**
acids, 293–295. *See also* **pH**
    amino acids, 203, 203*f*, 204, 243
    common examples of, 295*f*
    as electrolytes, 294, 294*f*
    in household products, 310–313
    lab on, 296
    properties of, 293
    safe handling of, 295
    in sour fruits, 293, 293*f*
    strong, 294, 294*f*, 295, 295*f*
    uses of, 295, 295*f*
    weak, 294, 294*f*, 295, 295*f*
    weathering of minerals by, 757, 757*f*, 758, 758*f*
action forces, 412–413, 412*f*, 413*f*
    conservation of momentum and, 417
    lab on, 414
active site, of enzyme, 241, 241*f*
additive primary colors, 565, 565*f*
aerobic organisms, 778
aerogel, 53
air. *See* **atmosphere**
air bags, 399
air conditioners, 489, 490
air masses, 789, 790, 790*f*
air pollution, 824, 825–827, 825*f*, 826*f*
    lab on, 827
    ozone in, 236, 827
    temperature inversion and, 774, 774*f*
airport security, 629
air pressure, 784–785, 784*f*, 785*f*. *See also* **pressure**
air resistance
    in free fall, 407, 407*f*
    mechanical energy lost to, 455, 456
    perpetual motion and, 460
    in projectile motion, 409
alcohols, 200, 200*f*
algal blooms, 828, 828*f*
algebraic rearrangements, 865. *See also* **equations**
alien life, 706
alkali metals, 157, 157*f*
    single-displacement reactions of, 234, 234*f*
alkaline-earth metals, 158, 158*f*
alkanes, 198–199, 198*f*, 199*f*
alkenes, 200, 200*f*
alloys, 266, 266*f*
alpha decay, 328, 330, 331
alpha particles, 328, 328*f*
    penetration of matter by, 328, 329*f*, 348
    in Rutherford's experiment, 117, 117*f*
    in smoke detectors, 346
alternating current, 634, 636, 636*f*
    transformer and, 638, 638*f*
altocumulus clouds, 783*f*, 784
altostratus clouds, 783*f*, 784
amalgam, 264
amino acids, 203, 203*f*, 204, 243
ammeters, 630
ammonia
    as base, 297, 310
    in household cleaners, 310, 310*f*
    manufacture of, 246–247, 247*f*
    in nitrogen cycle, 246
    products made from, 246, 246*f*, 247
amperes (A), 595
amplitude, 514, 514*f*, 515
anabolic reactions, 242–243
analogies, 112, 584
AND operator, 874
aneroid barometers, 785, 785*f*
angle of incidence, 561, 561*f*
angle of reflection, 561, 561*f*
angles, bond, 178, 178*f*
animals. *See also* **ecosystems**
    bioluminescence of, 223
    chemical energy for, 449
    gravitational force on, 404, 404*f*
anions. *See also* **ions**
    formation of, 153, 153*f*
    names of, 190, 190*f*, 192, 192*f*
    polyatomic, 189–190, 189*f*, 190*f*
anode, of vacuum tube, 115, 115*f*
antacids, 310, 311, 311*f*
    lab on, 312
antinodes, 529, 529*f*
    of guitar string, 547
antioxidants, 312, 312*f*
apparent weightlessness, 408, 408*f*
Archimedes' principle, 90, 90*f*
architect, career as, 426
area. *See also* **surface area**
    of geometric shapes, 864, 864*f*
    of rectangle, 10, 18, 864*f*
    units of, 18*f*
Aristotle, 672
arm, of lever, 439, 440, 443
arson investigator, career as, 214
ash, volcanic
    impact on humans, 747
    on ocean floor, 746
    venting of, 743, 743*f*, 744, 745
asteroids, 666, 666*f*, 675
    impacts on moon, 678
    meteorites derived from, 676, 677
    origin of, 674*f*
asthenosphere, 733, 734
astronauts
    apparent weightlessness of, 408, 408*f*
    career as, 688
    in empty space, 710, 710*f*
    on moon, 403, 403*f*, 404, 659
astronomical units (AU), 662
astronomy. *See also* **planets; solar system; stars; universe**
    early history of, 671–673, 671*f*, 672*f*
atmosphere, 663, 773–780. *See also* **air pollution; air resistance; clouds; greenhouse effect; weather; wind**
    of early Earth, 663, 777–778, 777*f*
    gases in, 50, 663, 773, 775, 775*f*, 776
    lab on, 796–797
    layers of, 773–777, 773*f*, 776*f*
    oxygen-carbon dioxide cycle and, 778, 778*f*
    ozone layer of, 236, 558, 773*f*, 775, 778
    refraction of light in, 567, 567*f*
    water in, 774, 781–784, 781*f*, 783*f*
    word origin of, 772

INDEX

atmospheric pressure, 784–785, 784*f*, 785*f*
atomic mass, 124
   average, 124, 124*f*, 125, 126
   Mendeleev's periodic table and, 145, 146, 147
   in radioactive decay, 330, 330*f*, 331
   unit of, 124
atomic mass units (amu), 124
atomic number, 121, 121*f*
   periodic table and, 147, 151
   in radioactive decay, 330–331
   in symbol of isotope, 124, 124*f*
atomic radius, lab on, 166–167
atoms. *See also* **chemical bonds; elements**
   Bohr model of, 128–129, 128*f*
   Dalton's theory of, 114, 114*f*
   of different elements, 46–47, 47*f*, 114, 120, 121
   earliest theories of, 113
   electric force and, 120
   energy levels of, 128, 128*f*, 130–131, 130*f*, 131*f*
   energy level transitions, 131–132, 132*f*
   kinetic energy of, 448
   labs on, 111, 114, 122, 131, 134–135
   magnetic properties of, 621, 628
   mass number of, 121–122, 121*f*, 124, 124*f*
   modern models of, 11, 128–129, 128*f*, 129*f*
   in molecules, 47, 47*f*, 48, 48*f*
   motion of, 77, 448
   particles in, 119–120, 119*f*, 120*f*
   properties of everyday things and, 113, 113*f*
   rearranged in chemical reactions, 220
   Rutherford's experiment on, 117–118, 117*f*
   Rutherford's model of, 117–118, 118*f*
   Thomson's model of, 115, 115*f*, 117
aurora australis, 777
aurora borealis, 79, 79*f*, 777, 777*f*
automobiles
   accident reconstruction, 378–379
   air bags, 399
   brakes, 383, 398
   car seats, 398, 398*f*
   catalytic converters, 240, 240*f*
   engines, 492–493, 492*f*, 493*f*
   friction acting on, 378–379, 382, 383–385, 385*f*
   seat belts, 398
   solar, 461, 461*f*
average acceleration, 374, 374*f*, 375
average atomic mass, 124, 124*f*, 125, 126
average speed, 368, 368*f*
Avogadro, Amedeo, 125
Avogadro's number, 125

B

background radiation, 344, 344*f*, 345, 345*f*
baking powder, 313, 313*f*
balance, triple-beam, 878
balanced chemical equations, 226–229, 226*f*, 228*f*
bar graphs, 23, 23*f*, 871
   of mechanical energy, 455
   of star colors, 720
barometers, 784, 784*f*, 785, 785*f*
barometric pressure, 784–785, 784*f*, 785*f*
basalt, 749
bases, 295–297. *See also* **pH**
   in acid-base reactions, 302–304, 302*f*, 303*f*, 311
   antacids, 310, 311, 311*f*, 312
   common examples of, 297*f*
   as electrolytes, 296
   in household products, 310, 310*f*, 311, 311*f*, 313, 313*f*
   labs on, 296, 312, 314–315
   properties of, 295
   safe handling of, 297
   strong, 296, 297, 297*f*
   uses of, 297*f*
   weak, 297, 297*f*
basilar membrane, 549, 549*f*
batteries, 594–595, 594*f*
   in circuits, 600, 601*f*, 602*f*
   environmental impact of, 830
   lab on, 595
beats, 528, 528*f*
bends, 279
Bernoulli's principle, 94, 94*f*
beta decay, 329, 330, 330*f*
beta particles, 328, 328*f*, 329
   penetration of matter by, 329, 329*f*, 348
bias
   on Internet, 834
   in science, 16

bicycles, 435, 443, 443*f*
big bang, 710, 712–713, 715
biochemical compounds, 202–205
   carbohydrates, 202, 202*f*
   DNA, 8, 8*f*, 202, 204–205, 204*f*
   in human body, 243
   proteins, 202, 203, 203*f*, 204, 262
biochemistry, 8
biology, 7*f*, 8
bioluminescence, 223
black holes, 411
   at center of galaxy, 411, 704
   as possible dark matter, 716
   of quasars, 707
   as supernova remnants, 411, 700
bleach, 310
block and tackle, 440
blood pressure, 405
blood substitutes, 274–275
blue shift, 710, 710*f*
Bohr, Niels, 128, 129
Bohr model, 128–129, 128*f*
boiling, 85
   lab on, 102–103
boiling points, 52, 85
   lab on, 86
   of solutions, 273
   structures of compounds and, 180, 180*f*, 181, 182*f*
bonds, chemical. *See* **chemical bonds**
booklet (FoldNote), 542
   instructions for, 848
books, numbering systems for, 875
Boolean operators, 874
Boolean search, 874
botany, 8
Boyle's law, 97–98, 97*f*
brakes, 383, 398
brass, 266, 266*f*
brightness
   of light, 555, 555*f*
   of stars, 695, 700–701, 701*f*
bromthymol blue, 304, 304*f*
brown dwarfs, 716
brushes, of motor, 631, 631*f*
buckminsterfullerene, 163
buoyant force, 90–91, 90*f*
   lab on, 91
   on submarine, 95
burning. *See also* **combustion reactions; fire**
   chemical energy released by, 451
   flammability and, 56

INDEX

C

calculus, 374
caloric theory, 10
Calorie, 451
carbohydrates, 202, 202f. See also photosynthesis
carbon, 163, 163f
carbon-14
    dating materials with, 336, 336f
    decay curve of, 333, 333f
    nuclear decay process in, 330, 330f
carbon dioxide
    in carbonated drinks, 244–245, 244f
    from cellular respiration, 815
    in early atmosphere, 663, 777
    from fossil fuels, 817, 825, 826
    as greenhouse gas, 779–780, 779f, 795, 826, 826f
    in oxygen-carbon dioxide cycle, 778, 778f
    in rainwater, 757, 758
carbonic acid, 757, 757f, 758, 758f
carbon monoxide, 232, 825, 825f
carburetors, 493
careers using chemistry, 214–215
careers using Earth science, 688–689
cars
    accident reconstruction, 378–379
    air bags, 399
    brakes, 383, 398
    catalytic converters, 240, 240f
    engines, 492–493, 492f, 493f
    friction acting on, 378–379, 382, 383–385, 385f
    seat belts, 398
    solar, 461, 461f
car seats, 398, 398f
catabolic reactions, 242–243
catalog, library, 875
catalysts, 240–241, 240f
    enzymes, 241, 241f, 242
catalytic converter, 240, 240f
catapults, 418–419
cathode, 115, 115f
cathode-ray tube, 5–6, 5f
    of television, 116
    Thomson's experiment, 115, 115f
cations. See also **ions**
    formation of, 153, 153f
    names of, 191, 191f, 192, 192f
    polyatomic, 189, 189f
cause-and-effect map (Graphic Organizer), 292
    instructions for, 855

cause-and-effect relationships, 396, 618
cell phones, 559
cells (atmospheric), 787
cells (biological), 268
cells (electrochemical), 594
    lab on, 595
cellular respiration, 243, 815
Celsius-Fahrenheit conversion, 475
Celsius-Kelvin conversion equation, 476
Celsius temperature scale, 475, 476, 476f, 477
centripetal acceleration, 373, 373f
Ceres, 666
chain-of-events chart (Graphic Organizer), 652
    instructions for, 854
chain reaction, nuclear, 337, 340–341, 340f
changes of state, 84–87, 84f, 85f, 86f
    conservation of mass and energy in, 87
    constant temperature during, 87, 87f, 487, 487f
    graphs of, 87f, 104
    labs on, 86, 102–103
charge, electric
    basic properties of, 585–586, 585f, 586f
    in charging by contact, 589, 589f
    in charging by friction, 589
    conservation of, 585
    force between objects and, 591
    Franklin's experiments on, 587
    induced, 588, 588f, 590, 590f
    on ions, 153, 153f, 208
    lab on, 590
    moving, magnetism and, 450, 626, 628
    of subatomic particles, 119, 119f, 120
    transfer of, 588–590, 588f, 589f, 590f
charged particles
    and electric fields, 450, 450f, 591–592, 591f, 592f
    subatomic, 119–120, 119f
Charles's law, 100, 100f
chef, career as, 215
chemical bonds, 177–179, 178f, 179f
    angles of, 178, 178f
    in chemical reactions, 220–221, 222, 449
    covalent, 183, 186–187, 186f, 187f, 189
    double, 187, 187f, 198, 200
    explanation for, 183
    hydrogen bonds, 182, 182f, 269, 269f

    ionic, 183, 184–185, 184f, 185f, 189
    lengths of, 178, 178f, 179
    metallic, 188, 188f
    triple, 187, 187f, 198
chemical changes, 61–62, 61f, 62f. See also **chemical reactions**
    compounds and, 61, 63, 64, 64f
    conservation of mass and energy in, 87–88, 88f
chemical energy, 449, 449f, 451
    converted to other energy forms, 456, 456f
    in heat engine, 492
    in reactions, 221, 222, 222f
chemical equations, 225–229
    balanced, 226–229, 226f, 228f
    lab on, 228
    mass calculations with, 228f, 229, 250
    mole ratios derived from, 228–229, 250
    reading, 218, 226, 226f
    as summaries of reactions, 225, 225f
chemical equilibrium, 245, 246–247
chemical formulas, 48, 48f, 208. See also **chemical equations**
    empirical, 194–196, 195f
    for ionic compounds, 192, 193
    molecular, 195, 195f
    structural, 178, 199, 199f
chemical properties, 56–58, 56f
    compared with physical properties, 58, 58f
    of groups in periodic table, 151
    identifying substances by, 57
    lab on, 58
chemical reactions. See also **chemical changes; chemical equations; combustion reactions**
    acid-base, 302–304, 302f, 303f, 311, 312, 314–315
    conservation of energy in, 88, 88f, 221
    conservation of mass in, 88, 220, 226
    definition of, 219
    electrons in, 235, 237
    endothermic, 222, 222f, 224, 224f
    energy changes in, 220–222, 221f, 224, 449, 449f
    equilibrium in, 245, 246–247
    exothermic, 222, 222f
    in human body, 242–243
    labs on, 222, 235, 239, 241, 248–249
    neutralization, 302–304, 302f, 303f, 311, 312, 314–315
    radioisotopes in, 346

Index **921**

INDEX

chemical reactions (*continued*)
   rates of, 238–241, 238f, 239f, 245, 248–249
   rearrangement of atoms in, 220
   types of, 230–237, 231f, 233f, 234f
   visible signs of, 219, 219f
chemical structure, 178–179, 178f. *See also* **chemical bonds**
   properties and, 180–182, 180f, 181f, 182f
chemical symbols, 208
chemical weathering, 750, 757–758, 757f, 758f
chemistry, 8, 45
   careers using, 214–215
   historical development of, 113
chlorofluorocarbons, 778
cinder cones, 744, 744f
circuit breakers, 606, 607, 607f
circuits, electric, 600–607
   basic features of, 600, 600f
   fuses and circuit breakers in, 606–607, 606f, 607f
   lab on, 608–609
   miniaturization of, 604
   parallel, 603, 603f
   power consumed in, 605–606, 605f
   schematic diagrams of, 601–602, 601f, 602f
   series, 603, 603f
   short, 606, 607
   switches in, 601, 601f, 602, 602f, 603
circular motion
   acceleration in, 373, 373f
   in orbit, 410
cirrostratus clouds, 783f, 784, 790, 790f
cirrus clouds, 783, 783f, 790, 790f
classification, 4, 292, 504
clay, 179
cleaning products, 307–310
   ammonia in, 310, 310f
   bleach, 310
   detergents, 309, 310, 311
   lab on, 309
   soaps, 307–309, 307f, 311
climate, 794–795, 795f
   ecosystem changes caused by, 812
   global changes in, 16, 780, 780f, 795, 826
closed circuits, 600, 600f, 601, 601f
closed systems, 457
clouds, 781f, 783–784, 783f. *See also* **precipitation**
   fronts and, 789, 790, 790f
   funnel cloud, 791, 791f
   of hurricane, 792, 792f
   international symbols for, 882
   lightning and, 791
   over mountains, 795
clusters, galactic, 703, 703f, 719f
coefficient of friction, 378–379
coefficients, in chemical equations, 226
cold fronts, 789, 789f, 790, 790f
collisions, 416–417, 417f
   kinetic energy in, 448
colloids, 261–262, 261f, 262f
colors, 564–565, 564f, 565f. *See also* **spectrum**
   of fireworks, 133
   frequencies of light and, 521, 521f
   lab on, 564
   of light emitted by atoms, 132, 132f
   of rainbow, 571, 571f
   separated by prism, 570, 570f
   in starlight, 695, 696, 696f
combustion reactions, 232
   air pollution caused by, 825, 825f, 826, 827
   in engine, 492
   as exothermic reactions, 222
   fire extinguishers and, 232
   incomplete, 232, 236
   as redox reactions, 237
comets, 675–676, 675f, 676f
   impacts with moon, 678
   impact with Earth, 677
   Stardust mission to, 53
communities, 808, 808f, 811
commutator, 631, 631f
comparisons
   with analogies, 112, 584
   signaling words for, 326
comparison table (Note Taking), 76, 472
   instructions for, 843
compass, 622, 622f, 623
   gyrocompass, 621
   lab on, 623
   near current-carrying wire, 626, 626f, 627
composite volcanoes, 743, 744f
compound machines, 443, 443f
compounds, 45, 47–48, 47f. *See also* **biochemical compounds; covalent compounds; ionic compounds; molecular compounds; network structures; organic compounds**
   chemical changes in, 61, 63, 64, 64f
   Dalton's atomic theory and, 114, 114f
   definition of, 47
   models of, 178, 178f
   molar masses of, 127, 127f
   nonpolar, 270, 270f
   as pure substances, 48
   structures and properties of, 180–182, 180f, 181f, 182f
compressions, of wave medium, 512, 512f
compression stroke, 492, 493, 493f
computer chips, 165
computer models, 11–12, 12f
computers, 8, 8f, 604
concave mirrors, 563
concentrated solution, 277, 280
concentration
   equilibrium and, 245, 246f
   reaction rates and, 238, 239–240
   of solutions, 277, 280
concept map (Graphic Organizer), 430, 728
   instructions for, 852
condensation, 84f, 86, 86f, 781f, 782–783
condensation point, 86
condensed structural formulas, 199, 199f
conduction, thermal, 480–481, 480f, 481f
conductors (electricity), 588, 588f
   acid solutions, 293, 294, 294f
   basic solutions, 296, 297
   ionic compounds, 185, 185f
   lab on, 598
   living things, 589
   metals, 188, 188f, 597, 599
   in periodic table, 154, 155f
   resistance of, 596–599, 603
   in schematic diagrams, 602f
conductors (heat), 484–485
   labs on, 66–67, 484, 494–495
   in periodic table, 154, 155f
cones, cinder, 744, 744f
cones (eye), 569, 569f
conglomerate rock, 750, 750f
conservation of charge, 585
conservation of energy
   in chemical reactions, 88, 88f, 221
   electromagnetic induction and, 633
   hydroelectric power and, 458
   lab on, 457
   law of, 87, 88, 456–457, 490, 491
conservation of mass
   in chemical reactions, 88, 220, 226
   law of, 87–88
conservation of momentum, 416–417
   lab on, 418–419
   with rockets, 416
conservator, career as, 215
constant acceleration, 376–377, 377f. *See also* **free fall**

constants, 865
constant speed, 368, 371
constellations, 654, 654*f*, 697
constructive interference, 527, 527*f*
    of light, 528, 528*f*, 552*f*
    of sound, 528, 528*f*
    standing waves and, 529, 529*f*
contact, charging by, 589, 589*f*
contact forces, 381
continental drift, 731–733, 731*f*, 733*f*
controlled experiment, 15, 876
convection, 480, 480*f*, 483
    plate tectonics and, 733
    in stars, 694
convection currents, 480, 480*f*, 482
    in air and ocean, 483, 486
    in homes, 488
conventional current, 595
convergent plate boundaries, 735–736, 735*f*, 736*f*, 745
converging lens, 568, 568*f*
conversion factors, 19, 19*f*, 68
convex mirrors, 563, 563*f*
cooling systems, 488–489, 490
Copernicus, Nicolaus, 672
core, 729*f*, 730, 730*f*
    seismic waves and, 741, 741*f*
Coriolis effect, 786, 786*f*
cornea, 569, 569*f*
cosmic background radiation, 712, 712*f*
coulombs (C), 586
counterfeit money, 572–573
covalent bonds, 183, 186–187, 186*f*, 187*f*
    nonpolar, 186*f*, 187
    polar, 187, 187*f*
    in polyatomic ions, 189
covalent compounds, 183, 183*f*, 186–187, 186*f*, 187*f*. *See also* **molecular compounds**
    naming, 194, 194*f*
craters
    on Earth, 677, 677*f*
    on moon, 678
creep, 761
crests, 512, 512*f*, 513
    amplitude and, 514, 514*f*
    frequency and, 516, 516*f*
    wavelength and, 515, 515*f*
critical mass, 341
critical temperature, of superconductor, 599
critical thinking, 14–15, 14*f*
crust, 729, 729*f*, 730*f*, 732
    at convergent boundaries, 735
    minerals in, 748

cumulonimbus clouds, 783*f*, 784, 790, 790*f*
cumulus clouds, 783, 783*f*
Curie, Marie, 332
Curie, Pierre, 332
current, electric
    in acid solutions, 293, 294, 294*f*
    alternating, 634, 636, 636*f*, 638, 638*f*
    in basic solutions, 296, 297
    in closed circuit, 600, 600*f*, 601
    conventional, 595
    definition of, 595
    direct, 595, 602*f*
    induced by magnetic field, 632–634, 632*f*, 634*f*, 636, 636*f*
    in ionic compounds, 185, 185*f*
    magnetism from, 626–629, 626*f*, 627*f*, 630, 631*f*
    measurement of, 630, 630*f*
    in metals, 188, 597, 599
    in overloaded circuit, 606, 607
    in parallel circuit, 603
    in plasma, 79, 82
    power and, 605, 606
    resistance and, 596–599
    in series circuit, 603
    in superconductor, 599
currents, convection, 480, 480*f*, 482
    in air and ocean, 483, 486
    in homes, 488
currents, ocean, 483, 654
cyclones, 792
cylinder, graduated, 877

D

Dalton, John, 114
damped harmonic motion, 509
dams, 458, 813, 820, 820*f*
dark matter, 716, 716*f*
data. *See also* **graphs; measurements**
    collection of, 15, 15*f*, 16, 16*f*, 17
    reporting of, 14, 22, 879
daughter isotope, 754
da Vinci, Leonardo, 13
dead spots (sound), 527
decanting, 261
decay, exponential, 335, 335*f*. *See also* **radioactive decay**
decay curve, 335, 335*f*
decibels, 545, 545*f*
decimal point
    in scientific notation, 866

significant figures and, 868
decimals, 862
decomposition reactions, 231, 231*f*
    in human body, 242
definite proportions, law of, 114, 114*f*, 228
deforestation, 761, 761*f*
deltas, 759, 759*f*
Democritus, 113, 114
density, 54–55, 55*f*
    floating and, 91, 91*f*
    of gases, 96
    labs on, 43, 55, 66–67
    submarines and, 95, 95*f*
    units of, 54, 68
    of various materials, 881
deoxyribonucleic acid (DNA), 8, 8*f*, 202, 204–205, 204*f*
dependent variable, 23, 869, 877
deposition, 759, 759*f*
derived units, 18, 880
destructive interference, 527, 527*f*
    of light, 528, 528*f*, 552*f*
    of sound, 528, 528*f*
    standing waves and, 529, 529*f*
detergents, 309, 310, 311
deuterons, 694
Dewey decimal system, 875
dew point, 783
diffraction, 525, 525*f*, 552*f*
diffuse reflection, 561, 561*f*
diffusion, 268, 272
digestion, 242
dilute solution, 277, 280
dinosaurs, 677
dioxin, 829
direct current, 595, 602*f*
direction of motion
    change in, 373, 373*f*, 375
    displacement and, 366, 370
    momentum and, 414
    reference points for, 365, 367
    work and, 431
direct relationship, 101
disaster preparedness, 793
disc brakes, 383
disinfectants, 310
dispersion, 570–571, 570*f*, 571*f*
displacement, 366, 366*f*, 370
displacement reactions, 233–234, 233*f*, 234*f*
dissociation, 296
dissolving. *See also* **solubility; solutions**
    forces between particles and, 268, 271, 277
    heating and, 272, 273*f*, 279

Index **923**

INDEX

dissolving (continued)
    of ionic compounds by water, 267–268, 268f
    lab on, 270
    like dissolves like, 270
    of molecular compounds by water, 269, 269f
    of nonpolar compounds, 270, 270f
    as physical change, 60, 60f
    process of, 271
    stirring or shaking and, 272, 272f, 273f
    surface area and, 271, 271f
distance, 365–366, 366f. *See also* **height; length**
    gravitational potential energy and, 445
    sonar measurement of, 551
    speed and, 367, 367f, 368–369, 371, 371f
    third-class lever and, 439, 439f
    work done by force and, 431–432, 434, 436–437, 437f
distance vs. time graph, 367, 367f, 370–371, 371f, 388
    acceleration and, 377, 377f
distillation, 264, 265
divergent plate boundaries, 734, 734f, 745
diverging lens, 568, 568f
DNA (deoxyribonucleic acid), 8, 8f, 202, 204–205, 204f
DNA fingerprinting, 205
domains, Internet, 168, 316, 610
domains, magnetic, 621
Doppler effect
    in Doppler radar, 523f
    with light, 710, 710f
    with sound, 522–523, 522f
dosimeters, 348, 348f
double bonds, 187, 187f, 198, 200
double-displacement reactions, 234
double-door fold (FoldNote), 618
    instructions for, 849
double helix, 204, 204f
drum brakes, 383
dual nature, of light, 554
dwarf planet, 666, 670, 670f

E

ear, 549, 549f
Earth. *See also* **atmosphere; climate; Earth's magnetic field; ecosystems; gravity; plate tectonics; weather**
    daily cycles on, 654, 654f
    in early astronomy, 672, 672f
    gravitational forces acting on, 405, 405f, 413, 413f
    hydrosphere of, 663
    impact craters on, 677, 677f
    interior of, 729–730, 729f, 730f, 741, 741f
    map of, 884–885
    as open system, 457
    orbit of, 655, 655f, 656, 661, 661f
    planetary characteristics of, 663, 663f
    radioactivity in interior of, 333, 730
    rotation of, 654, 786, 786f
    tilted axis of, 794, 794f, 795
    view from, 653–654, 653f, 654f
earthquakes, 738–743
    labs on, 739, 762–763
    magnitudes of, 742, 742f
    plate boundaries and, 738–739, 738f
    prediction of, 743
    transform fault boundaries and, 737
    waves of, 506, 515, 518, 739–741, 740f, 741f
Earth science, 7, 7f, 8
    careers using, 688–689
Earth's magnetic field, 622–623, 623f, 624, 624f
    animal navigation and, 624, 624f
    auroras and, 777, 777f
    bacterial orientation and, 637
    reversals of, 625, 732, 732f
eclipses, 658, 658f
ecology, 8
ecosystems, 807–814
    adaptation of organisms to, 808
    changes in, 811–814, 811f, 813f
    definition of, 807
    divisions of, 808, 808f
    elements of, 807–808, 807f
    sizes of, 808
    stability in, 809–811, 809f, 810f
efficiency, 459–461, 459f
Einstein, Albert, 339, 340, 717
elastic potential energy, 445, 455
    of mass-spring system, 508, 508f, 509
electrical energy. *See also* **energy resources**
    from coal-fired power plant, 821, 821f, 822
    electric fields and, 450, 450f
    from generator, 634, 634f, 636–637, 636f
    from hydroelectric plant, 458, 637, 820, 820f
    of lightning, 450, 450f, 791
    from nuclear reactor, 341, 343, 349–351, 349f, 818, 822
    power and, 605–606
    transmission from power plants, 639
    from wind, 788, 819, 819f, 822
electrical ground, 598
electrical meter, 605, 605f
electrical potential energy, 593–595, 593f, 594f
electrical resistance, 596–599, 603, 605
    calculation of, 597
    insulators and, 598
    lab on, 598
    in parallel circuits, 603
    in schematic diagrams, 602f
    superconductors and, 599
electric charge. *See also* **charged particles**
    basic properties of, 585–586, 585f, 586f
    in charging by contact, 589, 589f
    in charging by friction, 589
    conservation of, 585
    force between objects and, 591
    Franklin's experiments on, 587
    induced, 588, 588f, 590, 590f
    on ions, 153, 153f, 208
    lab on, 590
    moving, magnetism and, 450, 626, 628
    of subatomic particles, 119, 119f, 120
    transfer of, 588–590, 588f, 589f, 590f
electric circuits, 600–607
    basic features of, 600, 600f
    fuses and circuit breakers in, 606–607, 606f, 607f
    lab on, 608–609
    miniaturization of, 604
    parallel, 603, 603f
    power consumed in, 605–606, 605f
    schematic diagrams of, 601–602, 601f, 602f
    series, 603, 603f
    short, 606, 607
    switches in, 601, 601f, 602, 602f, 603
electric current
    in acid solutions, 293, 294, 294f
    alternating, 634, 636, 636f, 638, 638f
    in basic solutions, 296, 297
    in closed circuit, 600, 600f, 601
    conventional, 595
    definition of, 595
    direct, 595, 602f

induced by magnetic field, 632-634, 632*f*, 634*f*, 636, 636*f*
in ionic compounds, 185, 185*f*
magnetism from, 626-629, 626*f*, 627*f*, 630, 631*f*
measurement of, 630, 630*f*
in metals, 188, 597, 599
in overloaded circuit, 606, 607
in parallel circuit, 603
in plasma, 79, 82
power and, 605, 606
resistance and, 596-599
in series circuit, 603
in superconductor, 599

electric field lines, 591-592, 591*f*, 592*f*

electric fields
of charged particles, 591-592, 591*f*, 592*f*
charged particles in, 450, 450*f*, 591
in conductor, 597
of electromagnetic waves, 452, 506, 511, 637, 637*f*
energy in, 450, 450*f*, 452
potential energy associated with, 593, 594

electric force, 590-592
holding atoms together, 120
potential energy associated with, 593, 594

electric guitars, 635

electric motors, 450, 630, 630*f*, 631, 631*f*

electric potential, 450

electric power, 605-606. *See also* **electrical energy**

electrochemical cell, 594
lab on, 595

electrodes, 594

electrolysis, 229, 229*f*, 231

electrolytes
acids as, 294, 294*f*
bases as, 296, 297
in electrochemical cells, 594

electromagnetic energy, 637

electromagnetic force, 380, 381, 637

electromagnetic induction, 632-637, 632*f*
conservation of energy and, 633
electric guitars and, 635
Faraday's Law of, 632
generators and, 634, 634*f*, 636-637, 636*f*
lab on, 633
magnetic force and, 633-634, 634*f*
in transformers, 638

electromagnetic radiation, 451, 482, 482*f*, 557. *See also* **electromagnetic waves**

electromagnetic spectrum, 521, 521*f*, 556-558, 556-557*f*, 880

electromagnetic waves, 506, 506*f*, 637, 637*f*. *See also* **gamma rays; infrared light; light; radio waves; ultraviolet light**
cosmic background radiation, 712, 712*f*
energy of, 452, 452*f*, 482, 482*f*, 554, 554*f*
fields of, 452, 506, 511, 637, 637*f*
frequencies of, 521, 554, 554*f*
speed of, 521
from stars, 693, 694, 695-696, 696*f*
as transverse waves, 511, 637, 637*f*
vibrating charges and, 508

electromagnets, 628
labs on, 628, 640-641

electrons, 115, 119, 119*f*, 120, 120*f*. *See also* **orbitals; valence electrons**
atomic number and, 121
as beta particles, 328*f*, 329, 330
in chemical reactions, 235, 237
electric charge of, 115, 586
electric current composed of, 595
in electric field, 450
energy levels of, 128, 128*f*, 130-131, 130*f*, 131*f*
in Rutherford's atomic model, 118, 118*f*
shared, in covalent bonding, 186-187, 186*f*, 187*f*
Thomson's discovery of, 115
transferred between materials, 588-590, 589*f*
transferred in ionic bonding, 184, 184*f*
transitions between energy levels, 131-132, 132*f*
as waves, 129
word origin of, 112

electron spin, 628

elements, 45-47, 46*f*. *See also* **isotopes; periodic table**
atoms of, 46-47, 47*f*, 114, 120, 121
classification of, 154, 154*f*, 155*f*, 156, 156*f*
families of, 156, 156*f*
formation of compounds from, 177, 177*f*
in human body, 46, 46*f*
inert, 161
labs on, 158, 166-167
molecules of, 47, 47*f*
neutrons in, 121-122, 121*f*, 122*f*
origin of, 350, 714
protons in, 120, 121, 121*f*
as pure substances, 48
radioactive, 160, 160*f*
in sea water, 162
spectral analysis of, 132, 696, 696*f*
symbols for, 124, 124*f*, 208
synthetic, 160, 160*f*
wavelengths emitted by, 132, 132*f*

empirical formulas, 194-196, 195*f*

emulsions, 262, 262*f*
lab on, 262
soap and, 307, 307*f*, 308

endothermic reactions, 222, 222*f*, 224, 224*f*

energy, 444-452. *See also* **chemical energy; conservation of energy; electrical energy; heat; kinetic energy; potential energy; thermal energy; work**
changes of state and, 84-87, 84*f*, 87*f*
chemical reactions and, 220-222, 221*f*, 224, 449, 449*f*
definitions of, 80, 444
electromagnetic, 637
of electromagnetic waves, 452, 452*f*, 482, 482*f*, 554, 554*f*
in fields, 450, 450*f*, 452
mass equivalent to, 339-340, 450
mechanical, 449, 455, 455*f*, 456, 492
of nuclei, 339-340
to raise temperature, 485-486, 485*f*, 496
of sound waves, 543, 545
temperature difference and, 478-479, 479*f*, 490, 491
transformations of, 453-455, 454*f*, 455*f*, 456, 456*f*
units of, 444
usable, 491
wasted, 491, 821-822, 822*f*, 828
of waves, 505, 507, 509, 511, 515

energy levels, 128, 128*f*, 130-131, 130*f*, 131*f*
lab on, 131
transitions between, 131-132, 132*f*

energy resources, 815-820. *See also* **electrical energy; fossil fuels;** *specific alternative sources*
alternative, 818-820, 818*f*, 819*f*, 820*f*, 830
conservation of, 831
lab on, 832-833
solar origins of, 815, 816, 817

INDEX

energy resources (*continued*)
    United States map of, 886
    uses of, 815, 815*f*
    wasted, 821–822, 822*f*
engines, 492–493, 492*f*, 493*f*
entropy, 491, 491*f*
environmental engineer, career as, 689
enzymes, 241, 241*f*, 242
epicenter, 739, 739*f*, 741, 741*f*, 742
    lab on, 762–763
equations. *See also* **chemical equations**
    fractions in, 576
    of laws and theories, 10, 76
    for nuclear decay, 330–331
    rearranging, 420, 865
    symbols in, 208
equilibrium systems, 244–247, 244*f*, 246*f*
equivalence point, of titration, 304
Eris, 670
erosion, 759–761, 759*f*, 760*f*, 761*f*
ethnobotanist, career as, 214
eutrophication, 828
evaporation, 84*f*, 85, 781–783
    from oceans and continents, 781–782, 781*f*
    temperature and, 782–783, 783*f*
event data recorders, 379
examples, signal words in, 44, 258
excited state, 131
exhaust stroke, 492, 493*f*
exoplanets, 679
exosphere, 776
exothermic reactions, 222, 222*f*
experiments, 5–6, 5*f*, 8. *See also* **data; graphs; hypothesis; measurements**
    conducting, 877
    controlled, 15, 876
    laws and theories based on, 9, 10, 76
    planning, 14, 876
    variables in, 15, 16, 877
exponential decay, 335, 335*f*
exponents, 863
    in order of operations, 864
    powers of ten, 24–25, 866
    rules for, 863*f*
extraterrestrial intelligence, 706
extrusive igneous rock, 749, 749*f*
eye, 569, 569*f*

F

fab technician, career as, 426
facts, 728

Fahrenheit-Celsius conversion equations, 475
Fahrenheit temperature scale, 475, 476*f*, 477
falling objects. *See* **free fall**
families of elements, 156, 156*f*
Faraday, Michael, 632
Faraday's law, 632
faults, 737, 737*f*, 739. *See also* **earthquakes**
Fermi, Enrico, 337
fertilizers, 827, 828
field forces, 381. *See also* **electric fields; gravity; magnetic fields**
filament, 596, 596*f*
file extensions, 168
file names, 168
fire. *See also* **burning; combustion reactions**
    started with friction, 490, 490*f*
fire extinguishers, 232
fireworks, 133, 133*f*, 456, 456*f*
first law of thermodynamics, 456, 490
fish, mercury compounds in, 147
fission, nuclear, 339–341, 339*f*, 340*f*, 450
    chain reaction in, 337, 340–341, 340*f*
    electric power from, 341, 343, 349–350, 349*f*, 818, 822
    historical background of, 337, 337*f*
    lab on, 341
flammability, 56
Fleming, Alexander, 6
floating, 90–91, 90*f*, 91*f*
flow chart (Graphic Organizer), 472
    instructions for, 853
fluids, 79, 89–94. *See also* **convection currents; gases; liquids**
    buoyant force of, 90–91, 90*f*, 95
    motion of, 93–94, 93*f*, 94*f*
    Pascal's principle for, 92–93
    pressure of, 89, 89*f*, 90
fluoride ions, 153, 153*f*
    in drinking water, 281
focal point, 568
focus, of earthquake, 739, 739*f*, 740, 741, 742
FoldNotes
    booklet, 542, 848
    double-door fold, 618, 849
    four-corner fold, 326, 849
    instructions for, 848–851
    key-term fold, 76, 258, 396, 806, 848
    layered book, 176, 850
    pyramid, 112, 850
    table fold, 218, 850
    three-panel flip chart, 772, 851

    tri-fold, 364, 584, 692, 851
    two-panel flip chart, 851
forced vibrations, 548
forces. *See also* **friction; gravity**
    acceleration caused by, 381, 382, 400–402, 400*f*, 402*f*
    action and reaction, 412–414, 412*f*, 413*f*, 417
    balanced, 382
    buoyant, 90–91, 90*f*, 95
    change in momentum caused by, 415, 415*f*
    contact forces, 381
    definition of, 380
    direction of, 382, 434, 435
    electric, 120, 590–592, 593, 594
    electromagnetic, 380, 381, 637
    field forces, 381
    fundamental, 380–381, 380*f*
    inertia and, 398
    machines and, 434–437, 434*f*, 437*f*
    magnetic, 381, 620, 633–634
    multiplying, 434, 435, 436, 440
    net, 381–382, 397, 400, 402
    nuclear, 337–338, 338*f*, 380, 381
    in solution, 268, 271, 277
    unbalanced, 381*f*, 382, 400
    units of, 401
    work and, 431–432
forensics
    of automobile accidents, 378–379
    in counterfeit detection, 572–573
    DNA fingerprinting, 205
    in substance identification, 57
forensic scientists, 57
formulas, chemical, 48, 48*f*, 208. *See also* **chemical equations**
    empirical, 194–196, 195*f*
    for ionic compounds, 192, 193
    molecular, 195, 195*f*
    structural, 178, 199, 199*f*
formula unit, 185, 185*f*
fossil fuels, 816–817, 816*f*, 817*f*. *See also* **gasoline**
    acid precipitation and, 758
    air pollution from, 825, 825*f*, 826, 827
    distillation of petroleum, 264, 265
    global warming and, 780
    power plants using, 821–822, 821*f*
fossils
    Pangaea and, 731, 731*f*
    in sedimentary rocks, 750, 750*f*, 751, 753
four-corner fold (FoldNote), 326
    instructions for, 849
fractions, 576, 862, 862*f*

frame of reference, 365, 365*f*
Franklin, Benjamin, 587
free fall, 407–408, 408*f*
    action-reaction forces in, 413, 413*f*
    constant acceleration, *g*, in, 403, 407
    gravitational potential energy and, 445, 446
    of orbiting object, 408, 410, 410*f*
    in projectile motion, 409, 409*f*
free radicals, 235, 236
freezing, 84*f*, 86
    lab on, 102–103
freezing points, 86, 87*f*. *See also* **melting points**
    of solution, 273
frequency, 516, 516*f*
    definition of, 516
    Doppler effect and, 522–523, 522*f*
    of electromagnetic waves, 521, 554, 554*f*
    fundamental, 547
    of sound waves, 546, 546*f*
    units of, 516
    wave speed and, 518, 519
    words indicating, 176
friction, 382–385
    on automobiles, 378–379, 382, 383–385, 385*f*
    charging by, 589
    efficiency of machine and, 459
    electrical resistance as, 596
    electromagnetic force as basis of, 380
    fire started with, 490, 490*f*
    helpful, 384–385, 385*f*
    kinetic, 383
    labs on, 384, 386–387
    mechanical energy lost to, 455, 459, 460
    motion and, 382, 383, 384–385
    Newton's first law and, 397, 398
    rolling, 383, 386–387
    sliding, 383, 386–387
    static, 383, 386–387
    unwanted, 384, 384*f*
Frisch, Otto, 337
fronts, 789–790, 789*f*, 790*f*
    tornadoes on, 791
frost wedging, 756
ftp (file transfer protocol), 168
fulcrum, 439, 439*f*, 440, 443
fullerenes, 163
fundamental forces, 380–381, 380*f*
fundamental frequency, 547
funnel cloud, 791, 791*f*
fuses, 606–607, 606*f*
fusion, nuclear, 83, 342, 342*f*
    lab on, 695
    as power source, 350–351, 351*f*, 818
    in stars, 342, 694, 694*f*, 698, 699, 714
    in sun, 342, 450, 450*f*, 698

galaxies, 702–707, 702*f*
    clusters of, 703, 703*f*, 719*f*
    collisions of, 707, 716*f*
    contents of, 702
    evolution of, 706–707
    expansion of universe and, 710–711
    gravity and, 703, 705, 707, 716
    interstellar matter in, 704, 705
    Milky Way, 703, 704, 704*f*, 705, 705*f*
    number of, 702
    types of, 704–705, 705*f*, 718–719
Galileo, 667
Galle, Johann, 669
galvanometers, 630, 630*f*
gamma decay, 330, 338
gamma rays, 328, 328*f*, 329
    in electromagnetic spectrum, 557*f*, 558
    from nuclear fusion, 342
    penetration of matter by, 329, 329*f*, 348
    in radiotherapy, 346
gases. *See also* **atmosphere; fluids**
    changes of state, 84*f*, 85–86, 85*f*, 86*f*, 87*f*
    in galaxies, 704
    heat conduction by, 484
    kinetic energy of particles in, 80, 80*f*
    lab on, 99
    laws of, 97–101, 97*f*, 99*f*, 100*f*
    in mixtures, 50, 50*f*, 96, 264
    molecules of, 181
    noble gases, 161, 161*f*
    pressure of, 97–99, 97*f*, 99*f*, 101
    properties of, 97
    reaction rates of, 240
    solubility in liquids, 279, 279*f*, 282–283
    of stars, 693, 694, 696
    as state of matter, 78, 78*f*, 79, 79*f*
    wave speed in, 521
gas giants, 666–669, 666*f*
    Jupiter, 666, 666*f*, 667, 667*f*
    Jupiter's collision with comet, 675, 675*f*
    Neptune, 666, 666*f*, 669, 669*f*, 670
    satellites of, 656, 667, 668, 673
    Saturn, 654, 654*f*, 666–667, 668, 668*f*
    Uranus, 666, 666*f*, 667, 669, 669*f*
gas grills, 198
gas laws, 97–101, 97*f*, 99*f*, 100*f*
gasoline. *See also* **fossil fuels**
    burning of, 220–221, 221*f*
    isooctane in, 220–222, 220*f*, 221*f*
    separation from crude oil, 265
Gateway Arch, 29
Gay-Lussac's law, 99, 99*f*
gemologist, career as, 689
generators, 634, 634*f*, 636–637, 636*f*. *See also* **electrical energy**
geocentric model, 672, 672*f*
geodynamo, 625
geology, 8
geometrical optics, 560
geometry, 864, 864*f*
geophysics, 8
geothermal energy, 819, 819*f*
germanium, 146, 146*f*
glaciers, 760, 760*f*, 812, 812*f*
glass, 65
glass blowing, 65
global warming, 780, 780*f*, 795, 826
glycerol, 307
glycogen, 202
gradients, pressure, 785
graduated cylinder, 877
grams (g), 20*f*
    converting to/from moles, 126, 126*f*
granite, 748, 749, 749*f*, 752
Graphic Organizers
    cause-and-effect map, 292, 855
    chain-of-events chart, 652, 854
    concept map, 430, 728, 852
    flow chart, 472, 853
    instructions for, 852–857
    spider map, 4, 144, 856
    Venn diagram, 806, 857
graphs, 23–24, 869–872. *See also* **distance vs. time graph; line graphs; slope**
    bar graphs, 23, 23*f*, 455, 720, 871
    line graphs, 23, 23*f*, 388, 869
    pie graphs, 24, 24*f*, 284, 872
    scatter plots, 870
    of speed vs. time, 376–377, 377*f*
    of transverse wave, 532
gravitational constant, 405, 406, 407
gravitational potential energy, 445–446, 445*f*, 453–454, 454*f*
    electrical potential energy and, 593, 593*f*, 595
    hydroelectric power and, 458
    lab on, 462–463

INDEX

gravity, 403–411. *See also* **free fall; weight**
  of black holes, 411
  blood pressure and, 405
  distance and, 405, 406, 406*f*, 407, 445
  Earth's surface and, 403, 407, 409
  as field force, 381
  friction in opposition to, 385, 385*f*
  as fundamental force, 380, 380*f*, 381
  future of universe and, 715
  galaxies and, 703, 705, 707, 716
  living things and, 404, 404*f*
  mass and, 405–406, 406*f*, 407, 445, 446
  mass movement of landscape by, 761
  on moon, 403, 403*f*, 404
  projectile motion and, 408, 408*f*, 409, 410*f*
  in solar system, 655, 655*f*, 673, 674*f*
  stars and, 406, 694, 698, 699
  strength of, 381, 406
  sun and, 405, 405*f*, 698, 698*f*
  tides and, 660, 660*f*
  universal law of, 10, 405–406, 405*f*, 406*f*, 407, 673
grease. *See* **oil**
greenhouse effect
  on Earth, 451, 663, 779–780, 779*f*, 795, 826, 826*f*
  lab on, 779
  on Venus, 662
ground, electrical, 598
ground fault circuit interrupter, 607
ground state, 131
groups (categories)
  classification of, 4, 292, 504
  generalizations about, 144
groups (periodic table), 150
  electron arrangements in, 151, 151*f*, 152*f*
  ion formation and, 153
guitars, electric, 635
gyrocompass, 621

H

Haber process, 246–247
Hahn, Otto, 337, 339, 340
half-life, 333–336, 333*f*, 335*f*
  calculations with, 334, 354
halogens, 162, 162*f*
hard magnetic materials, 620
hard water, 309, 311

harmonic motion. *See also* **vibrations**
  damped, 509
  simple, 508
hearing, 508, 549, 549*f*
heat. *See also* **temperature**
  changes of state and, 487, 487*f*
  chemical reaction caused by, 222
  conduction of, 480–481, 480*f*, 481*f*
  conductors of, 154, 155*f*, 484–485, 494–495
  convection of, 480, 480*f*, 483
  definition of, 479
  dissolving process and, 272, 273*f*, 279
  from electric circuit, 605
  as energy transfer, 88, 456, 479, 479*f*
  from engine, 492
  from friction, 382, 382*f*, 459
  in homes, 488–489, 490, 491
  kinetic energy of particles and, 448, 490
  lab on, 482
  methods of transfer of, 480–483, 480*f*, 481*f*, 482*f*
  radiated, 482, 482*f*, 557
  second law of thermodynamics and, 490
  specific heat, 485–486, 485*f*, 496, 881
  temperature and, 84, 487, 487*f*, 490
  theories about, 9, 9*f*, 10
  as waste energy, 491, 821–822, 822*f*, 828
heat engines, 492–493, 492*f*, 493*f*
heating systems, 488, 491
height. *See also* **distance; length**
  gravitational potential energy and, 445–446
heliocentric model, 672
helium
  atoms of, 120, 120*f*
  in sun, 132
Herschel, William, 669
hertz (Hz), 516
Hertz, Heinrich, 516
Hertzsprung, Ejnar, 700
Hertzsprung-Russell diagram (H-R diagram), 700–701, 701*f*
heterogeneous mixtures, 49, 49*f*, 259–262, 259*f*
  colloids, 261–262, 261*f*, 262*f*
  suspensions, 260–261, 260*f*, 261*f*, 264
home heating and cooling, 488–489, 491
homogeneous mixtures, 49, 49*f*, 50, 263, 263*f*. *See also* **solutions**
hot spots, 746, 746*f*, 747
http (hypertext transfer protocol), 168

Hubble, Edwin, 703*f*, 705, 710
Hubble Space Telescope, 703, 703*f*
human body
  chemical reactions in, 242–243
  elements in, 46, 46*f*
  minerals needed by, 306
humidity, 782, 782*f*, 783
  relative, 782, 798
hurricane hunter, career as, 689
hurricanes, 12, 12*f*, 792, 792*f*
hydraulic devices, 92–93, 92*f*
hydraulic system, of brakes, 383
hydrocarbons, 198–201, 198*f*, 199*f*, 200*f*
hydroelectric power, 458, 637, 820, 820*f*
hydrogen
  abundance of, 164
  atomic structure of, 120, 121
  isotopes of, 122–123, 122*f*
  nuclear fusion of, 342, 342*f*
  properties of, 164
hydrogen bonds, 182, 182*f*, 269, 269*f*
hydrogen ions, 293
hydrolysis, 758
hydronium ions, 293, 294
  in neutralization reactions, 302–304, 303*f*
  pH as measure of, 298, 298*f*, 299, 300
hydrosphere, 663
hydrothermal vents, 732, 732*f*
hydroxide ions, 295, 296, 297
  in neutralization reactions, 302–304, 303*f*
  pH as measure of, 298, 298*f*
hydroxyl groups, 200
hypothesis, 15–16, 15*f*
  compared with facts and theories, 728
  forming, 34, 876
  model for testing of, 764
  observations and measurements about, 464
  plan for testing of, 876
  predictions based on, 136, 642, 876, 879
  stated in lab report, 879
  steps for testing of, 136

ice
  in clouds, 783, 784, 791
  erosion by, 759, 760, 760*f*
  models of, 11, 11*f*
  weathering of rocks by, 756

INDEX

ice ages, 812, 812*f*, 826
igneous rocks, 749, 749*f*, 752, 752*f*
images
    lab on, 574–575
    in mirrors, 562–563, 562*f*, 563*f*
    from refracted light, 567, 567*f*, 568, 568*f*, 569
immiscible liquids, 49, 261, 261*f*, 262, 262*f*
incidence, angle of, 561, 561*f*
inclined planes, 438, 438*f*, 441–442, 441*f*, 442*f*
    in building pyramids, 442
    lab on, 441
independent variable, 23, 869, 877
indicators
    in litmus paper, 293, 293*f*, 295
    in pH paper, 298*f*, 300
    for titration, 304, 304*f*
indigo, 48, 48*f*, 49
induced current, 632–634, 632*f*, 634*f*. *See also* **electromagnetic induction**
    in generator, 636, 636*f*
induced electric charge, 588, 588*f*, 590, 590*f*
inert elements, 161
inertia, 398
    air bags and, 399
infrared light (infrared radiation), 482, 482*f*, 554, 554*f*, 556*f*, 557
infrasound, 546
inhibitors, 240
ink, 264
inner planets. *See* **terrestrial planets**
insoluble substances, 276, 276*f*
instantaneous speed, 369
insulation, on electrical wire, 588, 588*f*, 598, 606
insulators (electricity), 154, 588, 588*f*
    dry skin as, 589
    induced charge on surface of, 590, 590*f*
    resistance of, 598
insulators (heat), 154
    energy transfer and, 484–485, 484*f*
    lab on, 484
intake stroke, 492, 493, 493*f*
intensity
    of light, 555, 555*f*
    of sound waves, 545, 545*f*
interference, 526–528, 526*f*, 527*f*, 528*f*
    of light, 528, 528*f*, 552–553, 552*f*, 554
    of sound, 527, 528, 528*f*
    standing waves and, 529, 529*f*

internal combustion engine, 492–493, 492*f*, 493*f*
International System of Units (SI), 17, 867
Internet
    bias on, 834
    reputable sources on, 316
    search engines on, 610, 682, 873–874
    terminology about, 610
    Web addresses on, 168, 316
interstellar matter, 704, 705
intrusive igneous rock, 749, 749*f*
inverse relationship, 101
ionic bonds, 183, 184–185, 184*f*, 185*f*, 189
ionic compounds, 183, 183*f*, 185, 185*f*
    dissolving in water, 267–268, 268*f*
    formulas for, 192, 193
    naming, 191–192, 191*f*, 192*f*
    network structure of, 180, 181, 181*f*
    solubilities in water, 276–277, 277*f*
ionization, 153, 153*f*
    of acids, 293, 294, 294*f*
    of bases, 297
    by nuclear radiation, 328, 329, 332, 348
    in plasmas, 79
ionization chamber, 332
ionosphere, 776–777, 776*f*, 777*f*
ions. *See also* **hydronium ions; hydroxide ions; salts**
    charge on, 153, 153*f*, 208
    definition of, 120
    in electrolytes, 294, 294*f*, 296, 297
    formation of, 153, 153*f*
    in living cells, 589
    names of, 191–192, 191*f*, 192*f*
    polyatomic, 189–190, 189*f*, 190*f*
    in space, 190
island arcs, 736
isolated systems, 457
isotopes, 122–124, 124*f*. *See also* **elements; radioisotopes**
    average atomic mass and, 124, 124*f*, 125
    of hydrogen, 122–123, 122*f*
    labs on, 122, 134–135
    symbols for, 124, 124*f*, 208

J

jack, car, 434, 434*f*, 437, 443
joules (J)
    of energy, 444
    of kinetic energy, 447

    of work, 432
Jupiter, 666, 666*f*, 667, 667*f*
    comet's collision with, 675, 675*f*

K

Kelvin temperature scale, 476–477, 476*f*
Kepler, Johannes, 672
keratin, 311
key-term fold (FoldNote), 76, 258, 396, 806
    instructions for, 848
kilocalories (kcal), 451
kilowatt-hours, 605
kilowatts (kW), 605
kinetic energy, 447–448, 447*f*
    definition of, 447
    in heat engine, 492
    increased by work, 490, 490*f*
    lab on, 462–463
    as mechanical energy, 449, 454, 455, 455*f*
    temperature and, 80–81, 80*f*, 473–474, 476, 479
    transformations of, 453, 454–455, 454*f*
    units of, 447
kinetic friction, 383
kinetic theory, 9*f*, 10, 77, 80
    dissolving process and, 272
    reaction rates and, 240
Kuiper Belt, 670, 676, 676*f*
KWL notes, 584

L

laboratory. *See* **experiments**
landslides, 761
lava
    human impact of, 747
    on ocean floor, 746
    venting of, 743, 743*f*, 744, 745
law of action and reaction, 412, 412*f*
    momentum and, 417
law of conservation of energy, 87, 88, 456–457, 490, 491
law of conservation of mass, 87–88
law of conservation of momentum, 416–417
    lab on, 418–419
law of definite proportions, 114, 114*f*, 228

INDEX

law of reflection, 561, 561*f*, 562
law of universal gravitation, 10, 405–406, 405*f*, 406*f*
   free fall and, 407
   Newton and, 405, 673
laws, scientific, 9, 10, 10*f*, 76
   predictions based on, 642
layered book (FoldNote), 176
   instructions for, 850
leaching, 758, 826
Le Châtelier's principle, 246, 247
Leibniz, Gottfried, 374
length. *See also* **distance; height**
   measurement of, 30
   units of, 18–19, 18*f*, 19*f*, 20*f*, 21, 21*f*
lenses, 568–569, 568*f*, 569*f*
   lab on, 574–575
Leonardo da Vinci, 13
levers, 438–440, 438*f*. *See also* **pulleys**
   brake pedal and, 383
   classes of, 439, 439*f*
   in compound machines, 443, 443*f*
   wheel and axle as, 438, 438*f*, 440, 440*f*
Library of Congress classification system, 875
library searches, 875
life science, 7, 7*f*, 8
lifting. *See* **machines**
light, 552–558. *See also* **colors; electromagnetic waves; photons; photosynthesis; reflection; refraction**
   atomic absorption or emission of, 131–132, 132*f*
   brightness of, 555, 555*f*
   chemical energy converted to, 449, 449*f*
   diffraction of, 525, 552*f*
   dispersion of, 570–571, 570*f*, 571*f*
   Doppler effect with, 710, 710*f*
   as electromagnetic wave, 506, 506*f*, 637, 637*f*
   energy of, 452, 452*f*, 482, 554, 554*f*
   interference of, 528, 528*f*, 552–553, 552*f*, 554
   labs on, 564, 574–575
   from living organisms, 223
   models of, 552–554, 553*f*, 560
   plasma emission of, 82
   polarized, 511
   scattered by colloid, 261, 261*f*
   spectroscopes and, 17
   speed of, 521, 555, 555*f*, 566, 570
   from stars, 693, 694, 695, 696, 696*f*
   visible spectrum of, 521, 521*f*, 556, 557*f*

light bulbs, 596, 596*f*
   in closed or open circuits, 600–601, 600*f*, 601*f*
   in schematic diagrams, 601, 601*f*, 602*f*
   in series or parallel circuits, 603, 603*f*
lighting designer, career as, 426
lightning
   electrical energy of, 450, 450*f*, 791
   Franklin's experiments on, 587
   magnetism and, 626
   as plasma, 79, 82
light rays
   as model, 560
   reflection of, 560–561, 561*f*, 562, 562*f*, 563
   refraction of, 566–567, 566*f*, 567*f*, 568, 568*f*
light-years (ly), 693, 709
like dissolves like, 270
limestone
   chemical weathering of, 757, 757*f*, 758
   formation of, 158, 158*f*, 750, 750*f*
   lime made from, 245, 245*f*
   marble derived from, 751, 751*f*
line graphs, 23, 23*f*, 869. *See also* **slope**
   calculating slope of, 370
   compared to scatter plots, 870
   of distance vs. time, 370, 388
   interpreting, 101
   making, 104
   of speed vs. time, 376
liquids. *See also* **fluids; solutions**
   changes of state, 84–85, 84*f*, 86–87, 86*f*, 87*f*
   immiscible, 49, 261, 261*f*, 262, 262*f*
   kinetic energy of particles in, 80, 80*f*
   miscible, 49, 264, 264*f*
   mixed with gases, 50, 50*f*
   as state of matter, 78, 78*f*
   viscosity of, 94
   volume measurement of, 20*f*, 32, 877
   wave speed in, 521
lithium ions, 153, 153*f*
lithosphere, 732, 733, 734, 735, 736
   faults in, 737, 737*f*
litmus paper, 293, 293*f*, 295
lodestones, 619, 619*f*, 620, 622
longitudinal waves, 511, 512, 512*f*. *See also* **sound waves**
   from earthquake, 518, 739–741, 741*f*
   wavelength of, 515, 515*f*
loudness, 545, 545*f*
lubricants, 384

luciferase, 223
lunar eclipse, 658, 658*f*

machines, 434–443. *See also* **inclined planes; levers; mechanical advantage**
   on bicycles, 435, 443, 443*f*
   compound, 443, 443*f*
   efficiency of, 459–461, 459*f*
   perpetual motion, 460, 460*f*, 461
   simple, 438–442, 438*f*, 439*f*
magma
   geothermal energy and, 819
   at plate boundaries, 734, 735, 736
   from volcano, 743, 744, 745, 749, 752
magnetic domains, 621
magnetic field lines, 622, 622*f*
   direction of force and, 633, 634, 634*f*
   electromagnetic induction and, 632
magnetic fields, 621–622, 622*f*. *See also* **Earth's magnetic field**
   from electric currents, 626–629, 626*f*, 627*f*, 630, 631*f*
   electromagnetic induction and, 632–634, 632*f*, 634*f*
   of electromagnetic waves, 452, 506, 511, 637, 637*f*
   energy in, 450
   of hydroelectric generators, 458
   lab on, 623
   of moving charges, 450, 626, 628
   right-hand rule for, 627, 627*f*
   of solenoid, 627–628, 627*f*
   of sun, 624
magnetic force, 381, 620, 633–634
magnetic poles, 619, 621
   of Earth, 623–624, 623*f*
   field lines and, 622, 622*f*
   lab on, 621
   of solenoid, 627
magnetite, 619, 637, 732
magnets, 619–620, 619*f*, 620*f*
   electromagnets, 628, 640–641
   labs on, 621, 628
   permanent, 620
   superconducting, 599, 599*f*
magnification, 568
main sequence stars, 700, 701, 701*f*
mantle, 729, 729*f*, 730, 730*f*, 732
   at convergent boundaries, 735, 736, 745
mantle plumes, 746

INDEX

marble, 158, 751, 751*f,* 758
maria, 657, 657*f,* 678
Mars, 664, 664*f,* 665, 666
    meteoroids from, 677
mass. See also **atomic masses**
    acceleration and, 400–402, 400*f,* 402*f*
    calculating from chemical equations, 228*f,* 229, 250
    conservation of, 87–88, 220, 226
    converting moles to, 126, 126*f*
    curving of space by, 717, 717*f*
    of dark matter, 716
    density and, 54–55, 55*f*
    energy equivalent to, 339–340, 450
    future of universe and, 715
    gravitational force and, 405–406, 406*f,* 407
    gravitational potential energy and, 445, 446
    inertia associated with, 398
    kinetic energy and, 447, 448
    kinetic theory and, 77
    measurement of, 31, 878
    molar, 125–127, 125*f,* 126*f*
    momentum and, 414, 415
    reaction rates and, 240
    of subatomic particles, 119, 119*f*
    units of, 18*f,* 20*f,* 21
    of universe, 87
    weight and, 21, 403–404
mass defect, 340
mass-energy equation, 339, 340
mass movement, 761
mass number, 121–122, 121*f*
    in radioactive decay, 330, 331
    in symbol of element, 124, 124*f*
matches, 382, 382*f,* 449, 449*f*
mathematics. See also **equations; exponents; fractions**
    of laws and theories, 10
    Math Skills, 862–868
    word problems in, 430
matter. See also **states of matter**
    changes of, 59–64
    classification of, 45–50
    definition of, 45
    kinetic theory of, 9*f,* 10, 77, 80
    properties of, 51–58, 66–67
measurements, 21, 21*f,* 464, 877–878. See also **units of measurement**
    labs on, 27, 30–33
    of length, 30
    of mass, 31, 878
    pitfalls of, 464, 877
    precision of, 26–28, 27*f,* 29, 868, 877
    of temperature, 30, 878

    of volume, 32, 877
mechanical advantage, 434–437, 434*f*
    of inclined plane, 441
    of pulleys, 440, 440*f*
    of third-class lever, 439*f*
mechanical energy. See also **kinetic energy; potential energy**
    changed to nonmechanical energy, 455, 455*f,* 456, 459
    conserved, 456
    definition of, 449
    graphing, 455
    produced by engine, 492
mechanical processes, 490
mechanical waves, 506, 506*f*
    vibrating medium of, 508
medical practitioner, career as, 214
medium, wave, 506, 506*f,* 508, 511
    speed and, 520–521, 520*f,* 526
Meitner, Lise, 337
melting, 60, 60*f,* 84*f,* 85
melting points, 52, 85, 86, 87*f.* See also **freezing points**
    structures of compounds and, 180, 180*f,* 181, 182*f*
Mendeleev, Dmitri, 145–147, 145*f,* 146*f*
meniscus, 32, 877
Mercury, 662, 662*f*
mercury, toxic compounds of, 147
mercury barometers, 784, 784*f*
mesosphere, 773*f,* 776
metabolism, 242–243
metal detectors, 629
metal hydroxides, 296, 297, 297*f*
metallic bonds, 188, 188*f*
metallic properties, 150, 150*f*
metalloids. See **semiconductors**
metallurgist, career as, 688
metals, 154, 154*f,* 155*f*
    alloys of, 266, 266*f*
    amalgam of, 264
    as electrical conductors, 188, 188*f,* 597, 599
    families of, 156*f,* 157–160, 157*f,* 158*f,* 159*f*
    as heat conductors, 154, 155*f,* 484, 494–495
    ions formed by, 184
    labs on, 66–67, 160, 188
    in ores, 755, 758
    single-displacement reactions of, 233–234, 233*f,* 234*f*
metamorphic rocks, 751, 751*f,* 752, 752*f*
meteorites, 675, 676, 676*f,* 677, 677*f*
meteoroids, 675, 677, 677*f*
meteorologists, 12, 789

meteorology, 8. See also **weather**
    computer models in, 12, 12*f*
meteors, 675
meter, electrical, 605, 605*f*
meters (m), 18, 20*f,* 867
microprocessors, 165
microscopes, 569, 569*f*
microwaves, 556*f,* 557
mid-oceanic ridges, 734, 734*f*
    magnetic bands adjacent to, 732
Milky Way, 703, 704, 704*f,* 705, 705*f*
Millennium Bridge, 11
minerals, 748. See also **rocks**
    animals' need for, 306
    chemical weathering of, 757–758, 757*f*
    in ores, 755, 758
minor planets. See **asteroids**
mirages, 567, 567*f*
mirrors, 560, 560*f,* 562–563, 562*f,* 563*f*
    lab on, 563
miscible liquids, 49, 264, 264*f*
mixtures, 45, 48–50. See also **heterogeneous mixtures; homogeneous mixtures; solutions**
    classification of, 49, 49*f*
    gases in, 50, 50*f,* 96, 264
    labs on, 48, 63
    separation of, 63, 63*f*
mnemonics
    for colors of spectrum, 542
    for order of planets, 652
models, 11–12, 11*f,* 12*f,* 764
molarity, 280
    pH of solution and, 299
molar mass, 125–127, 125*f,* 126*f*
molar ratio, 195–196
molecular compounds. See also **covalent bonds**
    dissolving in water, 269, 269*f*
    structures and properties of, 181–182, 181*f,* 182*f*
molecular formulas, 195, 195*f*
molecules, 47, 47*f.* See also **compounds; polar molecules**
    compounds composed of, 181–182, 181*f,* 182*f,* 186
    models of, 11, 11f, 178, 178*f*
    motion of, 77, 448
    in space, 190
mole ratios, 228–229, 250
moles (mol), 125–127, 125*f*
    converting to/from grams, 126, 126*f*
momentum, 414–417
    calculating, 415
    in collisions, 416–417, 417*f*

Index **931**

momentum (*continued*)
  conservation of, 416–417
  force causing change in, 415, 415*f*
  lab on, 418–419
  SI unit for, 414
monomers, 201
moon, 657–660. *See also* **satellites**
  astronauts on, 403, 403*f*, 404, 659
  eclipses and, 658, 658*f*
  formation of, 678, 678*f*
  gravitational forces acting on, 405, 405*f*
  gravity on surface of, 403, 403*f*, 404
  halo appearing around, 784
  meteoroids from, 677
  orbiting of, 410
  phases of, 657, 657*f*
  planned trip to, 659
  as satellite, 656
  surface appearance, 657, 657*f*
  tides and, 660, 660*f*
Moseley, Henry, 147
motion. *See also* **acceleration; direction of motion; distance; kinetic energy; Newton's first law; Newton's second law; Newton's third law; projectile motion; speed; velocity**
  detecting, 365
  displacement in, 366, 366*f*, 370
  energy associated with, 444, 444*f*, 447–448, 447*f*
  frame of reference for, 365, 365*f*
  friction and, 382, 383, 384–385
  momentum of, 414–417, 415*f*, 417*f*
  orbital, 408, 410, 410*f*
  work associated with, 431, 432
motors, electric, 450, 630, 630*f*, 631, 631*f*
mountain-bike suspension, 510
mountains. *See also* **volcanoes**
  climate and, 795, 795*f*
  colliding plates and, 736, 736*f*
  subduction zones and, 735, 735*f*
mudflows, 761
mudstone, 750, 751, 751*f*
musical instruments, 547–548

N

natural disasters, 793
natural frequencies, 548
natural resources. *See also* **energy resources**
  United States map of, 886

nebular model, 673, 674*f*
nebulas, 673
  star formation in, 693*f*, 698*f*, 702
  as supernova remnants, 700, 700*f*
negative charge, 585, 586. *See also* **electric charge**
Neptune, 656, 666, 666*f*, 669, 669*f*, 670
net force, 381–382
  Newton's first law and, 397
  Newton's second law and, 400, 402
network structures, 180–181, 180*f*, 181*f*, 185, 186
neutralization reactions, 302–304, 302*f*, 303*f*
  with antacids, 311
  labs on, 312, 314–315
neutral solutions, 298, 298*f*
  acid-base reactions and, 303, 304
neutrons, 119, 119*f*, 120, 120*f*
  calculating the number of, 124, 124*f*
  decay of, 329, 330
  of different isotopes, 122, 122*f*, 124, 124*f*
  emitted in radioactive decay, 328, 328*f*, 329
  mass number and, 121, 121*f*
  from nuclear fission, 339, 340, 341
  from nuclear fusion, 351
  nuclear stability and, 337–338, 338*f*
  in Rutherford's atomic model, 118
neutron stars, 700
Newton, Isaac, 374, 397, 405, 673
newtons (N), 401, 403
Newton's first law, 397–398, 397*f*, 398*f*
  lab on, 398
Newton's second law, 400–402
  calculating weight with, 403
  with gravitational force, 407
  rearranging equation for, 420
Newton's third law, 412–414, 412*f*
  conservation of momentum and, 416, 417
  with falling objects, 413, 413*f*
  labs on, 414, 418–419
  with rockets, 416
nimbostratus clouds, 783*f*, 784, 790, 790*f*
nitrogen cycle, 246
nitrogen oxides, 825*f*, 826, 827
noble gases, 161, 161*f*
nodes, 529, 529*f*
  of guitar string, 547
nonmechanical energy, 449, 455, 455*f*, 456, 456*f*
nonmetals, 154, 154*f*, 155*f*
  families of, 156*f*, 161–163, 161*f*–163*f*

nonnative species, 814, 814*f*
nonpolar compounds, 270, 270*f*
nonpolar covalent bonds, 186*f*, 187
nonrenewable resources, 817
normal, 561, 561*f*, 563
normal alkanes, 199, 199*f*
north pole
  of Earth's magnetic field, 623, 623*f*, 732
  of magnet, 619, 622
  of solenoid, 627
Note Taking
  comparison table, 76, 472, 843
  instructions for, 843–847
  outlining, 504, 844
  pattern puzzles, 845
  summarizing, 258, 846
  two-column notes, 44, 396, 847
NOT operator, 874
nuclear bomb, 341
nuclear chain reaction, 337, 340–341, 340*f*
nuclear fission, 339–341, 339*f*, 340*f*, 450
  chain reaction in, 337, 340–341, 340*f*
  electric power from, 341, 343, 349–350, 349*f*, 818, 822
  historical background of, 337, 337*f*
  lab on, 341
nuclear forces, 337–338, 338*f*, 380, 381
nuclear fusion, 83, 342, 342*f*
  lab on, 695
  as power source, 350–351, 351*f*, 818
  in stars, 342, 694, 694*f*, 698, 699, 714
  in sun, 342, 450, 450*f*, 698
nuclear medicine, 123, 346–347
nuclear pile, 337, 337*f*
nuclear radiation, 327–329, 327*f*, 328*f*, 329*f*. *See also* **radioactive decay**
  beneficial uses of, 346–347, 346*f*
  discovery of, 332
  dosimeters for measurement of, 348, 348*f*
  everyday sources of, 344–345, 344*f*, 345*f*
  ionization of matter by, 328, 329, 332, 348
  risks from, 348, 349, 350, 351
  units of human exposure to, 345, 345*f*
  unstable nuclei and, 338
nuclear waste, 350, 350*f*, 818, 822
nucleus, 119. *See also* **isotopes**
  changes in, from radioactive decay, 330–331, 330*f*
  energy decrease in, 330, 338
  forces in, 337–338, 338*f*, 380, 381

magnetic field of, 628
mass defect of, 340
Rutherford's discovery of, 118, 118*f*
size of, 118, 118*f*
stability of, 337–338, 338*f*

O

observations, 6, 14, 15–17, 15*f*
   in experiments, 876, 877
   hypotheses and, 34, 464, 876
   lab on, 16
obsidian, 749, 749*f*
ocean
   breezes coming from, 486
   currents in, 483, 654
   elements in, 162
   erosion by, 759, 759*f*
   evaporation from, 781, 781*f*
   mountains near, 795, 795*f*
   surfing in, 517
   waves in, 507, 507*f*, 517
ocean trenches, 735, 735*f*
Oersted, Hans Christian, 626
ohm, 596
Ohm's law, 596
oil. *See also* **fossil fuels**
   cleaning products for, 307–310, 307*f*, 310*f*, 311
   crude oil, 265
   as fossil fuel, 816–817, 816*f*, 817*f*
   solubility in water, 276, 276*f*
Oort cloud, 676, 676*f*
open circuits, 600, 601
open systems, 457
optics, geometrical, 560
orbital motion, 408, 410, 410*f*
orbitals, 129, 129*f*, 130–131, 130*f*, 131*f*
   periodic table and, 152, 152*f*
orbits of planets, 655, 655*f*, 656
   gas giants, 666*f*
   historical theories of, 672–673
   as projectile motion, 410
   terrestrial planets, 661, 661*f*
order of magnitude, 866
order of operations, 864, 864*f*
ores, 755, 758
organic compounds, 197–201. *See also* **biochemical compounds**
   definition of, 197
   hydrocarbons, 198–201, 198*f*, 199*f*, 200*f*
   sugarless sweeteners, 197, 197*f*
OR operator, 874

outgassing, 777, 777*f*
outlining (Note Taking), 504
   instructions for, 844
overloaded circuit, 606–607, 606*f*
oxidation, 237
oxidation-reduction reactions, 237. *See also* **combustion reactions**
   in human body, 243
oxidized substance, 237
oxygen
   in atmosphere, 773, 775, 775*f*, 776, 777–778
   in combustion reactions, 222, 232
   in redox reactions, 237, 243
oxygen–carbon dioxide cycle, 778, 778*f*
ozone, 236, 775, 775*f*, 827
ozone layer, 236, 558, 773*f*, 775, 778

P

Pangaea, 731, 731*f*
parallax, 877
parallel circuits, 603, 603*f*
parentheses, 864
parent isotope, 754
particle accelerators, 17
particle model, of light, 553–554, 553*f*
particulates, 825, 825*f*
Pascal's principle, 92–93
path, of computer file, 168
pattern puzzles instructions, 845
Pauling, Linus, 184
peer reviewed research, 16
pendulum, 457
penicillin, 6
Penzias, Arno, 712
percentages, 798, 862
   pie chart of, 872
perfluorocarbons, 275
perfumer, 215
period, of wave, 516, 516*f*, 518
periodic law, 147
periodic table, 46, 148–149*f*. *See also* **elements**
   arrangement of elements in, 147
   atomic masses in, 124, 126
   groups of, 150, 151, 152*f*, 153
   historical development of, 145–147, 145*f*, 146*f*
   lab on, 166–167
   main categories in, 154, 154*f*, 155*f*
   periods of, 150, 150*f*, 152, 152*f*
periods, of periodic table, 150, 150*f*, 152, 152*f*

permanent magnets, 620
perpetual motion machines, 460, 460*f*, 461
pesticides, 828
PET (positron emission tomography), 347
petroleum. *See also* **fossil fuels**
   distillation of, 264, 265
pH, 298–300, 298*f*
   of acid rain, 301
   antacids and, 311, 311*f*
   measurement of, 298*f*, 300, 300*f*
   neutralization reactions and, 303–304
   of shampoo, 311
   in titrations, 304, 304*f*
phases of moon, 657, 657*f*
pH meter, 300, 300*f*
phosphors, 116
photochemical smog, 827
photons, 131–132, 553
   energy of, 554, 554*f*
   of fireworks, 133
   gamma rays as, 329
   intensity of light and, 555
photosynthesis
   carbon-14 dating and, 336
   as endothermic reaction, 224, 224*f*
   energy storage in, 449, 451, 815
   evolution of, 663, 777
   in oxygen-carbon dioxide cycle, 778, 778*f*
pH paper, 298*f*, 300
physical changes, 59–60, 59*f*, 60*f*. *See also* **changes of state**
   conservation of mass and energy in, 87–88
   in separating mixtures, 63, 63*f*
   vs. chemical changes, 62
physical properties, 51–55, 51*f*, 52*f*
   compared to chemical properties, 58, 58*f*
   identifying substances by, 57
   lab on, 66–67
   structures of compounds and, 180–182, 180*f*, 181*f*, 182*f*
physical science, 7, 7*f*, 8
physics, 8
   careers using, 426–427
pickup, electric guitar, 635
pie graphs, 24, 24*f*, 284, 872
pigments, 264
pitch, 522, 523, 546, 546*f*, 547
pixels, 116
planes, inclined, 438, 438*f*, 441–442, 441*f*, 442*f*

INDEX

planes, inclined (*continued*)
   in building pyramids, 442
   lab on, 441
planets, 655–656, 656*f*, 661–670. *See also* **asteroids; Earth; gas giants; orbits of planets; satellites; terrestrial planets**
   beyond gas giants, 670
   definition of, 653
   dwarf planet, 666, 670, 670*f*
   exploration of, 664*f*, 665, 666
   formation of, 673, 674*f*
   free-fall acceleration on, 404
   gravitational forces acting on, 405, 406
   lab on, 668
   motion among constellations, 654, 654*f*
   names of, 652
   order of, 652
   of stars, 679, 702
   properties of, 882
plants. *See also* **ecosystems; photosynthesis**
   algal blooms, 828, 828*f*
   breaking of rocks by, 756
   gravitational force on, 404
   transpiration from, 781*f*, 782
plasmas, 79, 79*f*, 82–83
plate boundaries, 734–737, 734*f*, 735*f*, 736*f*, 737*f*
   earthquakes and, 738–739, 738*f*
   volcanoes at, 735, 735*f*, 736, 745, 745*f*
plate tectonics, 731–737, 733*f*
   labs on, 733, 736
plum-pudding model, 115
Pluto, 670, 670*f*
polar covalent bonds, 187, 187*f*
polarization
   of insulator, 590
   of transverse waves, 511
polar molecules, 269
   water as, 267–268, 267*f*, 268*f*, 269, 270
poles, magnetic, 619, 621
   of Earth, 623–624, 623*f*
   field lines and, 622, 622*f*
   lab on, 621
   of solenoid, 627
pollution, 824–831. *See also* **air pollution**
   causes of, 824–825
   labs on, 827, 829
   land, 829
   reduction of, 830–831, 830*f*, 831*f*
   water, 824*f*, 827–828, 827*f*, 828*f*, 829
polyatomic ions, 189–190, 189*f*, 190*f*

polyethene, 201, 201*f*, 230*f*, 231
polymers, 201, 201*f*. *See also* **proteins**
   carbohydrate, 202
   DNA as, 202, 204–205, 204*f*
   labs on, 201, 203, 206–207
   synthesis of, 231, 235
p orbitals, 130, 130*f*, 131*f*
position, energy of. *See* **potential energy**
positive charge, 585, 586. *See also* **electric charge**
positron emission tomography (PET), 347
positrons, 329
potential difference, 594–595, 594*f*. *See also* **voltage**
potential energy, 445–446. *See also* **gravitational potential energy**
   chemical energy as, 449, 449*f*, 451
   elastic, 445, 455, 508, 508*f*, 509
   electrical, 593–595, 593*f*, 594*f*
   lab on, 462–463
   of mass-spring system, 508, 508*f*, 509
   as mechanical energy, 449, 454, 455
   nuclear, 450
   transformations of, 453, 454–455, 454*f*
pounds (lb), 401
power, 433–434. *See also* **electrical energy**
   calculation of, 434
   definition of, 433
   electric, 605–606
   electrical resistance and, 596
   lab on, 433
   light intensity and, 555
powers, 863
   in order of operations, 864
   rules for, 863*f*
   of ten, 24–25, 866
power stroke, 492, 493*f*
precipitation, 781*f*, 782. *See also* **rain**
   acid, 301, 751, 758, 758*f*, 826, 826*f*
   lab on, 784
   weather fronts and, 789
precision, 26–28, 27*f*, 29, 877
predictions, 136, 642, 772, 876, 879
prefixes
   of SI units, 18–19, 18*f*, 867
   of words, 218, 472, 542, 772, 858
pressure
   barometric, 784–785, 784*f*, 785*f*
   Bernoulli's principle and, 94, 94*f*
   definition of, 89
   equilibrium and, 244, 245, 246*f*, 247
   of a fluid, 89, 89*f*, 90

   of a gas, 97–99, 97*f*, 99*f*, 101
   Pascal's principle and, 92–93
   reaction rates and, 238, 240
   solubility of gases and, 279, 279*f*
   units of, 89, 784
pressure gradients, 785
primary colors, 565, 565*f*
principle of superposition, 753, 753*f*
principles, scientific, 76
prisms, 570, 570*f*
   lab on, 570
products, 220
   in chemical equations, 226
   mole ratios and, 228–229
projectile motion, 408–410, 408*f*, 409*f*
propane, 198, 199, 199*f*
properties of matter. *See also* **chemical properties; physical properties**
   of groups in the periodic table, 150, 151, 153
proportional relationship, 101
proteins, 202, 203, 203*f*, 204
   colloids formed by, 262
   in human body, 243
protons, 119–120, 119*f*, 120*f*
   from decay of neutron, 329, 330
   electric charge of, 586
   nuclear stability and, 337–338, 338*f*
   number of, in an element, 120
   in Rutherford's atomic model, 118
protostars, 698, 698*f*
Ptolemy, 672
pulleys, 438, 438*f*, 440, 440*f*
   efficiency of, 459, 459*f*
pulsars, 700
pulse induction, 629
pupil, 569, 569*f*
pure science, 8
pure substances, 48, 49, 49*f*, 259
P waves, 518, 739–741, 741*f*
pyramid (FoldNote), 112
   instructions for, 850
pyramids, Egyptian, 442

qualitative information, 464
qualitative statements, 10
quantitative information, 464
quantitative statements, 10
quartz, 180, 180*f*
quasars, 707
questions, asking, 876

R

radar, 556, 556f
radiation, electromagnetic, 451, 482, 482f, 556–558. *See also* **electromagnetic waves**
radiation, nuclear, 327–329, 327f, 328f, 329f. *See also* **radioactive decay**
   beneficial uses of, 346–347, 346f
   discovery of, 332
   dosimeters for measurement of, 348, 348f
   everyday sources of, 344–345, 344f, 345f
   ionization of matter by, 328, 329, 332, 348
   risks from, 348, 349, 350
   units of human exposure to, 345, 345f
   unstable nuclei and, 338
radiation sickness, 348
radicals, free, 235, 236
radioactive decay, 327–336. *See also* **radiation, nuclear**
   calculations with, 334, 354
   dating materials with, 333, 336, 336f, 754, 754f
   definition of, 327, 327f
   discovery of, 332
   in Earth's interior, 333, 730
   equations for, 330–331
   labs on, 335, 352–353
   nuclear changes in, 330–331, 330f
   nuclear stability and, 338
   rates of, 333–336, 333f, 335f
   word origins relating to, 326
radioactive elements, 160, 160f
radioactive tracers, 346, 346f, 347
radioisotopes, 123, 327, 330–331, 333–336, 333f
   ages of rocks and, 333, 754, 754f
   beneficial uses of, 346–347, 346f
radiologist, 123
radio telescopes, 17, 695, 706, 707
radiotherapy, 346
radio waves, 506, 556, 556f
   reflected by ionosphere, 776, 776f
radon gas, 348
rain, 774, 781f, 782. *See also* **precipitation**
   fronts and, 789, 790
   of hurricane, 792
   lab on, 784
   topography and, 795
rainbows, 571, 571f
rain shadow, 795

ramp, 436, 437, 437f, 441, 441f
   lab on, 462–463
rarefactions, 512, 512f
rates. *See also* **speed**
   of chemical reactions, 238–241, 238f, 239f, 245, 248–249
   of radioactive decay, 333–336, 333f, 335f
ray diagrams
   of reflection, 560, 561, 561f, 562, 562f
   of refraction, 566f, 567, 567f, 568f
reactants, 220
   in chemical equations, 226
   mole ratios and, 228–229
reaction forces, 412–413, 412f, 413f
   conservation of momentum and, 417
   lab on, 414
reaction rates, 238–241, 238f, 239f
   balanced at equilibrium, 245
   catalysts and, 240–241
   labs on, 239, 248–249
reactivity, 56, 56f
   lab on, 58
   single-displacement reactions and, 233
Reading Toolbox, overview of, 842
real images, 563, 568, 569
rectangle, area of, 10, 18, 864f
recycling, 830, 831, 831f
red giants, 699, 699f, 700, 701, 701f
   at center of galaxy, 704
redox reactions, 235, 237. *See also* **combustion reactions**
   in human body, 243
red shift, 710, 710f
reduced substance, 237
reference points, 365, 367
reflection (light), 524, 524f, 560–561, 561f. *See also* **mirrors**
   angle of, 561, 561f
   colors and, 564, 564f
   in rainbow formation, 571, 571f
reflection (sound waves), 550, 551
refraction, 526, 526f, 566–567, 566f, 567f
   dispersion in, 570–571, 570f, 571f
   by lenses, 568–569, 569f
refrigerators, 489
   natural substitute for, 823
relative humidity, 782
   calculating with, 798
relative intensity, of sound, 545, 545f
relativity, theory of
   gravity in, 717, 717f
   mass-energy equivalence in, 339
rems, 345, 345f

renewable resources, 818–820, 818f, 819f, 820f. *See also specific energy sources*
resistors, 596, 597, 602f
   power dissipated by, 605
resonance, 548
respiration, cellular, 243, 815
retina, 569, 569f
Richter scale, 742, 742f
rift valleys, 734, 734f, 745
right-hand rule, 627, 627f
Ring of Fire, 745, 745f
rock cycle, 752, 752f
rockets, 416
rocks, 748–754. *See also* **erosion; minerals; sedimentary rocks; weathering**
   ages of, 333, 753–754, 753f, 754f
   human uses of, 749, 755
   igneous, 749, 749f, 752, 752f
   lab on, 753
   metamorphic, 751, 751f, 752, 752f
   in rock cycle, 752, 752f
rods, 569, 569f
Roentgen, Wilhelm, 6–7, 7f
rolling friction, 383, 386–387
roots
   of a number, 863
   of words, 144, 472, 504, 728, 772, 859
rounding numbers, 27–28, 868
rubbing alcohol, 264
Russell, Henry Norris, 700
rust, 56, 56f, 237
Rutherford, Ernest, 117–118, 117f, 118f, 328

S

salts, 305–306
   animals' need for, 306, 306f
   in the body, 306
   common examples of, 305, 305f
   formed in neutralization reactions, 303, 303f
   of halogens, 162
   in household products, 307, 309, 310, 313, 313f
   sources of, 305
   uses of, 305, 305f
sandstone, 750, 752
satellites, 656, 675. *See also* **moon**
   formation of, 673
   of gas giants, 656, 667, 668, 673
   of Pluto, 670, 670f

INDEX

saturated air, 782
saturated solutions, 278–279, 278f, 279f, 280
Saturn, 666–667, 668, 668f
    motion through Leo, 654, 654f
scatter plots, 870
schematic diagrams, 601–602, 601f, 602f
science
    bias in, 16
    branches of, 4, 7–8, 7f
    definition of, 7
    everyday words used in, 4, 292, 364, 430, 692, 860–861
    models in, 11–12, 11f, 12f, 764
    skills in, 14–17, 14f, 22
    technology and, 8, 8f, 13, 17
    tools in, 17, 20f, 21
scientific laws, 9, 10, 10f, 76
scientific methods, 15, 15f, 876–879. *See also* **data; experiments; hypothesis; observations**
scientific notation, 24–25, 866
scientific theories, 9, 9f, 10
    compared with facts and hypotheses, 728
    predictions based on, 642, 772
scintigrams, 123
scissors, 443
screws, 438, 438f, 442, 442f, 443
search engines, 610, 682, 873–874
seasons, 794, 794f, 811, 811f
    lab on, 812
seat belts, 398
sea water. *See* **ocean**
second law of thermodynamics, 490, 491
seconds (s), 20f
sediment
    deposition of, 759, 759f
    erosion of, 759, 760
    formation of, 750
sedimentary rocks, 750, 750f
    chemical changes in, 757, 757f
    principle of superposition and, 753, 753f
    in rock cycle, 752, 752f
seismic waves, 506, 515, 518, 739–741, 740f, 741f
    lab on, 739
seismographs, 740–741, 740f
seismology, 740
semiconductors, 154, 154f, 155f, 164, 164f
    electrical properties of, 155f, 598, 598f
    microprocessors made of, 165

series circuits, 603, 603f
shale, 750, 751
shampoos, 311
shield volcanoes, 743, 744f
shock absorbers, 510
short circuit, 606, 607
SI (International System of Units), 17, 867
SI units, 17–21, 19f, 18f, 20f, 867, 880
significant figures, 26–28, 877
    rules for determining, 868
silicon chips, 165. *See also* **semiconductors**
simple harmonic motion, 508
simple lever, 438, 438f
simple machines, 438–442, 438f, 439f
sine curves, 514
    lab on, 530–531
sine waves, 514, 514f
single-displacement reactions, 233–234, 233f, 234f
skid marks, 378–379
sky maps, 883
slate, 751, 751f
sliding friction, 383, 386–387
slope
    calculation of, 370, 370f
    of distance vs. time graph, 367f, 371, 371f, 388
    of speed vs. time graph, 376, 377
smog, 236, 827. *See also* **air pollution**
smoke detectors, 160, 346, 346f
snow, 774, 782. *See also* **precipitation**
    acidic, 826
    fronts and, 789, 790
soaps, 307–309, 307f, 311
soap scum, 309, 311
sodium chloride, 181, 181f, 184–185, 184f
    dissolving in water, 268, 268f
    solution of, 263, 263f, 273
sodium-potassium pumps, 268
soft magnetic materials, 620
solar eclipse, 658, 658f, 717
solar electric car, 461, 461f
solar energy. *See also* **photosynthesis**
    electricity from, 818, 818f
    at equator and poles, 794, 794f
    for living things, 449, 451, 491
    radiated back into space, 457
    as source of hydroelectric power, 820
    as source of winds, 483, 819
    trapped in fossil fuels, 816, 817
solar heating systems, 488

solar system, 655–656, 655f, 656f. *See also* **asteroids; comets; Earth; moon; planets; satellites; sun**
    age of, 673
    definition of, 655
    early ideas about, 671–673, 672f
    formation of, 673, 674f, 675, 676
    Kuiper Belt in, 670, 676, 676f
    labs on, 668, 672
    location of, in Milky Way, 704
    meteoroids and meteorites in, 675, 676, 676f, 677, 677f
    as part of universe, 709, 709f
solar wind, 82, 675
solenoids, 627–628, 627f
solids, 78, 78f
    changes of state, 84–85, 84f, 85f, 86–87, 87f
    dissolved in solids, 266, 266f
    kinetic energy of particles in, 80, 80f
    wave speed in, 521
solubility
    definition of, 276
    of gases, 279, 279f, 282–283
    insoluble substances, 276, 276f
    lab on, 282–283
    of solids in water, 276–277, 277f, 279
    temperature and, 279, 282–283
solutes. *See also* **dissolving; solubility**
    concentration of, 277, 280
    definition of, 263
    states of, 264
solutions, 263–264, 263f, 264f. *See also* **dissolving; neutral solutions; solubility**
    boiling points of, 273
    concentration of, 277, 280
    freezing points of, 273
    saturated, 278–279, 278f, 279f
    of solids in solids, 266, 266f
solvents. *See also* **dissolving; solubility**
    definition of, 263
    heating of, 272
    nonpolar, 270, 270f
    states of, 264
    water as, 267–270, 268f, 269f
sonar, 551
sonograms, 550
s orbitals, 130, 130f, 131f
sound waves, 543–551
    creation of, 508, 543, 543f
    dead spots in halls, 527
    diffraction of, 525
    Doppler effect with, 522–523, 522f
    energy of, 543, 545
    energy transfer by, 456, 459, 507

hearing and, 508, 549, 549*f*
intensity of, 545, 545*f*
interference of, 527, 528, 528*f*
labs on, 544, 547, 548, 551
as longitudinal waves, 512, 515
medium of, 506
of musical instruments, 547–548
pitch of, 522, 523, 546, 546*f*, 547
properties of, 543–546
reflection of, 550, 551
of sonar systems, 551
speed of, 520, 520*f*, 544, 544*f*
ultrasound, 546, 550, 551
wavelength of, 515
south pole
of Earth's magnetic field, 623, 623*f*, 732
of magnet, 619, 621, 622
of solenoid, 627
space, words and phrases for, 364, 692
space-filling model, 178, 178*f*
space shuttle
apparent weightlessness in, 408, 408*f*
orbital motion of, 408, 410*f*
spatial language, 692
speakers, 635
specific heat, 485–486, 485*f*
calculation of, 496
of various materials, 881
spectator ions, 302, 303
spectral analysis, 132
red shift in, 710, 710*f*
of starlight, 132, 696, 696*f*
spectroscopes, 17
spectrum
electromagnetic, 521, 521*f*, 556–558, 556–557*f*, 880
of visible light, 521, 521*f*, 556, 557*f*, 570
speed. *See also* **rates; velocity**
average, 368, 368*f*
calculation of, 368
change in, 372, 372*f*
constant, 368, 371
definition of, 367
of everyday objects, 366–367*f*
instantaneous, 369
kinetic energy and, 447–448, 447*f*
lab on, 368
of light, 521, 555, 555*f*, 566, 570
SI unit for, 368
as slope of graph, 367*f*, 371, 371*f*, 388
of sound waves, 520, 520*f*, 544, 544*f*
of waves, 518–521, 518*f*
speed vs. time graph, 376–377, 377*f*

spider map (Graphic Organizer), 4, 144
instructions for, 856
spin, electron, 628
spring, 508–509, 508*f*, 509*f*
longitudinal waves in, 512, 512*f*
spring scale, 414
square root, 863
stable nuclei, 337–338, 338*f*
standing waves, 529, 529*f*
of musical instruments, 547, 547*f*
stars, 693–701. *See also* **black holes; galaxies; sun; telescopes**
ancient observations of, 654
brightness of, 695, 700–701, 701*f*
colors of, 695, 696, 696*f*
constellations of, 654, 654*f*, 697
distances from Earth, 693
elements formed in, 350, 714
formation of, 693, 693*f*, 704, 707, 713
gravity and, 406, 694, 698, 699
life cycles of, 698–699*f*, 698–701, 701*f*
nuclear fusion in, 342, 694, 694*f*, 698, 699, 714
number of, in universe, 125
planets of, 679, 702
sky maps of, 883
spectral analysis of light from, 132, 696, 696*f*
structures of, 693, 694
telescope studies of, 695
states of matter, 52, 78–79, 78*f*, 79*f*. *See also* **changes of state;** *specific states of matter*
kinetic energy in, 80, 80*f*
kinetic theory and, 77
wave speed in, 521
static electricity, 589
static friction, 383, 386–387
stationary front, 790
Statue of Liberty, 237
steam, 80*f*, 84, 87*f*
step-down transformer, 638, 638*f*, 639, 639*f*
step-up transformer, 638, 638*f*, 639
Stonehenge, 671, 671*f*
Strassman, Fritz, 337, 339, 340
stratosphere, 773*f*, 775, 775*f*. *See also* **ozone layer**
stratus clouds, 783, 783*f*
strong acids, 294, 294*f*, 295, 295*f*
neutralization reactions of, 302–304, 303*f*
pH of, 298*f*, 299
strong bases, 296, 297, 297*f*
neutralization reactions of, 302–304, 303*f*

strong nuclear force, 338, 338*f*, 380, 381
structural formulas, 178
condensed, 199, 199*f*
structure, chemical, 178–179, 178*f*. *See also* **chemical bonds**
properties and, 180–182, 180*f*, 181*f*, 182*f*
subatomic particles, 119–120, 119*f*, 120*f*
subduction, 735–736, 735*f*, 745
sublimation, 84*f*, 85, 85*f*
submarines, 95
substances, pure, 48, 49, 49*f*, 259
substrate, 241, 241*f*
subtractive primary colors, 565, 565*f*
succession, 811
suffixes, 44, 176, 472, 618, 859
sulfur dioxide, 825*f*, 826
summarizing (Note Taking), 258
instructions for, 846
sun, 653–654, 654*f*. *See also* **solar energy; solar system; ultraviolet light**
curving of space by, 717, 717*f*
daily cycles on Earth and, 654, 654*f*
electromagnetic waves from, 452, 452*f*, 477, 482
gravity and, 405, 405*f*, 698, 698*f*, 717
halo appearing around, 784
harmful radiation from, 663
helium in, 132
hydrogen in, 123
lab on, 680–681
life cycle of, 698–700, 701
magnetic field of, 624
nuclear fusion in, 342, 450, 450*f*, 698
ozone layer and, 236, 558, 775, 778
plasma of, 82
power output of, 680–681
size of, 653, 653*f*, 680–681
spectral analysis of, 132
as a star, 653, 693
temperature of, 477
tides and, 660
superclusters, galactic, 703
superconductors, 599, 599*f*
supernova, 699–700, 699*f*, 700*f*, 714, 716
superposition, principle of, 753, 753*f*
supersaturated solution, 279, 279*f*
surface area
calculation of, 864
reaction rates and, 238, 239
surface waves, 513, 513*f*
from earthquake, 740, 740*f*, 741
surfing, 517
suspensions
as mixtures, 260–261, 260*f*, 261*f*, 264

INDEX

S waves, 518, 739–741, 741f
sweating, 85
swim bladders, 91
switches, 601, 601f, 602, 602f
   circuit breaker as, 607
   in series circuit, 603
symbols, 208
synthesis reactions, 231
   in human body, 243
systems
   closed, 457
   open, 457

T

table fold (FoldNote), 218
   instructions for, 850
tangent, to magnetic field lines, 622
tannic acid, 264
technetium-99m, 123
technology, 8, 8f, 13, 17
tectonic plates. *See* **plate boundaries; plate tectonics**
telescopes, 17, 17f, 695
   Hubble Space Telescope, 703, 703f
   new technology for, 715, 715f, 716, 716f
   radio telescopes, 17, 695, 706, 707
televisions, 116
temperature, 80–81, 473–479. *See also* **heat**
   buoyancy of air and, 796–797
   in changes of state, 87, 87f, 487, 487f
   climate and, 794
   energy transfer and, 478–479, 479f
   equilibrium and, 246f, 247
   evaporation and, 782–783, 783f
   everyday decisions based on, 473, 473f
   expansion caused by, 474–475, 475f
   gas pressure and, 99, 99f
   gas volume and, 99, 100–101, 100f
   heat and, 84, 487, 487f, 490
   kinetic energy and, 80–81, 80f, 473–474, 476, 479
   labs on, 81, 474, 478
   light spectrum and, 696, 696f
   measurement of, 30, 878
   motion of particles and, 9, 77, 80, 81
   reaction rates and, 238–239, 239f, 248–249
   second law of thermodynamics and, 490
   sensation of, 81, 474, 478, 479f
   solubility and, 279, 282–283
   in space, 477
   specific heat and, 485–486, 485f
   stars' life cycle and, 700, 701f
   thermometers and, 474, 474f, 475, 878
   thermostats and, 475, 475f
temperature inversions, 774, 774f
temperature scales, 475–477, 476f
temporal language, 806
terminals, of battery, 594–595, 594f
terminal velocity, 407, 407f
terrestrial planets, 661–667. *See also* **Earth**
   formation of, 673
   geologic features of, 661
   Mars, 664, 664f, 665, 666, 677
   Mercury, 662, 662f
   orbits of, 661, 661f
   Venus, 662, 662f
theories, scientific, 9, 9f, 10
   compared with facts and hypotheses, 728
   predictions based on, 642, 772
thermal conduction, 480–481, 480f, 481f
thermal energy, 81
   from sun, 451
thermodynamics
   first law of, 456, 490
   second law of, 490, 491
thermometers, 474, 474f, 475, 878
thermosphere, 773f, 776
thermostats, 475, 475f
Thomson, J. J., 115, 117
three-panel flip chart (FoldNote), 772
   instructions for, 851
thunder, 791
thunderstorms, 790, 795
tides, 660, 660f
time. *See also* **distance vs. time graph**
   in calculating speed, 368, 369
   change in momentum during, 415, 415f
   period of wave, 516, 516f, 518
   speed vs. time graphs, 376–377, 377f
   units of, 18f, 20f, 21
   words and phrases for, 364, 806
   work done in, 433, 434
titrations, 304, 304f
Tokamak Fusion Reactor, 83
topography, 795, 795f
tornadoes, 790, 791, 791f, 795
trace gases, 773
transceivers, 559
transformers, 638–639, 638f, 639f
transform fault boundaries, 737, 737f
transition metals, 159–160, 159f, 160f
   cations of, 192–193, 192f
transpiration, 781f, 782
transponders, 556
transverse waves, 511, 511f, 512. *See also* **electromagnetic waves**
   amplitude of, 514, 514f
   from earthquake, 739–741, 741f
   electromagnetic, 511, 637, 637f
   graphs of, 532
   lab on, 530–531
   light as, 553
   wavelength of, 515, 515f
tri-fold (FoldNote), 364, 584, 692
   instructions for, 851
triple-beam balance, 878
triple bonds, 187, 187f, 198
tropical depressions, 792
tropopause, 774, 775
troposphere, 773f, 774
   water cycle in, 781, 781f
troughs, 512, 512f, 513
   amplitude and, 514, 514f
   wavelength and, 515, 515f
tsunamis, 507, 507f
turns, of transformer, 638, 638f
two-column notes (Note Taking), 44, 396
   instructions for, 847
two-panel flip chart (FoldNote)
   instructions for, 851
Tyndall effect, 261, 261f
typhoons, 792

U

ultrasound, 546, 550, 551
ultraviolet light, 554, 554f, 557f, 558, 558f
   atmosphere and, 663, 775, 778
unified atomic mass units (u), 124
uniform circular motion, 373, 373f
units of measurement, 17–21, 18f, 20f, 867, 880. *See also* **measurements**
   conversions within SI, 19, 19f, 68
   for microscopic quantities, 21, 21f
universal gravitation equation, 10, 405, 407
universe, 708–717
   age of, 712
   beginning of, 710–713, 713f
   contents of, 708–709
   definition of, 708
   empty space in, 710

INDEX

expansion of, 710–713, 711f, 715, 715f
future of, 715–716, 715f
lab on, 711
mass of, 87
number of stars in, 125
seen as in the past, 709
sizes and distances in, 708, 708f–709f, 709
visible to unaided eye, 709
unsaturated solution, 278, 278f, 280
uranium, 121, 124
Uranus, 666, 666f, 667, 669, 669f

valence electrons, 130, 183, 186
    periodic table and, 151–152, 151f, 152f, 156, 156f
variables
    in algebraic equations, 865
    dependent, 23, 869, 877
    in experiments, 15, 16, 877
    independent, 23, 869, 877
    proportional, 101
velocity, 367. *See also* **acceleration; speed**
    calculation of, 369
    change in, 372–375
    definition of, 367
    momentum and, 414, 415, 416
    Newton's first law and, 397, 398
    resultant, 367
    terminal, 407, 407f
Venn diagram (Graphic Organizer), 806
    instructions for, 857
vents
    hydrothermal, 732, 732f
    of volcanoes, 743, 743f, 744
Venus, 662, 662f
vibrations, 508–509, 508f, 511
    amplitude of, 514
    forced, 548
    frequency of, 516
    period of, 516, 516f
    sound waves created by, 508, 543, 543f
video game programmer, career as, 427
virtual images
    in reflection, 562, 562f, 563
    in refraction, 567, 567f, 568, 568f, 569
viscosity, 94
visible light, 521, 521f, 556, 557f. *See also* **light**
volcanoes, 743–746

climate change and, 795
of early Earth, 777, 777f
at hot spots, 746, 746f, 747
human impact of, 747, 824
islands associated with, 736, 746
at plate boundaries, 735, 735f, 736, 745, 745f
rock formation after eruption of, 749, 752
solidified core of, 748, 748f
types of, 743–744, 744f
underwater, 744, 745, 746
vents of, 743, 743f
volcanologist, career as, 427
voltage, 594–595, 594f
    of household outlet, 596, 600, 600f
    measurement of, 630
    in parallel circuits, 603
    power and, 605, 606
    resistance and, 596–597, 599
    in series circuits, 603
    transformers and, 638–639, 638f, 639f
voltmeters, 630
volts (V), 594
volume
    calculation of, 21, 30
    density and, 54–55, 55f
    of gas, 97–98, 97f, 99, 100–101, 100f
    of geometric shapes, 864, 864f
    measurement of, 32, 877
    states of matter and, 78–79
    units of, 20f, 21

wafers, silicon, 165
warm fronts, 789, 789f, 790, 790f
water. *See also* **ice**
    in atmosphere, 774, 781–784, 781f, 783f
    changes of state, 84–87, 84f, 87f, 487, 487f
    cleaning products used with, 307–310, 307f, 310f
    electrolysis of, 229, 229f, 231
    erosion by, 759–760, 759f, 760f, 761, 761f
    formation from elements, 177, 177f
    hard, 309, 311
    hydrogen bonds of, 182, 182f, 269, 269f
    labs on, 55, 102–103
    in mixtures, 49, 49f, 50
    molar mass of, 127

molecules of, 47, 47f, 114, 114f, 178, 178f
pH of, 298, 298f, 299
as polar molecule, 267–268, 267f, 268f, 270
as pure substance, 48, 49, 49f
solubility of gases in, 279, 279f, 282–283
solubility of solids in, 276–277, 277f, 279
as solvent, 267–270, 268f, 269f
states of, 52
as steam, 80f, 84, 87f
weathering of rocks and, 756, 756f, 757–758, 757f, 758f
water cycle, 781–784, 781f
water pollution, 824f, 827–828, 827f, 828f
    lab on, 829
water waves, 505–506, 505f, 506f, 507, 507f
    as surface waves, 513, 513f
watts (W), 433, 605
wave fronts, 507
wavelength, 514, 515, 515f
    speed and, 518–519, 570
wave medium, 506, 506f, 508, 511
    speed and, 520–521, 520f, 526
wave model, of light, 553, 553f, 554
waves, 505–532. *See also* **electromagnetic waves; frequency; interference; longitudinal waves; mechanical waves; reflection; refraction; sound waves; transverse waves; wavelength**
    amplitude of, 514, 514f, 515
    definition of, 505
    diffraction of, 525, 525f, 552f
    Doppler effect with, 522–523, 522f, 710, 710f
    electron as, 129
    energy carried by, 505, 507, 509, 511, 515
    labs on, 509, 511, 520, 530–531
    ocean, 507, 507f, 517
    period of, 516, 516f, 518
    sine waves, 514, 514f
    speed of, 518–521, 518f
    standing, 529, 529f, 547, 547f
    surface, 513, 513f, 740, 740f, 741
    vibrations and, 508–509, 509f, 511, 514, 516
weak acids, 294, 294f, 295, 295f
    reaction with strong base, 303, 304

Index **939**

INDEX

weak bases, 297, 297f
    reaction with strong acid, 303, 304
weak nuclear force, 380
weather, 789–792. *See also* **clouds; lightning; precipitation; wind**
    barometric pressure and, 784
    climate and, 794
    computer models of, 12, 12f
    fronts and, 789–790, 789f, 790f, 791
    global warming and, 826
    hurricanes, 12, 12f, 792, 792f
    international symbols for, 882
    lab on, 791
    maps of, 886
    meteorology and, 8
    tornadoes, 790, 791, 791f, 795
    troposphere and, 774
weathering, 756–758
    chemical, 750, 757–758, 757f, 758f
    erosion and, 759, 760, 761
    physical, 750, 756, 756f, 759, 760
    in rock cycle, 752, 752f
wedges, 438, 438f, 442, 442f, 443
Wegener, Alfred, 731
weight, 404–405
    balanced by air resistance, 407
    calculation of, 403
    compared with density, 55
    compared with mass, 21, 403–404
    on different planets, 404
    gravitational potential energy and, 445
    law of universal gravitation and, 407
    on moon, 404
    unit of, 403
weightlessness, apparent, 408, 408f
wheel and axle, 438, 438f, 440, 440f
white dwarfs, 699, 699f, 700, 701, 701f
Wilson, Robert, 712
windsmith, career as, 427
wind, 483, 785–787, 786f, 787f
    erosion by, 760, 760f
    fronts and, 789, 790
    human uses of, 788, 819, 819f, 822
    of hurricane, 792, 792f
    lab on, 832–833
    surfing and, 517
    symbols for speed of, 789, 790
    of tornado, 791, 791f, 795
    troposphere and, 774
wind velocity, surfing and, 517
word parts, 858–859
word problems, 430
words
    in examples, 44, 258
    families of, 584
    frequency indicators, 176
    mnemonics, 542, 652
    for nuclear radiation, 326
    prefixes of, 218, 472, 542, 772, 858
    roots of, 144, 472, 504, 728, 772, 859
    scientific meanings of, 4, 292, 364, 430, 692, 860–861
    for space and time, 364, 692, 806
    spatial, 692
    suffixes of, 44, 176, 472, 618, 859
    temporal, 806
work, 431–432, 431f. *See also* **machines**
    calculation of, 432
    electrical, 605
    by electric motor, 450, 630
    energy and, 444–445, 444f, 450, 451
    energy conservation and, 456
    kinetic energy and, 447, 448, 490
    mechanical energy and, 449
    power and, 433–434
    units of, 432
    useful, 459, 460
    by waves, 507
World Wide Web
    addresses on, 168, 316
    bias on, 834
    reputable sources on, 316
    search engines on, 610, 682, 873–874
    terminology about, 610

X rays, 7, 7f, 557f, 558
    medical or dental, 345, 345f
    orbiting observatory for, 716, 716f

Young, Thomas, 552–553

Credits

Photography

Abbreviations used (t) top, (c) center, (b) bottom, (l) left, (r) right, (bkgd) background
Cover © Ed Honowitz/Stone/Getty Images
Table of Contents v (bl) Digital Vision/Getty Images; vi (cl) Expuesto- Nicolas Randall/Alamy; vii (tr) Alexander Hubrich/zefa/Corbis; vii (br) Sam Dudgeon/HRW; viii (tl) Gail Shumway/Getty Images; viii (bl) Sergio Purtell/Foca/HRW; ix (br) Tim Platt/Getty Images; x (cl) Ted Kinsman/Photo Researchers, Inc.; xi (tr) A. Ramey/PhotoEdit; xi (br) Richard Megna/Fundamental Photographs, New York; xii (tl) NASA; xii (bl) James Kay; xiii (r) Bernard Photo Productions//Animals Animals/Earth Scenes; xiv (tr) Buzz Pictures/Alamy; xvii (b) Scott B. Rosen/HRW Photo

Chapter One 2-3 (bkgd) Courtesy of Pagani Automobili, Italy; 2 (tl) © PhotoLink/PhotoDisc Red/gettyimages; 2 (cl) Sam Dudgeon/HRW; 2 (bl) Peter Van Steen/HRW; 3 (cr) Scott B. Rosen/HRW Photo; 5 (tr) Hulton Archive/Getty Images; 5 (br) Kari Marttila/Alamy; 7 (tr) AIP Emilio Segrè Visual Archives, Landé Collection; 8 (tl) © Dr. Tim Evans/SPL/Photo Researchers, Inc.; 8 (bl) Nicolas Russell/Getty Images; 8 (br) Volker Steger/Photo Researchers, Inc.; 9 (br) Sam Dudgeon/HRW; 10 (tl) © PhotoLink/PhotoDisc Red/gettyimages; 11 (tr) Kristian Hilsen/Getty Images/Stone; 11 (b) Ianni Dimitrov/Alamy; 11 (br) Courtesy Arup Photo Library; 12 (tl) NOAA; 12 (cl) NOAA; 12 (tr) NOAA; 13 (bkgd) © Ashley Cooper/CORBIS; 13 (tr) Scala/Art Resource, NY; 13 (tl) The Granger Collection, New York; 13 (cl) Scala/Art Resource, NY; 14 (bl) Scott B. Rosen/HRW Photo; 14 (bl) Scott B. Rosen/HRW Photo; 16 (br) Roger Ressmeyer/CORBIS; 17 (t) Bryan Allen/Corbis; 17 (tr) Fred A. Calvert/cold Spring Observatory/Adam Black/KPNO/AURA/NSF; 19 (tr) Hemera Technologies/Alamy; 20 (tr) Sam Dudgeon/HRW; 20 (cl) Peter Van Steen/HRW; 20 (cr) Image Copyright © Photodisc, Inc.; 20 (c) Sam Dudgeon/HRW; 20 (c) © Eyewire/gettyimages; 20 (bl) Peter Van Steen/HRW; 20 (tl) Scott B. Rosen/HRW Photo; 20 (cr) © Ragnar Schmuck/Getty Images; 20 (c) Ian M. Butterfield/Alamy; 20 (bl) PhotoDisc; 20 (br) Royalty-Free/Corbis; 20 (br) Scott B. Rosen/HRW Photo; 21 (tr) CNF, Cornell University; 22 (bl) Peter Van Steen/HRW; 24 (tl) BananaStock; 27 (tl) Sam Dudgeon/HRW; 27 (tc) Sam Dudgeon/HRW; 27 (tc) Sam Dudgeon/HRW; 27 (tr) Sam Dudgeon/HRW; 29 (bkgd) Andrea Pistolesi/Getty Images; 29 (cl) Jefferson National Expansion Memorial/National Parks Service; 29 (bl) Jefferson National Expansion Memorial/National Parks Service; 31 (b) HRW Owned; 32 (b) Scott B. Rosen/HRW Photo; 35 (tl) © PhotoLink/PhotoDisc Red/gettyimages; 35 (cl) Sam Dudgeon/HRW; 35 (bl) Peter Van Steen/HRW

Chemistry Unit Opener 41 (cl) Darren Higgins Photography; (tr) Adastra/Getty Images; (br) Edward Kinsman/Photo Researchers, Inc.

Chapter Two 42-43 (bkgd) James Caldwell/Alamy; 42 (br) Charles D. Winters/Photo Researchers, Inc.; 42 (cl) Aqua Image/Alamy; 42 (cl) Charles O'Rear/CORBIS; 43 (br) Scott B. Rosen/HRW Photo; 45 (br) Index Stock Imagery, Inc.; 46 (bl) David Muir/Masterfile; 46 (cl) Charles D. Winters/Photo Researchers, Inc.; 47 (b) David Madison/Getty Images; 48 (bl) Scott B. Rosen/HRW Photo; 49 (tl) Scott B. Rosen/HRW Photo; 49 (tl) Scott B. Rosen/HRW Photo; 50 (cr) FoodPix/Getty Images; 50 (c) Tudio Bonisolli-StockFood Munich/Stockfood America; 51 (cr) © Judith Collins/Alamy; 51 (b) Judith Collins/Alamy; 51 (br) Stockdisc Classis/Alamy; 52 (bl) © Photodisc/gettyimages; 53 (bkgd) NASA/Jet Propulsion Laboratory; 53 (cl) NASA; 53 (b) NASA/Jet Propulsion Laboratory; 55 (cr) Comstock; 55 (b) Scott B. Rosen/HRW Photo; 55 (tl) Scott B. Rosen/HRW Photo; 56 (bl) Rob Boudreau/Getty Images/Stone; 57 (bkgd) Charles Gupton/CORBIS; 57 (tl) Mauro Fermariello/Photo Researchers, Inc.; 57 (cl) Mauro Fermariello/Photo Researchers, Inc.; 57 (bl) Mauro Fermariello/Photo Researchers, Inc.; 58 (cl) Aqua Image/Alamy; 58 (c) Scott B. Rosen/HRW Photo; 58 (cr) Scott B. Rosen/HRW Photo; 59 (bc) Benelux Press/Index Stock Imagery, Inc.; 59 (bl) HRW Owned; 59 (br) Lance Schriner/HRW; 60 (cl) Sam Dudgeon/HRW; 60 (tl) Royalty Free/Corbis; 60 (tc) Charles O'Rear/CORBIS; 60 (tr) © PunchStock; 61 (bl) James Randklev/Corbis; 61 (bc) BSIP/Phototake; 61 (br) SuperStock; 62 (t) Scott B. Rosen/HRW Photo; 62 (bl) Ben Fink/FoodPix; 62 (tr) HRW Owned; 63 (br) Scott B. Rosen/HRW Photo; 63 (tr) David Buffington/Getty Images

64 (t) HRW Owned; 65 (bkgd) Steve Sant/Alamy; 65 (tl) Richard S. Huntrods; 65 (tr) Expuesto-Nicolas Randall/Alamy; 67 (r) Scott B. Rosen/HRW Photo; 69 (bl) Charles O'Rear/CORBIS; 69 (cl) Aqua Image/Alamy; 69 (tl) Charles D. Winters/Photo Researchers, Inc.; 70 (bl) Andrew Lambert Photography/Photo Researchers, Inc.

Chapter Three 74-75 (bkgd) John McAnulty/CORBIS; 74 (t) Johnny Johnson/Getty Images; 74 (tl) ImageState/Alamy; 74 (cl) Royalty-Free/Corbis; 74 (bl) David R. Frazier Photolibrary, Inc./Alamy; 75 (br) Sam Dudgeon/HRW Photo; 77 (br) Royalty-Free/Corbis; 78 (t) Sam Dudgeon/HRW; 79 (t) Scott Van Osdol/HRW; 79 (b) Johnny Johnson/Getty Images; 80 (br) Tony Freeman/PhotoEdit; 80 (bc) Galen Rowell/CORBIS; 80 (bl) John Langford/HRW; 81 (tl) Scott B. Rosen/HRW Photo; 82-83 (bkgd) © PunchStock; 82 (bl) Scott Stulberg/CORBIS; 83 (r) NASA; 85 (b) Digital Vision/Punchstock; 86 (b) ImageState/Alamy; 86 (tl) Scott B. Rosen/HRW Photo; 87 (l) John Langford/HRW; 87 (cr) Tony Freeman/PhotoEdit; 87 (bc) Galen Rowell/CORBIS; 88 (l) Fancy Photography/Veer; 91 (t) Scott B. Rosen/HRW Photo; 92 (b) Royalty-Free/Corbis; 93 (b) Brian Hagiwara/FoodPix; 95 (bkgd) CORBIS; 96 (bl) W.H. Muller/Zefa/Corbis; 99 (b) Scott B. Rosen/HRW Photo; 99 (t) David R. Frazier Photolibrary, Inc./Alamy; 100 (b) Charles D. Winters; 103 (bl) Scott B. Rosen/HRW Photo; 105 (t) Johnny Johnson/Getty Images; 105 (tl) ImageState/Alamy; 105 (bl) Royalty-Free/Corbis; 105 (b) David R. Frazier Photolibrary, Inc./Alamy

Chapter Four 110-111 (bkgd) © Eye of Science/SPL/Photo Researchers, Inc.; 110 (t) Sam Dudgeon/HRW; 110 (c) Sam Dudgeon/HRW; 110 (b) TZ Aviation/Airliners.net; 111 (b) Scott B. Rosen/HRW Photo; 113 (br) Scott B. Rosen/HRW Photo; 114 (bl) Michael Newman/Photo Edit; 115 (t) Charles D. Winters/Photo Researchers, Inc.; 115 (b) Sam Dudgeon/HRW; 118 (tr) Douglas Peebles/CORBIS; 118 (inset) CORBIS Images/HRW; 120 (tl) Mira/Alamy; 122 (tr) Scott B. Rosen/HRW Photo; 123 (r) GJLP/Photo Researchers, Inc.; 123 (bl) © Spencer Grant/SPL/Photo Researchers, Inc.; 125 (bc) Sam Dudgeon/HRW; 127 (t) Dynamic Graphics Group/IT Stock Free/Alamy; 129 (b) TZ Aviation/Airliners.net; 132 (c) PhotoDisc/Getty Images; 135 (r) Scott B. Rosen/HRW Photo; 137 (tl) Sam Dudgeon/HRW; 137 (cl) Sam Dudgeon/HRW; 137 (bl) TZ Aviation/Airliners.net

Chapter Five 142-143 (bkgd) Andrew Syred/Photo Researchers, Inc.; 142 (cl) Sam Dudgeon/HRW Photo; 142 (bl) PHOTOTAKE Inc./Alamy; 145 (br) Science Photo Library/Photo Researchers, Inc.; 145 (c) HRW Owned; 145 (bc) HRW Owned; 146 (b) The Granger Collection, New York; 146 (l) Richard Megna/Fundamental Photographs; 147 (b) Volvox/PictureQuest; 147 (bl) © Foodcollection/Alamy; 147 (cr) Russ Lappa/Photo Researchers, Inc.; 150 (tl) Tom Pantages Photography; 150 (tc) © Klaus Guldbrandsen/SPL/Photo Researchers, Inc.; 150 (tr) Richard Megna/Fundamental Photographs; 155 (tl) Sam Dudgeon/HRW Photo; 155 (cl) HRW Owned; 155 (tc) Sally Anderson-Bruce/HRW; 155 (c) Astrid & Hanns-Frieder Michler/Photo Researchers, Inc.; 155 (tr) Russ Lappa/Photo Researchers, Inc.; 155 (cr) Astrid & Hanns-Frieder Michler/Photo Researchers, Inc.; 156 (bl) Rob Lewine/CORBIS; 157 (br) Andrew Lambert Photography/Photo Researchers, Inc.; 157 (cr) © Andrew Lambert Photography/SPL/Photo Researchers, Inc.; 158 (bc) Richard Megna Fundamental Photographs; 158 (br) LADA/Photo Researchers, Inc.; 159 (tl) Peter Van Steen/HRW; 159 (cr) Phil Degginger/Alamy; 160 (bl) Oullette Theroux/Publiphoto/Photo Researchers, Inc.; 161 (bc) PHOTOTAKE Inc./Alamy; 161 (bl) Owaki-Kulla/CORBIS; 162 (bl) Martyn Chillmaid/Oxford Scientific; 162 (bc) Ric Frazier/Masterfile; 163 (cr) Charles D. Winters/Photo Researchers, Inc.; 163 (cl) © Imageshop/Alamy; 163 (bl) Horst Klemm/Masterfile; 165 (bkgd) Lawrence Manning/CORBIS; 165 (c) © John Maher/Index Stock Imagery, Inc.; 165 (bc) Richard T. Nowitz/CORBIS; 165 (cr) © Tetra Images/Alamy; 169 (cl) Sam Dudgeon/HRW Photo; 169 (bl) PHOTOTAKE Inc./Alamy

Chapter Six 174-175 (bkgd) Peter Arnold, Inc./Alamy; 174 (t) GC Minerals/Alamy; 174 (tl) Index Stock/Alamy; 174 (cl) Paul Silverman, Fundamental Photographs, NYC; 174 (bl) Alexander Hubrich/zefa/Corbis; 175 (br) HRW OWNED; 177 (bl) Sergio Purtell/Foca/HRW; 177 (br) Sergio Purtell/Foca/HRW; 179 (t) digitalvision/punchstock; 179 (cl) AAD Worldwide Travel Images/Alamy; 179 (bl) nagelestock/Alamy; 180 (br) GC Minerals/Alamy; 181 (tr) Sam Dudgeon/HRW; 181 (br) Profimedia.CZ s.r.o./Alamy; 182 (l) Furnald/Gray/Getty Images; 184 (br) Sam Dudgeon/HRW; 185 (bc) Richard Megna, Fundamental Photographs, NYC; 185 (br) Hrw Owned; 185 (bl) Richard Megna, Fundamental Photographs, NYC; 186 (l) Leslie Garland Picture Library/Alamy; 188 (bl) Scott B. Rosen/HRW Photo; 188 (cr) Index Stock/Alamy; 192 (bc) Paul Silverman, Fundamental Photographs, NYC; 192 (br) © Andrew Lambert Photography/SPL/Photo Researchers, Inc.; 194 (br) © Getty Images; 194 (br) © Getty Images; 194 (bl) © Getty Images; 194 (bl) © Getty Images; 197 (br) Peter Van Steen/HRW; 198 (b) Justin Kase/Alamy; 200 (t) Sam Dudgeon/HRW; 200 (bl) Scott B. Rosen/HRW Photo; 201 (tr) Royalty-free/CORBIS; 202 (tr) Alexander Hubrich/zefa/Corbis; 203 (br) Scott B. Rosen/HRW Photo; 205 (bkgd) Fritz Goro/Time & Life Pictures/Getty Images; 205 (tl) Andrew Brookes/Corbis; 205 (cl) © TEK Image/SPL/Photo Researchers, Inc.; 205 (bl) © James Holmes/Cellmark Diagnostics/SPL/Photo Researchers,

Inc.; 207 (br) Scott B. Rosen/HRW Photo; 209 (t) GC Minerals/Alamy; 209 (tl) Index Stock/Alamy; 209 (cl) Paul Silverman, Fundamental Photographs, NYC; 209 (bl) Alexander Hubrich/zefa/Corbis; 214-215 (bkgd) Ted Horowitz/CORBIS; 214 (tr) Gabe Palmer/CORBIS; 214 (cl) © Michael Donne/SPL/Photo Researchers, Inc.; 214 (br) Aurora/Getty Images; 215 (tr) Richard Levine/Alamy; 215 (cl) Gail Moone/CORBIS; 215 (bc) Royalty-Free/CORBIS

Chapter Seven 216-217 (bkgd) Ian Cartwright/Getty Images; 216 (t) Charles D. Winters; 216 (cl) Royalty-Free/CORBIS; 216 (cl) Royalty-Free/CORBIS; 216 (bl) Photo ITAR-TASS/Vladimir Malygin; 217 (br) Scott B. Rosen/HRW Photo; 219 (bl) Charles D. Winters; 219 (bc) Charles D. Winters; 219 (br) Charles D. Winters; 220 (br) Matt Rainey/Star Ledger/Corbis; 223 (bkgd) Jeff Rotman/Getty Images; 223 (cl) Gregory G. Dimijian/Photo Researchers, Inc.; 223 (tl) Gail Shumway/Getty Images; 223 (bl) © Ted Kinsman/SPL/Photo Researchers, Inc.; 224 (c) Dorling Kindersley/Getty Images; 225 (br) Royalty-Free/Corbis; 226 (tl) Sam Dudgeon/HRW; 228 (tl) Scott B. Rosen/HRW Photo; 229 (cr) Charlie Winters; 230 (br) Judith Haeusler/Getty Images; 231 (cr) © Paul Rapson/SPL/Photo Researchers, Inc.; 231 (br) Royalty-Free/Corbis; 231 (b) Royalty-Free/CORBIS; 232 (b) Syracuse Newspapers/Carl J. Single/The Image Works; 233 (bl) Sergio Purtell/Foca/HRW; 234 (br) Sergio Purtell/Foca/HRW; 234 (tl) Sergio Purtell/Foca/HRW; 235 (tr) Scott B. Rosen/HRW Photo; 236 (bkgd) Lester Lefkowitz/CORBIS; 236 (bl) NASA/Goddard Space Flight Center; 236 (bc) NASA/Goddard Space Flight Center; 238 (bl) StockTrek/Getty Images; 239 (tr) Sergio Purtell/Foca/HRW; 239 (c) Sergio Purtell/Foca/HRW; 239 (br) Scott B. Rosen/HRW Photo; 240 (bl) Dorling Kindersley Limited courtesy of Science Museum, London/Corbis; 242-243 (bkgd) © Simon Fraser/SPL/Photo Researchers, Inc.; 242 (bc) Virgo/zefa/Corbis; 243 (tl) David Stoecklein/CORBIS; 243 (c) Microworks/Phototake; 244 (bl) Scott B. Rosen/HRW Photo; 244 (br) Scott B. Rosen/HRW Photo; 245 (br) SuperStock; 246 (br) Visuals Unlimited/Tom J. Ulrich; 247 (tr) Photo ITAR-TASS/Vladimir Malygin; 249 (br) Scott B. Rosen/HRW Photo; 251 (t) Charles D. Winters; 251 (tl) Royalty-Free/CORBIS; 251 (cl) Royalty-Free/CORBIS; 251 (bl) Photo ITAR-TASS/Vladimir Malygin

Chapter Eight 256-257 (bkgd) Lester Lefkowitz/CORBIS; 256 (tl) Peter Van Steen/HRW; 256 (cl) PunchStock; 256 (bl) Charlie Winters/Photo Researchers Inc.; 257 (cr) Scott B. Rosen/HRW Photo; 259 (cr) Peter Van Steen/HRW; 259 (br) Peter Van Steen/HRW; 260 (tl) Sam Dudgeon/HRW; 260 (tr) Sam Dudgeon/HRW; 260 (tl) Sam Dudgeon/HRW; 260 (tr) Sam Dudgeon/HRW; 261 (b) HRW Owned; 262 (inset) Bruce Iverson; 262 (br) Peter Van Steen/HRW; 262 (b) Scott B. Rosen/HRW Photo; 263 (bl) Sergio Purtell/Foca/HRW; 263 (cr) Sergio Purtell/Foca/HRW; 263 (br) Sergio Purtell/Foca/HRW; 264 (tl) Scott B. Rosen/HRW Photo; 265 (bkgd) © PunchStock; 266 (t) Tim Pannell/Corbis; 267 (br) © PunchStock; 269 (tl) Richard Megna/Fundamental Photographs, New York; 270 (t) Sam Dudgeon/HRW; 270 (b) Scott B. Rosen/HRW Photo; 271 (br) Scott B. Rosen/HRW Photo; 272 (bl) Peter Van Steen/HRW; 272 (br) Peter Van Steen/HRW; 273 (tl) HRW Owned; 273 (tc) HRW Owned; 273 (tr) HRW Owned; 274-275 (bkgd) © Scimat/SPL/Photo Researchers, Inc.; 274 (bl) Lester Lefkowitz/CORBIS; 275 (cr) Black Star; 276 (br) Charlie D. Winters/Photo Researchers, Inc.; 278 (bl) Peter Van Steen/HRW; 278 (br) Peter Van Steen/HRW; 279 (tr) Charlie Winters/Photo Researchers, Inc.; 279 (bl) Charles D. Winters; 279 (br) Charles D. Winters; 279 (tr) Christina Kennedy/Getty Images; 283 (r) Scott B. Rosen/HRW Photo; 285 (t) Peter Van Steen/HRW; 285 (c) PunchStock; 285 (b) Charlie Winters/Photo Researchers, Inc.

Chapter Nine 290-291 (bkgd) Pat O'Hara/CORBIS; 290 (tl) Oliver Strewe/Getty Images; 290 (cl) CNR/Photo Researchers, Inc.; 290 (bl) © Jake Wyman/Getty Images; 291 (br) Scott B. Rosen/HRW Photo; 293 (br) Scott B. Rosen/HRW Photo; 294 (bl) Sergio Purtell/Foca/HRW; 294 (tl) Sergio Purtell/Foca/HRW; 295 (tr) Scott B. Rosen/HRW Photo; 296 (cl) John Morrison/Morrison Photography; 297 (br) Sam Dudgeon/HRW; 298 (bl) Charles D. Winters; 298 (bc) Charles D. Winters; 298 (c) Charles D. Winters; 298 (br) Charles D. Winters; 298 (r) Charles D. Winters; 298 (cl) Scott B. Rosen/HRW Photo; 298 (l) Royalty-Free/Corbis; 300 (tl) Charles D. Winters/Photo Researchers, Inc.; 301 (bkgd) © Oliver Strewe/Getty Images; 301 (tr) Ted Spiegel/CORBIS; 301 (cl) Michael S. Quinton/Getty Images; 301 (c) Sally A. Morgan; Ecoscene/CORBIS; 302 (bl) Leonard Lessin/Peter Arnold, Inc.; 303 (t) Charles D. Winters; 304 (tl) Charles D. Winters; 305 (tr) CNRI/Photo Researchers, Inc.; 305 (br) Scott B. Rosen/HRW Photo; 306 (tl) Frans Lanting/Minden Pictures; 306 (tr) David Whitten/PictureQuest; 307 (br) Bob Thomason/Getty Images/Stone; 308 (bkgd) Aaron Haupt/Photo Researchers, Inc.; 309 (bl) Scott B. Rosen/HRW Photo; 310 (tl) © Jake Wyman/Getty Images; 311 (tl) Peter Van Steen/HRW; 311 (tc) Peter Van Steen/HRW; 312 (tr) Scott B. Rosen/HRW Photo; 312 (br) Scott B. Rosen/HRW Photo; 313 (tr) Scott B. Rosen/HRW Photo; 313 (cr) Scott B. Rosen/HRW Photo; 313 (bl) Scott B. Rosen/HRW Photo; 315 (br) HRW Owned; 317 (tl) Oliver Strewe/Getty Images; 317 (cl) CNR/Photo Researchers, Inc.; 317 (bl) Jake Wyman/Getty Images; 322 (tr) The Granger Collection, New York; 322 (tc) Bettmann/CORBIS; 322 (tl) The Granger Collection, New York; 322 (cr) Mike Agliolo/Photo Researchers, Inc.; 322 (c) Oxford Science Archive/Heritage-Images/The Image Works; 322 (cl) Alfred Pasieka/Photo Researchers, Inc.; 322 (bl) Getty Images; 322 (br) Courtesy of DuPont; 322 (bc) Columbus Dispatch, Craig Holman/Associated Press, AP; 323 (tl) Albert Riethausen/Associated Press, AP; 323 (tc) Ron Sanford/CORBIS; 323 (tr) Underwood & Underwood/CORBIS; 323 (c) © NREL/US Department of Energy/SPL/Photo Researchers, Inc.; 323 (cl) © Dr. Tim Evans/SPL/Photo Researchers, Inc.; 323 (cr) Scott Olson/Getty Images/NewsCom; 323 (bl) © David Parker/SPL/Photo Researchers, Inc.; 323 (bc) Stone/Getty Images

Chapter Ten 324-325 (bkgd) Roger Ressmeyer/CORBIS; 324 (tl) Giani Dagli Orti/CORBIS; 324 (cl) Jason Hawkes/CORBIS; 324 (bl) US Department of Energy/Photo Researchers, Inc.; 325 (br) Scott B. Rosen/HRW Photo; 332 (bkgd) Bettmann/CORBIS; 332 (cl) Jean-loup Charmet/Photo Researchers, Inc.; 332 (bl) DK Limited/CORBIS; 335 (tr) Scott B. Rosen/HRW Photo; 336 (t) Giani Dagli Orti/CORBIS; 337 (br) Bettmann/CORBIS; 341 (tl) Peter Van Steen/HRW; 343 (bkgd) Jason Hawkes/CORBIS; 344 (br) SuperStock; 345 (t) Keith Brofsky; 346 (tl) Peter Van Steen/HRW; 346 (bl) Larry Lefever/Grant Heilman Photography, Inc.; 347 (bkgd) Lester Lefkowitz/CORBIS; 347 (bl) Roger Ressmeyer/CORBIS; 348 (bl) © Martyn F. Chillmaid/SPL/Photo Researchers, Inc.; 349 (tl) Colin Cuthbert/SPL/Photo Researchers, Inc.; 350 (tl) US Department of Energy/Photo Researchers, Inc.; 351 (r) ITER/Photo Researchers, Inc.; 355 (tl) Giani Dagli Orti/CORBIS; 355 (cl) Jason Hawkes/CORBIS; 355 (bl) US Department of Energy/Photo Researchers, Inc.

Physics Unit Opener 361 (cl) John McAnulty/CORBIS; (tr) James Caldwell/Alamy; (br) Andrew Syred/Photo Researchers, Inc.

Chapter Eleven 362-363 (bkgd) Adastra/Getty Images; 362 (cl) Duomo/CORBIS; 362 (bl) Mike Powell/Getty Images; 362 (tl) Josef Fankhauser/Getty Images; 363 (tr) David Muir/Masterfile; 365 (br) Sam Spurgeon; 366 (bc) Alan Levenson/Getty Images/Stone; 366 (br) Index Stock Photography, Inc.; 366 (bl) Rubberball/Jupiter Images; 367 (bc) Michael H. Dunn/Corbis Stock Market; 367 (bl) Courtesy of Amtrak; 367 (br) Thinkstock/Superstock; 368 (tl) Scott B. Rosen/HRW Photo; 368 (bl) Josef Fankhauser/Getty Images; 371 (tr) Transtock Inc./Alamy; 371 (tc) Zoomstock/Masterfile; 371 (tl) David A. Barnes/Alamy; 373 (br) © Royalty Free/Wernher Krutein/CORBIS; 373 (t) Duomo/CORBIS; 377 (t) AFP/Getty Images; 378-379 (bkgd) David Frazier/The Image Works; 379 (t) Courtesy of Vericom Computers, Inc.; 381 (bl) Scott B. Rosen/HRW Photo; 381 (br) Scott B. Rosen/HRW Photo; 382 (bl) Al Francekevich/CORBIS; 384 (tl) Scott B. Rosen/HRW Photo; 384 (bl) Mike Powell/Getty Images; 387 (b) Scott B. Rosen/HRW Photo; 389 (tl) Josef Fankhauser/Getty Images; 389 (cl) Duomo/CORBIS; 389 (bl) Mike Powell/Getty Images

Chapter Twelve 394-395 (bkgd) Duomo/CORBIS; 394 (tl) Dennis O'Clair/Getty Images; 394 (cl) NASA; 394 (bl) Brian Bailey/CORBIS; 395 (br) Scott B. Rosen/HRW Photo; 397 (br) Dennis O'Clair/Getty Images; 398 (tl) Scott B. Rosen/HRW Photo; 398 (bl) Phillip Kaake/CORBIS; 399 (bkgd) Rick Fischer/Masterfile; 400 (bl) Sam Dudgeon/HRW; 400 (br) Sam Dudgeon/HRW; 402 (tl) Sam Dudgeon/HRW; 402 (tr) Sam Dudgeon/HRW; 403 (br) NASA; 404 (br) Gavriel Jecan/Getty; 404 (bc) Jeremy Woodhouse/Getty Images; 404 (t) Royalty-Free/Corbis; 404 (tl) CORBIS; 404 (cl) Royalty Free/Corbis; 404 (bl) JPL/NASA; 407 (br) Toby Rankin/Masterfile; 408 (tl) NASA; 408 (bl) Michelle Bridwell/Frontera Fotos; 408 (b) Image Copyright © PhotoDisc, Inc./HRW; 409 (bl) Richard Megna/Fundamental Photographs; 411 (bkgd) NASA; 411 (tr) NASA; 411 (cl) NASA; 412 (tr) David Madison; 412 (bl) Tim Platt/Getty Images; 413 (cr) Tim Platt/Getty Images; 414 (tl) Scott B. Rosen/HRW Photo; 415 (tr) Brian Bailey/CORBIS; 416 (bl) Digital Vision/Getty Images; 417 (t) INSADCO Photography/Alamy; 419 (b) Scott B. Rosen/HRW Photo; 421 (tl) Dennis O'Clair/Getty Images; 421 (cl) NASA; 421 (bl) Brian Bailey/CORBIS; 422 (bl) Stefan Puetz/zefa/Corbis; 426-427 (bkgd) Royalty-Free/CORBIS; 426 (tr) David Zalubowski/Associated Press, AP; 426 (cl) Ronnie Kaufman/CORBIS; 426 (br) Lester Lefkowitz/CORBIS; 427 (tr) Reuters/CORBIS; 427 (cl) Ed Young/CORBIS; 427 (bc) Ric Francis/Associated Press, AP

Chapter Thirteen 428-429 (bkgd) Darren Higgins Photography; 428 (t) Shawn Frederick/Getty Images; 428 (tl) SuperStock; 428 (bl) Alec Ptylowany/Masterfile; 428 (b) Altera Stefano/NASC/GAMMA; 429 (tr) Scott B. Rosen/HRW Photo; 431 (br) Mike Powell/Getty Images; 433 (tl) Scott B. Rosen/HRW Photo; 434 (bl) Shawn

Frederick/Getty Images; 435 (bkgd) Reuters/Stefano Rellandini; 435 (tl) Philip Gatward (c) Dorling Kindersley; 435 (tc) photolibrary pty. ltd./NewsCom; 435 (tr) Image Farm Inc./Alamy; 437 (tl) Peter Van Steen/HRW; 437 (tr) Peter Van Steen/HRW; 438 (tl) Robert Wolf/HRW Photo; 438 (tc) Visuals Unlimited/A. J. Copley; 438 (bc) SuperStock; 438 (br) Dr. E. R. Degginger/Color-Pic, Inc.; 438 (tr) Peter Van Steen/HRW Photo; 438 (bl) Scott B. Rosen/HRW Photo; 439 (tl) Michelle Bridwell/HRW; 439 (tc) John P. Kelly/Getty Images/The Image Bank; 439 (r) Purestock; 440 (bl) Peter Van Steen/HRW Photo; 441 (tr) Scott B. Rosen/HRW Photo; 441 (bl) Scott B. Rosen/HRW Photo; 442 (tr) SuperStock; 442 (br) Dr. E. R. Degginger/Color Pic, Inc.; 443 (tc) Peter Van Steen/HRW; 443 (tl) Peter Van Steen/HRW; 443 (tr) Peter Van Steen/HRW; 444 (bl) Pulse Productions/SuperStock/PictureQuest; 445 (tr) Richard Bannister; 447 (b) Alec Pytlowany/Masterfile; 449 (r) Royalty-Free/Corbis; 449 (br) © Darwin Dale/SPL/Photo Researchers, Inc.; 450 (tl) NASA/Phototake; 450 (br) Steve Bloom Images; 451 (bkgd) David Trood/Getty Images; 451 (cl) Dennis MacDonald/Alamy; 452 (t) Garry Black/Masterfile; 453 (br) Six Flags/Splash News; 454 (t) Coaster Gallery/JAR Productions; 455 (tr) SuperStock; 456 (tl) P. Freytag/zefa/Corbis; 457 (br) Scott B. Rosen/HRW Photo; 458 (bkgd) Patrick Eden/Alamy; 459 (tr) Jouanneau Thomas/CORBIS SYGMA; 460 (tl) Hank Morgan/Rainbow Inc.; 461 (c) Altera Stefano/NASC/GAMMA; 463 (l) Peter Van Steen/HRW; 465 (t) Shawn Frederick/Getty Images; 465 (tl) SuperStock; 465 (c) Alec Pytlowany/Masterfile; 465 (b) Altera Stefano/NASC/GAMMA; 466 (cl) Peter Van Steen/HRW; 467 (r) Scott B. Rosen/HRW Photo; 467 (c) Scott B. Rosen/HRW Photo; 467 (c) Scott B. Rosen/HRW Photo

Chapter Fourteen 470-471 (bkgd) Edward Kinsman/Photo Researchers, Inc.; 470 (tl) Phanie/Photo Researchers, Inc.; 470 (cl) Steve Mason/Photodisc Green/Getty Images; 470 (bl) NativeStock; 471 (r) Thinkstock Images; 473 (bl) Steve Bloom Images/Alamy; 473 (bc) Michael Newman/PhotoEdit; 473 (br) Phanie/Photo Researchers, Inc.; 474 (tl) Scott B. Rosen/HRW Photo; 474 (bl) HRW Owned; 475 (tr) Scott B. Rosen/HRW Photo; 479 (tr) Burke/Triolo Productions; 479 (cr) Deborah Ory Photography/Stockfood America; 480 (b) © Steve Mason/Photodisc Green/gettyimages; 482 (tr) Sam Dudgeon/HRW; 482 (bl) Ted Kinsman/Photo Researchers, Inc.; 483 (bkgd) Masumi Nakada/zefa/Corbis; 484 (bl) Sam Dudgeon/HRW; 484 (tl) © Brian & Cherry Alexander/Alamy; 485 (tr) Charles D. Winters; 488-489 (bkgd) Robert Perron; 490 (bl) NativeStock; 491 (tr) Guy Grenier/Masterfile; 491 (cr) Lorcan/DigitalVision/gettyimages; 495 (b) Scott B. Rosen/HRW Photo; 497 (tl) Phanie/Photo Researchers, Inc.; 497 (cl) Steve Mason/Photodisc Green/Getty Images; 497 (bl) NativeStock

Chapter Fifteen 502-503 (bkgd) Courtesy of Patricia Levi; 502 (tl) Travelshots/Alamy; 502 (cl) Jim Sugar/CORBIS; 502 (bl) Michael Freeman/Bruce Coleman, Inc.; 503 (br) Scott B. Rosen/HRW Photo; 506 (br) Travelshots/Alamy; 506 (bl) SuperStock; 507 (tl) Art Resource, NY; 509 (bl) Scott B. Rosen/HRW Photo; 510 (bkgd) Davo Blair/Alamy; 515 (br) Jim Sugar/CORBIS; 517 (bkgd) Buzz Pictures/Alamy; 517 (tl) Buzz Pictures/Alamy; 517 (cl) Buzz Pictures/Alamy; 517 (bl) Buzz Pictures/Alamy; 517 (b) Buzz Pictures/Alamy; 518 (tr) ©Joe Devenney/Getty Images/The Image Bank; 520 (tl) Scott B. Rosen/HRW Photo; 520 (br) Brian J. Skerry/National Geographic Image Collection; 522 (bl) Peter Van Steen/HRW; 522 (br) Peter Van Steen/HRW; 523 (tl) © Jim Reed/SPL/Photo Researchers, Inc.; 523 (tr) Jim Reed/CORBIS; 524 (bl) Erich Schrempp/Photo Researchers, Inc.; 525 (tl) Richard Megna/Fundamental Photographs; 525 (tr) FP/Fundamental Photographers; 526 (tl) Peter Van Steen/HRW; 526 (br) E. R. Degginger/Color-Pic, Inc.; 528 (tl) Michael Freeman/Bruce Coleman, Inc.; 529 (tr) Richard Megna/Fundamental Photographs; 529 (tr) Richard Megna/Fundamental Photographs; 531 (b) Scott B. Rosen/HRW Photo; 533 (tl) Travelshots/Alamy; 533 (c) Jim Sugar/CORBIS; 533 (bl) Michael Freeman/Bruce Coleman, Inc.; 538-539 (bkgd) Aaron Horowitz/CORBIS; 538 (tr) The Granger Collection, New York; 538 (cr) The Granger Collection, New York; 538 (c) The Granger Collection, New York; 538 (cl) The Granger Collection, New York; 538 (bl) © Tony Craddock/SPL/Photo Researchers, Inc.; 538 (bc) Sheila Terry/Rutherford Appleton Laboratory/Photo Researchers, Inc.; 538 (br) Getty Images; 539 (tl) Hulton Archive/Getty Images; 539 (tc) Hulton Archive/Getty Images; 539 (cl) The Granger Collection, New York; 539 (cr) The Granger Collection, New York; 539 (br) FPG/Hulton Archive/Getty Images; 539 (c) J. R. Eyerman/Time Life Pictures/Getty Images; 539 (bl) Digital Vision/Getty Images Royalty Free; 539 (bc) Toyota/Getty Images

Chapter Sixteen 540-541 (bkgd) Jose Fuste Raga/CORBIS; 540 (t) © Andrew Lambert Photography/SPL/Photo Researchers, Inc.; 540 (tl) Royalty-Free/CORBIS; 540 (cl) Swerve/Alamy; 540 (bl) © Jeremy Woodhouse/PunchStock; 541 (cr) Scott B. Rosen/HRW Photo; 543 (bc) A. Ramey/PhotoEdit; 544 (tl) Scott B. Rosen/HRW Photo; 545 (cl) Outdoor Perspectives/Alamy; 545 (bl) Michael Newman/PhotoEdit; 545 (c) Getty Images Royalty Free; 545 (br) Comstock Royalty Free; 545 (cr) Mint Photography/Alamy; 546 (cl) Royalty-Free/CORBIS; 546 (c) HRW Owned; 546 (bl) PhotoDisc, Inc.; 546 (br) Doug Perrine; 547 (bl) Redferns Music Picture Library/Alamy; 547 (br) © Andrew Lambert Photography/SPL/Photo Researchers, Inc.; 548 (cl) Scott B. Rosen/HRW Photo; 550 (br) Taxi/Getty Images; 550 (b) Blend Images/Alamy; 555 (bl) Gukenter Rossenbach/zefa/CORBIS; 556 (br) E. R. Degginger/Animals Animals/Earth Scenes; 556 (bl) Telegraph Colour Library/Getty Images/Taxi; 556 (bc) Don Couch/HRW Photo; 557 (bc) Ron Chapple/Getty Images/Taxi; 557 (bl) ©Royalty-Free/CORBIS; 557 (br) Royalty-Free/CORBIS; 558 (tl) Sheila Terry/Photo Researchers, Inc.; 559 (tr) Royalty-Free/CORBIS; 559 (bl) Andersen Ross/Getty Images; 560 (bl) Claude Gazuit/Photo Researchers, Inc.; 561 (bl) Richard Megna/Fundamental Photographs, New York; 562 (b) John Langford/HRW; 563 (tl) Scott B. Rosen/HRW Photo; 563 (br) Swerve/Alamy; 564 (bl) Peter Van Steen/HRW; 564 (br) Peter Van Steen/HRW; 566 (bl) Richard Megna/Fundamental Photographs; 567 (bl) © Jeremy Woodhouse/PunchStock; 568 (tl) Richard Megna/Fundamental Photographs; 568 (tr) Richard Megna/Fundamental Photographs; 568 (br) Peter Van Steen/HRW; 570 (br) © Science Photo Library/Photo Researchers, Inc.; 571 (t) Graham French/Masterfile; 572-573 (bkgd) Scott B. Rosen/HRW Photo; 572 (c) Scott B. Rosen/HRW Photo; 572 (tr) Scott B. Rosen/HRW Photo; 572 (l) Scott B. Rosen/HRW Photo; 573 (tl) Scott B. Rosen/HRW Photo; 573 (b) Scott B. Rosen/HRW Photo; 577 (t) © Andrew Lambert Photography/SPL/Photo Researchers, Inc.; 577 (tl) Royalty-Free/CORBIS; 577 (cl) Swerve/Alamy; 577 (bl) © Jeremy Woodhouse/PunchStock

Chapter Seventeen 582-583 (bkgd) © Arthur S. Aubry/Getty Images; 582 (tl) Scott B. Rosen/HRW Photo; 582 (cl) Joseph Brignolo/Getty Images; 582 (bl) Brand X Pictures/Alamy; 583 (br) Scott B. Rosen/HRW Photo; 585 (br) Scott B. Rosen/HRW Photo; 586 (tl) Scott B. Rosen/HRW Photo; 586 (cl) Scott B. Rosen/HRW Photo; 587 (bkgd) Douglas E. Walker/Masterfile; 587 (tr) National Portrait Gallery, Smithsonian Institution/Art Resource, NY; 587 (cl) Bettman/CORBIS; 588 (cl) Scott B. Rosen/HRW Photo; 590 (bl) Scott B. Rosen/HRW Photo; 590 (tl) Scott B. Rosen/HRW Photo; 594 (bl) Sam Dudgeon/HRW; 595 (br) Scott B. Rosen/HRW Photo; 598 (bl) Royalty-Free/CORBIS; 599 (tr) Joseph Brignolo/Getty Images; 600 (bl) © Brand X Pictures/Alamy; 601 (bl) Sam Dudgeon/HRW; 601 (tr) Sam Dudgeon/HRW; 602 (tl) Sergio Purtell/Foca/HRW; 602 (c) Sergio Purtell/Foca/HRW; 602 (cl) Sam Dudgeon/HRW; 602 (bl) Sergio Purtell/Foca/HRW; 602 (bc) Sergio Purtell/Foca/HRW; 603 (tc) Sergio Purtell/Foca/HRW; 603 (cr) Sam Dudgeon/HRW; 603 (br) Sam Dudgeon/HRW; 604 (bkgd) CORBIS; 604 (c) SSPL/The Image Works; 604 (cl) Scott B. Rosen/HRW Photo; 604 (tr) Courtesy of Computer History Museum; 605 (br) Royalty-Free/CORBIS; 606 (bl) Paul Silverman/Fundamental Photographs; 607 (tr) Scott B. Rosen/HRW Photo; 609 (br) Scott B. Rosen/HRW Photo; 611 (tl) Scott B. Rosen/HRW Photo; 611 (cl) Joseph Brignolo/Getty Images; 611 (bl) © Brand X Pictures/Alamy

Chapter Eighteen 616-617 (bkgd) Mike Macri/Masterfile; 616 (tl) © G. Glatsmaaier, Los Alamos National Laboratory/P. Roberts, UCLA/SPL/Photo Researchers, Inc.; 616 (cl) Dynamic Graphics Group/Creatas/Alamy; 616 (bl) Tara Moore/Getty Images; 617 (tr) Victoria Smith/HRW; 619 (br) Breck P. Kent/Animals Animals/Earth Scenes; 620 (bl) Peter Van Steen/HRW; 621 (tr) Scott B. Rosen/HRW Photo; 622 (tl) © Cordelia Molloy/SPL/Photo Researchers, Inc.; 623 (br) Scott B. Rosen/HRW Photo; 624 (tl) Tim Davis/CORBIS; 625 (bkgd) Michael Carlowicz, Woods Hole Oceanographic Institute; 625 (t) © G. Glatsmaaier, Los Alamos National Laboratory/P. Roberts, UCLA/SPL/Photo Researchers, Inc.; 625 (cr) © G. Glatzmaaier, Los Alamos National Laboratory/P. Roberts, UCLA/SPL/Photo Researchers, Inc.; 626 (bl) Richard Megna/Fundamental Photographs, New York; 627 (tr) Scott B. Rosen/HRW Photo; 628 (tl) Scott B. Rosen/HRW Photo; 629 (bkgd) © PunchStock; 629 (cr) © Dynamic Graphics Group/Creatas/Alamy; 630 (tl) Take 2 Productions/Ken Kaminesky/CORBIS; 633 (cr) Mike Fager/HRW; 635 (bkgd) © Tara Moore/Getty Images; 639 (tr) Peter Casolino/Alamy; 641 (br) Sam Dudgeon/HRW Photo; 643 (tl) © G. Glatsmaaier, Los Alamos National Laboratory/P. Roberts, UCLA/SPL/Photo Researchers, Inc.; 643 (cl) Dynamic Graphics Group/Creatas/Alamy; 643 (bl) Tara Moore/Getty Images

Earth and Space Science Unit Opener
649 (cl) © Royal Observatory, Edinburgh/AAO/SPL/Photo Researchers, Inc.; (tr) George Steinmetz/Corbis; (br) Dan Rees/Nature Picture Library

Chapter Nineteen 650-651 (bkgd) NASA/JPL/Cornell; 650 (cl) NASA/JPL/Space Science Institute; 651 (b) Scott B. Rosen/HRW Photo; 651 (br) © Dr. Fred Espenak/SPL/Photo Researchers, Inc.; 654 (tl) Budd Titlow/Visuals Unlimited; 654 (cl) Science VU/Visuals Unlimited; 657 (tr) USGS/NASA; 657 (b) John Sanford/Photo Researchers, Inc.; 658 (tl) Scott B. Rosen/HRW Photo; 659 (r) NASA/John Frassanito and Associates; 659

(bkgd) NASA/John Frassanito and Associates; 659 (b) © US Geological Survey/SPL/Photo Researchers, Inc.; 660 (tl) Peter Gregg/Color-Pic, Inc.; 660 (tr) Peter Gregg/Color-Pic, Inc.; 662 (bl) © NASA/SPL/Photo Researchers, Inc.; 662 (tl) © NASA/SPL/Photo Researchers, Inc.; 663 (br) NASA; 664 (tl) Handout/Reuters/CORBIS; 664 (bl) © NASA/ESA/STScI/SPL/Photo Researchers, Inc.; 665 (bkgd) Illustration by Bob Sauls/JF&A, Inc.; 665 (tl) © Ria Novosti/SPL/Photo Researchers, Inc.; 665 (bl) NASA/JPL; 665 (b) © David Ducros/SPL/Photo Researchers, Inc.; 666 (tl) NASA/JPL; 667 (tr) © NASA/JPL/Photo Researchers, Inc.; 668 (br) NASA/JPL/Space Science Institute; 669 (tr) NASA. ESA, and M. Showalter (SETI Institute); 669 (br) NASA; 670 (tl) NASA; 671 (b) Hugh Sitton/Getty Images; 672 (bl) J-L Charmet/Science Photo Library/Photo Researchers, Inc.; 672 (cl) Scott B. Rosen/HRW Photo; 675 (tr) CORBIS; 675 (bl) John Gleason/Celestial Images; 676 (bl) E.R. Degginger/Bruce Coleman, Inc.; 676 (bc) Breck P. Kent/Animals Animals/Earth Scenes; 676 (br) Ken Nichols/Institute of Meteorites; 677 (br) USGS/Landsat Project; 677 (b) Karen Su/CORBIS; 677 (tr) Jonathan Blair/CORBIS; 679 (t) Roger Ressmeyer/CORBIS; 681 (r) HRW Owned; 683 (cl) NASA/JPL/Space Science Institute; 684 (c) © NASA/SPL/Photo Researchers, Inc.; 684 (b) © NASA/SPL/Photo Researchers, Inc.; 684 (cr) © Tom Van Sant/Geosphere Project, Santa Monica/SPL/Photo Researchers, Inc.; 684 (br) NASA/JPL; 688-689 (bkgd) Frank Krahmer/Masterfile; 688 (tr) Roger Ressmeyer/CORBIS; 688 (cl) NASA/Time Life Pictures/Getty Images; 688 (br) Courtesy of Aundra Nix; 689 (tr) NOAA/CORBIS; 689 (cl) Barry Lewis/Alamy; 689 (bc) John Chiasson/Liaison/Getty Images

Chapter Twenty 690-691 (bkgd) © Royal Observatory, Edinburgh/AAO/SPL/Photo Researchers, Inc.; 690 (tl) NASA, ESA, HEIC, and The Hubble Heritage Team; 690 (cl) Gemini Observatory, GMOS team; 690 (bl) NASA/WMAP Science Team; 691 (br) Scott B. Rosen/HRW Photo; 693 (bl) Canada-France-Hawaii Telescope/SPL/Photo Researchers, Inc.; 693 (br) NASA, ESA, HEIC, and The Hubble Heritage Team (STScI/AURA); 695 (tl) Scott B. Rosen/HRW Photo; 697 (bkgd) Jerry Schad/Photo Researchers, Inc.; 697 (bc) The Art Archive/South Australia Art Gallery; 697 (bl) ImageState/Alamy; 700 (bl) NASA. ESA, J. Hester, and A. Loll (Arizona State University); 702 (bl) John Gleason/Celestial Images; 703 (t) NASA; 703 (br) Gemini Observatory/Travis Rector, University of Alaska Anchorage; 704 (tl) Stephen & Donna O'Meara/Photo Researchers, Inc.; 705 (tl) NASA Gemini Observatory, GMOS team; 705 (tc) Anglo-Australian Observatory; 705 (tr) Dennis Di Cicco/Peter Arnold, Inc.; 706 (t) © David Nunuk/SPL/Photo Researchers, Inc.; 706 (cr) © NASA/SPL/Photo Researchers, Inc.; 706 (tl) Courtesy of SETI League; 707 (tr) NASA.ESA. S. Beckwith (STScI) and the HUDF Team; 708 (bl) Icon SMI; 708 (bc) Mike Yamashita/Woodfin Camp/Picture Quest; 708 (br) NASA; 710 (tr) CORBIS; Original Image courtesy of NASA/CORBIS; 711 (tl) Scott B. Rosen/HRW Photo; 711 (bl) Sam Dudgeon/HRW; 711 (br) Sam Dudgeon/HRW; 712 (bl) NASA/WMAP Science Team; 714 (bkgd) S. Points, C. Smith, R. Leiton, C. Aguilera and NOAO/AURA/NSF; 714 (bl) Stockbyte/Getty Images; 714 (cl) Judith Collins/Alamy; 714 (tl) Andrew Lambert Photography/Photo Researchers, Inc.; 714 (bc) © Hemera Technologies/Alamy; 715 (tr) © PHOTOTAKE Inc./Alamy; 716 (tl) NASA; 716 (cl) NASA Marshall Space Flight Center (NASA-MSFC); 721 (tl) NASA, ESA, HEIC, and The Hubble Heritage Team; 721 (cl) NASA Gemini Observatory, GMOS team; 721 (bl) NASA/WMAP Science Team

Chapter Twenty One 726-727 (bkgd) Dan Rees/Nature Picture Library; 726 (t) Chris Howes/Wild Places Photography/Alamy; 726 (tl) Douglas Peebles Photography/Alamy; 726 (cl) Gary Crabbe/Alamy; 726 (bl) Kristen Brochmann/Fundamental Photographs; 727 (tr) Scott B. Rosen/HRW Photo; 731 (br) Chris Howes/Wild Places Photography/Alamy; 732 (tl) Ralph White/CORBIS; 733 (tr) Scott B. Rosen/HRW Photo; 734 (tl) Wang Yuan-mao/AP/Wide World Photos; 734 (br) NASA; 735 (bl) Photographers Direct; 736 (cr) Scott B. Rosen/HRW Photo; 736 (bl) Roger Cracknell/Alamy; 737 (cl) David Parker/Science Photo Library/Photo Researchers, Inc.; 739 (br) HRW Owned; 740 (tl) Reuters/Corbis; 743 (br) Douglas Peebles Photography/Alamy; 746 (t) Volcano photos by photographer Jef Maion; 747 (bkgd) The Newark Museum/Art Resource, NY; 747 (cl) Picture Contact/Alamy; 747 (cr) Bridgeman Art Library; 747 (bl) NASA; 748 (bl) Bill Ross/CORBIS; 749 (tc) G. R. Roberts © Natural Sciences Image Library; 749 (tl) Pat Lanza/Bruce Coleman Inc.; 750 (cl) Grant Heilman Photography, Inc.; 750 (t) Gary Crabbe/Alamy; 750 (bl) Angie Sharp/Alamy; 751 (bl) Sam Dudgeon/HRW; 751 (bc) Sam Dudgeon/HRW; 751 (tr) Paul Edmondson/CORBIS; 753 (tr) Scott B. Rosen/HRW Photo; 753 (br) Deborah Long/Visuals Unlimited; 754 (l) © James King-Holmes/SPL/Photo Researchers, Inc.; 755 (bkgd) Jacques Jangoux/Alamy; 755 (tr) Dr. John D. Cunningham Visuals Unlimited; 755 (bl) Dale O'Dell/Alamy; 755 (cr) Scott B. Rosen/HRW Photo; 756 (bl) James Kay; 757 (tr) Larry Ulrich; 757 (bl) Chris Howed/Wild Places Photography/Alamy; 758 (tl) NYC Parks Photo Archive/Fundamental Photographs; 758 (tr) Kristen Brochmann/Fundamental Photographs; 759 (b) Jim Wark/Airphoto; 759 (tr) Elvele Images/Alamy; 760 (tl) Grant Heilman Photography, Inc.; 760 (tr) Visuals Unlimited/Bill Kamin; 760 (bl) Mark Tomalty/Masterfile; 761 (tr) © Gordon Garrado/SPL/Photo Researchers, Inc.; 765 (t) Chris Howes/Wild Places Photography/Alamy; 765 (tl) Douglas Peebles Photography/Alamy; 765 (cl) Gary Crabbe/Alamy; 765 (bl) Kristen Brochmann/Fundamental Photographs; 766 (br) G. R. Roberts © Natural Sciences Image Library; 766 (tl) Pat Lanza/Bruce Coleman Inc.; 766 (tr) Grant Heilman Photography, Inc.; 766 (bl) Sam Dudgeon/HRW

Chapter Twenty Two 770-771 (bkgd) Warren Faidler/Weatherstock; 770 (tl) Jon Arnold Images/Alamy; 770 (cl) TZ Aviation/Airliners.net; 770 (bl) Warren Faidley/Weatherstock; 771 (cr) Myrleen Ferguson Cate/PhotoEdit; 774 (bl) Jon Arnold Images/Alamy; 775 (t) Daniel Umana/Jetphotos.net; 777 (tl) George Lepp/Getty Images/Stone; 778 (br) Larry Lefever/Grant Heilman Photography, Inc.; 779 (tl) Scott B. Rosen/HRW Photo; 782 (l) Bernard Photo Productions//Animals Animals/Earth Scenes; 784 (bl) Tom Pantages Photography; 785 (tl) Peter Arnold, Inc./Alamy; 787 (tl) TZ Aviation/Airliners.net; 788 (cr) Roy Ooms/Masterfile; 788 (bl) Ed Young/CORBIS; 788 (br) Art Resource, NY; 788 (bkgd) Mark S Cosslett/Getty Images; 788 (cl) Boating Images Photo Library/Alamy; 789 (b) Courtesy of The Weather Channel; 791 (bl) Warren Faidley/Weatherstock; 791 (bc) Warren Faidley/Weatherstock; 791 (br) Warren Faidley/Weatherstock; 793 (tr) Courtesy of Louisiana Photos; 793 (bkgd) Scott B. Rosen/HRW Photo; 793 (cr) Courtesy of Louisiana Photos; 797 (r) Scott B. Rosen/HRW Photo; 799 (tl) Jon Arnold Images/Alamy; 799 (cl) TZ Aviation/Airliners.net; 799 (bl) Warren Faidley/Weatherstock

Chapter Twenty Three 804-805 (bkgd) George Steinmetz/Corbis; 804 (tl) M. Osf Gibbs/Animals Animals/Earth Scenes; 804 (cl) Stefan Schott/Panoramic Images, Ltd.; 804 (bl) Patti Murray/Animals animals Earth Scenes; 805 (br) Scott B. Rosen/HRW Photo; 809 (tr) M. Osf Gibbs/Animals Animals/Earth Scenes; 809 (bl) Visuals Unlimited/Tom J. Ulrich; 810 (cl) Craig Fugii/1988 The Seattle Times; 810 (bl) Raymond Gehman/National Geographic Society Image Collection; 811 (bl) E. R. Degginger/Animals Animals/Earth Scenes; 811 (br) E. R. Degginger/Animals Animals/Earth Scenes; 812 (tl) Scott B. Rosen/HRW Photo; 813 (bl) David R. Frazier Photolibrary, Inc./Alamy; 813 (bc) W. Geirsperger/CORBIS; 813 (br) Peter Bowater/Alamy; 814 (tl) Mike Wilkes/Nature Picture Library; 814 (cl) Read, Marie/Animals Animals; 817 (tl) WoodyStock/Alamy; 818 (cl) David L. Moore/Alamy; 819 (t) Stefan Schott/Panoramic Images, Ltd.; 819 (br) Inga Spence/Index Stock; 820 (t) © John Mead/SPL/Photo Researchers, Inc.; 821 (br) Simmons Aerofilms Ltd./Alamy; 822 (cl) Courtesy of the G.C. Broach Company; 823 (l) Rolex Awards/Tomas Bertelsen; 823 (tr) Rolex Awards/Tomas Bertelsen; 824 (bl) Warren Bolster/Getty Images/Stone; 826 (bl) © Simon Fraser/SPL/Photo Researchers, Inc.; 827 (br) Patti Murray/Animals animals Earth Scenes; 828 (t) © Michael Marten/SPL/Photo Researchers, Inc.; 829 (bl) Scott B. Rosen/HRW Photo; 830 (b) © Randy Faris/CORBIS; 830 (bl) Phil Degginger/Bruce Coleman, Inc.; 830 (bl) Kay Park - Rec. Corp; 831 (tr) Telegraph Colour Library/Getty Images/Taxi; 835 (tl) M. Osf Gibbs/Animals Animals/Earth Scenes; 835 (cl) Stefan Schott/Panoramic Images, Ltd.; 835 (bl) Patti Murray/Animals animals Earth Scenes; 836 (br) © John Mead/SPL/Photo Researchers, Inc.

Reference Section Title Page 841 (all) Sam Dudgeon/HRW

Reference Section 877 (br) HRW Photo; 878 (bl) Sam Dudgeon/HRW; 878 (br) Scott Rosen/Bill Smith Studio

HRW Staff

The people who contributed to *Holt Science Spectrum: Physical Science* are listed below. They represent editorial, design, production, eMedia, marketing, and permissions.

David Alvarado, Wesley M. Bain, Kimberly Barr, Angela Beckmann, Cindy Brooks, Sara Buller, Becky Calhoun, Soojinn Choi, Lorraine Cooper, Martize Cross, Eddie Dawson, Julie Dervin, Lydia Doty, Paul Draper, Sam Dudgeon, Sally Garland, Diana Goetting, Jessica Gonzalez, Jevara Jackson, Simon Key, Jane A. Kirschman, Liz Kline, Laura Likon, Jenifer Limb, Denise Mahoney, Richard Metzger, Mercedes Newman, Micah Newman, Cathy Paré, Jenny Patton, Peter D. Reid, Raegan Remington, Sara Rider, Kelly Rizk, Jeff Robinson, Tara Ross, Michelle Rumpf-Dike, Beth Sample, Kay Selke, Angela Senicz, Chris Smith, Victoria Smith, Dawn Marie Spinozza, Sherry Sprague, Jeff Streber, JoAnn Stringer, Jeannie Taylor, Lindsey Thomas, Bob Tucek, Kira J. Watkins, Aimee Wiley, Sara Zettner, Patricia Zepeda